SAUL BELLOW

Saul Bellow

NOVELS 1970–1982

Mr. Sammler's Planet
Humboldt's Gift
The Dean's December

THE LIBRARY OF AMERICA

The paper used in this publication meets the
minimum requirements of the American National Standard for
Information Sciences—Permanence of Paper for Printed
Library Materials, ANSI Z39.48—1984.

Distributed to the trade in the United States
by Penguin Group (USA) Inc.
and in Canada by Penguin Books Canada Ltd.

Library of Congress Control Number: 2010924272
ISBN 978-1-59853-079-7

First Printing
The Library of America—209

Manufactured in the United States of America

James Wood
wrote the notes for this volume

Contents

MR. SAMMLER'S PLANET

I

SHORTLY after dawn, or what would have been dawn in a normal sky, Mr. Artur Sammler with his bushy eye took in the books and papers of his West Side bedroom and suspected strongly that they were the wrong books, the wrong papers. In a way it did not matter much to a man of seventy-plus, and at leisure. You had to be a crank to insist on being right. Being right was largely a matter of explanation. Intellectual man had become an explaining creature. Fathers to children, wives to husbands, lecturers to listeners, experts to laymen, colleagues to colleagues, doctors to patients, man to his own soul, explained. The roots of this, the causes of the other, the source of events, the history, the structure, the reasons why. For the most part, in one ear out the other. The soul wanted what it wanted. It had its own natural knowledge. It sat unhappily on superstructures of explanation, poor bird, not knowing which way to fly.

The eye closed briefly. A Dutch drudgery, it occurred to Sammler, pumping and pumping to keep a few acres of dry ground. The invading sea being a metaphor for the multiplication of facts and sensations. The earth being an earth of ideas.

He thought, since he had no job to wake up to, that he might give sleep a second chance to resolve certain difficulties imaginatively for him, and pulled up the disconnected electric blanket with its internal sinews and lumps. The satin binding was nice to the fingertips. He was still drowsy, but not really inclined to sleep. Time to be conscious.

He sat and plugged in the electric coil. Water had been prepared at bedtime. He liked to watch the changes of the ashen wires. They came to life with fury, throwing tiny sparks and sinking into red rigidity under the Pyrex laboratory flask. Deeper. Blenching. He had only one good eye. The left distinguished only light and shade. But the good eye was dark-bright, full of observation through the overhanging hair of the brow as in some breeds of dog. For his height he had a small face. The combination made him conspicuous.

His conspicuousness was on his mind; it worried him. For

several days, Mr. Sammler returning on the customary bus late afternoons from the Forty-second Street Library had been watching a pickpocket at work. The man got on at Columbus Circle. The job, the crime, was done by Seventy-second Street. Mr. Sammler if he had not been a tall straphanger would not with his one good eye have seen these things happening. But now he wondered whether he had not drawn too close, whether he had also been seen seeing. He wore smoked glasses, at all times protecting his vision, but he couldn't be taken for a blind man. He didn't have the white cane, only a furled umbrella, British-style. Moreover, he didn't have the look of blindness. The pickpocket himself wore dark shades. He was a powerful Negro in a camel's-hair coat, dressed with extraordinary elegance, as if by Mr. Fish of the West End, or Turnbull and Asser of Jermyn Street. (Mr. Sammler knew his London.) The Negro's perfect circles of gentian violet banded with lovely gold turned toward Sammler, but the face showed the effrontery of a big animal. Sammler was not timid, but he had had as much trouble in life as he wanted. A good deal of this, waiting for assimilation, would never be accommodated. He suspected the criminal was aware that a tall old white man passing as blind had observed, had seen the minutest details of his crimes. Staring down. As if watching open-heart surgery. And though he dissembled, deciding not to turn aside when the thief looked at him, his elderly, his compact, civilized face colored strongly, the short hairs bristled, the lips and gums were stinging. He felt a constriction, a clutch of sickness at the base of the skull where the nerves, muscles, blood vessels were tightly interlaced. The breath of wartime Poland passing over the damaged tissues—that nerve-spaghetti, as he thought of it.

Buses were bearable, subways were killing. Must he give up the bus? He had not minded his own business as a man of seventy in New York should do. It was always Mr. Sammler's problem that he didn't know his proper age, didn't appreciate his situation, unprotected here by position, by privileges of remoteness made possible by an income of fifty thousand dollars in New York—club membership, taxis, doormen, guarded approaches. For him it was the buses, or the grinding subway, lunch at the automat. No cause for grave complaint, but his years as an "Englishman," two decades in London as correspondent for Warsaw papers and journals, had left him with attitudes not especially useful to a refugee in Manhattan. He had developed expressions suited to an Oxford common room; he had the face of a British Museum reader. Sammler as a schoolboy in Cracow before World War I fell in love with England. Most of that nonsense had been knocked out of him. He had reconsidered the whole question of Anglophilia, thinking skeptically about Salvador de Madariaga, Mario Praz, André Maurois and Colonel Bramble. He knew the phenomenon. Still, confronted by the elegant brute in the bus he had seen picking a purse—the purse still hung open—he adopted an English tone. A dry, a neat, a prim face declared that one had not crossed anyone's boundary; one was satisfied with one's own business. But under the high armpits Mr. Sammler was intensely hot, wet; hanging on his strap, sealed in by bodies, receiving their weight and laying his own on them as the fat tires took the giant curve at Seventy-second Street with a growl of flabby power.

He didn't in fact appear to know his age, or at what point of life he stood. You could see that in his way of walking. On the streets, he was tense, quick, erratically light and reckless, the elderly hair stirring on the back of his head. Crossing, he lifted the rolled umbrella high and pointed to show cars, buses, speeding trucks, and cabs bearing down on him the way he intended to go. They might run him over, but he could not help his style of striding blind.

With the pickpocket we were in an adjoining region of recklessness. He knew the man was working the Riverside bus. He had seen him picking purses, and he had reported it to the police. The police were not greatly interested in the report. It had made Sammler feel like a fool to go immediately to a phone booth on Riverside Drive. Of course the phone was smashed. Most outdoor telephones were smashed, crippled. They were urinals, also. New York was getting worse than Naples or Salonika. It was like an Asian, an African town, from this standpoint. The opulent sections of the city were not immune. You opened a jeweled door into degradation, from hypercivilized Byzantine luxury straight into the state of nature, the barbarous world of color erupting from beneath. It might well be barbarous on either side of the jeweled door. Sexually, for example. The thing evidently, as Mr. Sammler was beginning to grasp, consisted in obtaining the privileges, and the free ways of barbarism, under the protection of civilized order, property rights, refined technological organization, and so on. Yes, that must be it.

Mr. Sammler ground his coffee in a square box, cranking counterclockwise between long knees. To common-place actions he brought a special pedantic awkwardness. In Poland, France, England, students, young gentlemen of his time, had been unacquainted with kitchens. Now he did things that cooks and maids had once done. He did them with a certain priestly stiffness. Acknowledgment of social descent. Historical ruin. Transformation of society. It was beyond personal humbling. He had gotten over those ideas during the war in Poland—utterly gotten over all that, especially the idiotic pain of losing class privileges. As well as he could with one eye, he darned his own socks, sewed his buttons, scrubbed his own sink, winter-treated his woolens in the spring with a spray can. Of course there were ladies, his daughter, Shula, his niece (by marriage), Margotte Arkin, in whose apartment he lived. They did for him, when they thought of it. Sometimes they did a great deal, but not dependably, routinely. The routines he did himself. It was conceivably even part of his youthfulness—youthfulness sustained with certain tremors. Sammler knew these tremors. It was amusing—Sammler noted in old women wearing textured tights, in old sexual men, this quiver of vivacity with which they obeyed the sovereign youth-style. The powers are the powers—overlords, kings, gods. And of course no one knew when to quit. No one made sober decent terms with death.

The grounds in the little drawer of the mill he held above the flask. The red coil went deeper, whiter, white. The kinks had tantrums. Beads of water flashed up. Individually, the pioneers gracefully went to the surface. Then they all seethed together. He poured in the grounds. In his cup, a lump of sugar, a dusty spoonful of Pream. In the night table he kept a bag of onion rolls from Zabar's. They were in plastic, a transparent uterine bag fastened with a white plastic clip. The night table, copper-lined, formerly a humidor, kept things fresh. It had belonged to Margotte's husband, Ussher Arkin. Arkin, killed three years ago in a plane crash, a good man, was missed, was regretted, mourned by Sammler. When he was invited by the widow to occupy a bedroom in the large apartment on West Ninetieth Street, Sammler asked to have Arkin's humidor in his room. Sentimental herself, Margotte said, "Of course, Uncle. What a nice thought. You did love Ussher." Margotte was German, romantic. Sammler was something else. He was not even her uncle. She was the niece of his wife, who had died in Poland in 1940. His late wife. The widow's late aunt. Wherever you looked, or tried to look, there were the late. It took some getting used to.

Grapefruit juice he drank from a can with two triangular punctures kept on the window sill. The curtain parted as he reached and he looked out. Brownstones, balustrades, bay windows, wrought iron. Like stamps in an album—the dun rose of buildings canceled by the heavy black of grilles, of corrugated rainspouts. How very heavy human life was here, in forms of bourgeois solidity. Attempted permanence was sad. We were now flying to the moon. Did one have a right to private expectations, being like those bubbles in the flask? But then also people exaggerated the tragic accents of their condition. They stressed too hard the disintegrated assurances; what formerly was believed, trusted, was now bitterly circled in black irony. The rejected bourgeois black of stability thus translated. That too was improper, incorrect. People justifying idleness, silliness, shallowness, distemper, lust—turning former respectability inside out.

Such was Sammler's eastward view, a soft asphalt belly rising, in which lay steaming sewer navels. Spalled sidewalks with clusters of ash cans. Brownstones. The yellow brick of elevator buildings like his own. Little copses of television antennas. Whiplike, graceful thrilling metal dendrites drawing images from the air, bringing brotherhood, communion to immured apartment people. Westward the Hudson came between Sammler and the great Spry industries of New Jersey. These flashed their electric message through intervening night. SPRY. But then he was half blind.

In the bus he had been seeing well enough. He saw a crime committed. He reported it to the cops. They were not greatly shaken. He might then have stayed away from that particular bus, but instead he tried hard to repeat the experience. He went to Columbus Circle and hung about until he saw his man again. Four fascinating times he had watched the thing done, the crime, the first afternoon staring down at the masculine hand that came from behind lifting the clasp and tipping the pocketbook lightly to make it fall open. Sammler saw a polished Negro forefinger without haste, with no criminal tremor, turning aside a plastic folder with Social Security or credit cards, emery sticks, a lipstick capsule, coral paper tissues, nipping open the catch of a change purse—and there lay the green of money. Still at the same rate, the fingers took out the dollars. Then with the touch of a doctor on a patient's belly the Negro moved back the slope leather, turned the gilded scallop catch. Sammler, feeling his head small, shrunk with strain, the teeth tensed, still was looking at the patent-leather bag riding, picked, on the woman's hip, finding that he was irritated with her. That she felt nothing. What an idiot! Going around with some kind of stupid mold in her skull. Zero instincts, no grasp of New York. While the man turned from her, board-shouldered in the camel's-hair coat. The dark glasses, the original design by Christian Dior, a powerful throat banded by a tab collar and a cherry silk necktie spouting out. Under the African nose, a cropped mustache. Ever so slightly inclining toward him, Sammler believed he could smell French perfume from the breast of the camel's-hair coat. Had the man noticed him then? Had he perhaps followed him home? Of this Sammler was not sure.

He didn't give a damn for the glamour, the style, the art of criminals. They were no social heroes to him. He had had some talks on this very matter with one of his younger relations, Angela Gruner, the daughter of Dr. Arnold Gruner in New Rochelle, who had brought him over to the States in 1947, digging him out of the DP camp in Salzburg. Because Arnold (Elya) Gruner had Old World family feelings. And studying the lists of refugees in the Yiddish papers, he had found the names Artur and Shula Sammler. Angela, who was in Sammler's neighborhood several times a week because her psychiatrist was just around the corner, often stopped in for a visit. She was one of those handsome, passionate, rich girls who were always an important social and human category. A bad education. In literature, mostly French. At Sarah Lawrence College. And Mr. Sammler had to try hard to remember the Balzac he had read in Cracow in 1913. Vautrin the escaped criminal. From the hulks. *Trompe-la-mort.* No, he didn't have much use for the romance of the outlaw. Angela sent money to defense funds for black murderers and rapists. That was her business of course.

However, Mr. Sammler had to admit that once he had seen the pickpocket at work he wanted very much to see the thing again. He didn't know why. It was a powerful event, and illicitly—that is, against his own stable principles—he craved a repetition. One detail of old readings he recalled without effort—the moment in *Crime and Punishment* at which Raskolnikov brought down the ax on the bare head of the old woman, her thin gray-streaked grease-smeared hair, the rat's-tail braid fastened by a broken horn comb on her neck. That is to say that horror, crime, murder, did vivify all the phenomena, the most ordinary details of experience. In evil as in art there was illumination. It was, of course, like the tale by Charles Lamb, burning down a house to roast a pig. Was a general conflagration necessary? All you needed was a controlled fire in the right place. Still, to ask everyone to refrain from setting fires until the thing could be done in the right place, in a higher manner, was possibly too much. And while Sammler, getting off the bus, intended to phone the police, he nevertheless received from the crime the benefit of an enlarged vision. The air was brighter—late afternoon, daylight-saving time. The world, Riverside Drive, was wickedly lighted up. Wicked because the clear light made all objects so explicit, and this explicitness taunted Mr. Minutely-Observant Artur Sammler. All metaphysicians please note. Here is how it is. You will never see more clearly. And what do you make of it? This phone booth has a metal floor; smooth-hinged the folding green doors, but the floor is smarting with dry urine, the plastic telephone instrument is smashed, and a stump is hanging at the end of the cord.

Not in three blocks did he find a phone he could safely put a dime into, and so he went home. In his lobby the building management had set up a television screen so that the doorman could watch for criminals. But the doorman was always off somewhere. The buzzing rectangle of electronic radiance was vacant. Underfoot was the respectable carpet, brown as gravy. The inner gate of the elevator, supple brass diamonds folding, grimy and gleaming. Sammler went into the apartment and sat on the sofa in the foyer, which Margotte had covered with large squares of Woolworth bandannas, tied at the corners and pinned to the old cushions. He dialed the police and said, "I want to report a crime."

"What kind of crime?"

"A pickpocket."

"Just a minute, I'll connect you."

There was a long buzz. A voice toneless with indifference or fatigue said, "Yes."

Mr. Sammler in his foreign Polish Oxonian English tried to be as compressed, direct, and factual as possible. To save time. To avoid complicated interrogation, needless detail.

"I wish to report a pickpocket on the Riverside bus."

"O.K."

"Sir?"

"O.K. I said O.K., report."

"A Negro, about six feet tall, about two hundred pounds, about thirty-five years old, very good-looking, very well dressed."

"O.K."

"I thought I should call in."

"O.K."

"Are you going to do anything?"

"We're supposed to, aren't we? What's your name?"

"Artur Sammler."

"All right, Art. Where do you live?"

"Dear sir, I will tell you, but I am asking what you intend to do about this man."

"What do you think we should do?"

"Arrest him."

"We have to catch him first."

"You should put a man on the bus."

"We haven't got a man to put on the bus. There are lots of buses, Art, and not enough men. Lots of conventions, banquets, and so on we have to cover, Art. VIPs and Brass. There are lots of ladies shopping at Lord and Taylor, Bonwit's, and

Saks', leaving purses on chairs while they go to feel the goods."

"I understand. You don't have the personnel, and there are priorities, political pressures. But I could point out the man."

"Some other time."

"You don't want him pointed out?"

"Sure, but we have a waiting list."

"I have to get on *your* list."

"That's right, Abe."

"Artur."

"Arthur."

Tensely sitting forward in bright lamplight, Artur Sammler like a motorcyclist who has been struck in the forehead by a pebble from the road, trivially stung, smiled with long lips. America! (he was speaking to himself). Advertised throughout the universe as *the* most desirable, most exemplary of all nations.

"Let me make sure I understand you, officer—mister detective. This man is going to rob more people, but you aren't going to do anything about it. Is that right?"

It was right—confirmed by silence, though no ordinary silence. Mr. Sammler said, "Good-by, sir."

After this, when Sammler should have shunned the bus, he rode it oftener than ever. The thief had a regular route, and he dressed for the ride, for his work. Always gorgeously garbed. Mr. Sammler was struck once, but not astonished, to see that he wore a single gold earring. This was too much to keep to himself, and for the first time he then mentioned to Margotte, his niece and landlady, to Shula, his daughter, that this handsome, this striking, arrogant pickpocket, this African prince or great black beast was seeking whom he might devour between Columbus Circle and Verdi Square.

To Margotte it was fascinating. Anything fascinating she was prepared to discuss all day, from every point of view with full German pedantry. Who was this black? What were his origins, his class or racial attitudes, his psychological views, his true emotions, his aesthetic, his political ideas? Was he a revolutionary? Would he be for black guerrilla warfare? Unless Sammler had private thoughts to occupy him, he couldn't sit through these talks with Margotte. She was sweet but on the theoretical side very tedious, and when she settled down to an earnest theme, one was lost. This was why he ground his own coffee, boiled water in his flask, kept onion rolls in the humidor, even urinated in the washbasin (rising on his toes to a meditation on the inherent melancholy of animal nature, continually in travail, according to Aristotle). Because mornings could disappear while Margotte in her goodness speculated. He had learned his lesson one week when she wished to analyze Hannah Arendt's phrase The Banality of Evil, and kept him in the living room, sitting on a sofa (made of foam rubber, laid on plywood supported by two-inch sections of pipe, backed by trapezoids of cushion all covered in dark-gray denim). He couldn't bring himself to say what he thought. For one thing, she seldom stopped to listen. For another, he doubted that he could make himself clear. Moreover, most of her family had been destroyed by the Nazis like his own, though she herself had gotten out in 1937. Not he. The war had caught him, with Shula and his late wife, in Poland. They had gone there to liquidate his father-in-law's estate. Lawyers should have attended to this, but it was important to Antonina to supervise it in person. She was killed in 1940, and her father's optical-instrument factory (a small one) was dismantled and sent to Austria. No postwar indemnity was paid. Margotte received payment from the West German government for her family's property in Frankfurt. Arkin hadn't left her much; she needed this German money. You didn't argue with people in such circumstances. Of course he had circumstances of his own, as she recognized. He had actually gone through it, lost his wife, lost an eye. Still, on the theoretical side, they could discuss the question. Purely as a question. Uncle Artur, sitting, knees high in the sling chair, his pale-tufted eyes shaded by tinted glasses, the forked veins coming down from the swells of his forehead and the big mouth determined to be silent.

"The idea being," said Margotte, "that here is no great spirit of evil. Those people were too insignificant, Uncle. They were just ordinary lower-class people, administrators, small bureaucrats, or *Lumpenproletariat*. A mass society does not produce great criminals. It's because of the division of labor all over society which broke up the whole idea of general responsibility. Piecework did it. It's like instead of a forest with enormous trees, you have to think of small plants with shallow roots. Modern civilization doesn't create great individual phenomena any more."

The late Arkin, generally affectionate and indulgent, knew how to make Margotte shut up. He was a tall, splendid, half-bald, mustached man with a good subtle brain in his head. Political theory had been his field. He taught at Hunter College—taught women. Charming, idiotic, nonsensical girls, he used to say. Now and then, a powerful female intelligence, but very angry, very complaining, too much sex-ideology, poor things. It was when he was on his way to Cincinnati to lecture at some Hebrew college that his plane crashed. Sammler noticed how his widow tended now to impersonate him. She had become the political theorist. She spoke in his name, as presumably he would have done, and there was no one to protect his ideas. The common fate also of Socrates and Jesus. Up to a point, Arkin had enjoyed Margotte's tormenting conversation, it must be admitted. Her nonsense pleased him, and under the mustache he would grin to himself, long arms reaching to the ends of the trapezoidal cushions, and his stockinged feet set upon each other (he took off his shoes the instant he sat down). But after she had gone on a while, he would say, "Enough, enough of this Weimar *schmaltz.* Cut it, Margotte!" That big virile interruption would never be heard again in this cockeyed living room.

Margotte was short, round, full. Her legs in black net stockings, especially the underthighs, were attractively heavy. Seated, she put out one foot like a dancer, instep curved forward. She set her strong little fist on her haunch. Arkin once said to Uncle Sammler that she was a first-class device as long as someone aimed her in the right direction. She was a good soul, he told him, but the energetic goodness could be tremendously misapplied. Sammler saw this for himself. She couldn't wash a tomato without getting her sleeves wet. The place was burglarized because she raised the window to admire a sunset and forgot to lock it. The burglars entered the dining room from the rooftop just below. The sentimental value of her lockets, chains, rings, heirlooms was not appreciated by the insurance company. The windows were now nailed shut and draped. Meals were eaten by candlelight. Just enough glow to see the framed reproductions from the Museum of Modern

Art, and across the table, Margotte serving, spattering the tablecloth; her lovely grin, dark and tender with clean, imperfect small teeth, and eyes dark blue and devoid of wickedness. A bothersome creature, willing, cheerful, purposeful, maladroit. The cups and tableware were greasy. She forgot to flush the toilet. But all that one could easily live with. It was her earnestness that gave the trouble—considering everything under the sun with such German wrongheadedness. As though to be Jewish weren't trouble enough, the poor woman was German too.

"So. And what is your opinion, dear Uncle Sammler?" At last she asked. "I know you have thought a lot about this. You have experienced so much. And you and Ussher had such conversations about that crazy old fellow—King Rumkowski. The man from Lodz. . . . What do you think?"

Uncle Sammler had compact cheeks, his color was good for a man in his seventies, and he was not greatly wrinkled. There were, however, on the left side, the blind side, thin long lines like the lines in a cracked glass or within a cake of ice.

To answer was not useful. It would produce more discussion, more explanation. Nevertheless, he was addressed by another human being. He was old-fashioned. The courtesy of some reply was necessary.

"The idea of making the century's great crime look dull is not banal. Politically, psychologically, the Germans had an idea of genius. The banality was only camouflage. What better way to get the curse out of murder than to make it look ordinary, boring, or trite? With horrible political insight they found a way to disguise the thing. Intellectuals do not understand. They get their notions about matters like this from literature. They expect a wicked hero like Richard III. But do you think the Nazis didn't know what murder was? Everybody (except certain bluestockings) knows what murder is. That is very old human knowledge. The best and purest human beings, from the beginning of time, have understood that life is sacred. To defy that old understanding is not banality. There was a conspiracy against the sacredness of life. Banality is the adopted disguise of a very powerful will to abolish conscience. Is such a project trivial? Only if human life is trivial. This woman professor's enemy is modern civilization itself. She is only using the Germans to attack the twentieth century—to denounce it in terms invented by Germans. Making use of a tragic history to promote the foolish ideas of Weimar intellectuals."

Arguments! Explanations! thought Sammler. All will explain everything to all, until the next, the new common version is ready. This version, a residue of what people for a century or so say to one another, will be, like the old, a fiction. More elements of reality perhaps will be incorporated in the new version. But the important consideration was that life should recover its plenitude, its normal contented turgidity. All the old fusty stuff had to be blown away, of course, so we might be nearer to nature. To be nearer to nature was necessary in order to keep in balance the achievements of modern Method. The Germans had been the giants of this Method in industry and war. To relax from rationality and calculation, machinery, planning, technics, they had romance, mythomania, peculiar aesthetic fanaticism. These, too, were like machines—the aesthetic machine, the philosophic machine, the mythomanic machine, the culture machine. Machines in the sense of being systematic. System demands mediocrity, not greatness. System is based on labor. Labor connected to art is banality. Hence the sensitivity of cultivated Germans to everything banal. It exposed the rule, the might of Method, and their submission to Method. Sammler had it all figured out. Alert to the peril and disgrace of explanations, he was himself no mean explainer. And even in the old days, in the days when he was "British," in the lovely twenties and thirties when he lived in Great Russell Street, when he was acquainted with Maynard Keynes, Lytton Strachey, and H. G. Wells and loved "British" views, before the great squeeze, the human physics of the war, with its volumes, its vacuums, its voids (that period of dynamics and direct action upon the individual, comparable biologically to birth), he had never much trusted his judgment where Germans were concerned. The Weimar Republic was not attractive to him in any way. No, there was an exception—he had admired its Plancks and Einsteins. Hardly anyone else.

In any case, he was not going to be one of those kindly European uncles with whom the Margottes of this world could have day-long high-level discussions. She would have liked him trailing after her through the apartment while, for two hours, she unpacked the groceries, hunting for lunch a salami which was already on the shelf; while she slapped and smoothed the bed with short strong arms (she kept the bedroom piously unchanged, after the death of Ussher—his swivel chair, his footstool, his Hobbes, Vico, Hume, and Marx underlined), discussing things. He found that even if he could get a word in edgewise it was encircled and cut off right away. Margotte swept on, enormously desirous of doing good. And really she was good (that was the point), she was boundlessly, achingly, hopelessly on the right side, the best side, of every big human question: for creativity, for the young, for the black, the poor, the oppressed, for victims, for sinners, for the hungry.

A significant remark by Ussher Arkin, giving much to think of after his death, was that he had learned to do the good thing as if practicing a vice. He must have been thinking of his wife as a sexual partner. She had probably driven him to erotic invention, and made monogamy a fascinating challenge. Margotte, continually recalling Ussher, spoke of him always, Germanically, as her Man. "When my Man was alive . . . my Man used to say." Sammler was sorry for his widowed niece. You could criticize her endlessly. High-minded, she bored you, she made cruel inroads into your time, your thought, your patience. She talked junk, she gathered waste and junk in the flat, she bred junk. Look, for instance, at these plants she was trying to raise. She planted avocado pits, lemon seeds, peas, potatoes. Was there anything ever so mangy, trashy, as these potted objects? Shrubs and vines dragged on the ground, tried to rise on grocer's string hopefully stapled fanwise to the ceiling. The stems of the avocados looked like the sticks of fireworks falling back after the flash, and produced a few rusty, spiky, anthrax-damaged, nitty leaves. This botanical ugliness, the product of so much fork-digging, watering, so much breast and arm, heart and hope, told you something, didn't it? First of all, it told you that the individual facts were filled with messages and meanings, but you couldn't be sure what the messages meant. She wanted a bower in her living room, a screen of glossy leaves, flowers, a garden, blessings of freshness and beauty—something to foster as woman the germinatrix, the matriarch of reservoirs and gardens. Humankind, crazy for symbols, trying to utter what it doesn't know itself. Meantime the spreading fanlike featherless quills: no peacock purple, no sweet blue, no true green, but only spots before your eyes. Redeemed by a feeling of ready and available human warmth? No, you couldn't be sure. The strain of unrelenting analytical effort gave Mr. Sammler a headache. The worst of it was that these frazzled plants would not, could not respond. There was not enough light. Too much clutter.

But when it came to clutter, his daughter, Shula, was much worse. He had lived with Shula for several years, just east of Broadway. She had too many oddities for her old father. She passionately collected things. In plainer words, she was a scavenger. More than once, he had seen her hunting through Broadway trash baskets (or, as he still called them, dustbins). She wasn't old, not bad looking, not even too badly dressed, item by item. The full effect would have been no worse than vulgar if she had not been obviously a nut. She turned up in a miniskirt of billiard-table green, revealing legs sensual in outline but without inner sensuality; at the waist a broad leather belt; over shoulders, bust, a coarse strong Guatemalan embroidered shirt; on her head a wig such as a female impersonator might put on at a convention of salesmen. Her own hair had a small curl, a minute distortion. It put her in a rage. She cried out that it was thin, she had masculine hair. Thin it evidently was, but not the other. She had it straight from Sammler's mother, a hysterical woman, certainly, and anything but masculine. But who knew how many sexual difficulties and complications were associated with Shula's hair? And, from the troubled widow's peak, following an imaginary line of illumination over the nose, originally fine but distorted by restless movement, over the ridiculous comment of the lips (swelling, painted dark red), and down between the breasts to the middle of the body—what problems there must be! Sammler kept hearing how she had taken her wig to a good hairdresser to have it set, and how the hairdresser exclaimed, please! to take the thing away, it was too cheap for him to work on! Sammler did not know whether this was an isolated incident involving one homosexual stylist, or whether it had happened on several separate occasions. He saw many open elements in his daughter. Things that ought but failed actually to connect. Wigs for instance suggested orthodoxy; Shula in fact had Jewish connections. She seemed to know lots of rabbis in famous temples and synagogues on Central Park West and on the East Side. She went to sermons and free lectures everywhere. Where she found the patience for this Sammler could not say. He could bear no lecture for more than ten minutes. But she, with loony, clever, large eyes, the face full of white comment and skin thickened with concentration, sat on her rucked-up skirt, the shopping bag with salvage, loot, coupons, and throwaway literature between her knees. Afterward she was the first to ask questions. She became well acquainted with the rabbi, the rabbi's wife and family—involved in Dadaist discussions about faith, ritual, Zionism, Masada, the Arabs. But she had Christian periods as well. Hidden in a Polish convent for four years, she had been called Slawa, and now there were times when she answered only to that name. Almost always at Easter she was Catholic. Ash Wednesday was observed, and it was with a smudge between the eyes that she often came into clear focus for the old gentleman. With the little Jewish twists of kinky hair descending from the wig beside the ears and the florid lips dark red, skeptical, accusing, affirming something substantive about her life-claim, her right to be whatever—whatever it all came to. Full of comment always, the mouth completing the premises stated from an insane angle by the merging dark eyes. Not altogether crazy, perhaps. But she would come in saying that she had been run down by mounted policemen in Central Park. They were trying to recapture a deer escaped from the zoo, and she was absorbed, reading an article in *Look*, and they knocked her over. She was, however, quite cheerful. She was far too cheerful for Sammler. At night she typed. She sang at her typewriter. She was employed by cousin Gruner, the doctor, who had this work invented for her. Gruner had saved her (it amounted to that) from her equally crazy husband, Eisen, in Israel, sending Sammler ten years ago to bring Shula-Slawa to New York.

That had been Sammler's first journey to Israel. Brief. On a family matter.

Unusually handsome, brilliant-looking, Eisen had been wounded at Stalingrad. With other mutilated veterans in

Rumania, later, he had been thrown from a moving train. Apparently because he was a Jew. Eisen had frozen his feet; his toes were amputated. "Oh, they were drunk," said Eisen in Haifa. "Good fellows—*tovarischni*. But you know what Russians are when they have a few glasses of vodka." He grinned at Sammler. Black curls, a handsome Roman nose, shining sharp senseless saliva-moist teeth. The trouble was that he kicked and beat Shula-Slawa quite often, even as a newlywed. Old Sammler in the cramped, stone-smelling, whitewashed apartment in Haifa considered the palm branches at the window in warm, clear atmosphere. Shula was cooking for them out of a Mexican cookbook, making bitter chocolate sauce, grating coconuts over chicken breasts, complaining that you could not buy chutney in Haifa. "When I was thrown out," said Eisen cheerfully, "I thought I would go and see the Pope. I took a stick and walked to Italy. The stick was my crutch, you see."

"I see."

"I went to Castel Gandolfo. The Pope was very nice to us."

After three days Mr. Sammler saw that he would have to remove his daughter.

He could not stay long in Israel. He was unwilling to spend Elya Gruner's money. But he did visit Nazareth and took a taxi to Galilee, for the historical interest of the thing, as long as he was in the vicinity. On a sandy road, he found a gaucho. Under a platter hat fastened beneath the large chin, in Argentinian bloomers tucked into boots, with a Douglas Fairbanks mustache, he was mixing feed for small creatures racing about him in a chicken-wire enclosure. Water from a hose ran clear and pleasant in the sun over the yellow meal or mash and stained it orange. The little animals though fat were lithe; they were heavy, their coats shone, opulent and dense. These were nutrias. Their fur made hats worn in cold climates. Coats for ladies. Mr. Sammler, feeling red-faced in the Galilean sunlight, interrogated this man. In his bass voice of a distinguished traveler —a cigarette held between his hairy knuckles, smoke escaping past his hairy ears—he put questions to the gaucho. Neither spoke Hebrew. Nor the language of Jesus. Mr. Sammler fell back on Italian, which the nutria breeder in Argentine gloom comprehended, his heavy handsome face considering the greedy beasts about his boots. He was Bessarabian-Syrian-

South American—a Spanish-speaking Israeli cowpuncher from the pampas.

Did he butcher the little animals himself? Sammler wished to know. His Italian had never been good. "*Uccidere?*" "*Ammazzare?*" The gaucho understood. When the time came, he killed them himself. He struck them on the head with a stick.

Didn't he mind doing this to his little flock? Hadn't he known them from infancy—was there no tenderness for individuals—were there no favorites? The gaucho denied it all. He shook his handsome head. He said that nutrias were very stupid.

"*Son muy tontos.*"

"*Arrivederci,*" said Sammler.

"*Adios. Shalom.*"

Mr. Sammler's hired car took him to Capernaum, where Jesus had preached in the synagogue. From afar, he saw the Mount of the Beatitudes. Two eyes would have been inadequate to the heaviness and smoothness of the color, parted with difficulty by fishing boats—the blue water, unusually dense, heavy, seemed sunk under the naked Syrian heights. Mr. Sammler's heart was very much torn by feelings as he stood under the short, leaf-streaming banana trees.

> And did those feet in ancient time
> Walk upon . . .

But those were England's mountains green. The mountains opposite, in serpentine nakedness, were not at all green; they were ruddy, with smoky cavities and mysteries of inhuman power flaming above them.

The many impressions and experiences of life seemed no longer to occur each in its own proper space, in sequence, each with its recognizable religious or aesthetic importance, but human beings suffered the humiliations of inconsequence, of confused styles, of a long life containing several separate lives. In fact the whole experience of mankind was now covering each separate life in its flood. Making all the ages of history simultaneous. Compelling the frail person to receive, to register, depriving him because of volume, of mass, of the power to impart design.

Well, that was Sammler's first visit to the Holy Land. A decade later, for another purpose, he went again.

Shula had returned with Sammler to America. Rescued from Eisen, who walloped her, he said, because she went to Catholic priests, because she was a liar (lies infuriated him; paranoiacs, Sammler concluded, are more passionate for pure truth than other madmen), Shula-Slawa set up housekeeping in New York. Creating, that is, a great clutter-center in the New World. Mr. Sammler, a polite Slim-Jim (the nickname Dr. Gruner had given him), a considerate father, muttering appreciation of each piece of rubbish as presented to him, was in certain moods explosive, under provocation more violent than other people. In fact, his claim for indemnity from the Bonn government was based upon damage to his nervous system as well as his eye. Fits of rage, very rare but shattering, laid him up with intense migraines, put him in a postepileptic condition. Then he lay most of a week in a dark room, rigid, hands gripped on his chest, bruised, aching, incapable of an answer when spoken to. With Shula-Slawa, he had a series of such attacks. First of all, he couldn't bear the building Gruner had put them into, with its stone stoop slumping to one side, into the cellar stairway of the Chinese laundry adjoining. The lobby made him ill, tiles like yellow teeth set in desperate grime, and the slinking elevator shaft. The bathroom where Shula kept an Easter chick from Kresge's until it turned into a hen that squawked on the edge of the tub. The Christmas decorations which lasted into spring. The rooms themselves were like those dusty red paper Christmas bells, folds within folds. The hen with yellow legs in his room on his documents and books was too much one day. He was aware that the sun shone brightly, the sky was blue, but the big swell of the apartment house, heavyweight vaselike baroque, made him feel that the twelfth-story room was like a china cabinet into which he was locked, and the satanic hen-legs of wrinkled yellow clawing his papers made him scream out.

Shula-Slawa then agreed that he should move. She told everyone that her father's lifework, his memoir of H. G. Wells, made him too tense to live with. She had H. G. Wells on the brain, the large formation of a lifetime. H. G. Wells was the most august human being she knew of. She had been a small girl when the Sammlers lived in Woburn Square, Bloomsbury, and with childish genius accurately read the passions of her parents—their pride in high connections, their snobbery, how contented they were with the cultural best of England. Old Sammler thinking of his wife in prewar Bloomsbury days interpreted a certain quiet, bosomful way she had of conveying with a downward stroke of the hand, so delicate you had to know her well to identify it as a vaunting gesture: we have the most distinguished intimacy with the finest people in Britain. A small vice—almost nutritive, digestive—which gave Antonina softer cheeks, smoother hair, deeper color. If a little social-climbing made her handsomer (plumper between the legs—the thought rushed in and Sammler had stopped trying to repel these mental rushes), it had its feminine justification. Love *is* the most potent cosmetic, but there are others. And the little girl may actually have observed that the very mention of Wells had a combined social-erotic influence on her mother. Judging not, and recalling Wells always with respect, Sammler knew that he had been a horny man of labyrinthine extraordinary sensuality. As a biologist, as a social thinker concerned with power and world projects, the molding of a universal order, as a furnisher of interpretation and opinion to the educated masses—as all of these he appeared to need a great amount of copulation. Nowadays Sammler would recall him as a little lower-class Limey, and as an aging man of declining ability and appeal. And in the agony of parting with the breasts, the mouths, and the precious sexual fluids of women, poor Wells, the natural teacher, the sex emancipator, the explainer, the humane blesser of mankind, could in the end only blast and curse everyone. Of course he wrote such things in his final sickness, horribly depressed by World War II.

What Shula-Slawa said came back amusingly to Sammler through Angela Gruner. Shula visited Angela in the East Sixties, where her cousin had the beautiful, free, and wealthy young woman's ideal New York apartment. Shula admired this. Apparently without envy, without self-consciousness, Shula with wig and shopping bag, her white face puckering with continual inspiration (receiving and transmitting wild messages), sat as awkwardly as possible in the super comfort of

Angela's upholstery, blobbing china and forks with lipstick. In Shula's version of things her father had had conversations with H. G. Wells lasting several years. He took his notes to Poland in 1939, expecting to have spare time for the memoir. Just then the country exploded. In the geyser that rose a mile or two into the skies were Papa's notes. But (with *his* memory!) he knew it all by heart, and all you had to do was ask what Wells had said to him about Lenin, Stalin, Mussolini, Hitler, world peace, atomic energy, the open conspiracy, the colonization of the planets. Whole passages came back to Papa. He had to concentrate of course. Thus she turned about his moving in with Margotte until it became her idea. He had moved away to concentrate better. He said he didn't have much time left. But obviously he exaggerated. He looked so well. He was such a handsome person. Elderly widows were always asking her about him. The mother of Rabbi Ipsheimer. The grandmother of Ipsheimer, more likely. Anyway (Angela still reporting), Wells had communicated things to Sammler that the world didn't know. When finally published they would astonish everybody. The book would take the form of dialogues like those with A. N. Whitehead which Sammler admired so much.

Low-voiced, husky, a hint of joking brass in her tone, Angela (*just* this side of coarseness, a beautiful woman) said, "Her Wells routine is *so* great. Were you that close to H. G., Uncle?"

"We were well acquainted."

"But chums? Were you bosom buddies?"

"Oh? My dear girl, in spite of my years, I am a man of the modern age. You do not find David and Jonathan, Roland and Olivier bosom buddies in these days. The man's company was very pleasant. He seemed also to enjoy conversation with me. As for his views, he was just a mass of intelligent views. He expressed as many as he could, and at all times. Everything he said I found eventually in written form. He was like Voltaire, a graphomaniac. His mind was unusually active, he thought he should explain everything, and he actually said some things very well. Like 'Science is the mind of the race.' That's true, you know. It's a better thing to emphasize than other collective facts, like disease or sin. And when I see the wing of a jet plane I don't only see metal, but metal tempered by the agreement of many minds which know the pressure and velocity and weight, calculating on their slide rules whether they are Hindus or Chinamen or from the Congo or Brazil. Yes, on the whole he was a sensible intelligent person, certainly on the right side of many questions."

"And you used to be interested."

"Yes, I used to be interested."

"But she says you're composing that great work a mile a minute."

She laughed. Not merely laughed, but laughed brilliantly. In Angela you confronted sensual womanhood without remission. You smelled it, too. She wore the odd stylish things which Sammler noted with detached and purified dryness, as if from a different part of the universe. What were those, white-kid buskins? What were those tights—sheer, opaque? Where did they lead? That effect of the hair called frosting, that color under the lioness's muzzle, that swagger to enhance the natural power of the bust! Her plastic coat inspired by cubists or Mondrians, geometrical black and white forms; her trousers by Courrèges and Pucci. Sammler followed these jet phenomena in the *Times*, and in the women's magazines sent by Angela herself. Not too closely. He did not read too much of this. Careful to guard his eyesight, he passed pages rapidly back and forth before his eye, the large forehead registering the stimulus to his mind. The damaged left eye seemed to turn in another direction, to be preoccupied separately with different matters. Thus Sammler knew, through many rapid changes, Warhol, Baby Jane Holzer while she lasted, the Living Theater, the outbursts of nude display more and more revolutionary, Dionysus '69, copulation on the stage, the philosophy of the Beatles; and in the art world, electric shows and minimal painting. Angela was in her thirties now, independently wealthy, with ruddy skin, gold-whitish hair, big lips. She was afraid of obesity. She either fasted or ate like a stevedore. She trained in a fashionable gym. He knew her problems—he had to know, for she came and discussed them in detail. She did not know *his* problems. He seldom talked and she seldom asked. Moreover, he and Shula were her father's pensioners, dependents—call it what you like. So after psychiatric sessions, Angela came to Uncle Sammler to hold a seminar and analyze the preceding hour. Thus the old man knew what she did and with whom and how it felt. All that she knew how to say he had to hear. He could not choose but.

Sammler in his *Gymnasium* days once translated from Saint Augustine: "The Devil hath established his cities in the North." He thought of this often. In Cracow before World War I he had had another version of it—desperate darkness, the dreary liquid yellow mud to a depth of two inches over cobblestones in the Jewish streets. People needed their candles, their lamps and their copper kettles, their slices of lemon in the image of the sun. This was the conquest of grimness with the aid always of Mediterranean symbols. Dark environments overcome by imported religious signs and local domestic amenities. Without the power of the North, its mines, its industries, the world would never have reached its astonishing modern form. And regardless of Augustine, Sammler had always loved his Northern cities, especially London, the blessings of its gloom, of coal smoke, gray rains, and the mental and human opportunities of a dark muffled environment. There one came to terms with obscurity, with low tones, one did not demand full clarity of mind or motive. But now Augustine's odd statement required a new interpretation. Listening to Angela carefully, Sammler perceived different developments. The labor of Puritanism now was ending. The dark satanic mills changing into light satanic mills. The reprobates converted into children of joy, the sexual ways of the seraglio and of the Congo bush adopted by the emancipated masses of New York, Amsterdam, London. Old Sammler with his screwy visions! He saw the increasing triumph of Enlightenment—Liberty, Fraternity, Equality, Adultery! Enlightenment, universal education, universal suffrage, the rights of the majority acknowledged by all governments, the rights of women, the rights of children, the rights of criminals, the unity of the different races affirmed, Social Security, public health, the dignity of the person, the right to justice—the struggles of three revolutionary centuries being won while the feudal bonds of Church and Family weakened and the privileges of aristocracy (without any duties) spread wide, democratized, especially the libidinous privileges, the right to be uninhibited, spontaneous, urinating, defecating, belching, coupling in all positions, tripling, quadrupling, polymorphous, noble in being natural, primitive, combining the leisure and luxurious inventiveness of Versailles with the hibiscus-covered erotic ease of Samoa. Dark romanticism now took hold. As old at least as the strange Orientalism of the Knights Templar, and since then filled up with Lady Stanhopes, Baudelaires, de Nervals, Stevensons, and Gauguins—those South-loving barbarians. Oh yes, the Templars. They had adored the Muslims. One hair from the head of a Saracen was more precious than the whole body of a Christian. Such crazy fervor! And now all the racism, all the strange erotic persuasions, the tourism and local color, the exotics of it had broken up but the mental masses, inheriting everything in a debased state, had formed an idea of the corrupting disease of being white and of the healing power of black. The dreams of nineteenth-century poets polluted the psychic atmosphere of the great boroughs and suburbs of New York. Add to this the dangerous lunging, staggering crazy violence of fanatics, and the trouble was very deep. Like many people who had seen the world collapse once, Mr. Sammler entertained the possibility it might collapse twice. He did not agree with refugee friends that this doom was inevitable, but liberal beliefs did not seem capable of self-defense, and you could smell decay. You could see the suicidal impulses of civilization pushing strongly. You wondered whether this Western culture could survive universal dissemination—whether only its science and technology on administrative practices would travel, be adopted by other societies. Or whether the worst enemies of civilization might not prove to be its petted intellectuals who attacked it at its weakest moments—attacked it in the name of proletarian revolution, in the name of reason, and in the name of irrationality, in the name of visceral depth, in the name of sex, in the name of perfect instantaneous freedom. For what it amounted to was limitless demand—insatiability, refusal of the doomed creature (death being sure and final) to go away from this earth unsatisfied. A full bill of demand and complaint was therefore presented by each individual. Non-negotiable. Recognizing no scarcity of supply in any human department. Enlightenment? Marvelous! But out of hand, wasn't it?

Sammler saw this in Shula-Slawa. She came to do his room. He had to sit in his beret and coat, for she needed fresh air.

She arrived with cleaning materials in the shopping bag—ammonia, shelf paper, Windex, floor wax, rags. She sat out on the sill to wash the windows, lowering the sash to her thighs. Her little shoe soles were inside the room. On her lips—a burst of crimson asymmetrical skeptical fleshy business-and-dream sensuality—the cigarette scorching away at the tip. There was the wig, too, mixed yak and baboon hair and synthetic fibers. Shula, like all the ladies perhaps, was needy—needed gratification of numerous instincts, needed the warmth and pressure of men, needed a child for sucking and nurture, needed female emancipation, needed the exercise of the mind, needed continuity, needed interest—*interest!*—needed flattery, needed triumph, power, needed rabbis, needed priests, needed fuel for all that was perverse and crazy, needed noble action of the intellect, needed culture, demanded the sublime. No scarcity was acknowledged. If you tried to deal with all these immediate needs you were a lost man. Even to consider it all the way she did, spraying cold froth on the panes, swabbing it away, left-handed with a leftward swing of the bust (*ohne Büstenhalter*), was neither affection for her, nor preservation for her father. When she arrived and opened windows and doors the personal atmosphere Mr. Sammler had accumulated and stored blew away, it seemed. His back door opened to the service staircase, where a hot smell of incineration rushed from the chute, charred paper, chicken entrails, and burnt feathers. The Puerto Rican sweepers carried transistors playing Latin music. As if supplied with this jazz from a universal unfailing source, like cosmic rays.

"Well, Father, how is it going?"

"What is going?"

"The work. H. G. Wells?"

"As usual."

"People take up too much of your time. You don't get enough reading done. I know you have to protect your eyesight. But is it going all right?"

"Tremendous."

"I wish you wouldn't make jokes about it."

"Why, is it too important for jokes?"

"Well, it is important."

Yes. O.K. He was sipping his morning coffee. Today, this

very afternoon, he was going to speak at Columbia University. One of his young Columbia friends had persuaded him. Also, he must call up about his nephew. Dr. Gruner. It seemed the doctor himself was in the hospital. Had had, so Sammler was told, minor surgery. Cutting in the neck. One could do without that seminar today. It was a mistake. Could he back out, beg off? No, probably not.

Shula had hired university students to read to him, to spare his eyes. She herself had tried it, but her voice made him nod off. Half an hour of her reading, and the blood left his brain. She told Angela that her father tried to fence her out of his higher activities. As if they had to be protected from the very person who believed most in them! It was a very sad paradox. But for four or five years she had found student-readers. Some had graduated, now were in professions or business but still came back to visit Sammler. "He is like their guru," said Shula-Slawa. More recent readers were student activists. Mr. Sammler was quite interested in the radical movement. To judge by their reading ability, the young people had had a meager education. Their presence sometimes induced (or deepened) a long, still smile which had the effect more than anything else of blindness. Hairy, dirty, without style, levelers, ignorant. He found after they had read to him for a few hours that he had to teach them the subject, explain the terms, do etymologies for them as though they were twelve-year-olds. "*Janua*—a door. Janitor—one who minds the door." "*Lapis*, a stone. Dilapidate, take apart the stones. One cannot say it of a person." But if one could, one would say it of these young persons. Some of the poor girls had a bad smell. Bohemian protest did them the most harm. It was elementary among the tasks and problems of civilization, thought Mr. Sammler, that some parts of nature demanded more control than others. Females were naturally more prone to grossness, had more smells, needed more washing, clipping, binding, pruning, grooming, perfuming, and training. These poor kids may have resolved to stink together in defiance of a corrupt tradition built on neurosis and falsehood, but Mr. Sammler thought that an unforeseen result of their way of life was loss of femininity, of self-esteem. In their revulsion from authority they would respect no persons. Not even their own persons.

Anyhow, he no longer wanted these readers with the big dirty boots and the helpless vital pathos of young dogs with their first red erections, and pimples sprung to the cheeks from foaming beards, laboring in his room with hard words and thoughts that had to be explained, stumbling through Toynbee, Freud, Burckhardt, Spengler. For he had been reading historians of civilization—Karl Marx, Max Weber, Max Scheler, Franz Oppenheimer. Side excursions into Adorno, Marcuse, Norman O. Brown, whom he found to be worthless fellows. Together with these he took on *Doktor Faustus, Les Noyers d'Altenbourg*, Ortega, Valéry's essays on history and politics. But after four or five years of this diet, he wished to read only certain religious writers of the thirteenth century—Suso, Tauler, and Meister Eckhardt. In his seventies he was interested in little more than Meister Eckhardt and the Bible. For this he needed no readers. He read Eckhardt's Latin at the public library from microfilm. He read the Sermons and the Talks of Instruction—a few sentences at a time—a paragraph of Old German—presented to his good eye at close range. While Margotte ran the carpet sweeper through the rooms. Evidently getting most of the lint on her skirts. And singing. She loved Schubert lieder. Why she had to mingle them with the zoom of the vacuum eluded his powers of explanation. But then he could not explain a liking for certain combinations: for instance, sandwiches of sturgeon, Swiss cheese, tongue, steak tartare, and Russian dressing in layers—such things as one saw on fancy delicatessen menus. Yet customers seemed to order them. No matter where you picked it up, humankind, knotted and tangled, supplied more oddities than you could keep up with.

A combined oddity, for instance, which drew him today into the middle of things: One of his ex-readers, young Lionel Feffer, had asked him to address a seminar at Columbia University on the British Scene in the Thirties. For some reason this attracted Sammler. He was fond of Feffer. An ingenious operator, less student than promoter. With his florid color, brown beaver beard, long black eyes, big belly, smooth hair, pink awkward large hands, loud interrupting voice, hasty energy, he was charming to Sammler. Not trustworthy. Only charming. That is, it sometimes gave Sammler great pleasure to see Lionel

Feffer working out in his peculiar manner, to hear the fizzing of his vital gas, his fuel.

Sammler didn't know what seminar this was. Not always attentive, he failed to understand clearly; perhaps there was nothing clear to understand; but it seemed that he had promised, although he couldn't remember promising. But Feffer confused him. There were so many projects, such cross references, so many confidences and requests for secrecy, so many scandals, frauds, spiritual communications—a continual flow backward, forward, lateral, above, below; like any page of Joyce's *Ulysses*, always *in medias res*. Anyway, Sammler had apparently agreed to give this talk for a student project to help backward black pupils with their reading problems.

"You must come and talk to these fellows, it's of the utmost importance. They have never heard a point of view like yours," said Feffer. The pink oxford-cloth shirt increased the color of his face. The beard, the straight large sensual nose made him look like François Premier. A bustling, affectionate, urgent, eruptive, enterprising character. He had money in the stock market. He was vice-president of a Guatemalan insurance company covering railroad workers. His field at the university was diplomatic history. He belonged to a corresponding society called the Foreign Ministers' Club. Its members took up a question like the Crimean War or the Boxer Rebellion and did it all again, writing one another letters as the foreign ministers of France, England, Germany, Russia. They obtained very different results. In addition Feffer was a busy seducer, especially, it seemed, of young wives. But he found time as well to hustle on behalf of handicapped children. He got them free toys and signed photographs of hockey stars; he found time to visit them in the hospital. He "found time." To Sammler this was a highly significant American fact. Feffer led a high-energy American life to the point of anarchy and breakdown. And yet devotedly. And of course he was in psychiatric treatment. They all were. They could always say that they were sick. Nothing was omitted.

"The British Scene in the Thirties—you must. For my seminar."

"*That* old stuff?"

"Exactly. Just what we need."

"Bloomsbury? All of that? But why? And for whom?"

Feffer called for Sammler in a taxi. They went uptown in style. Feffer stressed the style of it. He said the driver must wait while Sammler gave his talk. The driver, a Negro, refused. Feffer raised his voice. He said this was a legal matter. Sammler persuaded him to drop it as he was about to call the police. "There is no need to have a taxi waiting for me," said Sammler.

"Go get lost then," said Feffer to the cabbie. "And no tip."

"Don't abuse him," Sammler said.

"I won't make any distinction because he's black," said Lionel. "I hear from Margotte that you've been running into a black pickpocket, by the way."

"Where do we go, Lionel? Now that I'm about to speak, I have misgivings. I feel unclear. What, really, am I supposed to say? The topic is so vast."

"You know it better than anyone."

"I know it, yes. But I am uneasy—somewhat shaky."

"You'll be great."

Then Feffer led him into a large room. He had expected a small one, a seminar room. He had come to reminisce, for a handful of interested students, about R. H. Tawney, Harold Laski, John Strachey, George Orwell, H. G. Wells. But this was a mass meeting of some sort. His obstructed vision took in a large, spreading, shaggy, composite human bloom. It was malodorous, peculiarly rancid, sulphurous. The amphitheater was filled. Standing room only. Was Feffer running one of his rackets? Was he going to pocket the admission money? Sammler mastered and dismissed this suspicion, ascribing it to surprise and nervousness. For he was surprised, frightened. But he pulled himself together. He tried to begin humorously by recalling the lecturer who had addressed incurable alcoholics under the impression that they were the Browning Society. But there was no laughter, and he had to remember that Browning Societies had been extinct for a long time. A microphone was hung on his chest. He began to speak of the mental atmosphere of England before the Second World War. The Mussolini adventure in East Africa. Spain in 1936. The Great Purges in Russia. Stalinism in France and Britain. Blum, Daladier, the Peoples' Front, Oswald Mosley. The mood of English intellectuals. For this he needed no notes, he could easily recall what people had said or written.

"I assume," he said, "you are acquainted with the background, the events of nineteen seventeen. You know of the mutinous armies, the February Revolution in Russia, the disasters that befell authority. In all European countries the old leaders were discredited by Verdun, Flanders Field, and Tannenberg. Perhaps I could begin with the fall of Kerensky. Maybe with Brest-Litovsk."

Doubly foreign, Polish-Oxonian, with his outrushing white back hair, the wrinkles streaming below the smoked glasses, he pulled the handkerchief from the breast pocket, unfolded and refolded it, touched his face, wiped his palms with thin elderly delicacy. Without pleasure in performance, without the encouragement of attention (there was a good deal of noise), the little satisfaction he did feel was the meager ghost of the pride he and his wife had once taken in their British successes. In his success, a Polish Jew so well acquainted, so handsomely acknowledged by the nobs, by H. G. Wells. Included, for instance, with Gerald Heard and Olaf Stapledon in the *Cosmopolis* project for a World State, Sammler had written articles for *News of Progress*, for the other publication, *The World Citizen*. As he explained in a voice that still contained Polish sibilants and nasals, though impressively low, the project was based on the propagation of the sciences of biology, history, and sociology and the effective application of scientific principles to the enlargement of human life; the building of a planned, orderly, and beautiful world society: abolishing natonal sovereignty, outlawing war; subjecting money and credit, production, distribution, transport, population, arms manufacture et cetera to world-wide collective control, offering free universal education, personal freedom (compatible with community welfare) to the utmost degree; a service society based on a rational scientific attitude toward life. Sammler, with growing interest and confidence recalling all this, lectured on *Cosmopolis* for half an hour, feeling what a kindhearted, ingenuous, stupid scheme it had been. Telling this into the lighted restless hole of the amphitheater with the soiled dome and caged electric fixtures, until he was interrupted by a clear loud voice. He was being questioned. He was being shouted at.

"Hey!"

He tried to continue. "Such attempts to draw intellectuals away from Marxism met with small success. . . ."

A man in Levi's, thick-bearded but possibly young, a figure of compact distortion, was standing shouting at him.

"Hey! Old Man!"

In the silence, Mr. Sammler drew down his tinted spectacles, seeing this person with his effective eye.

"Old Man! You quoted Orwell before."

"Yes?"

"You quoted him to say that British radicals were all protected by the Royal Navy? Did Orwell say that British radicals were protected by the Royal Navy?"

"Yes, I believe he did say that."

"That's a lot of shit."

Sammler could not speak.

"Orwell was a fink. He was a sick counterrevolutionary. It's good he died when he did. And what you are saying is shit." Turning to the audience, extending violent arms and raising his palms like a Greek dancer, he said, "Why do you listen to this effete old shit? What has he got to tell you? His balls are dry. He's dead. He can't come."

Sammler later thought that voices had been raised on his side. Someone had said, "Shame. Exhibitionist."

But no one really tried to defend him. Most of the young people seemed to be against him. The shouting sounded hostile. Feffer was gone, had been called away to the telephone. Sammler, turning from the lectern, found his umbrella, trench coat, and hat behind him and left the platform, guided by a young girl who had rushed up to express indignation and sympathy, saying it was a scandal to break up such a good lecture. She showed him through a door, down several stairs, and he was on Broadway at One hundred-sixteenth Street.

Abruptly out of the university.

Back in the city.

And he was not so much personally offended by the event as struck by the will to offend. What a passion to be *real.* But *real* was also brutal. And the acceptance of excrement as a standard? How extraordinary! Youth? Together with the idea of sexual potency? All this confused sex-excrement-militancy, explosiveness, abusiveness, tooth-showing, Barbary ape howling. Or like the spider monkeys in the trees, as Sammler once had read, defecating into their hands, and shrieking, pelting the explorers below.

He was not sorry to have met the facts, however saddening, regrettable the facts. But the effect was that Mr. Sammler did feel somewhat separated from the rest of his species, if not in some fashion severed—severed not so much by age as by preoccupations too different and remote, disproportionate on the side of the spiritual, Platonic, Augustinian, thirteenth-century. As the traffic poured, the wind poured, and the sun, relatively bright for Manhattan—shining and pouring through openings in his substance, through his gaps. As if he had been cast by Henry Moore. With holes, lacunae. Again, as after seeing the pickpocket, he was obliged to events for a difference, an intensification of vision. A delivery man with a floral cross filling both arms, a bald head dented, seemed to be drunk, fighting the wind, tacking. His dull boots small, and his short wide pants blowing like a woman's skirts. Gardenias, camellias, calla lilies, sailing above him under light transparent plastic. Or at the Riverside bus stop Mr. Sammler noted the proximity of a waiting student, used his eye-power to observe that he wore wide-wale corduroy pants of urinous green, a tweed coat of a carrot color with burls of blue wool; that sideburns stood like powerful bushy pillars to the head; that civilized tortoise-shell shafts intersected these; that he had hair thinning at the front; a Jew nose, a heavy all-savoring, all-rejecting lip. Oh, this was an artistic diversion of the streets for Mr. Sammler when he was roused to it by some shock. He was studious, he was bookish, and had been trained by the best writers to divert himself with perceptions. When he went out, life was not empty. Meanwhile the purposive, aggressive, business-bent, conative people did as mankind normally did. If the majority walked about as if under a spell, sleepwalkers, circumscribed by, in the grip of, minor neurotic trifling aims, individuals like Sammler were only one stage forward, awakened not to purpose but to aesthetic consumption of the environment. Even if insulted, pained, somewhere bleeding, not broadly expressing any anger, not crying out with sadness, but translating heartache into delicate, even piercing observation. Particles in the bright wind, flinging downtown, acted like emery on the face. The sun shone as if there were no death. For a full minute, while the bus approached, squirting air, it was like that. Then Mr. Sammler got on, moving like a good citizen toward the rear, hoping he would not be pushed past the back door, for he had only fifteen blocks to go, and there was a thick crowd. The usual smell of long-seated bottoms, of sour shoes, of tobacco muck, of stogies, cologne, face powder. And yet along the river, early spring, the first khaki—a few weeks of sun, of heat, and Manhattan would (briefly) join the North American continent in a day of old-time green, the plush luxury, the polish of the season, shining, nitid, the dogwood white, pink, blooming crabapple. Then people's feet would swell with the warmth, and at Rockefeller Center strollers would sit on the polished stone slabs beside the planted tulips and tritons and the water, all in a spirit of pregnancy. Human creatures under the warm shadows of skyscrapers feeling the heavy pleasure of their nature, and yielding. Sammler too would enjoy spring—one of those penultimate springs. Of course he was upset. Very. Of course all that stuff about Brest-Litovsk, all that old news about revolutionary intellectuals versus the German brass was in this context downright funny. Inconsequent. Of course those students were comical, too. And what was the worst of it (apart from the rudeness)? There were appropriate ways of putting down an old bore. He might well be, especially in a public manifestation, lecturing on *Cosmopolis*, an old bore. The worst of it, from the point of view of the young people themselves, was that they acted without dignity. They had no view of the nobility of being intellectuals and judges of the social order. What a pity! old Sammler thought. A human being, valuing himself for the right reasons, has and restores order, authority. When the internal parts are in order. They must be in order. But what was it to be arrested in the stage of toilet training! What was it to be entrapped by a psychiatric standard (Sammler blamed the Germans and their psychoanalysis for this)! Who had raised the diaper flag? Who had made shit a sacrament? What literary and psychological movement was that? Mr. Sammler, with bitter angry mind, held the top rail of his jammed bus, riding downtown, a short journey.

He certainly had no thought of his black pickpocket. Him

he connected with Columbus Circle. He always went uptown, not down. But at the rear, in his camel's-hair coat, filling up a corner with his huge body, he was standing. Sammler against strong internal resistance saw him. He resisted because at this swaying difficult moment he had no wish to see him. Lord! not now! Inside, Sammler felt an immediate descent; his heart sinking. As sure as fate, as a law of nature, a stone falling, a gas rising. He knew the thief did not ride the bus for transportation. To meet a woman, to go home—however he diverted himself—he unquestionably took cabs. He could afford them. But now Mr. Sammler was looking down at his shoulder, the tallest man in the bus, except for the thief himself. He saw that in the long rear seat he had cornered someone. Powerfully bent, the wide back concealed the victim from the other passengers. Only Sammler, because of his height, could see. Nothing to be grateful to height or vision for. The cornered man was old, was weak; poor eyes, watering with terror; white lashes, red lids, and a sea-mucus blue, his eyes, the mouth open with false teeth dropping from the upper gums. Coat and jacket were open also, the shirt pulled forward like detached green wallpaper, and the lining of the jacket ragged. The thief tugged his clothes like a doctor with a clinic patient. Pushing aside tie and scarf, he took out the wallet. His own homburg he then eased back (an animal movement, simply) slightly from his forehead, furrowed but not with anxiety. The wallet was long—leatherette, plastic. Open, it yielded a few dollar bills. There were cards. The thief put them in his palm. Read them with a tilted head. Let them drop. Examined a green federal-looking check, probably Social Security. Mr. Sammler in his goggles was troubled in focusing. Too much adrenalin was passing with light, thin, frightening rapidity through his heart. He himself was not frightened, but his heart seemed to record fear, it had a seizure. He recognized it—knew what name to apply: tachycardia. Breathing was hard. He could not fetch in enough air. He wondered whether he might not faint away. Whether worse might not happen. The check the black man put into his own pocket. Snapshots like the cards fell from his fingers. Finished, he then dropped the wallet back into the gray, worn, shattered lining, flipped back the old man's muffler. In ironic calm, thumb and forefinger took the knot of the necktie and yanked it approximately, but only approximately, into place. It was at this moment that, in a quick turn of the head, he saw Mr. Sammler. Mr. Sammler seen seeing was still in rapid currents with his heart. Like an escaping creature racing away from him. His throat ached, up to the root of the tongue. There was a pang in the bad eye. But he had some presence of mind. Gripping the overhead chrome rail, he stooped forward as if to see what street was coming up. Ninety-sixth. In other words, he avoided a gaze that might be held, or any interlocking of looks. He acknowledged nothing, and now began to work his way toward the rear exit, gently urgent, stooping doorward. He reached, found the cord, pulled, made it to the step, squeezed through the door, and stood on the sidewalk holding the umbrella by the fabric, at the button.

The tachycardia now running itself out, he was able to walk, though not at the usual rate. His stratagem was to cross Riverside Drive and enter the first building, as if he lived there. He had beaten the pickpocket to the door. Maybe effrontery would dismiss him as too negligible to pursue. The man did not seem to feel threatened by anyone. Took the slackness, the cowardice of the world for granted. Sammler, with effort, opened a big glass black-grilled door and found himself in an empty lobby. Avoiding the elevator, he located the staircase, trudged the first flight, and sat down on the landing. A few minutes of rest, and he recovered his oxygen level, although something within felt attenuated. Simply thinned out. Before returning to the street (there was no rear exit), he took the umbrella inside the coat, hooking it in the armhole and belting it up, more or less securely. He also made an effort to change the shape of his hat, punching it out. He went past West End to Broadway, entering the first hamburger joint, sitting in the rear, and ordering tea. He drank to the bottom of the heavy cup, to the tannic taste, squeezing the sopping bag and asking the counterman for more water, feeling parched. Through the window his thief did not appear. By now Sammler's greatest need was for his bed. But he knew something about lying low. He had learned in Poland, in the war, in forests, cellars, passageways, cemeteries. Things he had passed through once which had abolished a certain margin or leeway ordinarily taken for granted. Taking for granted that one will not be shot stepping into the street, nor clubbed to death as one stoops to relieve oneself, nor hunted in an alley like a rat. This civil margin once removed, Mr. Sammler would never trust the restoration totally. He had had little occasion to practice the arts of hiding and escape in New York. But now, although his bones ached for the bed and his skull was famished for the pillow, he sat at the counter with his tea. He could not use buses any more. From now on it was the subway. The subway was an abomination.

But Mr. Sammler had not shaken the pickpocket. The man obviously could move fast. He might have forced his way out of the bus in midblock and sprinted back, heavy but swift in homburg and camel's-hair coat. Much more likely, the thief had observed him earlier, had once before shadowed him, had followed him home. Yes, that must have been the case. For when Mr. Sammler entered the lobby of his building the man came up behind him quickly, and not simply behind but pressing him bodily, belly to back. He did not lift his hands to Sammler but pushed. There was no building employee. The doormen, also running the elevator, spent much of their time in the cellar.

"What is the matter? What do you want?" said Mr. Sammler.

He was never to hear the black man's voice. He no more spoke than a puma would. What he did was to force Sammler into a corner beside the long blackish carved table, a sort of Renaissance piece, a thing which added to the lobby melancholy, by the buckling canvas of the old wall, by the red-eyed lights of the brass double fixture. There the man held Sammler against the wall with his forearm. The umbrella fell to the floor with a sharp crack of the ferrule on the tile. It was ignored. The pickpocket unbuttoned himself. Sammler heard the zipper descend. Then the smoked glasses were removed from Sammler's face and dropped on the table. He was directed, silently, to look downward. The black man had opened his fly and taken out his penis. It was displayed to Sammler with great oval testicles, a large tan-and-purple uncircumcised thing—a tube, a snake; metallic hairs bristled at the thick base and the tip curled beyond the supporting, demonstrating hand, suggesting the fleshly mobility of an elephant's trunk, though the skin was somewhat iridescent rather than thick or rough. Over the forearm and fist that held him Sammler was required to gaze at this organ. No compulsion would have been necessary. He would in any case have looked.

The interval was long. The man's expression was not directly menacing but oddly, serenely masterful. The thing was shown with mystifying certitude. Lordliness. Then it was returned to the trousers. *Quod erat demonstrandum.* Sammler was released. The fly was closed, the coat buttoned, the marvelous streaming silk salmon necktie smoothed with a powerful hand on the powerful chest. The black eyes with a light of super candor moved softly, concluding the session, the lesson, the warning, the encounter, the transmission. He picked up Sammler's dark glasses and returned them to his nose. He then unfolded and mounted his own, circular, of gentian violet gently banded with the lovely Dior gold.

Then he departed. The elevator, with a bump, returning from the cellar opened simultaneously with the street door. Retrieving the fallen umbrella, lamely stooping, Sammler rode up. The doorman offered no small talk. For this sad unsociability one was grateful. Better yet, he didn't bump into Margotte. Best of all, he dropped and stretched on his bed, just as he was, with smarting feet, thin respiration, pain at the heart, stunned mind and—oh!—a temporary blankness of spirit. Like the television screen in the lobby, white and gray, buzzing without image. Between head and pillow, a hard rectangle was interposed, the marbled cardboard of a notebook, sea-green. A slip of paper was attached with Scotch tape. Drawing it into light, passing it near the eye, and with lips spelling mutely, bitterly, he forced himself to read the separate letters. The note was from S (either Shula or Slawa).

"Daddy: These lectures on the moon by Doctor V. Govinda Lal are on short loan. They connect with the Memoir." Wells of course, writing on the moon circa 1900. "This is the very latest. Fascinating. Daddy—you have to read it. A must! Eyes or no eyes. And soon, please! as Doctor Lal is guest-lecturing up at Columbia. He needs it back." Frowning terribly, patience, forbearance all gone, he was filled with revulsion at his daughter's single-minded, persistent, prosecuting, horrible-comical obsession. He drew a long, lung-racking, body-straightening breath.

Then, bending open the notebook, he read, in sepia, in rust-gilt ink, *The Future of the Moon*. "How long," went the first sentence, "will this earth remain the only home of Man?"

How long? Oh, Lord, you bet! Wasn't it the time—the very hour to go? For every purpose under heaven. A time to gather stones together, a time to cast away stones. Considering the earth itself not as a stone cast but as something to cast oneself from—to be divested of. To blow this great blue, white, green planet, or to be blown from it.

II

THE mean radius of the moon, 1737 kilometers; that of the earth, 6371 kilometers. The moon's gravity, 161 cm./sec.^{2}; the earth's, 981 cm./sec.^{2}. Faults and crevices in the lunar bedrock and mountains caused by extremes of temperature. Of course there is no wind. Five billion windless years. Except for solar wind. Stone crumbles but without the usual erosion. The split rock is slow to fall, the gravitational force being lower and the angle of fall correspondingly sharper. Moreover, in the moon's vacuum stones, sand, dust, or explorers' bodies would all have the same rate of fall, so before attempting to climb, it is essential to study the avalanche perils from all sides. Information organs are rapidly developing. Mass spectrometers. Solar batteries. Electricity produced by radioactive isotopes, strontium 90, polonium 210, by thermoelectric energy conversion. Dr. Lal had thoroughly considered telemetry, data transmission. Had he neglected anything? Supplies could be put in orbit and brought down as needed by a braking system. The computers would have to be exceedingly accurate. If you needed a ton of dynamite at point X, you didn't want to bring it down 800 kilometers away. And what if it were essential oxygen? And because of the greater curvature of the moon's surface the horizons are shorter and present apparatus cannot send order signals beyond the horizon. Even more precise coordination will be necessary. For the good of the moon personnel, to increase their inventiveness, and simply as a desirable stimulus to the mind, Dr. Lal recommended the brewing of beer in the pioneer colonies. For beer oxygen is necessary, for oxygen gardens, for gardens hothouses. A brief chapter was devoted to the selection of lunar flora. Well, tough members of the plant kingdom lived in Margotte's parlor. Open two doors, and there they were: potato vines, avocados, rubber plants. Dr. Lal had hops and sugar beets in mind.

Sammler thought, This is not the way to get out of spatial-temporal prison. Distant is still finite. Finite is still feeling through the veil, examining the naked inner reality with a gloved hand. However, one could see the advantage of getting away from here, building plastic igloos in the vacuum, dwelling in quiet colonies, necessarily austere, drinking the fossil waters, considering basic questions only. No question of it. Shula-Slawa had brought him this time a document worth his attention. She was always culling idiotic titles on Fourth Avenue, from sidewalk bins, books with bleached spines and rain spots—England in the twenties and thirties, Bloomsbury, Downing Street, Clare Sheridan. His shelves were stacked with eight-for-a-dollar rubbish bargains hauled in splitting shopping bags. And even the books he himself had bought were largely superfluous. After you had expended great effort on serious writers you found out little you hadn't known already. So many false starts, blind alleys, postulates which decayed before the end of the argument. Even the ablest thinkers groping as they approached their limits, running out of evidence, running out of certainties. But whether they were optimists or pessimists, whether the final vision was dark or bright, it was generally *terra cognita* to old Sammler. So Dr. Lal had a certain value. He brought news. Of course it should be possible still to follow truth on the inward track, without elaborate preparations, computers, telemetry, all the technological expertise and investment and complex organization required for visiting Mars, Venus, the moon. Nevertheless, it was perhaps for the same human activities that had shut us up like this to let us out again. The powers that had made the earth too small could free us from confinement. By the homeopathic principle. Continuing to the end the course of the Puritan revolution which had forced itself onto the material world, given all power to material processes, translated and exhausted religious feeling in so doing. Or, in the crushing summary of Max Weber, known by heart to Sammler, "Specialists without spirit, sensualists without heart, this nullity imagines that it has attained a level of civilization never before achieved." So conceivably there was no alternative but to push further in the same direction, to wait for a neglected force, left in the rear, to fly forward again and recover ascendancy. Perhaps by a growing agreement among the best minds, not unlike the Open Conspiracy of H. G. Wells. Maybe the old boy (Sammler, himself an old boy, considering this) was right after all.

But he laid aside the sea-textured cardboard notebook, the

gilt-ink sentences of V. Govinda Lal written in formal Edwardian pedantic Hindu English to go back—under mental compulsion, in fact—to the pickpocket and the thing he had shown him. What had *that* been about? It had given a shock. Shocks stimulated consciousness. Up to a point, true enough. But what was the object of displaying the genitalia? *Qu'est-ce que cela preuve?* Was it a French mathematician who had asked this after seeing a tragedy of Racine? To the best of Mr. Sammler's recollection. Not that he liked playing the old European culture game. He had had that. Still, unsummoned, sentences came to him in this way. At any rate, there was the man's organ, a huge piece of sex flesh, half-tumescent in its pride and shown in its own right, a prominent and separate object intended to communicate authority. As, within the sex ideology of these days, it well might. It was a symbol of superlegitimacy or sovereignty. It was a mystery. It was unanswerable. The whole explanation. This is the wherefore, the why. See? Oh, the transcending, ultimate, and silencing proof. We hold these things, man, to be self-evident. And yet, such sensitive elongations the anteater had, too, uncomplicated by assertions of power, even over ants. But make Nature your God, elevate creatureliness, and you can count on gross results. Maybe you can count on gross results under any circumstances.

Sammler knew a lot about such superstressed creatureliness without even wanting to know. For singular reasons he was much in demand these days, often visited, often consulted and confessed to. Perhaps it was a matter of sunspots or seasons, something barometric or even astrological. But there was always someone arriving, knocking at the door. As he was thinking of anteaters, of the fact that he had been spotted long ago and shadowed by the black man, there was a knock at his back door.

Who was it? Sammler may have sounded more testy than he felt. What he felt was rather that others had more strength for life than he. This caused secret dismay. And there was an illusion involved, for, given the power of the antagonist, no one had strength enough.

Entering was Walter Bruch, one of the family. Walter, Margotte's cousin, was related also to the Gruners.

Cousin Angela once had taken Sammler to a Rouault exhibition. Beautifully dressed, fragrant, subtly made up, she led Sammler from room to room until it seemed to him that she was a rolling hoop of marvelous gold and gem colors and that he, following her, was an old stick from which she needed only an occasional touch. But then, stopping together before a Rouault portrait, both had had the same association: Walter Bruch. It was a broad, low, heavy, ruddy, thick-featured, wool-haired, staring, bake-faced man, looking bold enough but obviously incapable of bearing his own feelings. The very man. There must be thousands of such men. But this was our Walter. In a black raincoat, in a cap, gray hair bunched before the ears; his reddish-swarthy teapot cheeks; his big mulberry-tinted lips—well, imagine the Other World; imagine souls there by the barrelful; imagine them sent to incarnation and birth with dominant qualities *ab initio.* In Bruch's case the voice would have been significant from the very first. He was a voice-man, from the soul barrels. He sang in choruses, in temple choirs. By profession he was a baritone and musicologist. He found old manuscripts and adapted or arranged them for groups performing ancient and baroque music. His own little racket, he said. He sang well. His singing voice was fine, but his speaking voice gruff, rapid, throaty. He gobbled, he quacked, grunted, swallowed syllables.

Approaching when Sammler was so preoccupied, Bruch, in his idiosyncrasy, got a very special reception. Roughly, this: Things met with in this world are tied to the forms of our perception in space and time and to the forms of our thinking. We see what is before us, the present, the objective. Eternal being makes its temporal appearance in this way. The only way out of captivity in the forms, out of confinement in the prison of projections, the only contact with the eternal, is through freedom. Sammler thought he was Kantian enough to go along with this. And he saw a man like Walter Bruch as wearing out his heart within the forms. This was what he came to Sammler about. This was what his clowning was about, for he was always clowning. Shula-Slawa would tell you how she was run down while absorbed in a *Look* article by mounted policemen pursuing an escaped deer. Bruch might very suddenly begin to sing like the blind man on Seventy-second Street, pulling along the seeing-eye dog, shaking pennies in his cup: "What a friend we have in Jesus—God bless you, sir." He also enjoyed mock funerals with Latin and music, Monteverdi, Pergolesi, the Mozart C Minor Mass; he sang "*Et incarnatus est*" in falsetto. In his early years as a refugee, he and another German Jew, employed in Macy's warehouse, used to hold Masses over each other, one lying down in a packing case with dime-store beads wound about the wrists, the other doing the service. Bruch still enjoyed this, loved playing corpse. Sammler had often enough seen it done. Together with other clown routines. Nazi mass meetings at the Sportspalast. Bruch using an empty pot for sound effects, holding it over his mouth to get the echo, ranting like Hitler and interrupting himself to cry "*Sieg Heil.*" Sammler never enjoyed this fun. It led, soon, to Bruch's Buchenwald reminiscences. All that dreadful, comical, inconsequent senseless stuff. How, suddenly, in 1937, saucepans were offered to the prisoners for sale. Hundreds of thousands, new, from the factory. Why? Bruch bought as many pans as he could. What for? Prisoners tried to sell saucepans to one another. And then a man fell into the latrine trench. No one was allowed to help him, and he was drowned there while the other prisoners were squatting helpless on the planks. Yes, suffocated in the feces!

"Very well, Walter, very well!" Sammler severely would say.

"Yes, I know, I wasn't even there for the worst part, Uncle Sammler. And you were in the middle of the whole war. But I was sitting there with diarrhea and pain. My guts! Bare *arschenloch.*"

"Very well, Walter, don't repeat so much."

Unfortunately, Bruch was obliged to repeat, and Sammler was sorry. He was annoyed and he was sorry. And with Walter, as with so many others, it was always, it was ever and again, it was still, interminably, the sex business. Bruch fell in love with women's arms. They had to be youngish, plump women. Dark as a rule. Often they were Puerto Ricans. And in the summer, above all in the summer, without coats, when women's arms were exposed. He saw them in the subway. He went along to Spanish Harlem. He pressed himself against a metal rod. Way up in Harlem, he was the only white passenger. And the whole thing—the adoration, the disgrace, the danger of swooning when he came! Here, telling this, he began to finger the hairy base of that thick throat of his. Clinical! At the same time, as a rule, he was having a highly idealistic and refined relationship with some lady. Classical! Capable of sympathy, of sacrifice, of love. Even of fidelity, in his own Cynara-Dowson fashion.

At present he was, as he said, "hung up" on the arms of a cashier in the drugstore.

"I go as often as I can."

"Ah, yes," said Sammler.

"It is madness. I have my attaché case under my arm. Very strong. First-class leather. I paid for it thirty-eight fifty at Wilt Luggage on Fifth Avenue. You see?"

"I get the picture."

"I buy something for a quarter, a dime. Gum. A package of Sight-Savers. I give a large bill—a ten, even a twenty. I go in the bank and get fresh money."

"I understand."

"Uncle Sammler, you have no idea what it is for me in that round arm. So dark! So heavy!"

"No, I probably do not."

"I put the attaché case against the counter, and I press myself. While she is making the change, I press."

"All right, Walter, spare me the rest."

"Uncle Sammler, forgive me. What can I do? For me it is the only way."

"Well, that is your business. Why tell me?"

"There is a reason. Why shouldn't I tell you? There must be a reason. Please don't stop me. Be kind."

"You should stop yourself."

"I can't."

"Are you sure?"

"I press. I have a climax. I wet myself."

Sammler raised his voice. "Can't you leave out anything?"

"Uncle Sammler, what shall I do? I am over sixty years old."

Then Bruch raised the backs of his thick short hands to his eyes. His flat nose dilated, his mouth open, he was spurting tears and, apelike, twisting his shoulders, his trunk. And with those touching gaps between his teeth. And when he wept he was not gruff. You heard the musician then.

"My whole life has been like that."

"I'm sorry, Walter."

"I am hooked."

"Well, you haven't harmed anybody. And really people take these things much less seriously than they once did. Couldn't you concentrate more on other interests, Walter? Besides, your plight is so similar to other people's, you are so contemporary, Walter, that it should do something for you. Isn't it a comfort that there is no more isolated Victorian sex suffering? Everybody seems to have these vices, and tells the whole world about them. By now you are even somewhat old-fashioned. Yes, you have an old nineteenth-century Krafft-Ebing trouble."

But Sammler stopped himself, disapproving of the light tone that was creeping into his words of comfort. But as to the past he meant what he said. The sexual perplexities of a man like Bruch originated in the repressions of another time, in images of woman and mother which were disappearing. He himself, born in the old century and in the Austro-Hungarian Empire, could discern these changes. But it also struck him as unfair to lie in bed making such observations. However, the old, the original Cracow Sammler was never especially kind. He was an only son spoiled by a mother who had herself been a spoiled daughter. An amusing recollection: When Sammler was a little boy he had covered his mouth, when he coughed, with the servant's hand, to avoid getting germs on his own hand. A family joke. The servant, grinning, red-faced, kindly, straw-haired, gummy (odd lumps in her gums) Wadja, had allowed little Sammler to borrow the hand. Then, when he was older, his mother herself, not Wadja, used to bring lean, nervous young Sammler his chocolate and croissants as he sat in his room reading Trollope and Bagehot, making an "Englishman" of himself. He and his mother had had a reputation for eccentricity, irritability in those days. Not compassionate people. Not easily pleased. Haughty. Of course all this, for Sammler, had changed considerably in the last thirty years. But then Walter Bruch with his old urchin knuckles in his eyes sat in his room and sobbed, having told on himself. And when was there nothing to tell? There was always something. Bruch told how he bought himself toys. At F. A. O. Schwarz or in antique shops he bought wind-up monkeys who combed their hair in a mirror, who banged cymbals and danced jigs, in little green jackets or red caps. Nigger minstrels had fallen in price.

He played in his room with the toys, alone. He also sent denunciatory, insulting letters to musicians. Then he came and confessed and wept. He didn't weep for display. He wept because he felt he had lost his life. Would it have been possible to tell him that he hadn't?

It was easier with a man like Bruch to transfer to broad reflections, to make comparisons, to think of history and themes of general interest. For instance, in the same line of sexual neurosis Bruch was exceeded by individuals like Freud's Rat Man, with his delirium of rats gnawing into the anus, persuaded that the genital also was ratlike, or that he himself was some sort of rat. By comparison an individual like Bruch had a light case of fetishism. If you had the comparative or historical outlook you would want only the most noteworthy, smashing instances. When you had those you could drop junk and forget the rest, which were only a burden or excess baggage. If you considered what the historical memory of mankind would retain, it would not bother to retain the Bruchs; nor, come to that, the Sammlers. Sammler didn't much mind his oblivion, not with such as would do the remembering, anyway. He thought he had found out the misanthropy of the whole idea of the "most memorable." It was certainly possible that the historical outlook made it easier to dismiss the majority of instances. In other words, to jettison most of us. But here was Walter Bruch, who had come to his room because he felt he could talk to him. And probably Walter, when his crying stopped, would be hurt by the Krafft-Ebing reference, by the assertion that his deviation was not too unusual. Nothing seemed to hurt quite so much as being ravaged by a vice that was not a top vice. And this brought to mind Kierkegaard's comical account of people traveling around the world to see rivers and mountains, new stars, birds of rare plumage, queerly deformed fishes, ridiculous breeds of men—tourists abandoning themselves to the bestial stupor which gapes at existence and thinks it has seen something. This could not interest Kierkegaard. He was looking for the Knight of Faith, the real prodigy. That real prodigy, having set its relations with the infinite, was entirely at home in the finite. Able to carry the jewel of faith, making the motions of the infinite, and as a result needing nothing but the finite and the usual. Whereas others sought the extraordinary in the world. Or wished to be what was gaped at. They themselves wanted to be the birds of rare plumage, the queerly deformed fishes, the ridiculous breeds of men. Only Mr. Sammler, extended, a long old body with brickish cheekbones and the often electrified back hair riding the back of the head—only Mr. Sammler was worried. He was concerned about the test of crime which the Knight of Faith had to meet. Should the Knight of Faith have the strength to break humanly appointed laws in obedience to God? Oh, yes, of course! But maybe Sammler knew things about murder which might make the choices just a little more difficult. He thought often what a tremendous appeal crime had made to the children of bourgeois civilization. Whether as revolutionists, as supermen, as saints, Knights of Faith, even the best teased and tested themselves with thoughts of knife or gun. Lawless. Raskolnikovs. Ah yes . . .

"Walter, I'm sorry—sorry to see you suffer."

The odd things occurring in Sammler's room, with its papers, books, humidor, sink, electric coil, Pyrex flask, documents.

"I'll pray for you, Walter."

Bruch stopped crying, clearly startled.

"What do you mean, Uncle Sammler? You pray?"

The baritone music left his voice, and it was gruff again, and he gruffly gobbled his words.

"Uncle Sammler, I have my arms. You have prayers?" He gave a belly laugh. He laughed and snorted, swinging his trunk comically back and forth, holding both his sides, blindly showing both his nostrils. He was not, however, mocking Sammler. Not really. One had to learn to distinguish. To distinguish and distinguish and distinguish. It was distinguishing, not explanation, that mattered. Explanation was for the mental masses. Adult education. The upswing of general consciousness. A mental level comparable with, say, that of the economic level of the proletariat in 1848. But distinguishing? A higher activity.

"I will pray for you," said Sammler.

After this the conversation sank for a while into mere sociability. Sammler had to look at letters Bruch had sent to the *Post*, *Newsday*, the *Times*, tangling with their music reviewers.

This again was the contentious, ludicrous side of things, the thick-smeared, self-conscious, performing loutish Bruch. Just when Sammler wanted to rest. To recover a little. To put himself in order. And Bruch's rollicking, guttural Dada routine was contagious. Go, Walter, go away so that I can pray for you, Sammler felt like saying, falling into Bruch's style. But then Bruch asked, "And when are you expecting your son-in-law?"

"Who? Eisen?"

"Yes, he's coming. He's maybe here already."

"I didn't know that. He's threatened to come, many times, to set up as an artist in New York. He doesn't want Shula at all."

"I know that," said Bruch. "And she is so afraid of him."

"Certainly it would not work. He is too violent. Yes, she will be frightened. She will also feel flattered, imagining that he has come to win her back. But he's not thinking of wives and marriage. He wants to show his paintings on Madison Avenue."

"He thinks he is that good?"

"He learned printing and engraving in Haifa and I was told in his shop that he was a dependable worker. But then he discovered Art, and began to paint in his spare time and make etchings. Then he sent each member of the family a portrait of himself copied from photographs. Did you see any? They were appalling, Walter. An insane mind and a frightening soul made those paintings. I don't know how he did it, but by using color he robbed every subject of color. Everybody looked like a corpse, with black lips and red eyes, with faces a kind of left-over cooked-liver green. At the same time it was like a little schoolgirl learning to draw pretty people, with cupid mouths and long eyelashes. Frankly, I was stunned when I saw myself like a kewpie doll from the catacombs. In that shiny varnish he uses, I looked really done for. It was as if one death was not enough for me, but I had to have a double death. Well, let him come. His crazy intuition about New York may be right. He is a cheerful maniac. Now so many highbrows have discovered that madness is higher knowledge. If he painted Lyndon Johnson, General Westmoreland, Rusk, Nixon, or Mr. Laird in that style he might become a celebrity of the art world. Power and money of course do drive people crazy. So why shouldn't people also gain power and wealth through being crazy? They should go together."

Sammler had taken off his shoes, and now the long frail feet in brown stockings felt cold and he laid over them the blanket with its frayed silk binding. Bruch took this to mean that he was going to sleep. Or was it that the conversation had taken a turn that didn't interest Sammler? The singer said good-by.

When Bruch bustled out—black coat, short legs, sack-wide bottom, cap tight, bicycle clips at the bottoms of his trousers (the suicidal challenge of cycling in Manhattan)—Sammler was again thinking of the pickpocket, the pressure of his body, the lobby and the hernial canvas walls, the two pairs of dark glasses, the lizard-thick curving tube in the hand, dusty stale pinkish chocolate color and strongly suggesting the infant it was there to beget. Ugly, odious; laughable, but nevertheless important. And Mr. Sammler himself (one of those mental invasions there was no longer any point in attempting to withstand) was accustomed to put his own very different emphasis on things. Of course he and the pickpocket were different. Everything was different. Their mental, characterological, spiritual profiles were miles apart. In the past, Mr. Sammler had thought that in this same biological respect he was comely enough, in his own Jewish way. It had never greatly mattered, and mattered less than ever now, in the seventies. But a sexual madness was overwhelming the Western world. Sammler now even vaguely recalled hearing that a President of the United States was supposed to have shown himself in a similar way to the representatives of the press (asking the ladies to leave), and demanding to know whether a man so well hung could not be trusted to lead his country. The story was apocryphal, naturally, but it was not a flat impossibility, given the President, and what counted was that it should spring up and circulate so widely that it reached even the Sammlers in their West Side bedrooms. Take as another instance the last exhibit of Picasso. Angela had brought him to the opening at the Museum of Modern Art. It was in the strictly sexual sense also an exhibition. Old Picasso was wildly obsessed by sexual fissures, by phalluses. In the frantic and funny pain of his farewell, creating organs by the thousands, perhaps tens of thousands. Lingam and Yoni. Sammler thought it might be enlightening to recall the Sanskrit words. Bring in a little perspective. But it didn't really do much for such a troubled theme. And it was very troubled. He fetched back, for example, a statement by Angela Gruner, blurted out after several drinks when she was laughing, gay, and evidently feeling free (to the point of brutality) with old Uncle Sammler. "A Jew brain, a black cock, a Nordic beauty," she had said, "is what a woman wants." Putting together the ideal man. Well, after all, she had charge accounts at the finest shops in New York, and access to the best of everything in the world. If Pucci didn't have what she wanted, she ordered from Hermès. All that money could buy, luxury could offer, personal beauty could bear upon the person, or that sexual sophistication could reciprocate. If she could find the ideal male, her divine synthesis—well, she was sure she could make it worth his while. The best was not too good for her. There seemed to be no question about that. At moments like this Mr. Sammler was more than ever pleasantly haunted by moon-visions. Artemis—lunar chastity. On the moon people would have to work hard simply to stay alive, to breathe. They would have to keep a strict watch over the gauges of all the devices. Conditions altogether different. Austere technicians—almost a priesthood.

If it wasn't Bruch forcing his way in with confessions, if it wasn't Margotte (for she was now beginning to think about affairs of the heart after three years of decent widowhood—more discussion than prospects, surely: discussion, earnest examination *ad infinitum*), if it wasn't Feffer with his indiscriminate bedroom adventures, it was Angela who came to confide. If confidence was the word for it. Communicating chaos. Getting to be oppressive. Especially since her father had recently been unwell, at this moment actually in the hospital. Sammler had ideas about this chaos—he had his own view of everything, an intensely peculiar one, but what else was there to go by? Of course he made allowances for error. He was a European, and these were American phenomena. Europeans often misunderstood America comically. He could remember that many refugees had packed their bags to take off for Mexico or Japan after Stevenson's first defeat, certain that Ike would bring a military dictatorship. Certain European importations were remarkably successful in the United States—psychoanalysis, existentialism. Both related to the sexual revolution.

In any case, a mass of sadness had been waiting for free, lovely, rich, ever-so-slightly coarse Angela Gruner, and she was now flying under thick clouds. For one thing she was having trouble with Wharton Horricker. She was fond of, she liked, probably she loved, Wharton Horricker. In the last two years Sammler had heard of few other men. Fidelity, strict and literal, was not Angela's dish, but she had an old-fashioned need for Horricker. He was from Madison Avenue, some sort of market-research expert and statistical wizard. He was younger than Angela. A physical culturist (tennis, weight lifting). Tall, from California, marvelous teeth. There was gymnastic apparatus in his house. Angela described the slanted board with footstraps for sit-ups, the steel bar in the doorway for chinning. And the chrome-metal, cold marble furniture, the leather straps and British folding officers' chairs, the op and pop *objets d'art*, the indirect lighting, and the prevalence of mirrors. Horricker was handsome. Sammler agreed. Cheerful, somewhat unformed as yet, Horricker was perhaps intended by nature to be rascally (what was all that muscle for? Health? Not banditry?). "And what a dresser!" said Angela with husky, comedienne's delight. With long California legs, small hips, crisp long hair with a darling curl at the back, he was a mod dandy. Extremely critical of other people's clothes. Even Angela had to submit to West Point inspection. Once when he thought her improperly dressed, he abandoned her on the street. He crossed to the other side. Custom-made shirts, shoes, sweaters were continually arriving from London and Milan. You could play sacred music while he had his hair cut (no, "styled!"), said Angela. He went to a Greek on East Fifty-sixth Street. Yes, Sammler knew a good deal about Wharton Horricker. His health foods. Horricker had even brought him bottles of yeast powder. Sammler found the yeast beneficial. Then there was the matter of neckties. Horricker's collection of beautiful neckties! By now the comparison with his own black pickpocket was unavoidable. This cult of masculine elegance must be thought about. Something important, still nebulous, about Solomon in all his glory versus the lilies of the field. We would see. Still, despite his self-pampering fastidiousness, his intolerance of badly clothed people, despite his dressy third-generation-Jew name, Wharton received serious consideration from Sammler. He sympathized with him, understanding the misleading and corrupting power of Angela, insidious without intending to be. What she intended to be was gay, pleasure-giving, exuberant, free, beautiful, healthy. As young Americans (the Pepsi generation, wasn't it?) saw the thing. And she told old Uncle Sammler everything—the honor of her confidences belonged to him. Why? Oh, she thought he was the most understanding, the most European-worldly-wise-nonprovincial-mentally-diversified-intelligent-young-in-heart of old refugees, and really interested in the new phenomena. To deserve this judgment had he perhaps extended himself a little? Hadn't he lent himself, played the game, acted the ripe old refugee? If so, he was offended with himself. And, yes, it was so. If he heard things he didn't want to hear, there was a parallel—on the bus he had seen things he didn't want to see. But hadn't he gone a dozen times to Columbus Circle to look for the black thief?

Without restraint, in direct terms, Angela described events to her uncle. Coming into his room, taking off the coat, the head scarf, shaking free the hair with its dyed streaks like raccoon fur, smelling of Arabian musk, an odor which clung afterward to the poor fabrics, seat cushions, to the coverlet, even to the curtains, as stubborn as walnut stain on one's fingers, she sat down in white textured stockings—*bas de poule* as the French called them. Cheeks bursting with color, eyes dark sexual blue, a white vital heat in the flesh of the throat, she carried a great statement to males, the powerful message of gender. In this day and age people felt obliged to temper all such powerful messages with comedy, and she provided that, too. In America certain forms of success required an element of parody, self-mockery, a satire on the-thing-itself. Mae West had this. Senator Dirksen had it. One caught glimpses of the strange mind-revenge on the alleged thing-itself in Angela. She crossed her legs on a chair too fragile to accommodate such thighs, too straight for her hips. She opened her purse for a cigarette, and Sammler offered a light. She loved his manners. The smoke came from her nose, and she looked at him, when she was in good form, cheerfully with a touch of slyness. The beautiful maiden. He was the old hermit. When she became hearty with him and laughed, she turned out to have a big mouth, a large tongue. Inside the elegant woman he saw a coarse one. The lips were red, the tongue was often pale. That tongue, a woman's tongue—evidently it played an astonishing part in her free, luxurious life.

To her first meeting with Wharton Horricker, she had come running uptown from East Village. Something she couldn't get out of. She had used no grass that night, only whisky, she said. Grass didn't turn her on as she best liked turning on. Four telephone calls she made to Wharton from a crowded joint. He said he had to get his sleep; it was after one a.m.; he was a crank about sleep, health. Finally she burst in on him with a big kiss. She cried, "We're going to fuck all night!" But first she had to have a bath. Because she had been longing all evening for him. "Oh, a woman is a skunk. So many odors, Uncle," she said. Taking off everything, but overlooking the tights, she fell into the tub. Wharton was astonished and sat on the commode cover in his dressing gown while she, so ruddy with whisky, soaped her breasts. Sammler knew quite well how the breasts must look. Little, after all, was concealed by her low-cut dresses. So she was soaped and rinsed, and the wet tights with joyful difficulty were removed, and she was led to the bed by the hand. Or did the leading. For Horricker walked behind her and kissed her on the neck and shoulders. She cried "Oh!" and was mounted.

Mr. Sammler was supposed to listen benevolently to all kinds of intimate reports. Curiously enough, though with more thought and decency, H. G. Wells had also talked to him about sexual passion. From such a superior individual one might have expected views more in line with those of Sophocles in old age. "Most gladly have I escaped the thing of which you speak; I feel as if I had escaped from the hands of a mad and furious master." No such thing. As Sammler remembered it, Wells in his seventies was still obsessed with girls. He had powerful arguments for a total revision of sexual attitudes to accord with the increased life span. When the average individual died at thirty, toil-ruined, ill-fed, sickly mankind was sexually finished before the third decade. Romeo and Juliet were adolescents. But as the civilized life expectancy approaches seventy, the old standards of brutal brevity, early exhaustion, and doom must be set aside. Rancor, and gradually even rage, came over Wells at a certain point as he talked about the powers of the brain, its expansive limits, the ability in old age to take a fresh interest in new events diminishing. Utopian, he didn't even imagine that the hoped-for future would bring excess, pornography, sexual abnormality. Rather, as the old filth and gloomy sickness were cleared away, there would emerge a larger, stronger, older, brainier, better-nourished, better-oxygenated, more vital human type, able to eat and drink sanely, perfectly autonomous and well regulated in desires, going nude while attending tranquilly to duties, performing his fascinating and useful mental work. Yes, gradually the long shudder of mankind at the swift transitoriness of mortal beauty, pleasure, would cease, to be replaced by the wisdom born of prolongation.

Oh, wrinkled faces, gray beards, eyes purging thick amber or gum, a plentiful lack of wit together with weak hams, out of the air, crabwise, into the grave: Hamlet had his own view of it. And Sammler on many occasions, listening to Angela as he lay in bed, considering two sets of problems (at least) with two different-looking eyes, a tense stitch between rib and hip making him draw up one leg for an ease he did not attain, had a slight look of rebuke as well as the look of receptivity. His daily tablespoon of nutritional yeast, a primary product from natural sugars, dissolved and shaken to a pink foam in fruit juice, kept him in fresh color. One result, possibly, of longevity was divine entertainment. You could appreciate God's entertainment from the formation of patterns which needed time for their proper development. Sammler had known Angela's grandparents. They had been Orthodox. This gave a queer edge to his acquaintance with her paganism. Somewhere he doubted the fitness of these Jews for this erotic Roman voodoo primitivism. He questioned whether release from long Jewish mental discipline, hereditary training in lawful control, was obtainable upon individual application. Although claims for erotic leadership had also been made by modern Jewish spiritual and mental doctors, Sammler had his doubts.

Accept and grant that happiness is to do what most other

people do. Then you must incarnate what others incarnate. If prejudices, prejudice. If rage, then rage. If sex, then sex. But don't contradict your time. Just don't contradict it, that's all. Unless you happened to be a Sammler and felt that the place of honor was outside. However, what was achieved by remoteness, by being simply a vestige, a visiting consciousness which happened to reside in a West Side bedroom, did not entitle one to the outside honors. Moreover, inside was so roomy and took in so many people that if you were in the West Nineties, if you were in fact here, you *were* an American. And the charm, the ebullient glamour, the almost unbearable agitation that came from being able to describe oneself as a twentieth-century American was available to all. To everyone who had eyes to read the papers or watch the television, to everyone who shared the collective ecstasies of news, crisis, power. To each according to his excitability. But perhaps it was an even deeper thing. Humankind watched and described itself in the very turns of its own destiny. Itself the subject, living or drowning in night, itself the object, seen surviving or succumbing, and feeling in itself the fits of strength and the lapses of paralysis—mankind's own passion simultaneously being mankind's great spectacle, a thing of deep and strange participation, on all levels, from melodrama and mere noise down into the deepest layers of the soul and into the subtlest silences, where undiscovered knowledge is. This sort of experience, in Mr. Sammler's judgment, might bring to some people fascinating opportunities for the mind and the soul, but a man would have to be unusually intelligent to begin with, and in addition unusually nimble and discerning. He didn't even think that he himself qualified by his own standard. Because of the high rate of speed, decades, centuries, epochs condensing into, months, weeks, days, even sentences. So that to keep up, you had to run, sprint, waft, fly over shimmering waters, you had to be able to see what was dropping out of human life and what was staying in. You could not be an old-fashioned sitting sage. You must train yourself. You had to be strong enough not to be terrified by local effects of metamorphosis, to live with disintegration, with crazy streets, filthy nightmares, monstrosities come to life, addicts, drunkards, and perverts celebrating their despair openly in midtown. You had to be able to bear the tangles of the soul, the sight of cruel dissolution. You had to be patient with the stupidities of power, with the fraudulence of business. Daily at five or six a.m. Mr. Sammler woke up in Manhattan and tried to get a handle on the situation. He didn't think he could. Nor, if he could, would he be able to convince or convert anyone. He could leave the handle to Shula in his will. She could disclose possession to Rabbi Ipsheimer. She could whisper to Father Robles in the confessional that she had it. What could the main thing be? Consciousness and its pains? The flight from consciousness into the primitive? Liberty? Privilege? Demons? The expulsion of those demons and spirits from the air, where they bad always been, by enlightenment and rationalism? And mankind had never lived without its possessing demons and had to have them back! Oh, what a wretched, itching, bleeding, needing, idiot, genius of a creature we were dealing with here! And how queerly it was playing (he, she) with all the strange properties of existence, with all varieties of possibility, with antics of all types, with the soul of the world, with death. Could it be condensed into a statement or two? Humankind could not endure futurelessness. As of now, death was the sole visible future.

A family, a circle of friends, a team of the living got things going, and then death appeared and no one was prepared to acknowledge death. Dr. Gruner, it was given out, had had minor surgery, a little operation. Was it so? An artery to the brain, the carotid, had begun to leak through weak walls. Sammler had been slow, reluctant to grasp what this might mean. He had perhaps a practical reason for such reluctance. Since 1947, he and Shula had been Dr. Gruner's dependents. He paid their rents, invented work for Shula, supplemented the Social Security and German indemnity checks. He was generous. Of course he was rich, but the rich were usually mean. Not able to separate themselves from the practices that had made the money: infighting, habitual fraud, mad agility in compound deceit, the strange conventions of legitimate swindling. To old Sammler, considering, with smallish ruddy face, the filmed bubble of the eye, and slightly cat-whiskered—a meditative island on the island of Manhattan—it was plain that the rich men he knew were winners in struggles of criminality, of permissible criminality. In other words, triumphant in forms of deceit and hardness of heart considered by the political order as a whole to be productive; kinds of cheating or thieving or (at best) wastefulness which on the whole caused the gross national product to increase. Wait a minute, though: Sammler denied himself the privilege of the high-principled intellectual who must always be applying the purest standards and thumping the rest of his species on the head. When he tried to imagine a just social order, he could not do it. A non-corrupt society? He could not do that either. There were no revolutions that he could remember which had not been made for justice, freedom, and pure goodness. Their last state was always more nihilistic than the first. So if Dr. Gruner had been corrupt, one should glance also at the other rich, to see what hearts they had. No question. Dr. Gruner, who had made a great deal of money as a gynecologist and even more, later, in real estate, was on the whole kindly and had a lot of family feeling, far more than Sammler, who in his youth had taken the opposite line, the modern one of Marx-Engels-private-property-the-origins-of-the-state-and-the-family.

Sammler was only six or seven years older than Gruner, his nephew by an amusing technicality. Sammler was the child of a second marriage, born when his father was sixty. (Evidently Sammler's own father had been sexually enterprising.) And Dr. Gruner had longed for a European uncle. He was elaborately deferential, positively Chinese in observing old forms. He had left the old country at the age of ten, he was sentimental about Cracow, and wanted to reminisce about grandparents, aunts, cousins with whom Sammler had never had much to do. He couldn't easily explain that these were people from whom he had thought he must free himself and because of whom he became so absurdly British. But Dr. Gruner himself after fifty years was still something of an immigrant. In spite of the grand Westchester house and the Rolls Royce glittering like a silver tureen, covering his courteous Jewish baldness. Dr. Gruner's wrinkles were mild. They expressed patience and sometimes even delight. He had large, noble lips. Irony and pessimism were also there. It was a pleasant, pleasantly illuminated face.

And Sammler, an uncle through his half-sister—an uncle really by courtesy, by Gruner's pious antiquarian wish—was seen (tall, elderly, foreign) as the last of a marvelous old generation. Mama's own brother, Uncle Artur, with big pale tufts over the eyes, with thin wrinkles augustly flowing under the big-brimmed perhaps romantically British hat. Sammler understood from his "nephew's" face with the grand smile and conspicuous ears that his historical significance for Gruner was considerable. Also his *experiences* were respected. The war. Holocaust. Suffering.

Because of his high color, Gruner always looked healthy to Sammler. But the doctor one day said, "Hypertension, Uncle, not health."

"Maybe you shouldn't play cards."

Twice a week, at his club, in very long sessions, Gruner played gin rummy or canasta for high stakes. So Angela said, and she was pleased with her father's vice. She had hereditary vices to point to—she and her younger brother, Wallace. Wallace was a born plunger. He had already gone through his first fifty thousand, investing with a Mafia group in Las Vegas. Or perhaps they were only would-be Mafia, for they hadn't made it. Dr. Gruner himself had grown up in a hoodlum neighborhood and sometimes dropped into the hoodlum manner, speaking out of the corner of his mouth. He was a widower. His wife had been a German Jewess, above him socially, so she thought. Her family had been 1848 pioneers. Gruner was an *Ostjude* immigrant. Her job was to refine him, to help him build his practice. The late Mrs. Gruner had been decent, proper, with thin legs, bouffant hair sprayed stiffly, and Peck & Peck outfits, geometrically correct to the millimeter. Gruner had believed in the social superiority of his wife.

"It's not the rummy that aggravates my blood pressure. If there were no cards, there would still be the stock market, and if there weren't the stock market, there would be the condominium in Florida, there would be the suit with the insurance company, or there would still be Wallace. There would be Angela."

Tempering his great glowing affection, mixing fatherly love with curses, Gruner would mutter "Bitch" when his daughter approached with all her flesh in motion—thighs, hips, bosom displayed with a certain fake innocence. Presumably maddening men and infuriating women. Under his breath, Gruner said "Cow!" or "Sloppy cunt!" Still, he had settled money on her so that she could live handsomely on the income. Millions of corrupt ladies, Sammler saw, had fortunes to live on. Foolish creatures, or worse, squandering the wealth of the land. Gruner would never have been able to bear the details that Sammler heard from Angela. She was always warning him, "Daddy would *die* if he knew this." Sammler did not agree; Elya probably knew plenty. The truth was naturally known by all concerned. It was all in Angela's calves, in the cut of her blouses, in the motions of her fingertips, the musical brass of her whispers.

Dr. Gruner had taken to saying, "Oh, yes, I know that broad. I know my Angela. And Wallace!"

Sammler didn't at first understand what an aneurysm meant; he heard from Angela that Gruner was in the hospital for throat surgery. The day after the pickpocket had cornered him, he went to the East Side to visit Gruner. He found him with a bandaged neck.

"Well, Uncle Sammler?"

"Elya—how are you? You look all right." And the old man, reaching beneath himself with a long arm, smoothing the underside of the trench coat, bending thin legs, sat down. Between the tips of cracked wrinkled black shoes he set the tip of his umbrella and leaned with both palms on the curved handle, stooping toward the bed with Polish-Oxonian politeness. Meticulously, the sickroom caller. Finely, intricately wrinkled, the left side of his face was like the contour map of difficult terrain.

Dr. Gruner sat straight, unsmiling. His expression after a lifetime of good-humored appearance was still mainly pleasant. This was not pertinent at present, merely habitual.

"I am in the middle of something."

"The surgery was successful?"

"There is a gimmick in my throat, Uncle."

"For what?"

"To regulate the flow of blood in the artery—the carotid."

"Is that so? Is it a valve or something?"

"More or less."

"It's supposed to reduce the pressure?"

"Yes, that's the idea."

"Yes. Well, it seems to be working. You look as usual. Normal, Elya."

Evidently there was something which Dr. Gruner had no intention of letting out. His expression was neither dire nor grim. Instead of hardness Mr. Sammler thought he could observe a curious kind of tight lightness. The doctor in the hospital, in pajamas, was a good patient. He said to the nurses, "This is my uncle. Tell him what kind of patient I am."

"Oh, the doctor is a wonderful patient."

Gruner had always insisted on having affectionate endorsements, approbation, the good will of all who drew near.

"I am completely in the surgeon's hands. I do exactly as he says."

"He is a good doctor?"

"Oh, yes. He's a hillbilly. A Georgia red-neck. He was a football star in college. I remember reading about him in the papers. He played for Georgia Tech. But he's professionally very able; and I take orders from him, and I never discuss the case."

"So you're satisfied completely with him?"

"Yesterday the screw was too tight."

"What did that do?"

"Well, my speech got thick. I lost some coordination. You know the brain needs its blood supply. So they had to loosen me up again."

"But you are better today?"

"Oh, yes."

The mail was brought, and Dr. Gruner asked Uncle Sammler to read a few items from the Market Letter. Sammler lifted the paper to his right eye, concentrating window light upon it. "The U.S. Justice Department will file suit to force Ling-Temco-Vought to divest its holdings of Jones and Laughlin Steel. Moving against the huge conglomerate . . ."

"Those conglomerates are soaking up all the business in the country. One of them, I understand, has acquired all the funeral parlors in New York. I hear reports that Campbell, Riverside, have been bought by the same company that publishes *Mad* magazine."

"How curious."

"Youth is big business. Schoolchildren spend fantastic

amounts. If enough kids get radical, that's a new mass market, then it's a big operation."

"I have a general idea."

"Very little is holding still. First making your money, then keeping your money from shrinking by inflation. How you invest it, whom you trust—you trust nobody—what you get with it, how you save it from those Federal taxation robbers, the gruesome Revenue Service. And how you leave it . . . wills! Those are the worst problems in life. Excruciating."

Uncle Sammler now understood fully how it was. His nephew Gruner had in his head a great blood vessel, defective from birth, worn thin and frayed with a lifetime of pulsation. A clot had formed from leakage. The whole jelly trembled. One was summoned to the brink of the black. Any beat of the heart might open the artery and spray the brain with blood. These facts shimmered their way into Sammler's mind. Was it the time? *The* time? How terrible! But yes! Elya would die of a hemorrhage. Did he know this? Of course he did. He was a physician, so he must know. But he was human, so he could arrange many things for himself. Both knowing and not knowing—one of the more frequent human arrangements. Then Sammler, making himself intensely observant, concluded after ten or twelve minutes that Gruner definitely knew. He believed that Gruner's moment of honor had come, that moment at which the individual could call upon his best qualities. Mr. Sammler had lived a long time and understood something about these cases of final gallantry. *If* there were time, occasionally good things were done. *If* one had a certain kind of luck.

"Uncle, try some of these fruit jellies. The lime and orange are the best. From Beersheba."

"Aren't you watching your weight, Elya?"

"No, I'm not. They're making terrific stuff in Israel these days." The doctor had been buying Israel bonds and real estate. In Westchester, he served Israeli wine and brandy. He gave away heavily embossed silver ball-point pens, made in Israel. You could sign checks with them. For ordinary purposes they were not useful. And on two occasions Dr. Gruner, as he was picking up his fedora, had said, "I believe I'll go to Jerusalem for a while."

"When are you leaving?"

"Now."

"Right away?"

"Certainly."

"Just as you are?"

"Just as I am. I can buy my toothbrush and razor when I land. I love it there."

He had his chauffeur drive him to Kennedy Airport.

"I'll cable you, Emil, when I'm coming back."

In Jerusalem were more old relatives like Sammler, and Gruner did genealogies with them, one of his favorite pastimes. More than a pastime. He had a passion for kinships. Sammler found this odd, especially in a physician. As one whose prosperity had been founded in the female generative slime, he might have had less specific sentiment about his own tribe. But now, seeing a fatal dryness in the circles under his eyes, Sammler better understood the reason for this. To each according to his intimations. Gruner had not worked in his profession for ten years. He had had a heart attack and retired on insurance. After a year or two of payments, the insurance company insisted that he was well enough to practice, and there had been a lawsuit. Then Dr. Gruner learned that insurance companies kept the finest legal talent in the city on retainer. The best lawyers were tied up, and the courts were deliberately choked with trivial suits by the companies, so that it was years before his case came to trial. But he won. Or was about to win. He had disliked his trade—the knife, blood. He had been conscientious. He had done his duty. But he hadn't liked his trade. He was still, however, fastidiously manicured like a practicing surgeon. Here in the hospital the manicurist was sent for, and during Sammler's visit Gruner's fingers were being soaked in a steel basin. The strange tinge of male fingers in the suds. The woman in her white smock, every single hair of the neckless head the same hue of dyed black, without variation, was gloomy, sloven-footed in orthopedic white shoes. Heavy-shouldered, she bent with instruments over his nails, concentrating on her work. She had quite a wide, tear-pregnant nose. Dr. Gruner had to woo reactions from her. Even from such a dismal creature.

As it might not be many times more for Elya the room was

filled with sunny light. In which familiar human postures were struck. From which no great results had come in the past. From which little could be expected at this late hour. What if the manicurist were to take a liking to Dr. Gruner? What if she should requite his longing? What was his longing? Mr. Sammler had a thing about these unprofitable instants of clarity. Seeing the singular human creature demand more when the sum of human facts could not yield more. Sammler did not like such instants, but they came nevertheless.

The woman pushed back the cuticle. She would not be tempted up from her own underground galleries. Intimacy was refused.

"Uncle Artur, can you tell me anything about my grandmother's brother in the old country?"

"Who?"

"Hessid was the man's name."

"Hessid? Hessid? Yes, there was a Hessid family."

"He had a mill for cornmeal, and a shop near the Castle. Just a small place with a few barrels."

"You must be mistaken. I remember no one in the family who ground anything. However, you have an excellent memory. Better than mine."

"Hessid. A fine-looking old man with a broad white beard. He wore a derby, and a very fancy vest with watch and chain. Called up often to read from the Torah, though he couldn't have been a heavy contributor to the synagogue."

"Ah, the synagogue. Well, you see, Elya, I didn't have much to do with the synagogue. We were almost freethinkers. Especially my mother. She had a Polish education. She gave me an emancipated name: Artur."

Sammler regretted that he was so poor at family reminiscences. Contemporary contacts being somewhat unsatisfactory, he would gladly have helped Gruner to build up the past.

"I loved old Hessid. You know, I was a very affectionate child."

"I'm sure you were," said Sammler. He could hardly remember Gruner as a boy. Standing, he said, "I won't tire you with a long visit."

"Oh, you aren't tiring me. But you probably have things to do. At the public library. One thing, before you go,

Uncle—you're in pretty good shape still. You took that last trip to Israel very well, and that was a tough one. Do you still like to run in Riverside Park, as you used to do?"

"Not lately. I feel too stiff for it."

"I was going to say, it's not safe to run down there. I don't want you mugged. When you're winded from running, some crazy sonofabitch jumps out and cuts your throat! Anyway, if you are too stiff to run you're far from feeble. I know you're not a sickly type, apart from your nervous trouble. You still get that small payment from the West Germans? And the Social Security? Yes, I'm glad we had the lawyer set that up, about the Germans. And I don't want you to worry, Uncle Artur."

"About what?"

"About anything at all. Security, in old age. Being in a home. You stay with Margotte. She's a good woman. She'll look after you. I realize Shula is a little too nutty for you. She amuses other people but not her own father. I know how that can be."

"Yes, Margotte is decent. You couldn't ask for better."

"So, remember, Uncle, no worries."

"Thank you, Elya."

A confusing, frowning moment, and, getting into the breast, the head, and even down into the bowels and about the heart, and behind the eyes—something gripping, aching, smarting. The woman was buffing Gruner's nails, and he sat straight in the fully buttoned pajama coat; above it, the bandage hiding the throat with its screw. His large ruddy face was mainly unhandsome, his baldness, his big-eared plainness, the large tip of the nose; Gruner belonged to the common branch of the family. It was, however, a virile face, and, when superficial objections were removed, a kindly face. Sammler knew the defects of his man. Saw them as dust and pebbles, as rubble on a mosaic which might be swept away. Underneath, a fine, noble expression. A dependable man—a man who took thought for others.

"You've been good to Shula and me, Elya."

Gruner neither acknowledged nor denied this. Perhaps by the rigidity of his posture he fended off gratitude he did not deserve in full.

In short, if the earth deserves to be abandoned, if we are

now to be driven streaming into other worlds, starting with the moon, it is not because of the likes of you, Sammler would have said. He put it more briefly, "I'm grateful."

"You're a gentleman, Uncle Artur."

"I'll be in touch."

"Yes, come back. It does me good."

Sammler, outside the rubber-silenced door, put on his Augustus John hat. A hat from the Soho that was. He went down the corridor in his usual quick way, favoring the sightful side slightly, putting forward the right leg and the right shoulder. When he came to the anteroom, a sunny bay with soft plastic orange furniture, he found Wallace Gruner there with a doctor in a white coat. This was Elya's surgeon.

"My dad's uncle—Dr. Cosbie."

"How do you do, Dr. Cosbie." The conceivably wasted fragrance of Mr. Sammler's manners. Who was there now to be aware of such Old World stuff! Here and there perhaps a woman might appreciate his style of greeting. But not a Doctor Cosbie. The ex-football star, famous in Georgia, struck Sammler as a sort of human wall. High and flat. His face was mysteriously silent, and very white. The upper lip was steep and prominent. The mouth itself thin and straight. Somewhat unapproachable, he kept his hands behind his back. He had the air of a general whose mind is on battalions in a bloody struggle, just out of sight over a hill. To a civilian pest who came up to him at that moment he had nothing to say.

"How is Dr. Gruner?"

"Makin' good progress, suh. A very fine patient."

Dr. Gruner was being seen as he wished to be seen. Every occasion had its propaganda. Democracy was propaganda. From government, propaganda entered every aspect of life. You had a desire, a view, a line, and you disseminated it. It took, everyone spoke of the event in the appropriate way, under your influence. In this case Elya, a doctor, a patient, made it known that he was the patient of patients. An allowable foible; boyish, but what of it? It had a certain interest.

Faced with a doctor, Sammler had his own foible, for he often wanted to ask about his symptoms. This was repressed of course. But the impulse was there. He wanted to mention that he woke up with a noise inside his head, that his good eye built up a speck at the corner which he couldn't scratch out, it stuck in the fold, that his feet burned intolerably at night, that he suffered from *pruritis ani*. Doctors loathed laymen with medical phrases. All, naturally, was censored. The tachycardia last of all. Nothing was shown to Cosbie but a certain cool, elderly rosiness. A winter apple. A busy-minded old man. Colored specs. A wide wrinkled hat brim. An umbrella on a sunny day—inconsequent. Long narrow shoes, cracked but highly polished.

Was he cold-hearted about Elya? No, he was grieving. But what could he do? He went on thinking, and seeing.

As usual, even in the midst of conversation, Wallace with round black eyes was dreaming away. Profoundly dreaming. He also had a very white color. In his late twenties he was still little brother with the curls, the lips of a small boy. A bit careless perhaps in his toilet habits, also like a small boy, he often transmitted to Sammler in warm weather (perhaps Sammler's nose was hypersensitive) a slightly unclean odor from the rear. The merest hint of fecal carelessness. This did not offend his great-uncle. It was simply observed, by a peculiarly delicate recording system. Actually, Sammler rather sympathized with the young man. Wallace fell into the Shula category. There was even a family resemblance, especially in the eyes—round, dark, wide, filling the big bony orbits, capable of seeing all, but adream, adream, dreamy, apparently drugged. He was a kinky cat, said Angela. With Dr. Cosbie he was discussing sports. Wallace took no common interest in any subject. With him all interests were uncommon. He caught a tearing fever. Horses, football, hockey, baseball. He knew averages, performance records, statistics. You could test him by the almanac. Dr. Gruner said that he would be up at four a.m. memorizing tables and jotting away left-handed at top speed across the body. With this, the intellectual if slightly pedomorphic forehead, the refinement of the nose, somewhat too small, and the middle of the face, somewhat too concave, and a look of mental power, virility, nobility, all slightly spoiled. Wallace nearly became a physicist, he nearly became a mathematician, nearly a lawyer (he had even passed the bar and opened an office, once), nearly an engineer, nearly a Ph.D. in behavioral science. He was a licensed pilot. Nearly an alcoholic, nearly a homosexual. At present he seemed to be a handicapper. He had yellow pages of legal foolscap covered with team names and ciphers, and he and Dr. Cosbie, who seemed to be a gambler, too, were going over these intricate, many-factored calculations, and plainly the doctor was fascinated, not simply humoring Wallace. Slender Wallace in the dark suit was very handsome. A young man with stunning gifts. It was puzzling.

"You may be out of line on the Rose Bowl," said the doctor.

"Not at all," said Wallace. "Just examine this yardage analysis. I broke down last year's figures and fitted them into my own special equation: Now look . . ."

This was as much of the conversation as Sammler could follow. He waited awhile at the window observing traffic, women with dogs, leashed and unleashed. A vacant building opposite marked for demolition. Large white X's on the windowpanes. On the plate glass of the empty shop were strange figures or nonfigures in thick white. Most scrawls could be ignored. These for some reason caught on with Mr. Sammler as pertinent. Eloquent. Of what? Of future nonbeing, Elya! But also of the greatness of eternity which shall lift us from this present shallowness. At this time forces, energies that might carry mankind up carried it down. For finer purposes of life, little was available. Terror of the sublime maddened all minds. Capacities, impressions, visions amassed in human beings from the time of origin, perhaps since matter first glinted with grains of consciousness, were bound up largely with vanities, negations, and revealed only in amorphous hints or ciphers smeared on the windows of condemned shops. All naturally were frightened of the future. Not death. Not that future. Another future in which the full soul concentrated upon eternal being. Mr. Sammler believed this. And in the meantime there was the excuse of madness. A whole nation, all of civilized society, perhaps, seeking the blameless state of madness. The privileged, the almost aristocratic state of madness. Meantime there spoke out those thick loops and open curves across an old tailor-shop window.

It was in Poland, in wartime, particularly during three or four months when Sammler was hidden in a mausoleum, that he first began to turn to the external world for curious ciphers and portents. The dead life of that summer and into autumn when he had been a portent watcher, and very childish, for many larger forms of meaning had been stamped out, and a straw, or a spider thread or a stain, a beetle or a sparrow had to be interpreted. Symbols everywhere, and metaphysical messages. In the tomb of a family called Mezvinski he was, so to speak, a boarder. The peacetime caretaker of the cemetery let him have bread. Water, too. Some days were missed, but not many, and anyway Sammler saved up a small bread reserve and did not starve. Old Cieslakiewicz was dependable. He brought bread in his hat. It smelled of scalp, of head. And during this period there was a yellow tinge to everything, a yellow light in the sky. In this light, bad news for Sammler, bad news for humankind, bad information about the very essence of being was diffused. Something hateful, and at times overwhelming. At its worst it seemed to go something like this: You have been summoned to be. Summoned out of matter. Therefore here you are. And though the vast over-all design may be of the deepest interest, whether originating in a God or in an indeterminate source which should have a different name, you yourself, a finite instance, are obliged to wait, painfully, anxiously, heartachingly, in this yellow despair. And why? But you must! So he lay and waited. There was more to this, when Sammler was boarding in the tomb. No time to be thinking, perhaps, but what else was there to do? There were no events. Events had stopped. There was no news. Cieslakiewicz with hanging mustache, swollen hands, palsy, his ugly blue eyes—Sammler's savior—had no news or would not give it. Cieslakiewicz had risked his life for him. The basis of this fact was a great oddity. They didn't like each other. What had there been to like in Sammler?—half-naked, famished, caked hair and beard, crawling out of the forest. Long experience of the dead, handling of human bones, had perhaps prepared the caretaker for the apparition of Sammler. He had let him into the Mezvinski tomb, brought him some rags for cover. After the war Sammler had sent money, parcels, to Cieslakiewicz. There was correspondence with the family. Then, after some years, the letters began to contain anti-Semitic sentiments. Nothing very vicious. Only a touch of the old stuff. This was no great surprise, or only a brief one. Cieslakiewicz had had his time of honor and charity. He had risked his life to save Sammler. The old Pole was also a hero. But the heroism ended. He was an ordinary human being and wanted again to be himself. Enough was enough. Didn't he have a right to be himself? To relax into old prejudices? It was only the "thoughtful" person with his exceptional demands who went on with self-molestation—responsible to "higher values," to "civilization," pressing forward and so on. It was the Sammlers who kept on vainly trying to perform some kind of symbolic task. The main result of which was unrest, exposure to trouble. Mr. Sammler had a symbolic character. He, personally, was a symbol. His friends and family had made him a judge and a priest. And of what was he a symbol? He didn't even know. Was it because he had survived? He hadn't even done that, since so much of the earlier person had disappeared. It wasn't surviving, it was only lasting. He had lasted. For a time yet he might last. A little longer, evidently, than Elya Gruner with the clamp or screw in his throat. *That* couldn't hold death off very long. A sudden escape of red fluid, and the man was gone. With all his will, purpose, his virtues, his good record as a physician, his enterprises, card games, his loyalty to Israel, dislike of de Gaulle, with all his kindness of heart, greediness of heart, with his mouth making passionate love to the manifest, with his money talk, his Jewish fatherhood, his love and despair over son and daughter. When his life—or this life, that life, the other life—was gone, taken away, there would remain for Sammler, while he lasted, that bad literalness, the yellow light of Polish summer heat behind the mausoleum door. It was the light also of that china-cabinet room in the apartment where he had suffered confinement with Shula-Slawa. Endless literal hours in which one is internally eaten up. Eaten because coherence is lacking. Perhaps as a punishment for having failed to find coherence. Or eaten by a longing for sacredness. Yes, go and find it when everyone is murdering everyone. When Antonina was murdered. When he himself underwent murder beside her. When he and sixty or seventy others, all stripped naked and having dug their own grave, were fired upon and fell in. Bodies upon his own body. Crushing. His dead wife nearby somewhere. Struggling out much later from the weight of corpses, crawling out of the loose soil. Scraping on his belly. Hiding in a shed. Finding a rag to wear. Lying in the woods many days.

Nearly thirty years after which, in April days, sunshine, springtime, another season, the rush and intensity of New York City about to be designated as spring; leaning on a soft, leatherlike orange sofa; feet on an umber Finnish rug with a yellow core or nucleus—with mitotic spindles; looking down to a street; in that street, a tailor's window on which the spirit of the time through the unconscious agency of a boy's hand had scrawled its augury.

Is our species crazy?

Plenty of evidence.

All of course seems man's invention. Including madness. Which may be one more creation of that agonizing inventiveness. At the present level of human evolution propositions were held (and Sammler was partly swayed by them) by which choices were narrowed down to sainthood and madness. We are mad unless we are saintly, saintly only as we soar above madness. The gravitational pull of madness drawing the saint crashwards. A few may comprehend that it is the strength to do one's duty daily and promptly that makes saints and heroes. Not many. Most have fantasies of vaulting into higher states, feeling just mad enough to qualify.

Take someone like Wallace Gruner. The doctor was gone and Wallace, with his yellow papers, was standing gracefully, handsomely, with his long lashes. How much normalcy, what stability was Wallace prepared to sacrifice to obtain the grace of madness?

"Uncle?"

"Ah, yes, Wallace."

The doctor had left the room.

Some were eccentric, some were histrionic. Probably Wallace was genuinely loony. For him it required a powerful effort to become interested in common events. This was possibly why sporting statistics cast him into such a fever, why so often he seemed to be in outer space. *Dans la lune*. Well, at least he didn't treat Sammler as a symbol, and he apparently had no use for priests, judges, or confessors. Wallace said that what he appreciated in Uncle Sammler was his wit. Sammler, especially when greatly irritated or provoked, when he felt galled, said witty things. In the old European style. Often these witticisms signaled the approach of a nervous fit.

But Wallace, when he began a conversation with Sammler, was immediately smiling, and sometimes he repeated the punch lines of Sammler's witticisms.

"Not a well-rounded person, Uncle?"

Referring to himself, Sammler once had observed, "I am more stupid about some things than about others; not equally stupid in all directions; I am not a well-rounded person."

Or else, a recent favorite with Wallace: "The billiard table, Uncle. The billiard table."

This had to do with Angela's trip to Mexico. She and Horricker had had an unhappy Mexican holiday. In January she had had enough of New York and winter. She wanted to go to Mexico, to a hot place, she said, where she could see something green. Then abruptly, before he could check himself, Sammler had said, "Hot? Something green? A billiard table in hell would answer the description."

"Oh, wow! That really cracked me up," said Wallace.

Later he would ask Sammler if he had the exact words. Sammler smiled, his small cheeks began to flush, but he refused to repeat his sayings. Wallace was not witty. He had no such sayings. But he did have experiences, he invented curious projects. Several years ago he flew out to Tangiers with the purpose of buying a horse and visiting Morocco and Tunisia on horseback. Not taking his Honda, he said, because backward people should be seen from a horse. He had borrowed Jacob Burckhardt's *Force and Freedom* from Sammler, and it affected him strongly. He wanted to examine peoples in various stages of development. In Spanish Morocco he was robbed in his hotel. By a man with a gun, hidden in his closet. He then flew on to Turkey and tried again. Somehow he managed to enter Russia on his horse. In Soviet Armenia he was detained by the police. After Gruner had gone five or six times to see Senator Javits, Wallace was released from prison. Then, once again in New York, Wallace, taking a young lady to see the film *The Birth of a Child*, fainted away at the actual moment of birth, struck his head on the back of a seat, and was knocked unconscious. Reviving, he was on the floor. He found that his date had moved away from him in embarrassment, changed her seat. He had a row with her for abandoning him. Wallace, borrowing his father's Rolls, let it somehow get away from him; carelessly parked, it ended up at the bottom of a reservoir somewhere near Croton. He drove a city bus crosstown to pay off debts. The Mafia was after him. His bookie gave him two months to pay. The handicapping hadn't worked. He flew with a friend to Peru to climb in the Andes. Said to be quite a good pilot. He offered to take Sammler into the air ("No, I believe not. Thank you just the same, Wallace"). He volunteered for the domestic Peace Corps. He wanted to be of use to little black children, to be a basketball coach in playgrounds.

"What does this surgeon really think of Elya's chances, Wallace?"

"He's going to take new X rays of his head."

"Are they planning brain surgery now?"

"It depends on whether they can get to the place. They may not be able to reach it. Of course if they can't reach it, they can't reach it."

"To look at him you'd never think . . . He looks so well."

"Oh, yes," said Wallace. "Why not?"

Sammler sighed at this. He guessed how well pleased the late Mrs. Gruner must have been with her Wallace, his shapely head, long neck, crisp hair, and fine eyebrows, the short clean line of the nose, and the neat nakedness of his teeth, the work of skilled orthodontia.

"It's hereditary, having an aneurysm. You happen to be born with a thin wall in an artery. I may have it. Angela may, too, though I'd be surprised if she had a thin place anywhere. But people, young people, too, perfect in every other respect sometimes, drop dead of it. Walking along strong, beautiful, full of beans, when it explodes inside. They die. There's a bubble first. Such as lizards blow from the throat, maybe. Then death. You've lived so long, you've probably come across this before."

"Even for me, there's always something a little new."

"I had a lot of trouble with last week's crossword puzzle, the Sunday one. Did you work on it?"

"No."

"You sometimes do."

"Margotte didn't bring home the *Times*."

"Amazing how you know words."

For some months Wallace had actually practiced law. His father had rented the office; his mother had furnished it, calling in Croze the interior decorator. For six months Wallace rose punctually like any commuter and went to business. But at business it came out that he worked on nothing but crossword puzzles, locking the door, taking the phone off the hook, lying on the leather sofa. That was all. No, one thing more: he unbuttoned the stenographer's dress and examined her breasts. This information came from Angela, who had it from the girl, direct. Why did the girl permit it? Maybe she thought it would lead to marriage. Placing hopes in Wallace? No sane woman would. But his interest in the breasts had evidently been scientific. Something about nipples. Like Jean Jacques Rousseau, who became so engrossed in the breasts of a Venetian whore that she pushed him away and told him to go study mathematics. (More of Uncle Sammler's wide reading, his European culture.)

"I don't like the people who make up the puzzles. They have low-grade minds," said Wallace. "Why should people know so much trash? Its Eastern-Seaboard-educated trash. Smart-ass Columbia University quiz-kid miscellaneous information. I actually telephoned you about an old English dance. Jig, reel, and hornpipe were all I could come up with. But this one began with an m."

"An m? Might it have been morrice?"

"Oh, damn! Of course it was morrice. Jesus, your mind is in good order. How do you happen to remember?"

"Milton, *Comus.* A wavering morrice to the moon."

"Oh, that's pretty. Oh, that's really lovely, a wavering morrice."

"'Now to the Moon in wavering Morrice move.' It's the fishes, by the billions, I believe, and the seas themselves, performing the dance."

"Why, that's splendid. You must be living right, to remember such pretty things. Your mind is not devoured by fool business. You're a good old guy, Uncle Artur. I don't like old people. I don't respect many individuals—a few physical scientists. But you—you're very austere in a way, but you have a good sense of humor. The only jokes I tell are the ones I hear from you. By the way, let me make sure I have the de Gaulle joke right. He said he didn't want to be buried under the Arc de Triomphe next to an unknown. *A côté d'un inconnu*. Right?"

"So far."

"My father has it in for de Gaulle because he woos the Arabs. I'm fond of de Gaulle because he's a monument. And he wouldn't go into the Invalides with Napoleon, who was only a lousy corporal."

"Yes."

"But the Israelis wanted to charge him a hundred thousand bucks for space in the Holy Sepulcher."

"That's the joke."

"And de Gaulle said, 'For three days? It's too much money.' '*Pour trois jours*?' He was going to be resurrected, right? Now that, I think, is very funny." Wallace's grave judgment. "Poles love to tell jokes," he said. He had no sense of humor. Sometimes he had occasion to laugh.

"Conquered people tend to be witty."

"You don't like Poles very much, Uncle?"

"I think on the whole I like them better than they liked me. Besides, a Pan once saved my life."

"And Shula in the convent."

"Yes, that too. Nuns hid her."

"I can remember Shula years ago in New Rochelle, coming downstairs in her nightgown, and she was no kid, she must have been twenty-seven or so, kneeling in front of everybody in the parlor and praying. Did she use Latin? Anyway that nightgown was damn flimsy. I thought she was trying to get your goat, with her Christian act. It was a put-down, wasn't it, in a Jewish house? Some Jews, anyhow! Is she still such a Christian?"

"At Christmas and Easter, somewhat."

"And she bugs you about H. G. Wells. But fathers are soft on daughters. Look how Dad favors Angela. He gave her ten times more. Because she reminded him of Mae West. He was always smiling at her boobs. He wasn't aware of it. Mother and I saw it."

"What do you think will happen, Wallace?"

"My dad? He won't make it. He's got about a two percent chance. What good is that screw?"

"He's struggling."

"Any fish will fight. A hook in the gill. It gets jerked into the wrong part of the universe. It must be like drowning in air."

"Ah, that is terrifying," said Sammler.

"Still, to some people death is very welcome. If they've spoiled their piece of goods, I'm sure many would rather be dead. What I'm finding out is that when the parents are living, they stand between you and death. They have to go first, so you feel pretty safe. But when they die, you're next, and there's nobody ahead of you in line. At the same time I see already that I'm taking the wrong slant emotionally, and I know I'll pay for it later. I'm part of the system, whether I like it or not." Another moment of silent aberrant reflection—Mr. Sammler felt the density and the unruliness of Wallace's thoughts. Then Wallace said, "I wonder why Dr. Cosbie is so keen on football pools."

"Aren't you?"

"Not the way I was. Dad told him how much I know about pro football. College football, too. That's all behind me now. But it was like Dad offering me to the surgeon, so I would do something for him, so that we would all be close and friendly."

"But it's something else you're keen on now?"

"Yes. Feffer and I have a business idea. It's practically all I can think about."

"Ah, Feffer. He abandoned me, and I haven't seen him since. I wondered even whether he was trying to make money on me."

"He's a terribly imaginative businessman. He'd con anyone. But maybe not you. Here's what we've come up with, as an enterprise. Aerial photographs of country houses. Then the salesman arrives with the picture—not just contacts but the fully developed picture—and offers you a package deal. We will identify the trees and shrubs on the place and band them handsomely, in Latin and English. People feel ignorant about the plants on their property."

"Does Feffer know trees?"

"In every neighborhood we'd hire a graduate student in botany. In Dutchess County, for instance, we could get someone from Vassar."

Mr. Sammler could not keep from smiling. "Feffer would seduce her, and also the lady of the house."

"Oh, no. I'd see he didn't get out of hand. I can control that character. He's a top salesman. Spring is a good time to start. Right now. Before the leaves are too thick for aerial photography. In the summer we could work Montauk, Chilmark, Wellfleet, Nantucket from the sea. My father won't give me the money."

"Is it a great deal?"

"A plane and equipment? Yes, it's considerable."

"You intend to buy a plane, not rent one?"

"Rent doesn't make sense. If you buy you get the tax write-off—depreciation. The secret of business is to make the government cover your risk. In Dad's bracket we'd save seventy cents on the dollar. The IRS is murder. He doesn't file a joint return and isn't head of a family since Mother died. He doesn't want to give me another lump sum. It's set up for me in trust so I'll have to live on the income. When I had my chance I dropped fifty thousand in that boutique."

"Gambling, I thought. Las Vegas."

"No, no, it was a motel complex in Vegas, and we had the clothing shop, the men's boutique."

A furious dresser and adorner of men's bodies, Wallace would have been.

"Uncle Artur, I'd like to put you on our payroll. Feffer agrees. Feffer loves you, you know. If you don't want to do it, we'll put Shula on at fifty bucks a week."

"And in return for this? You want me to talk to your father?"

"Use your influence."

"No, Wallace, I'm afraid I couldn't. Why, think what's going on. It's dreadful. I'm terrified."

"You wouldn't upset him. He thinks the same thoughts whether you talk to him or not. Six of one, half a dozen of the other. He's brooding about this anyway."

"No, no."

"Well, that's your decision. There is something else, though. There's money at home, in New Rochelle. In the house."

"Excuse me?" From curiosity, uncertainty, Sammler's voice went up.

"Hidden cash. A large amount. Never declared."

"It can't be, can it?"

"Oh yes it can, Uncle. You're surprised. If the inside of a person were only as simple as a watermelon—red meat, black seeds. Now and then, as a favor to highly placed people, Papa performed operations. Dilatation and curettage. Only when there was a terrific crisis, when some young socialite heiress got knocked up. Top secret. Only out of pity. My dad pitied famous families, and got big gifts of cash."

"Wallace, look. Let's talk straight. Elya is a good man. He stands close to the end. You're his son. You've been brought up to think that for your health you have to throw a father down. You've had a troubled life, I know. But this old-fashioned capitalistic-family-and-psychological struggle has to be given up, finally. I'm telling you this because you're basically intelligent. You've done a lot of peculiar things. No one can call you boring. But you may become boring if you don't stop. You could retire honorably now with plenty of interesting experience to point to. Enough. You should try something different."

"Well, Uncle Sammler, you have good manners. I know it. In some ways, you're aloof too. Sort of distant from life. But you put up with people's shenanigans and *shtick*. It's just your old-fashioned Polish politeness. All the same, there is also a practical question here. Nothing but practical."

"Practical?"

"My father has X thousands of dollars in the house, and he won't tell where it is. He's sore at us. *He's* in the capitalistic-family-psychology struggle. You're perfectly right—why should a person burn himself out with neurotic fever? There are higher aims in life. I don't think those are shit. Far from it. But you see, Uncle, if I have that plane, I can make a nice income with a few hours of flying. I can spend the rest of my time reading philosophy. I can finish up my Ph.D. in mathematics. Now listen to this. People are like simple whole numbers. Do you see?"

"No, of course not, Wallace."

"Numbers also bear an important relation to people. The series of numbers is like the series of human beings—infinite numbers of individuals. The characteristics of numbers are like the characteristics of matter, otherwise mathematical expressions could not tell us what matter will or may do.

Mathematical equations lead us to physical realities. Things not yet seen. Like the turbulence of heated gases. Do you see now?"

"Only in the vaguest way."

"The equations preceded the actual observations. So what we need is a similar system of signs for human beings. In this system, what is One? What is the human integer like? Now you see, you've made me talk seriously to you. But just for a minute or two, I want to go on with that other thing. There is money in the house. I think there are phony pipes through the attic in which he hid the bills. He borrowed a Mafia plumber once. I know it. You might just slip in a reference to pipes or to attics in your next conversation. See how he reacts. He may decide to tell you. I don't want to have to tear apart the house."

"No, certainly not," said Sammler.

What *is* One?

III

HOMEWARD.

On Second Avenue the springtime scraping of roller skates was heard on hollow, brittle sidewalks, a soothing harshness. Turning from the new New York of massed apartments into the older New York of brownstone and wrought-iron, Sammler saw through large black circles in a fence daffodils and tulips, the mouths of these flowers open and glowing, but on the pure yellow the fallout of soot already was sprinkled. You might in this city become a flower-washer. There was an additional business opportunity for Wallace and Feffer.

He walked once around Stuyvesant Park, an ellipse within a square with the statue of the peg-legged Dutchman, corners bristling with bushes. Tapping the flagstones with his ferrule every fourth step, Sammler held Dr. Govinda Lal's manuscript under his arm. He had brought it to read on the subway, though he didn't like being conspicuous in public, passing pages back and forth before the eye, pressing back the hat brim and his face intensely concentrated. He seldom did that.

Drop a perpendicular from the moon. Let it intersect a grave. Inside, a man till now tended, kept warm, manicured. Those heavy rainbow colors came. Decay. Mr. Sammler had once been on far more easy terms with death. He had lost ground, regressed. He was very full of his nephew, a man quite different from himself. He admired him, loved him. He could not cope with the full sum of facts about him. Remote considerations seemed to help—the moon, its lifelessness, its deathlessness. A white corroded pearl. By a sole eye, seen as a sole eye.

And Sammler had learned to be careful on public paths in New York, invariably dog-fouled. Within the iron-railed plots the green lights of the grass were all but put out, burned by animal excrements. The sycamores, blemished bark, but very nice, brown and white, getting ready to cough up leaves. Red brick, the Friends Seminary, and ruddy coarse warm stone, broad, clumsy, solid, the Episcopal church, St. George's. Sammler had heard that the original J. Pierpont Morgan had been an usher there. In Austro-Hungarian-Polish-Cracovian antiquity old fellows who had read of Morgan in the papers spoke of him with high regard as Piepernotter-Morgan. At St. George's, Sundays, the god of stockbrokers could breathe easy awhile in the riotous city. In thought, Mr. Sammler was testy with White Protestant America for not keeping better order. Cowardly surrender. Not a strong ruling class. Eager in a secret humiliating way, to come down and mingle with all the minority mobs, and scream against themselves. And the clergy? Beating swords into plowshares? No, rather converting dog collars into G strings. But this was neither here nor there.

Watching his steps (the dogs), looking for a bench for ten minutes, to think or avoid thinking of Gruner. Perhaps despite great sadness to read a few paragraphs of this fascinating moon manuscript. He noted a female bum drunkenly sleeping like a dugong, a sea cow's belly rising, legs swollen purple; a short dress, a mini-rag. At a corner of the fence, a wino was sullenly pissing on newspapers and old leaves. Cops seldom bothered about these old-fashioned derelicts. Younger people, autochthonous-looking, were also here. Bare feet, the boys like Bombay beggars, beards clotted, breathing rich hair from their nostrils, heads coming through woolen ponchos, somewhat Peruvian. Natives of somewhere. Innocent, devoid of aggression, opting out, much like Ferdinand the Bull. No *corrida* for them; only smelling flowers under the lovely cork tree. How similar also to the Eloi of H. G. Wells' fantasy *The Time Machine*. Lovely young human cattle herded by the cannibalistic Morlocks who lived a subterranean life and feared light and fire. Yes, that tough brave little old fellow Wells had had prophetic visions after all. Shula wasn't altogether wrong to campaign for a memoir. A memoir should be written. Only there was little time left for relaxed narration about this and that, about things fairly curious in themselves, like Wells at seventy-eight still bucking for the Royal Society—his work (on earthworms?) was not acceptable. Not earthworms. "The Quality of Illusion in the Continuity of Individual Life in the Higher Metazoa." They would not make him a Fellow. But to unscramble this would have taken weeks, and there were no free weeks for Sammler. He had other necessities, higher priorities.

He shouldn't even be reading this—this being the pages of

Govinda Lal in bronze ink and old-fashioned penmanship. He wrote a Gothic hand. But Mr. Sammler, having seen through so much, had no resistance to real fascination. On page seventy, Lal had begun to speculate on organisms possibly capable of adapting themselves in exposed lunar conditions. Were there no plants which might cover the moon's surface? Water and carbon dioxide would have to be present, extremes of temperature would have to be withstood. Lichens, thought Govinda, possibly could make it. Also certain members of the cactus family. The triumphant plant, a combination of lichen and cactus, certainly would look weird to the eyes of man. But life's capacities are even now inconceivably diverse. What impossibilities has it not faced? Who knows what the depths of the seas may yet yield? Creatures, perhaps even one to a species. A grotesque individual which has found its equilibrium under twenty miles of water. Small wonder, said Govinda, that human beings stress so fiercely the next realizable possibilities and are so eager to bound from the surface of the earth. The imagination is innately a biological power seeking to overcome impossible conditions.

Mr. Sammler raised his face, aware that someone was hastening toward him. He saw Feffer. Always in a rush. Feffer was stout, should have lost weight. He had trouble with his back, and wore at times an elastic orthopedic garment. Large, with fresh color, with the vivid brown François Premier beard and straight nose, Feffer always seemed to demand haste from his body, his legs. An all-but-running urgency. The hands, awkward and pink, were raised as if he feared to collide with another rush like his own. The brown eyes were key-shaped. As he grew older, the corners would be more elaborately notched.

"I *thought* you might stop here a minute," said Feffer. "Wallace said you had just left, so I ran down."

"Indeed? Well, the sun is shining, and I was in no hurry to go down into the subway. I haven't seen you since the lecture."

"That's right. I had to go to the telephone. I understand that you were wonderful. I genuinely apologize for the behavior of the students. That's my generation for you! I don't even know if they were real students or just tough characters—you know, militants, dropouts. It's not the kids who start the trouble. All the leaders are older. But Fanny looked after you, didn't she?"

"The young lady?"

"I didn't just disappear. I assigned a girl to look after you."

"I see. Your wife, by chance?"

"No, no." Feffer quickly smiled, and quickly went on, sitting on the edge of the bench. He wore a dark-blue velvet double-breasted jacket with large pearl buttons. His arm reached the backrest of the bench and lay affectionately near Sammler's shoulder. "Not my wife. Just a girl I fuck now and then, and look after."

"I see. It all seems so rapid. It strikes me that there is something electronic about your contacts. You shouldn't have left. I was your guest. Too late, I suppose, for you to learn manners. Still, she was very nice. She conducted me from the hall. I didn't expect such a large crowd. I thought you might be making money on me."

"I? No. Never. Believe me—no. It was a benefit for black children, just as I said. You must believe me, Mr. Sammler. I wouldn't put you into a con, I have too much regard for you. You may not know it, or it may not matter to you, but you have a special position with me, which is practically sacred. Your life, your experiences, your character, your views—plus your soul. There are relationships I would do anything to protect. And if I hadn't been called to the phone, I would have blasted that guy. I know that shit. He wrote a book about homosexuals in prison; he's like a poor man's Jean Genet. Buggery behind bars. Or being a pure Christian angel because you commit murder and have beautiful male love affairs. You know how it is."

"I have a general idea. But you misled me, Lionel."

"I didn't mean to. At the last minute a speaker didn't show for another student thing, and some of my graduate-school buddies who were frantic got hold of me. I saw a way to double the take. For the remedial-reading project. I assumed it wouldn't make so much difference to you, you would understand. I made a deal. I got the best of them."

"What was the subject of the missing speaker?"

"Sorel and Modern Violence, I think it was."

"And I talked about Orwell and what a sane person he was."

"Lots of young radicals see Orwell as part of the cold-war anti-Communist gang. You didn't really praise the Royal Navy, did you?"

"Is that what you heard?"

"If it hadn't been such an important call I would never have left. It was a question of buying or not buying a locomotive. The federal government creates these funny situations with tax breaks to encourage investment. Where it thinks dollars ought to go. You can buy a jet plane and lease it to the airlines. You can lease the locomotive to Penn Central or the B & O. Cattle investments get similar encouragement."

"Are you already making such sums that you need these deductions?"

Sammler didn't want to lead Feffer into dream conversation, exaggeration, fantasy, lying. He didn't know how much the poor young man made up simply to impress, to entertain. Feffer had a strange need to cover himself with the brocade of boasts. Money, brag—Jewish foibles. American too? Being deficient in contemporary American information, Sammler was tentative here. It was, however, no kindness to listen to this big talk. Sammler appreciated the degree of life in young Feffer, the marvelous rich color of his cheeks, the passion-sounds he made. The voice resembling an instrument played with higher and higher intensity but musically hopeless—the undertones appealing really for help.

But sometimes Mr. Sammler felt that the way he saw things could not be right. His experiences had been too peculiar, and he feared that he projected peculiarities onto life. Life was probably not blameless, but he often thought that life was not and could not be what he was seeing. And then again, most powerfully, he occasionally felt on the contrary that he was a million times exceeded in strangeness by the phenomena themselves. What oddities!

"Really, Lionel, you aren't about to buy a whole locomotive."

"Not alone. As part of a group. One hundred thousand dollars a share."

"And what about this other plan, with Wallace? Photographing houses and identifying trees."

"It does sound hokey, but it's really a very good business idea. I intend to experiment with it personally. I have a great gift for salesmanship, I'll say that for myself. If the thing pans out, I'll organize it nationally, with sales crews in every part of the country. We'll need regional plant specialists. The problems would be different in Portland, Oregon, from Miami Beach or Austin, Texas. 'All men by nature desire to know.' That's the first sentence of Aristotle's *Metaphysics.* I never got much farther, but I figured that the rest must be out of date anyway. However, if they desire to know, it makes them depressed if they can't name the bushes on their own property. They feel like phonies. The bushes belong. They themselves don't. And I'm convinced that knowing the names of things braces people up. I've gone to shrinkers for years, and have they cured me of anything? They have not. They have put labels on my troubles, though, which sound like knowledge. It's a great comfort, and worth the money. You say, 'I'm manic.' Or you say, 'I'm a reactive-depressive.' You say about a social problem, 'It's colonialism.' Then the dullest brain has internal fireworks, and the sparks drive you out of your skull. It's divine. You think you're a new man. Well, the way to wealth and power is to latch on to this. When you set up a new enterprise, you redescribe the phenomena and create a feeling that we're getting somewhere. If people want things named or renamed, you can make dough by becoming a taxonomist. Yes, I definitely intend to try out this idea of Wallace's."

"It's ill-timed. Does he have to have a plane?"

"I can't say if it's essential, but he seems to have a thing about piloting. Well, that's his bag. Other people have other bags."

This last statement about other people was injected with much significance. Sammler saw what was happening. Feffer was pretending to hold back, out of a delicacy he didn't have, a piece of information he couldn't wait to release. His eagerness shone from his face. In the eyes. Upon the ready lips.

"What are you referring to?"

"I'm really referring to a certain Hindu scientist. I believe that his name is Lal. I think that this Lal is a guest lecturer at Columbia University."

"What about him?"

"Several days ago, after his lecture, a woman approached him. She asked to see his manuscript. He thought she just wanted to glance at something in the text and he let her take it. There was a small crowd of people around. I believe H. G. Wells was mentioned. Then the lady disappeared with the manuscript."

Mr. Sammler removed his hat and placed it on his lap over the sea-marbled cardboard.

"She walked off with it?"

"Disappeared with the only copy of the work."

"Ah. How unfortunate. The only, eh? Quite bad."

"Yes, I thought you might think so. Dr. Lal expected her to come back with it, that she might be just an absent-minded person. He didn't say anything for twenty-four hours. But then he went to the authorities. Is it the department of astronomy? Or some space program Columbia has?"

"How is it that you always have information of this sort, Lionel?"

"I have to have these contacts in my way of life. Naturally I know the security people—the campus cops. Anyway, they weren't equipped to handle this. They had to call in investigators. The Pinkertons. The original Pinkerton was picked by Abraham Lincoln himself to organize the Secret Service, you know. You do know that, don't you?"

"It doesn't seem to me an item of great importance. I suppose these Pinkertons will know how to recover this article. Isn't it stupid to have only one copy? With all these Xeroxes and reproducing machines, and the man *is* a scientist."

"Well, I don't know. There was Carlyle. There was T. E. Lawrence. Brilliant people, weren't they? And they both lost the only copy of a masterpiece."

"Dear, dear."

"By now the campus is covered with posters. Manuscript missing. And there is a description of the lady. Often seen at public lectures. She wears a wig, carries a shopping bag, is associated somehow with H. G. Wells."

"Yes, I see."

"You wouldn't know anything about it, would you, Mr. Sammler? Naturally I want to help."

"I am astonished by the amount of information that sticks to you. You remind me of a frog's tongue. It flips out and comes back covered with gnats."

"I didn't think I was doing any harm. Where you are concerned, Mr. Sammler, I have only one interest, and that is protection. I have a protective instinct toward you. I am aware it might be Oedipal—the names, again—but I have a feeling of veneration toward you. You are the only person in the world with whom I would use a word like veneration. That's the kind of word you write down, not say."

"Yes, I understand that somewhat, Lionel." Mr. Sammler's forehead, grown damp, was itching. He touched it finely with his ironed pocket handkerchief. It was Shula who brought back his handkerchiefs ironed so smooth and flat.

"I know that you are trying to condense what you know, your life experience. Into a Testament."

"How do you know this?"

"You told me."

"Did I? I don't remember ever saying that. It is very private. If I am saying things unaware, it's a bad sign. I certainly never meant to mention it."

"We were standing in front of the Bretton Hall Hotel, that miserable bunch of decay, and you were leaning on the umbrella. And may I say"—there were signs of an upward expansion of feeling—"I may have doubts about other people, whether they're even human, but I love you without reservation. And to relieve your mind, you didn't discuss anything, you only said that you would like to boil down your experience of life to a few statements. Maybe just one single statement."

"Sydney Smith."

"Smith?"

"He said, 'Short views, for God's sake, short views.' An English clergyman."

To hear what Shula-Slawa had done (folly-devotion-to-Papa-comedy-theft) filled oppressively certain spaces for oppression which had opened and widened during the last three decades. Because of Elya, they were all agape today. Before 1939 Sammler could recall no such heaviness and darkness. Was there anywhere in the world a shrinking-tincture that could be prescribed for such openings? Mr. Sammler did try to turn toward the fun of the thing, imagining Shula in space shoes, disorderly crimson on the mouth, coming up like a little demon body from *Grimm's Fairy Tales*, making off with the treasure of a Hindu sage. Sammler himself was treated like some sort of Enchanter by Shula. She thought he was Prospero. He could make beautiful culture. Compose a memoir of the highest distinction, so magical that the world would long remember what a superior thing it was to be a Sammler. The answer of private folly to public folly (in an age of overkill) was more distinction, more high accomplishments, more dazzling brilliants strewn before admiring mankind. Pearls before swine? Mr. Sammler, thinking of Rabbi Ipsheimer, whom he had been dragged by Shula to hear, revised the old saying. Artificial pearls before real swine were cast by these jet-set preachers. To have thought this made him more cheerful. His nervously elegant hand made a shaking bridge over the tinted spectacles, adjusting them without need on the nose. Well, he was not what Shula believed him to be. Moreover, he was not what Feffer thought. How could he satisfy the needs of these imaginations? Feffer in the furious whirling of his spirit took him for a fixed point. In such hyperenergetic revolutions you fell in love with ideas of stability, and Sammler was an idea of stability. And how lavishly Feffer flattered him! Sammler was sorry about that. He made sure his large hat was covering the notebook entirely.

"Is there anything you would like me to do?" said Feffer.

"Why yes, Lionel." He rose. "Walk with me to the subway. I'm going to Union Square."

By the wrought-iron gate they left the little park, westward past the Quaker Meeting House, and then the cool sandstone buildings set back among trees. The chained bellies of garbage cans. One of the chains even wore a sheath. And there were dogs, more dogs. Devoted dog-tendance—by schoolchildren, by women in fairly high style, by certain homosexuals. One would have said that only the Eskimos had nearly so much to do with dogs as this local branch of mankind. The veterinarians must be sailing in yachts, surely. Their fees were high.

I shall get hold of Shula right away, Mr. Sammler decided. He hated scenes with his daughter. She might set her teeth, burst into screams. He cared too much for her. He cherished her. And really, his only contribution to the continuation of the species! It filled him with heartache and pity that he and

Antonina had not blended better. Since she was a child he had seen, especially in the slenderness of Shula's neck, so vulnerably valved, in the visible glands, and blue veins, in the big bluish eyelids and topheavy head, a pitiful legacy, loony, frail, touching him with a fear of doom. Well, the Polish nuns had saved her. When he came to the convent to get her, she was already fourteen years old. Now she was over forty, straying about New York with her shopping bags. She would have to return the manuscript immediately. Dr. Govinda Lal would be frantic. Who knew what Asiatic form that man's despair was taking.

Meantime too there was in Sammler's consciousness a red flush. Possibly due to Elya Gruner's condition. This assumed a curious form, that of a vast crimson envelope, a sky-filling silk fabric, the flap fastened by a black button. He asked himself whether this might not be what mystics meant by seeing a mandala, and believed the suggestion might have been implanted by association with Govinda, an Asiatic. But he himself, a Jew, no matter how Britannicized or Americanized, was also an Asian. The last time he was in Israel, and that was very recent, he had wondered how European, after all, Jews were. The crisis he witnessed there had brought out a certain deeper Orientalism. Even in German and Dutch Jewry, he thought. As for the black button, was it an after-image of the white moon?

Through Fifteenth Street ran a warm spring current. Lilacs and sewage. There were as yet no lilacs, but an element of the savage gas was velvety and sweet, reminiscent of blooming lilac. All about was a softness of perhaps dissolved soot, or of air passed through many human breasts, or metabolized in multitudinous brains, or released from as many intestines, and it got to one—oh, deeply, too! Now and then there came an appreciative or fanciful pleasure, apparently inconsequent, suggested by the ruddy dun of sandstone, by cool corners of the warmth. Bliss from his surroundings! For a certain period Mr. Sammler had resisted such physical impressions—being wooed almost comically by momentary and fortuitous sweetness. For quite a long time he had felt that he was not necessarily human. Had no great use, during that time, for most creatures. Very little interest in himself. Cold even to the thought of recovery. What was there to recover? Little regard for earlier forms of himself. Disaffected. His judgment almost blank. But then, ten or twelve years after the war, he became aware that this too was changing. In the human setting, along with everyone else, among particulars of ordinary life he *was* human—and, in short, creatureliness crept in again. Its low tricks, its doggish hind-sniffing charm. So that now, really, Sammler didn't know how to take himself. He wanted, with God, to be free from the bondage of the ordinary and the finite. A soul released from Nature, from impressions, and from everyday life. For this to happen God Himself must be waiting, surely. And a man who has been killed and buried should have no other interest. He should be perfectly disinterested. Eckhardt said in so many words that God loved disinterested purity and unity. God Himself was drawn toward the disinterested soul. What besides the spirit should a man care for who has come back from the grave? However, and mysteriously enough, it happened, as Sammler observed, that one was always, and so powerfully, so persuasively, drawn back to human conditions. So that these flecks within one's substance would always stipple with their reflections all that a man turns toward, all that flows about him. The shadow of his nerves would always cast stripes, like trees on grass, like water over sand, the light-made network. It was a second encounter of the disinterested spirit with fated biological necessities, a return match with the persistent creature.

Therefore, walking toward the BMT, Union Square Station, one hears Feffer explain why it is necessary to purchase a Diesel locomotive. A beautiful stroke of business. So apt! So congruent with spring, death, Oriental mandalas, sewer gas edged with opiate lilac sweetness. Bliss from bricks, from the sky! Bliss and mystic joy!

Mr. Artur Sammler, confidant of New York eccentrics; curate of wild men and progenitor of a wild woman; registrar of madness. Once take a stand, once draw a baseline, and contraries will assail you. Declare for normalcy, and you will be stormed by aberrancies. All postures are mocked by their opposites. This is what happens when the individual begins to be drawn back from disinterestedness to creaturely conditions. Portions or aspects of his earlier self revive. The former character asserts itself, and sometimes disagreeably, weakly, disgracefully. It was the earlier Sammler, the Sammler of London and Cracow, who had gotten off the bus at Columbus Circle foolishly eager to catch sight of a black criminal. He now had to avoid the bus, dreading another encounter. He had been warned, positively instructed, to appear no more.

"Just a minute, now," said Feffer. "I know you hate subways. Isn't there a switch here? I thought you were positively claustrophobic."

Feffer was extremely intelligent. He had been admitted to Columbia without a high-school certificate by obtaining unheard-of marks in the entrance examinations. He was sly, shrewd, meddling, as well as fresh, charming and vigorous. In his eyes a strangely barbed look appeared, a kind of hooking intensity. Sammler, the earlier Sammler, had had little power to resist such looks.

"It isn't because of the crook you saw on the bus, is it?"

"Who told you about him?"

"Your niece, Mrs. Arkin, did. I mentioned that before the lecture."

"So you did. And she told you, eh?"

"Yes, about the fancy dress, the Dior accessories, and all of that. What a terrific gas! So you're afraid of him. Why? Has he spotted you?"

"Something like that."

"Did he speak?"

"Not a word."

"There's something going on, Mr. Sammler. I think you'd better tell me about it. You may not understand the New York idiom. You may be in danger. You should tell a younger person."

"You confuse me, Feffer. There are moments when I am slightly not myself under your influence. I get muddled. You're very noisy, very turbulent."

"The man has done something to you. I just know it. What's he done? He may hurt you. You may be in trouble, and you shouldn't keep it to yourself. You're wise, but not hip, and this cat, Mr. Sammler, sounds like a real tiger. You've seen him in action?"

"Yes."

"And he's seen you looking?"

"That, too."

"That's serious. Now what has he done to scare you off the bus? You told the cops."

"I tried to. Come, Feffer, you're involving me in things I don't like."

"It's being driven from the bus that should bother you, interference with your customs, your habits, and so on. Are you afraid of him?"

"Well, I was aroused. My heart *did* beat awfully hard. The mind is so odd. Objectively I have little use for such experiences, but there is such an absurd craving for actions that connect with other actions, for coherency, for forms, for mysteries or fables. I may have thought that I had no more ordinary human curiosity left, but I was surprisingly wrong. And I don't like it. I don't like any of it."

"When he saw you, did he chase you?" said Feffer.

"He came after me, yes. Now let's drop the matter."

Feffer was unable to do that. His face was flaming. Within the old-fashioned frame of the beard, it prickled with wild modern passions. "He followed you but he didn't say anything? He must have gotten his message through, though. What did he do? He threatened you. Did he pull a switchblade on you?"

"No."

"A gun? Didn't he point a gun at you?"

"No gun." Had Sammler been in good balance he would have been able to resist Feffer. But his balance was not good. Descending to the subway was a trial. The grave, Elya, death, entombment, the Mezvinski vault.

"But he found out where you live?" said Feffer.

"Yes, Feffer, he tracked me. He must have had an eye on me for some time. He followed me into my lobby."

"But what did he do, Mr. Sammler! For God's sake, why won't you say!"

"What is there to say? It is ludicrous. It is not worth discussing. Simply nonsensical."

"Nonsensical? Are you sure it's nonsense? You'd better let a younger person judge. A different generation. A different . . ."

"Well, perhaps you have a natural claim to these bizarre nonsensical things. Such a hungry curiosity about them. I'll make it brief. The man exhibited himself to me."

"He didn't! That's just wild! To you? That's far out! Did he corner you?"

"Yes."

"In your own lobby, he pulled his thing on you? He flashed it?"

Sammler would say no more about it.

"Stupendous!" said Feffer. "What the devil was it like?" He was also laughing. How marvelous, what a . . . . a sudden glory. And if Sammler was any interpreter of laughter, Feffer was dying to see this phenomenon. To protect Sammler, yes. To guide him through the dangers of New York, yes. But to see, to meddle, to intrude, that was Lionel all over. Had to have a piece of the action—Sammler believed that was the current expression. "He yanked out his cock? Didn't say a word? Just flashed? Wow, Mr. Sammler! What the hell did he mean? How big a thing was it? You didn't say. I can imagine. It could be straight out of *Finnegans Wake*. 'Everyone must bare his crotch!' And he operates between Columbus Circle and Seventy-second Street in the rush hours? Well, what does one do about this? New York is really a gas city. And all those guys running for mayor like a bunch of lunatics. And Lindsay, just imagine Lindsay campaigning on his record. His *record*, no less, when they can't even send a cop to arrest a bandit. And the other guys with *their* record! Mr. Sammler, I know a guy at NBC television who has a talk show. It's really Fanny's husband. We ought to put you on that to discuss all this."

"Oh, come, Feffer."

"It would do everyone a hell of a lot of good to hear you. I know, I know, its as the man said, it's not the mind of the viewer you'll reach but his backsides. You'll tickle his backsides with beautiful feathers of deep thought."

"Absolutely."

"And yet, Mr. Sammler, to have influence and power. Or just confronting the phony with the real thing. You should denounce New York. You should speak like a prophet, like from another world. TV should be used. Used by *us*—and you might like coming out of isolation."

"We did that at Columbia yesterday, Feffer. I came out of isolation. You've already turned me into a performer."

"I'm thinking only of the good you could do."

"You're thinking of the arrangements you could promote, how you could get a finder's fee from Fanny's husband, and how close you could bring together the TV and that person's genitalia." Mr. Sammler was intensely smiling. Another moment, and he would actually have been laughing, drawn out of his preoccupations.

"Very well," said Feller. "I don't have the same ideals of privacy as you. I'm willing to drop it."

"By all means."

"I'll ride uptown on the bus with you."

"No, thanks."

"To make sure no one bothers you."

"What you want is to have me point him out."

"Really, I know how you dislike, you *hate*, subways."

"It's quite all right."

"Of course you've stirred up my curiosity, why should I deny it? I know you finally told me about him to get rid of me, and here I am pestering you still. You say he wears a camel's-hair coat?"

"I thought it was that."

"A homburg? Dior shades?"

"Homburg I'm certain of. The Dior is a guess."

"You're a good observer, I take your word for it. A mustache, also, fancy shirts and psychedelic neckties. He's a prince of some kind, or thinks he is."

"Yes," said Sammler. "A certain majesty is assumed."

"I have an idea about him."

"Let him be. Leave him alone, I advise you."

"I wouldn't actually tangle with him. I'd never do that. He wouldn't even suspect I was there. But cameras can be introduced anywhere. They even have photos of the child in the womb. Somehow they got a camera in. I just acquired a new Minox which is as small as a cigarette lighter."

"Don't be stupid, Lionel."

"He'd never know. I assure you. Wouldn't be aware. Pictures could be valuable. Catch a criminal, sell the story to *Look*.

Do a job on the police at the same time, and on Lindsay, who has no business being mayor while running for president. A triple killing."

The low wall of Union Square, the raised green platform of lawn parted by dry gray pathways, and the fast traffic circling —the foul, reckless, stinking automobiles. Sammler did not need Feller's hand on his elbow. He drew away.

"I go down here."

"This time of day you can't get a taxi. The shift is changing. I'll ride uptown with you."

Sammler, still holding hat and notebook by his side, the umbrella hooked on his wrist, pursued his way in the half-light of the corridors, in the smoke of grilled sausages. The quick turnstiles metered the tokens with a noise of ratchets. The bison-rumble of trains. Sammler wanted to ride alone. Feffer could not let him go. Feffer could not be quiet. His need was to be perpetually arresting, radiant with fresh interest. And, of course, because he respected Sammler so much he had to make tests or insert small notes or hints of disrespect, a little here, a bit there, liberties, familiarities, insinuations, exploring for spoilage. My dear fellow, why look so hard? There is corruption in many places. I could show you.

"This Fanny—the girl who guided you—she's very willing," said Feffer.

He ran on. "Nowadays girls are. Still somewhat shy. Not really so marvelous in the sack. In spite of big tits. Married of course. The husband works at night. He bosses the talk show I referred to . . ." And on: "I like companionship. We spend a lot of time together. Then when the insurance adjuster came . . ."

"What adjuster was that?" said Sammler.

"I put in a claim on a piece of luggage damaged at the airport. The fellow came over when Fanny was visiting me, and he fell in love with her—bang! Like that. He was a swinger, too, with chimpanzee teeth. Said he was a dropout from the Harvard School of Business. A real yellow face, and sweating. Awful. He looked like an oil filter that should have been changed five thousand miles ago."

"Ah, did he?"

"So I encouraged his interest in Fanny. That was good for my claim. Would I give him her phone number? I certainly did."

"With her permission?"

"I didn't think she'd mind. Then he phoned and said, 'This is Gus, honey. Meet me for a drink.' But her husband had picked up the phone. He works nights. And next time Gus came to see me I said, 'Boy, Gus, her husband is really sore. Stay away. He's tough, too.' Then Gus said . . ."

Was there no Eighteenth Street station? There was Twenty-third, Thirty-fourth. At Forty-second you changed to the IRT.

"Gus said, 'What am I afraid of? Look, I carry a gun.' He pulled out a pistol. I was flabbergasted. But it wasn't much of a gun either. I said, 'A thing like that? You couldn't shoot through a telephone book with it.' And before I knew it, he had the telephone book on a music stand and was aiming at it. That crazy sonofabitch. He was only five feet from it, and he fired, I never heard such a roar. The whole building heard. But I was right. The bullet went in only two inches. Couldn't pierce the Manhattan directory."

"Yes, a poor weapon."

"You know something about weapons?"

"Something."

"Well, you could just about wound a guy with that gun. Probably wouldn't kill unless you shot him in the head at short range. What a lot of lunatics around."

"Quite so."

"But I'm getting about two hundred bucks from insurance, which is more than the suitcase is worth, a piece of trash."

"Yes, clever business."

"Next day Gus came again and wanted me to write a recommendation for him."

"To whom?"

"To his superior in the adjuster's office."

At Ninety-sixth Street they ascended together into the full blast of Broadway. Feffer accompanied Sammler to his door.

"If you need assistance, Mr. Sammler . . ."

"I won't invite you up, Lionel. The fact is I'm feeling tired."

"It's spring. I mean it's the temperature change," said Feffer. "Even youth is susceptible to that."

Mr. Sammler in the elevator, extracting the Yale key from his change purse. He pushed into the foyer. In honor of spring, Margotte had set forsythia in Mason jars. One jar was overturned at once. Sammler brought a roll of paper towels from the kitchen, ascertaining as he went through the house that his niece had gone out. Soaking up the spilt water, watching the absorbent paper darken, he then lifted the telephone onto the maple arm of the sofa, sat on the bandanna covers, and dialed Shula. No reply. Perhaps she had turned off her telephone. Sammler had not seen her for several days. Now a thief, she very likely was in hiding. If Eisen was actually in New York, she had an added reason for locking herself away. Sammler could not imagine, however, that Eisen would actually want to molest her. He had other irons in the fire, he had other fish to fry (how fond old Sammler was of such expressions!).

Carrying the paper towels, the sopping and the dry, back to the kitchen, Sammler cut himself several slices of salami with the large chef's knife (Margotte seemed to have no small knives, she pared onions, even, with these great blades). He made a sandwich. Colman's English Mustard, still a favorite. Margotte's low-calorie cranberry juice. Unable to find clean glasses, he sipped from a paper cup. The feel of wax was disagreeable but he was on his way out of the house and had no time for washing and drying. He went at once across Broadway to Shula's apartment. He rang, he rapped, he raised his voice and said, "Shula, it's Father. Open. Shula?" He wrote a note and slipped it under the door. "Call me at once." Then, descending in the black elevator (how rusty and black it was!), he looked into her mailbox, which she never locked. It was full, and he sorted through the mail. Throwaway stuff. Personal letters, none. So she was evidently away, hadn't taken out her letters. Maybe she had caught a train to New Rochelle. She had a key to the Gruner house. Sammler had refused the offer of a key to her apartment. He didn't want to walk in when she was with a lover. Such a lover as she would have was surely to be dreaded. Undoubtedly she had one now and then. Perhaps for her complexion, when it was bad. He once had heard a woman say this. And Shula was proud of her clear skin. How could you know what people—individuals—were *really* doing!

When he returned, he asked Margotte, "You haven't seen Shula, have you?"

"No, Uncle Sammler, I haven't. You had a call, though, from your son-in-law."

"Eisen has called?"

"I told him you were at the hospital."

"What did he seem to want?"

"Why, to see the family. Though he said they don't come to see him when they're in Israel, not Elya and not you. He really sounded hurt."

Margotte's sympathies, so readily available, so full, made others feel stony-hearted.

"And Elya, how is he?" she said.

"Not well, I'm afraid."

"Oh, I must go and visit poor Elya."

"Perhaps you should, but very briefly."

"Oh, I wouldn't tire him. As for Shula, she's afraid to see Eisen. She thinks she did him a terrible injury when you forced her to leave."

"I never did. She was glad to go. He seemed glad, too. Did Eisen inquire for her?"

"Not a word. Didn't even mention her name. He talked about his work. His art. He's hunting for a studio."

"Yes . . . Well, it won't be easy to find in this city of artists. Lofts. But then of course he fought at Stalingrad, he could winter in a loft."

"He wanted to go to the hospital and do a drawing of Elya."

"A thing we should prevent, by any means."

"Uncle Sammler, would you join me for a cutlet? I'm cooking schnitzel."

"Thank you, I've eaten."

He went to his room.

With a reading glass held trembling in the long left hand, Sammler threw quivering transparencies on the writing paper. From the desk lamp, glassy nuclei of brightness followed the words he wrote.

Dear Professor Doctor:
Your manuscript is safe. The woman who borrowed it is my daughter. She meant no harm. It was only her thick-handed, clumsy way of helping me, advancing an imaginary project that obsesses her. She is pierced by an inspiration—H. G. Wells, the scientific future. She believes we share this inspiration. I am pierced sometimes from a different side by the vision of her activities. Psychologically archaic—all the fossils in her mental strata fully alive (the moon, too, is a kind of fossil)—she dreams about the future. Yet everyone grapples, each in his awkward muffled way, with a power, a Jacob's angel, to get a final satisfaction or glory that is withheld. In any case, kindly ask the authorities to call off their search. I beg you. My daughter evidently believed you were lending her this document, though it may point to treachery aforethought that she did not give you her name and address. However, I would be glad to bring *The Future of the Moon* to you. I have been reading it with fascination, though on the scientific side my qualifications are nil. More than thirty years ago, I enjoyed the friendship of H. G. Wells whose moon-fantasy you undoubtedly know—Selenites, subterranean moon-ocean, and all of that. As correspondent for Eastern European periodicals, I lived in England for many years. Woburn Square. Ah, it was lovely. But I apologize for my daughter. I can well imagine the anguish of spirit she must have caused you. In women the keenest sense of wrongdoing seems to be in a different place. The notebook lies before me at this moment. It is marbled green cardboard and the ink is brown and iridescent, almost bronze. I can be phoned at any hour of the night at the Endicott number under the date above.

Your obedient servant,
Artur Sammler

"Margotte," he said, leaving his desk.

She sat alone, eating in the dining room, under an imitation Tiffany shade of gay red-and-green paper. The tablecloth was an Indonesian print. All was really very dark, in the awkward room. She herself looked dark there, cutting the yellow-crusted veal on her dish. He should, more often, sit down to meals with her. A childless widow. He was sorry for her, the small face with its heavy black bangs. He took a chair. "Look here, Margotte, we have a problem with Shula."

"Let me set a place for you."

"No, thank you, I have no appetite. Please sit down. I'm afraid Shula stole something. Not a theft, really. That would be nonsense. She took something. A manuscript by a Hindu scientist at Columbia. It was, of course, done for me. That idiocy about H. G. Wells. You see, Margotte, this Indian book is about colonizing the moon and the planets. Shula took away the only copy."

"The moon. How fascinating, Uncle."

"Yes, industries on the moon. Manufacturing centers on the moon. How to build cities."

"I can see why Shula wanted it for you."

"But it must be returned. Why, it's stolen goods, Margotte, and detectives have been called in. And I can't find Shula. She knows she has done wrong."

"Oh, Uncle Sammler, would you call it a crime? Not by Shula. Poor creature."

"Yes, poor creature. To whom would this not apply, if you start to say poor creature?"

"I would never have said it about Ussher, I wouldn't say it about you, either."

"Really? Well, all right. I accept the correction. However, that Indian must be notified. Here I have a letter for him."

"Why not a telegram?"

"Useless. Telegrams are no longer delivered."

"That's what Ussher used to say. He said the messengers just threw them down the sewer."

"Mailing won't do. It might take three days for the letter to arrive. All these local communications are in decay," said Sammler. "Even Cracow in the days of Franz Josef was more efficient than the U.S. postal system. And Shula may be picked up by the police, that's what I'm afraid of. Could we send the doorman in a cab?"

"What's the matter with the telephone?"

"Yes, certainly, if I could be sure we would talk to Dr. Lal himself. A direct explanation. I hadn't thought of that. But how to get his number!"

"Couldn't you just take the manuscript to him?"

"Now that I know I have the only copy, I hesitate, Margotte, to go into the street with it, and especially at night, when people are being mugged. Suppose it were snatched out of my hands?"

"And the police?"

"They have given little satisfaction. I wish to avoid them. I did think perhaps of the security officers at Columbia, or even the Pinkerton people, but I would rather hand it over personally to Dr. Lal to make sure no charges will be brought against Shula. The Indian temperament is so excitable, you know. If he doesn't meet any of us, become personally acquainted, he will let the police advise him. Then we would need a lawyer. Don't suggest Wallace. In the past, Elya always had Mr. Widick take care of such matters."

"Well, perhaps handing him a letter is best. Better than the telephone. Maybe I should carry the letter to him, Uncle. Personally."

"Ah, yes, a woman. Coming from a woman, it might have a softening effect."

"Better than a doorman. It's still light. I can get a cab."

"I have a little money in my room. About ten dollars."

Then he heard Margotte on the telephone, making inquiries. He suspected that things were being done the least efficient way. But Margotte was prompt to help when difficulties were real. She didn't start discussions about Shula—the effects of the war or Antonina's death or puberty in a Polish convent or what terror could do to the psyche of a young girl. Elya was right. Ussher, too. Margotte was a good soul. Not persisting mechanically in her ways when the signal was given. As others did, jumping into their routines. Tumbling into their grooves.

In the bathroom there was a great rush of water. She was taking a shower, the usual sign that she was preparing to go out. If she had three occasions to leave the house, she took three showers in a day. He next heard her walking very rapidly in her bedroom, shoeless, but thumping quickly, opening closets and drawers. In about twenty minutes, dressed in her black basic and wearing a black straw hat, she was at his door and asking for the letter. She was a dear thing.

"You know where he is?" said Sammler. "Did you talk to him?"

"Not personally, he was out. But he's staying at Butler Hall, and the switchboard knew all about it."

Gloves, though the evening was warm. Perfume, quite a lot. Bare arms. Bruch might have liked those arms. They had a proper little heaviness of their own. She was at times a pretty woman. And Sammler saw that she was glad to have this errand. It saved her from an empty night at home. Ussher had been fond of late-late shows. Margotte rarely turned on the television set. It was often out of repair. Since Ussher's death, it had begun to look old-fashioned in its wood cabinet. Maybe it wasn't wood, but a woodlike wig of some dark and grained material.

"If I meet Dr. Lal—and should I wait for him at Butler Hall? Shall I bring him back with me?"

"I was planning to go again to the hospital," said Sammler. "You know, it's very bad for Elya."

"Oh, poor Elya. I know it's one thing on top of another. But don't make yourself too tired. You just got in."

"I'll lie down for fifteen minutes. Yes, if Dr. Lal wants to come, by all means, yes. Let him come."

Before she went, Margotte wanted to kiss the old man. He did not move away, although he felt that people were seldom in a fit state for kissing and that mostly it was done, in defilement, as a reminder of beatitude. But this kiss of Margotte's, reaching upward, getting on her toes and swelling her plump strong legs, was an appropriate one. She seemed grateful that he chose to live with her rather than with Shula, that he liked her so much, and that he turned to her also in trouble. Through him, moreover, she was going to meet a distinguished gentleman, a Hindu scientist. She was perfumed, she was wearing eye make-up.

He said, "I should be home by about ten."

"Then, if he is there, dear Uncle, I'll bring him back and he can wait here with me. He'll be so eager for his manuscript."

He saw her soon in the street. Touching the frieze curtain, he watched her going toward West End Avenue, up the pale width of the sidewalk, alert for a taxi. She was small, she was strong, and had a sort of compact female pride. Somewhat shaking as women do when they hurry. Gotten up strangely. And altogether odd. Females! The drafts must blow between their legs. Such observations originated mainly in kindly detachment, in farewell-detachment, in earth-departure-objectivity.

In daylight still, the white Spry sign across the Hudson began to flash against pale green and also down into the dark water; while in the sunset copper the asphalt belly of the street was softly disfigured, softly rank, with its manhole covers. And the cars always packed tightly into the street. Machines for going away.

Removing shoes and socks, Mr. Sammler raised a long foot to the sink. Wasn't he too old for such movements? Evidently not. In the privacy of his room he was actually less stiff in the limbs. He bathed the feet and did not dry them thoroughly, for it was a warm evening. Evaporation relieved the smarting. As evolutionary time went we had not long been bipeds, and the flesh of the feet suffered for it, especially in spring when organisms experienced a peculiar expansion. Tired and breathing quietly, Sammler lay down. He left his feet uncovered. He brought the coolness of the sheet over his flat, slender chest. He turned away his lamp to shine on the drawn curtain.

The luxury of nonintimidation by doom—that might describe his state. Since the earth altogether was now a platform, a point of embarkation, you could think with a very minimum of terror about going. Not to waive another man's terror for him (he was thinking of Elya with the calibrated metal torment in his throat). But often he felt himself very nearly out of it. And everything soon must change. Men would set their watches by other suns than this. Or time would vanish. We would need no personal names of the old sort in the sidereal future, nothing being fixed. We would be designated by other nouns. Days and nights would belong to the museums. The earth a memorial park, a merry-go-round cemetery. The seas powdering our bones like quartz, making sand, grinding our peace for us by the aeon. Well, that would be good—a melancholy good.

Ah. Before he had let go the curtain, when Margotte disappeared, before sitting to remove the shoes, before turning to wash his feet, he had seen, come to think of it, the moon not too remote from the Spry sign, and round as a traffic signal. This moon image or circular afterimage was still with him. And we know now from photographs the astronauts took, the beauty of the earth, its white and its blue, its fleeces, the great glitter afloat. A glorious planet. But wasn't everything being done to make it intolerable to abide here, an unconscious collaboration of all souls spreading madness and poison? To flush us out? Not so much Faustian aspiration, thought Mr.

Sammler, as a scorched-earth strategy. Ravage all, and what does death get? Defile, and then flee to the bliss of oblivion. Or bolt to other worlds.

He recognized by these thoughts that he was preparing to meet Govinda Lal. They would possibly discuss such matters. Dr. Lal, whose field seemed to he biophysics, and who might, like most experts, turn out to be a nonindividual, gave signs, in his writing anyway, of wider thoughtfulness. For after each technical section he offered remarks on the human aspects of future developments. He seemed aware, for instance, that the discovery of America had raised hopes in the sinful Old World of a New Eden. "A shared consciousness," Lal had written, "may well be the new America. Access to central data mechanisms may foster a new Adam." Well, it was very odd what Mr. Sammler found himself doing as he lay in his room, in an old building. Settling, the building had cracked its plaster, and along these slanted cracks he had mentally inscribed certain propositions. According to one of these he, personally, stood apart from all developments. From a sense of deference, from age, from good manners, he sometimes affirmed himself to be *out* of it, *hors d'usage*, not a man of the times. No force of nature, nothing paradoxical or demonic, he had no drive for smashing through the masks of appearances. Not "Me and the Universe." No, his personal idea was one of the human being conditioned by other human beings, and knowing that present arrangements were not, *sub specie aeternitatis*, the truth, but that one should be satisfied with such truth as one could get by approximation. Trying to live with a civil heart. With disinterested charity. With a sense of the mystic potency of humankind. With an inclination to believe in archetypes of goodness. A desire for virtue was no accident.

New worlds? Fresh beginnings? Not such a simple matter. (Sammler, reaching for diversion.) What did Captain Nemo do in *20,000 Leagues Under the Sea*? He sat in the submarine, the *Nautilus*, and on the ocean floor he played Bach and Handel on the organ. Good stuff, but old. And what of Wells' Time Traveler, when he found himself thousands of years in the future? He fell in square love with a beautiful Eloi maiden. To take with one, whether down into the depths or out into space and time, something dear, and to preserve it—that seemed to be the impulse. Jules Verne was quite right to have Handel on the ocean floor, not Wagner, though in Verne's day Wagner was avant-garde among the symbolists, fusing word and sound. According to Nietzsche the Germans, insufferably oppressed by being German, used Wagner like hashish. To Mr. Sammler's ears, Wagner was background music for a pogrom. And what should one have on the moon, electronic compositions? Mr. Sammler would advise against that. Art groveling before Science.

But Sammler was preoccupied by different matters, far from playful. Feffer, wishing to divert him, had told him the tale of the insurance adjuster who pulled out the pistol. It was no diversion. Feffer had said that with that rotten gun you would have to shoot a man at close range, and in the head. Killing point blank. This shooting in the head was what Sammler had been attempting to shut out, screen off. Hopeless. Diversion shriveled up. He was obliged to give in, to confront certain insufferable things. These things were not subject to control. They had to be endured. They had become a power within him which did not care whether he could bear them or not. Visions or nightmares for others, but for him daylight events, in full consciousness. Certainly Sammler had not experienced things denied to everyone else. Others had gone through the like. Before and after. Especially non-Europeans had a quieter way of taking such things. Surely some Navaho, Apache must have fallen into the Grand Canyon, survived, picked himself up, possibly said nothing to his tribe. Why speak of it? Things that happen, happen. So, for his part, it had happened that Sammler, with his wife and others, on a perfectly clear day, had had to strip naked. Waiting, then, to be shot in the mass grave. (Over a similar new grave Eichmann had testified that he had walked, and the fresh blood welling up at his shoes had sickened him. For a day or two, he had to lie in bed.) Sammler had already that day been struck in the eye by a gun butt and blinded. In contraction from life, when naked, he already felt himself dead. But somehow he had failed, unlike the others, to be connected. Comparing the event, as mentally he sometimes did, to a telephone circuit: death had not picked up the receiver to answer his ring. Sometimes, when he walked on Broadway today, and heard a phone ringing in a shop when doors were open, he tried to find, to intuit, the syllable one would hear from death. "Hello? Ah, you at last." "Hello." And the air of the street visibly vapored with lead, and also with a brass tinge. But if there were live New York bodies passing as there had once been dead ones piled on top of him, if there were this crowd strolling, lounging, dragging, capering (a Broadway rabble to which he belonged)—if there were this, there was also enough to feed every mouth: baked goods, raw meat, smoked meat, bleeding fish, smoked fish, barbecued pork and chicken, apples like ammunition, antihunger orange grenades. In the gutters, along curbs was much food, eaten, as he saw at three a.m., by night-emerging rats. Buns, chicken bones, which, once, he would have thanked God to have. When he was a partisan in Zamosht Forest, freezing, the dead eye like a ball of ice in his head. Envying fallen sticks from his nearness to their state. In a moldered frozen horse blanket and rag-wrapped feet. Mr. Sammler carried a weapon. He and other starved men chewing at roots and grasses to stay alive. They drifted out at night to explode bridges, unseat rails, kill German stragglers.

Sammler himself, shooting men. There was Feffer's mad insurance adjuster, clutched by impulse or desire for display, firing at the telephone book on the music stand. That had something comically fanatical about it. Putting a bullet through a million close-printed names—a parlor game. But Sammler was driven through the parlor and back to Zamosht Forest. There at very close range he shot a man he had disarmed. He made him fling away his carbine. To the side. A good five feet into snow. It landed flat and sank. Sammler ordered the man to take off his coat. Then the tunic. The sweater, the boots. After this, he said to Sammler in a low voice, "*Nicht schiessen.*" He asked for his life. Red-headed, a big chin bronze-stubbled, he was scarcely breathing. He was white. Violet under the eyes. Sammler saw the soil already sprinkled on his face. He saw the grave on his skin. The grime of the lip, the large creases of skin descending from his nose already lined with dirt—that man to Sammler was already underground. He was no longer dressed for life. He was marked, lost. Had to go. Was gone. "Don't kill me. Take the things." Sammler did not answer, but stood out of reach. "I have children." Sammler pulled the trigger. The body then lay in the snow. A second shot went through the head and shattered it. Bone burst. Matter flew out.

Sammler picked up as much as he could—gun, shells, food, boots, gloves. Two shots in winter air; the sound would carry for miles. He hurried, looking back once. The red hair and thick nose he could see from the bushes. Regrettably there was no chance to get the shirt. The stinking woolen socks yes. He had wanted those badly. He was too weak to carry his loot far. He sat down under winter-creaking trees and ate the German's bread. With it, he took snow into his mouth to help the swallowing, which was difficult. He had no saliva. The thing no doubt would have happened differently to another man, a man who had been eating, drinking, smoking, and whose blood was brimming with fat, nicotine, alcohol, sexual secretions. None of these in Sammler's blood. He was then not entirely human. Rag and paper, a twine-wound bundle, and those objects might have been blown where they liked, if the string had snapped. One would not have minded much. At that minimum we were. Not much there for human appeal, for the pleading of a distorted face and sinews spreading into the throat.

When Mr. Sammler hid later in the mausoleum, it was not from the Germans but from the Poles. In Zamosht Forest the Polish partisans turned on the Jewish fighters. The war was ending, the Russians advancing, and the decision seems to have been taken to reconstruct a Jewless Poland. There was therefore a massacre. The Poles at dawn came shooting. As soon as it was light enough for murder. There was fog, smoke. The sun tried to rise. Men began to drop, and Sammler ran. There were two other survivors. One played dead. The other, like Sammler, found a break and rushed through. Hiding in the swamp, Sammler lay under a tree trunk, in the mud, under scum. At night he left the forest. He took a chance with Cieslakiewicz next day. (Was it only a day? Perhaps it was longer.) He spent those summer weeks in the cemetery. Then he appeared in Zamosht, in the town itself, wild, gaunt, decaying, the dead eye bulging—like a whelk. One of the doomed who had lasted it all out.

Scarcely worth so much effort, perhaps. There are times when to quit is more reasonable and decent and hanging on is a disgrace. Not to go beyond a certain point in hanging on. Not to stretch the human material too far. The nobler choice. So Aristotle thought.

Mr. Sammler himself was able to add, to basic wisdom, that to kill the man he ambushed in the snow had given him pleasure. Was it only pleasure? It was more. It was joy. You would call it a dark action? On the contrary, it was also a bright one. It was mainly bright. When he fired his gun, Sammler, himself nearly a corpse, burst into life. Freezing in Zamosht Forest, he had often dreamed of being near a fire. Well, this was more sumptuous than fire. His heart felt lined with brilliant, rapturous satin. To kill the man and to kill him without pity, for he was dispensed from pity. There was a flash, a blot of fiery white. When he shot again it was less to make sure of the man than to try again for that bliss. To drink more flames. He would have thanked God for this opportunity. If he had had any God. At that time, he did not. For many years, in his own mind, there was no judge but himself.

In the privacy of his bed he turned very briefly to that rage (for reference, he did it). Luxury. And when he himself was nearly beaten to death. Had to lift dead bodies from himself. Desperate! Crawling out. Oh heart-bursting! Oh vile! Then he himself knew how it felt to take a life. Found it could be an ecstasy.

He got up. It was pleasant here—the lamplight, his own room. He had gathered a very pleasant sort of intimacy about himself. But he got up. He wasn't resting, and he might as well go to the hospital. His nephew Gruner needed him. That thing was fizzing in his brain. Soil was scattered on *his* face. Look hard. You must see some grains. So, rising, Sammler smoothed back the bedding, the coverlet. He never left a bed unmade. He drew on clean socks. Up to the knee.

Too bad! Too bad, that is, to be pounded back and forth so abnormally on the courts, like a ball between powerful players. Or subject to wild instances. Oh merciless! Thank you, no, no! I did not want to fall into the Grand Canyon. Nice not to have died? Nicer not to have fallen in. Too many inside things were ruptured. To some people, true enough, experience seemed wealth. Misery worth a lot. Horror a fortune. Yes. But I never wanted such riches.

After the socks his ten-year-old shoes. He kept having them resoled. Good enough for getting around Manhattan. He took excellent care of his things, he stuffed his good suit with tissue paper, put in shoe trees at night even though this leather was puckered with age and wear, streaming with wrinkles. These same shoes Mr. Sammler had worn in Israel, in the summer of 1967. Not Israel only but also Jordan, the Sinai Desert, and into Syrian territory during the Six-Day War. His second visit. If it was a visit. It was an expedition. At the beginning of the Aqaba crisis he had suddenly become excited. He could not sit still. He had written to an old journalist friend in London and said he was obliged to go, he absolutely must go, as a journalist, and cover the events. There was an association of Eastern European publications. All Sammler really wanted was credentials, a card to enable him to wire cables, a press pass to satisfy the Israelis. The money was supplied by Gruner. And so Sammler had been with the armies on the three fronts. It was curious, that. At the age of seventy-two on battlegrounds, wearing these shoes and a seersucker jacket and soiled white cap from Kresge's. Tankmen spotted him as an American because of the jacket, shouting, "Yank!" Coming up to them, he spoke to some in Polish, to others in French, English. He thought of himself at moments as a camel among the armored vehicles. No Zionist, Mr. Sammler, and for many years little interested in Jewish affairs. Yet, from the start of the crisis, he could not sit in New York reading the world press. If only because for the second time in twenty-five years the same people were threatened by extermination: the so-called powers letting things drift toward disaster; men armed for a massacre. And he refused to stay in Manhattan watching television.

Perhaps it was the madness of things that affected Sammler most deeply. The persistence, the maniacal push of certain ideas, themselves originally stupid, stupid ideas that had lasted for centuries, this is what drew the most curious reactions from him. The stupid sultanism of a Louis Quatorze reproduced in General de Gaulle—Neo-Charlemagne, someone said. Or the imperial ambition of the Czars in the Mediterranean. They wanted to be the dominant naval power in the Mediterranean, a stupid craving of two centuries, and this, under the "revolutionary" auspices of the Kremlin, was still worked at, in the same way—worked at! Did it make no difference that soon floating dominion by armed ships would be as obsolete as Ashurbanipal, as queer as the dog-headed gods of Egypt? Why, no, it made no difference. No more than the disappearance of Jews from Poland made a difference to the anti-Semitism of the Poles. This was the meaning of historical stupidity. And the Russians also, with their national tenacity. Give them a system, let them grasp some idea, and they would plunge to the depths with it, they would apply it to the end, pave the whole universe with hard idiot material. In any case, it had seemed to Sammler that he must reach the scene. He would be there, to send reports, to do something, perhaps to die in the massacre. Through such a thing he could not sit in New York. That! Quivering, riotous, lurid New York—Feffer's gas city! And Sammler himself went to an extreme, became perhaps too desperate, carried away, beginning to think of sleeping pills, poison. It was really the tangled nervous system, the "nerve-spaghetti." These were his old Polish nerves raging. It was his old panic, his peculiar affliction. He would not read a second day's reports on Shukairy's Arabs in Tel Aviv killing thousands. He told Gruner that. Gruner said, "If you feel so strongly about it, I think you should go." Now Sammler thought that he had been guilty of exaggeration. He had lost his head. Still he had been right to go.

Sammler, from keeping his own counsel for so long, from seven decades of internal consultation, had his own views on most matters. And even the greatest independence was insufficient, still not enough. And there were mental dry courses in his head, of no interest to anyone else, perhaps—wadis, he believed such things were called, small ravines made by the steady erosion of preoccupations. The taking of life was one of these. Just that. His life had nearly been taken. He had seen life taken. He had taken it himself. He knew it was one of the luxuries. No wonder princes had so long reserved the right to murder with impunity. At the very bottom of society there was also a kind of impunity, because no one cared what happened. Under that dark brutal mass blood crimes were often disregarded. And at the very top, the ancient immunities of kings and nobles. Sammler thought that this was what revolutions were really about. In a revolution you took away the privileges of an aristocracy and redistributed them. What did equality mean? Did it mean all men were friends and brothers? No, it meant that all belonged to the elite. Killing was an ancient privilege. This was why revolutions plunged into blood. Guillotines? Terror? Only a beginning—nothing. There came Napoleon, a gangster who washed Europe well in blood. There came Stalin, for whom the really great prize of power was unobstructed enjoyment of murder. That mighty enjoyment of consuming the breath of men's nostrils, swallowing their faces like a Saturn. This was what the conquest of power really seemed to mean. Sammler tied his shoelaces—continued dressing. He brushed at his hair. Trancelike. At several removes from the self in the glass, opposite. And for the middle part of society there was envy and worship of this power to kill. How those middle-class Sorels and Maurrases adored it—the hand that gripped the knife with authority. How they loved the man strong enough to take blood guilt on himself. For them an elite must prove itself in this ability to murder. For such people a saint must be understood as one who was equal in spirit to the fiery twisting of crime in the inmost fibers of his heart. The superman testing himself with an ax, crushing the skulls of old women. The Knight of Faith, capable of cutting the throat of his Isaac upon God's altar. And now the idea that one could recover, or establish, one's identity by killing, becoming equal thus to any, equal to the greatest. A man among men knows how to murder. A patrician. The middle class had formed no independent standards of honor. Thus it had no resistance to the glamour of killers. The middle class, having failed to create a spiritual life of its own, investing everything in material expansion, faced disaster. Also, the world becoming disenchanted, the spirits and demons expelled from the air were now taken inside. Reason had swept and garnished the house, but the last state might be worse than the first. Well, now, what would one carry out to the moon?

He brushed the felt hat with an elbow, backed into the vestibule, locked and tested the door, buzzed for the elevator, and descended. Mr. Sammler, back walking the streets, which now were dark blue, a bluish glow from the street lamps. Stooped, walking quickly. He had only two hours, and if he couldn't catch the Eighty-sixth Street Crosstown to Second

Avenue, he would be forced to take a cab. West End was very gloomy. He preferred even fuming, heaving, fool-heaped, quivering, stinking Broadway. With the tufts above his glasses silken, graying, tangled, rising as be faced the phenomenon. No use being the sensitive observer, the tourist (was there any land stable enough to tour?), the philosophical rambler out on Broadway, inspecting the phenomenon. The phenomenon had in some way achieved a sense of its own interest and observability. It was aware of being a scene of perversity, it knew its own despair. And fear. The terror of it. Here you might see the soul of America at grips with historical problems, struggling with certain impossibilities, experiencing violently states inherently static. Being realized but trying itself to realize, to act. Attempting to make interest. This attempt to make interest was, for Mr. Sammler, one reason for the pursuit of madness. Madness makes interest. Madness is the attempted liberty of people who feel themselves overwhelmed by giant forces of organized control. Seeking the magic of extremes. Madness is a base form of the religious life.

But wait—Sammler cautioning himself. Even this madness is also to a considerable extent a matter of performance, of enactment. Underneath there persists, powerfully too, a thick sense of what is normal for human life. Duties are observed. Attachments are preserved. There is work. People show up for jobs. It is extraordinary. They come on the bus to the factory. They open the shop, they sweep, they wrap, they wash, they fix, they tend, they count, they tend the computers. Each day, each night. And however rebellious at heart, however despairing, terrified, or worn bare, come to their tasks. Up and down in the elevator, sitting down to the desk, behind the wheel, tending machinery. For such a volatile and restless animal, such a high-strung, curious animal, an ape subject to so many diseases, to anguish, boredom, such discipline, such drill, such strength for regularity, such assumption of responsibility, such regard for order (even in disorder) is a great mystery, too. Oh, it is a mystery. One cannot mistake this for thorough madness, therefore. One thing, though, the disciplined hate the undisciplined to the point of murder. Thus the working class, disciplined, is a great reservoir of hatred. Thus the clerk behind the wicket finds it hard to forgive those who come and go their apparent freedom. And the bureaucrat, glad when disorderly men are killed. All of them, killed.

What one sees on Broadway while bound for the bus. All human types reproduced, the barbarian, redskin, or Fiji, the dandy, the buffalo hunter, the desperado, the queer, the sexual fantasist, the squaw; bluestocking, princess, poet, painter, prospector, troubadour, guerrilla, Che Guevara, the new Thomas à Becket. Not imitated are the businessman, the soldier, the priest, and the square. The standard is aesthetic. As Mr. Sammler saw the thing, human beings, when they have room, when they have liberty and are supplied also with ideas, mythologize themselves. They legendize. They expand by imagination and try to rise above the limitations of the ordinary forms of common life. And what is "common" about "the common life"? What if some genius were to do with "common life" what Einstein did with "matter"? Finding its energetics, uncovering its radiance. But at the present level of crude vision, agitated spirits fled from the oppressiveness of "the common life," separating themselves from the rest of their species, from the life of their species, hoping perhaps to get away (in some peculiar sense) from the death of their species. To perform higher actions, to serve the imagination with special distinction, it seems essential to be histrionic. This, too, is a brand of madness. Madness has always been a favorite choice of the civilized man who prepares himself for a noble achievement. It is often the simplest state of availability to ideals. Most of us are satisfied with that: signifying by a kind of madness devotion to, availability for, higher purposes. Higher purposes do not necessarily appear.

If we are about to conclude our earth business—or at least the first great phase of it—we had better sum these things up. But briefly. As briefly as possible.

Short views, for God's sake!

Then: a crazy species? Yes, perhaps. Though madness is also a masquerade, the project of a deeper reason, a result of the despair we feel before infinities and eternities. Madness is a diagnosis or verdict of some of our greatest doctors and geniuses, and of their man-disappointed minds. Oh, man stunned by the rebound of man's powers. And what to do? In the matter of histrionics, see, for instance, what that furious world-boiler Marx had done, insisting that revolutions were made in historical costume, the Cromwellians as Old Testament prophets, the French in 1789 dressed in Roman outfits. But the proletariat, he said, he declared, he affirmed, would make the first non-imitative revolution. It would not need the drug of historical recollection. From sheer ignorance, knowing no models, it would simply do the thing pure. He was as giddy as the rest about originality. And only the working class was original. Thus history would get away from mere poetry. Then the life of humankind would clear itself of copying. It would be free from Art. Oh, no. No, no, not so, thought Sammler. Instead, Art increased, and a sort of chaos. More possibility, more actors, apes, copycats, more invention, more fiction, illusion, more fantasy, more despair. Life looting Art of its wealth, destroying Art as well by its desire to become the thing itself. Pressing itself into pictures. Reality forcing itself into all these shapes. Just look (Sammler looked) at this imitative anarchy of the streets—these Chinese revolutionary tunics, these babes in unisex toyland, these surrealist warchiefs, Western stagecoach drivers—Ph.D.s in philosophy, some of them (Sammler had met such, talked matters over with them). They sought originality. They were obviously derivative. And of what—of Paiutes, of Fidel Castro? No, of Hollywood extras. Acting mythic. Casting themselves into chaos, hoping to adhere to higher consciousness, to be washed up on the shores of truth. Better, thought Sammler, to accept the inevitability of imitation and then to imitate good things. The ancients had this right. Greatness without models? Inconceivable. One could not be the thing itself—Reality. One must be satisfied with the symbols. Make it the object of imitation to reach and release the high qualities. Make peace therefore with intermediacy and representation. But choose higher representations. Otherwise the individual must be the failure he now sees and knows himself to be. Mr. Sammler, sorry for all, and sore at heart.

Before lighting out, before this hop to the moon and outward bound, we had better look into some of this. As for the Crosstown and at this time of night, it was a perfectly safe bus to take.

IV

Dr. Gruner had private nurses around the clock. Sammler entered and found the uniformed woman sitting by the bed. The patient was sleeping. Sammler in a careful whisper introduced himself. "His uncle—oh, yes, he said you'd probably come," said the nurse. She didn't make it sound like a pleasant prediction. Under her starched cap the dyed dry hair was puffed out. The face itself, middle-aged, was fleshy, healthy, bossy. The eyes had an expression of sovereignty. Patients would be brought along the way that they must go: recovery or death.

"Is he asleep for the night, or is he taking a nap?" said Sammler.

"He may be waking up soon, but that's a guess. Miss Gruner is in the visitors' room."

"I'll stand a bit," said Sammler, not invited to sit.

There were many flowers, baskets of fruit, candy boxes, best sellers. The television set was running, soundlessly. The nurse listened with an earpiece. Reflected light flickered on the wall behind the bed. Elya's hands were turned downward at his sides, as though he had arranged himself symmetrically before dropping off. The hairy hands were clean, strong, venous, with polished nails. The nails had the same shine as the shot glass from which Gruner had sipped his mineral oil. The Nujol bottle was there, too, and beside it the *Wall Street Journal*. Bald dignity. The cord of the electric razor was plugged in above. He always was clean-shaven. The priests of Apis the Bull, as described by Herodotus, with shaven heads and bodies. And with the sleeping mouth bulged out on one side as if Elya, who liked to say that he had grown up in Greenpoint among hoodlums, might have been dreaming about racketeers and gunfire. Under his chin the bandage was like a military collar. Sammler thought of him as a man who badly, even desperately, needed confirmation, support, and touch. Gruner was a toucher. His habit, even in passing through a room, was to touch, to take people's arms, even perhaps getting medical information about their muscles, glands, weight, or the growth of their hair. He also implanted his opinions, his hopes in their breasts, and then if he said, "Well, isn't it so?", it was indeed so. Like a modern General of the Army, an Eisenhower, he made his logistical preparations. This shrewdness was very childish. But easy to pardon. Especially at such a time. At such a time, how could he sleep?

Sammler backed through the door softly and went to the visitors' room. There Angela sat smoking but not in her usual sensual and elegant style. She had been crying, and her face was white and hot. Her figure was heavy, breasts a burden, knees bulging pale against the taut silk of the stockings. Was it only because of her father that she was weeping? Sammler sensed a combined cause for those tears. He sat opposite her and laid the Augustus John hat, mole-gray, on his lap.

"Sleeping still?"

"Yes," said Sammler.

Angela's large lips, as though to cool herself, were open; she breathed through her mouth. Hot, the slope face with close-textured skin seemed very tight. The heat rose also into the whites of the eyes. "Does he *really* understand the situation?"

"I wonder. But he is a doctor, and I think he does."

Angela cried again, and Sammler was even more convinced of a second cause for her tears. "And there's nothing else wrong with him," said Angela. "He's perfectly well except for that thing—that one tiny damned thing. And you think he knows, Uncle?"

"Yes, probably."

"But acting so normal. Talking about the family. He was so glad to see you and hoped you'd come back tonight. And he still keeps worrying about Wallace."

"One can see why."

"Wallace has been such a headache. At six, seven, he was such a beautiful gifted little boy. He put together mathematical things. We thought we had another Einstein. Daddy sent him to MIT. But next thing we knew he was a bartender in Cambridge, and he beat some drunk almost to death."

"I've heard."

"And now he's bugging Daddy to get him a plane. At such a time! A flying saucer would be more like it. Of course I share some of the blame for Wallace." Sammler knew that the conversation would take a tiresome psychiatric-pediatric turn, and that he would have to endure a certain amount of explanation.

"Of course I was resentful when they brought the kid home from the hospital. I asked Mother to put his crib in the garage. I'm sure he felt rejection, from the first. I never liked him. He was too gloomy. He just wasn't like a child. He had terrible fits of rage."

"Well, everybody has a history," said Sammler.

"I think I decided in adolescence that my brother was going to be a queer. I thought it was my fault, that I was so slutty that he became frightened of girls."

"Is that so? Well, I remember your confirmation," said Sammler. "You were quite studious. I was impressed that you were studying Hebrew."

"Just a front, Uncle. I was a dirty little bitch, really."

"I wonder. In retrospect, people exaggerate so."

"Neither Father nor I ever liked Wallace. We pushed him off on Mother, and that was like condemning him for life. Then it was one thing after another, his obese stage, his alcoholic stage. Well, now have you heard? He thinks there's money hidden in the house."

"Do you think so, too?"

"I'm not sure. There have been hints from Daddy about it. Mother too before she died. She seemed to believe that now and then Daddy would—he'd step out of line, as she used to say."

"To help out famous families from Dutchess County, as Wallace tells me?"

"Is that what he says? No, Uncle, what I heard was that Daddy did favors for the Mafia characters he grew up with. Top people in the Syndicate. He knew Lucky Luciano very well. You probably never heard of Luciano."

"Just vaguely."

"Luciano came out to New Rochelle now and then. And if Daddy did those things and they paid him in cash, it must have been embarrassing. He probably didn't know what to do with that money. But that's not what's weighing on my mind."

"No. Speaking of New Rochelle, you haven't seen Shula, have you, Angela?"

"I haven't. What is she up to?"

"She brought me a very interesting book. However, it wasn't hers to bring."

"I assume she's hiding from Eisen. She thinks he's come to claim her."

"A flattering fear. If only he were capable of coming on such a mission. If he didn't beat her, it would answer many needs. It would be a mercy. No, I don't think he wants her at all. He doesn't like it that she poses as a Catholic. That was his pretext. Although he did say he got along well with Pope Pius at Castel Gandolfo. And now Eisen is not the friend of Popes, he is an artist. I don't think he has much genius, though he's crazy enough to want great glory." But Angela didn't want to hear this now. Apparently she thought Sammler was trying to turn the subject in a theoretical direction—to discuss the creative psychotic.

"Well, he's been here."

"You saw Eisen? He's been annoying Elya? Did he go in?"

"He wanted to make drawings—to sketch him, you know."

"I don't like it. I wish he wouldn't bother Elya. What the devil does he want? Keep him away."

"Well, maybe I shouldn't have let him in. I thought he might entertain Daddy."

Sammler was about to answer, but several beats of comprehension passed through his head and made him see matters differently. Of course. Ah, yes. Angela was having her own troubles with Dr. Gruner. Angela was not one of your great weepers, not like Margotte with her high annual tearfall. If Angela was looking so wan that even the frosted hair, usually so glossy and powerful, seemed to bristle dryly and Sammler thought he saw the dark follicular spots on her scalp, it was because she had been wrangling with her father. Under stress, Sammler believed, the whole faltered, and parts (follicles, for instance) became conspicuous. Such at least was his observation. Elya must be furious with her, and she was trying to divert his attention. Visitors. Obviously this was why she had taken Eisen straight in. But Eisen was not diverting. He was one of those smiling gloomy maniacs. Very gloomy, really. A depressing fellow. The smart silk suit he had worn ten years ago in Haifa when he and his father-in-law had gone out in the street, to a café, to discuss Shula, might have made a satisfactory coffin lining. Eisen certainly deserved to be cared for, and that was one of the uses of Israel, to gather in these cripples. But now Eisen had broken out, had heard the jolly frantic music of America and wanted to get into the act. He made a beeline for the rich cousin. The rich cousin was in the hospital with some kind of fiddle-peg in his neck. Odd what an instinct they all had for molesting a dying man.

"Did Elya find Eisen amusing? I doubt it."

Angela wore a playful cap, matching the black and white shoes. Now that her head was lowered Sammler saw the large button of kid leather set in the radial creases.

"A while he did, I think," she said. "Eisen made sketches of Daddy. But then he tried to sell them to him. Daddy would hardly glance at them."

"Not surprising. I wonder where Eisen got the money to come to America."

"I don't know, maybe he saved up. He's put out with you, Uncle."

"I'm sure of that."

"For not coming to see him in Israel. You were there for the war. He says you cut him."

"That doesn't concern me much. I wasn't there to pay my respects to a son-in-law or to make social visits."

"He complained to Daddy about you."

"Horrible!" said Sammler. "Everybody hitting away with these stupidities. At this time!"

"But Daddy takes an interest in all kinds of things. If everything suddenly stopped, it would be abnormal. Of course it's bad to aggravate him. For instance, he's angry with me."

"I suppose there is really no good way for Elya to do this thing."

"I'd say that he should stop talking to Widick. You know his fat lawyer, Widick?"

"Of course, I've met the man."

"Four or five times a day on the telephone. And Daddy asks me to leave the room. They're still buying and selling, trading on the stock market. Also I assume they discuss his will, or he wouldn't send me outside."

"Evidently, Angela, in spite of the case you make against Mr.

Widick, you've crossed your father yourself, in some way. And you seem to want me to ask about it?"

"I think I should tell you."

"It doesn't sound good."

"It isn't. It was when Wharton Horricker and I went to Mexico."

"I believe Elya likes Horricker. He wouldn't have objected to that."

"No, he hoped that Wharton and I would get married."

"Won't you?"

Angela held a lighted cigarette in forked fingers before her face. Actions normally graceful, now distressingly heavy. She shook her head, her eyes filling, reddening. Ah, trouble with Horricker. Sammler had guessed something of the sort. It was a little hard for him to understand why she should always have so much trouble. Perhaps he put it to himself that she enjoyed so many privileges, what more did she want? She had the income from half a million to live on: tax-exempt Municipals, as Elya would repeat. She had this flesh, these sex attractions and talents—*volupté* she had. She brought back the French sex vocabulary Sammler had learned at the University of Cracow reading Emile Zola. That book about the fruit market. *Le Ventre de Paris.* Les Halles. And that appetizing woman there who was also something good to eat, a regular orchard. *Volupté, seins, épaules, hanches. Sur un lit de feuilles. Cette tiédeur satinée de femme.* Excellent, Emile! And—all right!—orchards suffering when there were earth tremors could drop all their pears; this too Sammler could sympathetically understand. But Angela was always unusually involved in difficulty and suffering, tripping on invisible obstructions, bringing forth complications of painful mischief which made him wonder whether this *volupté* was not one of the sorest strangest burdens that could be laid on a woman's soul. Saw the woman (by her own erotic account), as if in the actual bedroom. By invitation he was there, a perplexed bystander. Evidently she believed it necessary that he should know what went on in America. He did not need quite so much information. But better a surplus than ignorance. Both the U.S.A. and the U.S.S.R. were, for Sammler, utopian projects. There, in the East, the emphasis was on low-level goods, on shoes, caps, toilet-plungers, and tin basins for peasants and laborers. Here it fell upon certain privileges and joys. Here wading naked into the waters of paradise, et cetera. But always a certain despair underlining pleasure, death seated inside the health-capsule, steering it, and darkness winking at you from the golden utopian sun.

"So you've had a quarrel with Wharton Horricker?"

"He's angry with me."

"Aren't you angry with him?"

"Not exactly. I seem to be in the wrong."

"Where is he now?"

"He's supposed to be in Washington. He's doing something statistical on antiballistic missiles. For the Senate bloc against the ABM. I don't understand the thing."

"It's a pity to have such trouble now, to have a double difficulty."

"I'm afraid Daddy has found out about this."

In Angela's expression as in Wallace's there was something soft, a hint of infancy or of baby reverie. The parents must have longed overmuch for babies and so inhibited something in their children's cycle of development. Angela's last glance, before she began to sob, astonished Sammler. Open lips, wrinkled forehead, the skin expressing utter surrender, traits of the original person. An infant! But the eyes did not give up their look of erotic experience.

"Found out about what?"

"A thing that happened at Acapulco. I didn't think it was so very serious. Neither did Wharton. At the time, it was just a kick. I mean it was funny. We had a party with another couple."

"What sort of party was it?"

"Well, it was a sex thing for the four of us."

"With other people? Who were they?"

"They were perfectly all right. We met them on the beach. The wife suggested it."

"An exchange?"

"Well, yes. Oh, it is done now, Uncle."

"I hear it is."

"You are disgusted with me, Uncle."

"I? Not really. I knew all this long ago. I regret it when things become so stupid, that's true. It seems to me that things poor professionals once had to do for a living, performing for bachelor parties, or tourist sex-circuses on the Place Pigalle, ordinary people, housewives, filing-clerks, students, now do just to be sociable, And I can't really say what it's all about. Is it maybe some united effort to conquer disgust? Or to show that all the repulsive things in history are not so repulsive? I don't know. Is it an effort to 'liberalize' human existence and show that nothing that happens between people is really loathsome? Affirming the Brotherhood of Man? Ah, well—" Sammler steadied and restrained himself. He did not want to know the details of this incident in Acapulco, didn't want to hear that the man in the case was a municipal judge from Chicago, or a chiropractor or CPA or a dope-pusher or that he made perfume or formaldehyde.

"Wharton went along, he did his share, but afterward he turned sullen. Then on the plane, flying back, he told me how angry he was about it."

"Well, he's a fastidious young man. You can see from his shirts. I assume he was well brought up."

"He acted no better than the rest of us."

"If you expected to marry Wharton, it was certainly poor judgment to do this."

Sammler badly wanted to get this conversation over. Elya had told him not to worry about the future, a hint that he was provided for; but there were also practical considerations to bear in mind. What if he and Shula had to depend on Angela? Angela had always been generous—she spent easily. When they went to a gallery or to lunch, she, naturally, paid for cabs, paid the check, left the tip, everything. But it would not do to go too deeply with Angela into this life of hers. The facts were too bad, too bald, abominable, pitiful. To a degree such behavior was based on theory, on generational ideology, part of a liberal education, and was therefore to an extent impersonal. But Angela would later regret these confessions—regret, and resent his disapproval. On the whole he received her confidences in a disinterested way. He was not unsympathetic, unfeeling; he was (she had said it herself) objective, nonjudging. As they faced Elya's death, he decided that under no circumstances and on no account would he become involved in a perverse relationship with Angela in which he had to listen for his supper. His disinterestedness would never become one of her comforts, part of the furniture of her life. Not even his anxiety over Shula's future could force him into such a position. A receiver of sordid goods? His whole heart rose against this.

"Daddy is asking very pointed questions about Wharton."

"He has heard about this episode?"

"That's right, Uncle."

"Who would tell him such things? It seems unusually cruel."

"I don't know whether you understand about that fat Widick, the lawyer. He and Wharton are related somewhere along the line. He's a bastard."

"That's not my impression at all. Normally fraudulent, perhaps, but that is simply business."

"He's a shit. Daddy thinks the world of Widick. He won the big case for him against the insurance company. I told you they talk four or five times a day on the phone. And Widick hates me."

"How do you know that?"

"I feel it. I get the spoiled-daughter look from him. There have always been people around who thought that Daddy had a bad thing about me, made me financially too independent. You know—pampered me and let me hang too loose."

"Hasn't he been exceptionally indulgent?"

"Not just for my sake, Uncle Sammler. You don't just act for yourself, and he's also lived through me. You can believe it."

Men, thought Sammler, often sin alone; women are seldom companionless in sin. But although Angela might be trying to force this interpretation on her father's kindness, it was possible that Elya too had his own lustful tendencies. Who was Sammler to say no? Things in general were desperate. The arterial bulge in Elya's brain must have cast its shadow earlier —spatters before the cloudburst. Sammler believed in premonitions, and death was a powerful instigator of erotic ideas. Sammler's own sex impulses (perhaps even now not altogether gone) had been very different. But he knew how to respect differences. He didn't measure others by himself. Now Shula had no *volupté*. She had something else. Of course she was not a rich man's daughter, and money, the dollar, was certainly a terrific sexual additive. But even Shula, though a scavenger or magpie, had never actually stolen before. Then suddenly she too was like the Negro pickpocket. From the black side, strong currents were sweeping over everyone. Child, black, redskin—the unspoiled Seminole against the horrible Whiteman. Millions of civilized people wanted oceanic, boundless, primitive, neckfree nobility, experienced a strange release of galloping impulses, and acquired the peculiar aim of sexual niggerhood for everyone. Humankind had lost its old patience. It demanded accelerated exaltation, accepted no instant without pregnant meanings as in epic, tragedy, comedy, or films. He had an idea even that the very special development of the significance of prisons since the eighteenth century had some relation to this shrinking ability to endure restraint. Punishment must be fitted, closely tailored to the state of the spirit, adapted to the need of the soul. Where liberty had been promised most, they had the biggest, worst prisons. Then another question: Had Elya performed abortions to oblige old Mafia friends? As to that, Sammler had no opinion. He simply couldn't say. Elya had never wanted to be a physician. He disliked the practice of medicine. But he had done his duty. And even doctors nowadays made sexual gestures to their patients. Put women's hands on their parts. Sammler had heard of this. Physicians who rejected the Oath, who joined the Age. Also Shula, Shula stealing, was contemporary—lawless. She was experiencing the Age. In so doing, she drew her father along with her. And possibly Elya, with the screw in his throat, had not wished to be left behind either, and had delegated Angela to experience the Age for him.

Be all that as it might—life once had nearly ended. Someone ahead, carrying the light, stumbled, faltered, and Mr. Sammler had thought it was over. However, he was still alive. He had not come through, for the connotation of coming through was that of an accomplishment and little had been accomplished. He had been steered from Cracow to London, from London to the Zamosht Forest, and eventually into New York City. One result of such a history was that he had formed a habit of condensation. He was a specialist in short views. And in the short view, Angela had offended her dying father. He was angry, and she wanted Sammler to intercede for her. Maybe Elya would cut her out of his will, give his money to charity. He had made large contributions to the Weizmann Institute. That Think-tank, they called it, at Rehovoth. Or perhaps she was afraid that he himself, Sammler, who was so close to Elya, would become his heir.

"Will you talk to Daddy, Uncle?"

"About this . . . thing of yours? That would be up to him. I wouldn't introduce the subject. I don't think he's just become aware of your style of life. I can't say what he's gotten out of it—vicariously, as you suggest. But he's not stupid, and giving a young woman like you a capital of half a million dollars to live in New York City, he would have to be very dumb to think you were not amusing yourself."

Great cities are whores. Doesn't everyone know? Babylon was a whore. *Ô La Reine aux fesses cascadantes.* Penicillin keeps New York looking cleaner. No faces gnawed by syphilis, with gaping noseholes as in ancient times.

"Daddy has such respect for you."

"What use should I make of that respect?"

"All the oldest, deepest, worst sexual prejudices are mobilized against me."

"Lord only knows what's in his mind," said Sammler. "Perhaps it's only one pain among many."

"He's said cruel things to me."

"This Mexican event is not the first," said Sammler. "Surely your father has always known. He hoped you would marry Horricker and stop this sexual nonsense."

"I'll see if he's awake," said Angela, and rose. Her soft and heavy self was dressed in one of its costumes. Her legs, exposed to the last quarter of the thigh, were really very strong, almost clumsy. Her face was at this moment baby-pale, and soft under the little leather cap. As she detached herself from the plastic seat, and the evening was quite warm, an odor was released. Both low comic and high serious. Goddess and majorette. The Great Sinner! What a vexation for poor Elya. What overvaluation. What an atrocious mixture of feelings. Angela was displeased with Sammler. She walked away.

As she was going, he remembered where he had last seen a cap like hers. It was in Israel—the Six-Day War he had seen.

He had seen.

It was almost as if he had attended—among other spectators. Arriving in fast cars at a point before Mount Hermon, where a tank battle was taking place, he was one of a press group watching a fight, below. Down in the flat valley, as in Vista-Vision. Where they were standing, Mr. Sammler and the others, Israeli press officers and journalists, were safe enough. The battle was two miles or more beyond them. The tank columns were maneuvering in dust. Bombs were spilling from planes as remote as insects. You saw the wings when they spun into the light, then heard detonations, and shrubs of smoke rose briefly. Remotely, you heard machinery—distant tank treads. You heard tiny war sounds. Then two more cars came tearing up, joined the group, and cameramen leaped out. They were Italians, *paparazzi*, someone explained, and had brought with them three girls in mod dress. The girls might have come from Carnaby Street or from King's Road in their buskins, miniskirts, false eyelashes. They were indeed British, for Mr. Sammler heard them talking, and one of them had on just the sort of little cap that Angela wore, of houndstooth check. The young ladies had no idea where they were, what this was about, had been quarreling with their lovers, who were now lying in the road on their bellies. Photographing battle, the shirts fluttering on their backs. The girls were angry. Carried off from the Via Veneto, probably, without knowing clearly where the jet was going. Then, bare to the waist, a runt but muscular, a Swiss correspondent with small twisted kinky-blond beard and his chest hung with cameras began to complain to the Israeli captain that it was improper for these girls to be at the front. Sammler heard him give this protest through his teeth, which were bad and tiny. The place where they were standing had been bombed earlier. One could not see why. There seemed no military reason for it. But the ground was full of large holes, still black with fresh bomb soot.

"Put them at least in those holes," the Swiss insisted.

"What?"

"Foxholes, foxholes. Another shell may come. You can't have them walking on the road, like this. You can't have it, don't you understand?" He was an unbearable little man. His war was being ruined by these stupid girls in costume. The Israeli officer gave in. He made the girls get into the burnt holes. All you could see of them then was heads and shoulders. Not quite frightened out of their anger, but beginning to be. Somewhat stunned by now, in the paint of great amorousness, one beginning to sob a little, and another puffing up and growing red. Becoming middle-aged—a scrubwoman. Frills of glistening black rising about the girls, the cordite-shining grass.

Other things as strange were occurring. Father Newell, the Jesuit correspondent, was there. He wore the full battle dress of the Vietnam jungles—yellow, black, and green daubs and stripes of camouflage. Representing a newspaper in Tulsa, Oklahoma, was it, or Lincoln, Nebraska? Sammler still owed him ten dollars, his share of the taxi they had hired in Tel Aviv to drive to the Syrian front. But he didn't have Father Newell's address. He might have tried harder to find it. On his way home from Southeast Asia, the priest was a tourist in Athens, looking at the Acropolis, when he heard of the fighting and went at once. The big jungle boots were as ample as galoshes. Father Newell sweated in his green battle clothes. His hair cropped Marine-style, his eyes also green and the cheeks splendid meat-red. Down below the tanks raced and the smoke puffed yellow from the ground. Few sounds rose.

Mr. Sammler in the waiting room now stirred and stood up. Wallace, entering from the general light of the corridor into the lamplight of the visitors' room, was already speaking to him. "Dad is sleeping, Angela says. I don't suppose you've had a chance to talk to him about the attic?"

"I have not."

Wallace was not alone. Eisen entered at his back.

Wallace and Eisen knew each other. How well? A curious question. But quite long, at any rate. They had met when Wallace, after his attempted horse tour of Central Asia and his arrest by the Russian authorities, had visited Israel and stayed with Cousin Eisen. Wallace had then prepared a full set of notes (going to work at once) for an essay arguing that the modernization Israel was bringing to the Middle East was altogether too rapid for the Arabs. Pernicious. Wallace, of course, was bound to oppose Elya's Zionism. But Eisen, never comprehending, unaware of Wallace's sudden passion (soon vanishing) for Arab culture, brought him coffee in bed while he was working. Because Wallace was just out of a Soviet prison, thanks to Gruner and Senator Javits, and Eisen knew what it was to be in Russian hands. He had made Wallace rest, he waited on him. On his mutilated feet he had learned to move rapidly. Ingenious adaptation. The shuffle of his toeless feet in Haifa had put Sammler's teeth on edge. He couldn't have endured two hours alone with handsome, curly, smiling Eisen. But Wallace, with his great-orbited eyes and long lashes, reaching a skinny hairy arm from the bed and, without looking, accepting coffee in trembling fingers, coddled himself ten days in Eisen's bed after the jails of Soviet Armenia. The Russians had sent him to Turkey. From Turkey he went to Athens. From Athens, like Newell the Jesuit later, he flew to Israel. Tenderly, devotedly, Eisen had waited on him.

"Ah, here is my father-in-law."

Was it with pleasure at seeing him that Eisen beamed, or was it because the event (Eisen in New York for the first time in his life) was so splendid? He was gay but stiff, cramped under the arms and between the legs by his new American clothes. Wallace must have taken him to one of those execrable mod male shops, like Barney's. Perhaps to one of the unisex establishments. The madman wore a magenta shirt with a persimmon-colored necktie as thick as an ox tongue. The gloom of his never-ending laughter, the shining of his excellent teeth unharmed by the Stalingrad siege and unaffected by starvation when he hobbled over the Carpathians and the Alps. Teeth like that deserved a saner head.

"How nice to find you here," said Eisen to Sammler in Russian.

Sammler answered in Polish, "How are you, Eisen?"

"You wouldn't stop to visit me in my country, so I came to see you in yours," said Eisen.

In this reproach, a familiar and traditional Jewish opening, there was at least a vestige of normalcy. Not so in the next statement. "I have come to America to make myself a new career." *Karyera* was the word he employed. Dressed in the cramping narrow gray-denim garments, obviously old stock from the Ivy League period that had been palmed off on him, in magenta, persimmon, and tomato colors (the red Chelsea boots mounting to the ankles), his unbarbered curls fusing head and shoulders and brutally eliminating the neck, he was obviously getting a new image, revising his self-conception. No longer a victim of Hitler and Stalin; deposited starved to the bones on Israel's sands; lice, lunacy, and fever his only assets; taken from internment in Cyprus; taught a language and a trade. But you could not tell recovery where to stop. He had gone on to become an artist. Rising from negligibility, expendability, something that waited to be slaughtered with a trenching tool (Eisen said he had watched this before escaping from Nazi-occupied territory into the Russian zone—men too insignificant to waste bullets on, having their heads smashed by shovel blows); but rising and rising to heights of world mastery. By the divinity of art. Speaking, inspired, to mankind. Making signs in the universal language of charged pigments. Hurray, Eisen, flying from peak to peak! Though his colors were grayer than slate, blacker than coal, redder than disease, and his life studies were double dead, the bus that brought him in from Kennedy was a limousine; the expressways greeted him like a glorious astronaut, and he faced his *Karyera* with the moist laughing teeth, in most desperate ecstasy. (To pair with the Russian *Karyera*, you wanted the Russian *Extass*!)

He and Wallace were already doing business together. Eisen was designing labels for the trees and the bushes. They showed Sammler sample cards: QUERCUS and ULMUS, in thick blotchy letters of Gothic black. Other labels in the foreign cursive style Eisen had learned in the *Gymnasium* were neater. Poor Eisen had been a schoolboy when the war broke out and had no higher education. Sammler did his best to say something appropriate and harmless though he was repelled by everything that Eisen set on paper.

"These have got to be modified here and there," said Wallace. "But the idea is surprisingly right. For a greenie, you know."

"You are going into this business, really?"

Wallace said firmly, even with a slight jeer (forming about a dimple) at the old man's doubts, "Definitely, really, Uncle. In fact I'm going to test-fly some planes tomorrow, in Westchester. I'm going back this evening to spend the night at the old place."

"Is your pilot's license still good?"

"Why, of course it's good."

"Well, it must be an agreeable feeling of excitement—a new enterprise, with friends and relatives. What have you got there, Eisen?"

A heavy green baize bag hung from cords wound about Eisen's wrist. "Here? I have brought work of mine in a different medium." Eisen said. He clinked down the weight on the glass tabletop; the baize fell back.

"You've made some paperweights."

"Not paperweights. You could use them for that purpose, Father-in-law, but they are medallions." You couldn't offend Eisen because he took such pleasure in his accomplishments. As if he were inhaling some aromatic rarity, he began to close his eyes and to show those peerless bones, his teeth, and with both hands smoothed back the curls over his ears. "I have invented a new process in the foundry," he said. In technical Russian he began to explain, but Sammler said, "You are losing me, Eisen. I am not familiar with the vocabulary."

The metal was crude-looking, partly bronze but also pale yellow, tinged with sulfides like fool's gold. And Eisen had made the usual Stars of David, branched candelabra, scrolls and rams' horns, or inscriptions flaming away in Hebrew: *Nahamu!* "Comfort ye!" Or God's command to Joshua: *Hazak!* With a certain interest Sammler watched these crude, lunky pieces being laid out. After each, a pause, while the face of the connoisseur was intently examined for the beautiful reaction obviously due. These iron pyrites, belonging at the bottom of the Dead Sea.

"And what is this, Eisen, a tank, I take it, a Sherman tank?"

"Metaphor for a tank. Nothing is literal in my work."

"No one simply hallucinates any more," said Mr. Sammler in Polish. The remark was unnoticed.

"Shouldn't these be ground smoother?" said Wallace. "And what is this word?"

"*Hazak, hazak,*" said Sammler. "The order God gave before Jericho, to Joshua. 'Strengthen thyself.'"

"*Hazak, v'ematz,*" said Eisen.

"Yes, well . . . Why does God speak such a funny language?" said Wallace.

"I brought these medallions to show to Cousin Elya."

"Nonsense," said Sammler. "Elya's sick. He can't handle this rough heavy metal."

"No, no, I'll hold up one piece at a time. I want him to see what I accomplished. Twenty-five years ago I came to the

Eretz a broken man. But I wouldn't die. I couldn't shut my eyes—not before I did something like a human being, something important, beautiful."

Sammler ventured no comment. After all, his heart was not so hard to touch. Moreover, he had been trained in the ancient mode of politeness. Almost as, once, women had been brought up to chastity. Well-schooled in murmuring over the trash Shula found in wastebaskets, he made the necessary sounds and passes of the hand, but then he said again that Elya was very ill. These medallions might tire him.

"I differ," said Eisen. "On the contrary. How can art hurt?" He began to stow the clinking pieces in the baize bag.

Wallace then said to someone behind Sammler, "Yes, he is." The private nurse had come in.

"Who is?

"You, Uncle. This is Mr. Sammler here."

"Is Elya asking for me?"

"You're wanted on the telephone. You are Uncle Sammler?"

"Miss? I am Artur Sammler."

"A Mrs. Arkin. She wants you to call home."

"Oh, Margotte. Did she phone Elya's room? I hope she didn't wake him."

"The call was to the floor, not to the room."

"Thank you. Oh, yes, where is the public phone?"

"Do you need dimes, Uncle?" Sammler picked two warm coins out of Wallace's palm. Wallace had been clutching his money.

Margotte tried extraordinarily hard to speak firmly. "Uncle? Now listen. Where did you leave Dr. Lal's manuscript?"

"I left it on my desk."

"Are you sure?"

"Of course I am sure. On my desk."

"Is there no other place you might have put it? I know you aren't absent-minded, but the strain is unusual."

"It isn't on the desk? Is Dr. Lal with you?"

"I sat him down in the living room."

Among the pots of soil. What must this Lal be feeling!

"And does he know it's gone?"

"I couldn't very well lie to him. I had to tell him. He

wanted to wait here for you. We raced back from Butler Hall, of course. He was so anxious."

"Now, Margotte, we must keep our heads."

"He is in such distress. Really, Uncle, no one has the right to expose a person to such things."

"My apologies to Dr. Lal. I regret more than I can say . . . can imagine how upset he is. But Margotte, only one person in the world could have taken that notebook. You must find out from the elevator man. Has Shula been there?"

"Rodriguez lets her in as one of the family. She *is* one of the family."

Rodriguez had a giant ring of keys, practically a hoop. He fetched it at need from a nail in the brick wall of the cellar.

"Really, Shula is too stupid. Enough is enough. I've been too easy with her. The embarrassment is terrible. Being the father of the woman-lunatic who ambushes this unhappy Indian. You spoke to Rodriguez?"

"It was Shula."

"Ah."

"Dr. Lal had a report from the detective who visited her today, at noon. I think the man threatened her."

"As I feared."

"He said the manuscript must be back by ten a.m. tomorrow; otherwise he would come with a warrant."

"To search? Arrest?"

"I don't know. Neither does Dr. Lal. But she got very excited. What she said was that she would go to her priest. She would go to Father Robles and complain to the Church."

"Margotte, you had better check with that priest. A search warrant in that apartment? She has been filling it with trash for twelve years. If the police put down their hats, they'll never find them again. But I would say she has gone to New Rochelle."

"Do you think so?"

"If she's not with Father Robles, that's where she is." Sammler knew her ways; knew them as the Eskimo knows the ways of the seal. Its breathing-holes. "She is protecting me now, because the stolen property is in my hands. She must have been terrified by the detective, poor thing, and then waited till we had both gone out." Spying on my door like the black man. Feeling that she was not included by her father among his most serious concerns. Determined to regain the top priority. "I have let her go too far with this H. G. Wells nonsense. And now someone has been hurt."

This unlucky Lal, who must have been sick of earth to begin with if he had such expectations of the moon.

And partly he was right, for humankind kept doing the same stunts over and over. The old comical-tearful stuff. Emotional relationships. Desires incapable of useful fulfillment. Over and over, trying to vent and empty the breast of certain cries, of certain fervencies. What positive balance was possible? Was this passional struggle altogether useless? It was the energy bank also of noble purposes. Barking, hissing, ape-chatter, and spitting. But there were times when Love seemed life's great architect. Weren't there? Even stupidity might at times be hammered out as a golden background for great actions. Mightn't it? But for these weaknesses and these tenacious sicknesses were there true cures? Sometimes the idea of cures seemed to Sammler itself pernicious. What was cured? You could rearrange, you could orchestrate the disorders. But cure? Nonsense. Change Sin to Sickness, a change of words (Feffer was right), and then enlightened doctors would stamp the sickness out. Oh, yes! So, then, philosophers, men of science, of brilliant intellect, understanding this more and more clearly, are compelled to sue for divorce from all these human states. Then they launch outward, moonward, their flying arthropod hardware.

"I shall go to New Rochelle with Wallace," said Sammler. "She is certainly there. To be sure, we will check with Father Robles. If he knows where she is . . . I'll call back."

Because she was not an American he felt a certain solidarity with Margotte. From her he did not have to conceal his (foreign) mortification. And she had shown delicacy in remembering not to ring Elya's room.

"What shall I do with Dr. Lal?"

"Apologize," he said. "Reassure. Comfort him, Margotte. Tell him I'm sure the manuscript is safe. Explain Shula's respect for the written word. And please ask him to keep the detectives out of this."

"Wait a minute. He is here. He would like to say a word."

An Eastern voice enriched the wire.

"*Is* this Mr. Sammler?"

"It is."

"Dr. Lal, here. This is the second robbery. I cannot tolerate much more. Since Mrs. Arkin has appealed for patience, I can hold off just a very little longer. But very little. Then I must have the police detain your daughter."

"If only it would help to put her behind bars! Believe me, I am sorrier than I can say. But I am perfectly sure the manuscript is safe. I understand you have no other copy."

"Three years of composition."

"That is distressing. I had hoped it was more like six months. But I can see how much careful preparation it would need." Normally Sammler shunned flattery, but now he had no choice. Moisture formed upon the black instrument, against his ear, and on his cheek was a red pressure mark. He said, "The work is brilliant."

"I am glad you think so. Judge how it affects me."

I can judge. Anyone can clutch anyone, and whirl him off. The low can force the high to dance. The wise have to reel about with leaping fools. "Try not to be too anxious, sir. I can recover your manuscript, and will do it tonight. I don't use my authority often enough. Believe me, I can control my daughter, and I shall."

"I had hoped to publish by the time of the first moon landing," said Lal. "You can imagine how many bad paperbacks will be out. Confusing to the public. Meretricious."

"Of course." Sammler sensed that the Indian, probably passionate, resisting great internal pressure, was after all being decent, allowing for the frailty of an old man, the tightness of the situation. He thought, The fellow is a gentleman. Inclining his head within the soundproof metal enclosure, the dotted voile of insulation, Sammler yielded to Oriental suggestion: "May the sun brighten your face. Single you out among the multitude (imagining Hindus always in crowds: like mackerel-crowded seas) many years yet." Sammler was determined that Shula should hurt no one but himself. He had to put up with it, but no one else should.

"I shall be interested in your comments on my essay."

"Of course," said Sammler, "we will have a long talk about it. Please stand by. I will phone as soon as there is some news. Thank you for bearing with me."

Both parties hung up.

"Wallace," said Sammler, "I think I shall be driving to New Rochelle with you."

"Really? Then Dad did say something about the attic?"

"It has nothing to do with the attic."

"Then why? Is it something about Shula? It must be."

"Why, yes, in fact. Shula. Can we leave soon?"

"Emil is out there with the Rolls. Might as well use it while we can. What is Shula up to? She called me."

"When?"

"Not long ago. She wanted to put something in Dad's wall safe. Did I know the combination. Naturally I couldn't say I knew the combination. I'm not supposed to know."

"Where was she calling from?"

"I didn't ask. Of course you've seen Shula whispering to the flowers in the garden," said Wallace. Wallace was not observant and took little interest in the conduct of others. But for that very reason he prized highly the things he did notice. What he noticed he cherished. He had always been kind and warm to Shula. "What language does she speak to them, is it Polish?"

The language of schizophrenia, very likely.

"I used to read *Alice in Wonderland* to her. Those talking flowers. The garden of live flowers."

Sammler opened the patient's door and saw him sitting up, alone. Dr. Gruner in his large black spectacles was studying, or trying to study, a contract or legal document. He would sometimes say that he should have been a lawyer, not a doctor. Medical school had not been his choice but his mother's. Of his own free will he had probably done little. Consider his wife.

"Come in, Uncle, and shut the door. Let's make it fathers only. I don't want to see children tonight."

"I understand that feeling," said Sammler. "I've had it often."

"It's a pity about Shula, poor woman. But she is only wacky. My daughter is a dirty cunt."

"A different generation, a different generation."

"And my son, a high-IQ moron."

"He may come around, Elya."

"You don't believe it for a minute, Uncle. What, a ninth-inning rally? I ask myself what I spent so many years of my life on. I must have believed what America was telling me. I paid for the best. I never suspected that I wasn't getting the best."

Had Elya spoken in excitement, Sammler would have tried to calm him. He was, however, speaking factually and he sounded utterly level. In the goggles he looked particularly judicious. Like the chairman of a Senate committee hearing scandalous testimony without loss of composure.

"Where is Angela?"

"Gone to the ladies' to have a cry, I suppose. If she isn't Frenching an orderly, or in a daisy chain. When she goes around the corner, you never know."

"Oh, too bad. You ought not to be quarreling."

"Not quarreling. Just making things plainer, spelling them out. I figured this Horricker to marry her, but he'll never do it now."

"Is that certain?"

"Did she tell you what happened in Mexico?"

"Not in detail."

"That's just as well, if you don't know the details. The joke you made was right on the head, about the billiard table in hell, about something green where it's hot."

"It wasn't aimed at Angela."

"Of course I knew my daughter with twenty-five thousand tax-free dollars must be having herself a time. I expected that, and as long as she was handling herself maturely and sensibly I had no objections. All that, theoretically, is fine. You use the words 'mature' and 'sensible,' and they satisfy you. But then you take a close look, and when you take a close look, you see something else. You see a woman who has done it in too many ways with too many men. By now she probably doesn't know the name of the man between her legs. And she looks . . . Her eyes—she has fucked-out eyes."

"I'm sorry."

Something very odd in Elya's expression. There were tears

about, somewhere, but dignity would not permit them. Perhaps it was self-severity, not dignity. But they did not come out. They were rerouted, absorbed into the system. They were subdued, converted into tones. They were present in the voice, in the color of the skin, in the lights of the eye.

"I must go, Elya. I'll take Wallace with me. I'll be back tomorrow."

V

EMIL in the Rolls Royce may have had an enviable life. The silver limousine was his faucet. He had all that power to turn on. Also, he was outside the wretched, anxious rivalry, rancor, hatred, and warfare of ordinary drivers of lesser cars. Double-parked, he was not molested by cops. As he stood beside the grand machine, his buttocks, given a rectilinear projection by the formal breeches, were nearer to the ground than most people's. He seemed also to have a calm, serious spirit; heavy creases in the face; lips that turned inward and never showed the teeth; midparted hair like a cowl descending to the ears; a heavy Savonarola nose. The Rolls still carried MD on the license plate.

"Emil drove for Costello, for Lucky Luciano," said Wallace, smiling.

In the light of the padded gray interior, Wallace was beard-stippled. The large dark eyes in the big orbits wished to offer courteous entertainment. When you considered how profoundly Wallace was absorbed and preoccupied by business, by problems of character, by death, you recognized how generous and how difficult this was—how much trying, shaking, rousing, what an effort was required. Arranging a kindly smile for the old uncle.

"Luciano? Elya's friend? Yes. Eminent Mafia. Angela mentioned him."

"Connections from way back."

They drove out on the West Side Highway, along the Hudson. There was the water—how beautiful, unclean, insidious! and there the bushes and the trees, cover for sexual violence, knifepoint robberies, sluggings, and murders. On the water bridgelight and moonlight lay smooth, enjoyably brilliant. And when we took off from all this and carried human life outward? Mr. Sammler was ready to think it might have a sobering effect on the species, at this moment exceptionally troubled. Violence might subside, exalted ideas might recover importance. Once we were emancipated from telluric conditions.

In the Rolls was a handsome bar; it had a small light, within the mirror-lined cabinet. Wallace offered the old man liquor or Seven-Up, but he wanted nothing. Enclosing the umbrella between high knees, he was reviewing some of the facts. Outer-space voyages were made possible by specialist-collaboration. While on earth sensitive ignorance still dreamed of being separate and "whole." "Whole"? What "whole"? A childish notion. It led to all, this madness, mad religions, LSD, suicide, to crime.

He shut his eyes. Breathed out of his soul some bad, and breathed in some good. No, thank you, Wallace, no whisky. Wallace poured some for himself.

How could the ignorant nonspecialist be strong with strength adequate to confront these technical miracles which made him a sort of uncomprehending Congo savage? By vision, by archaic inner-preliterate purity, by natural force, nobly whole? The children were setting fire to libraries. And putting on Persian trousers, letting their sideburns grow. This was their symbolic wholeness. An oligarchy of technicians, engineers, the men who ran the grand machines, infinitely more sophisticated than this automobile, would come to govern vast slums filled with bohemian adolescents, narcotized, beflowered, and "whole." He himself was a fragment, Mr. Sammler understood. And lucky to be that. Totality was as much beyond his powers as to make a Rolls Royce, part by part, with his own hands. So perhaps, *perhaps!* colonies on the moon would reduce the fever and swelling here, and the passion for boundlessness *and* wholeness might find more material appeasement. Humankind, drunk with terror, calm itself, sober up.

Drunk with terror? Yes, and fragments (a fragment like Mr. Sammler) understood: this earth was a grave: our life was lent to it by its elements and had to be returned: a time came when the simple elements seemed to long for release from the complicated forms of life, when every element of every cell said, "Enough!". The planet was our mother and our burial ground. No wonder the human spirit wished to leave. Leave this prolific belly. Leave also this great tomb. Passion for the infinite caused by the terror, by *timor mortis*, needed material appeasement. *Timor mortis conturbat me. Dies irae. Quid sum miser tunc dicturus.*

The moon was so big tonight that it caught the eye of Wallace, drinking in the back seat, in the unlimited luxury of upholstery and carpets. Legs crossed, leaning back, he pointed moonward past Emil, above the smooth parkway north of the George Washington Bridge.

"Isn't the moon great? They're buzzing away, around it," he said.

"Who?"

"Spacecraft are. Modules."

"Oh, yes. It's in the papers. Would you go there?"

"Would I ever! In a minute," said Wallace. "Out—out? You bet I'd go. I'd fly. In fact, I'm already signed up with Pan Am."

"With whom?"

"With the airlines. I believe I was the five-hundred-twelfth person to phone for a reservation."

"Are they already taking reservations for moon excursions?"

"They most certainly are. Hundreds of thousands of people want to go. Also to Mars and Venus, jumping off from the moon."

"How very odd."

"What's odd about it? To go? It isn't odd at all. I tell you, the airlines get bales of applications. What about you, would you take the trip, Uncle?"

"No."

"Because of your age, maybe?"

"Possibly age. No, my travels are over."

"But the moon, Uncle! Of course you wouldn't physically be able to do it; but a man like you? I can't believe such a person wouldn't be raring to go."

"To the moon? But I don't even want to go to Europe," Mr. Sammler said. "Besides, if I had my choice, I'd prefer the ocean bottom. In Dr. Piccard's bathysphere. I seem to be a depth man rather than a height man. I do not personally care for the illimitable. The ocean, however deep, has a top and bottom, whereas there is no sky ceiling. I think I am an Oriental, Wallace. Jews, after all, are Orientals. I am content to sit here on the West Side, and watch, and admire these gorgeous Faustian departures for the other worlds. Personally, I require a ceiling, although a high one. Yes, I like ceilings, and the high better than the low. In literature I think there are low-ceiling masterpieces—*Crime and Punishment*, for instance—and high-ceiling masterpieces, *Remembrance of Things Past.*"

Claustrophobia? Death is confinement.

Wallace, continuing to smile, softly but definitely differed; yet took a subtle interest in Uncle Sammler's views. "Of course," he said, "the world looks different to you. Literally. Because of the eyes. How well do you see?"

"Partially only. You are right."

"And yet you described that Negro man and his thing."

"Ah, Feffer told you that. Your partner. I should have known he'd rush to tell. I hope he's not serious about snapping photographs on the bus."

"He thinks he can, with his Minox. He is sort of a nut. I suppose that when people are young and full of enthusiasm, you say, 'All that youth and enthusiasm,' but as they grow older you just say, about the same behavior, 'What a nut.' He was very excited by your experience. What actually did the man do, Uncle? He exhibited himself. Did he drop his trousers?"

"No."

"He opened them. And then he took out his tool. What was it like? I wonder . . . Did it occur to him that your eyesight wasn't good enough to see?"

"I don't know what occurred to him. He didn't say."

"Well, tell me about his thing. It wasn't actually black, was it? It must have been a purple kind of chocolate, or maybe the color of his palms?"

Wallace's scientific objectivity!

"I don't wish to talk about it, really."

"Oh, Uncle, suppose I were a zoologist who had never seen a live leviathan but you knew Moby Dick from the whaleboat? Was it sixteen, eighteen inches?"

"I couldn't say."

"Would you guess it weighed two pounds, three pounds, four?"

"I have no way to estimate. And you are not a zoologist. You just this minute became one."

"Uncircumcised?"

"That was my impression."

"I wonder if women really prefer that kind of thing."

"I assume they have other interests in addition."

"That's what they say. But you know you can't trust them. They're animals, aren't they."

"Temporarily there is an animal emphasis."

"I'm not taken in by the gentle-dainty-lady line. Women are lustful. They're raunchier than men in my opinion. With all respect for your experience and knowledge of life, Uncle Sammler, this is a field where I wouldn't be inclined to take your word. Angela would always say that if a man had a thick dick—excuse me, Uncle."

"Angela is perhaps a special case."

"You prefer to think she's off the continuum. What if she's not?"

"I'd like to drop the subject, Wallace."

"No, it's really too interesting. And this is pure objectivity, not a dirty conversation. Now, Angela gives a good report on Wharton Horricker. It seems he's a long, strong fellow. She says, however, that he takes too much exercise, he's too muscular. It's hard to get tender emotions from a man who has such steel cable arms and heavy thick weight-lifting pectorals. An iron man. She says it interferes with the flow of tender feeling."

"I hadn't thought about it."

"What does she know about tender feeling? Just some guy between her legs—Everyman is her lover. No, Anyman. They say that fellows that beef themselves up like that—'I was a ninety-pound weakling'—that such fellows are narcissistic pansies. I don't judge anybody. What if they are homosexuals? That's nothing any more. I don't think homosexuality is simply a different way of being human, I actually think it's a disease. I don't know why homosexuals fuss so much and proclaim themselves so normal. Such gentlemen. Of course they have *us* to point at—and we're not so great. I believe this boom in faggots was caused by modern warfare. One result of 1914, that slaughter in the trenches. The men were getting blasted. It was obviously healthier to be a woman than a man. It was better to be a child. Best of all is to be an artist, combining child, woman, or dervish—do I mean a dervish? A shaman? A necromancer is probably what I mean. Plus millionaire. Many a millionaire wants to be an artist, or a kid or woman and a necromancer. What was I talking about? Oh,

Horricker. I was saying that in spite of all that physical culture and weight lifting he was not a queer. But that he did have a fantastic image of male strength. A person making a determined self-effort. Angela's job seemed to be to take him down a few pegs. She's weepy about him today, but she's a pig, and he'll be forgotten tomorrow. I think my sister is a swine. If he's got too much muscle, she's got too much fat. What about that fat bust interfering with the flow of tender feeling? What did you say just now?"

"Not a word."

"Sometimes at night, last thing before sleeping, I go through a whole list of people and call them all swine. I find it's marvelous therapy. I clear my mind for the night. If you were in the room, you'd only hear me saying, 'Swine, swine, swine!' Not the names. Each name is mental. Don't you agree that she'll forget Horricker by tomorrow?"

"I think she may. But I trust she's not too lost."

"She's a female-power type, the *femme fatale.* Every myth has its natural enemies. The enemy of the distinguished-male myth is the *femme fatale.* Between those thighs, a man's conception of himself is just assassinated. If he thinks he's so special she'll show him. Nobody is so special. Angela represents the realism of the race, which is always pointing out that wisdom, beauty, glory, courage in men are just vanities and her business is to beat down the man's legend about himself. That's why she and Horricker are finished, why she let that twerp in Mexico ball her fore and aft in front of Wharton, with who-knows-what-else thrown in free by her. In a spirit of participation."

"I didn't know that Horricker had such a presumptuous image of himself."

"Let's get back to that other matter. What else did the man do, did he shake the thing at you?"

"Not at all. But the subject is becoming unpleasant. He was warning me not to defend the poor old man he robbed. Not to inform the police. I had already tried to inform them."

"You, naturally, would feel sorry for those people he robs."

"It's ugly. Not that I have such a tender heart."

"You've probably seen too much. Weren't you invited to testify at the Eichmann trial?"

"I was approached. I didn't feel up to it."

"If you wrote that article about that crazy character from Lodz—King Rumkowski."

"Yes."

"I often think a man's parts look expressive. Women's too. I think they're just about to say something, through those whiskers."

Sammler did not answer. Wallace sipped his whisky as a boy might sip Coca-Cola.

"Of course," Wallace said, "the blacks speak another language. A kid pleaded for his life—"

"What kid?"

"In the papers. A kid who was surrounded by a black gang of fourteen-year-olds. He begged them not to shoot, but they simply didn't understand his words. Literally not the same language. Not the same feelings. No comprehension. No common concepts. Out of reach."

I was begged, too. Sammler however did not say this.

"The child died?"

"The kid? After some days he died of the wound. But the boys didn't even know what he was saying."

"There is a scene in *War and Peace* I sometimes think about," said Sammler. "The French General Davout, who was very cruel, who was said, I think, to have torn out a man's whiskers by the roots, was sending people to the firing squad in Moscow, but when Pierre Bezhukov came up to him, they looked into each other's eyes. A human look was exchanged, and Pierre was spared. Tolstoy says you don't kill another human being with whom you have exchanged such a look."

"Oh, that's marvelous! What do you think?"

"I sympathize with such a desire for such a belief."

"You only sympathize."

"No, I sympathize deeply. I sympathize sadly. When men of genius think about humankind, they are almost forced to believe in this form of psychic unity. I wish it were so."

"Because they refuse to think themselves entirely exceptional. I see that. But you don't think this exchange of looks will work? Doesn't it happen?"

"Oh, it probably happens from time to time. Pierre Bezhukov was altogether lucky. Of course he was a person in a book. And of course life is a kind of luck, for the individual. Very booklike. But Pierre was exceptionally lucky to catch the eye of his executioner. I myself never knew it to work. No, I never saw it happen. It is a thing worth praying for. And it is based on something. It's not an arbitrary idea. It's based on the belief that there is the same truth in the heart of every human being, or a splash of God's own spirit, and that this is the richest thing we share in common. And up to a point I would agree. But though it's not an arbitrary idea, I wouldn't count on it."

"They say that you were in the grave once."

"Do they?"

"How was it?"

"How was it. Let us change the subject. We are already on the Cross County Highway. Emil is very fast."

"No traffic, this time of night. I had my life saved, one time. It was before New Rochelle. I cut school and roamed the park. The lagoon was frozen, but I fell through the ice. There was a Japanese type of bridge, and I was climbing the girders, underneath, and tumbled off. It was December, and the ice was gray. The snow was white. The water was black. I was hanging on to the ice, scared shitless, and my soul felt like a little marble rolling away, away. A bigger kid came and saved me. He was a truant, too, and he crawled out on the ice with a branch. I caught hold, and he dragged me out. Then we went to the men's toilet in the boathouse, and I stripped. He rubbed me with his sheepskin coat. I laid my clothes on the radiator, but they wouldn't dry. He said, 'Jeez kid, you're gonna catch hell.' My dear mother raised hell all right. She pulled my ears because my clothes were wet."

"Very good. She should have done it oftener."

"You know something? I agree. You're right. The memory is precious. It's much more vivid than chocolate cake, and much richer. But Uncle Sammler, the next day at school when I saw the kid I made up my mind to give him my allowance, which was ten cents."

"He took it?"

"He sure did."

"I like such stories. What did he say?"

"Not a word. He just nodded his head and took the dime.

He stuck it in his pocket and went back to his bigger pals. I guess he felt he had earned it on the ice. It was his fair reward."

"I see you have these recollections."

"Well, I need them. Everybody needs his memories. They keep the wolf of insignificance from the door."

And all this will continue. It will simply continue. Another six billion years before the sun explodes. Six billion years of human life! It lames the heart to contemplate such a figure. Six billion years! What will become of us? Of the other species, yes, and of us? How we ever make it? And when we have to abandon the earth, and leave this solar system for another, what a moving-day that will be. But by then humankind will have become very different. Evolution continues. Olaf Stapledon reckoned that each individual in future ages would be living thousands of years. The future person, a colossal figure, a beautiful green color, with a hand that had evolved into a kit of extraordinary instruments, tools strong and subtle, thumb and forefinger capable of exerting thousands of pounds of pressure. Each mind belonging to a marvelous analytical collective, thinking out its mathematics, its physics as part of a sublime whole. A race of semi-immortal giants, our green descendants, dear kin and brethren, inevitably containing still some of our bitter peculiarities as well as powers of spirit. The scientific revolution was only three hundred years old. Give it a million, give it a billion more. And God? Still hidden, even from this powerful mental brotherhood, still out of reach?

But now the Rolls was in the lanes. You could hear the new spring leaves brushing and stirring as the silver car passed. After many years, Sammler still did not know the way to Elya's house in the suburban woods, the small roads twisted so. But here was the building, half-timbered Tudor style, where the respectable surgeon and his home-making wife had brought up two children, and played badminton on this pleasant grass. In 1947 as a refugee Sammler had been astonished at their playfulness—adults with rackets and shuttlecocks. The lawn now was lighted by the moon, which seemed to Sammler clean-shaven; the gravel, fine, white, and small, made an amiable sound of grinding under the tires. The elms were thick, old—older than the combined ages of all the Gruners. Animal eyes appeared in the headlights, or beveled reflectors set out on the borders of paths shone: mouse, mole, woodchuck, cat, or glass bits peering from grass and bush. There were no lighted windows. Emil turned his brights on the front door. Wallace, as he hurried out, spilled his whisky on the carpet. Sammler groped for the glass and gave it to the chauffeur, explaining, "This fell." Then he followed Wallace over the rustling gravel.

As soon as Sammler entered, Emil backed away to the garage. That left only moonlight in the rooms. A house of misconceived purposes, as it had always seemed to Sammler, where nothing really functioned except the mechanical appliances. But Gruner had always taken care of it conscientiously, especially since the death of his wife, in a memorial spirit. Just as Margotte did for Ussher Arkin. That was fresh gravel in the drive. As soon as winter ended, Gruner ordered it laid down. The moon rinsed the curtains and foamed like peroxide on the nap of the white heavy carpets.

"Wallace?" Sammler believed he heard him below in the cellar. If he didn't turn on the lights, it was because he didn't want Sammler to know his movements. The poor fellow was demented. Mr. Sammler, forced by life, by fate, by what you like, to be disinterested, to think to the best of his ability on universal lines, was not about to stoop to policing Wallace in his father's house, to prevent him from digging out money—real or imaginary criminal abortion dollars.

Examining the kitchen, Sammler found no evidence that anyone had lately been here. The cupboards were shut, the stainless-steel sink and counters dry. As in a model exhibit. Cups on their hooks, none missing. But at the bottom of the garbage pail lined with a brown paper bag was an empty tunafish can; waterpacked, Geisha brand, freshly fish-smelly. Sammler held it to his nose. Aha! Had someone lunched? Emil the chauffeur, perhaps? Or Wallace himself, straight from the can without vinegar or dressing? Wallace would have left crumbs on the counter, and the soiled fork, disorderly signs of eating. Sammler put back the cut tin circle, released the pedal of the pail, and went to the living room. There he felt the chain mail of the fire screen, for Shula was fond of fires. It was cool. But the evening was warm. This proved nothing.

He then went on to the second floor, recalling how he and she had played hide-and-go-seek in London thirty-five years ago. He had been good at it, talking aloud to himself. "Is Shula in this broom closet? Let me see. Where can she be? She is not in the broom closet. How mystifying! Is she under the bed? No. My, what a clever little girl. How well she hides herself. She's simply disappeared." While the child, just five years old, thrilling with game fever, positively white, crouched behind the brass scuttle where he pretended not to see her, her bottom near the floor, her large kinky head with the small red bow—a whole life there. Melancholy. Even if there hadn't been the war.

However, theft! That was serious. And theft of intellectual property—even worse. And in the dark he yielded somewhat to elderly weakness. Too old for this. Toiling along the banister in the fatiguing luxury of the carpet. He belonged at the hospital. An old relative in the waiting-room. Much more appropriate. On the second floor, the bedrooms. He moved cautiously in darkness. In the housebound air were old odors of soap and eau de cologne. No one had lately ventilated the place.

A sound of water reached him, a slight movement in a full tub. A wallow. His hand reached in, wrist bent, sliding over the tile wall until he found the electric switch. In the light he saw Shula trying to cover her breasts with a washcloth. The enormous tub was only half occupied by her short body. The soles of her white feet, he saw, the black female triangle, and the white swellings with large rings of purplish brown. The veins. Yes, yes, she belonged to the club. The gender club. This was a female. That was a male. Much difference it could make to him.

"Father. Please. Please turn off the light."

"Nonsense. I'll wait in the bedroom. Wrap yourself up. Be quick about it."

He sat in Angela's old room. When she was a young girl. Or an apprentice whore. Well, people went to the wars. They took what weapons they had, and they advanced toward the front.

Sammler sat in a peach cretonne boudoir chair. Hearing no movements in the bathroom, he called, "I'm waiting," and she surged up from the water. He heard her feet, solid, rapid. In walking she always brushed objects with her body. She never simply walked. She touched things and claimed them. As property. Then she entered, quick-footed, wearing a man's woolen robe and a towel on her head, and she seemed to be gasping, shocked at being seen in the tub by her father.

"Well, where is it?"

"Daddy!"

"No. I am the one that is shocked, not you. Where is that document you have stolen twice?"

"It was not stealing."

"Other people may make new rules as they go along, but I will not, and you will not put me in that position. I was about to return the manuscript to Dr. Lal, and it was taken from my desk. Just as it was taken from his hands. Same method."

"That is not the way to look at it. But don't excite yourself too much."

"After all this, don't protect my heart or hint that I am an old man who may fall dead of apoplexy. You won't get away with anything like that. Now, where is this object?"

"It's really perfectly safe." She began to speak Polish. Severe, he denied her permission to speak that language. She was trying to invoke her terrible times of hiding—the convent, the hospital, the contagious ward when the German searching party came.

"None of that. Answer in English. Have you brought it here?"

"I've had a copy made. Daddy, I went to Mr. Widick's office . . ."

Sammler held himself in. Since be wouldn't allow her to speak Polish she was lapsing into something else, childishness. With small-girl softness, she lowered her mature, already fully middle-aged face. She was now meeting his look from one side, with only the one expanded childlike eye, and her chin shyly, slyly sinking toward the woolen robe.

"Yes? Well, what did you do in Mr. Widick's office?"

"He has one of those duplicating machines. I've used it for Cousin Elya. And Mr. Widick never goes home. He must hate home. He's always at the office, so I called and asked to use the machine, and he said, 'Sure.' I Xeroxed the whole thing."

"For me?"

"Or for Dr. Lal."

"You thought I might want the original?"

"If it's more convenient for you."

"Now, what have you done with these manuscripts?"

"I locked them in two lockers in Grand Central Station."

"In Grand Central. Good God. You have the keys, or have you lost the keys?"

"I have them, Father."

"Where are they?"

Shula was prepared for him. She produced two stamped and sealed envelopes. One was addressed to him, the other to Dr. Govinda Lal at Butler Hall.

"You were going to send these through the mails? The locker is for twenty-four hours only. These might take a week to arrive. Then what? And did you write down the numbers of the lockers? No. Then how would one know where they were if the letters got lost? You'd have to file a claim and prove ownership, authorship. Enough to drive a man out of his mind."

"Don't scold so hard. I did everything for you. You had stolen property in your house. The detective said it was stolen property, and anybody who had it was a receiver of stolen property."

"From now on, do me no such favors. It can't even be discussed with you. You seem to have no grasp of the matter."

"I brought it to you to show my faith in the memoir. I wanted to remind you how important it is. Sometimes you yourself forget. As if H. G. Wells were nothing so special. Well, maybe not to you, but to a great many people H. G. Wells is still important and very very special. I've been waiting for you to finish, and be reviewed in the papers. I wanted to see my father's picture in the bookshops, instead of all those foolish faces and unimportant stupid books."

The soiled rental keys in the envelopes. Mr. Sammler considered them. As well as exasperating, troubling, she was of course sadly amusing. If the lockers contained the manuscripts and not wads of paper in portfolios. No, he thought not. She was only a bit crazy. His poor child. A creature caused by him and adrift in a formless, boundless world. How had she come to be like this? Perhaps the inward, the intimate, the dear life—the thing that is oneself from earliest days—when it first learns of death is often crazed. Here magical powers must help, assuage, console, and for a woman, those marvelous powers so often are the powers of a man. As, Antony dying, Cleopatra cried she wouldn't abide in this dull world which "in thy absence is No better than a sty." And? A sty, and? He now remembered the end, fit for this night. "There is nothing left remarkable Beneath the visiting moon."

And he was supposed to be the remarkable thing, he who sitting on this glazed slipcover felt under him the tedium of its peach color and its fat red flowers. Such an article, meant to oppress and afflict the soul, was even now succeeding. He had remained touchable, vulnerable to trifles. But Mr. Sammler still received primordial messages too. And the immediate basic message was that she, this woman with her sexual female form plain in the light wrapping of the woolen robe (especially beneath the waist, where a thing was to make a lover gasp), this mature woman should not now be asking that her daddy make sublunary objects remarkable. For one thing, *he* never bestrode the world like a Colossus with armies and navies, dropping coronets from his pockets. He was only an old Jew whom they had hacked at, shot at, but missed killing somehow, murdering everyone else with their blasts. In their peculiar transformation: a people changed into uniform, masked in military cloth and helmets, and coming with machinery for the purpose of murdering boys, girls, men, women, making blood run, burying, and finally exhuming and burning rotten corpses. Man is a killer. Man has a moral nature. The anomaly can be resolved by insanity only, by insane dreams in which delusions of consciousness are maintained by organization, in states of mad perdition clinging to forms of business administration. Making it "government work." All of that! But in this world he, now *he*, dear God! was to supply his unhinged, wavering-witted daughter with high aims. And of course in Shula's view he had been getting too delicate for earthly life, too absorbed in unshared universals, excluding her. And by extravagance, by animal histrionics, by papers pinched, by goofy business with shopping bags, trash-basket neuroses, exotic heartburn cookery she wished to implicate him and bring him back, to bind him and keep him in the world beside her. Some world! Some her! Their elevation would be joint elevation. She would back him, and he would accomplish great things in the world of culture. For she was *kulturnaya*. Shula was so *kulturnaya*. Nothing was more suitable than this philistine Russian word. *Kulturny*. She might creep down on her knees and pray like a Christian; she might pull that on her father; she might crawl into dark confession boxes; she might run to Father Robles and invoke Christian protection against his Jewish anger; but in her nutty devotion to culture she couldn't have been more Jewish.

"Very well, my photograph in bookshops. A fine idea. Excellent. But stealing . . . ?"

"It wasn't actually stealing."

"Well, what word do you prefer, and what difference does it make? Like the old joke: what more do I learn about a horse if I know that in Latin it is called *equus*?"

"But I'm not a thief."

"Very well. In your mind you're not a thief. Only in fact."

"I thought if you were really, really serious about H. G. Wells you would have to know if he predicted accurately about the moon, or Mars, and that you'd pay any price to have the latest, most up-to-date scientific information. A creative person wouldn't stop at anything. For the creative there are no crimes. And aren't you a creative person?"

It seemed to Sammler that inside him (*faute de mieux*, in his mind) was a field in which many hunters at cross-purposes were firing bird shot at a feather apparition assumed to be a bird. Shula had meant to set him a test. Was he the real thing or wasn't he? Was he creative, a force of nature, a true original, or not? Yes, it was a fitness test, and this was very American of Shula. Did an American exist who was not morally didactic? Was there any crime committed which didn't punish the victim for "the greater good"? Was there any sinner who did not sin *pro bono publico*? So great was the evil of helpfulness, and so immense the liberal spirit of explanation. The psychopathology of teaching in the United States. So, then, was Papa a true creative intransigent—capable of bold theft for the sake of the memoir? Could he risk all for H. G.?

"Truthfully, my child, have you ever read a book of Wells'?"

"Yes, I have."

"Tell me—but the truth, just between you and me."

"I read one book, Father."

"One? One book by Wells is like trying to bathe in a single wave. What was the book?"

"It was about God."

"*God the Invisible King*?"

"That's the one."

"Did you finish it?"

"No."

"Neither did I."

"Oh, Father—you?"

"I just couldn't read it. Human evolution with God as Intelligence. I soon saw the point, then the rest was tedious, garrulous."

"But it was *so* intelligent. I read a few pages and was so thrilled. I knew he was a great man, even if I couldn't read the whole book. You know I can't read an entire book. I'm too restless. But you've read all his other books."

"No one could read them all. I've read many. Probably too many."

Smiling Sammler emptied the envelopes and tossed the crumpled ball into Angela's wastepaper basket of gilded Florentine leather. Acquired by her mother on a tour. The keys he dropped into his pocket, leaning far to one side in the boudoir chair to get at the flap.

Shula, observing silently, was smiling also, holding her wrists with her fingers, forearms crossing on her bosom to keep the robe from falling open. Sammler, despite the washrag, had seen the brown-purple tips, enriched with salient veins. At the corner of her mouth, now that she had done her mischief, there was a chaste twist of achievement. The flat black kinked hair was covered up, towel-swathed, except, as always, for the kosher sidelocks escaping at her ears. And smiling as if she had eaten a plateful of divine forbidden soup, and what was to be done about it now that it was down? At the back, the white nape of her neck was strong. Biological strength. Below the neck there was a mature dorsal hump. A grown woman. But the arms and legs were not proportionate. His only begotten child. He never doubted that she performed acts originating far beyond, in the past, of unconscious ancestral origin. He was aware how true this was of himself.

Especially in religious matters. She was a praying nut, but he, after all, was given to praying, too, often addressed God. Just now he asked to understand why he so much loved this fool woman with the thick, uselessly sensual cream skin, the painted mouth, and that towel turban.

"Shula, I know you did this for me—"

"You are more important than that man, Father. You needed it."

"But from now on, don't use me as an excuse. For your exploits . . ."

"We nearly lost you in Israel, in that war. I was afraid you wouldn't finish your lifework."

"Nonsense, Shula. What lifework! And killed? There? The finest death I could imagine. Besides, there was no danger, Ridiculous!"

Shula stood up. "I hear wheels," she said. "Somebody just drove up."

He had not heard. She had keen senses. Idiot ingenuous animal, she had ears like a fox. Rising so abrupt, standing silent to listen, queenly, dim-witted, alert. And the white feet. Her feet had not been disfigured by fashionable shoes.

"It probably is Emil."

"No, it's not Emil. I must get dressed."

She ran from the room.

Sammler went downstairs wondering where Wallace had gone. The doorbell began to chime and continued chiming. Margotte didn't know how to ring, when to stop pushing a button. He could see her, through the long narrow pane, in her straw hat, and Professor V. Govinda Lal was with her.

"We hired a Hertz car," she said. "The Professor couldn't bear to wait. We talked to Father Robles on the phone. He hadn't seen Shula in days."

"Professor Lal. Imperial College. Biophysics."

"I am Shula's father."

There were small bows, a handshake.

"We can sit in the living room. Shall I make a pot of coffee? Is Shula here?" said Margotte.

"She is."

"And my manuscript?" said Lal. "*The Future of the Moon*?"

"Safe," said Sammler. "Not actually in the house, but locked up safely. I have the keys. Professor Lal, please accept my apologies. My daughter has behaved very badly. Caused you pain."

Sammler under the foyer light saw the shocked and disappointed face of Lal: brown cheeks, black hair, neat, vivid, and gracefully parted, and a huge spreading beard. The inadequacy of words—the need for several simultaneous languages to address all parts of the mind at once, especially those parts left free by meager communication, functioning furiously on their own. Instead, as one were to smoke ten cigarettes simultaneously; while also drinking whisky; while also being sexually engaged with three or four other persons; while hearing bands of music; while receiving scientific notations—thus to capacity *engagé* . . . the boundlessness, the pressure of modern expectations.

Lal shouted, "Dear me! This is intolerable! Intolerable! Why am I sent this punishment!"

"Pour Dr. Lal a brandy, Margotte."

"I do not drink! I do not drink!"

In the dark setting of his beard the teeth were clenched. Then, aware of his own loudness, he said in more appropriate tones, "Normally I do not drink."

"But, Dr. Lal, you recommended beer on the moon. However—*I* am illogical. Go on, go on, Margotte, don't just look solicitous. Get the brandy. I'll have some if he won't. You know where the liquor is. Bring two glasses. Now, Professor, the anxiety will soon be over."

The living room was what they called "sunken." You had to descend. A well, a pool, a tank of carpet. It was furnished or decorated with professional completeness, densely arranged. This, if you allowed it to, gave pain. Sammler had known the late Mrs. Gruner's decorator. Or stultifier. Croze. Croze was petit, but had the strength of an art personality. He stood like a thrush. His little belly came far forward and lifted his trousers well above the ankles. His face had lovely color, his hair was barbered to the shapely little head, he had a rosebud mouth, and after you shook hands with Croze, your own hand was all day perfumed. He was creative. Capable of criminal acts, probably. All this was his creation. Here many boring hours had occurred, especially after family dinners. It wouldn't be a bad custom to send these furnishings into the tomb with the deceased, Egyptian style. However, here they all were, these spoils of silk, leather, glass, and antique wood. Here Sammler led the hairy Dr. Lal, a small man, very dark. Not black, sharp-nosed, the Dravidian type, dolichocephalic, but round-featured. Probably from Punjab. He had thin and hairy wrists, ankles, legs. He was a dandy. A macaroni (Sammler could not surrender the old words it had given him so much pleasure in Cracow to pick up from eighteenth-century books). Yes, Govinda was a beau. He was also sensitive, intelligent, nervous, keen, a handsome, elegant, birdy man. One major incongruity: the round face enlarged by soft but strong beard. Behind, thin shoulder blades stuck through the linen blazer. He had a stoop.

"Where is your daughter, may I ask?"

"Coming down. I will ask Margotte to fetch her. She was frightened by your detective."

"He was clever to find her at all. Ingenious work. He did his job."

"No doubt, but with my daughter Pinkerton methods did not apply. Because of Poland, you see, and the war—police. She was hidden. So she panicked. Too bad you have had to suffer for it. But what can one do if she is somewhat . . . ?"

"Psycho?"

"That's putting it strongly. She's not entirely out of touch. She made a copy of your manuscript, and she took two lockers in Grand Central Station for copy and original. Here are the keys."

Lal's hand, long and thin, accepted them. "How can I be sure it's really there, my book?" he said.

"Dr. Lal, I know my daughter. I feel quite certain. Safe in fireproof steel. In fact, I'm glad she didn't bring the book on the train. She might have lost it—forgotten it on the seat. Grand Central is well lighted, policed, and even if one lock were to be picked by thieves, there would still be the other. Have no further anxiety. I see you are on edge. You can consider this disagreeable misadventure over. The manuscript is safe."

"Sir, I hope so."

"Let us have a sip of brandy. We have had some trying days."

"Agonizing. Somehow the kind of terror I anticipated in America. My first visit. I had an intuition."

"Has America been all like that?"

"Not altogether. But almost."

Noisy in the kitchen, Margotte was opening cans, taking down bowls, slamming the icebox, clattering the flatware. Margotte's household doings were in continual transmission.

"I could take the train to New York," said Lal.

"Margotte can't drive. What will you do with the Hertz car?"

"Oh, damn! The car! Bloody machines!"

"I regret I can't drive," Sammler said. "Not to drive is the latest snobbery, I am told. But I am innocent of that. It is my eyesight."

"I'd have to come back for Mrs. Arkin."

"You might surrender your Hertz in New Rochelle, but I doubt that they are open at night. There must be a Penn Central timetable. However, it's close to midnight. We could ask Wallace to take you to the train, if he hasn't slipped out the back way—Wallace Gruner," he explained. "We are in the Gruner house. My relative—my nephew by a half-sister. But first let us have the supper Margotte is preparing. What you said before interested me, your presentiments about the U.S.? Twenty-two years ago, my own arrival was a relief."

"Of course in a sense the whole world is now U.S. Inescapable," said Govinda Lal. "It's like a big crow that has snatched our future from the nest, and we, the rest, are like little finches in pursuit trying to peck it. However, the Apollo flights are American. I have been employed by NASA. On other research. But this is where my ideas will count, if they are any use. . . . If I sound strange, excuse me. I've been distressed."

"With good reason. My daughter did you a real injury."

"I am beginning to feel easier. I don't think any hard feelings will remain."

Through the tinted lens and while breathing brandy fumes, Sammler provisionally approved of Govinda Lal, who reminded him in some ways of Ussher Arkin. Very often, oftener than he consciously knew, and vividly, he thought of Ussher underground, in this or that posture, of this or that color or physical condition. As he thought of Antonina, his wife. So far as he knew the enormous grave had never been touched again. From which he himself, scratching dirt, pushing the corpses, came out choked with blood, and crept away on his belly. This preoccupation therefore was only to be expected.

Now Margotte was chopping onions in a bowl. Something to eat. Life in its lighted droplet cells continued its enactments. Poor Ussher in that plane at the Cincinnati airport. Sammler missed him and acknowledged that he had moved into the apartment with Margotte because of the contact with Ussher it afforded.

But he noted some of the same qualities, Arkin's qualities, in this very different, duskier, smaller, bushier Lal, whose wrist was no wider than a ruler.

Then Shula-Slawa came down the stairs. Lal, who saw her first, had an expression which made Sammler immediately turn. She had dressed herself in a sari, or something like it, had found a piece of Indian material in a drawer. It couldn't have been correctly wrapped. It also covered her head. Especially at the bust there was an error. (Sammler with increased concern this evening for the sensitivity of that area; if there was danger of exposure or of hurt, he felt it in his own organs.) He wasn't sure that she was wearing undergarments. No, there was no *Büstenhalter*. She was extremely white—citrus-thick skin, cream cheeks—and her lips, looking fuller and softer than ever, were painted a peculiar orange color. Like the Neapolitan cyclamens Sammler had admired in the botanical garden. Also, she wore false eyelashes. On her forehead was a Hindu spot made with the lipstick. Exactly where the Ash Wednesday smudge had been. The general idea was to charm and appease this angry Lal. Her eyes as she hurried, without looking, into the well of the room were heated, and in the old man's words to himself, kookily dilated, sensuality-bent. Though ladylike, she made too many gestures, coming forward too much, wildly overprompt, having too much by far to say.

"Professor Lal!"

"My daughter."

"Yes, so I thought."

"I am sorry. So terribly sorry, Dr. Lal. There was a misunderstanding. You were surrounded by people. You must have thought you were just letting me look at the manuscript. But I thought you were letting me take it home to my father. As I said, you remember? That he was writing the book about H. G. Wells?"

"Wells? No. But my impression is that he is very obsolete."

"Still, for the sake of science, of science, and for the sake of literature and history, because my father is writing this important history, and you see I help him in his intellectual cultural work. There's nobody else to do it. I never meant to make trouble."

No. Not trouble. Only to dig a pit and cover it with brushwood, and when a man fell into it to lie flat on the ground and converse with him amorously. For Sammler now suspected that she had run away with *The Future of the Moon* in order to create this very opportunity, this meeting. Were he and Wells really secondary, then? Was it really done to provoke interest? Wasn't that a familiar stratagem? To him, Sammler remembered, women used sometimes to act insolent to get his attention and say stinging things imagining that it made them fascinating. Was this why Shula had taken the book? Out of female seductiveness? One species: but the sexes like two different savage tribes. In full paint. Surprising and shocking each other in the bush. This Govinda, this light spry whiskered dark frail, flying sort of a man—an intellectual. And intellectuals she was mad for. They kept the world remarkable beneath that visiting moon. They kindled up her womb. Even Eisen, perhaps, to recover her esteem (among other reasons), had left the foundry and turned artist. Had probably lost track of the original motive, to show that he was, like her father, a man of culture. And now he was a painter. Poor Eisen.

But Shula was sitting very close to Lal on the sofa, almost taking him by the hand, by the arm, as if bent upon having a touch of his limbs. She was assuring him that she had reproduced his manuscript with great care. She worried lest the Xerox take away the ink and wipe the pages blank. She did page one dying of anxiety. "Such a special ink you use, and what if there should be a bad reaction. I would have died." But it worked beautifully. Mr. Widick said it was lovely copying. And it was in the two lockers. The copy was in a legal binder. Mr. Widick said you could even leave ransom money in Grand Central. Perfectly safe. Shula wanted Govinda Lal to see that the orange circle between the eyes had lunar significance. She kept tilting her face, offering her brow.

"Now, Shula, my dear," said Sammler. "Margotte needs help in the kitchen. Go and help her."

"Oh, Father." She tried, speaking aside in Polish, to tell him she wished to stay.

"Shula! Go! Go on now—go!"

As she obeyed, her cheeks had a hot and bitter look. Before Lal she wanted to show filial submission, but her behind was huffy as she went.

I would never have recognized, never have identified her," said Lal.

"Yes? Without the wig. She often affects a wig."

He stopped. Govinda was thinking. Presumably about the recovery of his work from the locker. Yes. He felt his blazer pockets from beneath, making certain of the keys.

"You are Polish?" he said.

"I was Polish."

"Artur?"

"Yes. Like Schopenhauer, whom my mother read. Arthur, at that period, not very Jewish, was the most international, enlightened name you could give a boy. The same in all languages. But Schopenhauer didn't care for Jews. He called them vulgar optimists. Optimists? Living near the crater of Vesuvius, it is better to be an optimist. On my sixteenth birthday my mother gave me *The World as Will and Idea*. Naturally it was an agreeable compliment that I could be so serious and deep. Like the great Arthur. So I studied the system, and I still remember it. I learned that only Ideas are not overpowered by the Will—the cosmic force, the Will, which drives all things. A blinding power. The inner creative fury of the world. What we see are only its manifestations. Like Hindu philosophy—Maya, the veil of appearances that hangs over all human experience. Yes, and come to think of it, according to Schopenhauer, the seat of the Will in human beings is . . ."

"Where is it?"

"The organs of sex are the seat of the Will."

The thief in the lobby agreed. He took out the instrument of the Will. He drew aside not the veil of Maya itself but one of its forehangings and showed Sammler his metaphysical warrant.

"And you were a friend of the famous H. G. Wells—that much is true, isn't it?"

"I don't like to claim the friendship of a man who is not alive to affirm or deny it, but at one time, when he was in his seventies, I saw him often."

"Ah, then you must have lived in London."

"So we did, in Woburn Square near the British Museum. I took walks with the old man. In those days my own ideas didn't amount to much so I listened to his. Scientific humanism, faith in an emancipated future, in active benevolence, in reason, in civilization. Not popular ideas at the moment. Of course we have civilization but it is so disliked. I think you understand what I mean, Professor Lal."

"I believe I do, yes."

"Still, you know, Schopenhauer would not have called Wells a vulgar optimist. Wells had many dark thoughts. Take a book like *The War of the Worlds.* There the Martians come to get rid of mankind. They treat our species as Americans treated the bison and other animals, or for that matter the American Indians. Extermination."

"Ah, extermination. I assume you have personal acquaintance with the phenomenon?"

"I do have some, yes."

"Indeed?" said Lal. "I have seen some of it myself. As a Punjabi."

"You *are* a Punjabi?"

"Yes, and in nineteen forty-seven studying at the University in Calcutta and present at the terrible riots, the fighting of Hindus and Moslems. Since called the great Calcutta killing. I am afraid I have seen homicidal maniacs."

"Ah."

"Yes, and slaying with loaded sticks and sharp iron bars. And the corpses. Rape, arson, looting."

"I see." Sammler looked at him. An intelligent and sensitive man, this was, with an expressive face. Of course such expressiveness was sometimes a sign of subjectivity and of inward mental habits. Not an outgoing imagination. He was beginning to think, however, that this Lal was, like Ussher Arkin, a man he could talk to. "Then it is not a theoretical matter to you. Nor to me. But excellent good-hearted gentlemen, Mr. Arnold Bennett, Mr. H. G. Wells, lunching at the Savoy . . . Olympians of lowerclass origin. So nice. So serious. So English, Mr. Wells. I was flattered to be chosen to listen to his monologues. I was also fond of him. Of course since Poland, nineteen thirty-nine, my judgments are different. Altered. Like my eyesight. I see you trying to observe what is behind these tinted glasses. No, no, that's quite all right. One eye is functioning. Like the old saying about the one-eyed being King in the Country of the Blind. Wells wrote a story around this. Not a good story. Anyway, I am not in the Country of the Blind, but only one-eyed. As for Wells . . . he was a writer. He wrote and wrote and wrote."

Sammler thought that Govinda was about to speak. When be paused, several waves of silence passed, containing tacit questions: You? No, you, sir: You speak. Lal was listening. The sensitivity of a hairy creature; the animal brown of his eyes; the good breeding of his attentive posture.

"You wish me to say more about Wells, since Wells is in a way behind all this?"

"Would you, kindly?" said Lal. "You have doubts about the value of Wells's writing."

"Yes, of course I have. Grave doubts. Through universal education and cheap printing poor boys have become rich and powerful. Dickens, rich. Shaw, also. He boasted that reading Karl Marx made a man of him. I don't know about that, but Marxism for the great public made him a millionaire. If you wrote for an elite, like Proust, you did not become rich, but if your theme was social justice and your ideas were radical you were rewarded by wealth, fame, and influence."

"Most interesting."

"Do you find it so? Excuse me, I am heavy-hearted this evening. Both heavy-hearted and talkative. And when I meet someone I like, I am apt to be garrulous at first."

"No, no, please continue this explanation."

"Explanation? I have an objection to extended explanations.

There are too many. This makes the mental life of mankind ungovernable. But I have thought about the Wells matter—the Shaw matter, and about people like Marx, Jean-Jacques Rousseau, Marat, Saint-Just, powerful speakers, writers, starting out with no capital but mental capital and achieving an immense influence. And all the rest, little lawyers, readers, bluffers, pamphleteers, amateur scientists, bohemians, librettists, fortune tellers, charlatans, outcasts, buffoons. A crazy provincial lawyer demanding the head of the King, and getting it, too. In the name of the people. Or Marx, a student, a fellow from the University, writing books which overwhelm the world. He was really an excellent journalist and publicist. As I was a journalist myself, I am a judge of his ability. Like many journalists, he made things up out of other newspaper articles, the European press, but he made them up extremely well, writing about India or the American Civil War, matters of which he actually knew nothing. But he was marvelously shrewd, a guesser of genius, a powerful polemicist and rhetorician. His ideological hashish was very potent. Anyhow, you see what I mean—people become authoritative and plebeians of genius elevate themselves first to nobility and then to universal glory, and all because they had what all poor children got from literacy: the ABCs, the dictionary, the grammar books, the classics. Until, soaring from their slums or their little petit-bourgeois parlors, they were addressing worldwide millions. These are the people who set the terms, who make up the discourse, and then history follows their words. Think of the wars and revolutions we have been scribbled into."

"The Indian press had much responsibility for those riots, certainly," said Lal.

"One thing in Wells's favor was that because of personal disappointments he at least did not demand the sacrifice of civilization. He did not become a cult-figure, a royal personality, a grand art-hero or activist leader. He did not feel disgraced by words. Many did and do."

"Meaning what, sir?"

"Well you see," said Mr. Sammler, "in the great bourgeois period, writers became aristocrats. And having become aristocrats through their skill in words, they felt obliged to go into action. Evidently it's a disgrace for true nobility to substitute words for acts. You can see this in the career of Monsieur Malraux, or Monsieur Sartre. You can see it much farther back in Hamlet when he feels that humiliation, Dr. Lal, saying, 'I . . . must like a whore unpack my heart with words.' "

" 'And fall a-cursing like a very drab.' "

"Yes, that is the full quotation. Or to Polonius, 'Words, words, words.' Words are for the elderly, or for the young who are old-in-heart. Of course this is the condition of a prince whose father has been murdered. But when people out of a contempt for impotence and paralyzed *talk* throw themselves into noble actions, do they know what they are doing? When they begin to call for blood, and advocate terror, or proclaim a general egg-breaking to make a great historical omelet, do they know what they are calling for? When they have struck a mirror with a hammer, aiming to repair it, can they put the fragments together again? Well, Dr. Lal, I am not sure what good this examination or rebuke can do. It is not as if I were certain that human beings can be controlled at any level of complexity. I would not swear that mankind was governable. But Wells was inclined to believe that it was. He thought, most of the time, that the minority civilization could be transmitted to the great masses, and that orderly conditions for this transmission were possible. Decent, British-style, Victorian-Edwardian, nonoutcast, nonlunatic, *grateful* conditions. But in World War Two he despaired. He compared humankind to rats in a sack, desperately struggling and biting. Indeed it was ratlike and sacklike. Indeed so. But now I have exhausted my interest in Wells. Yours too, I hope, Dr. Lal."

"Ah, you did know the man well," said Lal. "And how clearly you put things. You are a first-rate condenser. I wish I had your talent. I lacked it sorely when I wrote my book."

"Your book, what I had time to read of it, is very clear."

"I hope you will read it all. Excuse me, Mr. Sammler, I am confused. I don't know quite where Mrs. Arkin has brought me, or where we are. You explained, but I did not follow."

"This is Westchester County, not far from New Rochelle, and the house of my nephew, Dr. Arnold Elya Gruner. At the moment, he is in the hospital."

"I see. Is he very sick?"

"There is an escape of blood in the brain."

"An aneurysm. It can't be reached for surgery?"

"It can't be reached."

"Dear, dear. And you are dreadfully disturbed."

"He will die in a day or two. He is dying. A good man. He brought us from a DP camp, Shula and me, and for twenty-two years he has taken care of us with kindness. Twenty-two years without a day of neglect, without a single irascible word."

"A gentleman."

"Yes, a gentleman. You can see that my daughter and I are not very competent. I did some journalism, until about fifteen years ago. It was never much. Recently I wrote a Polish report on the war in Israel. But it was Dr. Gruner who paid my way."

"He simply let you be a kind of philosopher?"

"If that is what I am. I am familiar with many explanations of things. To tell the truth, I am tired of most of them."

"Ah, you have an eschatological point of view, then. How interesting."

Sammler, not much caring for the word "eschatological," shrugged. "You think we should go into space, Dr. Lal?"

"You are very sad about your nephew. Perhaps you would prefer not to talk."

"Once you begin talking, once the mind takes to this way of turning, it keeps turning, and it dips through all events. And perhaps it makes matters slightly more tolerable to let it turn. Though I can't see why they should be tolerable. It is really a frightful moment. But what can one do? The thoughts continue turning."

"Like a Ferris wheel," said fragile, black-bearded Govinda Lal. "I should say that I have done work for Worldwide Technics, in Connecticut. Mine are highly sophisticated and theoretical assignments having to do with order in biological systems, how complex mechanisms reproduce themselves. Though it will not greatly signify to you, I am associated with the bang-bang hypothesis, related to the firing of simultaneous impulses, atomic theories of cellular conductivity. As you mentioned Rousseau, man may or may not have been born free. But I can say with assurance that he would not exist without his atomistic chains. I do hope you like my jokes. I enjoy your wit. If not mutual, that would be too bad. I refer to those chain structures of the cell. These are matters of order, Mr. Sammler.

Though I have not the full blueprint to present. I am not yet that universal genius. Ha, ha! In earnest, however, biological science is in an extraordinary state of progress. Oh, it is lovely, it is so beautiful! To participate is a privilege. This chemical order, which is a fundamental of life, is of great beauty. Oh, yes, very great. And what a high privilege! It occurred to me as you were speaking of another matter that to desire to live without order is to desire to turn from the fundamental biological governing principle. Which is widely presumed to be there only to free us, a platform for impulse. Are we crazy, or what? From order, from governing principle, the human being can tear himself to express his immense privilege of sheer liberty or unaccountability of impulse. The biological fundamentals are like the peasantry, the whole individual considering himself to be a prince. It is the *cigale* and the *fourmi*. The ant was once the hero, but now the grasshopper is the whole show. My father taught me maths and French. The chief anxiety of my father's life was that his students would cut up the *Encyclopedia Britannica* with razors and take the articles with them for home perusal. He was a simple person. Because of him, I have loved French literature. First in Calcutta, and then in Manchester, I studied it until my scientific interests matured. But as to your question about space. There is, of course, much objection to these expeditions. Accusation that it is money taken from school, slum, and so on, of course. Just as the Pentagon money is withheld from social improvements. What nonsense! It is propaganda by the social-science bureaucracy. *They* would hog the funds. Besides, money alone does not necessarily make the difference, does it? I think not. The Americans have always been reckless spenders. Bad, no doubt, but there is such a thing as fruitful *gaspillage*. Wastefulness can be justified if it permits inventiveness, originality, adventure. Unfortunately, the results are mostly and usually corrupt, making vile profits, playboy recreations, and building reactionary fortunes. As far as Washington is concerned, a moon expedition no doubt is superb PR. It is show biz. My slang may not be current." The rich and Oriental voice was very pleasing.

"I am not a good authority."

"You know, however, what I have in mind. Circuses.

Dazzlement. The U.S. becoming the greatest dispenser of science-fiction entertainments. As far as the organizers and engineers are concerned, it is a vast opportunity, but that is not of high theoretical value. Still, at the same time something serious happens within. The soul most certainly feels the grandeur of this achievement. Not to go where one can go may be stunting. I believe the soul feels it, and therefore it is a necessity. It may introduce new sobriety. Naturally the technology will impress minds more than the personalities. The astronauts may not seem so very heroic. More like superchimpanzees. Especially if they do not express themselves beautifully. But after all, this is the function of poets. If any. But even the technicians I venture to guess will be ennobled. But do you agree, sir, that we should go into space?"

"Well, why not? Up to a point, yes. Although I don't think it can be rationally justified."

"Why not? I can think of many justifications. I see it as a rational necessity. You should have finished my book."

"Then I would have found the irresistible proof?" Sammler smiled through the tinted glasses, and the blind eye attempted to participate. In the old black and neat suit, his stiff and slender body upright and his fingers, which trembled strongly under strain, lightly holding his knees. A cigarette (he smoked only three or four a day) burned between his awkward hairy knuckles.

"I simply mean you would be acquainted with my argument, which I base in part on U.S. history. After 1776 there was a continent to expand into, and this space absorbed all the mistakes. Of course I am not a historian. But if one cannot make bold guesses, one will have to surrender all to the experts. Europe after 1789 did not have the space for its mistakes. Result: war and revolution, with the revolutions ending up in the hands of the madmen."

"De Maistre said that."

"Did he? I don't know much about him."

"It may be enough to know that he agrees. Revolutions do end up in the hands of madmen. Of course there are always enough madmen for every purpose. Besides, if the power is great enough, it will make its own madmen by its own pressure. Power certainly corrupts, but that statement is humanly incomplete. Isn't it too abstract? What should certainly be added is the specific truth that having power destroys the sanity of the powerful. It allows their irrationalities to leave the sphere of dreams and come into the real world. But there—excuse me. I am no psychologist. As you say, however, one must be allowed to make guesses."

"Perhaps it is natural that an Indian should be supersensitive to a surplus of humanity. Calcutta is so teeming, so volcanic. A Chinese would be similarly sensitive. Any nation of vast multitudes. We are crowded in, packed in, now, and human beings must feel that there is a way out, and that the intellectual power and skill of their own species opens this way. The invitation to the voyage, the Baudelaire desire to get out—get out of human circumstances—or the longing to be a drunken boat, or a soul whose craving is to crack open a closed universe is still real, only the impulse does not have to be assigned to tiresomeness and vanity of life, and it does not necessarily have to be a death-voyage. The trouble is that only trained specialists will be able to take the trip. The longing soul cannot by direct impulse go because it has the boundless need, or the mind for it, or the suffering-power. It will have to know engineering and wear those peculiar suits, and put up with personal, organic embarrassments. Perhaps the problems of radiation will prove insuperable, or strange diseases will be contracted on other worlds. Still, there is a universe into which we can overflow. Obviously we cannot manage with one single planet. Nor refuse the challenge of a new type of experience. We must recognize the extremism and fanaticism of human nature. Not to accept the opportunity would make this earth seem more and more a prison. If we could soar out and did not, we would condemn ourselves. We would be more than ever irritated with life. As it is, the species is eating itself up. And now Kingdom Come is directly over us and waiting to receive the fragments of a final explosion. Much better the moon."

Sammler did not think that must necessarily happen.

"Do you think the species doesn't want to live?" he said.

"Many wish to end it," said Lal.

"Well, if as you say we are the kind of creature which is compelled to do what it is capable of doing, it would follow that we must demolish ourselves. But isn't that up to the species?

Could we say that at this point politics is anything but pure biology? In Russia, in China, and here, very mediocre people have the power to end life altogether. These representatives—not representatives of the best but Calibans or, in the jargon, creeps—will decide for us all whether we live or die. Man now plays the drama of universal death. Should all not die at once, together, like one great individual death, expressing freely all of man's passions toward his doom? Many *say* they wish to end it. Of course that may be only rhetoric."

"Mr. Sammler," said Lal, "I believe you intimate that there is an implicit morality in the will-to-live and that these mediocrities in office will do their duty by the species. I am not sure. There is no duty in biology. There is no sovereign obligation to one's breed. When biological destiny is fulfilled in reproduction the desire is often to die. We please ourselves in extracting ideas of duty from biology. But duty is pain. Duty is hateful—misery, oppressive."

"Yes?" said Sammler, in doubt. "When you know what pain is, you agree that not to have been born is better. But being born one respects the powers of creation, one obeys the will of God—with whatever inner reservations truth imposes. As for duty—you are wrong. The pain of duty makes the creature upright, and this uprightness is no negligible thing. No, I stand by what I first said. There is also an instinct against leaping into Kingdom Come."

The scene, for such a conversation, was itself curious—the green carpets, large pots, silk drapes of the late Hilda Gruner's living room. Here Govinda Lal, small, hunched, dusky, with his rusty-gilt complexion, his full face and beard, was like an Oriental ornament or painting. Sammler himself came under this influence, like a figure in Indian color—the red cheeks, the spreading white hair at the back, the circles of his specs, and the cigarette smoke about his hair. To Wallace he had insisted that he was an Oriental, and now felt that he resembled one.

"As for the present state of affairs," said Govinda, "I see that personal dissatisfaction, which is so great, may contribute energy to the biggest job which fate has secretly prepared—earth-departure. It may be the compression preceding the new expansion. To hurl yourself toward the moon, you may need an equal and opposite inertia. An inertia at least two hundred fifty thousand miles deep. Or more. We moreover seem to have it. Who knows how these things work? You know the famous Oblomov? He couldn't get out of bed. This phantom of inertia or paralysis. The opposite was frantic activism—bomb-throwing, civil war, a cult of violence? You have mentioned that. Do we always, always to the point of misery, do a thing? Persist until exhausted? Perhaps. Take my own temperament, for instance. I confess to you, Mr. Sammler (and how glad I am that your daughter's peculiarities have brought us together—I think we shall be friends) . . . I confess that I am originally—originally, you understand—of a melancholy, depressed character. As a child, I could not bear to be separated from Mother. Nor, for that matter, Father, who was, as I said, a teacher of French and mathematics. Nor the house, nor playmates. When visitors had to leave, I would make violent scenes. I was an often-sobbing little boy. All parting was such an emotional ordeal that I would get sick. I must have felt separation as far inward as my constituent molecules, and trembled in billions of nuclei. Hyperbole? Perhaps, my dear Mr. Sammler. But I have been convinced since my early work in biophysics of vascular beds (I will not trouble you with details) that nature, more than an engineer, is an artist. Behavior is poetry, is metaphorical order, is metaphysics. From the high-frequency tenths-of-millisecond brain responses in corticothalamic nets to the grossest of ecological phenomena, it is all the printing out, in mysterious code, of sublime metaphor. I am speaking of my own childhood passions, and the body of an individual is electronically denser than the tropical rain forest is dense with organisms. And all these existences are, it often suggests itself, poems. I do not even try to overcome this impression of universal poetry any more. But to return to the question of my own personality, I see now that I had set myself a task of distance from objects of closest attachment. In which, Mr. Sammler, outer space is an opposite—personally, an emotional pole. One is born between his mother's legs, afterward persisting outward. To see the sidereal archipelagoes is one thing, but to plunge into them, into a dayless, nightless universe, why that, you see, makes sea-depth petty, the leviathan no more than a polliwog—"

Margotte came in—short thick, rapid, efficient legs, but

drying her hands ineptly in both skirt and apron—saying, "We will all feel better when we eat something. For you, Uncle, we have lobster salad, and some Crosse and Blackwell onion soup and bauernbrot and butter, and coffee. Dr. Lal, I assume you are not a meat eater. Do you like cottage cheese?"

"If you please, no fish."

"But where is Wallace?" said Sammler.

"Oh, he went up with tools to fix something in the attic." She smiled as she returned to the kitchen, smiled especially at Govinda Lal.

Lal said, "I am very much taken with Mrs. Arkin."

Sammler thought, She intended, sight unseen, that you should be taken with her. I can give you pointers on being happy with her. I'll lose my sanctuary, perhaps, but I can give that up if this is serious. With an outer-space perspective perhaps immediate urgencies and egoism are lessened and marriage would be a kindly association—*sub specie aeternitatis*. Besides, though small, Govinda was in certain ways like Ussher Arkin. Women do not like too much change.

"Margotte is an excellent person," said Sammler.

"That is my impression. And exceedingly, highly attractive. Has her husband been dead long?"

"Three years, poor fellow."

"Poor fellow indeed, to die young, and with such a desirable wife."

"Come, I am hungry," said Sammler. Already he was considering how to take Shula out of this. She was smitten with this Indian. Had her desires. Needs. Was a woman, after all. What could one do for a woman? Little, very little. Or, for Elya, with the spray bubbling in his head? Terrible. Elya reappeared strangely and continually, as if his face were orbiting—as if he were a satellite.

However, they sat down to a little supper in Elya's kitchen, and the conversation continued.

Now that Sammler had been charmed by Govinda and seen, or imagined, a resemblance to Ussher Arkin, and was affectionately committed, it went with his habit of mind to see him also in another aspect, as an Eastern curiosity, a bushy little planet-buzzing Oriental demon, mentally rebounding from limits like a horse-fly from glass. Wondering if the fellow might be a charlatan, in some degree. No, no, not that. One had no time to make *funny* observations, or paltry ones; one must be decisive and trust one's instincts. Lal was the real thing. His conversation was conversation, it was not a line. This was no charlatan, only an oddity. He was excellent, solid. His one immediately apparent weakness was to want his credentials known. He let fall names and titles—the Imperial College, his intimate friend Professor Waddington, his position as hunch-consultant with Professor Hoyle, his connection with Dr. Feltstein of NASA, and his participation in the Bellagio conference on theoretical biology. This was pardonable in a little foreigner. The rest was perfectly straight. Of course it amused Sammler that he and Lal spoke such different brands of foreign English, and it was also diverting that they were tall and short. To him height meant pituitary hyperactivity and maybe vital wastage. The large sometimes seemed to have diminished minds, as if the shooting up cost the brain something. Strangest of all in the eighth decade of one's life, however, was a spontaneous feeling of friendship. At his age? That was for your young person, still dreaming of love, of meeting someone of the opposite sex who would cure you of all your troubles, heart and soul, and for whom you would cure and fulfill the same. From this came a disposition for sudden attachments such as you now saw in Lal, Margotte, and Shula. But for himself, at his time of life and because he had come back from the other world, there were no rapid connections. His own first growth of affections had been consumed. His onetime human, onetime precious, life had been burnt away. More green growth rising from the burnt black would simply be natural persistency, the Life Force working, trying to start again.

However, while this little supper in the kitchen (laid on with Margotte's maladroit bounty) lasted, the sad old man experienced the utmost joy, too. It seemed to him that the others also felt as he did: Shula-Slawa in her misbound sari following the conversation with devoted eyes and mumming every word with soft orange-painted lips, leaning her head on be palm; Margotte, delighted of course; she was gone on this little Hindu; the occasion was intellectual, and moreover she was feeding everyone. Could any instant of life be nicer? To Sammler these female oddities were endearing.

Dr. Lal was saying that we did not get much from our brains, considering what brains were, electronically, with billions of instantaneous connections. "What goes on within a man's head," he said, "is far beyond his comprehension, of course. In very much the same way as a lizard or a rat or a bird cannot comprehend being organisms. But a human being, owing to dawning comprehension, may well feel that he is a rat who lives in a temple. In his external development, as a thing, a creature, in cerebral electronics he enjoys an adaptation, a fitness which makes him feel the unfitness of his personal human efforts. Therefore, at the lowest, a rat in a temple. At best, a clumsy thing, with dawning awareness of the finesse of internal organization employed in crudities."

"Yes," said Mr. Sammler, "that is a very nice way to put it, though I am not sure that there are many people so fine that they can feel this light weight of being so much more than they can grasp."

"I should be extremely interested to hear your views," said Lal.

"My views?"

"Oh, yes, Papa."

"Yes, dear Uncle Sammler."

"My views."

A strange thing happened. He felt that he was about to speak his full mind. Aloud! That was the most striking part of it. Not the usual self-communing of an aged and peculiar person. He was about to say what he thought, and *viva voce.*

"Shula is fond of lectures, I am not," he said. "I am extremely skeptical of explanations, rationalistic practices. I dislike the modern religion of empty categories, and people who make the motions of knowledge."

"View it as a recital rather than a lecture," said Lal. "Consider the thing from a musical standpoint."

"A recital. It is Dr. Lal who should give it—he has a musical voice. A recital—that is more inviting," said Sammler putting his cup down. "Recitals are for trained performers. I am not ready for the stage. But there isn't much time. So, ready or not . . . I keep my own counsel much too much, and I *am* tempted to pass on some of my views. Or impressions. Of course, the old always fear they have decayed unaware. How do I know I have not? Shula, who thinks her papa is a powerful wizard, and Margotte, who likes discussion of ideas so much, they will deny it."

"Of course," said Margotte. "It simply is not so."

"Well, I have seen it happen to others, why not to me? One must live with all combinations of the facts. I remember a famous anecdote about a demented man: Someone said, 'You are a paranoiac, my dear fellow,' and he answered, 'Perhaps, but that doesn't prevent people from plotting against me.' That is an important ray of light from a dark source. I can't say that I have felt any weakness in the head, but it may be there. Luckily, my views are short. I suppose, Dr. Lal, that you are right. Biologically, chemically, the subtlety of the creature is beyond the understanding of the creature. We have an inkling of it, and feel how, by comparison, the internal state is so chaotic, such a hodgepodge of *odi et amo*. They say our protoplasm is like sea water. Our blood has a Mediterranean base. But now we live in a social and human sea. Inventions and ideas bathe our brains, which sometimes, like sponges, must receive whatever the currents bring and digest the metal protozoa. I do not say there is no alternative to such passivity, which is partly comical, but there are times, states, in which we lie under and feel the awful volume of cumulative consciousness, we feel the weight of the world. Not at all funny. The world is a terror, certainly, and mankind in a revolutionary condition becoming, as we say, modern—more and more mental, the realm of nature, as it used to be called, turning into a park, a zoo, a botanical garden, a world's fair, an Indian reservation. And then there are always human beings who take it upon themselves to represent or interpret the old savagery, tribalism, the primal fierceness of the fierce, lest we forget prehistory, savagery, animal origins. It is even said, here and there, that the real purpose of civilization is to permit us all to live like primitive people and lead a neolithic life in an automated society. That is a droll point of view. I don't want to lecture you, however. If one lives in his room, as I do, though Shula and Margotte take such excellent care of me, one has fantasies about addressing a captive audience. Very recently, I tried to give a speech at Columbia. It did not go well. I think I made a fool of myself."

"Oh, but please continue," said Dr. Lal. "We are most attentive."

"A person's views are either necessary or superfluous," said Sammler. "The superfluous irritates me sharply. I am an extremely impatient individual. My impatience sometimes borders on rage. It is clinical."

"No, no, Papa."

"However, it is sometimes necessary to repeat what all know. All mapmakers should place the Mississippi in the same location, and avoid originality. It may be boring, but one has to know where he is. We cannot have the Mississippi flowing toward the Rockies for a change. Now, as everyone knows, it has only been in the last two centuries that the majority of people in civilized countries have claimed the privilege of being individuals. Formerly they were slave, peasant, laborer, even artisan, but not person. It is clear that this revolution, a triumph for justice in many ways—slaves should be free, killing toil should end, the soul should have liberty—has also introduced new kinds of grief and misery, and so far, on the broadest scale, it has not been altogether a success. I will not even talk about the Communist countries, where the modern revolution has been most thwarted. To us the results are monstrous. Let us think only about our own part of the world. We have fallen into much ugliness. It is bewildering to see how much these new individuals suffer, with their new leisure and liberty. Though I feel sometimes quite disembodied, I have little rancor and quite a lot of sympathy. Often I wish to do something, but it is a dangerous illusion to think one can do much for more than a very few."

"What is one supposed to do?" said Lal.

"Perhaps the best is to have some order within oneself. Better than what many call love. Perhaps it *is* love."

"Please do say something about love," said Margotte.

"But I don't want to. What I was saying—you see I am getting old. I was saying that this liberation into individuality has not been a great success. For a historian of great interest, but for one aware of the suffering it is appalling. Hearts that get no real wage, souls that find no nourishment. Falsehoods, unlimited. Desire, unlimited. Possibility, unlimited. Impossible demands upon complex realities, unlimited. Revival in childish and vulgar form of ancient religious ideas, mysteries, utterly unconscious of course—astonishing. Orphism, Mithraism, Manichaeanism, Gnosticism. When my eye is strong, I sometimes read in the Hastings *Encyclopedia of Religion and Ethics.* Many fascinating resemblances appear. But one notices most a peculiar play-acting, an elaborate and sometimes quite artistic manner of presenting oneself as an individual and a strange desire for originality, distinction, *interest*—yes, *interest*! A dramatic derivation from models, together with repudiation of models. Antiquity accepted models, the Middle Ages—I don't want to turn into a history book before your eyes—but modern man, perhaps because of collectivization, has a fever of originality. The idea of the uniqueness of the soul. An excellent idea. A true idea. But in these forms? In these poor forms? Dear God! With hair, with clothes, with drugs and cosmetics, with genitalia, with round trips through evil, monstrosity, and orgy, with even God approached through obscenities? How terrified the soul must be in this vehemence, how little that is really dear to it it can see in these Sadic exercises. And even there, the Marquis de Sade in his crazy way was an Enlightenment philosophe. Mainly he intended blasphemy. But for those who follow (unaware) his recommended practices, the idea no longer is blasphemy, but rather hygiene, pleasure which is hygiene too, and a charmed and *interesting* life. An *interesting* life is the supreme concept of dullards.

"Perhaps I am not thinking clearly. I am very sad and torn today. Besides, I am aware of the abnormality of my own experience. Sometimes I wonder whether I have any place here, among other people. I assume I am one of you. But also I am not. I suspect my own judgments because my lot has been extreme. I was a studious young person, not meant for action. Suddenly, it was all action—blood, guns, graves, famine. Very harsh surgery. One cannot come out intact. For a long time I saw things with peculiar hardness. Almost like a criminal—a person who brushes aside flimsy ordinary arrangements and excuses, and simplifies everything brutally. Not exactly as Mr. Brecht said, *Erst kommt das Fressen, und dann kommt die Moral.* That is swagger. Aristotle said something like it and did not swagger or act like a bully. Anyway, by force of circumstances I have had to ask myself simple questions, like 'Will I kill him? Will he kill me? If I sleep, will I ever wake? Am I really alive, or is there nothing left but an illusion of life?' And I know now that humankind marks certain people for death. Against them there shuts a door. Shula and I have been in this written-off category. If you chance nevertheless to live, having been out leaves you with idiosyncrasies. The Germans attempted to kill me. Then the Poles also shot at me. I would have died without Mr. Cieslakiewicz. He was the one man with whom I was not written off. By opening the tomb to me, he let me live. Experience of this kind is deforming. I apologize to you for the deformity."

"But you are not deformed."

"I am of course deformed. And obsessed. You can see that I am always talking about play-acting, originality, dramatic individuality, theatricality in people, the forms taken by spiritual striving. It goes round and round in my head, all of this. I cannot tell you how often, for instance, I think about Rumkowski, the mad Jewish King of Lodz."

"Who is that?" said Lal.

"A person thrown into prominence in Lodz, the big textile city. When the Germans arrived, they installed in authority this individual. He is still often discussed in refugee circles. Rumkowski was his name. He was a failed businessman. Elderly. A noisy individual, corrupt, director of an orphanage, a fund-raiser, a bad actor, a distasteful fun-figure in the Jewish community. A man with a bit to play, like so many modern individuals. Have you ever heard of him?"

Lal had not heard of him.

"Well, you shall hear a little. The Nazis made him *Judenältester*. The city was fenced off. The ghetto became a labor camp. The children were seized and deported for extermination. There was famine. The dead were brought down to the sidewalk and lay there to wait for the corpse wagon. Amidst all this, Rumkowski was King. He had his own court. He printed money and postage stamps with his picture. He had pageants and plays organized in his honor. There were ceremonies to which he wore royal robes, and he drove in a broken coach of the last century, very ornate, gilded, pulled by a dying white nag. On one occasion he showed courage, protesting the arrest and deportation, in plain words the murder, of his council.

For this he was beaten up and thrown out into the street. But he was a terror to the Jews of Lodz. He was a dictator. He was their Jewish King. A parody of the thing—a mad Jewish King presiding over the death of half a million people. Perhaps his secret thought was to save a remnant. Perhaps his mad acting was meant to amuse or divert the Germans. These antics of failed individuality, the *grand seigneur* or dictatorial absurdities—this odd rancor against the evolution of human consciousness, bringing forth these struggling selves, horrible clowns, from every hole and corner. Yes, this would have appealed to those people. Humor seldom failed to appear in their murder programs. This harshness toward clumsy pretensions, toward the bad joke of the self which we all feel. The imaginary grandeur of insects. And besides, the door had been shut against these Jews; they belonged to the category written off. This theatricality of King Rumkowski evidently pleased the Germans. It further degraded the Jews to have a mock king. The Nazis liked that. They had a predilection for such *Ubu Roi* murder farces. They played at Pataphysics. It lightened or relieved the horror. Here at any rate one can see peculiarly well the question of the forms to be found for the actions of liberated consciousness, and the blood-minded hatred, the killers' delight taken in its failure and abasement."

"Excuse me, but I have failed to make this connection," said Lal.

"Yes, I am sure I could be more lucid. It is part of the self-communing obsession that I have. But in the Book of Job there is the complaint that God requires far too much. Job protests that he is magnified unbearably—'What is man, that thou shouldst magnify him? And that thou shouldst set thine heart upon him? And that thou shouldst visit him every morning and try him every moment? How long wilt thou not depart from me, nor let me alone till I swallow down my spittle?' And saying 'I would not live always.' 'Now I shall sleep in the dust.' This too great demand upon human consciousness and human capacities has overtaxed human endurance. I am not speaking only of moral demand, but also of the demand upon the imagination to produce a human figure of adequate stature. What is the true stature of a human being? This, Dr. Lal, was what I meant by speaking of the killers' delight in abasement in parody—in Rumkowski, King of rags and shit, Rumkowski, ruler of corpses. And this is what preoccupies me with the theatricality of the Rumkowski episode. Of course the player was doomed. Many other players, with less agony, have also a sense of doom. As for the others, the large mass of the condemned, I assume, as they were starving, that they felt less and less. Even starving mothers could not feel for more than a day or two the children torn from them. Hunger pains put out grief. *Erst kommt das Fressen*, you see.

"Perhaps my sense of connection is faulty. Please tell me if it seems so. My aim is to bring out . . . though the man was perhaps crazy from the start; perhaps shock even made him saner; in any case, at the end, he voluntarily stepped into the train for Auschwitz . . . to bring out the weakness of the outer forms which are at present available for our humanity, and the pitiable lack of confidence in them. The early result of our modern individuality boom. In such a figure we have the very worst of cases. The most monstrous kind of exaggeration. We see the disintegration of the worst ego ideas. Such ego ideas taken from poetry, history, tradition, biography, cinema, journalism, advertising. As Marx pointed out . . ." But he did not say what Marx had pointed out. He thought, and the others did not speak. His food had not been touched. "I understand that old man was very lewd," he said. "He fingered the young girls. His orphans, perhaps. He knew all would die. Then everything seemed to come out as an efflorescence, a spilling of his 'personality.' Perhaps when people are so desperately impotent they play that instrument, the personality, louder and wilder. It seems to me that I have seen this often. I remember reading in a book, but can't remember where, that when people had found a name for themselves, Human, they spent a lot of time Acting Human, laughing and crying and getting others to laugh and cry, seeking occasions, provoking, taking such relish in wringing their hands, in drawing tears from their glands, and swimming and boating in that cloudy, contaminated, confusing, surging medium of human feelings, taking the passion-waters, exclaiming over their fate. This exercise was condemned by the book, especially the lack of originality. The writer preferred intellectual strictness, hated emotion, demanded exalted tears only, tears shed at last, after much resistance, from the most high-minded of recognitions.

"But suppose one dislikes all this theater of the soul? I too find it tiresome to have to meet it so often and in such familiar forms. I have read many disagreeable accounts of it. I have seen it described as so much debris of the ages, historical junk, dead weight, as bourgeois property, as hereditary deformity. The Self may think it wears a gay new ornament, delightfully painted, but from outside we see that it is a millstone. Or again, this personality of which the owner is so proud is from the Woolworth store, cheap tin or plastic from the five-and-dime of souls. Seeing it in this way, a man may feel that being human is hardly worth the trouble. Where is the desirable self that one might be? *Dov'è sia*, as the question is sung in the opera? That depends. It depends in part on the will of the questioner to see merit. It depends on his talent and his disinterestedness. It is right that we should dislike contrived individuality, bad pastiche, banality, and the rest. It is repulsive. But individualism is of no interest whatever if it does not extend truth. As personal distinction, enhancement, glory, it is for me devoid of interest. I care for it only as an instrument for obtaining truth," said Sammler. "But setting this aside for the moment, I think we may summarize my meaning in terms like these: that many have surged forward in modern history, after long epochs of namelessness and bitter obscurity, to claim and to enjoy (as people enjoy things now) a name, a dignity of person, a life such as belonged in the past only to gentry, nobility, the royalty or the gods of myth. And that this surge has, like all such great movements, brought misery and despair, that its successes are not clearly seen, but that the pain of heart it makes many people feel is incalculable, that most forms of personal existence seem to be discredited, and that there is a peculiar longing for nonbeing. As long as there is no ethical life and everything is poured so barbarously and recklessly into personal gesture this must be endured. And there is a peculiar longing for nonbeing. Maybe it is more accurate to say that people want to visit all other states of being in a diffused state of consciousness, not wishing to be any given thing but instead to become comprehensive, entering and leaving at will.

Why should they be human? In most of the forms offered there is little scope for the great powers of nature in the individual, the abundant, generous powers. In business, in professions, in labor; as a member of the public; as an inhabitant of the cities, these strange pits; as experiencer of compulsions, manipulations; as endurer of strain; as father, husband obliging society by performing his quota of actions—the individual seems to feel these powers less, less and less. So it certainly seems to me that he wants a divorce from all the states that he knows.

"It was charged against the Christian that he wanted to get rid of himself. Those that brought the charge urged him to transcend his unsatisfactory humanity. But isn't transcendence the same disorder? Isn't that also getting rid of the human being? Well, maybe man should get rid of himself. Of course. If he can. But also be has something in him which he feels it important to continue. Something that deserves to go on. It is something that has to go on, and we all know it. The spirit feels cheated, outraged, defiled, corrupted, fragmented, injured. Still it knows what it knows, and the knowledge cannot be gotten rid of. The spirit knows that its growth is the real aim of existence. So it seems to me. Besides, mankind cannot be something else. It cannot get rid of itself except by an act of universal self-destruction. But it is not even for us to vote Yea or Nay. And I have not stated my arguments, for I argue nothing. I have stated my thoughts. They were asked for, and I wanted to express them. The best, I have found, is to be disinterested. Not as misanthropes dissociate themselves, by judging, but by not judging. By willing as God wills.

"During the war I had no belief, and I had always disliked the ways of the Orthodox. I saw that God was not impressed by death. Hell was his indifference. But inability to explain is no ground for disbelief. Not as long as the sense of God persists. I could wish that it did not persist. The contradictions are so painful. No concern for justice? Nothing of pity? Is God only the gossip of the living? Then we watch these living speed like birds over the surface of a water, and one will dive or plunge but not come up again and never be seen any more. And in our turn we will never be seen again, once gone though that surface. But then we have no proof that there is no depth under the surface. We cannot even say that our knowledge of death is shallow. There is no knowledge. There is longing, suffering, mourning. These come from need, affection, and love —the needs of the living creature, because it *is* a living creature. There is also strangeness, implicit. There is also adumbration. Other states are sensed. All is not flatly knowable. There would never have been any inquiry without this adumbration, there would never have been any knowledge without it. But I am not life's examiner, or a connoisseur, and I have nothing to argue. Surely a man would console, if he could. But that is not an aim of mine. Consolers cannot always be truthful. But very often, and almost daily, I have strong impressions of eternity. This may be due to my strange experiences, or to old age. I will say that to me this does not feel elderly. Nor would I mind if there were nothing after death. If it is only to be as it was before birth, why should one care? There one would receive no further information. One's ape restiveness would stop. I think I would miss mainly my God adumbrations in the many daily forms. Yes, that is what I should miss. So then, Dr. Lal, if the moon were advantageous for us metaphysically, I would be completely for it. As an engineering project, colonizing outer space, except for the curiosity, the ingenuity of the thing, is of little real interest to me. Of course the drive, the will to organize this scientific expedition must be one of those irrational necessities that make up life—this life we think we can understand. So I suppose we must jump off, because it is our human fate to do so. If it were a rational matter, then it would be rational to have justice on this planet first. Then, when we had an earth of saints, and our hearts were set upon the moon, we could get in our machines and rise up . . ."

"But what is this on the floor?" said Shula. All four rose about the table to look. Water from the back stairs flowed over the white plastic Pompeian mosaic surface. "Suddenly my feet were wet."

"Is it a bath overflowing?" said Lal.

"Shula, did you turn off the bath?"

"I'm sure and positive I did."

"I believe it is too rapid for bath water," said Lal. "A pipe presumably is burst." Listening, they heard a sound of spraying above, and a steady, rapid tapping, trickling, cascading, snaking of water on the staircase. "An open pipe. It sounds a flood." He broke from the table and ran through the large kitchen, the thin hairy fists laid on his chest, his head drawn down between thin shoulders.

"Oh, Uncle Sammler, what is it?"

The women followed. Necessarily slower, Sammler also climbed.

Wallace's theory that there were dummy pipes in the attic filled with criminal money had been put to the test. Sammler guessed, since Wallace was so mathematical, loved equations, spent nights working out gambling odds, that he had prepared a plumbing blueprint before taking up the wrench.

Treading carefully in dry places became pointless on the second floor. There the carpeted corridor was like a soaked lawn and sucked at Sammler's cracked shoes. The attic door was shut but water ran under it.

"Margotte," said Sammler. "Go down this instant. Call the plumber and the fire department. Call the firemen first and tell them you are calling in the plumber. Don't stand. Be quick." He took her arm and turned her toward the door.

Wallace had evidently tried to stuff his shirt into the break. When calculation failed, he fell apart. The garment lay underfoot and he and Lal were trying to bring together the open ends of pipe.

"There's something wrong with the coupling. I must have stripped the threads," said Wallace. He was astride the flowing pipe. Dr. Lal, trying to make the connection, was being sprayed, beard and chest. Shula stood close to him. If great eyes could be mechanical aids—if staring and proximity could lead to blending!

"Is there no shutoff? Is there no valve?" said Sammler. "Shula, don't get drenched. Stand back, my dear, you're in the way."

"I doubt we can accomplish anything by this means," said Lal. The water fizzed loudly.

"You don't think so?" said Wallace.

They spoke very politely.

"Well, no. For one thing there is too much water force. And as you see, this connecting metal cannot be advanced," said Lal. He lowered the pipe and stepped aside. At the waist his gray trousers were black with water. "Do you know the water system here?"

"In what sense do I know it?"

"I mean, is it city-supplied, or do you have a private source? If it is city water, the authorities will have to be called. However, if it is a driven well, the solution may lie in the cellar. If it is a well, there is a pump."

"The odd thing is I never knew."

"What of the sewage, is it municipal?"

"You got me there, too."

"If it is a well and there is a pump there is a switch also. I shall go down. Is there a flashlight?"

"I know the house," said Shula. "I'll go with you." In the sari, loosely bound, sandals dropping from her eager feet she hurried after Lal, who ran down the stairs.

Sammler said to Wallace, "Aren't there any buckets? The ceilings will come down."

"There's insurance. Don't worry about ceilings."

"Nevertheless . . ."

Sammler descended.

Under the kitchen sink and in the broom closet he found yellow plastic pails and climbed back. He recognized that he had the peculiar anxieties of the poor relation. He had certainly disliked this house, always. Found it hard while eating benefactor's bread to be natural here. Besides, all this dense comfort, the rooms crowded with conversation-pieces, attractions, stood on a foundation of nullity. The work of Mr. Croze, with his rosebud mouth, visible nostrils, Oscar Wilde hairdo, suave little belly, and perfumed fingers, who sent, as Elya bitterly said once, as tough and cynical a business statement as he had ever seen. Elya conceded he was being fittingly furnished, done right by, but he didn't like being upgraded by Mr. Croze, who dealt in beautiful rewards, in suburban dukedoms for slum boys who made good! Still—a flood! Sammler could not bear it. Besides, it was a typical Wallace production, like the sinking of the limousine in Croton Reservoir, the horse pilgrimage into Soviet Armenia, the furnishing of a law office to work crossword puzzles in—protests against his father's "valueless" success. There was nothing new in this. Regularly, now, for generations, prosperous families brought forth their anarchistic sons—these boy Bakunins, geniuses of liberty, arsonists, demolishers of prisons, property, palaces. Bakunin had loved fire so. Wallace worked in water, a different medium. And it was very curious (Sammler with the two plastic buckets, which were as yellow and as light as leaves or feathers, had time on the stairs, while the water ran, to entertain the curiosity) that in speaking of his father that afternoon Wallace had said he was hooked like a fish by the aneurysm and jerked into the wrong part of the universe, drowning in air.

"You brought some pails. Let's see if we can't fit them under the pipe. Won't do much good."

"It may do some. You can open a window and spill the water into the gutters."

"Down the spout. O.K. But how long can we keep bailing?"

"Till the fire department comes."

"You called the firemen?"

"Of course. I made Margotte call."

"They'll file a report. That's what the insurance people will go by. I'd better put away these tools. I mean I want this to seem accidental."

"That these pipes just dropped apart? Opened by themselves? Nonsense, Wallace, pipes only burst in winter."

"Yes, I suppose that's right."

"So you thought they were full of thousand-dollar bills. Ah, Wallace!"

"Don't scold me, Uncle. There's loot here somewhere. There is, I swear. I know my father. He's a hider. And what good is the money to him now? He couldn't afford to declare it even if—"

"Even if he were going to live?"

"That's right. And it's like he's turning away from us. Or like a dog in the manger."

"Do you think that's a suitable figure of speech?"

"It wouldn't be suitable for you, but when I say it it doesn't make much difference. I'm a different generation. I never had any dignity to start with. A different set of givens, altogether. No natural feeling of respect. Well, I certainly fucked these pipes up good and proper."

Sammler was considering how much alike Wallace and Shula

were, with their misdeeds. You had to stop and turn and wait for them. They would not be omitted. Sammler held the second bucket under the splashing pipe. Wallace had gone to empty the first from the dormer, turning back with grimy wet hands, bare-chested, the short black hairs neatly symmetrical like a clerical dickey. Arms were long, shoulders white, shapely to no purpose. And with a certain drop of the mouth, smiling at himself, transmitting to Sammler as he had done before the mother's sense of the graceful boy, the child's large skull and long neck, the clear-lined brows, crisp hair, fine small nose. But, as in certain old paintings, another world was also represented above, and one could imagine on a straight line over Wallace's head symbols of turbulence: smoke, fire, flying black things. Arbitrary rulings. A sealed judgment.

"If he would tell me where the dough is, it would at least cover the water damage. But he won't, and you won't ask him."

"No. I want no part of it."

"You think I should make my own dough."

"Yes. Label the trees and bushes. Earn your own."

"We will. In fact, that's all I want from the old man, a stake for the equipment. It's his last chance to show confidence in me. To wish me well. To give me like his blessing. Do you think he loved me?"

"Certainly he loved you."

"As a child. But did he love me as a man?"

"He would have."

"If I had ever been a man according to his idea. That's what you mean, isn't it?"

Sammler, having recourse to one of his blind looks, could always express his thought. Or if you had loved him, Wallace. These are very transitory opportunities. One must be nimble.

"I'm sorry that so late at night you have to be bailing. You must be tired."

"I suppose I am. Dry old people can go on and on. Still, I am beginning to feel it."

"I don't feel so hot myself. How is it downstairs, bad? A lot of water?"

No comment.

"It always turns out like this. Is that my message to the world from my unconscious self?"

"Why send such messages? Censor them. Put your unconscious mind behind bars on bread and water."

"No, it's just the mortal way I am. You can't hold it down. It must come out. I hate it too."

Lean Mr. Sammler, delicately applying the light pail to the pipe, while the rapid water splashed.

"I know that Dad had guys up here installing phony connections."

"I would have thought if it was a lot of money the false pipe would be a thick one."

"No, he wouldn't do an obvious thing. You have the wrong image of him. He has a lot of scientific cool. It could have been this pipe. He could have rolled the bills tight and small. He is a surgeon. He has the skill and the patience."

Suddenly the splashing stopped.

"Look! He's shut it off. It's down to a dribble. Hurray!" said Wallace.

"Dr. Lal!"

"What a relief. He found a turnoff. Who is that fellow?"

"Professor V. Govinda Lal."

"What is he a professor of?"

"Biophysics, I think, is his field."

"Well, he certainly uses his head. It never once occurred to me to find out where our water came from. There must be a well. Can you imagine that! And we've been here since I was ten. June 8, 1949. I'm a Gemini. Lily of the valley is my birth flower. Did you know the lily of the valley was very poisonous? We moved on my birthday. No party. The van got stuck between the gateposts on moving day. So it's not municipal water—I'm so astonished." With his usual lightness, he introduced general considerations. "It's supposed to be a sign of the Mass Man that he doesn't know the difference between Nature and human arrangements. He thinks the cheap commodities—water, electricity, subways, hot dogs—are like air, sunshine, and leaves on the trees."

"Just as simple as that?"

"Ortega y Gasset thinks so. Well, I'd better see what the damage is and get the cleaning woman in."

"You could mop up. Don't let the puddles stand all night."

"I don't know the first thing about mopping. I doubt that I

ever even held a mop in my hands. But I could spread newspapers. Old *Timeses* from the cellar. But just one thing, Uncle."

"What thing is that?"

"Don't dislike me on account of this."

"I don't."

"Well, don't look down on me—don't despise me."

"Well, Wallace . . ."

"I know you must. Well, this is like an appeal. I'd like to have your good opinion."

"Are you depressed, Wallace, when things go wrong like this?"

"Less and less."

"You mean you're improving," said Sannnler.

"You see, if Angela inherits the house that ends my chances for the money. She'll put the place up for sale, being unmarried. She doesn't have any sentiment about the old homestead. The roots. Well, neither do I, when you come right down to it. Dad doesn't really like the place himself. No, I don't feel any black gloom about the water damage. Everything is replaceable. At exorbitant prices. But the estate will pay the bill, which will be a real gyp. And there's insurance. Possessive emotions are in a transitional phase. I really think they are." Wallace could turn suddenly earnest, but his earnestness lacked weight. Earnestness was probably Wallace's ideal, his true need, but the young man was incapable of finding his own essences. "I'll tell you what I'm afraid of, Uncle," he said. "If I have to live on a fixed income from a trust it'll be the end of me. I'll never find myself then. Do you want me to rot? I need to crash out of the future my father has prepared for me. Otherwise, everything just goes on being possible, and all these possibilities are going to be the death of me. I have to have my own necessities, and I don't see those anywhere. All I see is ten thousand a year, like my father's life sentence on me. I have to bust out while he's still living. When he dies, I'll get so melancholy I won't be able to lift a finger."

"Shall we soak up some of this water?" said Sammler. "Shall we start spreading around the *Times*?"

"Oh, that can wait. The hell with it. We'll get screwed anyway on the repairs. You know, Uncle, I think I'm just half as smart as a man needs to be to work out these things, so I never get more than halfway there."

"So you have no connection with this house—no desire for roots, Wallace."

"No, of course not. Roots? Roots are not modern. That's a peasant conception, soil and roots. Peasantry is going to disappear. That's the real meaning of the modern revolution, to prepare world peasantry for a new state of existence. I certainly have no roots. But even I am out of date. What I've got is a lot of old wires, and even wires belong to the old technology. The real thing is telemetry. Cybernetics. I've practically decided, Uncle Sammler, if this enterprise doesn't pan out, with Feffer, that I'll go to Cuba."

"To Cuba, is it? But you aren't a Communist, too, Wallace?"

"Not at all. I do admire Castro, however. He has terrific style, he's a bohemian radical, and he's held his own against Washington superpower. He and his cabinet ride in jeeps. They meet in the sugar cane."

"What do you want to tell him?"

"It could be important, don't make fun of me, Uncle Sammler. I have ideas about revolution. When the Russians made their revolution, everybody said, 'A leap forward into a new stage of history.' Not at all. The Russian Revolution was a delaying action—ah, my God, what a noise. It's the fire trucks. I'd better run. They could just bash down the door. They have an orgy, these guys, with their axes. And I have to have an alibi for the insurance."

He ran.

In the yard the rotating lights swept through the trees, dark red over the lawn, the walls and windows. The bell was slamming, bangalang, and deeper down the road gulping passionate shrieks approached the mortal-sounding sirens. More engines were arriving. From the attic window Sammler watched as Wallace ran out, his hands raised, explaining to the helmeted men as they sprang in the soft gum boots from the trucks.

Water, they had brought.

Mr. Sammler had some wakeful hours that night. A predictable result of worry over Elya. Of the flood. Also of the conversation with Lal which had compelled him to state his views—historical, planetary, and universal. The order probably should be reversed: first there were the views, planetary or universal, and then there were hidden dollars, water pipes, firemen. Sammler went out and walked in the garden, behind the house, up and down the drive. He was dissatisfied. He had explained, he had taken positions, he had said things he hadn't meant, meant things he hadn't said. Indoors, there were activities, discussions, explanations, arrangements, rearrangements. In the house of a dying man. It was the turn again of certain minor things which people insisted on enlarging, magnifying, moving into the center: relationships, interior decorations, family wrangles, Minox photographs of thieves on buses, arms of Puerto Rican ladies on the Bronx Express, *odi-et-amo* need-and-rejection, emotional self-examinations, erotic businesses in Acapulco, fellatio with friendly strangers. Civilian matters. Civilian one and all! The high-minded, like Plato (now he was not only lecturing, but even lecturing himself), wished to get rid of such stuff—wrangles, lawsuits, hysterias, all such hole-and-corner pettiness. Other powerful minds denied that this could be done. They held (like Freud) that the mightiest instincts were bound up in just such stuff, each trifle the symptom of a deep disease in a creature whose whole fate was disease. What to do about such things? Absurd in form, but possibly real? But possibly not real? Relief from this had become imperative. And that was why, during the Aqaba crisis, Mr. Sammler had had to go to the Middle East.

At this moment, walking in white moonlight on Elya Gruner's washed gravel, which had been cut with black tracks by the fire engines, he recognized and again identified his motives. He had gone back to 1939. He wanted to refer again to Zamosht Forest, to more basic human characteristics. When had things seemed real, true? In Poland when blinded, in Zamosht when freezing, in the tomb when hungry. So he had persuaded Elya to let him go, to send him, and he had renewed his familiarity with a certain sort of fact. Which, as he was older and more fragile, had made his legs tremble more; the more he tried to stiffen himself up the more be faltered. Few outer signs of this were given. But wasn't he too old? Did he have any business to fly to a war?

It was announced in Athens, on the plane, that this flight would not continue because the fighting had already begun in Israel. Grounded! He must get out. The Greek heat was dizzy, in the airport. The public music circled through Mr. Sammler's unwilling head. The sugary coffee, the sticky drinks, also were a trial to him. The suspense, the delay, gnawed him intolerably. He went into the city and visited airline offices, he asked a business friend of Elya's, in oil or gasoline, to help, he visited the Israeli consulate and obtained a seat on the first El Al flight. He waited again at the airport until four a.m. among journalists and hippies. These young people—Dutch, German, Scandinavian, Canadian, American—had been encamped at Eilath on the Red Sea. The Bedouins on the ancient route from Arabia into Egypt had sold them hashish. It was a jolly place. Now with their guitars they wanted to go back. Responding to a primary event. Though recognizing no governments.

The jet was packed. One could not move. For lean old men, breathing was difficult. A television man beside Sammler offered him a pull from his whisky bottle. "Thank you," said Sammler, and accepted. He swallowed down Bell's scotch. Just then the sun ran up from the sea like a red fox. It was not round but long, not far but near. The metal of the engines, those shapely vats in which the freezing air was screaming—light into blackness, blackness into light—hung under the wings beside Sammler's window. Whisky from a bottle—he smiled at himself—made him a real war correspondent. An odd person to be rushing to this war, although no more odd than these Stone Age bohemians with their solemn beards. There were others besides who did not seem very useful in a crisis. Sammler would be filing his old-fashioned dispatches to Mr. Jerzy Zhelonski in London to be read by a very mixed Polish public.

Mr. Sammler had had no business, at his age, in a white cap and striped seersucker jacket, to be riding in a press bus behind those tanks to Gaza, to Al Arish and beyond. But he had managed it all himself. There was nothing accidental about it. In these American articles of dress he had perhaps passed for a younger man. Americans and Englishmen always looked a little younger. Anyway, there he was. He was one of the journalists. He walked about in conquered Gaza. They were sweeping broken glass. In the square, armor and guns. Just beyond, the cemetery walls, the domes of white tombs. In the dust, scraps of food baking, sour; odors of heating garbage and of urine. Broadcast Oriental jazz winding like dysentery through the bowels. Such deadly comical music. Women, oldish women only, went marketing; or set out to market; there couldn't have been much to buy. The black veils were transparent. You saw the heavy-boned mannish faces: underneath—large noses, the stern mouths projecting over stonelike teeth. There was nothing to keep you in Gaza for long. The bus stopped for Sammler, and young Father Newell in his Vietnam battle dress greeted him.

Knowing modern warfare, the Father was able to point things out which Sammler might have missed when they passed the last of the irrigated fields and entered the Sinai Desert. Then they began to see the dead, the unburied Arab bodies. Father Newell showed him the first. Sammler might never have noticed, might have taken the corpse for nothing but a greenish gunnysack, stuffed tight, dropped from a truck on the white sand.

Driven off the road, sunk in the sand, wrecked on the dunes, many burnt—all these vehicles, the personnel carriers, tanks, trucks, the light cars smashed flat, wheels freed, escaped; and very thick about these machines, the dead. There were dug positions, emplacements, trenches, and in them, too, there were hundreds of corpses. The odor was like damp cardboard. The clothes of the dead, greenish-brown sweaters, tunics, shirts were strained by the swelling, the gases, the fluids. Swollen gigantic arms, legs, roasted in the sun. The dogs ate human roast. In the trenches the bodies leaned on the parapets. The dogs came cringing, flattening up. The inhabitants had run away from the encampments you saw here and there—the low tents, Bedouin-style, but made of plastic crate wrappings dumped from ships, pieces of styrofoam, dirty sheets of cellulose like insect moltings, large cockroach cases. Poor folk! Ah, poor creatures!

"Well, they did a job, didn't they," said Father Newell. "How many casualties, would you say?"

"I have no idea."

"This was a small Russian experiment, I believe," Father Newell said. "Now they know."

In the sun the faces softened, blackened, melted, and flowed away. The flesh sank to the skull, the cartilage of the nose warping, the lips shrinking, eyes dissolving, fluids filling the hollows and shining on the skin. A strange flavor of human grease. Of wet paper pulp. Mr. Sammler fought his nausea. As he and Father Newell walked together, they were warned not to step off the road because of mines. Sammler read out for the priest the Russian letters stenciled white on the green tanks and trucks: GORKISKII AUTOZAVOD, most of them said. Father Newell seemed to know a lot about gun calibers, armor thickness, ranges. In a lowered voice, out of respect for the Israelis who denied its use, he identified the napalm. See all that reddish, all that mauve out there? Salmon-pink with a green tinge in the clinkers was the sure sign. Positively napalm. It was a real war. These Jews were tough. He spoke to Sammler as one American to another. The long blue seersucker stripes, the soiled white cap from Kresge's, the little spiral book in which Sammler made his notes for Polish articles, also from Kresge's, accounted for this. It was a real war. Everyone respected killing. Why not the priest? He walked in the big American battle boots as if he were not altogether a priest. He was not a chaplain. He was a newspaperman. He was not what he was assumed to be. Nor was Sammler. What Sammler was he could not clearly formulate. Human, in some altered way. The human being at the point where he attempted to obtain his release from being human. Wasn't this what Sammler had been getting at in the kitchen, talking to Lal and the ladies of divorce from every human state? Petitioning for a release from God's attention? My days are vanity. I would not live always. Let me alone. To be visited every morning, to be called upon, to be magnified. Let me alone.

Walking the narrow road with Father Newell, picking up curious objects, shells, bandages, Arab comic books and letters, stepping aside for trucks stacked high with bread, weighing down the springs, projecting at the rear. But really the main subject could not be changed, the subject of the dead. Bristling in the green-brown and gravy-colored woolens. The suffocating wet cardboard fumes they gave off. In the superhot, the crack light, the glassy persistency and distortion of the desert light, these swollen shapes were the main thing to be seen. They were the one subject the soul was sure to take seriously. And this perhaps was what Sammler's instinct had directed him to do. To go to Kennedy, to get on a jet, to land in Tel Aviv, to have snapshots taken, to obtain a press card, to find a bus to Gaza, to visit the great sun wheel of white desert in which these Egyptian corpses and machines were embedded, to make his primary contact. Certain desires thus were met, for which he could not account. And this war was, as human affairs went, a most minor affair. In modern experience, so very little. Nothing at all. And the people involved in it, the boys, after fighting, played soccer at Al Arish. They cleared a space, and they kicked and butted, they leaped up, they trotted on the sand. Or in the shade of the hangars they took out their books and read biology or chemistry, philosophy, preparing for exams perhaps. Then he and Father Newell were called over to look at captured snipers on the bed of a truck, trussed up and blindfolded. Below these eye rags, the desperate faces, as if it were *not* a most minor affair. One saw those, and then the next things, and then other things. And evidently Mr. Sammler had his own need for these sights, for which he mastered the trembling of his legs or the wish to cry which flashed through him when he saw the snipers' bandaged faces. He was taken down to the sea by some men. They entered the water to refresh themselves. He too went in and stood. In a broad band along the beaches the foam mixed with heat-shimmer for many miles, in varying deep curves of seething white between the sand and the great blue. For a little while, in the water, he did not smell rotting flesh, but soon had to tie a handkerchief over his face. The handkerchief quickly absorbed the smell. It tainted his clothing. His spittle tasted of it.

Via London, ten days later, he flew home. As if he had been on some sort of mission: self-assigned: fact-finding. He observed that modern London was very playful. He visited his old flat in Woburn Square. He noted that the traffic was very thick. He saw that there were more drunkards in the streets, that the British advertising industry had discovered the female nude, and that most posters along the escalators of the Underground were of women in undergarments. He found his acquaintances as old as himself. Then BOAC brought him back to Kennedy Airport, and soon afterward he was in the Forty-second Street Library reading, as always, Meister Eckhardt.

"Blessed are the poor in spirit. Poor is he who has nothing. He who is poor in spirit is receptive of all spirit. Now God is the Spirit of spirits. The fruit of the spirit is love, joy, and peace. See to it that you are stripped of all creatures, of all consolation from creatures. For certainly as long as creatures comfort and are able to comfort you, you will never find true comfort. But if nothing can comfort you save God, truly God will console you."

Mr. Sammler could not say that he literally believed what he was reading. He could, however, say that he cared to read nothing but this.

On the lawn before the half-timbered house the ground was damp, the grass was fragrant. Or was it the soil itself that smelled so fresh? In the clarified, moon-purged air, he saw Shula coming, looking for him.

"Why aren't you in bed?"

"I'm going."

She gave him Elya's own afghan to cover himself with, and he lay down.

Feeling what a strange species he belonged to, which had organized its planet to such an extent. Of this mass of ingenious creatures, about half had gone into the state of sleep, in pillows, sheeted, wrapped, quilted, muffled. The waking, like a crew, worked the world's machines, and all went up and down and round about with calculations accurate to the billionth of a degree, the skins of engines removed, replaced, million-mile trajectories laid out. By these geniuses, the waking. The sleeping, brutes, fantasists, dreaming. Then they woke, and the other half went to bed.

And that is how this brilliant human race runs this wheeling globe.

He joined the other sleepers for a while.

VI

THE washstand in the small lavatory off the den was dark onyx, the fittings gold, the faucets dolphins, the soap dish a scallop, the towel thick as mink. Mirrors on four walls showed Mr. Sammler to himself in more aspects than he wanted. The soap was spermy sandalwood. The blade was dull and had to be honed on the porcelain. Very likely ladies occasionally slipped in to trim their legs with this razor. Sammler did not want to look for another blade upstairs. The master bedroom was seriously water-damaged. The ladies had pulled the twin mattresses from the beds to a dry corner. Dr. Lal had slept in the guest room. Wallace? Perhaps he had spent the night on his head, like a yogi.

Suddenly Sammler stopped shaving, paused and stared at himself, his dry, small, "cured" face undergoing in the mirror a strong inrush of color. Even the left, the swelled, the opaque guppy eye, took up some light from this. Where were they all? Opening the door, he listened. There was no sound. He went into the garden. Dr. Lal's car was gone. He looked in the garage, and that was empty. Gone, fled!

He found Shula in the kitchen. "Everyone has left?" he said. "Now how do I get to New York?"

She was pouring coffee through the filter cone, having first boiled the grounds, French style.

"Took off," she said. "Dr. Lal wasn't able to wait. There was no room for me. He rented a two-seater. A gorgeous little Austin Healy, did you see it?"

"And Emil, where is he?"

"He had to take Wallace to the airport. Wallace has to fly—to test-fly. For his business, you know what I mean. They're going to take pictures and so on."

"And I am stuck. Is there a timetable? I've got to be in New York."

"Well, it's nearly ten o'clock now and there aren't so many trains. I'll phone. And then Emil should be back soon, and he can drive you. You were sleeping. Dr. Lal didn't want to disturb you."

"Extremely inconsiderate. You knew and Margotte knew that I had to get back."

"The little car was very pretty. Margotte didn't look right in it."

"I am annoyed."

"Margotte has thick legs, Father. You've probably never even noticed. Well, they won't show in the car. Dr. Lal will call later in the day. You'll see him all right."

"Whom, Lal? Why? The document is there, isn't it?"

"There?"

"Don't irritate me by repeating questions. I am already irritated. Why didn't you wake me? The document *is* in the locker, isn't it?"

"I locked it up myself, with the quarter, and took out the key. No, you'll see him because Margotte is out for him. Maybe you didn't notice that either. I really need to talk to you about this, Father."

"Yes, I'm sure you do. I did notice, yes, to tell the truth. Well, she's a widow, and she's had enough of mourning, and she needs somebody like that. We aren't much comfort to her. I don't know what she sees in that bushy black little fellow. It's just loneliness, I suppose."

"I can see what she sees. Dr. Lal is very distinguished. You know it. Don't pretend, after the way you talked in the kitchen. It was beautiful."

"Well, well. What will I do? This thing of Elya's is very bad, you know."

"Very?"

"The worst. And I should have realized that returning might present problems."

"Father, just leave it to me. And you haven't finished shaving. No, go on, and I'll bring you a cup of coffee."

He went, thinking how he had been feinted out of position. Outgeneraled. Like Pompey or Labienus by Caesar. He should not have left the city. He was cut off from his base. And now how was he to reach Elya, who needed him today? Picking up the phone in the den to call the hospital, he heard the busy signal Shula was getting from the Penn Central. Patience, waiting, now were necessary—things Mr. Sammler had no talent for. But he had studied, he had trained himself. One began with external composure. So he sat down on the hassock, looking at the sofa, and at the silken green luxurious wool of Elya's own afghan he had slept under. It was a lovely morning, too. The sun came in as he sipped the coffee Shula brought him. Glass tables on legs and semicircular struts of brass spattered the Oriental rug with light, brought out the colors and the figures.

"Busy signal," she said.

"Yes, I know."

"There's a telephone crisis, anyway, all over New York. The experts are working on it."

She went into the garden, and Sammler again tried dialing the hospital. All lines were busy in that dreary place, and he hung up the repetitious croaking instrument. Thinking of the colossal number of conversations, all those communings. Utilizing the invisible powers of the universe. Out in the garden, Shula was also engaged in conversation. It was warm. Tulips, daffodils, jonquils, and a paradise of gusts. Evidently she asked the flowers how they were today. No answers required. Brilliant instances sufficed. She herself was a brilliant instance of something organically strange. His glimpse of the entire Shula last night now made him feel her specific weight, as she trod the grass. The entire female body was evoked, white skin everywhere, the thighs, the trunk, the actual feet, the belly with its organs, together with the kinky hair straggling from the scarf. All visible and almost palpable. And even about plants, who knew the whole truth? On educational TV one night he and Margotte watched a singular botanist who had attached a polygraph machine—a lie-detector—to flowers and recorded the reactions of roses to gentle and violent stimuli. Stridency made them shrink, he said. A dead dog cast before them caused aversion. A soprano singing lullabies had the opposite effect. Sammler would have guessed that the investigator himself, his pale leer, his wild stern police nose would distress roses, African violets. Even without nerves these organisms were discerning. We with our oversupply of receptors were in a state of nervous chaos. Amid the tree shadows, pliant, and the window-frame shadows, rigid, and the brass and glass reflections, semi-steady, Mr. Sammler wiped his shoes with the paper towel Shula had placed under the coffee cup. The shoes were damp, still. They were soggy, unpleasantly so. Margotte also had her plants, and Wallace was about to found a plant business. It would be too bad if the first contacts of plants were entirely with the demented. Maybe I'd better have a word with them myself. Mr. Sammler was heavy-hearted and tried to divert himself. The heaviness was brutally persistent, however.

He came to the point. First, how apt it was that Wallace should flood the attic. Why, it was a metaphor for Elya's condition. In connection with that condition there arose other images—a blistering of the brain, a froth or rusty scum of blood over that other plant which lay in one's head. Something like convolvulus. No, like fatty cauliflower. The screw on the artery could not reduce the pressure, and where the vessel was varicose and weaker than cobweb it would open. A terrible flood! One might try to think of mitigating things— That, oh well! Life! Everyone who had it was bound to lose it. Or that this was Elya's moment of honor and that he called upon his best qualities. That was all very well, until death turned its full gaze on the individual. Then all such ideas were nothing. The point was that he, Sammler, should be at the hospital, now; to do what could be done; to say what might he said, and what should he said. Exactly what should or might be said Sammler did not know. He could not find the precise thing. Living as he did, in this inward style, working out his condensations or contractions, one became uncommunicative. To explain or expand his thoughts tired and vexed him, as he had learned last night. But he did not feel uncommunicative toward Elya. On the contrary, he wanted to say everything possible. He wanted to go to the hospital and *say* something! He loved his nephew, and he had something that Elya needed. All concerned ought to have had it. The first place at Elya's bedside belonged to Wallace or to Angela, but they were not about to take it.

Elya was a physician and a businessman. With his own family, to his credit, he had not been businesslike. Nevertheless, he had the business outlook. And business, in business America, was also a training system for souls. The fear of being unbusinesslike was very great. As he was dying Elya might conceivably draw strength from doing business. He had in fact done that. He kept talking to Widick. And Sammler had nothing with a business flavor to offer him. But at the very end business would not do for Elya. Some, many, would go on with business to the last breath, but Elya was not like that, not so limited. Elya was not finally ruled by business considerations. He was not in that insect and mechanical state—such a surrender, such an insect disaster for human beings. Even now (now perhaps more than ever) Elya was accessible. In fact Sammler had not seen this in time. Yesterday, when Elya began to speak of Wallace, when he denounced Angela, he, Sammler ought to have stayed with him. Any degree of frankness might have been possible. In the going phrase, a moment of truth. Meaning that most conversation was a compilation of lies, of course. But Elya's was not one of those sealed completed impenetrable systems, he was not one of your monstrous crystals or icicles. Feeling, or stroking the long green fibers of the afghan, Sammler put it to himself that because he and Antonina had been designated, part of a demonstration of the meaninglessness of this vivid shuffle with its pangs of higher intuition from the one side and the continual muddy suck of the grave underfoot—that because of this he himself, Artur Sammler, had put up obstinate resistance. And Elya, too, was devoted to ideas of conduct which seemed discredited, which few people explicitly defended. It was not the behavior that was gone. What was gone was the old words. Forms and signs were absent. Not honor but the word honor. Not virtuous impulse, but the terms beaten into flat nonsense. Not compassion; but what was a compassionate utterance? And compassionate utterance was a mortal necessity. Utterance, sounds of hope and desire, exclamations of grief. Such things were suppressed, as if illicit. Sometimes coming through in ciphers, in vague figures scrawled on the windows of condemned buildings (the empty tailor shop facing the hospital). At this stage of things there was a terrible dumbness. About essentials, almost nothing could be said. Still, signs could be made, should be made, must be made. One should declare something like this: "However actual I may seem to you and you to me, *we are not as actual as all that.* We will die. Nevertheless there is a bond. There is a bond." Mr. Sammler believed that if this was not said in so many words it should be said tacitly. In fact it *was* continually asserted, in many guises. And anyway, we know *what is what*. But Elya at this moment had a most particular need for a sign and he, Sammler, should be there to meet that need.

He again telephoned the hospital. To his surprise, he found himself speaking with Gruner. He had asked for the private nurse. One could get through? Elya must be molested by calls. With the mortal bulge in his head he was still in the game, did business.

"How are you?"

"How are you, Uncle?"

The actual meaning of this might have been, "Where are you?"

"How are you feeling?"

"There's been no change. I thought we would be seeing each other."

"I'm coming in. I'm sorry. When there's something important there is always some delay. It never fails, Elya."

"When you left yesterday, it was like unfinished business between us. We got sidetracked by Angela and such hopeless questions. There was something I was meaning to ask. About Cracow. The old days. And by the way, I bragged about you to a Polish doctor here. He wanted very much to see the Polish articles you sent from the Six-Day War. Do you have copies?"

"Certainly, at home. I have plenty."

"Aren't you at home now?"

"Actually I'm not."

"I wonder if you'd mind bringing the clippings. Would you mind stopping off?"

"Of course not. But I don't want to lose the time."

"I may have to go down for tests." Elya's voice was filled with unidentifiable tones. Sammler's interpretive skill was insufficient. He was uneasy. "Why shouldn't there be time?" Elya said. "There's time enough for everything." This had an odd ring, and the accents were strange.

"Yes?"

"Of course, yes. It was good you called. A while ago tied to phone you. There was no answer. You went out early."

Uneasiness somewhat interfered with Sammler's breathing. Long and thin, he held the telephone, concentrating, aware of the anxious intensity gathered in his face. He was silent. Elya said, "Angela is on her way over."

"I am coming too."

"Yes." Elya lingered somewhat on the shortest words. "Well, Uncle?

"Good-by, for now."

"Good-by, Uncle Sammler."

Rapping at the pane, Sammler tried to get Shula's attention. Among the wagging flowers she was conspicuously white. His Primavera. On her head she wore a dark-red scarf. Covering up, afflicted always by the meagerness of her hair. It was perhaps the natural abundance, growth power, exuberance that she admired in flowers. Seeing her among the blond open-mouthed daffodils, which were being poured back and forth by the wind, her father believed that she was in love. From the hang of her shoulders, the turn of the orange lips, he saw that she was already prepared to accept unrequited longing. Dr. Lal was not for her; she would never clasp his head or hold his beard between her breasts. You could seldom get people to long for what was possible—that was the cruelty of it. He opened the French window.

"Where is the timetable?" he said.

"I can't find it. The Gruners don't use the train. Anyway, you'll get to New York quicker with Emil. He's going to the hospital."

"I don't suppose he'd wait at the airport for Wallace. Not today."

"Why did you say that about Lal, that he was just a bushy black little fellow?"

"I hope you're not personally interested in him."

"Why not?"

"He's not at all suitable, and I'd never give my consent."

"You wouldn't?"

"No, no. He wouldn't make any kind of husband for you."

"Because he's an Asiatic? You wouldn't be so prejudiced. Not you, Father."

"Not the slightest objection to an Asiatic. There is much to be said for exotic marriages. If your husband is a bore, it takes years longer to discover it, in French. But scientists make bad husbands. Sixteen hours a day in the laboratory, absorbed in research. You'd be neglected. You'd be hurt. I wouldn't allow it."

"Not even if I loved him?"

"You also thought you loved Eisen."

"He didn't love me. Not enough to forgive my Catholic background. And I couldn't discuss anything with him. Besides, sexually, he was a very gross person. Things I wouldn't care to tell you about, Father. But he is extremely common and lousy. He's here in New York. If he comes near me, I'll stab him."

"You amaze me, Shula. You would actually stab Eisen with a knife?"

"Or with a fork. I often regret that I let him beat me in Haifa and didn't do anything back to him. He hit me really too hard, and I should have defended myself."

"All the more important that you should avoid future mistakes. I have to protect you from failures I can foresee. A father should."

"But what if I did love Dr. Lal? And I saw him first."

"Rivalry—a poor motive. Shula, we must take care of each other. As you look after me on the H. G. Wells side, I think about your happiness. Margotte is a much less sensitive person than you. If a man like Dr. Lal was mentally absent for weeks at a time, she'd never notice. Don't you remember how Ussher used to speak to her?"

"He would tell her to shut up."

"That's right."

"If a husband treated me like that, I couldn't bear it."

"Exactly. Wells also thought that people in scientific research made poor husbands."

"He didn't!"

"I seem to remember his saying that. Does Wallace really know the first thing about aerial photography?"

"He knows so many things. What do you think of his business idea?"

"He doesn't have ideas—he has delusions, brainstorms. However, he wouldn't be the first maniac to make money. And his scheme has charm, dealing in plant names . . . well, some of the plants do have beautiful names. Take one like Gazania Pavonia."

"Gazania Pavonia is darling. Well, come out in the sun and enjoy the weather. I feel much better when you take an interest in me. I'm glad you understand that I took the moon thing for you. You aren't going to give up the project, are you? It would be a sin. You were made to write the Wells book, and it would be a masterpiece. Something terrible will happen if you don't. Bad luck. I feel it inside."

"I may try again."

"You must."

"To find a place for it among my preoccupations."

"You should have no other preoccupations. Only creative ones."

Mr. Sammler, smelling of sandalwood soap, decided to sit in the garden to wait for Emil. Perhaps the soap odor would evaporate in the sun. He didn't have it in him to rinse again in the onyx bathroom. Too close in there.

"Bring your coffee out."

"I'd like that, Shula." He handed her the cup and stepped onto the lawn. "And my shoes are wet from last night."

Black fluid, white light, green ground, the soil heated and soft, penetrated by new growth. In the grass, a massed shine of particles, a turf-buried whiteness, and from this dew, wherever the sun could reach it, the spectrum flashed: like night cities seen from the jet, or the galactic sperm of worlds.

"Here. Sit. Take those things off. You'll catch cold. I can dry them in the oven." Kneeling, she removed the wet shoes. "How can you wear them? Do you want to catch pneumonia?"

"Is Emil coming straight back or waiting for that lunatic?"

"I don't know. Why do you keep calling him a lunatic? Why is Wallace a lunatic?"

To a lunatic, how would you define a lunatic? And was he himself a perfect example of sanity? He was certainly not. They were his people—he was their Sammler. They shared the same fundamentals.

"Because he flooded the house?" said Shula.

"Because he flooded it. Because now he's flying around with his cameras."

"He was looking for money. That's not crazy, is it?"

"How do you know about this money?"

"He told me. He thinks there's a fortune here. What do you think?"

"I wouldn't know. But Wallace *would* have such fantasies—Ali Baba, Captain Kidd, or Tom Sawyer treasure fantasies."

"But he says—no joking—there's a fortune of money in the house. He won't rest until he finds it. Wouldn't it be a little mean of Cousin Elya . . ."

"To die without saying where it is?"

"Yes." Shula seemed slightly ashamed, now that her meaning was explicit.

"It's up to him. Elya will do as he likes. I assume Wallace has asked you to help find this secret hoard."

"Yes."

"What did he do, promise a reward?"

"Yes, he did."

"I don't want you to meddle, Shula. Keep out of it."

"Shall I bring you a slice of toast, Father?"

He didn't answer. She went away, taking his wet shoes.

Above New Rochelle, several small planes snored and buzzed. Probably Wallace was piloting one of them. Unto himself a roaring center. To us, a sultry beetle, a gnat propelling itself through blue acres. Sammler set back his chair into the shade. What had been in the sun a mass of pine foliage now resolved itself into separate needles and trees. Then the silver-gray Rolls turned the corner of the high hedges. The geometrical, dignified, monogrammed radiator flashed its rods. Emil stepped out, looking upward. A yellow plane flew over the house.

"That must be Wallace for sure. He said he was going to fly a Cessna."

"I suppose it is Wallace."

"He wanted to try the equipment on a place he knows."

"Emil, I've been waiting to go to the station."

"Of course, Mr. Sammler. But right now there aren't many trains. How is Dr. Gruner, do you know?"

"I spoke to him," Sammler said. "No change."

"I'd be glad to take you to town."

"When?"

"Very soon."

"It would save time. I have to stop at home. You aren't going back to the airport for Wallace?"

"He was going to land at Newark and take the bus."

"Do you think he knows what he's doing, Emil?"

"Without a license they wouldn't let him fly."

"That's not what I mean."

"He's the type of kid who wants to put things together his own way."

"I'm not sure he'll ever know . . ."

"He finds out as he goes along. He says that's what Action painters do."

"I could have more confidence in the process. I don't think he should be flying about today. His feelings, whatever they are—rivalry with his father, grief, or whatever—may carry him away."

"If it was my dad, I'd be at the hospital right now. It's different, now. We old guys have to go along."

Lifting his cap to extend the shade over his eyes, he gazed after the speeding Cessna. He revealed his long, full-bottomed Lombard nose. He had the wolfish North Italian look. His skin was tight. Perhaps he had been, as Wallace insisted, Emilio, a fierce little driver for the Mafia. But he was now at the stage of life at which the once-compact person begins to show an elderly frailty. This appeared in the shoulders and at the back of the neck, where the creases were deep. He was connected with the very finest, the supreme land vehicle. No competition with aircraft. He leaned against the fender, arms folded, making sure that no button scratched the finish. He held the hair-fragrant cap and tapped himself. He lightly struck the descending terraces, the large wrinkles of his forehead.

"I figure he wants shots from every altitude. He's flying low, all right."

"If he doesn't hit the house, I'll be very pleased."

"He could rack up the perfect score, after flooding the joint. You wonder, will he want to top that?"

Mr. Sammler brought out the folded handkerchief to slip under the lenses before removing his glasses, covering his disfigurement from Emil. He was unable to stare up longer, his eyes were smarting.

"How can one guess?" said Sammler. "Yesterday he said that it was his unconscious self that opened the wrong pipe."

"Yes, he talks that way to me, too. But I've been eighteen years with the Gruners and know that character. He's very, very disturbed about the doctor."

"Yes, I think he is. I agree. But that little machine . . . Like an ironing board with an egg beater. Are you a family man, Emil—do you have children?"

"Two. Grown up and graduated."

"Do they love you?"

"They act like it."

"That's already a great deal."

He was beginning to consider that he might not reach New York in time. Even Elya's request for clippings might delay him too long. But—one thing at a time. Then Wallace's engine grew louder. The noise attacked one's skull. It gave Sammler a headache. The injured eye felt pressure. The air was parted. On one side nuisance, on the other a singular current, an insidious spring brightness.

Blasting, shining, clear yellow, the color of a bird's bill, the Cessna made another, lower pass at the house. The trees threshed under it.

"He's going to crash. He'll hit the roof next time."

"I don't think he can buzz it any closer while snapping pictures," Emil said.

"He must certainly be below the permissible point."

The plane, rising, banking, grew smaller; you could hardly hear it now.

"Wasn't he about to strike the chimney?"

"It looked close, but only from our angle," said Emil.

"They shouldn't let him fly."

"Well, he's gone. Maybe that's it."

"Shall we start?" said Sammler.

"I'm supposed to pick up the cleaning woman at eleven—I think the phone has been ringing."

"The cleaning woman? Shula's in the house. She will answer."

"She's not," said Emil. "When I drove up I saw her in the road, walking along with her purse."

"Going where?"

"I wouldn't know. To the store, maybe. I'll get the phone."

The call was for Sammler. It was Margotte.

"Hello, Margotte. Well—?"

"We opened the lockers."

"What did you find, what she said?"

"Not exactly, Uncle. In the first locker was one of Shula's shopping bags, and in it there was only the usual staff. *Chris-*

tian Science Monitors from way back, clippings, and some old copies of *Life*. Also a great deal of student-revolt literature. SDS. Dr. Lal was shocked. He was very upset."

"Come, what about the second locker?"

"Thank God! We found the manuscript there."

"Intact?"

"I think so. He's looking through it." She spoke away from the phone. "Are pages torn out? No, Uncle, he doesn't think so."

"Oh, I am very glad. For him, and for myself. Even for Shula. But where is the copy she made on Widick's machine? She must have misplaced or lost that. But Dr. Lal must be delighted."

"Oh, he is. He's just going to wait at the soda fountain. It's such a chaos in Grand Central."

"I wish you had knocked at my door. You knew I had to get to town."

"Dear Uncle Sammler, we thought of that, but there was no room in the car. Am I mistaken, or are you irritated? You sound annoyed. We could have dropped you at the station." What Sammler refrained from saying was that he and Lal might have dropped her, Margotte, at the station. Was he annoyed! But even now, with skull-pressure, eye-pangs, he did not want to be too hard on her. No. She had her own female vital aims. No sense of the vital aims of others. His tension now. "Govinda was so anxious to leave. He insisted. However, the trains are fast. Besides, I phoned the hospital and talked to Angela. Elya's condition is just the same."

"I know. I've spoken to him."

"Well, you see? And he has to have some tests, so you would only have to wait if you were here. Now I'm taking Dr. Lal home to lunch. There's so much he doesn't eat, and Grand Central is a madhouse. And it smells so of hot dogs. Because of him, I notice it now for the first time."

"Of course. Home is better. By all means."

"Angela talked to me in a very mature way. She was sad, but she sounded so calm, and so aware." Margotte's kind and considerate views of people were terribly trying to Sammler. "She said that Elya was asking for you. He very much wishes to see you."

"I might have been there now. . . ."

"Well, he's down below anyhow," she said. "So take your time. Have lunch with us."

"I have to stop at the house. But no lunch."

"You wouldn't be in the way. Govinda likes you so much. He admires you. Anyway, you are my family. We love you like a father. All of us. I know I am a pest to you. I was to Ussher, too. Still, we loved each other."

"Well, well, Margotte. All right. Now let's hang up."

"I know you want to get away. And you don't like long phone conversations. But Uncle, I'm insecure about my ability to interest a man like Dr. Lal on the mental level."

"Nonsense, Margotte, don't be a fool. Don't get on the mental level. You charm him. He finds you exotic. Don't have long discussions. Let him do the talking."

But Margotte went on talking. She was putting in more coins. There were bongs and chimes. He did not hang up. Neither did he listen.

Further tests for Elya he took to be a tactic of the doctors. They protected their prestige by appearing to make real moves. But Elya himself was a doctor. He had lived by such gestures and had to submit to them now and without complaint. That certainly he would do. Now what of Elya's unfinished business? Before the vessel wall gave out did he really want to go on about Cracow? To talk about Uncle Hessid, who ground cornmeal and wore a derby and fancy vest? Sammler could recall no such individual. No. Elya with strong family feelings he could not gratify, wanted Sammler there to represent the family. His thin, lean presence, his small ruddy face, wrinkled on the one side. It was even more than piety for kinship which the age, acting through his children ("high-IQ moron, fucked-out eyes"), had leveled with derision and knocked flat. And Gruner called upon Sammler as more than an old uncle, one-eyed, growling peculiarly in Polish-Oxonian. He must have believed that he had some unusual power, magical perhaps, to affirm the human bond. What had he done to generate this belief? How had he induced it? By coming back from the dead, probably.

Margotte had much to say. She did not notice his silence.

By coming back, by preoccupation with the subject, the

dying, the mystery of dying, the state of death. Also, by having been inside death. By having been given the shovel and told to dig. By digging beside his digging wife. When she faltered he tried to help her. By this digging, not speaking, he tried to convey something to her and fortify her. But as it had turned out, he had prepared her for death without sharing it. She was killed, not he. She had passed the course, and he had not. The hole deepened, the sand clay, and stones of Poland, their birthplace, opened up. He had just been blinded, he had a stunned face, and he was unaware that blood was coming from him till they stripped and he saw it on his clothes. When they were as naked as children from the womb, and the hole was supposedly deep enough, the guns began to blast, and then came a different sound of soil. The thick fall of soil. A ton, two tons, thrown in. A sound of shovel-metal, gritting. Strangely exceptional, Mr. Sammler had come through the top of this. It seldom occurred to him to consider it an achievement. Where was the achievement? He had clawed his way out. If he had been at the bottom, he would have suffocated. If there had been another foot of dirt. Perhaps others had been buried alive in that ditch. There was no special merit, there was no wizardry. There was only suffocation escaped. And had the war lasted a few months more, he would have died like the rest. Not a Jew would have avoided death. As it was, he still had his consciousness, earthliness, human actuality—got up, breathed his earth gases in and out, drank his coffee, consumed his share of goods, ate his roll from Zabar's, put on certain airs—all human beings put on certain airs—took the bus to Forty-second Street as if he had an occupation, ran into a black pickpocket. In short, a living man. Or one who had been sent back again to the end of the line. Waiting for something. Assigned to figure out certain things, to condense, in short views, some essence of experience, and because of this having a certain wizardry ascribed to him. There was, in fact, unfinished business. But how did business finish? We entered in the middle of the thing and somehow became convinced that we must conclude it. How? And since he had lasted—survived—with a sick headache—he would not quibble over words—was there an assignment implicit? Was he meant to do something?

"I never want to annoy Lal," said Margotte. "He's gentle and small. By the way, Uncle, is the cleaning woman there?"

"Who? Cleaning?"

"You say charwoman. So is that the char? I hear the vacuum running."

"No, my dear, what you hear is our relative Wallace in his airplane. Don't ask me more. Well see each other later."

He found his sodden shoes baking in the kitchen. Shula had set them on the open door of the electric oven and the toes were smoking. That, too! When he had cooled them, he labored to put them on with the handle of a tablespoon. The recovery of the manuscript helped him to be patient with Shula. She did not actually step over the line. The usefulness of these shoes, however, was at an end. They were ready for the dustbin. Not even Shula herself would want to retrieve them. And the immediate problem was not shoes, he could get to New York without shoes. Emil had already gone to fetch the charwoman. Taxis were listed in the Yellow Pages, but Sammler did not know which company to call, nor how much it might cost. He had only four dollars. Not to embarrass the Gruners you had to tip fifty cents at least. There was also fare to the city. Long-mouthed, silent, and with a hectic color, he tried to make the penny calculations. He saw himself, somewhere, eight cents short, trying to convince a policeman that he was not a panhandler. It would be better to wait. Perhaps Emil would meet Shula in the road, bringing her back with the char. Shula usually had money.

But Emil returned with the Croatian woman alone, and when he had shown her the water damage, he put on his cap, and, behaving to Sammler like a chauffeur, not at all treating him like a poor relation, he opened the silver door.

"Would you like the air conditioner, Mr. Sammler?"

"Thank you, Emil."

Examining the sky, Emil said, "It looks as if Wallace has all his pictures. He must be on his way to Newark."

"Yes, he's gone, thank God."

"I know the doctor wants to see you." Sammler was already seated. "What's the matter with your shoes?"

"I had trouble getting them on, and now I can't lace them. There's another pair at home. May we stop at the apartment?"

"The doctor talks about you all the time."

"Does he?"

"He's an affectionate fellow. I don't want to bad mouth Mrs. Gruner, but you know how she was."

"Not demonstrative."

Emil shut the door, and very correct, walked behind the car and let himself into the driver's seat. "Well, she was very organized," he said. "As lady of the house, first class. Like laid out with a ruler. Reserved. Fair. O.K. She ran the place like IBM—the gardener, the laundress, the cook, me. The doctor was grateful, being a kid from a rough neighborhood. She made him real Ivy. A gentleman." Emil backed the slow, silver high-bodied car, poor Elya's car, out of the drive. He gave Sammler the proper options of conversation or privacy. Sammler chose privacy and drew shut the glass panel.

Mr. Sammler's root feeling (a prejudice, if you like) was that women with exceedingly skinny legs could not be loving wives or passionate mistresses. Especially if with such legs they also had bouffant hairstyles. Hilda had been an agreeable person, cheerful, amiable, high-pitched, even at times breezy. But strictly correct. Often the doctor would demonstratively embrace her and say, "The world's best wife. Oh! I love you, Hil." He would clasp her from the side and kiss her on the cheek. This was permitted. It was allowed under a new dispensation which acknowledged the high value of warmth and impulsiveness. Undoubtedly Elya's feelings were strong, unlike Hilda's. But impulsive? There was in his conduct a strong element of propaganda. It came to him, perhaps, from the American system as a whole and showed his submissiveness. Everyone, to everyone, had a way of making propaganda for the good. Democracy was propagandistic in its style. Conversation was often nothing but the repetition of liberal principles. But Elya had certainly been disappointed in his wife. Sammler hoped that he had love affairs. With a nurse, perhaps? Or a patient who had become a mistress? Sammler did not recommend this for everyone, but in Elya's case it would have been beneficial. But no, probably the doctor was respectable. And it's a doomed man that woos affection so much.

It would soon be full spring. The Cross County, the Saw Mill River, the Henry Hudson thick with reviving grass and dandelions, the oven of the sun baking green life again. One was both sickened and strengthened by this swirling, this roughness and sweetness. Then—Mr. Sammler's elbow at rest on the gray cushion, and holding the back of one hand in the palm of the other—then there were the gray, yellow, homogeneous highways, from the engineering standpoint so impressive, from the moral, aesthetic, political something else. Staggering billions appropriated. But as someone had said about statesmen, the foremost of the Gadarene swine. Who had? He couldn't remember. Yet he was not cynical about these matters. He was not against civilization, nor against politics, institutions, nor against order. When the grave was dug, institutions and the rest had not been for him. No politics, no order intervened for Antonina. But there was no need to thrust oneself personally into every general question—to assail Churchill, Roosevelt, for having known (and surely they did know) what was happening and failing to bomb Auschwitz. Why not have bombed Auschwitz? But they didn't. Well, they didn't. They wouldn't. Emotions of justified reproach, supremacy in blame, made no appeal to Sammler. The individual was the supreme judge of nothing. Because he had to find things out for himself, he was necessarily the intermediate judge. But never final. Existence was not accountable to him. Indeed not. Nor would he ever put together the inorganic, organic, natural, bestial, human, and superhuman in any dependable arrangement but, however fascinating and original his genius, only idiosyncratically, a shaky scheme, mainly decorative or ingenious. Of course at the moment of launching from this planet to another something was ended, finalities were demanded, summaries. Everyone appeared to feel this need. Unanimously all tasted, and each in his own way, the flavor of the end of things-as-known. And by way of summary, perhaps, each accented more strongly his own subjective style and the practices by which he was known. Thus Wallace, on the day of destiny for his father, roared and snored in the Cessna snapping photographs. Thus Shula, hiding from Sammler, was undoubtedly going to hunt for treasure, for the alleged abortion dollars. Thus Angela, making more experiments in sensuality, in sexology, smearing all with her female fluids. Thus Eisen with his art, the Negro with his penis. And in the series, but not finally, himself with his condensed views. Eliminating the superfluous. Identifying the necessary.

Looking from the window, passing all in state, in an automobile costing upwards of twenty thousand dollars, Mr. Sammler still saw that together with the end of things-as-known the feeling for new beginnings was nevertheless very strong. Marriage for Margotte, America for Eisen, business for Wallace, love for Govinda. And away from this death-burdened, rotting, spoiled, sullied, exasperating, sinful earth but already looking toward the moon and Mars with plans for founding cities. And for himself . . .

He tapped the glass partition with a coin. The toll booth was approaching.

"It's O.K., Mr. Sammler."

Sammler insisted, "Here, Emil, take it, take it."

Measured by watch hands the trip was brief. In the off-hour, traffic moved quickly on the gray-and-yellow masterwork roads. Emil knew exactly how to drive. He was the faultless driver of the faultless car. He entered the city at One hundred twenty-fifth Street, under the ultrahigh railroad bridge that crossed the meat wholesalers' area. Sammler had some affection for this intricate bridge and the structural shadows it threw. Reflected in the shine of the meat trucks. The sides of beef and pork, gauze-wrapped, blood-spotted. Things edible would always be respected by a man who had nearly starved to death. The laborers, too, in white smocks, broad and heavy, a thickset personnel, butchers' men. By the river the smell was equivocal. You were not sure whether the rawness came from the tidewater or the blood. And here Sammler once saw a rat he took for a dachshund. The breeze out of this electric-lighted corner had the fragrance of meat dust. That was sprayed from the band saws that went through frozen fat, through marbled red or icy porphyry, and whizzed through bone. Try to stroll here. The pavements were waxed with fat.

Then a right turn, downtown on Broadway. The street rose while the subway was lowering. Up, the brown masonry; and down, the black shadow and steel tracks. Then tenements, the Puerto Rican squalor. Then the University, squalid in a different way. It was already too warm in the city. Spring lost the touch of winter and got the summer rankness. Between the pillars at One hundred-sixteenth Street Sammler looked into the brick quadrangles. He half expected Feffer to pass, or the bearded man in Levi's who had said he couldn't come. He saw growing green. But green in the city had lost its association with peaceful sanctuary. The old-time poetry of parks was banned. Obsolete thickness of shade leading to private meditation. Truth was now slummier and called for litter in the setting—leafy reverie? A thing of the past.

Except on special occasions (Feffer's lecture, twenty-four? forty-eight hours ago?), Sammler never came this way any more. Walking for exercise, he didn't venture this far uptown. And now, from Elya's Rolls Royce, he inspected the subculture of the underprivileged (terminology recently acquired in the *New York Times*), its Caribbean fruits, its plucked naked chickens with loose necks and eyelids blue, the wavering fumes of Diesel and hot lard. Then Ninety-sixth Street, tilted at all four corners, the kiosks and movie houses, the ramparts of wire-fastened newspaper bundles, and the colors of panic waving. Broadway, even when there was some urgency, hurrying to see Elya for possibly the last time, always challenged Sammler. He was never up to it. And why should there be any contest? But there was, every time. For something was stated here. By a convergence of all minds and all movements the conviction transmitted by this crowd seemed to be that reality was a terrible thing, and that the final truth about mankind was overwhelming and crushing. This vulgar, cowardly conclusion, rejected by Sammler with all his heart, was the implicit local orthodoxy, the populace itself being metaphysical and living out this interpretation of reality and this view of truth. Sammler could not swear that this was really accurate, but Broadway at Ninety-sixth Street gave him such a sense of things. Life, when it was like this, all question-and-answer from the top of intellect to the very bottom, was really a state of singular dirty misery. When it was all question-and-answer it had no charm. Life when it had no charm was entirely question-and-answer. The thing worked both ways. Also, the questions were bad. Also, the answers were horrible. This poverty of soul, its abstract state, you could see in faces on the street. And he too had a touch of the same disease—the disease of the single self explaining what was what and who was who. The results could be foreseen, foretold. So, then, brought down Broadway in high style, Sammler visited his own (what did Wallace call it?)

his own *turf*. As a tourist. And then Emil, by way of Riverside Drive, came round and set him down before the great, used, soiled mass of conveniences where he and Margotte lived. The time was half past twelve.

"It shouldn't take long. Elya asked for some papers."

There was a tightness at his heart. The remedy was fuller breathing, but he could not get his chest to rise and fall. Something had locked it. Margotte and Govinda were not back. The pin-up lamp burned needlessly in the foyer above the sofa with its maple armrests, the bandanna covers. There was a certain peace in the house. Or did it seem so because he had no time to sit down? He changed shoes, shook a few dollars from his jar, put the newspaper clippings into his wallet. On his desk was a bottle of vodka. Shula provided this out of the wages Elya paid her. It was excellent, Stolichnaya, imported from the Soviet Union. Sammler made use of it about once a month. He uncorked the bottle now and drank a glass. It went down burning, and he made a face. First aid for the old. Then he opened his door to the back stairs, slipping the latch lest one of the strong drafts there should come slamming and lock him out. He put his old shoes into the incinerator drop. He didn't want Shula arguing that she had done them no harm in the electric oven. They had had it.

For once the lobby television worked. Gray and whitish figures, unsteady on the vertical hold, wavered and fizzed. Sammler saw himself mortally pale on the screen. The shuddering image of an aged man. This lobby was like certain underground carpeted rooms in disused theaters—spaces to shun. It was less than two days ago that the pickpocket had forced him, belly-to-back, across this same brass-bolted rug into the corner beside the Florentine table. Unbuttoning his puma colored coat in puma silence to show himself. Was this the sort of fellow called by Goethe *eine Natur*? A primary force?

He stopped Emil from getting out of the car for him. "I can work the door myself."

"We're off, then. Open the bar, pour yourself a drink."

"I hope the traffic will not be too thick."

"We'll go straight down Broadway."

"Turn on the TV."

"Thanks. No TV."

Again Sammler smelled the enclosed, fabric-scented air. He did not make himself comfortable. The tightness of heart was greater than before. It went on contracting; he thought it could not be worse, and then it was worse. The traffic was unusually heavy, jammed up at the lights. Delivery trucks were double-parked, triple-parked. The use of private cars in Manhattan had never seemed so irrational and harmful. He was swept by impatience toward the drivers of these large, purposeless machines but then the sweeping feelings swept beyond him. Conveyed in air-conditioned silence by the roarless power of the engine, he sat forward with his thighs upon the backs of his hands. Evidently Elya thought that he owed it to himself to maintain this Rolls. He couldn't have had much use for such a prestigious machine. It wasn't as if he were a Broadway producer, an international banker, a tobacco millionaire. Where did it take him? To Widick's law office. To Hayden, Stone Incorporated, where he had an account. On High Holy Days, he went to the temple on Fifth Avenue. On Fifty-seventh Street were his tailors, Felsher and Kitto. The temple and the tailors had been selected by Hilda. Sammler would have sent him to another tailor. Elya had a tall figure and wide stiff shoulders, too wide, considering the flatness of his body. His buttocks were too high. Like my own, for that matter. Sammler, in the sound-deadened cabinet of the Rolls, saw the resemblance. Felsher and Kitto made Elya too dapper. The trousers were too narrow. The virile bulge that appeared when he sat was inappropriate. He used matching ties and handkerchiefs by Countess Mara, and sharp, swaggering shoes which connected him less with medicine than with La Vegas, with racing, broads, and singers in the rackets. Things equivocally related to his kindliness. Swaying his shoulders like a gunman. Wearing double-vented jackets. Playing gin and canasta for high stakes and talking out of the corner of the mouth. Detesting *Kulturny* physicians who wanted to discuss Heidegger or Wittgenstein. Real doctors had no time for that phony stuff. He was a keen spotter of phonies. He could easily afford this car, but had none of the life that went with it. No Broadway musicals, no private jet. His one glamorous eccentricity was to fly to Israel on short notice and stroll into the King David Hotel without baggage, his hands in his pockets. That struck him as a sporting thing to do. Of course, thought Sammler, Elya was also peculiar; surgery was psychically peculiar. To enter an unconscious body with a knife? To take out organs, sew in the flesh, splash blood? Not everyone could do that. And perhaps he kept the car for Emil's sake. What would Emil do if there were no Rolls? Now there was the likeliest answer of all. The protective instinct was strong in Elya. Undisclosed charities were his pleasure. He had many stratagems of benevolence. I have reason to know. How very odd—astonishing, the desire to relieve and protect us. It was astonishing because Elya the surgeon also despised incompetence and weakness. Only great and powerful instincts worked so deeply and deviously, coming out on the side of things despised. But how could Elya afford to have rigid ideas of strength? He himself was hooked man. Hilda had been far stronger than he. In the Mafioso swagger were pretensions of lawless liberty. But it was little Hilda with the rodlike legs and the bouffant hair and faultless hemlines and sweet refinements who was the real criminal. She had had her hook in Elya. And there had never been any help for Elya. Who was there to help him? He was the sort of individual from whom help emanated. There were no arrangements for return. However, it would soon be over. It was about to wash away.

As for the world, was it really about to change? Why? How? By the fact of moving into space, away from earth? There would be changes of heart? There would be new conduct? Why, because we were tired of the old conduct? That was not reason enough. Why, because the world was breaking up? Well, America, if not the world. Well, staggering, if not breaking.

Emil was driving more steadily again, below Seventy-second Street. The traffic had eased. There were no truck deliveries to impede it. Lincoln Center was approaching and, at Columbus Circle, the Huntington Hartford Building, which Bruch called the Taj Mahole. Wasn't that funny! said Bruch. At his own jokes he rolled with laughter. Apelike, he put his hands on his paunch and closed his eyes, letting the tongue hang out of his blind head. What a building! All holes. But that was some lunch they put down for only three bucks. He raved about the bill of fare—Hawaiian chicken and saffron rice. Finally he had taken the old man there. It was indeed a grand lunch. But

Lincoln Center Sammler had seen only from the outside. He was cold to the performing arts, and shunned large crowds. Exhibitions, electrical or nude, he had attended only because it amused Angela to keep him up to date. But he passed by the pages of the *Times* that dealt with painters, singers, fiddlers, or play actors. He saved his reading eye for better things. He had noted with hostile interest crews wrecking the nice old tenements and greasy-spoons, and the new halls rising.

But now, as they were nearing the Center, Emil stopped the car and pushed back the glass slide.

"Why are you stopping?"

Emil said, "There's something happening across the street." He looked, wrinkling his face deeply, as if this explanation must really be heeded. But why, at such a time, should he have stopped for anything? "Don't you recognize those people, Mr. Sammler?"

"Which? Has someone scraped someone? Is it a traffic thing?" Of course he lacked authority to tell Emil to drive on, but he gestured, nevertheless, with the back of his hand. He waved Emil forward.

"No, I think you'll want to stop, Mr. Sammler. I see your son-in-law there. Isn't that him, with the big green bag? And isn't that Wallace's partner?"

"Feffer?"

"That fat kid. The pink face, the beard. He's fighting. Can't you see?"

"Where is this? In the street? Is it Eisen?"

"It's the other fellow who's in trouble. The young guy, the beard. I think he's getting hurt."

On the east side of the slant street a bus had pulled to the curb at a wide angle, obstructing traffic. Sammler could see now that someone was struggling there, in the midst of a crowd.

"One of those is Feffer?"

"Yes, Mr. Sammler."

"Wrestling with someone—with the bus driver?"

"Not the driver, no. I think not. Somebody else."

"Then I must go and see what it is."

The craziness of these delays! Almost deliberate, almost intentional, they were breaking down every barrier of patience.

They got to you at last. Why this, why Feffer? But he could see now what Emil meant. Feffer was pinned to the front of a bus. That *was* Feffer against the wide bumper. Sammler began to pull at the handle of the door.

"Not on the street side, Mr. Sammler. You'll be hit."

But Sammler, his patience utterly lost, was already hurrying through traffic.

Feffer, in the midst of the crowd, was fighting the black man, the pickpocket. There were twenty people at least, and more were stopping, but no one was about to interfere. Struggling in the criminal's grip, Feffer was forced back against the big cumbersome machine. His head was knocking on the windshield below the empty driver's seat. The man was squeezing him, and Feffer was scared. He resisted, he defended himself, but he was inept. He was overmatched. Of course. How could it be otherwise? His bearded face was frightened. Upturned, the broad cheeks flamed, and his wide-spaced brown eyes appealed for help. Or were thinking what to do. What should he do? Like a man groping in a stream for a lost object, while staring into air, mouth gaping in his beard. But he would not give up the Minox. One arm was held straight up, out of reach. The weight of the big body in the fawn-colored suit crushed him. He had had the bad luck to get his candid shot. The black man was snatching at the Minox. To get the tiny camera, to give Feffer a few kicks in the ribs, in the belly—what else would he have had in mind? Leaving, without haste if possible, before the police arrived. But Feffer, near panic, still was obstinate. Shifting his grip, the Negro grabbed and twisted his collar, holding him as he had held Sammler with his forearm against the wall. He choked Feffer with the neckband. The Dior shades, round and bluish, had not moved from the low-bridged nose. Feffer had caught the spouting red necktie in his fist, but could do nothing with it.

How shall we save this prying, stupid idiotic boy? He may be hurt. And I must go. There's no time. "Some of you," Sammler ordered. "Here! Help him. Break this up." But of course "some of you" did not exist. No one would do anything, and suddenly Sammler felt extremely foreign—voice, accent, syntax, manner, face, mind, everything foreign.

Emil had seen Eisen. Sammler looked for him now. And there he was, smiling and very pale. He was evidently waiting to be discovered. Then he seemed delighted.

"What are you doing here?" said Sammler in Russian.

"And you, Father-in-law—what are you doing?"

"I? I am rushing to the hospital to see Elya."

"Yes. And I was with my young friend on the bus when he took the picture. Of a purse being opened. I saw it myself."

"What a stupid thing!"

Eisen held his green baize bag. It contained his sculptures or medallions. Those Dead Sea pieces—iron pyrites, or whatever they were.

"Let him give up the camera. Why doesn't he give it to him?" said Sammler.

"But how do we prevail upon him?" said Eisen in a tone of discussion.

"Get a policeman," Sammler said. He would have liked to say, too, "Stop this smiling."

"But I don't know English."

"Then help the boy."

"You help him, Father-in-law. I am a foreigner and a cripple. You're older, true. But I just got to this country."

Sammler said to the pickpocket, "Let go. Let him go."

The man's large face turned. New York was reflected in the lenses, under the stiff curves of the homburg. Perhaps he recognized Sammler. But nothing was said.

"Give him the camera, Feffer. Hand it over," Sammler said.

Feffer, with a stare of shock and appeal, looked as if he expected soon to lose consciousness. He did not bring down his arm.

"I say let him have that stupid thing. He wants the film. Don't be an idiot."

Feffer may have been holding out in expectation of a squad car, waiting for the police to save him. It was hard otherwise to explain his resistance. Considering the Negro's strength—his crouching, squeezing, intense animal pressing-power, the terrific swelling of the neck and the tightness of the buttocks as he rose on his toes. In straining alligator shoes! In fawn-colored trousers! With a belt that matched his necktie—a crimson belt! How consciousness was lashed by such a fact!

"Eisen!" said Sammler, furious.

"Yes, Father-in-law."

"I ask you to do something."

"Let them do something." He motioned with the baize bag to the bystanders. "I only came forty-eight hours ago."

Again Mr. Sammler turned to the crowd, staring hard. Wouldn't anyone help? So even now—now, *still!*—one believed in such things as help. Where people were, help might be. It was an instinct and a reflex. (An unexasperated hope?) So, briefly examining faces, passing from face to face to face among the people along the curb—red, pale, swarthy, lined taut or soft, grim or adream, eyes bald-blue, iodine-reddish, coal-seam black—how strange a quality their inaction had. They were expecting gratification, oh! at last! of teased, cheated, famished needs. Someone was going to get it! Yes. And the black faces? A similar desire. Another side. But the same. Though there was nothing to hear, Sammler had the sense that something was barking away. Then it struck him that what united everybody was a beatitude of presence. As if it were—yes—blessed are the present. They are here and not here. They are present while absent. So they were waiting in that ecstatic state. What a supreme privilege! And there was only Eisen to break up the fight. Which was, after all, an odd sort of fight. Sammler did not believe that the black man would choke Feffer into unconsciousness; he would only go on squeezing, screwing the collar tighter until Feffer surrendered the Minox. Of course, there was always a chance that he might strike him, pull a knife, stab him. But there was something worse here than this event itself, namely, the feeling that stole over Sammler.

It was a feeling of horror and grew in strength, grew and grew. What was it? How was it to be put? He was a man who had come back. He had rejoined life. He was near to others. But in some essential way he was also companionless. He was old. He lacked physical force. He knew what to do, but had no power to execute it. He had to turn to someone else—to an Eisen! a man himself very far out on another track, orbiting a different foreign center. Sammler was powerless. To be so powerless was death. And suddenly he saw himself not so much standing as strangely leaning, as reclining, and peculiarly in profile, and as a *past* person. That was not himself. It was someone—and this struck him—poor in spirit. Someone between the human and not-human states, between content and emptiness, between full and void, meaning and not-meaning, between this world and no world. Flying, freed from gravitation, light with release and dread, doubting his destination, fearing there was nothing to receive him.

"Eisen, separate them," he said. "He's been choked enough. The police will come, and then there will be arrests. And I must go. To stand here is crazy. Please. Just take the camera. Take it. That will stop this."

Then handsome Eisen, shrugging, grinning, making a crooked movement of the shoulders, working them free from the tight denim, stepped away from Sammler as though he were doing a very amusing thing at his special request. He drew up the sleeve of his right arm. The dark hairs were thick. Then shortening his grip on the cords of the baize bag he swung it very wide, swung with full force and struck the pickpocket on the side of the face. It was a hard blow. The glasses flew. The hat. Feffer was not immediately freed. The man seemed to rest on him. Obviously stunned. Eisen was a laborer, a foundry worker. He had the strength not only of his trade but also of madness. There was something limitless, unbounded, about the way he squared off, took the man's measure, a kind of sturdy viciousness. Everything went into that blow, discipline, murderousness, everything. What have I done! This is much worse! This is the worst thing yet. Sammler thought Eisen had crushed the man's face. And he was now about to hit him again, with his medallions. The black man took his hands from Feffer and was turning. His lips came away from his teeth. Eisen had gashed his skin and the cheek was bleeding and swelling. Eisen clinked the weights from his wrist, spread his legs. "He'll kill that cocksucker!" someone in the crowd said.

"Don't hit him, Eisen. I never said that. I tell you no!" said Sammler.

But the bag of weights was speeding from the other side, very wide but accurate. It struck more heavily than before and knocked the man down. He did not drop. He lowered himself as though he had decided to lie in the street. The blood ran in points on his cheek. The terrible metal had cut him through the baize.

Eisen now heaved his weapon back over the shoulder, prepared to slam it straight down on the man's skull. Sammler seized his arm and twisted him away. "You'll murder him. Do you want to beat out his brains?"

"You *said*, Father-in-law!"

They quarreled in Russian before the crowd.

"You said I had to do something. You said you had to go. I must do something. So I did."

"I didn't say to hit him with these damned irons. I didn't say to hit him at all. You're crazy, Eisen, crazy enough to murder him."

The pickpocket had tried to brace himself on his elbows. His body now rested on his doubled arms. He bled thickly on the asphalt.

"I am horrified!" Sammler said.

Eisen, still handsome, curly, still with the smile, though now panting, and the peculiar set of the toeless feet, seemed amused at Sammler's ludicrous inconsistency. He said, "You can't hit a man like this just once. When you hit him you must really hit him. Otherwise he'll kill you. You know. We both fought in the war. You were a Partisan. You had a gun. So don't you know?" His laughter, his logic, laughing and reasoning at Sammler's absurdities, made him repeat until he stuttered. "If in—in. No? If out—out. Yes? No? So answer."

It was the reasoning that sank Sammler's heart completely. "Where is Feffer?" he said, and turned away.

Feffer, resting his forehead against the bus, was getting back his breath. Putting it on, no doubt. To Sammler this exaggeration was revolting.

Damn these—these *occasions!* he was thinking. Damn them, it was Elya who needed him. It was only Elya he wanted to see. To whom there was something to say. Here there was nothing to say.

Now he heard someone ask, "Where are the cops?"

"Busy. On the take. Writing tickets, someplace. Those shits. When you need 'em."

"There's plenty of blood. They better bring an ambulance."

The light upon the dull kinks, the porous carbon-cake of the man's head, still dropping blood, showed his eye shut. But he wished to get to his feet. He made efforts.

Eisen said to Sammler, "This is the man, isn't it? The man you told about who followed you? Who showed you his jinjik?"

"Get away from me, Eisen."

"What should I do?"

"Go away. Get away from here. You're in trouble," said Sammler. He spoke to Feffer, "What have you to say now?"

"I caught him in the act. Please wait awhile, he hurt my throat."

"Nonsense, don't put on agony with me. *This* is the man. *He's* badly hurt."

"I swear he was picking the purse, and I got two shots of him."

"*Did* you, now!"

"You seem angry, sir. Why are you so angry with me?"

Sammler now saw the squad car, the whirling roof light, and the policemen coming out at a saunter, pushing away the crowd. Emil drew Sammler away to the side of the bus and said, "You don't want any of this. We have to go."

"Yes, Emil, of course."

They crossed the street. Avoid getting mixed up with the police. They might detain him for hours. He should never have stopped at the flat. He should have gone directly to the hospital.

"I think I would like to sit in the front with you, Emil."

"Why, sure. Are you all shook up?" He helped him in. Emil's own hand was shaking, and Sammler himself had trembling arms and legs. An extraordinary weakness came up the legs from beneath.

The great engine ignited. Coolness poured from the air conditioner. Then the Rolls entered traffic.

"What was all that about?"

"I wish I knew," said Sammler.

"Who was that black character?"

"Poor man, I can't really say who he is."

"He took two mean wallops, there."

"Eisen is brutal."

"What did he have in that bag?"

"Pieces of metal. I feel responsible, Emil, because I appealed to Eisen, because I wanted so badly to get to Dr. Gruner."

"Well, maybe the guy has a thick skull. I guess you never saw anybody hitting to kill. You want to lie down in back for ten minutes? I can stop."

"Do I look sick? No, Emil. But I think I will shut my eyes."

Sammler was sick with rage at Eisen. The black man? The black man was a megalomaniac. But there was a certain—a certain princeliness. The clothing, the shades, the sumptuous colors, the barbarous-majestical manner. He was probably a mad spirit. But mad with an idea of noblesse. And how much Sammler sympathized with him—how much he would have done to prevent such atrocious blows! How red the blood was, and how thick—and how terrible those crusted, spiny lumps of metal were! And Eisen? He counted as a war victim, even though he might anyhow have been mad. But he belonged in the mental hospital. A homicidal maniac. If only, thought Sammler, Shula and Eisen had been a little less crazy. Just a little less. They would have gone on playing casino in Haifa, those two cuckoos, in their whitewashed Mediterranean cage. For they used to get the cards out when they weren't scandalizing the neighborhood with their screams and slaps. But no. Such individuals had the right to be considered normal. They had liberty of movement, on top of it. They had passports, tickets. So then, poor Eisen flew across with his works. Poor soul, poor dog-laughing Eisen.

They all had such fun: Wallace, Feffer, Eisen, Bruch, too, and Angela. They laughed so much. Dear brethren, let us all be human together. Let us all be in the great fun fair, and do this droll mortality with one another. Be entertainers of your near and dear. Treasure hunts, flying circuses, comical thefts, medallions, wigs and saris, beards. Charity, all of it, sheer charity, when you consider the state of things, the blindness of the living. It is fearful! Not to be borne! Intolerable! Let us divert each other while we live!

"I'll park here and go up with you," said Emil. "They can give me a ticket if they like."

"The doctor is not back?" said Emil.

Obviously not. Angela sat alone in the hospital room.

"Then O.K. I'll be standing by if you want me."

"I seem to be smoking three packs a day. I'm out of cigarettes, Emil. I can't even concentrate on a newspaper."

"Benson and Hedges, right?"

When he left she said, "I don't like to send an elderly person on errands."

Sammler made no reply. The Augustus John hat was in his hand. He didn't lay it on the clean newmade bed.

"Emil is part of Daddy's gang. They're very attached."

"What's happening?"

"I wish I knew. He was taken down for tests, but two hours is a long time. I assume Dr. Cosbie knows his stuff. I don't like the man. I don't go for the magnolia charm. He acts as if he ran a military academy in the South. But I'm not one of the boys. Drill is not my dish. He's cross, cold, and repulsive. One of those good-looking men who don't realize that women dislike them. Take the straight chair, Uncle. You like those better. I have to talk to you."

Sammler drew the seat under him, and out of the light—he couldn't bear to face windows through which nothing but blue sky was visible. He saw trouble. Himself aroused, he was sensitive to all the signs. Another woman would have had a hectic color; Angela was candle-white. The amusing husky voice, copying Tallulah's perhaps, fell short of amusement. Her throat was prominent, it looked swollen, and the light brown brows, penciled out like wings, kept rising. She tried at times to give a look of appeal. She was angry, too. It was heavy going. Even wrinkling her forehead seemed difficult. Something was obstructed. With a low-necked satin blouse she wore a miniskirt. No, Sammler changed that, it was a microskirt, a band of green across the thighs. The frosted hair was pulled back tightly; the skin was full of female qualities (the hormones). On her cheeks large gold earrings lay. A big, shapely woman childishly dressed, erotically playing the kid, she was not likely to be taken for a boy. Sitting near her, Sammler could not smell the usual Arabian musk. Instead her female effluence was very strong, a salt odor, similar to tears or tidewater, something from within the woman. Elya's words had taken effect strongly—his "Too much sex." Even the white lipstick suggested perversion. But this was curiously without prejudice. Sammler felt no prejudice about persuasion, about sexual matters. Nothing. It was too late in the day for that. Too much heat was on. Much larger powers of distortion were at work. The smash of Eisen's medallions on the pickpocket's face was still with Sammler. His own nerves, in the elementary way of nerves, connected this with the crushing of his eye under the rifle butt thirty years ago. The sensations of choking and falling—one *could* live through that again. If it was worth living through. He waited for the rubber bump of Elya's wheeled stretcher against the door.

"Has Wallace shown up? He was supposed to land at Newark."

"He didn't. I've got to tell you about Brother. When did you see him? I heard from Margotte about the pipes."

"In the flesh? I saw him last night. And this morning in the sky."

"Oh, so you watched him looping around, that idiot."

"Has he had an accident?"

"Oh, don't worry, he isn't hurt. I wish he had given himself a good bang, but he's like a Hollywood stunt man."

"He hasn't crashed, has he?"

"What do you think! It's already an item on the radio. He scraped his wheels off on a house."

"Dear Lord! Did he have to parachute? Was it your house?"

"He made a crash landing. It was some big place in Westchester. God alone knows why that creep should be out buzzing houses when we're in this predicament. It's enough to drive me mad."

"You don't mean that Elya heard this on the radio!"

"No, he didn't hear. He was already going down in the elevator."

"You say Wallace isn't hurt?"

"Wallace is in seventh heaven. Overjoyed. He had to have stitches in his cheek."

"I see. He'll have a scar. All this is terrible!"

"You have too much sympathy for him."

"I do admit that all this feeling sorry for people can be wearing. I also am provoked by him."

"You should be. They really ought to put my kid brother away. Lock him up in an asylum. You should have heard him babbling."

"Then you've spoken to him?"

"He had some guy to describe the beautiful landing. Then he took the phone in person. Something terrific. As if he had reached the North Pole by bicycle. You know we'll be sued for damages to the house. The plane is wrecked. Civil Aeronautics will take away his license. I wish they'd take him away, too. But he was very high. He said, 'Shouldn't we tell Dad?' "

"No!"

"Yes," said Angela. She was furious. With Dr. Cosbie, with Wallace, with Widick, Horricker. And she was bitter with Sammler, too. And he himself was far from normal. Far! The injured black man. The blood. And now, confronted by all that superfemininity, sensuality, he saw everything with heightened, clarity. As he had seen Riverside Drive, wickedly illuminated, after watching the purse being picked on the bus. That was how he was seeing now. To see was delicious. Oh, of course! An extreme pleasure! The sun may shine, and be a blessing, but sometimes shows the fury of the world. Brightness like this, the vividness of everything, also dismayed him. The soft clearness of Angela's face, the effort of her brows—the full mixture of fineness and rankness he saw there. And the sun was squarely at the window. The streaked glass ran with light like honey. A barrage of sweetness and intolerable brightness was laid down. Sammler did not really want to experience this. It all rose against him, too dizzy, too turbulent.

"I can see that you and Elya went on talking about that event."

"He won't let it alone. It's cruel. Both to himself and to me. I can't stop him."

"What is there for you to do but give in? He's the one with the thing to do. There should be no arguments. Perhaps young Mr. Horricker should come up. Why doesn't he come? Show that he doesn't take it too much to heart. Does he, by the way?"

"He says so."

"Maybe he loves you."

"Him? Who knows. But I wouldn't ask him to come. That would be using Daddy's illness."

"You don't want him back?"

"Want him? Maybe. I'm not sure."

Was there a successor in view? Human attachments being so light, there were probably lists of alternates, preconscious reserves—men met in the park while walking the dog; people one had chatted with at the Museum of Modern Art; this fellow with the sideburns; that one with dark sexy eyes; the person with the child in a sanitarium, the wife with multiple sclerosis. To go with quantities of ideas and purposes there were quantities of people. And all this came from Angela's conversation. He heard and remembered everything, every drab fact, every crimson touch. He didn't want to listen, but she told him things. He had no wish to remember, but he remembered it all. And Angela really was a beauty. She was big, but a beauty, a healthy young woman. Healthy young women have their needs. Her legs were—her thighs nearly all shown down from the green ribbon of skirt—she was, beautiful. Horricker would suffer, knowing he had lost her. Sammler was still thinking things through. Tired, dizzy, despairing, he still thought. Still in touch. With reality, that is.

"Wharton is no kid. He knew what he was getting into, down in Mexico," said Angela.

"Ah, I don't understand any of that. I assume he's read some of those books you lent me—Bataille and other theorists—about transgression and pain and sex; lust, crime, and desire; murder and erotic pleasure. It didn't mean much to me, any of that stuff."

"I know it's not your kind of thing. But Wharton got his kicks out of that little broad. He liked her. Better than I liked the other man. I'd never see *him* again. But then on the plane Wharton perversely became jealous. Wouldn't let it alone."

"My only thought is that Elya might feel more at peace with you if he saw Horricker."

"I'm furious that Wharton should blab to Widick, and Widick to Father."

"I'm not prepared to believe that Mr. Widick would speak to Elya of this. He's decent enough in most ways. I don't know him well, of course. My main impression is of a stout lawyer. Not a villain. A big soft face."

"That fat sonofabitch. I'll curse him when I see him. I'll tear his hair out."

"Don't be so sure that it was some evil-doer. You may be wrong. Elya's extremely intelligent and quick to pick up hints."

"Who could it be, then? Wallace? Emil? But whoever dropped the hint, it began with Wharton, too weak to keep his mouth shut. Well, if he wants to visit Father that's all right. But I'm offended. I'm furious."

"You do have a feverish look, Angela. I don't want to agitate you. But in view of your father's preoccupation with all this, with Mexico, do you think you should arrive in such a costume?"

"This skirt, you mean?"

"It's very short. My opinion may be worthless, but it seems bad judgment to wear that kind of sexual kindergarten dress."

"Now it's my clothes! Are you speaking for him, or for yourself?"

The sunlight was yellow, sweet. It was horrible.

"Oh yes, I know I may be out of order, with bad puritanical attitudes from the sick past which have damaged civilization so much. I did read your books. We've discussed all this. But really, how do you expect your father not to be excited, to feel bitter, when he sees this provoking Baby Doll costume?"

"Really? My skirt? It never occurred to me. I dressed quickly and ran out. This is a strange thing to take up with me now. Everybody wears these skirts. I don't think I care for the way you put it."

"Undoubtedly I could have put it better. I don't want to be disagreeable. There are other things to think about."

"That's right. And I'm under a terrible burden. It is terrible."

"I'm sure of it."

"I'm in despair, Uncle."

"Yes, you must be. Of course you are. Yes."

"Yes, what? It sounds as if there's something more."

"There is. I'm in a state, too, about your father. He's been a great friend to me. I am sick, too, about him."

"We don't have to beat around the bush, Uncle."

"No. He's going to die."

"That's coming out with it all right," she said. She was for plain speaking, was this too plain?

"It's as terrible to say as to hear."

"I'm sure you love Daddy," she said.

"I do."

"Apart from the practical reasons, I mean."

"Of course Shula and I have been supported by him. I never concealed my gratitude. I hope that has been no secret," said Sammler. As he was dry and old, the beating of his heart, even violent beating, would not be evident. "If I were practical, if I were very practical, I would be careful not to antagonize you. I think there are reasons other than the practical ones."

"Well, I hope we're not going to quarrel."

"That's right," said Sammler. She was angry with Wallace, with Cosbie, Horricker. He did not want to add himself to the list. He needed no victory over Angela. He only wanted to persuade her of something, and didn't know whether even that was feasible. But he was certainly not about to make war on suffering females. He began to talk. "I'm feeling very jumpy, Angela. There are certain damaged nerves you don't hear from for years, and then they act up, they flare up. They're burning now, very painfully. Now I'd like to say something about your father, as long as we're waiting for him. On the surface, I don't have much in common with Elya. He's a sentimental person. He makes a point, too much of a point, of treasuring certain old feelings. He's on an old system. I've always been skeptical of that myself. One might ask, where is the new system? But we don't have to get into that. I never had much natural liking for people who make open declarations of affection. Being a 'Britisher' was one of my foibles. Cold? But I still appreciate a certain restraint. I didn't care for the way Elya courted everyone, tried to make contact with people, winning their hearts, engaging their interest, getting personal even with waitresses, lab technicians, manicurists. It was always too easy for him to say 'I love you.' He was forever saying it to your mother in public, embarrassing her. I don't intend to discuss her with you. She had her good points. But as I was a snob about the British, she was a German Jewess who cultivated the Wasp style (now outmoded, by the way), and I recognized it. She was going to refine your father, an *Ostjude*. He was supposed to be the expressive one, the one with the heart. Isn't that about right? So your father was assigned to be expressive. He certainly had his work cut out for him with your mother. I think it would have been easier to love a theorem in geometry than your poor mother. Excuse me, Angela, for going on like this."

She said, "It's like we're sitting on the edge of a cliff anyway, waiting here."

"All right, Angela. One might as well talk, then. Not to add to your difficulties . . . I just saw something peculiarly nasty, on my way over. Partly my fault. I feel distressed. But I was saying that your father has had his assignments. Husband, medical man—he was a good doctor—family man, success, American, wealthy retirement with a Rolls Royce. We have our assignments. Feeling, outgoingness, expressiveness, kindness, heart—all these fine human things which by a peculiar turn of opinion strike people now as shady activities. Openness and candor about vices seem far easier. Anyway, there is Elya's assignment. That's what's in his good face. That's why he has such a human look. He's made something of himself. He hasn't done badly. He didn't like surgery. You know that. He dreaded those three- and four-hour operations. But he performed them. He did what he disliked. He had an unsure loyalty to certain pure states. He knew there had been good men before him, that there were good men to come, and he wanted to be one of them. I think he did all right. I don't come out nearly so well myself. Till forty or so I was simply an Anglophile intellectual Polish Jew and person of culture—relatively useless. But Elya, by sentimental repetition and by formulas if you like, partly by propaganda, has accomplished something good. Brought himself through. He loves you. I'm sure he loves Wallace. I believe he loves me. I've learned much from him. I have no illusions about your father, you understand. He's touchy, boastful, he repeats himself. He's vain, grouchy, proud. But he's done well, and I admire him."

"So he's human. All right, he's human." She was, perhaps, only half following him, though she looked straight at him, full-face, knees apart so that he saw the pink material of her undergarment. Seeing that pink band, he thought, Why argue? What is the point? But he replied.

"Well, everybody's human only in some degree. Some more than others."

"Some very little?"

"That's the way it seems. Very little. Faulty. Scanty. Dangerous."

"I thought everybody was born human."

"It's not a natural gift at all. Only the capacity is natural."

"Well, Uncle, why are you putting me through this? What have you got in mind? You're after something."

"Yes, I suppose I am."

"You're criticizing me."

"No, I'm praising your father."

Angela's gaze was dilated, brilliant, smeary, angry. No fights, for God's sake, with a despairing woman. Still, he was getting at something. He held his thin body rigid; the ginger-gray brows overhung the tinted dimness of the shades.

"I don't like the opinion I think you have of me," she said.

"Why should that matter on a day like this? Well, perhaps I do feel that today there ought to be a difference. Perhaps if we were in India or Finland we might not be in quite the same mood. New York makes one think about the collapse of civilization, about Sodom and Gomorrah, the end of the world. The end wouldn't come as surprise here. Many people already bank on it. And I don't know whether humankind is really all that much worse. In one day, Caesar massacred the Tencteri, four hundred and thirty thousand souls. Even Rome was appalled. I am not sure that this is the worst of all times. But it is in the air now that things are falling apart, and I am affected by it. I always hated people who declared that it was the end. What did they know about the end? From personal experience, from the grave if I may say so, *I* knew something about it. But I was flat, dead wrong. Anybody may feel the truth. But suppose it to be true—true, and not a mood, not ignorance or destructive pleasure or the doom desired by people who have botched everything. Suppose it to be so. There is still such a thing as a man—or there was. There are still human qualities. Our weak species fought its fear, our crazy species fought its criminality. We are an animal of genius."

This was a thing he often thought. At the moment it was only a formula. He did not thoroughly feel it.

"O.K., Uncle."

"But we don't have to decide whether the world is ending. The point is that for your father it *is* the end."

"Why are you pushing that, as if I didn't know. What do you want from me?"

Indeed what? From her, sitting there, breasts shown, diffusing woman-odors, big eyes practically merged; tormented, and at this moment strangely badgered by Caesar and the Tencteri, by ideas. Let the poor creature be. For now she was claiming to be a poor creature. And she was. But he could not let her be—not yet.

"As a rule these aneurysms cause instant death," he said. "With Elya there has been a delay, which gives an opportunity."

"An opportunity? What do you mean?"

"A chance to resolve some things. And it has made your father realistic—facing up to facts that were obscure."

"Facts about me, for instance? He didn't really want to know about me."

"Yes."

"What are you getting at?"

"You've got to do something for him. He has a need."

"What something am I supposed to do?"

"That's up to you. If you love him, you can make some sign. He's grieving. He's in a rage. He's disappointed. And I don't really think it is the sex. At this moment that might well be a trivial consideration. Don't you see, Angela? You wouldn't need to do much. It would give the man a last opportunity to collect himself."

"As far as I can see, if there is anything at all in what you say, you want an old-time deathbed scene."

"What difference does it make what you call it?"

"I should ask him to forgive me? Are you serious?"

"I am perfectly serious."

"But how could I— It goes against everything. You're talking to the wrong person. Even for my father it would be too hokey. I can't see it."

"He's been a good man. And he's being swept out. Can't you think of something to say to him?"

"What is there to say? And can't you think of anything but death?"

"But that's what we have before us."

"And you won't stop. I know you're going to say something more. Well, say it."

"In so many words?"

"In so many words. The fewer the better."

"I don't know what happened in Mexico. The details don't matter. I only note the peculiarity that it is possible to be gay, amorous, intimate with holiday acquaintances. Diversions, group intercourse, fellatio with strangers—one can do that but not come to terms with one's father at the last opportunity. He's put an immense amount of feeling into you. Probably most of his feeling has gone toward you. If you can in some way see this and make some return . . ."

"Uncle Sammler!" She was furious.

"Ah. You're angry. Naturally."

"You've insulted me. You've been trying hard enough. Well, now you have—you've insulted me, Uncle Sammler."

"It was not the object. I only believe that there are things everyone knows, and must know."

"For God's sake, quit this."

"I shall mind my own business."

"You lead a special life in that dumpy room. Charming, but what's it got to do with anything! I don't think you understand people's business. What do you mean about fellatio? What do *you* know about it?"

Well, it hadn't worked. What she threw at him was what the young man at Columbia had also cried out. He was out of it. A tall, dry, not agreeable old man, censorious, giving himself airs. Who in hell was he? *Hors d'usage*. Against the wall. *A la lanterne!* Very well. That was little enough. He ought not perhaps to have provoked Angela so painfully. By now he himself was shaking.

The gray nurse at this moment came and called Sammler to the telephone. "You are Mr. Sammler, aren't you?"

He started. Quickly he got to his feet. "Ah! Who wants me? Who is it?" He didn't know what to expect.

"The phone wants you. Your daughter. You can take it outside, at the desk."

"Yes, Shula, yes?" her father said. "Speak up. What is it? Where are you?"

"In New Rochelle. Where is Elya?"

"We are waiting for him. What do you want now, Shula?"

"Have you heard about Wallace?"

"Yes, I've heard."

"He did a really great thing when he brought in that plane without wheels."

"Yes, magnificent. He's certainly marvelous. Now, Shula, I want you out of there. You are not to prowl around that house, you have no business there. I wanted you to come back with me. You are not supposed to disobey me."

"I wouldn't dream of it."

"But you did."

"I didn't. If we differ, it's in your interest."

"Shula, don't fool with me. Enough of my interests. Let them alone. You called with a purpose. I'm afraid I begin to understand."

"Yes, Father."

"You succeeded!"

"Yes, Father, aren't you pleased? In the—guess where? In the den where you slept. In the hassock you sat on this morning. When I brought in the coffee and saw you on it, I said, 'That's where the money is.' I was just about sure. So when you went away, I came back and opened it up, and it was filled—filled with money. Would you think that about Cousin Elya? I'm surprised at him. I didn't want to believe it. The hassock was upholstered with packages of hundred-dollar bills. Money was the stuffing."

"Dear God."

"I haven't counted it," she said.

"I will not have you lying."

"All right, I did count. But I don't really know about money. I don't understand business."

"Did you speak to Wallace on the phone?"

"Yes."

"And did you tell him about this?"

"I didn't say one single word."

"Good, very good, Shula. I expect you to turn it over to Mr. Widick. Call him to come and get it, and tell him you want a receipt for it."

"Father!"

"Yes, Shula."

He waited. He knew that, gripping one of those New Rochelle white telephones, she was marshaling her arguments, she was mastering her resentment at his ancient-father's stubbornness and stupid rectitude. At her expense. He knew quite well what she was feeling. "What will you live on, Father, when Elya is gone?" she said.

An excellent question, a shrewd, relevant question. He had lost out with Angela, he had infuriated her. He knew what she would say. "I'll never forgive you, Uncle." And what's more she never would.

"We will live on what there is."

"But suppose he doesn't leave any provision?"

"That's as he wishes. Up to him, entirely."

"We are part of the family. You are the closest to him."

"You will do as I tell you."

"Listen to me, Father. I have to look out for you. You haven't even said anything to me about finding this."

"It was damn clever of you, Shula. Yes. Congratulations. That was clever."

"It really was. I noticed how the hassock bulged under you, not like other hassocks, and when I felt around I heard the money rustle. I knew from the rustle, what it was. Of course I didn't say anything to Wallace. He'd squander it in a week. I thought I'd buy some clothes. If I was dressed at Lord and Taylor, maybe I'd be less of an eccentric type, and I'd have a chance with somebody."

"Like Govinda Lal."

"Yes, why not? I've made myself as interesting as I could within my means."

Her father was astonished by this. Eccentric type? She *was* aware of herself, then. There *was* a degree of choice. Wig, scavenging, shopping bags, were to an extent deliberate. Was that what she meant? How fascinating!

"And I think," she was saying, "that we should keep this. I think Elya would agree. I'm a woman without a husband, and I've never had children, and this money comes from preventing children, and I think it's only right that I should take it. For you, too, Father."

"I'm afraid not, Shula. Elya may already have told Mr.

Widick about this hoard. I'm sorry. But we're not thieves. It's not our money. Tell me how much it was?"

"Each time I count, it's different."

"How much was it the last time?"

"Either six or eight thousand. I laid it all out on the floor. But I was too excited to count straight."

"I assume it's much, much more, and I can't allow you to keep any."

"I won't."

Of course she would, he was certain of it. As a trash-collector, treasure-hunter, she would be unable to surrender it all.

"You must give Widick every cent."

"Yes, Father. It's painful, but I will. I'll hand it over to Widick. I think you're making a mistake."

"No mistake. And don't take off as you did with Govinda's manuscript."

Too late to be tempted. One more desire gone. He very nearly smiled at himself.

"Good-by, Shula. You're a good daughter. The best of any. No better daughter."

Wallace, then, had been right about his father. He had done favors for the Mafia. Performed some operations. The money did exist. There was no time to think about all this, however. He put up the phone and left the marble counter to find that Dr. Cosbie had been waiting for him. The one-time football star in his white coat held his upper lip pressed by the nether one. The bloodless face and gas-blue eyes had been trained to transmit surgeons' messages. The message was plain. It was all over.

"When did he die?" said Sammler. "Just now?"

While I was stupidly urging Angela!

"A little while back. We had him down in the special unit, doin' the maximum possible."

"You couldn't do anything about a hemorrhage, I see, yes."

"You are his uncle. He asked me to say good-by to you."

"I wish I had been able to say it also to him. So it didn't happen in one rush?"

"He knew it was startin'. He was a doctor. He knew it. He asked me to take him from the room."

"He asked you to?"

"It was obvious he wanted to spare his daughter. So I said tests. It's Miss Angela?"

"Yes, Angela."

"He said he preferred downstairs. He knew I'd take him anyway."

"Of course. As a surgeon, Elya knew. He certainly knew the operation was futile, all that torture of putting a screw in his throat." Sammler removed his glasses. His eyes, one a sightless bubble, under the hair of overhanging brows, were level with Dr. Cosbie's. "Of course it was futile."

"The procedure was correct. He knew it was."

"My nephew wished always to agree. Of course he knew. It might have been kinder though not to make him go through it."

"I suppose you want to go in and tell Miss Angela?"

"Please tell Miss Angela yourself. What I want is to see my nephew. How do I get to him? Give me directions."

"You'll have to wait and see him at the chapel, sir. It's not allowed."

"Young man, it is important and you had better allow me. Take my word for it. I am determined. Let us not have a bad scene out here in the corridor. You would not want that, would you?"

"Would you make one?"

"I would."

"I'll send his nurse with you," said the doctor.

They went down in the elevator, the gray woman and Mr. Sammler, and through lower passages paved in speckled material, through tunnels, up and down ramps, past laboratories and supply rooms. Well, this famous truth for which he was so keen, he had it now, or it had him. He felt that be was being destroyed, what was left of him. He wept to himself. He walked at the habitual rapid sweeping pace, waiting at the crossways for the escorting nurse. In stirring air flavored with body-things, sickness, drugs. He felt that be was breaking up, that irregular big fragments inside were melting, sparkling with pain, floating off. Well, Elya was gone. He was deprived of one more thing, stripped of one more creature. One more reason to live trickled out. He lost his breath. Then the women came up. More hundreds of yards in this winding underground smelling of serum, of organic soup, of fungus, of cell-brew. The nurse took Sammler's hat and said, "In there." The door sign read P.M. That would mean post-mortem. They were ready to do an autopsy as soon as Angela signed the papers. And of course she would sign. Let's find out what went wrong. And then cremation.

"To see Dr. Gruner. Where?" said Sammler.

The attendant pointed to the wheeled stretcher on which Elya lay. Sammler uncovered his face. The nostrils, the creases were very dark, the shut eyes pale and full, the bald head high-marked by gradients of wrinkles. In the lips bitterness and an expression of obedience were combined.

Sammler in a mental whisper said, "Well, Elya. Well, well, Elya." And then in the same way he said, "Remember, God, the soul of Elya Gruner, who, as willingly as possible and as well as he was able, and even to an intolerable point, and even in suffocation and even as death was coming was eager, even childishly perhaps (may I be forgiven for this), even with a certain servility, to do what was required of him. At his best this man was much kinder than at my very best I have ever been or could ever be. He was aware that he must meet, and he did meet—through all the confusion and degraded clowning of this life through which we are speeding—he did meet the terms of his contract. The terms which, in his inmost heart, each man knows. As I know mine. As all know. For that is the truth of it—that we all know, God, that we know, that we know, we know, we know."

HUMBOLDT'S GIFT

THE book of ballads published by Von Humboldt Fleisher in the Thirties was an immediate hit. Humboldt was just what everyone had been waiting for. Out in the Midwest I had certainly been waiting eagerly, I can tell you that. An avant-garde writer, the first of a new generation, he was handsome, fair, large, serious, witty, he was learned. The guy had it all. All the papers reviewed his book. His picture appeared in *Time* without insult and in *Newsweek* with praise. I read *Harlequin Ballads* enthusiastically. I was a student at the University of Wisconsin and thought about nothing but literature day and night. Humboldt revealed to me new ways of doing things. I was ecstatic. I envied his luck, his talent, and his fame, and I went east in May to have a look at him—perhaps to get next to him. The Greyhound bus, taking the Scranton route, made the trip in about fifty hours. That didn't matter. The bus windows were open. I had never seen real mountains before. Trees were budding. It was like Beethoven's *Pastorale.* I felt showered by the green, within. Manhattan was fine, too. I took a room for three bucks a week and found a job selling Fuller Brushes door to door. And I was wildly excited about everything. Having written Humboldt a long fan letter, I was invited to Greenwich Village to discuss literature and ideas. He lived on Bedford Street, near Chumley's. First he gave me black coffee, and then poured gin in the same cup. "Well, you're a nice-looking enough fellow, Charlie," he said to me. "Aren't you a bit sly, maybe? I think you're headed for early baldness. And such large emotional handsome eyes. But you certainly do love literature and that's the main thing. You have sensibility," he said. He was a pioneer in the use of this word. Sensibility later made it big. Humboldt was very kind. He introduced me to people in the Village and got me books to review. I always loved him.

Humboldt's success lasted about ten years. In the late Forties he started to sink. In the early Fifties I myself became famous. I even made a pile of money. Ah, money, the money! Humboldt held the money against me. In the last years of his life when he wasn't too depressed to talk, wasn't locked up in a loony bin, he went about New York saying bitter things about me and my "million dollars." "Take the case of Charlie Citrine. He arrived from Madison, Wisconsin, and knocked on my door. Now he's got a million bucks. What kind of writer or intellectual makes that kind of dough—a Keynes? Okay. Keynes, a world figure. A genius in economics, a prince in Bloomsbury," said Humboldt. "Married to a Russian ballerina. The money follows. But who the hell is Citrine to become so rich? We used to be close friends," Humboldt accurately said. "But there's something perverse with that guy. After making this dough why does he bury himself in the sticks? What's he in Chicago for? He's afraid to be found out."

Whenever his mind was sufficiently clear he used his gifts to knock me. He did a great job.

And money wasn't what I had in mind. Oh God, no, what I wanted was to do good. I was dying to do something good. And this feeling for good went back to my early and peculiar sense of existence—sunk in the glassy depths of life and groping, thrillingly and desperately, for sense, a person keenly aware of painted veils, of Maya, of domes of many-colored glass staining the white radiance of eternity, quivering in the intense inane and so on. I was quite a nut about such things. Humboldt knew this, really, but toward the end he could not afford to give me any sympathy. Sick and sore, he wouldn't let up on me. He only stressed the contradiction between the painted veils and the big money. But such sums as I made, made themselves. Capitalism made them for dark comical reasons of its own. The world did it. Yesterday I read in *The Wall Street Journal* about the melancholy of affluence, "Not in all the five millennia of man's recorded history have so many been so affluent." Minds formed by five millennia of scarcity are distorted. The heart can't take this sort of change. Sometimes it just refuses to accept it.

In the Twenties kids in Chicago hunted for treasure in the March thaw. Dirty snow hillocks formed along the curbs and when they melted, water ran braided and brilliant in the gutters and you could find marvelous loot—bottle tops, machine gears, Indian-head pennies. And last spring, almost an elderly fellow now, I found that I had left the sidewalk and that I was following the curb and looking. For what? What was I doing? Suppose I found a dime? Suppose I found a fifty-cent piece? What then? I don't know how the child's soul had gotten back, but it was back. Everything was melting. Ice, discretion, maturity. What would Humboldt have said to this?

When reports were brought of the damaging remarks he made I often found that I agreed with him. "They gave Citrine a Pulitzer prize for his book on Wilson and Tumulty. The Pulitzer is for the birds—for the pullets. It's just a dummy newspaper publicity award given by crooks and illiterates. You become a walking Pulitzer ad, so even when you croak the first words of the obituary are 'Pulitzer prizewinner passes.'" He had a point, I thought. "And Charlie is a double Pulitzer. First came that schmaltzy play. Which made him a fortune on Broadway. Plus movie rights. He got a percentage of the gross! And I don't say he actually plagiarized, but he did steal something from me—my personality. He built my personality into his hero."

Even here, sounding wild, he had grounds, perhaps.

He was a wonderful talker, a hectic nonstop monologuist and improvisator, a champion detractor. To be loused up by Humboldt was really a kind of privilege. It was like being the subject of a two-nosed portrait by Picasso, or an eviscerated chicken by Soutine. Money always inspired him. He adored talking about the rich. Brought up on New York tabloids, he often mentioned the golden scandals of yesteryear, Peaches and Daddy Browning, Harry Thaw and Evelyn Nesbit, plus the Jazz Age, Scott Fitzgerald, and the Super-Rich. The heiresses of Henry James he knew cold. There were times when he himself schemed comically to make a fortune. But his real wealth was literary. He had read many thousands of books. He said that history was a nightmare during which he was trying to get a good night's rest. Insomnia made him more learned. In the small hours he read thick books—Marx and Sombart, Toynbee, Rostovtzeff, Freud. When he spoke of wealth he was in a position to compare Roman *luxus* with American Protestant riches. He generally got around to the Jews—Joyce's silk-hatted Jews outside the Bourse. And he wound up with the gold-plated skull or death mask of Agamemnon, dug up by Schliemann. Humboldt could really talk.

His father, a Jewish Hungarian immigrant, had ridden with Pershing's cavalry in Chihuahua, chasing Pancho Villa in a Mexico of whores and horses (very different from my own father, a small gallant person who shunned such things). His old man had plunged into America. Humboldt spoke of boots, bugles, and bivouacs. Later came limousines, luxury hotels, palaces in Florida. His father had lived in Chicago during the boom. He was in the real-estate business and kept a suite at the Edgewater Beach Hotel. Summers, his son was sent for. Humboldt knew Chicago, too. In the days of Hack Wilson and Woody English the Fleishers had a box at Wrigley Field. They drove to the game in a Pierce-Arrow or a Hispano-Suiza (Humboldt was car-crazy). And there were lovely John Held, Jr., girls, beautiful, who wore step-ins. And whisky and gangsters and the pillared doom-dark La Salle Street banks with railroad money and pork and reaper money locked in steel vaults. Of this Chicago I was completely ignorant when I arrived from Appleton. I played Piggie-move-up with Polish kids under the El tracks. Humboldt ate devil's-food coconut-marshmallow layer cake at Henrici's. I never saw the inside of Henrici's.

I did, once, see Humboldt's mother in her dark apartment on West End Avenue. Her face was like her son's. She was mute, fat, broad-lipped, tied up in a bathrobe. Her hair was white, bushy, Fijian. The melanin was on the back of her hands and on her dark face still darker spots as large as her eyes. Humboldt bent over to speak to her, and she answered nothing but stared out with some powerful female grievance. He was gloomy when we left the building and he said, "She used to let me go to Chicago but I was supposed to spy on the old man and copy out bank statements and account numbers and write down the names of his hookers. She was going to sue him. She's mad, you see. But then he lost everything in the crash. Died of a heart attack down in Florida."

This was the background of those witty cheerful ballads. He was a manic depressive (his own diagnosis). He owned a set of Freud's works and read psychiatric journals. Once you had read the *Psychopathology of Everyday Life* you knew that everyday life *was* psychopathology. That was all right with Humboldt. He often quoted me *King Lear*: "In cities, mutinies; in countries, discord; in palaces, treason; and the bond cracked 'twixt son and father. . . ." He stressed "son and father." "Ruinous disorders follow us disquietly to our graves."

Well, that's where ruinous disorders followed him seven years ago. And now as new anthologies came out I went down to Brentano's basement and checked them. Humboldt's poems were omitted. The bastards, the literary funeral directors and politicians who put together these collections had no use for old-hat Humboldt. So all his thinking, writing, feeling counted for nothing, all the raids behind the lines to bring back beauty had no effect except to wear him out. He dropped dead in a dismal hotel off Times Square. I, a different sort of writer, remained to mourn him in prosperity out in Chicago.

The noble idea of being an American poet certainly made Humboldt feel at times like a card, a boy, a comic, a fool. We lived like bohemians and graduate students in a mood of fun and games. Maybe America didn't need art and inner miracles. It had so many outer ones. The USA was a big operation, very big. The more *it*, the less *we*. So Humboldt behaved like an eccentric and a comic subject. But occasionally there was a break in his eccentricity when he stopped and thought. He tried to think himself clear away from this American world (I did that, too). I could see that Humboldt was pondering what to do between *then* and *now*, between birth and death, to satisfy certain great questions. Such brooding didn't make him any saner. He tried drugs and drink. Finally, many courses of shock treatment had to be administered. It was, as he saw it, Humboldt versus madness. Madness was a whole lot stronger.

I wasn't doing so well myself recently when Humboldt acted from the grave, so to speak, and made a basic change in my life. In spite of our big fight and fifteen years of estrangement he left me something in his will. I came into a legacy.

HE was a great entertainer but going insane. The pathologic element could be missed only by those who were laughing too hard to look. Humboldt, that grand erratic handsome person with his wide blond face, that charming fluent deeply worried man to whom I was so attached, passionately lived out the theme of Success. Naturally he died a Failure. What else can result from the capitalization of such nouns? Myself, I've always held the number of sacred words down. In my opinion Humboldt had too long a list of them—Poetry, Beauty, Love, Waste Land, Alienation, Politics, History, the Unconscious. And, of course, Manic and Depressive, always capitalized. According to him, America's great Manic Depressive was Lincoln. And Churchill with what he called his Black Dog moods was a classic case of Manic Depression. "Like me, Charlie," said Humboldt. "But think—if Energy is Delight and if Exuberance is Beauty, the Manic Depressive knows more about Delight and Beauty than anyone else. Who else has so much Energy and Exuberance? Maybe it's the strategy of the Psyche to increase Depression. Didn't Freud say that Happiness was nothing but the remission of Pain? So the more Pain the intenser the Happiness. But there is a prior origin to this, and the Psyche makes Pain on purpose. Anyway, Mankind is stunned by the Exuberance and Beauty of certain individuals. When a Manic Depressive escapes from his Furies he's irresistible. He captures History. I think that aggravation is a secret technique of the Unconscious. As for great men and kings being History's slaves, I think Tolstoi was off the track. Don't kid yourself, kings are the most sublime sick. Manic Depressive heroes pull Mankind into their cycles and carry everybody away."

Poor Humboldt didn't impose his cycles for very long. He never became the radiant center of his age. Depression fastened on him for good. The periods of mania and poetry ended. Three decades after *Harlequin Ballads* made him famous he died of a heart attack in a flophouse in the West Forties, one of those midtown branches of the Bowery. On that night I happened to be in New York. I was there on Business—i.e., up to no good. None of my Business was any good. Estranged from everybody, he was living in a place called the Ilscombe. I went later to have a look at it. Welfare lodged old people there. He died on a rotten hot night. Even at the Plaza I was uncomfortable. Carbon monoxide was thick. Throbbing air conditioners dripped on you in the street. A bad night. And on the 727 jet, as I was flying back to Chicago next morning, I opened the *Times* and found Humboldt's obituary.

I knew that Humboldt would soon die because I had seen him on the street two months before and he had death all over him. He didn't see me. He was gray stout sick dusty, he had bought a pretzel stick and was eating it. His lunch. Concealed by a parked car, I watched. I didn't approach him, I felt it was impossible. For once my Business in the East was legitimate and I was not chasing some broad but preparing a magazine article. And just that morning I had been flying over New York in a procession of Coast Guard helicopters with Senators Javits and Robert Kennedy. Then I had attended a political luncheon in Central Park at the Tavern on the Green, where all the celebrities became ecstatic at the sight of one another. I was, as they say, "in great shape" myself. If I don't look well, I look busted. But I knew that I looked well. Besides, there was money in my pockets and I had been window-shopping on Madison Avenue. If any Cardin or Hermès necktie pleased me I could buy it without asking the price. My belly was flat, I wore boxer shorts of combed Sea Island cotton at eight bucks a pair. I had joined an athletic club in Chicago and with elderly effort kept myself in shape. I played a swift hard game of paddle ball, a form of squash. So how could I talk to Humboldt? It was too much. While I was in the helicopter whopping over Manhattan, viewing New York as if I were passing in a glass-bottomed boat over a tropical reef, Humboldt was probably groping among his bottles for a drop of juice to mix with his morning gin.

I became, after Humboldt's death, an even more intense physical culturist. Last Thanksgiving Day I ran away from a mugger in Chicago. He jumped from a dark alley and I beat it. It was pure reflex. I leaped away and sprinted down the middle of the street. As a boy I was not a remarkable runner. How was it that in my middle fifties I became inspired with flight and capable of great bursts of speed? Later that same night I boasted, "I can still beat a junkie in the hundred-yard dash." And to whom did I brag of this power of my legs? To a young woman named Renata. We were lying in bed. I told her how I took off—I ran like hell, I flew. And she said to me, as if on cue (ah, the courtesy, the gentility of these beautiful girls), "You're in terrific shape, Charlie. You're not a big fellow but you're sturdy, solid, and you're elegant also." She stroked my naked sides. So my pal Humboldt was gone. Probably his very bones had crumbled in potter's field. Perhaps there was nothing in his grave but a few lumps of soot. But Charlie Citrine was still outspeeding passionate criminals in the streets of Chicago, and Charlie Citrine was in terrific shape and lay beside a voluptuous friend. This Citrine could now perform a certain Yoga exercise and had learned to stand on his head to relieve his arthritic neck. About my low cholesterol Renata was well informed. Also I repeated to her the doctor's comments about my amazingly youthful prostate and my supernormal EKG. Strengthened in illusion and idiocy by these proud medical reports, I embraced a busty Renata on this Posturepedic mattress. She gazed at me with love-pious eyes. I inhaled her delicious damp, personally participating in the triumph of American civilization (now tinged with the Oriental colors of Empire). But in some phantom Atlantic City boardwalk of the mind I saw a different Citrine, this one on the border of senility, his back hooked, and feeble. Oh very, very feeble, pushed in a wheelchair past the little salt ripples, ripples which, like myself, were puny. And who was pushing my chair? Was it Renata—the Renata I had taken in the wars of Happiness by a quick Patton-thrust of armor? No, Renata was a grand girl, but I couldn't see her behind my wheelchair. Renata? Not Renata. Certainly not.

Out in Chicago Humboldt became one of my significant dead. I spent far too much time mooning about and communing with the dead. Besides, my name was linked with Humboldt's, for, as the past receded, the Forties began to be valuable to people fabricating cultural rainbow textiles, and the word went out that in Chicago there was a fellow still alive who used to be Von Humboldt Fleisher's friend, a man named Charles Citrine. People doing articles, academic theses, and books wrote to me or flew in to discuss Humboldt with me. And I must say that in Chicago Humboldt was a natural subject for reflection. Lying at the southern end of the Great Lakes—twenty percent of the world's supply of fresh water—Chicago with its gigantesque outer life contained the whole problem of poetry and the inner life in America. Here you could look into such things through a sort of fresh-water transparency.

"How do you account, Mr. Citrine, for the rise and fall of Von Humboldt Fleisher?"

"Young people, what do you aim to do with the facts about Humboldt, publish articles and further your careers? This is pure capitalism."

I thought about Humboldt with more seriousness and sorrow than may be apparent in this account. I didn't love so many people. I couldn't afford to lose anyone. One infallible sign of love was that I dreamed of Humboldt so often. Every time I saw him I was terribly moved, and cried in my sleep. Once I dreamed that we met at Whelan's Drugstore on the corner of Sixth and Eighth in Greenwich Village. He was not the stricken leaden swollen man I had seen on Forty-sixth Street, but still the stout normal Humboldt of middle life. He was sitting beside me at the soda fountain with a Coke. I burst into tears. I said, "Where have you been? I thought you were dead."

He was very mild, quiet, and he seemed extremely well pleased, and he said, "Now I understand everything."

"Everything? What's everything?"

But he only said, "Everything." I couldn't get more out of him, and I wept with happiness. Of course it was only a dream such as you dream if your soul is not well. My waking character is far from sound. I'll never get any medals for character. And all such things must be utterly clear to the dead. They have finally left the problematical cloudy earthly and human sphere. I have a hunch that in life you look outward from the ego, your center. In death you are at the periphery looking inward. You see your old pals at Whelan's still struggling with the heavy weight of selfhood, and you hearten them by intimating that when their turn comes to enter eternity they too will begin to comprehend and at last get an idea of what has happened. As none of this is Scientific, we are afraid to think it.

All right, then, I will try to summarize: at the age of twenty-two Von Humboldt Fleisher published his first book of ballads. You would have thought that the son of neurotic immigrants from Eighty-ninth and West End—his extravagant papa hunting Pancho Villa and, in the photo Humboldt showed me, with a head so curly that his garrison cap was falling off; his mama, from one of those Potash and Perlmutter yapping fertile baseball-and-business families, darkly pretty at first, then gloomy mad and silent—that such a young man would be clumsy, that his syntax would be unacceptable to fastidious goy critics on guard for the Protestant Establishment and the Genteel Tradition. Not at all. The ballads were pure, musical, witty, radiant, humane. I think they were Platonic. By Platonic I refer to an original perfection to which all human beings long to return. Yes, Humboldt's words were impeccable. Genteel America had nothing to worry about. It was in a tizzy—it expected Anti-Christ to burst out of the slums. Instead this Humboldt Fleisher turned up with a love-offering. He behaved like a gentleman. He was charming. So he was warmly welcomed. Conrad Aiken praised him, T. S. Eliot took favorable notice of his poems, and even Yvor Winters had a good word to say for him. As for me, I borrowed thirty bucks and enthusiastically went to New York to talk things over with him on Bedford Street. This was in 1938. We crossed the Hudson on the Christopher Street ferry to eat clams in Hoboken and talked about the problems of modern poetry. I mean that Humboldt lectured me about them. Was Santayana right? Was modern poetry barbarous? Modern poets had more wonderful material than Homer or Dante. What they didn't have was a sane and steady idealization. To be Christian was impossible, to be pagan also. That left you-know-what.

I had come to hear that great things might be true. This I was told on the Christopher Street ferry. Marvelous gestures had to be made and Humboldt made them. He told me that poets ought to figure out how to get around pragmatic America. He poured it on for me that day. And there I was, having raptures, gotten up as a Fuller Brush salesman in a smothering wool suit, a hand-me-down from Julius. The pants were big in the waist and the shirt ballooned out, for my brother Julius had a fat chest. I wiped my sweat with a handkerchief stitched with a J.

Humboldt himself was just beginning to put on weight. He was thick through the shoulders but still narrow at the hips. Later he got a prominent belly, like Babe Ruth. His legs were restless and his feet made nervous movements. Below, shuffling comedy; above, princeliness and dignity, a certain nutty charm. A surfaced whale beside your boat might look at you as he looked with his wide-set gray eyes. He was fine as well as thick, heavy but also light, and his face was both pale and dark. Golden-brownish hair flowed upward—two light crests and a dark trough. His forehead was scarred. As a kid he had fallen on a skate blade, the bone itself was dented. His pale lips were prominent and his mouth was full of immature-looking teeth, like milk teeth. He consumed his cigarettes to the last spark and freckled his tie and his jacket with burns.

The subject that afternoon was Success. I was from the sticks and he was giving me the low-down. Could I imagine, he said, what it meant to knock the Village flat with your poems and then follow up with critical essays in the *Partisan* and the *Southern Review*? He had much to tell me about Modernism, Symbolism, Yeats, Rilke, Eliot. Also, he was a pretty good drinker. And of course there were lots of girls. Besides, New York was then a very Russian city, so we had Russia all over the place. It was a case, as Lionel Abel said, of a metropolis that yearned to belong to another country. New York dreamed of leaving North America and merging with Soviet Russia. Humboldt easily went in his conversation from Babe Ruth to Rosa Luxemburg and Béla Kun and Lenin. Then and there I realized that if I didn't read Trotsky at once I wouldn't be worth conversing with. Humboldt talked to me about Zinoviev, Kamenev, Bukharin, the Smolny Institute, the Shakhty engineers, the Moscow trials, Sidney Hook's *From Hegel to Marx*, Lenin's *State and Revolution*. In fact, he compared himself to Lenin. "I know," he said, "how Lenin felt in October when he exclaimed, '*Es schwindelt!*' He didn't mean that he was *schwindling* everyone but that he felt giddy. Lenin, tough as he was, was like a young girl waltzing. Me too. I have vertigo from success, Charlie. My ideas won't let me sleep. I go to bed without a drink and the room is whirling. It'll happen to you, too. I tell you this to prepare you," Humboldt said. In flattery he had a marvelous touch.

Madly excited, I looked diffident. Of course I was in a state of intense preparation and hoped to knock everybody dead. Each morning at the Fuller Brush sales-team pep meeting we said in unison, "I'm fine and dandy, how are you?" But I actually was fine and dandy. I didn't have to put it on. I couldn't have been more eager—eager to greet housewives, eager to come in and see their kitchens, eager to hear their tales and their complaints. The passionate hypochondria of Jewish women was new to me then, I was keen to hear about their tumors and their swollen legs. I wanted them to tell me about marriage, childbirth, money, sickness, and death. Yes, I tried to put them into categories as I sat there drinking coffee. They were petty bourgeois, husband-killers, social climbers, hysterics, etcetera. But it was no use, this analytical skepticism. I was too enthusiastic. So I eagerly peddled my brushes, and just as eagerly I went to the Village at night and listened to the finest talkers in New York—Schapiro, Hook, Rahv, Huggins, and Gumbein. Under their eloquence I sat like a cat in a recital hall. But Humboldt was the best of them all. He was simply the Mozart of conversation.

On the ferryboat Humboldt said, "I made it too young, I'm in trouble." He was off then. His spiel took in Freud, Heine, Wagner, Goethe in Italy, Lenin's dead brother, Wild Bill Hickok's costumes, the New York Giants, Ring Lardner on grand opera, Swinburne on flagellation, and John D. Rockefeller on religion. In the midst of these variations the theme was always ingeniously and excitingly retrieved. That afternoon the streets looked ashen but the deck of the ferry was bright gray. Humboldt was slovenly and grand, his mind undulating like the water and the waves of blond hair rising on his head, his face with widely separated gray eyes white and tense, his hands deep in his pockets, and his feet in polo boots set close together.

If Scott Fitzgerald had been a Protestant, said Humboldt, Success wouldn't have damaged him so much. Look at Rockefeller Senior, he knew how to handle Success, he simply said that God had given him all his dough. Of course that was stewardship. That was Calvinism. Once he had spoken of Calvinism, Humboldt was bound to go on to Grace and Depravity. From Depravity he moved to Henry Adams, who said that in a few decades mechanical progress would break our necks anyway, and from Henry Adams he went into the question of eminence in an age of revolutions, melting pots, and masses, and from this he turned to Tocqueville, Horatio Alger, and Ruggles of Red Gap. Movie-mad Humboldt followed *Screen Gossip* magazine. He personally remembered Mae Murray like a goddess in sequins on the stage of Loew's inviting kids to visit her in California. "She starred in *The Queen of Tasmania* and *Circe the Enchantress*, but she ended as a poorhouse crone. And what about what's-his-name who killed himself in the hospital? He took a fork and hammered it into his heart with the heel of his shoe, poor fellow!"

This was sad. But I didn't really care how many people bit the dust. I was marvelously happy. I had never visited a poet's house, never drunk straight gin, never eaten steamed clams, never smelled the tide. I had never heard such things said about business, its power to petrify the soul. Humboldt spoke wonderfully of the wonderful, abominable rich. You had to view them in the shield of art. His monologue was an oratorio in which he sang and played all parts. Soaring still higher he began to speak about Spinoza and of how the mind was fed with joy by things eternal and infinite. This was Humboldt the student who had gotten A's in philosophy from the great Morris R. Cohen. I doubt that he would have talked like this to anyone but a kid from the sticks. But after Spinoza Humboldt was a bit depressed and said, "Lots of people are waiting for me to fall on my face. I have a million enemies."

"You do? But why?"

"I don't suppose you've read about the Cannibal Society of the Kwakiutl Indians," said learned Humboldt. "The candidate when he performs his initiation dance falls into a frenzy and eats human flesh. But if he makes a ritual mistake the whole crowd tears him to pieces."

"But why should poetry make you a million enemies?"

He said this was a good question but it was obvious that he didn't mean it. He turned gloomy and his voice went flat—plink—as though there were one note of tin in his brilliant keyboard. He struck it now. "I may think I'm bringing an offering to the altar, but that's not how they see it." No, it was not a good question, for the fact that I asked it meant that I didn't know Evil, and if I didn't know Evil my admiration was worthless. He forgave me because I was a boy. But when I heard the tinny plink I realized that I must learn to defend myself. He had tapped my affection and admiration, and it was flowing at a dangerous rate. This hemorrhage of eagerness would weaken me and when I was weak and defenseless I would get it in the neck. And so I figured, ah ha! he wants me to suit him perfectly, down to the ground. He'll bully me. I'd better look out.

On the oppressive night when I achieved *my* success, Humboldt picketed the Belasco Theatre. He had just been let out of Bellevue. A huge sign, *Von Trenck by Charles Citrine*, glittered above the street. There were thousands of electric bulbs. I arrived in black tie, and there was Humboldt with a gang of pals and rooters. I swept out of the taxi with my lady friend and was caught on the sidewalk in the commotion. Police were controlling the crowd. His cronies were shouting and rioting and Humboldt carried his picket sign as though it were a cross. In streaming characters, mercurochrome on cotton, was written, "The Author of this Play is a Traitor." The demonstrators were pushed back by the police, and Humboldt and I did not meet face to face. Did I want him run in? the producer's assistant asked me.

"No," I said, wounded, trembling. "I used to be his protégé. We were pals, the crazy son of a bitch. Let him alone."

Demmie Vonghel, the lady who was with me, said, "Good man! That's right, Charlie, you're a good man!"

Von Trenck ran for eight months on Broadway. I had the attention of the public for nearly a year, and I taught it nothing.

Now as to Humboldt's actual death: he died at the Ilscombe around the corner from the Belasco. On his last night, as I have reconstructed it, he was sitting on his bed in this decayed place, probably reading. The books in his room were the poems of Yeats and Hegel's *Phenomenology*. In addition to these visionary authors he read the *Daily News* and the *Post*. He kept up with sports and with night life, with the jet set and the activities of the Kennedy family, with used-car prices and want ads. Ravaged as he was he maintained his normal American interests. Then at about 3 a.m.—he wasn't sleeping much toward the end—he decided to take his garbage down and suffered a heart attack in the elevator. When the pain struck he seems to have fallen against the panel and pressed all the buttons, including the alarm button. Bells rang, the door opened, he stumbled into a corridor and fell, spilling cans, coffee grounds, and bottles from his pail. Fighting for breath, he tore off his shirt. When the cops came to take the dead man to the hospital his chest was naked. The hospital didn't want him now, so they carried him on to the morgue. At the morgue there were no readers of modern poetry. The name Von Humboldt Fleisher meant nothing. So he lay there, another derelict.

I visited his uncle Waldemar not long ago in Coney Island. The old horse-player was in a nursing home. He said to me, "The cops rolled Humboldt. They took away his watch and his dough, even his fountain pen. He always used a real pen. He didn't write poetry with a ball-point."

"Are you sure he had money?"

"He never went out without a hundred dollars minimum in his pocket. You ought to know how he was about money. I miss the kid. How I miss him!"

I felt exactly as Waldemar did. I was more moved by Humboldt's death than by the thought of my own. He had built himself up to be mourned and missed. Humboldt put that sort of weight into himself and developed in his face all the graver, all the more important human feelings. You'd never forget a face like his. But to what end had it been created?

Quite recently, last spring, I found myself thinking about this in an odd connection. I was in a French train with Renata, taking a trip which, like most trips, I neither needed nor desired. Renata pointed to the landscape and said, "Isn't that beautiful out there!" I looked out, and she was right. Beautiful was indeed there. But I had seen Beautiful many times, and so I closed my eyes. I rejected the plastered idols of the Appearances. These idols I had been trained, along with everybody else, to see, and I was tired of their tyranny. I even thought, The painted veil isn't what it used to be. The damn thing is wearing out. Like a roller-towel in a Mexican men's room. I was thinking of the power of collective abstractions, and so forth. We crave more than ever the radiant vividness of boundless love, and more and more the barren idols thwart this. A world of categories devoid of spirit waits for life to return.

Humboldt was supposed to be an instrument of this revival. This mission or vocation was reflected in his face. The hope of new beauty. The promise, the secret of beauty.

In the USA, incidentally, this sort of thing gives people a very foreign look.

It was consistent that Renata should direct my attention to the Beautiful. She had a personal stake in it, she was linked with Beauty.

Still, Humboldt's face clearly showed that he understood what was to be done. It showed, too, that he had not gotten around to doing it. And he, too, directed my attention to landscapes. Late in the Forties, he and Kathleen, newlyweds, moved from Greenwich Village to rural New Jersey, and when I visited them he was all earth, trees, flowers, oranges, the sun, Paradise, Atlantis, Rhadamanthus. He talked about William Blake at Felpham and Milton's Eden, and he ran down the city. The city was lousy. To follow his intricate conversation you had to know his basic texts. I knew what they were: Plato's *Timaeus*, Proust on Combray, Virgil on farming, Marvell on gardens, Wallace Stevens' Caribbean poetry, and so on. One reason why Humboldt and I were so close was that I was willing to take the complete course.

So Humboldt and Kathleen lived in a country cottage. Humboldt several times a week came to town on business—poet's business. He was at the height of his reputation though not of his powers. He had lined up four sinecures that I knew of. There may have been more. Considering it normal to live on fifteen bucks a week I had no way of estimating his needs and his income. He was secretive but hinted at large sums. And now he got himself appointed to replace Professor Martin Sewell at Princeton for a year. Sewell was off to give Fulbright lectures on Henry James in Damascus. His friend Humboldt was his substitute. An instructor was needed in the program and Humboldt recommended me. Making good use of my opportunities in the postwar cultural boom I had reviewed bushels of books for *The New Republic* and the *Times*. Humboldt said, "Sewell has read your pieces. Thinks you're pretty good. You *seem* pleasant and harmless with your dark ingenu eyes and your nice Midwestern manners. The old guy wants to look you over."

"Look me over? He's too drunk to find his way out of a sentence."

"As I said, you *seem* to be a pleasant ingenu, till your touchiness is touched. Don't be so haughty. It's just a formality. The fix is already in."

"Ingenu" was one of Humboldt's bad words. Steeped in psychological literature, he looked quite through my deeds. My mooning and unworldliness didn't fool him for a minute. He knew sharpness and ambition, he knew aggression and death. The scale of his conversation was as big as he could make it, and as we drove to the country in his secondhand Buick Humboldt poured it on as the fields swept by—the Napoleonic disease, Julien Sorel, Balzac's *jeune ambitieux*, Marx's portrait of Louis Bonaparte, Hegel's World Historical Individual. Humboldt was especially attached to the World Historical Individual, the interpreter of the Spirit, the mysterious leader who imposed on Mankind the task of understanding him, etcetera. Such topics were common enough in the Village, but Humboldt brought a peculiar inventiveness and a manic energy to such discussions, a passion for intricacy and for Finneganesque double meanings and hints. "And in America," he said, "this Hegelian individual would probably come from left field. Born in Appleton, Wisconsin, maybe, like Harry Houdini or Charlie Citrine."

"Why start on me? With me you're way off."

I was annoyed with Humboldt just then. In the country, one night, he had warned my friend Demmie Vonghel against me, blurting out at dinner, "You've got to watch it with Charlie. I know girls like you. They put too much into a man. Charlie is a real devil." Horrified at what he had blurted out, he then heaved himself up from the table and ran out of the house. We heard him pounding heavily on the pebbles of the dark country road. Demmie and I sat awhile with Kathleen. Kathleen finally said, "He dotes on you, Charlie. But there's something in his head. That you have a mission—some kind of secret thing—and that people like that are not exactly trustworthy. And he likes Demmie. He thinks he's protecting her. But it isn't even personal. You aren't sore, are you?"

"Sore at Humboldt? He's too fantastic to be sore at. And especially as a protector of maidens."

Demmie appeared amused. And any young woman would find value in such solicitude. She asked me later in her abrupt way, "What's this mission stuff about?"

"Nonsense."

"But you once said something to me, Charlie. Or is Humboldt only talking through his hat?"

"I said I had a funny feeling sometimes, as if I had been stamped and posted and they were waiting for me to be delivered at an important address. I may contain unusual information. But that's just ordinary silliness."

Demmie—her full name was Anna Dempster Vonghel—taught Latin at the Washington Irving School, just east of Union Square, and lived on Barrow Street. "There's a Dutch corner in Delaware," said Demmie. "And that's where the Vonghels came from." She had been sent to finishing school, studied classics at Bryn Mawr, but she had also been a juvenile delinquent and at fifteen she belonged to a gang of car thieves. "Since we love each other, you have a right to know," she said. "I have a record—hubcap-stealing, marijuana, sex offenses, hot cars, chased by cops, crashing, hospital, probation officers, the whole works. But I also know about three thousand Bible verses. Brought up on hellfire and damnation." Her Daddy, a backwoods millionaire, raced around in his Cadillac spitting from the window. "Brushes his teeth with kitchen cleanser. Tithes to his church. Drives the Sunday-school bus. The last of the old-time Fundamentalists. Except that there are scads of them down there," she said.

Demmie had blue eyes with clean whites and an upturned nose that confronted you almost as expressively and urgently as the eyes. The length of her front teeth kept her mouth slightly open. Her long elegant head grew golden hair and she parted it evenly, like the curtains of a neat house. Hers was the sort of face you might have seen in a Conestoga wagon a century ago, a pioneer face, a very white sort of face. But I fell first for her legs. They were extraordinary. And these beautiful legs had an exciting defect—her knees touched and her feet were turned outward so that when she walked fast the taut silk of her stockings made a slight sound of friction. In a cocktail crowd, where I met her, I could scarcely understand what she was saying, for she muttered in the incomprehensible fashionable Eastern lockjaw manner. But in her nightgown she was the perfect country girl, the farmer's daughter, and pronounced her words plainly and clearly. Regularly, at about 2 a.m., her nightmares woke her. Her Christianity was the delirious kind. She had unclean spirits to cast out. She feared hell. She moaned in her sleep. Then she sat up sobbing. More than half asleep myself, I tried to calm and reassure her. "There is no hell, Demmie."

"I know there is hell. There *is* a hell—there *is*!"

"Just put your head on my arm. Go back to sleep."

On a Sunday in September 1952 Humboldt picked me up in front of Demmie's apartment building on Barrow Street near the Cherry Lane Theatre. Very different from the young poet with whom I went to Hoboken to eat clams, he now was thick and stout. Cheerful Demmie called down from the third-floor fire escape where she kept begonias—in the morning there was not a trace of nightmare. "Charlie, here comes Humboldt driving the four-holer." He charged down Barrow Street, the first poet in America with power brakes, he said. He was full of car mystique, but he didn't know how to park. I watched him trying to back into an adequate space. My own theory was that the way people parked had much to do with their intimate self-image and revealed how they felt about their own backsides. Humboldt twice got a rear wheel up on the curb and finally gave up, turning off the ignition. Then in a checked sport jacket and strap-fastened polo boots he came out, swinging shut a door that seemed two yards long. His greeting was silent, the large lips were closed. His gray eyes seemed more widely separated than ever—the surfaced whale beside the dory. His handsome face had thickened and deteriorated. It was sumptuous, it was Buddhistic, but it was not tranquil. I myself was dressed for the formal professorial interview, all too belted furled and buttoned. I felt like an umbrella. Demmie had taken charge of my appearance. She ironed my shirt, chose my necktie, and brushed flat the dark hair I still had then. I went downstairs. And there we were, with the rough bricks, the garbage cans, the sloping sidewalks, the fire escapes, Demmie waving from above and her white terrier barking at the window sill.

"Have a nice day."

"Why isn't Demmie coming? Kathleen expects her."

"She has to grade her Latin papers. Make lesson plans," I said.

"If she's so conscientious she can do it in the country. I'd take her to the early train."

"She won't do it. Besides, your cats wouldn't like her dog."

Humboldt did not insist. He was devoted to the cats.

So from the present I see two odd dolls in the front seat of the roaring, grinding four-holer. This Buick was all over mud and looked like a staff car from Flanders Field. The wheels were out of line, the big tires pounded eccentrically. Through the thin sunlight of early autumn Humboldt drove fast, taking advantage of the Sunday emptiness of the streets. He was a terrible driver, making left turns from the right side, spurting, then dragging, tailgating. I disapproved. Of course I was much better with a car but comparisons were absurd, because this was Humboldt, not a driver. Steering, he was humped huge over the wheel, he had small-boy tremors of the hands and feet, and he kept the cigarette holder between his teeth. He was agitated, talking away, entertaining, provoking, informing, and snowing me. He hadn't slept last night. He seemed in poor health. Of course he drank, and he dosed himself with pills, lots of pills. In his briefcase he carried the *Merck Manual*. It was bound in black like the Bible, he consulted it often, and there were druggists who would give him what he wanted. This was something he had in common with Demmie. She too was an unauthorized pill-taker.

The car walloped the pavement, charging toward the Holland Tunnel. Close to the large form of Humboldt, this motoring giant, in the awful upholstered luxury of the front seat, I felt the ideas and illusions that went with him. He was always accompanied by a swarm, a huge volume of notions. He said how changed the Jersey swamps were, even in his lifetime, with roads, dumps, and factories, and what would a Buick like this with power brakes and power steering have meant even fifty years ago. Imagine Henry James as a driver, or Walt Whitman, or Mallarmé. We were off: he discussed machinery, luxury, command, capitalism, technology, Mammon, Orpheus and poetry, the riches of the human heart, America, world civilization. His task was to put all of this, and more, together.

The car went snoring and squealing through the tunnel and came out in bright sunlight. Tall stacks, a filth artillery, fired silently into the Sunday sky with beautiful bursts of smoke. The acid smell of gas refineries went into your lungs like a spur. The rushes were as brown as onion soup. There were sea-going tankers stuck in the channels, the wind boomed, the great clouds were white. Far out, the massed bungalows had the look of a necropolis-to-be. Through the pale sun of the streets the living went to church. Under Humboldt's polo boot the carburetor gasped, the eccentric tires thumped fast on the slabs of the highway. The gusts were so strong that even the heavy Buick fluttered. We plunged over the Pulaski Skyway while the stripes of girder shadows came at us through the shuddering windshield. In the back seat were books, bottles, beer cans, and paper bags—Tristan Corbière, I remember, *Les Amours Jaunes* in a yellow jacket, *The Police Gazette*, pink, with pictures of vulgar cops and sinful kittycats.

Humboldt's house was in the Jersey back country, near the Pennsylvania line. This marginal land was good for nothing but chicken farms. The approaches were unpaved and we drove in dust. Briars lashed the Roadmaster as we swayed on huge springs through rubbishy fields where white boulders sat. The busted muffler was so loud that though the car filled the lane there was no need to honk. You could hear us coming. Humboldt yelled, "Here's our place!" and swerved. We rolled over a hummock or earth-wave. The front of the Buick rose and then dived into the weeds. He squeezed the horn, fearing for his cats, but the cats lit out and found safety on the roof of the woodshed which had collapsed under the snow last winter.

Kathleen was waiting in the yard, large, fair-skinned, and beautiful. Her face, in the feminine vocabulary of praise, had "wonderful bones." But she was pale, and she had no country color at all. Humboldt said she seldom went outside. She sat in the house reading books. It was exactly like Bedford Street, here, except that the surrounding slum was rural. Kathleen was glad to see me, and gave my hand a kind touch. She said, "Welcome, Charlie." She said, "Thank you for coming. But where's Demmie, couldn't she come? I'm very sorry."

Then in my head a white flare went off. There was an illumination of curious clarity. I saw the position into which Humboldt had placed Kathleen and I put it into words: Lie there. Hold still. Don't wiggle. My happiness may be peculiar, but once happy I will make you happy, happier than you ever dreamed. When I am satisfied the blessings of fulfillment will flow to all mankind. Wasn't this, I thought, the message of modern power? This was the voice of the crazy tyrant speaking, with peculiar lusts to consummate, for which everyone must hold still. I grasped it at once. Then I thought that Kathleen must have secret feminine reasons for going along. I too was supposed to go along, and in another fashion I too was to hold still. Humboldt had plans also for me, beyond Princeton. When he wasn't a poet he was a fanatical schemer. And I was peculiarly susceptible to his influence. Why that was I have only recently begun to understand. But he thrilled me continually. Whatever he did was delicious. Kathleen seemed aware of this and smiled to herself as I came out of the car. I stood on the down-beaten grass.

"Breathe the air," Humboldt said. "Different from Bedford Street, hey?" He then quoted, "This castle hath a pleasant seat. Also, The heaven's breath smells wooingly here."

We then started to play football. He and Kathleen played all the time. This was why the grass was trampled. Kathleen spent most of the day reading. To understand what her husband was talking about she had to catch up, she said, on James, Proust, Edith Wharton, Karl Marx, Freud, and so on. "I have to make a scene to get her out of the house for a little football," said Humboldt. She threw a very good pass—a hard, accurate spiral. Her voice trailed as she ran barelegged and made the catch on her breast. The ball in flight wagged like a duck's tail. It flew under the maples, over the clothesline. After confinement in the car, and in my interview clothes, I was glad to play. Humboldt was a heavy choppy runner. In their sweaters he and Kathleen looked like two rookies, big, fair, padded out. Humboldt said, "Look at Charlie, jumping like Nijinsky."

I was as much Nijinsky as his house was Macbeth's castle. The crossroads had eaten into the small bluff the cottage sat on, and it was beginning to tip. By and by they'd have to prop it up. Or sue the county, said Humboldt. He'd sue anyone. The neighbors raised poultry on this slummy land. Burdocks, thistles, dwarf oaks, cottonweed, chalky holes, and whitish puddles everywhere. It was all pauperized. The very bushes might have been on welfare. Across the way, the chickens were throaty—they sounded like immigrant women—and the small trees, oaks sumacs ailanthus, were underprivileged, dusty, orphaned-looking. The autumn leaves were pulverized and the fragrance of leaf-decay was pleasant. The air was empty but good. As the sun went down the landscape was like the still frame of an old movie on sepia film. Sunset. A red wash spreading from remote Pennsylvania, sheep bells clunking, dogs in the brown barnyards. I was trained in Chicago to make something of such a scant setting. In Chicago you became a connoisseur of the near-nothing. With a clear eye I looked at a clear scene, I appreciated the red sumac, the white rocks, the rust of the weeds, the wig of green on the bluff over the crossroads.

It was more than appreciation. It was already an attachment. It was even love. The influence of a poet probably contributed to the feeling for this place that developed so quickly. I'm not referring to the privilege of being admitted to the literary life, though there may have been a touch of that. No, the influence was this: one of Humboldt's themes was the perennial human feeling that there was an original world, a home-world, which was lost. Sometimes he spoke of Poetry as the merciful Ellis Island where a host of aliens began their naturalization and of this planet as a thrilling but insufficiently humanized imitation of that home-world. He spoke of our species as castaways. But good old peculiar Humboldt, I thought (and I was peculiar enough in my own right), now has taken on the challenge of challenges. You needed the confidence of genius to commute between this patch, Nowhere, New Jersey, and the home-world of our glorious origin. Why did the crazy son of a bitch make things so hard for himself? He must have bought this joint in a blaze of mania. But now, running far into the weeds to catch the waggle-tailed ball as it flew over the clotheslines in the dusk, I was really very happy. I thought, Maybe he can swing it. Perhaps, being lost, one should get loster; being very late for an appointment, it might be best to walk slower, as one of my beloved Russian writers advised.

I was dead wrong. It wasn't a challenge, and he wasn't even trying to swing it.

When it grew too dark to play we went inside. The house was Greenwich Village in the fields. It was furnished from thrift shops, rummage sales, and church bazaars, and seemed to rest on a foundation of books and papers. We sat in the parlor drinking from peanut-butter glasses. Big fair wan lovely pale-freckled Kathleen with that buoyant bust gave kindly smiles but mostly she was silent. Wonderful things are done by women for their husbands. She loved a poet-king and allowed him to hold her captive in the country. She sipped beer from a Pabst can. The room was low pitched. Husband and wife were large. They sat together on the Castro sofa. There wasn't enough room on the wall for their shadows. They overflowed onto the ceiling. The wallpaper was pink—the pink of ladies' underclothing or chocolate creams—in a rose-and-lattice pattern. Where a stovepipe had once entered the wall there was a gilt-edged asbestos plug. The cats came and glared through the window, humorless. Humboldt and Kathleen took turns letting them in. There were old-fashioned window pins to pull. Kathleen laid her chest to the panes, lifting the frame with the heel of her hand and boosting also with her bosom. The cats entered bristling with night static.

Poet, thinker, problem drinker, pill-taker, man of genius, manic depressive, intricate schemer, success story, he once wrote poems of great wit and beauty, but what had he done lately? Had he uttered the great words and songs he had in him? He had not. Unwritten poems were killing him. He had retreated to this place which sometimes looked like Arcadia to him and sometimes looked like hell. Here he heard the bad things being said of him by his detractors—other writers and intellectuals. He grew malicious himself but seemed not to hear what he said of others, how he slandered them. He brooded and intrigued fantastically. He was becoming one of the big-time solitaries. And he wasn't meant to be a solitary. He was meant to be in active life, a social creature. His schemes and projects revealed this.

At this time he was sold on Adlai Stevenson. He thought that if Adlai could beat Ike in the November election, Culture would come into its own in Washington. "Now that America is a world power, philistinism is finished. Finished and politically dangerous," he said. "If Stevenson is in, literature is in—we're in, Charlie. Stevenson reads my poems."

"How do you know that?"

"I'm not free to tell you how, but I'm in touch. Stevenson carries my ballads with him on the campaign trail. Intellectuals are coming up in this country. Democracy is finally about to begin creating a civilization in the USA. That's why Kathleen and I left the Village."

He had become a man of property by now. Moving into the barren backlands, among the hillbillies, he felt that he was entering the American mainstream. That at any rate was his cover. Because there were other reasons for the move—jealousy, sexual delusions. He told me once a long and tangled story. Kathleen's father had tried to get her away from him, Humboldt. Before they were married the old man had taken her and sold her to one of the Rockefellers. "She disappeared one day," said Humboldt. "Said she was going to the French bakery, and was gone for almost a year. I hired a private detective but you can guess what kind of security arrangements the Rockefellers with their billions would have. There are tunnels under Park Avenue."

"Which of the Rockefellers bought her?"

"Bought is the word," said Humboldt. "She was sold by her father. Never again smile when you read about White Slavery in the Sunday supplements."

"I suppose it was all against her will."

"She's very pliant. You see what a dove she is. One-hundred-percent obedient to that vile old man. He said 'Go,' and she went. Maybe that was her real pleasure, which her pimp father only authorized. . . ."

Masochism, of course. This was part of the Psyche Game which Humboldt had studied under its modern masters, a game far more subtle and rich than any patented parlor entertainment. Out in the country Humboldt lay on his sofa reading Proust, pondering the motives of Albertine. He seldom allowed Kathleen to drive to the supermarket without him. He hid the ignition key from her and kept her in purdah.

He was a handsome man still, Kathleen adored him. He, however, suffered keen Jewish terrors in the country. He was an Oriental, she a Christian maiden, and he was afraid. He expected the KKK to burn a cross in his yard or shoot at him through the window as he lay on the Castro sofa reading Proust or inventing scandal. Kathleen told me that he looked under the hood of the Buick for booby traps. More than once Humboldt tried to get me to confess that I had similar terrors about Demmie Vonghel.

A neighboring farmer had sold him green logs. These smoked in the small fireplace as we sat after dinner. On the table was the stripped skeleton of a turkey. The wine and beer were going fast. There was an Ann Page coffee cake and melting maple-walnut ice cream. A slight cesspool smell rose to the window, and the Skellgas cylinders resembled silver artillery shells. Humboldt was saying that Stevenson was a man of real culture, the first really since Woodrow Wilson. But Wilson was inferior in this respect to Stevenson and Abraham Lincoln. Lincoln knew Shakespeare well and quoted him at the crises of his life. "There's nothing serious in mortality, All is but toys. . . . Duncan is in his grave; After life's fitful fever he sleeps well . . ." These were Lincoln's premonitions just as Lee was about to surrender. Frontiersmen were never afraid of poetry. It was Big Business with its fear of femininity, it was the eunuchoid clergy capitulating to vulgar masculinity that made religion and art sissy things. Stevenson understood that. If you could believe Humboldt (and I couldn't) Stevenson was Aristotle's great-souled man. In his administration cabinet members would quote Yeats and Joyce. The new joint Chiefs would know Thucydides. Humboldt would be consulted about each State of the Union message. He was going to be the Goethe of the new government and build Weimar in Washington. "You be thinking what you might like to do, Charlie. Something in the Library of Congress, for a start."

Kathleen said, "There's a good program on the *Late Late Show*. An old Bela Lugosi movie."

She saw that Humboldt was overexcited. He would not sleep tonight.

Very good. We tuned in the horror picture. Bela Lugosi was a mad scientist who invented synthetic flesh. He daubed it on himself, making a fearful mask, and he broke into the rooms of beautiful maidens who screamed and fell unconscious. Kathleen, more fabulous than scientists, more beautiful than any of the ladies, sat with a hazy absent freckled half-smile. Kathleen was a somnambulist. Humboldt had surrounded her with the whole crisis of Western Culture. She went to sleep. What else could she do? I understand these decades of sleep. This is a subject I know well. Meantime Humboldt kept us from going to bed. He took Amytal to overcome the Benzedrine, on top of which he drank gin.

I went out and walked in the cold. Light poured from the cottage into ruts and gullies, over the tangled road-crown of wild carrot and ragweed. Yapping dogs, foxes maybe, piercing stars. The late-late spooks jittered through the windows, the mad scientist shot it out with the police, his lab exploded, and he died in flames, the synthetic flesh melting from his face.

Demmie on Barrow Street would be watching this same picture. She didn't have insomnia. She dreaded sleep and preferred horror movies to bad dreams. Toward bedtime Demmie always grew restless. We would take in the 10 o'clock news and walk the dog and play backgammon and double solitaire. Then we would sit on the bed and watch Lon Chaney throwing knives with his feet.

I hadn't forgotten that Humboldt tried to make himself into Demmie's protector, but I no longer had it in for him. As soon as they met, Demmie and Humboldt would begin at once to talk about old movies and new pills. When they discussed Dexamil so passionately and learnedly they lost me. But it pleased me that they had so much in common. "He's a grand man," said Demmie.

And Humboldt said of Demmie, "This girl really knows her pharmaceuticals. This is an exceptional girl." But not to tamper was more than he could bear, so he added, "She's got a few things to get out of her system."

"Bunk. What things? She's already been a juvenile delinquent."

"That's not enough," said Humboldt. "If life is not intoxicating, it's nothing. Here it's burn or rot. The USA is a romantic country. If you want to be sober, Charlie, it's only because you're a maverick and you'll try anything." Then he lowered his voice and spoke looking at the floor. "What about Kathleen, does she look wild? But she let herself be stolen and sold by her father to Rockefeller. . . ."

"I still don't know which Rockefeller bought her."

"I wouldn't make any plans about Demmie, Charlie. That girl has a lot of agony to get through yet."

He was meddling, just meddling. Still, I took this to heart. For there was a lot of agony in Demmie. Some women wept as softly as a watering can in the garden. Demmie cried passionately, as only a woman who believes in sin can cry. When she cried you not only pitied her, you respected her strength of soul.

Humboldt and I were up talking half the night. Kathleen lent me a sweater; she saw that Humboldt would sleep very little and maybe she took advantage of my visit to get a little rest, foreseeing an entire week of manic nights when there would be no guest to spell her.

As a foreword to this Evening of Conversation with Von Humboldt Fleisher (for it was a sort of recital) I should like to offer a succinct historical statement: There came a time (Early Modern) when, apparently, life lost the ability to arrange itself. It had to *be* arranged. Intellectuals took this as their job. From, say, Machiavelli's time to our own this arranging has been the one great gorgeous tantalizing misleading disastrous project. A man like Humboldt, inspired, shrewd, nutty, was brimming over with the discovery that the human enterprise, so grand and infinitely varied, had now to be managed by exceptional persons. He was an exceptional person, therefore he was an eligible candidate for power. Well, why not? Whispers of sane judgment plainly told him why not and made this comical. As long as we were laughing we were okay. At that time I was more or less a candidate myself. I, too, saw great opportunities, scenes of ideological victory, and personal triumph.

Now a word about Humboldt's conversation. What was the poet's conversation actually like?

He wore the look of a balanced thinker when he began, but he was not the picture of sanity. I myself loved to talk and kept up with him as long as I could. For a while it was a double concerto, but presently I was fiddled and trumpeted off the stage. Reasoning, formulating, debating, making discoveries

Humboldt's voice rose, choked, rose again, his mouth went wide, dark stains formed under his eyes. His eyes seemed blotted. Arms heavy, chest big, pants gathered with much belt to spare under his belly, the loose end of leather hanging down, he passed from statement to recitative, from recitative he soared into aria, and behind him played an orchestra of intimations, virtues, love of his art, veneration of its great men—but also of suspicion and skulduggery. Before your eyes the man recited and sang himself in and out of madness.

He started by talking about the place of art and culture in the first Stevenson administration—his role, *our* role, for we were going to make hay together. He began this with an appreciation of Eisenhower. Eisenhower had no courage in politics. See what he allowed Joe McCarthy and Senator Jenner to say about General Marshall. He had no guts. But he shone in logistics and public relations, and he was no fool. He was the best type of garrison officer, easygoing, a bridge-player, he liked girls and read Zane Grey Westerns. If the public wanted a relaxed government, if it had recovered sufficiently from the Depression and now wanted a holiday from war, and felt strong enough to get along without New Dealers and prosperous enough to be ungrateful, it would vote for Ike, the sort of prince who could be ordered from a Sears Roebuck catalogue. Maybe it had had enough of great personalities, like FDR and energetic men like Truman. But he didn't wish to underrate America. Stevenson might make it. Now we would see where art would go in a liberal society, whether it was compatible with social progress. Meantime, having mentioned Roosevelt, Humboldt hinted that FDR might have had something to do with the death of Bronson Cutting. Senator Cutting's plane had crashed while he was flying from his home state after a vote recount. How did that happen? Maybe J. Edgar Hoover was involved. Hoover kept his power by doing the dirty work of presidents. Remember how he tried to damage Burton K. Wheeler of Montana. From this Humboldt turned to Roosevelt's sex life. Then from Roosevelt and J. Edgar Hoover to Lenin and Dzerzhinsky of the GPU. Then back to Sejanus, and the origins of secret police in the Roman Empire. Next he spoke of Trotsky's literary theories and how heavy a load great art made in the baggage train of the Revolution. Then he went back to Ike and the peacetime life of professional soldiers in the Thirties. The drinking habits of the military. Churchill and the bottle. Confidential arrangements to protect the great from scandal. Security measures in the male brothels of New York. Alcoholism and homosexuality. The married and domestic lives of pederasts. Proust and Charlus. Inversion in the German Army before 1914. Late at night Humboldt read military history and war memoirs. He knew Wheeler-Bennett, Chester Wilmot, Liddell Hart, Hitler's generals. He also knew Walter Winchell and Earl Wilson and Leonard Lyons and Red Smith, and he moved easily from the tabloids to General Rommel and from Rommel to John Donne and T. S. Eliot. About Eliot he seemed to know strange facts no one else had ever heard. He was filled with gossip and hallucination as well as literary theory. Distortion was inherent, yes, in all poetry. But which came first? And this rained down on me, part privilege, part pain, with illustrations from the classics and the sayings of Einstein and Zsa Zsa Gabor, with references to Polish socialism and the football tactics of George Halas and the secret motives of Arnold Toynbee, and (somehow) the used-car business. Rich boys, poor boys, jewboys, goyboys, chorus girls, prostitution and religion, old money, new money, gentlemen's clubs, Back Bay, Newport, Washington Square, Henry Adams, Henry James, Henry Ford, Saint John of the Cross, Dante, Ezra Pound, Dostoevski, Marilyn Monroe and Joe DiMaggio, Gertrude Stein and Alice, Freud and Ferenczi. With Ferenczi he always made the same observation: nothing could be further from instinct than rationality and therefore, according to Ferenczi, rationality was also the height of madness. As proof, how crazy Newton became! And at this point Humboldt generally spoke of Antonin Artaud. Artaud, the playwright, invited the most brilliant intellectuals in Paris to a lecture. When they were assembled there was no lecture. Artaud came on stage and screamed at them like a wild beast. "Opened his mouth and screamed," said Humboldt. "Raging screams. While those Parisian intellectuals sat frightened. For them it was a delicious event. And why? Artaud as the artist was a failed priest. Failed priests specialize in blasphemy. Blasphemy is aimed at a community of believers. In this case, what kind of belief? Belief only in intellect, which a Ferenczi has now charged with madness. But what does it mean in a larger sense? It means that the only art intellectuals can be interested in is an art which celebrates the primacy of ideas. Artists must interest intellectuals, this new class. This is why the state of culture and the history of culture become the subject matter of art. This is why a refined audience of Frenchmen listens respectfully to Artaud screaming. For them the whole purpose of art is to suggest and inspire ideas and discourse. The educated people of modern countries are a thinking rabble at the stage of what Marx called primitive accumulation. Their business is to reduce masterpieces to discourse. Artaud's scream is an intellectual thing. First, an attack on the nineteenth-century 'religion of art,' which the religion of discourse wants to replace. . . .

"And you can see for yourself, Charlie," said Humboldt after more of this, "how important it is for the Stevenson administration to have a cultural adviser like me who understands this worldwide process. Somewhat."

Above us, Kathleen was getting into bed. Our ceiling was her floor. The boards were bare and you heard every movement. I rather envied her. I was now shivering and would have liked to get under the covers myself. But Humboldt was pointing out that we were only fifteen minutes from Trenton and two hours from Washington by train. He could shoot right in. He confided that Stevenson had already been in touch with him and that a meeting was being arranged. Humboldt asked me to help him prepare notes for this conversation, and until three in the morning we discussed this. Then I went to my room and left Humboldt pouring himself a last cup of gin.

Next day he was still going strong. It made me giddy to hear so much subtle analysis and to have so much world history poured over my head at breakfast. He hadn't slept at all.

To calm himself he took a run. With slovenly shoes he pounded the gravel. Waist-high in dust, his arms bunched against his chest, he descended the road. He seemed to sink down into it under the sumacs and small oaks, between banks of brittle crab grass, thistle, milkweed, puffballs. Burrs were sticking to his pants when he returned. For running, too, he had a text. When Jonathan Swift was secretary to Sir Wm. Temple he ran miles every day to blow off steam. Thoughts too rich, emotions too dense, dark expressive needs? You could do some roadwork. That way, you sweated out the gin, too.

He took me for a stroll and the cats accompanied us through the dead leaves and brush. They practiced pouncing. They attacked ground gossamers. With grenadier tails they bounded to sharpen their claws on trees. Humboldt was extremely fond of them. The morning air was infused with something very nice. Humboldt went in and shaved and then we drove in the fateful Buick to Princeton.

My job was in the bag. We met Sewell for lunch—a muttering subtle drunken backward-leaning hollow-faced man. He had little to say to me. At the French restaurant he wanted to gossip with Humboldt about New York and Cambridge. Sewell, a cosmopolitan if there ever was one (in his own mind), had never gone abroad before. Humboldt didn't know Europe either. "If you'd like to go, old friend," said Sewell, "we could arrange that."

"I don't feel quite ready," said Humboldt. He was afraid that he would be kidnaped by former Nazis or by GPU agents.

And as Humboldt walked me to the train, he said, "I told you it was just a formality, this interview. We've known each other for years, and we've written about each other, Sewell and I. But there are no hard feelings at all. Only I wonder why Damascus wants to know about Henry James. Well, Charlie, it should be a cheerful season for us. And if I should have to go to Washington, I know I can count on you to run things here."

"Damascus!" I said. "Among those Arabs he'll be the Sheik of Apathy."

Pale Humboldt opened his mouth. Through small teeth he gave his near-silent laugh.

At that time I was an apprentice and a bit player and Sewell had treated me like one. He had seen, I expect, a soft-fibered young man, handsome enough but slack, with large sleepy-looking eyes, a bit overweight, and with a certain reluctance (it showed in his glance) to become enthusiastic about other people's enterprises. That he failed to appreciate me made me sore. But such vexations always filled me with energy as well. And if I later became such a formidable mass of credentials it was because I put such slights to good use. I avenged myself by making progress. So I owed Sewell quite a lot and it was ungrateful of me, years later when I read in the Chicago paper that he was dead, to say, as I sipped my whisky, what I occasionally did say at such moments—death is good for some people. I remembered then the wisecrack I had made to Humboldt as we walked to the Princeton Dinkey connecting with the Junction. People die and the stinging things I said about them come winging back to attach themselves to me. What *about* this apathy? Paul of Tarsus woke up on the road to Damascus but Sewell of Princeton would sleep even deeper there. Such was my wicked meaning. I confess I am sorry now that I had said such a thing. I should add, about that interview, that it was a mistake to let Demmie Vonghel send me down dressed in charcoal gray, in a button-down collar, a knitted maroon necktie, and maroon cordovan shoes, an instant Princetonian.

Anyway, it was not long after I read Sewell's obituary in the Chicago *Daily News*, leaning on the kitchen counter at 4 p.m. with a glass of whisky and a snack of pickled herring, that Humboldt, who had been dead for five or six years, re-entered my life. He came from left field. I shan't be too exact about the time of this. I was then becoming careless about time, a symptom of my increasing absorption in larger questions.

AND now the present. A different side of life—entirely contemporary.

It was in Chicago, and not very long ago by the calendar, that I left the house one morning in December to see Murra, my accountant, and when I got downstairs I found that my Mercedes-Benz had been attacked in the night. I don't mean that it had been banged and scraped by a reckless or drunken driver who ran away without leaving a note under my wipers. I mean that my car had been pounded all over, I assume with baseball bats. This elite machine, no longer new but worth eighteen thousand dollars three years ago, had been mauled with a ferocity difficult to grasp—to grasp, I mean, even in an esthetic sense, for these Mercedes coupes are beautiful, the silver-gray ones in particular. My dear friend George Swiebel had even said once, with a certain bitter admiration, "Murder

Jews and make machines, that's what those Germans really know how to do."

The attack on this car was hard on me also in a sociological sense, for I always said that I knew my Chicago and I was convinced that hoodlums, too, respected lovely automobiles. Recently a car was sunk in the Washington Park lagoon and a man was found in the trunk who had tried to batter his way out with tire-tools. Evidently he was the victim of robbers who decided to drown him—get rid of the witness. But I recall thinking that his car was only a Chevrolet. They would never have done such a thing to a Mercedes 280-SL. I said to my friend Renata that *I* might be knifed or stomped on an Illinois Central platform but that this car of mine would never be hurt.

So on this morning I was wiped out as an urban psychologist. I recognized that it hadn't been psychology but only swagger, or perhaps protective magic. I knew that what you needed in a big American city was a deep no-affect belt, a critical mass of indifference. Theories also were very useful in the building of such a protective mass. The idea, anyway, was to ward off trouble. But now the moronic inferno had caught up with me. My elegant car, my shimmering silver motor tureen which I had had no business to buy—a person like me, hardly stable enough to drive this treasure—was mutilated. Everything! The delicate roof with its sliding panel, the fenders, hood, trunk, doors, locks, lights, the smart radiator emblem had been beaten and clubbed. The shatterproof windows had held up, but they looked spat on all over. The windshield was covered with white fracture-blooms. It had suffered a kind of crystalline internal hemorrhage. Appalled, I nearly broke down, I felt like swooning.

Someone had done to my car as rats, I had heard, did when they raced through warehouses by the thousands and tore open sacks of flour for the hell of it. I felt a similar rip at my heart. The machine belonged to a time when my income was in excess of a hundred thousand dollars. Such an income had attracted the attention of the IRS, which now examined all my returns, yearly. I had set out this morning to see William Murra, that well-dressed marvelous smooth expert, the CPA who was defending me in two cases against the federal government. Although my income had now dropped to its lowest level in many years they were still after me.

I had really bought this Mercedes 280-SL because of my friend Renata. When she saw the Dodge compact I was driving when we met she said, "What kind of car is this for a famous man? There's some kind of mistake." I tried to explain to her that I was too susceptible to the influence of things and people to drive an eighteen-thousand-dollar automobile. You had to live up to such a grand machine, and consequently you were not yourself at the wheel. But Renata dismissed this. She said that I didn't know how to spend money, that I neglected myself, and that I shirked the potentialities of my success and was afraid of it. She was an interior decorator by trade, and style or panache came natural to her. Suddenly I got the idea. I went into what I called an Antony and Cleopatra mood. Let Rome in Tiber melt. Let the world know that such a mutual pair could wheel through Chicago in a silver Mercedes, the engines ticking like wizard-made toy millipedes and subtler than a Swiss Accutron—no, an Audemars Piguet with jeweled Peruvian butterfly wings! In other words, I had allowed the car to become an extension of my own self (on the folly and vanity side), so that an attack on it was an attack on myself. It was a moment terribly fertile in reactions.

How could such a thing happen on a public street? The noise must have been louder than rivet guns. Of course the lessons of jungle guerrilla tactics were being applied in all the great cities of the world. Bombs were exploding in Milan and London. Still, mine is a relatively quiet Chicago neighborhood. I was parked around the corner from my high-rise, in a narrow side street. But wouldn't the doorman have heard such clattering in the middle of the night? No, people generally hide under the covers when there are disturbances. Hearing pistol shots they say, "Backfire," to one another. As for the night-man he locks up at 1 a.m. and washes the floors. He changes in the cellar into a gray denim suit saturated with sweat. Entering the lobby late you smell the combined odors of soap powder and the musk of his denims (like rotting pears). No, the criminals who battered my car would have had no problems with the doorman. Nor with the police. As soon as the squad car had passed, knowing that it wouldn't return for fifteen minutes, they had jumped out of hiding and fallen on my car with bats, clubs, or hammers.

I knew perfectly well who was responsible for this. I had been warned over and over again. Late at night the phone often rang. Stumbling toward consciousness I picked it up and even before I could bring it to my ear I already heard my caller yelling, "Citrine! You! Citrine!"

"Yes? Yes, this is Citrine. Yes?"

"You son of a bitch. Pay me. Look what you're doing to me."

"Doing to you?"

"To me! Fucking-A-right. The check you stopped was to me. Make good, Citrine. Make that lousy check good. Don't force me to do something."

"I was fast asleep—"

"*I'm* not sleeping, why should you be?"

"I'm trying to wake up, Mr.—"

"No names! All we have to talk about is a stopped check. No names! Four hundred and fifty bucks. That's our only subject."

These gangster threats in the night against me—me! of all people! a peculiar soul and, in my own mind, almost comically innocent—made me laugh. My way of laughing has often been criticized. Well-disposed people are amused by it. Others can be offended.

"Don't laugh," said my night caller. "Knock it off. That's not a normal sound. Anyhow, who the hell do you think you're laughing at? Listen, Citrine, you lost the dough to me in a poker game. You'll say it was just a family evening, or you were drunk, but that's a lot of crap. I took your check, and I won't hold still for a slap in the face."

"You know why I stopped payment. You and your buddy were cheating."

"Did you see us?"

"The host saw. George Swiebel swears you were flashing cards to each other."

"Why didn't he speak up, that dumb prick. He should have thrown us out."

"He may have been afraid to tackle you."

"Who, that health fiend, with all the color in his face? For

Christ sake he looks like an apple, with all that jogging five miles a day, and the vitamins I saw in his medicine chest. There were seven, eight people at the game. They could have bounced us. Your friend has no guts."

I said, "Well, it wasn't a good evening. I was high, though you don't believe it. Nobody was rational. Everyone was out of character. Let's be sensible."

"What, I have to hear from my bank about your stop order, which is like a kick in the ass, and then be sensible? You think I'm a punk? It was a mistake to get into all that talk about education and colleges. I saw the look you gave when I told the name of the cow-college I went to."

"What's colleges got to do with it?"

"Don't you understand what you're doing to me? You've written all that stuff. You're in *Who's Who.* But you dumb asshole you don't understand anything."

"At two in the morning it's hard for me to understand. Can't we meet in the daytime when my head is clear?"

"No more talk. Talk is finished."

He said this many times, however. I must have received ten such calls from Rinaldo Cantabile. The late Von Humboldt Fleisher had also used the dramatic properties of night to bully and harass people.

George Swiebel had ordered me to stop the check. My friendship with George goes back to the fifth grade, and to me such pals are a sacred category. I have been warned often against this terrible weakness or dependency on early relationships. Once an actor, George had given up the stage decades ago and become a contractor. He was a wide-built fellow with a ruddy color. There was nothing subdued about his manner, his clothing, his personal style. For years he had been my self-designated expert on the underworld. He kept me informed about criminals, whores, racing, the rackets, narcotics, politics, and Syndicate operations. Having been in radio and television and journalism, his connections were unusually extensive, "from putrid to pure," he would say. And I was well up among the pure. I make no such claims for myself. This is to explain how George saw me.

"You lost that money at my kitchen table, and you'd better listen," he said. "Those punks were cheating."

"Then you should have called them on it. Cantabile has a point."

"He's got nothing, and he's nobody. If he owed you three bucks, you'd have to chase him for it. Also he was spaced out on drugs."

"I didn't notice."

"You didn't notice anything. I gave you the high sign a dozen times."

"I didn't see. I can't remember. . . ."

"Cantabile was working on you every minute. He snowed you. He was smoking pot. He was talking art and culture and psychology and the Book-of-the-Month Club and bragging about his educated wife. You bet every hand you were dealt. And every single subject I ever asked you not to mention you were discussing freely."

"George, these night calls of his are wearing me down. I'll pay him. Why not? I pay everybody. I have to get rid of this creep."

"No pay!" Trained as an actor, George had learned to swell his voice theatrically, to glare, to seem startled and to have a startling effect. He shouted at me, "Charlie, you listen!"

"But I'm dealing with a gangster."

"There are no Cantabiles in the rackets any more. They all got thrown out years ago. I told you. . . ."

"He puts on a damned good imitation then. At two a.m. I'm convinced that he's a real hoodlum."

"He's seen *The Godfather* or something and he's grown a dago mustache. He's only a confused big-mouth kid and a dropout. I shouldn't have let him and his cousin into the house. Now you forget this. They were playing gangster and they cheated. I tried to stop you giving him the check. Then I made you stop payment. I won't let you give in. Anyhow, the whole thing—take it from me—is over."

So I submitted. I couldn't challenge George's judgment. Now Cantabile had hit my car with everything he had. The blood left my heart when I saw what he had done. I dropped back against the building for support. I had gone out one evening to amuse myself in vulgar company and I had fallen into the moronic inferno.

Vulgar company was not my own expression. What I was in

fact hearing was the voice of my ex-wife. It was Denise who used terms like "common clay" and "vulgar company." The fate of my poor Mercedes would have given her very deep satisfaction. This was something like war, and she had an intensely martial personality. Denise hated Renata, my lady friend. She correctly identified Renata with this automobile. And she loathed George Swiebel. George, however, took a complex view of Denise. He said that she was a great beauty but not altogether human. Certainly Denise's huge radial amethyst eyes in combination with a low-lined forehead and sharp sibylline teeth supported this interpretation. She is exquisite, and terribly fierce. Down-to-earth George is not without myths of his own, especially where women are concerned. He has Jungian views, which he expresses coarsely. He has fine feelings which frustrate him because they fiddle his heart, and he overreacts grossly. Anyway, Denise would have laughed with happiness at the sight of this ruined car. And I? You would have thought that being divorced I had escaped the marital "I-told-you-so." But here I was, supplying it myself.

For Denise continually spoke to me about myself. She would say, "I just can't believe the way you are. The man who's had all those wonderful insights, the author of all these books, respected by scholars and intellectuals all over the world. I sometimes have to ask myself, 'Is that *my* husband? The man *I* know?' You've lectured at the great Eastern universities and had grants and fellowships and honors. De Gaulle made you a knight of the Legion of Honor and Kennedy invited us to the White House. You had a successful play on Broadway. *Now* what the hell do you think you're doing? Chicago! You hang around with your old Chicago school chums, with freaks. It's a kind of mental suicide, death wish. You'll have nothing to do with really interesting people, with architects or psychiatrists or university professors. I tried to make a life for you when you insisted on moving back here. I put myself out. You wouldn't have London or Paris or New York, you had to come back to this—this deadly, ugly, vulgar, dangerous place. Because at heart you're a kid from the slums. Your heart belongs to the old West Side gutters. I wore myself out being a hostess. . . ."

There were large grains of truth in all of this. My old

mother's words for Denise would have been "*Edel, gebildet, gelassen*," for Denise was an upper-class person. She grew up in Highland Park. She went to Vassar College. Her father, a federal judge, also came from the West Side Chicago gutters. *His* father had been a precinct captain under Morris Eller in the stormy days of Big Bill Thompson. Denise's mother had taken the judge when he was a mere boy, only the son of a crooked politician, and straightened him out and cured him of his vulgarity. Denise had expected to do as much with me. But oddly enough her paternal inheritance was stronger than the maternal. On days when she was curt and tough, in her high tense voice you heard that old precinct captain and bagman, her grandfather. Because of this background, perhaps, she hated George fiercely. "Don't bring him to the house," she said. "I can't bear to see his ass on my sofa, his feet on my rug." Denise said, "You're like one of those overbred race horses that must have a goat in his stall to calm his nerves. George Swiebel is your billy goat."

"He's a good friend to me, an old friend."

"Your weakness for your school chums isn't to be believed. You have the *nostalgie de la boue*. Does he take you around to the whores?"

I tried to give a dignified answer. But as a matter of fact I wanted the conflict to increase, and I provoked Denise. On the maid's night out I once brought George home to dinner. Maid's night out threw Denise into an anguish of spirit. Housework was insufferable. It killed her to have to cook. She wanted to go to a restaurant, but I said I didn't feel like dining out. So at six o'clock, she hastily mixed ground meat with tomatoes, kidney beans, and chili powder. I said to George, "Share our chili con carne tonight. We can open a few bottles of beer."

Denise signaled me to come into the kitchen. She said, "I won't have this." She was warlike and shrill. Her voice was clear, thrilling, and minutely articulate—the rising arpeggios of hysteria.

"Oh, come on. Denise, he can hear you." I lowered my voice and said, "Let George have some of this chili con carne."

"There's not enough. It's just half a pound of hamburger. But that's not the point. The point is I won't serve him."

I laughed. Partly from embarrassment. I am normally a low baritone, almost basso profundo, but under certain kinds of provocation my voice disappears into the higher registers, perhaps into the bat range.

"Listen to that screeching," said Denise. "You give yourself away when you laugh like this. You were born in a coal scuttle. Brought up in a parrot-house."

Her great violet eyes were unyielding.

"All right," I said. I took George to the Pump Room. We ate shashlik brought in flaming by turbaned Moors.

"I don't want to interfere in your marriage, but I notice you've stopped breathing," said George.

George feels that he can speak for Nature. Nature, instinct, heart guide him. He is biocentric. To see him rub his large muscles, his Roman Ben Hur chest and arms with olive oil is a lesson in piety toward the organism. Concluding, he takes a long swig from the bottle. Olive oil is the sun and the ancient Mediterranean. Nothing is better for the bowels, the hair, the skin. He holds his own body in numinous esteem. He is a priest to the inside of his nose, his eyeballs, his feet. "You're not getting enough air with that woman. You look as if you're suffocating. Your tissues aren't getting any oxygen. She'll give you cancer."

"Oh," I said. "She may think she's offering me the blessings of an American marriage. Real Americans are supposed to suffer with their wives, and wives with husbands. Like Mr. and Mrs. Abraham Lincoln. It's the classic US grief, and a child of immigrants like me ought to be grateful. For a Jew it's a step up."

Yes, Denise would be overjoyed to hear of this atrocity. She had seen Renata speeding past in the silver Mercedes. "And you, the passenger," said Denise, "getting to be as bald as a barber pole, even if you comb your side-hair over to hide it, and grinning. She'll give you something to grin about, that fat broad." From insult Denise went into prophecy. "Your mental life is going to dry out. You're sacrificing it to your erotic needs (if that's the term for what you have). After sex, what can you two talk about. . . ? Well, you wrote a few books, you wrote a famous play, and even that was half ghosted. You associated with people like Von Humboldt Fleisher. You took it into your head that you were some kind of artist. *We* know better, don't we. And what you really want is to get rid of everybody, to tune out and be a law unto yourself. Just you and your misunderstood heart, Charlie. You couldn't bear a serious relationship, that's why you got rid of me and the children. Now you've got this tramp with the fat figure who wears no bra and shows her big nipples to the world. You've got ignorant kikes and hoodlums around you. You're crazy with your own brand of pride and snobbery. There's nobody good enough for you. . . . *I* could have helped you. Now it's too late!"

I would not argue with Denise. I felt a certain sympathy with her. She said I was living badly. I agreed. She thought I wasn't all there, and I would have had to be completely crazy to deny it. She said I was writing stuff that made sense to no one. Maybe so. My last book, *Some Americans*, subtitled *The Sense of Being in the USA*, was quickly remaindered. The publishers had begged me not to print it. They offered to forget a debt of twenty thousand dollars if I would shelve it. But now I was perversely writing Part II. My life was in great disorder.

I was, however, loyal to something. I had an idea.

"Why did you ever bring me back to Chicago?" said Denise. "Sometimes I think you did it because your dead are buried here. Is that the reason? Land where my Jewish fathers died? And you dragged me to your graveyard so you could get into the anthem? And what's it about? All because you have delusions about being a marvelous noble person. Which you are—like hell!"

Such abuse does Denise more good than vitamins. As for me, I find that certain kinds of misunderstanding are full of useful hints. But my final though silent answer to Denise was always the same. Despite her intelligence, she *had* been bad for my idea. From that standpoint, Renata was the better woman—better for me.

Renata had forbidden me to drive a Dart. I tried to negotiate with the Mercedes salesman for a secondhand 250-C, but in the showroom Renata—roused, florid, fragrant, large—had put her hand on the silver hood and said, "This one—the coupe." The touch of her palm was sensual. Even what she did to the car I felt in my own person.

BUT now something had to be done about this wreck. I went to the Receiving Room and fetched Roland the doorman—skinny, black, elderly, never-shaven Roland. Roland Stiles, unless I deceived myself (a strong likelihood), was on my side. In my fantasies of solitary death it was Roland whom I saw in my bedroom filling a flight bag with a few articles before calling the police. He did so with my blessing. He particularly needed my electric razor. His intensely black face was pitted and spiky. Shaving with a blade must have been nearly impossible.

Roland, in the electric-blue uniform, was perturbed. He had seen the ruined car when he came to work in the morning but, he said, "I couldn't be the one to tell you, Mist' Citrine." Tenants on their way to work had seen it, too. They knew of course to whom it belonged. "This is a real bitch," said Roland soberly, his lean old face twisted and his mouth and mustache puckered. Quickwitted, he had always kidded me about the beautiful ladies who called on me. "They come in Volkswagens and Cadillacs, on bikes and motorcycles, in taxis and walkin'. They ask when you went out, and when you comin' back, and they leave notes. They come, they come, they come. You some ladies' man. Plenty of husbands got it in for you, I bet." But the amusement was gone. Roland hadn't been a black man sixty years for nothing. He knew moronic infernos. I had lost the immunity which made my ways so entertaining. "You in trouble," he said. He muttered something about "Miss Universe." He called Renata Miss Universe. Sometimes she paid him to entertain her little boy in the Receiving Room. The child played with parcels while his mother lay in my bed. I didn't like it, but you can't be a ridiculous lover by halves.

"Now what?"

Roland twisted his hands outward. He lifted his shoulders. Shrugging, he said, "Call the cops."

Yes, a report had to be filed, if only because of the insurance. The insurance company would find this a very queer case. "Well, flag the squad car when it passes. Have those useless fellows look at this ruin," I said. "And then send them up."

I gave him a dollar for his trouble. I usually did that. And now the flow of malevolence had to be reversed.

Through my apartment door I heard the telephone. It was Cantabile.

"All right, smart-ass."

"Insane!" I said. "Vandalism! Beating a machine. . . . !"

"You've seen your car—you saw what you made me do!" He yelled. He forced his voice. Nevertheless it shook.

"What's that? You're blaming me?"

"You were warned."

"*I* made you hammer that beautiful automobile?"

"You made me. Yes, you. You sure did. You think I don't have feelings? You wouldn't believe how I feel about a car like that. You're stupid. This is nobody's fault but yours." I tried to answer but he shouted me down. "You forced me! You made me! Okay, last night was only step one."

"What does that mean?"

"Don't pay me and you'll see what it means."

"What kind of threat is that? This is getting out of hand. Do you mean my daughters?"

"I'm not going to a collection agency. You don't know what you're into. Or who I am. Wake up!"

I often said "Wake up!" to myself, and many people also have cried, "Wake, wake!" As if I had a dozen eyes, and stubbornly kept them sealed. "Ye have eyes and see not." This, of course, was absolutely true.

Cantabile was still speaking. I heard him say, "So, go and ask George Swiebel what to do. He gave you the advice. *He*, like, smashed your car."

"Let's stop all this. I want to settle."

"No settle. Pay. Make good the check. The full amount. And cash. No money orders, no cashier's check, no more fucking around. Cash. I'll call you later. We'll make a date. I want to see you."

"When?"

"Never mind when. You stick by the telephone till I call."

Next instant I heard the interminable universal electronic miaow of the phone. And I was desperate. I had to tell what had happened. I needed to consult.

A sure sign of distress: telephone numbers stormed through my head—area codes, digits. I must telephone someone. The first person I called was George Swiebel, of course; I had to tell him what had happened. I also had to warn him. Cantabile might attack him, too. But George was out with a crew. They were pouring a concrete footing somewhere, said Sharon, his secretary. George, before he became a businessman, was, as I have said, an actor. He started out in the Federal Theater. Afterward he was a radio announcer. He had tried television and Hollywood as well. Among business people he spoke of his show-business experience. He knew his Ibsen and his Brecht and he often flew to Minneapolis to see plays at the Guthrie Theatre. In South Chicago he was identified with Bohemia and the Arts, with creativity, with imagination. And he was vital, generous, had an open nature. He was a good guy. People formed strong attachments to him. Look at this little Sharon, his secretary. She was a hillbilly, dwarfish and queer-faced, and looked like Mammy Yokum in the funnies. Yet George was her brother, her doctor, her priest, her tribe. She had, as it were, surveyed South Chicago and found only one man there, George Swiebel. When I spoke to her, I had enough presence of mind to dissemble, for if I had told Sharon how shocking things were she would not have given George the message. George's average day, as he and his people saw it, was one crisis after another. Her job was to protect him. "Ask George to call me," I said. I hung up thinking of the crisis-outlook in the USA, a legacy from old frontier times, etcetera. I thought these things from force of habit. Just because your soul is being torn to pieces doesn't mean that you stop analyzing the phenomena.

I restrained my real desire, which was to scream. I recognized that I would have to recompose myself unassisted. I didn't dial Renata. Renata is not especially good at giving consolation over the phone. You have to get it from her in person.

Now I had Cantabile's ring to wait for. And the police as well. I had to explain to Murra the CPA that I wouldn't be coming in. He'd charge me for the hour anyway, after the manner of psychiatrists and other specialists. That afternoon I was to have taken my small daughters Lish and Mary to their piano teacher. For, as the Gulbransen Piano Co. used to say on the brick walls of Chicago, "The richest child is poor without a musical education." And mine were rich man's daughters, and it would be a disaster if they grew up unable to play "Für Elise" and the "Happy Farmer."

I had to recover my calm. Seeking stability, I did the one Yoga exercise I know. I took the small change and the keys out of my pockets, I removed my shoes, took a position on the floor, advancing my toes, and, with a flip, I stood on my head. My loveliest of machines, my silver Mercedes 280, my gem, my love-offering, stood mutilated in the street. Two thousand dollars' worth of bodywork would never restore the original smoothness of the metal skin. The headlights were crushed blind. I hadn't the heart to try the doors, they might be jammed shut. I tried to concentrate on hatred and fury—revenge, revenge! But I couldn't get anywhere with that. I could only see the German steward at the shop in his long white smock, like a dentist, telling me that parts would have to be imported. And I, clutching my half-bald head in both hands as if in despair, fingers interlocked, had my trembling aching legs in the air, tufts of side-hair sticking out, and the green Persian carpet flowing under me. I was heart-injured. I was desolate. The beauty of the carpet was one of my comforts. I have become deeply attached to carpets, and this one was a work of art. The green was soft and varied with great subtlety. The red was one of those surprises that seem to spring straight from the heart. Stribling, my downtown expert, told me that I could get far more than I had paid for this rug. Everything that wasn't mass-produced was zooming in value. Stribling was an obese excellent man who kept horses but now was too heavy to ride. Few people seemed to be consummating anything good, these days. Look at me. I couldn't be serious, becoming involved in this sort of grotesque comic Mercedes-and-Underworld thing. As I stood on my head, I knew (I *would* know!) that there was a sort of theoretical impulse behind this grotesqueness too, one of the powerful theories of the modern world being that for self-realization it's necessary to embrace the deformity and absurdity of the inmost being (we *know* it's there!). Be healed by the humiliating truth the Unconscious contains. I didn't buy this theory, but that didn't mean that I was free from it. I had a talent for absurdity, and you don't throw away any of your talents.

I was thinking that I'd never get a penny from the insurance company on a queer claim like this. I had bought every kind of protection they offered, but somewhere in the small print they were sure to have the usual foxy clauses. Under Nixon the great corporations became drunk with immunity. The good old bourgeois virtues, even as window dressing, are gone forever.

It was from George that I had learned this upside-down position. George warned that I was neglecting my body. Several years ago he began to point out that my throat was becoming crepy, my color was poor, and I was easily winded. At a certain point in middle age you had to make a stand, he argued, before the abdominal wall gives, the thighs get weak and thin, the breasts female. There was a way to age that was physically honorable. George interpreted this for himself with peculiar zeal. Immediately after his gall-bladder operation he got out of bed and did fifty push-ups—his own naturopath. From this exertion, he got peritonitis and for two days we thought he was dying. But ailments seemed to inspire him, and he had his own cures for everything. Recently he told me, "I woke up day before yesterday and found a lump under my arm."

"Did you go to the doctor?"

"No. I tied it with dental floss. I tied it tight, tight, tight. . . ."

"What happened?"

"Yesterday when I examined it, it had swelled up to the size of an egg. Still I didn't call the doctor. To hell with that! I took more dental floss and tied it tight, tight, even tighter. And now it's cured, it's gone. You want to see?"

It was when I told him of my arthritic neck that he prescribed standing on my head. Though I threw up my palms and shrieked with laughter (looking like one of Goya's frog caricatures in the *Visión Burlesca*—the creature with the locks and bolts) I did as he advised. I practiced and learned the headstand, and I was cured of the neck pains. Next, when I had a stricture, I asked George for a remedy. He said, "It's the prostate gland. You start, then you stop, then you trickle again, it burns a bit, you feel humiliated?"

"All correct."

"Don't worry. Now as you stand on your head, tighten your

buttocks. Just suck them in as if you were trying to bring the cheeks together."

"Why must this be done as you stand on your head? I already feel like Old Father William."

But he was adamant and said, "On your head."

Again his method worked. The stricture went away. Others may see in George a solid high-colored good-humored building contractor; I see a hermetical personage; I see a figure from the tarot deck. If I was on my head now I was invoking George. When I'm in despair he's always the first person I telephone. I've reached an age at which you can see your neurotic impulses advancing on you. There's not much that I can do when the dire need of help comes over me. I stand at the edge of a psychic pond and I know that if crumbs are thrown in, my carp will come swimming up. You have, like the external world, your own phenomena inside. At one time I thought the civilized thing to do was to make a park and a garden for them, to keep these traits, your quirks, like birds, fishes, and flowers.

However, the fact that I had no one but myself to turn to was awful. Waiting for bells to ring is a torment. The suspense claws at my heart. Actually, standing on my head did relieve me. I breathed again. But I saw, when I was upside-down, two large circles in front of me, very bright. These occasionally appear during this exercise. Reversed on your cranium, of course you do think of being caught by a cerebral hemorrhage. A physician advising against the headstand said to me that a chicken held upside-down would die in seven or eight minutes. But that's obviously because of terror. The bird is scared to death. I figure that the bright rings are caused by pressure on the cornea. The weight of the body set upon the skull buckles the cornea and produces an illusion of big diaphanous rings. Like seeing eternity. Which, believe me, I was ready for on this day.

Behind me, I had a view of the bookcase, and when my head was readjusted, with more weight shifted to the forearms, the pellucid rings swam away, the shades of a fatal hemorrhage with them. In reverse, I saw rows and rows of my own books. I had stacked them at the back of my closets, but Renata had brought them out again to make a display. I prefer, when I'm on my head, to have a view of the sky and the clouds. It's good fun to study the clouds upside-down. But now I was looking at the titles which had brought me money, recognition, prizes, my play, *Von Trenck*, in many editions and languages, and a few copies of my favorite, the failure *Some Americans: The Sense of Being in the USA*. *Von Trenck* while it was running brought in about eight thousand dollars a week. The government, which had taken no previous interest in my soul, immediately claimed seventy percent in the result of its creative efforts. But this was not supposed to affect me. You rendered unto Caesar what was Caesar's. At least you knew that you should. Money belonged to Caesar. There was also *Radix malorum est cupiditas.* I knew all that, too.

I knew everything I was supposed to know and nothing I really needed to know. I had bungled the whole money thing. It was highly educational, of course, and education has become the great and universal American recompense. It has even replaced punishment in the federal penitentiaries. Every great prison is now a thriving seminar. The tigers of wrath are crossed with the horses of instruction, making a hybrid undreamed of in the Apocalypse. Not to labor the matter too much, I had lost most of the money that Humboldt had accused me of making. The dough came between us immediately. He put through a check for thousands of dollars. I didn't contest this. I didn't want to go to law. Humboldt would have been fiercely delighted with a trial. He was very litigious. But the check he cashed was actually signed by me, and I would have had a hard time explaining this in court. Besides, courts kill me. Judges, lawyers, bailiffs, stenotypists, the benches, the woodwork, the carpets, even the water glasses I hate like death. Moreover, I was actually in South America when he cashed the check. He was then running wild in New York, having been released from Bellevue. There was no one to restrain him. Kathleen had gone into hiding. His nutty old mother was in a nursing home. His uncle Waldemar was one of those eternal kid brothers to whom responsibilities are alien. Humboldt was jumping and prancing about New York being mad. Perhaps he was aware dimly of the satisfaction he was giving to the cultivated public which gossiped about his crack-up. Frantic desperate doomed crazy writers and suicidal painters are dramatically and socially valuable. And at that time he was a fiery

Failure and I was a newborn Success. Success baffled me. It filled me with guilt and shame. The play performed nightly at the Belasco was not the play I had written. I had only provided a bolt of material from which the director had cut shaped basted and sewn his own Von Trenck. Brooding, I muttered to myself that after all Broadway adjoins the garment district and blends with it.

Cops have their own way of ringing a doorbell. They ring like brutes. Of course, we are entering an entirely new stage in the history of human consciousness. Policemen take psychology courses and have some feeling for the comedy of urban life. The two heavy men who stood on my Persian carpet carried guns, clubs, cuffs, bullets, walkie-talkies. Such an unusual case—a Mercedes beaten in the street—amused them. This pair of black giants had a squad-car odor, the smell of close quarters. Their hardware clinked, their hips and bellies swelled and bulged.

"I never saw such massacre on an automobile," said one of them. "You in trouble with some real bad actors." He was probing, hinting. He didn't actually want to hear about the Mob, about juice men or gang-entanglements. Not one word. But it was all obvious. I didn't *look* like a fellow in the rackets, but maybe I was one. Even the cops had seen *The Godfather*, *The French Connection*, *The Valachi Papers*, and other blast-and-bang thrillers. I was drawn to this gang stuff, myself, as a Chicagoan, and I said, "I don't know anything." I dummied up, and I believe the police approved of this.

"You keep your car in the street?" said one of the cops—he had volumes of muscle and a great slack face. "If I didn't have a garage, I wouldn't own but a piece of junk." Then he saw my medal, which Renata had framed in plush on the wall, and he said, "Were you in Korea?"

"No," I said. "The French government gave me that. The Legion of Honor. I'm a knight, a *chevalier*. Their ambassador decorated me."

On that occasion, Humboldt had sent me one of his unsigned post cards. "*Shoveleer! Your name is now lesion!*"

He had been on a *Finnegans Wake* kick for years. I remembered our many discussions of Joyce's view of language, of the poet's passion for charging speech with music and meaning, of the dangers that hover about all the works of the mind, of beauty falling into abysses of oblivion like the snow chasms of the Antarctic, of Blake and Vision versus Locke and the *tabula rasa.* As I saw the cops out I was remembering with sadness of heart the lovely conversations Humboldt and I used to have. Humanity divine incomprehensible!

"You better square this thing," the cop advised me, low and kindly. His great black weight moved toward the elevator. The Shoveleer inclined politely. I felt my eyes ache with a helpless craving for help.

Yes, the medal reminded me of Humboldt. Yes, when Napoleon gave the French intellectuals ribbons stars and baubles, he knew what he was doing. He took a boatload of scholars with him to Egypt. He ditched them. They came up with the Rosetta stone. From the time of Richelieu and earlier, the French had been big in the culture business. You'd never catch De Gaulle wearing one of these ridiculous trinkets. He had too much self-esteem. The fellows who bought Manhattan from the Indians didn't wear beads themselves. I would gladly have given this gold medal to Humboldt. The Germans tried to honor him. He was invited to Berlin in 1952 to lecture at the Free University. He wouldn't go. He was afraid of being abducted by the GPU or the NKVD. He was a longtime contributor to the *Partisan Review* and a prominent anti-Stalinist, so he was afraid that the Russians would try to kidnap and kill him. "Also, if I spent a year in Germany I'd be thinking of one thing only," he stated publicly (I was the only one listening). "For twelve months I'd be a Jew and nothing else. I can't afford to give an entire year to that." But I think a better explanation is that he was having a grand time being mad in New York. He was seeing psychiatrists and making scenes. He invented a lover for Kathleen and then he tried to kill the man. He smashed up the Buick Roadmaster. He accused me of stealing his personality for the character of Von Trenck. He drew a check on my account for six thousand seven hundred and sixty-three dollars and fifty-eight cents and bought an Oldsmobile with it, among other things. Anyway, he didn't want to go to Germany, a country where no one could follow his conversation.

From the papers he later learned that I had become a Shoveleer. I had heard that he was living with a gorgeous black girl who studied the French horn at the Juilliard School. But when I last saw him on Forty-sixth Street I knew that he was too destroyed to be living with anyone. He was destroyed—I can't help repeating this. He wore a large gray suit in which he was floundering. His face was dead gray, East River gray. His head looked as if the gypsy moth had gotten into it and tented in his hair. Nevertheless I should have approached and spoken to him. I should have drawn near, not taken cover behind the parked cars. But how could I? I had had my breakfast in the Edwardian Room of the Plaza, served by rip-off footmen. Then I had flown in a helicopter with Javits and Bobby Kennedy. I was skirring around New York like an ephemerid, my jacket lined with jolly psychedelic green. I was dressed up like Sugar Ray Robinson. Only I didn't have a fighting spirit, and seeing that my old and close friend was a dead man I beat it. I went to La Guardia and took a 727 back to Chicago. I sat afflicted in the plane, drinking whisky on the rocks, overcome with horror, ideas of Fate and other humanistic lah-de-dah—compassion. I had gone around the corner and gotten lost on Sixth Avenue. My legs trembled and my teeth were set hard. I said to myself, Humboldt good-by, I'll see you in the next world. And two months after this in the Ilscombe Hotel, which has since collapsed, he started down at 3 a.m. with his garbage pail and died in the corridor.

At a Village cocktail party in the Forties I heard a beautiful girl tell Humboldt, "Do you know what you're like? You're like a person from a painting." Sure, women dreaming of love might have visions of Humboldt at twenty stepping down from a Renaissance or an Impressionist masterpiece. But the picture on the obituary page of the *Times* was frightful. I opened the paper one morning and there was Humboldt, ruined, black and gray, a disastrous newspaper face staring at me from death's territory. That day, too, I was flying from New York to Chicago—wafting back and forth, not always knowing why. I went to the can and locked myself in. People knocked but I was weeping and wouldn't come out.

ACTUALLY Cantabile didn't make me wait too long. He phoned just before noon. Maybe he was getting hungry. I remembered that someone or other in Paris toward the end of the nineteenth century used to see Verlaine drunken and bloated pounding his cane wildly on the sidewalk as he went to lunch, and shortly afterward the great mathematician Poincaré, respectably dressed and following his huge forehead while describing curves with his fingers, also on his way to lunch. Lunchtime is lunchtime, whether you are a poet or a mathematician or a gangster. Cantabile said, "All right, you dumb prick, we're going to meet right after lunch. Bring cash. And that's all you bring. Don't make any more bad moves."

"I wouldn't know what or how," I said.

"That's true, as long as you don't cook up anything with George Swiebel. You come alone."

"Of course. It never even occurred to me—"

"Well now I've said it, but it better not occur. Alone, and bring new bills. Go to the bank and get clean money. Nine bills of fifty. New. I don't want any grease stains on those dollars. And be glad if I don't make you eat that fucking check."

What a fascist! But maybe he was only priming or haranguing himself to keep up the savagery level. By now, however, my only object was to get rid of him by submission and agreement. "Any way you want it," I said. "Where shall I bring this money?"

"The Russian Bath on Division Street," he said.

"That old joint? For the love of God!"

"You be in front, there, at one-forty-five and wait. And alone!" he said.

I answered, "Right." But he hadn't waited for agreement. Again I heard the dial tone. I identified this interminable squalling with the anxiety level of the disengaged soul.

I had to put myself into motion. And I couldn't expect Renata to do anything for me. Renata, at business today, was attending an auction, and she'd have been miffed if I had called the auction rooms to ask her to take me to the Northwest Side. She's an obliging and beautiful woman, she has marvelous breasts, but she takes offense at certain kinds of slights and quickly flares up. Well, I'd manage it all somehow. Perhaps the Mercedes could be driven to the shop. A tow truck might not be needed. And then I'd have to find a taxi or call the Emery Livery Service or Rent-a-Car. I wouldn't ride the bus. There are too many armed drunkards and heroin users on the buses and trains. But, no, wait! First, I must call Murra and then run to the bank. Also I had to explain that I couldn't drive Lish and Mary to their piano lesson. This made my heart particularly heavy, because I'm somewhat afraid of Denise. She still wields a certain power. Denise made a great production of these lessons. But with her everything was a production, everything was momentous, critical. All psychological problems relating to the children were presented with great intensity. Questions of child development were desperate, dire, mortal. If these kids were ruined it would be my fault. I had abandoned them at a most perilous moment in the history of civilization to take up with Renata. "That whore with fat tits"—was what Denise regularly called her. She spoke of beautiful Renata always as a gross tough broad. The trend of her epithets, it seemed, was to make a man of Renata and a woman of me.

Denise, like my wealth, goes back to the Belasco Theatre. Trenck was played by Murphy Verviger and the star had a retinue (a dresser, a press agent, an errand boy). Denise, who was living with Verviger at the St. Moritz, arrived with his other attendants daily, carrying his script. Dressed in a plum velvet jump-suit she wore her hair down. Elegant, slender, slightly flat-chested, high-shouldered, wide across the top like an old-fashioned kitchen chair, she had large violet eyes, a marvelously rich subtle color in her face and a mysterious, seldom visible down, even over her nose. Because of the August heat the great doors offstage were open on the cement alleys and the daylight stealing in showed the appalling baldness and decay of the antique luxury. The Belasco was like a gilded cake-platter with grimed frosting. Verviger, his face deeply grooved at the mouth, was big and muscular. He resembled a skiing instructor. Some concept of intense refinement was eating at him. His head was shaped like a busby, a high solid arrogant rock covered with thick moss. Denise kept rehearsal notes for him. She wrote with terrible concentration, as if she were the smartest pupil in the class and the rest of the fifth grade were in pursuit. When she came to ask a question she held the script to her chest and spoke to me in a condition of operatic crisis. Her voice seemed to make her own hair bristle and to dilate her astonishing eyes. She said, "Verviger wants to know how you'd like him to pronounce this word"—she printed it out for me, FINITE. "He says he can do it *fin*-it, or *fine*-it, or *fine-ite*. He doesn't take my word for it—fine-ite!"

I said, "Why so fancy? . . . I don't care what he does with it." I didn't add that I despaired of Verviger anyway. He had the play wrong from top to bottom. Maybe he was getting things right at the St. Moritz. That didn't concern me then. I went home and told my friend Demmie Vonghel about the glaring bristling beauty at the Belasco, Verviger's girlfriend.

Well, ten years later Denise and I were husband and wife. And we were invited to the White House by the President and Mrs. Kennedy in black tie for a cultural evening. Denise consulted twenty or thirty women about dresses, shoes, gloves. Very intelligent, she always read up on national and world problems at the beauty parlor. Her hair was heavy and worn high. It wasn't easy to be sure when she had had it done, but I could always tell from her dinner conversation whether she'd been to the hairdresser that afternoon, because she was a speed reader and covered every detail of world crisis under the dryer. "Do you realize what Khrushchev did in Vienna?" she said. So at the beauty salon, to prepare for the White House, she mastered *Time* and *Newsweek* and *The U.S. News and World Report*. On the flight to Washington we reviewed the Bay of Pigs and the Missile Crisis and the Diem problem. Her nervous intensity is constitutional. After dinner she got hold of the President and spoke to him privately. I saw her cornering him in the Red Room. I knew that she was driving urgently over the tangle of lines dividing her own terrible problems—and they were all terrible!—from the perplexities and disasters of world politics. It was all one indivisible crisis. I knew that she was saying, "Mr. President, what can be done about this?" Well, we woo one another with everything we've got. I tittered to myself when I saw them together. But JFK could take care of himself, and he liked pretty women. I suspected that he read *The U.S. News and World Report*, too, and that his information might not be much better than her own. She'd have made him an excellent Secretary of State, if some way could be found to wake her before 11 a.m. For she's quite marvelous. And a real beauty. And much more litigious than Humboldt Fleisher. He mainly threatened. But from the time of the divorce I have been entangled in endless ruinous lawsuits. The world has seldom seen a more aggressive subtle resourceful plaintiff than Denise. Of the White House I mainly remembered the impressive hauteur of Charles Lindbergh, the complaint of Edmund Wilson that the government had made a pauper of him, the Catskill resort music played by the Marine Corps orchestra, and Mr. Tate keeping time with his fingers on the knee of a lady.

One of Denise's big grievances was that I wouldn't allow her to lead this kind of life. The great captain Citrine who once had burst the buckles of his armor in heroic scuffles now cooled gypsy Renata's lust and in his dotage had bought a luxury Mercedes-Benz. When I came to call for Lish and Mary, Denise told me to make sure the car was well aired. She didn't want it smelling of Renata. Butts stained with her lipstick had to be emptied from the ashtray. She once marched out of the house and did this herself. She said there must be no Kleenexes smeared with God-knows-what.

Apprehensive, I picked out Denise's number on the telephone. I was in luck, the maid answered, and I told her, "I can't fetch the girls today. I've got car trouble."

Downstairs I found that I could squeeze into the Mercedes and though the windshield was bad, I thought I could manage the driving if the police didn't stop me. I tested this by going to the bank where I drew the new money. It was given to me in a plastic envelope. I didn't fold this packet but laid it next to my wallet. Then from a phone booth I made an appointment at the Mercedes shop. You've got to have an appointment—you don't barge in to the garage as you did in the old mechanic days. Then, still on the pay phone, I tried again to get hold of George Swiebel. Apparently I had said, while sounding off during the card game, that George enjoyed going with his old father to the Baths on Division Street near what used to be Robey Street. Probably Cantabile hoped to catch George there.

As a kid I went to the Russian Bath with my own father. This old establishment has been there forever, hotter than the tropics and rotting sweetly. Down in the cellar men moaned on the steam-softened planks while they were massaged abrasively with oak-leaf besoms lathered in pickle buckets. The wooden posts were slowly consumed by a wonderful decay that made them soft brown. They looked like beaver's fur in the golden vapor. Perhaps Cantabile hoped to trap George here naked. Could there be any other reason why he had named this rendezvous? He might beat him, he might shoot him. Why had I talked so much!

I said to George's secretary, "Sharon? He's not back? Now listen, tell him not to go to the *schwitz* on Division Street today. *Not!* It's serious."

George said of Sharon, "She digs emergencies." This is understandable. Two years ago she had her throat cut by a total stranger. This unknown black man stepped into George's South Chicago office with an open razor. He swept it over Sharon's throat like a virtuoso and disappeared forever. "The blood fell like a curtain," said George. He knotted a towel about Sharon's neck and rushed her to the hospital. George digs emergencies himself. He's always looking for something basic, "honest," "of the earth," primordial. When he saw blood, a vital substance, he knew what to do. But of course George is also theoretical; he is a primitivist. This ruddy, big-muscled, blunt-handed George with his brown, humanly comprehensive eyes is not stupid except when he proclaims his ideas. He does this loudly, fiercely. And then I only grin at him because I know how kindly he is. He takes care of his old parents, of his sisters, of his ex-wife and their grown children. He denounces eggheads, but he really loves culture. He spends whole days trying to read difficult books, knocking himself out. Not with great success. And when I introduce him to intellectuals like my learned friend Durnwald, he shouts and baits them and talks dirty, his face gets red. Well, it's that sort of curious moment in the history of human consciousness when the mind universally awakens and democracy originates, an era of turmoil and ideological confusion, the principal phenomenon of the present age. Humboldt, boyish, loved the life of the mind and I shared his enthusiasm. But the intellectuals one meets are something else again. I didn't behave well with the mental beau monde of Chicago. Denise invited superior persons of all kinds to the house in Kenwood to discuss politics and economics, race, psychology, sex, crime. Though I served the drinks and laughed a great deal I was not exactly cheerful and hospitable. I wasn't even friendly. "You despise these people!" Denise said, angry. "Only Durnwald is an exception, that curmudgeon." This accusation was true. I hoped to lay them all low. In fact it was one of my cherished dreams and dearest hopes. They were against the True, the Good, the Beautiful. They denied the light. "You're a snob," she said. This was not accurate. But I wouldn't have a thing to do with these bastards, the lawyers, Congressmen, psychiatrists, sociology professors, clergy, and art-types (they were mostly gallery-owners) she invited.

"You've got to meet real people," George said to me later. "Denise surrounded you with phonies, and now day in, day out you're alone with tons of books and papers in that apartment and I swear you're going to go nuts."

"Why no," I said, "there's yourself and Alec Szathmar, and my friend Richard Durnwald. And also Renata. And what about the people at the Downtown Club."

"Lots of good this guy Durnwald will do you. He's the professor's professor. And nobody can interest him. He's heard it or read it all. When I try to talk to him I feel that I'm playing the ping-pong champion of China. I serve the ball, he smashes it back, and that's the end of that. I have to serve again and pretty soon I'm out of balls."

He always came down heavily on Durnwald. There was a certain rivalry. He knew how attached I was to Dick Durnwald. In crude Chicago Durnwald, whom I admired and even adored, was the only man with whom I exchanged ideas. But for six months Durnwald had been at the University of Edinburgh, lecturing on Comte, Durkheim, Tönnies, Weber, and so on. "This abstract stuff is poison to a guy like you," said George. "I'm going to introduce you to guys from South Chicago." He began to shout. "You're too exclusive, you're going to dry out."

"Okay," I said.

So the fateful poker game was organized around me. But the guests knew that they had been invited as low company. Nowadays the categories are grasped by those who belong to them. It would have been obvious to them that I was some sort of mental fellow even if George hadn't advertised me as such, boasting that my name was in reference books and that I was knighted by the French government. So what? It wasn't as if I had been a Dick Cavett, a true celebrity. I was just another educated nut and George was showing me off to them and exhibiting them to me. It was nice of them to forgive me this great public-relations buildup. I was brought there by George to relish their real American qualities, their peculiarities. But they enriched the evening with their own irony and reversed the situation so that in the end my peculiarities were far more conspicuous. "As the game went on they liked you more and more," said George. "They thought you were pretty human. Besides, there was Rinaldo Cantabile. He and his cousin were flashing cards to each other, and you were getting drunk and didn't know what the hell was happening."

"So I was merely a contrast-gainer," I said.

"I thought contrast-gainer was just your term for married couples. You like a lady because she's got a husband, a real stinker, who makes her look good."

"It's one of those portmanteau expressions."

I am not a great poker-player. Besides, I was interested in the guests. One was a Lithuanian in the tuxedo-rental business, another a young Polish fellow getting computer training. There was a plainclothes detective from the homicide squad. Next to me sat a Sicilian-American undertaker, and last there were Rinaldo Cantabile and his cousin Emil. These two, said George, had crashed the party. Emil was a small-time hoodlum, born to twist arms and throw bricks through show windows. He must have taken part in the attack on my car. Rinaldo was extremely good-looking with a dark furry mustache as fine as mink, and he was elegantly dressed. He bluffed madly, spoke loudly, knocked the table with his knuckles, and pretended to be a cast-iron lowbrow. Still, he kept talking about Robert Ardrey, the territorial imperative, paleontology in the Olduvai Gorge, and the views of Konrad Lorenz. He said loudly and harshly that his educated wife left books around. The Ardrey book he had picked up in the toilet. God knows why we are drawn to others and become attached to them. Proust, an author to whom Humboldt introduced me and in whose work he gave me heavy instruction, said that he often was attracted to people whose faces had something in them of a hawthorn hedge in bloom. Hawthorn was not Rinaldo's flower. White calla lily was more like it. His nose was particularly white and his large nostrils, correspondingly dark, reminded me of an oboe when they dilated. People so distinctly seen have power over me. But I don't know which comes first, the attraction or the close observation. When I feel gross, dull, damaged in sensibility, a refined perception, coming suddenly, has great influence.

We sat at a round pedestal table and as the clean cards flew and flickered George got the players to talk. He was the impresario and they obliged him. The homicide cop talked about killings in the street. "It's all different, now they kill the sonofabitch if he doesn't have a dollar in his pocket and they kill the sonofabitch if he gives them fifty dollars. I tell 'em, 'You bastards kill for money? For money? The cheapest thing in the world. I killed more guys than you but that was in the war.' "

The tuxedo man was in mourning for his lady friend, a telephone ad-taker at the *Sun Times.* He spoke with a baying Lithuanian accent, joking, bragging, but gloomy, too. As he got into his story he blazed with grief, he damn-near cried. On Mondays he collected his rented tuxedoes. After the weekend they were stained, he said, with sauce, with soup, with whisky or semen, "You name it." Tuesdays he drove in his station wagon to a joint near the Loop where the suits were put to soak in vats of cleaning fluid. Then he spent the afternoon with a girl friend. Ah, they couldn't even make it to the bed, they were so hot for each other. They fell to the floor. "She was a good family type of girl. She was my kind of people. But she'd do anything. I told her how, and she did it, and no questions."

"And you saw her on Tuesdays only, never took her to dinner, never visited her at home?" I said.

"She went home at five o'clock to her old mother and cooked dinner. I swear I didn't even know her last name. For twenty years I never had but her phone number."

"But you loved her. Why didn't you marry her?"

He seemed astonished, looking at the other players as if to say, What's with this guy? Then he answered, "What, marry a hot broad who turns on in hotel rooms?"

While everyone laughed the Sicilian undertaker explained to me in the special tone in which you tell the facts of life to educated dummies, "Look, professor, you don't mix things up. That's not what a wife is about. And if you have a funny foot you have to look for a funny shoe. And if you find the right fit you just let it alone.

"Anyhow, my honey is in her grave."

I am always glad to learn, grateful for instruction, good under correction, if I say so myself. I may avoid opposition, but I know when it's true friendship. We sat with whisky, poker chips, and cigars in this South Chicago kitchen penetrated by the dark breathing of the steel mills and refineries, under webs of power lines. I often note odd natural survivals in this heavy-industry district. Carp and catfish still live in the benzine-smelling ponds. Black women angle for them with dough-bait. Woodchucks and rabbits are seen not far from the dumps. Red-winged blackbirds with their shoulder tabs fly like uniformed ushers over the cattails. Certain flowers persist.

Grateful for this evening of human company I let myself go. I dropped nearly six hundred dollars, counting the check to Cantabile. But I'm so used to having money taken from me that I didn't really mind. I had great pleasure that evening, drinking, laughing a good deal, and talking. I talked and talked. Evidently I discussed my interests and projects in some detail, and later I was told that I alone failed to understand what was going on. The other gamblers dropped out when they saw how the Cantabile cousins were cheating. They were flashing cards, finagling the deck, and pouncing on each pot.

"They don't get away with that on my turf," shouted George in one of his theatrical bursts of irrationality.

"But Rinaldo is dangerous."

"Rinaldo is a punk!" George yelled.

Possibly so, but in the Capone era the Cantabiles had been bad eggs. At that time the entire world identified Chicago with blood—there were the stockyards and there were the gang wars. In the Chicago blood-hierarchy the Cantabiles had stood in about the middle rank. They worked for the Mob, they drove whisky trucks, and they beat and shot people. They were average minor hoodlums and racketeers. But in the Forties a weak-minded Cantabile uncle on the Chicago police force brought disgrace upon the family. He got drunk in a bar and two playful punks took away his guns and had fun with him. They made him crawl on his belly and forced him to gobble filth and sawdust from the floor, they kicked his buttocks. After they had tormented and humiliated him and while he lay crying with rage they ran away, full of glee, throwing down the guns. This was their big mistake. He pursued them and shot them dead in the street. Since then, said George, no one would take the Cantabiles seriously. Old Ralph (Moochy) Cantabile, now a lifer at Joliet, ruined the family with the Mob by murdering two adolescents. This was why Rinaldo could not afford to be brushed off by a person like me, well known in Chicago, who lost to him at poker and then stopped his check. Rinaldo, or Ronald, may have had no standing in the underworld but he had done terrible things to my Mercedes. Whether his rage was a real hoodlum's rage, natural or contrived, who could say? But he was evidently one of those proud sensitive fellows who give so much trouble because they are passionate about internal matters of very slight interest to any sensible person.

I was not so completely unrealistic that I failed to ask myself whether by a sensible person I meant myself. Returning from the bank I shaved, and I noticed how my face, framed to be cheerful, taking a metaphysical premise of universal helpfulness, asserting that the appearance of mankind on this earth was on the whole a good thing—how this face, filled with premises derived from capitalist democracy, was now depressed, retracted in unhappiness, sullen, unpleasant to shave. Was I the aforementioned sensible person?

I performed a few impersonal operations. I did a little ontogeny and phylogeny on myself. Recapitulation: the family was called Tsitrine and came from Kiev. The name was Anglicized at Ellis Island. I was born in Appleton, Wisconsin, the birthplace also of Harry Houdini with whom I think I have some affinities. I grew up in Polish Chicago, I went to the Chopin Grammar School, I spent my eighth year in the public ward of a TB sanatorium. Good people donated piles of colored funny papers to the sanatorium. These were stacked high beside each bed. The children followed the adventures of Slim Jim and Boob McNutt. In addition, day and night, I read the Bible. One visit a week was allowed, my parents taking turns, my mother with her bosom in old green serge, big-eyed, straight-nosed, and white with worry—her deep feelings inhibited her breathing—and my father the immigrant desperate battler coming from the frost, his coat saturated with cigarette smoke. Kids hemorrhaged in the night and choked on blood and were dead. In the morning the white geometry of made-up beds had to be coped with. I became very thoughtful here and I think that my disease of the lungs passed over into an emotional disorder so that I sometimes felt, and still feel, poisoned by eagerness, a congestion of tender impulses together with fever and enthusiastic dizziness. Owing to the TB I connected breathing with joy, and owing to the gloom of the ward I connected joy with light, and owing to my irrationality I related light on the walls to light inside me. I appear to have become a Hallelujah and Glory type. Furthermore (concluding) America is a didactic country whose people always offer their personal experiences as a helpful lesson to the rest, hoping to hearten them and to do them good—an intensive sort of personal public-relations project. There are times when I see this as idealism. There are other times when it looks to me like pure delirium. With everyone sold on the good how does all the evil get done? When Humboldt called me an ingenu, wasn't this what he was getting at? Crystallizing many evils in himself, poor fellow, he died as an example, his legacy a question addressed to the public. The death question itself, which Walt Whitman saw as the question of questions.

At all events I didn't care a bit for the way I looked in the mirror. I saw angelic precipitates condensing into hypocrisy, especially around my mouth. So I finished shaving by touch and only opened my eyes when I started to dress. I chose a quiet suit and necktie. I didn't want to provoke Cantabile by appearing showy.

I didn't have to wait long for the elevator. It was just past dog time in my building. During dog-walking hours it's hopeless, you have to use the stairs. I went out to my dented car which, in maintenance alone, ran me fifteen hundred dollars per annum. In the street the air was bad. It was the pre-Christmas season, dark December, and a brown air, more gas than air, crossed the lake from the great steel-and-oil complex of South Chicago, Hammond, and Gary, Indiana. I got in and started the engine, also turning on the radio. When the music began I wished that there might be more switches to turn on, for it was somehow not enough. The cultural FM stations offered holiday concerts of Corelli, Bach, and Palestrina—Music Antiqua, conducted by the late Greenberg, with Cohen on the viola da gamba and Levi on the harpsichord. They performed pious and beautiful cantatas on ancient instruments while I tried to look through the windshield bashed by Cantabile. I had the fresh fifty-dollar bills in a packet together with my specs, billfold, and handkerchief. I hadn't yet decided in what order to proceed. I never decide such things but wait for them to be revealed and, on the Outer Drive, it occurred to me to stop at the Downtown Club. My mind was in one of its Chicago states. How should I describe this phenomenon? In a Chicago state I infinitely lack something, my heart swells, I feel a tearing eagerness. The sentient part of the soul wants to express itself. There are some of the symptoms of an overdose of caffeine. At the same time I have a sense of being the instrument of external powers. They are using me either as an example of human error or as the mere shadow of desirable things to come. I drove. The huge pale lake washed forward. To the east was a white Siberian sky and McCormick Place, like an aircraft carrier, moored at the shore. Life had withdrawn from the grass. It had its wintry buff color. Motorists swerved up alongside to look at the Mercedes, so incredibly mutilated.

I wanted to speak to Vito Langobardi at the Downtown Club to get his views, if any, on Rinaldo Cantabile. Vito was a big-time hoodlum, a pal of the late Murray the Camel and the Battaglias. We often played racquet ball together, I liked Langobardi. I liked him very much, and I thought him fond of me. He was a most important underworld personality, so high in the organization that he had become rarefied into a gentleman and we discussed only shoes and shirts. Among the members only he and I wore tailored shirts with necktie loops on the underside of the collar. By these loops we were in some sense joined. As in a savage tribe I once read about in which, after childhood, brother and sister do not meet until the threshold of old age because of a terrific incest taboo, when suddenly the prohibition ends . . . no, the simile is no good. But I had known many violent kids at school, terrible kids whose adult life was entirely different from mine, and now we could chat about fishing in Florida and custom-made shirts with loops or the problems of Langobardi's Doberman. After games, in the nude democracy of the locker room we sociably sipped fruit juice, and chatted about X-rated movies. "I never go to them," he said. "What if the show got raided and they arrested me? How would it look in the papers?" What you need for quality is a few million dollars, and Vito with millions salted away was straight quality. Rough talk he left to the commodity brokers and lawyers. On the court he tottered just a little when he ran, for his calf muscles were not strongly developed, a defect common also in nervous children. But his game was subtle. He outgeneraled me always because he always knew exactly what I was doing behind his back. I was attached to Vito.

Racquet ball or paddle ball to which I was introduced by George Swiebel is an extremely fast and bruising game. You collide with other players or run into the walls. You are hit in the backswing, you often catch yourself in the face with your own racquet. The game has cost me a front tooth. I knocked it out myself and had to have a root-canal and a crown job. First I was a puny child, a TB patient, then I strengthened myself, then I degenerated, then George forced me to recover muscle tone. On some mornings I am lame, hardly able to straighten my back when I get out of bed but by midday I am on the court playing, leaping, flinging myself full length on the floor to scoop dead shots and throwing my legs and spinning entrechats like a Russian dancer. However, I am not a good player. I am too tangled about the heart, overdriven. I fall into a competitive striving frenzy. Then, walloping the ball, I continually say to myself, "Dance, dance, dance, dance!" Convinced that mastery of the game depends upon dancing. But gangsters and businessmen, translating their occupational style into these matches, outdance me and win. I tell myself that when I achieve mental and spiritual clarity and translate these into play nobody will be able to touch me. Nobody. I'll beat everyone. Meantime, notwithstanding the clouded spiritual state that prevents me from winning, I play violently because I get desperate without strenuous action. Just desperate. And now and then one of the middle-aged athletes keels over. Rushed to the hospital, some players have never come back. Langobardi and I played Cut-Throat (the three-man game) with a man named Hildenfisch, who succumbed to a heart attack. We had noticed that Hildenfisch had been panting. Afterward he went to rest in the sauna and someone ran out saying, "Hildenfisch has fainted." When the black attendants laid him on the floor he spurted water. I knew what this loss of sphincter control meant. Mechanical resuscitation equipment was sent for but nobody knew how to operate it.

At times when I pushed too hard at the game, Scottie, the athletic director, told me to quit. "Stop and look at yourself, Charlie. You're purple." In the mirror I was gruesome, gushing sweat, dark, black, my heart clubbing away inside. I felt slightly deaf. The eustachian tubes! I made my own diagnosis. Owing to the blood pressure my tubes were crinkling. "Walk it off," said Scottie. I walked back and forth on the patch of carpet forever identified with poor Hildenfisch, surly inferior Hildenfisch. In the sight of death I was no better than Hildenfisch. And once when I had overdone things on the court and lay panting on the red plastic couch, Langobardi came over and gave me a look. When he brooded he squinted. One eye seemed to cross over like a piano-player's hand. "Why do you push it, Charlie?" he said. "At our age one short game is plenty. Do you see me play more? One of these days you could seven out. Remember Hildenfisch."

Yes. Seven out. Right. I could roll bad dice. I must stop this tease-act with death. I was touched by Langobardi's concern. Was it personal solicitude, however? These health-club fatalities were bad, and two coronaries in a row would make this a gloomy place. Still Vito wished to do what he could for me.

There was little of substance that we could tell each other. When he was on the telephone I sometimes observed him. In his own way he was an American executive. Handsome Langobardi dressed far better than any board chairman. Even his coat sleeves were ingeniously lined, and the back of his waistcoat was made of beautiful paisley material. Calls came in the name of Finch, the shoeshine man "—Johnny Finch, Johnny Finch, telephone, extension five—" and Langobardi took these Finch calls. He was manly, he had power. In his low voice he gave instructions, made rulings, decisions, set penalties, probably. Now then, could he say anything serious to me? But could I tell him what was on my mind? Could I say that that morning I had been reading Hegel's *Phenomenology*, the pages on freedom and death? Could I say that I had been thinking about the history of human consciousness with special emphasis on the question of boredom? Could I say that for years now I had been preoccupied with this theme and that I had discussed it with the late poet Von Humboldt Fleisher? Never. Even with astrophysicists, with professors of economics or paleontology, it was impossible to discuss such things. There were beautiful and moving things in Chicago, but culture was not one of them. What we had was a cultureless city pervaded nevertheless by Mind. Mind without culture was the name of the game, wasn't it? How do you like that! It's accurate. I had accepted this condition long ago.

Langobardi's eyes seemed to have the periscope power of seeing around corners.

"Get smart, Charlie. Do it the way I do," he said.

I had thanked him sincerely for his kindly interest. "I'm trying," I said.

So I parked today under the chill pillars at the rear of the club. Then I rose in the elevator and came out at the barbershop. There, the usual busy sight—the three barbers: the big Swede with dyed hair, the Sicilian, always himself (not even shaved), and the Japanese. Each had the same bouffant coiffure, each wore a yellow vest with golden buttons over a short-sleeved shirt. All three were using hot-air guns with blue muzzles and shaping the hair of three customers. I entered the club through the washroom where bulbs were bleaking over the sinks and Finch, the real Johnny Finch, was filling the urinals with heaps of ice cubes. Langobardi was there, an early bird. Lately he had taken to wearing his hair in a little fringe, like an English country churchwarden. He sat nude, glancing at *The Wall Street Journal* and gave me a short smile. Now what? Could I throw myself into a new relationship with Langobardi, hitch a chair forward and sit with my elbows on my knees, looking into his face and opening my own features to the warmth of impulse? Eyes dilated with doubt, with confidentiality, might I say, "Vito, I need a little help"? Or, "Vito, how bad is this fellow Rinaldo Cantabile?" My heart knocked violently—as it had knocked decades earlier when I was about to proposition a woman. Langobardi had now and then done me small favors, booking tables in restaurants where reservations were hard to get. But to ask him about Cantabile would be a professional consultation. You didn't do that at the club. Vito had once bawled out Alphonse, one of the masseurs, for asking me a bookish question. "Don't bug the man, Al. Charlie doesn't come here to talk about his trade. We all come to forget business." When I told this to Renata she said, "So you two have a relationship." Now I saw that Langobardi and I had a relationship in the same way that the Empire State Building had an attic.

"You want to play a short game?" he said.

"No, Vito, I came to get something from my locker."

The usual casting about, I was thinking as I went back to the beat-up Mercedes. How typical of me. The usual craving. I looked for help. I longed for someone to do the stations of the cross with me. Just like Pa. And where was Pa? Pa was in the cemetery.

AT the Mercedes shop the distinguished official and technician in the white smock was naturally curious but I refused to answer questions. "I don't know how this happened, Fritz. I found it this way. Fix it. I don't want to see the bill, either. Just send it to the Continental Illinois. They'll pay it." Fritz charged like a brain surgeon.

I flagged a taxi in the street. The driver was wild-looking with an immense Afro like a shrub from the gardens at Versailles. The back of his cab was dusty with cigarette ashes and had a tavern odor. There was a bullet-proof screen between us. He made a fast turn and charged due west on Division Street. I could see little, because of the blurred Plexiglas and the Afro, but I didn't really need to look, I knew it all by heart. Large parts of Chicago decay and fall down. Some are rebuilt, others just lie there. It's like a film montage of rise fall and rise. Division Street where the old Bath stands used to be Polish and now is almost entirely Puerto Rican. In the Polish days, the small brick bungalows were painted fresh red, maroon, and candy green. The grass plots were fenced with iron pipe. I always thought that there must be Baltic towns that looked like this, Gdynia for instance, the difference being that the Illinois prairie erupted in vacant lots and tumbleweed rolled down the streets. Tumbleweed is so melancholy.

In the old days of ice wagons and coal wagons householders used to cut busted boilers in half, set them out on the grass plots, and fill them with flowers. Big Polish women in ribboned caps went out in the spring with cans of Sapolio and painted these boiler-planters so that they shone silver against the blaring red of the brick. The double rows of rivets stood out like the raised-skin patterns of African tribes. Here the women grew geraniums, sweet William, and other low-grade dusty flowers. I showed all of this to Humboldt Fleisher years ago. He came to Chicago to give a reading for *Poetry* magazine and asked me for a tour of the city. We were dear friends then. I had come back to see my father and to put the last touches on my book, *New Deal Personalities*, at the Newberry Library. I took Humboldt on the El to the stockyards. He saw the Loop. We went to the lakeshore and listened to the foghorns. They bawled melancholy over the limp silk fresh lilac drowning water. But Humboldt responded mostly to the old neighborhood. The silvered boiler rivets and the blazing Polish geraniums got him. He listened pale and moved to the buzzing of roller-skate wheels on the brittle cement. I too am sentimental about urban ugliness. In the modern spirit of ransoming the commonplace, all this junk and wretchedness, through art and poetry, by the superior power of the soul.

Mary, my eight-year-old daughter, has discovered this about

me. She knows my weakness for ontogeny and phylogeny. She always asks to hear what life was like way-back-when.

"We had coal stoves," I tell her. "The kitchen range was black, with a nickel trim—huge. The parlor stove had a dome like a little church, and you could watch the fire through the isinglass. I had to carry up the scuttle and take down the ashes."

"What did you wear?"

"A leatherette war-ace cap with rabbit-fur flaps, high-top boots with a sheath for a rusty jackknife, long black stockings, and plus fours. Underneath, woolly combinations which left lint in my navel and elsewhere."

"What else was it like?" my younger daughter wanted to know. Lish, who is ten years old, is her mother's child and such information would not interest her. But Mary is less pretty, though to my mind she is more attractive (more like her father). She is secretive and greedy. She lies and steals more than most small girls, and this is also endearing. She hides chewing gum and chocolates with stirring ingenuity. I find her candy buried under the upholstery or in my filing cabinet. She has learned that I don't often look at my research materials. She flatters and squeezes me precociously. And she wants to hear about old times. She has her own purposes in evoking and manipulating my emotions. But Papa is quite willing to manifest the old-time feelings. In fact I must transmit these feelings. For I have plans for Mary. Oh, nothing so definite as plans, perhaps. I have an idea that I may be able to pervade the child's mind with my spirit so that she will later take up the work I am getting too old or too weak or too silly to continue. She alone, or perhaps she and her husband. With any luck. I worry about the girl. In a locked drawer of my desk I keep notes and memos for her, many of them written under the influence of liquor. I promise myself to censor these one day, before death catches me off base on the racquet-ball court or on the Posturepedic mattress of some Renata or other. Mary is sure to be an intelligent woman. She interprets "Für Elise" much better than Lish. She feels the music. My heart is often troubled for Mary, however. She will be a straight-nosed thin broad who feels the music. And personally I prefer plump women with fine breasts. So I felt sorry for her already. As for the project or purpose I want her to carry on, it is a very personal overview of the Intellectual Comedy of the modern mind. No one person could do this comprehensively. By the end of the nineteenth century what had been the ample novels of Balzac's Comedy had already been reduced to stories by Chekhov in his Russian *Comédie Humaine*. Now it's even less possible to be comprehensive. I never had a work of fiction in mind but a different kind of imaginative projection. Different also from Whitehead's *Adventures of Ideas*. . . . This is not the moment to explain it. Whatever it was, I conceived of it while still a youngish man. It was actually Humboldt who lent me the book of Valéry that suggested it. Valéry wrote of Leonardo, "*Cet Apollon me ravissait au plus haut degré de moi-même.*" I too was ravished with permanent effect—perhaps carried beyond my mental means. But Valéry had added a note in the margin: "*Trouve avant de chercher.*" This finding before seeking was my special gift. If I had any gift.

However, my small daughter would say to me with deadly accuracy of instinct, "Tell me what your mother used to do. Was she pretty?"

"I think she was very pretty. I don't look like her. And she did cooking, baking, laundry and ironing, canning and pickling. She could tell fortunes with cards and sing trembly Russian songs. She and my father took turns visiting me at the sanatorium, every other week. In February the vanilla ice cream they brought was so hard you couldn't cut it with a knife. And what else—ah yes, at home when I lost a tooth she would throw it behind the stove and ask the little mouse to bring a better one. You see what kind of teeth those bloody mice palmed off on me."

"You loved your mother?"

Eager swelling feeling suddenly swept in. I forgot that I was talking to a child and I said, "Oh, I loved them all terribly, abnormally. I was all torn up with love. Deep in the heart. I used to cry in the sanatorium because I might never make it home and see them. I'm sure they never knew how I loved them, Mary. I had a TB fever and also a love fever. A passionate morbid little boy. At school I was always in love. At home if I was first to get up in the morning I suffered because they were still asleep. I wanted them to wake up so that the whole marvelous thing could continue. I also loved Menasha the boarder and Julius, my brother, your Uncle Julius."

I shall have to lay aside these emotional data.

At the moment money, checks, hoodlums, automobiles preoccupied me.

Another check was on my mind. It had been sent by my friend Thaxter, the one whom Huggins accused of being a CIA agent. You see Thaxter and I were preparing to bring out a journal, *The Ark*. We were all ready. Wonderful things were to be printed in it—pages from my imaginative reflections on a world transformed by Mind, for example. But meantime Thaxter had defaulted on a certain loan.

It's a long story and one that I'd rather not go into at this point. For two reasons. One is that I love Thaxter, whatever he does. The other is that I actually do think too much about money. It's no good trying to conceal it. It's there and it's base. Earlier when I described how George saved Sharon's life when her throat was cut, I spoke of blood as a vital substance. Well, money is a vital substance, too. Thaxter was supposed to repay part of the defaulted loan. Broke but grandiose he had ordered a check from his Italian bank for me, the Banco Ambrosiano of Milan. Why the Banco? Why Milan? But all of Thaxter's arrangements were out of the ordinary. He had had a transatlantic upbringing and was equally at home in France and in California. You couldn't mention a region so remote that Thaxter didn't have an uncle there, or an interest in a mine, or an old château or villa. Thaxter with his exotic ways was another of my headaches. But I couldn't resist him. However, that too must wait. Only one last word: Thaxter wanted people to believe that he was once a CIA agent. It was a wonderful rumor and he did everything to encourage it. It greatly added to his mysteriousness, and mystery was one of his little rackets. This was harmless and in fact endearing. It was even philanthropic, as charm always is—up to a point. Charm always is a bit of a racket.

The cab pulled up at the Bath twenty minutes early and I wasn't going to loiter there so I said through the perforations of the bulletproof screen, "Go on, drive west. Take it easy, I just want to look around." The cabbie heard me and nodded his Afro. It was like an enormous black dandelion in seed, blown, all its soft spindles standing out.

In the last six months more old neighborhood landmarks had been torn down. This shouldn't have mattered much. I can't say why it made such a difference. But I was in a state. It almost seemed to me that I could hear myself rustling and fluttering in the back seat like a bird touring the mangroves of its youth, now car dumps. I stared with pulsatory agitation through the soiled windows. A whole block had gone down. Lovi's Hungarian Restaurant had been swept away, plus Ben's Pool Hall and the old brick carbarn and Gratch's Funeral Parlor, out of which both my parents had been buried. Eternity got no picturesque interval here. The ruins of time had been bulldozed, scraped, loaded in trucks, and dumped as fill. New steel beams were going up. Polish kielbasa no longer hung in butchers' windows. The sausages in the *carnicería* were Caribbean, purple and wrinkled. The old shop signs were gone. The new ones said HOY. MUDANZAS. IGLESIA.

"Keep going west," I said to the driver. "Past the park. Turn right on Kedzie."

The old boulevard now was a sagging ruin, waiting for the wreckers. Through great holes I could look into apartments where I had slept, eaten, done my lessons, kissed girls. You'd have to loathe yourself vividly to be indifferent to such destruction or, worse, rejoice at the crushing of the locus of these middle-class sentiments, glad that history had made rubble of them. In fact I know such tough guys. This very neighborhood produced them. Informers to the metaphysical-historical police against fellows like me whose hearts ache at the destruction of the past. But I had *come* here to be melancholy, to be sad about the wrecked walls and windows, the missing doors, the fixtures torn out, and the telephone cables ripped away and sold as junk. More particularly, I had come to see whether the house in which Naomi Lutz had lived was still standing. It was not. That made me feel very low.

In my highly emotional adolescence I had loved Naomi Lutz. I believe she was the most beautiful and perfect young girl I have ever seen, I adored her, and love brought out my deepest peculiarities. Her father was a respectable chiropodist.

He gave himself high medical airs, every inch the Doctor. Her mother was a dear woman, slipshod, harum-scarum, rather chinless, but with large glowing romantic eyes. Night after night I had to play rummy with Dr. Lutz, and on Sundays I helped him to wash and simonize his Auburn. But that was all right. When I loved Naomi Lutz I was safely *within life*. Its phenomena added up, they made sense. Death was an after all acceptable part of the proposition. I had my own little Lake Country, the park, where I wandered with my Modern Library Plato, Wordsworth, Swinburne, and *Un Cœur Simple*. Even in winter Naomi petted behind the rose garden with me. Among the frozen twigs I made myself warm inside her raccoon coat. There was a delicious mixture of coon skin and maiden fragrance. We breathed frost and kissed. Until I met Demmie Vonghel many years later, I loved no one so much as Naomi Lutz. But Naomi, while I was away in Madison, Wisconsin, reading poetry and studying rotation pool at the Rathskeller, married a pawnbroker. He dealt also in rebuilt office machinery and had plenty of money. I was too young to give her the charge accounts she had to have at Field's and Saks, and I believe the mental burdens and responsibilities of an intellectual's wife had frightened her besides. I had talked all the time about my Modern Library books, of poetry and history, and she was afraid that she would disappoint me. She told me so. I said to her, if a tear was an intellectual thing how much more intellectual pure love was. It needed no cognitive additives. But she only looked puzzled. It was this sort of talk by which I had lost her. She did not look me up even when her husband lost all his money and deserted her. He was a sporting man, a gambler. He had to go into hiding at last, because the juice men were after him. I believe they had even broken his ankles. Anyway, he changed his name and went or limped to the Southwest. Naomi sold her classy Winnetka house and moved to Marquette Park, where the family owned a bungalow. She took a job in the linen department at Field's.

As the cab went back to Division Street I was making a wry parallel between Naomi's husband's Mafia troubles and my own. He had muffed it, too. I couldn't help thinking what a blessed life I might have led with Naomi Lutz. Fifteen thousand nights embracing Naomi and I would have smiled at the solitude and boredom of the grave. I would have needed no bibliography, no stock portfolios, no medal from the Legion of Honor.

So we drove again through what had become a tropical West Indies slum, resembling the parts of San Juan that stand beside lagoons which bubble and smell like stewing tripe. There was the same crushed plaster, smashed glass, garbage in the streets, the same rude amateur blue chalk lettering on the shops.

But the Russian Bath where I was supposed to meet Rinaldo Cantabile stood more or less unchanged. It was also a proletarian hotel or lodging house. On the second floor there had always lived aged workingstiffs, lone Ukrainian grandfathers, retired car-line employees, a pastry cook famous for his icings who had to quit because his hands became arthritic. I knew the place from boyhood. My father, like old Mr. Swiebel, had believed it was healthful, good for the blood to be scrubbed with oak leaves lathered in old pickle buckets. Such retrograde people still exist, resisting modernity, dragging their feet. As Menasha the boarder, an amateur physicist (but mostly he wanted to be a dramatic tenor and took voice lessons: he had worked at Brunswick Phonograph Co. as a punch-press operator), once explained to me, human beings could affect the rotation of the earth. How? Well, if the whole race at an agreed moment were to scuff its feet the revolution of the planet would actually slow down. This might also have an effect on the moon and on the tides. Of course Menasha's real topic was not physics but concord, or unity. I think that some through stupidity and others through perversity would scuff the wrong way. However, the old guys at the Bath do seem to be unconsciously engaged in a collective attempt to buck history.

These Division Street steam-bathers don't look like the trim proud people downtown. Even old Feldstein pumping his Exercycle in the Downtown Club at the age of eighty would be out of place on Division Street. Forty years ago Feldstein was a swinger, a high roller, a good-time Charlie on Rush Street. In spite of his age he is a man of today, whereas the patrons of the Russian Bath are cast in an antique form. They have swelling buttocks and fatty breasts as yellow as buttermilk. They stand on thick pillar legs affected with a sort of creeping verdigris or blue-cheese mottling of the ankles. After steaming, these old fellows eat enormous snacks of bread and salt herring or large ovals of salami and dripping skirt-steak and they drink schnapps. They could knock down walls with their hard stout old-fashioned bellies. Things are very elementary here. You feel that these people are almost conscious of obsolescence, of a line of evolution abandoned by nature and culture. So down in the super-heated subcellars all these Slavonic cavemen and wood demons with hanging laps of fat and legs of stone and lichen boil themselves and splash ice water on their heads by the bucket. Upstairs, on the television screen in the locker room, little dudes and grinning broads make smart talk or leap up and down. They are unheeded. Mickey who keeps the food concession fries slabs of meat and potato pancakes, and, with enormous knives, he hacks up cabbages for coleslaw and he quarters grapefruits (to be eaten by hand). The stout old men mounting in their bed sheets from the blasting heat have a strong appetite. Below, Franush the attendant makes steam by sloshing water on the white-hot boulders. These lie in a pile like Roman ballistic ammunition. To keep his brains from baking Franush wears a wet felt hat with the brim torn off. Otherwise he is naked. He crawls up like a red salamander with a stick to tip the latch of the furnace, which is too hot to touch, and then on all fours, with testicles swinging on a long sinew and the clean anus staring out, he backs away groping for the bucket. He pitches in the water and the boulders flash and sizzle. There may be no village in the Carpathians where such practices still prevail.

Loyal to this place, Father Myron Swiebel came every day of his life. He brought his own herring, buttered pumpernickel, raw onions, and bourbon whisky. He drove a Plymouth, though he had no driver's license. He could see well enough straight ahead, but because there were cataracts on both eyes he sideswiped many cars and did great damage in the parking lot.

I went in to reconnoiter. I was quite anxious about George. His advice had put me in this fix. But then I knew that it was bad advice. Why did I take it? Because he had raised his voice with such authority? Because he had cast himself as an expert on the underworld and I had let him do his stuff? Well, I hadn't used my best mind. But my best mind was now alert and I believed I could handle Cantabile. I reckoned that Cantabile had already worked off his rage against the car and I thought the debt was largely paid.

I asked the concessionaire, Mickey, who stood in the smoke behind the counter searing fatty steaks and frying onions, "Has George come in? Does his old man expect him?"

I thought that if George were here it was not likely that Cantabile would rush fully dressed into the steam to punch or beat or kick him. Of course Cantabile was an unknown quantity. You couldn't guess what Cantabile might do. Either in rage or from calculation.

"George isn't here. The old man is steaming."

"Good. Is he expecting his son?"

"No. George was here Sunday, so he won't come again. He's only once a week with his father."

"Good. Excellent!"

Built like a bouncer with huge bar arms and an apron tied very high under his oxters, Mickey has a twisted lip. During the Depression he had to sleep in the parks and the cold ground gave him a partial paralysis of the cheek. This makes him seem to scoff or jeer. A misleading impression. He is a gentle earnest and peaceful person. A music-lover, he takes a season ticket at the Lyric Opera.

"I haven't seen you in a long time, Charlie. Go steam with the old man, he'll be glad for the company."

But I hurried out again past the cashier's cage with its little steel boxes where patrons left their valuables. I passed the squirming barber pole, and when I got to the sidewalk, which was as dense as the galaxy with stars of broken glass, a white Thunderbird pulled up in front of the Puerto Rican sausage shop across the street and Ronald Cantabile got out. He sprang out, I should say. I saw that he was in a terrific state. Dressed in a brown raglan coat with a matching hat and wearing tan kid boots, he was tall and good-looking. I had noted his dark dense mustache at the poker game. It resembled fine fur. But through the crackling elegance of dress there was a current, a desperate sweep, so that the man came out, so to speak, raging from the neck up. Though he was on the other side of the street I could see how furiously pale he was. He had worked himself up to intimidate me, I thought. But also he was making unusual steps. His feet behaved strangely. Cars and trucks came between us just then so that he could not cross over. Beneath the cars I could see him trying to dodge through. The boots were exquisite. At the first short break in the traffic Cantabile held open his raglan to me. He was wearing a magnificent broad belt. But surely it wasn't a belt that he wanted to display. Just beside the buckle something was sticking out. He clapped his hand to it. He wanted me to know that he was carrying a gun. More traffic came, and Cantabile was jumping up and down, glaring at me over the tops of automobiles. Under the utmost strain he called out to me when the last truck had passed, "You alone?"

"Alone. I'm alone."

He drew himself up toward the shoulders with peculiar twisting intensity. "You got anybody hiding?"

"No. Just me. Nobody."

He threw open the door and brought up two baseball bats from the floor of the Thunderbird. A bat in each hand, he started toward me. A van came between us. Now I could see nothing but his feet moving rapidly in the fancy boots. I thought, He sees I've come to pay. Why should he clobber me? He's got to know I wouldn't pull anything. He's proved his point on the car. And I've seen the gun. Should I run? Since I had discovered on Thanksgiving Day how fast I could still run, I seemed oddly eager to use this ability. Speed was one of my resources. Some people are too fast for their own good, like Asahel in the Book of Samuel. Still it occurred to me that I might dash up the stairs of the Bath and take shelter in the cashier's office where the little steel boxes were. I could crouch on the floor and ask the cashier to pass the four hundred and fifty dollars through the grille to Cantabile. I knew the cashier quite well. But he'd never let me in. He couldn't. I wasn't bonded. He had once referred to this special circumstance when we were having a chat. But I couldn't believe that Cantabile would batter me down. Not in the street. Not as I waited and bowed my head. And just at that moment I remembered Konrad Lorenz's discussion of wolves. The defeated wolf offered his throat, and the victor snapped but wouldn't bite. So I was bowing my head. Yes, but damn my memory! What did Lorenz say next? Humankind was different, but in what respect? How! I couldn't remember. My brain was disintegrating. The day before, in the bathroom, I hadn't been able to find the word for the isolation of the contagious, and I was in agony. I thought, whom should I telephone about this? My mind is going! And then I stood and clutched the sink until the word "quarantine" mercifully came back to me. Yes, quarantine, but I was losing my grip. I take such things hard. In old age my father's memory also failed. So I was shaken. The difference between man and other species such as the wolves never did come back to me. Perhaps the lapse was excusable at a time like this. But it served to show how carelessly I was reading, these days. This inattentiveness and memory-failure boded no good.

As the last of a string of cars passed, Cantabile took a long stride with both bats as if to rush upon me without a pause. But I yelled, "For Christ's sake, Cantabile!"

He paused. I held up open hands. Then he flung one of the bats into the Thunderbird and started for me with the other.

I called out to him, "I brought the money. You don't have to beat my brains out."

"You got a gun?"

"I've got nothing."

"You come over here," he said.

I started willingly to cross the street. He made me stop in the middle.

"Stay right there," he said. I was in the center of heavy traffic, cars honking and the provoked drivers rolling down their windows, already fighting mad. He tossed the second bat back into the T-bird. Then he strode up and took hold of me roughly. He treated me as if I deserved the extreme penalty. I held out the money, I offered it to him on the spot. But he refused to look at it. Furious he pushed me onto the sidewalk and toward the stairs of the Bath and past the squirming barbershop cylinders of red white and blue. We hurried in, past the cashier's cage and along the dirty corridor.

"Go on, go on," said Cantabile.

"Where do you want to go?"

"To the can. Where is it?"

"Don't you want the dough?"

"I said the can! The can!"

I then understood, his bowels were acting up, he had been caught short, he had to go to the toilet, and I was to go with him. He wouldn't allow me to wait in the street. "Okay," I said, "just take it easy and I'll lead you." He followed me through the locker room. The john entrance was doorless. Only the individual stalls have doors. I motioned him forward and was about to sit down on one of the locker-room benches nearby but he gave me a hard push on the shoulder and drove me forward. These toilets are the Bath at its worst. The radiators put up a stunning dry heat. The tiles are never washed, never disinfected. A hot dry urine smell rushes to your eyes like onion fumes. "Jesus!" said Cantabile. He kicked open a stall, still keeping me in front of him. He said, "You go in first."

"The both of us?" I said.

"Hurry up."

"There's space only for one."

He tugged out his gun and shook the butt at me. "You want this in your teeth?" The black fur of his mustache spread as the lip of his distorted face stretched. His brows were joined above the nose like the hilt of a large dagger. "In the corner, you!" He slammed the door and panting, took off his things. He thrust the raglan and the matching hat into my arms, although there was a hook. There was even a piece of hardware I had never before noticed. Attached to the door was a brass fitting, a groove labeled *Cigar*, a touch of class from the old days. He was seated now with the gun held in both palms, his hands between his knees, his eyes first closing then dilating greatly.

In a situation like this I can always switch out and think about the human condition over-all. Of course he wanted to humiliate me. Because I was a *chevalier* of the *Légion d'honneur*? Not that he actually knew of this. But he was aware that I was as they would say in Chicago a *Brain*, a man of culture or intellectual attainments. Was this why I had to listen to him rumbling and slopping and smell his stink? Perhaps fantasies of savagery and monstrosity, of beating my brains out, had loosened his bowels. Humankind is full of nervous invention of this type, and I started to think (to distract myself) of all the volumes of ape behavior I had read in my time, of Kohler and

Yerkes and Zuckerman, of Marais on baboons and Schaller on gorillas, and of the rich repertory of visceral-emotional sensitivities in the anthropoid branch. It was even possible that I was a more limited person than a fellow like Cantabile in spite of my concentration on intellectual achievement. For it would never have occurred to me to inflict anger on anyone by such means. This might have been a sign that his vital endowment or natural imagination was more prodigal and fertile than mine. In this way, thinking improving thoughts, I waited with good poise while he crouched there with his hardened dagger brows. He was a handsome slender man whose hair had a natural curl. It was cropped so close that you could see the roots of his curls and I observed the strong contraction of his scalp in this moment of stress. He wanted to inflict a punishment on me but the result was only to make us more intimate.

As he stood and then wiped, and then pulled his shirttails straight, belting his pants with the large oval buckle and sticking back the gun (I hoped the safety catch was on), as I say, when he pulled his shirttails straight and buckled his stylish belt on the hip-huggers, thrusting the gun in, flushing the toilet with his pointed soft boot, too fastidious to touch the lever with his hand—he said, "Christ, if I catch the crabs here . . . !" As if that would be my fault. He was evidently a violent reckless blamer. He said, "You don't know how I hated to sit here. These old guys must piss on the seats." This too he entered on the debit side against me. Then he said, "Who owns this joint?"

Now this was a fascinating question. It had never occurred to me, you know. The Bath was so ancient, it was like the Pyramids of Egypt, the Gardens of Ashurbanipal. It was like water seeking its level, or like gravitational force. But who in fact was its proprietor? "I've never heard of an owner," I said. "For all I know it's some old party out in British Columbia."

"Don't get smart. You're too fucking smart. I only asked for information. I'll find out."

To turn the faucet he used a piece of toilet paper. He washed his hands without soap, none was provided by the management. At this moment I offered him the nine fifty-dollar bills, again. He refused to look at them. He said, "My hands are wet." He wouldn't use the roller towel. It was, I must admit, repulsively caked, filthy, with a certain originality in the way of filth. I held out my pocket handkerchief, but he ignored it. He didn't want his anger to diminish. Spreading his fingers wide he shook them dry. Full of the nastiness of the place he said, "Is this what they call a Bath?"

"Well," I said, "the bathing is all downstairs."

They had two long rows of showers, below, which led to the heavy wooden doors of the steam room. There also was a small cistern, the cold plunge. The water was unchanged from year to year, and it was a crocodile's habitat if I ever saw one.

Cantabile now hurried out to the lunch counter, and I followed him. There he dried his hands with paper napkins which he pulled from the metal dispenser angrily. He crumpled these embossed flimsy papers and threw them on the floor. He said to Mickey, "Why don't you have soap and towels in the can? Why don't you wash the goddamn place out? There's no disinfectant in there."

Mickey was very mild, and he said, "No? Joe is supposed to take care of it. I buy him Top Job, Lysol." He spoke to Joe. "Don't you put in mothballs any more?" Joe was black and old, and he answered nothing. He was leaning on the shoeshine chair with its brass pedestals, the upside-down legs and rigid feet (reminiscent of my own feet and legs during the Yoga headstand). He was there to remind us all of some remote, grand considerations and he would not answer any temporal questions.

"You guys are gonna buy supplies from me," said Cantabile. "Disinfectant, liquid soap, paper towels, everything. The name is Cantabile. I've got a supply business on Clybourne Avenue." He took out a long pitted ostrich-skin wallet and threw several business cards on the counter.

"I'm not the boss," said Mickey. "All I have is the restaurant concession." But he picked up a card with deference. His big fingers were covered with black knife-marks.

"I better hear from you."

"I'll pass it along to the Management. They're downtown."

"Mickey, who owns the Bath?" I said.

"All I know is the Management, downtown."

It would be curious, I thought, if the Bath should turn out to belong to the Syndicate.

"Is George Swiebel here?" said Cantabile.

"No."

"Well, I want to leave him a message."

"I'll give you something to write on," said Mickey.

"There's nothing to write. Tell him he's a dumb shit. Tell him I said so."

Mickey had put on his specs to look for a piece of paper, and now he turned his spectacled face toward us as if to say that his only business was the coleslaw and skirt-steaks and whitefish. Cantabile did not ask for old Father Myron, who was steaming himself below.

We went out into the street. The weather had suddenly cleared. I couldn't decide whether gloomy weather suited the environment better than bright. The air was cold, the light was neat, and the shadows thrown by blackened buildings divided the sidewalks.

I said, "Well, now let me give you this money. I brought new bills. This ought to wrap the whole thing up, Mr. Cantabile."

"What—just like that? You think it's so easy?" said Rinaldo.

"Well, I'm sorry. It shouldn't have happened. I really regret it."

"You regret it! You regret your hacked-up car. You stopped a check on me, Citrine. Everybody blabbed. Everybody knows. You think I can allow it?"

"Mr. Cantabile, who knows—who is everybody? Was it really so serious? I was wrong—"

"Wrong, you fucking ape. . . !"

"Okay, I was stupid."

"Your pal George tells you to stop a check, so you stop it. Do you take that asshole's word for everything? Why didn't he catch Emil and me in the act? He has you pull this sneaky stunt and then you and he and the undertaker and the tuxedo guy and the other dummies spread around the gossip that Ronald Cantabile is a punk. Man! You could never get away with that. Don't you realize!"

"Yes, now I realize."

"No, I don't know what you realize. I was watching at the game, and I don't dig you. When are you going to do something *and know what you're doing*?" Those last words he spaced, he accented vehemently and uttered into my face.

Then he snatched away his coat, which I was still holding for him, the rich brown raglan with its large buttons. Circe might have had buttons like those in her sewing box. They were very beautiful, really, rather Oriental-treasure buttons.

The last garment I had seen resembling this one was worn by the late Colonel McCormick. I was then about twelve years old. His limousine had stopped in front of the Tribune Tower, and two short men came out. Each man held two pistols, and they circled on the pavement, crouching low. Then, in this four-gun setting, the Colonel stepped out from his car in just such a tobacco-colored coat as Cantabile's and a pinch hat with gleaming harsh fuzz. The wind was stiff, the air pellucid, the hat glistened like a bed of nettles.

"You don't think I know what I'm doing, Mr. Cantabile?"

"No you don't. You couldn't find your ass with both hands."

Well, he may have been right. But at least I wasn't crucifying anyone. Apparently life had not happened to me as it had happened to other people. For some indiscernible reason it happened differently to them, and so I was not a fit judge of their concerns and desires. Aware of this I acceded to more of these desires than was practical. I gave in to George's low-life expertise. Now I bent before Cantabile. My only resource was to try to remember useful things from my ethological reading about rats, geese, sticklebacks, and dancing flies. What good is all this reading if you can't use it in the crunch? All I asked was a small mental profit.

"Anyway, what about these fifty-dollar bills?" I said.

"I'll let you know when I'm ready to take them," he said. "You didn't like what happened to your car, did you?"

I said, "It's a beautiful machine. It was really heartless to do that."

Apparently the bats he had threatened me with were what he had used on the Mercedes and there were probably more assault weapons in the back seat of the Thunderbird. He made me get into this showy auto. It had leather bucket seats red as spilt blood and an immense instrument panel. He took off at top speed from a standstill, like an adolescent drag-racer, the tires wildly squealing.

In the car I got a slightly different impression of him. Seen in profile, his nose ended in a sort of white bulb. It was intensely, abnormally white. It reminded me of gypsum and it was darkly lined. His eyes were bigger than they ought to have been, artificially dilated perhaps. His mouth was wide, with an emotional underlip in which there was the hint of an early struggle to be thought full grown. His large feet and dark eyes also hinted that he aspired to some ideal, and that his partial attainment or nonattainment of the ideal was a violent grief to him. I suspected that the ideal itself might be fitful.

"Was it you or your cousin Emil that fought in Vietnam?"

We were speeding eastward on Division Street. He held the wheel in both hands as though it were a pneumatic drill to chop up the macadam. "What! Emil in the Army? Not that kid. He was 4-F, practically psycho. No, the most action Emil ever saw was during the 1968 riots in front of the Hilton. He was twigged out and didn't even know which side he was on. No, I was in Vietnam. The folks sent me to that smelly Catholic college near St. Louis that I mentioned at the game, but I dropped out and enlisted. That was sometime back."

"Did you fight?"

"I'll tell you what you want to hear. I stole a tank of gasoline—the truck, trailer, and all. I sold it to some blackmarket guys. I got caught but my folks made a deal. Senator Dirksen helped. I was only eight months in jail."

He had a record of his own. He wished me to know that he was a true Cantabile, a throwback to the Twenties and no mere Uncle Moochy. A military prison—he had a criminal pedigree and he could produce fear on his own credentials. Also the Cantabiles were evidently in small rackets of the lesser hoodlum sort, as witness the toilet-disinfectant business on Clybourne Avenue. Perhaps also a currency exchange or two —currency exchanges were often owned by former small-time racketeers. Or in the extermination business, another common favorite. But he was obviously in the minor leagues. Perhaps he was in no league at all. As a Chicagoan I had some sense of this. A real big shot used hired muscle. No Vito Langobardi would carry baseball bats in the back seat of his car. A Langobardi went to Switzerland for winter sports. Even his dog traveled in class. Not in decades had a Langobardi personally taken part in violence. No, this restless striving smoky-souled Cantabile was on the outside trying to get in. He was the sort of unacceptable entrepreneur that the sanitation department still fished out of the sewers after three months of decomposition. Certain persons of this type were occasionally found in the trunks of automobiles parked at O'Hare. The weight of the corpse at the back was balanced by a cinderblock laid on the motor.

Deliberately, at the next corner, Rinaldo ran a red light. He rode the bumper of the car ahead and he made other motorists chicken out. He was elegant, flashy. The seats of the T-bird were specially upholstered in soft leather—so soft, so crimson! He wore the sort of gloves sold to horsemen at Abercrombie & Fitch. At the expressway he swept right and gunned up the slope, running into merging traffic. Cars braked behind us. His radio played rock music. And I recognized Cantabile's scent. It was Canoe. I had once gotten a bottle of it for Christmas from a blind woman named Muriel.

In the squalid closet at the Bath when his pants were down and I was thinking about Zuckerman's apes at the London Zoo it had been clear that what was involved here were the plastic and histrionic talents of the human creature. In other words I was involved in a dramatization. It wouldn't have done much for the image of the Cantabiles, however, if he had actually shot off the gun that he held between his knees. It would make him too much like the crazy uncle who disgraced the family. That, I thought, was the whole point.

WAS I afraid of Cantabile? Not really. I don't know what he thought, but what I thought was perfectly clear to me. Absorbed in determining what a human being is, I went along with him. Cantabile may have believed that he was abusing a passive man. Not at all. I was a man active elsewhere. At the poker game, I received a visionary glimpse of this Cantabile. Of course, I was very high that night, if not downright drunk, but I saw the edge of his spirit rising from him, behind him. So when Cantabile yelled and threatened I didn't make a stand on grounds of proper pride—"Nobody treats Charlie Citrine like this, I'm going to the police," and so forth. No, the police had no such things to show me. Cantabile had made a very peculiar and strong impression on me.

What a human being is—I always had my own odd sense of this. For I did not have to live in the land of the horses, like Dr. Gulliver, my sense of mankind was strange enough without travel. In fact I traveled not to seek foreign oddities but to get away from them. I was drawn also to philosophical idealists because I was perfectly sure that *this* could not be *it*. Plato in the Myth of Er confirmed my sense that this was not my first time around. We had all been here before and would presently be here again. There was another place. Maybe a man like me was imperfectly reborn. The soul is supposed to be sealed by oblivion before its return to earthly life. Was it possible that my oblivion might be slightly defective? I never was a thorough Platonist. I never could believe that you could be reincarnated a bird or a fish. No soul once human was locked into a spider. In my case (which I suspect is not so rare as all that) there may have been an incomplete forgetting of the pure soul-life, so that the mineral condition of re-embodiment seemed abnormal, so that from an early age I was taken aback to see eyes move in faces, noses breathe, skins sweat, hairs grow, and the like, finding it comical. This was sometimes offensive to people born with full oblivion of their immortality.

This leads me to recall and reveal a day of marvelous spring and a noontime full of the most heavy silent white clouds, clouds like bulls, behemoths, and dragons. The place is Appleton, Wisconsin, and I am a grown man standing on a crate trying to see into the bedroom where I was born in the year 1918. I was probably conceived there, too, and directed by divine wisdom to appear in life as so-and-so, such-and-such (C. Citrine, Pulitzer Prize, Legion of Honor, father of Lish and Mary, husband of A, lover of B, a serious person, and a card). And why should this person be perched on a box, partly hidden by the straight twigs and glossy leaves of a flowering lilac? And without asking permission of the lady of the house? I had knocked and rung but she did not answer. And now her husband was standing at my back. He owned a gas station. I told him who I was. At first he was very hard-nosed. But I explained that this was my birthplace and I asked for old neighbors by name. Did he remember the Saunderses? Well, they were his cousins. This saved me a punch in the nose as a Peeping Tom. I could not say, "I am standing on this crate among these lilacs trying to solve the riddle of man, and not to see your stout wife in her panties." Which was indeed what I saw. Birth is sorrow (a sorrow that may be canceled by intercession) but in the room where my birth took place I beheld with sorrow of my own a fat old woman in underpants. With great presence of mind she pretended not to see my face at the screen but slowly left the room and phoned her husband. He ran from the gas pumps and nabbed me, laying oily hands on my exquisite gray suit—I was at the peak of my elegant period. But I was able to explain that I was in Appleton to prepare that article on Harry Houdini, also a native—as I have obsessively mentioned—and I experienced a sudden desire to look into the room where I was born.

"So what you got was an eyeful of my Missus."

He didn't take this hard. I think he understood. These matters of the spirit are widely and instantly grasped. Except of course by people who are in heavily fortified positions, mental opponents trained to resist what everyone is born knowing.

As soon as I saw Rinaldo Cantabile at George Swiebel's kitchen table I was aware that a natural connection existed between us.

I WAS now taken to the Playboy Club. Rinaldo was a member. He walked away from his supercar, the Bechstein of automobiles, leaving it to the car jockey. The checkroom Bunny knew him. From his behavior here I began to understand that my task was to make amends publicly. The Cantabiles had been defied. Maybe Rinaldo had been ordered at a family council to go out and repair the damage to their good bad name. And this matter of his reputation would consume a day—an entire day. And there were so many pressing needs, I had so many headaches already that I might justifiably have begged fate to give me a pass. I had a pretty good case.

"Are the people here?"

He threw over his coat. I also dropped mine. We stepped into the opulence, the semidarkness, the thick carpets of the bar where bottles shone, and sensual female forms went back and forth in an amber light. He took me by the arm into an elevator and we rose immediately to the top. Cantabile said, "We're going to see some people. When I give you the high sign, then you pay me the money and apologize."

We were standing before a table.

"Bill, I'd like to introduce Charlie Citrine," said Ronald to Bill.

"Hey, Mike, this is Ronald Cantabile," Bill said, on cue.

The rest was, Hey how are you, sit down, what'll you drink.

Bill was unknown to me, but Mike was Mike Schneiderman the gossip columnist. He was large heavy strong tanned sullen fatigued, his hair was razor styled, his cuff links were as big as his eyes, his necktie was a clumsy flap of silk brocade. He looked haughty, creased and sleepy, like certain oil-rich American Indians from Oklahoma. He drank an old-fashioned and held a cigar. His business was to sit with people in bars and restaurants. I was much too volatile for sedentary work like this, and I couldn't understand how it was done. But then I couldn't understand office jobs, either, or clerking or any of the confining occupations or routines. Many Americans described themselves as artists or intellectuals who should only have said that they were incapable of doing such work. I had many times discussed this with Von Humboldt Fleisher, and now and then with Gumbein the art critic. The work of sitting with people to discover *what was interesting* didn't seem to agree with Schneiderman either. At certain moments he looked blank and almost ill. He knew me, of course, I had once appeared on his television program, and he said, "Hello, Charlie." Then he said to Bill, "Don't you know Charlie? He's a famous person who lives in Chicago incognito."

I began to appreciate what Rinaldo had done. He had gone to great trouble to set up this encounter, pulling many strings. This Bill, a connection of his, perhaps owed the Cantabiles a favor and had agreed to produce Mike Schneiderman the columnist. Obligations were being called in all over the place. The accountancy must be very intricate, and I could see that Bill was not pleased. Bill had a Cosa Nostra look. There was something corrupt about his nose. Curving deeply at the nostrils it was powerful yet vulnerable. He had a foul nose. In a different context I would have guessed him to be a violinist who had become disgusted with music and gone into the liquor business. He had just returned from Acapulco and his skin was dark, but he was not exactly shining with health and well-being. He didn't care for Rinaldo; he appeared contemptuous of him. My sympathy at this moment was with Cantabile. He had attempted to organize what should have been a beautiful spirited encounter, worthy of the Renaissance, and only I appreciated it. Cantabile was trying to crash Mike's column. Mike of course was used to this. The would-be happy few were always after him and I suspected that there was a good deal of trading behind the scenes, *quid pro quo.* You gave Mike an item of gossip and he printed your name in bold type. The Bunny took our drink order. Up to the chin she was ravishing. Above, all was commercial anxiety. My attention was divided between the soft crease of her breasts and the look of business difficulty on her face.

We were on one of the most glamorous corners of Chicago. I dwelt on the setting. The lakeshore view was stupendous. I couldn't see it but I knew it well and felt its effect—the shining road beside the shining gold vacancy of Lake Michigan. Man had overcome the emptiness of this land. But the emptiness had given him a few good licks in return. And here we sat amid the flatteries of wealth and power with pretty maidens and booze and tailored suits, and the men wearing jewels and using scent. Schneiderman was waiting, most skeptically, for an item he could use in his column. In the right context, I was good copy. People in Chicago are impressed with the fact that I am taken seriously elsewhere. I have now and then been asked to cocktail parties by culturally ambitious climbing people and have experienced the fate of a symbol. Certain women have said to me, "You *can't* be Charles Citrine!" Many hosts are pleased by the contrast I offer. Why, I look like a man intensely but incompletely thinking. My face is no match for their shrewd urban faces. And it's especially the ladies who can't mask their disappointment when they see what the well-known Mr. Citrine actually looks like.

Whisky was set before us. I drank down my double Scotch

eagerly and, being a quick expander, started to laugh. No one joined me. Ugly Bill said, "What's funny?"

I said, "Well, I just remembered that I learned to swim just down the way at Oak Street before all these skyscrapers went up, the architectural pride of P.R. Chicago. It was the Gold Coast then, and we used to come from the slums on the streetcar. The Division car only went as far as Wells. I'd come with a greasy bag of sandwiches. My mother bought me a girl's bathing suit at a sale. It had a little skirt with a rainbow border. I was mortified and tried to dye it with India ink. The cops used to jab us in the ribs to hurry us across the Drive. Now I'm up here, drinking whisky. . . ."

Cantabile gave me a shove under the table with his whole foot, leaving a dusty print on my trousers. His frown spread upward into his scalp, rippling under the close-cut curls, while his nose became as white as candle wax.

I said, "By the way, Ronald . . ." and I took out the bills. "I owe you money."

"What money?"

"The money I lost to you at that poker game—it was some time back. I guess you forgot about it. Four hundred and fifty bucks."

"I don't know what you're talking about," said Rinaldo Cantabile. "What game?"

"You can't remember? We were playing at George Swiebel's apartment."

"Since when do you book guys play poker?" said Mike Schneiderman.

"Why? We have our human side. Poker has always been played at the White House. Perfectly respectable. President Harding played. Also during the New Deal. Morgenthau, Roosevelt, and so on."

"You sound like a West Side Chicago boy," said Bill.

"Chopin School, Rice and Western," I said.

"Well, put away your dough, Charlie," said Cantabile. "This is drink time. No business. Pay me later."

"Why not now, while I think of it and have the bills out? You know the whole thing slipped my mind, and last night I woke up with a start thinking, 'I forgot to pay Rinaldo his dough.' Christ, I could have blown my brains out."

Cantabile said violently, "Okay, okay, Charlie!" He snatched the money from me and crammed it without counting into his breast pocket. He gave me a look of high irritation, a flaming look. What for? I could not imagine why. What I did know was that Mike Schneiderman had power to put you in the paper and if you were in the paper you hadn't lived in vain. You were not just a two-legged creature, seen for a brief hour on Clark Street, sullying eternity with nasty doings and thoughts. You were—

"What'cha doing these days, Charlie," said Mike Schneiderman. "Another play maybe? A movie? You know," he said to Bill, "Charlie's a real famous guy. They made a terrific flick out of his Broadway hit. He's written a whole lot of stuff."

"I had my moment of glory on Broadway," I said. "I could never repeat it, so why try?"

"Now I remember. Somebody said you were going to publish some kind of highbrow magazine. When is it coming out? I'll give you a plug."

But Cantabile glared and said, "We've got to go."

"I'll be glad to phone when I have an item for you. It would be helpful," I said with a meaning glance toward Cantabile.

But he had already gone. I followed him and in the elevator he said, "What the fuck is the matter with you?"

"I can't think what I did wrong."

"You said you wanted to blow your brains out, and you know damn well, you creep, that Mike Schneiderman's brother-in-law blew *his* brains out two months ago."

"No!"

"You must have read it in the paper—that whole noise about the phony bonds, the counterfeit bonds he gave for collateral."

"Oh, *that* one, you mean Goldhammer, the fellow who printed up his own certificates, the forger!"

"You knew it, don't pretend," said Cantabile. "You did it on purpose, to louse me up, to wreck my plan."

"I didn't, I swear I didn't. Blowing my brains out? That's a commonplace expression."

"Not in a case like this. You knew," he said violently, "you knew. You knew his brother-in-law killed himself."

"I didn't make the connection. It must have been a Freudian slip. Absolutely unintentional."

"You always pretend you never know what you're doing. I suppose you didn't know who that big-nosed fellow was."

"Bill?"

"Yes! Bill! Bill is Bill Lakin, the banker who was indicted with Goldhammer. He took the forged bonds as security."

"Why should he be indicted for that? Goldhammer put them over on him."

"Because, you bird-brain, don't you understand what you read in the news? He bought Lekatride from Goldhammer for a buck a share when it was worth six dollars. Haven't you heard of Kerner either? All these grand juries, all these trials? But you don't care about the things that other people knock themselves out over. You have contempt. You're arrogant, Citrine. You despise us."

"Who's us?"

"Us! People of the world . . ." said Cantabile. He spoke wildly. It was no time for argument. I was to respect and to fear him. It would be provoking if he didn't think I feared him. I didn't think that he would shoot me but a beating was surely possible, perhaps even a broken leg. As we left the Playboy Club he thrust the money again into my hand.

"Do we have to do this over?" I said. He explained nothing. He stood with his head angrily hooked forward until the Thunderbird came around. Once more I had to get in.

Our next stop was in the Hancock Building, somewhere on the sixtieth or seventieth story. It looked like a private apartment, and yet it seemed also to be a place of business. It was furnished in decorator style with plastic, trick art objects hanging on the walls, geometrical forms of the *trompe l'œil* type that intrigue business people. They are peculiarly vulnerable to art racketeers. The gentleman who lived here was elderly, in a brown hopsack sports jacket with gold threads and a striped shirt on his undisciplined belly. White hair was slicked back upon his narrow head. The liver stains on his hands were large. Under the eyes and about the nose he did not look altogether well. As he sat on the low sofa which, judging by the way it gave under him, was stuffed with down, his alligator loafers extended far into the ivory shag carpet. The pressure of his belly brought out the shape of his phallus on his thigh. Long nose, gaping lip, and wattles went with all this velvet, the gold-threaded hopsack, brocade, satin, the alligator skin, and the *trompe l'œil* objects. From the conversation I gathered that his line was jewelry and that he dealt with the underworld. Perhaps he was also a fence—how would I know? Rinaldo Cantabile and his wife had an anniversary coming and he was shopping for a bracelet. A Japanese houseboy served drinks. I am not a great drinker but today I understandably wanted whisky and I took another double shot of Black Label. From the skyscraper I could contemplate the air of Chicago on this short December afternoon. A ragged western sun spread orange light over the dark shapes of the town, over the branches of the river and the black trusses of bridges. The lake, gilt silver and amethyst, was ready for its winter cover of ice. I happened to be thinking that if Socrates was right, that you could learn nothing from trees, that only the men you met in the street could teach you something about yourself, I must be in a bad way, running off into the scenery instead of listening to my human companions. Evidently I did not have a good stomach for human companions. To get relief from uneasiness or heaviness of heart I was musing about the water. Socrates would have given me a low mark. I seemed rather to be on the Wordsworth end of things—trees, flowers, water. But architecture, engineering, electricity, technology had brought me to this sixty-fourth story. Scandinavia had put this glass in my hand, Scotland had filled it with whisky, and I sat there recalling certain marvelous facts about the sun, namely, that the light of other stars when it entered the sun's gravitational field, had to bend. The sun wore a shawl made of this universal light. So Einstein, sitting thinking of things, had foretold. And observations made by Arthur Eddington during an eclipse proved it. Finding before seeking.

Meantime the phone rang continually and not a single call seemed local. It was all Las Vegas, L.A., Miami, and New York. "Send your boy over to Tiffany and find out what they get for an item like that," our host was saying. I then heard him speak of estate-jewels, and of an Indian prince who was trying to sell a whole lot of stuff in the USA and inviting bids.

At one interval, while Cantabile was fussing over a tray of diamonds (nasty, that white stuff seemed to me), the old gentleman spoke to me. He said, "I know you from somewhere, don't I?"

"Yes," I said. "From the whirlpool at the Downtown Health Club, I think."

"Oh yeah sure, I met you with that lawyer fellow. He's a big talker."

"Szathmar?"

"Alec Szathmar."

Cantabile said, fingering diamonds and not lifting his face from the dazzle of the velvet tray, "I know that son of a bitch Szathmar. He claims to be an old buddy of yours, Charlie."

"True," I said, "we were all boys at school. Including George Swiebel."

"In the old stone age that must have been," said Cantabile.

Yes, I had met this old gentleman in the hot chemical bath at the club, the circular bubbling whirlpool where people sat sweating, gossiping about sports, taxes, television programs, best sellers, or chatting about Acapulco and numbered bank accounts in the Cayman Islands. I didn't know but what this old fence had one of those infamous *cabañas* near the swimming pool to which young chicks were invited for the siesta. There had been some scandal and protest over this. What was done behind drawn drapes in the *cabañas* was no one's business, of course, but some of the old guys, demonstrative and exhibitionistic, had been seen fondling their little dolls on the sun-terrace. One had removed his false teeth in public to give a girl soul kisses. I had read an interesting letter in the *Tribune* about this. A retired history teacher living high up in the club building had written a letter saying that Tiberius—the old girl was showing off—Tiberius in the grottoes of Capri had had nothing on these grotesque lechers. But what did these old characters, in the rackets or in First Ward politics, care about indignant school-mams and classical allusions. If they had gone to see Fellini's *Satyricon* at the Woods Theater it was only to get more sex ideas not because they were studying Imperial Rome. I myself had seen some of these spider-bellied old codgers on the sundeck taking the breasts of teen-age hookers into their hands. It occurred to me that the Japanese houseboy was also a judo or karate expert as in 007 movies, there were so many valuables in the apartment. When Rinaldo said he'd like to see more Accutron watches, the fellow brought out a few dozen, flat as wafers. These may or may not have been stolen. My heated imagination couldn't be relied upon for guidance here. I was excited, I admit, by these currents of criminality. I could feel the need to laugh rising, mounting, always a sign that my weakness for the sensational, my American, Chicagoan (as well as personal) craving for high stimuli, for incongruities and extremes, was aroused. I knew that fancy thieving was a big thing in Chicago. It was said that if you knew one of these high-rise superrich Fagin-types you could obtain luxury goods at half the retail price. The actual shoplifting was done by addicts. They were compensated in heroin. As for the police, they were said to be paid off. They kept the merchants from making too much noise. Anyway there was insurance. There was also the well-known "shrinkage" or annual loss reported to the Internal Revenue Service. Such information about corruption, if you had grown up in Chicago, was easy to accept. It even satisfied a certain need. It harmonized with one's Chicago view of society. Naïveté was something you couldn't afford.

Item by item, I tried to assess what Cantabile wore as I sat there in soft upholstery with my scotch on the rocks, his hat coat suit boots (the boots may have been unborn calf) his equestrian gloves, and I made an effort to imagine how he had obtained these articles through criminal channels, from Field's, from Saks Fifth Avenue, from Abercrombie & Fitch. He was not, so far as I could judge, taken absolutely seriously by the old fence.

Rinaldo was intrigued with one of the watches and slipped it on. His old watch he tossed to the Japanese who caught it. I thought the moment had come to recite my piece and I said, "Oh, by the way, Ronald, I owe you some dough from the other night."

"Where from?" said Cantabile.

"From the poker game at George Swiebel's. I guess it slipped your mind."

"Oh I know that guy Swiebel with all the muscles," said the old gentleman. "He's terrific company. And you know he cooks a great bouillabaisse, I'll give him that."

"I inveigled Ronald and his cousin Emil into this game," I said. "It really was my fault. Anyhow, Ronald cleaned up on us. Ronald is one of the poker greats. I ended up about six hundred dollars in the hole and he had to take my IOU—I've got the dough on me, Ronald, and I better give it to you while we both remember."

"Okay." Again Cantabile, without looking, crumpled the notes into his jacket pocket. His performance was better than mine, though I was doing my very best. But then he had the honor side of the deal, the affront. To be angry was his right and that was no small advantage.

When we were out of the building again I said, "Wasn't that okay?"

"Okay—yes! Okay!" he said loud and bitter. Clearly he wasn't ready to let me off. Not yet.

"I figure that old pelican will pass the word around that I paid you. Wasn't that the object?"

I added, almost to myself, "I wonder who makes pants like the pants the old boy was wearing. The fly alone must have been three feet long."

But Cantabile was still stoking his anger. "Christ!" he said. I didn't like the way he was staring at me under those straight bodkin brows.

"Well, then, that does it," I said. "I can get a cab."

Cantabile caught me by the sleeve. "You wait," he said. I didn't really know what to do. After all, he carried a gun. I had for a long time thought about having a gun too, Chicago being what it is. But they'd never give me a license. Cantabile, without a license, packed a pistol. There was one index of the difference between us. Only God knew what consequences such differences might bring. "Aren't you enjoying our afternoon?" said Cantabile, and grinned.

Attempting to laugh this off I failed. The globus hystericus interfered. My throat felt sticky.

"Get in, Charlie."

Again I sat in the crimson bucket seat (the supple fragrant leather kept reminding me of blood, pulmonary blood) and fumbled for the seat belt—you never can find those cursed buckles.

"Don't fuck with the belt, we're not going that far."

Out of this information I drew what relief I could. We were on Michigan Boulevard, heading south. We drew up beside a skyscraper under construction, a headless trunk swooping up, swarming with lights. Below the early darkness now closing with December speed over the glistening west, the sun like a bristling fox jumped beneath the horizon. Nothing but a scarlet afterglow remained. I saw it between the El pillars. As the tremendous trusses of the unfinished skyscraper turned black, the hollow interior filled with thousands of electric points resembling champagne bubbles. The completed building would never be so beautiful as this. We got out, slamming the car doors, and I followed Cantabile over some plank-bedding laid down for the trucks. He seemed to know his way around. Maybe he had clients among the hard-hats. If he was in the juice racket. Then again if he was a usurer he wouldn't come here after dark and risk getting pushed from a beam by one of these tough guys. They must be reckless. They drink and spend recklessly enough. I like the way these steeplejacks paint the names of their girlfriends on inaccessible girders. From below you often see DONNA or SUE. I suppose they bring the ladies on Sunday to point to their love-offerings eight hundred feet up. They fall to death now and then. Anyway Cantabile had brought his own hard hats. We put them on. Everything was prearranged. He said he was related by blood to some of the supervisory personnel. He also mentioned that he did lots of business hereabouts. He said he had connections with the contractor and the architect. He told me things much faster than I could discount them. However, we rose in one of the big open elevators, up, up.

How should I describe my feelings? Fear, thrill, appreciation, glee—yes I appreciated his ingenuity. It seemed to me, however, that we were rising too high, too far. Where were we? Which button had he pressed? By daylight I had often admired the mantis-like groups of cranes, tipped with orange paint. The tiny bulbs, which seemed so dense from below, were sparsely strung through. I don't know how far we actually went, but it was far enough. We had as much light about us as the time of day had left to give, steely and freezing, keen, with the wind ringing in the empty squares of wound-colored rust and beating against the hanging canvases. On the east, violently rigid was the water, icy, scratched, like a plateau of solid stone, and the other way was a tremendous effusion of low-lying color, the last glow, the contribution of industrial poisons to the beauty of the Chicago evening. We got out. About ten hard-hats who had been waiting pushed into the elevator at once. I wanted to call to them "Wait!" They went down in a group, leaving us nowhere. Cantabile seemed to know where he was going, but I had no faith in him. He was capable of faking anything. "Come on," he said. I followed, but I was going slowly. He waited for me. There were a few windbreaks up here on the fiftieth or sixtieth floor, and those, the wind was storming. My eyes ran. I held on to a pillar and he said, "Come on Granny, come on check-stopper."

I said, "I have leather heels. They skid."

"You better not chicken out."

"No, this is it," I said. I put my arms around the pillar. I wouldn't move.

Actually we had come far enough to suit him. "Now," he said, "I want to show you just how much your dough means to me. You see this?" He held up a fifty-dollar bill. He rested his back on a steel upright and stripping off his fancy equestrian gloves began to fold the money. It was incomprehensible at first. Then I understood. He was making a child's paper glider of it. Hitching back his raglan sleeve, he sent the glider off with two fingers. I watched it speeding through the strung lights with the wind behind it out into the steely atmosphere, darker and darker below. On Michigan Boulevard they had already put up the Christmas ornaments, winding tiny bubbles of glass from tree to tree. They streamed down there like cells under a microscope.

My chief worry now was how to get down. Though the papers underplay it people are always falling off. But however scared and harassed, my sensation-loving soul also was gratified. I knew that it took too much to gratify me. The gratification-threshold of my soul had risen too high. I must bring it down again. It was excessive. I must, I knew, change everything.

He sailed off more of the fifties. Tiny paper planes. Origami (my knowledgeable mind, keeping up its indefatigable pedantry—my lexical busybody mind!), the Japanese paper-folder's art. An international congress of paper-aircraft freaks had been held, I think, last year. It seemed last year. The hobbyists were mathematicians and engineers.

Cantabile's green bills went off like finches, like swallows and butterflies, all bearing the image of Ulysses S. Grant. They brought crepuscular fortune to people down in the streets.

"The last two I'm going to keep," said Cantabile. "To blow them on drinks and dinner for us."

"If I ever get down alive."

"You did fine. Go on, lead the way, start back."

"These leather heels are awfully tricky. I hit an ordinary piece of wax paper in the street the other day and went down. Maybe I should take my shoes off."

"Don't be crazy. Go on your toes."

If you didn't think of falling, the walkways were more than adequate. I crept along, fighting paralysis of the calves and the thighs. My face was sweating faster than the wind could dry it as I took hold of the final pillar. I thought that Cantabile had been treading much too close behind. More hard-hats waiting for the elevator probably took us for union guys or architect's men. It was night now and the hemisphere was frozen all the way to the Gulf. Gladly I fell into the seat of the Thunderbird when we got down. He removed his hard hat and mine. He cocked the wheel and started the motor. He should really let me go now. I had given him enough satisfaction.

But he was off again, driving fast. He sped away toward the next light. My head hung back over the top of the seat in the position you take to stop a nosebleed. I didn't know exactly where we were. "Look, Rinaldo," I said. "You've made your point. You bashed my car, you've run me all day long, and you've just given me the scare of my life. Okay, I see it wasn't the money that upset you. Let's stuff the rest of it down a sewer so I can go home."

"You've had it with me?"

"It's been a whole day of atonement."

"You've seen enough of the whatchamacallems?—I learned some new words at the poker game from you."

"Which words?"

"Proles," he said, "*Lumps. Lumpenproletariat.* You gave us a little talk about Karl Marx."

"My lord, I did carry on, didn't I. Completely unbuttoned. What got into me!"

"You wanted to mix with riffraff and the criminal element. You went slumming, Charlie, and you had a great time playing cards with us dumbheads and social rejects."

"I see. I was insulting."

"Kind of. But you were interesting, here and there, about the social order and how obsessed the middle class was with the *Lumpenproletariat*. The other fellows didn't know what in hell you were talking about." For the first time, Cantabile spoke more mildly to me. I sat up and saw the river flashing night-lights on the right, and the Merchandise Mart decorated for Christmas. We were going to Gene and Georgetti's old steak house, just off the spur of the Elevated train. Parking among other sinister luxury cars we went into the drab old building where—hurrah for opulent intimacy!—a crash of jukebox music fell on us like Pacific surf. The high-executive bar was crowded with executive drinkers and lovely companions. The gorgeous mirror was peopled with bottles and resembled a group photograph of celestial graduates.

"Giulio," Rinaldo told the waiter. "A quiet table, and we don't want to sit by the rest rooms."

"Upstairs, Mr. Cantabile?"

"Why not?" I said. I was shaky and didn't want to wait at the bar for seating. It would lengthen the evening, besides.

Cantabile stared as if to say, Who asked you! But he then consented. "Okay, upstairs. And two bottles of Piper Heidsieck."

"Right away, Mr. Cantabile."

In the Capone days hoodlums fought mock battles with champagne at banquets. They jigged the bottles up and down and shot each other with corks and foaming wine, all in black tie, and like a fun-massacre.

"Now I want to tell you something," said Rinaldo Cantabile, "and it's a different subject altogether. I'm married, you know."

"Yes, I remember."

"To a marvelous beautiful intelligent woman."

"You mentioned your wife in South Chicago. That night . . . Do you have children? What does she do?"

"She's no housewife, buddy, and you'd better know it. You think I'd marry some fat-ass broad who sits around the house in curlers and watches TV? This is a real woman, with a mind, with knowledge. She teaches at Mundelein College and she's working on a doctoral thesis. You know where?"

"No."

"At Radcliffe, Harvard."

"That's very good," I said. I emptied the champagne glass and refilled it.

"Don't brush it off. Ask me what her subject is. Of the thesis."

"All right, what is it?"

"She's writing a study of that poet who was your friend."

"You're kidding. Von Humboldt Fleisher? How do you know he was my friend? . . . I see. I was talking about him at George's. Someone should have locked me in a closet that night."

"You didn't have to be cheated, Charlie. You didn't know what you were doing. You were talking away like a nine-year-old kid about lawsuits, lawyers, accountants, bad investments, and the magazine you were going to publish—a real loser, it sounded like. You said you were going to spend your own money on your own ideas."

"I never discuss these things with strangers. Chicago must be giving me arctic madness."

"Now, listen, I'm very proud of my wife. Her people are rich, upper class. . . ." Boasting gives people a wonderful color, I've noticed, and Cantabile's cheeks glowed. He said, "You're asking yourself what is she doing with a husband like me."

I muttered, "No, no," though that certainly was a natural question. However, it was not exactly news that highly educated women were excited by scoundrels criminals and lunatics, and that these scoundrels etcetera were drawn to culture, to thought. Diderot and Dostoevski had made us familiar with this.

"I want her to get her PhD," said Cantabile. "You understand? I want it bad. And you were a pal of this Fleisher guy. You're going to give Lucy the information."

"Now wait a minute—"

"Look this over." He handed me an envelope and I put on my glasses and glanced over the document enclosed. It was signed

Lucy Wilkins Cantabile and it was the letter of a model graduate student, polite, detailed, highly organized, with the usual academic circumlocutions—three single-spaced pages, dense with questions, painful questions. Her husband kept me under close observation as I read. "Well, what do you think of her?"

"Terrific," I said. The thing filled me with despair. "What do you two want of me?"

"Answers. Information. We want you to write out the answers. What's your opinion of her project?"

"I think the dead owe us a living."

"Don't horse around with me, Charlie. I didn't like that crack."

"I couldn't care less," I said. "This poor Humboldt, my friend, was a big spirit who was destroyed . . . never mind that. The PhD racket is a very fine racket but I want no part of it. Besides, I never answer questionnaires. Idiots impose on you with their documents. I can't bear that kind of thing."

"Are you calling my wife an idiot?"

"I haven't had the pleasure of meeting her."

"I'll make allowances for you. You got hit in the guts by the Mercedes and then I ran you ragged. But don't be unpleasant about my wife."

"There are things I don't do. This is one of them. I'm not going to write answers. It would take weeks."

"Listen!"

"I draw the line."

"Just a minute!"

"Bump me off. Go to hell."

"All right, easy does it. Some things are sacred. I understand. But we can work everything out. I listened at the poker game and I know that you're in plenty of trouble. You need somebody tough and practical to handle things for you. I've given this a lot of thought, and I have all kinds of ideas for you. We'll trade off."

"No, I don't want to trade anything. I've had it. My heart is breaking and I want to go home."

"Let's have a steak and finish the wine. You need red meat. You're just tired. You'll do it."

"I won't."

"Take the order, Giulio," he said.

I WISH I knew why I feel such loyalty to the deceased. Hearing of their deaths I often said to myself that I must carry on for them and do their job, finish their work. And that of course I couldn't do. Instead I found that certain of their characteristics were beginning to stick to me. As time went on, for instance, I found myself becoming absurd in the manner of Von Humboldt Fleisher. By and by it became apparent that he had acted as my agent. I myself, a nicely composed person, had had Humboldt expressing himself wildly on my behalf, satisfying some of my longings. This explained my liking for certain individuals—Humboldt, or George Swiebel, or even someone like Cantabile. This type of psychological delegation may have its origins in representative government. However, when an expressive friend died the delegated tasks returned to me. And as I was also the expressive delegate of other people, this eventually became pure hell.

Carry on for Humboldt? Humboldt wanted to drape the world in radiance, but he didn't have enough material. His attempt ended at the belly. Below hung the shaggy nudity we know so well. He was a lovely man, and generous, with a heart of gold. Still his goodness was the sort of goodness people now consider out of date. The radiance he dealt in was the old radiance and it was in short supply. What we needed was a new radiance altogether.

And now Cantabile and his PhD wife were after me to recall the dear dead days of the Village, and its intellectuals, poets, crack-ups, its suicides and love affairs. I didn't care much for that. I had no clear view of Mrs. Cantabile as yet, but I saw Rinaldo as one of the new mental rabble of the wised-up world and anyway I didn't feel just now like having my arm twisted. It wasn't that I minded giving information to honest scholars, or even to young people on the make, but I just then was busy, fiercely, painfully busy—personally and impersonally busy: personally, with Renata and Denise, and Murra the accountant, and the lawyers and the judge, and a multitude of emotional vexations; impersonally, participating in the life of my country and of Western Civilization and global society (a mixture of reality and figment). As editor of an important magazine, *The Ark*, which would probably never come out, I was always thinking of statements that must be made and truths of which the world must be reminded. The world, identified by a series of dates (1789–1914–1917–1939) and by key words (Revolution, Technology, Science, and so forth), was another cause of busyness. You owed your duty to these dates and words. The whole thing was so momentous, overmastering, tragic, that in the end what I really wanted was to lie down and go to sleep. I have always had an exceptional gift for passing out. I look at snapshots taken in some of the most evil hours of mankind and I see that I have lots of hair and am appealingly youthful. I am wearing an ill-fitting double-breasted suit of the Thirties or Forties, smoking a pipe, standing under a tree, holding hands with a plump and pretty bimbo—and I am asleep on my feet, out cold. I have snoozed through many a crisis (while millions died).

This is all terrifically relevant. For one thing, I may as well admit that I came back to settle in Chicago with the secret motive of writing a significant work. This lethargy of mine is related to that project—I got the idea of doing something with the chronic war between sleep and consciousness that goes on in human nature. My subject, in the final Eisenhower years, was boredom. Chicago was the ideal place in which to write my master essay—"Boredom." In raw Chicago you could examine the human spirit under industrialism. If someone were to arise with a new vision of Faith, Love, and Hope, he would want to understand to whom he was offering it—he would have to understand the kind of deep suffering we call boredom. I was going to try to do with boredom what Malthus and Adam Smith and John Stuart Mill or Durkheim had done with population, wealth, or the division of labor. History and temperament had put me in a peculiar position, and I was going to turn it to advantage. I hadn't read those great modern boredom experts, Stendhal, Kierkegaard, and Baudelaire, for nothing. Over the years I had worked a lot on this essay. The difficulty was that I kept being overcome by the material, like a miner by gas fumes. I wouldn't stop, though. I'd say to myself that even Rip Van Winkle had slept for only twenty years, I had gone him at least two decades better and I was determined to make the lost time yield illumination. So I kept doing advanced mental work in Chicago, and also joined a gymnasium, playing ball with commodity brokers and gentleman-hoodlums in an effort to strengthen the powers of consciousness. Then my respected friend Durnwald mentioned, kiddingly, that the famous but misunderstood Dr. Rudolf Steiner had much to say on the deeper aspects of sleep. Steiner's books, which I began to read lying down, made me want to get up. He argued that between the conception of an act and its execution by the will there fell a gap of sleep. It might be brief but it was deep. For one of man's souls was a sleep-soul. In this, human beings resembled the plants, whose whole existence is sleep. This made a very deep impression on me. The truth about sleep could only be seen from the perspective of an immortal spirit. I had never doubted that I had such a thing. But I had set this fact aside quite early. I kept it under my hat. These beliefs under your hat also press on your brain and sink you down into the vegetable realm. Even now, to a man of culture like Durnwald, I hesitated to mention the spirit. He took no stock in Steiner, of course. Durnwald was reddish, elderly but powerful, thickset and bald, a bachelor of cranky habits but a kind man. He had a peremptory blunt butting even bullying manner, but if he scolded it was because he loved me—he wouldn't have bothered otherwise. A great scholar, one of the most learned people on earth, he was a rationalist. Not narrowly rationalistic, by any means. Nevertheless, I couldn't talk to him about the powers of a spirit separated from a body. He wouldn't hear of it. He had simply been joking about Steiner. I was not joking, but I didn't want to be thought a crank.

I had begun to think a lot about the immortal spirit. Still, night after night, I kept dreaming that I had become the best player in the club, a racquet demon, that my backhand shot skimmed the left wall of the court and fell dead in the corner, it had so much English on it. I dreamed that I was beating all the best players—all those skinny, hairy, speedy fellows who in reality avoided playing with me because I was a dud. I was badly disappointed by the shallow interests such dreams betrayed. Even my dreams were asleep. And what about money? Money is necessary for the protection of the sleeping. Spending drives you into wakefulness. As you purge the inner film from the eye and rise into higher consciousness, less money should be required.

Under the circumstances (and it should now be clearer what I mean by circumstances: Renata, Denise, children, courts, lawyers, Wall Street, sleep, death, metaphysics, karma, the presence of the universe in us, our being present in the universe itself) I had not paused to think about Humboldt, a precious friend hid in death's dateless night, a camerado from a former existence (almost), well-beloved but dead. I imagined at times that I might see him in the life to come, together with my mother and my father. Demmie Vonghel, too. Demmie was one of the most significant dead, remembered every day. But I didn't expect him to come at me as in life, driving ninety miles an hour in his Buick fourholer. First I laughed. Then I shrieked. I was transfixed. He bore down on me. He struck me with blessings. Humboldt's gift wiped out many immediate problems.

The role played by Ronald and Lucy Cantabile in this is something else again.

Dear friends, though I was about to leave town and had much business to attend to, I decided to suspend all practical activities for one morning. I did this to keep from cracking under strain. I had been practicing some of the meditative exercises recommended by Rudolf Steiner in *Knowledge of the Higher Worlds and Its Attainment.* As yet I hadn't attained much, but then my soul was well along in years and very much stained and banged up, and I had to be patient. Characteristically, I had been trying too hard, and I remembered again that wonderful piece of advice given by a French thinker: *Trouve avant de chercher*—Valéry, it was. Or maybe Picasso. There are times when the most practical thing is to lie down.

And so the morning after my day with Cantabile I took a holiday. The weather was fine and clear. I drew the openwork drapes which shut out the details of Chicago and let in the bright sun and the high blue (which in their charity shone and towered even over a city like this). Cheerful, I dug out my Humboldt papers. I piled notebooks, letters, diaries, and manuscripts on the coffee table and on the covered radiator behind the sofa. Then I lay down, sighing, pulling off my shoes.

Under my head I put a needlepoint cushion embroidered by a young lady (what a woman-filled life I always led. Ah, this sexually-disturbed century!), a Miss Doris Scheldt, the daughter of the anthroposophist I consulted now and then. She had given me this handmade Christmas gift the year before. Small and lovely, intelligent, strikingly strong in profile for such a pretty young woman, she liked to wear old-fashioned dresses that made her look like Lillian Gish or Mary Pickford. Her footwear, however, was provocative, quite far out. In my private vocabulary she was a little *noli me tangerine.* She did and did not wish to be touched. She herself knew a great deal about anthroposophy and we spent a lot of time together last year, when Renata and I had a falling-out. I sat in her bentwood rocking chair while she put her tiny patent-leather boots up on a hassock, embroidering this red-and-green, fresh-grass-and-hot-embers cushion. We chatted, etcetera. It was an agreeable relationship, but it was over. Renata and I were back together.

This is by way of explaining that I took Von Humboldt Fleisher as the subject of my meditation that morning. Such meditation supposedly strengthened the will. Then, gradually strengthened by such exercises, the will might become an organ of perception.

A wrinkled postcard fell to the floor, one of the last Humboldt had sent me. I read the phantom strokes, like a fuzzy graph of the northern lights:

Mice hide when hawks are high;
Hawks shy from airplanes;
Planes dread the ack-ack-ack;
Each one fears somebody.
Only the heedless lions
Under the Booloo tree
Snooze in each other's arms
After their lunch of blood—
I call that living good!

Eight or nine years ago, reading this poem, I thought, Poor Humboldt, those shock-treatment doctors have lobotomized him, they've ruined the guy. But now I saw this as a communication, not as a poem. The imagination must not pine away—

that was Humboldt's message. It must assert again that art manifests the inner powers of nature. To the savior-faculty of the imagination sleep was sleep, and waking was true waking. This was what Humboldt now appeared to me to be saying. If that was so, Humboldt was never more sane and brave than at the end of his life. And I had run away from him on Forty-sixth Street just when he had most to tell me. I had spent that morning, as I have mentioned, grandly dressed up and revolving elliptically over the city of New York in that Coast Guard helicopter, with the two US Senators and the Mayor and officials from Washington and Albany and crack journalists, all belted up in puffy life jackets, each jacket with its sheath knife. (I've never gotten over those knives.) And then, after the luncheon in Central Park (I am compelled to repeat), I walked out and saw Humboldt, a dying man eating a pretzel stick at the curb, the dirt of the grave already sprinkled on his face. Then I rushed away. It was one of those ecstatically painful moments when I couldn't hold still. I had to run. I said, "Oh, kid, good-by. I'll see you in the next world!"

There was nothing more to be done for him in this world, I had decided. But was that true? The wrinkled postcard now made me reconsider. It struck me that I had sinned against Humboldt. Lying down on the goose-down sofa in order to meditate, I found myself getting hot with self-criticism and shame, flushing and sweating. I pulled Doris Scheldt's pillow from behind my head and wiped my face with it. Again I saw myself taking cover behind the parked cars on Forty-sixth Street. And Humboldt like a bush tented all over by the bagworm and withering away. I was stunned to see my old pal dying and I fled, I went back to the Plaza and phoned Senator Kennedy's office to say that I had been called to Chicago suddenly. I'd return to Washington next week. Then I took a cab to La Guardia and caught the first plane to O'Hare. I return again and again to that day because it was so dreadful. Two drinks, the limit in flight, did nothing for me—nothing! When I landed I drank several double shots of Jack Daniel's in the O'Hare bar, for strength. It was a very hot evening. I telephoned Denise and said, "I'm back."

"You're days and days early. What's up, Charles?"

I said, "I've had a bad experience."

"Where's the Senator?"

"Still in New York. I'll go back to Washington in a day or two."

"Well, come on home, then."

Life had commissioned an article on Robert Kennedy. I had now spent five days with the Senator, or rather near him, sitting on a sofa in the Senate Office Building, observing him. It was, from every point of view, a singular inspiration, but the Senator had allowed me to attach myself to him and even seemed to like me. I say "seemed" because it was his business to leave such an impression with a journalist who proposed to write about him. I liked him, too, perhaps against my better judgment. His way of looking at you was odd. His eyes were as blue as the void, and there was a slight lowering in the skin of the lids, an extra fold. After the helicopter trip we drove from La Guardia to the Bronx in a limousine, and I was in there with him. The heat was dismal in the Bronx but we were in a sort of crystal cabinet. His desire was to be continually briefed. He asked questions of everyone in the party. From me he wanted historical information—"What should I know about William Jennings Bryan?" or, "Tell me about H. L. Mencken" —receiving what I said with a kind of inner glitter that did not tell me what he thought or whether he could use such facts. We pulled up at a Harlem playground. There were Cadillacs, motorcycle cops, bodyguards, television crews. A vacant lot between two tenements had been fenced in, paved, furnished with slides and sandboxes. The playground director in his Afro and dashiki and beads received the two Senators. Cameras stood above us on trestles. The black director, radiant, ceremonious, held a basketball between the two Senators. A space was cleared. Twice the slender Kennedy, carelessly elegant, tossed the ball. He nodded his ruddy, foxy head high with hair and smiled when he missed. Senator Javits could not afford to miss. Compact and bald he too was smiling but squared off at the basket drawing the ball to his breast and binding himself by strength of will to the objective. He made two smart shots. The ball did not arch. It flew straight at the hoop and went in. There was applause. What vexation, what labor to keep up with Bobby. But the Republican Senator managed very well.

And this was what Denise wanted me to occupy myself with.

Denise had arranged all this for me, phoning the people at *Life*, supervising the whole deal. "Come on home," she said. But she was displeased. She didn't want me in Chicago now.

Home was a grand house in Kenwood on the South Side. Rich German Jews had built Victorian-Edwardian mansions here early in the century. When the mail-order tycoons and other nobs departed, university professors, psychiatrists, lawyers, and Black Muslims moved in. Since I had insisted on returning to become the Malthus of boredom, Denise bought the Kahnheim house. She had done this under protest, saying, "Why Chicago! We can live wherever we like, can't we? Christ!" She had in mind a house in Georgetown, or in Rome, or in London SW3. But I was obstinate, and Denise said she hoped it wasn't a sign that I was headed for a nervous breakdown. Her father the federal judge was a keen lawyer. I know she often consulted him downtown about property, joint-tenancy, widows' rights in the State of Illinois. He advised us to buy Colonel Kahnheim's mansion. Daily at breakfast Denise asked when I was going to make my will.

Now it was night and she was waiting for me in the master bedroom. I hate air conditioning. I kept Denise from installing it. The temperature was in the nineties, and on hot nights Chicagoans feel the city body and soul. The stockyards are gone, Chicago is no longer slaughter-city, but the old smells revive in the night heat. Miles of railroad siding along the streets once were filled with red cattle cars, the animals waiting to enter the yards lowing and reeking. The old stink still haunts the place. It returns at times, suspiring from the vacated soil, to remind us all that Chicago had once led the world in butcher-technology and that billions of animals had died here. And that night the windows were open wide and the familiar depressing multilayered stink of meat, tallow, blood-meal, pulverized bones, hides, soap, smoked slabs, and burnt hair came back. Old Chicago breathed again through leaves and screens. I heard fire trucks and the gulp and whoop of ambulances, bowel-deep and hysterical. In the surrounding black slums incendiarism shoots up in summer, an index, some say, of psychopathology. Although the love of flames is also religious. However, Denise was sitting nude on the bed rapidly and strongly brushing her hair. Over the lake, steel mills twinkled. Lamplight showed the soot already fallen on the leaves of the wall ivy. We had an early drought that year. Chicago, this night, was panting, the big urban engines going, tenements blazing in Oakwood with great shawls of flame, the sirens weirdly yelping, the fire engines, ambulances, and police cars—mad-dog, gashing-knife weather, a rape and murder night, thousands of hydrants open, spraying water from both breasts. Engineers were staggered to see the level of Lake Michigan fall as these tons of water poured. Bands of kids prowled with handguns and knives. And—dear-dear—this tender-minded mourning Mr. Charlie Citrine had seen his old buddy, a dead man eating a pretzel in New York, so he abandoned *Life* and the Coast Guard and helicopters and two Senators and rushed home to be comforted. For this purpose his wife had taken off everything and was brushing her exceedingly dense hair. Her enormous violet and gray eyes were impatient, her tenderness was mixed with glowering. She was asking tacitly how long I was going to sit on the chaise longue in my socks, heart-wounded and full of obsolete sensibility. A nervous and critical person, she thought I suffered from morbid aberrations about grief, that I was pre-modern or baroque about death. She often declared that I had come back to Chicago because my parents were buried here. Sometimes she said with sudden alertness, "Ah, here comes the cemetery bit!" What's more she was often right. Soon I myself could hear the chain-dragging monotony of my low voice. Love was the remedy for these death moods. And here was Denise, impatient but dutiful, sitting stripped on the bed, and I didn't even take off my necktie. I know this sorrow can be maddening. And it tired Denise to support me emotionally. She didn't take much stock in these emotions of mine. "Oh, you're on *that* kick again. You must quit all this operatic bullshit. Talk to a psychiatrist. Why are you hung up on the past and always lamenting some dead party or other?" Denise pointed out with a bright flash of the face, a sign that she had had an insight, that while I shed tears for my dead I was also patting down their graves with my shovel. For I did write biographies, and the deceased were my bread and butter. The deceased had earned my French decoration and got me into the White House. (The loss of our White House connections after the death of JFK was one of Denise's bitterest vexations.) Don't get me wrong, I know that love and scolding often go together. Durnwald did this to me, too. Whom the Lord loveth He chasteneth. The whole thing was mixed with affection. When I came home in a state over Humboldt, she was ready to comfort me. But she had a sharp tongue, Denise did. (I sometimes called her Rebukah.) Of course my lying there so sad, so heart-injured, was provoking. Besides, she suspected that I would never finish the *Life* article. There she was right again.

If I was going to feel so much about death, why didn't I *do* something about it. This endless sensibility was awful. Such was Denise's opinion. I agreed with that, too.

"So you feel bad about your pal Humboldt!" she said. "But how come you haven't looked him up? You had years to do it in. And why didn't you speak to him today?"

These were hard questions, very intelligent. She didn't let me get away with a thing.

"I suppose I could have said, 'Humboldt, it's me, Charlie. What about some real lunch? The Blue Ribbon is just around the corner.' But I think he might have thrown a fit. A couple of years ago he tried to hit some dean's secretary with a hammer. He accused her of covering his bed with girlie magazines. Some kind of erotic plot against him. They had to put him away again. The poor man is crazy. And it's no use going back to Saint Julien or hugging lepers."

"Who said anything about lepers? You're always thinking what nobody else has remotely in mind."

"Well okay, then, but he looked gruesome and I was all dressed up. And I'll tell you a curious coincidence. In the helicopter this morning I was sitting next to Dr. Longstaff. So naturally I thought of Humboldt. It was Longstaff who promised Humboldt a huge grant from the Belisha Foundation. This was when we were still at Princeton. Haven't I ever told you about that disaster?"

"I don't think so."

"The whole thing came back to me."

"Is Longstaff still so handsome and distinguished? He must be an old man. And I'll bet you pestered him about those old times."

"Yes, I reminded him."

"You would. And I suppose it was disagreeable."

"The past isn't disagreeable to the fully justified."

"I wonder what Longstaff was doing in that Washington crowd."

"Raising money for his philanthropies, I expect."

THUS went my meditation on the green sofa. Of all the meditative methods recommended in the literature I liked this new one best. Often I sat at the end of the day remembering everything that had happened, in minute detail, all that had been seen and done and said. I was able to go backward through the day, viewing myself from the back or side, physically no different from anyone else. If I had bought Renata a gardenia at an open-air stand, I could recall that I had paid seventy-five cents for it. I saw the brass milling of the three silver-plated quarters. I saw the lapel of Renata's coat, the white head of the long pin. I remembered even the two turns the pin took in the cloth, and Renata's full woman's face and her pleased gaze at the flower, and the odor of the gardenia. If this was what transcendence took, it was a cinch, I could do it forever, back to the beginning of time. So, lying on the sofa, I now brought back to mind the obituary page of the *Times.*

The *Times* was much stirred by Humboldt's death and gave him a double-column spread. The photograph was large. For after all Humboldt did what poets in crass America are supposed to do. He chased ruin and death even harder than he had chased women. He blew his talent and his health and reached home, the grave, in a dusty slide. He plowed himself under. Okay. So did Edgar Allan Poe, picked out of the Baltimore gutter. And Hart Crane over the side of a ship. And Jarrell falling in front of a car. And poor John Berryman jumping from a bridge. For some reason this awfulness is peculiarly appreciated by business and technological America. The country is proud of its dead poets. It takes terrific satisfaction in the poets' testimony that the USA is too tough, too big, too much, too rugged, that American reality is overpowering. And to be a poet is a school thing, a skirt thing, a church thing. The weakness of the spiritual powers is proved in the childishness, madness, drunkenness, and despair of these martyrs. Orpheus moved stones and trees. But a poet can't perform a hysterectomy or send a vehicle out of the solar system. Miracle and power no longer belong to him. So poets are loved, but loved because they just can't make it here. They exist to light up the enormity of the awful tangle and justify the cynicism of those who say, "If *I* were not such a corrupt, unfeeling bastard, creep, thief, and vulture, I couldn't get through this either. Look at these good and tender and soft men, the *best* of us. They succumbed, poor loonies." So this, I was meditating, is how successful bitter hard-faced and cannibalistic people exult. Such was the attitude reflected in the picture of Humboldt the *Times* chose to use. It was one of those mad-rotten-majesty pictures—spooky, humorless, glaring furiously with tight lips, mumpish or scrofulous cheeks, a scarred forehead, and a look of enraged, ravaged childishness. This was the Humboldt of conspiracies, putsches, accusations, tantrums, the Bellevue Hospital Humboldt, the Humboldt of litigations. For Humboldt was litigious. The word was made for him. He threatened many times to sue me.

Yes, the obituary was awful. The clipping was somewhere amongst these papers that surrounded me, but I didn't want to look at it. I could remember verbatim what the *Times* said. It said, in its tinkertoy style of knobs and sticks, that Von Humboldt Fleisher had made a brilliant start. Born on New York's Upper West Side. At twenty-two set a new style in American poetry. Appreciated by Conrad Aiken (who once had to call the cops to get him out of the house). Approved by T. S. Eliot (about whom, when he was off his nut, he would spread the most lurid improbable sexual scandal). Mr. Fleisher was also a critic, essayist, writer of fiction, teacher, prominent literary intellectual, a salon personality. Intimates praised his conversation. He was a great talker and wit.

Here, no longer meditative, I took over myself. The sun still shone beautifully enough, the blue was wintry, of Emersonian haughtiness, but I felt wicked. I was as filled with harsh things to say as the sky was full of freezing blue. Very good, Humboldt, you made it in American Culture as Hart Schaffner & Marx made it in cloaks and suits, as General Sarnoff made it in communications, as Bernard Baruch made it on a park bench.

As, according to Dr. Johnson, dogs made it on their hind legs and ladies in the pulpit—exceeding their natural limits curiously. Orpheus, the Son of Greenhorn, turned up in Greenwich Village with his ballads. He loved literature and intellectual conversation and argument, loved the history of thought. A big gentle handsome boy he put together his own combination of symbolism and street language. Into this mixture went Yeats, Apollinaire, Lenin, Freud, Morris R. Cohen, Gertrude Stein, baseball statistics, and Hollywood gossip. He brought Coney Island into the Aegean and united Buffalo Bill with Rasputin. He was going to join together the Art Sacrament and the Industrial USA as equal powers. Born (as he insisted) on a subway platform at Columbus Circle, his mother going into labor on the IRT, he intended to be a divine artist, a man of visionary states and enchantments, Platonic possession. He got a Rationalistic, Naturalistic education at CCNY. This was not easily reconciled with the Orphic. But all his desires were contradictory. He wanted to be magically and cosmically expressive and articulate, able to say *anything*; he wanted also to be wise, philosophical, to find the common ground of poetry and science, to prove that the imagination was just as potent as machinery, to free and to bless humankind. But he was out also to be rich and famous. And of course there were the girls. Freud himself believed that fame was pursued for the sake of the girls. But then the girls were pursuing something themselves. Humboldt said, "They're always looking for the real thing. They've been had and had by phonies, so they pray for the real thing and they rejoice when the real thing appears. That's why they love poets. This is the truth about girls." Humboldt was the real thing, certainly. But by and by he stopped being a beautiful young man and the prince of conversationalists. He grew a belly, he became thick in the face. A look of disappointment and doubt appeared under his eyes.

Brown circles began to deepen there, and he had a bruised sort of pallor in the cheeks. That was what his "frantic profession" did to him. For he always had said that poetry was one of the frantic professions in which success depends on the opinion you hold of yourself. Think well of yourself, and you win. Lose self-esteem, and you're finished. For this reason a persecution complex develops, because people who don't speak well of you are killing you. Knowing this, or sensing it, critics and intellectuals *had* you. Like it or not you were dragged into a power struggle. Then Humboldt's art dwindled while his frenzy increased. The girls were dear to him. They took him for the real thing long after he had realized that nothing real was left and that he was imposing on them. He swallowed more pills, he drank more gin. Mania and depression drove him to the loony bin. He was in and out. He became a professor of English in the boondocks. There he was a grand literary figure. Elsewhere, in one of his own words, he was zilch. But then he died and got good notices. He had always valued prominence, and the *Times* was tops. Having lost his talent, his mind, fallen apart, died in ruin, he rose again on the cultural Dow-Jones and enjoyed briefly the prestige of significant failure.

To Humboldt the Eisenhower landslide of 1952 was a personal disaster. He met me, the morning after, with heavy depression. His big blond face was madly gloomy. He led me into his office, Sewell's office, which was stuffed with books—I had the adjoining room. Leaning on the small desk, the *Times* with the election results spread over it, he held a cigarette but his hands were also clasped in despair. His ashtray, a Savarin coffee can, was already full. It wasn't simply that his hopes were disappointed or that the cultural evolution of America was stopped cold. Humboldt was afraid. "What are we going to do?" he said.

"We'll have to mark time," I said. "Maybe the next administration will let us into the White House."

Humboldt would allow no light conversation this morning.

"But look," I said. "You're poetry editor of *Arcturus*, you're on the staff of Hildebrand & Co. and a paid advisor to the Belisha Foundation, and teaching at Princeton. You have a contract to do a textbook in modern poetry. Kathleen told me that if you lived to be a hundred and fifty you'd never be able to make good on all the advances you've drawn from publishers."

"You wouldn't be jealous, Charlie, if you knew how hard my position is. I seem to have a lot going for me, but it's all a bubble. I'm in danger. You, without any prospects at all, are in a much stronger position. And now there's this political disaster." I sensed that he was afraid of his back-country neighbors. In his nightmares they burned his house, he shot it out with them, they lynched him and carried off his wife. Humboldt said, "What do we do now? What's our next move?"

These questions were asked only to introduce the scheme he had in mind.

"Our move?"

"Either we leave the US during this administration, or we dig in."

"We could ask Harry Truman for asylum in Missouri."

"Don't joke with me, Charlie. I have an invitation from the Free University of Berlin to teach American literature."

"That sounds grand."

He quickly said, "No, no! Germany is dangerous. I wouldn't take a chance on Germany."

"That leaves digging in. Where are you going to dig?"

"I said 'we.' The situation is very unsafe. If you had any sense you'd feel the same. You think because you're such a pretty-boy, and so bright and big-eyed, that nobody would hurt you."

Humboldt now began to attack Sewell. "Sewell really is a rat," he said.

"I thought you were old friends."

"Long acquaintance isn't friendship. Did *you* like him? He *received* you. He condescended, he was snotty, you were treated like dirt. He didn't even talk to you, only to me. I resented it."

"You didn't say so."

"I didn't want to rouse you right away and make you angry, start you under a cloud. Do you think he's a good critic?"

"Can the deaf tune pianos?"

"He's subtle, though. He's a subtle man, in a dirty way. Don't underrate him. And he's a rough infighter. But to become a professor without even a BA . . . it speaks for itself. His father was just a lobsterman. His mother took in washing. She did Kittredge's collars in Cambridge and she wangled library privileges for her son. He went down into the Harvard stacks a weakling and he came up a regular titan. Now he's a Wasp gentleman and lords it over us. You and I have raised his status. He comes on with two Jews like a mogul and a prince."

"Why do you want to make me sore at Sewell?"

"You're too lordly yourself to take offense. You're an even bigger snob than Sewell. I think you may be psychologically one of those Axel types that only cares about inner inspiration, no connection with the actual world. The actual world can kiss your ass," said Humboldt wildly. "You leave it to poor bastards like me to think about matters like money and status and success and failure and social problems and politics. You don't give a damn for such things."

"If true, why is that so bad?"

"Because you stick *me* with all these unpoetic responsibilities. You lean back like a king, relaxed, and let all these human problems happen. There ain't no flies on Jesus. Charlie, you're not place bound, time bound, goy bound, Jew bound. What *are* you bound? Others abide our question. Thou art free! Sewell was stinking to you. He snubbed you and you're sore at him, too, don't deny it. But you can't pay attention. You're always mooning in your private mind about some kind of cosmic destiny. Tell me, what is this great thing you're always working on?"

I was now still lying on my broccoli plush sofa engaged in a meditation on this haughty freezing blue December morning. The heating engines of the great Chicago building made a strong hum. I could have done without this. Though I was beholden to modern engineering, too. Humboldt in the Princeton office stood before my mind, and my concentration was intense.

"Come to the point," I said to him.

His mouth seemed dry but there was nothing to drink. Pills make you thirsty. He smoked some more instead, and said, "You and I are friends. Sewell brought me here. And I brought you."

"I'm grateful to you. But you aren't grateful to him."

"Because he's a son of a bitch."

"Perhaps." I didn't mind hearing Sewell called that. He had snubbed me. But with his depleted hair, his dry-cereal mustache, the drinker's face, the Prufrock subtleties, the would-be elegance of his clasped hands and crossed legs, with his involved literary mutterings he was no wicked enemy. Although I seemed to be restraining Humboldt I loved the way he loused up Sewell. Humboldt's wayward nutty fertility when he let himself go gratified one of my shameful appetites, no doubt about it.

"Sewell is taking advantage of us," Humboldt said.

"How do you figure that?"

"When he comes back we'll be turned out."

"But I always knew it was a one-year job."

"Oh, you don't mind being like a rented article from Hertz's, like a trundle bed or a baby's potty?" said Humboldt.

Under the shepherd's plaid of the blanket-wide jacket his back began to look humped (a familiar sign). That massing of bison power in his back meant that he was up to no good. The look of peril grew about his mouth and eyes and the two crests of hair stood higher than usual. Pale hot radiant waves appeared in his face. Pigeons, gray-and-cream-feathered, walked with crimson feet on the sandstone window sills. Humboldt didn't like them. He saw them as Princeton pigeons, Sewell's pigeons. They cooed for Sewell. At times Humboldt seemed to view them as his agents and spies. After all this was Sewell's office and Humboldt sat at Sewell's desk. The books on the walls were Sewell's. Lately Humboldt had been throwing them into boxes. He pushed off a set of Toynbee and put up his own Rilke and Kafka. Down with Toynbee; down with Sewell, too. "You and I are expendable here, Charlie," Humboldt said. "Why? I'll tell you. We're Jews, shonickers, kikes. Here in Princeton, we're no threat to Sewell."

I remembered thinking hard about this, knitting my forehead. "I'm afraid I still haven't grasped your point," I said.

"Try thinking of yourself as Sheeny Solomon Levi, then. It's safe to install Sheeny Solomon and go to Damascus for a year to discuss *The Spoils of Poynton*. When you come back, your classy professorship is waiting for you. You and I are no threat."

"But I don't want to be a threat to him. And why should Sewell worry about threats?"

"Because he's at war with these old guys, all the billy whiskers, the Hamilton Wright Mabie genteel crappers who never accepted him. He doesn't know Greek or Anglo-Saxon. To them he's a lousy upstart."

"So? He's a self-made man. Now I'm for him."

"He's corrupt, he's a bastard, he's covered you and me with contempt. I feel ridiculous when I walk down the street. In Princeton you and I are Moe and Joe, a Yid vaudeville act. We're a joke—Abie Kabibble and Company. Unthinkable as members of the Princeton community."

"Who needs their community?"

"Nobody trusts that little crook. There's something human he just hasn't got. The person who knew him best, his wife—when she left him she took her birds. You saw all those cages. She didn't even want an empty cage to remind her of him."

"Did she go away with birds sitting on her head and arms? Come on, Humboldt, what do you want?"

"I want you to feel as insulted as I feel, not stick me with the whole thing. Why don't you have any indignation, Charlie—Ah! You're not a real American. You're grateful. You're a foreigner. You have that Jewish immigrant kiss-the-ground-at-Ellis-Island gratitude. You're also a child of the Depression. You never thought you'd have a job, with an office, and a desk, and private drawers all for yourself. It's still so hilarious to you that you can't stop laughing. You're a Yiddisher mouse in these great Christian houses. At the same time, you're too snooty to look at anyone."

"These social wars are nothing to me, Humboldt. And let's not forget all the hard things you've said about Ivy League kikes. And only last week you were on the side of Tolstoi—it's time we simply refused to be inside history and playing the comedy of history, the bad social game."

It was no use arguing. Tolstoi? Tolstoi was last week's conversation. Humboldt's big intelligent disordered face was white and hot with turbulent occult emotions and brainstorms. I felt sorry for us, for both, for all of us, such odd organisms under the sun. Large minds abutting too close on swelling souls. And banished souls at that, longing for their home-world. Everyone alive mourned the loss of his home-world.

Sunk into the pillow of my green sofa it was all clear to me. Ah, what this existence was! What being human was!

Pity for Humboldt's absurdities made me cooperative. "You've been up all night thinking," I said.

Humboldt said with an unusual emphasis, "Charlie, you trust me, don't you?"

"Christ, Humboldt! Do I trust the Gulf Stream? What am I supposed to trust you in?"

"You know how close I feel to you. Interknitted. Brother and brother."

"You don't have to soften me up. Spill it, Humboldt, for Christ's sake."

He made the desk seem small. It was manufactured for lesser figures. His upper body rose above it. He looked like a three-hundred-pound pro linebacker beside a kiddie car. His nail-bitten fingers held the ember of a cigarette. "First we're going to get me an appointment here," he said.

"You want to be a Princeton prof?"

"A chair in modern literature, that's what I want. And you're going to help. So that when Sewell comes back he finds me installed. With tenure. The US Gov has sent him to dazzle and oppress those poor Syrian wogs with *The Spoils of Poynton*. Well, when he's wound up a year of boozing and mumbling long sentences under his breath he'll come back and find that the old twerps who wouldn't give him the time of day have made me full professor. How do you like it?"

"Not much. Is that what kept you up last night?"

"Call on your imagination, Charlie. You're overrelaxed. Grasp the insult. Get sore. He hired you like a spittoon-shiner. You've got to cut the last of the old slave-morality virtues that still bind you to the middle class. I'm going to put some hardness in you, some iron."

"Iron? This will be your fifth job—the fifth that *I* know of. Suppose I were hard—I'd ask you what's in it for me. Where do I come in?"

"Charlie!" He intended to smile; it was not a smile. "I've got a blueprint."

"I know you have. You're like what's-his-name, who couldn't drink a cup of tea without a stratagem—like Alexander Pope."

Humboldt seemed to take this as a compliment, and laughed between his teeth, silently. Then he said, "Here's what you do. Go to Ricketts and say: 'Humboldt is a very distinguished person—poet, scholar, critic, teacher, editor. He has an international reputation and he'll have a place in the literary history of the United States'—all of which is true, by the way. 'And here's your chance, Professor Ricketts, I happen to know that Humboldt's tired of living like a hand-to-mouth bohemian. The literary world is going fast. The avant-garde is a memory. It's time Humboldt led a more dignified settled life. He's married now. I know he admires Princeton, he loves it here, and if you made him an offer he'd certainly consider it. I might talk him into it. I'd hate for you to miss this opportunity, Professor Ricketts. Princeton has got Einstein and Panofsky. But you're weak on the literary creative side. The coming trend is to have artists on the campus. Amherst has Robert Frost. Don't fall behind. Grab Fleisher. Don't let him get away, or you'll end up with some third-rater.'"

"I won't mention Einstein and Panofsky. I'll start right out with Moses and the prophets. What a cast-iron plot! Ike has inspired you. This is what I call high-minded low cunning."

However, he didn't laugh. His eyes were red. He'd been up all night. First he watched the election returns. Then he wandered about the house and yard gripped by despair, thinking what to do. Then he planned out this putsch. Then filled with inspiration he drove in his Buick, the busted muffler blasting in the country lanes and the great long car skedaddling dangerously on the curves. Lucky for the woodchucks they were already hibernating. I know what figures crowded his thoughts—Walpole, Count Mosca, Disraeli, Lenin. While he thought also, with uncontemporary sublimity, about eternal life. Ezekiel and Plato were not absent. The man was noble. But he was all asmolder, and craziness also made him vile and funny. Heavy-handed, thick-faced with fatigue, he took a medicine bottle from his briefcase and fed himself a few little pills out of the palm of his hand. Tranquilizers, perhaps. Or maybe amphetamines for speed. He swallowed them dry. He doctored himself. Like Demmie Vonghel. She locked herself in the bathroom and took many pills.

"So you'll go to Ricketts," Humboldt told me.

"I thought he was only a front man."

"That's right. He's a stooge. But the old guard can't disown him. If we outsmart him, they'll have to back him up."

"But why should Ricketts pay attention to what I say?"

"Because, friend, I passed the word around that your play is going to be produced."

"You did?"

"Next year, on Broadway. They look on you as a successful playwright."

"Now why the hell did you do that? I'm going to look like a phony."

"No, you won't. We'll make it true. You can leave that to me. I gave Ricketts your last essay in the *Kenyon* to read, and he thinks you're a comer. And don't pretend with me. I know you. You love intrigue and mischief. Right now your teeth are on edge with delight. Besides, it's not just intrigue. . . ."

"What? Sorcery! *Fucking sortilegio!*"

"It's not *sortilegio*. It's mutual aid."

"Don't give me that stuff."

"First me, then you," he said.

I distinctly remember that my voice jumped up. I shouted, "What!" Then I laughed and said, "You'll make me a Princeton professor, too? Do you think I could stand a whole lifetime of this drinking, boredom, small talk, and ass-kissing? Now that you've lost Washington by a landslide, you've settled pretty fast for this academic music box. Thank you, I'll find misery in my own way. I give you two years of this goyish privilege."

Humboldt waved his hands at me. "Don't poison my mind. What a tongue you have, Charlie. Don't say those things. I'll expect them to happen. They'll infect my future."

I paused and considered his peculiar proposition. Then I looked at Humboldt himself. His mind was executing some earnest queer labor. It was swelling and pulsating oddly, painfully. He tried to laugh it all off with his nearly silent panting laugh. I could hardly hear the breath of it.

"You wouldn't be lying to Ricketts," he said. "Where would they get somebody like me?"

"Okay, Humboldt. That is a hard question."

"Well, I am one of the leading literary men of this country."

"Sure you are, at your best."

"Something should be done for me. Especially in this Ike moment, as darkness falls on the land."

"But why this?"

"Well, frankly, Charlie, I'm out of kilter, temporarily. I have to get back to a state in which I can write poetry again. But where's my equilibrium? There are too many anxieties. They dry me out. The world keeps interfering. I have to get the enchantment back. I feel as if I've been living in a suburb of reality, and commuting back and forth. That's got to stop. I have to locate myself. I'm here" (here on earth, he meant) "to do something, something good."

"I know, Humboldt. Here isn't Princeton, either, and everyone is waiting for the good thing."

Eyes reddening still more, Humboldt said, "I know you love me, Charlie."

"It's true. But let's only say it once."

"You're right. I'm a brother to you, too, though. Kathleen also knows it. It's obvious how we feel about one another, Demmie Vonghel included. Humor me, Charlie. Never mind how ridiculous this seems. Humor me, it's important. Call up Ricketts and say you have to talk to him."

"Okay. I will."

Humboldt put his hands on Sewell's small yellow desk and thrust himself back in the chair so that the steel casters gave a wicked squeak. The ends of his hair were confused with cigarette smoke. His head was lowered. He was examining me as if he had just surfaced from many fathoms.

"Have you got a checking account, Charlie? Where do you keep your money?"

"What money?"

"Haven't you got a checking account?"

"At Chase Manhattan. I've got about twelve bucks."

"My bank is the Corn Exchange," he said. "Now, where's your checkbook?"

"In my trench coat."

"Let's see."

I brought out the flapping green blanks, curling at the edges. "I see my balance is only eight," I said.

Then Humboldt reaching into his plaid jacket brought out his own checkbook and unclipped one of his many pens. He was bandoliered with fountain pens and ball-points.

"What are you doing, Humboldt?"

"I'm giving you *carte blanche* power to draw on my

account. I'm signing a blank check in your name. And you make one out to me. No date, no amount, just 'Pay to Von Humboldt Fleisher.' Sit down, Charlie, and fill it out."

"But what's it about? I don't like this. I have to understand what's going on."

"With eight bucks in the bank, what do you care?"

"It's not the money. . . ."

He was very moved, and he said, "Exactly. It isn't. That's the whole point. If you're ever up against it, fill in any amount you need and cash it. The same applies to me. We'll take an oath as friends and brothers never to abuse this. To hold it for the worst emergency. When I said mutual aid you didn't take me seriously. Well, now you see." Then he leaned on the desk in all his heaviness and in a tiny script he filled in my name with trembling force.

My control wasn't much better than his. My own arm seemed full of nerves and it jerked as I was signing. Then Humboldt, big delicate and stained, heaved himself up from his revolving chair and gave me the Corn Exchange check. "No, don't just stick it in your pocket," he said. "I want to see you put it away. It's dangerous. I mean it's valuable."

We now shook hands—all four hands. Humboldt said, "This makes us blood-brothers. We've entered into a covenant. This is a covenant."

A year later I had a Broadway hit and he filled in my blank check and cashed it. He said that I had betrayed him, that I, his blood-brother, had broken a sacred covenant, that I was conspiring with Kathleen, that I had set the cops on him, and that I had cheated him. They had lashed him in a strait jacket and locked him in Bellevue, and that was my doing, too. For this I had to be punished. He imposed a fine. He drew six thousand seven hundred and sixty-three dollars and fifty-eight cents from my account at Chase Manhattan.

As for the check he had given me, I put it in a drawer under some shirts. In a few weeks it disappeared and was never seen again.

HERE meditation began to get really tough. Why? Because of Humboldt's invectives and denunciations which now came back to me, together with fierce distractions and pelting anxieties, as dense as flak. Why was I lying here? I had to get ready to fly to Milan. I was supposed to go with Renata to Italy. Christmas in Milan! And I had to attend a hearing in Judge Urbanovich's chambers, conferring first with Forrest Tomchek, the lawyer who represented me in the action brought by Denise for every penny I owned. I needed also to discuss with Murra the CPA the government's tax case against me. Also Pierre Thaxter was due from California to talk to me about *The Ark*—really, to show why he had been right to default on that loan for which I had put up collateral—and to bare his soul and in so doing bare my soul, too, for who was I to have a covered soul? There was even a question about the Mercedes, whether to sell it or pay for repairs. I was almost ready to abandon it for junk. As for Ronald Cantabile, claiming to represent the new spirit, I knew that I could expect to hear from him any minute.

Still, I was able to hold out against this nagging rush of distractions. I fought off the impulse to rise as if it were a wicked temptation. I stayed where I was on the sofa sinking into the down for which geese had been ravished, and held on to Humboldt. The will-strengthening exercises I had been doing were no waste of time. As a rule I took plants as my theme: either a particular rosebush summoned from the past, or plant anatomy. I obtained a large botany book by a woman named Esau and sank myself into morphology, into protoplasts and ergastic substances, so that my exercises might have real content. I didn't want to be one of your idle hit-or-miss visionaries.

Sewell an anti-Semite? Nonsense. It suited Humboldt to hoke that up. As for blood-brotherhood and covenants, they were somewhat more genuine. Blood-brotherhood dramatized a real desire. But not genuine enough. And now I tried to remember our endless consultations and briefings before I called on Ricketts. I said, at last, to Humboldt, "Enough. I know how to do this. Not another word." Demmie Vonghel coached me too. She thought Humboldt very funny. On the morning of the interview she made sure that I was correctly dressed and took me to Penn Station in a cab.

This morning in Chicago I found that I could recall Ricketts without the slightest difficulty. He was youthful but white-haired. His crew cut sat low on his forehead. He was thick, strong, and red-necked, a handsome furniture-mover sort of man. Years after the war, he still clung to GI slang, this burly winsome person. A bit heavy for frolic, in his charcoal-gray flannels, he tried to take a light manner with me. "I hear you guys are going great in Sewell's program, that's the scuttlebutt."

"Ah, you should have heard Humboldt speak on *Sailing to Byzantium*."

"People have said that. I couldn't make it. Administration. Tough titty for me. Now what about you, Charlie?"

"Enjoying every minute here."

"Terrific. Keeping up your own work, I hope? Humboldt tells me you're going to have a Broadway production next year."

"He's a little ahead of himself."

"Ah, he's a great guy. Wonderful thing for us all. Wonderful for me, my first year as chairman."

"Is it, now?"

"Why yes, it's my shakedown cruise, too. Glad to have both of you. You look very cheerful, by the way."

"I feel cheerful, generally. People find fault with it. A drunken lady last week asked me what the hell my problem was. She said I was a compulsive-*heimischer* type."

"Really? I don't think I ever heard that expression."

"It was new to me too. Then she told me I was existentially out of step. And the last thing she said was, 'You're apparently having a hell of a good time, but life will crush you like an empty beer can.'"

Under the crew-cut crown Rickett's eyes were shame-troubled. Perhaps he too was oppressed by my good spirits. In reality I was only trying to make the interview easier. But I began to realize that Ricketts was suffering. He sensed that I had come to do mischief. For why was I here, what sort of call was this? That I was Humboldt's emissary was obvious. I brought a message, and a message from Humboldt meant nothing but trouble.

Sorry for Ricketts, I made my pitch as quickly as possible. Humboldt and I were pals, great privilege for me to be able to spend so much time with him down here. Oh, Humboldt! Wise warm gifted Humboldt! Poet, critic, scholar, teacher, editor, original. . . .

Eager to help me through this, Ricketts said, "He's just a man of genius."

"Thanks. That's what it amounts to. Well, this is what I want to say to you. Humboldt wouldn't say it himself. It's my idea entirely. I'm only passing through, but it would be a mistake not to keep Humboldt here. You shouldn't let him get away."

"That's a thought."

"There are things that only poets can tell you about poetry."

"Yes, Dryden, Coleridge, Poe. But why should Humboldt tie himself down to an academic position?"

"That's not the way Humboldt sees things. I think he needs an intellectual community. You can imagine how overpowering the great social structure of the country would be to inspired men of his type. Where to turn, is the question. Now the trend in the universities is to appoint poets, and you'll do it, too, sooner or later. Here's your chance to get the best."

Making my meditation as detailed as possible, no fact too small to be remembered, I could see how Humboldt had looked when he coached me on the way to handle Ricketts. Humboldt's face, with a persuasive pumpkin smile, came so close to mine that I felt the warmth or fever of his cheeks. Humboldt said, "You have a talent for this kind of errand. I know it." Did he mean I was a born meddler? He said, "A man like Ricketts didn't make it big in the Protestant establishment. Not fit for the important roles—corporation president, board chairman, big banks, Republican National Committee, Joint Chiefs, Budget Bureau, Federal Reserve. To be a prof. of his kind means to be the weak kid brother. Or maybe even sister. They get taken care of. He's probably a member of the Century Club. Okay to teach *The Ancient Mariner* to young Firestones or Fords. Humanist, scholar, scoutmaster, nice but a numbskull."

Maybe Humboldt was right. I could see that Ricketts was unable to cope with me. His sincere brown eyes seemed to ache. He waited for me to get on with this, to finish the interview. I didn't like backing him into a corner, but behind me I had Humboldt. Because Humboldt didn't sleep on the night Ike was elected, because he was drugged with pills and booze or toxic with metabolic wastes, because his psyche didn't refresh itself by dreaming, because he renounced his gifts, because he lacked spiritual strength, or was too frail to stand up to the unpoetic power of the USA, I had to come here and torment Ricketts. I felt pity for Ricketts. And I couldn't see that Princeton was such a big deal as Humboldt made out. Between noisy Newark and squalid Trenton it was a sanctuary, a zoo, a spa, with its own choochoo and elms and lovely green cages. It resembled another place I was later to visit as a tourist—a Serbian watering place called Vrnatchka Banja. But maybe what Princeton was not counted for more. It was not the factory or department store, not the great corporation office or bureaucratic civil service, it was not the routine job-world. If you could arrange to avoid that routine job-world, you were an intellectual or an artist. Too restless, tremorous, agitated, too mad to sit at a desk eight hours a day, you needed an institution—a higher institution.

"A chair in poetry for Humboldt," I said.

"A chair in poetry! A chair! Oh!—What a grand idea!" said Ricketts. "We'd love it. I speak for everyone. We'd all vote for it. The only thing is the dough! If only we had enough dough! Charlie, we're real poor. Besides, this outfit, like any outfit, has its table of organization."

"Table of organization? Translate, please."

"A chair like that would have to be created. It's a big deal."

"How would a chair be set up?"

"Special endowment, as a rule. Fifteen or twenty grand a year, for about twenty years. Half a million bucks, with the retirement fund. We just ain't got it, Charlie. Christ, how we'd love to get Humboldt. It breaks my heart, you know that." Ricketts was now wonderfully cheerful. Minutely observant, my memory brought back, without my especially asking for it, the white frieze of his vigorous short hair, his brownish oxheart cherry eyes, the freshness of his face, his happy full cheeks.

I figured that was that, when we shook hands. Ricketts,

having gotten rid of us, was rapturously friendly. "If only we had the money!" he kept saying.

And though Humboldt was waiting for me in a fever, I claimed a moment for myself in the fresh air. I stood under a brownstone arch, on foot-hollowed stone, while panhandling squirrels came at me from all directions across the smooth quadrangles, the lovely walks. It was chilly and misty, the blond dim November sun binding the twigs in circles of light. Demmie Vonghel's face had such a blond pallor. In her cloth coat with the marten collar, with her sublime sexual knees that touched, and the pointed feet of a princess, and her dilated nostrils presented almost as emotionally as her eyes, and breathing with a certain hunger, she had kissed me with her warm face, and pressed me with her tight-gloved hand, saying, "You'll do great, Charlie. Just great." We had parted at Penn Station that morning. Her cab had waited.

I didn't think that Humboldt would agree.

But I was astonishingly wrong. When I showed up in the doorway he sent away his students. He had them all in a state of exaltation about literature. They were always hanging around, waiting in the corridor with their manuscripts. "Gentlemen," he announced, "something has come up. Appointments are canceled—moved up one hour. Eleven is now twelve. Two-thirty is three-thirty." I came in. He locked the door of the hot book-crammed smoky office. "Well?" he said.

"He hasn't got the money."

"He didn't say no?"

"You're famous, he loves you, admires you, desires you, but he can't create a chair without the dough."

"And that's what he said?"

"Exactly what he said."

"Then I think I've got him! Charlie, I've got him! We've done it!"

"How have you got him? How have we done it?"

"Because—ho, ho! He hid behind the budget. He didn't say, 'no dice.' Or 'under no circumstances.' Or 'get the hell out of here.'" Humboldt was laughing that nearly silent, panting laugh of his, through tiny teeth, while a scarf of smoke flowed about him. He looked Mother-Goosey when he did this. The cow jumped over the moon. The little dog laughed to see such fun. Humboldt said, "Monopoly capitalism has treated creative men like rats. Well, that phase of history is ending. . . ." I didn't quite see how that was relevant, even if true. "We're going places."

"Tell me, then."

"I'll tell you later. But you did great." Humboldt had started to pack, to stuff his briefcase, as he did at all decisive moments. Unbuckling, he threw back the slack flap and began to pull out certain books and manuscripts and pill bottles. He made odd foot movements, as though his cats were clawing at his trouser cuffs. He restuffed the scraped leather case with other books and papers. He lifted his broad-brimmed hat from the coat tree. Like a silent-movie hero taking his invention to the big city, he was off for New York. "Put a note up for the kids. I'll be back tomorrow," he said.

I walked him to the train but he told me nothing more. He sprang into the antique Dinkey car. He wagged his fingers at me through the dirty window. And he left.

I might have gone back to New York with him, because I had come down only for the interview with Ricketts. But he was Manic and it was best to let him be.

So I, Citrine, comfortable, in the midst of life, extended on a sofa, in cashmere socks (considering how the feet of those interred shredded away like leaf tobacco—Humboldt's feet), reconstructed the way in which my stout inspired pal declined and fell. His talent had gone bad. And now I had to think what to do about talent in this day, in this age. How to prevent the leprosy of souls. Somehow it appeared to be up to me.

I meditated like anything. I followed Humboldt in my mind. He was smoking on the train. I saw him passing quick and manic through the colossal hall of Penn Station with its dusty dome of single-colored glass. And then I saw him get into a cab—the subway was good enough, as a rule. But today each move was unusual, without precedent. This was because he couldn't count on reason. Reason was coming and going in shorter cycles, and one of these days it might go for good. And then what would he do? Should he lose it once and for all, he and Kathleen would need lots of money. Also, as he had said to me, you could be gaga in a tenured chair at Princeton, and would anybody notice? Ah, poor Humboldt! He might have been—no, he *was* so fine!

He was soaring now. His present idea was to go straight to the top. When he got there, this blemished spirit, the top saw the point. Humboldt met with interest and consideration.

Wilmoore Longstaff, the famous Longstaff, archduke of the higher learning in America, was the man Humboldt went to see. Longstaff had been appointed the first head of the new Belisha Foundation. The Belisha was richer than Carnegie and Rockefeller, and Longstaff had hundreds of millions to spend on science and scholarship, on the arts, and on social improvement. Humboldt already had a sinecure with the Foundation. His good friend Hildebrand had gotten it for him. Hildebrand the playboy publisher of avant-garde poets, himself a poet, was Humboldt's patron. He had discovered Humboldt at CCNY, he admired his work, adored his conversation, protected him, kept him on the payroll at Hildebrand & Co. as an editor. This caused Humboldt to lower his voice when he slandered him. "He steals from the blind, Charlie. When the Blind Association mails in pencils, Hildebrand keeps those charity pencils. He never donates a penny."

I remembered saying, "Stingy-rich is just ordinary camp."

"Yes, but he overdoes it. Try eating dinner at his house. He starves you. And why did Longstaff hire Hildebrand for thirty thousand to plan a program for writers? He hired him because of me. If you're a Foundation you don't deal with poets, you go to the man who owns a stable of poets. So I do all the work and get only eight thousand."

"Eight for a part-time job isn't bad, is it?"

"Charlie, it's cheap of you to pull this fair-mindedness on me. I say I'm an underdog and then you slip it in that I'm so privileged, meaning that you're an under-underdog. Hildebrand gets full value from me. He never reads a manuscript. He's always on a cruise or skiing in Sun Valley. Without my advice he'd publish toilet paper. I save him from being a millionaire Philistine. He got to Gertrude Stein because of me. Also to Eliot. Because of me he has something to offer Longstaff. But I'm forbidden absolutely to talk to Longstaff."

"No."

"Yes! I tell you," said Humboldt. "Longstaff has a private elevator. No one gets to his penthouse from the lower ranks. I see him from a distance as he comes and goes but my instructions are to stay away from him."

Years afterward, I, Citrine, sat next to Wilmoore Longstaff on that Coast Guard helicopter. He was quite old then, finished, fallen from glory. I had seen him when the going was good, and he had looked like a movie star, like a five-star general, like Machiavelli's Prince, like Aristotle's great-souled man. Longstaff had fought technocracy and plutocracy with the classics. He forced some of the most powerful people in the country to discuss Plato and Hobbes. He made airline presidents, chairmen, governors of the Stock Exchange perform *Antigone* in board rooms. Truth, however, is truth and Longstaff was in many respects first rate. He was a distinguished educator, he was even noble. His life would perhaps have been easier if his looks had been less striking.

At any rate, Humboldt did the bold thing, just as we had all seen it done in the old go-getter movies. Unauthorized, he entered Longstaff's private elevator and pushed the button. Materializing huge and delicate in the penthouse, he gave his name to the receptionist. No, he had no appointment (I saw the sun on his cheeks, on his soiled clothes—it was shining as it shines through the purer air in skyscrapers), but he *was* Von Humboldt Fleisher. The name was enough. Longstaff had him shown in. He was very glad to see Humboldt. This he told me during the flight, and I believed him. We sat in the helicopter belted up in orange puffy life jackets, and we were armed with those long knives. Why the knives? Perhaps to fight sharks if one fell into the harbor. "I had read his ballads," Longstaff told me. "I considered him to have great talent." I knew of course that for Longstaff *Paradise Lost* was the last real poem in English. Longstaff was a greatness-freak. What he meant was that Humboldt was undoubtedly a poet and a charming man. That he was. In Longstaff's office Humboldt must have been swooning with wickedness and ingenuity, swollen with manic energy, with spots before his eyes and maculations of the heart. He was going to persuade Longstaff, do in Sewell, outfox Ricketts, screw Hildebrand, and bugger fate. At the moment he looked like the Roto Rooter man come to snake out the drains. Yet he was bound for a chair at Princeton. Ike had conquered, Stevenson had gone down, but Humboldt was vaulting into penthouses and beyond.

Longstaff too was riding high. He bullied his trustees with Plato and Aristotle and Aquinas, he had the whammy on them. And probably Longstaff had old scores to settle with Princeton, a pillbox of the educational establishment at which he aimed his radical flame thrower. I knew from Ickes' *Diaries* that Longstaff had made up to FDR. He wanted Wallace's place on the ticket, and Truman's, later. He dreamed of being Vice President and President. But Roosevelt had strung him along, had kept him waiting on tiptoes but never kissed him. That was Roosevelt all over. In this I sympathized with Longstaff (an ambitious man, a despot, a czar in my secret heart).

So as the helicopter tilted back and forth over New York I studied this handsome aged Dr. Longstaff trying to understand how Humboldt must have looked to him. In Humboldt he perhaps had seen Caliban America, heaving and yapping, writing odes on greasy paper from the fish shop. For Longstaff had no feeling for literature. But he had been delighted when Humboldt explained that he wanted the Belisha Foundation to endow a chair for him at Princeton. "Exactly right!" said Longstaff. "Just the thing!" He buzzed his secretary and dictated a letter. Then and there Wilmoore Longstaff committed the Foundation to an extended grant. Soon Humboldt, palpitating, held a signed copy of the letter in his hand, and he and Longstaff drank martinis, gazing at Manhattan from the sixtieth floor, and talked about Dante's bird imagery.

As soon as he left Longstaff, Humboldt rushed downtown by cab to visit a certain Ginnie in the Village, a Bennington girl to whom Demmie Vonghel and I had introduced him. He pounded on her door and said, "It's Von Humboldt Fleisher. I have to see you." Stepping into the vestibule, he propositioned her immediately. Ginnie said, "He chased me around the apartment, and it was a scream. But I was worried about the puppies underfoot." Her dachshund had just had a litter. Ginnie locked herself in the bathroom. Humboldt shouted, "You don't know what you're missing. I'm a poet. I have a big cock." And Ginnie told Demmie, "I was laughing so hard I couldn't have done it anyway."

When I asked Humboldt about this incident he said, "I felt I had to celebrate, and I understood these Bennington girls went for poets. Too bad about this Ginnie. She's very pretty but she's honey from the icebox, if you know what I mean. Cold sweets won't spread."

"Did you go elsewhere?"

"I gave up on erotic relief. I went around and visited lots of people."

"And showed them Longstaff's letter."

"Of course."

In any case, the scheme worked. Princeton couldn't refuse the Belisha gift. Ricketts was outgeneraled. Humboldt was appointed. The *Times* and the *Herald Tribune* both carried the story. For two or three months things were smoother than velvet and cashmere. Humboldt's new colleagues gave cocktail and dinner parties for him. Nor did Humboldt in his happiness forget that we were blood-brothers. Almost daily he would say, "Charlie, today I had a terrific idea for you. For the title role in your play . . . Victor McLaglen is a fascist of course. Can't have him. But . . . I'm going to get in touch with Orson Welles for you. . . ."

But then, in February, Longstaff's trustees rebelled. They had had enough, I guess, and rallied for the honor of American monopoly-capital. Longstaff's proposed budget was rejected, and he was forced to resign. He was not sent away quite empty-handed. He got some money, about twenty million, to start a little foundation of his own. But in effect they gave him the ax. The appropriation for Humboldt's chair was a tiny item in that rejected budget. When Longstaff fell, Humboldt fell with him. "Charlie," Humboldt said when he was at last able to talk about it, "it was just like my father's experience when he was wiped out in the Florida boom. One year more and we would have made it. I've even asked myself, I've wondered, whether Longstaff knew when he sent the letter that he was on his way out . . . ?"

"I can't believe that," I said. "Longstaff is certainly mischievous, but he isn't mean."

The Princeton people behaved well and offered to do the gentlemanly thing. Ricketts said, "You're one of us now, Hum, you know? Don't worry, we'll find the dough for your chair somehow." But Humboldt sent in his resignation. Then in March, on a back road in New Jersey, he tried to run Kathleen down in the Buick. She jumped into a ditch to save herself.

AT this moment I must say, almost in the form of deposition, without argument, that I do not believe my birth began my first existence. Nor Humboldt's. Nor anyone's. On esthetic grounds, if on no others, I cannot accept the view of death taken by most of us, and taken by me during most of my life—on esthetic grounds therefore I am obliged to deny that so extraordinary a thing as a human soul can be wiped out forever. No, the dead are about us, shut out by our metaphysical denial of them. As we lie nightly in our hemispheres asleep by the billions, our dead approach us. Our ideas should be their nourishment. We are their grainfields. But we are barren and we starve them. Don't kid yourself, though, we are watched by the dead, watched on this earth, which is our school of freedom. In the next realm, where things are clearer, clarity eats into freedom. We are free on earth because of cloudiness, because of error, because of marvelous limitation, and as much because of beauty as of blindness and evil. These always go with the blessing of freedom. But this is all I have to say about the matter now, because I'm in a hurry, under pressure—all this unfinished business!

As I was meditating on Humboldt, the hall-buzzer went off. I have a dark little hall where I press the button and get muffled shouts on the intercom from below. It was Roland Stiles, the doorman. My ways, the arrangements of my life, diverted Stiles a lot. He was a skinny witty old Negro. He was, so to speak, in the semifinals of life. In his opinion, so was I. But I didn't seem to see it that way, for some strange white man's reason, and I continued to carry on as if it weren't yet time to think of death. "Plug in your telephone, Mr. Citrine. Do you read me? Your number-one lady friend is trying to reach you." Yesterday my car was bashed. Today my beautiful mistress couldn't get in touch. To him I was as good as a circus. At night Stiles's missus liked stories about me better than television. He told me so himself.

I dialed Renata and said, "What is it?"

"What is it! For Christ's sake! I've called ten times. You have to see Judge Urbanovich at half past one. Your lawyer's been trying to get you, too. And he finally phoned Szathmar, and Szathmar phoned me."

"Half past one! They changed the time on me! For months they ignore me, then they give me two hours' notice, curse them." My spirit began to jump up and down. "Oh hell, I hate them, those crap artists."

"Maybe you can wind the whole thing up now. Today."

"How? I've surrendered five times. Each time I surrender Denise and her guy up their demands."

"In just a few days thank God I'm getting you out of here. You've been dragging your feet, because you don't want to go, but believe me, Charlie, you'll bless me for it when we're in Europe again."

"Forrest Tomchek doesn't even have time to discuss the case with me. Some lawyer Szathmar recommended."

"Now Charlie, how will you get downtown without your car? I'm surprised that Denise hasn't tried to hitch a ride to court with you."

"I'll get a cab."

"I have to take Fannie Sunderland to the Mart, anyway, for her tenth look at upholstery material for one fucking sofa." Renata laughed, but she was unusually patient with her clients. "I must take care of this before we pull out for Europe. We'll pick you up at one o'clock sharp. Be ready, Charlie."

Long ago I read a book called *Ils Ne M'auront Pas* (*They Aren't Going to Get Me*) and at certain moments I whisper, "*Ils ne m'auront pas.*" I did that now, determined to finish my exercise in contemplation or Spirit-recollection (the purpose of which was to penetrate into the depths of the soul and to recognize the connection between the self and the divine powers). I lay down again on the sofa. To lie down was no small gesture of freedom. I am only being factual about this. It was a quarter of eleven, and if I left myself five minutes for a container of plain yoghurt and five minutes to shave I could continue for two hours to think about Humboldt. This was the right moment for it.

Well, Humboldt tried to run down Kathleen in his car. They were driving home from a party in Princeton, and he was punching her, steering with the left hand. At a blinking light, near a package store, she opened the door and made a run for it in her stocking feet—she had lost her shoes in Princeton. He chased her in the Buick. She jumped into a ditch and he ran into a tree. The state troopers had to come and release him because the doors were jammed by the collision.

Anyhow, the trustees had risen up against Longstaff, and the Poetry chair had disintegrated. Kathleen later told me that Humboldt had kept this from her all that day. He put down the phone and with his shuffling feet and sumo-wrestler's belly came into the kitchen and poured himself a large jam-jar full of gin. Standing beside the dirty sink in his sneakers he drank this as if it had been milk.

"What was that call?" said Kathleen.

"Ricketts called."

"What did he want?"

"Nothing. Just routine," said Humboldt.

"He turned a funny color under the eyes when he drank all that gin," Kathleen told me. "A kind of light greeny purple. You sometimes see that shade of purple in artichoke hearts."

A little later on the same morning he seems to have had another talk with Ricketts. This was when Ricketts told him that Princeton would not renege. Money would be found. But this put Ricketts in the morally superior position. A poet could not allow a bureaucrat to surpass him. Humboldt locked himself in his office with the gin bottle and all day long wrote drafts of a letter of resignation.

But that evening, on the road as they were driving in to attend a party at the Littlewoods' he went to work on Kathleen. Why did she let her father sell her to Rockefeller? Yes the old guy was supposed to be just a pleasant character, a bohemian antique from Paris, one of the gang from the Closerie des

Lilas, but he was an international criminal, a Dr. Moriarty, a Lucifer, a pimp and didn't he try to have sexual relations with his own daughter? Well, how was it with Rockefeller? Did Rockefeller's penis thrill her more? Did the billions enter in? Did Rockefeller have to take a woman away from a poet in order to get it up? So they drove in the Buick skidding on the gravel and booming through clouds of dust. He began to shout that her great calm-and-lovely act didn't take him in at all. He knew all about these things. From a bookish viewpoint he actually did know a lot. He knew the jealousy of King Leontes in *The Winter's Tale*. Mario Praz he knew. And Proust —caged rats tortured to death, Charlus flogged by some killer-concierge, some slaughterhouse brute with a scourge of nails. "I know all that lust garbage," he said. "And I know the game has to be played with a calm face like yours. I know all about this female masochistic business. I understand your thrills, and you're just using me!"

So they got to the Littlewoods' and Demmie and I were there. Kathleen was white. Her face looked heavily powdered. Humboldt walked in silent. He wasn't talking. This was in fact his last night as the Belisha Professor of Poetry at Princeton. Tomorrow the news would be out. Maybe it was out already. Ricketts behaved honorably but he might not have been able to resist telling everyone. But Littlewood seemed not to know anything. He was trying hard to make his party a success. His cheeks were red and jolly. He looked like Mr. Tomato with a top hat in the juice ad. He had wavy hair and a fine worldly manner. When he took a lady's hand you wondered just what he was going to do with it. Littlewood was an upper-class bad boy, a minister's randy son. He knew London and Rome. He especially knew Shepheard's famous bar in Cairo, and had acquired his British Army slang there. He had friendly endearing spaces between his teeth. He loved to grin, and at every party he did imitations of Rudy Vallee. To cheer up Humboldt and Kathleen I got him to sing "I'm Just a Vagabond Lover." It did not go over well.

I was present in the kitchen when Kathleen made a serious mistake. Holding her drink and an unlit cigarette she reached into a man's pocket for a match. He was not a stranger, we knew him well, his name was Eubanks, and he was a Negro composer. His wife was standing near him. Kathleen was beginning to recover her spirits and was slightly drunk herself. But just as she was getting the matches out of Eubanks's pocket Humboldt came in. I saw him coming. First he stopped breathing. Then he clutched Kathleen with sensational violence. He twisted her arm behind her back and ran her out of the kitchen into the yard. A thing of this sort was not unusual at a Littlewood party, and others decided not to notice, but Demmie and I hurried to the window. Humboldt punched Kathleen in the belly, doubling her up. Then he pulled her by the hair into the Buick. As there was a car behind him he couldn't back out. He wheeled over the lawn and off the sidewalk, hacking off the muffler on the curb. I saw it there next morning like the case of a super-insect, flaky with rust, and a pipe coming out of it. Also I found Kathleen's shoes stuck by the heels in the snow. There was fog, ice, dirty cold, the bushes glassy, the elm twigs livid, the March snow brocaded with soot.

And now I recalled that the rest of the night had been a headache because Demmie and I were overnight guests, and when the party broke up Littlewood took me aside and proposed man to man that we do a swap. "An Eskimo wife deal. What say we have a romp," he said. "A wingding."

"Thanks, no, it isn't cold enough for this Eskimo stuff."

"You're refusing on your own? Aren't you even going to ask Demmie?"

"She'd haul off and hit me. Perhaps you'd like to try her. You wouldn't believe how hard she can punch. She looks like a fashionable broad, and elegant, but she's really a big honest hick."

I had my own reasons for giving him a soft answer. We were overnight guests here. I didn't want to go at 2 a.m. to sit in the Pennsylvania waiting room. Entitled to my eight hours of oblivion and determined to have them, I got into bed in the smoky study through which the party had swirled. But now Demmie had put on her nightgown and was a changed person. An hour ago in a black chiffon dress and the hair brushed gold and long on her head and fastened with an ornament she was a young lady of breeding. Humboldt, when he was in a balanced state, loved to cite the important American social categories, and Demmie belonged to them all. "She's pure Main Line. Quaker schools, Bryn Mawr. Real class," Humboldt said. She had chatted with Littlewood, whose subject was Plautus, about Latin translation and New Testament Greek. I didn't love the farmer's daughter in Demmie less than the society girl. She now sat on the bed. Her toes were deformed by cheap shoes. Her large collarbones formed hollows. When they were children, she and her sister, similarly built, filled up these collarbone hollows with water and ran races.

Anything to stave off sleep. Demmie took pills but she deeply feared to sleep. She said she had a hangnail and sat on the bed filing away, the long flexible file going zigzag. Suddenly lively, she faced me cross-legged with round knees and a show of thigh. In this position she released the salt female odor, the bacterial background of deep love. She said, "Kathleen shouldn't have reached for Eubanks's matches. I hope Humboldt didn't hurt her, but she shouldn't have done it."

"But Eubanks is an old friend."

"Humboldt's old friend? He's known him a long time—there's a difference. It means something if a woman goes into a man's pocket. And we saw her do it. . . . I don't completely blame Humboldt."

Demmie was often like this. Just as I was ready to close my eyes for the night, having had enough of my conscious and operating self, Demmie wanted to talk. At this hour she preferred exciting topics—sickness, murder, suicide, eternal punishment, and hellfire. She got into a state. Her hair bristled and her eyes deepened with panic and her deformed toes twisted in all directions. She then closed her long hands upon her smallish breasts. With baby tremors of the lip she sank at times into a preverbal baby stammer. It was now three o'clock in the morning and I thought I heard the depraved Littlewoods carrying on above us in the master bedroom, perhaps to give us an idea of what we were missing. This was probably imaginary.

I rose, anyway, and took away Demmie's nail file. I tucked her in. Her mouth was naïvely open as she gave up the file. I got her to lie down but she was disturbed. I could see that. As she laid her head on the pillow, in profile, one large lovely eye stared out childishly. "Off you go," I said. She shut the staring eye. Her sleep was instantaneous and seemed deep.

But in a few minutes I heard what I expected to hear—her night voice. It was low hoarse and deep almost mannish. She moaned. She spoke broken words. She did this almost every night. The voice expressed her terror of this strange place, the earth, and of this strange state, being. Laboring and groaning she tried to get out of it. This was the primordial Demmie beneath the farmer's daughter beneath the teacher beneath the elegant Main Line horsewoman, Latinist, accomplished cocktail-sipper in black chiffon, with the upturned nose, this fashionable conversationalist. Thoughtful, I listened to this. I let her go on awhile, trying to comprehend. I pitied her and loved her. But then I put an end to it. I kissed her. She knew who it was. She pressed her toes to my shins and held me with powerful female arms. She cried "I love you" in the same deep voice, but her eyes were still shut blind. I think she never actually woke up.

IN May, when the Princeton term was ended, Humboldt and I met, as blood-brothers, for the last time.

As deep as the huge cap of December blue behind me entering the window with thermal distortions from the sun, I lay on my Chicago sofa and saw again everything that had happened. One's heart hurt from this sort of thing. One thought, How sad, about all this human nonsense which keeps us from the large truth. But perhaps I can get through it once and for all by doing what I am doing now.

Very good, Broadway was the word then. I had a producer, a director, and an agent. I was part of the theater world, in Humboldt's eyes. There were actresses who said "dahling" and kissed you when you met. There was a Hirschfeld caricature of me in the *Times*. Humboldt took much credit for this. By bringing me to Princeton he had put me in the majors. Through him I met useful people in the Ivy League. Besides, he felt I had modeled Von Trenck, my Prussian hero, on him. "But look out, Charlie," he said. "Don't be taken in by the Broadway glamour and the commercial stuff."

Humboldt and Kathleen descended on me in the repaired Buick. I was in a cottage on the Connecticut shore, down the road from Lampton, the director, making revisions under his guidance—writing the play he wanted, for that was what it amounted to. Demmie was with me every weekend, but the Fleishers arrived on a Wednesday, when I was alone. Humboldt had just given a reading at Yale and they were going home. We sat in the small stone kitchen drinking coffee and gin, having a reunion. Humboldt was being "good," serious, high-minded. He had been reading *De Anima* and was full of ideas about the origins of thought. I noticed, however, that he didn't let Kathleen out of his sight. She had to tell him where she was going. "I'm just getting my cardigan." Even to go to the bathroom, she needed permission. Also he seemed to have punched her in the eye. She sat quietly and low in her chair, arms folded and long legs crossed, but she had a shiner. Humboldt finally spoke of it himself. "It wasn't me this time," he said. "You won't believe it, Charlie, but she fell against the dashboard when I made a fast stop. Some clunk in a truck came barreling out of a side road and I had to jump the brakes."

Perhaps he hadn't hit her, but he did watch her; he watched like a bailiff escorting a prisoner from one jail to another. He moved his chair all the while he was lecturing about *De Anima*, to make sure we didn't exchange eye-signals. He laid it on so thick that we were bound to try to outwit him. And we did. We managed at last to have a few words at the clothesline in the garden. She had rinsed her stockings and came out into the sunshine to hang them. Humboldt was probably satisfying a natural need.

"Did he sock you or not?"

"No, I fell on the dashboard. But it's hell, Charlie. Worse than ever."

The clothesline was old and dark gray. It had burst open and was giving up its white pith.

"He says I'm carrying on with a critic, a young, unimportant, completely innocent fellow named Magnasco. Very nice, but my God! And I'm tired of being treated like a nymphomaniac and told how I'm doing it on fire escapes or standing up, in clothes closets, every chance I get. And at Yale he made me sit on the platform during his reading. Then he blamed me for showing my legs. At every service station he forces his way into the ladies' room with me. I can't go back to New Jersey with him."

"What will you do?" said eager, heart-melting, concerned Citrine.

"Tomorrow when we get back to New York I'm going to get lost. I love him but I can't take any more. I'm telling you to prepare you, because you guys love each other, and you'll have to help him. He has some money. Hildebrand fired him. But he did get a Guggenheim, you know."

"I didn't even know he applied."

"Oh he puts in for everything. . . . Now he's watching us from the kitchen."

And there indeed was Humboldt bulging out the coppery webbing of the screen door like a fisherman's strange catch.

"Good luck."

As she went back to the house her legs were eagerly beaten by the grass of May. Through stripes of shrub shadow and country sunshine, the cat was strolling. The clothesline surrendered the pith of its soul, and Kathleen's stockings, hung at the wide end, now suggested lust. Such was Humboldt's effect. He came straight to me at the clothesline and ordered me to tell him what we had been talking about.

"Oh lay off, will you Humboldt? Don't force me into this neurotic superdrama." I was appalled by what I foresaw. I wished they would go—pile into their Buick (more than ever the muddy Flanders Field staff car) and pull out, leaving me with my Trenck troubles, the tyranny of Lampton, and the clean Atlantic shore.

But they stayed over. Humboldt didn't sleep. The wooden treads of the backstairs creaked all night under his weight. The tap ran and the refrigerator door slammed. When I came into the kitchen in the morning I found that the quart of Beefeater's gin, the house present they had brought, was empty on the table. The cotton wads of his pill bottles were all over the place, like rabbit droppings.

So Kathleen disappeared from Rocco's Restaurant on Thompson Street and Humboldt went wild. He said she was with Magnasco, that Magnasco kept her hidden in his room at the Hotel Earle. Somewhere Humboldt obtained a pistol and he hammered on Magnasco's door with the butt until he shredded the wood. Magnasco called the desk, and the desk sent for the cops, and Humboldt took off. But next day he jumped Magnasco on Sixth Avenue in front of Howard Johnson's. A group of lesbians gotten up as longshoremen rescued the young man. They had been having ice-cream sodas, and they came out and broke up the fight, pinning Humboldt's arms behind him. It was a blazing afternoon and the women prisoners at the detention center on Greenwich Avenue were shrieking from the open windows and unrolling toilet-paper streamers.

Humboldt phoned me in the country and said, "Charlie, where is Kathleen?"

"I don't know."

"Charlie, I think you do know. I saw her talking to you."

"But she didn't tell me."

He hung up. Then Magnasco called. He said, "Mr. Citrine? Your friend is going to hurt me. I'll have to swear out a warrant."

"Is it really that bad?"

"You know how it is, people go further than they mean to, and then where are you? I mean, where am I? I'm calling because he threatens me in your name. He says you'll get me if he doesn't—his blood-brother."

"I won't lay a hand on you," I said. "Why don't you leave town for a while?"

"Leave?" said Magnasco. "I only just got here. Down from Yale."

I understood. He was on the make, had long prepared for his career.

"The *Trib* is trying me out as a book reviewer."

"I know how it is. I have a show opening on Broadway. My first."

When I met Magnasco, he proved to be overweight, round-faced, young in calendar years only, steady, unflappable, born to make progress in cultural New York. "I won't be driven out," he said. "I'll put him on a peace bond."

"Well, do you need my permission?" I said.

"It won't exactly make me popular in New York to do this to a poet."

I then said to Demmie, "Magnasco is afraid of getting in bad with the New York culture crowd by calling the cops."

Night-moaning, hell-fearing, pill-addicted Demmie was also a most practical person, a supervisor and programmer of genius. When she was in her busy mood, domineering and protecting me, I used to think what a dolls' generalissimo she must have been in childhood. "And where you're concerned," she would say, "I'm a tiger-mother and a regular Fury. Isn't it about a month since you saw Humboldt? He's staying away. That means he's beginning to blame you. Poor Humboldt, he's flipped out, hasn't he! We have to help him. If he keeps attacking this Magnasco character they're going to lock him up. If the police put him in Bellevue, what you have to do is get ready to bail him out. He'll have to be sobered up, calmed down, and cooled off. The best place for that is Payne Whitney. Listen, Charlie, Ginnie's cousin Albert is the admitting physician at Payne Whitney. Bellevue is hell. We should raise some money and transfer him to Payne Whitney. Maybe we could get him a sort of scholarship."

She went into this with Ginnie's cousin Albert, and, in my name, she telephoned people and collected money for Humboldt, taking over because I was busy with *Von Trenck*. We had come back from Connecticut and were going into rehearsal at the Belasco. Efficient Demmie soon raised about three thousand dollars. Hildebrand alone contributed two thousand but he was still sore at Humboldt. He stipulated that the money was for psychiatric treatment and for bare necessities only. A Fifth Avenue lawyer, Simkin, held this fund in escrow. Hildebrand knew, by now we all knew, that Humboldt had hired a private detective, a man named Scaccia, and that this Scaccia had already gotten most of Humboldt's Guggenheim grant. Kathleen herself had done an uncharacteristic thing. Leaving New York at once she headed for Nevada to file for divorce. But Scaccia kept telling Humboldt that she was still in New York and doing lascivious things. Humboldt elaborated a new Proustian sensational scandal involving, this time, a vice ring of Wall Street brokers. If he could catch her in adultery, he would get the "property," the shack in New Jersey, worth about eight thousand dollars, with a mortgage of five, as Orlando Huggins told me—Orlando was one of those radical bohemians who knew money. In avant-garde New York everybody knew money.

The summer went quickly. In August rehearsals began. The

nights were hot, tense, and tiring. Each morning I rose already worn out and Demmie gave me several cups of coffee and at the breakfast table also a good deal of counsel about the theater and Humboldt and the conduct of life. The little white terrier, Cato, begged for crusts and snapped his teeth while dancing backward on his hind legs. I thought that I too would prefer sleeping all day on his cushion by the window, near Demmie's begonias, than sit in the antique filth of the Belasco and listen to dreary actors. I began to hate the theater, the feelings wickedly distended by histrionics, all the old gestures, clutchings, tears, and supplications. Besides, *Von Trenck* was no longer my play. It belonged to goggled Harold Lampton for whom I obligingly wrote new dialogue in the dressing rooms. His actors were a bunch of sticks. All the talent in New York seemed to be in the melodrama enacted by feverish, delirious Humboldt. Pals and admirers were his audience at the White Horse on Hudson Street. There he lectured and hollered. He also consulted lawyers and was seeing a psychiatrist or two.

Demmie, I felt, could understand Humboldt better than I because she too swallowed mysterious pills. (There were other affinities as well.) An obese child, she had weighed two hundred and eighty pounds at the age of fourteen. She showed me pictures I could hardly believe. She was given hormone injections and pills and she grew slender. Judging by the exophthalmic bulge, it must have been thyroxine that they put her on. She thought her pretty breasts disfigured by the rapid weight loss. The insignificant wrinkles in them were a grief to her. She sometimes cried, "They hurt my titties with their goddamn medicine." Brown-paper packets were still arriving from the Mount Coptic Drugstore. "But I am attractive, though." Indeed she was. Her Dutch hair positively gave light. She wore it sometimes combed to the side, sometimes with bangs, depending on what she had done to herself at the hairline with her nails. She often scratched herself. Her face was either childishly circular or like a frontierwoman's, gaunt. She was sometimes a van der Weyden beauty, sometimes Mortimer Snerd, sometimes a Ziegfeld girl. The slight silken scrape of her knock-knees when she walked quickly was, I repeat, highly prized by me. I thought that if I were a locust such a sound would send me soaring over mountain ranges. When Demmie's face with the fine upturned nose was covered with pancake make-up her big eyes, all the more mobile and clear because she had laid on so much dust, revealed two things: one was that she had a true heart and the other that she was a dynamic sufferer. More than once I rushed into Barrow Street to flag down a cab and take Demmie to the emergency room at St. Vincent's. She sun-bathed on the roof and was burned so badly that she became delirious. Then, slicing veal, she cut her thumb to the bone. She went to throw garbage down the incinerator and a gush of flame from the open chute singed her. As a good girl, she did her Latin lesson-plans for an entire term, she laid away scarves and gloves in labeled boxes, she scrubbed the house. As a bad girl she drank whisky, she had hysterics, or took up with thieves and desperadoes. She stroked me like a fairy princess or punched me in the ribs like a cowhand. In hot weather she stripped herself naked to wax the floors on her knees. Then there appeared big tendons, lanky arms, laboring feet. And when it was seen from behind the organ I adored in a different context as small, fine, intricate, rich in delightful difficulties of access, stood out like a primitive limb. But after the waxing, a seizure of sweating labor, she sat with lovely legs in a blue frock having a martini. Fundamentalist Father Vonghel owned Mount Coptic. He was a violent man. There was a scar on Demmie's head where he had banged the child's head on a radiator, there was another on her face where he had jammed a wastepaper basket over it—the tinsmith had to cut her free. With all this she knew the gospels by heart, she had been a field-hockey star, she could break Western horses, and she wrote charming bread-and-butter notes on Tiffany paper. Still, when she took a spoonful of her favorite vanilla custard, she was again the fat child. She savored the dessert at the tip of her tongue, open-mouthed, and the great blue mid-summer ocean-haze eyes in a trance, so that she started when I said, "Swallow your pudding." Evenings we played backgammon, we translated Lucretius, she expounded Plato to me. "People take credit for their virtues. But *he* sees—what else *can* you be but virtuous? There *is* nothing else."

Just before Labor Day Humboldt threatened Magnasco again, and Magnasco went to the police and persuaded a plainclothesman to come back to the hotel with him. They waited in the lobby. Then Humboldt roared in and went for Magnasco. The dick got between them, and Humboldt said, "Officer, he has my wife in his room." The reasonable thing was to make a search. They went upstairs, all three. Humboldt looked in all the closets, he searched under the pillows for her nightgown, he ran his hand under the lining papers of the drawers. There were no underthings. Nothing.

The plainclothesman said, "So, where is she? Was it you who banged hell out of this door with the butt of your gun?"

Humboldt said, "I have no gun. You want to frisk me?" He lifted his arms. Then he said, "Come to my room and look, if you like. See for yourself."

But when they got to Greenwich Street, Humboldt put the key in the lock and said, "You can't come in." He shouted, "Have you got a search warrant?" Then he whirled in and slammed and bolted his door.

This was when Magnasco filed the complaint or took a peace bond—I don't know which—and on a smoggy and stifling night the police came for Humboldt. He fought like an ox. He struggled also in the police station. An anointed head rolled on the filthy floor. Was there a strait jacket? Magnasco swore there wasn't. But there were handcuffs, and Humboldt wept. On the way to Bellevue he had diarrhea, and they locked him away for the night in a state of filth.

Magnasco let it transpire that he and I together had decided to do this, to prevent Humboldt from committing a crime. Everyone then said that the man responsible was Charles Citrine, Humboldt's blood-brother and protégé. I suddenly had many detractors and enemies, unknown to me.

And I'll tell you how I saw it from the plush decay and heated darkness of the Belasco Theatre. I saw Humboldt whipping his team of mules and standing up in his crazy wagon like an Oklahoma land-grabber. He rushed into the territory of excess to stake himself a claim. This claim was a swollen and quaking heart-mirage.

I didn't mean, The poet is off his nut. . . . Call the cops and damn the clichés. No, I suffered when the police laid hands on him, it threw me into despair. What then *did* I mean? Something perhaps like this: suppose the poet had been wrestled to the ground by the police, strapped into a strait jacket or handcuffed, and rushed off dingdong in a paddy wagon like a mad dog, arriving foul, and locked up raging! Was this art versus America? To me Bellevue was like the Bowery: it gave negative testimony. Brutal Wall Street stood for power, and the Bowery, so near it, was the accusing symbol of weakness. And so with Bellevue, where the poor and busted went. And so even with Payne Whitney where the monied derelicts lay. And poets like drunkards and misfits or psychopaths, like the wretched, poor or rich, sank into weakness—was that it? Having no machines, no transforming knowledge comparable to the knowledge of Boeing or Sperry Rand or IBM or RCA? For could a poem pick you up in Chicago and land you in New York two hours later? Or could it compute a space shot? It had no such powers. And interest was where power was. In ancient times poetry was a force, the poet had real strength in the material world. Of course, the material world was different then. But what interest could a Humboldt raise? He threw himself into weakness and became a hero of wretchedness. He consented to the monopoly of power and interest held by money, politics, law, rationality, technology because he couldn't find the next thing, the new thing, the necessary thing for poets to do. Instead he did a former thing. He got himself a pistol, like Verlaine, and chased Magnasco.

From Bellevue he phoned me at the Belasco Theatre. I heard his voice shaking, raging but rapid. He yelled, "Charlie, you know where I am, don't you? All right, Charlie, this isn't literature. This is life."

In the theater I was in the world of illusion while he, Humboldt, had broken out—was that it?

But no, instead of being a poet he was merely the figure of a poet. He was enacting "The Agony of the American Artist." And it was not Humboldt, it was the USA that was making its point: "Fellow Americans, listen. If you abandon materialism and the normal pursuits of life you wind up at Bellevue like this poor kook."

He now held court and made mad-scenes at Bellevue. He openly blamed me. Scandal-lovers were tisking when my name was mentioned.

Then Scaccia the private eye came to the Belasco with a note from Humboldt. He wanted the money I had raised and wanted it right now. So Mr. Scaccia and I faced each other in the gloomy musty cement exit alley outside the stage door. Mr. Scaccia wore open sandals and white silk socks, very soiled. At the corners of his mouth was a grimy deposit.

"The fund is held in escrow by a lawyer, Mr. Simkin, on Fifth Avenue. It's for medical expenses only," I said.

"You mean psychiatric. You think Mr. Fleisher is off his nut?"

"I don't make diagnoses. Just tell Humboldt to talk to Simkin."

"We're speaking of a man of genius. Who says a genius needs treatment?"

"You've read his poems?" I said.

"Fucking right. I won't take a put-down from you. You're supposed to be his friend? The man loves you. He loves you still. Do you love him?"

"And where do you come in?"

"I'm retained by him. And for a client I go all out."

If I didn't give the private eye the money he would go to Bellevue and tell Humboldt that I thought he was insane. My impulse was to kill Scaccia in this back alley. Natural justice was on my side. I could grab this blackmailer by the throat and strangle him. O, that would be delicious! And who could blame me! A gust of murderous feeling made me look modestly at the ground. "Mr. Fleisher will have to explain to Simkin what he wants the money for," I said. "It wasn't raised for you."

After this there came a series of calls from Humboldt. "The cops put me in a strait jacket. Did you have anything to do with that? My blood-brother? They manhandled me, too, you fucking Thomas Hobbes!"

I understand the reference. He meant that I cared only for power.

"I'm trying to help," I said. He hung up. Immediately the phone rang again.

"Where's Kathleen?" he said.

"I don't know."

"She talked to you out by the clothesline. You know where she is all right. Listen to me, handsome, you're sitting on this money. It's mine. You want to put me away with the little guys in the white coats?"

"You need calming down, that's all."

He called later in the day when the afternoon was gray and hot. I was having a tinny-tasting sandwich of crumbling wet tuna fish at the Greek's across the street when they summoned me to the telephone. I took the call in the star's dressing room.

"I've talked to a lawyer," shouted Humboldt. "I'm prepared to sue you for that money. You're a crook. You're a traitor, a liar, a phony, and a Judas. You had me locked up while that whore Kathleen was going to orgies. I'm charging you with embezzlement."

"Humboldt, I only helped to raise that money. I haven't got it. It's not in my hands."

"Tell me where Kathleen is and I'll call off my suit."

"She didn't tell me where she was going."

"You've broken your oath to me, Citrine. And now you want to put me away. You envy me. You always envied me. I'll put you in jail if I can. I want you to know what it's like when the police come for you, and what a strait jacket is like." Then, bam! he hung up, and I sat sweating in the star's grimy dressing room, the rotten tuna salad coming up on me, and a green ptomaine sensation, a cramp, a very sore spot in my side. Actors were trying on costumes that day and passed the door in their knickers, dresses, and cocked hats. I desired help but I felt like an arctic survivor in a small boat, an Amundsen hailing ships on the horizon which turned out to be icebergs. Trenck and Lieutenant Schell passed with their rapiers and wigs. They couldn't tell me that I was *not* an obvious phony, a crook, and a Judas. I couldn't tell them what I thought was really wrong with me: namely that I suffered from an illusion, perhaps a marvelous illusion, or perhaps only a lazy one, that by a kind of inspired levitation I could rise and dart straight to the truth. Straight to the truth. For I was too haughty to bother with Marxism, Freudianism, Modernism, the avant-garde, or any of these things that Humboldt, as a culture-Jew, took so much stock in.

"I'm going to the hospital to see him," I told Demmie.

"You are not. That's the worst thing you can do."

"But look at the state he's in. I've got to go there, Demmie."

"I won't allow it. He'll attack you. I couldn't bear for you to fight, Charlie. He'll hit you, and he's twice your size and crazy and strong. Besides, I won't have you disturbed when you're doing the play. Listen," she deepened her voice, "I'll take care of it. I'll go there myself. And I forbid you."

She never actually got to see him. Dozens of people were in the act by now. The drama at Bellevue drew crowds from Greenwich Village and Morningside Heights. I compared them to the residents of Washington who drove out in carriages to watch the Battle of Bull Run and then got in the way of the Union troops. Since I was no longer his blood-brother, bearded stammering Orlando Huggins became Humboldt's chief friend. Huggins obtained Humboldt's release. Then Humboldt went to Mount Sinai Hospital and signed himself in. Acting on my instructions, lawyer Simkin paid a week in advance for his private care. However, Humboldt checked out again on the very next day and collected from the hospital an unused balance of about eight hundred dollars. Out of this he paid Scaccia's latest bill. Then he started legal actions against Kathleen, against Magnasco, against the Police Department, and against Bellevue. He continued to threaten me but didn't actually file suit. He was waiting to see whether *Von Trenck* would make money.

I was still at the primer level in my understanding of money. I didn't know that there were many people, persistent ingenious passionate people, to whom it was perfectly obvious that *they* should have all your money. Humboldt had the conviction that there was wealth in the world—not his—to which he had a sovereign claim and that he was bound to get it. He had told me once that he was fated to win a big lawsuit, a million-dollar suit. "With a million bucks," he said, "I'll be free to think of nothing but poetry."

"How will this happen?"

"Somebody will wrong me."

"Wrong you a million dollars' worth?"

"If I'm obsessed by money, as a poet shouldn't be, there's a reason for it," was what Humboldt had told me. "The reason is that we're Americans after all. What kind of American would

I be if I were innocent about money, I ask you? Things have to be combined as Wallace Stevens combined them. Who says 'Money is the root of evils'? Isn't it the Pardoner? Well the Pardoner is the most evil man in Chaucer. No, I go along with Horace Walpole. Walpole said it was natural for free men to think about money. Why? Because money *is* freedom, that's why."

In the enchanting days we had had such marvelous talks, only touched a little by manic depression and paranoia. But now the light became dark and the dark turned darker.

Still reclining, holding tight on my padded sofa, I saw those gaudy weeks in review.

Humboldt riotously picketed *Von Trenck* but the play was a hit. To be closer to the Belasco and my celebrity, I took a suite at the St. Regis. The *art nouveau* elevators had gilded gates. Demmie taught Virgil. Kathleen played blackjack in Nevada. Humboldt had returned to his command post at the White Horse Tavern. There he held literary, artistic, erotic, and philosophic exercises till far into the night. He coined a new epigram which was reported to me uptown: "I never yet touched a fig leaf that didn't turn into a price tag." This gave me hope. He could still get off a good wisecrack. It sounded as if normalcy might be returning.

But no. Each day Humboldt gave himself a perfunctory shave, drank coffee, took pills, studied his notes, and went to midtown to see his lawyers. He had lots of lawyers—he collected lawyers and psychoanalysts. Treatment was not the object of his visits with the analysts. He wanted to talk, to express himself. The theoretical climate of their offices stimulated him. As to lawyers, he had them all preparing papers and discussing strategies. Lawyers didn't often meet writers. How was any lawyer to know what was going on? A famous poet calls for an appointment. Referred by so-and-so. The entire office is excited, the typists put on make-up. Then the poet arrives, stout and ill but still handsome pale hurt-looking terrifically agitated, timid in a way, and with strikingly small gestures or tremors for such a large man. Even seated he has leg tremors, his body is vibrating. At first the voice is from another world. Trying to smile, the man can only wince. Odd small stained teeth control a trembling lip. Although thickset, really a big bruiser, he is also a delicate plant, an Ariel, and so on. Can't make a fist. Never heard of aggression. And he unfolds a tale—you'd think it was Hamlet's father: fraud, deceit, betrayal of pledges; finally, as he slept in his garden, someone crept up with a vial and tried to pour stuff into his ear. At first he refuses to name his false friends and would-be murderers. They are only X and Y. Then he refers to "This Person." "I went along with this X-Person," he says. In his innocence he entered into agreements, exchanged promises with X, this Claudius Person. He said yes to everything. He signed a paper without reading it, about joint tenancy of the New Jersey house. He was also disappointed in a blood-brother who turned fink. Shakespeare was right, There's no art to find the mind's construction in the face: he was a gentleman on whom I built an absolute trust. But now recovering from shock he's building a case against the said gentleman. Building cases is one of the master preoccupations of human beings. He has Citrine dead to rights—Citrine grabbed his money. But restitution is all he asks. And he fights, or seems to fight, the rising fury. This Citrine is a deceptively handsome fellow. But Jakob Boehme was wrong, the outer is not the inner visible. Humboldt says he is struggling for decency. His father had no friends, he has no friends—so much for the human material. Fidelity is for phonographs. But let's be restrained. Not all turn into poisoned rats biting one another. "I don't want to hurt the son of a bitch. All I want is justice." Justice! He wanted the fellow's guts in a shopping bag.

Yes, he spent much time with lawyers and doctors. Lawyers and doctors would best appreciate the drama of wrongs and the drama of sickness. He didn't want to be a poet now. Symbolism, his school, was used up. No, at this time he was a performing artist who was being *real.* Back to direct experience. Into the wide world. No more art-substitute for real life. Lawsuits and psychoanalysis were real.

As for the lawyers and the shrinkers, they were delighted with him not because he represented the real world but because he was a poet. He didn't pay—he threw the bills out. But these people, curious about genius (which they had learned from Freud and from movies like *Moulin Rouge* or *The Moon and Sixpence* to esteem), were hungry for culture. They listened with joy as he told his tale of unhappiness and persecution. He spilled dirt, spread scandal, and uttered powerful metaphors. What a combination! Fame gossip delusion filth and poetic invention.

Even then shrewd Humboldt knew what he was worth in professional New York. Endless conveyor belts of sickness or litigation poured clients and patients into these midtown offices like dreary Long Island potatoes. These dull spuds crushed psychoanalysts' hearts with boring character problems. Then suddenly Humboldt arrived. Oh, Humboldt! He was no potato. He was a papaya a citron a passion fruit. He was beautiful deep eloquent fragrant original—even when he looked bruised in the face, hacked under the eyes, half-destroyed. And what a repertory he had, what changes of style and tempo. He was meek at first—shy. Then he became childlike, trusting, then he confided. He knew, he said, what husbands and wives said when they quarreled, bickerings so important to them and so tiresome to everyone else. People said ho-hum and looked at the ceiling when you started this. Americans! with their stupid ideas about love, and their domestic tragedies. How could you bear to listen to them after the worst of wars and the most sweeping of revolutions, the destruction, the death camps, the earth soaked in blood and fumes of cremation still in the air of Europe. What did the personal troubles of Americans amount to? Did they really suffer? The world looked into American faces and said, "Don't tell me these cheerful well-to-do people are suffering!" Still, democratic abundance had its own peculiar difficulties. America was God's experiment. Many of the old pains of mankind were removed, which made the new pains all the more peculiar and mysterious. America didn't like special values. It detested people who represented these special values. And yet, *without* these special values—you see what I mean, said Humboldt. Mankind's old greatness was created in scarcity. But what may we expect from plenitude? In Wagner the giant Fafnir—or is it a dragon?—sleeps on a magical ring. Is America sleeping, then, and dreaming of equal justice and of love? Anyway, I'm not here to discuss adolescent American love-myths—this was how Humboldt talked. Still, he said, I'd like you to listen to this. Then he began to narrate in his original style. He described and intricately embroidered. He worked in Milton on divorce and John Stuart Mill on women. After this came disclosure, confession. Then he accused, fulminated, stammered, blazed, cried out. He crossed the universe like light. He struck off X-ray films of the true facts. Weakness, lies, treason, shameful perversion, crazy lust, the viciousness of certain billionaires (names were named). The truth! And all of this melodrama of impurity, all these erect and crimson nipples, bared teeth, howls, ejaculations! The lawyers had heard this thousands of times but they wanted to hear it again, from a man of genius. Had he become their pornographer?

Ah Humboldt had been great—handsome, high-spirited, buoyant, ingenious, electrical, noble. To be with him made you feel the sweetness of life. We used to discuss the loftiest things—what Diotīma said to Socrates about love, what Spinoza meant by the *amor dei intellectualis.* To talk to him was sustaining, nourishing. But I used to think, when he mentioned people who had been his friends, that it could be only a question of time before I too was dropped. He had no old friends, only ex-friends. He could become terrible, going into reverse without warning. When this happened, it was like being caught in a tunnel by the Express. You could only cling to the walls, or lie between the rails, praying.

To meditate, and work your way behind the appearances, you have to be calm. I didn't feel calm after this summary of Humboldt, but thought of something he himself liked to mention when he was in a good humor and we were finishing dinner, a scramble of dishes and bottles between us. The late philosopher Morris R. Cohen of CCNY was asked by a student in the metaphysics course, "Professor Cohen, how do I know that I exist?" The keen old prof replied, "And *who* is asking?"

I directed this against myself. After entering so deeply into Humboldt's character and career it was only right that I should take a deeper look also at myself, not judge a dead man who could alter nothing but keep step with him, mortal by mortal, if you know what I mean. I mean that I loved him. Very well, then, *Von Trenck* was a triumph (I shrank from the shame of it) and I was a celebrity. Humboldt now was only a crazy sans-culotte picketing drunkenly with a mercurochrome sign while malicious pals cheered. At the White Horse on

Hudson Street, Humboldt won hands down. But the name in the papers, the name that Humboldt stifling with envy saw in Leonard Lyons' column, was Citrine. It was my turn to be famous and to make money, to get heavy mail, to be recognized by influential people, to be dined at Sardi's and propositioned in padded booths by women who sprayed themselves with musk, to buy Sea Island cotton underpants and leather luggage, to live through the intolerable excitement of vindication. (I was right all along!) I experienced the high voltage of publicity. It was like picking up a dangerous wire fatal to ordinary folk. It was like the rattlesnakes handled by hillbillies in a state of religious exaltation.

Demmie Vonghel who had coached me all along steered me now, acting as my trainer, my manager, my cook, my lover, and my strawboss. She had her work cut out for her and was terribly busy. She wouldn't let me see Humboldt at Bellevue. We quarreled over it. She needed a little help with all this and felt it would be a good idea for me to consult a psychiatrist also. She said, "To look as collected as you look when I know you're falling apart and dying of excitement just isn't good." She sent me to a man named Ellenbogen, a celebrity himself, appearing on many talk shows, the author of liberating books on sex. Ellenbogen's dry lean long face had big grinning sinews, redskin cheekbones, teeth like the screaming horse in Picasso's *Guernica*. He hit a patient hard in order to free him. The rationality of pleasure was his ideological hammer. He was tough, New York tough, but he smiled, and how it all added up he told you with New York emphasis. Our span is short and we must make up for the shortness of the human day in frequent, intense sexual gratification. He was never sore, never offended, he repudiated rage and aggression, the bondage of conscience, et cetera. All such things were bad for copulation. Bronze figurines of amatory couples were his bookends. The air in his office was close. Dark paneling, the comfort of deep leather. During sessions he lay fully extended, shoeless feet on a hassock, his long hand under his waistband. Was he fondling his own parts? Utterly relaxed he released a lot of gas which dissolved and impregnated the confined air. His plants anyway thrived on it.

He lectured me as follows: "You are a guilty anxious man.

Depressive. An ant longing to be a grasshopper. Can't bear success. Melancholia, I'd say, interrupted by fits of humor. Women must be chasing you. Wish I had your opportunities. Actresses. Well, give the women a chance to give you pleasure, that's really what they want. To them the act itself is far less important than the occasion of tenderness." Perhaps to increase my self-confidence he told me of his own wonderful experiences. A woman in the Deep South had seen him on television and came straight north to be laid by him, and when she got what she came for said with a sigh of luxury, "When I saw you on the box I knew you'd be good. And you *are* good." Ellenbogen was no friend of Demmie Vonghel when he heard of her ways. He sucked sharply and said, "Bad, a bad case. Poor kid. Pushing to get married, I bet. Development immature. A pretty baby. And weighed three hundred pounds when she was thirteen. One of those greedy parties. Domineering. She'll swallow you."

Demmie was unaware that she had sent me to the enemy. She said daily, "We must get married, Charlie," and she planned a big church wedding. Fundamentalist Demmie became an Episcopalian in New York. She talked to me about a wedding dress and veil, calla lilies, ushers, photographs, engraved announcements, morning coats. As best man and maid of honor she wanted the Littlewoods. I never had told her of the wingding Eskimo-style private party Littlewood had proposed to me in Princeton saying, "We can have a good show, Charlie." Demmie, if I had told her, would have been vexed with Littlewood rather than shocked. By now she had fitted herself into New York. The miraculous survival of goodness was the theme of her life. Dangerous navigation, monsters attracted by her boundless female magnetism—spells charms prayers divine protection secured by inner strength and purity of heart—this was how she saw things. Hell breathed from doorways over her feet as she passed, but she did pass safely. Boxes of pills still came in the mail from the home-town pharmacy. The delivery kid from Seventh Avenue came more and more and more often with bottles of Johnnie Walker Black Label. She drank the best. After all, she was an heiress. Mount Coptic belonged to her Daddy. She was a Fundamentalist princess who liked to drink. After a few highballs Demmie was grander, statelier, her eyes great circles of blue, her love stronger. She growled in Louis Armstrong style, "You are mah man." Then she said in earnest, "I love you with my heart. No other man better try and touch me." When she made a fist it was surprisingly big.

Attempts to touch were often made. Her dentist as he worked on her fillings took her hand and placed it on what she assumed to be the armrest of the chair. It was no such thing. It was his excited member. Her physician concluded an examination by kissing her violently wherever he could reach. "I can't say that I blame the man for being carried away, Demmie. You have a bottom like a white valentine greeting."

"I punched him right in the neck," she said.

On a warm day when the air conditioning had broken down, her psychiatrist said to her, "Why don't you take off your dress, Miss Vonghel." A millionaire host on Long Island spoke through the ventilator of his bathroom into hers. "I need you. Give me your bod. . . ." He said in a choking perishing voice, "Give me! I am dying. Save, save . . . save me!" And this was a burly strong jolly man who piloted his own airplane.

Sexual ideas had distorted the minds of people who were under oath, who were virtually priests. Were you inclined to believe that mania and crime and catastrophe were the destiny of mankind in this vile century? Demmie by her innocence, by beauty and virtue, drew masses of evidence from the environment to support this. A strange demonism revealed itself to her. But she was not intimidated. She told me that she was sexually fearless. "And they've tried to pull everything on me," she said. I believed her.

Dr. Ellenbogen said that she was a bad marriage-risk. He was not amused by the anecdotes I related about Mother and Daddy Vonghel. The Vonghels had made a bus tour of the Holy Land, obese Mother Vonghel bringing her own peanut-butter jars and Daddy his cans of Elberta cling peaches. Mother squeezed into the tomb of Lazarus but could not get out again. Arabs had to be sent for to free her. But I was delighted, despite Ellenbogen's warnings, with the oddities of Demmie and her family. When she lay suffering, her deep eye sockets filled with tears and she gripped the middle finger of her left hand convulsively with the other fingers. She was strongly drawn to sickbeds, hospitals, terminal cancers, and funerals. But her goodness was genuine and deep. She bought me postage stamps and commuter tickets, she cooked briskets of beef and pots of *paella* for me, lined my dresser drawers with tissue paper, put away my scarf in moth-flakes. She couldn't do elementary arithmetic but she could repair complicated machines. Guided by instinct she went into the colored wires and tubes of the radio and made it play. It seldom stopped broadcasting hillbilly music and religious services from everywhere. She received from home *The Upper Room, A Devotional Guide for Family and Individual Use*, with its Thought of the Month: "Christ's Renewing Power." Or "Read and consider: Habakkuk 2:2–4." I read this publication myself. The Song of Solomon 8:7: "Many waters cannot quench love, neither can the floods drown it." I loved her clumsy knuckles, her long head growing gold hair. We sat on Barrow Street playing gin rummy. She gripped and shuffled the deck, growling, "I'm going to clean you out, sucker." She snapped down the cards and shouted, "Gin! Count 'em up!" Her knees were apart.

"It's the open view of Shangri-La that takes my mind off these cards, Demmie," I said.

We also played double solitaire hearts and Chinese checkers. She led me to antique-jewelry shops. She loved old brooches and rings all the more because dead ladies once had worn them, but what she mostly wanted of course was an engagement ring. She made no secret of that. "Buy me this ring, Charlie. Then I can show my family that it's on the up-and-up."

"They won't like me no matter how big an opal you get," I said.

"No, that's true. They'll hit the roof. There's all kinds of sin in you. They wouldn't be impressed by Broadway. You write things that aren't so. Only the Bible is true. But Daddy is flying down to South America to spend Christmas at his Mission. The one he's such a big giver to, down in Colombia, near Venezuela. I'm going with him and tell him that we're getting married."

"Ah, don't go, Demmie," I said.

"Down in that jungle with savages all around you'll seem a lot more normal to him," she said.

"Tell him what I'm making. The money should help do it all," I said. "But I don't want you to go. Is your mother coming too?"

"Not here. I couldn't take that. No, she's staying back in Mount Coptic, giving a Christmas party for the kids in the hospital. *They'll* be sorry."

These meditations were supposed to make you tranquil. To look behind the appearances you had to cultivate an absolute calm. And I didn't feel very calm now. The heavy shadow of a jet from Midway airport crossed the room, reminding me of the death of Demmie Vonghel. Just before Christmas in the year of my success she and Daddy Vonghel died in a plane crash in South America. Demmie was carrying my Broadway scrapbook. Perhaps she had just begun to show it to him when the crash occurred. No one ever knew quite where this was—somewhere in the vicinity of the Orinoco River. I spent several months in the jungle looking for her.

It was at this time that Humboldt put through the blood-brother check I had given him. Six thousand seven hundred and sixty-three dollars and fifty-eight cents was a smashing sum. But it wasn't the money that mattered much. What I felt was that Humboldt should have respected my grief. I thought, What a time he chose to make his move! How could he do that! To hell with the money. But he reads the papers. He knows she's gone!

I NOW lay there grieving. Again! This wasn't what I was looking for when I lay down. And I was actually grateful when a brassy hammering at the door made me get up. It was Cantabile on the knocker, forcing his way into my sanctuary. I was annoyed with old Roland Stiles. I paid Stiles to keep intruders and pests away while I was meditating but he wasn't at his post in the receiving room today. Just before Christmas tenants wanted help with trees and such. He was much in demand, I suppose.

Cantabile had brought a young woman with him.

"Your wife, I presume?"

"Don't presume. She's not my wife. This is Polly Palomino. She's a friend. Of the family, she's a friend. She was Lucy's roommate at the Woman's College in Greensboro. Before Radcliffe."

White-skinned, wearing no brassiere, Polly entered the light and began strolling about my parlor. The red of her hair was entirely natural. Stockingless (in December, in Chicago), minimally dressed, she walked on platform shoes of maximum thickness. Men of my generation never have gotten used to the strength, size, and beauty of women's legs, formerly covered up.

Cantabile and Polly examined my flat. He touched the furniture, she stooped to feel the carpet, turning over a corner to read the label. Yes, it was a genuine Kirman. She studied the pictures. Cantabile then sat down on the silky plush bolstered sofa, saying, "*This* is whorehouse luxury."

"Don't make yourself too comfortable. I have to go to court."

Cantabile said to Polly, "Charlie's ex-wife goes on suing and suing him."

"For what?"

"For everything. You've given her a lot already, Charlie?"

"A lot."

"He's shy. He's ashamed to say how much," Cantabile told Polly.

I said to Polly, "Apparently I told Rinaldo the whole story of my life at a poker game."

"Polly knows it. I told her about yesterday. You did most of the talking after the poker game." He turned toward Polly. "Charlie was too smashed to drive his 280-SL so I took him home and Emil brought the T-bird. You told me plenty, Charlie. Where do you get these fancy goose-quill toothpicks? They're scattered all over. You seem very neurotic about having crumbs between your teeth."

"They're sent from London."

"Like your cashmere socks, and your face soap from Floris?"

Yes, I must have been eager to talk. I had given Cantabile plenty of information and he had made extensive inquiries besides, obviously intending to develop a relationship with me. "Why do you let your Ex bug you like this? And you have a lousy big-shot lawyer. Forrest Tomchek. You see I asked around. Tomchek is top-drawer in the divorce-establishment. He divorces corporation biggies. But you're nothing to him. It was your pal Szathmar who put you on to this prick, isn't that right? Now, who is your wife's lawyer?"

"A fellow named Maxie Pinsker."

"Yiy! Pinsker, that man-eating kike! She's picked the worst there is. He'll chop up your liver with egg and onion. Yuch, Charlie! this side of your life is disgusting. You refuse to be alert about your interests. You let people dump on you. It starts with your pals. I know something about your friend Szathmar. Nobody asks you to dinner, they invite him and he puts on his louse-up Charlie routine. He feeds confidential information about you to gossip columnists. Always kissing Schneiderman's ass, which is so low to the ground you have to stand in a foxhole to reach it. He'll get a kickback from Tomchek. Tomchek will sell you to that cannibal Pinsker. Pinsker will throw you to the judge. The judge will give your wife . . . what's her name?"

"Denise," I said, habitually helpful.

"He'll give Denise your skin and she'll hang it in the den.— Well, Polly, does Charles look like Charles is supposed to look?"

Of course Cantabile couldn't bear his elation. Last night he naturally had to tell someone what he had done. As Humboldt after his triumph with Longstaff ran straight to the Village to get on top of Ginnie so Cantabile had roared off in his Thunderbird to spend the night with Polly, to celebrate his triumph and my abasement. It made me think what a tremendous force the desire to be interesting has in the democratic USA. This is why Americans can't keep secrets. In WW II we were the despair of the British because we couldn't shut our mouths. Luckily the Germans couldn't believe we were so gabby. They figured we were deliberately leaking false information. And it's all done to prove that we're not so tedious as we seem but are running over with charm and inside information. So I said to myself, Okay, be elated, you mink-mustached bastard. Brag about what you did to me and the 280-SL. I'll catch up with you. At the same time I was glad that Renata was taking me away, forcing me to go abroad again. Renata had the right idea. For Cantabile obviously was making plans for our future. I wasn't at all sure that I could defend myself from his singular attack.

Polly was considering how to answer Cantabile's question and he himself, pale and handsome, was studying me almost with affection. Still buttoned in the raglan coat and wearing the pinch hat, his beautiful boots on my Chinese lacquer coffee table, he was dark-bristled and wore a look of fatigue and satisfaction. He was not fresh now, he was smelly, but he was flying high.

"I think Mr. Citrine is still a good-looking man," Polly said.

"Thank you, dear girl."

"He must have been. Slim but solid, with big Oriental eyes and probably a thick dick. Now he's a faded beauty," said Cantabile. "I know it's killing him. He's losing the clean jawline. Notice the dewlaps and the neck wrinkles. His nostrils are getting big and hungry-like, and they have white hair. It's a sign with beagles and horses too, turning white around the muzzle. Oh, he's unusual all right. A rare animal. Like the last of the orange flamingos. He should be protected as a national resource. And a sexy little bastard. He's slept with everything under the sun. Awfully vain, too. Charlie and his pal George jog and train like a couple of adolescent jocks. They stand on their heads, take vitamin E, and play racquet ball. Though they tell me you're a dog on the courts, Charlie."

"It's a bit late for the Olympics."

"He has a sedentary trade and needs the exercise," said Polly. She had a slightly bent nose as well as the fresh, shining red hair. I was growing fond of her—disinterestedly, for her human qualities.

"The main reason for all the fitness is that he has a young broad, and young broads, unless they have a terrific sense of humor, don't like being squeezed by a potbelly."

I explained to Polly, "I exercise because I suffer from an arthritic neck. Or did. As I grew older my head seemed to become heavier, my neck weaker."

The strain was largely at the top. In the crow's-nest from which the modern autonomous person keeps watch. But of course Cantabile was right. I was vain, and I hadn't reached the age of renunciation. Whatever that is. It wasn't entirely vanity, though. Lack of exercise made me feel ill. I used to hope that there would be less energy available to my neuroses as I grew older. Tolstoi thought that people got into trouble because they ate steak and drank vodka and coffee and smoked cigars. Overcharged with calories and stimulants and doing no useful labor they fell into carnality and other sins. At this point I always remembered that Hitler had been a vegetarian, so it wasn't necessarily the meat that was to blame. Heart-energy, more likely, or a wicked soul, maybe even karma—paying for the evil of a past life in this one. According to Steiner, whom I was now reading heavily, the spirit learns from resistance—the material body resists and opposes it. In the process the body wears out. But I had not gotten good value for my deterioration. Seeing me with my young daughters, silly people sometimes asked if these were my grandchildren. Me! Was it possible! And I saw that I was getting that look of a badly stuffed trophy or mounted specimen that I always associated with age, and was horrified. Also I recognized from photographs that I wasn't the man I had been. I should have been able to say, "Yes, maybe I do seem about to cave in but you should see my spiritual balance sheet." But as yet I was in no position to say that, either. I look better than the dead, of course, but at times only just.

I said, "Well, thanks for dropping in, Mrs. Palomino. You'll have to excuse me, though. I'm being called for and I haven't shaved or eaten lunch."

"How do you shave, electric or steel?"

"Remington."

"The electric Abercrombie & Fitch is the only machine. I think I'll shave, too. And what's for lunch?"

"I'm having yoghurt. But I can't offer you any."

"We've just eaten. Plain yoghurt? Do you put anything in it? What about a hard-boiled egg? Polly will boil you an egg. Polly, go in the kitchen and boil Charlie an egg. How did you say you were getting downtown?"

"I'm being called for."

"Don't be upset about the Mercedes. I'll get you three 280-SLs. You're too big a man to hold a mere car against me.

Things are going to be different. Look, why don't we meet after court and have a drink? You'll need it. Besides, you should talk more. You listen too much. It's not good for you."

He relaxed even more conspicuously, supporting both arms on the round back of the sofa as if to show that he was not a man I could shoo out. He wished also to transmit a sense of luxurious intimacy with pretty and fully gratified Polly. I had my doubts about that. "This kind of life is very bad for you," he said. "I've seen guys come out of solitary confinement and I know the signs. Why do you live South, surrounded by the slums? Is it because you have egghead friends on the Midway? You spoke about this Professor Richard What's-His-Face."

"Durnwald."

"That's the man. But you also told how some pork-chop chased you down the middle of the street. You should rent near-North in a high-security building with an underground garage. Or are you here because of these professors' wives? The Hyde Park ladies are easy to knock over." Then he said, "Do you own a gun at least?"

"No I don't."

"Christ, here's another example of what I mean. All you people are soft about the realities. This is a Fort Dearborn situation, don't you know that? And only the redskins have the guns and tomahawks. Did you read about the cabbie's face last week, blown off with a shotgun? It'll take a year for plastic surgery to rebuild. Don't you want revenge when you hear about that? Or have you really become so flattened out? If you have, then I don't see how your sex life can be any good either! Don't tell me you wouldn't be thrilled to waste the buffalo that chased you—just turning around and shooting him through the fucking head. If I give you a gun, will you carry it? No? You liberal Jesuses are disgusting. You'll go downtown today and it'll be more of the same with this Forrest Tomchek and this Cannibal Pinsker. They'll eat your ass. But you tell yourself they're gross, while you have class. You want a gun?" He thrust his quick hand under the raglan. "Here's a gun."

I had a weakness for characters like Cantabile. It was no accident that the Baron Von Trenck of my Broadway hit, the source of the movie-sale money—the blood-scent that attracted the sharks of Chicago who were now waiting for me downtown—

had also been demonstrative exuberant impulsive destructive and wrong-headed. This type, the impulsive–wrong-headed, was now making it with the middle class. Rinaldo was ticking me off for my decadence. Damaged instincts. I wouldn't defend myself. His ideas probably went back to Sorel (acts of exalted violence by dedicated ideologists to shock the bourgeoisie and regenerate its dying nerve). Although he didn't know who Sorel was, these theories do get around and find people to exemplify them—highjackers, kidnapers, political terrorists who murder hostages or fire into crowds, the Arafats one reads of in the papers and sees on television. Cantabile was manifesting these tendencies in Chicago, wildly exalting some human principle—he knew not what. In my own fashion I myself knew not what. Why was it that I enjoyed no relations with anyone of my own mental level? I was attracted instead by these noisy bumptious types. They did something for me. Maybe this was in part a phenomenon of modern capitalist society with its commitment to personal freedom for all, ready to sympathize with and even to subsidize the mortal enemies of the leading class, as Schumpeter says, actively sympathetic with real or faked suffering, ready to accept peculiar character-distortions and burdens. It was true that people felt it gave them moral distinction to be patient with criminals and psychopaths. To understand! We love to understand, to have compassion! And there I was. As for the broad masses, millions of people born poor now had houses and power tools and other appliances and conveniences and they endured the social turbulence, lying low, hanging on to their worldly goods. Their hearts were angry but they put up with the disorders and formed no mobs in the streets. They took all the abuse, doggedly waiting it out. No rocking the boat. Apparently I shared in their condition. But I couldn't see what good it would do me to fire a gun. As if I could shoot my way out of my perplexities—the chief perplexity being my character!

Cantabile had invested much boldness and ingenuity in me and now he seemed to feel that we must never part. Also he wanted me to draw him upward, to lead him to higher things. He had reached the stage reached by bums, con men, freeloaders, and criminals in France in the eighteenth century, the stage of the intellectual creative man and theorist. Maybe he thought he was Rameau's nephew or even Jean Genet. I didn't see this as the wave of the future. I wanted no part of it. In creating Von Trenck of course I had contributed my share to this. On the *Late Late Show* Von Trenck was still often seen fighting duels, escaping from prison, seducing women, lying and bragging, trying to set fire to his brother-in-law's villa. Yes, I had done my bit. Possibly, too, I continually gave hints of a new interest in higher things, of a desire to advance in the spirit, so that it was only fair that Cantabile should ask me to tell him something of this, to share with him, to give him a hint at least. He was here to do me good, he told me. He was eager to help me. "I can put you into a good thing," he said. He began to describe some of his enterprises to me. He had money in this and money in that. He was president of a charter-flight company, perhaps one of those that had stranded thousands of people in Europe last summer. He had also a little abortion-referral racket and advertised in college newspapers all over the country as a disinterested friend. "*Call us if this misfortune occurs. We will advise and help free of charge.*" This was quite accurate, said Cantabile. There was no charge but the doctors kicked back a percentage of the fee. It was normal business.

Polly did not seem bothered by this. I thought her far too good for Cantabile. But then in every couple there is a contrast-gainer. I could see that he amused Polly, with her white skin, red hair, fine legs. That was why she was with him. He really amused her. For his part he pushed me to admire her. He also boasted about his wife's education—what an achiever she was—and he showed me off to Polly. He was proud of us all. "Watch Charlie's mouth," he told Polly. "You'll notice that it moves even when he isn't talking. That's because he's thinking. He thinks all the time. Here, I'll show you what I mean." He grabbed up a book, the biggest on the table. "Take this monster—*The Hastings Encyclopedia of Religion and Ethics*—Jesus Christ, what the hell is that! Now Charlie tell us, what were you reading here?"

"I was checking something about Origen of Alexandria. Origen's opinion was that the Bible could not be a collection of mere stories. Did Adam and Eve really hide under a tree while God walked in the Garden in the cool of the day? Did angels really climb up and down ladders? Did Satan bring Jesus to the top of a high mountain and tempt him? Obviously these tales must have a deeper meaning. What does it mean to say 'God walked'? Does God have feet? This was where the thinkers began to take over, and—"

"Enough, that's enough. Now what's this book say, *The Triumph of the Therapeutic*?"

For reasons of my own I wasn't unwilling to be tested in this way. I actually did read a great deal. Did I know what I was reading? We would see. I shut my eyes, reciting, "It says that psychotherapists may become the new spiritual leaders of mankind. A disaster. Goethe was afraid the modern world might turn into a hospital. Every citizen unwell. The same point in *Knock* by Jules Romains. Is hypochondria a creation of the medical profession? According to this author, when culture fails to deal with the feeling of emptiness and the panic to which man is disposed (and he does say 'disposed') other agents come forward to put us together with therapy, with glue, or slogans, or spit, or as that fellow Gumbein the art critic says, poor wretches are recycled on the couch. This view is even more pessimistic than the one held by Dostoevski's Grand Inquisitor who said: mankind is frail, needs bread, cannot bear freedom but requires miracle, mystery, and authority. A natural disposition to feelings of emptiness and panic is worse than that. Much worse. What it really means is that we human beings are insane. The last institution which controlled such insanity (on this view) was the Church—"

He stopped me again. "Polly, you see what I mean. Now what's this, *Between Death and Rebirth*?"

"Steiner? A fascinating book about the soul's journey past the gates of death. Different from Plato's myth—"

"Whoa, hold it," said Cantabile, and he pointed out to Polly: "All you have to do is ask him a question and he turns on. Can you see this as an act in a night club? We could book him into Mr. Kelly's."

Polly glanced past him at me with full and reddish-brown eyes and said, "He wouldn't go for that."

"It depends how they sock it to him downtown today. Charlie, I had another idea on the way out here. We could tape you reading some of your essays and articles and rent the tapes to colleges and universities. You'd get a pretty nice little income out of that. Like that piece on Bobby Kennedy which I read at Leavenworth, in *Esquire.* And the thing called 'Homage to Harry Houdini.' But not 'Great Bores of the Modern World.' I couldn't read that at all."

"Well, don't get ahead of yourself, Cantabile," I said.

I was perfectly aware that in business Chicago it was a true sign of love when people wanted to take you into money-making schemes. But I couldn't lay hold of Cantabile in this present mood or get a navigational fix or reading of his spirit, which was streaming all over the place. He was a highly excited and, in that Goethean hospital, a sick citizen. I wasn't perhaps in such great shape myself. It occurred to me that yesterday Cantabile had taken me up to a high place, not exactly to tempt me, but to sail away my fifty-dollar bills. Wasn't he facing a challenge of the imagination now—I mean, how was he going to follow such an act? However, he seemed to feel that yesterday's events had united us in a near-mystical bond. There were Greek words for this—*philia*, *agape*, and so on (I had heard a famous theologian, Tillich the Toiler, expound their various meanings, so that now I was permanently confused about them). What I mean was that the *philia*, at this particular moment in the career of mankind, expressed itself in American promotional ideas and commercial deals. To this, along the edges, I added my own peculiar embroidery. I elaborated people's motives all too profusely.

I looked at the clock. Renata wouldn't be here for forty minutes yet. She would arrive fragrant painted fresh and even majestic in one of her large soft hats. I didn't want Cantabile to meet her. For that matter I didn't know that it was such a good idea for her to meet Cantabile. When she looked at a man who interested her she had a slow way of detaching her gaze from him. It didn't mean much. It was only her upbringing. She was schooled in charm by her mama, the Señora. Though I suppose that if you are born with such handsome eyes you work out your own methods. In Renata's method of womanly communication piety and fervor were important. The main point, however, was that Cantabile would see an old guy with a young chick and that he might try, as they say, to get leverage out of this.

I want it to be clear, however, that I speak as a person who had lately received or experienced light. I don't mean "The light." I mean a kind of light-in-the-being, a thing difficult to be precise about, especially in an account like this, where so many cantankerous erroneous silly and delusive objects actions and phenomena are in the foreground. And this light, however it is to be described, was now a real element in me, like the breath of life itself. I had experienced it briefly, but it had lasted long enough to be convincing and also to cause an altogether unreasonable kind of joy. Furthermore, the hysterical, the grotesque about me, the abusive, the unjust, that madness in which I had often been a willing and active participant, the grieving, now had found a contrast. I say "now" but I knew long ago what this light was. Only I seemed to have forgotten that in the first decade of life I knew this light and even knew how to breathe it in. But this early talent or gift or inspiration, given up for the sake of maturity or realism (practicality, self-preservation, the fight for survival), was now edging back. Perhaps the vain nature of ordinary self-preservation had finally become too plain for denial. Preservation for what?

For the moment Cantabile and Polly were not paying a great deal of attention to me. He was explaining to her how a convenient little corporation might be set up to protect my income. He spoke of "estate-planning," with a one-sided grimace. In Spain working-class women give themselves a three-fingered prod in the cheek and twist their faces to denote the highest irony. Cantabile grimaced in the same way. It was a question of keeping assets from the enemy, Denise, and her lawyer, Cannibal Pinsker, and maybe even Judge Urbanovich himself.

"My sources tell me the judge is in the lady's corner. How do we know he isn't on the take? There's plenty of funny business at the crossroads. In Cook County is there anything else? Charlie, have you thought of making a move to the Cayman Islands? That's the new Switzerland, you know. I wouldn't put my dough in Swiss banks. After the Russians have gotten what they want out of us in this détente, they'll make their move into Europe. And you know what'll happen to the dough stashed in Switzerland—all that Vietnam dough and Iranian dough and Greek colonels' and Arab oil dough. No, get yourself an air-conditioned condominium in the Caymans. Lay in a supply of underarm antiperspirant and live happy."

"And where's the dough for this?" said Polly. "Has he got it?"

"That I don't know. But if he has no money why are they peeling his toes downtown? Without an anesthetic? I can put you onto a good thing, Charlie. Buy some contracts in commodity futures. I've cleaned up."

"On paper you have. If this fellow Stronson is straight," Polly said.

"What are you talking about—Stronson? A multimillionaire. Didn't you see his big house in Kenilworth? The marketing degree from the Harvard Business School on his wall? Besides, he's been trading for the Mafia and you know how those fellows resent being took. They alone would keep him in line. But he's completely kosher. He has a seat on the Mid America Commodity Exchange. The twenty Gs I gave him five months ago he doubled for me. I'll bring you his company's literature. Anyway, Charlie only has to lift his hand to make a pile. Don't forget he had a Broadway hit and a big box-office movie, once. Why not again? Look at all this paper lying around. These scripts and shit could be worth plenty. There's probably a gold mine right here, you want to bet? For instance, I know that you and your pal Von Humboldt Fleisher once wrote a movie scenario together."

"Who told you that?"

"My researcher wife."

I laughed at this, quite loudly. A movie scenario!

"You remember it?" said Cantabile.

"Yes, I remember. How did your wife hear of it? From Kathleen. . . ?"

"Mrs. Tigler in Nevada. Lucy is in Nevada now interviewing her. Has been for about a week, staying at this Mrs. Tigler's dude ranch. She's running it alone."

"Why, where's Tigler, did he take off?"

"For good, he took off. The guy is dead."

"Dead, is he? She's a widow. Poor Kathleen. She's got no luck, poor woman. I'm sorry about Kathleen."

"She's sentimental about you, too. Lucy told her that I

knew you, and she sent you regards. You got any message for her? Lucy and I talk on the telephone every day."

"How did Tigler die?"

"Shot in a hunting accident."

"That figures. He was a sporting man. Used to be a cowboy."

"And a pain in the ass?" said Cantabile.

"Could be."

"You knew him personally, then. Not much regret, hey? All you say is poor Kathleen. Now what about this movie that you and Fleisher wrote?"

"Oh yes, tell us," said Polly. "What was all that about? Two minds like yours, collaborating—wow!"

"It was piffle. Nothing to it. At Princeton we diverted ourselves that way. Simply horseplay."

"Haven't you got a copy of it? You might be the last to know, commercially, what there was in it," said Cantabile.

"Commercially? The Hollywood big-money days are over. No more of those fancy prices."

"That side of it you can leave to me," said Cantabile. "If we have a real property, I'll know how to promote it—director, star, financing, the whole ball of wax. You have a track record, don't forget, and Fleisher's name hasn't been completely forgotten yet. We'll get Lucy's thesis published, and that'll revive it."

"But what was the story?" said Polly, bent-nosed, fragrant, idling her legs.

"I have to shave. I need my lunch. I have to go to court. I'm expecting a friend from California."

"Who's that?" said Cantabile.

"His name is Pierre Thaxter, and we edit a journal together called *The Ark*. It's really none of your business anyway. . . ."

But of course it was his business, because he was a demon, an agent of distraction. His job was to make noise and to deflect and misdirect and send me foundering into bogs.

"Well, tell us a little about the movie," said Cantabile.

"I'll try. Just to see how good my memory is," I said. "The thing started with Amundsen the polar explorer and Umberto Nobile. In Mussolini's time Nobile was an Air Force officer, an engineer, a dirigible commander, a brave man. In the Twenties he and Amundsen headed an expedition over the North Pole, and flew from Norway to Seattle. But they were rivals and came to hate each other. On the next expedition, with Mussolini's backing, Nobile went it alone. Only his lighter-than-air ship crashed in the Arctic and his crew were scattered over the ice floes. When Amundsen heard of this, he said, 'My comrade Umberto Nobile'—whom he detested, mind you—'is down at sea. I shall rescue him.' So he chartered a French plane and filled it with equipment. The pilot warned him it was overloaded and wouldn't fly. Like Sir Patrick Spens, I remember saying to Humboldt."

"What Spens?"

"Just a poem," Polly told Cantabile. "And Amundsen was the fellow who beat the Scott expedition to the South Pole."

Pleased to have an educated dolly to brief him, Cantabile took the patrician attitude that drudges and bookworms would give him what trifling historical information he needed.

"The French pilot warned him, but Amundsen said, 'Don't teach me how to run a rescue expedition.' So the plane rose from the runway but it fell into the sea. Everyone was killed."

"Is that the picture? But what about the guys on the ice?"

"The men on the ice sent out radio messages and these were picked up by the Russians. An icebreaker named the *Krassin* was sent to find them. It cruised among the floes and rescued two men, an Italian and a Swede. There had been a third survivor—where was he? The explanations given were fishy and the Italian was suspected of cannibalism. The Russian doctor aboard the *Krassin* pumped his stomach and under the microscope he identified human tissue. Well, there was a frightful scandal. A jar containing the contents of this fellow's stomach was put on display in Red Square with a huge sign: "This is how fascist imperialist capitalist dogs devour each other. Only the proletariat knows morality brotherhood and self-sacrifice!' "

"What the hell kind of movie would this make," said Cantabile. "So far it's a real dumdum idea."

"I told you."

"Yes, but now you're sore at me, and you're glaring. You think I'm a moron, in your department. I'm not artistic and I'm unfit to have an opinion."

"This is only background," I said. "The picture, as Humboldt and I worked it out, opened in a Sicilian village. The cannibal, whom Humboldt and I called Signor Caldofreddo, is now a kindly old man and sells ice cream, the kids love him, he has an only daughter who's a beauty and a darling. Here nobody remembers the Nobile expediton. But a Danish journalist turns up to interview the old guy. He's writing a book about the *Krassin* rescue. The old man meets him in secret and says, 'Leave me alone. I've been a vegetarian for fifty years. I churn ice cream. I am an old man. Don't disgrace me now. Find a different subject. Life is full of hysterical situations. You don't need mine. Lord, let now thy servant depart in peace.'"

"So the Amundsen and Nobile part of it is worked around this?" said Polly.

"Humboldt admired Preston Sturges. He loved *The Miracle of Morgan's Creek* and also *The Great McGinty*, with Brian Donlevy and Akim Tamiroff, and Humboldt's idea was to work in Mussolini, Stalin, Hitler, and even the Pope."

"How the Pope?" said Cantabile.

"The Pope gave Nobile a large cross to drop on the North Pole. And we saw the movie as a vaudeville and farce but with elements of *Oedipus at Colonus* in it. Violent spectacular sinners in old age acquire magical properties, and when they come to die they have the power to curse and to bless."

"If it's supposed to be funny, leave the Pope out of it," said Cantabile.

"Backed into a corner, the old Caldofreddo flares up. He makes an attempt on the journalist's life. He pries loose a boulder on a mountainside. But then he has a change of heart and throws himself on the rock and fights it till the man's car passes in the road below. After this Caldofreddo blows his ice-cream vendor's bugle in the village square, he summons everyone and makes a public confession to the townspeople. Weeping, he tells them that he's a cannibal. . . ."

"Which punctures his daughter's romance, I suppose," said Polly.

"Just the reverse," I said. "The villagers hold a public hearing. The daughter's young man says, 'Think of what our ancestors ate. As apes, as lower animals, as fishes. Think what animals have eaten since the beginning of time. And we owe our existence to them.'"

"No, it doesn't sound like a winner to me," said Cantabile.

I said it was time to shave, and they both accompanied me to the bathroom.

"No," Cantabile said again. "I don't think it's any good. But have you got a copy of this thing?"

I had started the electric shaver but Cantabile took it from me. He said to Polly, "Don't sit down. Go fix that egg for Charlie's lunch. Go on, now, go to the kitchen." Then he said, "I'll shave first. I don't like to use the machine when it's heated up. The temperature of the other guy upsets me." He ran the buzzing shining machine up and down, pulling at his skin and twisting his face. "She'll fix your lunch. Pretty, isn't she! What do you make of her, Charlie?"

"A stunning girl. Signs of intelligence, too. I see by the left hand that she's married."

"Yes, to a drip who makes TV commercials. He's a hard worker. Never at home. I see a lot of Polly. Every morning when Lucy leaves for her job at Mundelein, Polly arrives and gets in bed with me. I see this makes a bad impression on you. But don't put on with me, you lit up when you saw her, and you've been trying to make a hit with her, showing off. That extra little try. You don't have it when you're among men."

"I admit I like to shine when there are ladies."

He lifted his chin to get at his neck with the razor. The bulb of his pale nose was darkly lined. "Would you like to make it with Polly?" he said.

"I? Is that an abstract question?"

"Nothing abstract. You do things for me, I do things for you. Yesterday I bashed your car, I ran you around town. Now we're on a different basis. I know you're supposed to have a pretty lady friend. But I don't care who she is and what she knows, compared to Polly she's a bush leaguer. Polly makes other girls look sick."

"In that case, I ought to thank you."

"That means you don't want to. You're refusing. Take your razor, I'm finished." He put the warm small machine into my hand with a slap. Then he stood away from the basin and leaned against the bathroom wall with his arms crossed and one foot posed on its toe. He said, "You'd better not reject me."

"Why not?"

His face, the colorless-intense type, filled with pale heat. But he said, "There's a thing the three of us can do together. You lie on your back. She gets on top of you and at the same time goes down on me."

"Let's not have any more filth. Stop it. I can't even visualize this."

"Don't put on with me. Don't be superior." He explained again. "I'm at the head of the bed, standing. You lie down. Polly straddles you, leaning forward to me."

"Stop these disgusting propositions. I want no part of your sexual circuses."

He gave me a bloody-murder look but I couldn't have cared less. There were lots of people ahead of him in the bloody-murder line—Denise and Pinsker, Tomchek and the court, the Internal Revenue Service. "You're no puritan," said Cantabile, sullen. But sensing my mood he changed the subject. "Your friend George Swiebel was talking at the game about a beryllium mine in East Africa—what is this beryllium stuff?"

"It's needed for hard alloys used in space ships. George claims he has friends in Kenya. . . ."

"Oh, he has an inside track with some jungle-bunnies. I bet they all love him. He's so natural healthy and humane. I bet he's a lousy businessman. You'd be better off with Stronson and the commodity futures. There's a real smart guy. I know you can't believe it but I'm trying to help you. They're going to mangle you in court. Haven't you stashed something away? You can't be as dumb as all that. Haven't you got a bagman somewhere?"

"I never thought of one."

"You want me to believe you have nothing in your thoughts except angels on ladders and immortal spirits but I can see from the way you live that it can't be true. First of all you're a dude. I know your tailor. Secondly you're an old sex-pot. . . ."

"Did I talk to you that night about the immortal spirit?"

"You sure as hell did. You said that after it gets through the gates of death—this is a quote—your soul spreads out and looks back at the world. Charlie, I had a thought this morning about you—shut the door. Go on, shut it. Now, listen, we could pretend to kidnap one of your kids. You pay the ransom, and I put the dough away in the Cayman Islands for you."

"Let me see that gun of yours now," I said.

He handed it to me and I pointed it at him. I said, "I'll certainly use this on you if you try any such thing."

"Put that Magnum down. It's only an idea. Don't get all shook up."

I removed the bullets and threw them in the wastepaper basket, handing back the pistol. That he made such suggestions to me was, I recognized, my own fault. The arbitrary can become the pets of the rational. Cantabile seemed to recognize that he was my pet arbitrary. In some sense he played up to this. Maybe it was better to be a pet arbitrary than a mere nut. But *was* I so rational?

"The kidnap idea is too gaudy. You're right," he said. "Well, how about getting to the judge? After all, a county judge has to be put on the ballot for re-election. Judges are in politics, too, and you'd better know it. There are little characters in the Organization who put 'em on and take 'em off the ballot. For thirty or forty Gs, the right guy will call on Judge Urbanovich."

I puffed, and blew the tiny clippings out of the shaver.

"You don't go for that either?"

"No."

"Maybe the other side has already gotten to him. Why be such a gentleman? It's like a kind of paralysis. Absolutely unreal. Behind the glass in the Field Museum, that's where you belong. I believe you got stuck in your childhood. If I said to you, 'Liquidate and go abroad,' what would you answer?"

"I'd say that I wouldn't leave the USA just because of money."

"That's right. You're no Vesco. You love your country. Well, you're not fit to have this money. Maybe the other guys should get it from you. People like the President pretended to be fine clean Americans from *The Saturday Evening Post.* They were boy scouts, they delivered the newspaper at dawn. But they were fakes. The real American is a freak like you, a highbrow Jew from the West Side of Chicago. *You* ought to be in the White House."

"I'm inclined to agree."

"You'd love the Secret Service protection." Cantabile opened the bathroom door to check on Polly. She was not eavesdropping. He shut it again and said, low-voiced, "We could put a contract on your wife. Does she wanna fight? Let her have it. There could be a car accident. She could die in the street. She could be pushed in front of a train, dragged into an alley and stabbed. Crazy buffaloes are doing women in left and right, so who's to know. She's bugging *you* to death—well, how would it be if *she* died? I know you'll say no, and treat it as a joke—Wildass Cantabile, a joker."

"You'd better be joking."

"I'm only reminding you this is Chicago, after all."

"Ninety-eight-percent nightmare, so you think I should total it? I'll just assume that you're kidding. I'm sorry Polly wasn't listening to this. Okay, I appreciate your great interest in my welfare. Don't offer any more suggestions. And don't make me a horrible Christmas present, Cantabile. You're casting about to make a dynamic impression. Don't make any more criminal offers, you understand? If I hear another whisper of this I'll tell the homicide squad."

"Relax. I wouldn't lift a finger. I just thought I'd point out the whole range of options. It helps to see them from end to end. It clears your head. You know she'll be damn glad when you're dead, you rascal you."

"I don't know any such thing," I said.

I was lying. She had told me exactly that herself. Really, to be having a conversation like this served me right. I had brought it on myself. I had rooted and sorted my way through mankind experiencing disappointment upon disappointment. What was my disappointment? I had, or assumed that I had, needs and perceptions of a Shakespearian order. But they were only too sporadically of that high order. And so I found myself now looking into the moony eyes of a Cantabile. Ah my higher life! When I was young I believed that being an intellectual assured me of a higher life. In this Humboldt and I were exactly alike. He too would have respected and adored the learning, the rationality, the analytical power of a man like Richard Durnwald. For Durnwald the only brave, the only passionate, the only manly life was a life of thought. I had agreed, but I no longer thought in the same way. I had decided to listen to the voice of my own mind speaking from within, from my own depths, and this voice said that there was my body, in nature, and that there was also me. I was related to nature through my body, but all of me was not contained in it.

Because of this kind of idea I now found myself under Cantabile's gaze. He examined me. He also looked tender concerned threatening punitive and even lethal.

I said to him, "Years ago there was a little kid in the funnies called Desperate Ambrose. Before your time. Now don't you play Desperate Ambrose with me. Let me out of here."

"Just a minute. What about Lucy's thesis?"

"Curse her thesis."

"She's coming back from Nevada in a few days."

I made no answer. In a few days' time I'd be safely abroad—away from this lunatic, though probably mixed up with others.

"One more thing," he said. "You can make it with Polly through me. Only. Don't try on your own."

"Rest easy," I said.

He remained in the bathroom. I suppose he was getting his bullets out of the wastepaper basket.

Polly had the yoghurt and the egg ready for me.

"I'll tell you," she said, "don't get mixed up in the commodity market. He's losing his shirt."

"Does he know that?"

"What do you think," she said.

"Then he's bringing in new investors perhaps to make a deal to recover some of his losses?"

"I couldn't say. That's beyond me," said Polly. "He's a very intricate person. What is that beautiful medal on the wall?"

"It's my French decoration, framed by my lady friend. She's an interior decorator. Actually, the medal is a kind of phony. Major decorations are red, not green. They gave me the sort of thing they give to pig-breeders and to people who improve the garbage cans. A Frenchman told me last year that my green ribbon must be the lowest rank of the Legion of Honor. In fact he had never actually seen a green ribbon before. He thought it might be the Mérite Agricole."

"I don't think it was very nice of him to tell you that," said Polly.

RENATA was punctual, and she had the engine of the old yellow Pontiac idling, waiting to be off. I shook hands with Polly and told Cantabile, "I'll be seeing you." I didn't introduce them to Renata. They tried hard to get a look at her but I got in, slammed the door, and said, "Go!" She went. The crown of Renata's large hat touched the roof of the car. It was amethyst felt and of the seventeenth-century cut you see in portraits by Frans Hals. She was wearing her long hair down. I preferred it in a bun, showing the shape of her neck.

"Who are your pals, and what's the big hurry?"

"That was Cantabile, who did in my car."

"Him? I wish I'd known. Was that his wife?"

"No, his wife is out of town."

"I watched you coming through the lobby. She's quite a number. And he's a good-looking man."

"He was dying to meet you—trying to get a load of you through the window."

"Why should you be so flustered by that?"

"Just now he offered to have Denise rubbed out for me."

Renata, laughing, shouted, "What?"

"A hit man, a mechanic, he suggested a contract. Everybody knows the lingo now."

"It must have been a put-on."

"I'm sure it was. On the other hand there's my 280-SL in the shop."

"It's not as though Denise didn't deserve it," said Renata.

"She is a maddening pest, that's true enough, and I always laughed when I read how old Mr. Karamazov rushed into the street when he heard that his wife was gone shouting, 'The bitch is dead!'—But Denise," said Citrine the lecturer, "is a comical, not a tragic personality. Besides, she shouldn't die to gratify *me*. Most important are the girls, they need a mother. Anyhow it's idiotic to hear people say kill, murder, die, death —they haven't the faintest idea what they're talking about. There isn't one person in ten thousand that understands the first thing about death."

"What do you suppose will happen downtown today?"

"Oh, the usual thing. They'll mobbalize me, as we used to

say in grammar school. I'll represent human dignity, and they'll give me hell."

"Well, must you do the dignity bit? You're stuck with it, while they have all the fun. If you could find some way to crush 'em, it would be so nice. . . . Well, here's my client on the corner. Isn't she built like a bouncer in a clip joint! You don't have to take part in the conversation, it's enough that she bores and badgers me. You just tune out and meditate. If she doesn't choose her upholstery material today I'll cut her throat."

Immense and fragrant in black and white silk, large polka dots covering her bosom (which I could, and did, visualize), Fannie Sunderland got in. I withdrew to the back seat, warning her about the hole in the floor, covered by a square of tin. The heavy samples carried by her salesman ex-husband had actually worn out the metal of Renata's Pontiac. "Unfortunately," said Renata, "our Mercedes is in the shop for repairs."

In the mental discipline I had recently begun, and of which I already felt the good effects, stability equipoise and tranquillity were the prerequisites. I said to myself, "Tranquillity, tranquillity." As on the racquet ball court I said, "Dance, dance, dance!" And it always had some result. The will is a link which connects the soul to the world as-it-is. Through the will the soul frees itself from distraction and mere dreams. But when Renata told me to tune out and meditate she struck a note of malice. She was needling me about Doris, the daughter of Dr. Scheldt, the anthroposophist from whom I had been getting instruction. Renata was terribly jealous of Doris. "That baby bitch!" Renata cried. "I know she couldn't wait to jump into your bed." But this was Renata's own fault, her very own doing. She and her mother, the Señora, had decided that I needed a lesson. They shut the door in my face. By invitation, I came to Renata's apartment for dinner one night and found myself locked out. Someone else was with her. For several months I was too depressed to be alone. I moved in with George Swiebel and slept on his sofa. I would sit up suddenly in the night with a crying fit, sometimes waking George who came out and turned on a lamp, his wrinkled pajamas baring powerful legs. He made this measured statement: "A man in his fifties who can break up and cry over a girl is a man I respect."

I said, "Oh hell! What are you talking about! I'm a moron. It's disgraceful to carry on like this."

Renata had taken up with a man named Flonzaley. . . .

But I'm getting ahead of myself. I sat behind the two fragrant chatting ladies. We turned into Forty-seventh Street, the boundary between rich man's Kenwood and poor man's Oakwood, passing the locked tavern which lost its license because a fellow had gotten twenty stab wounds there over a matter of eight dollars. This was what Cantabile meant by "crazy buffaloes." Where was the victim? He was buried. Who was he? Nobody could tell you. And now others, casually regardant, passed the place in automobiles still thinking of an "I," and of the past and the prospects of this "I." If there was nothing in this but some funny egoism, some illusion that fate was being outwitted, avoidance of the reality of the grave, perhaps it was scarcely worth the trouble. But that remained to be seen.

George Swiebel, that vitality-worshiper, thought it was a wonderful thing that an elderly man should still keep up an active erotic and vivid fluent emotional life. I did not agree. But when Renata called me up, weeping on the phone, and said she had never cared for this Flonzaley, she wanted me back, I said, "Oh, thank God, thank God!" and hurried straight over. That was the end of Miss Doris Scheldt, of whom I had been very fond. But fond was not enough. I was a nymph-troubled man and a person of frenzied longings. Perhaps the longings were not even specifically for nymphs. But whatever they were, a woman like Renata drew them out. Other ladies were critical of her. Some said she was gross. Maybe so, but she was also gorgeous. And one must bear in mind the odd angle or slant that the rays of love have to take in order to reach a heart like mine. From George Swiebel's poker game, at which I drank so much and became so garrulous, I carried away one useful idea—for an atypical foot you need an atypical shoe. If in addition to being atypical you are fastidious—well, you have your work cut out for you. And is there still any typical foot? I mean by this that such emphasis has fallen on the erotic that all the eccentricity of the soul pours into the foot. The effects are so distorting, the flesh takes such florid turns that nothing will fit. So deformity has overtaken love and love is a power that can't let us alone. It can't because we owe our existence to acts of love performed before us, because love is a standing debt of the soul. This is the position as I saw it. The interpretation given by Renata, something of an astrologer, was that my sign was to blame for my troubles. She had never come across a more divided screwed-up suffering Gemini, so incapable of pulling himself together. "Don't smile when I talk about the stars. I know that to you I'm a beautiful palooka, a dumb broad. You'd like me to be your *Kama Sutra* dream-girl."

But I hadn't been smiling at her. I smiled only because I had yet to read any account of the Gemini type in Renata's astrological literature which was not entirely correct. One book in particular impressed me; it spoke of Gemini as a mental feeling-mill, where the soul is sheared and shredded. As to her being my *Kama Sutra* girl, she was a very fine woman, I still say that, but she was by no means fully at ease in sex. There were times when she was sad and quiet and spoke of her "hang-ups." Now we were going to Europe on Friday, our second trip this year. There were serious personal reasons for these European flights. And if I couldn't offer mature sympathy to a young woman, what did I have to offer? As it happened I took a genuine interest in her problems, I sympathized fully with her.

Still, I owed it to common realism to see the thing as others might see it—an old troubled lecher was taking a gold-digging floozy to Europe to show her a big time. Behind this, to complete the classic picture, was the scheming old mother, the Señora, who taught commercial Spanish in a secretarial college on State Street. The Señora was a person of some charm, one of those people who thrive in the Midwest because they are foreign and dotty. Renata's beauty was not inherited from her. And on the biological or evolutionary side Renata was perfect. Like a leopard or a race horse, she was a "noble animal" (see Santayana, *The Sense of Beauty*). Her mysterious father (and our trips to Europe were made to discover just who this was) must have been one of those old-time strongmen who bent iron bars, pulled locomotives with his teeth, or supported twenty people on a plank across his back, a grand figure of a man, a model for Rodin. The Señora I believe was really a Hungarian. When she told family anecdotes I could see her transposing from the Balkans to Spain. I was convinced that I understood her, and for this claim I gave myself a strange reason; this was that I understood my mother's Singer sewing machine. At the age of ten I had dismantled the machine and put it together again. You pushed the wrought-iron treadle. This moved the smooth pulley, the needle went up and down. You pried up a smooth steel plate and there found small and intricate parts that gave off an odor of machine oil. To me the Señora was a person of intricate parts and smelled slightly of oil. It was on the whole a positive association. But certain bits were missing from her mind. The needle went up and down, there was thread on the bobbin, but the stitching failed to occur.

The Señora's chief claim to sanity was founded upon motherhood. She had many plans for Renata. These were extravagant in the distant reaches, but near at hand they were quite practical. She had invested a lot in Renata's upbringing. She must have spent a fortune on orthodontia. The results were of a very high order. It was a privilege to see Renata open her mouth, and when she kidded me and laughed brilliantly I was struck with admiration. All my mother could do for my teeth in the ignorant old days was to wrap a lid from the coal stove in flannel, or to put hot dry buckwheat in a Bull Durham tobacco sack to apply to my face when I had toothaches. Hence my respect for those beautiful teeth. Also, for a big girl, Renata had a light voice. When she laughed she ventilated her entire being—down to the uterus, I thought. She put up her hair with silk scarves, showing the line of a wonderfully graceful feminine neck, and she walked about—how she walked about! No wonder her mother didn't want to waste her on me with my dewlaps and my French medal. But since Renata did have a weakness for me, why not set up housekeeping? The Señora was for this. Renata was going on thirty, divorced, with a nice little boy named Roger, of whom I was very fond. The old woman (like Cantabile, come to think of it) urged me to buy a condominium on the near-North Side. She omitted herself from these suggested arrangements. "I need privacy. I have my *affaires de cœur.*" "But," said the Señora, "Roger should be in a household that has a male figure in it."

Renata and the Señora collected news items about May–December marriages. They sent me clippings about old husbands and interviews with their brides. In one year they lost Steichen, Picasso, and Casals. But they still had Chaplin and Senator Thurmond and Justice Douglas. From the sex columns of the *News* the Señora even culled scientific statements about sex for the aging. And even George Swiebel said, "Maybe this would be a good deal for you. Renata wants to settle down. She's been around and seen a lot. She's had it. She's ready."

"Well, she's certainly not one of those little *noli me tangerines,*" I said.

"She's a good cook. She's lively. She has plants and knickknacks and the lights are on and the kitchen is steaming and goy music plays. Does she flow for you? Does she get wet when you lay a hand on her? Stay away from those dry mental broads. I have to be basic with you otherwise you'll shilly-shally. You'll be trapped again by a woman who says she shares your mental interests or understands your higher aims. That type already has shortened your life. One more will kill you! Anyhow, I know you want to make it with Renata."

I most certainly did! It's hard for me to stop praising her. In her hat and fur coat she drove the Pontiac, her outthrust leg in spangled textured panty hose bought in a theatrical-specialty house. Her personal emanations affected even the skins of the animals which composed her coat. They not only covered her body but were still in there trying. There was a certain similarity here. I too was trying. Yes, I longed to make it with Renata. She was helping me to consummate my earthly cycle. She had her irrational moments but she was also kindly. True, as a carnal artist she was disheartening as well as thrilling, because, thinking of her as wife-material, I had to ask myself where she had learned all this and whether she had taken the PhD once and for all. Furthermore our relationship made me entertain vain and undignified ideas. An ophthalmologist told me in the Downtown Club that a simple incision would remove the bags under my eyes. "It's just a hernia of one of the tiny muscles," Dr. Klosterman said, and described the plastic surgery and how the skin would be sliced and tucked back. He added that I had plenty of backhair left which could be transplanted to the top. Senator Proxmire had it done and for a time wore a turban on the Senate floor. He had claimed a deduction, disallowed by the IRS—but one could try again. I considered these suggestions but realized presently that I must stop this foolishness! I must fix my whole attention on the great and terrible matters that had put me to sleep for decades. Besides, something might be done at the front of a person but what about the rear? Even if the baggy eyes were fixed and the hair was fixed, wasn't there still the back of my neck? I was trying on a fancy check overcoat at Saks not long ago and in the triple mirror I saw how fissured, how deeply hacked I was between the ears.

I bought the coat anyway, Renata urged me to, and I was wearing it today. When I got out at the county building, giant Mrs. Sunderland said, "Golly, what a jazzy coat!"

RENATA and I had met in this same skyscraper, the new county building, while doing jury duty.

There was, however, an earlier, indirect connection between us. George Swiebel's father, old Myron, knew Gaylord Koffritz, Renata's ex-husband. These two had had an unusual encounter in the Russian Bath on Division Street. George had told me about it.

He was a simple modest person, George's father. All he wanted was to live forever. George came by his vitalism directly. He got it from Myron who had it in a more primitive form. Myron declared that he owed his longevity to heat and vapor, to black bread raw onion bourbon whisky herring sausage cards billiards race horses and women.

Now in the steam room with its wooden bleachers and its sizzling boulders and buckets of ice water the visual distortion was considerable. From the rear if you saw a slight figure with small buttocks you thought it to be a child, but there were no children here and from the front you discovered a rosy and shrunken old man. Father Swiebel, clean-shaven and seen from the back just like a little boy, met a bearded man in the steam and because of the glittering beard took *him* to be much older. He was however only in his thirties, and very well built. They sat down together on the wooden trestles, two bodies covered with drops of moisture, and Father Swiebel said, "What do you do?"

The bearded man was unwilling to say what he did. Father Swiebel urged him to talk. This was wrong. It was, in the demented jargon of the educated, against the "ethos" of the place. Here, as at the Downtown Club, business was not discussed. George liked to say that the steam bath was like the last refuge in the burning forest where hostile animals observed a truce and the law of fang and claw was suspended. I'm afraid he got this from Walt Disney. The point he wanted to remind me of was that it was wrong to ply your trade or make a pitch while steaming. Father Swiebel was to blame and admitted it. "This fellow with the hair didn't want to talk. I egged him on. So then he let me have it."

Where men are as nude as the troglodytes of Stone Age Adriatic caverns and sit together dripping and red, like sunset in a mist, and, as in this case, one has a full brown sparkling beard, and eyes are meeting eyes through streaming sweat and vapor, strange things are apt to be spoken. It turned out that the stranger was a salesman whose line was crypts tombs and mausoleums. When Father Swiebel heard this he wanted to back off. But now it was too late. With arched brows, with white teeth and living lips within the dense fell of the beard, the man spoke:

Has your last rest been arranged? Is there a family plot? Are you provided? No? But why not? Can you afford such neglect? Do you know how they will bury you? Amazing! Has anybody talked to you about conditions in the new cemeteries? Why, they're nothing but slums. Death deserves dignity. Out there the exploitation is terrible. It's one of the biggest real-estate swindles going. They cheat you. They don't give the statutory number of feet. You have to lie cramped forever. The disrespect is ferocious. But you know what politics and rackets are. High and low, everybody is on the take. One of these days there'll be a grand-jury investigation and a scandal. Guys will go to jail. But it'll be too late for the dead. They aren't going to open your grave and rebury you. So you'll lie there short-sheeted. Frogged. As kids do to each other in summer camp. And there you are with hundreds of thousands of bodies in a flattened-out death-tenement, with your knees up. Aren't you entitled to a full stretch? And in these cemeteries they don't allow you a headstone. You have to settle for a brass plate with your name and your dates. Then machines come to cut the grass. They use a gang-mower. You might as well be buried in a public golf course. The blades nick away the brass letters. Pretty soon they're obliterated. Then you can't even be located. Your kids can't find the place. You're lost forever—

"Stop!" Myron said. The fellow continued:

Now in a mausoleum it's different. It doesn't cost as much as you think. These new jobs are prefabricated but they're copies from the best models, starting with Etruscan tombs, up through Bernini and finally there's Louis Sullivan, *art nouveau*. People are mad now for *art nouveau*. They'll pay thousands for a Tiffany lamp or ceiling fixture. By comparison, an *art nouveau* prefab tomb is cheap. And then you're out of the crowd. You're on your own property. You don't want to get caught for eternity in a kind of expressway traffic jam or subway rush.

Father Swiebel said that Koffritz looked very sincere and that he saw in the steam only a respectful sympathetic troubled bearded face—an expert, a specialist, fair-minded, sensible. But the by-intimations were devastating. The vision got me, too—death seething under the treeless fairway, and the glitterless brass of nameless name plates. This Koffritz with his devilish sales-poetry clutched the heart of Father Swiebel. He grabbed mine as well. For at the time this was reported to me I was suffering intense death-anxieties. I wouldn't even attend funerals. I couldn't bear to see the coffin shut and the thought of being screwed into a box made me frantic. This was aggravated when I read a newspaper account of some Chicago children who found a heap of empty caskets near the crematory of a cemetery. They dragged them down to a pond and boated in them. Because they were reading *Ivanhoe* at school they tilted like knights, with poles. One kid was capsized and caught in the silk lining. They saved him. But there gaped in my mind a display of coffins lined with puffy rose taffeta and pale green satin, all open like crocodiles' jaws. I saw myself put down to suffocate and rot under the weight of clay and stones—no, under sand; Chicago is built on Ice Age beaches and marshes (Late Pleistocene). For relief, I tried to convert this into serious intellectual subject matter. I believe I did this kind of thing rather well—thinking how the death problem is *the* bourgeois problem, relating to material prosperity and the conception of life as pleasant and comfortable, and what Max Weber had written about the modern conception of life as an infinite series of segments, gainful advantageous and "pleasant," failing to provide the feeling of a life cycle, so that one couldn't die "full of years." But these learned high-class exercises didn't take the death-curse off for me. I could only conclude how bourgeois it was that I should be so neurotic about stifling in the grave. And I was furious with Edgar Allan Poe for writing so accurately about this. His tales of catalepsy and live burial poisoned my childhood, and still killed me. I couldn't even bear to have the sheet over my face at night or my feet tucked in. I spent a lot of time figuring out how to be dead. Burial at sea might be the answer.

The samples that had worn a hole in Renata's Pontiac were, then, models of crypts and tombs. When I met her I not only had been brooding over death (would it help to have a wooden partition in the grave, a floor just above the coffin to keep off the direct smothering weight?) but I had also developed a new oddity. On business errands on La Salle Street, zooming or plunging in swift elevators, every time I felt a check in the electrical speed and the door was about to open, my heart spoke up. Entirely on its own. It exclaimed, "My Fate!" It seems I expected some woman to be standing there. "At last! You!" Becoming conscious of this hungry demeaning elevator phenomenon I tried to do the right thing and get back on a mature standard. I even attempted to be scientific. But all science can do for you is to affirm again that when something like this happens there must be a natural necessity for it. This being sensible got me nowhere. What was there to be so sensible about if, as I felt, I had waited many thousands of years for God to send my soul to this earth? Here I was supposed to capture a true and clear word before I returned, as my human day ended. I was afraid to go back empty-handed.

Being sensible could do absolutely nothing to mitigate this fear of missing the boat. Anyone can see that.

Called to jury duty I grumbled at first that it was a waste of time. But then I became a happy eager juror. To leave the house in the morning like everybody else was bliss. Wearing a numbered steel badge I sat joyfully with hundreds of others in the jury pool, high up in the new county skyscraper, a citizen among fellow citizens. The glass walls, the russet and plum steel beams were very fine—the large sky, the ruled space, the faraway spools of storage tanks, the orange delicate distant filthy slums, the green of the river strapped by black bridges. Looking out from the jurors' hall I began to have Ideas. I brought books and papers downtown (so it shouldn't be a total loss). For the first time I read through the letters my colleague Pierre Thaxter had been sending me from California.

I am not a careful letter reader and Thaxter's letters were very long. He composed and dictated them in his orange grove near Palo Alto where he sat thinking in a canvas officer's chair. He wore a black carabiniere cloak, his feet were bare, he drank Pepsi-Cola, he had eight or ten children, he owed money to everyone, and he was a cultural statesman. Adoring women treated him like a man of genius, believed all that he told them, typed his manuscripts, gave birth to his kids, brought him Pepsi-Cola to drink. Reading his voluminous memoranda which dealt with the first number of *The Ark* (in the planning stage for three years, and the costs were staggering), I realized that he had been pressing me to complete a group of studies on "Great Bores of the Modern World." He kept suggesting possible lines of approach. Certain types were obvious, of course—political, philosophical, ideological, educational, therapeutic bores—but there were others frequently overlooked, for instance innovative bores. I however had lost interest in the categories and came presently to care only for the general and theoretical aspect of the project.

I had a lively time in the vast jurors' hall going over my boredom notes. I saw that I had stayed away from problems of definition. Good for me. I didn't want to get mixed up with theological questions about *accidia* and *tedium vitae*. I found it necessary to say only that from the beginning mankind experienced states of boredom but that no one had ever approached the matter front and center as a subject in its own right. In modern times the question had been dealt with under the name of *anomie* or Alienation, as an effect of capitalist conditions of labor, as a result of leveling in Mass Society, as a consequence of the dwindling of religious faith or the gradual using up of charismatic or prophetic elements, or the neglect of Unconscious powers, or the increase of Rationalization in a technological society, or the growth of bureaucracy. It seemed to me, however, that one might begin with this belief of the modern world—either you burn or you rot. This I connected with the finding of old Binet the psychologist that hysterical people had fifty times the energy, the endurance, the power of performance, the keenness of faculties, the creativity in their hysterical fits as they had in their quiet periods. Or as William James put it, human beings really lived when they lived at the top of their energies. Something like the *Wille zur Macht*. Suppose then that you began with the proposition that boredom was a kind of pain caused by unused powers, the pain of wasted possibilities or talents, and was accompanied by expectations of the optimum utilization of capacities. (I try to guard against falling into the social-science style on these mental occasions.) Nothing actual ever suits pure expectation and such purity of expectation is a great source of tedium. People rich in abilities, in sexual feeling, rich in mind and in invention—all the highly gifted see themselves shunted for decades onto dull sidings, banished exiled nailed up in chicken coops. Imagination has even tried to surmount the problems by forcing boredom itself to yield interest. This insight I owe to Von Humboldt Fleisher who showed me how it was done by James Joyce, but anyone who reads books can easily find it out for himself. Modern French literature is especially preoccupied with the theme of boredom. Stendhal mentioned it on every page, Flaubert devoted books to it, and Baudelaire was its chief poet. What is the reason for this peculiar French sensitivity? Can it be because the *ancien régime*, fearing another Fronde, created a court that emptied the provinces of talent? Outside the center, where art philosophy science manners conversation thrived, there was nothing. Under Louis XIV, the upper classes enjoyed a refined society, and, whatever else, people didn't need to be alone. Cranks like Rousseau made solitude glamorous, but sensible people agreed that it was really terrible. Then in the eighteenth century being in prison began to acquire its modern significance. Think how often Manon and Des Grieux were in jail. And Mirabeau and my own buddy Von Trenck and of course the Marquis de Sade. The intellectual future of Europe was determined by people impregnated with boredom, by the writings of prisoners. Then, in 1789, it was young men from the sticks, provincial lawyers scribblers and orators, who assaulted and captured the center of interest. Boredom has more to do with modern political revolution than justice has. In 1917, that boring Lenin who wrote so many boring pamphlets and letters on organizational questions was, briefly, all passion, all radiant interest. The Russian revolution promised mankind a permanently interesting life. When Trotsky spoke of permanent revolution he really meant permanent interest. In the early days the revolution was a work of inspiration. Workers peasants soldiers were in a state of excitement and poetry. When this short brilliant phase ended, what came next? The most boring society in history. Dowdiness shabbiness dullness dull goods boring buildings boring discomfort boring supervision a dull press dull education boring bureaucracy forced labor perpetual police presence penal presence, boring party congresses, et cetera. What was permanent was the defeat of interest.

What could be more boring than the long dinners Stalin gave, as Djilas describes them? Even I, a person seasoned in boredom by my years in Chicago, marinated, *mithridated* by the USA, was horrified by Djilas's account of those twelve-course all-night banquets. The guests drank and ate, and ate and drank, and then at 2 a.m. they had to sit down to watch an American Western. Their bottoms ached. There was dread in their hearts. Stalin, as he chatted and joked, was mentally picking those who were going to get it in the neck and while they chewed and snorted and guzzled they knew this, they expected shortly to be shot.

What—in other words—would modern boredom be without terror? One of the most boring documents of all time is the thick volume of Hitler's *Table Talk*. He too had people watching movies, eating pastries, and drinking coffee with

Schlag while he bored them, while he discoursed theorized expounded. Everyone was perishing of staleness and fear, afraid to go to the toilet. This combination of power and boredom has never been properly examined. Boredom is an instrument of social control. Power is the power to impose boredom, to command stasis, to combine this stasis with anguish. The real tedium, deep tedium, is seasoned with terror and with death.

There were even profounder questions. For instance, the history of the universe would be very boring if one tried to think of it in the ordinary way of human experience. All that time without events! Gases over and over again, and heat and particles of matter, the sun tides and winds, again this creeping development, bits added to bits, chemical accidents—whole ages in which almost nothing happens, lifeless seas, only a few crystals, a few protein compounds developing. The tardiness of evolution is so irritating to contemplate. The clumsy mistakes you see in museum fossils. How could such bones crawl, walk, run? It is agony to think of the groping of the species—all this fumbling, swamp-creeping, munching, preying, and reproduction, the boring slowness with which tissues, organs, and members developed. And then the boredom also of the emergence of the higher types and finally of mankind, the dull life of paleolithic forests, the long long incubation of intelligence, the slowness of invention, the idiocy of peasant ages. These are interesting only in review, in thought. No one could bear to experience this. The present demand is for a quick forward movement, for a summary, for life at the speed of intensest thought. As we approach, through technology, the phase of instantaneous realization, of the realization of eternal human desires or fantasies, of abolishing time and space the problem of boredom can only become more intense. The human being, more and more oppressed by the peculiar terms of his existence—one time around for each, no more than a single life per customer—has to think of the boredom of death. O those eternities of nonexistence! For people who crave continual interest and diversity, O! how boring death will be! To lie in the grave, in one place, how frightful!

Socrates tried to soothe us, true enough. He said there were only two possibilities. Either the soul is immortal or, after death, things would be again as blank as they were before we were born. This is not absolutely comforting either. Anyway it was natural that theology and philosophy should take the deepest interest in this. They owe it to us not to be boring themselves. On this obligation they don't always make good. However, Kierkegaard was not a bore. I planned to examine his contribution in my master essay. In his view the primacy of the ethical over the esthetic mode was necessary to restore the balance. But enough of that. In myself I could observe the following sources of tedium: 1) The lack of a *personal* connection with the external world. Earlier I noted that when I was riding through France in a train last spring I looked out of the window and thought that the veil of Maya was wearing thin. And why was this? I wasn't seeing what was there but only what everyone sees under a common directive. By this is implied that our world-view has used up nature. The rule of this view is that I, a subject, see the phenomena, the world of objects. They, however, are not necessarily in themselves objects as modern rationality defines objects. For in spirit, says Steiner, a man can step out of himself and let things speak to him about themselves, to speak about what has meaning not for him alone but also for them. Thus the sun the moon the stars will speak to nonastronomers in spite of their ignorance of science. In fact it's high time that this happened. Ignorance of science should not keep one imprisoned in the lowest and weariest sector of being, prohibited from entering into independent relations with the creation as a whole. The educated speak of the disenchanted (a boring) world. But it is not the world, it is my own head that is disenchanted. The world *cannot* be disenchanted. 2) For me the self-conscious ego is the seat of boredom. This increasing, swelling, domineering, painful self-consciousness is the only rival of the political and social powers that run my life (business, technological-bureaucratic powers, the state). You have a great organized movement of life, and you have the single self, independently conscious, proud of its detachment and its absolute immunity, its stability and its power to remain unaffected by anything whatsoever—by the sufferings of others or by society or by politics or by external chaos. In a way it doesn't give a damn. It is asked to give a damn, and we often urge it to give a damn but the curse of noncaring lies upon this painfully free consciousness. It is free from attachment to beliefs and to other souls. Cosmologies, ethical systems? It can run through them by the dozens. For to be fully conscious of oneself as an individual is also to be separated from all else. This is Hamlet's kingdom of infinite space in a nutshell, of "words, words, words," of "Denmark's a prison."

These were some of the notes that Thaxter wanted me to expand. I was however in too unstable a condition. Several times a week I went downtown to see my lawyers and discuss my problems. They told me how complex my predicament was. Their news was worse and worse. I soared in elevators looking for salvation in female form whenever a door opened. A person in my condition should lock himself in his room, and if he hasn't the strength of character to take Pascal's advice to stay put he ought to throw the key out of the window. Then the door rolled open in the county building and I saw Renata Koffritz. She too wore a numbered steel badge. We were both taxpayers, voters, citizens. But oh, what citizens! And where was the voice that said, "My Fate!"? It was silent. Was she, then, it? She certainly was all woman, soft and beautifully heavy in a miniskirt and nursery-school shoes fastened with a single strap. I thought, God help me. I thought, Better think twice about this. I even thought, At your age a Buddhist would already be thinking of disappearing forever into the forest. But it was no use. She may not have been the Fate I was looking for but she was nevertheless a Fate. She even knew my name. "You must be Mr. Citrine," she said.

The year before I had been given an award by the Zig-Zag Club, a Chicago cultural society of bank executives and stockbrokers. I was not invited to become a member. I did however receive a plaque for the book I wrote about Harry Hopkins and my picture was in the *Daily News.* Perhaps the lady had seen it there. But she said, "Your friend Mr. Szathmar is my divorce lawyer and he thought we should get to know each other."

Ah, she had me. How quickly she informed me that she was being divorced. Those love-pious eyes were already sending messages of love and depravity to the Chicago-boy sector of my soul. A gust of the old West Side sex malaria came over me.

"Mr. Szathmar is devoted to you. He adores you. He practically closes his eyes and looks poetic when he discusses you. And he's such a stout man, you don't expect it. He told me about your love who crashed in the jungle. And also about your first romance—with the doctor's daughter."

"Naomi Lutz."

"That's a crazy name."

"Yes, it is, isn't it."

It was true that my boyhood friend Szathmar loved me but he loved matchmaking or procuring also. He had a passion for arranging affairs. This was useful to him professionally, as it tied many clients to him. In special cases he took over all the practical details for them—the rent of a mistress's apartment, her car, and her charge accounts, her dental bills. He even covered suicide attempts. Even funerals. Not the law but fixing people up was his real calling. And we two boyhood pals were going to continue lustful to the end, if he had his way. He made this decorous. He did it all with philosophy, poetry, ideology. He quoted, he played records, and he theorized about women. He tried to keep up with the rapidly changing erotic slang of successive generations. So were we to end our lives as cunt-struck doddering wooers left over from a Goldoni farce? Or like Balzac's Baron Hulot d'Ervy whose wife on her deathbed hears the old man propositioning the maid?

Alec Szathmar a few years ago, while under great stress in the vaults of the First National Bank, suffered a heart attack. I loved foolish Szathmar. I worried terribly about him. As soon as he was out of the intensive care unit, I ran down to see him and found that he was already being sexual. After heart attacks this is common, apparently. Under the powerful crown of white hair, bushy on the cheekbones in the new style of adornment, his gloomy eyes dilated as soon as a nurse entered his room though he still looked purple in the face. My old friend who now was stout, massive, was restless in bed. He threw himself about, kicked away the sheets, and exposed himself as if by fretful accident. If I was making a sympathy call he didn't need my goddamn sympathy. Those eyes of his were grim and alert. At last I said, "Now Alec stop this flashing. You know what I'm talking about—stop uncovering your parts every time some poor old lady comes to mop under the bed."

He glared. "What? You're stupid!" he said.

"That's all right. Quit pulling up your gown."

Bad examples can be elevating—you can win a quick promotion in taste and say, "Poor old Alec, flashing. By the grace of God, there never goes me." Yet here I was in the jury box with an erection for Renata. I was excited, amused, I was slightly mortified. Before us was a personal-injury case. In fairness I should have gone to the judge and asked to be disqualified. "Your honor, I can't keep my mind on the trial because of the glorious lady juror next to me. I'm sorry to be such an adolescent. . . ." (Sorry! I was in seventh heaven.) Besides, the case was only one of those phony whiplash suits against the insurance company filed by the lady passenger in a taxi collision. My personal business was more important. The trial was only background music. I kept the time with metronomic pulsations.

Two floors below, I myself was defendant in a post-decree action to deprive me of all my money. You might have thought that this would sober me. Not in the least!

Excused for lunch I hurried to La Salle Street to get information from Alec Szathmar about this wonderful girl. As I ran into the Chicago crowd I felt my pegs slipping, the strings slacker, my tone going lower. But what was I to do single-handed about a force that had seized the whole world?

There was a genteel and almost Harvard air about Alec's office, though he was a night-school lawyer. The layout was princely, sets of torts and statutes, an atmosphere of high jurisprudence, photographs of Justice Holmes and Learned Hand. Before the Depression Alec had been a rich kid. Not big-rich, only neighborhood-rich. But I knew rich kids. I had studied rich kids at the very top of society—as in the case of Bobby Kennedy. Von Humboldt Fleisher who always claimed that he had been one was not a real rich boy while Alec Szathmar who had been a rich boy told everyone that he was really a poet. In college he proved this by possession. He owned the works of Eliot, Pound, and Yeats. He memorized "Prufrock," which became one of his assets. But the Depression hit the Szathmars hard and he didn't get the silk-stocking education his doting scheming old father hoped to give him. However, just as Alec in boyhood had had bikes and chemistry sets and

BB guns and fencing foils and tennis rackets and boxing gloves and skates and ukuleles, he now owned all the latest IBM equipment, conference phones, desk computers, transistor wristwatches, Xerox machines, tape recorders, and hundreds of thick law books.

He had gained weight after his coronary, when he should have thinned down. Always a conservative dresser he tried to cover his broad can with double-vented jackets. So he looked like a giant thrush. The exceedingly human face of this bird was framed with stormy white sideburns. The warm brown eyes full of love and friendship were not especially honest. One of C. G. Jung's observations helped me to make sense of Szathmar. Some minds, said Jung, belong to earlier periods of history. Among our contemporaries there are Babylonians and Carthaginians or types from the Middle Ages. To me Szathmar was an eighteenth-century cavalryman, a follower of Pandour von Trenck, the cousin of my lucky Trenck. His padded swarthy cheeks, his Roman nose, his mutton-chop whiskers, his fat chest wide hips neat feet and virile cleft chin attracted women. Whom women will embrace is one of the unfathomable mysteries. But of course the race has to keep going. Anyway, here was Szathmar waiting to receive me. In his chair his posture suggested clumsy but unshakable sexual horsemanship atop pretty ladies. His arms were crossed, like the arms of Rodin's *Balzac*. Unfortunately he still looked a bit ill. Almost everyone downtown seemed to me a touch sick these days.

"Alec, who is this Renata Koffritz? Brief me." Szathmar took a warm interest in his clients, especially the attractive women. They got sympathy from him, psychiatric guidance practical advice and even touches of art and philosophy. And he briefed me: only child; kooky mother; no father in sight; ran away to Mexico with her high-school art teacher; fetched back; ran away later to Berkeley; found in one of those California touch-therapy groups; married off to Koffritz, a salesman whose line was crypts and tombs—

"Hold it. Have you seen him? A tall fellow? Brown beard? Why, he's the man who gave old Myron Swiebel a sales pitch in the Russian Bath on Division Street!"

Szathmar was not impressed by the coincidence. He said, "She's just about the finest piece I ever got a divorce for. She's got a little boy who's quite sweet. I thought of you. You can see action with this woman."

"Have you already seen some?"

"What, her lawyer?"

"Don't give me the ethical bit. If you haven't made a pass it's because she hasn't paid the retainer."

"I know your view of my profession. To you all business is fraud."

"Since Denise went on the warpath I've seen plenty of business. You fixed me up with Forrest Tomchek, one of the biggest names in this branch of law. It was like laying a speck of confetti in front of a jumbo vacuum cleaner."

Gigantically glowering, Szathmar said, "Poo!" He spat air to the side, symbolically. "You stupid prick, I had to beg Tomchek to take the case. He did me a favor as a colleague. A man like that! Why he wouldn't put you in his fish tank for an ornament. Board chairmen and bank presidents beg for his time, you twerp. Tomchek! Tomchek belongs to a family of legal statesmen. And an ace fighter-pilot in the Pacific."

"He's a crook all the same and he's incompetent besides. Denise is a thousand times smarter. She studied the documents and caught him in a minute. He didn't even make a routine check of titles to see who legally owned what. Don't give *me* the dignity of the bar, friend! But let's not hassle. Tell me about this girl."

He rose from his office chair. I've been in the White House, I've sat in the President's chair in the Oval Room, and Szathmar's, I swear, is finer leather. Framed pictures of his father and his grandfather on the wall reminded me of old days on the West Side. My feeling toward Szathmar was after all family feeling.

"I picked her for you as soon as she came through that door. I keep you in mind, Charlie. Your life hasn't been happy."

"Don't exaggerate."

"Unhappy," he insisted. "Wasted talent and advantages, obstinate as hell, perverse proud and pissing everything away. All those connections of yours in New York Washington Paris London and Rome, all your achievements, your knack with words, your luck—because you've been lucky. What I could have done with that! And you had to marry that yenta West

Side broad from a family of ward politicians and punchboard gamblers of candy-store kikes and sewer inspectors. That pretentious Vassar girl! Because she talked like a syllabus, and you were dying for understanding and conversation and she had culture. And I who love you, who always loved you, you stupid son of a bitch, I who have had this big glow for you since we were ten years old, and lie awake nights thinking: how do I save Charlie now; how do I protect his dough; find him tax shelters; get him the best legal defense; fix him up with good women. Why you nitwit, you low-grade moron, you don't even know what such love means."

I must tell you that I enjoyed Szathmar in this vein. As he was giving me the works like this his eyes kept turning to the left, where no one stood. If someone were standing there, some objective witness, he would support indignant Szathmar. Szathmar's dear mother had this same trait. She too summoned justice from empty space in this outraged way, laying both hands on her bosom. In Szathmar's breast there was a large true virile heart whereas I had no heart at all, only a sort of chicken giblet—that was how he saw things. He pictured himself as a person of heroic vitality, mature, wise, pagan, Tritonesque. But his real thoughts were all of getting on top, of intromission and all the dirty tricks that he called sexual freedom. But he also had to think how to make his monthly nut. His expenses were high. How to combine these different needs was the question. He told me once, "I was into the sexual revolution before anybody even heard of it."

But I have another thing to tell you. I was ashamed of us both. I had no business to look down on Szathmar. All this reading of mine has taught me a thing or two, after all. I understand a little the middle-class endeavor of two centuries to come out looking well, to preserve a certain darling innocence—the innocence of Clarissa defending herself against the lewdness of Lovelace. Hopeless! Even worse is the discovery that one has been living out certain greeting-card sentiments, with ribbons of middle-class virtue tied in a bow around one's heart. This sort of abominable American innocence is rightly detested by the world, which scented it in Woodrow Wilson in 1919. As schoolchildren we were taught boy-scout honor and goodness and courtesy; strange ghosts of Victorian gentility still haunt the hearts of Chicago's children, now in their fifties and sixties. This appeared in Szathmar's belief in his own generosity and greatness of heart, and also in my thanking God that I would never be as gross as Alec Szathmar. To atone I let him go on denouncing me. But when I thought that he had ranted long enough, I said to him, "How's your health?"

He didn't like this. He acknowledged no infirmities. "I'm fine," he said. "Not that you ran from court to ask me that. I just have to lose some weight."

"Shave your sideburns, too, while you're making improvements. They make you look like the bad guy in an old Western—one of those fellows who sold guns and firewater to the redskins."

"Okay, Charlie, I'm nothing but a would-be swinger. I'm a decaying squaw man, while you think only of higher things. You're noble. I'm a creep. But did you or did you not come to ask about this broad!"

"That's true, I did," I said.

"Don't knock yourself out for that. It's at least a sign of life, and you haven't got all that many. I just about gave up on you when you turned down that Felicia with the beautiful knockers. She's a nice middle-aged woman and would have been grateful to you. Her husband plays around. She adored you. She would have blessed you to the end of her days for treating her right. This is a decent housewife and mother who would have taken care of you from top to bottom, and washed and cooked and baked and shopped, and even done your accounts, and nice in the sack. She would have kept her mouth shut because she's married. Perfect. But to you it was only another of my vulgar ideas." He stared angrily. Then he said, "Okay, I'll fix it with this chick. Take her for a drink at the Palmer House tomorrow. I'll arrange the details."

If I was susceptible to the West Side sex malaria, Szathmar could not resist the arranging fever. His one aim now was to get Renata and me into bed, where he would be present in spirit. Maybe he hoped it would eventually develop into a threesome. He, like Cantabile, occasionally suggested fantasy combinations. "Now, listen," he said. "During daylight hours you can get a hotel room at what they call Conference Rates.

I'll reserve one. I'm holding money for you in escrow and they can bill me."

"If we're only having a drink, how do you know it'll get as far as the room?"

"That's up to you. The bartender will be holding the room key. Slip him five bucks and he'll hand over the envelope."

"In what name will the envelope be?"

"Not the stainless name of Citrine, hey?"

"What about Crawley as a name."

"Our old Latin teacher. Old Crawley! *Est avis in dextra melior quam quattuor extra.*"

So the next day Renata and I went to have a drink in the dark bar below street level. I promised myself that this would be absolutely my last idiocy. To myself I put it all as intelligently as possible: that we couldn't evade History, and that this was what History was doing to everybody. History had decreed that men and women had to become acquainted in these embraces. I was going to find out whether or not Renata was really my Fate, whether the true Jungian anima was in her. She might turn out to be something far different. But one sexual touch would teach me that, for women had peculiar effects on me, and if they didn't make me ecstatic they made me ill. There were no two ways about it.

On this wet gloomy day the Wabash El was dripping but Renata redeemed the weather. She wore a plastic raincoat divided into red, white, and black bands, a Rothko design. In this gleamy hard-surfaced coat she sat fully buttoned in the dark booth. A broad, bent-brim hat was part of the costume. The banana-fragrant lipstick of her beautiful mouth matched the Rothko red. Her remarks made little sense but then she spoke little. She laughed considerably and quickly turned extremely pale. A candle in a round-bottomed glass wrapped in a fishnet kind of thing gave a small quantity of light. Presently her face settled low on the hard buckling glamorous plastic of her coat and became very round. I couldn't believe that the kind of broad described by Szathmar—so ready for action, so experienced, would down four martinis and that her face would grow so white, whiter than the moon when seen at 3 p.m. I wondered at first whether she might not be feigning timidity out of courtesy to a man of an older generation, but a cold gin moisture came out on her beautiful face and she appeared to be appealing to me to do something. In all this so far there was an element of *déjà vu*, for after all I had been through this more than once. What was different now was that I felt sympathetic and even protective toward this young woman in her unexpected weakness. I thought I understood simply enough why I was in the black and subcellar bar. Conditions were very tough. One couldn't make it without love. Why not? I was unable to budge this belief. It had perhaps the great weight of stupidity in it. This need for love (in such a generalized state) was an awful drag. If it should ever become publicly known that I whispered "My Fate!" as elevator doors were opening the Legion of Honor might justifiably ask to have its medal back. And the most constructive interpretation I could find at the time was the Platonic one that Eros was using my desires to lead me from the awful spot I was in toward wisdom. That was nice, it had class, but I don't think it was a bit true (for one thing there was not perhaps all that much Eros left). The big name if I must have one, if any supernatural powers troubled themselves about me, was not Eros, it was probably Ahriman, the principal potentate of darkness. Be that as it might, it was time to get Renata out of this joint.

I went to the bar and leaned over discreetly. I interposed myself among the drinkers. On any ordinary day I would have described these people as barflies and lushes but now their eyes all seemed to me as big as portholes and shed a moral light. The bartender came over. Between the knuckles of my left hand was folded a five-dollar bill. Szathmar had told me exactly how to do this. I asked the bartender whether there was an envelope in the name of Crawley. Immediately he took the five bucks. He had the kind of alertness you find only in a big town. "Now," he said, "what's this envelope?"

"Left for Crawley."

"I got no Crawley."

"Crawley must be there. Look again, if you don't mind."

He rattled through his envelopes again. Each contained a room key.

"What's your first name, buddy? Give me another clue."

Tormented, I said in a low voice, "Charles."

"That's better. Could this be you—C-I-T-R-I-N-E?"

"I know how to spell it, for Christ's sake," I said, faint but furious. I muttered, "Stupid fucking baboon Szathmar. Never did anything right in all his life. And me!—still depending on him to make my arrangements." Then I became aware that someone was trying to get my attention from behind, and I turned. I saw a middle-aged person smiling. She obviously knew me and was bursting with gladness. This lady was stout and gentle, snub-nosed, high in the bust. She appealed for recognition but at the same time tacitly confessed that the years had changed her. But was she as changed as all that? I said, "Yes?"

"You don't know me, I see. But you're still the same old Charlie."

"I can never understand why bars have to be dark as all this," I said.

"But Charlie, it's Naomi—your school-days' sweetheart."

"Naomi Lutz!"

"How wonderful to run into you, Charlie."

"How do you happen to be at the bar of this hotel?"

A woman alone at a bar is, as a rule, a hooker. Naomi was too old for that trade. Besides, it was inconceivable that Naomi who had been my girl at fifteen should have turned into a bar broad.

"Oh, no," she said. "My Dad is here. He'll be right back. I bring him downtown from the nursing home at least once a week for a drink. You remember how he always adored to be in the Loop."

"Old Doc Lutz—just think!"

"Yes, alive. Very old. And he and I've been watching you with that lovely thing in the booth. Forgive me Charlie, but how you men keep going is unfair to females. How marvelous for you. Daddy was saying that he shouldn't have interfered with us, child sweethearts."

"I was more than your childhood sweetheart," I said. "I loved you with my soul, Naomi." Saying this I was aware that I had brought one woman to the bar and was making a passionate declaration to another. However, this was the truth, involuntary spontaneous truth. "I've often thought, Naomi, that I lost my character altogether because I couldn't spend my life with you. It distorted me all over, it made me ambitious cunning complex stupid vengeful. If I had been able to hold you in my arms nightly since the age of fifteen I would never have feared the grave."

"Oh Charlie, tell it to the Marines. It always was wonderful the way you talked. But off-putting too. You've had lots and lots of women. I can see by your behavior in that booth."

"Ah, yes—to the Marines!" I was grateful for this antique slang. First of all it checked my effusion, which would have led to nothing. Secondly it relieved me of the weight of another impression that had been gathering in the dark bar. I traced this to the idea that soon after death, when the lifeless body fell into decay and became a lot of minerals again, the soul awoke to its new existence, and an instant after death I expected to find myself in a dark place similar to this bar. Where all who had ever loved each other might meet again, etcetera. And this was my impression here in the bar. With the "Conference Room" key in my hand, the links clinking, I knew I must get back to Renata. If she was still drinking her martini she would be too bombed to rise to her feet and get out of the booth. But I had to wait now for Dr. Lutz. And here he came from the men's room, very weak and bald, and snub-nosed like his daughter. His Twenties Babbittry had faded into old-fashioned courtliness. He had demanded a strange courtesy from us, for though he had never been a real doctor, only a foot-doctor (he had kept offices downtown and at home too), he insisted on being called Doctor and flew into a rage if anyone said Mr. Lutz. Fascinated by being a doctor he treated diseases of many kinds, up to the knee. If feet, why not legs? I recalled that he asked me in to assist him when he was laying a purple jelly of his own mixture on horrible sores that punctured the legs of a lady who worked at the National Biscuit factory. I held the jar and the applicators for him and as he filled these holes he made confident quack conversation. I valued this woman for she always brought the doctor a shoe box filled with chocolate-marshmallow puffs and devil's-food bars. As I remembered this, pulsations of chocolate sweetness came into the roof of my mouth. And then I saw myself sitting ecstatic in Dr. Lutz's treatment chair while a snowstorm blackened the tiny offices painted clinical white and I read *Herodias.* Moved by the decapitation of John the Baptist I went into Naomi's room. We were alone during the blizzard. I took off her warm terrycloth blue pajamas and saw her naked. These were the recollections that closed in on my heart. Naomi was no foreign body to me. That was just it. There was nothing alien in Naomi. My feeling for her went into her cells, into the very molecules that, being hers, all had her properties. Because I had conceived of Naomi without otherness, because of this passion, I was trapped by old Doc Lutz in a Jacob-Laban relationship. I had to help him wash his Auburn, a celestial blue car with white-wall tires. I poured from the hose and rubbed with the shammy while the Doctor in white linen golf knickers stood smoking a Cremo cigar.

"Oh Charlie Citrine, you surely have gone places," said the old gentleman. His voice was still lyrical, high, and quite empty. He never had been able to make you feel that he was saying anything at all substantial. "Though I was a Coolidge and Hoover Republican myself, still when the Kennedys had you to the White House I was so proud."

"Is that young woman your speed?" said Naomi.

"I can't honestly say that I know. And what are you doing with yourself, Naomi?"

"My marriage was no good at all and my husband went on the loose. I think you know that. I brought two kids up anyway. You didn't happen to read some articles by my son in the *Southwest Township Herald*?"

"No. I wouldn't have known they were by your son."

"He wrote about kicking the drug habit, based on personal experience. I wish you would give me an opinion on his writing. My daughter is a doll but the boy is a problem."

"And you, Naomi, my dear?"

"I don't do much any more. I have a man friend. Part of the day I'm a crossing guard at the grammar school."

Old Doc Lutz seemed to hear none of this.

"It's a pity," I said.

"About you and me? No it's not. You and your mental life would have been a strain on me. I'm into sports. My bag is football on TV. It's a big outing when we get passes to

Soldiers' Field or to the hockey game. Early dinner at the Como Inn, we take the bus to the stadium, and I actually wait for fights on the ice and holler when they knock out their teeth. I'm afraid I'm just a common woman."

When Naomi said "common" and Doc Lutz said "Republican" they meant that they had joined the great American public and thus found contentment and fulfillment. To have been a foot doctor in the Loop during the Thirties gave the old fellow joy. His daughter delivered a similar message about herself. They were pleased with themselves and with each other and happy in their likeness. Only I, mysteriously a misfit, stood between them with my key. Obviously what ailed me was my unlikeness. I was an old friend, only I was not wholly American.

"I've got to go," I said.

"Couldn't we have a beer together sometime? I'd love to see you," said Naomi. "You could advise me about Louie better than anybody. You haven't got hippie kids yourself have you?" And as I took her number she said, "Oh, look Doc, what a neat little book he writes in. Everything about Charlie is so elegant. What a handsome old guy you're turning into. But you're not the type any woman could ever tie down." As they watched I went back to the booth and raised up Renata. I put on my hat and coat and pretended that we were going outside. I felt the dishonor of everybody.

The conference-rate room was just what lechers and adulterers deserved. Not much bigger than a broom closet it opened on the air shaft. Renata dropped into a chair and ordered two more martinis from room service. I pulled the shade, not for privacy—there were no windows opposite—and not as a seducer, but only because I hate to look into brick air shafts. Against the wall was a sofa bed covered in green chenille. As soon as I saw this object I knew it would defeat me. I was sure I would never be able to get it open. Once anticipated this challenge would not leave my head. I had to meet it at once. The trapezoid foam-rubber bolsters weighed nothing. I pushed them away and pulled off the fitted spread. The sheets under it were perfectly clean. Then I knelt and groped under the sofa frame for a lever. Renata watched silent as my face grew tight and reddened. I crouched and pulled, furious with manufacturers who made such junk, and with the management for taking money from afternoon conferees and crucifying them in spirit.

"This thing is like an IQ test," I said.

"So?"

"I'm flunking. I can't get the thing to open."

"So? Leave it."

There was room for only one on this narrow bed. To tell the truth however I had no desire to lie down.

Renata went into the bathroom. There were two chairs. I sat in the *fauteuil.* It had wings. Between my shoes was a square of colonial American hooked rug. The blood rustled circulating over my eardrums. Surly room service brought the martinis. A dollar tip was taken without thanks. Then Renata came out, the gleamy coat still fully buttoned. She sat on the sofa bed, sipped once or twice at her martini, and passed out. Through the plastic I tried to listen to her heart. She didn't have a cardiac condition, did she? Suppose this were serious. Could one call an ambulance? I felt her pulse, stupidly studying my watch, losing count. For comparison I took my own pulse. I couldn't coordinate the results. Her pulse seemed no worse than mine. Unconscious she had, if anything, the better of it. She was damp and felt cold. I wiped the chill from her with a corner of the sheet and tried to think what George Swiebel, my health counselor, would do in an emergency like this. I knew exactly what he'd do—straighten her legs remove her shoes and unbutton her coat to help the breathing. I did just that.

Under the coat Renata was naked. She had gone into the bathroom and taken off her clothes. After undoing the top button I might have stopped, but I didn't. Of course I had appraised Renata and tried to guess how she might be. My generous guesses had been far behind the facts. I hadn't expected everything to be so large and faultless. I had observed in the jury box that the first joint of her fingers was fleshy and began to swell slightly before it tapered. My conjecture was that her beautiful thighs must also swell toward each other in harmony with this. I found that to be the case, absolutely, and felt more like an art lover than a seducer. My quick impression, for I didn't keep her uncovered very long, was that every tissue was perfect, every fiber of hair was shining. The deep female odor arose from her. When I saw how things were I buttoned her up from sheer respect. I got things back into place as well as I knew how. Next I raised the window. Unfortunately it drove off her wonderful odor but she had to have fresh air. I took her clothing from behind the bathroom door and stuffed it into her large handbag, checking to make sure that we didn't lose her juror's badge. Then in my overcoat, with hat and gloves in hand, I waited for her to come to.

The same things are done by us, over and over, with terrible predictability. One may be forgiven, in view of this, for wishing at least to associate with beauty.

AND now—with her fur coat and her wonderful, soft, versatile, flexible amethyst hat, with belly and thighs under an intermediate sheath of silk—Renata dropped me in front of the county building. And she and her client, the big potent-looking lady in the polka-dot poplin, said, "*Ciao*, so long." And there was the handsome russet and glass skyscraper, and there was the insignificant Picasso sculpture with its struts and its sheet metal, no wings, no victory, only a token, a reminder, only the *idea* of a work of art. Very similar, I thought, to the other ideas or reminders by which we lived—no more apples but the idea, the pomologist's reconstruction of what an apple once was, no more ice cream but the idea, the recollection of something delicious made of substitutes, of starch, glucose, and other chemicals, no more sex but the idea or reminiscence of that, and so with love, belief, thought, and so on. On this theme I rose in an elevator to see what the court, with its specters of equity and justice, wanted of me. When the door of the elevator opened, it merely opened, no voice said, "My Fate!" Either Renata really filled the bill, or the voice had become too discouraged to speak.

I got out and saw my lawyer Forrest Tomchek and his junior associate Billy Srole waiting at the end of the wide open light gray corridor outside Judge Urbanovich's courtroom—two honest-looking deceitful men. According to Szathmar (Szathmar who couldn't even remember a simple name like Crawley), I was represented by Chicago's finest legal talent.

I said, "Then why don't I feel safe with Tomchek?"

"Because you're hypercritical, nervous, and a damn fool," said Szathmar. "In his branch of the law nobody has more respect and clout. Tomchek is one of the most powerful guys in the legal community. In Divorce and Post-Decree these guys form a club. They commute, they play golf, they fly to Acapulco together. Behind the scenes, he tells the other guys how it's all going to be done. Understand? That includes the fees, the tax consequences. Everything."

"You mean," I said, "they'll study my tax returns and so forth and then decide how to cut me up."

"My God!" said Szathmar. "Keep your opinion of lawyers to yourself." He was deeply offended, infuriated really, by my disrespect for his profession. Oh, I agreed with him that I must keep my feelings to myself. I made every effort to be pleasant and deferential to Tomchek, but I wasn't very good at this. The harder I tried, murmuring at Tomchek's pretensions, saying the right thing, the more he mistrusted and disliked me. He kept score. In the end I would pay a heavy price, an enormous fee, I knew that. So here was Tomchek. With him stood Billy Srole, the associate. Associate is a wonderful word, a wonderful category. Srole was chubby, pale, his attitude highly professional. He wore his hair long and kept it flowing by stroking it with a heavy white palm and looping it behind the ears. His fingers bent backward at the tips. He was a bully. These were bully refinements. I know bullies.

"What's up," I said.

Tomchek put his arm about my shoulder and we went into a brief huddle.

"Nothing to worry about," said Tomchek. "Urbanovich was suddenly free to meet with both parties."

"He wants to wrap the thing up. He's proud of his record as a negotiator," Srole told me.

"Look, Charlie," said Tomchek. "Here's the technique Urbanovich uses. He'll throw a scare into you. He'll tell you how much harm he can do and stampede you into an agreement. Don't panic. Legally we've put you in a good position."

I saw the healthy grim folds of Tomchek's close-shaven face. His breath was sourly virile. He gave off an odor which I associated with old-fashioned streetcar brakes, and with metabolism, and with male hormones. "No, I won't give any more ground," I said. "It doesn't work. If I meet her demands she makes brand-new ones. Since the Emancipation Proclamation there's been a secret struggle in this country to restore slavery by other means." This was the sort of statement that caused Tomchek and Srole to be suspicious of me.

"Okay, draw the line and hold it," said Srole. "And leave the rest to us. Denise makes things tough for her own lawyer. Pinsker doesn't want a hassle. He only wants his dough. He doesn't like this situation. She's getting legal advice on the side from that fellow Schwirner. Completely unethical."

"I hate Schwirner! That son of a bitch," said Tomchek, violent. "If I could prove that he was banging the plaintiff and interfering in my case I'd fix his clock for him. I'd have him before the Ethics Committee."

"Is Gumballs Schwirner still carrying on with Charlie's wife?" said Srole. "I thought he just got married."

"So what if he got married? He still hasn't stopped meeting this crazy broad in motels. She gets strategy ideas from him in the sack, then she bugs Pinsker with them. They're confusing the hell out of Pinsker. How I'd love to get that Schwirner."

I offered no comment and scarcely seemed to hear what they were saying. Tomchek wanted me to suggest that we hire a private investigator to get the goods on Schwirner. I recalled Von Humboldt Fleisher and Scaccia, the private eye. I was having no part of this. "I expect you guys to restrain Pinsker," I said. "Don't let him tear at my guts."

"What, in chambers? He'll behave himself. He rags you on the witness stand but in conference it's different."

"He's an animal," I said.

They answered nothing.

"He's a beast, a cannibal."

This made an unpleasant impression. Tomchek and Srole, like Szathmar, were touchy about the profession. Tomchek remained silent. It was for Srole, the associate and stooge, to deal with captious Citrine. Mild, distant, Srole said, "Pinsker is a very tough man. Tough opponent. A gut fighter."

Okay, they weren't going to let me knock lawyers. Pinsker belonged to the club. Who, after all, was I? A filmy transient figure, eccentric and snooty. They disliked my style entirely.

They hated it. But then why should they like it? Suddenly I saw the thing from their viewpoint. And I was extremely pleased. In fact I was illuminated. Maybe these sudden illuminations of mine were an effect of the metaphysical changes I was undergoing. Under the recent influence of Steiner I seldom thought of death in the horrendous old way. I wasn't experiencing the suffocating grave or dreading an eternity of boredom, nowadays. Instead I often felt unusually light and swift-paced, as if I were on a weightless bicycle and sprinting through the star world. Occasionally I saw myself with exhilarating objectivity, literally as an object among objects in the physical universe. One day that object would cease to move and when the body collapsed the soul would simply remove itself. So, to speak again of the lawyers, I stood between them, and there we were, three naked egos, three creatures belonging to the lower grade of modern rationality and calculation. In the past the self had had garments, the garments of station, of nobility or inferiority, and each self had its carriage, its looks, wore the sheath appropriate to it. Now there were no sheaths and it was naked self with naked self burning intolerably and causing terror. I saw this now, in a fit of objectivity. It felt ecstatic.

What was I to these fellows anyway? An oddball and a curiosity. To build himself up Szathmar bragged about me, he oversold me, and people became horribly annoyed because he told them to look me up in reference books and read about my prizes and my medals and Zig-Zag awards. He hammered them with this, he said they should be proud to have a client like me so of course they detested me sight unseen. The quintessence of their prejudice was once expressed by Szathmar himself when he lost his temper and shouted, "You're nothing but a prick with a pen!" He was so sore that he surpassed himself and yelled even louder, "With or without a pen you're a prick!" But I wasn't offended. I thought this was a whopping epithet and I laughed. If you only put it right you could say what you liked to me. However, I knew exactly how I made Tomchek and Srole feel. From their side they inspired me with an unusual thought. This was that History had created something new in the USA, namely crookedness with self-respect or duplicity with honor. America had always been very upright and moral, a model to the entire world, so it had put to death the very idea of hypocrisy and was forcing itself to live with this new imperative of sincerity, and it was doing an impressive job. Just consider Tomchek and Srole: they belonged to a prestigious honorable profession; that profession had its own high standards and everything was hotsy-totsy until some impossible exotic like me who couldn't even keep a wife in line, an idiot with a knack for stringing sentences together, came and disseminated a sense of wrongdoing. I carried an old accusing smell. It was, if you see what I mean, totally unhistorical of me. Owing to this I got a filmy side glance from Billy Srole, as if he were bemused by all the things he could do to me, under law or near the law, if I should ever step out of line. Watch out! He'd hack me up, he'd chop me into bits with his legal cleaver. Tomchek's eyes, unlike Srole's, needed no film, for his deeper opinions never reached his gaze. And I was completely dependent upon this fearful pair. In fact this was part of my ecstasy. It was terrific. Tomchek and Srole were just what I deserved. It was only right that I should pay a price for coming on so innocent and expecting the protection of those less pure, of people completely at home in the fallen world. Where did I get off, laying the fallen world on everyone else! Humboldt had used his credit as a poet when he was a poet no longer, but only crazy with schemes. And I was doing much the same thing, for I was really far too canny to claim such unworldliness. I believe the word is disingenuous. But Tomchek and Srole would set me straight. They had the assistance of Denise, Pinsker, Urbanovich, and a cast of thousands.

"I wish I knew what the hell made you look so pleased," said Srole.

"Only a thought."

"Lucky you, with your nice thoughts."

"But when do we go in?" I said.

"When the other side comes out."

"Oh, are Denise and Pinsker talking to Urbanovich now? Then I think I'll go and relax in the courtroom, my feet are beginning to hurt." A little of Tomchek and Srole went a long way. I wasn't going to stand chatting with them until we were summoned. My consciousness couldn't take much more of them. They quickly tired me.

I refreshed myself by sitting on a wooden bench. I had no book to read, I took this opportunity to meditate briefly. The object I chose for meditation was a bush covered with roses. I often summoned up this bush, but sometimes it made its appearance independently. It was filled, it was dense, it was choked with tiny dark garnet roses and fresh healthy leaves. So for the moment I thought "rose"—"rose" and nothing else. I visualized the twigs, the roots, the harsh fuzz of the new growth hardening into spikes, plus all the botany I could remember: phloem xylem cambium chloroplasts soil sun water chemistry, attempting to project myself into the very plant and to think how its green blood produced a red flower. Ah, but new growth in rosebushes was always red before it turned green. I recalled very accurately the inset spiral order of rose petals, the whitey faint bloom over the red and the slow opening that revealed the germinating center. I concentrated all the faculties of my soul on this vision and immersed it in the flowers. Then I saw, next to these flowers, a human figure standing. The plant, said Rudolf Steiner, expressed the pure passionless laws of growth, but the human being, aiming at higher perfection, assumed a greater burden—instincts, desires, emotions. So a bush was a sleeping life. But mankind took a chance on the passions. The wager was that the higher powers of the soul could cleanse these passions. Cleansed, they could be reborn in a finer form. The red of the blood was a symbol of this cleansing process. But even if all this wasn't so, to consider the roses always put me into a kind of bliss.

After a while I contemplated something else. I visualized an old black iron Chicago lamppost from forty years back, the type with a lid like a bullfighter's hat or a cymbal. Now it was night, there was a blizzard. I was a young boy and I watched from my bedroom window. It was a winter gale, the wind and snow banged the iron lamp, and the roses rotated under the light. Steiner recommended the contemplation of a cross wreathed with roses but for reasons of perhaps Jewish origin I preferred a lamppost. The object didn't matter as long as you went out of the sensible world. When you got out of the sensible world, you might feel parts of the soul awakening that never had been awake before.

I had made quite a lot of progress in this exercise when Denise came out of the chambers and passed through the swinging gate to join me.

This woman, the mother of my children, though she made so much trouble for me, often reminded me of something Samuel Johnson had said about pretty ladies: they might be foolish, they might be wicked, but beauty was of itself very estimable. Denise was in this way estimable. She had big violet eyes and a slender nose. Her skin was slightly downy—you could see this down when the light was right. Her hair was piled on top of her head and gave it too much weight. If she hadn't been beautiful you wouldn't have noticed the disproportion. The very fact that she wasn't aware of the top-heavy effect of her coiffure seemed at times a proof that she was a bit nutty. At court, having dragged me here with her suit, she always wanted to be chummy. And as she was unusually pleasant today I figured she had had a successful session with Urbanovich. The fact that she was going to beat me like a dog released her affections. For she was fond of me. She said, "Ah, you're waiting?" and her voice was high and tremulous, breaking slightly, but also militant. The weak, at war, never know how hard they are hitting you. She wasn't of course so weak. The strength of the social order was on her side. But she always felt weak, she was a burdened woman. Getting out of bed to make breakfast was almost more than she could face. Taking a cab to the hairdresser was also very hard. The beautiful head was a burden to the beautiful neck. So she sat down beside me, sighing. She hadn't been to the beauty salon lately. When her hair was thinned out by the hairdresser she didn't look quite so huge-eyed and goofy. There were holes in her stockings, for she always wore rags to court. "I'm absolutely exhausted," she said. "I never get any sleep before these court days."

I muttered, "Dreadfully sorry."

"You don't seem so well yourself."

"The girls tell me sometimes, 'Daddy, you look like a million dollars—green and wrinkled.' How are they, Denise?"

"As well as they can be. They miss you."

"That's normal, I suppose."

"Nothing is normal for them. They miss you painfully."

"You are to sorrow what Vermont is to syrup."

"What do you want me to say?"

"Only 'okay,' or 'not okay,'" I said.

"Syrup! As soon as something enters your head you blurt it out. That's your big weakness, your worst temptation."

This was my day to see the other fellow's point of view. How does anyone strengthen himself? Denise had it right, you know —by overcoming the persistent temptation. There've been times when just because I kept my mouth shut and didn't say what I thought, I felt my strength increasing. Still, I don't seem to know what I think till I see what I say.

"The girls are making Christmas plans. You're supposed to take them to the pageant at the Goodman Theater."

"No, nothing doing. That's your idea."

"Are you too big a figure to take them to a show like any ordinary father? You told them you would."

"Me? Never. You did that yourself, and now you imagine that I told them."

"You're going to be in town, aren't you?"

I wasn't in fact. I was leaving on Friday. I hadn't gotten around to informing Denise of this, and I said nothing now.

"Or are you planning a trip with Renata Fat-Tits?"

On this level, I was no match for Denise. Again, Renata! She wouldn't even allow the children to play with little Roger Koffritz. She once said, "Later they'll become immune to that kind of whore influence. But they came home once shaking their little behinds and I knew you had broken your promise to keep them away from Renata." Denise's information network was unusually effective. She knew all about Harold Flonzaley, for instance. "How is your rival the undertaker?" she sometimes asked me. For Renata's suitor Flonzaley owned a chain of funeral parlors. One of her ex-husband's business connections, Flonzaley had a ton of money, but his degree from the state university, it couldn't be denied, was in embalming. This gave our romance a gloomy tinge. I quarreled once with Renata because her apartment was filled with flowers and I knew that they were surplus funeral flowers abandoned by heartbroken mourners and delivered in Flonzaley's special flower-Cadillac. I made her throw them down the rubbish chute. Flonzaley was still wooing her.

"Are you working at all?" said Denise.

"Not too much."

"Just playing paddle ball with Langobardi, relaxing with the Mafia? I know you aren't seeing any of your serious friends on the Midway. Durnwald would give you what-for but he's in Scotland. Too bad. I know he doesn't like Fat-Tits much more than I do. And he told me once how he disapproved of your buddy Thaxter, and your being involved in *The Ark*. You've spent a barrel of money probably on that magazine, and where is the first issue? *Nessuno sa.*" Denise was an opera lover and she took a season ticket at the Lyric and quoted often from Mozart or from Verdi. *Nessuno sa* was from *Così Fan Tutte*. Where does one find the fidelity of women, sings Mozart's worldly wiseman—*dove sia? dove sia? Nessu-no sa!* Again she was referring to the curious delinquency of Renata, and I knew it perfectly well.

"As a matter of fact, I'm expecting Thaxter. Maybe today."

"Sure, he'll blow into town like the entire cast of *A Midsummer Night's Dream*. You'd rather foot his bills than give the money to your children."

"My children have plenty of money. You have the house and hundreds of thousands. You got all the *Trenck* money, you and the lawyers."

"I can't keep that barn going. The fourteen-foot ceilings. You haven't seen the fuel bills. But then again you could squander your money on worse people than Thaxter, and you do. Thaxter at least has some style. He took us to Wimbledon in plenty of style. Remember? With a hamper. With champagne and smoked salmon from Harrods. From what I understand, it was the CIA that was picking up his tab in those days. Why not get the CIA to pay for *The Ark*?"

"Why the CIA?"

"I read your prospectus. I thought this was just the kind of serious intellectual magazine the CIA could use abroad for propaganda. You imagine you're some kind of cultural statesman."

"All I wanted to say in the prospectus was that America didn't have to fight scarcity and we all felt guilty before people who still had to struggle for bread and freedom in the old way, the old basic questions. We weren't starving, we weren't bugged by the police, locked up in madhouses for our ideas, arrested, deported, slave laborers sent to die in concentration camps. We were spared the holocausts and nights of terror. With our advantages we should be formulating the new basic questions for mankind. But instead we sleep. Just sleep and sleep, and eat and play and fuss and sleep again."

"When you get solemn you're a riot, Charlie. And now you're going in for mysticism, as well as keeping that fat broad, as well as becoming an athlete, as well as dressing like a dude—all symptoms of mental and physical decline. I'm so sorry, really. Not just because I'm the mother of your children, but because you once had brains and talent. You might have stayed productive if the Kennedys had lived. Their kind of action kept you responsible and sane."

"You sound like the late Humboldt. He was going to be Czar of Culture under Stevenson."

"The old Humboldt hang-up, too. You've still got that. He was the last serious friend you had," she said.

In these conversations, always somewhat dreamlike, Denise believed that she was concerned, solicitous, even loving. The fact that she had gone into judge's chambers and dug another legal pit for me was irrelevant. In her view we were like England and France, dear enemies. For her it was a special relationship, permitting intelligent exchanges.

"People tell me about this Dr. Scheldt, your anthroposophist guru. They say he's very kind and nice. But his daughter is a real little popsie. A small opportunist. She wants you to marry her, too. You're a fearful challenge to females who have dreams of glory about you. But you can always hide behind poor Demmie Vonghel."

Denise was pelting me with the ammunition she stored up daily in her mind and heart. Again, however, her information was accurate. Like Renata and the old Señora, Miss Scheldt also spoke of May–December marriages, of the happiness and creativity of Picasso's declining years, of Casals and Charlie Chaplin and Justice Douglas.

"Renata doesn't want you to be a mystic, does she?"

"Renata doesn't meddle that way. I'm not a mystic. Anyway I don't know why mystic should be such a bad word. It doesn't mean much more than the word religion, which some people still speak of with respect. What does religion say? It says that there's something in human beings beyond the body and brain and that we have ways of knowing that go beyond the organism and its senses. I've always believed that. My misery comes, maybe, from ignoring my own metaphysical hunches. I've been to college so I know the educated answers. Test me on the scientific world-view and I'd score high. But it's just head stuff."

"You're a born crank, Charlie. When you said you were going to write that essay on boredom, I thought, There he goes! Now you're degenerating quickly, without me. Sometimes I feel you might be certifiable or committable. Why don't you go back to the Washington-in-the-Sixties book? The stuff you published in magazines was fine. You've told me lots more that never got into print. If you've lost your notes, I could remind you. I can still straighten you out, Charlie."

"You think you can?"

"I understand the mistakes we both made. And the way you live is too grotesque—all these girls, and the athletics and trips, and now the anthroposophy. Your friend Durnwald is upset about you. And I know your brother Julius is worried. Look, Charlie, why don't you marry me again? For starters we could stop the legal fight. We should become reunited."

"Is this a serious proposition?"

"It's what the girls want more than anything. Think it over. You're not exactly leading a life of joy. You're in bad shape. I'd be taking a risk." She stood up and opened her purse. "Here are a few letters that came to the old address."

I looked at the postmarks. "They're months old. You might have turned them over before, Denise."

"What's the difference? You get too much mail as it is. You don't answer most of it, and what good does it do you?"

"You've opened this one and resealed it. It's from Humboldt's widow."

"Kathleen? They were divorced years before he died. Anyway, here comes your legal talent."

Tomchek and Srole entered the courtroom, and from the other side came Cannibal Pinsker in a bright yellow double-knit jazzy suit and a large yellow cravat that lay on his shirt like a cheese omelette, and tan shoes in two tones. His head was brutally hairy. He was grizzled and he carried himself like an old prizefighter. What might he have been in an earlier incarnation, I wondered. I wondered about us all.

WE were not meeting with Denise and Pinsker after all, only with the judge. Tomchek, Srole, and I entered his chambers. Judge Urbanovich, a Croatian, perhaps a Serbian, was plump and bald, a fatty, and somewhat flat-faced. But he was cordial, he was very civilized. He offered us a cup of coffee. I referred his cordiality to the Department of Vigilance. "No, thanks," I said.

"We've now had five sessions in court," Urbanovich began. "This litigation is harmful to the parties—not to their lawyers, of course. Being on the stand is frightful for a sensitive creative person like Mr. Citrine. . . ." The judge meant me to feel the ironic weight of this. Sensitivity in a mature Chicagoan, if genuine, was a treatable form of pathology, but a man whose income passed two hundred thousand dollars in his peak years was putting you on about sensitivity. Sensitive plants didn't make that kind of dough. "It can't be pleasant," Judge Urbanovich now said to me, "to be examined by Mr. Pinsker. He belongs to the hard-edge school. He can't pronounce the titles of your works, or the names of French, Italian, or even English companies you deal with. Besides, you don't like his tailor, his taste in shirts and ties. . . ."

In short it was too bad to turn this ugly violent moron Pinsker loose on me but if I remained uncooperative, the judge would unleash him.

"Three, four, five separate times we've negotiated with Mrs. Citrine," said Tomchek.

"Your offers weren't good enough."

"Your honor, Mrs. Citrine has received large amounts of money," I said. "We offer more and she always increases her demands. If I capitulate, will you guarantee that I won't be back in court next year?"

"No, but I can try. I can make it *res judicata*. Your problem, Mr. Citrine, is your proven ability to earn big sums."

"Not lately."

"Only because you're upset by the litigation. If I end the litigation, I set you free and there's no limit to what you can make. You'll thank me. . . ."

"Judge, I'm old-fashioned and maybe even obsolete. I never learned mass-production methods."

"Don't be so nervous about this, Mr. Citrine. We have confidence in you. We've seen your articles in *Look* and in *Life*."

"But *Life* and *Look* have gone out of business. They're obsolete, too."

"We have your tax returns. They tell a different story."

"Still," said Forrest Tomchek. "In terms of reliable business forecast. How can my client promise to produce?"

Urbanovich said, "It's inconceivable, whatever happens, for Mr. Citrine ever to fall below the fifty-percent tax bracket. So if he pays Mrs. Citrine thirty thousand per annum it only costs him fifteen thousand in real dollars. Until the majority of the littlest daughter."

"So for the next fourteen years, or until I'm about seventy, I must earn one hundred thousand dollars a year. I can't help being a little amused by this, your Honor. Ha ha! I don't think my brain is strong enough, it's my only real asset. Other people have land, rent, inventories, management, capital gains, price supports, depletion allowances, federal subsidies. I have no such advantages."

"Ah but you're a clever person, Mr. Citrine. Even in Chicago that's obvious. So there's no need to put this on a special-case basis. In the property division under the decree Mrs. Citrine got less than half and she alleges that records were falsified. You are a bit dreamy and probably were not aware of this. Perhaps the records were falsified by others. Nevertheless you are responsible under the law."

Srole said, "We deny any kind of fraud."

"Well, I don't think fraud is a great issue here," said the judge—and made an "out-the-window" gesture with open hands. Pisces was evidently his astrological sign. He wore tiny fish cuff links, tail to head.

"As for Mr. Citrine's lowered productivity of recent years, this may be deliberate to balk the plaintiff. Or it may actually be that he is mentally in transition." The judge was having a good time, I could see that. Evidently he disliked Tomchek the Divorce Statesman, he agreed that Srole was only a stooge, and he was diverting himself with me. "I am sympathetic to the problems of intellectuals and I know you may get into special preoccupations that aren't lucrative. But I understand that this Maharishi fellow by teaching people to turn their tongues backward past the palate so that they can get the tip of the tongue into their own sinuses has become a multimillionaire. Many ideas are marketable and perhaps your special preoccupations are more lucrative than you realize," he said.

Anthroposophy was having definite effects. I couldn't take any of this too hard. Other-worldliness tinged it all and every little while my spirit seemed to disassociate itself. It left me and passed out of the window to float a bit over the civic plaza. Or else the meditative roses would start to glow in my head, set in dewy green. But the judge was giving me a going-over, reinterpreting the twentieth century for me, lest I forget, deciding how the rest of my life was to be spent. I was to quit being an old-time artisan and adopt the methods of soulless manufacture (Ruskin). Tomchek and Srole, at either side of the desk, in their hearts consented and agreed. They said almost nothing. Feeling deserted, vexed, I therefore spoke up for myself.

"So it's about half a million dollars more. And even if she remarries she wants a guaranteed income of ten thousand dollars?"

"True."

"And Mr. Pinsker is asking for a fee of thirty thousand—ten thousand dollars for each month he spent on the case?"

"That's not really so unreasonable," said the judge. "You haven't been hurt hard in the way of fees."

"It doesn't come to more than five hundred dollars an hour. That's what I figure my own time to be worth, especially when I have to do what I dislike," I said.

"Mr. Citrine," the judge said to me, "you've led a more or less bohemian life. Now you've had a taste of marriage, the family, middle-class institutions, and you want to drop out. But we can't allow you to dabble like that."

Suddenly my detachment ended and I found myself in a

state. I understood what emotions had torn at Humboldt's heart when they grabbed him and tied him up and raced him to Bellevue. The man of talent struggled with cops and orderlies. And, up against the social order, he had had to fight his Shakespearian longing, too—the longing for passionate speech. This had to be resisted. I could have cried aloud now. I could have been eloquent and moving. But what if I were to burst out like Lear to his daughters, like Shylock telling off the Christians? It would get me nowhere to utter burning words. The daughters and the Christians understood. Tomchek, Srole, and the judge didn't. Suppose I were to exclaim about morality, about flesh and blood and justice and evil and what it felt like to be me, Charlie Citrine? Wasn't this a court of equity, a forum of conscience? And hadn't I tried in my own confused way to bring some good into the world? Yes, and having pursued a higher purpose although without even getting close, now that I was aging, weakening, disheartened, doubting my endurance and even my sanity, they wanted to harness me to an even heavier load for the last decade or so. Denise was not correct in saying that I blurted out whatever entered my head. No sir. I crossed my arms on my chest and kept my mouth shut, taking a chance on heartbreak through tongue-holding. Besides, as suffering went, I was only in the middle rank or even lower. So out of respect for the real thing I clammed up. I shunted my thoughts onto a different track. At least I tried to. I wondered what Kathleen Fleisher Tigler was writing to me about.

These were very tough guys. I had their attention because of my worldly goods. Otherwise I would already have been behind the steel meshes of the county jail. As for Denise, that marvelous lunatic with the great violet eyes, the slender downy nose, the breaking martial voice—suppose I were to offer her all of my money? It would make no difference whatever, she would want to get more. And the judge? The judge was a Chicagoan and a politician, and his racket was equal justice under the law. A government of laws? This was a government of lawyers. But no, no, inflammation of the heart and burning words would only aggravate matters. No, the name of the game was silence, hardness and silence. I wasn't going to talk. A rose, or something that glowed like a rose, intruded itself, it wagged for an instant in my skull, and I felt that my decision was endorsed.

The judge now began to strafe me in earnest. "I understand that Mr. Citrine has been leaving the country often and is planning to go abroad again."

"This is the first I hear of it," said Tomchek. "Are you going anywhere?"

"For the Christmas holidays," I said. "Is there any reason why I shouldn't go?"

"None," said the judge, "if you're not trying to escape jurisdiction. The plaintiff and Mr. Pinsker have suggested that Mr. Citrine is planning to leave the country for good. They say he hasn't renewed his apartment lease and is selling his valuable collection of Oriental rugs. I assume that there are no numbered Swiss accounts. But what's to prevent him taking his head, which is his big asset, to Ireland or to Spain, countries that have no reciprocal agreements with us?"

"Is there any evidence for this, your honor?" I said.

The lawyers began to discuss the matter and I wondered how Denise had come to know that I was going away. Renata of course told the Señora everything and the Señora, singing for her supper all over Chicago, needed bright items to sing about. If she couldn't find something interesting to say at the dinner table, she might as well be dead. However, it was also possible that Denise's spy network had a contact in Poliakoff's Travel Bureau.

"These frequent flights to Europe are thought to have a purpose." Judge Urbanovich had his hand on the valve now and increased the heat still more. His genial glance said brilliantly, "Look out!" And suddenly Chicago was not my town at all. It was totally unrecognizable. I merely imagined that I had grown up here, that I knew the place, that I was known by it. In Chicago my personal aims were bunk, my outlook a foreign ideology, and I made out what the judge was telling me. It was that I had avoided all the Cannibal Pinskers and freed myself from unpleasant realities. He, Urbanovich, as clever a man as myself, with as much sensibility and better looks, bald or not, had paid his social dues in full, had played golf with all the Pinskers, had lunched with them. He had had to put up with this as man and citizen while I was at liberty to sail up and down elevator shafts expecting that a lovely being—"My Fate!"—would be smiling at me the next time the door opened. They'd give me Fate.

"Plaintiff has asked for an order of *ne exeat.* I am considering whether a bond should not be posted," said Urbanovich. "Two hundred thousand, say."

Indignant, Tomchek said, "With no evidence that my client is running out?"

"He's a very absent-minded fellow, your honor," said Srole. "Not signing a lease is a normal oversight, for him."

"If Mr. Citrine owned a little retail business, a little factory, if he had a professional practice or a position in an institution," said Urbanovich, "there would be no question of sudden flight." With round-eyed terrible lightness he was gazing at me, speculative.

Tomchek argued, "Citrine is a lifetime Chicagoan, a figure in this city."

"I understand that a great deal of money has slipped away this year. I hesitate to use the word squandered—it's his money." Urbanovich consulted a memo. "Large losses in a publishing enterprise called *The Ark.* A colleague, Mr. Thaxter . . . bad debts."

"Is it suggested these are not genuine losses and he's been squirreling away money? These are Mrs. Citrine's allegations and suspicions," said Tomchek. "Does the court believe them to be facts?"

The judge said, "This is a private conversation in chambers and only that. I feel, however, in view of the one indisputable fact that so much money is suddenly taking wing, Mr. Citrine should give me a full and current financial statement so that I can determine a bond figure, should that be necessary. You won't refuse me that, will you, Mr. Citrine?"

Oh bad! Very bad! What if Cantabile had the right idea after all—run her down in a truck, kill the bitch.

"I'll have to sit down with my accountant, your honor," I said.

"Mr. Citrine, you have a slightly persecuted look. I hope you understand that I am impartial, that I shall be fair to both parties." When the judge smiled certain muscles which unsubtle people never develop at all became visible. That was interesting. What did nature originally intend such muscles for? "I myself don't think you intend to run away. Mrs. Citrine admits you're a very affectionate father. Still, people do get desperate, and then they can be persuaded to do rash things."

He wanted me to know that my relations with Renata were no secret.

"I hope that you and Mrs. Citrine and Mr. Pinsker will leave me a little something to live on, Judge."

Then we, the defendant's group, were in the light gray speckled heavy polished stone corridor again and Srole said, "Charles, just as we told you, it's the man's technique. Now you're supposed to be terrified and beg us to settle and save you from being butchered and hacked to pieces."

"Well, it's working," I said. I wished that I could spring from this official skyscraper with its multiple squares into another life, never to be seen again. "I am terrified," I said. "And I'm dying to settle."

"Yes, but you can't. She won't accept it," said Tomchek, "she'll only pretend. She won't hear of settle. It's all in the books and at every dinner table every psychoanalyst I ever discussed it with told me the same thing—castration, that's all it is, when a woman is after the money."

"It isn't clear to me why Urbanovich is so keen to assist her."

"With him it seems a terrific fun thing," said Srole. "I often think so."

"And in the end most of the money will go for legal fees," I said. "I have asked myself sometimes why not give up and take a vow of poverty. . . ." But this was idle theorizing. Yes, I might surrender my small fortune and live and die in a hotel room like Humboldt. I was better equipped to lead a mental life as I was not a manic depressive and it might suit me very well. Only it wouldn't suit me well enough. For then there would be no more Renatas, no more erotic life, and no more of the exciting anxieties associated with the erotic life, which were perhaps even more important to me than sex itself. A vow of poverty was not the vow Renata was looking for.

"The bond—the bond is what's bad. That's a low blow," I said. "I really felt that you should have objected more. Put up a fight."

"But what was there to fight?" said Billy Srole. "It's all a bluff. He's got nothing to hang it on. You forgot to sign a lease. You're taking trips to Europe. Those might be professional trips. And listen, how come that woman knows every single move you're going to make?"

I was sure that Mrs. Da Cintra at the travel bureau, the one with the paisley turban, gave Denise information because Renata was impolite to her, even overbearing. As to Denise's knowledge of my actions, I had an analogy for it. Last year I took my little girls to the Far West camping and we visited a beaver lake. Along the shore the Forest Service had posted descriptions of the beaver's life cycle. The beavers were unaware of this and went on gnawing damming feeding and breeding. My own case was quite similar. With Denise it was, in the Mozartian Italian that she liked, *Tutto tutto già si sa.* Everything, everything about me was known.

I now realized that I had offended Tomchek by criticizing his handling of the bond question. No, I had incensed him. However, to protect the client relationship, he took it out on Denise. "How could you marry such a vile bitch!" he said. "Where the hell was your judgment! You're supposed to be a clever man. And if a woman like that decides to bug you to death what do you expect a couple of lawyers to do?" Already out of breath with exasperation he could say no more but snapped his attaché case under his arm and left us. I wished that Srole would go too, but he felt that he must tell me how strong my legal position really was (thanks to him). He stood in my way repeating that Urbanovich couldn't impound my money. He had no grounds for it. "But if it *should* come to the worst and he does lay a bond on you I know a guy who can give you a real buy in tax-exempt municipals so you don't lose the income of the frozen money."

"Good thinking," I said.

To get away I went to the men's room. As he followed me there I entered one of the stalls and was free at last to read Kathleen's letter.

As expected, Kathleen informed me of the death of her second husband, Frank Tigler, in a hunting accident. I knew him well, for while putting in my six weeks in Nevada to qualify for a divorce I had been a paying guest at the Tigler dude ranch. This was a lonely rundown god-forsaken place on Volcano Lake. My relations with Tigler were memorable. I had even the right to claim that I had saved his life, for when he fell out of a boat I jumped into the water to rescue him. Rescue? This event never seemed to deserve such a description. But he was a nonswimming cowboy, a cripple when he was not on horseback. On the ground in boots and Western hat he looked injured in the knees, and when he toppled into the water—the bold bronze face with ginger tufted brows, the bent horse-disfigured legs—I went after him immediately because water was not his element. He was a dry-land man of the extreme type. Then why were we in a boat? Because Tigler was keen to catch fish. He was not so much a fisherman as he was intent always on getting something for nothing. And it was spring and the toobie-fish were running. The toobies, a biological antiquity related to the coelacanth of the Indian Ocean, lived in Volcano Lake, coming up from a great depth to spawn. Crowds of people, Indians mostly, gaffed them in. The fish were awkward, strange to look at, living fossils. They were cured in the sun and stank up the Indian village. Words like "pellucid" and "voltaic" can be applied to the waters of Volcano Lake. When Tigler fell in I was instantly afraid that I might never see him again, the Indians having told me that the lake was miles deep and that bodies seldom were recovered. So I jumped and the cold was electrifying. I boosted Tigler into the boat again. He did not admit that he couldn't swim. He admitted nothing, he said nothing, but caught up the gaff and hooked in his floating hat. His cowboy boots had filled with water. Acknowledgments were neither asked nor given. It was an incident between two men. I mean, I felt it to be the manly silent West. The Indians would surely have let him drown. They didn't want white men coming in their boats, filled with the something-for-nothing fever, and taking their toobies. Besides, they hated Tigler for price-gouging and cheating, and for letting his horses graze everywhere. Furthermore, and Tigler himself had said this to me, the redskins didn't interfere with death but seemed simply to let it happen. Once, he told me, he was present when an Indian named Winnemucca was shot down in front of the post office. No one called a doctor. The man had bled to death in the road while men women and children, sitting on benches and in their old automobiles, watched silently. But at the present moment, high in the county building, I could see the late Tigler's Western figure as if it were cast in bronze, turning over and over in the electrical icy water, and then I saw myself, who had learned swimming in a small chlorinated tank in Chicago, pursuing him like an otter.

From Kathleen's letter I learned that he died in action. "Two fellows from Mill Valley California wanted to hunt deer with crossbows," wrote Kathleen. "Frank was guiding and took them into the hills. There was a run-in with the game warden. I think you met this warden, an Indian named Tony Calico, a Korean War veteran. One of the hunters turned out to have a criminal record. Poor Frank, you know, loved to be a little outside the law. He wasn't, in this case, but still there was a touch of it. There were shotguns in the Land Rover. I won't go into the details, they're too painful. Frank didn't fire but he was the only one shot. He bled to death before Tony could get him to the hospital.

"It hit me very hard, Charlie," she continued. "We were married twelve years, you know. At any rate, not to dwell on this too long, there was a big funeral. Quarter-horse people came from three states. Business associates from Las Vegas and Reno. He was very well liked."

I knew that Tigler had been a rodeo-rider and bronco-buster, winner of many prizes, and that he enjoyed some esteem in the horse world, but I doubt that he was dear to anyone except Kathleen and his old mother. The income from the dude ranch, such as it was, he put into his quarter horses. Some of these horses were registered under phony papers, their sires having been ruled off the track as doped or doctored. The hereditary attainder rule was very strict. Tigler was bound to try to get around it with forged documents. So he was on the move from track to track and left Kathleen to manage the business. There wasn't much business to manage. He milked it of income to buy feed and trailers. The guest cabins folded and fell. They reminded me of Humboldt's collapsing chicken farm. Kathleen was in exactly the same fix in Nevada. Fate—fate within—was too strong for her. Tigler put her in charge of the ranch and told her to pay nothing but essential horse-bills, and those only on violent demand.

I had plenty of troubles of my own, but the double solitude of Kathleen's life—first in New Jersey, then in the West—moved me strongly. I leaned against the partition of the biffy in the county building trying to get light from above on her letter, typed with a faded ribbon. "I know you liked Tigler, Charlie. You had such a good time trout fishing with him and playing poker. It took your mind off your troubles."

That was so, although he was furious when I caught the first trout. We were trawling from his boat and I was using his lure, so he said it was his trout. He made a scene and I tossed the fish into his lap. The surroundings were unearthly. It was not a fish setting—only bare rock, no trees, pungent sagebrush, and marl dust floating when a truck passed.

However, it was not to discuss Tigler that Kathleen wrote to me. She wrote because Orlando Huggins was asking for me. Humboldt had left me something. Huggins was his executor. Huggins, that old left-wing playboy, was a decent man, at bottom an honorable person. He too cherished Humboldt. After I was denounced as a false blood-brother Huggins was called in to sort out Humboldt's business affairs. He eagerly rushed into the act. Then Humboldt accused him of cheating and threatened to sue him, too. But Humboldt's mind had evidently cleared toward the last. He had identified his true friends, naming Huggins as administrator of his estate. Kathleen and I were remembered in the will. What she got from him she didn't say, but he couldn't have had much to give. Kathleen mentioned, however, that Huggins had turned over to her a posthumous letter from Humboldt. "He talked about love, and the human opportunities he missed," she wrote. "He mentioned old friends, Demmie and you, and the good old days in the Village and out in the country."

I can't think what made those old days so good. I doubt that Humboldt had had a single good day in all his life. Between fluctuations and the dark qualms of mania and depression, he had had good spells. Perhaps not so many as two consecutive hours of composure. But Humboldt would have appealed to Kathleen in ways in which I was too immature twenty-five years ago to understand. She was a big substantial woman whose deep feelings were invisible because her manner was so quiet. As for Humboldt he had some nobility even when he was crazy. Even then he was constant to some very big things indeed. I remember the shine of his eyes when he dropped his voice to pronounce the word "relume" spoken by a fellow about to commit a murder, or when he spoke Cleopatra's words "I have immortal longings in me." The man loved art deeply. We loved him for it. Even when the decay was raging there were incorruptible places in Humboldt that were not rotted out. But I think he wanted Kathleen to protect him when he entered the states a poet needed to be in. These high dreaming states, always being punctured and torn by American flak, were what he wanted Kathleen to preserve for him. Enchantment. She did her best to help him with the enchantment. But he could never come up with enough enchantment or dream material to sheathe himself in. It would not cover. However, I saw what Kathleen had tried to do and admired her for it.

The letter went on. She reminded me of our long talks under the trees at Rancho Tigler. I suppose I had been telling her about Denise, busy with self-justification. I can recall the trees she referred to, a few box elders and cottonwoods. Tigler advertised the gaiety of his resort, but the bleached boards were sprung and falling from the bunkhouses, the swimming pool was all cracks and covered with leaves and scum. The fences were down and Tigler's mares strolled about freely like beautiful naked matrons. Kathleen wore dungarees and her gingham shirt was laundered to an ectoplasmic degree. I can remember Tigler squatting, repainting his decoy ducks. He wasn't speaking at that time, for his jaw had been broken by someone in anger over a feed bill and was now wired shut. Also that week the utilities were cut off, the guests were freezing, the water was not running. Tigler said that this was the West the dudes really loved. They didn't come out here to be pampered. They wanted it rough and ready. But to me Kathleen said, "I can only handle this a day or two more."

Luckily a movie company turned up to make a picture about

the Mongol hordes and Tigler was hired to be the horse expert. He recruited Indians to wear quilted Asiatic costumes and to gallop shrieking and do stunts in the saddle. It was a big thing for Volcano Lake. Credit for this windfall was claimed by Father Edmund, the Episcopal minister who in his youth had been a silent-movie star and very beautiful. In the pulpit he wore marvelous old negligees. The Indians were all film-fans. They whispered that his garments had been donated by Marion Davies or Gloria Swanson. He, said Father Edmund, with his Hollywood connections, had induced the company to come to Volcano Lake. Anyway, Kathleen became acquainted with movie people. I mention this because in her letter she spoke of selling the ranch, putting Mother Tigler out to board with people in Tungsten City while she took a job in the picture industry. People in transition often develop an interest in the movies. Either that or they begin to talk about going back to school for a degree. There must be twenty million Americans who dream of returning to college. Even Renata was forever about to enroll herself at De Paul.

I went back to the courtroom to pick up my primrose path youthful check overcoat deeply considering what to do for money if Urbanovich laid a bond on me. What a bastard he was, this Croatian American bald judge. He knew neither the children nor Denise nor me, and what right had he to take away money earned in thought and fever by such peculiar operations of the brain! Oh yes I knew how to be high-minded about money too. Yea let them take all! And I could fill out a psychological questionnaire with the best of them, certain of being in the top ten percent for magnanimity. But Humboldt—I was full of Humboldt today—used to accuse me of trying to spend my whole life in the upper stories of higher consciousness. Higher consciousness, Humboldt said, lecturing me, was "innocent, aware of no evil in itself." When you tried to live entirely in high consciousness, purely reasonable, you saw evil in other people only, never in yourself. From this Humboldt went on to insist that in the unconscious, in the irrational core of things money was a vital substance like the blood or fluids that bathed the brain tissues. Since he was always so earnest about the higher significance of money, had he perhaps returned my six thousand seven hundred and sixty-odd bucks in his last will and testament? Of course he hadn't, how could he? He had died broke in a flophouse. But six thousand bucks wouldn't go far now. Szathmar alone owed me more than that. I had lent Szathmar money to buy a condominium. Then there was Thaxter. Thaxter, by defaulting on a loan, had cost me fifty shares of IBM stock posted as collateral. After many letters of warning, the bank, with ethical gestures and regrets, almost weeping to see me so cruelly stung by a conniving friend, took away those shares. Thaxter pointed out that this was a deductible loss. Both he and Szathmar often comforted me in this way. By appealing also to dignity and to absolute value. (Didn't I, myself, aim at magnanimity, and wasn't friendship a far bigger thing than money?) People kept me broke. And now what was I to do? I owed publishers about seventy thousand dollars in advances for books I was too paralyzed to write. I had lost interest in them utterly. I could sell my Oriental rugs. I had told Renata that I was tired of them, and she knew an Armenian dealer who was willing to take them on commission. Now that foreign currencies were booming and the oil-rich Persians no longer wished to work at the loom, German and Japanese buyers and even Arabs were raiding the Midwest and carrying off the carpets. As for the Mercedes, perhaps it would be better to get rid of it. I was always greatly shaken when forced to fret about money. I felt like a falling rigger or dangling window washer, caught under the arms by his safety harness. I was strained across the chest and seemed to be deprived of oxygen. I considered sometimes storing a cylinder of oxygen in the clothes closet for just such spells of worry. I should of course have opened a numbered Swiss bank account. How was it, that having lived most of my life in Chicago, I hadn't thought to provide myself with a bagman? And now what had I to sell? Thaxter was sitting on two articles of mine, a reminiscence of Kennedy Washington (now as far behind us as the founding of the Capuchin Order) and an article from the unfinished series "Great Bores of the Modern World." There was no money there. It was excellent, but who would publish a serious study of bores?

I was even willing now to consider George Swiebel's scheme for mining beryllium in Africa. I had scoffed at this when George proposed it but wilder ideas were commercially sound and no man ever knew what form his Dick Whittington's cat might take. A man named Ezekiel Kamuttu, George's guide to the Olduvai Gorge two years ago, claimed to own a mountain of beryllium and semiprecious stones. A sack of exotic burlap was at this moment lying under George's bed, filled with peculiar minerals. George had given me a sweat sock filled with these and asked me to get them assayed at the Field Museum by Ben Isvolsky, one of our schoolmates, now a geologist. Sober Ben said they were the real thing. At once he lost his scholar's air and began to put business questions to me. Could we get these stones in marketable quantities on a regular basis? And with what machinery, and how get into the bush and out? And who was this Kamuttu? Kamuttu, George said, would lay down his life for him. He had invited George to marry into his family. He wanted to sell him his sister. "But," I said to Ben, "you know George's boon-companion complex. He has a few drinks with natives, they see how real he is and that his heart is bigger than the Mississippi. It really is, too. But how can we be sure that this Kamuttu hasn't got some con? Maybe he's stolen these beryllium samples. Or maybe he's bonkers. There's no world shortage of that."

Knowing Isvolsky's domestic troubles, I understood why he dreamed of making a killing in minerals. "Anything," he told me, "to get away from Winnetka for a while." Then he said, "Okay, Charlie, I know what's on your mind. When you come back here to see me you want to be shown those birds." He referred to the museum's great collection of birds, hoarded up over decades and stored in classified drawers. The huge workshops and laboratories behind the scenes, the sheds, storerooms, and caverns were infinitely more fascinating than the museum's public exhibits. The preserved birds were collapsed, their legs tagged. And mainly I liked to see the hummingbirds, thousands upon thousands of little bodies, some no bigger than my fingertip, endless varieties of them, all spattered minutely with a whole Louvre of iridescent colors. So Ben took me to inspect them again. He had full cheeks and woolly hair, a bad skin but an agreeable face. The museum treasures now bored him and he said, "If this Kamuttu really has a mountain of beryllium we should go there and grab it."

"I'm leaving soon for Europe," I said.

"Ideal. George and I can pick you up. We can all fly to Nairobi together."

Thoughts of beryllium and Oriental rugs showed how nervous I was, and impractical. When I was in this state only one man in all the world could help me, my practical brother Julius, a real-estate operator in Corpus Christi, Texas. I loved my stout and now elderly brother. Perhaps he loved me too. In principle he was not in favor of strong family bonds. Possibly he saw brotherly love as an opening for exploitation. My feelings for him were vivid, almost hysterically intense, and I could not blame him for trying to resist them. He wished to be a man entirely of today, and he had forgotten or tried to forget the past. Unassisted he could remember nothing, he said. For my part there was nothing that I could forget. He often said to me, "You inherited the old man's terrific memory. And before him there was that old bastard, his old man. Our grandfather was one of ten guys in the Jewish Pale who knew the Babylonian Talmud by heart. Lots of good that did. I don't even know what it is. But that's where you get your memory." The admiration was not unmixed. I don't think he was always grateful to me for remembering so well. My own belief was that without memory existence was metaphysically injured, damaged. And I couldn't conceive of my own brother, irreplaceable Julius, having metaphysical assumptions different from mine. So I would talk to him about the past, and he would say, "Is that so? Is that a fact? And you know I can't remember a thing, not even the way Mama looked, and I was her favorite, after all."

"You must remember how she looked. How could you forget her? I don't believe that," I said. My family sentiments tormented my stout brother sometimes. He thought me some sort of idiot. He himself, a wizard with money, built shopping centers, condominiums, motels, and contributed greatly to the transformation of his part of Texas. He wouldn't refuse to help me. But this was purely theoretical, for although the idea of help was continually in the air between us, I never actually asked him to give me any. In fact I was extremely reserved about making such a request. I was, if I may say so, merely obsessed, filled by the need to make it.

As I was picking up my coat, Urbanovich's bailiff came up to me and took a piece of paper from the pocket of his cardigan. "Tomchek's office phoned this message in," he said. "There's a fellow with a foreign name—is it Pierre?" said the old man.

"Pierre Thaxter?"

"I wrote down what they gave me. He wants you to meet him at three at the Art Institute. Also a couple came to ask for you. Fellow with a mustache. Girl with red hair, mini-skirt."

"Cantabile," I said.

"He didn't leave no name."

It was now half past two. Much had happened in a short time. I went to Stop and Shop and bought sturgeon and fresh rolls, also Twining's breakfast tea and Cooper's vintage marmalade. If Thaxter was staying overnight I wanted to give him the breakfast he was accustomed to. He always fed me extremely well. He took pride in his table and told me in French what I was eating. I ate no mere tomatoes but *salade de tomates*, no bread and butter but *tartines*, and so it went with *bouilli*, *brûlé*, *farci*, *fumé*, and excellent wines. He dealt with the best tradespeople and nothing disagreeable to eat or drink was ever set before me.

As a matter of fact I looked forward to Thaxter's visit. I was always delighted to see him. Perhaps I even had the illusion that I could open my oppressed heart to him, although I really knew better than that. He would blow in from California wearing his hair long like a Stuart courtier and, under his carabiniere cloak, dressed in a charming blue velvet lounging suit from the King's Road. His broad-brimmed hat was bought in a shop for black swingers. About his neck would be apparently valuable chains, and also a piece of knotted, soiled, but uniquely tinted silk. His light-tan boots, which came up to the ankle, were ingeniously faced with canvas, and on each of the canvas sides there was an ingenious fleur-de-lis of leather. His nose was strongly distorted, his dark face flaming, and when I saw his leopard eyes I'd give a secret cheer. There was a reason why, when the bailiff told me that he was in town, I immediately laid out five dollars on sturgeon. I was extremely fond of Thaxter. Now, then, the great question: did he or did he not know what he was doing? In a word, was he a crook? This was a question a shrewd man should be able to answer, and I couldn't answer. Renata, when she did me the honor of treating me as her future husband, often said, "Don't drop any more money on Thaxter. Charm? All charm. Talent? Buckets of talent. But a phony."

"He's really not."

"What? Have a little self-respect, Charlie, about what you swallow. All that Social Register stuff of his?"

"Oh that! Yes, but people have to boast. They're dead if they can't say good things about themselves. Good things *have* to be said. Have a heart."

"All right then, his special wardrobe. His special umbrella. The only umbrella with class is a natural-hook umbrella. You don't buy an umbrella with a manufactured steam-bent hook. For Christ's sake it's got to grow that way. Then there's his special wine cellar, and his special attaché case which you can buy only in one shop in London, and his special water bed with special satin sheets, where he was lying in Palo Alto with his special tootsie-roll and they were watching Davis Cup tennis on a special color TV. Not to mention a special putz named Charlie Citrine who pays for everything. Why the guy's delirious."

The above conversation had taken place when Thaxter telephoned to say that he was en route to New York to sail on the *France* and would stop in Chicago to discuss *The Ark.*

"What's he going to Europe for?" said Renata.

"Well, he is a crack journalist, you know."

"Why is a crack journalist sailing First Class on the *France*? That's five days. Has he got all that time to kill?"

"He must have a little, yes."

"And we're flying Economy," said Renata.

"Yes, but he has a cousin who's a director of the French Line. His mother's cousin. They never pay. The old woman knows all the plutocrats in the world. She brings out their debutante daughters."

"I notice he doesn't stick those plutocrats for fifty shares of anything. The rich know their deadbeats. How could you do such a dumb thing?"

"Really, the bank might have waited a few days more. His check was on the way from the Banco Ambrosiano of Milano."

"How did the Italians get in the act? He told you his family funds were in Brussels."

"No, in France. You see his share of his aunt's estate was in the Crédit Lyonnais."

"First he swindles you, then he fills you with garbage explanations which you go around repeating. All those high European connections are straight out of old Hitchcock movies. So now he's coming to Chicago, and what does he do, he has his office girl get you on the phone. It's beneath him to dial a number or answer a ring. But you answer in person and the chick says, 'Hold the line, Mr. Thaxter is coming,' so you stand waiting with the phone to your ear. And the whole thing, mind you, is charged to your bill. Then he tells you he's arriving but later he'll let you know when."

As far as it went this was all true. By no means did I tell Renata everything about Thaxter. There were also blacklists and scandals at country clubs and gossip about larceny charges. My friend's taste in trouble was old-fashioned. There were no more bounders unless, from pure love of antiquity, someone like Thaxter revived the type. But I also felt that something deep was at work and that Thaxter's eccentricities would eventually reveal a special spiritual purpose. I knew it was risky to put up the collateral because I had seen him do other people in the eye. But not me, I thought. There has to be *one* exception. Thus I gambled on immunity and I lost. He was a dear friend. I loved Thaxter. I knew also that I was the last man in the world he would wish to harm. But it came to that, finally. He had run out of harmable men. As there was no one else left, it was friendship versus his life-principle. Besides, I could now call myself a patron of Thaxter's form of art. Such things must be paid for.

He had just lost his house in the Bay Area with the swimming pool and the tennis court, the orange grove he had had put in, the formal garden, the MG, the station wagon, and the wine cellar.

Last September I flew to California to find out why our magazine, *The Ark*, was not appearing. It was a wonderfully pleasant affectionate visit. We walked out to inspect his estate under the California sunshine. At the time I was beginning to develop a new cosmological feeling for the sun. That it was in part our Creator. That there was a sun-band in our spirits.

That light rose within us and came forward to meet the sun's light. That this sun light was not just an external glory revealed to our dark senses and that as light was to the eye, thought was to the mind. So here we were. A happy blessed day. The sky was giving its marvelous temperate pulsating blue heat, while oranges hung about us. Thaxter wore his favorite outdoor garment, the black cloak, and the toes of his bare feet were pressed together like Smyrna figs. He was now having roses put in and asked me not to talk to the Ukrainian gardener. "He was a concentration-camp guard and still insanely anti-Semitic. I don't want him to start raving." So in this beautiful place I felt that demon-selves and silly-selves and loving-selves were intermingling. Some of Thaxter's newest children, fair and innocent, were allowed to play with dangerous knives and poisonous rose-dust containers. Nobody came to harm. Lunch was a big production, served beside the sparkling swimming pool with two wines poured by himself in somber dignity and intense connoisseurship, with cloak and curved pipe and bare toes writhing. His darkly pretty young wife gladly attended to all preparations and presided practically in the background. She was utterly delighted with her life and there was no dough, absolutely none. The gas station at the corner refused to take his check for five dollars. I had to pay with my credit card. And behind the scenes the young woman was holding off the tennis-court and swimming-pool people, the wine people, the car people, the grand-piano people, the bank people.

The Ark was going to be produced on new IBM equipment without expensive compositors. Never has any country given its people so many toys to play with or sent such highly gifted individuals to the remotest corners of idleness, as close as possible to the frontiers of pain. Thaxter was building a wing to house *The Ark*. Our magazine had to have its own premises and not interfere with his private life. He recruited some college students on a Tom Sawyer basis to dig a foundation. He went about in his MG visiting building sites to get construction hints from the hard-hats and scrounge pieces of plywood. This was an expansion I refused to subsidize. "I predict your house will slide into this hole," I said. "Are you sure you're within the building code?" But Thaxter had that willingness to try that makes field marshals and dictators. "We'll throw twenty thousand men into this sector, and if we lose more than half, we'll take a different tack."

In *The Ark* we were going to publish brilliant things. Where were we to find such brilliancy? We knew it must be there. It was an insult to a civilized nation and to humankind to assume that it was not. Everything possible must be done to restore the credit and authority of art, the seriousness of thought, the integrity of culture, the dignity of style. Renata, who must have had an unauthorized look at my bank statements, apparently knew how much I was spending as a patron. "Who needs this *Ark* of yours, Charlie, and who are these animals you're gonna save? You're not really such an idealist—you're full of hostility, dying to attack a lot of people in your very own magazine and insult everyone right and left. Thaxter's arrogance is nothing compared to yours. You let him think he's getting away with murder, but that's really because you can double his arrogance in spades."

"My money is running out anyhow. I'd rather spend it on this—"

"Not spend but squander," she said. "Why do you finance this California setup?"

"Better than giving it to lawyers and to the government."

"When you start to talk about *The Ark* you lose me. For once tell me simply—what, why?"

I was grateful for such a challenge really. As an aid to concentration I shut my eyes to answer. I said, "The ideas of the last few centuries are used up."

"Who says! See what I mean by arrogance," Renata interrupted.

"But so help me, they are used up. Social ideas, political, philosophical theories, literary ideas (poor Humboldt!), sexual ones, and, I suspect, even scientific ones."

"What do you know about all these things, Charlie? You've got brain fever."

"As the world's masses arrive at the point of consciousness, they take these exhausted ideas for new ones. How should they know? And people's parlors are papered with these projections."

"This is too serious for tongue twisters."

"I *am* serious. The greatest things, the things most necessary for life, have recoiled and retreated. People are actually dying of this, losing all personal life, and the inner being of millions, many many millions, is missing. One can understand that in many parts of the world there is no hope for it because of famine or police dictatorships, but here in the free world what excuse have we? Under pressure of public crisis the private sphere is being surrendered. I admit this private sphere has become so repulsive that we are glad to get away from it. But we accept the disgrace ascribed to it and people have filled their lives with so-called 'public questions.' What do we hear when these public questions are discussed? The failed ideas of three centuries. Anyhow the end of the individual, whom everyone seems to scorn and detest, will make our destruction, our superbombs, superfluous. I mean, if there are only foolish minds and mindless bodies there'll be nothing serious to annihilate. In the highest government positions almost no human beings have been seen for decades now, anywhere in the world. Mankind must recover its imaginative powers, recover living thought and real being, no longer accept these insults to the soul, and do it soon. Or else! And this is where a man like Humboldt, faithful to failed ideas, lost his poetry and missed the boat."

"But he went insane. You can't lay all the blame on him. I never knew the guy but sometimes I think you're too hard when you attack him. I know," she said, "you feel that he lived out the poet's awful life in just the way the middle class expected and approved. But nobody makes the grade with you. Thaxter is just your private pet. He certainly doesn't make it."

Of course she was right. Thaxter was always saying, "What we want is a major statement." He suspected that I had a major statement up my sleeve.

I told him, "You mean something like a life reverence, or Yogis and Commissars. You have a weakness for such terrible stuff. You'd give anything to be a Malraux and talk about the West. What is it with you and these seminal ideas? Major statements are hot air. The disorder is here to stay." And so it is—rich, baffling, agonizing, and diverse. As for striving to be exceptional, everything was already strange enough.

Pierre Thaxter was absolutely mad for Culture. He was a

classicist, heavily trained by monks in Latin and Greek. He learned French from a governess, and studied it in college as well. He had taught himself Arabic also, and read esoteric books, and hoped to astonish everyone by publishing in learned journals in Finland or Turkey. He spoke with peculiar respect of Panofsky or Momigliano. He saw himself also as Burton of Arabia or T. E. Lawrence. Sometimes he was a purple genius of the Baron Corvo type, sordidly broke in Venice, writing something queer and passionate, rare and distinguished. He could not bear to leave anything out. He played Stravinsky on the piano, knew much about the Ballets Russes. On Matisse and Monet he was something of an authority. He held views on ziggurats and Le Corbusier. He could tell you, and often did, what sort of articles to buy and where to buy them. This was what Renata was talking about. No proper attaché case, for instance, fastened at the top, the clasps had to be on the side. He was bugs about attaché cases and umbrellas. There were plantations in Morocco where proper umbrella handles grew. And on top of it all Thaxter described himself as a Tolstoyan. If you pressed him he would say that he was a Christian pacifist anarchist and confess his faith in simplicity and purity of heart. So of course I loved Thaxter. How could I help it? Besides, the fever that afflicted his poor head made him an ideal editor. The diversity of interests, you see, and his cultural nosiness. He was an excellent journalist. This was widely recognized. He had worked on good magazines. Each and every one of them had fired him. What he needed was an ingenious and patient editor to send him on suitable assignments.

He was waiting between the lions in front of the Institute, exactly as expected in the cloak and blue velvet suit and boots with canvas sides. The only change was in his hair which he was now wearing in the Directoire style, the points coming down over his forehead. Because of the cold his face was deep red. He had a long mulberry-colored mouth, and impressive stature, and warts, and the distorted nose and leopard eyes. Our meetings were always happy and we hugged each other. "Old boy, how are you? One of your good Chicago days. I've missed the cold air in California. Terrific! Isn't it. Well, we may as well start right with a few of those marvelous Monets." We left attaché case, umbrella, sturgeon, rolls, and marmalade in the checkroom. I paid two dollars for admission and we mounted to the Impressionist collection. There was one Norwegian winter landscape by Monet that we always went to see straightaway: a house, a bridge, and the snow falling. Through the covering snow came the pink of the house, and the frost was delicious. The whole weight of snow, of winter, was lifted effortlessly by the astonishing strength of the light. Looking at this pure rosy snowy dusky light, Thaxter clamped his pince-nez on the powerful twisted bridge of his nose with a gleam of glass and silver and his color deepened. He knew what he was doing. With this painting his visit began on the right tone. Only, familiar with the whole span of his thoughts, I was sure that he was also thinking how a masterpiece like this might be stolen from the museum, and that his mind quickly touched upon twenty daring art thefts from Dublin to Denver, complete with getaway cars and fences. Maybe he even dreamed up some multimillionaire Monet fanatic who had built a secret shrine in a concrete bunker and would be willing to pay a ton of money for this landscape. Scope was what Thaxter longed for (me, too, for that matter). Still he was a puzzle to me. He was either a kindly or a brutal man, and deciding which was a torment. But now he collapsed the trick pince-nez, and turned toward me with the ruddy swarthy face, his big-cat gaze heavier than before, gloomy, and even a touch cross-eyed.

"Before the shops close," he said, "I have an errand in the Loop. Let's go out. I can't take in anything more after this picture." So we retrieved our things and passed through the revolving door. In the Mallers Building there was a dealer named Bartelstein, who sold antique fish knives and forks. Thaxter wanted to obtain a set. "There's a controversy over the silver," he said decisively. "Fish on silver is now supposed to give a bad flavor. But I believe in the silver."

Why fish knives? And with what, and for whom? The bank was putting him out of his Palo Alto house, still he never ran out of resources. He occasionally spoke of other houses that he owned, one in the Italian Alps, one in Brittany.

"The Mallers Building?" I said.

"This Bartelstein has a world reputation. My mother knows him. She needs the knives for one of her Social Register clients."

At this moment Cantabile and Polly approached us, both breathing December vapor, and I saw the white Thunderbird idling at the curb, its door hanging open, and the blood-red upholstery. Cantabile was smiling and his smile was somewhat unnatural, less an expression of pleasure than something else. Perhaps it was a reaction to Thaxter's cloak and hat and zooty shoes and flaming face. I, too, felt red in the face. Cantabile, on the other hand, was peculiarly white. He breathed the air as if he were stealing it. He had a look of eagerness and of distemper. The Thunderbird, puffing fumes, was beginning to block traffic. Because I had been immersed for much of the day in Humboldt's life and because Humboldt had in turn been immersed in T. S. Eliot, I thought as he might have done of the violet hour when the human engine waits like a taxi throbbing, waiting. But I cut this out. The moment required my full presence. I made quick introductions left and right: "Mrs. Palomino Mr. Thaxter—and Cantabile."

"Hurry, quick, jump in," said Cantabile, a man to be obeyed.

I wasn't having any of this. "No," I said. "We've got lots to discuss and I'd just as soon walk two blocks to the Mallers Building than be stuck in traffic with you."

"For Christ's sake get in the car." He had been stooping over me. But then he cried this out so loud that he jerked himself straight.

Polly lifted her pleasant face. She enjoyed it all. Her straight hair, Japanese in texture but very red and cut like a fall, showed thick and even against her green loden coat. The pleasant cheeks meant that one could be sexually pleasant with Polly. It would gratify, it would be a success. Why was it that some men knew how to find women who naturally pleased and could be pleased? By their cheeks and smiles, even I could identify them—after they had been found. Meantime bits of snow fell from the gray invisibility that lay upon the skyscrapers and something like soft thunder occurred behind us. This might have been sonic boom or jet noise over the lake, for thunder meant warmth and the chill was biting at our reddened faces. In this deepening dusky gray the lake surface would be pearly, and its polar fringe had formed early this winter, white—soiled but white. In the matter of natural beauty

Chicago had its piece of the action despite the fact that its over-all historical destiny made it materially coarse, the air coarse, the soil coarse. The trouble was that such pearly water with its arctic edging and the gray air snowing could not be appreciated while these Cantabiles were carrying on, pushing me toward the Thunderbird and gesturing with the finest of fox-hunter's gloves. Nevertheless, one goes to a concert to think one's thoughts against the fine background of chamber music and one may make similar use of a Cantabile. A man who had been for years closely shut up and sifting his inmost self with painful iteration, deciding that the human future depended on his spiritual explorations, frustrated utterly in all his efforts to reach an understanding with those representatives of modern intellect whom he had tried to reach, deciding instead to follow the threads of spirit he had found within himself to see where they might lead, found a peculiar stimulus in a fellow like this Cantabile fellow.

"Let's go!" he bawled at me.

"No. Mr. Thaxter and I have our own business to discuss."

"Oh, there's time for that—plenty of time," said Thaxter.

"And what about the fish knives? Suddenly you're not so keen on the fish knives," I said to Thaxter.

Cantabile's voice was jagged and high with exasperation. "I'm trying to do you some good, Charlie! Fifteen minutes of your time is all, and then I'll whip you back to the Mallers Building for these fucking knives. How'd you do in court, pal? I know how you did! They've got a case full of nice clean bottles waiting for your blood. You already look drained. You've got a damn haggard look. You've aged ten years since lunchtime. But I've got the answer for you and I'll prove it. Charlie, ten grand today will get you fifteen by Thursday—if not, I'll let you beat me on the head with the bat I used on your Mercedes. I've got Stronson waiting. He needs cash badly."

"I want no part of that. I'm not a juice man," I said.

"Don't be stupid. We've got to move fast."

I glanced at Polly. She had warned me against Cantabile and Stronson and I checked silently with her. Her smile confirmed the caution she had given me. But she was highly amused by Cantabile's determination to drive us into the Thunderbird, to cram us into the red leather upholstery of the throbbing open car. He made it seem like a kidnap. We were on the broad sidewalk in front of the Institute, and lovers of criminal legend could tell you that the celebrated Dion O'Banion used to drive his Bugatti at a hundred mph over the very spot where we were standing while pedestrians fled. I had in fact mentioned this to Thaxter. Wherever he went, Thaxter wished to experience the characteristic thing, the essence. Getting the essence of Chicago, he was delighted, he was grinning, and he said, "If we miss Bartelstein now we can stop in the morning en route to the airport."

"Poll," said Cantabile, "get behind the wheel. I see the squad car." Buses were trying to squeeze past the parked Thunderbird. Traffic was tied up. The cops were already spinning their blue lights at Van Buren Street. Thaxter followed Polly to the car and I said to Cantabile, "Ronald, go away. Let me alone."

He gave me a look of open and terrible disclosure. I saw a spirit striving with complications as dense as my own, in another, faraway division. "I didn't want to spring this on you," he said, "but you force me to twist your arm." His fingers in the horseman's gloves, skin-tight, took me by the sleeve. "Your lifelong friend Alec Szathmar is in hot trouble, or could be in hot trouble—that's up to you."

"Why? How come?"

"I'm telling you. There's this pretty young woman—her husband is one of my people—and she's a kleptomaniac. She was caught in Field's pinching a cashmere cardigan. And Szathmar is her lawyer, dig? It was me that recommended Szathmar. He went to court and told the judge not to send her to jail, she needed psychiatric treatment and he'd see that she got it. So the court released her in his custody. Then Szathmar brought this chick straight to a motel and took her clothes off, but before he could screw her she escaped. She didn't have more on than the strip of paper they stretch across the toilet seat when she streaked out. There are plenty of witnesses. Now this girl is straight. She doesn't go for the motel bit. Her only bag is stealing. For your sake, I'm restraining the husband."

"All I hear from you, Cantabile, is nonsense, more and more and more nonsense. Szathmar can act like a jerk, but he's not a monster."

"All right, I'll unleash the husband. You think your buddy wouldn't be disbarred? He would be—fucking-A-right."

"You've hoked up all this for some goofy reason," I said. "If you had anything on Szathmar you'd be blackmailing him right now."

"So have it your way, don't cooperate, I'll slaughter and butcher the son of a bitch."

"I don't care."

"You don't have to tell me that. You know what you are? You're an isolationist, that's what you really are. You don't want to know what other people are into."

Everyone is forever telling me what my faults are, while I stand with great hungry eyes, believing and resenting all. Without metaphysical stability a man like me is the Saint Sebastian of the critical. The odd thing is that I hold still for it. As now, clutched by the sleeve of my checked coat, with Cantabile steaming intrigues and judgments at me from the flues of his white nose. With me it's not how all occasions do inform against me, but how I employ occasions to extract buried information. The latest information seemed to be that I was by inclination the sort of person who needed microcosmic-macrocosmic ideas, or the belief that everything that takes place in man has world significance. Such a belief warmed the environment for me, and brought out the sweet glossy leaves, the hanging oranges of the groves where the unpolluted self was virginal and gratefully communed with its Maker, and so on. It was possible that this was the only way for me to be my own true self. But in the actual moment we were on the wide freezing pavement, on Michigan Boulevard, the Art Institute behind us, and over against us all the colored lights of Christmas traffic and the white façades of Peoples Gas and other companies.

"Whatever I am, Cantabile, my friend and I aren't going with you." I hurried to the Thunderbird to try to stop Thaxter, who was getting in. He was already pulling in his cloak about him, sinking into the supple upholstery. He looked very pleased. I put my head in and said, "Come out of there. You and I are walking."

But Cantabile shoved me in to the car beside Thaxter. He put his hands on my rear and thrust me in. Then he jammed the front seat back to keep me there. In the next motion he pulled the door shut with a slam and said, "Take off, Polly." Polly did just that.

"Now what the hell do you think you're doing, pushing and trapping me in here," I said.

"The cops are right on top of us. I didn't have time to argue," Cantabile said.

"Well, this is nothing but a kidnap," I told him. And as soon as I pronounced the word "kidnap" my heart was instantly swollen with a childish sense of terrible injury. But Thaxter was laughing, chuckling through his wide mouth, and his eyes were wrinkling and twinkling. He said, "Hee-hee, don't take it so hard, Charlie. It's a very funny moment. Enjoy it."

Thaxter couldn't have been happier. He was having a real Chicago treat. For his sake, the city was living up to its reputation. Observing this, I cooled off somewhat. I guess I really love to entertain my friends. Hadn't I brought sturgeon and fresh rolls and marmalade when the bailiff said that Thaxter was in town? I was still holding the paper bag from Stop and Shop.

Traffic was thick but Polly's mastery of the car was extraordinary. She worked the white Thunderbird into the left lane without touching the brake, without a jolt, with fearless competency, a marvelous driver.

Restless Cantabile twisted about to the rear to face us and said to me, "Look what I've got here. An early copy of tomorrow morning's paper. I bought it from a guy in the press room. It cost me plenty. You want to know something? You and I made Mike Schneiderman's column. Listen," he read. " 'Charlie Citrine, the Chevrolet of the French Legion and Chicago scribe, who authored the flick *Von Trenck*, made a card-debt payoff to an underworld figure at the Playboy Club. Better go take a poker seminar at the University, Charles.' What do you say, Charlie. It's a pity Mike didn't know all the facts about your car and the skyscraper and all the rest of it. *Now* what do you think?"

"What do I think? I won't accept author as a verb. I also want to get out at Wabash Avenue."

Chicago was more bearable if you didn't read the papers. We had turned west on Madison Street and passed under the black frames of the El. "Don't pull up, Polly," said Cantabile. We moved on toward the Christmas ornaments of State Street, the Santa Clauses and the reindeer. The only element of stability in this moment lay in Polly's wonderful handling of the machine.

"Tell me about the Mercedes," said Thaxter. "What happened to it? And what was the skyscraper thing, Mr. Cantabile? Is the underworld figure at the Playboy Club you yourself?"

"Those in the know will know," said Cantabile. "Charlie, how much will they charge for the bodywork on your car? Did you take it back to the dealer? I hope you keep away from those rip-off specialists. Four hundred bucks a day for one grease monkey. What crooks! I know a good cheap shop."

"Thank you," I said.

"Don't be ironical with me. But the least I can do is make you back some of the money this will cost."

I made no answer. My heart hammered upon a single theme: I urgently desired to be elsewhere. I simply didn't want to be here. It was utter misery. This was not the moment to remember certain words of John Stuart Mill, but I remembered them anyway. They went something like this: The tasks of noble spirits at a time when the works which most of us are appointed to do are trivial and contemptible—da-da-*da*, da-da-*da*, da-da-*da*. Well the only thing valuable in these contemptible works is the spirit in which they are done. I couldn't see any values in the vicinity at all. But if the tasks of the *durum genus hominum*, said the great Mill, were performed by a supernatural agency and there was no demand for wisdom or virtue O! then there would be little that man could prize in man. This was exactly the problem America had set for itself. The Thunderbird would do as the supernatural agency. And what else was man prizing? Polly was transporting us. Under that mass of red hair lay a brain which certainly knew what to prize, if anyone cared to ask. But no one was asking, and she didn't need much brain to drive this car.

We now passed the towering upswept frames of the First National Bank, containing layer upon layer of golden lights. "What's this beautiful structure?" asked Thaxter. No one answered. We charged up Madison Street. At this rate, and due west, we would have reached the Waldheim Cemetery on the outskirts of the city in about fifteen minutes. There my parents lay under snow-spattered grass and headstones; objects would still be faintly visible in the winter dusk, etcetera. But of course we were not bound for the cemetery. We turned into La Salle Street where we were held up by taxicabs and newspaper trucks and the Jaguars and Lincolns and Rolls-Royces of stockbrokers and corporation lawyers—of the deeper thieves and the loftier politicians and the spiritual elite of American business, the eagles in the heights far above the daily, hourly, and momentary destinies of men.

"Hell, we're going to miss Stronson. That fat little son of a bitch is always tearing off in his Aston-Martin as soon as he can lock his office," said Cantabile.

But Polly sat silent at the steering wheel. Traffic was jammed. Thaxter succeeded at last in getting Cantabile's attention. And I sighed and, left to myself, tuned out. Just as I had done yesterday when forced, practically at gunpoint, into the stinking closet of the Russian Bath. This is what I thought: certainly the three other souls in the warm darkness of this glowing, pulsating and lacquered automobile had thoughts just as peculiar as my own. But they were apparently less aware of them than I. And what was it that I was so aware of? I was aware that I used to think that I knew where I stood (taking the universe as a frame of reference). But I was mistaken. However, I could at least say that I had been spiritually efficient enough not to be crushed by ignorance. However, it was now apparent to me that I was neither of Chicago nor sufficiently beyond it, and that Chicago's material and daily interests and phenomena were neither actual and vivid enough nor symbolically clear enough to me. So that I had neither vivid actuality nor symbolic clarity and for the time being I was utterly nowhere. This was why I went to have long mysterious conversations with Professor Scheldt, Doris's father, on esoteric subjects. He had given me books to read about the etheric and the astral bodies, the Intellectual Soul and the Consciousness Soul, and the unseen Beings whose fire and wisdom and love created and guided this universe. I was far more thrilled by Dr. Scheldt's talks than by my affair with his daughter. She was a good kid actually. She was attractive and lively, a fair, sharp-profiled, altogether excellent small young woman. True, she insisted on serving fancy dishes like Beef Wellington and the pastry crust was always underdone, and so was the meat, but those were minor matters. I had taken up with her only because Renata and her mother had expelled me and put Flonzaley in my place. Doris couldn't hold a candle to Renata. Renata? Why, Renata didn't need an ignition key to start a car. One of her kisses on the hood would turn it on. It would roar for her. Moreover, Miss Scheldt was ambitious socially. In Chicago, husbands with higher mental interests aren't easy to find, and it was obvious that Doris wanted to be Madame Chevalier Citrine. Her father had been a physicist at the old Armour Institute, an executive of IBM, a NASA consultant who improved the metal used in space ships. But he was also an anthroposophist. He didn't wish to call this mysticism. He insisted that Steiner had been a Scientist of the Invisible. But Doris, with reluctance, spoke of her father as a crank. She told me many facts about him. He was a Rosicrucian and a Gnostic, he read aloud to the dead. Also at a time when girls have to do erotic things whether or not they have the talent for them, the recent situation being what it is, Doris behaved quite bravely with me. But it was all wrong, I was simply not myself with her and at the wrongest possible time I cried out, "Renata! Oh Renata!" Then I lay there shocked with myself and mortified. But Doris didn't take my outcry at all hard. She was thoroughly understanding. That was her main strength. And when my talks with the Professor began she was decent about that as well, understanding that I was not going to sleep with the daughter of my guru.

Sitting in the Professor's clean parlor—I have seldom sat in a room so utterly clean, the parquet floors of light wood limpid with wax and the Oriental scatter rugs lint-free, and the park below with the equestrian statue of General Sherman prancing on clean air—I was entirely happy. I respected Dr. Scheldt. The strange things he said were at least deep things. In this day and age people had ceased to say such things. He was from another time, entirely. He even dressed like a country-club member of the Twenties. I had caddied for men of this type. A Mr. Masson, one of my regulars at Sunset Ridge in Winnetka, had been the image of Professor Scheldt. I assumed that Mr. Masson had long ago joined the hosts of the dead and that in all the universe there was only me to remember how he had looked when he was climbing out of a sand trap.

"Dr. Scheldt. . . ." The sun is shining clear, the water beyond is as smooth as the inner peace I have not attained, as wrinkled as perplexity, the lake is strong with innumerable powers, flexuous, hydromuscular. In the parlor is a polished crystal bowl filled with anemones. These flowers are capable of nothing except grace and they are colored with an untranslatable fire derived from infinity. "Now Dr. Scheldt," I say. I'm speaking to his interested and plain face, calm as a bull's face and trying to determine how dependable his intelligence is—i.e., whether we are real here or crazy here. "Let me see if I understand these things at all—thought in my head is also thought in the external world. Consciousness in the self creates a false distinction between object and subject. Am I getting it right?"

"Yes, I think so, sir," the strong old man says.

"The quenching of my thirst is not something that begins in my mouth. It begins with the water, and the water is out there, in the external world. So with truth. Truth is something we all share. Two plus two for me is two plus two for everyone else and has nothing to do with my ego. That I understand. Also the answer to Spinoza's argument that if the dislodged stone had consciousness it could think, 'I am flying through the air,' as if it were freely doing it. But if it were conscious, it would not be a mere stone. It could also originate movement. Thinking, the power to think and to know, is a source of freedom. Thinking will make it obvious that spirit exists. The physical body is an agent of the spirit and its mirror. It is an engine and a reflection of the spirit. It is the spirit's ingenious memorandum to itself and the spirit sees itself in my body, just as I see my own face in a looking glass. My nerves reflect this. The earth is literally a mirror of thoughts. Objects themselves are embodied thoughts. Death is the dark backing that a mirror needs if we are to see anything. Every perception causes a certain amount of death in us, and this darkening is a necessity. The clairvoyant can actually see that when he learns how to obtain the inward view. To do this, he must get out of himself and stand far off."

"All this is in the texts," says Dr. Scheldt, "I can't be sure that you have grasped it all, but you're fairly accurate."

"Well, I understand in part, I think. When our understanding wants it, divine wisdom will flow toward us."

Then Dr. Scheldt begins to speak on the text, *I am the light of the world*. To him that light is understood also as the sun itself. Then he speaks of the gospel of Saint John as drawing upon the wisdom-filled Cherubim, while the gospel of Saint Luke draws upon the fiery love of the Seraphim—Cherubim, Seraphim, and Thrones being the three highest spiritual hierarchy. I am not at all certain that I am following. "I have no experience of any of this advanced stuff, Dr. Scheldt, but I still find it peculiarly good and comforting to hear it all said. I don't at all know where I'm at. One of these days when life is quieter I'm going to buckle down to the training course and do it in earnest."

"When will life be quieter?"

"I don't know. But I suppose people have told you before this how much stronger the soul feels after such a conversation."

"You shouldn't wait for things to become quieter. You must decide to make them quieter."

He saw that I was fairly skeptical still. I couldn't make my peace with things like the Moon Evolution, the fire spirits, the Sons of Life, with Atlantis, with the lotus-flower organs of spiritual perception or the strange mingling of Abraham with Zarathustra, or the coming together of Jesus and the Buddha. It was all too much for me. Still, whenever the doctrine dealt with what I suspected or hoped or knew of the self, or of sleep, or of death, it always rang true.

Moreover, there were the dead to think of. Unless I had utterly lost interest in them, unless I were satisfied to feel only a secular melancholy about my mother and my father or Demmie Vonghel or Von Humboldt Fleisher, I was obliged to investigate, to satisfy myself that death *was* final, that the dead *were* dead. Either I conceded the finality of death and refused to have any further intimations, condemned my childish sentimentality and hankering, or I conducted a full and proper investigation. Because I simply didn't see how I could refuse to investigate. Yes, I could force myself to think of it all as the irretrievable loss of shipmates to the devouring Cyclops. I could think of the human scene as a battlefield. The fallen are put into holes in the ground or burned to ash. After this, you are not supposed to inquire after the man who gave you life, the woman who bore you, after a Demmie whom you had last seen getting into a plane at Idlewild with her big blond legs and her make-up and her earrings, or after the brilliant golden master of conversation Von Humboldt Fleisher, whom you had last beheld eating a pretzel in the West Forties. You could simply assume that they had been forever wiped out, as you too would one day be. So if the daily papers told of murders committed in the streets before crowds of neutral witnesses, there was nothing illogical about such neutrality. On the metaphysical assumptions about death everyone in the world had apparently reached, everyone would be snatched, ravished by death, throttled, smothered. This terror and this murdering were the most natural things in the world. And these same conclusions were incorporated into the life of society and present in all its institutions, in politics, education, banking, justice. Convinced of this, I saw no reason why I shouldn't go to Dr. Scheldt to talk about Seraphim and Cherubim and Thrones and Dominions and Exousiai and Archai and Angels and Spirits.

I said to Dr. Scheldt at our last meeting, "Sir, I have studied the pamphlet called *The Driving Force of Spiritual Powers in World History*, and it contains a fascinating passage about sleep. It seems to say that mankind doesn't know how to sleep any more. That something should be happening during sleep that simply isn't happening and that this is why we wake up feeling so stale and unrested, sterile, bitter, and all the rest of it. So let me see if I've got it right. The physical body sleeps, and the etheric body sleeps, but the soul goes off."

"Yes," said Professor Scheldt. "The soul, when you sleep, enters the supersensible world, or at least one of its regions. To simplify, it enters its own element."

"I'd like to think that."

"Why shouldn't you?"

"Well, I will, just to see if I understand it. In the supersensible world the soul meets the invisible forces which were known by initiates in the ancient world in their Mysteries. Not all the beings of the hierarchy are accessible to the living, only some of them, but these are indispensable. Now, as we sleep, the pamphlet says, the words that we have spoken all day long are vibrating and echoing about us."

"Not literally, the words," Dr. Scheldt corrected.

"No, but the feeling-tones, the joy or pain, the purpose of the words. Through the vibrations and echoes of what we have thought and felt and said we commune as we sleep with the beings of the hierarchy. But now, our daily monkeyshines are such, our preoccupations are so low, language has become so debased, the words so blunted and damaged, we've said such stupid and dull things, that the higher beings hear only babbling and grunting and TV commercials—the dog-food level of things. This says nothing to them. What pleasure can these higher beings take in this kind of materialism, devoid of higher thought or poetry? As a result, all that we can hear in sleep is matter creaking and hissing and washing, the rustling of plants, and the air conditioning. So we are incomprehensible to the higher beings. They can't influence us and they themselves suffer a corresponding privation. Have I got it right?"

"Yes, by and large."

"It makes me wonder about a late friend of mine who used to complain of insomnia. He was a poet. And I can see now why he may have had such a problem about sleeping. Maybe he was ashamed. Out of a sense that he had no words fit to carry into sleep. He may actually have preferred insomnia to such a nightly shame and disaster."

Now the Thunderbird pulled up beside the Rookery on La Salle Street. Cantabile jumped out. As he was holding the door open for Thaxter I said to Polly, "Now Polly—tell me something helpful, Polly."

"This Stronson fellow is in big trouble," she said, "big, big, big trouble. Look in tomorrow's paper."

We went through the tiled, balustraded Rookery lobby and up in a swift elevator, Cantabile repeating, as though he wanted to hypnotize me, "Ten grand today will get you fifteen by Thursday. That's fifty percent in three days. Fifty percent." We came out into a white corridor and then up against two grand cedar doors lettered *Western Hemisphere Investment Corporation*. On these doors Cantabile gave a coded set of knocks: three times; pause; once; then a final once. It was odd that this should be necessary, but after all a man who could give such a return on money must be fighting off investors. A beautiful receptionist let us in. The anteroom was carpeted heavily. "He's here," said Cantabile. "Just wait a few minutes, you guys."

Thaxter sat down on a low orange loveseat sort of thing. A man was vacuuming loudly around us, wearing a gray porter's jacket. Thaxter removed his wide dude hat and smoothed the Directoire points over his irregularly formed forehead. He took the stem of his curved pipe into his straight lips and said, "Sit down." I gave him the sturgeon and marmalade to hold and overtook Cantabile at the door to Stronson's private office. I pulled tomorrow's paper from under his arm. He grabbed at it and we both tugged. His coat came open and I saw the pistol in his belt but this no longer deterred me. "What do you want?" he said.

"I just want to have a look at Schneiderman's column."

"Here, I'll tear it out for you."

"You do that and I'm leaving."

He pushed the paper at me violently and went into Stronson's office. Rapidly leafing, I found an article in the financial section describing the difficulties of Mr. Stronson and the Western Hemisphere Investment Corporation. A complaint had been filed by the Securities and Exchange Commission against him. He was charged with violation of the federal securities regulations. He had used the mails to defraud and had dealt in unregistered securities. An explanatory affidavit filed by the SEC alleged that Guido Stronson was a complete phony, not a Harvard graduate, but only a New Jersey high-school dropout and gas-station attendant, until recently a minor employee in a bill-collecting agency in Plainfield. He had abandoned a wife and four children. They were now on welfare in the East. Coming to Chicago, Guido Stronson had opened a grand office on La Salle Street and produced glittering credentials, including a degree from the Harvard Business School. He said he had been conspicuously successful in Hartford as an insurance executive. His investment company soon had a very large clientele for hog bellies, cocoa, gold ore. He had bought a mansion on the North Shore and said he wanted to go in for fox hunting. Complaints lodged by clients had led to these federal investigations. The report concluded with the

La Salle Street rumor that Stronson had many Mafia clients. He had apparently cost these clients several millions of dollars.

By tonight Greater Chicago would know these facts and tomorrow this office would be mobbed by cheated investors and Stronson would need police protection. But who would protect him the day after tomorrow from the Mafia? I studied the man's photograph. Newspapers distort faces peculiarly—I knew that from personal experience, but this photograph, if it did Stronson justice in any degree, inspired no sympathy. Some faces gain by misrepresentation.

Now why had Cantabile brought me here? He promised me fast profits, but I knew *something* about modern life. I mean, I could read a little in the great mysterious book of urban America. I was too fastidious and skittish to study it closely—I had used the conditions of life to test my powers of immunity; the sovereign consciousness trained itself to avoid the phenomena and to be immune to their effects. Still, I did know, more or less, how swindlers like Stronson operated. They hid away a good share of their stolen dollars, they were sentenced to prison for eight or ten years, and when they got out, they retired quietly to the West Indies or the Azores. Maybe Cantabile was now trying to get his hands on some of the money Stronson had stashed—in Costa Rica, perhaps. Or maybe if he was losing twenty thousand dollars (some of it possibly Cantabile family money) he intended to make a big scene. He would want me to see such a scene. He liked me to be present. Because of me he had gotten into Mike Schneiderman's column. He must have been thinking of something even more brilliant, more sensationally inventive. He needed me. And why was I so often involved in such things? Szathmar too did this to me; George Swiebel had staged a poker party in order to show me a thing or two; this afternoon even Judge Urbanovich had acted up in chambers for my sake. I must have been associated in Chicago with art and meaning, with certain upper values. Wasn't I the author of *Von Trenck* (the movie), honored by the French government and the Zig-Zag Club? I still carried in my wallet a thin wrinkled length of silk ribbon for the buttonhole. And O! we poor souls, all of us so unstable, ignorant, perturbed, so unrested. Couldn't even get a good night's sleep. Failing in the night to make contact with the merciful, regenerative angels and archangels who were there to strengthen us with their warmth and their love and wisdom. Ah, poor hearts that we were, how badly we were all doing and how I longed to make changes or amends or corrections. Something!

Cantabile had shut himself up in conference with Mr. Stronson, and this Stronson, represented in the paper with a brutally thick face and hair done in pageboy style, was probably frantic. Maybe Cantabile was offering him deals—deals upon deals upon deals. Advice on how to come to terms with his furious Mafia customers.

Thaxter was lifting his legs to let the porter vacuum under them.

"I think we'd better go," I said.

"Leave? Now?"

"I think we should get out of here."

"Oh, come on, Charlie, don't make me leave. I want to see what happens. There'll never be another occasion like this. This man Cantabile is absolutely wild. He's fascinating."

"I wish you hadn't rushed into his Thunderbird without asking me. So excited by gangland Chicago you just couldn't wait. I suppose you expect to make use of this experience, send it to the *Reader's Digest* or something nonsensical like that—you and I have all kinds of things to discuss."

"They can wait, Charles. You know I'm sort of impressed by you. You always complain that you're isolated, then I come to Chicago and find you bang in the middle of things." He flattered me. He knew how much I liked to be thought a Chicago expert. "Is Cantabile one of the ballplayers at your club?"

"I don't think Langobardi would let him join. He doesn't suffer minor hoodlums gladly."

"Is that what Cantabile is?"

"I don't know exactly what he is. He carries on like a Mafia Don. He's some sort of silly-billy. He has a wife who's getting a PhD."

"You mean that smashing redhead with the platform shoes?"

"She's not the one."

"Wasn't it grand how he gave that code knock on the door? And the pretty receptionist opened? Notice these glass cases with the pre-Columbian art and the collection of Japanese fans. I tell you, Charles, nobody actually knows this country. This is some country. The leading interpreters of America stink. They do nothing but swap educated formulas about it. *You*, yes *you!* Charles, should write about it, describe your life day by day and apply some of your ideas to it."

"Thaxter, I told you how I took my little girls to see the beavers out in Colorado. All around the lake the Forestry Service posted natural-history placards about the beaver's life cycle. The beavers didn't know a damn thing about this. They just went on chewing and swimming and being beavers. But we human beavers are all shook up by descriptions of ourselves. It affects us to hear what we hear. From Kinsey or Masters or Erikson. We read about identity crisis, alienation, etcetera, and it all affects us."

"And you don't want to contribute to the deformation of your fellow man with new inputs?—God, how I loathe the word 'input.' But you yourself continually make high-level analyses. What about the piece for *The Ark* you sent me—I think it's right here in my attaché case—in which you offer an economic interpretation of personal eccentricities. Let's see, I'm sure I've got it here. You argue that there may be a connection at this particular stage of capitalism between the shrinking of investment opportunities and the quest for new roles or personality investments. You even quoted Schumpeter, Charlie. Yes, here it is: 'These dramas may appear purely internal but they are perhaps economically determined . . . when people think they are being so subtly inventive or creative they merely reflect society's general need for economic growth.'"

"Put away that paper," I said. "For God's sake, don't quote my big ideas at me. If there's one thing I can't take today, it's that."

It was really very easy for me to generate great thoughts of this sort. Instead of regretting this glib weakness with me, Thaxter envied it. He longed to be a member of the intelligentsia, to stand in the pantheon and to make a Major Statement like Albert Schweitzer or Arthur Koestler or Sartre or Wittgenstein. He didn't see why I distrusted this. I was too grand; too snobbish, even, he said, sharply resentful. But there it was, I simply did not wish to be a leader of the world intelligentsia. Humboldt had pursued it with all his might. He believed in victorious analysis, he preferred "ideas" to poetry, he was prepared to give up the universe itself for the subworld of higher cultural values.

"Anyway," said Thaxter, "you should go around Chicago like Restif de la Bretonne in the streets of Paris and write a chronicle. It would be sensational."

"Thaxter, I want to talk to you about *The Ark*. You and I were going to give a new impulse to the mental life of the country and outdo the *American Mercury* and *The Dial*, or the *Revista de Occidente*, and so on. We discussed and planned it for years. I've spent a pot of money on it. I've paid all the bills for two and a half years. Now where is *The Ark*? I think you're a great editor, a born editor, and I believe in you. We announced our magazine and people sent in material. We've been sitting on their manuscripts for ages. I've gotten bitter letters and even threats. You've made me the fall guy. They all blame me, and they all quote you. You've set yourself up as a Citrine expert and interpret me all over the place—how I function, how little I understand women, all the weaknesses of my character. I don't take that too hard. I'd be glad though, if you didn't interpret me quite so much. And the words you put into my mouth—that X is a moron, or Y is an imbecile. *I* have no prejudices against X or Y. The one who's out to get 'em is you."

"Frankly, Charles, the reason why our first number isn't out is that you sent me so much anthroposophical material. You're no fool so there must be something to anthroposophy. But for God's sake, we can't come out with all this stuff about the soul."

"Why not? People talk about the psyche, why not the soul?"

"Psyche is scientific," said Thaxter. "You have to accustom people gradually to these terms of yours."

I said, "Why did you buy such a huge supply of paper?"

"I wanted to be ready to publish five issues in succession without worrying about supplies. Besides, we got a good buy."

"Where are all these tons of paper now?"

"In the warehouse. But I don't think that it's *The Ark* that bothers you. It's really Denise that's eating at you, the courts and the dollars and all that grief and harassment."

"No, that's not what it is," I said. "Sometimes I'm grateful to Denise. You think I should be like Restif de la Bretonne, in the streets? Well, if Denise weren't suing me, I'd never get out of the house. Because of her I have to go downtown. It keeps me in touch with the facts of life. It's been positively enlightening."

"How so?"

"Well, I realize how universal the desire to injure your fellow man is. I guess it's the same in the democracies as in dictatorships. Only here the government of laws and lawyers puts a palisade up. They can injure you a lot, make your life hideous, but they can't actually do you in."

"Your love of education really does you credit, Charles. No kidding. I can tell you after a friendship of twenty years," said Thaxter. "Your character is a very peculiar one but there is a certain—I don't know what to call it—dignity that you do have. If you say soul and I say psyche, you have your reason for it, probably. You probably do have a soul, Charles. And it's a pretty startling fact about anyone."

"You have one yourself. Anyway, I think we had better give up our plan to publish *The Ark* and liquidate our assets remaining if any."

"Now, Charles, don't be hasty. We can straighten this business out very easily. We're almost there."

"I can't put any more money into it. I'm not doing well, financially."

"You can't compare your situation to mine," said Thaxter. "I've been wiped out in California."

"How bad is it there?"

"Well, I've kept your obligations down to a minimum. You promised to pay Blossom her salary. Don't you remember Blossom, the secretary? You met her in September?"

"My obligations? In September we agreed to lay Blossom off."

"Ah, but she was the only one who really knew how to operate all the IBM machinery."

"But the machinery was never operated."

"That wasn't her fault. We were prepared. I was ready to go at any time."

"What you mean, really, is that you're too grand a personage to do without a staff."

"Have a heart, Charles. Just after you left, her husband was killed in a car crash. You wouldn't want me to fire her at such a time. I know your heart, whatever else, Charles. So I took it on myself to interpret your attitude. It's only fifteen hundred bucks. There is actually another thing I must mention, the lumber bill for the wing we started."

"I didn't tell you to build the wing. I was dead against it."

"Why, we agreed there was to be a separate office. You didn't expect me to bring all of that editorial confusion into my house."

"I definitely said I'd have no part of it. I warned you even, that if you dug that big hole next to your house you'd undermine the foundations."

"Well, it isn't very serious," said Thaxter. "The lumber company can damn well dismantle it all and take back their wood. Now, as for the slip-up between banks—I'm damn sorry about that, but it was not my fault. The payment from the Banco Ambrosiano di Milano was delayed. It's these damn bureaucracies! Besides, it's just anarchy and chaos now in Italy. Anyway, you have my check. . . ."

"I have not."

"You haven't? It's got to be in the mail. Postal service is outrageous. It was my last installment of twelve hundred dollars to the Palo Alto Trust. They had already closed me out. They owe you twelve hundred."

"Is it possible that they never received it? Maybe it was sent out from Italy by dolphin."

He did not smile. The moment was solemn. We were speaking, after all, of his money. "Those California crumbs were supposed to reissue it and send you their cashier's check."

"Maybe the Banco Ambrosiano's check hasn't cleared yet," I said.

"Now, then," he took a legal pad from his attaché case. "I've worked out a schedule to repay the money you lost. You must have the original cost of the stock. I absolutely insist. I believe you bought it at four hundred. You overpaid, you know, it's way down now. However, that's not your fault. Let's say that when you posted it for me it was worth eighteen thousand. Nor will I forget the dividends."

"You don't have to do dividends, Thaxter."

"No, I insist. It's easy enough to find out what sort of

dividend IBM is paying. You send me the figure and I'll send you the check."

"In five years you paid off less than one thousand dollars on this loan. You kept up the interest payments and little else."

"The interest rate was out of sight."

"In five years you reduced the amount of the principal by two hundred dollars a year."

"The exact figures don't come to me now," said Thaxter. "But I know that the bank will owe you something after it sells the stock."

"IBM is now under two hundred a share. The bank gets hurt, too. Not that I care what happens to banks."

But Thaxter was now busy explaining how he would return the money, dividends and all, over a five-year period. The split black pupils of his long grape-green eyes moved over the figures. He was going to do the whole thing handsomely, with dignity, aristocratically, fully sincere, shirking no part of his obligation to a friend. I could see that he entirely meant what he said. But I also knew that this elaborate plan to do right by me would be, in his mind, tantamount to doing right. These long yellow sheets from the legal pad filled with figures, these generous terms of repayment, the care for detail, the expressions of friendship, settled our business fully and forever. This was magically it.

"It's a good idea to be scrupulously precise with you in these petty deals. To you the small sums are more important than big ones. What sometimes surprises me is that you and I should be fooling around with trifles. You could make any amount of money. You don't know your own resources. Odd, isn't it? You could turn a crank and money would fall into your lap."

"What crank?" I said.

"You could go to a publisher with a project and name your own advance."

"I've already taken big advances."

"Peanuts. You could get lots more. I've come up with some ideas myself. For starters you and I could do that cultural Baedeker I'm always after you about, a guide for educated Americans who go to Europe and get tired of shopping for Florentine leather and Irish linen. They're fed up with the thundering herd of common rubbernecks. Are these cultivated Americans in Vienna, for instance? In our guide they can find lists of research institutes to visit, small libraries, private collections, chamber-music groups, the names of cafés and restaurants where one can meet mathematicians or fiddlers, and there would be listings of the addresses of poets, painters, psychologists, and so on. Visit their studios and labs. Have conversations with them."

"You might as well bring over a firing squad and shoot all these poets dead as put such information into the hands of culture-vulture tourists."

"There isn't a ministry of tourism in Europe that wouldn't get excited by this. They'd all cooperate fully. They might even kick in some money. Charlie, we could do this for every country in Europe, for all major cities as well as the capitals. This idea is worth a million dollars to you and me. I would take charge of the organization and research. I'd do most of the work. You'd cover atmospheric stuff and ideas. We'll need a staff for the details. We could start in London and move on to Paris and Vienna and Rome. Say the word and I'll go to one of the big houses. Your name will pull down an advance of two hundred and fifty thousand. We split it two ways and your worries are over."

"Paris and Vienna! Why not Montevideo and Bogotá? There's just as much culture there. Why are you sailing and not flying to Europe?"

"It's my favorite way to travel, deeply restful. One of my old mother's remaining pleasures in life is to arrange these trips for her only child. She's done more, this time. The Brazilian football champions are touring Europe, and she knows I love football. I mean superb football. So she's wangled me tickets for four matches. Besides, I have business reasons for going. And I want to see some of my children."

I refrained from asking how he could travel first class on the *France* when he was dead broke. Asking got me nowhere. I never succeeded in assimilating his explanations. I did remember being told, however, that the velvet suit with a blue silk scarf knotted in the Ronald Colman manner made perfectly acceptable evening wear. In fact the black-tie millionaires looked tacky by comparison. And women adored Thaxter.

One evening during his last crossing an old Texas lady, if you could believe him, dropped a chamois sack full of gems into his lap, under the tablecloth. He discreetly passed them back to her. He would not service rich old Texas frumps, he told me. Not even those who were magnanimous in Oriental or Renaissance style. Because after all, he continued, this was a big gesture suitable to a big ocean and a big character. But he was remarkably dignified, virtuous, and faithful to his wife—to all his wives. He was warmly devoted to his extended family, the many children he had had by several women. If he didn't make a Major Statement he would at least leave his genetic stamp upon the world.

"If I had no cash, I'd ask my mother to put me in steerage. How much do you tip when you get off the *France* in Le Havre?" I asked him.

"I give the chief steward five bucks."

"You're lucky to leave the boat alive."

"Perfectly adequate," said Thaxter. "They bully the American rich and despise them for their cowardice and ignorance."

He told me now, "My business abroad is with an international consortium of publishers for whom I'm developing a certain idea. Originally, I got it from you, Charlie, but you won't remember. You said how interesting it would be to go around the world interviewing a lot of second-, third-, and fourth-rank dictators—the General Amins, the Qaddafis, and all that breed."

"They'd have you drowned in their fishpond if they thought you were going to call them third-rate."

"Don't be silly, I'd never do such a thing. They're leaders of the developing world. But it's actually a fascinating subject. These shabby foreign-student-bohemians a few years ago, future petty blackmailers, now they're threatening the great nations, or formerly great nations, with ruin. Dignified world leaders are sucking up to them."

"What makes you think they'll talk to you?" I said.

"They're dying to see somebody like me. They're longing for a touch of the big time, and I have impeccable credentials. They all want to hear about Oxford and Cambridge and New York and the London season, and discuss Karl Marx and Sartre. If they want to play golf or tennis or ping-pong, I can do all of that. To prepare myself for writing these articles I've been reading some good things to get the right tone—Marx on Louis Napoleon is wonderful. I've also looked into Suetonius and Saint-Simon and Proust. Incidentally, there's going to be an international poets' congress in Taiwan. I may cover that. You have to keep your ear to the ground."

"Whenever I try that I get nothing but a dirty ear," I said.

"Who knows, I may get to interview Chiang Kai-shek before he kicks off."

"I can't imagine that he has anything to tell you."

"Oh, I can take care of that," said Thaxter.

"How about getting out of this office?" I said.

"Why don't you, for once, go along with me and do the thing my style. Not to overprotect. Let the interesting thing happen. How bad can it be? We can talk just as well here as anywhere. Tell me what's going on personally, what's with you?"

Whenever Thaxter and I met we had at least one intimate conversation. I spoke freely to him and let myself go. In spite of his eccentric nonsense, and my own, there was a bond between us. I was able to talk to Thaxter. At times I told myself that talking to him was as good for me as psychoanalysis. Over the years, the cost had been about the same. Thaxter could elicit what I was really thinking. A more serious learned friend like Richard Durnwald would not listen when I tried to discuss the ideas of Rudolf Steiner. "Nonsense!" he said. "Simply nonsense! I've looked into that." In the learned world anthroposophy was not respectable. Durnwald dismissed the subject sharply because he wished to protect his esteem for me. But Thaxter said, "What is this Consciousness Soul, and how do you explain the theory that our bones are crystallized out of the cosmos itself?"

"I'm glad you asked me that," I said. But before I could begin I saw Cantabile approaching. No, he didn't approach, he descended on us in a peculiar way, as if he weren't using the floor with its carpeting but had found some other material basis.

"Let me borrow this," he said, and took up the black dude hat with the swerving brim. "All right," he said, promotional and tense. "Get up, Charlie. Let's go and visit the man." He gave my body a rough lift. Thaxter also rose from the orange loveseat but Cantabile pushed him down again and said, "Not you. One at a time." He took me with him to the presidential door. There, he paused. "Look," he said, "you let me do the talking. It's a special situation."

"This is one more of your original productions, I see. But no money is going to change hands."

"Oh, I wouldn't really have done that to you. Who else but a guy in bad trouble would give you three for two? You saw the item in the paper, hey?"

"I certainly did," I said. "And what if I hadn't?"

"I wouldn't let you get hurt. You passed my test. We're friends. Come meet the guy anyway. I figure it's like your duty to examine American society from White House to Skid Row. Now all I want you to do is stand still while I say a few words. You were a terrific straight man yesterday. There was no harm in that, was there?" He belted my coat tightly as he spoke and put Thaxter's hat on my head. The door to Stronson's office opened before I could get away.

The financier was standing beside his desk, one of those deep executive desks of the Mussolini type. The picture in the paper was misleading in one respect only—I had expected a bigger man. Stronson was a fat boy, his hair light brown and his face sallow. In build he resembled Billy Srole. Brown curls covered his short neck. The impression he made was not agreeable. There was something buttocky about his cheeks. He wore a turtleneck shirt, and swinging ornaments, chains, charms hung on his chest. The pageboy bob gave him a pig-in-a-wig appearance. Platform shoes increased his height.

Cantabile had brought me here to threaten this man. "Take a good look at my associate, Stronson," he said. "He's the one I told you about. Study him. You'll see him again. He'll catch up with you. In a restaurant, in a garage, in a movie, in an elevator." To me he said, "That's all. Go wait outside." He faced me toward the door.

I had turned to ice. Then I was horrified. Even to be a dummy impersonating a murderer was dreadful. But before I could indignantly deny, remove the hat, stop Cantabile's bluff, the voice of Stronson's receptionist came, enormously amplified and room-filling, from the slotted box on the desk. "Now?" she said.

And he answered, "Now!"

Immediately the porter in the gray jacket entered the office, pushing Thaxter before him. His I.D. card was open in his hand. He said, "Police, Homicide!" and he pushed all three of us against the wall.

"Wait a minute. Let's see that card. What do you mean, homicide?" said Cantabile.

"What do you think, I was just going to let you make threats and hold still? After you said how you'd have me killed I went to the State's Attorney and swore a warrant," said Stronson. "Two warrants. One John Doe for the hit man, your friend."

"Are you supposed to be Murder Incorporated?" said Thaxter to me. Thaxter seldom laughed aloud. His deepest delight was always more than half-silent, and his delight at this moment was wonderfully deep.

"Who's the hit man, me?" I said, trying to smile.

No one replied.

"Who has to threaten you, Stronson?" said Cantabile. His brown eyes, challenging, were filled with moisture, while his face turned achingly dry and pale. "You lost more than a million bucks for the guys in the Troika, and you're finished, kid. You're dead! Why should anybody else get in the act? You've got no more chance than a shit-house rat. Officer, this man is unreal. You want to see the story in tomorrow's paper. Western Hemisphere Investment Corporation is wiped out. Stronson wants to pull a few people down with him. Charlie, go and get the paper. Show it to the man."

"Charlie ain't going anywhere. Everybody just lean on the wall. I hear you carry a gun, and your name is Cantabile. Bend over, sweetheart—that's the way." We all obeyed. His own weapon was under his arm. His harness creaked. He took the pistol from Cantabile's ornate belt. "No ordinary .38, a Saturday-Night Special. It's a Magnum. You could kill an elephant with this."

"There it is, just as I told you. That's the gun he shoved under my nose," said Stronson.

"It must run in the Cantabile family to be silly with guns.

That was your Uncle Moochy, wasn't it, who wasted those two kids? No effing class at all. Goofy people. Now we'll see if you've got any grass on you. It would also be nice if there was a little parole violation to go with this too. We'll fix you fine, buddy boy. Goddamn bunch of kid-killers."

Thaxter was now being frisked under the cloak. His mouth was wide and his nose strongly distorted and flaming across the bridge with all the mirth, the joy of this marvelous Chicago experience. I was angry with Cantabile. I was furious. The detective ran his hands over my sides, under the arms, up between my legs and said, "You two gentlemen can turn around. You're quite a pair of dressers. Where did you get those shoes with the canvas sides?" he asked Thaxter. "Italy?"

"The King's Road," said Thaxter pleasantly.

The detective took off the gray porter's jacket—under it he wore a red turtlenecked shirt—and emptied Cantabile's long black ostrich-skin wallet on the desk. "And which one is supposed to be the hit man? Errol Flynn in the cape, or the check coat?"

"The coat," said Stronson.

"I should let you make a fool of yourself and arrest him," said Cantabile, still facing the wall. "Go ahead. On top of the rest."

"Why, is he somebody?" said the policeman. "A big shot?"

"Fucking-A-right," said Cantabile. "He's a well-known distinguished man. Look in tomorrow's paper and you'll see his name in Schneiderman's column—Charles Citrine. He's an important Chicago personality."

"So what, we're sending important personalities to jail by the dozen. Governor Kerner didn't even have the brains to get a smart bagman." The detective was enjoying himself. He had a plain seamed face, now jolly, a thoroughly experienced police face. Under the red shirt his breasts were fat. The dead hair of his wig did not agree with his healthy human color and was lacking in organic symmetry. It took off from his head in the wrong places. You saw such wigs on the playful, gaily-colored seats of the changing booths at the Downtown Club—hair pieces like Skye terriers waited for their masters.

"Cantabile came to see me this morning with wild propositions," said Stronson. "I said, no way. Then he threatened he'd murder me, and he showed me the gun. He's really crazy. Then he said he'd be back with his hit man. He described how the hit would be done. The guy would track me for weeks. Then he'd shoot half my face off like a rotten pineapple. And the smashed bone and the brains and blood running out of my nose. He even told me how the murder weapon, the evidence, would be destroyed, how the killer would saw it up with a power hacksaw and hammer the pieces out and drop them down different manholes in all the suburbs. Every little detail!"

"You're dead anyway, fat-ass," said Cantabile. "They'll find you in a sewer in a few months and they'll have to scrape an inch of shit off your face to see who it was."

"There's no permit for a gun. Beautiful!"

"Now take these guys out of here," said Stronson.

"Are you going to charge everybody? You only got two warrants."

"I'm going to charge everybody."

I said, "Mr. Cantabile himself has just told you that I had nothing to do with this. My friend Thaxter and I were coming out of the Art Institute and Cantabile made us come here to discuss an investment, supposedly. I can sympathize with Mr. Stronson. He's terrified. Cantabile is out of his mind with some kind of vanity, eaten up with conceit, violent egomania—bluff. This is just one of his original hoaxes. Maybe the officer can tell you, Mr. Stronson, that I'm not the Lepke type of hired killer. I'm sure he's seen a few."

"This man never killed anybody," said the cop.

"And I have to leave for Europe and I have lots of things to attend to."

This last point was the main one. The worst of this situation was that it interfered with my anxious preoccupations, my complicated subjectivity. It was my inner civil war versus the open life which is elementary, easy for everyone to read, and characteristic of this place, Chicago, Illinois.

As a fanatical reader, walled in by his many books, accustomed to look down from his high windows on police cars, fire engines, ambulances, an involuted man who worked from thousands of private references and texts, I now found relevance in the explanation T. E. Lawrence had given for enlisting in the RAF—"To plunge crudely among crude men and find for myself . . ." How did it go, now? ". . . for these remaining years of my prime life." Horseplay, roughhouse, barracks obscenity, garbage detail. Yes, many men, Lawrence said, would take the death-sentence without a whimper to escape the life-sentence which fate carries in her other hand. I saw what he meant. So it was time that someone—and why not someone like me?—did more with this baffling and desperate question than had been done by other admirable men who attempted it. The worst thing about this absurd moment was that my stride was broken. I was expected at seven o'clock for dinner. Renata would be upset. It vexed her to be stood up. She had a temper, her temper always worked in a certain way; and also, if my suspicions were correct, Flonzaley was never far off. Substitutes are forever haunting people's minds. Even the most stable and balanced individuals have a secretly chosen replacement in reserve somewhere, and Renata was not one of the stablest. As she often fell spontaneously into rhymes, she had surprised me once by coming out with this:

When the dear
Disappear
There are others
Waiting near.

I doubt that anyone appreciated Renata's wit more deeply than I did. It always opened breath-taking perspectives of candor. But Humboldt and I had agreed long ago that I could take anything that was well said. That was true. Renata made me laugh. I was willing to deal later with the terror implicit in her words, the naked perspectives suddenly disclosed. She had for instance also said to me, "Not only are the best things in life free, but you can't be too free with the best things in life."

A lover in the lockup gave Renata a classic floozy opportunity for free behavior. Because of my habit of elevating such mean considerations to the theoretical level it will surprise no one that I started to think about the lawlessness of the unconscious and its independence from the rules of conduct. But it was only antinomian, not free. According to Steiner, true freedom lived in pure consciousness. Each microcosm had been separated from the macrocosm. In the arbitrary division between Subject and Object the world had been lost. The zero self sought diversion. It became an actor. This was the situation of the Consciousness Soul as I interpreted it. But there now passed through me a qualm of dissatisfaction with Rudolf Steiner himself. This went back to an uncomfortable passage in Kafka's *Diaries* pointed out to me by my friend Durnwald, who felt that I was still capable of doing serious intellectual work and wanted to save me from anthroposophy. Kafka too had been attracted by Steiner's visions and found the clairvoyant states he described similar to his own, feeling himself on the outer boundaries of the human. He made an appointment with Steiner at the Victoria Hotel on Jungmannstrasse. It is recorded in the *Diaries* that Steiner was wearing a dusty and spotted Prince Albert and that he had a terrible head cold. His nose ran and he kept working his handkerchief deep into his nostrils with his fingers while Kafka, observing this with disgust, told Steiner that he was an artist stuck in the insurance business. Health and character, he said, prevented him from following a literary career. If he added theosophy to literature and the insurance business, what would become of him? Steiner's answer is not recorded.

Kafka himself of course was crammed to the top with this same despairing fastidious mocking Consciousness Soul. Poor fellow, the way he stated his case didn't do him much credit. The man of genius trapped in the insurance business? A very banal complaint, not really much better than a head cold. Humboldt would have agreed. We used to talk about Kafka and I knew his views. But now Kafka and Steiner and Humboldt were together in death where, presently, all the folk in Stronson's office would join them. Reappearing, perhaps, centuries hence in a more sparkling world. It wouldn't have to sparkle much to sparkle more than this one. Nevertheless, Kafka's description of Steiner upset me.

While I was engaged in these reflections, Thaxter had gotten into the act. He came on with malice toward none. He was going to straighten matters out most amiably, not patronizing people too much. "I really don't think you want to take Mr. Citrine away on this warrant," he said, gravely smiling.

"Why not?" said the cop, with Cantabile's pistol, the fat nickel-plated Magnum, stuck in his belt.

"You agreed that Mr. Citrine doesn't resemble a killer."

"He's tired-out and white. He should go to Acapulco for a week."

"It's preposterous, a hoax like this," said Thaxter. He was showing me the beauty of his common touch, how well he understood and got around his fellow Americans. But it was obvious to me how exotic the cop found Thaxter, his elegance, his Peter Wimsey airs. "Mr. Citrine is internationally known as an historian. He really *was* decorated by the French government."

"Can you prove that?" said the cop. "You wouldn't have your medal on you by any chance, would you?"

"People don't carry medals around," I said.

"Well, what kind of proof have you got?"

"All I have is this bit of ribbon. I have the right to wear it in my buttonhole."

"Let's have a look at that," he said.

I drew out the tangled faded insignificant bit of lime green silk.

"That?" said the cop. "I wouldn't tie it on a chicken leg."

I agreed with the cop completely, and as a Chicagoan I scoffed inwardly with him at these phony foreign honors. I was the Shoveleer, burning with self-ridicule. It served the French right, too. This was not one of their best centuries. They were doing everything badly. What did they mean by handing out these meager bits of kinky green string? Because Renata insisted in Paris that I must wear it in my buttonhole, we had been exposed to the insults of the real *chevalier* whom Renata and I met at dinner, the man with the red rosette, the "hard scientist," to use his own term. He gave me the snubbing of my life. "American slang is deficient, nonexistent," he said. "French has twenty words for 'boot.'" Then he was snooty about the Behavioral Sciences—he took me for a behavioral scientist—and he was very rough on my green ribbon. He said, "I am sure you have written some estimable books but this is the kind of decoration given to people who improve the *poubelles*." Nothing but grief had ever come of my being honored by the French. Well, that would have to pass. The only real distinction at this dangerous moment in human history and cosmic development has nothing to do with medals and ribbons. Not to fall asleep is distinguished. Everything else is mere popcorn.

Cantabile was still facing the wall. The cop, I was glad to note, had it in for him. "You just hold it, there," he said. It seemed to me that we in this office were under something like a huge transparent wave. This enormous transparent thing stood still above us, flashing like crystal. We were all within it. When it broke and detonated we would be scattered for miles and miles along some far white beach. I almost hoped that Cantabile would have his neck broken. But, no, when it happened I saw each of us cast up safe and separate on a bare white pearly shore.

As all parties continued—Stronson, stung by Cantabile's evocation of his corpse fished from the sewer, crying in a kind of pig's soprano voice, "I'll see that *you* get it, anyway!" while Thaxter was coming in underneath, trying to be persuasive—I tuned out and gave my mind to one of my theories. Some people embrace their gifts with gratitude. Others have no use for them and can think only of overcoming their weaknesses. Only their defects interest and challenge them. Thus those who hate people may seek them out. Misanthropes often practice psychiatry. The shy become performers. Natural thieves look for positions of trust. The frightened make bold moves. Take the case of Stronson, a man who entered into desperate schemes to swindle gangsters. Or take myself, a lover of beauty who insisted on living in Chicago. Or Von Humboldt Fleisher, a man of powerful social instincts burying himself in the dreary countryside.

Stronson didn't have the strength to carry through. Seeing how self-deformed he was, fat but elegant; short of leg and ham, on platform shoes; given to squealing, but sending his voice deep, I was sorry, oh! deeply sorry for him. It seemed to me that his true nature was quickly reclaiming him. Had he forgotten to shave that morning or did terror make his beard suddenly rush out? And long awful bristles were coming up from his collar. A woodchuck look was coming over him. The pageboy wave went lank with sweat. "I want all these guys handcuffed," he said to the plainclothesman.

"What, with one pair of cuffs?"

"Well, put 'em on Cantabile. Go, put 'em on."

I completely agreed with him, in silence. Yes, manacle the son of a bitch, twist his arms behind him, and cut into the flesh. But having said these savage things to myself, I didn't necessarily wish to see them happen.

Thaxter drew the cop aside and said a few words in an undertone. I wondered later whether he hadn't passed him a secret CIA code word. You couldn't be sure with Thaxter. To this day I have never been able to decide whether or not he had ever been a secret agent. Years ago he invited me to be his guest in Yucatán. Three times I changed planes to get there, and then I was met at a dirt landing strip by a peon in sandals who drove me in a new Cadillac to Thaxter's villa, fully staffed with Indian servants. There were cars and jeeps, and a wife and little children, and Thaxter had already mastered the local dialect and ordered people around. A linguistic genius, he quickly learned new languages. But he was having trouble with a bank in Mérida, and there was, of all things, a country club in his neighborhood where he had run up a tab. I arrived just as he was completing the invariable pattern. He said on the second day that we were leaving this damn place. We packed his steamer trunks with fur coats and tennis equipment, with temple treasures and electrical appliances. As we drove away I was holding one of his babies on my lap.

The cop took us out of Stronson's office. Stronson called after us, "You bastards are going to get it. I promise you. No matter what happens to me. Especially you, Cantabile."

Tomorrow he himself would get it.

As we waited for the elevator, Thaxter and I had time to confer. "No, I'm not being booked," said Thaxter. "I'm almost sorry about that. I'd love to go along, really."

"I expect you to get busy," I said. "I felt that Cantabile was going to pull something like this. And Renata's going to be very upset, that's the worst of it. Don't go off and forget me now, Thaxter."

"Don't be absurd, Charles. I'll get the lawyers right on this. Give me some names and numbers."

"First thing is to call up Renata. Take Szathmar's number. Also Tomchek and Srole."

Thaxter wrote the information on an American Express receipt form. Could it be that he was still a cardholder?

"You'll lose that flimsy bit of paper," I said.

Thaxter spoke to me rather seriously about this. "Watch it, Charlie," he said. "You're being a nervous Nellie. This is a trying moment, sure. Exactly why you have to watch it all the more. *A plus forte raison.*"

You knew that Thaxter was in earnest when he spoke French. And whereas George Swiebel always shouted at me not to abuse my body, Thaxter forever warned me about my anxiety level. Now there was a man whose nerves were strong enough for his chosen way of life. And notwithstanding his weakness for French expressions, Thaxter was a real American in that, like Walt Whitman, he offered himself as an archetype —"What I assume you will assume." At the moment, that didn't particularly help. I was under arrest. My feelings toward Thaxter were those of a man with many bundles trying to find the doorkey and hampered by the house cat. But the truth was that the people from whom I looked for help were by no means my favorites. Nothing was to be expected from Thaxter. I even suspected that his efforts to help might be downright dangerous. If I cried out that I was drowning, he would come running and throw me a life preserver of solid cement. If odd feet call for odd shoes, odd souls have odd requirements and affection comes to them in odd modes. A man who longed for help was fond of someone incapable of giving any.

I suppose that it was the receptionist who had sent for the blue-and-white squad car now waiting for us. She was a very pretty young woman. I had looked at her as we were leaving the office and thought, Here's a sentimental girl. Well brought up. Lovely. Distressed to see people arrested. Tears in her eyes.

"In the back seat, you," said the plainclothesman to Cantabile, who, in his pinch hat, white in the face, hair sticking out at the sides, got in. At this moment, disheveled, he seemed for the first time genuinely Italian.

"The main thing is Renata. Get in touch with Renata," I told Thaxter as I got into the front seat. "I'll be in trouble if you don't—trouble!"

"Don't worry. People won't let you disappear from sight forever," said Thaxter.

His words of comfort gave me my first moment of deeper anxiety.

He did indeed try to get in touch with Renata and with Szathmar. But Renata was still at the Merchandise Mart with her client, picking fabrics, and Szathmar had already closed his office. Somehow Thaxter forgot what I had told him about Tomchek and Srole. To kill time, therefore, he went to a Black Kung Fu movie on Randolph Street. When the show let out he reached Renata at home. He said that since she knew Szathmar so well he thought he could leave things to her, entirely. After all, he was a stranger in town. The Boston Celtics were playing the Chicago Bulls and Thaxter bought a ticket to the basketball game from a scalper. En route to the Stadium the cab stopped at Zimmerman's and he bought a bottle of Piesporter. He couldn't get it chilled properly, but it went well with the sturgeon sandwiches.

Cantabile's dark form was riding before me in the front seat of the squad car. I addressed my thoughts to it. A man like Cantabile took advantage of my inadequate theory of evil, wasn't that it? He filled all the gaps in it to the best of his histrionic ability with his plunging and bluffing. Or did I, as an American, *have* a theory of evil? Perhaps not. So he entered the field from that featureless and undemarcated side where I was weak, with his ideas and conceits. This pest delighted the ladies, it seemed—he pleased Polly and, apparently, his wife the graduate student as well. It was my guess that he was an erotic lightweight. But after all it's the imagination that counts for most with women. So he made his progress through life with his fine riding gloves and his calfskin boots, and the keenly gleaming fuzz of his tweeds, and the Magnum he carried in his waistband, threatening everybody with death. Threats were what he loved. He had called me in the night to threaten me. Threats had affected his bowels yesterday on Division Street. This morning he had gone to threaten Stronson. In the afternoon he offered, or threatened, to have Denise knocked off. Yes, he was a queer creature, with his white face, his long ecclesiastical-wax nose with its dark flues. He was very restless in the front seat. He seemed to be trying to get a look at me. He was almost limber enough to twist his head about and preen his own back feathers. What might it mean that he had tried to pass me off as a murderer? Did he find the original suggestion for that in me? Or was he trying in his own way to bring me out, to carry me into the world, a world from which I had the illusion that I was withdrawing? On the Chicago level of judgment I dismissed him as ready for the bughouse. Well, he was ready for the bughouse, certainly. I was sophisticated enough to recognize that in what he proposed that we two should do with Polly there was a touch of homosexuality, but that wasn't very serious. I hoped that they would send him back to prison. On the other hand I sensed that he was doing something for me. In his gleaming tweed fuzz, the harshness of which suggested nettles, he had materialized in my path. Pale and crazy, with his mink mustache, he seemed to have a spiritual office to perform. He had appeared in order to move me from dead center. Because I came from Chicago no normal and sensible person could do anything of this sort for me. I couldn't be myself with normal sensible people. Look at my relations with a man like Richard Durnwald. Much as I admired him, I couldn't be mentally comfortable with Durnwald. I was slightly more successful with Dr. Scheldt the anthroposophist, but I had my troubles with him too, troubles of a Chicago nature. When he spoke to me of esoteric mysteries I wanted to say to him, "Don't give me that spiritual hokum, friend!" And after all, my relations with Dr. Scheldt were tremendously important. The questions I raised with him couldn't have been more serious.

All this went to my head, or flowed to my head, and I recalled Humboldt in Princeton quoting to me, "*Es schwindelt!*" The words of V. I. Lenin at the Smolny Institute. And things were *schwindling* now. Now was it because, like Lenin, I was about to found a police state? It was from a flux or inundation of sensations, insights, and ideas.

Of course the cop was right. Strictly speaking, I was no killer. But I did incorporate other people into myself and consume them. When they died I passionately mourned. I said I would continue their work and their lives. But wasn't it a fact that I added their strength to mine? Didn't I have an eye on them in the days of their vigor and glory? And on their women? I could already see the outline of my soul's purgatorial tasks, when it entered the next place.

"Watch it, Charlie," Thaxter had admonished me. He wore his cape and held the ideal attaché case and the natural hook umbrella, as well as the sturgeon sandwiches. I watched it. *A plus forte raison*, I watched it. Watching, I was aware that in the squad car I was following in Humboldt's footsteps. Twenty years ago in the hands of the law, he had wrestled with the cops. They had forced him into a strait jacket. He had had diarrhea in the police wagon as they rushed him to Bellevue. They were trying to cope, to do something with a poet. What did the New York police know about poets! They knew drunks and muggers, they knew rapists, they knew women in labor and hopheads, but they were at sea with poets. Then he had called me from a phone booth in the hospital. And I had answered from that hot grimy flaking dressing room at the Belasco. And he had yelled, "This is life, Charlie, not literature!" Well, I don't suppose the Powers, Thrones and Dominions, the Archai, the Archangels and the Angels read poetry. Why should they? They are shaping the universe. They're busy. But when Humboldt cried, "Life!" he didn't mean the Thrones, Exousiai, and Angels. He only meant realistic, naturalistic life. As if art hid the truth and only the sufferings of the mad revealed it. *This* was impoverished imagination?

We arrived and Cantabile and I were separated. They kept him at the desk, I went inside.

Anticipating the job I had cut out for me in purgatory, I didn't find it necessary to take jail too seriously. What was it, after all? A lot of bustle, and people who specialized in giving you a hard time. They photographed me, front and sides. Good. After these mug shots I was fingerprinted too. Very well. Following this, I expected to go into the lockup. There was a fat domestic-looking policeman waiting to take me to the slammer. Inside duties make these cops obese. There he was, housewifely, in a coat sweater and slippers, with belly and gun, a big pouting lip, and fat furrows at the back of his head. He was steering me in when someone said, "You! Charles Citrine! Outside!" I went back into the main corridor. I wondered how Szathmar had gotten here so fast. But it wasn't Szathmar who was waiting for me, it was Stronson's young receptionist. This beautiful girl said that her employer had decided to drop the case against me. He was going to concentrate on Cantabile.

"And did Stronson send you over?"

She explained, "Well, I really wanted to come. I knew who you were. As soon as I found out your name, I did. So I explained it to my boss. He's been like in shock these days. You can't exactly blame Mr. Stronson, when people come and say he's going to be murdered. But I finally got him to understand that you were a famous person, not a hit man."

"Ah, I see. And you're a dear girl as well as a beautiful one. I can't tell you how grateful I am. Talking to him couldn't have been easy."

"He really was scared. Now he's mostly depressed. Why are your hands so dirty?" she said.

"Fingerprinting. The ink they used."

She was upset. "My God! Imagine fingerprinting a man like you!" She opened her purse and began to moisten paper tissues and to rub my stained fingertips.

"No, thank you. No, no, don't do that," I said. Such attentions always get to me, and it seemed a dreadfully long time since anyone had done me any intimate kindness like this. There are days when one wants to go to the barber, not for a haircut (there's not much hair to cut) but just for the sake of the touch.

"Why not?" said the girl. "I feel that I've always known you."

"From books?"

"Not books. I'm afraid I never read any of your books. I understand they're history books and history has never been my bag. No, Mr. Citrine, through my mother."

"Do I know your mother?"

"Since I was a kid, I've heard you were her school-days' sweetheart."

"Your mother isn't Naomi Lutz!"

"Yes, she was. I can't tell you how thrilled she and Doc were when they ran into you at that bar downtown."

"Yes, Doc was with her."

"When Doc passed away, Mother was going to call you. She says now you're the only one she can talk old times with.

There are things she wants to remember and can't place. Just the other day she couldn't recall the name of the town where her Uncle Asher lived."

"Her Uncle Asher lived in Paducah, Kentucky. Of course I'll call her. I loved your mother, Miss. . ."

"Maggie," she said.

"Maggie. You've inherited her curves from the waist down. I never saw another back-curve so lovely till this moment, and in jail, of all places. You also have her gums and teeth, a bit short in the teeth, and the same smile. Your mother was beautiful. You'll excuse me for saying this, it's an exciting moment, but I always felt that if I could have embraced your mother every night for forty years, as her husband, of course, my life would have been completely fulfilled, a success—instead of this. How old are you, Maggie?"

"Twenty-five."

"O Lord!" I said as she washed my fingers in the freezing drinking water. My hand is very sensitive to a feminine touch. A kiss in the palm can send me out of my head.

She took me home in her Volkswagen, weeping a little as she drove. She was thinking perhaps of the happiness her mother and I had missed. And when, I wondered, would I rise at last above all this stuff, the accidental, the merely phenomenal, the wastefully and randomly human, and be fit to enter higher worlds?

So before leaving town I paid a visit to Naomi. Her married name was Wolper.

But I didn't go immediately to see her. I had a hundred chores to do first.

The last days in Chicago were crowded. As if to make up for the hours Cantabile's mischief had cost me, I followed a busy schedule. My accountant, Murra, gave me a whole hour of his time. In his smooth offices, decorated by the famous Richard Himmel and overlooking the lightest green part of the Chicago River, he told me that he had failed to convince the IRS that it had no case against me. His own bill was high. I owed him fifteen hundred dollars for getting nowhere. When I left his building I found myself in the gloom of Michigan Avenue in front of the electric-light shop near Wacker Drive. Always drawn to this place, with its ingenious new devices, the tints and shapes of bulbs and tubes, I bought a 300-watt flood reflector. I had no use for this article. I was going away. What did I need it for? The purchase only expressed my condition. I was still furnishing my retreat, my sanctuary, my Fort Dearborn deep in Indian (Materialistic) Territory. Also I was in the grip of departure anxieties—jet engines would tear me from the ground at two thousand miles per hour but where was I going, and what for? The reasons for this terrific speed remained unclear.

No, buying a bulb didn't help much. What did give me comfort was to talk with Dr. Scheldt. I questioned him about the Spirits of Form, the Exousiai, known in Jewish antiquity by another name. These shapers of destiny should long ago have surrendered their functions and powers to the Archai, the Spirits of Personality who stand one rank closer to man in the universal hierarchy. But a number of dissident Exousiai, playing a backward role in world history, had for centuries refused to let the Archai take over. They obstructed the development of a modern sort of consciousness. Refractory Exousiai belonging to an earlier phase of human evolution were responsible for tribalism and the persistence of peasant or folk consciousness, hatred of the West and of the New, they nourished atavistic attitudes. I wondered whether this might not explain how Russia in 1917 had put on a revolutionary mask to disguise reaction; and whether the struggle between these same forces might not lie behind Hitler's rise to power as well. The Nazis also adopted the modern disguise. But you couldn't entirely blame these Russians, Germans, Spaniards, and Asiatics. The terrors of freedom and modernity were fearful. And this was what made America appear so giddy and monstrous in the eyes of the world. It also made certain countries seem, to American eyes, desperately, monumentally dull. Fighting to retain their inertias the Russians had produced their incomparably boring and terrifying society. And America, under the jurisdiction of the Archai, or Spirits of Personality, produced autonomous modern individuals with all the giddiness and despair of the free, and infected with a hundred diseases unknown during the long peasant epochs.

After visiting with Dr. Scheldt I took my small daughters, Lish and Mary, to the Christmas pageant after all, outmaneuvered by Denise, who had put them on the phone in tears. Unexpectedly, however, the pageant was very stirring. I do love theatricals, with their breaking voices, missed cues, and silly costumes. All the fine costumes were in the audience. Hundreds of excited kiddies were brought by their Mamas, many of those Mamas being tigresses of the subtlest sort. And dressed, arrayed, perfumed to a degree! *Rip Van Winkle* was given as a curtain raiser. To me it was immensely relevant. It was all very well to blame the dwarfs for making Rip drunk, but he had his own good reasons for passing out. The weight of the sense world is too heavy for some people, and getting heavier all the time. His twenty years of sleep, let me tell you, went straight to my heart. My heart was sensitive today—worry, anticipated problems, and remorse made it tender and vulnerable. An idiotic old lecher was leaving two children to follow an obvious gold digger to corrupt Europe. As one of the few fathers in the audience I felt how wrong this was. I was encompassed by feminine judgment. The views of all these women were unmistakably expressed. I saw for instance that the mothers resented the portrayal of Mrs. Van Winkle, clearly the American Bitch in an early version. Myself, I reject all such notions about American Bitches. The mothers, however, were angry, they smiled but were hostile. The kids, though, were innocent, and they clapped and cheered when Rip was told that his wife had died of apoplexy during a fit of rage.

I was thinking of the higher significance of these things—naturally. For me the real question was how Rip would have spent his time if the dwarfs had not put him to sleep. He had an ordinary human American right, of course, to hunt and fish and roam the woods with his dog—much like Huckleberry Finn in the Territory Ahead. The following question was more intimate and difficult: what would I have *done* if I hadn't been asleep in spirit for so long? Amid the fluttering and squealing and clapping and writhing of little children, so pure of face, so fragrant (even the small gases released, inevitably, by a crowd of children were pleasant if you breathed them in a paternal spirit), so *savable*, I forced myself to stop and answer—I was *obliged* to do it. If you believed one of the pamphlets Dr. Scheldt had given me to read, this sleeping was no trifling matter. Our unwillingness to come out of the state of sleep was the result of a desire to evade an impending revelation. Certain spiritual beings must achieve their development through men, and we betray and abandon them by this absenteeism, this will-to-snooze. Our duty, said one bewitching pamphlet, is to collaborate with the Angels. They appear within us (as the Spirit called the *Maggid* manifested himself to the great Rabbi Joseph Karo). Guided by the Spirits of Form, Angels sow seeds of the future in us. They inculcate certain pictures into us of which we are "normally" unaware. Among other things they wish to make us see the concealed divinity of other human beings. They show man how he can cross by means of thought the abyss that separates him from Spirit. To the soul they offer freedom and to the body they offer love. These facts must be grasped by waking consciousness. Because, when he sleeps, the sleeper *sleeps.* Great world events pass him by. Nothing is momentous enough to rouse him. Decades of calendars drop their leaves on him just as the trees dropped leaves and twigs on Rip. Moreover, the Angels themselves are vulnerable. Their aims must be realized in earthly humanity itself. Already the brotherly love they put into us has been corrupted into sexual monstrosity. What are we doing with each other in the sack? Love is being disgracefully perverted. Then, too, the Angels send us radiant freshness and we, by our own sleeping, make it all dull. And in the political sphere we can hear, semiconscious though we are, the grunting of the great swine empires of the earth. The stink of these swine dominions rises into the upper air and darkens it. Is it any wonder that we invite slumber to come quickly and seal our spirits? And, said the pamphlet, the Angels, thwarted by our sleep during waking hours, have to do what they can with us in the night. But then their work cannot touch our feeling or thinking, for these are absent during sleep. Only the unconscious body and the sustaining vital principle, the ether body, lie there in bed. The great feelings and the thoughts are gone. So also in the day, sleepwalking. And if we will not awaken, if the Spiritual Soul can't be brought to participate in the work of the Angels, we will be sunk. For me the clinching argument was that the impulses of higher love were corrupted into sexual degeneracy. That really went home. Perhaps I had more basic, ultimate reasons for going off with Renata, leaving two little girls in dangerous Chicago, than I was aware enough to produce at a moment's notice. I might, just possibly, justify what I was doing. After all, Christian in *Pilgrim's Progress* had taken off, too, and left his family to pursue salvation. Before I could do the children any real good, I had to wake up. This muddiness, this failure to focus and to concentrate, was very painful. I could see myself as I had been thirty years ago. I didn't need to look in the picture album. That damning photograph was unforgettable. There I was, a pretty young man under a tree, holding hands with an attractive girl. But I might as well have been wearing flannel pajamas as that flapping double-breasted suit—the gift of my brother Julius—for in the flower of my youth and at the height of my powers I was out cold.

As I sat in the theater I allowed myself to imagine that there were spirits near, that they wished to reach us, that their breathing enlivened the red of the little dresses the kids were wearing, just as oxygen brightened fire.

Then the children started to scream. Rip was staggering up from the mass of leaves that had dropped on him. Knowing what he was up against, I groaned. The real question was whether he could stay awake.

During intermission I ran into Dr. Klosterman from the Downtown Club. He was the one who had urged me in the sauna to go to a plastic surgeon and do something about the bags under my eyes—a simple operation to make me look years younger. All I had for him was a cold nod when he came forward with his children. He said, "We haven't seen you around lately."

Well, I hadn't been around lately. But only last night, unconscious in Renata's arms, I had dreamed again that I was playing paddle ball like a champion. My dream-backhand skimmed the left wall of the court and dropped with deadly english into the corner. I beat Scottie the club-player, and also the unbeatable Greek chiropractor, a skinny athlete, very hairy, pigeon-toed but a fiery competitor from whom in real life I could never win a single point. But on the court of my dreams I was a tiger. So in dreams of pure wakefulness and forward intensity I overcame my inertia, my mooning and muddiness. In dreams at any rate I had no intention of quitting.

As I was thinking of all this in the lobby, Lish remembered that she had brought a note for me from her mother. I opened the envelope and read, "Charles: my life has been threatened!"

There was no end to Cantabile. Before kidnaping Thaxter and me on Michigan Boulevard, perhaps at the very moment when we were admiring the beautiful Monet Sandvika winter scene, Cantabile was on the telephone with Denise, doing what he loved best, i.e., making threats.

Once when he was speaking of Denise, George Swiebel had explained to me (although knowing his Nature System I could have provided this explanation myself), "Denise's struggle with you is her whole sex life. Don't talk to her, don't argue with her, unless you still want to give her kicks." Undoubtedly he would have interpreted Cantabile's threats in the same way. "This is how the son of a bitch gets his nuts off." But it was just possible that Cantabile's death-dealing fantasy, his imaginary role as Death's highest-ranking deputy, was intended also to wake me up—"*Brutus, thou sleep'st*," etcetera. This had occurred to me in the squad car.

But he had really done it now. "Does your mother expect an answer?" I asked the kid.

Lish looked at me with her mother's eyes, those wide amethyst circles. "She didn't say, Daddy."

Denise had certainly reported to Urbanovich that there was a plot to murder her. This would clinch the matter with the judge. He didn't trust or like me anyway, and he could impound my money. I could forget about those dollars, they were gone. What now? I began again with the usual haste and inaccuracy to tot up my fluid resources, twelve hundred here, eighteen hundred there, the sale of my beautiful carpets, the sale of the Mercedes, very disadvantageous given its damaged condition. So far as I knew, Cantabile was locked up at Twenty-sixth and California. I hoped he would get it in the neck. Lots of people were killed in jail. Perhaps someone would do him in. But I didn't believe that he would spend much time behind bars. Getting out was very easy now and he'd probably draw another suspended sentence. The courts now gave them as freely as the Salvation Army gave out doughnuts. Well, it didn't really matter, I was leaving for Milan.

So, as I said, I paid a sentimental visit to Naomi Lutz, now Wolper. I hired a limousine from the livery service to take me out to Marquette Park—why stint myself now? It was wintry. wet, sleety, a good day for a schoolboy to fight the weather with his satchel and feel dauntless. Naomi was at her post, stopping traffic while kids trotted, straggled, dragged their raincapes and stamped through the puddles. Under the police uniform she wore layers of sweaters. On her head was a garrison cap and a Sam Browne belt crossed her chest—the works: fleece boots, mittens, her neck protected by an orange havelock, her figure obliterated. She waved her coat-hampered wet arms, gathering kids about her, she stopped the traffic and then, heavy in the back, she turned and footed slowly to the curb on her thick soles. And this was the woman for whom I once felt perfect love. She was the person with whom I should have been allowed to sleep for forty years in my favorite position (the woman backed up to me and her breasts in my hands). In a city like brutal Chicago could a man really expect to survive without such intimate, such private comfort? When I came up to her I saw the young woman within the old one. I saw her in the neat short teeth, the winsome gums, the single dimple in the left cheek. I thought I could still breathe in her young woman's odor, damp and rich, and I heard the gliding and drawling of her voice, an affectation she and I had both thought utterly charming once. And even now, I thought, Why not? The rain of the Seventies looked to me like the moisture of the Thirties when our adolescent lovemaking brought out tiny drops in a little band, a Venetian mask across the middle of her face. But I knew better than to try to touch her, to take off the police coat and the sweaters and the dress and the underclothes. Nor would she want me to see what had happened to her thighs and her breasts. That was all right for her friend Hank—Hank and Naomi had grown old together—but not for me, who knew her way-back-when. There was no prospect of this. It was not indicated, not hinted, not possible. It was only one of those things that had to be thought.

We drank coffee in her kitchen. She had invited me to brunch and served fried eggs, smoked salmon, nutbread, and comb honey. I felt completely at home with her old ironware and hand-knitted pot holders. The house was all that Wolper left her, she said. "When I saw how fast he was losing money on the horses I insisted that he should make the title over."

"Smart thinking."

"A little later my husband's nose and ankle were broken, just as a warning, by a juice man. Till then I didn't know Wolper was paying the gangsters juice. He came home from the hospital with his face all purple around the bandages. He said I shouldn't sell the bungalow to save his life. He cried and said he was no damn good and he decided to disappear. I know you're surprised that I live in this Czech neighborhood. But my father-in-law, a smart old Jew, bought investment property in this nice safe Bohunk district. So this was where we wound up. Well, Wolper was a jolly man. He didn't give me trouble the way you would have. For a wedding present he made me a present of my own convertible and a charge account at Field's. That was what I wanted most in life."

"I always felt it would have given me strength to be married to you, Naomi."

"Don't idealize so much. You were a violent kid. You almost choked me to death because I went to a dance with some basketball player. And once, in the garage, you put a rope on your neck and threatened to hang yourself if you didn't get your way. Do you remember?"

"I'm afraid I do, yes. Superkeen needs were swelling up in me."

"Wolper is married again and has a bikeshop in New Mexico. He may feel safer near the border. Yes, you were thrilling but I never knew where you were at with your Swinburne and your Baudelaire and Oscar Wilde and Karl Marx. Boy, you certainly did carry on."

"Those were intoxicating books and I was in the thick of beauty and wild about goodness and thought and poetry and love. Wasn't that merely adolescence?"

She smiled at me and said, "I don't really think so. Doc told Mother that your whole family were a bunch of greenhorns and aliens, too damn emotional, the whole bunch of you. Doc died last year."

"Your daughter told me that."

"Yes, he fell apart finally. When old men put two socks on one foot and pee into the bathtub I suppose it's the end."

"I'm afraid so. I myself think that Doc overdid the Yankee Doodle stuff. Being a Babbitt inspired him almost the way Swinburne did me. He was dying to say good-by to Jewry, or to feudalism. . . ."

"Do me a favor—I still freeze when you use a word like feudalism on me. That was the trouble between us. You came down front Madison raving about that poet named Humboldt Park or something and borrowed my savings to go to New York on a Greyhound bus. I really and truly loved you, Charlie, but when you rolled away to see this god of yours, I went home and painted my nails and turned on the radio. Your father was furious when I told him you were a Fuller Brush salesman in Manhattan. He needed your help in the wood business."

"Nonsense, he had Julius."

"Jesus, your father was handsome. He looked like—what the girls used to say—The Spaniard Who Ruined My Life. And Julius?"

"Julius is disfiguring south Texas with shopping centers and condominiums."

"But you people all loved each other. You were like real primitive that way. Maybe that's why my father called you greenhorns."

"Well, Naomi, my father became an American too and so did Julius. They stopped all that immigrant loving. Only I persisted, in my childish way. My emotional account was always overdrawn. I never have forgotten how my mother cried out when I fell down the stairs or how she pressed the lump on my head with the blade of a knife. And what a knife—it was her Russian silver with a handle like a billy club. So there you are. Whether it was a lump on my head, or Julius's geometry, or how Papa could raise the rent, or poor Mama's toothaches, it was the most momentous thing on earth for us all. I never lost this intense way of caring—no, that isn't so. I'm afraid the truth is that I did lose it. Yes, sure I lost it. But I still required it. That's always been the problem. I required it and apparently I also promised it. To women, I mean. For women I had this utopian emotional love aura and made them feel I was a cherishing man. Sure, I'd cherish them in the way they all dreamed of being cherished."

"But it was a phony," said Naomi. "You yourself lost it. You didn't cherish."

"I lost it. Although anything so passionate probably remains in force somewhere."

"Charlie, you put it over on lots of girls. You must have made them awfully unhappy."

"I wonder whether mine is such an exceptional case of longing-heart-itis. It's unreal, of course, perverse. But it's also American, isn't it? When I say American I mean uncorrected by the main history of human suffering."

Naomi sighed as she listened to me and then said, "Ah, Charlie, I'll never understand how or why you reach your conclusions. When you used to lecture me, I never could follow you at all. But at the time your play opened on Broadway, you were in love with a girl, they tell me. What happened to her?"

"Demmie Vonghel. Yes. She was the real thing, too. She was killed in South America with her father. He was a millionaire from Delaware. They took off from Caracas in a DC-3 and crashed in the jungle."

"Oh how sad and terrible."

"I went down to Venezuela to look for her."

"I'm glad you did that. I was going to ask."

"I took the same flight out of Caracas. They were old planes and patched up. Indians flying around with their chickens and goats. The pilot invited me to sit in the cockpit. There was a big crack in the windshield and the wind rushed in. Flying over the mountains I was afraid we wouldn't make it either, and I thought, O Lord, let it happen to me the way it happened to Demmie. Looking at those mountains I frankly didn't care much for the way the world was made, Naomi."

"What do you mean by that?"

"Oh I don't know, but you get disaffected from nature and all its miracles and stupendous achievements, from subatomic to galactic. Things play too rough with human beings. They chafe too hard. They stick you in the veins. As we came over the mountains and I saw the Pacific throwing a fit of epilepsy against the shore I thought, To hell with *you,* then. You can't always like the way in which the world was molded. Sometimes I think, Who wants to be an eternal spirit and have more existences! Screw all that! But I was telling you about the flight. Up and down about ten times. We landed on bare earth. Strips of red dirt on coffee plantations. Waving at us under the trees were little naked kids with their brown bellies and bent dinguses hanging."

"You never found anything? Didn't you search in the jungle?"

"Sure I searched. We even found a plane, but not the missing DC-3. This was a Cessna that went down with some Japanese mining engineers. Vines and flowers were growing all over their bones, and God knows what spiders and other animals were making themselves at home in their skulls. I didn't want to discover Demmie in that condition."

"You didn't like the jungle much."

"No. I drank lots of gin. I developed a taste for straight gin, like my friend Von Humboldt Fleisher."

"The poet! What happened to him?"

"He's dead, too, Naomi."

"Isn't all this dying something, Charlie!"

"The whole thing is disintegrating and reintegrating all the time, and you have to guess whether it's always the same cast of characters or a lot of different characters."

"I suppose you finally got to the mission," said Naomi.

"Yes, and there were lots of Demmies there, about twenty Vonghels. They were all cousins. All with the same long heads golden hair knock-knees and upturned noses, and the same mumbling style of speech. When I said that I was Demmie's fiancé from New York they thought I was some sort of nut. I had to attend services and sing hymns, because the Indians wouldn't understand a white visitor who was not a Christian."

"So you sang hymns while your heart was breaking."

"I was glad to sing the hymns. And Dr. Tim Vonghel gave me a bucket of gentian violet to sit in. He told me I had a bad case of *tinia crura.* So I stayed among these cannibals, hoping that Demmie would show up."

"Were they cannibals?"

"They had eaten the first group of missionaries that came there. As you sang in the chapel and saw the filed teeth of somebody who had probably eaten your brother—Dr. Timothy's brother was eaten, and he knew the fellows who had done it—well, Naomi, there's lots of peculiar merit in people. I wouldn't be surprised if my experiences in the jungle put me in a forgiving frame of mind."

"Who was there to forgive?" said Naomi.

"This friend of mine, Von Humboldt Fleisher. He drew a check on my account while I was knocking myself out over Demmie in the jungle."

"Did he forge your signature?"

"I had given him a blank check, and he put it through for more than six thousand dollars."

"No! But you, of course, you didn't expect a poet to act that way about money, did you? Excuse me for laughing. But you always did provoke people into doing the dirty human thing to you by insisting that they should do the Goody Two-Shoes bit. I'm awfully sorry you lost that girl in the jungle. She sounds to me like your type. She was like you, wasn't she? You could both have been out of it together, and perfectly happy."

"I see what you mean, Naomi. I failed to understand the deeper side of human nature. Until recently I couldn't bear to think of it."

"Only you could get mixed up with this goofy fellow that threatened Stronson. This Italian Maggie described to me."

"You may be right," I said. "And I must try to analyze my motives for going along with people of the Cantabile type. But think how I felt to have a child of yours, that beautiful girl, come and get me out of jail—the daughter of the woman I loved."

"Don't get sentimental, Charlie. Please!" she said.

"I have to tell you, Naomi, that I loved you cell by cell. To me you were a completely nonalien person. Your molecules were my molecules. Your smell was my smell. And your daughter reminded me of you—same teeth, same smile, same everything, for all I know."

"Don't get carried away. You'd marry her, wouldn't you, you old sex pot. Are you testing to see if I'd say go ahead? It's a real compliment that you're ready to marry her because she reminds you of me. Well, she's a wonderful kid, but what you need is a woman with a heart as big as a washing machine, and that's not my daughter. Anyway, you're still with that chick I saw in the bar—the gorgeous kind of Oriental one, built like a belly dancer, and big dark eyes. Aren't you?"

"Yes, she is gorgeous, and I'm still the boyfriend."

"A boyfriend! I wonder what it is with you—a big important clever man going around so eager from woman to woman. Haven't you got anything more important to do? Boy, have women ever sold you a bill of goods! Do you think they're really going to give you the kind of help and comfort you're looking for? As advertised?"

"Well, it is advertised, isn't it?"

"It's like an instinct with women," she said. "You communicate to them what you have to have and right away they tell you they've got exactly what you need, although they never even heard of it until just now. They're not even necessarily lying. They just have an instinct that they can supply everything that a man can ask for, and they're ready to take on any size or shape or type of man. That's what they're like. So you go around looking for a woman like yourself. There ain't no such animal. Not even his Demmie could have been. But the girls tell you, 'Your search is ended. Stop here. I'm it.' Then you award the contract. Of course nobody can deliver and everybody gets sore as hell. Well, Maggie isn't your type. Why don't you tell me about your wife?"

"Don't put temptation before me. Just pour me another cup."

"What's the temptation?"

"Oh, the temptation? The temptation is to complain. I could tell you how bad Denise is with the kids, how she dumps them when she can, has the court tie me in knots and the lawyers rip me off, and so on. Now that's a Case, Naomi. A Case can be a work of art, the beautiful version of one's sad life. Humboldt the poet used to perform his Case all over New York. But these Cases are bad art, as a rule. How will all this complaining seem when the soul has flowed out into the universe and looks back on the complete scene of earthly suffering?"

"You've only changed physically," said Naomi. "This is how you used to talk. What do you mean, 'the soul flows out into the universe'? . . . When I was an ignorant girl and loved you, you tried out your ideas on me."

"I found when I made my living by writing people's personal memoirs that no successful American had ever made a real mistake, no one had sinned or ever had a single thing to hide, there have been no liars. The method practiced is concealment through candor to guarantee duplicity with honor. The writer would be drilled by the man who hired him until he believed it all himself. Read the autobiography of any great American—Lyndon Johnson for instance—and you'll see how faithfully his brainwashed writers reproduce his Case. Many Americans—"

"Never mind many Americans," said Naomi. How comfortable she looked in slippers, smiling in the kitchen, her fat arms crossed. I kept repeating that it would have been bliss to sleep with her for forty years, that it would have defeated death, and so on. But could I really have borne it? The fact was that I became more and more fastidious as I grew older. So now I was honor-bound to face the touchy question: could I really have embraced this faded Naomi and loved her to the end? She really didn't look good. She had been beaten about by biological storms (the mineral body is worn out by the developing spirit). But this was a challenge that I could have met. Yes, I could have done it. Yes, it would have worked. Molecule for molecule she was still Naomi. Each cell of those stout arms was still a Naomi cell. The charm of those short teeth still went to my heart. Her drawl was as effective as ever. The Spirits of Personality had done a real job on her. For me the Anima, as C. G. Jung called it, was still there. The counterpart soul, the missing half described by Aristophanes in the *Symposium*.

"So you're going away to Europe with that young broad?" she said.

I was astonished. "Who told you that?"

"I ran into George Swiebel."

"I wish George wouldn't tell my plans to everyone."

"Oh, come, we've all known each other a lifetime."

"These things get back to Denise."

"You think you have secrets from that woman? She could see through a wall of steel, and you're no wall of steel. She doesn't have to figure you, anyway, she only has to figure out what the young lady wants you to do. Why are you going twice a year to Europe with this broad?"

"She's got to find her father. Her mother isn't certain which of two men . . . . And last spring I had to be in London on business. So we stopped in Paris, too."

"You must be right at home, over there. The French made you a knight. I kept the clipping."

"I'm the cheapest type of low-grade *chevalier.*"

"And did it tickle your vanity to travel with a great big beautiful doll? How did she make out with your high-class European friends?"

"Do you know that Woodrow Wilson sang 'Oh You Beautiful Doll' on the honeymoon train with Edith Bolling? The Pullman porter saw him dancing and singing in the morning when he came out."

"That's just the sort of fact you'd know."

"And he was just about our most dignified President," I added. "No, Renata wasn't a big hit with women abroad. I took her to a fancy dinner in London and the hostess thought her terribly vulgar. It wasn't the beige lace see-through dress. Nor even her wonderful coloring, her measurements, her vital emanations. She was just Sugar Ray Robinson among the paraplegics. She turned on the Chancellor of the Exchequer. He compared her to a woman in the Prado, by one of the Spanish masters. But the ladies were rough on her and she cried afterward and said it was because we weren't married."

"So next day you bought her thousands of dollars' worth of gorgeous clothes instead, I bet. But be you what you may, I get a big kick out of seeing you. You're a sweet fellow. This visit is a wonderful treat for a poor plain old broad. But would you humor me about one thing?"

"Sure, Naomi, if I can."

"I was in love with you, but I married a regular kind of Chicago person because I never really knew what you were talking about. However, I was only eighteen. I've often asked myself, now that I'm fifty-three, whether you'd make more sense today. Would you talk to me the way you talk to one of your intelligent friends—better yet, the way you talk to yourself? Did you have an important thought yesterday, for instance?"

"I thought about sloth, about how slothful I've been."

"Ridiculous. You've worked hard. I know you have, Charlie."

"There's no real contradiction. Slothful people work the hardest."

"Tell me about this. And remember, Charlie, you're not going to tone this down. You're going to say it to me as you would to yourself."

"Some think that sloth, one of the capital sins, means ordinary laziness," I began. "Sticking in the mud. Sleeping at the switch. But sloth has to cover a great deal of despair. Sloth is really a busy condition, hyperactive. This activity drives off the wonderful rest or balance without which there can be no poetry or art or thought—none of the highest human functions. These slothful sinners are not able to acquiesce in their own being, as some philosophers say. They labor because rest terrifies them. The old philosophy distinguished between knowledge achieved by effort (*ratio*) and knowledge received (*intellectus*) by the listening soul that can hear the essence of things and comes to understand the marvelous. But this calls for unusual strength of soul. The more so since society claims more and more and more of your inner self and infects you with its restlessness. It trains you in distraction, colonizes consciousness as fast as consciousness advances. The true poise, that of contemplation or imagination, sits right on the border of sleep and dreaming. Now, Naomi, as I was lying stretched out in America, determined to resist its material interests and hoping for redemption by art, I fell into a deep snooze that lasted for years and decades. Evidently I didn't have what it took. What it took was more strength, more courage, more stature. America is an overwhelming phenomenon, of course. But that's no excuse, really. Luckily, I'm still alive and perhaps there's even some time still left."

"Is this really a sample of your mental processes?" asked Naomi.

"Yes," I said. I didn't dare mention the Exousiai and Archai and the Angels to her.

"Oh Christ, Charlie," said Naomi, sorry for me. She pitied me, really, and reaching over and breathing kindly into my face she patted my hand. "Of course you've probably become even more peculiar with time. I see now it's lucky for us both that we never got together. We would have had nothing but maladjustment and conflict. You would have had to speak all this high-flown stuff to yourself, and everyday gobbledygook to me. In addition, there may be something about me that provokes you to become incomprehensible. Anyway you already took one trip to Europe with your lady and you didn't find Daddy. But when you go away, there are two more little girls with a missing father."

"I've had that very thought."

"George says that the little one is your favorite."

"Yes, Lish is just like Denise. I do love Mary more. I fight my prejudice, however."

"I'd be surprised if you didn't love those children a lot in your dippy way. Like everybody else I have my own child worries."

"Not with Maggie."

"No, I didn't like the job she had with Stronson, but now that he's washed up she'll get another, easy. It's my son that upsets me. Did you ever get around to reading his articles in the neighborhood paper on kicking the drug habit? I sent them to you for your opinion."

"I didn't read them."

"I'll give you another set of clippings. I want you to tell me if he has talent. Will you do that for me?"

"I wouldn't dream of refusing."

"You ought to dream of it oftener. People lay too much on you. I know I shouldn't be doing this. You're leaving town and must have plenty to do. But I want to know."

"Is the young man like his sister?"

"No, he isn't. He's more like his dad. You could do something for him. As a good man who's led a cranky life, you might reach him. He's already begun a cranky career."

"So what's missing is the goodness I'm alleged to have."

"Well, you are a crackpot, but you do have a real soul. The kid grew up without a father," said Naomi, tears coming to her eyes. "You don't have to do much. Just let him get to know you. Take him to Africa with you."

"Ah, did George sound off about the beryllium mine?"

This was all that I needed to add to my other enterprises

and commitments, to Denise and Urbanovich, to the quest for Renta's father and the exploratory study of anthroposophy, and to Thaxter and *The Ark.* A hunt for valuable minerals in Kenya or Ethiopia. Just the thing! I said, "There's really nothing in this beryllium stuff, Naomi."

"I didn't actually think there was. But how wonderful it would be for Louie to go with you on safari. It isn't that I buy *King Solomon's Mines* or anything like that. And before you go, let me suggest something, Charlie. Don't wear yourself out proving something with these giant broads. Remember, your great love was for me, just five feet tall."

WE were accompanied to O'Hare by the gloomy Señora. In the cab she coached Renata in whispers and stayed with us as we checked in, went through skyjacking inspection. At last we took off. Renata told me in the plane not to worry about leaving Chicago. "At last, you're doing something for yourself," she said. "It's funny about you. You're self-absorbed but you don't know the ABC of selfishness. Think of it this way, without a me, there's neither thee nor we." Renata was a perfect whiz at rhymed sayings. Her couplet for Chicago was, "Without O'Hare, it's sheer despair." And when I asked her once what she thought of another fascinating woman she said, "Would Paganini pay to hear Paganini play?" I often wished that the London hostess who thought her so gross, such a slob, could have heard her when she got going. When we reached the take-off position and suddenly began to race, tearing from the runway with an adhesive-plaster sound, she said, "So long, Chicago. Charlie, you wanted to do this town some good. Why that bunch of low bastards, they don't deserve a man like you here. They know fuck-all about quality. A lot of ignorant crooks are in the papers. The good guys are ignored. I only hope when you write your essay on boredom that you'll let this city have it right in the teeth."

We tilted backward as the 727 climbed and heard the grinding of the retracted landing gear. The dark wool of clouds and mist came between us and the bungalows, industries, the traffic, and the parks. Lake Michigan gave one glint and became invisible. I said to her, "Renata, it's sweet of you to stand up for me. The truth is that my attitude toward the USA—and Chicago is just the USA—hasn't been one hundred percent either. I've always hunted for some kind of cultural protection. When I married Denise I thought I had an ally."

"Because of her college degrees, I suppose."

"She turned out to be the head of the Fifth Column. But now I can see why this was. Here was this beautiful slender girl."

"Beautiful?" said Renata. "She's witchy-looking."

"This beautiful slender aspiring martial bookish young woman. She told me that her mother once saw her in the bath and gave a cry, 'You are a golden girl.' And then her mother burst into tears."

"I understand the disappointment of such women," Renata said. "That's the upper-middle-class Chicago scene, with the driving mothers. What are those daughters supposed to rise to? They can't all marry Jack Kennedy or Napoleon or Kissinger or write masterpieces or play the harpsichord at Carnegie Hall dressed in gold lamé with a purple backdrop."

"So Denise would start up in the night and sob and say that she was *nothing*."

"Were you supposed to make her something?"

"Well, there was an ingredient missing."

"You never found it," said Renata.

"No, and she went back to the faith of her fathers."

"Who were the fathers?"

"A bunch of ward-heelers and tough guys. But I'm bound to say that. I didn't have to be such a sensitive plant. After all, Chicago is my own turf. I should have been able to take it."

"She cried in the night about her wasted life and that was what did it. You've got to have your sleep. You could never forgive a woman who kept you awake with her conflicts."

"I'm thinking about sensitive plants in Business America because we're headed for New York to find out about Humboldt's will."

"A complete waste of time."

"And I ask myself, Must Philistinism hurt so much?"

"I talk to you, and you lecture me. All our Milan arrangements had to be changed. And for what! He had nothing to leave you. He died in a flophouse, out of his mind."

"He was sane again before he died. I know that from Kathleen. Don't be a bad sport."

"I'm the best sport you'll ever know. You've got me confused with that up-tight bitch who drags you to court."

"To get back to the subject, Americans had an empty, continent to subdue. You couldn't expect them to concentrate on philosophy and art as well. Old Doc Lutz, because I read poetry to his daughter, called me a damn foreigner. To pare corns in a Loop office was an American calling."

"Please fold my coat and lay it on the rack. I wish stewardesses would stop gossiping and take our drink orders."

"Certainly, my darling. But let me finish what I was saying about Humboldt. I know you think I'm talking too much, but I am excited, and I feel remorseful about the children besides."

"Just what Denise wants you to be," said Renata. "When you go away and won't leave a forwarding address she tells you, 'Okay, if the kids get killed you can read about it in the paper.' But don't get into a tragic bind about this, Charlie. Those kids will have their Christmas fun, and I'm sure Roger will have a marvelous time with his Milwaukee grandparents. How children love that square family stuff."

"I hope he is all right," I said. "I'm very fond of Roger. He's an engaging kid."

"He loves you too, Charlie."

"To get back to Humboldt then."

Renata's face took on an I'm-going-to-let-you-have-it-straight look and she said, "Charlie, this will is just a gag from the grave. You said yourself, once, that it could be a posthumous prank. The guy died nuts."

"Renata, I've read the textbooks. I know what clinical psychologists say about manic depressives. But they didn't know Humboldt. After all, Humboldt was a poet. Humboldt was noble. What does clinical psychology know about art and truth?"

For some reason this provoked Renata. She became huffy. "You wouldn't think he was so wonderful if he was alive. It's only because he's dead. Koffritz sold mausoleums, so he had business reasons for his death hang-up. But what is it with you?"

I had it in mind to reply, "What about yourself? The men in your life have been, were, or are Mausoleum Koffritz, Flonzaley the Undertaker, and Melancholy Citrine." But I bit my tongue.

"What you do," she said, "is invent relationships with the dead you never had when they were living. You create connections they wouldn't allow, or you weren't capable of. I heard you say once that death was good for some people. You probably meant that you got something out of it."

This made me thoughtful and I said, "That's occurred to me, too. But the dead are alive in us if we choose to keep them alive, and whatever you say I loved Humboldt Fleisher. Those ballads moved me deeply."

"You were just a boy," she said. "It was that glorious time of life. He only wrote ten or fifteen poems."

"It's true he didn't write many. But they were most beautiful. Even one is a lot, for certain things. You should know that. His failure is something to think about. Some say that failure is the only real success in America and that nobody who 'makes it' is ever taken into the hearts of his countrymen. This lays the emphasis on the countrymen. Maybe that's where Humboldt made his big mistake."

"Thinking about his fellow citizens?" said Renata. "When will they bring our drinks?"

"Be patient and I'll entertain you till they come. There are a few things I have to get off my chest about Humboldt. Why should Humboldt have bothered himself so much? A poet is what he is in himself. Gertrude Stein used to distinguish between a person who is an 'entity' and one who has an 'identity.' A significant man is an entity. Identity is what they give you socially. Your little dog recognizes you and therefore you have an identity. An entity, by contrast, an impersonal power, can be a frightening thing. It's as T. S. Eliot said of William Blake. A man like Tennyson was merged into his environment or encrusted with parasitic opinion, but Blake was naked and saw man naked, and from the center of his own crystal. There was nothing of the 'superior person' about him, and this made him terrifying. That is an entity. An identity is easier on itself.

An identity pours a drink, lights a cigarette, seeks its human pleasures, and shuns rigorous conditions. The temptation to lie down is very great. Humboldt was a weakening entity. Poets have to dream, and dreaming in America is no cinch. God 'giveth songs in the night,' the Book of Job says. I've devoted lots of thought to all these questions and I've concentrated hard on Humboldt's famous insomnia. But I think that Humboldt's insomnia testified mostly to the strength of the world, the human world and all its wonderful works. The world was interesting, really interesting. The world had money, science, war, politics, anxiety, sickness, perplexity. It had all the voltage. Once you had picked up the high-voltage wire and were *someone*, a known name, you couldn't release yourself from the electrical current. You were transfixed. Okay, Renata, I'm summarizing: the world has power, and interest follows power. Where are the poets' power and interest? They originate in dream states. These come because the poet is what he is in himself, because a voice sounds in his soul which has a power equal to the power of societies, states, and regimes. You don't make yourself interesting through madness, eccentricity, or anything of the sort but because you have the power to cancel the world's distraction, activity, noise, and become fit to hear the essence of things. I can't tell you how terrible he looked last time I saw him."

"You've told me."

"I can't get over it. You know the color of rivers that run through cities—the East River, the Thames, the Seine? He was that shade of gray."

Renata had nothing to say to this. As a rule her own reflections satisfied her perfectly and she used my conversation as a background to think her own thoughts. These thoughts, so far as I could tell, had to do with her desire to become Mrs. Charles Citrine, the wife of a Pulitzer *chevalier*. I therefore turned the tables on her and used her thoughts as a background for my thoughts. The Boeing tore off through shawls of cloud, the hurtling moment of risk and death ended with a musical *Bing!* and we entered the peace and light above. My head lay on the bib and bosom of the seat and when the Jack Daniel's came I strained it through my irregular multicolored teeth, curling my forefinger over the top of the glass to hold back the big perforated ice cubes—they always put in too many. The thread of whisky burned pleasantly in the gullet and then my stomach, like the sun outside, began to glow, and the delight of freedom also began to expand within me. Renata was right, I was away! Once in a while, I get shocked into upper wakefulness, I turn a corner, see the ocean, and my heart tips over with happiness—it feels so free! Then I have the idea that, as well as beholding, I can also be beheld from yonder and am not a discrete object but incorporated with the rest, with universal sapphire, purplish blue. For what is this sea, this atmosphere, doing within the eight-inch diameter of your skull? (I say nothing of the sun and the galaxy which are also there.) At the center of the beholder there must be space for the whole, and this nothing-space is not an empty nothing but a nothing reserved for everything. You can feel this nothing-everything capacity with ecstasy and this was what I actually felt in the jet. Sipping whisky, feeling the radiant heat that rose inside, I experienced a bliss that I knew perfectly well was not mad. They hadn't done me in back there, Tomchek, Pinsker, Denise, Urbanovich. I had gotten away from them. I couldn't say that I knew really what I was doing, but did it matter so much? I felt clear in the head nevertheless. I could find no shadow of wistful yearning, no remorse, no anxiety. I was with a beautiful bim. She was as full of schemes and secrets as the Court of Byzantium. Was that so bad? I was a goofy old chaser. But what of it?

Before leaving Chicago I had had a long talk about Renata with George Swiebel. We were exactly of an age, and approximately in the same physical condition. George was wonderfully kind. He said, "You've got to blow now. Get out of town. I'll take care of the details for you. You just sit on that plane, pull off your shoes, order a drink, and take the fuck off. You'll be okay. Don't worry." He sold the Mercedes for four thousand dollars. He took charge of the Persian carpets and made me an advance of another four. They must have been worth fifteen because they had been appraised by the insurance company at ten. But although George was in the building-repairs racket, he was utterly honorable. You couldn't find a single cheating fiber in his heart.

We drank a bottle of whisky together and he made me a

parting speech about Renata. It was full of his own kind of Nature-wisdom. He said, "All right, friend, you're going away with this gorgeous chick. She belongs to the new swinging generation and in spite of the fact that she's so developed she just isn't a grown-up woman. Charlie, she doesn't know a prick from a popsicle. Her mother is a gloomy sinister old character, a real angler. That mother is not my kind of people at all. She figures you for a cunt-crazy old man. You were once a winner with a big reputation. Now you're staggering a bit and here's a chance to marry you, grab off a piece of you before Denise gets it all. Maybe even rebuild you as a name and a money-maker. You're a bit mysterious to those types because there aren't many of you around. Now Renata is her mother's big, big, big prize apple from the Washington State Fair, a perfect Wenatchee, raised under scientific conditions, and she's hell-bent on cashing in while she's in her prime."

Working himself up, George got to his feet, a broad healthy figure of a man, rosy and vigorous, his nose bent like an Indian's, and his thin hair centered like a scalp lock. As always when he expounded his Nature-philosophy he started to shout. "This is no ordinary cunt. She's worth taking a chance on. All right, you might be humiliated, you might have to take a lot of shit, you might be robbed and plundered, you might lie sick with nobody looking after you or have a coronary or lose a leg. Okay, but you're alive, a flesh and blood brave instinct person. You've got guts. And I'll be standing by you. Cable me from anywhere and I'll arrive. I liked you all right when you were younger, but not the way I love you now. When you were younger you were on the make. You may not realize it but you were damn clever and canny about your career. But now, thank God, you're in a real dream and a fever over this young woman. You don't know what you're doing. And that's just what's great about it."

"You make it sound much too romantic, George."

"Never mind," he said. "Now Renata's 'real father' bit is baloney. Let's figure this out together. What does a broad like that need with a real father? She's already got this old pimp mother. Renata wouldn't know what to do with a father. She's got just the daddy she needs, a sex daddy. No, the whole thing was hoked up to get these trips to Europe. But that's just the finest part of it. Go on and blow all your money. Go broke, and the hell with the whole courthouse gang. Now you told me before about April in Paris with Renata but brief me again."

"Here it is," I said. "Until Renata was twelve she thought her father was a certain Signor Biferno, a fancy leather-goods dealer from the Via Monte Napoleone, in Milan. That's the big luxury-goods street. But when she was thirteen or so the old girl told her that Biferno might not be the man. The Señora and Biferno had been skiing in Cortina, she broke her ankle, her foot was in a cast, she quarreled with Biferno and he went home to his wife and kids. She revenged herself on him with a young Frenchman. Now when Renata was ten her mother had taken her to Milan to confront Biferno. They got all dressed up and made a scene on the Via Monte Napoleone."

"That old broad is one of the big-time troublemakers."

"The real Mrs. Biferno called the police. And much later, back in Chicago, her mother told Renata, 'Biferno may not be your father after all.'"

"So you went to Paris to see the young Frenchman, who is now an old Frenchman? That was a hell of a thing for a mother to tell a girl just as she enters adolescence."

"I had to be in London anyway and we were at the Ritz. Then Renata said she must go to Paris to look over this man who was perhaps her father and she wanted to go alone. She planned to come back three days later. So I took her to Heathrow. She was carrying a large bag, which was open. Right at the top, like a large compact, was her diaphragm case."

"Why was she taking her birth control?"

"You can never tell when the chance of a lifetime may present itself."

"Tactics, Charlie, just stupid tactics. Keep the fellow guessing. She was putting you off balance. I think she's really okay. She just does certain stupid things. One thing I want to say, Charlie. I don't know what your habits are but don't let her blow you. You'll be dead in a year. Now tell me the rest about Paris."

"Well, the man was homosexual, elderly, tedious, and garrulous. When she didn't return to London on the fourth day I went to look for her at the Hotel Meurice. She said she hadn't had the nerve to face him yet and she'd been shopping and going to the Louvre and seeing Swedish films—*I Am Curious Yellow* or something. The old guy remembered her mother and he was pleased to think that he might have a daughter but he was cagey and said that legal recognition was absolutely out of the question. His family would disinherit him. But he wasn't the man anyway. Renata said there was no resemblance. I looked him over myself. She was right. Of course, there's no way of knowing how nature does its stuff. An angry woman with a cast on her ankle gets a gay skier to make an exception for her, and they beget this beautiful daughter with the perfect skin and dark eyes and those eyebrows. Think of an El Greco beauty raising her eyes to heaven. Then substitute sex for heaven. That's Renata's pious look."

"Well, I know you love her," said George. "When she locked you out because she had another guy in there with her and you came to me crying—you remember what I said? A man your age sobbing over a girl is a man I respect. Furthermore, you've still got all your strength."

"I should have, I never used any of it."

"Well, okay, you saved it. Now you're coming down the stretch and it's time to pull ahead. Maybe you should marry Renata. Only don't get faint on your way to the license bureau. Do the whole thing like a man. Otherwise she'll never forgive you. Otherwise she'll turn you into an old errand boy. Poor old Charlie with a watering eye going out to buy cigars for his missus."

WE made our approach over the steely patch of evening water and landed at La Guardia in the tawny sundown. We then rode to the Plaza Hotel imprisoned in the low seats in one of New York's dog-catcher taxis. They make you feel that you have bitten someone and are being rushed to the pound, frothing with rabies, to be put down. I said this to Renata and she appeared to feel that I was using my imagination to spoil her pleasure, already somewhat damaged by the fact that we traveled, unlicensed, as a married pair. The doorman helped her out at the

Plaza and, in her high boots, she strode under the heated marquee with its glowing, orange rods. Over her mini-skirt she wore a long suède Polish coat lined with lambskin. I had bought it for her from Cepelia. Her beautifully pliant velvet hat inspired by seventeenth-century Dutch portrait painters was pushed off from her forehead. Her face, evenly and purely white, broadened toward the base. This gourdlike fullness was her only defect. Her throat was ever so slightly ringed or rippled by some enriching feminine deposit. This slight swell appears also on her hips and on the inside of her thighs. The first joint of her fingers revealed the same signs of sensual superabundance. Following her, admiring, thinking, I walked in the checked coat. Cantabile and Stronson had agreed that it gave me the cut of a killer. But I couldn't have looked less killer-like than I now did. My hair was blown out of position so that I felt the radiant heat of the marquee on my bald spot. The winter air swept into my face and made my nose red. Under my eyes the pouches were heavy. Teatime musicians in the Palm Court played their swooning, ingratiating, kiss-ass music. I registered Mr. and Mrs. Citrine under a false Chicago address, and we went up in the elevator with a crowd of charming college girls down for the holidays. They seemed to give out a wonderful fragrance of unripeness, a sort of green-banana odor.

"You certainly got a load of those darling kids," said Renata, perfectly good-humored again—we were in an endless corridor of golden carpet, endlessly repeating its black scrolls and flourishes, flourishes and scrolls. My manner of observing people entertained her. "You're such an eager looker," she said.

Yes, but for decades I had neglected my innate manner of doing it, my personal way of looking. I saw no reason why I shouldn't resume it now. Who cared?

"But what's this?" said Renata as the bellhop opened the door. "What kind of room did they give us?"

"These are the accommodations with mansard windows. The very top of the Plaza. The best view in the house," I said.

"We had a marvelous suite last time. What the hell are we doing in the attic? Where's our suite?"

"Oh, come, come, my darling. What's the difference? You

sound like my brother, Julius. He gets into such a state when hotels don't give him the best—so haughty and furious."

"Charles, are you having one of your stingy fits? Don't forget what you told me once about the observation car."

I was sorry now that I had ever made her familiar with Gene Fowler's saying that money was something to throw off the back end of a train. That was journalistic Hollywood of the golden age, the boozy night-club magnificence of the Twenties, the Big-Spender Syndrome. "But they're right, Renata. This is the best spot in the whole hotel for seeing Fifth Avenue."

Indeed the view, if you cared for views, was remarkable. I was very good myself at putting other people on to views for the purpose of absenting myself. Below, Fifth Avenue glowed with Christmas decorations and the headlights of the jammed traffic, solid between the Seventies and the Thirties, and shop illuminations, multicolored, crystalline, and like the cells in a capillary observed through a microscope, elastically changing shape, bumping and pulsatory. All this I saw in a single instant. I was like a deft girl, scooping all the jacks before the ball bounced back. It was as it had been with Renata last spring when we took the train to Chartres, "Isn't that beautiful out there!" she had said. I looked and yes, it was indeed beautiful. No more than a glance was necessary. You saved yourself a lot of time that way. The question was what you were going to do with the minutes gained by these economies. This, I may say, was all due to the operation of what Steiner describes as the Consciousness Soul.

Renata didn't know that Urbanovich was about to rule on the impounding of my money. By the movement of her eyes, however, I saw that money thoughts were on her mind. Her brows often were tilted heavenward with love but now and then a strongly practical look swept over her which, however, I also liked very much. But then she gave her head a quick lift and said, "As long as you're in New York, you may as well see a few editors and peddle your essays. Did Thaxter give them back?"

"Reluctantly. He still expects to bring out *The Ark*."

"Sure. He himself is every kind of animal."

"He called me yesterday and invited us to a Bon Voyage party on the *France*."

"His aging mother is throwing him a party too? She must be quite an old dame."

"She understands style. For generations she's arranged the coming out of debutantes and she's connected with the Rich. She always knows where there's a chalet vacant for her boy or a shooting box or a yacht. If he feels run-down she sends him to the Bahamas or the Aegean. You ought to see her. She's skinny clever capable and she glowers at me, I'm low company for Pierre. She stands on guard for monied families defending their right to drink themselves to death, their ancient privilege to amount to nothing."

Renata laughed and said, "Spare me his party. Let's get your Humboldt business over and go on to Milan. I have a deep anxiety about it."

"Do you think this Biferno really is your father? Better he than that queer Henri."

"Honestly I wouldn't think about a father if we were married. My insecure position forces me to look for solid ground. You'll say I have been married, but the ground with Koffritz wasn't very solid. And now there's my responsibility for Roger. By the way, we must send out toys to all the kids from F. A. O. Schwarz and I haven't got a cent. Koffritz is six months behind in payments. He says I have a rich man-friend. I will not drag him into court though, or throw him in jail. As for you, you carry so many freeloaders and I don't want to come under that heading. If I may say so, though, I at least care for you and do you some good. If you fell into the hands of that anthroposophist's daughter, that little blonde fox, you'd soon known the difference. She's a toughie."

"What has Doris Scheldt got to do with anything?"

"What? You wrote her a note before we left Chicago. I read the impression on your note pad. Don't look so truthful, Charlie. You're the world's worst liar. I wish I knew how many ladies you had in reserve."

I was not indignant over her spying. I no longer made scenes. Pleasant in themselves, our European trips also took me away from Miss Scheldt. Renata considered her a dangerous person and even the Señora had tried to scold me about her.

"But Señora," I had replied, "Miss Scheldt didn't enter the picture until the Flonzaley incident."

"Now, Charles, the matter of Mr. Flonzaley must be dropped. You are not just a middle-class provincial person but a man of letters," said the old Spanish lady. "Flonzaley belongs to the past. Renata is very sensitive to pain and when the man was in agony what could you expect her to do? She cried the entire night he was there. He is in a vulgar business and there is no comparison between you. She simply felt she owed him the consideration. And as you are an *homme de lettres* and he is an undertaker, the higher person must be more tolerant."

I couldn't argue with the Señora. I had seen her one morning before she was made up, hurrying toward the bathroom, completely featureless, a limp and yellow banana skin, without brows or lashes and virtually without lips. The sorrow of this sight took me by the heart, I never again wanted to win a point from the Señora. When I played backgammon with her I cheated against myself.

"The main thing about Miss Scheldt," I told Renata at the Plaza, "is her father. I couldn't have a love affair with the daughter of a man who was teaching me so much."

"He fills you with such bunk," she said.

"Renata, let me quote you a text: 'Though you are said to be alive you are dead. Wake up and put some strength into what is left, which must otherwise die.' That's from the Revelation of Saint John, more or less."

Indulgently smiling, Renata rose and straightened her miniskirt, saying, "You'll wind up with bare feet in the Loop carrying one of those where-will-you-spend-eternity signs. Get on the phone, for God's sake, and talk to this man Huggins, Humboldt's executor. And for dinner don't try to take me to Rumpelmayer's again."

Huggins was going to an opening at the Kootz Gallery and invited me to meet him there when I mentioned my business.

"Is there anything to this? What is this legacy stuff?" I said.

"There is something," said Huggins.

In the late Forties when Huggins was a celebrity in Greenwich Village I was a very minor member of the group that discussed politics, literature, and philosophy in his apartment. There were people like Chiaromonte and Rahv and Abel and Paul

Goodman and Von Humboldt Fleisher. What Huggins and I had in common was our love for Humboldt. There wasn't much else. In many respects we irritated each other. Some years ago at the Democratic convention in Atlantic City, that old pleasure-slum, we watched Hubert Humphrey pretending to relax with his delegation while Johnson dangled him, and something about the dinky desolation, the torn fibers of holiday gaiety provoked Huggins against me. We went out on the boardwalk and as we faced the horrid Atlantic, tamed here to saltwater taffy and the foam-like popcorn pushed by the sweeper's brush, Huggins became disagreeable to me. Fearing no man and urging home his arguments with his white billy-goat beard, he made hostile comments on the book about Harry Hopkins I had published that spring. Huggins was covering the convention for the *Women's Wear Daily.* A better journalist than I would ever be, he was also a famous bohemian dissenter and revolutionist. Why had I been so kind to the New Deal and seen so much merit in Hopkins? I was forever sneaking praises of the American system of government into my books. I was an apologist, a front man and stooge, practically, an Andrei Vishinsky. At Atlantic City as elsewhere, he was informal in chino wash pants and tennis sneakers, tall, rosy, bearded, stammering, and argumentative.

I could actually see myself as I studied him on the boardwalk. In my eyes were specks of green and amber in which he might have seen whole aeons of sleep and waking. If he thought I disliked him he was wrong. I liked him better and better all the time. He was quite old now, and the unkind forces of human hydrostatics were beginning to make a strained and wrinkled bag of his face, but his color remained fresh and he was still the Harvard radical of the John Reed type, one of those ever-youthful lightweight high-spirited American intellectuals, faithful to his Marx or his Bakunin, to Isadora, Randolph Bourne, Lenin and Trotsky, Max Eastman, Cocteau, André Gide, the Ballets Russes, Eisenstein—the beautiful avant-garde pantheon of the good old days. He could no more give up his delightful ideological capital than the bonds he had inherited from his father.

In Kootz's crowded gallery he was talking with several

people. He knew how to carry on a conversation at a noisy cocktail party. Din and drink stimulated him. He was not perhaps too clear in the head, but the actual head I always appreciated. It was long and high, banked with well-brushed silver hair, the uneven ends of long strands giving a spiky effect at the back. Over his tall-man's belly was a shirt of Merrymount stripes, broad crimson and diabolical purple, like the ribbons of the revelers' Maypole. It came back to me that more than twenty years ago I had found myself at a beach party in Montauk, on Long Island, where Huggins, naked at one end of the log, discussed the Army McCarthy hearings with a lady sitting naked and astride opposite him. Huggins was speaking with a cigarette holder in his teeth, and his penis which lay before him on the water-smooth wood, expressed all the fluctuations of his interest. And while he was puffing and giving his views in a neighing stammer, his genital went back and forth like the slide of a trombone. You could never feel unfriendly toward a man of whom you kept such a memory.

He was uncomfortable with me at the gallery. He sensed the peculiarities of my perspective. I was not proud of the same. Moreover, I was more warmly friendly than he wanted me to be. If he was not too clear in the head, neither was I. I was full of unmastered intimations and transitional thoughts and I judged no one. As a matter of fact I was fighting the judgments I had made in my days of rashness. I told him I was glad to see him and that he looked well. This was no lie. His color was fresh and despite the increased grossness of his nose, the distortions of age, and the bee-stung swelling of his lips, I still liked his looks. The rube-constable chin beard he could have done without.

"Ah, Citrine, they let you out of Chicago? Going somewhere?"

"Abroad," I said.

"Nice young lady you're with. Terribly att-att-ractive." Huggins' fluency was increased, not impeded, by his stammer. The boulders in a mountain stream show you how fast the water is flying. "So you want to collect your leg-leg. . . ?"

"Yes, but first I want you to tell me why you're so uncordial. We've known each other more than thirty years."

"Well, apart from your political views—"

"Most political views are like old newspapers chewed up by wasps—faded clichés and buzzing."

Huggins said, "Some people care where mankind is going. Beside, you can't expect me to be cor-cor-cor when you make such cracks about me. You said I was the Tommy Manville of the left and that I espoused cau-causes the way he ma-married broads. A couple of years ago-go you insulted me on Madison Avenue because of the protest buttons I was wearing. You said I used to have i-i-ideas and now I had only buttons." Aggrieved, inflamed, facing me with my own effrontery, he waited to hear what I could say for myself.

"I'm sorry to say that you quote me correctly. I admit this low vice. In the sticks, away from the Eastern scene, I think up wicked things to say. Humboldt brought me around in the Forties, but I never became part of your gang. When everybody was on Burnham or on Koestler I was somewhere else. The same for the *Encyclopedia of Unified Science*, or Trotsky's Law of Combined Development, or Chiaromonte's views on Plato or Lionel Abel on theater or Paul Goodman on Proudhon, or almost everybody on Kafka or Kierkegaard. It was like poor old Humboldt's complaint about girls. He wanted to do them good but they wouldn't hold still for it. I wouldn't hold still either. Instead of being grateful for my opportunity to get into the cultural life of the Village at its best—"

"You were reserved," said Huggins. "But what were you re-re-reserving yourself for? You had the star attitude, but where was the twi-twi-twink. . . ."

"Reserved is the right word," I said. "If other people had a bad content, I had a superior emptiness. My sin was that I thought in secret that I was more intelligent than all you enthusiasts for 1789, 1848, 1870, 1917. But you all had a much nicer and gayer time with your parties and all-night discussions. All I had was the subjective, anxious pleasure of thinking myself so smart."

"Don't you still think so?" said Huggins.

"No, I don't. I've given up on that."

"Well, you're out in Chicago where they think the earth is flat and the moon is made of green cheese. You've returned to your mental home," he said.

"Have it your way. That's not what I came to see you about. We still have one bond, anyway. We both adored Humboldt. Maybe we have something else in common, we're both amorous old dogs. We don't take each other seriously. But women seem to, still. Now what about the legacy?"

"Whatever it is, it's in an envelope labeled 'Citrine,' and I haven't read it because old Wald-Waldemar, Humboldt's uncle, grabbed it off. I don't know how I became exec-executor."

"Humboldt gave you lumps too, didn't he, after you joined the gang at Bellevue and he said I stole his money. You may have been at the Belasco when he picketed me."

"No, but it had a certain ch-cha-charm."

Laughing, Huggins puffed at his holder. Was it the old Russian actress, Ouspenskaya, who had made these holders popular in the Thirties, or FDR, or John Held, Jr.? Like Humboldt, like myself for that matter, Huggins was an old-movie buff. Humboldt's picketing and his own behavior at the White House he might see as moments from René Clair.

"I never thought you stole his money," said Huggins. "I understand he got into you for a few thousand. Did he forge a check?"

"No. We once exchanged blank checks sentimentally. He used his," I said. "And it wasn't a few, it was nearly seven."

"I took care of finances for him. I got Kathleen to way-way-waive rights. But he said I took kickbacks. Sore as a boil. So I didn't see him ever again, poor Humboldt. He accused some switch-switch-board old woman at a hotel of covering his bed with cen-centerfold girls from *Playboy*. Grabbed a hammer and tried to hit the old broad. Took him away. More shock-shock therapy! Enough to make you cry when you think how viv-viv, how fresh, handsome, wonderful, and what masterpieces. Ah! This society has a lot to an-answer for."

"Yes, he was wonderful and generous. I loved him. He was good." Strange words these at a clamorous cocktail party. "He wanted with all his heart to give us something exquisite and delicate. He put a heavy demand on himself. But you say that his horse-playing uncle took most of his papers?"

"And clothes and valuables."

"He must have been hit very hard, losing his nephew, and frightened, probably."

"He came running in from Co-Coney Island. Humboldt kept him in a nursing home. The old bookie must have figured that the pa-papers of a man who rated such a long obituary in the *Times* must be valuable."

"Did Humboldt leave him some money?"

"There was an insurance policy, and if he didn't drop it all on the horses he's okay."

"Was Humboldt in his right mind toward the end or am I mistaken?"

"He wrote me a beauti-beauti-beautiful letter. He copied out some poems for me on good paper. The one about his Hungarian Pa, riding with Pershing's cavalry to capture Pancho."

"The toothy horses, the rattler's castanet, the cactus thorn, and the banging guns . . ."

"You're not quoting quite right," said Huggins.

"And it was you that gave Kathleen Humboldt's bequest?"

"It was, and she's in New York right now."

"Is she? Where is she? I'd love to see her."

"On her way to Europe, like you. I don't know where she's stay-staying."

"I must find out. But first I have to get on to Uncle Waldemar in Coney Island."

"He may not give you anything," said Huggins. "He's can-cantankerous. And I've written him and phoned him. No soap."

"Probably a phone call isn't good enough. He's holding out for a real visit. You can't blame him for that, if nobody comes. Wasn't Humboldt's mother the last of his sisters? He wants somebody to go to Coney Island. He's using Humboldt's papers as a bait. Maybe he'll give them to me."

"I'm sure you'll be irre-ree. You'll be irresistible," said Huggins.

RENATA was greatly annoyed when I said that she must come to Coney Island with me.

"What, go to a nursing home? On the subway? Don't drag me into this. Go alone."

"You've got to do it. I need you, Renata."

"You're wrecking my day. I have a professional thing I need to do. It's business. Homes for the aged depress me. Last time I set foot in one I became hysterical. At least spare me the subway."

"There's no other transportation. And give old Waldemar a break. He's never seen a woman like you, and he was a sporting man."

"Save the sweet talk. I didn't hear any when the girl at the switchboard called me Mrs. Citrine. You clammed up."

Later on the boardwalk she was still vexed, and strode ahead of me. The subway had been awful, the filth, the spray-can graffiti were not to be believed. She kicked out the skirts of her maxi-coat as she marched, and the hanging fleeces fluttered at the front. The high-crowned Netherlands hat was pushed back. Henri, the Señora's old friend in Paris, the man who was clearly not Renata's father, had been impressed by her forehead. "*Un beau front!*" he said, over and over again. "*Ah, ce beau front!*" A fine brow. But what was behind it? Now I couldn't see it. She was striding away, offended, ruffled. She wished to punish me. But really I couldn't lose on Renata. I was pleased with her even when she was cross. People looked after her as she passed. Walking behind her I admired the action of her hips. I might not have cared to know what went on behind that *beau front*; and her dreams might have shocked me but her odor alone was a great solace in the night. The pleasure of sleeping with her went far beyond the ordinary pleasure of sharing a bed. Even to lie unconscious beside her was a distinct event. As for insomnia, Humboldt's complaint, she made that agreeable, too. Energizing influences passed into my hands from her breasts during the night. I allowed myself to imagine that these influences entered my finger bones like a sort of white electricity and surged upward to the very roots of my teeth.

A white December sky overlay the Atlantic gloom. The message of Nature seemed to be that conditions were severe, that things were tough, very tough, and that people should console one another. In this Renata thought I was not doing my part, for when the operator at the Plaza had called her Mrs. Citrine, Renata had put down the phone and turned to me, her face lighted, saying, "She called me Mrs. Citrine!" I failed to answer. People are really far more naïve and simple-hearted than we commonly suppose. It doesn't take much to make them glow. I'm that way myself. Why withhold your kindliness from them when you see the glow appearing? To increase Renata's happiness, I might have said, "Why of course, kid. You'd make a wonderful Mrs. Citrine. And why not?" What would that have cost me . . . ? Nothing but my freedom. And I wasn't, after all, doing much with this precious freedom. I was assuming that I had world enough and time to do something with it later. And which was more important, this pool of unused freedom or the happiness of lying beside Renata at night which made even unconsciousness special, like a delectable way to be stricken? When that cursed operator called her "Mrs." my silence seemed to accuse her of being just a whore, no Mrs. at all. This burned her up. The pursuit of her ideal made Renata intensely touchy. But I too pursued ideals—freedom, love. I wanted to be loved for myself alone. Noncapitalistically, as it were. This was one of those American demands or expectations which, as a native of Appleton and a kid from the Chicago streets, I had all too many of. What caused me a certain amount of anguish was that I suspected that the time had passed when I might still have been loved for myself alone. Oh with what speed conditions had worsened!

I had told Renata that marriage would have to wait until my case with Denise was settled.

"Ah, come on, she'll quit suing when you're out in Waldheim beside your Pa and your Ma. She's good for the rest of the century," said Renata. "Are you?"

"Of course solitary old age would be horrible," I said. Then I ventured to add, "But you can see yourself pushing my wheelchair?"

"You don't understand real women," said Renata. "Denise wanted to knock you out of action. Because of me she hasn't succeeded. It wasn't that pale little fox Doris, in the Mary Pickford getup. It's all me—*I've* kept your sex powers alive. I know how. Marry me and you'll still be balling me at eighty. By ninety, when you can't, I'll love you still."

Thus we were walking on the Coney Island boardwalk. And as I, when a boy, had rattled my stick on fence palings, so Renata, when she passed the popcorn men, the caramel-corn and hot-dog men, got a rise out of each one. I followed her, elderly but fit, wrinkled with anxieties yet smiling. In fact I was feeling unusually high. I'm not altogether sure why I was in this glorious condition. It couldn't have been only the result of physical well-being, of sleeping with Renata, of good chemistry. Or of the temporary remission of difficulties which, according to certain grim experts, is all that people need to make them happy and is, in fact, the only source of happiness. No, I was inclined to think as I vigorously walked behind Renata that I owed it to a change in my attitude toward death. I had begun to entertain other alternatives. This in itself was enough to make me soar. But even more joyful was the possibility that there might be something to soar into, a space unused, neglected. All this while the vastest part of the whole had been missing. No wonder human beings went mad. For suppose that we—as we are in this material world—are the highest of all beings. Suppose that the being-series ends with us and there is nothing more beyond us. On such assumptions who can blame us for going into convulsions! Assume a cosmos, however, and it's metaphysically a more spacious situation.

Then Renata turned and said, "Are you sure the old dodo knows you're coming?"

"Sure. We're expected. I phoned him," I said.

We entered one of the alley-like streets, where garment workers used to pass their summer holidays, and found the address. An old brick building. On its wooden stoop were wheelchairs and walking frames for invalids who had had strokes.

At another time I might have been astonished by what happened next. But now that the world was being reconstituted and the old structure, death and all, was no more solid than a Japanese lantern, human matters came over me with the greatest vividness, naturalness, even with gaiety—I mustn't leave out the gaiety. The saddest of sights might have it. Anyway, we were indeed expected. Leaning on a stick someone was watching for us between the door and the storm door of the nursing home and came out shouting, "Charlie, Charlie," as soon as we reached the stairs.

I said to this man, "You're not Waldemar Wald, are you?"

"No, Waldemar is here. But I'm not Waldemar, Charlie. Now look at me. Listen to my voice." He began to sing something in an old raven tenor. He took me by the hand and sang "La donna è mobile" in the style of Caruso, but miserably, poor old boy. I took him in, I studied his hair, once kinky and red, the busted nose and eager nostrils, the dewlaps, the Adam's apple, the skinny stoop of his figure. Then I said, "Ah yes, you're Menasha! Menasha Klinger! Chicago Illinois 1927."

"That's right." For him this was sublime. "It's me. You recognized me!"

"Holy mackerel! What a pleasure! I swear I don't deserve such a surprise." In putting off my search for Humboldt's uncle it seems that I had been avoiding good luck, wonderful things, miracles almost. Immediately I met a person whom I loved way-back-when. "It's dreamlike," I said.

"No," said Menasha. "For an ordinary guy, maybe it would be. But when you turn into a personage, Charlie, it's much less of a coincidence than you think. There must be friends and acquaintances like me all over the place who used to know you but are too shy to approach and remind you. I would have been too shy myself if it wasn't that you were coming to see my buddy Waldemar." Menasha turned to Renata. "And this is Mrs. Citrine," he said.

"Yes" I said, looking her in the face. "This is Mrs. Citrine."

"I knew your husband as a kid. I boarded with his family when I came down from Ypsilanti, Michigan, to work at Western Electric as a punch-press operator. What I really came for was to study singing. Charlie was a wonderful boy. Charlie was the best-hearted little kid on the whole Northwest Side. I could talk to him when he was only nine or ten, and he was my only friend. I'd take him downtown with me Saturdays for my music lesson."

"Your teacher," I said, "was Vsevelod Kolodny, room eight sixteen in the Fine Arts Building. Basso profundo with the Imperial Opera, Petersburg, bald, four-feet-ten, wore a corset and Cuban heels."

"He recognized me, too," said Menasha, infinitely pleased.

"You were a dramatic tenor," I said. I had only to say this to see how he rose on his toes, clasping his punch-press-callused palms and singing "In questa tomba oscura," tears of ardor filling up his eyes, and his voice so roosterish, with so much heart, so much cry and hackle and hope—tuneless. Even as a boy I knew he'd never make stardom. I did believe, however, that he might have become a singer but for the fact that on the Ypsilanti YMCA boxing team someone had hit him in the nose and this had ruined his chances in art. The songs that were sung through this disfigured nose would never be right.

"Tell me, my boy, what else do you remember?"

"I remember Tito Schipa, Titta Ruffo, Werrenrath, McCormack, Schumann-Heink, Amelita Galli-Curci, Verdi, and Boito. And when you heard Caruso sing *Pagliacci*, life was never the same again, right?"

"Oh, yes!"

Love made these things unforgettable. In Chicago fifty years ago, we had been passengers on the double-deck open-topped bus down to the Loop on Jackson Boulevard, Menasha explaining to me what bel canto was, telling me, radiant, about *Aida*, envisioning himself in brocade robes as a priest or warrior. After his singing lesson he took me to Kranz's for a chocolate-fudge sundae. We went to hear Paul Ash's sizzling band, we also heard vaudeville seals who played "Yankee Doodle" by nipping the syringe bulbs of automobile horns. We swam at Clarendon Beach, where everyone peed in the water. At night he taught me astronomy. He explained Darwin to me. He married his high-school sweetheart from Ypsilanti. Her name was Marsha. She was obese. She was homesick and she lay in bed and cried. I once saw her sitting in the bathtub trying to wash her hair. She took water in her hands but her arms were too fat to raise it in her palms as high as the head. This dear girl was dead. Menasha had been an electrician in Brooklyn for most of his life. Of his dramatic tenor nothing was left but the yelping of an old man, greatly moved. Of his stiff red hair there remained only this orange-whitey cirrus formation. "Very kind people, the Citrines. Maybe not Julius. He was rough. Is Julius still Julius? Your mother was so helpful to Marsha. Your kind poor mother. . . . But let's go and see Waldemar. I'm only the greeting committee and he's waiting. They keep him in a back room by the kitchen."

We found Waldemar sitting on the edge of his bed, a man with wide shoulders, and his hair wet-brushed very like Humboldt's, the same broad face, and the eyes gray and set wide. Within ten miles of Coney Island, perhaps, sucking in and straining tons of water, puffing vapor from his head, there was a whale with eyes similarly positioned.

"So you were my nephew's buddy," said the old gambler.

"This is Charlie Citrine," said Menasha. "You know, Waldemar, he recognized me. The boy recognized me all right. Gosh, Charlie, you should, you know. I paid out a fortune on sodas and treats. There ought to be some justice."

Through Humboldt I knew Uncle Waldemar, of course. He was an only son, with four older sisters and a doting mother, much pampered, idle, a poolroom bum, a dropout, mooching from his sisters and stealing from their purses. Eventually he placed Humboldt in the senior position as well. Becoming rather a brother than an uncle. The kid role was the only role he understood.

I was thinking that life was a hell of a lot more bounteous than I had ever realized. It rushed over us with more than our senses and our judgment could take in. One life with its love affairs, its operatic ambitions, its dollars and horse races and marriage-designs and old people's homes is, after all, only a tin dipperful of this superabundance. It rushes up also from within. Take a room like Uncle Waldemar's, smelling of wieners boiling for lunch, with Waldemar squatting on the edge of the bed, all dressed up for a visit, his face, his head blearily similar to Humboldt's, but with the effect of a blown dandelion, all the yellow gone gray; take the old gentlemen's green shirt, buttoned to the collar; take his good suit on the wire hanger in the corner (he would have a dressy funeral); take the satchels under his bed and the pin-ups of horses and prizefighters and the book-jacket photograph of Humboldt in the days when Humboldt was impossibly beautiful. If this is literally all what life is, then Renata's little rhyme about Chicago is right on the head: "Without O'Hare, it's sheer despair." And all O'Hare can do is change the scene for you and take you from dismal to dismal, from boredom to boredom. But why did a kind of faintness come over me at the start of this interview with Uncle Waldemar in the presence of Menasha and Renata? Because there is far more to any experience, connection, or relationship than ordinary consciousness, the daily life of the ego, can grasp. Yes. You see, the soul belongs to a greater, an all-embracing life outside. It's got to. Learning to think of this existence of mine as merely the present existence, one in a series, I was not really surprised to meet Menasha Klinger. He and I obviously held permanent membership in some larger, more extended human outfit, and his desire to stand in brocade and sing Rhadames in *Aida*, was like my eagerness to go far, far beyond fellow intellectuals of my generation who had lost the imaginative soul. Oh, I admired some of these intellectuals without limits. Especially the princes of science, astrophysicists, pure mathematicians, and the like. But nothing had been done about the main question. The main question, as Walt Whitman had pointed out, was the death question. And music drew me toward Menasha. By means of music a man affirmed that the logically unanswerable was, in a different form, answerable. Sounds without determinate meaning became more and more pertinent, the greater the music. This was such a man's assignment. I, too, in spite of lethargy and weakness, was here for a big reason. Just what this was I would consider later, when I looked back on my life in the twentieth century. Calendars would disintegrate under the gaze of the spirit. But there would be a December spot for a subway ride in cars disfigured by youth gangs, and a beautiful woman whom I followed on the boardwalk while hearing the peppery pang of shooting galleries and smelling popcorn and hot dogs, thinking of the sex of her figure, the consumerism of her garments, and of my friendship with Von Humboldt Fleisher which had brought me to Coney Island. In my reflective purgatory I would see it all, from a different perspective and know, perhaps, how all these peculiarities added up—know why an emotional estuary should have opened up in me when I laid eyes on Waldemar Wald.

Waldemar was now saying, "What a dog's age since anybody visited. I've been forgot. Humboldt would never have stuck me in a dump like this. It was temporary. The chow is awful, and the help is rough. They say, 'Shut up, you're gaga.' They're all from the Caribbean. Everybody else is a kraut. Menasha and me are practically the only Americans. Humboldt once made a joke, 'Two is company, three is a kraut!'"

"But he did put you here," said Renata.

"Just till he could iron out some problems. The whole week before he died he was looking for an apartment for us both.

Once we lived together for three months and that was heaven. Up in the morning like a real family, bacon and eggs, and then we'd talk baseball. I made a real fan of him, you know that? Fifty years ago I bought him a first-baseman's mitt. I taught him to field a grounder and throw a guy out. Football, too. I showed him how to toss a forward pass. My mother's railroad apartment had a long, long corridor where we played. When his dad took off it was a houseful of women and it was up to me to make an American boy out of him. Those women did plenty of damage. Look at the names they gave us—Waldemar! The kids called me Walla-Walla. And he had it rough, too. Humboldt! My goofy sister named him after a statue in Central Park."

All this was familiar to me from Humboldt's charming poem "Uncle Harlequin." Waldemar Harlequin, in the old days on West End Avenue, after his wage-earning sisters went to business, rose at eleven, bathed for an hour, shaved with a new Gillette blade, and then lunched. His mother sat beside him to butter his rolls, or skin his whitefish and bone it, to pour his coffee while he read the papers. Then he took a few bucks from her and went out. He talked at the dinner table about Jimmy Walker and Al Smith. He, in Humboldt's opinion, was his family's American. This was his function among the ladies and with his nephew. When the national conventions were broadcast on the radio he could call the roll of the states together with the announcer—"Idaho, Illinois, Indiana, Iowa"—and patriotic tears filled his eyes.

"Mr. Wald, I've come to see you about the papers Humboldt left. I told you on the phone. I have a note from Orlando Huggins."

"Yes, I know Huggins, that long drink of water. Now I want to ask you about the papers. Is this stuff valuable or ain't it?"

"Sometimes we see in the *Times*," said Menasha, "a letter by Robert Frost fetches eight hundred bucks. As for Edgar Allen Poe, don't ask."

"What's actually in those papers, Mr. Wald?" asked Renata.

"Well, I have to tell you," said Waldemar. "*I* never understood any of his stuff. I'm not a big reader. What he wrote was way over my head. Humboldt could hit like a sonofabitch on the sandlot. With his shoulders, just imagine how much beef there went into his swing. If I had my way he would have ended up in the majors. But he started in to hanging around the Forty-second Street library and bull-shitting with those bums on the front steps. First thing I knew he was printing highbrow poems in the magazines. I mean, the kind of magazines without pictures."

"Come on, Waldemar," said Menasha. His chest was high with feeling and his voice rose and rose. "I've known Charlie from a kid. I want to tell you you can trust Charlie. Long ago, soon as I laid eyes on him, I said to myself, This kid's heart is right up there in his face. He's getting along in years himself. Although compared to us he's a strong fellow still. Now Waldemar, whyn't you come clean and tell him what's on your mind?"

"In Humboldt's papers, as papers, there probably isn't much money," I said. "One might try to sell them to a collector. But perhaps there is something in what he left that could be published."

"It's mostly the sentiment," said Renata. "Like a message from an old friend in the next world."

Waldemar looked at her, obstinate. "But suppose it *is* valuable, why should I get screwed? Am I entitled to get something out of it or not? I mean, why should I stick in this lousy home here? As soon as they showed me Humboldt's obituary in the *Times*—Christ! Imagine what that did to me! Like my own kid, the last of the family, my own flesh and blood! I got on the BMT as fast as I could and went up to his room. His stuff was half gone already. The cops and the hotel management were grabbing it off. The cash and the watch and his fountain pen and the typewriter disappeared."

"What's the use of sitting on this stuff and dreaming you'll make a killing?" said Menasha. "Hand it over to somebody who knows."

"Don't fink on me," said Waldemar to Menasha. "We're in here together. This much I'm willing—I'll level with you, Mr. Citrine. I could have peddled this stuff long ago. If you ask me there is a real property in this."

"You have read it then," I said.

"Hell, sure I've read it. What the hell else have I got to do? I couldn't make heads or tails out of it."

"I wouldn't dream of doing you out of anything," I said. "If it has got value I'll tell you honestly."

"Why don't we get a lawyer to draw up a legal document?" said Waldemar.

He was Humboldt's uncle all right. I became very persuasive. I am never so reasonable as when I badly want something. I can make it seem natural justice itself that I should have it. "We can make things as legal as you like," I said. "But shouldn't I read it all? How can I tell without examining it?"

"Then read it here," said Waldemar.

Menasha said, "You've always been a sport, Charlie. Take a gamble."

"Along that line my record isn't so hot," said Waldemar. I thought he would cry, he sounded so shaky. So little stood between him and death, you see. On the bald harsh crimson of the threadbare carpet, a pale patch of weak December warmth said, "Don't cry, old boy." Inaudible storms of light, ninety-three million miles away, used a threadbare Axminster, a scrap of human manufacture, to deliver a message through the soiled window of a nursing home. My own heart became emotional. I wished to convey something important. We have to go through the bitter gates of death, I wanted to say to him, and give back those loaned minerals that comprise us, but I want to tell you, brother Waldemar, that I deeply suspect things do not end there. The thought of the life we are now leading may pain us as greatly later on as the thought of death pains us now.

Well, finally I got around him with my good sense and honesty and we all went down on our knees and began to pull all sorts of stuff from under his bed—bedroom slippers, an old bowling ball, a toy baseball game, playing cards, odd dice, cardboard boxes, and valises, and, finally, a relic that I could identify—Humboldt's briefcase. It was Humboldt's old bag with the frayed straps, the one that was always riding, crammed with books and pill bottles, in the back seat of his Buick.

"Wait, I've got my files in there," Waldemar said, fussing. "You'll screw it all up. I'll do this."

Renata, on the floor with the rest of us, wiped the dust with paper tissues. She was always saying, "Here's a Kleenex," and producing paper tissues. Waldemar removed several insurance policies and a bundle of computer-perforated Social Security cards. There were several horse photographs, which he identified as an almost complete set of Kentucky Derby winners. Then like a blindish postman, he went through numerous envelopes. "Quicker!" I wanted to say.

"This is the one," he said.

There was my name written in Humboldt's tight, scratchy hand.

"What's in it? Let me see," said Renata.

I took it from him, an outsized heavy manila envelope.

"You'll have to give me a receipt," said Waldemar.

"Certainly I will. Renata, would you mind making out a form? Like, received from Mr. Waldemar Wald, papers willed to me by Von Humboldt Fleisher. I'll sign it."

"Papers of what kind? What's actually here?"

"What's in them?" said Waldemar. "One thing is a long personal letter to Mr. Citrine. Then a couple of sealed envelopes which I never broke open at all because there are instructions that say if you open them something goes wrong with the copyright. Anyhow, they're duplicates, or duplicates of duplicates. I can't tell you. Most of it doesn't add up, to me. Maybe for you it will. Anyhow, if I, the last member of my family, can tell you what's on my mind, my dead are all over the place, one grave here, and the other to hell and gone, my sister in that joint they call Valhalla for the German Jews and my nephew buried in potter's field. What I really want is to reunite the family again."

Menasha said, "It bugs Waldemar that Humboldt is buried in a bad place. Way out in no man's land."

"If there's any value in this legacy, the first money should be spent to dig the kid up and move him. It doesn't have to be the Valhalla. That was my sister keeping up with the Joneses. She had a thing about them German Jews. But I want to bring us all together. Gather up my dead," the old horse-player said.

This solemnity was unexpected. Renata and I looked at each other.

"Count on Charlie to do right by you," said Menasha.

"I'll write and tell you what I find in these papers," I said. "And just as soon as we get back from Europe, I promise you we'll attend to everything. You can start lining up a cemetery.

Even if these papers have no commercial value I'd be perfectly willing to pick up the burial tab."

"Just what I told you," said Menasha to Waldemar. "A kid like this kid was bound to grow up into a gentleman."

We now went out. I held each of the old boys by a wasted arm, by the big double knobs of the elbow where radius and ulna meet, promising to stay in touch. Sauntering behind us, Renata with her white face and great hat was incomparably more substantial in person than any of us. She said unexpectedly, "If Charles says it, Charles'll do it. We'll go away and he'll be thinking of you."

In a corner of the cold porch stood the wheelchairs, glittering, lightweight, tubular, stainless metal, with batlike folds. "I wonder if anyone would object if I sat in one of these wheelchairs," I said.

I got into one of them and said to Renata, "Give us a ride." The old men didn't quite know what to make of my being trundled back and forth on the stoop by this large, laughing, brilliant woman with the wonderful teeth. "Don't carry on like a fool. You'll offend them, Renata," I said. "Just push."

"These damn handles are damn cold," she said.

She drew on the long gloves with charming swagger, I must say.

In the racketing speed of the howling, weeping subway I began to read the long letter, the preface to Humboldt's gift, handing on the onionskin pages to Renata. Incurious after she had glanced at a few of these, she said, "When you get to the story, let me know. I'm not big on philosophy." I can't say that I blame her. He was not *her* precious friend hid in death's dateless night. There was no reason why she should be moved, as I was. She made no effort to enter into my feelings, nor did I want her to try.

"Deer Shoveleer," wrote Humboldt. "I am in a bad position, getting more sane as I become weaker. By a damn peculiar arrangement, lunatics always have energy to burn. And if old William James was right, and happiness is living at the energetic top and we are here to pursue happiness, then madness is pure bliss and also has supreme political sanction." This was the sort of thing that Renata objected to. I agree that it was not a restful habit of mind. "I am living in a bad place," he went on. "And eating bad meals. I've now eaten sixty or seventy delicatessen dinners in a row. You can't get sublime art on a diet like this. On the other hand pastrami and peppery potato salad seem to nourish calm judgment. I don't go out to dinner. I stay in my room. There is a colossal interval between supper and bedtime and I sit beside a drawn window shade (who can look out eighteen hours a day?) correcting certain old mistakes. It occurs to me sometimes that I may be petitioning death to lay off because I am deep in good works. Would I be trying, also, to keep the upper hand in dying as in the sexual act?—Do this, do that, hold still, wriggle now, kiss my ear, graze my back with your nails, but don't touch my testicles. However, death is the passionate party in this case."

"Poor fellow, I can see him now. I understand his type," said Renata.

"So, Charlie, as these weaker saner days come and go I think often about you, and think with end-of-the-line lucidity. That I wronged you is very true. I knew even when I loused you up so elaborately and fiercely that you were in Chicago trying to do me good, consulting people behind my back to get me jobs. I called you a sell-out, Judas, fink, suck-ass, climber, hypocrite. I had first a deep black rage against you, and then a red hot rage. Both were very luxurious. The fact is that I was remorseful about the blood-brother check. I knew you were mourning the death of Demmie Vonghel. I was panting with cunning and I put one over on you. You were a Success. And if that weren't enough and you wanted to be a big moral figure as well, then the hell with you, it was going to cost you a few thousand bucks. It was entrapment. I was going to give you a chance to forgive me. In forgiving you would be lying your head off. This fool kindliness would damage your sense of reality, and with your sense of reality damaged you'd be suffering what I suffered. All this crazy intricacy was unnecessary, of course. You were going to suffer anyway because you were stricken with the glory and the gold. Your giddy flight through the florid heavens of success, and so on! Your innate sense of truth, if nothing else, would make you sick. But my 'reasoning,' in endless formulae like chemistry formulae on a college blackboard, put me into swoons of rapture. I was manic. I was chattering from the dusty top of my crazy head. Afterward I was depressed and silent for long, long days. I lay in the cage. Grim gorilla days.

"I ask myself why you figured so prominently in my obsessions and fixations. You may be one of those people who arouse family emotions, you're a son-and-brother type. Mind, you want to arouse feeling but not necessarily to return it. The idea is that the current should flow your way. You stimulated the blood-brother oath. I was certainly wild, but I acted on a suggestion emanating from you. Nevertheless, in the words of the crooner, 'With all your faults, I love you still.' You are a promissory nut, that's all.

"Let me say a word about money. When I used your blood-brother check, I didn't expect it to clear the bank. I put it through, outraged because you didn't come to see me at Bellevue. I was suffering; you didn't draw near, as a loving friend should. I decided to punish hurt and fine you. You accepted the penalty, and therefore the sin, too. You borrowed my spirit to put into Trenck. My ghost was a Broadway star. All this daylight delusion, cracked, spoiled, and dirty! I don't know how else to put it. Your girl died in the jungle. She wouldn't let you come to Bellevue—I found that out. Oh! the might of money and the entanglement of art with it—the dollar as the soul's husband: a marriage nobody has had the curiosity to study.

"And do you know what I did with the six thousand bucks? I bought an Oldsmobile with part of it. What I thought I was going to do with this big powerful car on Greenwich Street, I can't tell you. It cost me lots of dough to keep it in a garage, more than the rent in my fifth-floor walk-up. And what happened to this automobile? I had to be hospitalized and when I got out, after a course of shock treatments, I couldn't remember where I left it. I couldn't find the claim check, or the registration either. I had to forget about it. But for a while I drove a hell of a car. I became capable of observing some of my own symptoms. My eyelids became deep violet with manic insomnia. Late at night I drove past the Belasco Theatre with some buddies and I said, 'There's the hit that paid for this powerful machine.' I declare I had it in for you because you thought I was going to be the great American poet of the century. You came down from Madison, Wisconsin, and told me so. But I wasn't! And how many people were waiting for that poet! How many souls hoped for the strength and sweetness of visionary words to purge consciousness of its stale dirt, to learn from a poet what had happened to the three-fourths of life that are obviously missing! But during these last years I haven't been able to even read poetry, much less write it. Opening the *Phaedrus* a few months ago, I just couldn't do it. I broke down. My gears are stripped. My lining is shot. It is all shattered. I didn't have the strength to bear Plato's beautiful words, and started to cry. The original, fresh self isn't there any more. But then I think, Maybe I can recover. If I play it smart. Playing it smart means simpler kinds of enjoyment. Blake had it right with Enjoyment the food of Intellect. And if the intellect can't digest meat (the *Phaedrus*) you coddle it with zwieback and warm milk."

When I read his words about the original fresh self, I began to cry myself, and big benign Renata shook her head when she observed this as if to say, "Men!" As if to say, "These poor mysterious monsters. You work your way down into the labyrinth and there you find the minotaur breaking his heart over a letter." But I saw Humboldt in the days of his youth, covered in rainbows, uttering inspired words, affectionate, intelligent. In those days his evil was only an infinitesimal black point, an amoeba. The mention of zwieback brought back to me, also, the pretzel he was chewing on the curb on that hot day. On that day I made a poor showing. I behaved very badly. I should have gone up to him. I should have taken his hand. I should have kissed his face. But is it true that such actions are effective? And he was dreadful. His head was all gray webbing, like an infested bush. His eyes were red and his big body was floundering in the gray suit. He looked like an old bull bison on his last legs, and I beat it. Maybe that was the very day on which he wrote this beautiful letter to me. "Now come on, kid," said Renata, kindly. "Dry your eyes." She gave me a fragrant hankie, oddly redolent, as if she kept it not in her pocketbook but between her legs. I put it to my face and curiously enough it did something, it gave me some comfort. That young woman had a good understanding of certain fundamentals.

"This morning," Humboldt went on, "the sun was bright. For certain of the living it was a very fine day. Though without sleep for several nights I remembered how it used to be to bathe and shave and breakfast and go into the world. A mild lemon light rinsed the streets. (Hope for this wild combined human operation called America?) I thought I would stroll to Brentano's and look into a copy of Keats's *Letters.* During the night I had thought of something Keats had said about Robert Burns. How a luxurious imagination deadens its delicacy in vulgarity and in things attainable. For the first Americans were surrounded by thick forests, and then they were surrounded by things attainable, and these were just as thick. The problem became one of faith—a faith in the equal sovereignty of the imagination. Standing at Brentano's I stopped to copy out this sentence but a clerk came up to me and took the Keats *Letters* away. He thought I was from the Bowery. So I went out, and that was the end of the fine day. I felt like Emil Jannings in one of his pictures. The former tycoon ruined by drink and whores comes home an old bummer and tries to peep into the window of his own house where his daughter's wedding is being celebrated. The cop makes him move on, and so he shuffles away and a cello plays Massenet's 'Elégie.'

"Now, Charles, I come to the zwieback and warm milk. Big enterprises are beyond me, obviously, but my wit oddly enough is intact. This wit, developed to cope with the disgraces of life, real or imaginary, is like a companion to me these days. It stands by me and we are on good terms. In short, my sense of humor has not disappeared and now that bigger ambitious passions have worn themselves out it has been coming before me with an old-fashioned bow out of Molière. A relationship has developed.

"You remember how we amused ourselves in Princeton with the movie scenario about Amundsen and Nobile and Caldofreddo the Cannibal? I always thought it would make a classic. I handed it to a fellow named Otto Klinsky in the RCA Building. He promised to get it to Sir Laurence Olivier's hairdresser's cousin who was the sister of a scrubwoman at Time and Life who was the mother of the beautician who did Mrs. Klinsky's hair. Somewhere in these channels our script got lost. I still have a copy of this. You will find it among these papers." Indeed I did. I was curious to read it again. "But that is not my gift to you. After all, we collaborated, and it would be chintzy of me to call it a gift. No, I have dreamed up another story and I believe it is worth a fortune. This small work has been important to me. Among other things it has given me hours of sane enjoyment on certain nights and brought relief from thoughts of doom. The fitting together of the parts gave me the pleasure of a good intricacy. The therapy of delight. I tell you as a writer—we have had some queer American bodies to fit into art's garments. Enchantment didn't have enough veiling material for this monstrous mammoth flesh, for such crude arms and legs. But this preface is getting too long. On the next page begins my Treatment. I've tried to sell it. I've offered it to some people but they weren't interested. I haven't got the strength to follow through. People don't want to see me. You remember how I went to see Longstaff? No more. Receptionists turn me away. I guess I look like the sheeted dead who squeaked and gibbered in the streets of Rome. Now, Charlie, you are still in the midst of life and are rich in contacts. People will pay attention to the Shoveleer, the author of *Trenck*, the chronicler of Woodrow Wilson and Harry Hopkins. This will not reach you unless I kick the bucket. But then it will be a fabulous legacy and I want you to have it. For you are, at one and the same time, no good at all and also a darling man.

"Good old Henry James, of whom Mrs. Henry Adams said that he chewed more than he bit off, tells us that the creative mind is better off with hints than with extensive knowledge. I have never suffered from a knowledge handicap. The *donnée* for this treatment comes from the gossip columns, which I have always read faithfully. *Verbum sapientiae*—I think that's the dative. The original is apparently true.

TREATMENT

I.

A fellow named Corcoran, a successful author, has been barren for many years. He has tried skin diving and parachute jumping as subjects but nothing has resulted. Corcoran is married to a strong-minded woman. A woman of her sort might have made Beethoven a powerful wife, but Beethoven wasn't having any of that. To play the part of Corcoran I have in mind someone like Mastroianni.

II.

Corcoran meets a beautiful young woman with whom he has an affair. Had she lived, poor Marilyn Monroe would have been ideal for this role. For the first time in many years Corcoran tastes happiness. Then in a fit of enterprise, ingenuity, daring, he escapes with her to a faraway place. His disagreeable wife is nursing a sick father. Taking advantage of this, he and his girl go off. I don't know where. To Polynesia, to New Guinea, to Abyssinia, with dulcimers, wonderful and far off. The place is still quite pure in its beauty and enchanting weeks follow. Chieftains receive Corcoran and his girl. Hunts occur, and dances and banquets are laid on. The girl is an angel. They bathe in pools together, they float among gardenias and hibiscus. At night the spots of heaven draw near. The sensors open. Life is renewed. Dross and impurities evaporate.

III.

Returning, Corcoran writes a marvelous book—a book of such potency and beauty that it must not be kept from the world. But

IV.

He cannot publish. It would hurt his wife and destroy his marriage. He himself had a mother and few people have character enough to cast off their new supersitions about mothers and sons. He would have no identity, he would not even be an American without this bitch-affliction. If Corcoran hadn't been a writer he would not have sullied the heart of this angelic girl by writing a book about their adventure. Unfortunately, he is one of those writing fellows. He is a mere writer. Not to publish would kill him. And he is comically afraid of his wife. This wife should be matronly, jolly, frank, a bit tough but not altogether forbidding. In her own way rather attractive. A good broad, a bossy all-American girl. I think she should be a food faddist who drinks Tiger's Milk and eats Queen-Bee Jelly. You may be able to do something with that.

V.

Corcoran takes the book to his agent, a Greek American named Zane Bigoulis. This is a most important role. It should be played by Zero Mostel. He is a comedian of genius. But if he isn't restrained, he runs away with everything. At all events, I have him in mind for this part. Zane real the book and cries "Magnificent." "But I can't publish it, it would finish my marriage." Now Charlie, *My Marriage*! Marriage having become one of the idols-of-the-tribe (Francis Bacon), the source of this comedy is the low seriousness which has succeeded the high seriousness of the Victorians. Corcoran has enough imagination to write a wonderful book, but he is enslaved by middle-class attitudes. As the wicked flee when none pursueth, so does the middle-class wrestle when none contendeth. They cried out for freedom, it came down on them in a flood. Nothing remains but a few floating timbers of psychotherapy. "What shall I do?" Corcoran cries. They deliberate. Then Bigoulis says, "All you can do is take the same trip with Hepzibah that you took with Laverne. Exactly the same trip, following the book faithfully, at the same season. Having reproduced the trip, you can publish the book."

VI.

"I won't let a word be changed," says Corcoran. "No impurity, no betrayal of the Experience." "Leave it to me," says Bigoulis. "I will precede you everywhere with transistors, panty hose, pocket computers, and so on, and bribe the chieftains. I'll get them to put on the same hunts and banquets and duplicate the dances. When your publisher sees this manuscript he'll be glad to pick up the tab." "It's really a frightful idea to do all this with Hepzibah. And I'll have to lie to Laverne. She feels as I do about our miraculous month on the Island. There's something sacred about it." But, Charlie, as *The Scarlet Letter* shows, love and lying have always gone together in this country. Truth is actually fatal. Dimmesdale tells it and dies. But Bigoulis argues, "You want the book published? You don't want Hepzibah to leave you, and you want to hang on to Laverne as well? From a male viewpoint the whole thing makes complete sense. So . . . we go to the Island. I can swing it for you. If you bury this book I lose a hundred grand in commissions, with picture-rights maybe more."

I see, Charlie, that I have now made the place an Island. Thinking of *The Tempest.* Prospero is a Hamlet who gets his revenge through art.

VII.

Thus Corcoran repeats with Hepzibah the journey he made with Laverne. Oh what a difference! All now is parody, desecration, wicked laughter. Which must be suffered. To the high types of Martyrdom the twentieth century has added the farcical martyr. This, you see, is the artist. By wishing to play a great role in the fate of mankind he becomes a bum and a joke. A double punishment is inflicted on him as the would-be representative of meaning and beauty. When the artist-agonist has learned to be sunk and shipwrecked, to embrace defeat and assert nothing, to subdue his will and accept his assignment to the hell of modern truth perhaps his Orphic powers will be restored, the stones will dance again when he plays. Then heaven and earth will be reunited. After long divorce. With what joy on both sides, Charlie! What joy!

But this has no place in our picture. In the picture, Corcoran and his wife are bathing in a pool covered with hibiscus. She adores it. He fights his depression and prays for strength to play his role. Meantime, Bigoulis goes ahead staging each event, bribing chieftains, and hiring musicians and dancers. In this Island he sees also, on his own score, the investment opportunity of a lifetime. He is already planning to build the world's greatest resort here. At night he sits in his tent with a map, laying out a pleasure dome. The natives will become waiters, cooks, porters, and caddies on his golf course.

VIII.

The terrible trip over, Corcoran comes back to New York and publishes his book. It is a great success. His wife leaves him and sues for divorce. She knows she is not the heroine of those tender scenes. Laverne is outraged when she discovers that he repeated the same trip, sacred to her, with Hepzibah. She can never, she says, love a man capable of such a betrayal. To make love with another woman among those flowers, by moonlight! She knew he was a married man. That, she was willing to tolerate. But not this, not the breaking of the faith. She never wants to see him again.

He is therefore alone with his success, and his success is enormous. You know what that means. . . .

"Charles, here is my gift to you. It is worth a hundred times more than the check I put through. A picture like this should gross millions and fill Third Avenue with queues for a year. Insist on a box-office percentage.

"You will make a good script of this outline if you will remember me as I kept remembering you in plotting this out. You took my personality and exploited it in writing your *Trenck*. I have borrowed from you to create this Corcoran. Don't allow the caricatures to get out of hand. Let me call your attention to the opinion of Blake on this subject. 'Fun I love,' he says, 'but too much Fun is of all things the most loathsome. Mirth is better than Fun, & Happiness is better than Mirth. I feel that a Man may be happy in This World. And I know that This World Is a World of Imagination & Vision. . . . The tree which moves some to tears of joy is in the Eyes of others only a Green thing which stands in the way. Some see Nature all Ridicule & Deformity, & by these I shall not regulate my proportions.' "

Humboldt added a few sentences more. "I have explained why I wrote such a Treatment. I wasn't really strong enough to bear the great burdens. I haven't made it here, Charlie. Not to be guilty of a final failure of taste, I will avoid the heavy declaration. Let's say I have a leg already over the last stile and I look back and see you far back laboring still in fields of ridicule.

"Help my Uncle Waldemar all you can. Be sure that if there is a hereafter I will be pulling for you. Before you sit down to work at this scenario play a few sides of *The Magic Flute* on the phonograph, or read *The Tempest.* Or E. T. A. Hoffmann. You are lazy, disgraceful, tougher than you think but not yet a dead loss. In part you are humanly okay. We are supposed to do something for our kind. Don't get frenzied about money. Overcome your greed. Better luck with women. Last of all—remember: we are not natural beings but supernatural beings.

Lovingly, Humboldt"

"So now I know why we missed the Scala," said Renata. "We had tickets for tonight. All that glow—that gorgeous performance of *The Barber of Seville*—a chance to be part of the greatest musical audience in Europe! And we sacrificed it. And for what? To go to Coney Island. Coming back with what? A goofy outline. I could laugh about it," she said. In fact she was laughing. She was in a good humor and had seldom been more beautiful, the dark hair drawn back and secured at the top, giving a sense—well, a sense of rescue, silken and miraculous. The dark hues with the red suited Renata best. "*You* don't mind missing out on the Scala. In spite of all your credentials you don't really care much for culture. Deep down, you're from Chicago after all."

"Let me make it up to you. What's at the Met tonight?"

"No, it's Wagner, and that 'Liebestod' drags me. Actually, as everybody is talking about it, let's see if we can get in to see *Deep Throat.* All right, I can see you getting ready to make a remark about sex films. Don't do it. I'll tell you what your attiude is—When it's done it's fun, but when it's seen it's unclean. And remember that your wisecracks show no respect for me. First I do things for you, and then I become a woman of a certain class."

Still, she was in good heart, chatty and highly affectionate. We were lunching at the Oak Room, far from the beans and wieners of the nursing home. We should have given those two old geezers a treat and taken them out. At lunch Menasha might have told me much about my mother. She died when I was an adolescent and I longed to hear her described by a mature man, if such Menasha was. She had come to be a sacred person. Julius always insisted that he couldn't remember her at all. He had his doubts about my memory altogether. Why such keenness (approaching hysteria) for the past? Clinically speaking, I guess the problem was hysteria. Philosophically, I came out better. Plato links recollection with love. But I couldn't ask Renata creep to along with two old boys to some seafood joint on boardwalk and spend a whole afternoon helping them to read the menu and to deal with clams, wiping butter from their pants, looking away when they popped out their detachable bridges, just so I could discuss my mother. To her it was odd that elderly fellow like me should be so eager to hear reminiscences of his mother. Contrast with these very old guys might make me look a bit younger, still it was also possible that she would lump us all together in her irritation. Thus Menasha and Waldemar were deprived of a treat.

In the Oak Room she ordered Beluga caviar. She said it was her reward for taking the subway. "And after that," she told the waiter, "lobster salad. For dessert, the *profiterole.* Mr. Citrine will have the *omelette fines-herbes*. I'll let him order the wine." And so I did, having been told what she wanted. I commanded a bottle of Pouilly-Fuissé. When the waiter left, Renata said, "I notice that your eye goes from right to left as you read the menu. There is no reason for the poor-boy bit. You can always make money, piles of it. Especially if you team up with me, I promise we'll be Lord and Lady Citrine. I know the visit to Coney Island has made you downhearted. So I'll give you a blessing to count. Look around this dining room and look at the women—see what kind of dogs important brokers, corporation executives, and big-time lawyers get stuck with. Then compare."

"You are certainly right. My heart bleeds for all parties."

The wine waiter came and made the usual phony passes, showed the label, and ducked down with his corkscrew. He then poured some wine for me to taste, and harassed me with perfunctory courtesies that had to be acknowledged.

"Still, coming to New York was right, I now agree," she said. "Your mission here is accomplished, and that's all to the good because it's about time your life was set on a real basis and you cleared away a few tons of rubbish. Your sentiments and deep feelings may do you credit, but you're like a mandolin-player. You tickle every note ten times. It's cute, but a little goes a long way. Were you about to say something?"

"Yes, the strangeness of life on this earth is very oppressive."

"You're always saying 'on this earth.' It gives me a creepy feeling. This old Professor Scheldt, the father of your pussycat Doris, has filled you up with his esoteric higher worlds and when you talk to me about this I feel we're both going bonkers: knowledge that doesn't need a brain, hearing without real ears, sight without eyes, the dead are with us, the soul leaves the body when we sleep. Do you believe all this stuff?"

"I take it seriously enough to examine it. As to the soul leaving the body when we sleep, my mother absolutely believed that. She told me so when I was a kid. I find nothing strange in that. Only my head-culture opposes it. My hunch is that Mother was right. This can't lead me into oddity, I already am in oddity. People as ingenious, as fertile in wishes as I am, and also my wonderful betters, have gone to their death. And what is this death? Again, *nessuno sa*. But ignorance of death is destroying us. And this is the field of ridicule in which Humboldt sees me still laboring. No honorable person can refuse to lend his mind, to give his time, to devote his soul to this problem of problems. Death now has no serious challenge from science or from philosophy or religion or art. . . ."

"So you think crank theories are the best bet?"

I muttered something to myself, for she had heard this quotation from Samuel Daniel before, and her mandolin-playing figure prevented me from repeating it aloud. It was, "While timorous knowledge stands considering, audacious ignorance hath done the deed." My thought was that life on this earth was actually everything else as well, provided that we learned how to apprehend it. But, not knowing, we were oppressed to the point of heartbreak. *My* heart was breaking all the time, and I was sick and tired of it.

Renata said, "Really, what do I care—worship as you please is American and fundamental. It's just that when you open your eyes there's a sort of gloony gleam in them. That's a made-up word, gloony. I loved it, by the way, when Humboldt said you were a promissory nut. I just loved that."

For my part, I loved Renata's cheerfulness. Her roughness and frankness were infinitely better than her loving-pious bit. I had never bought that—never. But her cheerfulness as she laid caviar, chopped egg, and onion on Melba toast for me gave me wonderful extravagant comfort. "Only," she went on, "you've got to stop twittering like a ten-year-old girl. And now let's take this Humboldt thing straight on. He thought he was leaving you a valuable property. Poor character. What a gas! Who'd buy such a story? What's it got? You'd have to do everything twice, first with the girl and then with the wife. It would drive an audience nuts. Producers are looking to go beyond *Bonnie and Clyde*, *The French Connection*, *The Godfather*. Murder on an El train. Naked lovers who bounce up and down when machine-gun slugs tear into their bodies. Dudes on massage tables who get bullets straight through their eyeglasses." Ruthless, perfectly good-natured Renata laughed, sipping Pouilly-Fuissé, aware of how I admired her throat and the feminine subtlety of its white rings (here the veil of Maya was as vivid as ever). "Well, isn't that it, Charles? And how does Humboldt compete? He dreamed about having magic with his public. But you didn't have it either. Without your director, *Trenck* could never have made a big box office. You told me so yourself. What did you get for those *Trenck* movie rights?"

"The price was three hundred thousand. The producer took half, the agent took ten percent, the government took sixty percent of the rest, I put fifty into the house in Kenwood which now belongs to Denise. . . ." Renata's face, when I recited figures and percentages, was wonderfully at peace. "That's how my commercial success breaks down," I said. "And I would never have been capable of doing it on my own, I agree. It was all Harold Lampton and Kermit Bloomgarden. As for Humboldt he was not the first man to go down trying to combine worldly success with poetic integrity, blasted with poetic fire, as Swift says, and consequently unfit for Church or Law or State. But he thought of me, Renata. His scenario gives his opinion of me—foolishness, intricacy, wasted subtlety, a loving heart, some kind of disorganized genius, a certain elegance of construction. His legacy is also his affectionate opinion of me. And he did its very best. It was an act of love—"

"Charlie, look, they're bringing you the telephone," said Renata. "It's terrific!"

"You're Mr. Citrine?" said the waiter.

"Yes."

He plugged in the instrument and I spoke to Chicago. The call was from Alec Szathmar. "Charlie, you're in the Oak Room?" he said.

"I am."

He laughed with excitement. We two who had sparred in the alley with boxing gloves as children hitting each other in the face until we were winded and dazed were now men, and had risen in the world. I was lunching elegantly in New York; he was phoning me from a paneled office on La Salle Street. Unfortunately, the messages he gave me did not suit the plush occasion. Or did it? "Urbanovich is going along with Denise and Pinsker. The court says you must post a bond. The figure is two hundred thousand dollars. This is what happens when you ignore my advice. I told you to hide some money in Switzerland. No, you had to be aboveboard. You weren't going to do anything gross. That's the kind of snobbery that does you in. You want austerity? Well, you're two hundred grand closer to it than you were yesterday."

A slight echo told me that he was using an amplifier. My replies were heard on the squawk box in his office. This meant that his secretary, Tulip, was listening. Because of the affectionate interest this woman took in my doings, Szathmar, always the showman, sometimes invited her to listen in on our conversations. She was a fine woman, somewhat pale and heavy, and carried herself in the sad high-hearted style of the old West Side. She was devoted to Szathmar, whose weaknesses she knew and forgave. Only Szathmar himself was conscious of no weaknesses. "What will you do for dough, Charlie?" he said.

The first thing to do was to conceal the facts from Renata.

"There's no immediate problem. I've got a small balance with you, still, haven't I?"

"We agreed that I would repay the condominium loan in five annual installments, and you've already gotten this year's payment. I suppose the decades of free legal advice I gave you don't count for a thing."

"You also put me on to Tomchek and Srole."

"The finest domestic-relations people in Chicago. They couldn't work with you. No one could."

Renata passed me another bit of Melba toast with caviar, grated egg, onion, and sour cream.

"Now I've given you message number one," said Szathmar. "Message number two is to call your brother in Texas. His wife has been trying to reach you. Nothing has happened. Don't lose your head. Julius is going to have open-heart surgery. Your sister-in-law says they're going to transplant a few arteries for the angina. She thought his only brother should know. They're going up to Houston for the operation."

"Your face is completely changed, what is it?" said Renata as I put down the telephone.

"My brother is going to have open-heart surgery."

"Oh-oh!" she said.

"Quite right. I must go there."

"You're not asking me to postpone this trip again?"

"We can easily fly from Texas."

"You've got to go?"

"Of course, I must."

"I've never met your brother, but I know he's a rough man. He wouldn't cancel his plans for you."

"Now Renata he's my only brother, and these are frightful operations. As I understand it, they break into your chest, remove the heart, lay it on a towel or something, while they circulate the blood by machine. It's one of those demonic modern technological things. Poor humankind, we're all hurled down into the object world now. . . ."

"Ugh," said Renata, "I hope they never make such a jigsaw puzzle of me."

"Darling Renata, in your case the very thought is blasphemous." Renata's breasts, when the support of clothing was removed, fell slightly to the right and to the left, owing to a certain enchanting fullness at the base of each and perhaps because of their connection with the magnetic poles of the earth. You did not think of Renata as having a chest in the usual human way—certainly not my brother's human way, gray-haired and stout.

"You want me to go to Texas with you, don't you," she said.

"It would mean a great deal to me."

"And to me, too, if we were husband and wife. I'd go there twice a week if you needed support. But don't expect to take me in tow and show me off to a dirty old man as your floozy. Don't go by my behavior as a single woman."

This last was a reference to the night she locked me out and lay beside Flonzaley the mortuary king. She had been weeping, to hear her tell it, while I telephoned frantically. "Marry me," she said to me now. "Change my status. That's what I need. I'll make you a wonderful wife."

"I should do it. You're a glorious woman. Why should I bandy arguments with you?"

"There's nothing to argue about. I'm going to Italy tomorrow, and you can meet me in Milan. But I'll be walking into the Biferno leather shop in a weak position. As a divorced woman who floats around with a lover I can't expect my father to be enthusiastic, and, practically speaking it'll be harder for him to have an emotional catharsis over me than if I were an innocent girl. As for me, I still remember how Mother and I were put out on the street—right on the Via Monte Napoleone, and how I stood in front of his show window with all the beautiful leather and cried. To this day when I go into Gucci and see the luxury luggage and handbags I feel almost like fainting from rejection and heartbreak."

Some statements are meant to pass, some to echo. The words "my behavior as a single woman" continued to reverberate, as it was her tactical intention that they should. But it was impossible to marry her just to keep her honest for a few days in Milan.

I went up to the mansard room and got the operator to connect me with my brother in Corpus Christi.

"Ulick?" I said, using his family name.

"Yes, Chuckie."

"I'm coming down to Texas tomorrow."

"Ah, they've told you," he said. "They're going to hack me open on Wednesday. Well, come along if you haven't got anything else to do. I thought I heard that you were going to Europe."

"I can leave the country from Houston."

He was of course pleased that I wanted to come but he was distrustful, and he wondered whether I might not be angling for some advantage. Julius in fact loved me but affirmed and even believed that he didn't. My brotherly intensity flattered him. But he was too clear-headed to deceive himself. He was not a lovable man and if he held an important place in my feelings, and those feelings were intricate and keen, the reason was either that I was queerly undeveloped, immature, or that possibly without knowing what I was doing I was involved in a con. Ulick saw rackets everywhere. A stout character, sharp-faced, handsome, his eyes were big alert and shrewd. A mustache in the style of the late Secretary Acheson mitigated the greediness of his mouth. He was a strutting heavy graceful rapacious man who wore checks, stripes, gaudy but elegantly fitted. Somewhere between business and politics he had once made a fortune in Chicago, connected with the underworld although without being a part of it. But he fell in love and left his wife for the other woman. In the divorce he was wiped out, losing his Chicago possessions. However, he made a second fortune in Texas and raised a second family. It was impossible to think of him without his wealth. It was necessary for him to be in the money, to have dozens of suits and hundreds of pairs of shoes, shirts beyond inventory, cuff links, pinkie rings, large houses, luxury automobiles, a grand-ducal establishment over which he ruled like a demon. Such was Julius, my big brother Ulick, whom I loved.

"For the life of me," said Renata, "I can't figure why you're so crazy about this brother of yours. The more he puts you down, the more you worship the ground. Let me recall a few of the things you told me about him. When you were a kid playing with toys on the floor he would step on your fingers. He rubbed your eyes with pepper. He hit you on the head with a bat. When you were an adolescent he burned your collection of Marx and Lenin pamphlets. He had fist fights with everyone, even a colored maid."

"Yes, that was Bama, she was six feet tall and she gave him a hard punch on the ear, which he had coming."

"He's been in a hundred scandals and lawsuits. He fired ten years ago at a car that used his driveway to turn around."

"He only meant to shoot out a tire."

"Yes, but he hit the windows, and he was being sued for assault with a deadly weapon—didn't you tell me? He sounds like one of those crazy brutes who get entangled in your life. Or was it the other way around?"

"The odd thing is that he isn't a brute, he's charming, a gentleman. But mainly he's my brother Ulick. Some people are so actual that they beat down my critical powers. Once they're there—inarguable, incontestable—nothing can be done about them. Their reality matters more than my practical interests. Beyond a certain point of vividness I become passionately attached."

Obviously Renata herself belonged to this category. I was passionately attached to her because she was Renata. She had an additional value, too—she knew a lot about me. I had a vested interest in her because I had told her so much about myself. She was educated in the life and outlook of Citrine. You needed no such education in the life of Renata. All you had to do was look at her. And conditions were such that I had to purchase her consideration. The more facts I put into her the more I needed her, and the more I needed her the more her price increased. In the life to come there will be no such personal or erotic bondage. You won't have to bribe another soul to listen while you explain what you're about, and what you had meant to do, and what you had done, and what others had done, et cetera. (Although the question naturally arises, why should anyone listen gratis to such stuff?) Spiritual science says that in the life to come the moral laws have the priority, and they are as powerful there as the laws of nature are in the physical world. Of course I was just a beginner, in theosophical kindergarten.

But I was serious about it. I meant to make a strange jump and plunge into the truth. I had had it with most contemporary ways of philosophizing. Once and for all I was going to find out whether there was anything behind the incessant hints of immortality that kept dropping on me. Besides, this was the biggest and most revolutionary thing one could undertake to do, and of the greatest value. Socially, psychologically, politically, the very essence of human institutions was an extract of what we assumed about death. Renata said I was furious and arrogant and vengeful toward intellectuals. I always said that they were wasting their time and ours, and that I wanted to trample and clobber them. Possibly so, though she exaggerated my violence. I had the strange hunch that nature itself was not *out there*, an object world eternally separated from subjects, but that everything external corresponded vividly with something internal, that the two realms were identical and interchangeable, and that nature was my own unconscious being. Which I could come to know through intellectual work, scientific study, and intimate contemplation. Each thing in nature was an emblem for something in my own soul. At this moment in the Plaza, I took a rapid reading on my position. I had a slightly outer-space feeling. The frame of reference was tenuous and shuddering all around me. So it was necessary to be firm and to put metaphysics and the conduct of life together in some practical way.

Suppose, then, that after the greatest, most passionate vividness and tender glory, oblivion is all we have to expect, the big blank of death. What options present themselves? One option is to train yourself gradually into oblivion so that no great change has taken place when you have died. Another option is to increase the bitterness of life so that death is a desirable release. (In this the rest of mankind will fully collaborate.) There is a further option seldom chosen. That option is to let the deepest elements in you disclose their deepest information. If there is nothing but nonbeing and oblivion waiting for us, the prevailing beliefs have not misled us, and that's that. This would astonish me, for the prevailing beliefs seldom satisfy my need for truth. Still the possibility must be allowed. Suppose, however, that oblivion is *not* the case? What, then, have I been doing for about six decades? I think that I never believed that oblivion *was* the case and by five and a half decades of distortion and absurdity have challenged and disputed the alleged rationality and finality of the oblivion view.

Those were the thoughts whirling through my head in the top story of the Plaza Hotel. Renata was still criticizing the mansard room. I always gave her a grand time in New York, spent magnificently, blew my money like a Klondike miner. Urbanovich had grounds for his opinion that I was a wild old guy, that I was jettisoning the capital to keep it out of enemy hands, and he was restraining me. But it wasn't his money, was it? However, the matter was very odd, for all kinds of people with whom I was scarcely acquainted had claims on it. There was, for instance, Pinsker, Denise's lawyer, the hairy man with the cheese-omelette cravat. I didn't even know the man, we had never exchanged a single personal word. How did he get his hand into my pocket?

"What arrangements are we going to make?" said Renata.

"For you, in Italy? Will a thousand dollars hold you for a week?"

"The most awful things are said about you back in Chicago, Charlie. You should hear what a reputation you have. Of course Denise sees to that. She even works on the kids and they spread her view, too. You're supposed to be unbearable. Mother hears that everywhere. But when a person gets to know you, you turn out to be sweet—as sweet a guy as I ever knew. What do you say we make love? We don't have to take off all our clothes. I know you sometimes like it half-and-half." She removed her bottom garments, unhooking her bra for easy access, and settled herself on a corner of the bed in all the fullness, smoothness, and beauty of her nether half, her face white and her brows going up with piety. I faced her in my shirttails. She said, "Let's store up a little comfort for our separation."

Then, behind us on the night table, the small light of the telephone began to beat silently, to pulsate. Someone was trying to reach me. Whose pulsations came first, was the question.

Renata began to laugh. "You know the most talented nuisances," she said. "They always know when to bother you. Well? Answer it. The occasion is ruined anyway. You look anxious. You probably are thinking about the kids."

The caller was Thaxter. He said, "I'm downstairs. Are you busy? Can you come to the Palm Court? I have important news."

"To be continued," said Renata, cheerful enough. We put our clothing on and went downstairs to find Thaxter. I didn't recognize him at first, for he was wearing a new outfit, a Western hat and his velvet trousers were tucked into cowboy boots.

"What's this?" I said.

"The good news is that I've just signed a contract for that book on the temperamental dictators," he said. "Qaddafi, Anin, and those other types. What's more, Charlie, we can get another contract. Today. Tonight, if you like. And I think we should. It would be a really good deal for you. And oh, by the way, on the house phone next to me there was a lady also asking for you. She's the widow of the poet Fleisher, I believe, or his divorced wife."

"Kathleen? Where has she gone? Where is she?" I said.

"I told her we had urgent business and she said she had some shopping to do anyway. She said you could meet in the Palm Court in about an hour."

"You sent her away?"

"Before you get sore, remember that I'm giving a cocktail party on the *France*. I'm a little pressed for time."

"What's the Western get-up about?" said Renata.

"Well, I thought it would be a good idea to look more American, like a guy from the heartland. I felt I should show that I had nothing to do with the liberal media and the Eastern Establishment."

"You'll pretend to take those fellows from the Third World seriously," I said, "and then you'll write them up as vulgarians, imbeciles, blackmailers, and killers."

"No, there's a serious side to it," said Thaxter. "I plan to avoid out-and-out satire. This question has its serious side. I want to examine them not just as soldier-demagogues and bad-boy buffoons but also as leaders defying the West. I want to say something about their resentment over the failure of civilization to lead the world beyond technology and banking. I intend to analyze the crisis of values—"

"Don't tamper with that stuff. Stay away from the values, Thaxter. I'd better give you a few words of advice. First of all, don't push forward, don't intrude yourself into these interviews, and don't ask long questions. Secondly, don't fool around with these dictators and stay away from competitive games. If you play backgammon or ping-pong or bridge with them you'll get carried away—you'll be sunk. You don't know Thaxter," I said to Renata, "until you've seen him with a cue in his hand or a paddle or a racquet or golf club. He's vicious, he leaps, he cheats, he gets fiery in face, and he'll trounce everybody without pity, man woman or child—are you getting a big advance?"

He was prepared, of course, for such a question.

"Not bad, considering. But there are so many liens against me in California that my lawyers have advised me to take monthly installments, not a lump sum, so I'm drawing five hundred a month."

The Palm Court was silent, the musicians were taking their break. Renata, reaching under the table, began to rub my leg. She took my foot into her lap and slipped off the loafer, stroking my sole and caressing the instep. Presently she applied the foot to herself, unremittingly sensual, secretly making love to me—or to herself with me. This had happened before, at dinner parties where the company annoyed or bored her. She was wearing the beautiful velour hat copied from the *Syndics of Amsterdam*, under it the dreaming white face, full toward the bottom, expressed its amusement, its affection, its comment upon my relations with Thaxter, its enjoyment of secrecy. How easy and natural she made everything seem—goodness, badness, lustfulness. I envied her this. At the same time I didn't really believe that it was all so very natural or easy. I suspected—no, I actually *knew* better.

"So if you're thinking about payment, I haven't got anything to give you on account," said Thaxter. "Instead I'm going to do better by you. I'm here to make a practical proposal. You and I should do that cultural Baedeker of Europe. There's an idea that really turns my editor on. Stewart really went for it. Frankly, your name is important in a deal like this. But I'd organize the whole project. You know I have a talent for that. And you wouldn't have a thing to worry about. I'd definitely be the junior partner and you'd get fifty thousand bucks on signing. All you have to do is put down your name."

Renata didn't seem to hear our conversation. She entirely missed the mention of the fifty thousand dollars. She had now left us, as it were, and was pressing me closer and closer. Her need was strong. She was gross, brilliant, endearing, and if she had to suffer fools she knew what measures to take to compensate herself. I loved her for this. The conversation meantime continued. I was glad to hear that I could still command big advances.

Thaxter was not an especially observant man. He entirely missed what Renata was doing, the dilation of her eyes and the biological seriousness in which her fine joke ended. She went from fun to mirth to happiness and finally to a climax, her body straightening in the French provincial Palm Court chair. She nearly passed out with a fine long quiver. This was almost fishlike in its delicacy. Then her eyes shone at me as she smoothed my foot, gentle and calm.

Thaxter meantime was saying, "Of course you worry about working with me. Of course you're afraid I'll run off with my end of the advance, and you'll either have to refund your end or do the book alone. That would be a nightmare to a man with an anxious character like yours."

"I could use the money," I said, "but don't ask me to commit suicide. If I got stuck with a responsibility like that, if you were to beat it and I had to do work alone, my head would go off like a bomb."

"Well, you'd be fully covered. You could protect yourself contractually. It would be stipulated that your only obligation by contract would be to do the major essay on each of the countries. There'll be six countries—England, France, Spain, Italy, Germany, and Austria. The serial rights to those would be yours, completely. Those alone, if you handle them right, might be worth fifty thousand dollars. So my proposal is this, Charlie, we start with Spain, the simplest country, and see how it goes. Now listen to this, Stewart says he'll stake you to a month at the Ritz in Madrid. On approval. You couldn't ask anything fairer. You'd both love it. The Prado is right around the corner. The Michelin Guide lists quite a few first-class restaurants now, like the Escuadrón. I'll set up all the interviews. There'll be a stream of painters, poets, critics, historians, sociologists, architects, musicians, and underground leaders coming to you at the Ritz. You could sit there all day conversing with excellent people and eating and drinking fantastically and making a fortune besides. In three weeks' time you could write a piece called 'Contemporary Spain, a Cultural Overview' or something like that."

Renata, returning to consciousness, was now listening with interest to what Thaxter was saying. "Would this publisher really pick up the tab? Madrid sounds like a wonderful deal," she said.

"You know what these giant conglomerates are," said Thaxter. "What would a few thousand bucks mean to Stewart?"

"I'll think about it."

"It generally means 'No' when Charlie says he'll think about it."

Thaxter bent toward me in his Stetson hat. "I can follow your train of thought," he said. "You're thinking that I better do my book on the dictators first. Thaxter, *avec tout ce qu'il a sur son assiette*? Too many irons in the fire. But that's just it. Other people would burn themselves but with me, the more irons the better I function. I can wrap up five dictators in three months," Thaxter asserted.

"Madrid sounds enchanting," said Renata.

"The old country for your mother, isn't it?" I said.

"Let me give you the rundown on the international Ritz Hotel situation," said Thaxter. "The London Ritz is played out—soiled, run-down. The Paris Ritz belongs to the Arab oil billionaires, the Onassis types, and the Texas barons. No waiter will pay attention to you there. Right now, with those Portuguese upheavals, the Lisbon Ritz isn't a restful place. But Spain is still stable and feudal enough to give the real old-fashioned Ritz treatment."

Thaxter and Renata had this in common: they fancied themselves to be Europeans, Renata because of the Señora, Thaxter because of his French governess, his international family connections, his BA in French at Olivet College, Michigan.

Money apart, Renata saw in me the hope of an interesting life, Thaxter saw the hope of a higher one leading perhaps to a Major Statement. We were sipping tea and sherry and eating pastries iced in beautiful colors while I waited for Kathleen to arrive.

"Trying to keep up with your interests," said Thaxter, "I've been reading your man Rudolf Steiner, and he's fascinating. I expected something like Madame Blavatsky, but he turns out to be a very rational kind of mystic. What's his angle on Goethe?"

"Don't start that, Thaxter," said Renata.

But I needed a serious conversation. I longed for it. "It isn't mysticism," I said. "Goethe simply wouldn't stop at the boundaries drawn by the inductive method. He let his imagination pass over into objects. An artist sometimes tries to see how close he can come to being a river or a star, playing at becoming one or the other—entering into the forms of the phenomena painted or described. Someone has even written of an astronomer keeping droves of stars, the cattle of his mind, in the meadows of space. The imaginative soul works in that way, and why should poetry refuse to be knowledge? For Shelley, Adonais in death became part of the loveliness he had made more lovely. So according to Goethe the blue of the sky *was* the theory. There was a thought in blue. The blue became blue when human vision received it. A wonderful man like my late friend Humboldt was overawed by rational orthodoxy, and because he was a poet this probably cost him his life. Isn't it enough to be a poor naked forked creature without also being a poor naked forked spirit? Must the imagination be asked to give up its own full and free connection with the universe—the universe as Goethe spoke of it? As the living garment of God? And today I found out that Humboldt really believed that human beings were supernatural beings. He too!"

"There he goes," said Renata. "What did you want to start him spouting for?"

"Thought is a real constituent of being," I tried to continue.

"Charlie! Not now," said Renata.

Thaxter who was normally polite to Renata spoke stiffly to her when she barged into these higher conversations. He said, "I take a real interest in the way Charles's mind works." He was smoking his pipe, his mouth drawn wide and dark, under the big Western brim.

"Try living with it," said Renata. "Charlie's kinky theorizing puts together combinations nobody else could imagine, like the way the US Congress does its business, with Immanuel

Kant, Russian Gulag camps, stamp collecting, famine in India, love and sleep and death and poetry. The less said about the way his mind works, the better. But if you do have to be a guru, Charlie, go the whole distance—wear a silk gown, get a turban, grow a beard. You'd make a hell of a good-looking spiritual leader with a beard and those paisley nostrils of yours. I'd dress up with you, and we'd be a smash. The way you carry on and for free! I sometimes have to pinch myself. I think I've taken fifty Valiums and am hearing things."

"People of powerful intellect never are quite sure whether or not it's all a dream."

"Well, people who don't know whether they're awake or dreaming don't necessarily have that powerful intellect," Renata answered. "My theory is that you're punishing me with this anthroposophy. You know what I mean. That blonde runt introduced you to her dad, and since then it's all been really spooky."

"I wish you'd finish what you started to say," Thaxter turned again to me.

"It comes to this, that the individual has no way to prove out what's in his heart—I mean the love, the hungering for the external world, the swelling excitement over beauty for which there are no acceptable terms of knowledge. True knowledge is supposed to be a monopoly of the scientific world view. But human beings have all sorts of knowledge. They don't have to apply for the right to love the world. But to see what goes on in this respect, take the career of someone like Von Humboldt Fleisher. . . ."

"Ah, that guy again," said Renata.

"Is it true that as big-time knowledge advances poetry must drop behind, that the imaginative mode of thought belongs to the childhood of the race? A boy like Humboldt, full of heart and imagination, going to the public library and finding books, leading a charmed life bounded by lovely horizons, reading old masterpieces in which human life has its full value, filling himself with Shakespeare, where there is plenty of significant space around each human being, where words mean what they say, and looks and gestures also are entirely meaningful. Ah, that harmony and sweetness, that art! But there it ends. The significant space dwindles and disappears. The boy enters the world and learns its filthy cutthroat tricks, the enchantment stops. But is it the world that is disenchanted?"

"No," said Renata. "I know the answer to that one."

"It's rather our minds that have allowed themselves to be convinced that there is no imaginative power to connect every individual to the creation independently."

It occurred to me suddenly that Thaxter in his home-on-the-range outfit might as well have been in church and that I was behaving like his minister. This was not a Sunday, but I was in my Palm Court pulpit. As for Renata, smiling—her dark eyes, red mouth, white teeth, smooth throat—though she interrupted and heckled during these sermons she got a kick out of the way I delivered them. I knew her theory well. Whatever was said, whatever was done, either increased or diminished erotic satisfaction, and this was her practical test for any idea. Did it produce a bigger bang? "We could have been at the Scala tonight," she said, "and part of a brilliant audience hearing Rossini. Instead, do you know what we were doing today, Thaxter? We went out to Coney Island so Charlie could collect his inheritance from his dear dead old pal Humboldt Fleisher. It's been Humboldt, Humboldt, Humboldt, like 'Figaro, Figaro.' Humboldt's eighty-year-old uncle gave Charlie a bunch of papers, and Charlie read 'em and wept. Well, for a month now I've heard nothing but Humboldt and death and sleep and metaphysics and how the poet is the arbiter of the diverse and Walt Whitman and Emerson and Plato and the World Historical Individual. Charlie is like Lydia the Tattooed Lady, covered with information. You remember that song, 'You Can Learn a Lot from Lydia'?"

"Could I see those papers?" said Thaxter.

"Come with me to Italy tomorrow," said Renata to me.

"Darling, I'll join you there in a few days."

The Palm Court Trio, returning, began to play Sigmund Romberg, and Renata said, "Why, it's four o'clock. I don't want to miss *Deep Throat*. It starts at four-twenty."

"Yes, and I've got to go to the dock," said Thaxter. "You are coming, aren't you, Charlie?"

"I hope to. I've got to wait here for Kathleen."

"I've written out my itinerary for the dictators," said Thaxter, "so you can get in touch if you have a mind to go to Madrid and start our project. Say the word, and I'll begin organizing. I know people are giving you the business in Chicago. I'm sure you'll be needing lots of money. . . ." He glanced at Renata, who was organizing herself to leave. "And there's real dough in my proposal."

"I've got to run," said Renata. "I'll see you back here later." She slung the bag over her shoulder and preceded Thaxter across the vast luxurious carpet, part of the Christmas display, a blast of gold within the bristling green, and through the swinging doors.

In her large bag Renata carried off my shoe. I realized this when I looked under the table for it. Gone! She had taken it. By means of this prank she told me how she felt about going to the movies alone while I visited sentimentally with an old friend, recently widowed and possibly available. I couldn't go upstairs now, Kathleen would arrive any minute, so I sat waiting, feeling the chill in one foot while the music played. Renata in high spirits had symbolic reasons for pinching my loafer; I was hers. Was she correspondingly mine? When she was proprietary I became uneasy. I felt that as soon as she was sure of one man she became free to contemplate her future with another. And I? Evidently I longed most to possess most the woman that threatened me most.

"Ah, Kathleen, I'm glad to see you," I said as Kathleen came up. I rose, my peculiar foot missing its peculiar shoe. She kissed me—an old friend's warm kiss on the cheek. The Nevada sun hadn't given her an outdoor color. Her fair hair was lighter from the admixture of gray. She hadn't grown stout but she was fleshier, a big woman. This was only the normal effect of the decades, a slackening and softening and a saddening of the cheeks, an attractive melancholy or hollowing. She had once had pale freckles. Now her face had larger spots. Her upper arms were heavier, her legs were thicker, her back wider, her hair paler. Her dress was black chiffon, thinly trimmed with gold at the neck.

"Lovely to see you," I said, for so it was.

"And to see you, Charlie."

She sat down but I remained standing. I said, "I took off a shoe to be more comfortable and now the thing is gone."

"How odd. Maybe the busboy took it. Why don't you try Lost and Found?" So for form's sake I beckoned to the waiter. I made a distinguished inquiry but then I said, "I'll have to go up and get another pair."

Kathleen offered to come with me but as Renata's underclothes were all over the floor and the bed was unmade at one corner in a way that I thought baldly telling, I said, "No, no, why don't you wait for me. This lousy high-toned pimble-pamble music is driving me nuts. I'll come right down and we'll go out for a drink. I want to get my coat, anyway."

So I went up again in the luxurious cage of the elevator thinking what a bold original Renata was and what a struggle she made continually against the threat of passivity, the universal threat. If I thought it, it had to be universal. I wasn't fooling around these days. This universalizing was becoming a craze with me, I suspected, as I put on my other pair of shoes. These were light, weightless red shoes from Harrods, a little short in the toe, but admired by the black shoeshine man at the Downtown Club for their weightlessness and style. In these, a little cramped but fine, I went down again.

This day belonged to Humboldt, it was charged with his spirit. I realized how emotional I was becoming under this influence when, tying to adjust my hat, I felt uncontrollable tremors in my arms. As I approached Kathleen, one side of my face also twitched. I thought, Old Dr. Galvani has got me. I saw two men, husbands, in their graves, decomposing. This beautiful lady's affections had not saved them from death. Next a vision of Humboldt's shade went through my head in the form of a dark gray cloud. His cheeks were fat and the abundant hair was piled on his head. I walked toward Kathleen as the three-piece group played what Renata called "frill-paper cup-cake music." They had dipped into *Carmen* now and I said, "Let's go to a dark, quiet bar. Above all, quiet." I signed the waiter's staggering check and Kathleen and I walked up and down in the cold streets until we found an agreeable place on West Fifty-sixth, dark enough for any taste and not too Christmasy.

We had a lot of catching up to do. First of all we had to

speak of poor Tigler. I couldn't bring myself to say what a nice man he had been, for he hadn't been nice at all. The old wrangler could stamp his foot like Rumpelstiltskin and flew into tantrums when he was crossed. It gave him keen satisfaction to stick and screw people. He despised them all the more if they were too timid to complain. His dudes, and I had been one of them, got no hot water. The lights went out and they sat in the dark. If they went to Kathleen to beef they came away pitying and forgiving, hating him and loving her. She was not, however, one of my contrast-gainers. Her own merits were clear, this large-limbed pale freckled quiet woman. Her quietness was most important. While Humboldt played the Furious Turk she was his Christian Captive, reading in the book-stuffed cottage parlor set in the barren thicken country while the ruddy sun persisted in trying to force color through the soiled small-framed windows. Then Humboldt ordered her to put on a sweater and come outside. They chased a football like two fair-haired rookies. Staggering backward on clumsy heels he threw passes over the clothesline and through the autumn maples. My recollection of this was complete—how as Kathleen ran to make the catch her voice trailed and she reached out her arms and brought the wagging ball to her bosom, and how she and Humboldt had sat together on the Castro sofa drinking beer. I recalled this so fully that I saw the cats, one with a Hitler mustache, at the window. I heard my own voice. Twice now she had been a sleeping maiden under the spell of demon lovers. "You know what my hillbilly neighbors say," Humboldt told me, "they say, keep 'em in their stocking feet. Sometimes," he said, "I think of Eros and Psyche." He flattered himself. Eros was beautiful and he came and went in dignity. Where was Humboldt's dignity? He confiscated Kathleen's driver's license. He hid the car keys. He wouldn't allow her to keep a garden because, he said, gardening expressed the Philistine-improving impulse of city people when they bought a dream house in the country. A few tomatoes grew at the kitchen door but these had reseeded themselves when raccoons overturned the garbage cans. He said seriously, "Kathleen and I have mental work to do. Besides, if we had fruits and flowers it would make us conspicuous out here." He was afraid of sheeted night-riders and of burning crosses in his yard.

I sympathized greatly with Kathleen because she was a sleeper. I wondered about her dreaminess. Was she born to be kept in the dark? Not to reach consciousness was a condition of Psyche's bliss. But perhaps there was a more economical explanation. Tigler's tight denims had revealed an enormous sexual lump in front, and Humboldt, when he pursued Demmie's friend to her apartment, among the dachshund puppies, had shouted, "I'm a poet, I have a big cock!" But my guess was that Humboldt had the character of a tyrant who wanted a woman to hold still and that his lovemaking was frenzied dictatorship. Even his last letter to me confirmed this interpretation. Still, how was one to know? And a woman without secrets was no woman at all. And probably Kathleen had decided to marry Tigler only because life in Nevada was so lonely. Enough of this ingenious analysis.

Giving in to my weakness for telling people what they wish to hear, I said to Kathleen, "The West has agreed with you." It was, however, more or less true.

"You look well but a little drawn, Charlie."

"Life is too vexatious. Maybe I should try the West myself. When the weather was nice I did like lying under the elder trees at your ranch watching the mountains all day long. Anyway, Huggins says you've got some sort of job in the picture business and you're on your way to Europe."

"Yes. You were there when that company came out to Volcano Lake to make a movie about Outer Mongolia and all the Indians were hired to ride their ponies."

"And Tigler was technical consultant."

"And Father Edmund—you remember him, the silent-film-star Episcopal minister—was so excited. Poor Father Edmund never got ordained. He hired somebody to take his written exam in theology and they were caught. It's too bad because the Indians loved him and they were so proud that his robes were those stars' negligees. But yes, I'm going to Yugoslavia and then to Spain. Those are big for film-making these days. You can hire Spanish soldiers by the regiment, and Andalusia is perfect for Westerns."

"It's odd that you should mention Spain. I've thought of going there myself."

"Have you? Well, from March first I'm going to be in the

Grand Hotel of Almería. Wouldn't it be wonderful to see you there."

"It's a good change for you," I said.

"You always wished me well, Charlie. I know that," said Kathleen.

"This has been a big Humboldt day, a major day, an accelerating spiral since this morning and I'm in a very emotional state. At Uncle Waldemar's nursing home, to add to the excitement, I met a man I've known since I was a kid. Now you're here I'm all worked up."

"I heard from Huggins that you were going to Coney Island. You know, Charlie, there were times in Nevada when I thought you were overdoing your attachment to Humboldt."

"That's possible, and I've tried to check it. I ask myself, why so much enthusiasm? As a poet or thinker his record wasn't all that impressive. And I'm not longing for the good old days. Is it that the number of people who got serious about Art and Thought in the USA is so small that even those who flunked out are unforgettable?" Here we were closer to the real topic. I meant to interpret the good and evil of Humboldt, understand his ruin, translate the sadness of his life, find out why such gifts produced negligible results, and so forth. But these were aims difficult to discuss even when I was flying high, full of affection for Kathleen and of wonderful pangs. "For me he had charm, he had the old magic," I said.

"I guess you loved him," she said. "Of course I was crazy about him. We went to New Jersey—that would have been hell even if he had had no crazy spells. The little cottage seems now like part of a terrible frame-up. But I would have gone to the Arctic with him. And the college girl's thrill at getting into the literary life was only a small part of it. I didn't care for most of his literary friends. They came to watch the show Humboldt put on, his routines. When they left, and he was still inspired, he'd go after me. He was a sociable person. He used to say how much he would like to move in brilliant circles, be a part of the literary world."

"That's just it. There never was such a literary world," I said. "In the nineteenth century there were several solitaries of the highest genius—a Melville or a Poe had no literary life. It was the customhouse and the barroom for them. In Russia,

Lenin and Stalin destroyed the literary world. Russia's situation now resembles ours—poets, in spite of everything against them, emerge from nowhere. Where did Whitman come from, and where did he get what he had? It was W. Whitman, an irrepressible individual, that had it and that did it."

"Well, if there had been a rich literary life, and if he had been able to drink tea with Edith Wharton and see Robert Frost and T. S. Eliot twice a week, poor Humboldt would have felt supported and appreciated and rewarded for his talent. He just didn't feel able to fill up all the vacancy he felt around him," said Kathleen. "Of course he was a wizard. He made me feel so slow, slow slow! He invented the most ingenious things to accuse me of. All that invention should have gone into his poetry. Humboldt had too many personal arrangements. Too much genius went into the arrangements. As his wife I had to suffer the consequences. But let's not go on talking about it. Let me ask . . . you two wrote a scenario once. . . ?"

"Just some nonsense to pass the time in Princeton. You said something about it to that young woman, Mrs. Cantabile. What is Mrs. Cantabile like?"

"She's pretty. She's polite in an old-fashioned Emily Post way, and sends proper notes to thank you for a delicious lunch. At the same time she paints her nails in gaudy colors, wears flashy clothes, and has a harsh voice. When she chats with you she's screaming. She sounds like a gun-moll but asks graduate-student questions. Anyway I'm getting into the film business now, and I'm curious about something that you and Humboldt did together. After all a successful movie was made of your play."

"Oh, our scenario could never have made a picture. Our cast included Mussolini, the Pope, Stalin, Calvin Coolidge, Amundsen, and Nobile. Our hero was a cannibal. We had a dirigible and a Sicilian village. W. C. Fields might have loved it, but only a mad producer would ever have put a penny into it. Of course no one ever does know about these things. In 1913, who would have looked twice at an advance-scenario of World War One? Or if, before I was born, you had submitted the tale of my own life to me and invited me to live with it, wouldn't I have turned you down flat?"

"But what about your hit play?"

"Kathleen, believe me. I was just the worm that spit out the silk thread. Other people created the Broadway garment. Now tell me, what did Humboldt leave you?"

"Well, first all, he wrote me an extraordinary letter."

"Me too. And a perfectly sane one."

"Mine is more mixed. It's too personal to show, even now. He spelled out all the crimes I was supposed to have committed. His purpose was to forgive me, whatever I had done, but he forgave in full detail and he was still talking about the Rockefellers. But there were patches of perfect sanity. Really moving, true things."

"Was that all you got from him?"

"Well, no, Charlie, there was something else he gave me. A document. Another idea for a movie. This is why I was asking you about the thing you two invented in Princeton. Tell me, what did he leave you, apart from this letter?"

"Astonishing!" I said.

"What's astonishing?"

"What Humboldt did. Sick as he was, dying, decaying, but still so ingenious."

"I don't understand you."

"Tell me, Kathleen, is this document, this film idea, about a writer? And does the writer have a domineering wife? And does he also have a beautiful young mistress? And do they take a journey? And does he then write a book he can't publish?"

"Ah, yes. I see. Of course. That's it, Charlie."

"What a son of a bitch. How marvelous! He duplicated everything. The same journey with the wife. And the same document for us both."

Silent, she studied me. Her mouth moved. She smiled. "Why do you suppose he gave the same gift to each of us?"

"Are you perfectly sure that we're his only heirs? Ha-ha, well, let's drink to his crazy memory. He was a dear man."

"Yes, he was a dear man. And how I wish—you think it was all done according to plan?" said Kathleen.

"Who was it, Alexander Pope, who couldn't drink a cup of tea without a stratagem? That was Humboldt, too. And he kept dreaming about miraculous money until the end. He was dying and still he wanted to make us both rich. Anyway, if he kept his sense of humor, or traces of it, to the last, that was astonishing. And crazy as he was he wrote two sane letters at least. I'm going to make an odd comparison—Humboldt had to break out of his case of hardened madness to do that. You might say that he had emigrated into this madness long ago. Became a settler there. For us, maybe, he managed a visit to the Old Country. To see his friends once more? And it may have been as hard for him to do it as it might be for someone —myself, for instance—to go from this world to the spirit world. Or, another odd comparison—he made a Houdini escape from the hardened projections of paranoia, or manic depression, or whatever it was. Sleepers do awaken. Exiles and emigrants do make it back, and dying genius can revive. 'End-of-the-line lucidity,' he wrote in my letter."

"I don't think at the end he had the strength for two separate gifts, one for each of us," she said.

"Or look at it this way," I said. "He showed us what he had most of—scheming, plotting, and paranoia. He did as much with it as any man could. Don't you remember the famous Longstaff scheme?"

"Do you think he might have had anything else in mind?" said Kathleen.

"One single thing?" I said.

"A kind of posthumous character test," she said.

"He was absolutely sure that my character was hopeless. Yours, too, maybe. Well, he's given us a very lively moment. Here we are laughing and admiring, and how sad it is. I'm very touched. We both are."

Quiet and large, Kathleen was mildly smiling, but the color of her large eyes suddenly changed. Tears came into them. Still she sat passive. That was Kathleen. It was not appropriate to mention this, but possibly Humboldt's idea was to bring us together. Not to become man and wife necessarily, but perhaps to combine our feelings for him and create a sort of joint memorial. For after he died, we would continue (for a time) to be active in life in this deluded human scene, and perhaps it would be a satisfaction to him and ease the boredom of the grave to think that we were busy with his enterprises. For when a Plato or a Dante or Dostoevski argued for immortality, Humboldt, a deep admirer of these men, couldn't say, "They were geniuses, but we don't have to take their ideas seriously."

But did he himself take immortality seriously? He didn't say. What he said was that we were supernatural, not natural. I would have given anything to find out what he meant.

"These scenarios or treatments are very hard to copyright," Kathleen explained. "And Humboldt must have gotten professional advice about legal protection. . . . He sealed a copy a his script in an envelope and went to the post office and registered it and had it delivered to himself by registered mail. So that it's never been opened. We've read the duplicates."

"That's right. I have two such sealed envelopes."

"Two?"

"Yes," I said. "The other is the one we'd dreamed up at Princeton. Now I know how Humboldt was amusing himself in that rotten hotel. He spent his time working all this out in meticulous detail and with ceremonious formalities. That was right up his alley."

"Listen, Charles, we must go fifty-fifty," Kathleen said.

"Bless you, commercially it's zero," I told her.

"On the contrary," Kathleen said firmly. I looked again at her, hearing this. It was out of character for Kathleen, normally diffident, to be so positively contradictory. "I submitted this to people in the business and I actually signed a contract and took an option payment of three thousand dollars. Half of that is yours."

"You mean that someone has actually paid out money for this?"

"I had two offers to choose from. I accepted the one from Steinhals Productions. Where shall I send your check?"

"At the moment I have no address. I'm in transit. But no, Kathleen, I won't take any of this money." I was thinking how I would give this news to Renata. She had ridiculed Humboldt's gift so brilliantly, and on behalf of our vanishing generation, Humboldt's and mine, I had felt hurt. "And is a script being written?"

"It's receiving serious consideration," said Kathleen. Occasionally her voice soared into a girlish treble. It broke.

"How interesting. How goofy. A solid mass of improbabilities," I said. "Although I've always been a little proud of my personal oddities, I've begun to suspect that they may be only faint images of a thousand real and much more powerful oddities out there, somewhere—that they may not be so personal after all and that maybe this is a general condition. That's why Humboldt's burlesque of love and ambition and all the rest of those monkeyshines can sound plausible to business people."

"I had good legal advice and my contract with Steinhals is for a minimum of thirty thousand dollars if the option is picked up. We could go over seventy thousand, depending on the budget. We should know in about two months. End of February. And what I feel now, Charlie, is that as joint owners you and I should draw a separate contract."

"Now, Kathleen, let's not add to the unreality of things. No contracts. And I don't need this money."

"I would have thought so too, before today, with everybody talking about your million-dollar fortune. But before you signed the check at the Palm Court you added it twice from top to bottom and again from the bottom. You lost your color. And then I saw you struggling to decide on a tip. Now don't be embarrassed, Charles."

"No, no, Kathleen. I've got plenty. It's only one of my Depression hang-ups. Besides, what a rip-off! It makes old-timers indignant."

"But I know you're being sued. I know what happens when the judges and lawyers get after a man. I haven't run a Nevada dude ranch for nothing."

"Hanging on to money is hard, of course. It's like clutching an ice cube. And you can't just make it and then live easy. There's no such thing. That's what Humboldt probably didn't understand. I wonder, did he think money made the difference between success and failure? Then he didn't understand. When you get money you go through a metamorphosis. And you have to contend with terrific powers inside and out. There's almost nothing personal in success. Success is always money's own success."

"You're merely trying to change the subject. You've always been a great observer. For years I've watched you looking at people cannily. As if you saw them but they didn't see you. But come now, Charlie, you aren't the only observer."

"Would I be staying at the Plaza if I were going broke?"

"With a young lady you might, yes."

This large, altered but still handsome woman with the occasionally breaking piercing voice, her cheeks looped inward with attractive melancholy, had been studying me. Her glance, though still a bit averted and oblique from the long habit of passivity, was warm and kindly. I am quickly and deeply touched when people take the trouble to note my situation.

"I understand you're on your way to Europe with this lady. So Huggins told me."

"True," I said, "that's right."

"To. . . ?"

"To what?" I said, "God knows." I might have told her more. I might have confessed that I no longer took seriously questions taken seriously by many serious people, questions of metaphysics or of politics, wrongly formulated. Was there then any reason why I should have a precise or practical motive for flying to Italy with a beautiful creature? I was pursuing a special tenderness, I was pursuing love and gratification from motives that would have been appropriate thirty years ago. What would it be like to overtake in my sixties what I had longed for in my twenties? What would I do with it when I got it? I had half a mind to open my heart to this fine woman. I believed that I saw signs that she too was coming out of a state of spiritual sleep. We might have discussed lots of fascinating subjects—for instance, why slumber sealed people's spirits, why waking was so convulsive, and whether she thought that the spirit could move independently of the body and if she felt that there might not be a kind of consciousness that needed no biological footing. I was tempted to tell her that I, personally, had some notion of doing something about the problem of death. I considered whether to discuss with her seriously the assignment set for writers by Walt Whitman, who was convinced that democracy would fail unless its poets gave it great poems of death. I felt that Kathleen was a woman to whom I could talk. But the position was an embarrassing one. An old chaser who had lost his head over a beautiful gold-digging palooka, a romancer who was going to fulfill the dreams of his youth, suddenly wanting to discuss supersensible consciousness and democracy's great poem of death! Come, Charlie, let's not make the world queerer than it already is. It was precisely because Kathleen *was* a woman to whom I could talk that I kept silent. Out of respect. I thought I would wait until I had considered all these questions more ripely, until I knew more.

She said, "I'll be at the Metropol in Belgrade next week. Let's stay in touch. I'm going to have a contract drawn, and I'll sign it and send it to you."

"No, no, let's not bother."

"Why, because I'm a widow you won't accept your own money from me? But *I* don't want *your* share. Think of it that way."

She was a kind woman. And she recognized the truth—I was spending big money on Renata and I was quickly going broke.

"My dear, why did you steal my shoe?"

"I couldn't resist," said great Renata. "How did you hobble upstairs on one shoe? What did your friend think? I bet it was a riot. Charlie, humor is a bond we have. That I know for a fact."

Humor had an edge over love in this relationship. My character and my ways entertained Renata. This entertainment was so extensive that I thought it might merge by degrees with love. For I didn't under any circumstances propose to do without love.

"You also took off my boot under the table in Paris."

"Yes, that was the night that horrible fellow told you how worthless your Legion ribbon was and put you in a class with garbage collectors and pig breeders. It was like revenge, consolation, kicks, all at the same time," said Renata. "Do you remember what I said afterward, that I thought was so funny?"

"Yes, I remember."

"What did I say, Charlie?"

"You said, to air it is human."

"To air it is human, to bare it divine." All made up, dark-haired and dressed in a crimson traveling costume, she laughed. "Oh, Charlie, give up this dumb trip to Texas. I need you in Milan. It isn't going to be easy for me with Biferno. Your brother doesn't want your visit and you don't owe him anything. You love him but he bullies you, and you have no defenses against bullies. You go to them with an aching heart and they always kick you in the ass. You know and I know what he's going to think. He's going to think that you're flying down at a tender moment to con him into putting you in one of his profitable deals. Let me ask you something, Charlie, will he be partly right? I want to pry into your present situation, but I suspect you need a break financially right now. There's one thing more: it'll be nip and tuck between you and his wife as to who has the right to be chief mourner if something happens, and why should he want to face both of his chief mourners just as he goes under the knife? In short, you're wasting your time. Come with me. I dream of marrying you in Milan under my true maiden name, Biferno, with my real father giving me away."

I wanted to humor Renata. She deserved to have things her way. We were at Kennedy now and, in her incomparable hat and the suède maxi-coat, her Hermès scarves, her elegant boots, she was no more to be privately possessed than the Tower of Pisa. And yet she claimed her private rights, the right to an identity-problem, the right to a father, a husband. How silly, what a comedown! However, from the next hierarchical level, and to an invisible observer, I might appear to be making similar claims to order, rationality, prudence, and other middle-class things.

"Let's have a drink in the VIP Lounge. I don't want to drink where it's so noisy and the glasses are sticky."

"But I don't belong any more."

"Charles," she said, "there is that guy Zitterbloom—the one who lost you twenty thousand dollars in oil wells a year ago when he was supposed to be buying you tax shelter. Get him on the phone and have him fix it. He suggested it himself last year. 'Anytime at all, Charlie.' "

"You make me feel like the fisherman in *Grimm's Fairy Tales*, the one whose wife sent him to the seashore to ask the magic fish for a palace."

"Watch how you talk. I'm no nag," she said. "We have a right to our last drink with a little class, not pushed around by a lousy crowd."

So I telephoned Zitterbloom, whose secretary easily

arranged the matter. It made me think how much a man might salvage from his defeats and losses if he wanted to put his mind to it. In a gloomy farewell spirit, I sipped my bloody mary, thinking what a risk I was running for my brother's sake and how little he would appreciate it. Still, I *must* have confidence in Renata. Ideal manhood demanded it and practical judgment would have to live with the demand of ideal manhood. I did not, however, wish to be asked on the spot to predict how it would all come out, for if I had to predict, everything would disappear in a whirlwind. "What about a bottle of 'Ma Griffe,' duty-free?" she said. I bought her a large-sized bottle, saying, "They'll deliver it on the plane, and I won't be there to smell it."

"Don't you worry, we're going to save everything for the reunion. Don't let your brother fix you up with women in Texas."

"That would be about the last thing on his mind. But what about you, Renata, when was the last time you spoke with Flonzaley?"

"You can forget Flonzaley. We've made a clean break. He's a nice man, but I can't go along with the undertaking business."

"He's very rich," I said.

"He's worth his wreaths in wraiths," she said, in the style I loved her for. "As president he doesn't have to handle corpses anymore but I can never help remembering his embalming background. Of course I don't hold with this guy Fromm, when he says how necrophilia has crept up on civilization. To be perfectly serious, Charlie, with a build like mine if I don't stay strictly normal where am I at?"

I was quite sad, nevertheless, wondering what part of the truth she was telling me and even whether we would see each other again. But despite the many pressures I was under I felt that I was making progress spiritually. At the best of times, separations and departures unnerve me and I experienced great anxiety now but felt I had something reliable within.

"So good-by, darling. I'll phone you from Milan tomorrow in Texas," said Renata, and we kissed many times. She seemed on the point of crying, but there were no tears.

I walked through the TWA tunnel, like an endless arched gullet or a corridor in an expressionistic film, and then I was searched for weapons and got on a plane to Houston. All the way to Texas I read occult books. There were many stirring passages in them, to which I shall come back in a while. I reached Corpus Christi in the afternoon and checked into a motel. Then I went over to Julius's house, which was large and new and surrounded by palms and jacarandas and loquats and lemon trees. The lawns looked artificial, like green excelsior or packing material. Expensive automobiles were parked in the driveway, and when I rang the bell there was a great gonging and tolling and dogs began to bark inside. The security arrangements were elaborate. Heavy locks were undone and then my sister-in-law, Hortense, opened the wide door covered with Polynesian carvings. She hollered at the dogs but with underlying affection. Then she turned to me. She was a blunt, decent person with blue eyes and chub lips. A bit blinded by the smoke of her own cigarette, which she did not remove from her mouth, she said, "Charles! How did you get here?"

"Hired a car from Avis. How are you, Hortense?"

"Julius is expecting you. He's dressing. Go on in."

The dogs were not much smaller than horses. She restrained them and I went toward the master bedroom, greeting the children, my nephews, who answered nothing. I wasn't altogether sure that for them I was a full member of the family. Entering, I found Ulick, my brother, in candy-striped boxer shorts reaching to his knees. "I thought that must be you, Chuckie," he said.

"Well, Ulick, here we are," I said. He did not look well. His belly was large and his titties were pointed. Between them grew profuse gray silk. He was, however, in full control, as usual. His long head was masterful with its straight nose and well-barbered smooth white hair, the commanding mustache and witty, hard-glinting pouchy eyes. He had always worn roomy shorts, he liked them better. Mine were as a rule shorter and snugger. He gave me one of his undershot glances. A whole lifetime was between us. With me it was continuous, but Ulick was the sort of man who wanted to renegotiate the terms again and again. Nothing was to be assumed permanently. The brotherly emotions brought with me mystified and embarrassed him, flattered and filled him with suspicion. Was I a nice fellow? Was I really innocent? And was I really any good? Ulick had, with me, the difficulties of a final determination which I myself had with Thaxter.

"If you had to come, you could have gone direct to Houston," he said. "That's where we go tomorrow." I could see that he was fighting his brotherly feelings. They were heavily present still. Ulink had by no means gotten rid of them all.

"Oh, I didn't mind the extra trip. And I had nothing special to do in New York."

"Well, I have to go and look at some property this afternoon. You want to come with me or do you want to swim in the pool? It's heated." Last time I slid into his pool one of his great dogs had bitten me in the ankle and drawn quite a lot of blood. And I hadn't come for the bathing, he knew that. He said, "Well, I'm pleased you're here." He turned away his powerful face and stared elsewhere while his brain, intensely trained in calculation, calculated his chances. "This operation is fucking up the kids' Christmas," he said, "and you're not even going to be with yours."

"I sent them a load of toys from F. A. O. Schwarz. I'm sorry to say I didn't think of bringing presents for your boys."

"What would you give them? They've got everything. It's a goddamn guessing game to buy them a toy. I'm set for the operation. They kept me in bed for all the tests, up in Houston. I made a twenty-thousand-dollar donation to that joint in memory of Papa and Mama. And I'm ready for the operation except that I'm a few pounds overweight. Chuck, they saw you open and I even think the bastards lift the heart right out of your chest. Their team does these heart jobs by the thousands. I expect to be back in my office by the first of February. Are you fluid? Have you got about fifty thousand? I may be able to put you into something."

From time to time Ulick telephoned me from Texas and said, "Send me a check for thirty, no, make it forty-five." I simply wrote the check and mailed it. There were no receipts. Occasionally a contract arrived six months later. Invariably my money was doubled. It pleased him to do this for me, although it also irritated him that I failed to understand the details of these deals and that I didn't appreciate his business subtlety. As for my profits, they had been entrusted to Zitterbloom, they paid Denise, they subsidized Thaxter, they were taken by the IRS, they kept Renata in the Lake Point Towers, they went to Tomchek and Srole.

"What have you got in mind?" I said.

"A few things," he said. "You know what bank rates are. I'd be surprised if they didn't hit eighteen percent before long." Three different television sets were turned on, adding to the streaming colors of the room. The wallpaper was gold-embossed. The carpet seemed a continuation of the dazzling lawn. Indoors and outdoors fell into each other through a picture window, garden and bedroom mingling. There was a blue Exercycle, and there were trophies on the shelves, for Hortense was a famous golfer. Enormous closets, specially built, were thick with suits and with dozens of pairs of shoes arranged on long racks and with hundreds of neckties and stacks of hatboxes. Showy, proud of his possessions, in matters of taste he was a fastidious critic and he reviewed my appearance as if he were the Douglas MacArthur of dress. "You were always a slob, Chuckie, and now you spend money on clothes and go to a tailor, but you're still a slob. Who sold you those goddamn shoes? And that horse-blanket overcoat? Hustlers used to sell shoes like that to the greenhorns fifty years ago with a buttonhook for a bonus. Now take this coat." He threw into my arms a black vicuna with a Chesterfield collar. "Down here it's too warm to get much use out of it. It's yours. The boys will take your coat to the stable, where it belongs. Take it off, put this on." I did as I was ordered. This was the form his affection took. When it was necessary to resist Ulick, I did it silently. He put on a pair of double-knit slacks, beautifully cut, with flaring cuffs, but he couldn't fasten them over his belly. He shouted to Hortense in the next room that the cleaner had shrunk them.

"Yah, they shrank," she answered.

This was the style of the house. None of your Ivy League muttering and subdued statement.

I was given a pair of his shoes, too. Our feet were exactly the same. So were the big extruded eyes and the straight noses. I don't clearly know what these features did for me. His gave him an autocratic look. And now that I was beginning to think of every earthly life as one of a series, I puzzled over Ulick's spiritual career. What had he been before? Biological evolution and Western History could never create a person like Ulick in sixty-five lousy years. He had brought his deeper qualities here with him. Whatever his earlier form, I was inclined to believe that in this life, as a rich rough American, he had lost some ground. America was a harsh trial to the human spirit. I shouldn't be surprised if it set everyone back. Certain higher powers seemed to be in abeyance, and the sentient part of the soul had every thing its own way, with its material conveniences. Oh the creature comforts, the animal seductions. Now which journalist was it that had written that there were countries in which our garbage would have been delicatessen?

"So you're going to Europe. Any special reason? Are you on a job? Or just running, as usual? You never go alone, always with some bim. What kind of cunt is taking you this time? . . . I can force myself into these slacks, but we're going to do a lot of driving and I won't be comfortable." He pulled them off angrily and threw them on the bed. "I'll tell you where we're going. There's a gorgeous piece of property, forty or fifty acres of peninsula into the Gulf and it belongs to some Cubans. Some general who was dictator before Batista ripped it off years ago. I'll tell you what his racket was. When currency wore out, the old bills were picked up at the Havana banks and trucked away to be destroyed. But this currency was never burned. No sir, it was shipped out of the country and deposited to the old general's account. With this he bought US property. Now the descendants are sitting on it. They're no damn good, a bunch of playboys. The daughters and daughters-in-law are after these playboy heirs to act like men. All they do is sail and drink and sleep and whore and play polo. Drugs, fast cars, planes—you know the scene. The women want a developer to size this property up. Bid on it. It'll take millions, Charlie, it's a whole damn peninsula. I've got some Cubans of my own, exiles who knew these heirs in the old country. I believe we have the inside track. By the way, I got a letter about you from Denise's lawyer. You owned one point in my Peony Condominiums and they wanted to know what it was worth. Did you have to tell them everything? Who is this fellow Pinsker?"

"I had no choice. They subpoenaed my tax returns."

"Ah, you poor nut, you overeducated boob. You come from good stock, and you weren't born dumb, you thrust it on yourself. And if you had to be an intellectual, why couldn't you be the tough type, a Herman Kahn or a Milton Friedman, one of those aggressive guys you read in *The Wall Street Journal*! You with your Woodrow Wilson and other dead numbers. I can't read the crap you write. Two sentences and I'm yawning. Pa should have slapped you around the way he did me. It would have woken you up. Being his favorite did you no good. Then you up and marry this fierce broad. She'd fit in with the Symbionese or the Palestine Liberation terrorists. When I saw her sharp teeth and the way her hair grew twisty at the temples I knew you were bound for outer space. You were born trying to prove that life on this earth was not feasible. Okay, your case is practically complete. Christ I wish I had your physical condition. You still play ball with Langobardi? Christ they say he's a gentleman now. Tell me, how is your lawsuit?"

"Pretty bad. The court ordered me to post a bond. Two hundred thousand."

The figure made him pale. "They tied up your money? You'll never see it again. Who's your lawyer, still your boyhood chum that fat-ass Szathmar?"

"No, it's Forrest Tomchek."

"I knew Tomchek at law school. The legal-statesman type of crook. He's smoother than a suppository, only his suppositories contain dynamite. And the judge is who?"

"A man named Urbanovich."

"Him I don't know. But he's been ruling against you and it's all clear to me. They've gotten to him. Dirty work at the crossroads. He's using you to make some payoff. He owes somebody something and he's settling the score with your dough. I'll check it out for you right now. You know a guy named Flanko, in Chicago?"

"Solomon Flanko? He's a Syndicate lawyer."

"He'll know." Ulick rapidly punched out the numbers on the telephone. "Flanko," he said when he got through, "this is Julius Citrine down in Texas. There's a guy in domestic-relations court caused Urbanovich. Is he on the take?" He listened keenly. He said, "Thanks, Flanko, I'll get back to you later." After hanging up, he chose a sport shirt. He said, "No,

Urbanovich doesn't seem to be on the take. He wants to make a record on the bench. He's very slick. He's callous. If he is after you, you and that money are going to be separated like yolks and whites. Okay, write it off. We'll make you some more. Did you put anything inside?"

"No."

"Nothing in a box? No numbered account anywhere? No bagman?"

"No."

He stared at me sternly. And then his face, grooved with age with worry and with indurated attitudes, relented somewhat and he smiled under the Acheson mustache. "To think that we should be brothers," he said. "It's positively a subject for a poem. You ought to suggest it to your pal Von Humboldt Fleisher. What ever happened, by the way, to your sidekick the poet? I came in a cab and took you night-clubbing in New York once in the fifties. We had fun at the Copacabana, you remember?"

"That night on the town was great. Humboldt loved it. He's dead," I said.

Ulick put on a shirt of flame-blue Italian silk, a beautiful garment. It seemed to hunger for an ideal body. He drew it over his chest. On my last visit Ulick was slender and wore magnificent hip-huggers, melon-striped and ornamented on the seams with Mexican silver pesos. He had achieved this new figure in a crash diet. But even then the floor of his Cadillac was covered with peanut shells, and now he was fat again. I saw the fat old body which I had always known and which was completely familiar to me—the belly, the freckles on his undisciplined upper arms, and his elegant hands. I still saw in him the obese, choked-looking boy, the lustful conniving kid whose eyes continually pleaded not guilty. I knew him inside-out, even physically, remembering how he gashed open his thigh on a broken bottle in a Wisconsin creek fifty years ago and that I stared at the yellow fat, layers and layers of fat through which the blood had to well. I knew the mole on the back of his wrist, his nose broken and reset, his fierce false look of innocence, his snorts, and his smells. Wearing an orange football jersey, breathing through the mouth (before we could afford the nose-job), he held me on his shoulders so that I could watch the GAR parade on Michigan Boulevard. The year must have been 1923. He held me by the legs. His own legs were bulky in ribbed black stockings and he wore billowing, bloomer like golf knickers. Afterward he stood behind me in the men's room of the Public Library, the high yellow urinals like open sarcophagi, helping me to fish my child's thing out from the complicated underclothes. In 1928 he became a baggage-smasher at American Express. Then he worked at the bus terminal changing the huge tires. He slugged it out with bullies in the street, and was a bully himself. He put himself through the Lewis Institute, nights, and through law school. He made and lost fortunes. He took his own Packard to Europe in the early Fifties and had it airlifted from Paris to Rome because driving over mountains bored him. He spent sixty or seventy thousand dollars a year on himself alone. I never forgot any fact about him. This flattered him. It also made him sore. And if I put so much heart into remembering, what did it prove? That I loved Ulick? There are clinical experts who think that such completeness of memory is a hysterical symptom. Ulick himself said he had no memory except for the business transactions.

"So that screwball friend of yours Von Humboldt is dead. He talked complicated gobbledygook and was worse dressed than you, but I liked him. He sure could drink. What did he die of?"

"Brain hemorrhage." I had to tell this virtuous lie. Heart disease was taboo today. "He left me a legacy."

"What, he had dough?"

"No. Just papers. But when I went to the nursing home to get them from his old uncle, whom should I run into but Menasha Klinger."

"Don't tell me—Menasha! The dramatic tenor, the redhead! The fellow from Ypsilanti who boarded with us in Chicago? I never saw such a damn deluded crazy bastard. He couldn't carry a tune in a bucket. Spent his factory wages on lessons and concert tickets. The one time he tried to do himself some good he caught a dose, and then the clap-doctor shared his wages with the music teacher. Is he old enough to be in a nursing home? Well, I'm in my middle sixties and he was about eight years ahead of me. You know what I found the other day? The deed to the family burial plots in Waldheim. There are two graves left. You wouldn't want to buy mine, would you? I'm not going to lie around. I'm having myself cremated. I need action. I'd rather go into the atmosphere. Look for me in the weather reports."

He too had a thing about the grave. He said to me on the day of Papa's funeral, "The weather is too damn warm and nice. It's awful. Did you ever see such a perfect afternoon?" The artificial grass carpet was rolled back by the diggers and under it in the tan sandy ground was a lovely cool hole. Aloft, far behind the pleasant May weather stood something like a cliff of coal. Aware of this coal cliff bearing down on the flowery cemetery—lilac time!—I broke out into a sweat. A small engine began to lower the coffin on smooth-running canvas bands. There never was a man so unwilling to go down, to pass through the bitter gates as Father Citrine—never a man so unfit to lie still. Papa, that great sprinter, that, broken-field runner, and now brought down by the tackle of heavy death.

Ulick wanted to show me how Hortense had redecorated the children's rooms, he said. I knew that he was looking for candy bars. In the kitchen the cupboards were padlocked, and the refrigerator was out of bounds. "She's absolutely right," he said, "I must stop eating. I know you always said it was all false appetite. You advised me to put my finger down my throat and gag when I thought I was hungry. What's that supposed to do, reverse the diaphragm muscle or something? You were always a strong-willed fellow and a jock, chinning yourself and swinging clubs and dumbbells and punching the bag in the closet and running around the block and hanging from the trees like Tarzan of the Apes. You must have had a bad conscience about what you did when you locked yourself in the toilet. You're a sexy little bastard, never mind your big-time mental life. All this fucking art! I never understood the play you wrote. I went away in the second act. The movie was better, but even that had dreary parts. My old friend Ev Dirksen had a literary period, too. Did you know the Senator wrote poems for greeting cards? But he was a deep old phony—he was a real guy, as cynical as they come. He at least kidded his own hokum. Say, listen, I knew the country was headed for trouble as soon as there began to be big money in art."

"I don't know about that," I said. "To make capitalists of artists was a humorous idea of some depth. America decided to test the pretensions of the esthetic by applying the dollar measure. Maybe you read the transcript of Nixon's tape where he said he'd have no part of this literature and art shit. That was because he was out of step. He lost touch with the spirit of Capitalism. Misunderstood it completely."

"Here, here, don't start one of your lectures on me. You were always spouting some theory to us at the table—Marx, or Darwin, or Schopenhauer, or Oscar Wilde. If it wasn't one damn thing it was another. You had the biggest collection of Modern Library books on the block. And I'd bet you fifty to one you're ass-deep in a crank theory this minute. You couldn't live without it. Let's get going. We have to pick up the two Cubans and that Boston Irishman who's coming along. *I* never went for this art stuff, did I?"

"You tried becoming a photographer," I said.

"Me? When was that?"

"When they had funerals in the Russian Orthodox church —you remember, the stucco one with the onion dome on Leavitt, corner of Haddon?—they opened the coffins on the front steps and took pictures of the family with the corpse. You tried to make a deal with the priest and be appointed official photographer."

"Did I? Good for me!" It pleased Ulick to hear this. But somehow he smiled quietly, with mild fixity, musing at himself. He felt his hanging cheeks and said that he had shaved too close today, his skin was tender. It must have been a rising soreness from the breast that made him touchy about the face. This visit of mine, with its intimations of final parting, bothered him. He acknowledged that I had done right to come but he loathed me for it, too. I could see it his way. Why did I come flapping around him with my love, like a death-pest? There was no way for me to win, because if I hadn't come here he'd have held it against me. He needed to be wronged. He luxuriated in anger, and he kept accounts.

For fifty years, ritualistically, he had been repeating the same jokes, laughing at them because they were so infantile and stupid. "You know who's in the hospital? Sick people"; and, "I took first prize in history once, but they seen me taking it and made me put it back." And in the days when I still argued with him I would say, "You're a real populist and know-nothing, you've given your Russian Jewish brains away out of patriotism. You're a self-made ignoramus and a true American." But I had long ago stopped saying such things. I knew that he shut himself up in his office with a box of white raisins and read Arnold Toynbee and R. H. Tawney, or Cecil Roth and Salo Baron on Jewish history. When any of this reading cropped up in conversation he made sure to mispronounce the key words.

He drove his Cadillac under the glittering sun. Shadows that might have been cast by all the peoples of the earth flickered over if. He was an American builder and millionaire. The souls of billions fluttered like spooks over the polish of the great black hood. In distant Ethiopia people with dysentery as they squatted over ditches, faint and perishing, opened copies of *Business Week*, abandoned by tourists, and saw his face or faces like his. But it seemed to me that there were few faces like his, with the ferocious profile that brought to mind the Latin word *rapax* or one of Rouault's crazed death-dealing arbitrary kings. We passed his enterprises, the Peony Condominiums, the Trumbull Arms. We reviewed his many building projects. "Peony almost did me in. The architect talked me into putting the swimming pool on the roof. The concrete estimate was short by tons and tons, to say nothing of the fact that we overran the lot by a whole foot. Nobody ever found out, and I got rid of the damn thing. I had to take lots of paper." He meant a large second mortgage. "Now listen, Chuck, I know you need income. That crazy broad won't be satisfied until she's got your liver in her deepfreeze. I'm astonished, really astonished, that you didn't put away some dough. You must be bananas. People must be into you for some pretty good sums. You've invested plenty with this fellow Zitterbloom in New York who promised to shelter you, protect your income from Uncle Sam. He screwed you good. You'll never get a penny out of him. But others must owe you thousands. Make them offers. Take half, but in cash. I'll show you how to launder your money and we'll make it disappear. Then you go to Europe and stay there. What the hell do you want to be in Chicago for? Haven't you had enough of that boring place? For me it wasn't boring, because I went out and saw action. But you?

You get up, look out, it's gray, you pull the curtain, and pick up a book. The town is roaring, but you don't hear it. If it hasn't killed your fucking heart you must be a man of iron, living like that. Listen, I have an idea. We'll buy a house on the Mediterranean together. My kids ought to learn a foreign language, have a little culture. You can tutor them. Listen, Chuck, if you can scrape together fifty thousand bucks I'll guarantee you a twenty-five-percent return, and you can live abroad on that."

So he talked to me, and I kept thinking about his fate. His fate! And I couldn't tell him my thoughts they were not transmissible. Then what good were they? Their oddity and idiosyncrasy was a betrayal. Thoughts should be real. Words should have a definite meaning and a man should believe what he said. This was Hamlet's complaint to Polonius when he said, "Words, words, words." The words are not *my* words, the thoughts not *my* thoughts. It's wonderful to have thoughts. They can be about the starry heavens and the moral law, the majesty of the one, the grandeur of the other. Ulick was not the only one that took lots of paper. We were all taking paper, plenty of it. And I wasn't about to pass any paper off on Ulick at a time like this. My new ideas, yes. They were more to the point. But I wasn't ready to mention them to him. I should have been ready. In the past, thoughts were too real to be kept like a cultural portfolio of stocks and bonds. But now we have mental assets. As many world views as you like. Five different epistemologies in an evening. Take you choice. They're all agreeable, and not one is binding or necessary or has true strength or speaks straight to the soul. It was this paper-taking, this passing of highbrow currency that had finally put my back up. But my back had gone up slowly, reluctantly. So now I wasn't ready to tell Ulick anything of genuine interest. I had nothing to offer my brother, bracing himself for death. He didn't know what to think about it and was furious and frightened. It was my business as the thoughtful brother to tell him something. And actually I had important intimations to communicate as he faced the end. But intimations weren't much use. I hadn't done my homework. He'd say, "What do you mean, Spirit! Immortality? You mean that?" And I wasn't yet prepared to explain. I was just about to go into it seriously myself. Maybe Renata and I would take a train to Taormina and there I could sit in a garden and concentrate on this, giving it my whole mind.

Our serious Old World parents certainly had produced a pair of American clowns—one demonic millionaire clown, and one higher-thought clown. Ulick had been a fat boy I adored, he was a man precious to me, and now the fatal coastline was in view before him and I wanted to say, as he sat looking sick behind the wheel, that this brilliant, this dazing shattering delicious painful thing (I was referring to life) when it concluded, concluded only what we knew. It did not conclude the unknown, and I suspected that something further would ensue. But I couldn't prove a thing to this hardheaded brother of mine. He was terrified by the approaching blank, the flowering pleasant-day-in-May conclusion with the cliff of coal behind it, the nice cool hole in the ground. So all I could really say to him if I spoke would go as follows: "Listen here, do you remember when we moved down to Chicago from Appleton and lived in those dark rooms on Rice Street? And you were an obese boy and I a thin boy? And mama doted on you with black eyes, and papa flew into a fit because you dunked your bread in cocoa? And before he escaped into the wood business he slaved in the bakery, the only work he could find, a gentleman but laboring at night? And came home and hung his white overalls behind the bathroom door so that the can always smelled like a bakeshop and the stiff flour fell off in scales? And he slept handsome and angry, on his side all day, with one hand under his face and the other between his drawn-up knees? While mama boiled the wash on the coal stove, and you and I disappeared to school? Do you remember all that? Well, I'll tell you why I bring it up—there are good esthetic reasons why this should not be wiped from the record eternally. No one would put so much heart into things doomed to be forgotten and wasted. Or so much love. Love is gratitude for being. This love would be hate, Ulick, if the whole thing is nothing but a gyp." But a speech like this was certainly not acceptable to one of the biggest builders of southeast Texas. Such communications were prohibited under the going mental rules of a civilization that proved its right to impose such rules by the many practical miracles it performed, such as bringing me to Texas from New York in four hours, or sawing open his sternum and grafting new veins into his heart. To accept the finality of death was part of his package, however. There was to be no sign of us left. Only a few holes in the ground. Only the dirt of certain mole-runs cast up by extinct creatures that once burrowed here.

Meantime Ulick was saying that he was going to help me. For fifty thousand dollars he would sell me two points in an already completed project. "That ought to throw off between twenty-five and thirty percent. So if you got an income of fifteen thousand, plus what you picked up by your scribbles, you could be comfortable in one of the cheap countries like Yugoslavia or Turkey, and tell the Chicago gang to fuck itself."

"Lend me the fifty grand, then," I said. "I can raise that much in a year's time and repay you."

"I'd have to go to the bank for it myself," he said. But I was a Citrine, the same blood ran in our veins, and he couldn't expect me to accept so obvious a lie. He then said, "Charlie, don't ask me to do such an unbusinesslike thing."

"You mean that if you advanced me the dough, and if you didn't make a little something on me, your self-respect would suffer."

"With your gift for putting things succinctly, what things *I* could write," he said, "seeing that I know a thousand times much as you. Of course I have to take a little advantage. After all, I'm the guy who puts the thing together—the whole ball of wax. But it would be the minimum basic. On the other hand, if you're tired of your way of life, and you sure ought to be, you could settle here in Texas and become filthy rich yourself. This place has big dimensions, Charlie, it's got scale."

But this reference to scale, to large dimensions, didn't fill me with business ambitions, it only reminded me of a stirring lecture by a clairvoyant that I had read on the plane. Now that did impress me deeply and I tried to comprehend it. After the two Cubans and the man from Boston got into the Cadillac with us and began to smoke cigars, so that I became carsick, to think about clairvoyance was as good a thing to do as any other. The car tore out of town, following the coastline. "There's a great fish place along here," said Ulick. "I want to stop and buy Hortense some smoked shrimp and smoked marlin." We pulled in and got some. Starving, Ulick ate pieces of marlin before the fish was removed from the scale. Before it could be wrapped he had already pulled off the tail-end.

"Don't gorge," I said.

He paid no attention to this, and he was quite right. He gorged. Gaspar, his Cuban crony, took the wheel and Ulick sat in the back with his fish. He kept it under the seat. "I want to save this for Hortense, she dotes on it," he said. But at this rate nothing would be left for Hortense. It wasn't for me to conjure away a whole lifetime of such extraordinary greed, and I should have let him be. But I had to put in my brotherly two cents, giving him just the touch of remorse you wanted from your family on the eve of open-heart surgery as you crammed yourself with smoked fish.

At the same time I was concentrating on the vision the clairvoyant had described in such extraordinary detail. Just as soul and spirit left the body in sleep, they could also be withdrawn from it in full consciousness with the purpose of observing the inner life of man. The first result of this conscious withdrawal is that everything is reversed. Instead of seeing the external world as we normally do with senses and intellect, initiates can see the circumscribed self from without. Soul and spirit are poured out upon the world which normally we perceive from within—mountains clouds forests seas. This external world we no longer see, for we are *it*. The outer world is now the inner. Clairvoyant, you are in the space you formerly beheld. From this new circumference you look back to the center, and at the center is your own self. That self, your self, is now the external world. Dearest God, there you see the human form, your own form. You see your own skin and the blood inside, and you see this as you see an external object. But what an object! Your eyes are now two radiant suns, filled with light. Your eyes are identified by this radiance. Your ears are identified by sound. From the skin comes a glow. From the human form emanate light, sound, and sparkling electrical forces. This is the physical being when the Spirit looks at it. And even the life of thought is visible within this radiance. Your thoughts can be seen as dark waves passing through the body of light, says this clairvoyant. And with this glory comes also a knowledge of stars which exist in the space where we formerly felt ourselves to stand inert. We are not inert but in motion together with these stars. There is a star world within us that can be seen when the Spirit takes a new vantage point outside its body. As for the musculature it is a precipitate of Spirit and the signature of the cosmos is in it. In life and in death the signature of the cosmos is within us.

We were now driving tough swampy, reefy places. There were mangroves. Here was the Gulf sparkling alongside. There was also a great deal of clutter, for the peninsula was a dumping ground and an old-car cemetery. The afternoon was hot. The great black Cadillac opened and we got out. The men, excited, striding off in all directions, studying the ground, trying to get the lay of the land and already struggling with future building problems. Gorgeous palaces, stunning towers, and thrilling gardens of crystal dew arose from their flaming minds.

"Solid rock," said the Boston Irishman, scraping the ground with his white calfskin shoe.

He had confided to me that he wasn't an Irishman at all, he was a Pole. His name, Casey, was shortened from Casimirz. Because I was Ulick's brother, he took me for a businessman. With a name like Citrine what else would I be? "This guy is a real creative entrepreneur. Your brother Julius is imaginative—a genius builder," said Casey. As he spoke, his flat freckled face gave me the false smile that swept the country about fifteen years ago. To achieve it, you drew your upper lip away from the teeth, while looking at your interlocutor with charm. Alec Szathmar did it better than anyone. Casey was a large, almost monumental and hollow-looking person who resembled a plainclothes dick from Chicago—same type. His ears were amazingly crinkled, like Chinese cabbage. He spoke with pedantic courtliness, as if he had taken a correspondence course originating in Bombay. I rather liked that. I saw that he wanted me to put in a good word for him with Ulick, and I understood his need. Casey was retired, a partial invalid, and he was seeking ways to protect his fortune from inflationary shrinkage. Also he was looking for action. Action or death. Money can't mark time. Now that I was committed to spiritual investigation, many matters presented themselves to me in a clearer light. I saw, for instance, what volcanic emotions Ulick was dissembling. He stood on a rubble elevation, eating smoked shrimps from the paper bag, and pretended to take a cool view of this peninsula as a development site. "It's promising," he said. "It's got possibilities. But there'd be some terrible headaches here. You'd have to start by blasting. There'll be a hell of a water problem. Sewage, too. And I don't even know how this is zoned."

"Why, what you could do with this is a first-class hotel," said Casey. "Apartment houses on each side, with ocean frontage, beaches, a yacht basin, tennis courts."

"It sounds easy," said Ulick. Oh cunning Ulick, my darling brother! I could see that he was in an ecstasy of craftiness. This was a place that might be worth hundreds of millions, and he came upon it just as the surgeons were honing up for him. A fat cumbered clogged ailing heart threatened to lay him in the grave just as his soul came into its most brilliant opportunity. You could be sure that when you were dreaming your best somebody would start banging at the door—the famous Butcher Boy from Porlock. In this case, the kid's name was Death. I understood Ulick and his passions. Why not? I was a lifetime Ulick subscriber. So I knew what a paradise he saw in this dumping ground—the towers in a sea-haze, the imported grass gemmy with moisture, the pools surrounded by gardenias where broads sunned their beautiful bodies, and all the dark Mexican servitors in embroidered shirts murmuring "*Si, señor*"—there were plenty of wetbacks crossing the border.

I also knew how Ulick's balance sheets would look. They'd read like Chapman's *Homer*, illuminated pages, realms of gold. If zoning ordinances interfered with this opportunity he was prepared to lay out a million bucks in bribes. I saw that in his face. He was the positive, I the negative sinner. He might have been wearing sultry imperial colors. I might have been buttoned into a suit of Dr. Denton's Sleepers. Of course I had a big thing to wake up to, a very big challenge. Now I was only simmering, still, and it would be necessary at last to come to a full boil. I had business on behalf of the entire human race—a responsibility not only to fulfill my own destiny but to carry on for certain failed friends like Von Humboldt Fleisher who had never been able to struggle through into higher wakefulness. My very fingertips rehearsed how they would work the keys of the trumpet, imagination's trumpet, when I got ready to blow it at last. The peals of that brass would be heard beyond the earth, out in space itself. When that Messiah, that savior faculty the imagination was roused, finally we could look again with open eyes upon the whole shining earth.

The reason why the Ulicks of this world (and also the Cantabiles) had such sway over me was that they knew their desires clearly. These desires might be low but they were pursued in full wakefulness. Thoreau saw a woodchuck at Walden, its eyes more fully awake than the eyes of any farmer. Of course that woodchuck was on his way to wipe out some hard-working farmer's crop. It was all very well for Thoreau to build up woodchucks and fume at farmers. But if society is a massive moral failure farmers have something to sleep about. Or look at the present moment. Ulick was awake to money; I, with a craving to do right swelling in my heart, was aware that the good liberal sleep of American boyhood had lasted half a century. And even now I had come to get something from Ulick—I was revisiting the conditions of childhood under which my heart had been inspired. Traces of the perfume of that sustaining time, that early and sweet dream-time of goodness still clung to him. Just as his face was turning toward (perhaps) his final sun, I still wanted something from him.

Ulick treated his two Cubans as deferentially as the Polish Casey treated him. These were his indispensable negotiators. They had gone to school with the proprietors. At times they hinted that they were all cousins. To me they looked like Caribbean playboys, a recognizable type—strong fatty men with fresh round faces and blue, not especially kindly, eyes. They were golfers, water-skiers, horsemen, polo-players, racing-car drivers, twin-engine pilots. They knew the Riviera, the Alps, Paris, and New York as well as the night clubs and gambling joints of the West Indies. I said to Ulick, "These are sharp guys. Exile hasn't dulled them any."

"I know they're sharp," said Ulick. "I'll have to find a way to put them into the deal. This is no time to be petty—my God, Chuckie, there's plenty here for everybody this time," he whispered.

Before this conversation occurred we had made two stops. As we were returning from the peninsula, Ulick said he wanted to stop at a tropical fruit farm he knew. He had promised

Hortense to bring home persimmons. The fish had been eaten. We sat with him under a tree sucking at the breast-sized, flame-colored fruit. The juice spurted over his sport shirt, and seeing that it now had to go to the cleaner anyway he wiped his fingers on it as well. His eyes had shrunk, and moved back and forth rapidly in his head. He was not, just then, with us. The Cubans took Hortense's golf bag from the trunk of the car and began to amuse themselves by driving balls across the fields. They were superb powerful golfers, despite their heavy bottoms and the folds of flesh that formed under their chins as they addressed the ball. They took turns, and with elastic strength whacked the elastic balls—crack!—into the unknown. It was pleasing to watch this. But when we were ready to leave it turned out that the ignition keys had gotten locked up in the trunk. Tools were borrowed from the persimmon farmer, and in half an hour the Cubans had punched out the lock. Of course they damaged the paint of new Cadillac. But that was nothing. "Nothing, nothing!" said Ulick. He was burned up, too, naturally, but these Gonzalez cousins could not be freely hated now. Ulick said, "What is it—some hardware, a touch of paint?" He rose, heavy, and said, "Let's stop now and get a drink and something to eat."

We went to a Mexican restaurant where he devoured an order of chicken breasts with *molé* sauce—a bitter spicy chocolate gravy. I could not finish mine. He took my plate. He ordered pecan pie à la mode, and then a cup of Mexican chocolate.

When we got home I said I would go to my motel and lie down; I was very tired. We stood together in his garden for a while.

"Do you even begin to get the picture of this peninsula?" he said. "With this land I could do the most brilliant piece of business in my life. These smart-ass Cubans will have to go along. I'll sweep those bastards with me. I'll develop a plan—while I'm convalescing I'll get a survey done, and a map, and when I make my pitch to those lazy Spanish jet-set bastards, I'll be prepared with architect's models and all my financing ready. I mean *if*, you know. Do you want to try some of these loquats?" He reached gloomily into one of his trees and picked handfuls of fruit.

"I'm bilious now," I said, "from all I've eaten."

He stood plucking and eating, spitting out stones and, skins, his gaze fixed beyond me. He wiped at his Acheson mustache from time to time. Arrogant, haggard, he was filled with incommunicable thoughts. These were written dense and small on every inch of his inner surface. "I won't see you in Houston before the operation, Charlie," he said. "Hortense is against it. She says you'll make me too emotional, and she's a woman who knows what she's talking about. Now this is what I want to say to you, Charlie. If I die, you marry Hortense. She's a better woman than you'll ever find by yourself. She's straight as they come. I trust her one hundred percent, and you know what that means. She acts a little rough but she's made me a wonderful life. You'll never have another financial problem, I can tell you that."

"Have you discussed this with Hortense?"

"No, I've written it in a letter. She probably guesses that I want her to marry a Citrine, if I die on the table." He stared hard at me and said, "She'll do what I tell her. So will you."

Late noon stood like a wall of gold. And a mass of love was between us, and neither Ulick nor I knew what to do with it. "Well, all right, good-by." He turned his back on me. I got into the rented car and took off.

HORTENSE, on the telephone, said, "Well, he made it. They took veins from his leg and attached them to his heart. He's going to be stronger than ever now."

"Thank God for that. He's out of danger?"

"Oh, sure, and you can see him tomorrow."

During the operation Hortense hadn't wanted my company. I attributed this to wife/brother rivalry, but later I changed my mind. I recognized a kind of boundlessness or hysteria in my affection which, in her place, I would have avoided, too. But on the phone there was a tone in her voice I had never heard before. Hortense raised exotic flowers and hollered at dogs and men—that was her style. This time, however, I felt that I shared what as a rule she reserved for the flowers and my attitude toward her changed entirely. Humboldt used to tell me, and he was a harsh judge of character himself, that far from being mild I was actually too tough. My reform (if it was one) would have pleased him. In this critical age, following science (fantasy-science is really what it is) people think they are being "illusionless" about one another. The law of parsimony makes detraction more realistic. Therefore I had had my reservations about Hortense. Now I thought she was a good broad. I had been lying on the king-sized motel bed reading some of Humboldt's papers and books by Rudolf Steiner and his disciples, and I was in a state.

I don't know what I expected to see when I entered Ulick's room—bloodstains, perhaps, or bone-dust from the power saw; they had pried open the man's rib cage and taken out his heart; they had shut it off like a small motor and laid it aside and started it up again when they were ready. I couldn't get over this. But I came into a room filled with flowers and sunlight. Over Ulick's head was a small brass plate engraved with the names of Papa and Mama. His color was green and yellow, the bone of his nose stuck out, his white mustache grew harshly under it. His look, however, was happy. And his fierceness was still there, I was glad to see. He was weak, of course, but he was all business again. If I had told him that I thought he looked a shade other-worldly he would have listened with contempt. Here was the polished window, here were the grand roses and dahlias, and here was Mrs. Julius Citrine in a knitted trouser-suit, her legs plump, low to the ground, an attractive short strong woman. Life went on. What life? This life. And what was this life? But now was not a time to be metaphysical. I was very eager, very happy. I kept things under my peculiar hat, however.

"Well, kid," he said, his voice still thin. "You're glad, aren't you?"

"That's right, Ulick."

"A heart can be fixed like a shoe. Resoled. Even new uppers. Like Novinson on Augusta Street . . ."

I suppose that I was Ulick's nostalgia-man. What he couldn't himself remember, he loved to hear from me. Tribal chieftains in Africa had had official remembrancers about them; I was Ulick's remembrancer. "Novinson in his window had trench souvenirs from 1917," I said. "He had brass shell casings and a helmet with holes in it. Over his bench was a colored cartoon made by his son Izzie of a customer squirted in the face and leaping into the air yelling, '*Hilp!*' The message was, *Don't Get Soaked for Shoe Repairs.*"

Ulick said to Hortense, "All you have to do is turn him on."

She smiled from her upholstered chair, her legs crossed. The color of her knitted suit was old rose, or young brick. She was as white-faced as a powdered Kabuki dancer, for despite her light eyes her face was Japanese—the cheekbones and the chub lips, painted crimson, did that.

"Well, Ulick, I'll be going, now that you're out of the woods."

"Listen, Chuck, there's something I've always wanted that you can buy for me in Europe. A beautiful seascape. I've always loved paintings of the sea. Nothing but the sea. I don't want to see a rock, or a boat, or any human beings. Only mid-ocean on a terrific day. Water water everywhere: Get me that, Chuckie, and I'll pay five grand, eight grand. Phone me if you come across the right thing and I'll wire the money."

It was implied that I was entitled to a commission— unofficial, of course. It would be unnatural for me not to chisel a little. This was the form his generosity sometimes took. I was touched.

"I'll go to the galleries," I said.

"Good. Now what about the fifty thousand—have you thought about my offer?"

"Oh, I'd certainly like to take you up on that. I need the income badly. I've already cabled a friend of mine—Thaxter. He's on his way to Europe on the *France.* I told him that I was willing to go to Madrid to try my hand at a project he dreamed up. A cultural Baedeker . . . So I'm going to Madrid now."

"Fine. You need projects. Get back to work. I know you. When you stop work you're in trouble. That broad in Chicago has brought your work to a standstill, with her lawyers. She knows what the stoppage does to you—Hortense, we have to look after Charlie a little, now."

"I agree we should," said Hortense. From moment to moment I more and more admired and loved Hortense. What a wonderful and sensitive woman she was, really, and what emotional versatility the Kabuki mask concealed. Her gruffness had put me off. But behind the gruffness, what goodness, what a rose garden. "Why not make more of an effort to settle with Denise?" she said.

"She doesn't want to settle," said Ulick. "She wants his gizzard in a glass on her mantelpiece. When he offers her more dough she raises the ante again. It's no use. The guy is pissing against the wind in Chicago. He needs broads, but he picks women who cripple him. So get back to business, Chuck, and start turning the stuff out. If you don't keep your name before the public people will assume you're gone and they missed your obituary. How much can you get out of this culture-guide deal? Fifty? Hold out for a hundred. Don't forget the taxes. Did you get caught in the stock market too? Of course you did. You're an America expert. You have to experience what the whole country experiences. You know what I'd do? I'd buy old railroad bonds. Some of them are selling for forty cents on the dollar. Only railroads can move the coal, and the energy crisis is bringing coal back strongly. We ought to acquire some coal-lands, too. Under Indiana and Illinois, the whole Midwest is a solid mass of coal. It can be crushed, mixed with water, and pumped through pipelines, but that's not economical. Even water is getting to be a scarce commodity," said Ulick, off on one of his capitalistic fugues. On this subject of coal he was a romantic poet, a Novalis speaking of earth-mysteries. "You get together some dough. Send it and I'll invest for you."

"Thank you, Ulick," I said.

"Right. Bug off. Stay in Europe, what the hell do you want to come back for? Get me a seascape."

He and Hortense went back to their development plans for the Cubans' peninsula. He fiercely applied his genius to maps and blueprints while Hortense dialed bankers for him on the telephone. I kissed my brother and his wife and drove my Avis to the airport.

ALTHOUGH I was full of joy, I knew that things were not going well in Milan. Renata troubled my mind. I didn't know what she was up to. From the motel last night I had talked with her on the telephone. I asked her what was happening. She said, "I'm not going into this on a transatlantic call, Charlie, it's too expensive." But then she wept for two solid minutes. Even Renata's intercontinental sobs were fresher than other women's close at hand. After this, still tearful, she laughed at herself and said, "Well, that was two-bits a tear, at least. Yes, I'll meet you in Madrid, you bet I will."

"*Is* Signor Biferno your father?" I said.

"You sound as if the suspense is killing you. Imagine what it's doing to me. Yes, I think Biferno is my dad. I *feel* he is."

"What does he feel? He must be a glorious-looking man. No punk could beget a woman like you, Renata."

"He's old and caved in. He looks like somebody they forgot to take off from Alcatraz. And he hasn't talked to me. He won't do it."

"Why?"

"Before I left, Mother didn't tell me that she was all set to sue him. Her papers were served on him the day before I arrived. It's a paternity suit. Child support. Damages."

"Child support? You're almost thirty. And the Señora didn't tell you that she was plotting this?" I said.

"When you sound incredulous, when you take that I-can't-believe-it tone I know you're really in a furious rage. You're sore about the money this trip is costing."

"Renata, why did the Señora have to sock Biferno with summonses just as you're about to solve the riddle of your birth?—to which she should have the answer, by the way. You go on this errand for the sake of your heart, or your identity—you've spent weeks fretting about your identity crisis—and then your own mother pulls this. You can't blame me for being baffled. It's wild. What a plan for conquest the old girl has hatched. All this—fire-bombing, victory, unconditional surrender."

"You can't bear to hear of women suing men. You don't know what I owe my mother. Bringing up a girl like me was a pretty tough project. As for what she pulled on me, remember what people pull on you. This Cantabile, may he rot in hell, or

Szathmar or Thaxter. Watch out for Thaxter. Take the month at the Ritz but don't sign any contract or anything. Thaxter will take his money and stick you with all the work."

"No, Renata, he's peculiar, but he is basically trustworthy."

"Good-by, darling," she said. "I've missed you like mad. Remember what you once said to me about the British lion standing up with his paw on the globe? You said that when you set your paw on my globe it was better than an empire. The sun never sets on Renata! I'll be waiting in Madrid."

"You seem to be washed up in Milan," I said.

She answered by telling me, like Ulick, that I must begin to work again. "Only for God's sake don't write that pedantic stuff you're unloading on me lately," she said.

But now the whole Atlantic must have surged between us; or perhaps the communications satellite was peppered with glittering particles in the upper air. Anyway, the conversation crumpled and ended.

But when the plane took off I felt unusually free and light—trundled out on the bowed eagle legs of the 747, lifted into flight on the great wings, the machine passing from level to level into brighter and brighter atmospheres while I gripped my briefcase between my feet like a rider and my head lay on the bosom of the seat. On balance I believed that the Señora's wicked and goofy lawsuit improved my position. She discredited herself. My kindliness, my patience, my sanity, my superiority would gain on Renata. All I had to do was to keep my mouth shut and to sit tight. Thoughts about her came thick and fast—all kinds of things connecting what-beautiful-girls-contributed-to-the-unfolding-destiny-of-capitalist-Democracy to, far beyond this, deeper questions. Let me see if I can clarify any of it. Renata was very nearly aware, as many people now are, of "leading a life in history." Now Renata was, as a biologically noble beauty, in a false category—Goya's *Maja* smoking a cigar, or Wallace Stevens' Fretful Concubine who whispered "Pfui!" That is she wished to defy and outsmart the category to which she was assigned by common opinion. But with this she also collaborated. And if there is one historical assignment for us it is to break with false categories. Vacate the personae. I once suggested to her, "A woman like you can be called a dumb broad only if Being and Knowledge are entirely separate. But if Being is also a form of Knowledge, one's own Being is one's own accomplishment in some degree. . . ."

"Then I'm not a dumb broad after all. I can't be, if I'm so beautiful. That's super! You've always been kind to me, Charlie."

"Because I really love you, kid."

Then she wept a little because, sexually, she was not all that she was cracked up to be. She had her hang-ups. Sometimes she accused herself wildly, crying, "The truth! I'm a phony! I like it better under the table." I told her not to exaggerate. I explained to her that the Ego had emancipated itself from the Sun and it must undergo the pain of this emancipation (Steiner). The modern sexual ideology could never counteract this. Programs of uninhibited natural joy could never free us from the universal tyranny of selfhood. Flesh and blood never could live up to such billing. And so on.

Anyway, we were lofted to an altitude of six miles in a great 747, an illuminated cavern, a theater, a cafeteria, the Atlantic in pale daylight raging below. According to the pilot, ships were taking hard punishment in the storm. But from this altitude the corrugations of the seas looked no higher to the eye than the ridges of our palate feel to the tongue. The stewardess served whisky and Hawaiian macadamia nuts. We plunged across the longitudinal lines of the planet, this deep place that I was learning to think of as the great school of souls, the material seat of the spirit. More than ever I believed that the soul with its occasional glimmers of the Good couldn't expect to get anywhere in a single lifetime. Plato's theory of immortality was not, as some scholars tried to make it, a metaphor. He literally meant it. A single span could only make virtue desperate. Only a fool would try to reconcile the Good with one-shot mortality. Or as Renata, that dear girl, might put it, "Better none than only one."

In a word, I allowed myself to think what I pleased and let my mind go in every direction. But I felt that the plane and I were headed the right way. Madrid was a smart choice. In Spain I could begin to set myself straight. Renata and I would enjoy a quiet month. I put it to myself—thinking of the carpenter's level—that maybe our respective bubbles could be coaxed back to the center. Then the things that really satisfied, naturally satisfied, all hearts and minds might be attempted. If people felt like fakers when they spoke of the True and the Good this was their bubble was astray, because they believed they were following the rules of scientific thought, which they didn't understand one single bit. But I had no business to be toying with fire either, or playing footsie with the only revolutionary ideas left. Actuarially speaking, I had only a decade left to make up in a life-span largely misspent. There was no time to waste even on remorse and penitence. I felt also that Humboldt, out there in death, stood in need of my help. The dead and the living still formed one community. This planet was still the base of operations. There was Humboldt's bungled life, and my bungled life, and it was up to me to do something, to give a last favorable turn to the wheel, to transmit moral understanding from the earth where you can get it to the next existence where you needed it. Of course I had my other dead. It wasn't Humboldt alone. I also had a substantial suspicion of lunacy. But why should my receptivity fall under such suspicion? On the contrary, etcetera. I concluded, We'll see what we shall see. We flew through unshadowed heights, and in the pure upper light I saw that the beautiful brown booze in my glass contained many crystalline corpuscles and thermal lines of heat-generating cold fluid. This was how I entertained myself and passed the time. We were held up in Lisbon for quite a while and reached Madrid hours off schedule.

The 747, with its whale's anterior hump, opened, and passengers poured out, eager Charlie Citrine among them. Tourists in this year, I had read in the airline magazine, outnumbered the Spanish population by about ten million. Still, what American could believe that his arrival in the Old World was not a special event? Behavior under these skies meant more than in Chicago. It had to. There was significant space here. I couldn't help feeling this. And Renata, also surrounded by significant space, was waiting at the Ritz. Meantime, my charter-flight countrymen, a party of old folks from Wichita Falls shuffled fatigued down the long corridors and resembled ambulatory patients in a hospital. I passed them like a streak. I was first at the passport window, first at the baggage conveyor. And then—my bag was the last bag of all. The Wichita Falls party was gone and I was beginning to think my bag with its elegant wardrobe, its Hermès neckties, its old chaser's monkey-jackets, and so forth was lost when I saw it wobbling, solitary, on the long, long trail of rollers. It came toward me like an uncorseted woman sauntering over cobblestones.

Then in the cab to the hotel I was pleased with myself again and thought I had done well to arrive late at night when the roads were empty. There was no delay; the taxi drove furiously fast, I could go to Renata's room at once and get out of my clothes and into bed with her. Not from lust but from eagerness. I was full of a boundless need to give and take comfort. I can't tell you how much I agreed with Meister Eckhardt about the eternal youth of the soul. From first to last, he says, it remains the same, it has only one age. The rest of us, however, is not so stable. So overlooking this discrepancy, denying decay, and always starting life over and over doesn't make much sense. Here, with Renata, I wanted to have another go at it, swearing up and down that I would be more tender and she would be more faithful and humane. It didn't make sense, of course. But it mustn't be forgotten that I had been a complete idiot until I was forty and a partial idiot after that. I would always be something of an idiot. Still, I felt that there was hope and raced in the cab toward Renata. I was entering the final zones of mortality, expecting that here in Spain of all places, here in a bedroom, all the right human things would—at last!—happen.

Dignified flunkies in the circular reception hall of the Ritz took my bag and briefcase and I came through the revolving door looking for Renata. Certainly she would not be waiting for me in one of those stately chairs. A queenly woman couldn't sit in the lobby with the night staff at 3 a.m. No, she must be lying wake, beautiful, humid, breathing quietly, and waiting for her extraordinary, her one-and-only Citrine. There were other suitable men, handsomer, younger, energetic, but of me Charlie there was only one, and Renata I believed was aware of this.

For reasons of sell-respect she had objected on the telephone to sharing a suite with me. "It doesn't matter in New York but in Madrid, with different names on our passports, it's just too whorey. I know it's going to cost double but that's the way it's got to be."

I asked the man at the switchboard to ring Mrs. Koffritz.

"We have no Mrs. Koffritz," was his answer.

"A Mrs. Citrine, then?" I said.

These was no Mrs. Citrine either. That was a wicked disappointment. I walked across the circular carpet under the dome to the concierge. He handed me a wire from Milan. SLIGHT DELAY. BIFERNO DEVELOPING. PHONING TOMORROW. I ADORE YOU.

I was then shown to my room, but I was in no condition to admire its effects: richly Spanish, with carved chests and thick drapes, with Turkish carpets and *fauteuils*, a marble bathroom and old-fashioned electrical fixtures in the grand old *Wagon-Lit* style. The bed stood in a curtained alcove and was covered in watered silk. My heart was behaving badly as I crept in naked and laid my head on the bolster. There was no word from Thaxter, either, and he should have reached Paris by now. I had to communicate with him. Thaxter would have to inform Stewart in New York that I was accepting his invitation to stay in Madrid for a month as his guest. This was a fairly important matter. I was down to four thousand dollars and couldn't afford two suites at the Ritz. The dollar was taking a beating, the peseta was unrealistically high, and I didn't believe that Biferno was developing into anything.

My heart was dumbly aching. I refused to give it the words it would have uttered. I condemned the state I was in. It was idle, idle, idle. Many thousands of miles from my last bed in Texas I lay stiff and infinitely sad, my body temperature at least three degrees below normal. I had been brought up to detest self-pity. It was part of my American training to be energetic, and positive, and a thriving energy system, and an achiever, and having achieved two Pulitzer prizes and the Zig-Zag medal and a good deal of money (of which I was robbed by a Court of Equity), I had set myself a final and ever higher achievement, namely, an indispensable metaphysical revision, a more correct way of thinking about the question of death! And now I remembered a quotation from Coleridge, cried by Von Humboldt Fleisher in the papers he had left me, about quaint metaphysical opinions. How did it go? Quaint metaphysical opinions, in an hour of anguish, were playthings by the bedside of a child deadly sick. I got up then to rummage in the briefcase for the exact quotation. But then I stopped. I recognized that to be afraid that Renata was ditching me was far different from being deadly sick. Besides, damn her, why should she give me an hour of anguish and make me stoop and rummage naked, pulling out a dead man's papers by the light of the *Wagon-Lit* lamp. I decided that I was only overtired and suffering from jet lag.

I turned from Humboldt and Coleridge to the theories of George Swiebel. I did what George would have done. I ran myself a hot bath and stood on my head while the tub was filling. I went on to do a wrestler's bridge, resting all my weight on my heels and on the back of my head. After this I performed some the exercises recommended by the famous Dr. Jacobsen, the relaxation and sleep expert. I had studied his manual. You were supposed to cast out tension toe by toe and finger by finger. This was not a good idea, for it brought back to me what Renata did with toes and fingers in moments of erotic ingenuity. (I never knew about the toes until Renata taught me.) After all this I simply went back to bed and prayed my upset soul to go out for a while, please, and let the poor body have some rest. I picked up her telegram, fixing my eyes on I ADORE YOU. Studying this hard, I decided to believe that she was telling the truth. As soon as I performed this act of faith I slept. For many hours I was out cold in the curtained alcove.

Then my telephone rang. In the shuttered curtained blackness I felt for the switch. It was not to be found. I picked up the phone and asked the operator, "What time is it?"

It was twenty minutes after eleven. "A lady is on her way up to your room," the switchboard told me.

A lady! Renata was here. I dragged the drapes aside from the windows and ran to brush my teeth and wash my face. I pulled on a bathrobe, gave a swipe at my hair to cover the bald spot, and was drying myself with one of the heavy luxurious towels when the knocker ticked many times, like a telegraph key, only more delicately, suggestively. I shouted, "Darling!" I swept the door open and found Renata's old mother before me. She was wearing her dark travel costume, with many of her own arrangements, including the hat and the veil. "Señora!" I said.

She entered in her medieval garments. Just over the threshold she reached a gloved hand behind her and brought in Renata's little boy, Roger. "Roger!" I said. "Why is Roger in Madrid? What you doing here, Señora?"

"Poor baby. He was sleeping on the plane. I had them carry him off."

"But Christmas with the grandparents in Milwaukee—what about that?"

"His grandfather had a stroke. May die. As for his father, we can't locate the man. I couldn't keep Roger with me, my apartment is small."

"What about Renata's apartment?"

No, the Señora, with her *affaires de cœur*, couldn't take care of a small child. I had met some other gentlemen friends. It was wise not to expose the child to them. As a rule I avoided thinking about her romances.

"Does Renata know?"

"Of course she knows we're coming. We discussed it on the telephone. Please order breakfast for us, Charles. Will you eat some nice Frosted Flakes, Roger darling? For me, hot chocolate and also some *croissants* and a glass of brandy."

The child sat bowed over the arm of the tall Spanish chair.

"Come on, kid," I said, "lie on my bed." I pulled off his small shoes and led him into the alcove. The Señora watched as I covered him and drew the curtains. "So Renata told you to bring him here."

"Of course. You may be here for months. It was the only thing to do."

"When is Renata arriving?"

"Tomorrow is Christmas," said the Señora.

"Terrific. What does your statement mean? Will she be here for Christmas or is she having Christmas with her father in Milan? Is she getting anywhere? How can she, if you're suing Mr. Biferno?"

"We've been in the air for ten hours, Charles. I'm not strong enough to answer questions. Please order breakfast. I wish you would shave also. I really can't bear a man's unshaven face across the table."

This made me consider the Señora's own face. She had wonderful dignity. She sat in her wimple like Edith Sitwell. Her power with her daughter, whom I so badly needed, was very great. There was a serpentine dryness about her eyes. Yes, the Señora was bananas. However, her composure, with its large content of furious irrationality, was unassailable.

"I'll shave while you're waiting for your cocoa, Señora. Why, I wonder, did you choose such a time to sue Signor Biferno?"

"Isn't that my own business?"

"Isn't it Renata's business also?"

"You speak like Renata's husband," she said. "Renata went to Milan to give that man a chance to acknowledge his daughter. But there is a mother in the case too. Who brought the girl up and made such an extraordinary woman of her? Who taught her class and all the important lessons of a woman? The whole injustice should be dealt with. The man has three plain ugly daughters. If he wants this marvelous child he had by me, let him settle his bill. Don't try to teach a Latin woman about such things, Charles."

I sat in my not entirely clean beige silk robe. The sash was too long and the tassels had dragged on the floor for many years. The waiter came, the tray was uncovered with a flourish, and we breakfasted. As the Señora snuffed up her cognac I observed the grain of her skin, the touch of whisker on her lip, the arched nose with its operatic nostrils and the peculiar chicken luster of her eyeballs. "I got the TWA tickets from your travel agent, that Portuguese lady who wears a paisley turban, Mrs. Da Cintra. Renata told me to charge them. I didn't have a cent." The Señora was like Thaxter in this regard—people who could tell you with pride, even with delight, how broke they were. "And I've taken a room here for Roger and me. My institute is closed this week. I will have a holiday."

At the mention of institute, I thought of a loony bin, but no, she was speaking of the secretarial school where she taught commercial Spanish. I had always suspected that she was actually a Magyar. Be that as it might, the students appreciated her. No school without spectacular eccentrics and crazy hearts is worth attending. But she would have to retire soon, and who would push the Señora's wheelchair? Was it possible that she now saw me in that capacity? But perhaps the old woman, like

Humboldt, dreamed that she could make her fortune in a lawsuit. And why not? Perhaps there was a judge in Milan like my Urbanovich.

"So we will have Christmas together," said the Señora.

"The kid is very pale. Is he sick?"

"It's only fatigue," said the Señora.

Roger, however, came down with the flu. The hotel sent an excellent Spanish doctor, a graduate of Northwestern who reminisced with me about Chicago and soaked me. I paid him an American fee. I gave the Señora money for Christmas presents and she bought all kinds of objects. On Christmas Day, thinking of my own girls, I felt quite low. I was glad to have Roger there and kept him company, reading him fairy tales and cutting and pasting long chains from the Spanish newspapers. There was a humidifier in the room which heightened the odors of paste and paper. Renata did not telephone.

I recalled that I had spent the Christmas of 1924 in the TB sanatorium. The nurses gave me a thick-striped peppermint candy cane and a red openwork Christmas stocking filled with chocolate coins wrapped in gilt, but it was depressing joy and I longed for Papa and Mama and for my wicked stout brother, Julius, even. Now I had survived this quaking and heartsickness and was an elderly fugitive, the prey of Equity, sitting in Madrid, cutting and pasting with sighs. The kid was pale with fever, his breath flavored with the chocolate and paste, and he was absorbed in a paper chain that went twice about the room and had to be strung over the chandelier. I tried to be nice and calm but now and then my feelings gave a wash (oh those lousy feelings) like the water in a ferry slip when the broad-beamed boat pushes in and the backing engines churn up the litter and drowned orange rinds. This happened when my controls failed and I imagined what Renata might be doing in Milan, the room she was in, the man who was with her, the positions they took , the other fellow's toes. I was determined that no, I wouldn't tolerate being wrung abandoned sea-sick ship-wrecked castaway. I tried quoting Shakespeare to myself —words to the effect that Caesar and Danger were two lions whelped on the same day, and Caesar the elder and more terrible. But that was aiming too high and it didn't work. In addition the twentieth century is not easily impressed by pains of this nature. It has seen everything. After the holocausts, you can't blame it for lacking interest in private difficulties of this sort. I myself recited a brief list of the real questions before the world—the oil embargo, the collapse of Britain, famines in India and Ethiopia, the future of democracy, the fate of humankind. This did no more good than Julius Caesar. I remained personally downhearted.

It wasn't until I was sitting in a French brocade armchair of the Ritz's private eighteenth-century barber's cubicle—I was here not because I needed a haircut but, as so often, only because I longed for a human touch—that I began to have clearer ideas about Renata and the Señora. How was it, for instance, that as soon as grandfather Koffritz had suffered his stroke and became paralyzed on one side Roger was ready to go? How did that old broad get him a passport so quickly? The answer was that the passport, when I went up and examined it on the quiet, proved to have been issued back in October. The ladies were very thorough planners. Only I failed to think ahead. So now it occurred to me take the initiative.

It would be a clever move to marry Renata before she could learn that I was broke. This should not be done merely to hit back. No, in spite of her shenanigans I was mad about her. Loving her, I was willing to overlook certain trifles. She had provoked me by locking me out one night and by the conspicuous display of her birth-control device at the top of her open bag in Heathrow last April when we were parting for three days. But was that, after all, very significant? Did it mean more than that one never knew when one was going to meet an interesting man? The serious question was whether I, with all my thoughts, or because of them, would ever be able to understand what sort of girl Renata was. I wasn't like Humboldt, given to jealous seizures. I recalled how he had looked in Connecticut, when he quoted me King Leontes in my yard by the sea. "I have tremor cordis on me: my heart dances; but not for joy, not joy." That heart-dancing was classic jealousy. I didn't suffer from classic jealousy. Renata did gross things, to be sure. But perhaps these were war measures. She was campaigning to get me and would be different when we were settled down as husband and wife. No doubt she was a dangerous person but I would never be greatly interested in any woman incapable of harm, in any woman who didn't threaten me with loss. Mine was the sort of heart that had to overcome melancholy and free itself from many depressing weights. The Spanish setting was right for this. Renata was acting like Carmen, and Flonzaley, for it probably was Flonzaley, was being Escamillo the Toreador, while I, at two and a half times the age for the role, was cast as Don José.

Quickly I sketched the immediate future. Civil marriages probably didn't exist in this Catholic country. The knot could be tied at the American Embassy by the military attaché, perhaps, or even a notary public for all I knew. I would go to the antique shops (I loved the Madrid antique shops) to look for two wedding bands and I could throw a champagne supper at the Ritz, no questions asked about Milan. After we had sent the Señora back to Chicago, the three of us might move to Segovia, a town I knew. After Demmie's death I traveled widely, so I had been to Segovia before. I was beguiled by the Roman aqueduct, I recalled that I had really gone for those tall knobby stone arches—stone whose nature was to fall or sink were sitting there lightly in the air. That was an achievement that had gone home—an example to me. For purposes of meditation Segovia couldn't be beat. We could live there *en famille* in one of the old back streets, and while I tried to see if I could really move from mental consciousness to the purer consciousness of spirit, it might amuse Renata to comb the town for antiques she could sell to decorators in Chicago. Perhaps she would even make a buck. Roger could attend nursery school and eventually my little girls might join us, because when Denise won her case and collected her money she'd want to get rid of them immediately. I had just enough cash left to settle in Segovia and give Renata a commercial start. Perhaps I would even write the essay on contemporary Spanish culture suggested by Thaxter, if that could be done without too much faking. And how would Renata take my deception? She would take it as good comedy, which she valued more highly than anything in the world. And when I told her after the marriage that we were down to our last few thousand dollars she would laugh brilliantly, larger than life, and say, "Well, *there's* a twist." I evoked Renata laughing brilliantly because I was in reality undergoing a major attack of my lifelong trouble—the longing, the swelling heart, the tearing eagerness of the deserted, the painful keenness or infinitizing of an unidentified need. This condition was apparently stretching from earliest childhood to the border of senescence. I thought, Hell, let's settle this once and for all. Then, not wanting the nosy Ritz staff to talk, I went to central post office of Madrid, with its sonorous halls and batty-looking steeples (Spanish bureaucratic Gothic) and sent a cable to Milan. MARVELOUS IDEA, RENATA DARLING. MARRY ME TOMORROW. YOUR TRULY LOVING FAITHFUL CHARLIE.

After this I lay awake all night because I had used the word faithful. This might queer the whole deal, with its implied accusation and the hint or shadow of forgiveness. But I had really meant no harm. I was betwixt and between. I mean, if I were a true hypocrite I wouldn't forever be putting my foot in my mouth. On the other hand, if I were a real innocent, pure in heart, I wouldn't have to fret the night out over Renata's conduct in Milan or her misinterpretation of my wire. But I lost a night's sleep for nothing. The wording of the message didn't matter. She didn't reply at all.

So that night, in the romantic dining room of the Ritz where every bite cost a fortune, I said to the Señora, "You'll never guess who's been on my mind today." Without waiting for an answer I then uttered the name "Flonzaley!" as a surprise assault on her defenses. But the Señora was made of terribly hard material. She seemed hardly to notice. I repeated the name. "Flonzaley! Flonzaley!" Flonzaley!"

"What is this loudness, what is the matter, Charles?"

"Maybe you'd better tell me what's the matter. Where is Mr. Flonzaley?"

"Why should his whereabouts be my problem? Would you mind asking the *camarero* to pour the wine?" It was not only because she was the lady and I the gentleman that the Señora wished me to speak to waiters. She was fluent in Spanish all right, but her accent was pure Hungarian. Of this there was no doubt now. I learned a thing or two from the Señora. For instance, did I think that people concluding their lives would all be in a fever to come to terms with their souls? I went through agonies of preparation before I blurted out Flonzaley's name and then she asked for more wine. And yet it must have been she that masterminded the plan to bring Roger to Madrid. It was she who made certain that I was pinned down here and prevented me from rushing to Milan to burst in on Renata. For Flonzaley was there with her, all right. He was mad for her and I didn't blame him. A man who met more people on the mortuary slab than he met socially could not be blamed for losing his head that way. A body like Renata's was not often seen in the living flesh. As for Renata, she complained of the morbid element in his adoration, but could I be altogether sure that it was not one of his attractions? I was certain of nothing. I sat trying to make myself drunk on a bottle of acid wine, but I made no headway against my bitter sobriety. No I didn't understand.

The activities of higher consciousness didn't inevitably improve the understanding. The hope of such understanding was raised by my manual—*Knowledge of the Higher Worlds and Its Attainment*. This gave specific instruments. One suggested exercise was to try to enter into the intense desire of another person on a given occasion. To do this one had to remove all personal opinions, all interfering judgments; one should be neither for nor against this desire. In this way one might come gradually to feel what another soul was feeling. I had made this experiment with my own child Mary. For her last birthday she desired a bicycle, the ten-speed type. I wasn't convinced that she was old enough to have one. When we went to the shop it was by no means certain that I would buy it. Now what was her desire, and what did she experience? I wanted to know this, and tried to desire in the way that she desired. This was my kid, whom I loved, and it should have been elementary to find out what a soul in its fresh state craved with such intensity. But I couldn't do this. I tried until I broke into a sweat, humiliated, disgraced by my failure. If I couldn't know this kid's desire could I know any human being? I tried it on a large number of people. And then, defeated, I asked where was I anyway? And what did I really know of anyone? The only desires I knew were my own and those of nonexistent people like Macbeth or Prospero. These I knew because the insight and language of genius made them clear. I bought Mary the bike and then shouted at her, "For Christ's sake, don't ride over the curbs, you'll bust hell out of the wheel." But this was an explosion of despair over my failure to know the kid's heart. And yet I was prepared to know. I was all set up to know in the richest colors, with the deepest feelings, and in the purest light. I was a brute, packed with exquisite capacities which I was unable to use. There's no need to go into this yet once again and tickle each mandolin note ten times as that dear friend of mine accused me of doing. The job, once and for all, was to burst from the fatal self-sufficiency of consciousness and put my remaining strength over into the Imaginative Soul. As Humboldt too should have done.

I don't know who the other gentlemen in the Ritz may have been dining with, the human scene was too pregnant and dense in complications for me at this moment, and all I can say was that I was glad the aims of the pimping old bitch across the table were merely conventional aims. If she had gone after my soul, what was left of it, I would have been sunk. But all she wanted was to market her daughter at her finest hour. And was I through? And was it over? For a few years I had had it good with Renata—the champagne cocktails, the table set with orchids, and this warm beauty serving dinner in feathers and G string while I ate and drank and laughed till I coughed at her erotic teasing, the burlesque of the amorous greatness of heroes and kings. Good-by, good-by to those wonderful sensations. Mine at least had been the real thing. And if hers were not, she had at least been a true and understanding pal. In her percale bed. In her heaven of piled pillows. All that was probably over.

And what could you be at the Ritz but a well-conducted diner? You were attended by servitors and chefs and *maîtres* and grooms, waiters, and the little *botónes* who was dressed like an American bellhop and was filling the glasses with crystalline ice water and scraping crumbs from the linen with a broad silver blade. Him I liked best of all. There was nothing I could do under the circumstances about my desire to give a sob. It was my heartbreak hour. For I didn't have the dough and the old woman knew it. This tunicate withered bag the Señora had my financial number. Flonzaley with his corpses would never run out of money. The course of nature itself was behind him. Cancers and aneurysms, coronaries and hemorrhages stood behind his wealth and guaranteed him bliss. All these dead, like the glorious court of Jerusalem, chanting, "Live forever, Solomon Flonzaley!" And so Flonzaley was getting Renata while I yielded a moment to bitter self-pity and saw myself very old and standing dazed in the toilet of some tenement. Perhaps like old Doc Lutz I would put two socks on one foot and pee in the bathtub. That, as Naomi said, was the end. It was just as well that the title to those graves in Waldheim had turned up in Julius's desk. I might just need them, untimely. Tomorrow, heavy of heart, I was going to the Prado to look for the Velásquez, or was it the Murillo that resembled Renata—the one mentioned by the Chancellor of the Exchequer in Downing Street. So I sat in this scene of silver service and brandy flames and the superb flash of chafing dishes.

"I wired Renata yesterday and asked her to marry me," I said.

"Did you? How nice. That should have been done long ago," said the relentless Señora. "You can't treat proud women like this. But I would be happy to have such a distinguished son-in-law and Roger loves you like his own daddy."

"But she hasn't answered me."

"The postal system isn't working. Haven't you heard, Italy is breaking down?" she said. "Did you telephone too?"

"I tried, Señora. I hesitate to call in the middle of the night. Anyway there's never an answer."

"She may have gone with her father for the holiday. Maybe Biferno still owns his house in the Dolomites."

"Why don't you use your influence for me, Señora," I said. This capitulation was a mistake. To appeal to certain peculiar powers is the worst thing you can do. These vulcanized hearts, they only become more resistant when you ask for mercy. "You know I'm in Spain to work on a new type of Baedeker. After Madrid Renata and I, if we got married, would be going on to Vienna, Rome, and Paris. I'm going to buy a new Mercedes-Benz. We could hire a governess for the boy. There's a great deal of money in this." I now dropped names, I bragged of my connections in European capitals, I babbled. She was less and less impressed. Maybe she had had a talk with Szathmar. I don't know why, but Szathmar loved to give my secrets away. Then I said. "Señora, why don't we go to the Flamenco Cabaret—the whatchamacallit that advertises all over the place? I really love strong voices and people hammering with their heels. We can get a sitter for Roger."

"Oh, very good," she said.

So we spent the evening with gypsies, and I splurged and behaved like a man with plenty of money. I discussed rings and wedding gifts with the crazy old woman at every interval in the guitar music and hand-clapping.

"What have you seen, going back and forth in Madrid, that might appeal to Renata?" I asked her.

"Oh, the most elegant leather and suède. Coats and gloves and bags and shoes," she said. "But I found a street where they sell exquisite cloaks and I talked with the president of the International Cloak Society, Los Amigos de la Capa, and he showed me, with hoods and without hoods, the most stunning velvet dark-green items."

"I'll buy one for her first thing tomorrow," I said.

If the Señora had given even the slightest hint of discouragement I might have known where I stood. But she gave me only a dry look. A blink crossed the table. It even seemed to come from the bottom of her eye upward, like a nictitating membrane. My impression was of a forest, and of a clearing from which a serpent departed just as I got to it on a dry and golden autumn afternoon fragrant with leaf mold. I mention this for what it may be worth. Nothing, probably. But I had been going around to the Prado, around the corner from the Ritz, looking at some strange pictures every free moment and especially the burlesque visions of Goya and the paintings of Hieronymus Bosch. My mind was prepared therefore for visiting images and even hallucinations.

"I congratulate you on finally making sense," said the old woman. She didn't say, mind you, that I had done this in time. She said, "I brought Renata up to make a perfect wife to a serious man."

A born patsy, I concluded from this that I was the serious man she meant and that these women had not yet reached an irrevocable decision. I celebrated this possibility by drinking a large amount of Lepanto brandy. As a result I slept soundly and woke rested. In the morning I opened the high windows and enjoyed the traffic wheeling in the sun, the dignified plaza with the white Palace Hotel on the far side. Delicious rolls and coffee were brought with sculptured butter and Hero jam. For ten years I had lived in style, well tailored, with custom-made shirts and cashmere stockings and silk neckties, esthetically satisfying. Now this silly splendor was ending but I, with my experience of the great Depression, knew austerity perfectly well. I had spent most of my life in it. The hardship was not living in a rooming house but becoming just another old guy, no longer capable of inspiring the minds of pretty ladies with May–December calculations or visions of being mistress of a castle like Mrs. Charlie Chaplin, having ten children by an autumnal-to-wintry husband of great stature. Could I bear to live without having this effect on women? And then possibly, just possibly, Renata loved me well enough to accept conditions of austerity. On an income of fifteen thousand dollars, promised by Julius if I were to invest fifty thousand with him, something very nice could be arranged in Segovia. I could even put up with the Señora for the rest of her life. Which I hoped would not be long. No hard feelings, you understand, but it would be nice to lose her soon.

I tried to reach Thaxter in Paris—the Hotel Pont-Royal his address there. I also put in a call for Carl Stewart in York. I wanted to discuss the cultural Baedeker with Thaxter's publisher myself. I also wanted to make certain that he would pay my bill at the Ritz. Thaxter was not registered at the Pont-Royal. Maybe he was staying with his mother's friend, the Princesse de Bourbon-Sixte. I was not disturbed. Having discussed the details of my New York call with the switchboard I gave myself ten minutes of tranquillity by the window. I enjoyed the winter freshness and the sun. I tried to experience the sun not as a raging thermonuclear pile of gases and fissions but as a being, an entity with a life and meanings of its own, if you know what I mean.

Thanks to penicillin, Roger was well enough to go to the Retiro with his grandma, so I had no responsibility for him this morning. I performed thirty push-ups and stood on my head: then I shaved and dressed and strolled out. I left the grand boulevards and found my way into the back streets of the old city. My object was to buy a beautiful cloak for Renata but I remembered Julius's request for a marine painting and since I had lots of time I went into antique shops and art galleries to have a look. But in all the blue and green, foam and sun, calm and storm, there was always a rock, a sail, a funnel and Julius wasn't having any of that. Nobody cared to paint the pure element, the inhuman water, the middle of the ocean, the formless deep, the world-enfolding sea. I kept thinking of Shelley among the Euganean Hills:

> Many a green isle needs must be
> In the deep wide sea of Misery . . .

But Julius didn't see why there needs must be anything in any sea whatever. Like a reverse Noah he sent out his dove brother, beautifully dressed, greatly troubled, anguishing over Renata, to find him water only. Shop assistants, girls, all of them, in black smocks, were bringing up old seascapes from the cellars because I was an American on the loose with traveler's checks in his pocket. I didn't feel foreign among Spaniards. They resembled my parents and my immigrant aunts and cousins. We were parted when the Jews were expelled in 1492. Unless you were very stingy with time, that wasn't really so long ago.

And I wondered how American my brother Ulick was after all. From the first he had taken the view that America was that materially successful happy land that didn't need to trouble its mind, and he had dismissed the culture of the genteel and their ideas and aspirations. Now the famous Santayana agreed, in a way, with Ulick. The genteel couldn't attain their ideals and were very unhappy. Genteel America was handicapped by meagerness of soul, thinness of temper, paucity of talent. The new America of Ulick's youth only asked for comfort and speed and good cheer, health and spirits, football games, political campaigns, outings, and cheerful funerals. But this new America now revealed a different bent, new kinks. The period of pleasant hard-working exuberance and of practical arts and technics strictly in the service of material life was also ending. Why did Julius want to celebrate the new veins grafted to his heart by miraculous medical technology by buying a water painting? Because even he was no longer all business. He now felt metaphysical impulses too. Maybe he had had it with the ever-alert practical American soul. In six decades he had spotted all the rackets, smelled all the rats, and he was tired of being the absolute and sick master and boss of the inner self.

What did a seascape devoid of landmarks signify? Didn't it signify elemental liberty release from the daily way and the horror of tension? O God, liberty!

I knew that if I went to the Prado and asked around, I could find a painter to paint me a seascape. If he charged me two thousand dollars, I could get five from Julius. But I rejected the idea of making a buck on a brother with whom I had bonds of such unearthly satin. I looked over all the marine paintings in one corner of Madrid and then went on to the cape shop.

There I did business with the president of the international society Los Amigos de la Capa. He was swarthy and small, stood somewhat lopsided, like a jammed accordion, had tooth problems and bad breath. On his dark face were white sycamore patches. As Americans do not tolerate such imperfections in themselves, I felt that I was in the Old World. The shop itself had a broken wooden floor. Cloaks hung from the ceiling everywhere. Women with long poles brought down these beautiful garments, velvet-lined, brocaded, and modeled them for me. Thaxter's carabiniere costume looked sick by comparison. I bought a black cloak lined with red (black and red—Renata's best colors) and forked over two hundred dollars in American Express checks. Many thanks and courtesies were exchanged. I shook hands with everyone and couldn't wait to get back to the Ritz with my parcel to show the Señora.

But the Señora wasn't there. In my room I found Roger on the settee, his feet resting on his packed bag. A chambermaid was keeping an eye on him. "Where's Grandma?" I said. The maid told me that about two hours before the Señora had been called away urgently. I phoned the cashier, who told me that my guest, the lady in Room 482, had checked out and that her charges would appear on my bill. Then I dialed the concierge. Oh yes, he said, a limousine had taken Madam to the airport. No, Madam's destination was not known. They had not been asked to arrange tickets for her.

"Charlie, have you got chocolate?" said Roger.

"Yes, kid, I brought you some." He needed all the sweet he could get, and I handed him the entire bar. *There* was someone whose desire I understood. He desired his Mama. We desired the same person. Poor little guy, I thought, as he peeled the foil from the chocolate and filled his mouth. I had a true feeling for this kid. He was in that feverish beautiful state of pale childhood when we are beating all over with pulses—nothing but a craving defenseless greedy heart. I remembered the condition very well. The chambermaid, when she found that I knew a little Spanish, asked whether Rogelio were my grandson. "No!" I said. It was bad enough that he had been dumped on me, must I be a grandfather, too? Renata was on her honeymoon with Flonzaley. Never having been married herself, the Señora was mad to achieve respectability for her daughter. And Renata, for all of her erotic development, was an obedient child. Perhaps the Señora, when she schemed on her daughter's behalf, felt herself more youthful. To do me in the eye must have made her decades younger. As for me, I now saw the connection between eternal youth and stupidity. If I was not too old to chase Renata, I was young enough to suffer adolescent heartache.

So I told the maid that Rogelio and I were not related although I was certainly old enough to be his *abuelo*, and I gave her a hundred pesetas to mind him for another hour. Even though I was going broke I still had money enough for certain refined needs. I could afford to suffer like a gentleman. Just now I couldn't cope with the kid. I had an urge to go to the Retiro, where I could abandon myself and beat my breast or stamp my feet or curse or weep. As I was leaving my room the phone rang and I snatched it up, hoping to hear Renata's voice. It was, however, New York calling.

"Mr. Citrine? This is Stewart in New York. We've never met. I know of you, of course."

"Yes, I wanted to ask you. You are publishing a book by Pierre Thaxter on dictators?"

"We have great hopes for it," he said.

"Where is Thaxter now, in Paris?"

"At the last moment he changed his plans and flew to South America. So far as I know he's in Buenos Aires interviewing Perón's widow. Very exciting. The country's being torn apart."

"You know, I suppose," I said, "that I'm in Madrid to explore the possibility of doing a cultural guide to Europe."

"Is that so?" he said.

"Didn't Thaxter tell you that? I thought we had your blessing."

"I don't know the first thing about it."

"You're sure now? You have no recollection?"

"What's this all about, Mr. Citrine?"

"To be brief," I said. "Only this question: Am I in Madrid as your guest?"

"Not that I know of."

"*¡Ay, que lío!*"

"Sir?"

In the curtained alcove, suddenly cold, I crawled into bed with the telephone. I said, "It's a Spanish expression like *malentendu* or *snafu* or screwed again. Excuse the emphasis. I am under stress."

"Perhaps you would be so kind as to explain this in a letter," said Mr. Stewart. "Are you at work on a book? We'd be interested, you know."

"Nothing," I said.

"But if you should get started . . ."

"I'll write you a letter," I said.

I was paying for this call.

Now very stormy, I asked the operator to try Renata again. I'll tell that bitch a thing or two, I thought. But when I got through, Milan said that she had gone and left no address. By the time I got to the Retiro, intending to express myself, there was nothing to express. I took a meditative walk. I reached the same conclusions I had reached in Judge Urbanovich's chambers. What good would it do me to tell Renata off? Fierce and exquisite speeches, perfect in logic, mature in judgment, deep wise rage, heavenly in poetry, were all right for Shakespeare but they wouldn't do a damn bit of good for me. The desire for emission still existed but reception was lacking for my passionate speech. Renata didn't want to hear it, she had other things on her mind. Well, at least she trusted me with Rogelio and in her own good time she'd send for him. By brushing me off like this she had probably done me a service. At least she would see it in that way. I should have married her long ago. I was a man of little faith, my hesitancy was insulting, and it was quite right that I should be left to mind her kid. Furthermore, I suppose the ladies figured that Rogelio would tie me down and prevent pursuit. Not that I had any intention of pursuing. By now I couldn't even afford it. For one thing, the bill at the Ritz was enormous. The Señora had made many telephone calls to Chicago to keep in touch with a certain young man whose business was to repair television sets, her present *affaire de cœur*. Moreover, Christmas in Madrid, counting Roger's illness and his presents, gourmet dining, and Renata's cloak, had reduced my assets by nearly a third. For many years, since the success of *Von Trenck*, or about the time of Demmie Vonghel's death, I had spent freely, lived it up, but now I must go back to the old rooming-house standard. To stay at the Ritz I would have to hire a governess. It was impossible anyway. I was going broke. My best alternative was to move into a *pensión*.

I had to account somehow for this child. If I described myself as his uncle it would raise suspicions. If I called myself his grandfather, I would have to behave like a grandfather. To be a widower was best. Rogelio called me Charlie, but in American children this was normal. Besides, the boy was in a sense an orphan, and I was without exaggeration bereaved. I went out and bought myself mourner's handkerchiefs and some very fine black silk neckties and a little black suit for Rogelio. I gave the American Embassy an extremely plausible account of a lost passport. It luckily happened that the young man who took care of such matters knew my books on Woodrow Wilson and on Harry Hopkins. A history major from Cornell, he had heard me once when I gave a paper at a meeting of the American Historical Association. I told him my wife had died of leukemia and that my wallet had been stolen on a bus here in Madrid. The young fellow told me that this town had always been notorious for its pickpockets. "Priests' pockets are picked under the soutane. They really are slick here. Many Spaniards boast that Madrid is a world center for this picking of pockets. To change the subject—maybe you'd lecture for the USIA."

"I'm too depressed," I said. "Besides, I'm here to do research. I'm preparing a book on the Spanish–American War."

"We've had leukemia cases in my family," he said. "These lingering deaths leave you wrung out."

At the Pensión La Roca I told the landlady that Roger's mother had been killed by a truck when she stepped off a curb in Barcelona.

"Oh, what a horrible thing."

"Yes," I said. I had prepared myself fully, consulting the Spanish dictionary. I added with great fluency, "My poor wife—her chest was crushed, her face was destroyed, her lungs were punctured. She died in agony."

Leukemia, I felt, was much too good for Renata.

In the *pensión* were any number of sociable people. Some spoke English, some French, and communication was possible. An Army captain and his wife lived there, and also some ladies from the Danish Embassy. One of these, the most outstanding, was a gimpy blond of about fifty. Occasionally, a sharp face and protruding teeth can be pleasant, and she was a rather agreeable-looking person, although the skin of her temples had gone a little silky (the veins), and she was even slightly hunchbacked. But hers was one of those commanding personalities that takes over a dining room or a drawing room not because they say much but because they know the secret of proclaiming their pre-eminence. As for the staff, the chambermaids who doubled as waitresses, they were extremely kind. Black means much less in the Protestant north. In Spain mourning still carries a lot of weight. Rogelio's little black suit was even more effective than my bordered handkerchief and my armband. When I fed him his lunch we brought the house down. It was not unusual for me to cut up the kid's meat. I did this normally in Chicago. But somehow, in the small, windowless dining room of the *pensión*, it was an eye opener—this unexpected disclosure of the mothering habits of American men got to people. My fussing over Roger must have been unbearably sad. Women began to help me. I put the *empleadas del hogar* on my payroll. In a few days' time he was speaking Spanish. Mornings, he attended a nursery school. Late every afternoon, one of the maids took him to the park. I was free to walk about Madrid or to lie on my bed and meditate. My life was quieter. Full quietude was something I couldn't expect, under the circumstances.

This was not the life I had pictured in the little plush seat of the 747, rushing over the deep Atlantic stream. Then, I had put it to myself, the little bubble in the carpenter's level might be coaxed back into the center. Now I wasn't sure that I had a bubble at all. Then there was Europe, too. For knowledgeable Americans, Europe was not much good these days. It led the world in nothing. You had to be a backward sort of person (a vulgar broad, a Renata—not to beat about the bush) to come here with serious cultural expectations. The sort of thing propagated by ladies' fashion magazines. I am obligated to confess, however, that I too had come this time with pious ideals, or the remnants of such ideals. People had once done great things here, inspired by the spirit. There were still relics of holiness and of art here. You wouldn't find Saint Ignatius, Saint Teresa, John of the Cross, El Greco, the Escorial on Twenty-sixth and California or at the Playboy Club in Chicago. But then there was no little Citrine family group in Segovia with the Daddy trying to achieve the separation of consciousness from its biological foundation, while the sexual, rousing Mommy busied herself with the antiques trade. No, Renata had given me my lumps and she had done it in such a way that my personal dignity was badly damaged. The mourning I wore helped me to recover, somewhat. Black garments put me on polite and courteous terms with the Spanish. A suffering widower and a pale foreign orphan touched the shop assistants, especially the women. At the *pensión*, the secretary from the Danish Embassy took a particular interest in us. She was very pale, and her pallor had origins very different from Roger's. She had a dry, hectic look and she was so white that the lipstick raged on her mouth. She applied it after dinner with a violent effect. Yet her intentions weren't bad. She took me for a walk one Sunday afternoon, when I was not at my best. She put on a cloche or bucket hat and we walked slowly, for she had a hip ailment. As we followed the paths with the holiday crowds, she gave me a talking-to about sorrow.

"Was your wife beautiful?"

"Oh, she was very beautiful."

"You Americans are so self-indulgent about grief. How long has she been dead?"

"Six weeks."

"Last week you said three."

"You can see for yourself, I've lost all sense of time."

"Well now, you've got to get back on your feet. There are times when you have to cut—cut your losses. What's the expression? Spin the thing off. I've got some good brandy in my room. Come have a drink when the boy is asleep. You have to share a double bed with him, don't you?"

"They're trying to find us two singles."

"Isn't he restless? Children kick a lot."

"He's a quiet sleeper. I can't sleep anyway. I lie there reading."

"We can find you something better than that to do at night," she said. "What's the use of brooding. She's gone."

She was certainly gone. That was fully confirmed now. She had written me from Sicily. On Saturday, only yesterday, when I stopped at the Ritz to ask for mail, I was given her letter. This was why I was not at my best on Sunday; I'd been up all night studying Renata's words. If I couldn't attend very closely to Miss Rebecca Volsted, this furiously white limping woman, it was because I was suffering. I might almost have wished that Roger weren't such a good child. He did not even kick in his sleep. He gave me no headaches. He was a dear little boy.

Renata and Flonzaley had gotten married in Milan and they were honeymooning in Sicily. I suppose they went to Taormina. She didn't specify. She wrote, "You are the best person to leave Roger with. You've proved often that you love him for his own sake and never used him to get at me. Mother is too busy to look after him. You don't think so now, but you'll get over this and remain a good friend. You'll be sore and bitter and call me a scheming dirty cunt—that's how you talk when you're burned up. But you've got justice in your heart, Charles. You owe me something and you know it. You had your chance to do right by me. You missed it! Oh, you missed it! I couldn't get you started doing right!" Renata burst into mourning. I had spoiled it. "The role you got me into was the palooka role. I was your marvelous sex-clown. You had me cooking dinner in a top hat, and my behind bare." Not so, not so, that was her own idea. "I was a good sport and let you have your fun. I enjoyed myself, too. I didn't deny you anything. You denied me plenty, though. You wouldn't remember that I was the mother of a boy. You showed me off in London as your spectacular lay from Chicago, that toddling town. The Chancellor of the Exchequer gave me a private feel. He did, the bastard. I let it pass because of the former greatness of Britain. But he wouldn't have done it if I had been your wife. You put me in the whore position. I don't think you have to be a professor of anatomy to connect the ass with the heart. If you had acted as though I had a heart in my breast just like your distinguished highness the Chevalier Citrine, we might have made it. Ah Charlie, I'll never forget how you smuggled Cuban cigars for me from Montreal. You put *Cyrus the Great* bands on them. You were kind and funny. I believed you when you said that a peculiar foot needed a peculiar shoe and that we were shoe and foot, foot and shoe together. Why, if you had only thought the obvious thing, 'This is a kid who grew up in hotel lobbies, and her mother never was married,' you would have married me in every city hall and church in America and given me some protection finally. This Rudolf Steiner you've been driving me crazy with says, I think, that if you're a man this time, you'll be reincarnated as a woman, and that the ether body (not that I'm sure what an ether body is; it's the vital part that makes the lady live, isn't it?) is always of the other sex. But if you're going be a woman in your next life, you've got a lot to learn in between. I'll tell you something anyway. Many a woman would admit, if she was honest, that what she'd really adore is a man made up of many men, a composite lover or husband. She loves this in X and that in Y and something else again in Z. Now you are charming, delightful, touching, usually a pleasure to be with. You could have been my X and partly my Y, but you were a complete dud in the Z department.

"I miss you this minute, and what's more Flonzaley knows it. But one advantage of his business is that it's made him very basic. You once said to me that Flonzaley's point of view must be Plutonian—whatever that meant. I put it that his trade is gloomy but his character is roomy. He doesn't insist that I shouldn't love you. Don't forget that I didn't run away with a stranger. I went back to him. When we parted at Idlewild, I didn't know I was going to do it. But I got out of patience with you. There are too many zigzags in your temperament. Both of us need more serious arrangements."

Wait a minute. She said this and she said that, but was she giving me up because I was about to go broke? That would never be a problem with Flonzaley. Probably Renata knew that I was beginning to think about a more austere sort of life. I hadn't renounced my money out of principle. Urbanovich was taking it from me, and that was just as well. But I was beginning to see the American dollar-drive for what it was. It had assumed the proportions of a cosmic force. It stood between us and the real forces. But no sooner had I thought this than I understood one of Renata's reasons for giving me up—she gave me up because I thought such thoughts as this. In her own way, she was telling me so.

"Now you can write your big essay on boredom, and maybe the human race will be grateful. It's suffering, and you want to help. It's a wonderful thing to knock yourself out over these deep problems, but personally I don't care to be around when you're doing it. I admit you're smart. That's all right with me. *You* should be as tolerant toward undertakers as *I* am toward intellectuals. When it comes to men, my judgments are completely female-human, regardless of race, creed, or previous condition of servitude, as Lincoln said. Congratulations, your intelligence is terrific. Still I agree with your old sweetie Naomi Lutz. I don't want to get involved in all this spiritual, intellectual, universal stuff. As a beautiful woman and still young, I prefer to take things as billions of people have done throughout history. You work, you get bread, you lose a leg, kiss some fellows, have a baby, you live to be eighty and bug hell out of everybody, you get hung or drowned. But you don't spend years trying to dope your way out of the human condition. To me that's boring." Yes, when she said this, I saw thinkers of genius throwing skeins of belief and purpose over the heads of the multitude. I saw them molesting the race with their fancies, programs, and world-perspectives. Not that the race itself was guiltless. But it had incredible abilities to work, to feel, to believe, which it was asked to bestow here, bestow there by those who were convinced that they knew best and abused mankind with projects. "And you never asked me," she went on, "but I have my own beliefs. I believe I live in nature. I think that when you're dead you're dead, and that's that. And this is what Flonzaley stands for. Dead is dead, and the man's trade is with stiffs, and I'm his wife now. Flonzaley performs a practical service for society. Like the plumber, the sewage department, or the garbage collector, he says. But you do people good and then they turn around and have a prejudice against you. In a way it's like my own personal situations. Flonzaley accepts the occupational stigma but there's a slight charge for that, and he adds it to the bill. Some of your ideas are spookier than his business. He keeps things in their compartments. The color of one frame doesn't leak into the next."

Here she wasn't being straight. This glowing person Renata, so wonderful to me because she was in the Biblical sense unclean, had made my life richer with the thrills of deviation and broken laws. If Flonzaley, because of pollution by the dead, was comparably wonderful to her, why didn't she just say so—I took it that in the Z department, and Renata never told me what this was, he was all that I was not. This hurt me very deeply, it made my heart ache. In the old expression, she hit me where I lived. But she might have spared me Flonzaley's rationalizations for soaking the bereaved. I knew Chicago's business thinkers. I had heard many a rich Chicagoan philosophizing. I knew all of that would-be Shavian wit you could hear at dinner tables on Lake Shore Drive: they wanted to make an untouchable and a chandala of Flonzaley, a scavenger, but he would take their gold into the gloom with him, and he would be a Prince there—that sort of stuff I could do without. Still, Renata was wonderful. Naturally she wanted to say grand things to me and show how well she had done. I had lost a wonderful woman. I was suffering over Renata. She marched off in boots and plumes, as it were, and left me figuring, in pain, what was what, and how, and what to do. And trying to guess what Z was.

"You always said that the way life happened to you was so different that you weren't in a position to judge the desires of other people. It's really true that you don't know people from inside or understand what they want—like you didn't understand that I wanted stability—and you never may know. You gave this away when you told me how you tried to feel your way into little Mary's emotions over the ten-speed bicycle but couldn't. Well, I'm lending you Roger. Look after him till I can send for him and study his desires. It's him you need now, not me. Flonzaley and I are going over to North Africa. Sicily hasn't been as warm as I like it. Let me suggest, as long as you're going back to fundamentals of feeling, that you give some thought to your friends Szathmar, Swiebel, and Thaxter. Your passion for Von Humboldt Fleisher speeded the deterioration of our relationship."

She didn't say just when she'd be sending for the boy.

"If you think you're on earth for such a very special purpose I don't know why you cling to the idea of happiness with a woman or a happy family life. This is either dumb innocence or else the last word in kinkiness. You're really far out and you take up with a person who's far out in her own way, and then you tell yourself that what you really want is a simple affectionate relationship. Well, you had the warmth and charm to make me think you wanted and needed me. Always your affectionate friend." She had filled up the paper, and the letter ended.

I couldn't help crying when I read this. On the night when Renata locked me out George Swiebel had told me how much he respected me for being able to suffer agonies of love at my age. He took off his hat to me for it. But this was the vitalist youth attitude which Ortega, one of the Madrid authors I had been reading, disparaged in *The Modern Theme*. I agreed with him. However, in the back bedroom of this third-rate *pensión* I was just the kind of old fool who carried on like an adolescent. I was balder and more wrinkled than ever and the white hairs had begun to grow long and wild from my eyebrows. Now I was a forsaken codger snuffling disgracefully from a beautiful floozy's abuse. I was forgetting that I might also be a World Historical Individual (of a sort), that perhaps I was supposed to scatter the intellectual nonsense of an age or must do something to help the human spirit burst from its mental coffin. She didn't think much of these aspirations, did she, if you took her running off with Flonzaley, who dealt in stiffs, as an expression of opinion. And even as I wept I glanced at the clock and realized that Roger would be back from his walk in fifteen minutes. We were supposed to play dominoes. Suddenly life goes into reverse. You're in first grade again. Approaching sixty you must start from the beginning and see whether you can understand another's desires. The woman you love is making mature progress in life, advancing independently in Marrakech, or somewhere. She doesn't need a primrose path. Wherever she treads the primroses start growing.

She was right, of course. In taking up with her I had asked for trouble. Why? Maybe the purpose of such trouble was to turn me deeper into realms of peculiar but necessary thought. One of these peculiar thoughts occurred now. It was that the beauty of a woman like Renata was not entirely appropriate. It was out of season. Her physical perfection was of the Classical Greek or High Renaissance type. And why was this sort of beauty historically inappropriate? Well, it went back to a time when the human spirit was just beginning to disengage itself from nature. Until that moment it hadn't occurred to man to think of himself separately. He hadn't distinguished his own being from natural being but was a part of it. But as soon as intellect awoke he became separated from nature. As an individual, he looked and saw the beauty of the external world, including human beauty. This a moment sacred in history—the golden age. Many centuries later, the Renaissance tried to recover this first sense of beauty. But even then it was too late. Intellect and spirit had moved on. A different sort of beauty, more internal, had begun its development. This internal beauty, manifested in romantic art and poetry, was the result of a free union of the human spirit with the spirit of nature. So Renata really was a peculiar phantom. My passion for her was an antiquarian passion. She seemed to be aware of this herself. Look at the way she swaggered and clowned. Attic or Botticellian loveliness doesn't smoke cigars. It doesn't stand up and do vulgar things in the bathtub. It doesn't stop in a picture gallery and say, "There's a painter with balls." It doesn't talk like that. But what a pity! How I missed her! What a darling woman she was, that crook! But she was a holdover from another time. I couldn't say that *I* had the new sort of internal beauty. I was a dumb old silly. But I had heard of this beauty, I got advance notice of it. What did I propose to do about this new beauty? I didn't know yet. At the moment I was waiting for Roger. He was eager to play dominoes. I was eager to get a glimpse of his mother in his face as I sat opposite with the dotted bones.

THE haggard Danish lady, Rebecca Volsted, came and walked with me in the Retiro. I walked slowly and she limped along side. Her cloche hat was pulled low on her face. Her face with its bitter flashes was lightning-pale. She questioned me very closely. She asked why I spent so much time in my room. She felt snubbed by me. Not socially. Socially I was very friendly. I only snubbed her—well, essentially. She seemed to be saying that if I wrestled passionately with her in bed she could, bad hip or no bad hip, cure me of what ailed me. On the contrary, experience had finally taught me that if I followed her suggestion I would only acquire one more (and possibly demented) dependent.

"What do you do all day long in your room?"

"I have to catch up on my correspondence."

"I suppose you have to notify people of your wife's death. How did she die, anyway?"

"She died of tetanus."

"You know, Mr. Citrine, I've taken the trouble of looking you up in *Who's Who in the United States.*"

"Why ever did you do that?"

"Oh, I don't know," she said. "A hunch. For one thing, though you have an American passport, you don't behave like a real American. I felt there must be something to you."

"So you found out that I was born in Appleton, Wisconsin. Just like Harry Houdini, the great Jewish escape artist—I wonder why he and I chose Appleton to be born in."

"Is there an element of choice?" said Rebecca. In her cloche hat, fire-pale, and limping beside me in the Spanish park she spoke up for rationality. I slowed my pace for her as we talked.

I said, "Of course, science is on your side. Still, it's rather strange, you know. People who have been on earth for only ten years or so are suddenly beginning to compose fugues and prove subtle theorems in mathematics. It may be that we may bring a great many powers here with us, Miss Volsted. The chronicles say that before Napoleon was born his mother enjoyed visiting battlefields. But isn't it possible that the little hoodlum, years before his birth, was already looking for a carnage-loving mother? So with the Bach family and the Mozart family and the Bernoulli family. Such family groups may have attracted musical or mathematical souls. As I explained in an article I wrote about Houdini, Rabbi Weiss, the magician's father, was a perfectly orthodox Jew from Hungary. But he had to leave the old country because he fought a duel with sabers and he certainly was an oddball. Besides, how is it that Houdini and I, both from Appleton, Wisconsin, struggle so hard with the problem of death?"

"Did Houdini do that?"

"Yes, this Houdini defied all forms of restraint and confinement, including the grave. He broke out of everything. They buried him and he escaped. They sank him in boxes and he escaped. They put him in a strait jacket and manacles and hung him upside-down by one ankle from the flagpole of the Flatiron Building in New York. Sarah Bernhardt came to watch this and sat in her limousine on Fifth Avenue looking on while he freed himself and climbed to safety. A friend of mine, a poet, wrote a ballad about this called 'Harlequin Harry.' Bernhardt was already very old and her leg had been amputated. She sobbed and hung on Houdini's neck as they were driven away in the car and begged him to give back her leg. He could do anything! In czarist Russia the Okhrana stripped him naked and locked him in the steel van it used for Siberian deportations. He freed himself from that too. He escaped from the most secure prisons in the world. And whenever he came home from a triumphal tour he went straight to the cemetery. He lay down on his mother's grave and on his belly through the grass he told her in whispers about his trips, where he had been, and what he had done. Later he spent years debunking spiritualists. He exposed all the tricks of the medium-racket. In an article I once speculated whether he hadn't had an intimation of the holocaust and was working out ways to escape from the death camps. Ah! If only European Jewry had learned what he knew. But then Houdini was punched experimentally in the belly by a medical student and died of peritonitis. So you see, nobody can overcome the final fact of the material world. Dazzling rationality, blazing of consciousness, the most ingenious skill—nothing can be done about death. Houdini worked out one line of inquiry completely. Have you looked into an open grave lately, Miss Volsted?"

"At this point in your life, such a morbid obsession is understandable," she said. She looked up, her face burning white. "There's only one thing to do. It's obvious."

"Obvious?"

"Don't play dumb," she said. "You know the answer. You and I could do very well together. With me you'd stay free—no strings attached. Come and go as you like. We are not in America. But what *do* you do in your room? *Who's Who* says you've won prizes in biography and history."

"I'm preparing to write about the Spanish-American War," I said. "And I'm catching up on my correspondence. Actually, I have this letter to post. . . ."

I had written to Kathleen in Belgrade. I didn't mention money but I hoped she wasn't going to forget my share of the option payment on Humboldt's scenario. The sum she had mentioned was fifteen hundred dollars and I was going to need it soon. I was being dunned in Chicago—Szathmar was forwarding my mail. It turned out that the Señora had flown to Madrid First Class. The travel bureau was asking me to remit, promptly. I had written to George Swiebel to ask whether the money for my Kirman rugs had been paid yet, but George was not a prompt correspondent. I knew that Tomchek and Stole would send in a staggering bill for losing my case and that Judge Urbanovich would let Cannibal Pinsker help himself from the impounded funds.

"You seem to be muttering to yourself in your room," said Rebecca Volsted.

"I'm sure you haven't been listening at the door," I said.

She flushed—that is, she turned even paler—and answered, "Pilar tells me that you're talking to yourself in there."

"I read fairy tales to Roger."

"You don't when he's at school. Or maybe you rehearse the big bad wolf. . . ."

WHAT was this muttering? I couldn't tell Miss Rebecca Volsted of the Danish Embassy in Madrid that I was making esoteric experiments, that I was reading to the dead. I already seemed odd enough. Supposedly a widower from the Midwest and father of a small boy, I turned out, according to *Who's Who*, to be a prize-winning biographer and playwright and a *chevalier* of the Legion of Honor. The *chevalier* widower rented the worst room in the *pensión* (across the air shaft from the kitchen). His brown eyes were red from weeping, he dressed with high elegance although the kitchen smells made his clothing noticeably rancid, he tried with persistent vanity to comb his thin and graying hair over the bald middle of his head and was always disheartened when he realized that in the lamplight his scalp was glistening. He had a straight nose like John Barrymore, but the resemblance went no further. He was a man whose bodily case was fraying. He was beginning to wrinkle under the chin, beside the ears, and below the sad, warm-hearted eyes that gazed intelligently in the wrong direction. I had always counted hygienically on regular intercourse with Renata. I apparently agreed with George Swiebel that you were headed for trouble if you neglected to have normal sexual relations. In all civilized countries this is the basic creed. There was, of course, a text to the contrary—I always had a text to the contrary. This text was from Nietzsche and took the interesting view that the mind was greatly strengthened by abstinence because the spermatazoa were reabsorbed into the system. Nothing was better for the intellect. Be that as it might, I became aware that I was developing tics. I missed my paddle ball games at the Downtown Club—the conversation of my fellow members I must say that I didn't miss at all. To them I could never say what I was really thinking. They didn't speak their thoughts to me either but those thoughts were at least speakable. Mine were incomprehensible and becoming more so all the time.

I was going to move out of here when Kathleen sent that check, but meantime I had to live on a tight budget. The IRS, Szathmar informed me, had reopened my 1970 return. I wrote to say that this was now Urbanovich's problem.

Every morning powerful coffee odors woke me. Afterward

came ammoniac smells of frying fish and also of cabbage garlic saffron, and of pea soup boiled with a ham bone. Pensión La Roca used a heavy grade of olive oil which took some getting used to. At first it went through me quickly. The water closet in the hall was lofty and very cold with a long chain pull of green brass. When I went there I carried the cape I had bought for Renata over my arm and put it over my shoulders when I was seated. To sit down on the freezing board was a sort of Saint Sebastian experience. Returning to my room I did fifty push-ups and stood on my head. When Roger was at nursery school I walked in the back streets or went to the Prado or sat in cafés. I devoted long hours to Steiner meditation and did my best to draw close to the dead. I had very strong feelings about this and could no longer neglect the possibility of communication with them. Ordinary spiritualism I dismissed. My postulate was that there was a core of the eternal in every human being. Had this been a mental or logical problem I would have dealt logically with it. However, it was no such thing. What I had to deal with was a lifelong intimation. This intimation must be either a tenacious illusion or else the truth deeply buried. The mental respectability of good members of educated society was something I had come to despise with all my heart. I admit that I was sustained by contempt whenever the esoteric texts made me uneasy. For there were passages in Steiner that set my teeth on edge. I said to myself, this is lunacy. Then I said, this is poetry, a great vision. But I went on with it, laying out all that he told us of the life of the soul after death. Besides, did it matter what I did with myself? Elderly, heart-injured, meditating in kitchen odors, wearing Renata's cloak in the biffy—should it concern anyone what such a person did with himself? The strangeness of life, the more you resisted it, the harder it bore down on you. The more the mind opposed the sense of strangeness, the more distortions it produced. What if, for once, one were to yield to it? Moreover I was convinced that there was nothing in the material world to account for the more delicate desires and perceptions of human beings. I concurred with the dying Bergotte in Proust's novel. There was no basis in common experience for the Good, the True, and the Beautiful. And I was too queerly haughty to take stock in the respectable empiricism in which I had been educated. Too many fools subscribed to it. Besides, people were not really surprised when you spoke to them about the soul and the spirit. How odd! No one was surprised. Sophisticated people were the only ones who expressed surprise. Perhaps the fact that I had learned to stand apart from my own frailties and the absurdities of my character might mean that I was a little dead myself. This detachment was a sobering kind of experience. I thought sometimes how much it must sober the dead to pass through the bitter gates. No more eating, bleeding, breathing. Without the pride of physical existence the shocked soul would surely become more sensible.

It was my understanding that the untutored dead blundered and suffered in their ignorance. In the first stages especially, the soul, passionately attached to its body, stained with earth, suddenly severed, felt cravings much as amputees feel their missing legs. The newly dead saw from end to end all that had happened to them, the whole of lamentable life. They burned with pain. The children, the dead children especially, could not leave their living but stayed invisibly close to those they loved and wept. For these children we needed rituals—something for the kids, for God's sake! The elder dead were better prepared and came and went more wisely. The departed worked in the unconscious part of each living soul and some of our highest designs were very possibly instilled by them. The Old Testament commanded us to have no business with the dead at all and this was, the teachings said, because in its first phase, the soul entered a sphere of passionate feeling after death, of something resembling a state of blood and nerves. Base impulses might be mobilized by contact with the dead in this first sphere. As soon as I began to think of Demmie Vonghel, for instance, I received violent impressions. I always saw her handsome and naked as she had been and looking as she had looked during her climaxes. They had always been convulsive, a series of them, and she used to go violently red in the face. There always was a trace of crime in the way that Demmie did the thing and there had always been a trace of the accessory in me, wickedly collaborating. Now I was flooded with sexual associations. Take Renata, there was never any violence with Renata, she always smiled and behaved like a courtesan. Take Miss

Doris Scheldt, she was a small girl, almost a blond child, although her profile hinted that there was a Savonarola embedded in her and that she would turn into a masterful little woman. The most charming thing about Miss Scheldt was her lighthearted bursting into laughter during the conclusion of the sexual act. The least charming was her dark feat of pregnancy. She worried when you hugged her naked in the night lest a stray spermatozoon ruin her life. It seems, after all, that there are no nonpeculiar people. This was why I looked forward to acquaintance with the souls of the dead. They *should* be a little more stable.

As I was only in a state of preparation, not an initiate, I couldn't expect to reach my dead. Still, I thought I would try, as their painful experience of life sometimes does qualify some people to advance more rapidly in spiritual development. So I tried to put myself in a proper state for such contact, concentrating especially on my parents and on Demmie Vonghel and Von Humboldt Fleisher. The texts said that actual communication with an individual who had died was possible though difficult but demanded discipline and vigilance and a keen awareness that the lowest impulses might break out and raise hell with you. A pure intention must police these passions. So far as I knew my intention was pure. The souls of the dead hungered for a completion of their purgatory and for the truth. I, in the Pensión La Roca, sent my intensest thoughts thoughts toward them with all the warmth I had. And I said to myself that unless you conceive Death to be a violent guerrilla and kidnaper who snatches those you love, and if you are not cowardly and cannot submit to such terrorism as civilized people now do in every department of life, you must pursue and inquire and explore every possibility and seek everywhere and try everything. Real questions to the dead have to be imbued with true feeling. By themselves abstractions will not travel. They must pass through the heart to be transmitted. The time to ask the dead something is in the last instant of consciousness before sleeping. As for the dead they reach us most easily just as we awaken. These are successive instants in the time-keeping of the soul, the eight intervening clock hours in bed being only biological. The one occult peculiarity that I couldn't get used to was that the questions we asked originated not with us but with the dead to whom they were addressed. When the dead answered it was really your own soul speaking. Such a mirror-image reversal was difficult to grasp. I spent a long time pondering that.

And this was the way I spent January and February in Madrid, reading helpful texts, *sotto voce*, to the departed, and trying to draw near to them. You might have thought that this hope of getting next to the dead would weaken my mind, if it didn't actually originate in mental debility. No. Although I have only my own authority for saying so, my mind appeared to become more stable. For one thing I seemed to be recovering an independent and individual connection with the creation, the whole hierarchy of being. The soul of a civilized and rational person is said to be free but is actually very closely confined. Although he formally believes that he ranges with perfect freedom everywhere and is thus quite a thing, he feels in fact utterly negligible. But to assume, however queerly, the immortality of the soul, to be free from the weight of death that everybody carries upon the heart presents, like the relief from any obsession (the money obsession or the sexual obsession), a terrific opportunity. Suppose that one doesn't think of death as all sensible people in their higher realism have agreed to think of it? The first result is a surplus, an overflow to be good with. Terror of death ties this energy up but when it is released one can attempt the good without feeling the embarrassment of being unhistorical, illogical, masochistically passive, feebleminded. Good then is nothing like the martyrdom of certain Americans (you will recognize whom I mean), illuminated by poetry in high school, and then testifying to the glory of their (unprovable, unreal) good by committing suicide —in high style, the only style for poets.

Going broke in a foreign country I felt little or no anxiety. The problem of money was almost nonexistent. It did bother me that I was a phony widower, indebted to the ladies of the pensión for their help with Rogelio. Rebecca Volsted, with her face of scalding white, was breathing down my neck. She wanted to sleep with me. But I simply went on with my exercises. Sometimes I thought, Oh, that stupid Renata, didn't she so know the difference between a corpse-man and a would-be seer? I wrapped myself in her cloak, a warmer garment than the vicuña Julius had given me, and I stepped out. As soon as I hit the open air, Madrid was all jewelry and art to me, the smells inspiring, the perspectives lovely, the faces attractive, the winter colors of the park frosty green and filled with vertical strokes of the lightly hibernating trees and the mouth and muzzle vapors of people and animals visible up and down the streets. Renata's little boy and I walked, holding hands. He was a remarkably composed and handsome little boy. When we wandered in the Retiro together and all the lawns were a dark and chill Atlantic green, this little Roger could very nearly convince me that up to a point the soul was the artist of its own body and I thought I could feel him at work within himself. Now and then you almost sense that you are with a person who was conceived by some wonderful means before he was physically conceived. In early childhood this invisible work of the conceiving spirit may still be going on. Pretty soon little Roger's master-building would stop and this extraordinary creature would begin to behave in the most ordinary or dull manner or perniciously, like his mother and grandma. Humboldt was forever talking about something he called "the home-world," Wordsworthian, Platonic, before the shades of the prison house fell. This is very possibly when boredom sets in, the point of advent. Humboldt had become boring in the vesture of a superior person, in the style of high culture, with all of his conforming abstractions. Many hundreds of thousands of people were now wearing this costume of the higher misery. A terrible breed, the educated nits, mental bores of the heaviest caliber. The world had never seen the likes of them. Poor Humboldt! What a mistake! Well, perhaps he could have another go at it. When? Oh, in a few hundred years his spirit might return. Meantime, I could remember him as a lovely man and generous, a heart of gold. Now and then I shuffled through the papers he had left me. He had believed so greatly in their value. I gave a skeptical sigh and was sad and put them back in his briefcase.

THE world checked in with me occasionally, reports arrived in from various parts of the globe. Renata's was the letter I most wanted. I longed to hear that she was sorry, that she was bored with Flonzaley and horrified at what she had done, that he had vile mortician's habits, and I rehearsed in my head the magnanimous moment when I took her back. When I was less nice I gave the bitch a month with her millionaire embalmer. When I was angrily depressed I thought that after all frigidity and money, as everyone has known since antiquity, made a stable combination. Add death, the strongest fixative in the world, and you had something remarkably durable. I figured by now that they had left Marrakech and were honeymooning in the Indian Ocean. Renata always did say that she wanted to winter in the Seychelles Islands. My secret belief had always been that I could cure Renata of what ailed her. Then I remembered, turning the point of recollection against myself, that Humboldt had always wanted to do the girls good but that they wouldn't hold still for it, and how he had said about Demmie's friend, Ginnie, in the Village, "Honey from the icebox . . . Cold sweets won't spread." No, Renata didn't write. She was concentrating on the new relationship and she didn't have to worry about Roger while I was looking after him. At the Ritz I picked up picture postcards addressed to the kid. I had guessed right. Morocco didn't detain the couple long. Her cards now bore Ethiopian and Tanzanian postmarks. He received some also from his father, who was skiing in Aspen and Vail. Koffritz knew where his child was.

Kathleen wrote from Belgrade to say how glad it made her to hear from me. Everything was going extremely well. Seeing me in New York had been unforgettably marvelous. She longed to talk to me again and she expected soon to pass through Madrid on her way to Almería to work on a film. She hoped to have very pleasant things to tell me. There was no check enclosed with her letter. Evidently she didn't suspect that I badly needed money. I had been prosperous for so many years that no such thought occurred to anyone. Toward the middle of February a letter arrived from George Swiebel, and George, who knew good deal about my financial condition, made no mention of money either. This was understandable because his letter came from Nairobi, so he couldn't have received my appeals for help and my questions about the sale of the Oriental rugs. He had been in Kenya for a month hunting for a beryllium mine in the bush. Or was it a lode? I preferred to think of a mine. Had George found such a mine, I as a full partner would be free forever from money anxieties. Unless, of course, the court found a way to take that too away from me. Judge Urbanovich had for some reason chosen to become my mortal enemy. He was out to strip me naked. I don't know why this was, but it was so.

George wrote as follows: "Our buddy from the Field Museum was unable to make this trip with me. Ben simply couldn't swing it. The suburbs wouldn't give him a release. He invited me for Sunday dinner so I could see for myself what a hell his life was. It didn't look too terrible to me. His wife is fat but she looks good-natured and there's a nice kid and a sort of standard mother-in-law and an English bulldog and a parrot. He says his mother-in-law lives on nothing but almond rings and cocoa. She must eat in the night because he's never yet seen her taking a bite, not in fifteen years. Well, I thought, a lot he's got to holler. His twelve-year-old boy is a Civil War buff and he and Daddy and the parrot and the bulldog have a kind of club. Besides, he has a nice profession looking after his fossils, and every summer he and the kid take a trip in the camper and fetch home more rocks. So what is he beefing? For old times' sake I let him into our deal, but he was not the one I took to East Africa with me.

"To tell the truth I didn't want to make that long trip alone. Then Naomi Lutz invited me to dinner to meet her son, the one who wrote those articles for the Southtown paper about how he kicked the drug habit. I read them and developed a real interest in this young fellow. Naomi said why not let him come with you? And I actually began to think he would be good company."

I interrupt to observe that George Swiebel conceived himself to be especially gifted with young people. They never saw *him* as a funny old fellow. He took pride in his readiness to understand. He had many special and privileged relationships. He was accepted by youth, by the blacks, by gypsies and bricklayers, by Arabs in the desert, and by tribesmen in every remote place he had ever visited. With exotics he was a hit, making instantaneous human contact, invited to their tents and their cellars and their most intimate private circles. As Walt Whitman did with the draymen, clam diggers, and roughs, as Hemingway did with the Italian infantry and Spanish bullfighters, so George always did in Southeast Asia or in the Sahara or in Latin America, or wherever he went. He made his trips of this sort as often as he could manage, and the natives were always his brothers and were mad about him.

His letter went on: "Naomi really wanted the boy to be with you. Remember we were going to meet in Rome? But when I was ready to leave, Szathmar still hadn't heard from you. My contact in Nairobi was waiting and when Naomi begged me to take her son, Louie—he needed adult masculine influences and her own boy friend, with whom she drinks beer and goes to the hockey game, was not the type to help and, in fact, was part of the kid's problem—I was sympathetic. I thought I would like to learn about the dope scene anyway, and the boy must have some character, you know, if he got the monkey off his back (as they use to say in our time) without outside help. Naomi sets a good table, there was lots to eat and drink, I got pretty mellow, and I said to this Louie with the beard, 'Okay, kid, meet me at O'Hare, TWA flight so and so, Thursday, half past five.' I told Naomi I'd drop him off with you on the return trip. She's a good old broad. I think you should have married her thirty years ago. She's our kind of people. She gave me a thank-you hug and cried quite a bit. So Thursday at flight time this skinny young character with the beard is hanging around near the gate in his sneakers and shirt sleeves. I say to him, 'Where's your coat?' and he says, 'What do I need a coat for in Africa?' And, 'Where's your luggage?' I said. He told me he liked to travel light. Naomi provided his ticket but nothing else. I outfitted him from my own duffel bag. He needed a windbreaker in London. I took him to a sauna to warm him up and gave him a Jewish dinner in East End. So far the boy was good company and told me a whole lot about the drug scene. Damn interesting. We went on to Rome and from Rome to Khartoum and from Khartoum to Nairobi where my friend Ezekiel was supposed to meet me. But Ezekiel didn't show. He was in the bush, collecting beryllium. Instead, we were met by his cousin Theo, this marvelous tall black man, built like a whippet, and black, black, shining deep black. Louie said, 'I dig this Theo. I'm gonna learn Swahili and rap with him.' Okay, fine. The next day we rented a Volks Minibus from the German Tourist Agency lady Ezekiel had worked for. She organized the trip I took with him four years ago. Then I bought clothing for the bush and even a pair of suède desert boots for Louie and railroad caps and smoked glasses and lots of other stuff, and we took off into the bush. Where we were bound for I didn't know, but I developed a relationship with Theo very quickly. To tell the truth, I was happy. You know I always had the feeling that Africa was the place where the human species got its start. That was the feeling that came to me when I visited the Olduvai Gorge and met Professor Leakey on my last trip. He absolutely convinced me that this was where man came from. I knew from my own intuition, like a sense of homecoming, that Africa was my place. And even if it wasn't, it was better than South Chicago anytime and I'd rather meet up with lions than use public transportation. For the weekend before I left Chicago, twenty-five murders were reported. I hate to think what the real figure must be. Last time I took a ride on the Jackson Park El, two cats were slicing off a guy's pants pocket with razor blades while he pretended to be asleep. I was one of twenty people watching. Couldn't do a thing.

"Before leaving Nairobi we visited the game park and saw a lioness jumping on wild pigs. The whole thing was really glorious. Then we drove off and before long we were wallowing in the deep red dust of the back roads and driving under the shade of marvelous big trees, like with roots in the air, and all the black people looked to be sleepwalking because of their nightgown- and pajama-type of costume. We'd enter some village where a whole lot of natives would be working on old foot-pedal Singer sewing machines under the open sky, and out again among the giant anthills like nipples all over the landscape. You know how I love sociable, affectionate situations and I was having the time of my life with this marvelous black man Theo. It wasn't long before we really became very close. The trouble was with Louie. In the city he was bearable but as soon as we got into the bush, he was something else again. I don't know what's with these kids. Are they feeble, sick, or what? The generation of the Sixties, now about twenty-eight years old, already are invalids and basket cases. He'd lie there all day long, acting dazed. Dog-tired we'd arrive in some village in the Minibus and the young fellow who had been pissing and moaning for two hours would begin to cry for his milk. Yes, that's right. Bottled, homogenized American milk. He'd never been without it and it made him frantic. It was easier to kick the heroin habit than the milk. It sounded innocent enough, and even amusing, why shouldn't a kid from Cook County, Illinois, have his lousy milk? But I tell you, Charlie, the thing got desperate two days out of Nairobi. He learned the Swahili word for milk from Theo, and when we drove into any little cluster of huts, he leaned out of the window and began to shout for it. '*Mizuah! Mizuah! Mizuah! Mizuah!*' as we bumped over the ruts. You would have thought he was in agony for his fix. What did the natives know about this damn *mizuah* of his? They kept a few little cans for the Britishers' tea and couldn't understand what he meant, had never even seen a glass of milk. They did their best with a trickle of evaporated stuff, while I felt—to tell the truth, I was humiliated. This was no way to travel in the wilds. After a few days this skinny character with his hair and beard and sharp nose and completely unreasonable eyes—there was just no rapport. My health went into reverse. I began to have a bad stitch in the side of my belly so that I couldn't sit comfortably or even lie down. The whole middle of me became inflamed, sensitive—horrible! I was trying to relate to the natural surroundings and the primitive life, the animals, etc. This should have been bliss for me. I could almost see the bliss ahead of me like heat waves in the road and couldn't catch up with it. I had fucked myself out of it by being such a do-gooder. And it only got worse. Ezekiel had left messages along the way and Theo said we should be catching up with him in a few days. I hadn't seen any beryllium yet. Ezekiel was supposedly making a tour of all the beryllium locations. We couldn't reach these in our Minibus. You had to have a Land Rover or a Jeep. Ezekiel had a Jeep. So we went along like this and every once in a while we hit a tourist hotel where Louie demanded *mizuah* and grabbed off the best food. If there were sandwiches, he seized the meat and left me nothing but cheese and Spam. If there was a little hot water, he bathed first and left nothing but dirt for me. The sight of his skinny ass as he toweled himself filled me with one complete hot passion, either to hit him on the butt with a two by four or give him a terrific boot.

"The payoff was when he got after Theo to teach him Swahili words and the first thing he asked for, naturally, was 'motherfucker.' Charlie, there is absolutely no such thing in Swahili. Louie couldn't accept the fact that in the very heart of Africa this expression should not exist. He said to me, 'Man, after all this is Africa. This Theo has got to be kidding. Is it a secret they won't tell the white man?' He swore he wasn't coming back to America without being able to say it. The truth was that Theo couldn't even grasp the concept. He had no difficulty with part one, the sex act. And of course he understood part two, the mother. But bringing them together was beyond him. Several long days Louie worked to get it out of him. Then one evening Theo at last understood. He put these two things together. When the idea became clear, he jumped up, he grabbed the jack handle out of the Minibus and swung at Louie's head. He landed a pretty bad hit on the shoulder and lamed him. This gave me a certain amount of satisfaction but I had to break it up. I had to pull Theo to the ground and get my knees on his arm and hold his head while I reasoned with him. I said it was a misunderstanding. However, Theo was all shook up and never talked to Louie again after this mother-blasphemy had struck home. As for Louie, he griped and bitched about his shoulder so long that I couldn't continue to follow Ezekiel. I decided that we would go back to town and wait for him. Actually we had been making an enormous circle and were now only fifty or sixty miles from Nairobi. It didn't look to me like any beryllium mine. I concluded that Ezekiel had been collecting or perhaps even stealing beryllium here and there. In Nairobi we X-rayed the young fellow. Nothing was broken but the Dr. did tie his arm in a sling. Before I took him to the airport we sat at an outdoor café while he drank several bottles of milk. He had had it with Africa. The place had become phony under civilized influence and denied its heritage. He said, 'I'm all shook up. I'm going straight home.' I took from him the outfit I had bought for his use in the bush and gave it to Theo. Then Louie said he had to bring African souvenirs home for Naomi. We went to tourist shops where he bought his mother a deadly ugly Masai spear. He was due to reach Chicago at 3 a.m. I knew he had no money in his pocket. 'How are you getting home from O'Hare?' I said. 'Why of course I'll phone Mother.' 'Don't wake Mother. Take a taxi. You can't hitchhike on Mannheim Road with that fucking spear.' I gave him a twenty-dollar bill and drove him to the airport. Happy for the first time in a month, I watched him in shirt sleeves and sling climbing up the stairs and carrying the Assegai for Mother into the plane. Then at about a thousand miles an hour ground speed, he took off for Chicago.

"As for the beryllium, Ezekiel showed up with a barrel of it. We went to an English lawyer whose name I had from Alec Szathmar and tried to set up a deal. Ezekiel needed about five thousand dollars worth of equipment, a Land Rover, a truck, etc. 'Good,' I said. 'We've got ourselves a partnership and I'm leaving this check in escrow and he'll pay it over as soon as you give him a title to the mine.' There was no title forthcoming nor any way to prove these semiprecious stones were legally come by. I'm going down to the coast now to visit the old slave towns and try to recover something from this double-disaster of Naomi's kid and our sour beryllium deal. I'm sorry to say that some kind of African con was going on. I don't think Ezekiel and Theo were on the level. Szathmar sent me your address, in care of his colleague in Nairobi. Nairobi is fancier than ever. Downtown it looks more like Scandinavia than East Africa. I'm getting on the night train to Mombasa. Coming home via Addis Ababa and maybe even Madrid. Yours with love."

WHILE I was absorbed in boning a slice of *merluza* for Roger, Pilar came into the dining room and whispered as she leaned over me with her high-aproned bosom, that an American gentleman was asking for me. I was delighted. Stirred, anyway. No one had called on me before, not in ten weeks. Could this be George? Or Koffritz, come to fetch Roger? Also Pilar, with cool apron, warm white face, large brown eyes leaning toward me with her powder fragrance, was being extremely discreet. Had she swallowed the widower story? Did she nevertheless know that had a deep legitimate sorrow and good reason to dress in black? "Shall I ask the señor to come to the *comedor* to take coffee?" said Pilar, and moved her eyes from me to the kid and back to me. I said that I would talk with my visitor in the salon if she would sit with the orphan for me and make him eat his fish.

Then I went to the salon, a room seldom used and crowded with old plushy dusty objects. It was kept dark, like a chapel, and I had never seen the sun in it before. Light now poured in, revealing many religious pictures and treasures of bric-a-brac on the wainscoting. Underfoot were rubbishy ensnaring scatter rugs. It all gave the effect of a period vanishing together with the emotions one had had for this period and the individuals who had felt such emotions. My caller stood by the window, aware that I was catching the dust-filled sunlight straight in the eyes and couldn't see his face. The dust swirled everywhere. I was as dense in these motes as an aquarium fish in bubbles. My caller was still pulling at the drapes to let in more sun and he sent down the dust of a whole century.

"You?" I said.

"Yes," said Rinaldo Cantabile, "that's who. You thought I was in jail."

"Thought, and wished. And hoped. How did you track me here, and what do you want?"

"You're sore at me. Okay, I admit that was a bad scene. But I'm here to make up for it."

"Was that your purpose in coming here? What you can do for me is go away. I'd like that best."

"Honestly I came to do you good. You know," he said, "when I was a little kid my grandmother on Taylor Street was laid out in a parlor like this with a ton of flowers. Wow, I never thought I'd see another roomful of such old-time crap. But leave it to Charlie Citrine. Look at these branches from Palm Sunday fifty years back. It stinks on the staircase and you're a fastidious guy. But it must agree with you here. You look okay —better, in fact. You haven't got those brown circles you had under your eyes in Chicago. You know what my guess is? That paddle ball game put too much strain on you. You here alone?"

"No, I've got Renata's little boy."

"The boy? And where is she?" I didn't answer. "She blew you off. I see. You're broke, and she's not the type for a tacky boardinghouse like this. She took up with somebody else and left you to be the sitter. You're what limeys call the nanny. That's a riot. And what's the black armband for?"

"Here I'm a widower."

"You're an impostor," said Cantabile. "Now that I like."

"I couldn't think what else to do."

"I won't give you away. I think it's terrific. I can't figure how you get yourself into these situations. You're a superintelligent high-grade person, the friend of poets, a kind of poet yourself. But being a widower in a dump like this is a two-day gag at most and you've been here two months, that's what I don't understand. You're a lively type of guy. When you and me were tiptoeing on the catwalk of that skyscraper in a high wind sixty stories up, hey, wasn't that something? Honestly, I wasn't sure you had the guts."

"I was intimidated."

"You entered into the spirit of the thing. But I want to tell you something a little more serious—you and that poet Fleisher, you really were a quality team."

"When did you get out of jail?"

"Are you kidding? When was I in jail? You don't know your own town at all. Any little Polish girl on confirmation day knows more than you, with all your books and prizes."

"You had a smart lawyer."

"Punishment is on the way out. The courts don't believe in it. Judges understand that no realistic sane person goes around Chicago without protection."

Well here he was. He arrived in a sort of torrent as if the tail wind that drove his jet had gotten into him somehow. He was high, exuberant, showing off, and he transmitted the usual sense of boundlessness, of cranky dangers—chanciness I called it. "I just now blew in from Paris," he said, pale, dark-haired, happy. His chancy eyes glittered under the dagger-hilt brows, his nose was full at the bottom and white. "You know neckties. What's your opinion of this one I bought on the rue de Rivoli?"

He was dressed with brilliant elegance in a double-knit sort of whipcord pattern and black lizard shoes. He was laughing, nerves were beating in his cheeks and temples. He had only two moods, this and the threatening one.

"Did you trace me through Szathmar?"

"If Szathmar could get you into a pushcart he'd sell you by the slice on Maxwell Street."

"Szathmar is a good fellow in his own way. From time to time I speak harshly of Szathmar, but I really love him, you know. You invented all that stuff about the kleptomaniac girl."

"Yes, but what of it? It could have been true. No, I didn't get your address from him. Lucy got it from Humboldt's widow. She phoned her in Belgrade to check out some facts. She's almost done with the thesis."

"She's very tenacious."

"You should read her dissertation."

"Never," I said.

"Why not?" He was offended. "She's smart. You might even learn something."

"I might."

"But you don't want to hear any more about your pal, is that it?"

"Something like that."

"Why, because he blew it—he goofed? This big jolly character with so many talents caved in, just a fucking failure, crazy and a deadbeat, so enough of him?"

I wouldn't reply. I saw no point in discussing such a thing with Cantabile.

"What would you say if I told you that your friend Humboldt scored a success from the grave. I talked to that woman Kathleen myself. There were some points I had to discuss with her and I thought she might have some answers. Incidentally, she's real keen on you. You've got a friend there."

"What is this about a success from the grave? What did you talk to her about?"

"A certain movie scenario. The one you described to Polly and me just before Christmas in your apartment."

"The North Pole? Amundsen, Nobile, and Caldofreddo?"

"Caldofreddo is what I mean. Caldofreddo. You wrote that? Or Humboldt? Or both?"

"We did it together. It was horseplay. A vein of humor we used to have. Kid stuff."

"Charlie, listen, you and I need to reach a preliminary agreement, have an understanding between us. I've already taken a certain amount of responsibility, put out money and effort, made arrangements. I'm entitled to ten percent, minimum."

"In a minute I'll ask what the devil you're talking about. But tell me first about Stronson. What happened to him?"

"Never mind Stronson now. Forget Stronson." Cantabile then shouted, "Fuck Stronson!" This must have been heard all over the *pensión*. After that his head shook a few times as if with vibration or recoil. But he collected himself, fetched his shirt-cuffs from under the coat sleeves, and said in quite a different tone, "Oh, Stronson. Well, there was a riot in his office by people who got screwed. But he wasn't even there. His big worry should be obvious to you. He lost a lot of Mafia money. They owned him. He had to do anything they said. So about a month ago they called the obligation in. Did you read about the Fraxo burglary in Chicago? No? Well, it was a sensational heist. And who should be flying afterward to Costa Rica with a bag, a big valise full of dollars to stash away?"

"Stronson was caught?"

"The Costa Rican officials put him in jail. He's in jail now. Charlie, can you actually prove that you and Von Humboldt Fleisher actually wrote this thing about Caldofreddo? That's what I asked Kathleen. Have you got any proof?"

"I think so."

"But you want to know why. The why is kind of strange Charlie, and you'll hardly believe it. However, you and I have to have an understanding before I explain things. It's complicated. I've taken a hand in this. I've laid out a plan. I've got people standing by. And I've really done it mostly out of friendship. Now take a look at this. I've prepared a paper that I want you to sign." He laid a document before me. "Take your time," he said.

"This is a regular contract. I can't bear to read these things. What do you want, Cantabile? I've never read a contract through in all my life."

"But you've signed them, haven't you? By the hundreds, I bet. So sign this one too."

"Oh God! Cantabile, you're back again to hassle me. I was beginning to feel so well here in Madrid. And calmer. And stronger. Suddenly you're here."

"When you get into a tizzy, Charlie, you're hopeless. Try to check yourself. I'm here to do you a major favor, for Christ's sake. Don't you trust me?"

"Von Humboldt Fleisher once asked me that and I said, 'Do I trust the Gulf Stream or the South Magnetic Pole or the orbit of the moon?'"

"Charles" (to calm me he addressed me formally) "what's to get so excited? To begin with this is a one-shot deal. For me it provides like a regular agent's fee—ten percent of your gross up to fifty thousand dollars, fifteen percent of the next twenty-five, and twenty percent on the balance, with a ceiling of one hundred and fifty thousand. So I can't get more than twenty grand out of this any way you look at it. Is that a colossal fortune? And I'm doing it more for you, and for a few kicks, you poor dimwit. A lot you got to lose. You're a fucking baby-sitter in a Spanish boardinghouse."

These last weeks I had been far from the world, beholding it from a considerable altitude and rather strangely. This white-nosed, ultranervous, overreaching, gale-force Cantabile had brought me back, one hundred percent. I said, "For just an instant I was almost glad to see you, Rinaldo. I always like people who seem to know what they want and behave boldly. But I am very happy to tell you now that I will not sign any paper."

"You won't even read it?"

"Definitely not."

"If I were really a bad guy I'd go away and let you miss out on a fortune of money, you creep. Well, let's have a verbal agreement. I put you on to one hundred thousand dollars. I manage the whole deal and you promise me ten percent."

"But of what?"

"You never read *Time* or *Newsweek*, I suppose, unless you're waiting to have a tooth drilled. But there is a sensational movie out, the biggest hit of the year. On Third Avenue the ticket line is about three blocks long and in London and Paris the same. Do you know the name of this hit? It's called *Caldofreddo*, and it's based on the scenario you and Humboldt wrote. It's got to be grossing millions."

"And is it the same? Are you certain?"

"Polly and I went to see it in New York and we both remembered what you described to us in Chicago. You don't have to take my word for it. You can see it yourself."

"Is it showing in Madrid?"

"No, you'll have to fly back to Paris with me."

"Well, Caldofreddo is the name we gave our protagonist all right. He's one of the survivors of the crash of Umberto Nobile's dirigible in the Arctic?"

"Eats human flesh! Exposed by the Russians as a cannibal! Goes back to his Sicilian village! An ice-cream vendor! All kids in town love him."

"You mean someone made something of such a farrago?"

Cantabile cried, "They're crooks, crooks, crooks! Those fuckers have stolen you blind! They've made a film out of your idea. How did they ever get it?"

"Well," I said, "all I know is that Humboldt gave the outline to a man named Otto Klinsky in the RCA building. He had an idea that he could reach Sir Laurence Olivier's hairdresser through a relative of some scrubwoman who was the mother of a friend of Mrs. Klinsky. Did they actually reach Olivier? Does he play the role?"

"No, it's some other Englishman, like the Charles Laughton or Ustinov type. Charlie, this is a hell of a good picture. Now, Charlie, if we can prove your authorship, we've really got those guys. I told them, you know, I'm ready to slaughter them. I'm in a position to throw their balls into the Osterizer."

"You can't have many equals when it comes to threatening," I said.

"Well, I had to put heat on them if I didn't want a long business in court. We're looking for a fast settle. What kind of proof have you got?"

"What Humboldt did," I explained, "was to send himself a copy of the scenario by registered mail. This has never been opened."

"You've got it?"

"Yes, I found it among the papers he left me with a note that tells all."

"Why didn't he copyright the idea?"

"There is no other way in these cases. But the method is

perfectly legal. Humboldt would have known. He always had more lawyers than the White House."

"Those movie bastards didn't have the time of day for me. Now we'll see. Our next move is this," he said. "We fly to Paris. . . ."

"We?"

"I am advancing expense money."

"But I don't want to go. I shouldn't even be here now. After lunch I generally sit in my room."

"What for? You just sit?"

"I sit and withdraw into myself."

"A hell of an egotistical thing to do," he said.

"On the contrary, I try to see and hear the outer world with no static whatever from within, an empty vessel, and completely silent."

"What is that supposed to do for you?"

"Well, according to my manual, if you sit quiet enough, everything in the outer world, every flower, every animal, every action, will eventually unveil secrets undreamed of—I'm quoting."

He stared at me with venturesome eyes and dagger brows. He said, "Damn it, you're not going to turn into one of those transcendental-type weirdos. You don't enjoy that, do you, just sitting quiet?"

"I enjoy it deeply."

"Come to Paris with me."

"Rinaldo, I don't want to come to Paris."

"You put your back up in the wrong place and you're passive in the wrong place. You've got everything arsy-versy. You come along to Paris and look at that picture. It'll only take a day or two. You can stay at the George V or the Meurice. It'll add strength to our case. I hired two good lawyers, one French and one American. We'll have to open that sealed envelope before witnesses under oath. Maybe we should get it done in the US Embassy and have the commercial attaché and the military attaché. So come on, pack your bag, Charlie. There's a plane in two hours."

"No I don't think I will. It's true I've got no money left, but I've been doing better without money than I ever did with it. And I don't want to leave the kid."

"Don't act like a granny about that kid."

"Anyway, I don't like Paris."

"You don't like Paris? What have you got against Paris?"

"A prejudice. For me Paris is a ghost town."

"You're out of your head. You should see the lines on the Champs-Elysées waiting to get into *Caldofreddo*. And it's your achievement. That should give you a feeling of secret power—a kick. I know you're sore because the French made a phony knight of you and you took it like an insult. Or maybe you hate them because of Israel. Or their record in the last war."

"Don't talk nonsense."

"When I try to guess what you're thinking I have to try nonsense. Otherwise it would take me a million years to figure out why to you Paris is a ghost town. Would old Chicago aldermen retire to a ghost town to spend their graft-money? Come on Charlie, we'll eat pressed duck tonight at the Tour d'Argent."

"No, that kind of food makes me ill."

"Well then give me the stuff to take back with me—the envelope Humboldt mailed to himself."

"No, Cantabile, I won't do that either."

"Why the hell not?"

"Because you're not trustworthy. I've got another copy of it, though. You can have that. And I'm willing to write a letter. A notarized letter."

"That won't do it."

"If your friends want to see the original they can come to me in Madrid."

"You irritate the shit out of me," said Cantabile. "I'm about to hit the ceiling." Incensed, he glared at me. Then he made a further effort to be reasonable. "Humboldt has some family yet, doesn't he? I asked Kathleen. There's an old uncle in Coney Island."

I had forgotten Waldemar Wald. Poor old man, he lived in kitchen odors, too, in a back room. He needed rescuing, certainly, from the nursing home. "You're right, there is an uncle," I said.

"What about his interest? What, just because you have a mental thing against Paris? You can pay a maid to look after the kid. This is a big deal, Charlie."

"Well, perhaps I should go," I said.

"Now you're talking."

"I'll pack a bag."

So we flew. That same evening Cantabile and I were on the Champs-Elysées waiting with our tickets to get into the vast movie house near the rue Marbeuf. Even for Paris the weather was bad. It was sleeting. I felt thinly dressed and became aware that my shoe soles had worn through and that my feet were getting wet. The queue was dense, the young people in the crowd were cheerful enough but Cantabile and I were both displeased. Humboldt's sealed envelope had been locked in the hotel vault and I had the claim check. Rinaldo had quarreled with me about possession of this brass disc. He wanted it in his pocket as a sign that he was my bona-fide representative.

"Give it to me," he said.

"No. Why should I?"

"Because I'm the natural one to take care of it. That's my kind of thing."

"I'll take care of it."

"You'll pull out your hankie and lose that check," he said. "*You* don't know what you're doing. You're absent-minded."

"I'll keep it."

"You were ornery about the contract, too. You wouldn't even read it," he said.

The ice beat on my hat and shoulders. I disliked intensely the smoke of French cigarettes. Above us in the lights were colossal posters of Otway as Caldofreddo and of the Italian actress, Silvia Sottotutti, or something of the sort, who played the role of his daughter. Cantabile was right, in a way, it was a curious experience to be the unrecognized source of this public attraction and to be standing in the sleet—it made one feel like a phantom presence. After two months of what was virtually a retreat in Madrid it felt like backsliding to be here, in the fog and glitter of the Champs-Elysées, under this icy pelting. At the Madrid airport I had picked up a copy of Baudelaire's *Intimate Journals* to read on the plane and to insulate me from Cantabile's frantic conversation. In Baudelaire I had found the following piece of curious advice: Whenever you receive a letter from a creditor write fifty lines upon some extraterrestrial subject and you will be saved. What this implied was that the *vie quotidienne* drove you from the globe, but the deeper implication was that real life flowed between *here* and *there*. Real life was a relationship between *here* and *there*. Cantabile, one thousand percent *here*, bore this out. He was acting up. He was feverish with me about the claim-check. He fought with the *ouvreuse* who took us to our seats. She was enraged by the small tip he gave her. She took his hand and slapped the coin into his palm.

"You bitch!" he yelled at her, and wanted to chase her up the aisle.

I caught him by the arm and said, "Cool it."

Again I was part of a French audience. Last April Renata and I had come to this very theater. In fact I had lived in Paris in 1955. I quickly learned that this was no place for me. I need a little more fondness from people than a foreigner is likely to get here, and I was then still suffering from Demmie's death. However, there was no time now to think of such things. The picture was beginning. Cantabile said, "Feel in your pocket, make sure you've still got that check. We're screwed if you've lost it."

"It's here. Easy, boy," I said.

"Hand it over. Let me enjoy the picture," he said. I ignored him.

Then with great crashes of music the film began to roll. It opened with shots from the Twenties in the old newsreel manner—the first conquest of the North Pole by Amundsen and Umberto Nobile who flew in a dirigible from Scandinavia to Alaska. This was played by excellent comedians, highly stylized. I was enormously pleased. They were delicious. We saw the Pope blessing the expedition and Mussolini haranguing from his balcony. The competition between Amundsen and Nobile increased in hostility. When a little girl presented Amundsen with a bouquet, Nobile snatched it away; Amundsen gave orders, Nobile countermanded them. The Norwegians bickered with the Italians on the airship. Gradually we recognized, behind the *Time Marches On* style of these events, the presence of old Mr. Caldofreddo now in his ancient

Sicilian village. These flashes of recollection were superimposed upon the daily existence of this amiable old gent, the ice-cream vendor who is loved by the kiddies, the affectionate father of Silvia Sottotutti. In his youth Caldofreddo had served with Nobile on two transpolar flights. The third, under Nobile's sole command, ended in a disaster. The dirigible went down in the Arctic seas. The crew was scattered over the ice floes. Receiving radio signals from the survivors, the Russian icebreaker *Krassin* came to the rescue. Amundsen was handed a cable telling of the disaster while he was drinking deeply at a banquet—according to Humboldt, who had private information about everything, the man had been drinking like a fish. Immediately he announced that he was organizing an expedition to save Nobile. It was all as we had laid it out in Princeton years and years ago. Amundsen chartered a plane. He quarreled violently with his French pilot, who warned him that the aircraft was dangerously overloaded. He commanded him to take off, anyhow. They crashed into the sea. I was shocked to see how effective the comic interpretation of this disaster was. I remembered now that Humboldt and I had disagreed on this. He had insisted that it would be extremely funny. And so it was. The plane sank. Thousands of people were laughing. I wondered how he would have liked that.

The next portion of the film was all mine. It was I who did the research and wrote the scenes in which the rescued Caldofreddo ran wild aboard the *Krassin*. The sin of eating human flesh was too much for him to bear. To the astonishment of the Russian crew, he ran amuck, shouting gibberish. He hacked at a table with a large knife, he tried to drink scalding water, he hurled his body against the bulkheads. The sailors wrestled him to the ground. The suspicious ship's doctor emptied his stomach with a pump and found human tissue under the microscope. I was responsible also for the big scene in which Stalin directs the contents of Caldofreddo's stomach to be exhibited in a jar on Red Square under great banners denouncing cannibalistic capitalism. I added also the rage of Mussolini at this news, the calm of Calvin Coolidge in the White House as he prepared to get into bed for his daily siesta. All this I watched in a state of elation. Mine! All had originated in my head in Princeton, New Jersey, twenty years ago. It was not a big achievement. It didn't ring bells in the far universe. It did nothing about brutality, inhumanity, it didn't clarify much or prevent anything. Nevertheless there was something in it. It was pleasing hundreds of thousands, millions of spectators. Of course, it was ingeniously directed and George Otway as Caldofreddo gave a wonderful performance. This Otway, an Englishman in his thirties, strongly resembled Humboldt. At the moment when he threw himself at the cabin walls, as I have seen maddened apes do in the monkey house, battering the partitions with heart-rending recklessness, I was stabbed with the thought of how Humboldt had fought the police when they took him away to Bellevue. Ah, poor character, poor fighting furious weeping hollering Humboldt. His flowers were aborted in the bulb. The colors never came into the light, they rotted in his chest. And the resemblance between Otway in the cabin and Humboldt was so uncanny that I began to cry. As the whole theater rocked with delight, shouting with laughter, I sobbed aloud. Cantabile said in my ear, "What a picture, hey? What did I tell you? Even you're laughing your head off."

Yes, and now Humboldt was spread out somewhere, his soul in some other part of the creation, there where souls waited for sustenance that only we, the living, could send from the earth, like grain to Bangla Desh. Alas for us, born by the millions, the billions, like the bubbles of effervescent drink. I had a world-wide dizzy glimpse of the living and the dead, of humanity either laughing its head off as pictures of man-eating comedy unrolled on the screen or vanishing in great waves of death, in flames and battle agonies, in starving continents. And then I had a partial vision of flying blind through darkness and then coming through a break above a metropolis. It glittered on the ground in icy drops, far below. I tried to divine whether we were landing or flying on. We flew on.

"Are they following your outline? Are they using it?" said Cantabile.

"Yes. They're doing it very well. They've added lots of their own ideas," I said.

"Try not to be so big about it. I want you in a fighting mood tomorrow."

I told Cantabile, "The Russians proved their case, according to the Doctor's statement, not only by pumping the stomach but also by examination of the man's excrement. The stools of the starving are hard and dry. This man claimed he had eaten nothing. But it was clear that he hadn't missed many meals, on the ice floe."

"They could have put that in. Stalin wouldn't have hesitated to put a crock of shit on Red Square. And you can do that nowdays in a picture."

The scene had changed to Caldofreddo's little town in Sicily where no one knew his sin, where he was just a jolly old man who peddled ice cream and played in the village band. As I listened to him tootle, I felt that there was something important about the contrast between his little arpeggios and the terrible modern complexity of his position. Lucky the man who has nothing more to say or play than these easy melodies. Are there still such people around? It was disconcerting also to see, as Otway was puffing at the trumpet, a face so much like Humboldt's. And since Humboldt had gotten into the film, I looked for myself as well. I thought that something in my nature might be seen in Caldofreddo's daughter, played by Silvia Sottotutti. Her personality expressed a sort of painful willingness or joyful anxiety which I thought that I had, too. I didn't care for the man in the role of her fiancé, with his short legs and his wide-angled jaw and flat face and lowish brow. It was possible that I identified him with Flonzaley. A man had once followed us at the Furniture Show who must have been Flonzaley. Signals had passed between Renata and him. . . . I had figured out, incidentally, that as Mrs. Flonzaley Renata was going to have a very limited social life in Chicago. Undertakers couldn't be very popular dinner guests, except with other undertakers. To be free from this occupational curse she'd have to travel a lot with him, and even on a Caribbean cruise, at the Captain's Table, they'd have to hope and pray that no one would turn up from the home town to ask, "You don't happen to be Flonzaley of Flonzaley Mortuaries, do you?" Thus Renata's happiness would be impaired, as the splendor of the Sicilian sky was stained for Caldofreddo by his dark act in the Arctic. Even in his trumpet-playing I detected this. I thought that there was one key of his trumpet which, when pushed down, drove right against the man's heart.

Now the Scandinavian journalist came to town, doing research for a book on Amundsen and Nobile. He tracked down poor Caldofreddo and began to molest him. The old fellow said, "You've got the wrong party. That was never me." "No, you're the man all right," said the journalist. He was one of those emancipated people from northern Europe who have expelled shame and darkness from the human breast, an excellent piece of casting. The two men had a conversation on a mountainside. Caldofreddo begged him to go away and leave him in peace. When the journalist refused, he fell into a fit similar to the one he had had on the *Krassin*. But this one, forty years later, was an old man's frenzy. It contained more strength and wickedness of soul than of body. In this seizure of pleading and rage, weakness and demonic despair, Otway was simply extraordinary.

"Was this the way you had it in your scenario?" said Cantabile.

"More or less."

"Give me that claim check," he said. He thrust his hand into my pocket. I realized that he was inspired by Caldofreddo's fit. He was so stirred that he had lost his head. More to defend myself than to keep the disc, I clutched his arm. "Get your hand out of my pocket, Cantabile."

"I have to take care of it. You're not responsible. A man who's been pussy-whipped. Not in your right mind."

We were openly fighting. I couldn't see what the maniac on the screen was doing because this other maniac was all over me. As one of my authorities said, the difference between the words "command" and "convince" is the difference between democracy and dictatorship. Here was a man who was crazy because he never had to persuade himself of anything! Suddenly it gave me as much despair to have thought this as to fight Cantabile off. This thinking would make a nitwit of me. As when Cantabile threatened me with baseball bats and I thought of Lorenz's wolves or of sticklebacks, or when he forced me into a toilet stall, I thought . . . All occasions were translated into thoughts and then the thoughts informed against me. I would die of these intellectual quirks. People began to cry out behind us, "*Dispute! Bagarre! Emmerdeurs!*" They roared, "*Dehors . . . !*" or "*Flanquez les à la porte!*"

"They're calling for the bouncer, you fool!" I said. Cantabile took his hand out of my pocket and we turned our attention to the screen again in time to see a boulder pried loose by Caldofreddo hurtling down the mountainside toward the journalist in his Volvo while the old man, appalled at himself, cried warnings and then fell on his knees and thanked the Virgin when the Scandinavian was spared. After this attempted murder Caldofreddo made a public confession in the village square. Finally he was given a hearing by a jury of townspeople in the ruins of the Greek theater on a Sicilian hillside. This ended with a choric scene of forgiveness and reconciliation—just as Humboldt, with *Oedipus at Colonus* in mind, would have wanted it.

When the lights came on and Cantabile turned toward the near aisle I made my exit by the far one. He caught up with me on the Champs-Elysées, saying, "Don't be sore, Charlie. That's just the breed of dog I am, to protect things like that claim check. What if you're mugged and rolled? Then who even knows what box the envelope is in? And five people are coming tomorrow morning to inspect the evidence. All right, I'm a high-strung fellow. I just want everything to go right. And you've been so hurt by that broad you're a hundred times more out of it than you ever were in Chicago. That's what I meant by pussy-whipped. Now why don't we pick up a couple of French hookers. I'll treat. Rebuild your ego a little."

"I'm going to sleep."

"I'm just trying to make up. I know it's hard for somebody like you having to share the earth with nuts like me. Well, let's go and have a drink. You're all ruffled and upset."

But I wasn't upset at all, really. A hard full day, even full of nonsense, acquits me of nonfeasance, satisfies my conscience. After four glasses of Calvados in the hotel bar I went to bed and slept soundly.

In the morning we met with Maître Furet and the American lawyer, a terribly aggressive man named Barbash, just the sort of representative that Cantabile would choose. Cantabile was deeply pleased. He had promised to deliver me and the evidence—I could see now why he had had such a fit about the check—and here we were, as prearranged, all beautifully coordinated.

The producers of *Caldofreddo* knew that one Charles Citrine, author of a Broadway play, *Von Trenck*, later made into a successful film, claimed to be the source of the original story on which their worldwide hit was based. They sent a couple of Harvard Business School types to meet with us. Poor Stronson now in jail in Miami hadn't come within miles of the image. These two clean, well-spoken, knowledgeable, moderate, completely bald, extremely firm young men were waiting in Barbash's office.

"Are you two gentlemen fully authorized to deal?" Barbash said to them.

"The last word will have to come from our principals."

"Then bring the principals, the guys with the clout. Why are you wasting our time!" said Cantabile.

"Easy, easy does it," Barbash said.

"Citrine is more important than your fucking principals, any day," Cantabile shouted at them. "He's a leader in his field, a Pulitzer winner, a *chevalier* of the Legion of Honor, a friend of the late President Kennedy and the late Senator Kennedy, the late Von Humboldt Fleisher the poet was his buddy and collaborator. Don't give us any shit here! He's busy with important research in Madrid. If he can spare the time to come up here so can your crummy principals. He won't throw his weight around, I'm here to throw it for him. Do this right or you'll see us in court."

To utter his threat relieved him wonderfully of something. His lips (not often silent) were lengthened by a silent smile when one of the young men said, "We've all heard of Mr. Citrine before."

Mr. Barbash now got control of the conversation. His problem, of course, was to subdue Cantabile. "Here are the facts. Mr. Citrine and his friend Mr. Fleisher wrote the outline for this film back in 1952. We are prepared to prove this. Mr. Fleisher mailed a copy of the scenario to himself in January 1960. We have this piece of evidence right here in a sealed envelope, postmarked and receipted."

"Let's go to the US Embassy and open it before witnesses," said Cantabile. "And let the principals get their asses down to the Place de la Concorde, too."

"Have you seen the film *Caldofreddo*?" said Barbash to me.

"I saw it last night. Beautiful performance by Mr. Otway."

"And does it resemble the original story by you and Mr. Fleisher?"

I now saw that a stenotypist sat in the corner at her tripod making a record of this conversation. Shades of Urbanovich's court! I became Citrine the witness. "It couldn't have had any other source," I said.

"Then how did these guys get it? They stole it," said Cantabile. "They might have to face a plagiarism rap."

As the envelope was handed around to be examined, a pang passed through my lower bowel. What if distracted, mad Humboldt had stuffed an envelope with letters, with old bills, with lines on an extraterrestrial subject?

"You are satisfied," said Maître Furet, "that this is the unopened, original object? It will be so deposed."

The Harvard business types agreed that it was on the up. Then the envelope was slit open—it contained a manuscript headed, "An original movie treatment.—Co-authors, Charles Citrine and Von Humboldt Fleisher." As the pages passed from hand to hand I breathed again. The case was proven. There was no doubt about the authenticity of this manuscript. Scene by scene, shot by shot, the picture followed our outline. Barbash made an elaborate and detailed statement for the record. He had obtained a copy of the shooting script. There were almost no departures from our plot.

Humboldt, bless him, had done things right this time.

"This is thoroughly legitimate," said Barbash. "Authentic beyond dispute. I take it you people are insured against such claims?"

"What do we care about that!" said Cantabile.

There was, of course, an insurance policy.

"I don't think our writers ever said anything, one way or another, about an original story," one of the young remarked.

Only Cantabile carried on. His idea was that everybody should be in a fever. But to business people it was just one of those things. I hadn't expected such coolness and decorum. Messrs. Furet, Barbash, and the Harvard Business graduates agreed that long costly lawsuits ought to be avoided.

"And what of Mr. Citrine's co-author?"

So that was all that the name Von Humboldt Fleisher meant to these MBAs from one of our great universities!

"Dead!" I said. This word reverberated with feeling for me.

"Any heirs?"

"One, that I know of."

"We'll take this matter to our principals. What sort of figure have you gentlemen in mind?"

"A big one," said Cantabile. "A percentage of your gross."

"I think we're in a position to ask for a statement of earnings," Barbash argued.

"Let's be more realistic. This will be viewed mainly as a minor nuisance claim."

"What do you mean minor nuisance? It's the whole picture," Cantabile shouted. "We can kill your group!"

"A little calmer, Mr. Cantabile, please. We have a serious claim here," said Barbash. "We'd like to hear what you say after serious consideration."

"Would there be any interest," I said, "in another idea for a screenplay from the same source?"

"Is there one?" said one of the Harvard businessmen. He answered me smoothly, unsurprised. I couldn't help admiring his admirable schooling. You couldn't catch a man like this out.

"*Is* there? You just heard it. We're telling you so," said Cantabile.

"I have here a second sealed envelope," I said. "It contains another original proposal for a picture. Mr. Cantabile, by the way, has nothing to do with this. He's never even heard of the existence of this. His participation is limited to *Caldofreddo* only."

"Let's hope you know what you're doing," said Ronald, angry.

This time I knew perfectly well. "I'm going to ask Mr. Barbash and Maître Furet to represent me also in this matter."

"Us!" Cantabile said.

"Me," I repeated.

"You, of course," Barbash quickly said.

I hadn't lost tons of money for nothing. I had mastered the commercial lingo at least. And as Julius had observed I was a Citrine by birth. "This sealed envelope contains a plot from the same brain that conceived *Caldofreddo*. Why don't you gentlemen ask the people you represent whether they'd like to have a look at it. My price for looking—for looking only, mind you—is five thousand dollars."

"That is what we want," said Cantabile.

But he was ignored. And I felt very much in command. So this was business. Julius, as I've mentioned before, was forever urging me to recognize what he liked to call the Romance of Business. And was this the famous Romance of Business? Why it was nothing but pushiness, rapidity, effrontery. The sense it gave of getting your way was shallow. Compared with the satisfaction of contemplating flowers or of something really serious—trying to get in touch with the dead, for instance—it was nothing, nothing at all.

Paris was not at its most attractive as Cantabile and I walked the Seine. The bankside was now a superhighway. The water looked like old medicine.

"Well, I got 'em for you, didn't I? I promised I'd make you money. What's your Mercedes now? Peanuts. I want twenty percent."

"We agreed on ten."

"Ten if you cut me into that other script. Thought you'd hold out on me, didn't you?"

"I'm going to write to Barbash to say that I want you to be paid ten percent. For *Caldofreddo*."

He said, "You're ungrateful. You never read the paper, you schmuck, and the whole thing would have passed you by without me. Just like the Thaxter business."

"What Thaxter business?"

"You see? You don't know anything. I didn't want to rattle you by telling you about Thaxter till the negotiations got started. You don't know what happened to Thaxter? He was kidnaped in Argentina."

"He wasn't! By whom, terrorists? But why? Why Thaxter? Have they hurt him?"

"America should thank God for its gangsters. The Mafia at least makes sense. These political guys don't know what the hell they're doing. They're snatching and murdering all over South America without rhyme and reason. How should I know why they picked on him. He must have acted like a big shot. They let him send out one letter and he mentioned your name in it. And you didn't even know you were all over the world press."

"What did he say?"

"He appealed to the internationally famous historian and playwright Charles Citrine for help. He said you'd vouch for him."

"Those fellows don't know what they're doing. I hope they won't harm Thaxter."

"They'll be sore as hell when they find out he's a phony."

"I don't understand. What was he pretending? Whom did they take him to be?"

"They're very confused in all those countries," said Cantabile.

"Ah, my old friend Professor Durnwald is probably right when he says how nice it would be to hack off the Western Hemisphere at the isthmus and let the southern part drift away. Only there are so many parts of the earth of which that holds true now."

"Charles, the more commission you pay me, the less you'll have left for those terrorists."

"Me? Why me?"

"Oh, it'll be you all right," said Cantabile.

THAXTER'S captivity by terrorists oppressed me. It made me grieve at heart to imagine him locked in a black cellar with rats and terrified of torture. He was, after all, an innocent sort of person. True, he was not perfectly upright but much of his wrongdoing was simply delirium. Restless, seeking a piece of the action, he had now been cast among even more violently hallucinated parties who cut off ears and planted bombs in mailboxes or hijacked jet planes and slaughtered passengers. The last time I troubled to read a newspaper I noted that an oil company, after paying a ransom of ten million dollars, was still unable to obtain the release of one of its executives from his Argentine kidnapers.

That afternoon from the hotel I wrote to Carl Stewart, Thaxter's publisher. I said, "I understand Pierre has been abducted and that in his appeal for help he has named me. Well, of course, I will give everything I've got to save his life. In a way all his own, he is a wonderful man and I do love him; I have been his faithful friend for more than twenty years. I assume you have been in touch with the State Department and also with the US Embassy in Buenos Aires. Despite the fact that I have written on political matters I am not a political person. Let me put it this way, that for forty years during the worst crises of civilization I read the papers faithfully and this faithful reading did no one any good. Nothing was prevented thereby. I gradually stopped reading the news. It now appears to me, however, and I say this as a dispassionate observer, that between gunboat diplomacy at one extreme and submission to acts of piracy at the other, there ought to be some middle ground for a great power. In this regard, the flabbiness of the United States is disheartening. Are we only now catching up with the lessons of World War I? We learned from Sarajevo not to let acts of terrorism precipitate wars and from Woodrow Wilson that small nations have rights that great ones must respect. But that's it and we have gotten stuck some six decades back and set the world a miserable example by allowing ourselves to be bullied.

"To come back to Thaxter, however, I am wildly anxious about him. As recently as three months ago I would have been able to offer a ransom of $250,000. But that has been swept away by an unfortunate litigation. There is now more money on the horizon. I may soon be able to come up with ten or even twenty thousand and I am prepared to put up that much. I don't see how I can go beyond twenty-five. You would have to advance it. I would give you my note. Perhaps some way could be found to repay me out of Pierre's royalties. If these South American bandits let him go he'll write a whopping account of his experiences. That's the twist things have taken. Formerly life's bitterest misfortunes enriched only the hearts of wretches or were of spiritual value exclusively. But now any frightful event may be a gold mine. I'm sure that if and when poor Thaxter makes it, if they release him, he will strike it rich by writing a book. Hundreds of thousands of people who at this moment don't give a single damn about him will suffer with him intensely. Their souls will be wrung and they will gasp and cry. This is actually very important. I mean that the powers of compassion are now being weakened by an impossible volume of demands. We don't need to go into that, however. I'd be very grateful to you for information, and you may regard this letter as binding on me to come up with dollars for Thaxter. He must have swaggered and put on the dog in his Stetson and Western boots till he impressed those Latin Maoists or Trotskyists. Well, I suppose it's one of those World Historical things, peculiar to our times."

I got this letter off to New York and then flew back to Spain. Cantabile took me to Orly in a cab, now arguing for fifteen percent and beginning to make threats.

As soon as I reached Pensión La Roca I was handed a note on Ritz stationery. It was from the Señora. She wrote, "Kindly deliver Roger to me at 10:30 a.m. tomorrow in the lobby. We are going back to Chicago." I understood why she stipulated lobby. I wouldn't lay violent hands on her in a public place. In her room I might go for her throat or try to drown her in the toilet bowl. So, in the morning, with the kid, I met the old woman, that extraordinary condensation of wild prejudices. In the great circle of the Ritz lobby under the dome, I handed the kid to her. I said, "Good-by, Roger darling, you're going home."

The kid began to cry. The Señora couldn't calm him and accused me of corrupting him, attaching him to myself with chocolates. "You've bribed the boy with sweets."

"I hope Renata is happy in her new state," I said.

"She certainly is. Flonzaley is a high type of man. His IQ is out if this world. Writing books is no proof that you're smart."

"Oh how true that is," I said. "And after all burial was a great step forward. Vico said there was a time when corpses were allowed to rot on the ground and dogs and rats and vultures ate your near and dear. You can't have the dead all over the place. Although Stanton, a member of Lincoln's cabinet, kept his dead wife for nearly a year."

"You look worn out. You have too much on your mind," she said.

Intensity does that to me. I know it's true, but I hate to hear it said. Despair rises up. "*Adiós*, Roger. You're a fine boy and I love you. I'll see you in Chicago soon. Have a good flight with Grandma. Don't cry, kid," I said. I was threatened by tears myself. I left the lobby and walked toward the park. The danger of being struck by speeding cars, masses of them battering from all directions, prevented me from shedding more tears.

At the *pensión* I said that I had sent Roger home to his grandparents until I could readjust myself. The Danish lady from the embassy, Miss Volsted, was still standing by to do the humane thing for my sake. Depressed by Roger's leaving I was almost demoralized enough to take her up on it.

Cantabile telephoned every day from Paris. It was of the greatest importance for him to figure in these deals. I should have thought that Paris, with the many opportunities it offered a man like Cantabile, would distract him from business. Not a bit. He was all business. He kept after Maître Furet and Barbash. He irritated Barbash greatly by going over his head and trying to negotiate independently. Barbash complained to me from Paris. The producers, Cantabile told me, were now offering twenty thousand dollars in settlement. "They should be ashamed of themselves. And what kind of impression did Barbash make on them to get such a puny, insulting offer! He's no good. Our figure is two hundred thousand." Next day he reported, "They're up to thirty now. I've changed my mind again. This Barbash is real tough. I think he's sore at me and taking it out on them. What's two hundred to them, with such a box office? A pimple on the ass. One thing—we have to think about the taxes, and whether we should take payment in foreign currency. I know we can get more in lire. *Caldofreddo* is doing a tremendous business in Milan and Rome. The suckers are standing ten deep. I wonder why the cannibalism gets the Italians, raised on *pasta*. Anyhow, if you'll take lire you can get a lot more money. Of course, Italy is falling apart."

"I'll take dollars. I have a brother in Texas who can invest them in a good thing for me."

"You're lucky to have a kind brother. Are you feeling antsy down there in spic-land?"

"Not a bit. I'm very much at home. I read anthroposophy and I meditate. I'm doing the Prado inch by inch. What about our second scenario?"

"I'm not in on that, so why ask me?"

I said, "No, you're not."

"Then I don't see why I should tell you a damn thing. But I'll tell you anyway, out of courtesy. They are interested. They are damn interested. They've offered Barbash three thousand dollars for a three-week option. They say they need time to show it to Otway."

"Otway and Humboldt look very much alike. Maybe resemblance means something. Some invisible link. I'm convinced that Otway will be attracted by Humboldt's story."

Next afternoon Kathleen Tigler arrived in Madrid. She was on her way to Almería to begin work on a new film. "I'm sorry to tell you," she said. "that the people to whom I sold the option on Humboldt's scenario have decided not to take it up."

"What's that?"

"You remember the outline that Humboldt bequeathed to both of us?"

"Of course."

"I should have sent you your share of the three thousand. Part of my purpose in coming to Madrid was to talk to you about it and draw a contract, settle with you. You've probably forgotten all about it."

"No, I hadn't forgotten," I said. "But it just occurred to me that I've been trying on my own to sell the same property to another group."

"I see," she said. "Selling the same thing to two parties. It would have been very awkward."

All this while, you see, business was going on. Business, with the peculiar autonomy of business, went its own way. Like it or not, we thought its thoughts, spoke its language. What did it matter to business that I suffered a defeat in love, or that I resisted Rebecca Volsted with her urgently blazing face, that I investigated the doctrines of anthroposophy? Business, sure of its own transcendent powers, got us all to interpret life through its practices. Even now, when Kathleen and I had so many private matters to consider, matters of the greatest human importance, we were discussing contracts options producers and sums of money.

"Of course," she said, "you couldn't be bound legally by an agreement I entered into."

"When we met in New York we spoke about a film outline Humboldt and I concocted in Princeton—"

"The one Lucy Cantabile asked me about? Her husband also phoned me in Belgrade and pestered me with mysterious questions."

"—to divert ourselves while Humboldt was scheming to get the chair in poetry."

"You told me it was all nonsense, and I thought no more about it."

"It was lost for twenty years or so, and then someone got around to stealing our original story and turned it into the picture called *Caldofreddo*."

"No! Is that where *Caldofreddo* comes from! You and Humboldt?"

"Have you seen it?"

"Of course I have. Otway's big, big hit was created by the two of you? It's not to be believed."

"Yes, indeed. I've just come from a meeting in Paris at which I proved our authorship to the producers."

"Will they settle with you? They should. You've got a real case against them, haven't you?"

"I die when I think of a lawsuit. Ten more years in the courts? That would be worth fees of four or five hundred thousand to my lawyers. But for me, a man approaching sixty and heading for seventy, there wouldn't be a penny left. I'll take my forty or fifty thousand now."

"Like a mere nuisance claim?" said Kathleen, indignant.

"No, like a man lucky enough to have his higher activities subsidized for a few years. I'll divide the money with Uncle Waldemar, of course. Kathleen, when I heard of Humboldt's will I thought it was just his posthumous way of carrying on more of the same touching tomfoolery. But the legal steps he took were all sound and he was right, damn it, about the value of his papers. He always had a wild hope of hitting the big time. And what do you know? He did! And it wasn't his serious work that the world found a use for. Just these capers."

"Also your capers," said Kathleen. When she smiled quietly she showed a great many small lines in her skin. I was sorry to see these signs of age in a woman whose beauty I remembered well. But you could live with such things if you took the right view of them. After all, these wrinkles were the result of many many many years of amiability. They were the mortal toll taken by a good thing. I was beginning to understand how one reconciled to such alterations. "But to be taken seriously, what do you suppose Humboldt should have done?"

"How can I say that, Kathleen? He did what he could, and lived and died more honorably than most. Being crazy was the conclusion of the joke Humboldt tried to make out of his great disappointment. He was so intensely disappointed. All a man of that sort really asks for is a chance to work his heart out at some high work. People like Humboldt—they express a sense of life, they declare the feelings of their times or they discover meanings or find out the truths of nature, using the opportunities their time offers. When those opportunities are great, then there's love and friendship between all who are in the same enterprise. As you can see in Haydn's praise for Mozart. When the opportunities are smaller, there's spite and rage, insanity. I've been attached to Humboldt for nearly forty years. It's been an ecstatic connection. The hope of having poetry—the joy of knowing the kind of man that created poetry. You know? There's the most extraordinary, unheard-of poetry buried in America, but none of the conventional means known to culture can even begin to extract it. But now this is true of the world as a whole. The agony is too deep, the disorder too big for art enterprises undertaken in the old way. Now I begin to understand what Tolstoi was getting at when he called on mankind to cease the false and unnecessary comedy of history and begin simply to live. It's become clearer and clearer to me in Humboldt's heartbreak and madness. He performed all the stormy steps of that routine. That performance was conclusive. That—it's perfectly plain, now—can't be continued. Now we must listen in secret to the sound of the truth that God puts into us."

"And that's what you call the higher activity—and this is what the money you get from *Caldofreddo* will subsidize. . . . I see," said Kathleen.

"On the assumption commonly made the commonest events of life can only be absurd. Faith *was* called absurd. But now faith will perhaps move these mountains of commonsense absurdity."

"I was going to suggest that you leave Madrid and come down to Almería."

"I see. You're worried about me. I look bad."

"Not exactly. But I can tell you've been under a huge strain. It'll be pleasant weather on the Mediterranean now."

"The Mediterranean, yes. How I'd love a month of blessed peace. But I haven't got much money to maneuver with."

"You're broke? I thought you were loaded."

"I've been unloaded."

"It was bad of me then not to send the fifteen hundred dollars. I assumed it would be a trifle."

"Well, until a few months ago it was a trifle. Can you find something for me to do in Almería?"

"You wouldn't want that."

"I don't know what 'that' is."

"To take a job in this picture—*Memoirs of a Cavalier*. Based on Defoe. There are sieges and such."

"I'd wear a costume?"

"It's not for you, Charlie."

"Why not? Listen, Kathleen. If I may speak good English for a moment. . . ."

"Be my guest."

"To efface the faults or remedy the defects of five decades I'm prepared to try anything. I am not too good to work in the movies. You little know how much it would please me to be an extra in this historical picture. Could I wear boots and bloomers? A casque, or a hat with plumes? It would do me a world of good."

"Wouldn't it be too distracting, mentally? You have . . . things to do."

"If these things I have to do can't find their way around those mountains of absurdity there's no hope for them. It's not as though my mind were free, you know. I worry about my daughters, and I worry terribly about my friend Thaxter. He was kidnaped by Argentine terrorists."

"I wondered about him," said Kathleen. "I read it in the *Herald-Tribune.* Is that the same Mr. Thaxter I met in Plaza? He wore a ten-gallon hat and asked me to come back later. Your name was mentioned in the article. He appealed to you for help."

"I'm upset by this. Poor Thaxter. If the scenarios do earn money I may have to pay it out to ransom him. I don't care too much. My own romance with wealth is over. What I intend to do now isn't very expensive. . . ."

"You know, Charles, Humboldt used to say wonderful things. You remind me of that. Tigler was lots of fun. He was an engaging person. We were always out hunting and fishing —doing something. But he wasn't much for conversation and nobody had talked to me like this in a long, long, long time, and I'm out of listening practice. I love it when you sound off. But it isn't very clear to me."

"I'm not surprised, Kathleen. It's my fault. I talk too much to myself. But human beings are far too deep in that false unnecessary comedy of history—in events, in developments, in politics. The common crisis is real enough. Read the papers— all that criminality and filth, murder, perversity, and horror. We can't get enough of it—we call it the human thing, the human scale."

"But what else is there?"

"A different scale. I know Walt Whitman compared us unfavorably to the animals. They don't whine about their condition. I see his point. I used to spend lots of time watching sparrows. I always adored sparrows. I do to this day. I spend hours in the park watching them bob and hop around and take dust baths. But I know they have less mental life than apes do. Orangutans are very charming. An orangutan friend sharing my apartment would make me very happy. But I know that he would understand less than Humboldt did. The question is this: why should we assume that the series ends with us? The fact is, I suspect, that we occupy a point within a great hierarchy that goes far far beyond ourselves. The ruling premises deny this. We feel suffocated and don't know why. The existence of a soul is beyond proof under the ruling premises, but people go on behaving as though they had souls, nevertheless. They behave as if they came from another place, another life, and they have impulses and desires that nothing in this world, none of our present premises, can account for. On the ruling premises the fate of humankind is a sporting event, most ingenious. Fascinating. When it doesn't become boring. The specter of boredom is haunting this sporting conception of history."

Kathleen again said that she had missed conversations of this kind in her married life with Tigler, the horse-wrangler. She certainly hoped I would come to Almería and work as a halberdier. "It's such an agreeable town."

"I'm about ready to get out of the *pensión*, too. People are breathing down my neck. But I'd better stay in Madrid so that I can keep track of everything—Thaxter, Paris. I may even have to go back to France for a while. I now have two attorneys there and that's double trouble."

"You haven't much confidence in lawyers."

"Well, Abraham Lincoln was a lawyer and I always venerated him. But he's nothing now but a name they put on license plates in the state of Illinois."

There was, however, no need to go to Paris. A letter came from Stewart, the publisher.

He wrote: "I see you haven't followed the papers for some time. It's true that Pierre Thaxter was abducted in Argentina. How or why or whether he's still in their hands I'm in no position to say. But I tell you in confidence, since you're his old pal, that it all puzzles me and sometimes I wonder if its really on the level. Mind you, I don't care to suggest that it's a phony kidnap, out-and-out. I'm ready to believe that the people who grabbed Thaxter off the sidewalk were convinced of his importance. Nor is there any indication of a prearranged snatching as may possibly have been the case with Miss Hearst and the Symbionese. But I enclose an article from the Op Ed page of *The New York Times* by our friend Thaxter. It's suppose to have been sent from the secret place or dungeon where they keep him. How come, I ask you, was he able to write and send to the *Times* this little essay on being kidnaped? Perhaps you will note, as I did, that he even makes a pitch for ransom funds. I am told that sympathetic readers have already sent checks to the US Embassy in Argentina to reunite him with his nine children. Far from being harmed, he is even crashing the big time and, if I'm not mistaken, the experience has also sharpened his literary style. This is publicity beyond price. Your guess that he may have fallen into a gold mine is probably correct. If his neck isn't broken, he'll be rich and famous."

Thaxter wrote, in part, "Three men held pistols to my head as I was leaving a restaurant in a busy street in Buenos Aires. In these three muzzles I saw the vanity of all the mental strategies for outwitting violence that I had ever entertained. Until that moment I had never realized how very often a modern man anticipates this critical moment. My head, now perhaps about to be blown open, had been full of schemes for saving myself. As I got into the waiting car I thought, I'm done for. I was not subjected to physical abuse. It soon became apparent that I was in the hands of sophisticated individuals advanced in their political thinking and utterly devoted to the principles of liberty and justice as they understood them. My captors believe that they have a case to present to civilized opinion and have chosen me to state it for them, having ascertained that I was sufficiently well known as an essayist and journalist to command attention." (Even now he gave himself a plug.) "As guerrillas and terrorists they would like it known that they are not heartless and irresponsible fanatics but that they have a high tradition of their own. They invoke Lenin and Trotsky as founders and builders who discovered that force was their indispensable instrument. They know the classics of this tradition, from nineteenth-century Russia to twentieth-century France. I have been brought up from the cellar to attend seminars on Sorel and Jean-Paul Sartre. These people are, in their own fashion, most high principled and serious. They have, furthermore, the quality to which Garcìa Lorca applied the term *Duende*, an inner power which burns the blood like powdered glass, a spiritual intensity that does not suggest, but commands."

I met Kathleen at a café and showed her the clippings. There was more in the same vein. I said, "Thaxter has a terrible weakness for making major statements. I think I might just ask for the three guns to be applied to the back of my head and the triggers pulled rather than sit through those seminars."

"Don't be too hard on him. The man is saving his life," she said. "Also it's a fascinating thing, really. Where does he make the ransom pitch?"

"Here. '. . . a price of fifty thousand dollars which I am allowed to take this occasion to request my friends and members of my family to contribute. In the hope of seeing my young children again,' and so forth. The *Times* treats its readers to plenty of thrills. That's a really pampered public that gets the Op Ed page."

"I don't suppose that the terrorists would get him to write

an apology to world opinion and then bump him off," she said.

"Well, it wouldn't be a hundred percent consistent. Who knows what those fellows will do. But I am a bit relieved. I think he's going to be all right."

Kathleen had questioned me closely, asking what I would like to do if Thaxter were out of the woods, if life became calmer and more settled. I answered her that I would probably spend a month at Dornach, near Basel, at the Swiss Steiner Center, the Goetheanum. Perhaps I could rent a house there where Mary and Lish could spend the summer with me.

"You should get quite a lot of money from the *Caldofreddo* people," she said. "And it seems that Thaxter is wiggling out of it, if he ever was really in it. For all you know he's free now."

"That's right. I still intend to split with Uncle Waldemar and give him Humboldt's full share."

"And how much would you estimate the settlement to be?"

"Oh, thirty thousand dollars," I said, "forty at the most."

But this guess was far too conservative. Barbash ended by bidding the producers up to eighty thousand dollars. They paid five thousand also to read Humboldt's scenario and eventually took an option on that as well. "They couldn't afford to pass it by," said Barbash, on the telephone. Cantabile was at that moment in the lawyer's office, talking loudly and urgently. "Yes, he's with me," said Barbash. "He's the most difficult bastard I ever had to deal with. He went over my head, he's been noisy, and lately he's begun to make threats. He's a real pain in the ass and if he weren't your authorized representative, Mr. Citrine, I'd have thrown him out long ago. Let me pay his ten percent and get him off my back."

"Mr. Barbash, you have my permission to disburse his eight thousand dollars immediately," I said. "What sort of terms are being offered for the second scenario?"

"They started at fifty thousand. But I argued that it was obvious the late Mr. Fleisher really had something. Contemporary, you know what I mean? Just the stuff the public was hungry for right now. You may have it yourself, Mr. Citrine. If you don't mind my saying so, I believe you shouldn't quit now. If you want to write the screenplay for the new vehicle I can make you one hell of a deal. Would you do it for two thousand a week?"

"I'm afraid I'm not interested, Mr. Barbash. I have other plans."

"What a pity. Won't you reconsider? They've asked many times."

"No thanks. No, I'm engaged in a very different kind of activity," I said.

"What about consultation?" said Mr. Barbash. "These people have got nothing but money and they'd be glad to pay twenty thousand bucks just because you understood the mind of Von Humboldt Fleisher. *Caldofreddo* is sweeping the world."

"Don't say no to everything." This was Cantabile who had taken the phone. "And listen, Charlie, I should get a cut on the other thing because if it wasn't for me none of this would have started. Besides, you owe me for planes, taxis, hotels, and meals."

"Mr. Barbash will settle your bill," I said. "Now go away, Cantabile, our relationship has drawn to a close. Let's become strangers again."

"Oh, you ungrateful, intellectual, ass-hole bastard," he said.

Barbash recovered the phone. "Where shall we be in touch? Are you staying in Madrid for a while?"

"I may fly down to Almería for a week or so, and then return to the USA," I said. "I've got a houseful of things in Chicago to dispose of. Children to see, and I've got to talk to Mr. Fleisher's uncle. When I've taken care of these necessary items and tied up a few loose ends I'm coming back to Europe. To take up a different kind of life," I added.

Inquire a little and I'll tell you all. I was still explaining myself in full to people who couldn't have cared less.

So this was how, in warm April, it happened that Waldemar Wald and I, together with Menasha Klinger, reburied Humboldt and his mother side by side in new graves at the Valhalla Cemetery. I took a very sad pleasure in doing this handsomely, in real style. Humboldt had been buried not in potter's field but far out in Deathsville, New Jersey, one of those vast, necropolitan developments described by Koffritz, Renata's first husband, to old Myron Swiebel in the steam room of the Division Street Bath. "They cheat," he had said about those places, "they skimp, they don't give the statutory number of feet. You lie there with your legs short-sheeted. Aren't you entitled to a full stretch for eternity?"

Investigating, I found that Humboldt's funeral had been arranged by someone at the Belisha Foundation. Sensitive person there, subordinate to Longstaff, recalling that Humboldt had once been an employee, had gotten him out of the morgue and had given him a send-off from the Riverside Chaple.

So Humboldt was exhumed and brought in a new casket over the George Washington Bridge. I had stopped for the old boys at their recently rented flat on the Upper West Side. A woman came to cook and clean for them and they were properly fixed up. Turning over a large sum to Uncle Waldemar made me uneasy and I told him so. He answered, "Charlie, my boy, listen—all the horses I ever knew became spooks years ago. And I wouldn't even know how to contact a bookie. It's all Puerto Rican up there in the old neighborhood now. Anyway, Menasha is keeping an eye on me. I want to tell you, kid, not many younger fellows would have given me the full split the way you did. If anything is left over at the end, you'll get it back."

We waited in the hired limousine at the New York end of the cabled bridge, the Hudson before us, till the hearse crossed over and we followed it to the cemetery. A blustery day might have been easier to tolerate than this heavy watered-silk blue close day. In the cemetery we wound about among dark trees. These should have been giving shade already but they stood brittle and schematic among the graves. For Humboldt's mother a new coffin also was provided, and this was already in position, ready to be lowered. Two attendants were opening the hearse as we came around to the back, moving slowly. Waldemar was wearing all the mourning he could find in his gambler's wardrode. Hat, trousers, and shoes were black, but his sport coat had large red houndstooth checks and in the sunshine of a delayed overwarm spring the fuzz was shining. Menasha, sad, smiling in thick glasses, felt his way over grass and gravel, his feet all the more cautious because he was looking up into the trees. He couldn't have been seeing much, a few sycamores and elms and birds and the squirrels coming and going in their fits-and-starts fashion. It was a low moment. There was a massive check threatened, as if a general strike against nature might occur. What if blood should not circulate, if food should not digest, breath fail to breathe, if the sap should not overcome the heaviness of the trees? And death, death, death, death, like so many stabs, like murder—the belly, the back, the breast and heart. This was a moment I could scarcely bear. Humboldt's coffin was ready to move. "Pallbearers?" said one of the funeral directors. He looked the three of us over. Not much manpower here. Two old fuddy-duddies and a distracted creature not far behind them in age. We took honorific positions along the casket. I held a handle—my first contact with Humboldt. There was very little weight within. Of course I no longer believed that any human fate could be associated with such remains and superfluities. The bones were very possibly the signature of spiritual powers, the projection of the cosmos in certain calcium formations. But perhaps even such elegant white shapes, thigh bones, ribs, knuckles, skull, were gone. Exhuming, the grave diggers might have shoveled together certain tatters and sooty lumps of human origin, not much of the charm, the verve and feverish invention, the calamity-making craziness of Humboldt. Humboldt, our pal, our nephew and brother, who loved the Good and the Beautiful, and one of whose slighter inventions was entertaining the public on Third Avenue and the Champs-Elysées and earning, at this moment, piles of dollars for everyone.

The laborers took over from us, setting Humboldt's coffin on the canvas bands of the electrical lowering device. The dead were now side by side in their bulky boxes.

"Did you know Bess?" said Waldemar.

"Once I saw her, on West End Avenue," I said.

He may have been thinking of money taken from her purse and lost in horse races long ago, of quarrels and scandalous scenes and curses.

In the long years since I had last attended a burial, many mechanical improvements had been made. There stood a yellow compact machine which apparently did the digging and bulldozed back the earth. It was also equipped as a crane. Seeing this, I started off on the sort of reflection Humboldt himself had trained me in. The machine in every square inch of metal was a result of collaboration of engineers and other artificers. A system built upon the discoveries of many great minds was always of more strength than what is produced by the mere workings of any one mind, which of itself can do little. So spoke old Dr. Samuel Johnson, and added in the same speech, that the French writers were superficial because they were not scholars and had proceeded upon the mere power of their own minds. Well, Humboldt had admired these same French writers and he too had proceeded for some time upon the mere power of his own mind. Then he began to look, himself, toward the collective phenomena. As his own self, he had opened his mouth and uttered some delightful verses. But then his heart failed him. Ah, Humboldt, how sorry I am. Humboldt, Humboldt—and this is what becomes of us.

The funeral director said, "Does anybody have a prayer to say?"

Nobody seemed to have or to know a prayer. But Menasha said he would like to sing something. He then did so. His style had not changed.

He announced, "I'm going to sing a selection from *Aida*, 'In questa tomba oscura.'" Aged Menasha now prepared himself. He turned up his face. The Adam's apple thus revealed was not what it had been when he was a young man operating a punch press in a Chicago factory, but it was there still. So was the old excitement. He clasped his hands, rising on his toes, and as emotionally as in our kitchen on Rice Street, weaker in voice, missing the tune still, and crowing but moved, terribly moved, he sang his aria. But this was only the warm-up. When he was done, he declared that he was going to perform "Goin' Home," an old American spiritual—used by Dvořák in the *New World* Symophony, he added as a program note. Then, oh Lord! I remembered that he had been homesick for Ypsilanti, and that he had pined for his sweetheart, back in the Twenties, longing for his girl, singing "Goin' home, goin' home, I'm a'goin' home," until my mother said, "For heaven's sake, go then." And when he came back with his obese, gentle, weeping bride, this girl sat in the tub, her arms too fat and defeating her efforts to bring the water as high as her head, Mama came into bathroom and washed her hair for her, and toweled it.

They were all gone but ourselves.

And looking into open graves was no pleasanter than it had ever been. Brown clay and lumps and pebbles—why must it all be so heavy. It was too much weight, oh, far too much to bear. I observed, however, another innovation in burials. Within the grave was an open concrete case. The coffins went down and then the yellow machine moved forward and the little crane, making a throaty whir, picked up a concrete slab and laid it atop the concrete case. So the coffin was enclosed and the soil did not come directly upon it. But then, how did one get out? One didn't, didn't, didn't! You stayed, you stayed! There was a dry light grating as of crockery when contact was made, a sort of sugar-bowl sound. Thus, the condensation of collective intelligences and combined ingenuities, its cables silently spinning, dealt with the individual poet. The same was done to the poet's mother. A gray lid was set upon her too and then Waldemar took the spade and weakly dug out clods and threw one into each grave. The old gambler wept and we turned aside to spare him. He stood beside the graves while the bulldozer began its work.

Menasha and I went toward the limousine. The side of his foot brushed away some of last autumn's leaves and he said, looking through his goggles, "What's this, Charlie, a spring flower?"

"It is. I guess it's going to happen after all. On a warm day like this everything looks ten times deader."

"So it's a little flower," Menasha said. "They used to tell one about a kid asking his grumpy old man when they were walking in the park, 'What's the name of this flower, Papa?' and the old guy is peevish and he yells, 'How should I know? Am I in the millinery business?' Here's another, but what do you suppose they're called, Charlie?"

"Search me," I said. "I'm a city boy myself. They must be crocuses."

THE DEAN'S DECEMBER

i

CORDE, who led the life of an executive in America—wasn't a college dean a kind of executive?—found himself six or seven thousand miles from his base, in Bucharest, in winter, shut up in an old-fashioned apartment. Here everyone was kind—family and friends, warmhearted people—he liked them very much, to him they were "old Europe." But they had their own intense business. This was no ordinary visit. His wife's mother was dying. Corde had come to give support. But there was little he could do for Minna. Language was a problem. People spoke little French, less English. So Corde, the Dean, spent his days in Minna's old room sipping strong plum brandy, leafing through old books, staring out of the windows at earthquake-damaged buildings, winter skies, gray pigeons, pollarded trees, squalid orange-rusty trams hissing under trolley cables.

Corde's mother-in-law, who had had first a heart attack and then a stroke, was in the hospital. Only the Party hospital had the machines to keep her alive, but the rules were rigid there. She was in intensive care, and visits were forbidden. Corde and Minna had flown a day and a night to be with her but in five days had seen her only twice—the first time by special dispensation, the second without official permission. The hospital superintendent, a colonel in the secret police, was greatly offended because his rules had been broken. He was a tough bureaucrat. The staff lived in terror of him. Minna and her aunt Gigi had decided (Corde took part in their discussions) that it would be polite to ask for an appointment. "Let's try to have a sensible talk with him."

On the telephone the Colonel had said, "Yes, come."

Minna, when she went to see him, brought her husband along—perhaps an American, a dean from Chicago, not quite elderly but getting there, would temper the Colonel's anger. No such thing happened. The Colonel was a lean, hollow-templed, tight-wrapped, braided-whip sort of man. Clearly, he wasn't going to give any satisfaction. An institution must keep its rules. Corde put in his two cents; he mentioned that he was an administrator himself—he had worked for many years on the Paris *Herald*, so he spoke French well enough. The Colonel politely let him speak his piece; he darkly, dryly listened, mouth compressed. He received, tolerated, the administrative comparison, despised it. He did not reply, and when the Dean was done he turned again to Minna.

There had been an impropriety. Under no circumstances could the administration tolerate that. Outraged, Minna was silent. What else could she be? Here only the Colonel had the right to be outraged. His high feeling—and he allowed it to go very high—was moderated in expression only by the depth of his voice. How sharp could a basso sound? Corde himself had a deep voice, deeper than the Colonel's, vibrating more. Where the Colonel was tight, Corde was inclined to be loose. The Colonel's sparse hair was slicked straight back, military style; Corde's baldness was more random, a broad bay, a straggling growth of back hair. From this enlarged face, the brown gaze of an intricate mind of an absent, probably dreamy tendency followed the conversation. You could not expect a Communist secret police colonel to take such a person seriously. He was only an American, a dean of students from somewhere in the middle of the country. Of these two visitors, Minna was by far the more distinguished. This beautiful woman, as the Colonel was sure to know, was a professor of astronomy, had an international reputation. A "hard" scientist. It was important for the Colonel to establish that he was not moved by such considerations. He was in as hard a field as she. Harder.

Minna spoke emotionally about her mother. She was an only child. The hearing the Colonel gave her was perfectly correct. A daughter who had come such a distance; a mother in intensive care, half paralyzed. Without knowing the language, Corde could understand all this easily enough, and interpreted the Colonel's position: Where you had hospitals, you had dying people, naturally. Because of the special circumstances an exception had been made for the *doamna* and her husband on their arrival. But there had been a second visit (here the incensed emphasis again), without permission.

Minna, in terse asides, translated for her husband. It wasn't really necessary. He loosely sat there in wrinkled woolen trousers and sports jacket, the image of the inappropriate

American—in all circumstances inappropriate, incapable of learning the lessons of the twentieth century; spared, or scorned, by the forces of history or fate or whatever a European might want to call them. Corde was perfectly aware of this.

He nodded, his brown eyes, bulging somewhat, in communion with the speckled activity of the floor, uniformly speckled over the entire hospital. The director's office was tall but not much roomier than a good-sized closet—a walk-in closet at home. The desk, too, was small. Nothing was big except the Colonel's authority. The electric fixture was hung very high, remote. Here, as everywhere in Bucharest, the light was inadequate. They were short on energy in Rumania—something about subnormal rainfall and low water in the dams. That's right, blame nature. December brown set in at about three in the afternoon. By four it had climbed down the stucco of old walls, the gray of Communist residential blocks: brown darkness took over the pavements, and then came back again from the pavements more thickly and isolated the street lamps. These were feebly yellow in the impure melancholy winter effluence. Air-sadness, Corde called this. In the final stage of dusk, a brown sediment seemed to encircle the lamps. Then there was a livid death moment. Night began. Night was very difficult here, thought Albert Corde. He sat slumped and heavy-headed, his wide head seeking the support it could not get from its stem. This brought his moody eyes forward all the more, the joined brows, the bridge of his spectacles out of level. It was his wife with her fine back, her neck, her handsome look, who made the positive impression. But that was nothing to the whiplash Colonel. Perhaps it only reminded him that this distinguished lady had defected twenty years ago, when she had been allowed out to study in the West, was here only because her mother was dying, arriving under the protection of her husband, this American dean; landing without a visa, met by a U.S. official (this meant a certain degree of influence). The Colonel would have all this information, of course. And Minna was not in a strong position; she had never formally renounced her Rumanian citizenship. If it had a mind to, the government could make trouble for her.

Valeria, the old woman, was not a Party member now,

hadn't been one since, as Minister of Health, she fell in disgrace. That had happened thirty years ago. She was then denounced publicly by press and radio, expelled, threatened with prison, with death, too. Before he could come to trial, one of her colleagues who fell in the same shake-up had his head hacked off in his cell. This old militant who had survived Antonescu and also the Nazis was butchered with an ax or a meat cleaver. Dr. Valeria somehow came through. Dr. Valeria herself had founded this very hospital, the Party hospital. Three weeks ago, probably feeling the first touches of sickness (Corde thought of it as the advance death thrill, the final presage; each of us in peculiar communication with his own organs and their sick-signals), she began to make the rounds, out all day on the buses and trolley cars, said Gigi, calling on old acquaintances, arranging to be admitted. She had been rehabilitated late in the fifties, her pension restored, and she had quiet connections of her own among the old-timers of the bureaucracy.

So she was hooked in now to the respirator, scanner, monitor. The stroke had knocked out the respiratory center, her left side was paralyzed. She couldn't speak, couldn't open her eyes. She could hear, however, and work the fingers of her right hand. Her face was crisscrossed every which way with tapes, like the Union Jack. Or like windowpanes in cities under bombardment. Corde, an old journalist before he became a dean, knew these wartime scenes—sandbags, window tapes. Never saw the crisscross on a face like hers, though; too delicate for it. Still, the next step, a tracheotomy, was even worse. He was an experienced man. He knew the stages.

Before you were allowed to approach Valeria you had to put on a sterile gown and oversocks, huge and stiff. Also a surgical cap and mask. Valeria understood that her daughter had come, and her eyes moved under the lids. Minna was there. And protected by her husband—further proof of his dependability. When Corde spoke to her, she answered by pressing his fingers. Her son-in-law then noticed for the first time a deformity of one of her knuckles. Had it been broken once, was it arthritic? It was discolored. He had never before seen her hair down, only braided and pinned. He would never have guessed this fine white hair to be so long. There was also her big belly. Beneath it her thin legs. That, too, was painful to see. Every bit of it moved him—more than that, it worked him up; more than that, it made him wild, drove him into savage fantasies. He wanted to cry, as his wife was doing. Tears did come, but also an eager violence, a kind of get-it-over ecstasy mingling pity and destructiveness. Part of him was a monster. What else could it be?

These reactions were caused by exhaustion, partly. They must have been. The trip had been long. He was fagged, dried out. His guts were strained. He felt plugged in the rear. Circulation to the face and scalp seemed insufficient. And a kind of demonic excitement rose up, for which no resolution seemed possible. Like evil forces, frantic, foul, working away. At the same time, his tears for the old woman were genuine, too. For the moment, he could suppress nothing, force nothing. Equally helpless before good and bad. On the electronic screen of the monitor, symbols and digits shimmied and whirled, he heard a faint scratching and ticking.

The Colonel, towards the last of the interview, put on a long, judicious look—cunning, twisting the knife—and said that if Valeria was removed from the intensive care unit, Minna might come as often as she liked. Unhooked from the machines, the old woman would die in fifteen minutes. This of course he did not spell out. But there was your choice, madam. This was the man's idea of a joke. You delivered it at the point of a knife.

That part of the conversation Corde had missed. Minna had told him about it. "My homecoming," she said after the interview, as they were going down the cement walk to the parking lot.

"Like tying a plastic bag over your face and telling you to breathe deep."

"I could kill him." Perhaps she could, from the set of her face—big eyes, intaken lips. "What should I do now, Albert? She'll be expecting us, waiting for us."

They were riding home in Petrescu's Russian compact, one of those strong dreary cars they drive in the satellite countries.

Mihai Petrescu had been *chef de cabinet* to Minna's father and to Valeria when she succeeded her late husband in the Ministry. He was attached to the family. Not himself a physician, he must have been the Party watchdog. He couldn't have had much to report. Dr. Raresh had been naively ideological, a

Christian and moral Communist, praying for God's help before he opened a patient's skull. The country's first neurosurgeon, trained in Boston by the famous Cushing, he had been too emotional, too good, too much the high-principled doctor to make a Communist official. Minna said she could never understand how he could have been taken in so completely. In the thirties he had brushed aside as bourgeois propaganda what he had read in the world press about the Great Terror, Stalin's labor camps, the Communists in Spain, the pact with Hitler. Enthusiastic when Russian troops reached Bucharest, he went into the streets with roses for the soldiers. Within a week they had taken the watch from his wrist, put him out of his little Mercedes and driven it away. But he made no complaints. He did not move into a villa like other ministers. His colleagues disliked this. His austerity was too conspicuous. Before he died, the regime had already decided the man was a fool and kicked him upstairs. He was named ambassador to the U.S.A. They didn't want him around protesting the disappearance of his medical friends one after another. He didn't live to go to Washington. He lasted only a year.

When he died Valeria was offered the Ministry. She probably thought it might be dangerous to refuse. Minna was then a small girl. Petrescu stayed on as *chef de cabinet*. Lower-echelon KGB was how Corde figured him. Mihai seemed to have converted the official connection into familial intimacy. He told Corde when they had a schnapps together, "*Elle a été une mère, une consolatrice pour moi.*" And for others, by the dozens. Valeria was a matriarch. Corde was well aware of that.

But sometimes Petrescu stayed away for years. He had not been seen for many months before Valeria's stroke. And even now he disappeared, reappeared unpredictably. Petrescu was squat, small-eyed; his fedora was unimpeded by hair so that the fuzz of the hat brim mingled with the growth of his ears in all-revealing daylight. In every conversation about Valeria his sentences had a way of creeping upwards, his pitch climbed as high as his voice could bring it, and then there was a steep drop, a crack of emotion. He was dramatically fervent about Valeria. Studying his face, Corde at the same time estimated that something like three-fourths of his creases were the creases of a very tough character, a man you could easily imagine slamming the table during an interrogation, capable perhaps of pulling a trigger. It wasn't just in Raymond Chandler novels that you met tough guys. All kinds of people are tough. But with the ladies Petrescu was wonderful, he behaved with gallantry, or else with saintly delicacy, he jumped up, moved chairs, tumbled out of the driver's seat to open the doors of his Soviet car. Today he was standing by, upstairs, with advice, telephoning, volunteering, murmuring, as silken with Minna and Tanti Gigi as the long fleshy lobes of his ears were silken. His underlip was full of a fervent desire to serve. Before he disappeared—for he soon did disappear—he played a leading part in the emotional composition whose theme was Valeria's last days. Great Valeria's end. For she was great—this was the conclusion Corde finally reached.

The apartment was shared by Valeria and Tanti Gigi. Corde and Minna were staying there. Visiting nieces, cousins, had to go to hotels. But under the special consanguinity regulations, the Cordes were permitted to move in with Gigi. Something of an invalid, Tanti Gigi managed the household with hysterical efficiency. She seemed to do it all in bathrobe and slippers and from her bed. When he knew the problems of the city better—the queues forming at daybreak, the aged women with oilcloth shopping bags waiting throughout the day—Corde was able to appreciate Gigi's virtuosity. The flat was as tentatively heated as it was electrically dim. Radiators turned cold after breakfast. The faucets went dry at 8 A.M. and did not run again until evening. The bathtub had no stopper. You flushed the toilet with buckets of water. Corde was not a man to demand comforts. He merely observed all this—a hungry observer. The parlor, once the brain surgeon's waiting room, was furnished with aging corpulent overstuffed chairs of bald, peeling leather. There were openwork brass lamps which resembled minarets. It was all quality stuff from the bourgeois days. The Biedermeier cabinets were probably despised in the twenties by young revolutionists, but in old age they clung to these things as relics of former happiness. Very odd, thought Corde, how much feeling went into these sofas, old orange brocade and frames with mother-of-pearl inlay; and the bric-a-brac and thin carpets, gilt-framed pictures, fat editions of Larousse, antiquated medical books in German and English. After her disgrace and loss of pension, during the period of ostracism, Valeria sold off the best of the silver and china. The last of the Baccarat had been smashed in the recent earthquake. While they were lying on the floor Tanti Gigi had heard the crystal minutely crumbling and tinkling, dancing on the floor, she said. The objects that remained were of no terrific value, but they were obviously consecrated—they were the family's old things: Dr. Raresh's worktable, Minna's bed, the pictures in her room, even her undergraduate notebooks.

Much better this old flat—it was a Balkan version of the Haussmann style—than the Intercontinental Hotel and the Plaza Athénée with their deluxe totalitarian comforts and the goings-on of the secret police—*securitate*: devices behind the draperies, tapes spinning in the insulated gloom. But you were bugged in the flat, too, probably with the latest American bugs. You name it, the manufacturing U.S. would sell it. Or else the French, the Japanese, the Italians would sell it. So if you wanted to talk privately you went outside, and in the streets, too, Minna would nudge you, directing your attention to certain men lounging, walking slowly or chatting. "Yup, I can spot 'em myself," said Corde. The fat concierge, Ioanna, was in continual conversation with these loungers. She reported to them. But she was also a friend of the family. That was how it went. Valeria and Tanti Gigi had more than once explained matters to him.

Corde knew the old girls very well. Valeria had visited the States, and he and Minna had often met them both abroad. When they were eligible for visas, the old sisters flew to Paris, Frankfurt, London. Of course they had to be sent for—no dollars, no passports—and they came out of the country without a penny, not even cab fare. Only last spring Valeria had joined Corde and Minna in England.

Valeria studied people closely, but she may not have been aware of the important place she held in Corde's feelings. How could she be? The deep-voiced slouching Dean would sit with his legs stretched out and his neck resting on the back of his chair like a reporter on a story, killing time patiently in a waiting room. His nonchalant way of looking at you, the extruded brown eyes, that drowned-in-dreams look, was probably the source of his reputation as a swinger, a chaser. Minna and Valeria had been warned against him. Erotic instability, womanizing, was the charge. Judged by the standards of perfect respectability, Corde had not been a good prospect for marriage. "It's true he's been married before, but so have I," said Minna to her mother. Valeria's influence was great, but in this instance Minna made her own decision. It was a sound decision. There was no instability. Corde proved to be entirely straight. After several years of observation Valeria gave him a clearance. She said to her daughter, "You were perfectly right about Albert." She was not after all one of your parochial Balkan ladies. She had studied Freud, Ferenczi, she was a psychiatrist—Corde forgave her the psychiatry; maybe psychiatry was different in the Balkans. He certainly wasn't kinky enough to be written up as a case history.

So there they were, in Minna's old room. It was still a schoolgirl's room. Valeria had kept it that way. There were textbooks, diplomas, group photographs. This was obviously Valeria's favorite place, where she read, sewed, wrote letters. Corde was curious about the books that crammed the shelves. Many were English and French. He found an old collection of Oscar Wilde published by some British reader's society in red cardboard, faded to weeping pink, and looked up some of the poems he had learned by heart as an adolescent, melodramatic pieces like "The Harlot's House," the puppet prostitute and the clockwork lover, the scandals of Greek love, the agonies of young men who had done so well at school but woke up beside their murdered mistresses in London with blood and wine upon their hands. Why had they killed them? That's what love does to you. An unsatisfactory proposition. Corde particularly wanted to find the lines about the red hell to which a man's sightless soul might stray. He found it, it amused him—the earth reeling underfoot, and the weary sunflowers—but not for long. He put down the not-so-amusing book. He found the street more interesting.

Earthquake damage was still being repaired. A machine, a wheeled crane, worked its way down the block. A crew of two stood in the large bucket to patch cracks in stucco, working around the open porches. Women in kerchiefs whacked their carpets in the morning. From all sides one heard the percussion of carpet beaters. Give it to them! The dust went off in the sunlight. A dog barked, whined as if a beater had given him a whack, then barked again. The barking of the dog, a protest against the limits of dog experience (for God's sake, open the universe a little more!)—so Corde felt, being shut in. He might have gone rambling about the city, but Minna was afraid the *securitate* would pick him up. What if he were accused of selling dollars illegally? She had heard stories about this. Friends warned her. All right, she had worries enough, and he stayed put.

She was busy in the parlor. Friends she hadn't seen in twenty years came to call—Viorica, Doina, Cornelia. Corde was asked to present himself in the parlor, the American husband. The telephone rang all the time. As soon as possible he went back to the room, his retreat. For three days he thought how much good it would do him to go out and walk off the tensions he had brought from Chicago (cramps in his legs), then he stopped thinking about it.

Back to the shelves. He pulled away the beds to see what titles they concealed. Pedagogy was one of Valeria's interests. He found an unpublished primer with pictures of cows, piglets, ponies. Curious about Minna's adolescence, he leafed through albums, studying snapshots. In the drawers he turned up coins from former regimes, embossed buttons, documents from the time of the monarchy, stopped watches, Byzantine crosses on thin silver chains, newspaper clippings, letters from Dr. Cushing to Raresh, one of his best pupils. There were also items about Corde—installed as dean, receiving an honorary degree from Grinnell. Minna had sent her mother a copy of the first installment of his long article on Chicago, the one that had stirred up so much trouble. Trouble was still raging. That was some of what he had brought with him. Valeria had obviously read his piece closely, making check marks in the margin where he had described the crazy state of the prisoners in County Jail—the rule of the barn bosses, the rackets, beatings, sodomizings and stabbings in the worst of the tiers: in "Dodge City," "H-1"; the prisoners who tucked trouser bottoms into socks to keep the rats from running up their legs in the night. Now there *was* a red hell for the soul to stray into.

Obviously it intrigued Valeria the psychiatrist to study the personality of her son-in-law as it was revealed in his choice of topics; his accounts of beatings and buggerings, of a murder with the sharp-honed metal of a bed leg, were underscored in red. He pored over these passages, hunched under his coat, noting how often he had mentioned the TV in each dayroom, the soaps and the sporting events, "society's alternatives continually in view," and "how strangely the mind of the criminal is stocked with images from that other anarchy, the legitimate one." Valeria had circled these sentences. She hadn't received the second installment. Mainly about the Rufus Ridpath scandal, the Spofford Mitchell case, it was filled with disobliging remarks about City Hall, the press, the sheriff, the governor. Corde had let himself go, indignant, cutting, reckless. He had made the college unhappy. One of its deans taking everybody on? A bad scene, an embarrassment. The administration behaved with restraint, but it was jittery. It was especially upset by Part Two. What would Valeria have thought of Part Two?

Valeria had never made Corde feel that she objected to the marriage; she had too much breeding for that, she was too tactful to antagonize him. She did study him, yes, but without apparent prejudice. Really, she was fair-minded. Although he hadn't much liked being under observation, he conceded that it wasn't unreasonable. "But Christ, do I need a parole officer?" Of course he was uncomfortable, and when he was uncomfortable he grew more silent, speaking only in a brief rumble. What was most distressing about being watched was that it made him see himself—a dish-faced man, long in the mouth. You could hardly blame him for being sensitive to close scrutiny. In giving his order to a waiter once, asking for an *omelette fines herbes*, he was pointedly corrected by Valeria. "The *s* is sounded—*feenzerbes.*" He was stunned, the abyss of pettiness opened. It *was* an abyss.

Nevertheless he was strongly drawn to the old woman. Last spring the three of them had stayed together at Durrants in George Street, and he was always in their company, didn't care to go off by himself. He tagged along to Liberty's, Jaeger's, Harrods. He enjoyed that. And last April great London had been wide open and the holiday gave him the kind of human "agreement" (he could find no other term for it) he very badly needed, was evidently looking for continually. He gladly followed the two ladies through Harrods ("Harrods of Jewry" to him, but now filled with Arabs). The parcels were heaped up in Valeria's room. He said to Minna, "Why not buy her something she can't give away, for herself only?"

"She doesn't seem to need . . . ." Minna began. "It's enough for her to be with—with us. And especially here, in London. She adores London."

No one understood better than the English how to build coziness in a meager setting. You polished up old tables, you framed dinginess in margins of gilt; without apology, you dignified worn corners, brushed up the bald nap of your velours—these were the Dickensian touches that Corde approved. He wasn't quite sure how Valeria viewed this less than luxurious hotel. Couldn't her American son-in-law do better? Coming out of Bucharest, you probably would have preferred the Ritz. But he was a dean, merely, not the governor of Texas—no, the governor wouldn't have been good enough for Minna, nor a member of the board of Chase Manhattan. Still, the feeling of human "agreement" would not have been possible without the old woman's acceptance. She accepted him, soon enough. He was all right. They were both all right. If his manner was quiet (the parolee on good behavior), hers was undemonstratively accommodating. In the morning she went down early to buy the *Times* for Corde (by half past eight the porter was likely to tell him, "Sorry, sir, sold out"). She made sure that there was a copy of the paper on her son-in-law's chair. Then she sat in her neat suit, waiting in the breakfast room, the green silk scarf about her neck—lovely blue-green. Until Minna joined her, Valeria did not accept so much as a cup of tea from the Spanish waiters. As breakfast drew to an end, Corde turned his chair aside slightly. The Dean, drawing back his head peculiarly—his neck was thin—focused his gaze on the *Times* (a foreign paper printed in his own language). Reading, he omitted no item of politics, the experienced newspaperman making his own swift observations. "I know these guys," was his attitude. As the ladies discussed their plans for the day, the Dean glanced also at the currency rates, the obituaries of civil servants and retired soldiers, the Court Calendar, items from Wimbledon—matters of minimal interest. He experienced alternate waves of bleakness and of warmth towards Valeria for her admirable control over such a diversity of factors—doubts (about him), love for her daughter, embarrassment at being without a penny of her own. Of course the daughter had a good income. But the son-in-law wanted very much to buy her coats, dresses, hats, purses, tickets, excursions, dinners, music, airline tickets. Then he would note her level look. She was wondering quietly about him. What sort of man is Albert—what is his quality? When he and Minna returned to their tight, small, neat Durrants room after breakfast, he said, "Here's a hundred pounds. Buy the old girl some kid gloves. Take her to Bond Street." Minna laughed at him.

Then he made an independent discovery, one it was impossible for Minna to make.

Minna, you see, had her astrophysical, mathematical preoccupations. Minna, in Corde's metaphor, was bringing together a needle from one end of the universe with a thread from the opposite end. Once this was accomplished, Corde couldn't say what there was to be sewn—this was his own way of concentrating his mind on the *mysterium tremendum*. Face it, the cosmos was beyond him. His own special ability was to put together for the general reader such pieces as this one from *Harper's*. Its topics (in Minna's schoolgirl room, he turned the pages) were the torments and wildness of black prisoners under the jurisdiction of the disabled sheriff of Cook County, who had himself broken his neck in a patriotic street brawl with rampaging Weathermen in the Loop, when he missed a flying tackle; and . . . no, there the Dean checked it, cooled it. He would stop with his ability to describe a scene for the common reader; or to deal with undergraduates—he did that fairly well, too. Or with his more important ability to engage (inexplicably) the affections of a woman like his wife, who had chosen him to share her planetary life. (Forgiving him his defects, his sins. But she would never regret it.) The county sheriff who campaigned from his wheelchair was, for the moment, set aside.

Corde's discovery in London was that Valeria no longer had the strength to travel, to fly back and forth. She was too old. The diagnosis was sudden but it was complete: "She can't hack it." She was sick, she doctored herself (he had seen pill bottles when she opened her pocketbook). Pushing eighty, she flew to England. Unless Minna formally renounced her Rumanian citizenship, she couldn't go to see her mother. It might not be safe. Hard to say why Minna balked at this formal renunciation. She found excuses. "I can't stand those people. I can't bear to correspond with them. Yes, I *will* go through with it. I've already got the forms filled in." True, she concentrated mostly on her science, couldn't be bothered with government papers, but that was a superficial explanation, considering the strength of her feeling for Valeria. But she preferred to assume that her mother was strong and well. That Valeria should be too sick to go abroad was inadmissible. As for Valeria, she would rather die in an airport than tell her daughter, "My dear, I'm too weak for suitcases, and I can't manage taxis, and I can't stand in line for customs, I'm too old for the jets." No, she came to London, her head full of lists—and every day she told Minna, "I have to bring dress material for Floara. I promised to get computer manuals for Ionel." And so with boots for Doina, tea from Fortnum's for Gigi. For herself she bought colored postcards of Westminster Abbey.

Corde was called upstairs to strap her boxy rawhide valises. To squeeze them shut took some doing. How did the old woman manage to haul these two fat trunks?—they *were* almost trunks.

"It must take plenty of wangling to get these damn things through customs."

"She's got what it takes," said Minna. She shrugged.

She had to read a paper before a scientific meeting in Copenhagen, and for two days Corde was in charge of Valeria. He entertained her at the Étoile on Charlotte Street. She loved the Étoile. He took her to a Rowlandson exhibition at Burlington House. That meant standing in a queue outside, and then making your way through crowded halls. The old woman smiled calmly at the stout, rosy, frilling ladies of fashion, at the fops, but Corde soon saw that the outing was too much for her. Strange to watch, troubling. He was upset for her. She couldn't keep her balance; she was tipping, listing, seemed unable to coordinate the movements of her feet. He said, "I've had enough Rowlandson, do you mind?" As he led her down the large staircase, the lightness and the largeness of her elbow surprised him. Why was the joint so big? It felt like dry sponge. She removed his hand. They emerged in the Piccadilly jam of vehicles and people. She said, "You have things to do, Albert. I'm going back to the hotel." He doubted even that she could hail a cab. He flagged one down and got in with her, saying, "I left my appointment book at the hotel; I don't remember where I'm supposed to go next." She made a place for him on the buttoned black leather seat and sat in the corner silent, even severe.

Corde's father had been an old-fashioned American, comfortable, calm, a "Pullman car type," his son called him. (The old guy had been a sort of playboy too, a man about town, but that was something else again.) Corde could reproduce his manner. That obtuse style was helpful now. He gave Valeria no sign that he had found her out. When he took her that night to a Turkish dinner in Wardour Street, she seemed stronger, she said how pleasant London was; she talked Communist politics, reminisced about Ana Pauker, in whose government she had served. He told her a little about life in Chicago. With red meat and a bottle of wine, she picked up somewhat. She said she had been tired that afternoon. Between three o'clock and five the body ran out of blood sugar.

"Yes, I go into an afternoon slump myself. Often."

But he said quietly to Minna when they had seen Valeria off at Heathrow, "Did the old girl say how good a time she had? I don't think she can make the trip again."

"You're not serious. Her only pleasure is coming out. These holidays in a civilized place. And seeing us. She lives for it."

He did not pursue the subject. He had gone on record. Minna would have to follow up in her own way.

ii

It was an instinct with Corde—maybe it was a weakness—always to fix attention on certain particulars, in every situation to grasp the details. If he took Valeria to dine at the Étoile, he brought away with him a clear picture of the wine waiter. That a bald man had triple creases at the back of his skull could not be left out of account, nor could the shape of his thumbs, the health of his face, the spread of his nose, the strength of his stout Italian body in the waiter's suit. Corde's eyes took in also the dishes on the hors d'oeuvre cart, the slices of champignons à la Grecque, the brown sauce, the pattern of the table silver. With him, exclusively mental acts seldom occurred. He was temperamentally an image man. To observe so much was not practical, sometimes it was disabling, often downright painful, but actualities could not be left out.

So when he left Chicago, it had to be remembered that he packed his dusty black zippered garment bag. As he carried it, it rubbed against his leg with a slithering sound (the synthetic material expressing itself). In the bag, his undistinguished clothing—shirts spotted and scorched in the hand laundry, trousers that should have gone to the cleaner (he could shut his eyes and locate those spots exactly). Another item: in the fever of departure, he saw the floating ice blocks in Lake Michigan, gray-white and tan, the top layer of snow stained with sand blown from the beaches by the prevailing wind. Item: the red thermal undershirt he removed from his luggage because he imagined that Bucharest would be a Mediterranean sort of place, a light city not a heavy one; rococo. Rococo! It was mass after mass of socialist tenements and government office buildings. Now he regretted that thermal shirt. Item: the tube of salve he needed for the rash about his ankles was squeezed dry, rolled up to the neck—he should have ordered another before leaving. Item: his pots of African violets. What good would it do to let the rods of ultra-violet light burn on? A crisis—how to save his plants! He had heard that if you put one end of a rope in a bucket of water, the other end would deliver sufficient moisture, but there was no time to set this up. Item: the can of Earl Grey tea on the kitchen counter, and the bananas. He took those with him to Europe. Essential documents were left on his desk. He hadn't been able to find his address book; he had most likely hidden it from himself. He wouldn't be writing letters anyway. His instinct was to cut, to drop everything and fly away unencumbered. It was only the violets he regretted leaving. Item: Minna packed her valise with astronomical papers, giving them priority over dresses. On the trip she couldn't be separated from these books and reprints. They weren't checked through but had to be carried as cabin luggage. Her eyes seemed to have been displaced by stress; they looked like the fruit in an eccentric still life. As soon as Gigi's wire came she stopped eating. In a matter of hours she was looking gaunt, and sallow; her face had a kind of negative color. Her underlip was retracted, and her chin filled with pressure marks. Corde was a close watcher of his wife. Item: the cab to the airport ran between levees of snow. Winter's first blizzard had struck Chicago. The cab was overheated and stank of excrement. Of dogs? Of people? It was torrid, also freezing; Arctic and Sahara, mixed. Also, the driver was sloshed with eau de cologne. The ribbed rubber floor was all filth and grit. Corde said, "People have even stopped wiping themselves." He took the precaution of saying this in French, and there was something false about that—raunchy gaiety (and disgust) in a foreign language. Anyhow it fell flat, as Minna scarcely heard him.

More items were checked on the way to O'Hare. The alarm system? The keys? The windows? Instructions to the super to remove the mail from the box, the newspapers from the front door? Had he gone to the bank for dollars? Talked to de Prima, the lawyer? Left Valeria's telephone number with Miss Porson at the office? The college might need to reach them. Minna was thinking not of the Dean's special problems but of the time reserved for her on the telescope at Mount Palomar. She had been due there Christmas week, but that was now canceled, of course. "Yes, they know where to find us," he said. With his dense eyebrows, the plain length of his mouth, his low voice, his usual posture was one of composure, and now and then students told him that it was wonderful how "laid back" he was. A handsome compliment but undeserved. He was engaged in a sharp rearguard action against the forces of agitation. When they took off from O'Hare, he felt that all the Chicago perplexities were injected into his nerves. Yet when he went into the lavatory of the Lufthansa 747 and the light went on, he seemed well enough to himself, with a mouth like a simple declarative sentence, although there were so many complex-compound things to be said.

Then, after making an air loop of thousands of miles, he found himself stuck. But alien as they were, his surroundings offered him intimacy, the instant intimacy of Minna's old room. For much of the day he lounged among Rumanian cushions on a divan, drinking peasant brandy and eating grapes, brownish green and heavy on the seeds, brought from the country by Tanti Gigi's far-flung agents. Because Gigi's heart was irregular, she was in bed much of the time, but women were coming and going all day, reporting to her, taking instructions. Corde was on her mind. He could drink only real coffee and, deprived of whiskey, he needed *pálinca*, at least. He was used to having meat (meat was virtually unobtainable), and a bottle of wine with it (you *could* get inferior wine on the black market). He had sacrificed his comforts to bring Minna here, and Gigi was therefore determined that he should have the best. ("What a rich, wonderful country we are," she said. "If only you could see the real Rumania.")

Despite doorbells and telephones, conferences, despite the developing struggle with the Colonel, despite the weight of a large totalitarian mass of life on the outside (the city was terrible!), he was quiet. No urgent calls, decisions, no hateful letters, no awkward conferences, infighting, or backbiting—people getting at him one way or another. After lunch he took off his clothing, pulled back the heavy gaudy bed cover (almost a rug) and went to sleep. Sometimes he did that after breakfast, too. He did not feel quite steady even in brilliant healthful weather; consciousness reeling as if he had been driving a car over endless plains and whole continents. He was eyesick, head-sick, seat-sick, motion-sick, gut-sick, wheel-weary. So he rested after breakfast. The nights were not easy. Minna wasn't sleeping. She seemed to lie there rerunning in her mind all the worst sequences of the day. To these were added thoughts for which there hadn't been sufficient time. The room was cold, the nights unnaturally black—or was this Corde's own intensity working outward, blacker than night. He put out his fingers and fetched the covers over his bony shoulders, but when he heard Minna stirring he knew that he must get up and offer her comfort. Lying down with her usually helped. But not now.

She didn't turn when he entered her small bed and put his arms around her from behind. They held a whispered conversation.

Minna said, "What does she think? Days go by and I'm not there."

"What, she? She can't open her eyes, and in that room you

couldn't tell days from nights anyway—besides, she understands why you're not there."

"Does she?"

"Are you kidding? With her experience? Inside the government? And/or private life? They've been under the Russians since 1945. That's a long, long time. She's got to know every wrinkle. You can be sure she thought it through even before we arrived."

"Yes, that may be."

He lowered his voice still more. "Even after a few days you feel them sitting on your face. And at this rate we may be looking at our own future."

"You shouldn't say that. . . ."

"It's not me that says it. *I* don't believe it, but it's what you hear and see. You should read what they say on the Russian New Right. Like, it's the weak democracies that produce dictatorships. Or that our decadence is heading full speed towards collapse. Of course, they overdo it. But you can't help thinking about it."

Minna let him go on, and he stopped himself. It wasn't exactly the time to develop such views. Evil visions. The moronic inferno. He read too many articles and books. If the night hadn't been so black and cold, none of this would have been said. The night made you exaggerate. Between them on the pillow was the float of her hair.

"They want to do a tracheotomy," she said.

"Do they have to?"

"Dr. Moldovanu said on the telephone that it had to be done. He also told me that he wrote a report to the Colonel about the visits. He suggested they were good for my mother."

"They're all afraid of that bastard. He scares them to death."

"Ileana told me that when Dr. Moldovanu's mother had an infarct, he wasn't allowed to bring her to the Party hospital. The request was refused."

"They call it an infarct here? There might be a way to go over the man's head, if this were Chicago or Honduras, or some such place."

"How can he not allow me . . . !"

It was Corde's habit to explain matters to his unworldly wife. It gave him pleasure and was sometimes instructive even to himself. "This gives the man an opportunity to test the efficiency of his controls. This is fine tuning," said Corde. "Yesterday I sent a note to a guy at the American embassy."

"Did you?"

"I asked Gigi to have it delivered for me. It's only a couple of blocks, she said. You see, just before we left Chicago I phoned my old friend Walter, in Washington, and explained where we were going, told him about this. He got back to me with some names here—contacts. I don't expect great results, but I did tell this guy in the information branch I wanted to visit him."

"Could he do us any good?"

"It's worth a try. I might suggest he ask the State Department to put in its oar."

"No! Do you think they might . . . ?"

"There's an election coming, and this would be one of those humane Christian things from the White House. Make good copy."

"Do they do such things?"

"Those people are sweet, and mostly air, like Nabisco wafers. Still, I did ask Walter to get to the right desk in the State Department. I've been worried all along about your dual citizenship."

"I should have attended to that long ago." She changed the subject. In science she was scientific; in other matters her methods were more magical, Corde believed. By giving up the dual citizenship, she would be admitting her mother's mortality, and that in itself might have weakened the old woman. That kind of primitive reasoning.

"Tanti Gigi wants me to get in touch with Dr. Gherea," she said.

"Gherea?"

"You remember who he is? You *don't* remember."

"Yes, I do. I do so. Your father's pupil, the one he trained in brain surgery."

"That's the man. He's the big neurosurgeon here, practically the only one. My father made him. After my father died he became a big shot."

"Is he good?"

"They say he's a genius."

"We'll have to think about it."

Her schoolgirl bed was too narrow for them both, and he returned to the divan. Several times during the night he got up to stroke her head or kiss her on the shoulders. These remedies had always given Corde a sense of useful power, but they were ineffectual now. The night pangs were too bad. He had them himself. He listened to Minna's breathing. She appeared to hold her breath. He waited, listening until she exhaled. He said at last, "Let's get out the bottle and have a shot or two. No use lying here like dummies." He switched on the light. They sat side by side in their coats, drinking plum brandy. The stuff was slightly oily and rank, but went down smooth and warm. Then up came the fermented fumes.

"It won't be easy to approach Gherea."

"Why not?" said Corde. "Don't you know him?"

"Thirty years ago he was like one of the family. But he's turned into a savage."

"In what way savage?"

"He knocks people down—assistants, anesthetists, nurses. He even hits his colleagues, doesn't give a damn for anybody. They have to take it from him. He punches and kicks them if they hand him the wrong instrument. And he won't operate without money. 'You don't give me five hundred thousand lei, I don't remove your brain tumor.'"

"A brute. You don't have to tell me about brutes. And the only game in town."

"That's it, Albert. Even the dictator's son, when he had a skull fracture and they brought him to Gherea, they say Gherea had him put in bed with another patient."

"Are they two to a bed here?"

"In lots of hospitals they are. This was Gherea's way of pointing out to *him* that he had to spend more on hospitals."

"So even the dictator has to put up with him. And what does Gherea do with the dough he squeezes from people—does he live it up?"

"I guess he must. But I don't see how—he never leaves the country. How do you live it up here? He doesn't have a second language. Maybe Russian. I think he comes from Bessarabia. He never goes abroad."

". . . Pictures, music?"

"They say he has no use for such stuff."

"Just himself and his knives and saws? Him and death? Only interested in the basic facts? What about sex?"

"That's just it; he has a lady friend and I happen to know her. I met the woman in Zurich eight or ten years ago. She's very decent, divorced. They're together."

"And you want her to persuade him to examine Valeria?"

"What's your picture of Gherea?"

"Your people had class, and he was a boor. They took him up because he had a knack for surgery. He despised them. Thought it was idiotic that with all their advantages they should be Communists. A peasant mentality. He concentrated on learning the Cushing techniques from your father, and then to hell with him."

"That's about right," said Minna. Corde's speed in making connections never failed to please her. She counted on him to spell things out.

"Sure, I see him. He's the tough glory type who goes into people's heads with his tools and his fingers. The brain has got to be hell to work in. Save 'em or kill 'em. Hates sentiment, dramatizes himself as a beast . . . maybe there's a peasant mother who still pines for him out in the bush. He never sees her. There's only this devoted woman with access to his softer side."

"I'm going to talk to her. Tanti Gigi got the number for me."

"Can't hurt."

"You think I should?"

"Of course. Let Gherea look at the X-rays."

The X-rays would show a cloud over the brain of the sort Corde had once seen on a film. A smart microphotographer had managed to insert a tiny lens into the carotid artery and push it up to the skull, capturing a cerebral hemorrhage on his camera. What you saw was the blood beginning to fizz out. At first it wavered in a thick, black, woolly skein. Then it suddenly filled in, thickened, a black rush, the picture of death itself. The memory of this television documentary was something Corde preferred to avoid.

He thought, Sure, let Minna get this surgeon character to look at the clot, make his gesture. It won't do any good. But let her put up a fight. Valeria fought for her. Minna when she was brought back to earth could be a tigress. He had seen that. Fighting was quite unrealistic, of course. Under the circumstances it would get her nowhere. The Colonel had them all in chancery, like John L. Sullivan. But it was necessary emotionally to do battle.

Corde had heard anecdotes about Valeria's dignified refusal to rejoin the Party after she was "forgiven." She told the Central Committee that she had loved her late husband, and that if he had been unfaithful she would have loved him still but she would never have taken him back. In matters of self-respect she was the model for her daughter, her sister and all the ladies of her circle. Had she made serious trouble, it would have been easy enough for the regime to put her away, but this would have upset many old academicians and physicians and educators of her own dying generation. Why stir up the codgers? Besides, she had been a sensible old character, and circumspect, and knew exactly how far she could go, so they were letting her die in the best of their hospitals. But they weren't about to be agreeable to the daughter. The daughter came flying in from the U.S. trailing her streamers of scientific prestige, arriving with this dean of hers and demanding special treatment. She had forgotten how things were here. Maybe she had never known. They would give the daughter a few lumps. This was the score, as her brooding husband saw it. Naive Gigi considered herself to be next in line and came forward to carry on in her fallen sister's place. She was protecting Minna, too, as Valeria had done. All these fighters. Corde reviewed the situation as though he were browsing over it, but his conclusions were sharp enough. The ladies were getting nowhere. They couldn't get anywhere. But they were bound to try. He would try too.

"Let's drink up and get some sleep," he said.

"You haven't heard from Chicago?" she said. "Nothing from Miss Porson?"

"Not yet."

"Not from Vlada, or from Sam Beech?"

Minna took an interest in the Beech project. Beech was a colleague at the college, a celebrated, a notable, a pure scientist, very high in the pantheon, who had asked the Dean for help in putting some of his ideas before the general public. Vlada was a Serbian friend of Minna's. They had been at

Harvard graduate school together. Lifelong students, both of them. Minna's old lycée was nearby. You might see the shape of it up the street even now if you could bear to open the door to the stucco porch (it couldn't be much colder than the room). That lycée had specialized in the "hard" disciplines, apparently. Behind the iron curtain, history and literature were phony subjects, but mathematics and the physical sciences were incorruptible.

Vlada was a member of Beech's research group, the famous geologist's chief chemist. In Minna's view the planet was a far better subject than slums, crimes and prisons. Why bother with that sort of thing if you could write instead about a geophysicist like Beech? She confessed she couldn't understand why the *Harper's* articles had disturbed so many people. What was in them? Corde had watched her rattle through the glossy pages, impatient, trying to do right by him. He doubted that she had read them. She admitted that she found the language hard, the spin he gave words was odd. She was told that the Dean was a journalist of unusual talent. That was good enough for her. The Dean said, "Don't you believe it. There is no such thing. That's just the way journalists pump, promote, gild and bedizen themselves, and build up their profession, which is basically a bad profession." The Cordes had a language problem. When he let himself go she didn't understand what he was saying. (What was *bedizen*?) In all essentials, of course, he was perfectly straight with her, an erratic person, a strange talker, but a secure husband—a crystallized, not an accidental husband.

It meant a lot to her that Corde was approached by Professor Beech after the first of his two articles in *Harper's*. The collaboration was Beech's idea. Corde then said to Minna, "You think this is the greatest, don't you? You look as if you just swallowed a double dose of delight." Yes, she was extremely pleased. Beech, you see, was a scientist. A joint article, when it was published, would remove Corde from the uproar he had somehow stirred up. "You think some of his class will rub off on me," said Corde.

When he understood what Beech was really after, he said that he might be willing to do the job. "Not so innocuous, either," he said to Minna, but she was too pleased to take this in.

Vlada herself was flying over from Chicago and was expected at Christmas. She had an only brother in Rumania whom she visited every year.

"If she actually *does* come," said Minna (there were often arbitrary delays over visas), "she'll bring a bundle of stuff for us from home. A mixed blessing. Bad as it is here, it's just as well for you to be away from Chicago."

"Yes," he said. "Quite a string of lesser evils."

"At least you haven't got that kid on your back."

He decided not to reply. He only said, "Better have some sleep. Drink up. I can always sack out for an hour, but you're on your feet all day."

iii

THE kid, Mason Zaehner, was the Dean's only nephew, the son of his widowed sister, Elfrida. Mason was a dropout, still connected with the college but drifting about the city. For a while he had taken special courses in computer science. Those were only a cover, apparently—but for what? More recently he had been a busboy; and in the kitchen of the delicatessen-restaurant that employed him, he became intimate with a black dishwasher, a parolee. Corde had seen this man's rap sheet. His crimes were the familiar ones—theft, possession of stolen property, et cetera. He was now charged with homicide. The young man he was accused of killing was a student, Rickie Lester. The Dean himself had had to identify the body. This was unusual, but it was August; the college's top security man was up in Eagle River, everybody was out of town. It was Corde's impression that the young man's wife, Lydia, was under sedation.

So the cops rang the Dean and at four o'clock in the morning called for him in their blue-and-white car. It was a rotten night. The air was heavy with the smell of malting grain from the kilns of Falstaff beer, near Calumet Harbor. This was better than the hot sulfur and sewer gases vented by U.S. Steel. *That* acid stink made you get out of bed to shut the windows. Through an ectoplasmic darkness—night was lifting—the Dean rode to the hospital. There he viewed the murdered boy.

Rick Lester's face had the subtracted look of the just dead. He had crashed through the window of his own third-floor apartment, and his skull was broken on the cement. His longish hair was damp (with blood?) and hung backwards. His slender feet were dirty. The cops said he had gone out barefoot earlier in the night. Making the rounds of the bars, he had driven his car without shoes. Many young people removed their shoes in hot weather—as if they were surrounded by woods and fields, not these broken-bottle, dog-fouled streets. What did these charmed-life children think Chicago was? The expression on Rick Lester's face suggested that he would have given up this sort of caper if he had lived. The folds of his mouth, his settled chin, gave him a long white mature look of dignity. More adult, more horsey, a different kind of human being altogether. Corde was inclined to think that his hurry-up death had taught him something. Since he had been subtracted once and for all from the active human sum, you could only try to guess when that lesson had been given. Illumination while falling? A ten-second review of his life?

An experienced man and far from young, Corde had not expected to feel this death so much. He couldn't see why. His feelings took him by surprise. Something seemed to be working its way upward, treading on his stomach and his guts. The pressure on his heart was especially heavy, unpleasantly hot and repulsively melting. He had no use for such sensations; he certainly didn't want the kid's death bristling over him like this. He had seen plenty of corpses. This one got to him, though. Corde believed that it was the evil that had overtaken the boy that did it. For he was a boy, with those slender feet curling apart. Corde didn't know him well enough to weep for him. So perhaps it wasn't the boy, entirely, but some other influence. After the identification was made and the face covered again, Corde's revulsion-depression, or whatever it was, took a different turn. He was unwilling to let the administration take over and follow its usual pattern, depending upon the homicide police, who would investigate at their own pace. It was beyond him to explain why he became so active in this case. He had had to handle student deaths before, mostly suicides, and to deal with parents. He wasn't particularly good at this, never saying what people expected of him although he chose his words with care. His pallor and the dish face and deep voice were not effectively combined into a manner. He wanted to say what he meant sensibly or warmly, but he was so unsuccessful with horrified families that he horrified himself—"I can't make sense of this senseless death," was what he tacitly confessed—and the odd phrases that came out only puzzled grieving parents and probably depressed them further.

What had happened? As yet the cops had little to say. They told the Dean that Rick Lester had gone out on the town that night. His wife was with him for a while, but he took her home and then was too restless to stay put. At two in the morning he turned up in a bar they described as flaky. There "he made a pest of himself, acted up, just about the only white person in the place, making sex signals, according to the bartender." The cops rumbled on, doing their heavy minimum for this dean. It wasn't so much that they were cynical, but their big-city-homicide outlook was summed up in the thickness of their cheeks and bodies more than by their words. The words were only a kind of stuffing. Maybe this boy had hot pants, or drank more than he could hold, or was freaked out on Quaaludes. Blood tests would tell. He may have known the party or parties who pushed him from the window. But although they sounded knowledgeable, the professional work of the cops wasn't too good. They moved slowly, indifferent. The mobile crime lab didn't do its job. And then it turned out that the coroner's report was incomplete. It all became worse, not better, as summer ended. The undertaker didn't do what he was supposed to do. The young wife broke down. Then she said that she must go away for a while at least.

One of the homicide cops had advised Corde to post a reward, and Corde moved quickly to find the money. He had run into trouble with the Provost about this. They had never had trouble before. The Provost, Alec Witt, was generally cooperative, and Corde had had a good opinion of him; but Witt seemed to think that Corde was moving too fast. This smooth man, Witt, whose manner was ultraconsiderate and solicitous, all mildness, wondered whether the college might not be well advised to keep a low profile. There was a tricky racial angle to the case, and no telling what disagreeable facts digging might bring out. But Corde persisted. He had in his hand a list of funds from which money could be taken. It was available, all right. He kept bringing forward his wide head, sinking it so that the glasses slipped away from his eyes and from his light-haired, dense joined brows. He was low-keyed but refused to accept a refusal. The college could afford it, should do it. The Provost began to think the man would resign if he couldn't have his way. Corde had gotten his back up. For what reason? That the shrewd Provost could not make out. He smiled one of his not-quite-pleasant smiles of understanding gentleness, but he was a rough Chicago man; his neck, his chest, told you that, not big but brutal, definitely—charging linebacker's strength packed into those muscles. Corde had never had occasion to take this in before. The physical Provost was revealed to him today. "I guess I can come up with a few thousand bucks if you absolutely have to offer money," Witt said at last.

"That's what it takes to get the information; the cops are definite about it," Corde said.

As soon as the reward was announced, witnesses came forward, sure enough, and within twenty-four hours two suspects were arrested on their evidence. One of these was Lucas Ebry, Mason's friend, and the other a prostitute with a long criminal record. After this, the case developed quickly. Student reaction was also quick. That was Mason's doing. Immediately, he organized something; Corde couldn't tell you what that something was—a resistance movement, a defense campaign. The radical student line was that the college waged a secret war against blacks and that the Dean was scheming with the prosecution, using the college's clout to nail the black man. Resolutions were passed and published in the student daily, which took up the case in a big way.

Mason argued that there had been no murder. Rick Lester hadn't been pushed from the window, he had stumbled, he fell. Anyway, it was all his fault, he went out that night looking for trouble, had been asking for it. Campus militants developed the ideological aspects of the case—the college was trying to restrict black housing in the neighborhood, it refused to divest itself of South African investments, it was slow on Affirmative Action. Himself a campus radical forty years ago, the Dean saw how little things had changed. The same meetings, agitprop slogans, fanaticism, pressure methods the same. The

Provost said, "This will die down by and by; it always does." What he really meant was, "See what you've stirred up." Corde's head came forward silently. His sober nod conceded nothing. He had Witt's number now—not that he knew what to do with it.

Mason had the nerve to drop in on his uncle. From her anteroom Corde's secretary, Miss Porson, said discreetly on the telephone—she was Corde's ally, but she loved the excitement, too—"Your nephew has just stopped by; wants a few minutes of your time."

"Tell him you're squeezing him in between appointments," said Corde.

His door was already opening, and there was his nephew, busy-minded, scheming Mason, in the usual youth drag—the worn narrow jeans, sprigged shirt, ponytail. What to make of Mason! Corde had always disliked puzzles and people who contrived to puzzle you. Did he dislike his nephew? No, but his feelings towards him were terribly mixed. Skinny, lanky, ambling, with pointed elbows, Mason gave himself graces, seemed even to fancy that there was a valuable kind of fragrance coming from him. What were his views? He was sometimes seen with the Workers' World International Marxist-Leninists, the ones who carried small red flags as they peddled their papers in the streets, but he wasn't one of them. A definite ideology would have made him easier to deal with, and Mason didn't intend to make anything easy. No, Corde couldn't identify the young man's position, if he had a position. Maybe there wasn't really any.

Mason came in with a light, bright Huckleberry Finn air. It made the Dean heavy-hearted. Behind the lightness there was supposed to be something dangerous, equivocal, what-have-you. Corde silently asked (and it was as much a prayer as a question), Must we go through this? Well, yes, we must. Accepting, he settled back in the Dean's chair and crossed his arms, his ankles. Leaning somewhat to the side, he composed himself. He said, "I've got somebody coming any minute, but sit down."

Mason when he sat was about as graceful as a driller's rig—a long frame, a remote head. You could see it going up and down rhythmically in a field of similar rigs. In time the boy would fill out, certainly, and the added weight might reduce his nervous intensity. His father had been bearish in build, anything but a nervous type. Mason senior, a high-powered Loop lawyer with connections in the Daley machine, had been tough, arrogant, a bulldozing type. Brutal people, those Chicago insiders, a special breed. Mason hadn't inherited his father's bulk—not yet. What had he inherited from him?

His nephew, as Corde saw him, was at an uncomfortable stage of development. Uncomfortable? Bright, light, he was also bristling, writhing. The young racket wasn't doing him a bit of good. Well, the field was very crowded; he was one of global millions. How to rise above the rest, grab the lead—that was the challenge, and he hadn't yet figured out how this was to be done. Hence the equivocal menace, a sort of announcement: "Watch this space." Corde looked down on these crowded fields packed with contenders; he was prepared to admit that. He was prepared to admit quite a lot about himself. For instance, you would not need to press hard to get him to concede that his patient air was only assumed, a pis aller and a burden. But it would have been a terrible mistake to try to discuss things with Mason frankly, or (still worse) on a theoretical level: youth, age, mass tendencies, self-presentation, demagogy. Corde had observed to Minna not long ago that although people talked to themselves all the time, never stopped communing with themselves, nobody had a good connection or knew what racket he was in—his *real* racket. Did Corde actually know? For most of his life he had had a bad connection himself. There was just a chance, however, that he might, at last, be headed in the right direction. Just a chance. He would have liked to tell his nephew that men and women were shadows, and shadows within shadows, to one another. Given encouragement, Corde would have liked being kindly, candid, affectionate, but Mason gave no encouragement, wasn't buying any kindly candor, and Corde was careful with him, never uncled him, never lectured. He was glad enough, *de minimis* (Mason senior used to say *de minimis*; he was fond of kidding—growling—in Latin), to make plain sense. Given the intricacy of these shadow-framed shadows, plain sense was plenty.

Corde was put off by puzzles, and here was Mason bent on puzzling him, and smiling at his uncle. It wasn't much of a smile. Mason's lips were set high across his face, they were puffy, they swelled, and between them were his ingenuous front teeth. His mother had darker coloring. Mason's hair was fair and brassy. Youthfully vital, it seemed also to have a mineral luster. In the length of his profile and the narrowness of his forehead, he resembled Elfrida. Corde was strongly attached to his sister, he loved her, so it was all the more painful to see the same features adapted to—well, to mischief, contrariness, contemporary expressions of face badly interpreted. This was tough luck—a pity. The pity took hold of Corde. It dragged his heart with sorrow—the skinny, ill-assembled, innerly weak kid taking the field against his uncle the Dean. But the sorrow was excessive, too. There was no call for heavy sorrow, it dragged him in the wrong direction. Corde put a stop to it.

The Dean's office was in a Brown Decade building. They had tried to move him to new quarters, but he fought that. The new rooms were too low, and the long modern lighting tubes hurt his eyes. Also, he preferred not to run into the Provost and other administrative personnel in the corridors or the men's room. The brownstone was more like his idea of a college building. He was not exactly deanlike in appearance. He wore a three-piece suit; the vest wasn't buttoned right somehow (no up-to-date official courting favor with undergraduates would dress in this style). He was something of a stand-in, a journalist passing for a dean. His wide face, a sphere enlarged by baldness, looked simple and calm but also a little dusty, with an on-the-shelf effect. There was something out of kilter in his look (the big glasses? the eyes themselves?). Long silky hairs at the base of his throat didn't sort well with the three-piece suit. The deep voice came from a man who after all didn't look very strong—a misleading appearance; he was strong enough.

"What's with your mother?" he said.

"I haven't seen much of her lately . . . sorry about that. But how's your beautiful wife? I have to tell you, you really got lucky with this one, Uncle Albert."

Corde made no answer. It was not possible to misinterpret this silence. But Mason went on, "She's not only very smart, she's also warm and cheerful. You're livelier, too, with her. The other ladies must have depressed you. That's just about impossible with Minna. And she's got class. Mother loves her."

"What's on your mind, Mason?"

"You won't accept this as a social visit? You're busy? I'm making trouble for you?"

"I assume it's trouble you want to discuss."

"I wrote twice to you about it. You didn't answer."

"There was no way to answer those muddled, boiling, murky letters."

"You could have asked me to come in and have a talk."

"After you blasted me publicly, what was there to talk about?"

"The real facts of the case."

"I can tell you in short order just how I see those facts. A student is dead. I'm dean of students. I had to take a hand in this. And I did. Two people were arrested, indicted, charged with homicide. That just about describes it."

"You put up a reward for information."

"Of course."

"Witnesses bought and paid for."

Corde absolutely refused to go along with this bright bitterness, the barrels-of-fun line that Mason tried to take with him. It was clearly rejected by his silence. He lowered his eyes to the simple gilt border of his desk—a straight line of stamped arabesques into which he would have liked to read sanity and order.

Mason said, "I have a special interest, too. Lucas Ebry is my friend."

"How close a friend is he?"

"You're suggesting that black street people don't have friendships? Especially with whites? Also, as soon as a reward was posted, 'friends' of Ebry and Riggie Hines came running with information? They wanted the money. Sure. As if white people from the bungalow belt wouldn't do the same for a buck."

"No doubt about it," said Corde.

"The blacks on food stamps, they're the *underclass*—that's what your sociologists around here call them. They're hoping that drugs and killings and prison will eliminate that lousy, trouble-making underclass."

"I'm not the sociologists. They're not my sociologists."

"No, you're my Uncle Albert, telling me not to put words in your mouth. Okay. But you're pushing for a conviction. You've made up your mind to get this one black man."

"Your friend Ebry is on trial for homicide. I didn't indict him, and I won't be trying him."

"You're buddy-buddy with all those Irish characters out of Notre Dame, Loyola and the Machine, the prosecutor, the State's Attorney's people."

"Naturally, I've talked to them."

Assume that there was nothing too rum to be true—could we say also that there was nobody too rum to be liked? The Dean and his nephew were family and so presumably liked or at least tried to like each other. The Dean would have made the effort (it would have been an effort), but liking was not what Mason wanted. He was here on a mature basis (to fight), meanwhile shuffling and grinning. His ultra-bright hey-presto look was insolent. Yes, he had a cause. But mostly he was eager to needle his uncle and he hoped—craved, longed—to drive his needle deep. He was here as a representative of the street people but he intended also to teach his ignorant uncle some lessons about Chicago's social reality. He had earned the right to speak for the oppressed because he and Lucas Ebry had worked together in the grease and garbage of the kitchen, sweat rags tied on their foreheads.

Mason was saying, "Week after week in that damn sewer. That's not a relationship an outside person can judge."

"Petty bourgeois and white, you mean."

"You said it."

There had been the army—mess halls, KP—but it would be foolish to bandy experiences with Mason. Corde let this pass. He waited while the second hand of the electric clock on the wall made one full cycle, like the long-legged fly. Mason's message was clear: Lucas Ebry was real, others (Uncle Albert, for instance) were not. Uncle Albert had no business to be messing with people who were wrapped up in an existence, in a reality that was completely beyond him. For those people the stakes were life and death. What did Uncle Albert stake? Let him stick to his fancy higher education—seminars in Plato and the Good. Those people of the *underclass*, dopers or muggers or whores: what were they, mice? To the "thinking population," to establishment intellectuals, they were nothing but mice! Thus Corde spelled out, parsed, his nephew's message. He even agreed, in part.

"But what about the boy who was killed?" he said.

"Who says he was killed!"

"Let's not quibble over words. He died. . . ."

"But you can't prove he was killed."

Steady in spite of the rise of unwanted anger, Corde said, "He was tied and gagged. He didn't first gag and then tie himself with strips from the drapes, did he? Or cut himself—slash his own ear with the kitchen knife? He went through the glass on the third floor with one of his arms still tied tight and the gag in his mouth. Then the police came . . . but what do we need to go over this for? There's the testimony of Mrs. Lester and the black woman."

"Are you going to put that whore in front of a jury? You never will. Her rap sheet goes back ten years. She's plea-bargaining. Her evidence isn't worth a damn. And the other lady, Lydia, what do you expect her to say? She and her husband went out that night looking for action. It was the kind of hot weather when people get raunchy, and that's what Lester was. He went to the bar and brought home Lucas Ebry and this black whore. Why do you think he did that?"

"Why do you think, if his wife was at home?"

"Lester went out twice, once with Lydia for a beer—at least that's what she said—and again after she went to bed. He took off alone in his car, no shoes on his feet. He went to this other bar, which is all black, and he didn't know how to behave. He got on everybody's nerves. He was damn loud, dumb and offensive. He tried to pick up Lucas Ebry and this black chick."

"It was they who picked him up."

The conversation here became painful to Corde for the motives it brought into question. He couldn't say what Lester had been looking for that night. Whatever the boy had done led, as if by prearranged stages, to his destruction and it was not impossible that all those wrong moves were made because they were wrong. An event had picked him to happen to. The gates of death were opening for the kid. Why shouldn't he himself have had some sense of this?

"You think he was just being nice and friendly," Mason said.

Corde conceded, "What he did that night seems out of character, but I don't believe it should have been punishable by death. Nothing he deserved to die for."

"I read what you said to the press about him, that he was a disciplined student and all that. He used to go to early mass."

"I didn't make it up," said Corde. "Two priests paid me a call. I didn't solicit the information. They told me he was religious. Why couldn't he have been?"

"No comment," said Mason, but the expression that worked about his mouth was nothing but comment. For a moment he was tough and mature in the manner of his late father, an artist in this sort of thing, an overbearing rude man. The late Zaehner had just such bulges in the lower cheek, and the identical bullying lusterless put-down stare. And Mason was still very young, only twenty-two. His brassy hair subsided on his jaws, towards the chin, in light streaks of down. You could almost see the pollen of adolescence over the bridge of his nose. Why did he have to be so very tall? His quiddity was overstretched.

"Whether he was religious is neither here nor there. His life was decently organized. He studied, worked, he was a married young man."

"Yeah? Well, let's continue with what happened. He acted like a loudmouth that night. He went up and down the bar, and forced people to shake hands with him. They could have cared less. A white student saying he understood their life and was *for* them. Big deal! They were turned off completely."

"This sounds like Ebry—the 'turned off.'"

"Never mind all the decent stuff," said Mason. "A nice clean boy and an Eagle Scout? You weren't born a dean, Uncle. Lester was as kinky as they come."

"Well, get to the point."

"He picked up Ebry and this Riggie Hines at the bar, and they went together to his apartment."

"That's from Ebry, too."

"Well, there were three people to begin with. One of them is dead. One is plea-bargaining—lying. What does that leave?"

Ebry, without bail money, was being held in County Jail. Riggie Hines was in prison, too.

Mason said, "How did they get into the apartment if Lester didn't invite them? So? Why did he?"

"For a sexual purpose? With his wife asleep? Why would he bring two people there? . . ."

"Riggie Hines is as tough as they come, and all whore. Ready for any damn thing. What's a white wife to her? You've seen her yourself. She goes around in a workshirt, wide open, and wears her jeans like a man. She spits on the floor like a trucker; and if a guy didn't pay her, she'd slug him. You don't bring home a broad like that at three in the morning to discuss academic subjects. She's a bad cunt."

Mason sketched all this for his uncle with an air of "You tell *me* how it happened, if not this way," and Corde had to agree that it wasn't easy to explain. It was like trying to see through a barrier of vapor or gas. Reconstruction was all the more problematic because of the emotional heaviness of all the circumstances, even time and weather. It had been one of those choking, peak-of-summer, urban-nightmare, sexual and obscene, running-bare times, and death panting behind the young man, closing in. But the evidence suggested that some unconscious choice had been made, some mixture, an emulsion of silliness and doom shaken up and running over. The younger generation didn't seem to understand who the people around them were, with whom they had to do.

Mason said, "He wanted Riggie Hines to go into the toilet with him."

"What for?"

"To go down on him while she was shitting."

Corde rejected this, hated it. He said violently, "Don't come to me with such talk. And you don't have to unload this kind of thing on that dead kid."

"Well, Uncle, I heard you saying to my mother once that we were living through some kind of sexual epidemic. You made quite a speech at the dinner table. Maybe you weren't aware that I was there. It happened about ten years ago, and I must have been about twelve, but I remember what you said. A kind of demon had ahold of us, was your idea. But here's an illustration and you don't accept it. You want him to be that dead kid, so nice, just an object of pity."

"According to the police, there was a dog shut up in the toilet."

"It was Lester's dog. He could have taken him to the kitchen."

"More Ebry. He's your one and only source."

"The woman says the same."

"I doubt that Lester had anything definite in mind," said Corde. "There was a melon in the icebox. He was going to entertain his visitors. He brought the melon and a carving knife into the parlor. Ebry grabbed the knife."

"That's not the way I heard it. That's Riggie's plea-bargaining. She's plenty familiar with knives. There's a stabbing on her rap sheet. Did she ever say how many people she cut? No, why should she?"

"I suppose," said Corde, "if you could get into that tight skull of hers you'd find it packed with grotesque ideas, deeds or pictures." It wasn't so much what he said that made Mason stare at him; it was the odd but characteristic lapse into abstruseness or into images by which grieving parents were also put off when the Dean was trying to console them.

"So he was just entertaining them with some nice cantaloupe."

"They held the knife on him," said Corde. "I suppose he put up some resistance, so they cut his ear to prove they meant business. They tore strips from the drapes and tied him up, they pushed a gag down his throat, and then they started to burglarize the apartment, which was what they had come for —hi-fi, tape recorder, earphones: those were stacked by the back door. Riggie pulled off Rick Lester's gold wedding band. That's in evidence, too, so we don't have to quibble about it. All right. Then Ebry dropped the TV set, and that woke up Mrs. Lester, and she came out in her short summer nightie. Till then she hadn't heard anything because of the noisy air conditioner in her bedroom. When his wife came in, Lester began to struggle. That's what seems to have happened. Riggie held him down, while Ebry jumped at Mrs. Lester from behind and forced her to the floor."

"Yes," said Mason. "So what have you got? A white woman, practically naked, and the black man on top of her with the knife. The classic rape fantasy."

"There was no rape."

"You bet not. What would he want that skinny broad for? He had his choice of women. At the restaurant they would come around to the kitchen and ask for him, plenty of white ones. And furthermore, Ebry wasn't the guy who was in Lester's apartment when the hassle started. He got disgusted long before, because Lester was patronizing the shit out of him."

"So he said in one of his statements. It was two other guys. Only Mrs. Lester picked him out in the lineup."

"How could she identify him if he was behind her? But all right, I'll go along with your reconstruction, Uncle. The husband saw the wife in her short nightie, on the floor, and he started to struggle. He got one arm free, and he managed to hop to his feet."

"Then he was pushed through the window, broke the glass and fell three stories. One arm was still tied and the gag was in his mouth. . . ."

"You really are hung up on that gag. Would it have been more humane if he wasn't gagged, so he could speak his last words? He fell, and he was killed. What else is there?" Mason scowled as he smiled.

"So that's your summary . . . what he had in mind was an orgy. Instead there was a fight, and if he was killed he had death coming to him."

"What do you want to add? 'Appalled'? 'Aghast'? 'All shook up'?"

For Corde this was the worst moment of their conversation. Strange interviews took place in a dean's office, stranger than you might think possible. Students who sought you out sometimes made curious requests or confessions, or boasts. But this interview, with the weight of his own family behind it, made his head ache, sent a pang through his eyeballs. Depressed, the Dean rose and opened the door to Miss Porson's outer office. Was there a student waiting? There was no one. The old girl's chair was empty. She was demonstratively sympathetic, his ally—she made a big thing of that—plenty of flourishes—but her instinct was to take off when the heat was on. She had gone to the ladies' room to smoke a cigarette and gossip with the other girls. So he was stuck with Mason. He saw no way to get rid of him. He longed to say, "I don't feel well. Beat it. Come back some other time." But that would have been weak. This was serious. It was crime and punishment, life and death for Ebry. Corde was furious with Miss Porson; gabby old bag, not worth a damn. But the real trouble, as he recognized, was that he was in a wrong relation to the sum of things—he himself. A sign of this was that he was in a useless debate—hopeless! all the premises were wrong—with this adolescent whose head was so remote. As he went back to his seat, Mason watched him.

The Dean understood only too well what the kid was transmitting when he said, "'Appalled'? 'All shook up'?" He was saying, Let's not fuck around with all these high sentiments and humane teachings and pieties and poetry, and the rest of that jazz. You keep going back to the knife and the gag and the blood and the corpse and the prostrated wife, and you do it to stir yourself with horror. Stones advertising how "human" they are.

The truth of this, even if it was not more than a particle, was a poisonous particle.

The true voice of Chicago—the spirit of the age speaking from its lowest register; the very bottom.

For Mason was never more like his father than when he thought he had you dead to rights. There were no two ways about Mason senior; he was either for you or against. If he didn't approve, then he despised you. Corde had long ago decided that Chicago was the contempt center of the U.S.A. And he heard the contempt note in his nephew's voice—the true, buzzing, bullying, braying La Salle Street brass. "Hold their feet to the fire," Mason senior liked to say. Or, if it was your own feet to the fire, "Got to bite the bullet." He chose to speak in platitudes; but he interpreted them powerfully, virile bruiser that he was. You were tough or you were nothing. In realism and cunning these La Salle Street characters were impressive because they had the backing of the pragmatic culture of the city, the state, the region, the country. In his brother-in-law's view, the Dean had given up the real world to take refuge with philosophy and art. Academics were hacks and phonies.

Old Mason could seem ponderously respectful, following polite protocol for liberals, but the bottom line was this: he said, or growled, with narrowed eyes, "I make my living by tipping over garbage cans, but at least I go in the alley and tip them over myself." Up in Lake Forest, Corde had been a subject of jokes at the Zaehner dinner table: "the dud dean." Elfrida didn't join in this fun, Corde was certain of that. But she had married an extroverted, assertive man, she preferred a husband who was altogether different from her brother. Her brother, as she had once told Corde, was strong-minded but at the same time withdrawn, seemed to have a minimum of common ground with the people about him, and seldom "gave out" except on paper.

Seated again, and facing Mason, the Dean felt bleak—bleakest of all about himself. A gap had opened. No, a vacuum. A vacuum was there. He said, "Yes, when I looked at the boy's body in the morgue, it shook me up." He might have added: This one time, I *was* shaken.

Mason said, "I read the story in the *Trib.* The wife was in shock, and Dean Albert Corde identified the victim. . . . You probably swore you'd get the sonsofbitches who did it."

"It's true I wanted them caught."

"You went to lots of trouble."

"It's also true that if they hadn't been found it would have upset me."

"What makes you so sure you got the right party? Okay, you made your own investigation. I know all about it. You went to the restaurant where we worked. You even went to see Toby Winthrop, that guy who runs the detoxification center, about Ebry."

"As a matter of fact, we didn't discuss him."

"You're like a mastermind nemesis when you get started. I bet if you had discussed him, Winthrop would have put Ebry down. Winthrop is one of these glamorous black types, a fund-raising personality."

Corde said, "Now I want to tell you something, Mason. I don't want you bothering Mrs. Lester. You paid her a visit to warn her not to push the case. You threatened that lots of ugly stuff would come out about her husband. Stay away from her. She's a good young woman."

"What does that mean, 'good young woman'?"

"It means that she has decent instincts. She feels, in earnest."

"Jesus-Cheesus," said Mason.

The Dean now had a swelling, pulsating, exorbitant headache. He had struck it rich this time. It was a beauty, right through the eyes. If he had been alone he would have gone to lie down. He kept an old aluminum lawn chair in the corner. Miss Porson had knitted an afghan for him. He often made use of this green and blue afghan, took comfort from it.

"Furthermore, Mason, you've been spreading stories on campus against the Lesters. No more of that, and knock off the threats."

"Does the relationship embarrass you—nephew against uncle?"

"It would surprise you how little that part of it affects me."

"Oh, this is just hysterical kid stuff?"

Corde, with swelling headache, a great balloon, but still patient, dropped his gaze to the desk. "Look, you came to have it out with me and settle all kinds of scores, put the whole mess on one square, like roulette. God knows what-all. It's too bad. . . ."

To Mason this earnestness was simply a ploy, Uncle Albert trying a softer approach. His smile said as much.

Corde now made a super effort to be fair, to reconsider. (Maybe he did have a blind spot.) He put his imagination to work once more on the circumstances of Rick Lester's death. For this purpose he had to absent himself briefly. He turned his swivel chair away from Mason and stared through the blue window and the fringe of autumn ivy. Let's try again. Begin by setting in place that boyish man's death. Begin with the crying ugliness of the Chicago night. Put that in the center. It had to be in the middle. Now then, who were the people involved? There was a business connection between Lucas Ebry and Riggie Hines. He pimped for her, steered students to her room. This information was from the cops. Very likely Mason knew it, too, if the friendship was as close as he claimed. But he'd see no special disgrace in pimping. It wasn't even pimping, only procuring. Those kids had to get themselves laid. So what? She didn't need Ebry's protection; she protected herself.

She had the build of a boxer and a boxer's compact tough

head. Even the way she tucked back the mannish shirt to show the tops of her breasts was pugilistic—this must have worked sexually on the boy. Ebry! She could floor Ebry with a punch. He was a shrunken, twisting figure, burnt out; his small beard was twisted, too. He drooped at the knees, he was a sheared-off man. Those hands of his hung down looking gorged, and with loose skin. The orgy was another clumsy invention, like vice in the toilet, like Rick staggering around until he went through the window. Those were the people who had come to see Rickie Lester off. Now imagine this gang breaking into Lydia's bedroom to wake her with a proposition. She would have burst into tears.

No, the whole purpose was robbery. This was what Ebry had come for. When the two jumped Lester and grabbed the kitchen knife, they must have cut his ear only to make him lie still. Probably he stopped struggling then and they tied him up. Riggie must have yanked off his gold wedding band first thing. They weren't going to kill him. Neither had ever been booked for homicide, although Riggie was once an accessory. It was the dropped TV set (was Ebry too puny to lift it?) that set off the panic, when Lydia Lester ran from bed and Ebry threw her to the floor. Rick Lester struggled to his feet, and then either one or both of the robbers reached the murder point. Lucas Ebry was chaotic enough to do it, scared, desperate; the night hot enough, bad enough; Riggie Hines was tough enough. You saw women like that in police court for scalding a man with boiling grease, or for cutting him. So, to go to the evil conclusion, Lester was pushed. He couldn't have broken the window by staggering against it. The frames were old but they were wood, not cardboard. He would have had to be pushed.

As soon as he fell, Ebry began to run around wiping the fingerprints—from the TV, from the knife. But clean prints were found in Lester's Toyota. Experienced killers would have done something about Lydia—she was a witness—but these two took off. They left the loot and escaped down the back stairs. These were ancient Chicago open back stairs and porches clapped together of gray lumber, held up by crude cross-trusses. There was a jumbled yard, a fence, and then the alley. In the alley Riggie and Ebry split.

Corde's upper lip when he was reflecting turned inward. His big open forehead rose bare towards the crown, his Irish nose was short (he had Irish blood from his mother), his eyes were large, his mouth plain and wide. So, then, they split. After splitting, Riggie got rid of the wedding ring. She passed it to a man, one of the street people, and asked him to keep it for her. But as soon as the reward was announced, this fellow went to the police, made a statement, turned over the ring, which was now in evidence, and claimed his dough. He said he was willing to take the witness stand, but he dropped out of sight later. Grady, the assistant State's Attorney, had the cops looking for him. So there were your facts. Corde wanted to be as impartial as possible, severely, even passionately impartial, saying to himself various things of characteristic oddity: Objectivity begins at home; harden yourself some more; it's no good without a hard spirit; by telling yourself normal-sounding stories, all you do is cling to nonexistent normalcy; then life is no more than you're "inclined to understand," and you're nowhere.

But the fact of facts was the body Corde had identified at the hospital, the kid on the slab, the long soiled feet, the face with the only-just-subtracted expression and the hint of mature knowledge. And then the sequel (another set of facts, framed in fire): Grady had ordered the body exhumed for further tests, but these could not be made because the boy hadn't been embalmed, and it was hot summer. However, the family had been charged for embalming, and the bill had been paid. But this was ordinary business practice, built-in fraud, nothing to get worked up about (although he was worked up). This last consideration, the decomposed body, was not mentioned by Corde. It would have given an opening for deeper nastiness.

Mason said, "Well, you've been sitting there for about five minutes without a word, only your lips moving. You want me to go. You're sore at me."

"Not exactly," said Corde in his low voice.

"I had a few things to say and wasn't sure you'd give me an appointment."

"Why not?"

"Maybe you don't want to see your antagonist face to face."

"What makes you think you're my antagonist?"

"Because if you aim to crucify this black dishwasher, you're going to have to fight me. Yes!" Corde was shaking his head. "If some black had fallen through the window, there wouldn't have been any damn reward or investigation or case. How many black people were killed in the same week? No big deals, no State's Attorney Grady, no press coverage."

"I'm sorry to say that's probably true. But it's my responsibility on this job to oversee the students. That's why we're discussing Rick Lester in the Dean's office, this nice autumn day." The nightmare fury of summer was behind them, and the (decomposing) heat had abated. As if the mad spell were over. But it had only been transposed. The same rotten music continued. This was its cooler key.

Corde understood very well what his nephew was saying to him. He said it to himself, and this was how it went: You meddle in things you have no sympathy with. These people do what they can in the space they've been confined to. Yes, they scrounge and they rob and they fuck; they drink and take drugs, they cut and shoot each other and die young. And what you, a man of routine, can't forgive is that they have no structure. They don't plan, and don't "do"; they only hang out. That's what disgusts you most.

He said to Mason, "It's odd how little you feel for Rick. He was a student like yourself."

"He wasn't like myself. He was your kind, not mine."

"He was a young man who went out on a hot night . . ."

"And ran into some blacks who murdered him. That's all you can see. You gave yourself away when you talked about the case to Mother. She told me how you described it. When the warrant went out for Riggie Hines, she was hiding out with a dope pusher in South Shore. The cops had to break down a door with baseball bats and drag her out from under the bed. That wasn't in the paper—she got it from you. You also said that witnesses came *running* to claim the dough. These people don't know what solidarity is. What's-his-name from Robert Taylor Homes, who described himself as a buddy, fingered Lucas Ebry and repeated what he claimed he heard. Those are my people, and you made them all seem subhuman to my mother—wild-ass savages from the Third World. And now I see that you are writing something about County Jail. It was advertised in the *Times.* Read Albert Corde in *Harper's* for

November. With a complete Chicago background. You think *you* have anything to say about the people of this city?"

"The subject of those articles isn't the jail. There is—there happens to be—a description of the jail in them."

"Uncle Albert, you don't know a damn about what goes on."

"Because I haven't lived the life, like yourself?"

"You went to see County, and still you want to send people to prison? What the hell good is that?"

Corde agreed. "The prisons certainly are awful."

"Why, the Swedish government refused extradition in the case of one American because of the Attica riots and those other stinking places. We have one of the worst right next door in Pontiac." Mason had still more to say. "According to Mother, you got your angle on County Jail from Rufus Ridpath, whom they threw out of there."

"Ridpath is as straight as they come."

"Your kind of black man."

"He seems to me a decent, intelligent public servant."

"Public servant! What kind of civics shit is that? A sadist and a fink."

The conversation was leaking, sinking, capsizing. But here with a raging headache was steady Corde, still on the bridge, looking calm and responsible. Really, he was fed up now. He wanted to run Mason out by the seat of the pants.

Mason said, "A warden who beat up on prisoners."

"He was acquitted. You don't know damn-all about it. Acquitted but still disgraced. And there's a man who *genuinely* felt for the street people, worked to improve the prison. Until he took over, it was run by the criminals. . . ." Here Corde stopped and passed the edge of his hand over his forehead, shading his eyes from the overhead light. Mason was within easy reach of the switch, but he made no move towards it. If he rose from his seat, he would be on his way out. And Mason was going. Only he had more to say. Apparently he followed a prepared mental outline. Corde longed to be rid of him—an acute longing. No bum's rush; kicking him out was just a fantasy. Those greeny-blue eyes and long eyelashes, and the youth pollen sprinkled over the Huck Finn cheekbones, the cheerful pleasant conventions of his suburban upbringing, the ingenuous teeth representing ten thousand dollars' worth of orthodontia, the brassy hair pulled back, the sallow face, shaky pride, the distemper, infection, sepsis. You could almost smell the paste odor of fever. Corde's anger, when this odor reached him, began to pass off in pulsations. He sat there feeling sorry.

"You'll probably go back to Mother and raise hell with her because she repeated what you said."

"I won't do that."

"That's right. I gave you your favorite opening. I'm the one who makes her unhappy. You're the one that protects her. Love your sister."

Corde loved Elfrida. He did, in fact. And this, too, was held against him.

"I was always having you rubbed into me," Mason continued. "Uncle Albert this and Uncle Albert that. A big man, and smart, and a notable. Uncle Albert wrote those pieces on the Potsdam Conference in *The New Yorker*. Uncle Albert saw Harry Truman play poker, and came face to face with Joe Stalin."

"I sympathize with you there. You can get to hate the absent model. But still there was your father to keep the balance. . . ."

"Yes, he put you down some."

"He thought I was a jerk," said Corde, quite neutral.

"You don't seem very sore about that."

"I'm not, very. Your father never did things by halves. There were those he liked, all out, and those he despised, the same."

Mason said, "Off and on you tried to make like a good uncle. You took me fishing on the Cape once."

"I remember very well. We went to catch porgies in the channel, and I fell in."

"You arrived in the night, and then in the morning you put on shorts and you said we should go and fish off the rocks. I thought your legs were very ugly."

"I'm no ballet dancer—Bugayev or Nureyev or whatever. Well, I wasn't very graceful. I lost my footing on those slanting rock slabs. They were covered with seaweed. First thing I knew, I was falling."

"You took a flop and slid down your side over the barnacles."

"And was cut in about fifty slices. Those cuts were thin, but they were nasty."

"That's what it was. It left a nasty memory."

"I went into the drink, rod and all. There was quite a heavy swell." Corde smiled, almost as if it was a pleasant recollection.

He recalled the great weight of the dark green water, and the sky upside down, vast clouds, bottoms up, all white, and the fishing line curving on the current in a long fluid pleat. The rod was lost, like his eyeglasses. Then he couldn't get a grip in the slime of the breakwater, and the boy was too small to help. After Corde at last got himself out, he pulled off his sea-heavy shirt and wrapped it around his thigh. "Those barnacles were hard little bastards." The scars they made were like hash marks. "So that left an impression," he said.

"It was the first time I saw anybody bleed like that."

A porgy or a flounder, if they had managed to hook one in the channel, would have been less memorable, threshing and thrilling on the line, than Uncle Albert. Dumb and inept Uncle Albert, who wrote about Stalin and Churchill at Potsdam, didn't know how to fish. Distortion underfoot because of his big bifocals. The channel caught *him*. Nothing but a deep voice, a bulging eye, an opinionated manner, long hairs growing from his Adam's apple and, when he took off his pants, disgusting shanks. Plus the blood. Odd, I never thought my legs were so bad. Minna likes them well enough. The way I'm put together entertains her. But then she has a cosmic perspective. Not like this ornery kid—really, a cruel kid. He might have judged me with more charity if he had foreseen that he himself would grow up looking two-dimensional, like a drawing of a driller's rig. You had to study Mason to find the humanity in him. It was as hard to see as the thin line of mercury in some thermometers. But if you turned your thermometer in the light and found the lucky angle, you'd be sure to get a reading.

Miss Porson now looked in. Aware that she had stayed away too long (and you couldn't pry into the secret feminine reasons for these irritating absences), she put some melody into her voice, announcing, "There's somebody waiting, Mr. Corde."

"One last thing," said Mason as he rose. "My mother refused to underwrite a bond for Lucas Ebry. . . ."

"She didn't discuss it with me. I didn't advise her," said Corde.

iv

EACH of the long days in Minna's room was a succession of curious states. The first was the state of rising, pulling on your Chicago socks and sweaters (good cashmere, but thinning at the heels and elbows), assembling a dean who was less and less a dean within. The room was dark, the cold mortifying. The toilet, located in a small cell apart from the bathroom, was Gothic. The toilet paper was rough. A long aeruginous pipe only gave an empty croak when you pulled the chain. No water above. You poured from one of the buckets into the bowl. Corde himself now took charge and filled them when the water was running. The buckets were far too heavy for Gigi with her cardiac condition. The bathtub might have been a reservoir if the stopper had worked. All this was like old times in the States, before the age of full convenience. It took you back.

On the dining room table, Turkish coffee was ready in a long-handled brass pitcher, lots of chicory, together with boiled milk, grilled bread in place of toast, brown marmalade with shreds of orange in it—ersatz, but the best that conscientious Tanti Gigi could furnish. Ladies with parcels reported to her. Her bed was a command post. Kindly acquaintances did the errands. Aged women rose at four to stand in line for a few eggs, a small ration of sausages, three or four spotted pears. Corde had seen the shops and the produce, the gloomy queues—brown, gray, black, mud colors, and an atmosphere of compulsory exercise in the prison yard. The kindly ladies were certainly buying on the black market, since Corde and Minna gave Gigi all the lei, bought with dollars at the preposterous rate of exchange. Corde ate grapes and tangerines and other black market luxuries. From time to time he was served meat. It was the general opinion of the ladies that there should be good things in the house of death. Especially for people from the blessed world outside, foreigners who took steaks and tangerines for granted, who would feel the privation, who were as fastidious as dragons. It was outrageous what they devoured, in their innocence. Feeding an American must have diverted these elderly women. But they had forgotten, apparently, how to cook a steak. The meat was served dry, and even scorched. Maybe the cooking oil was no good. Anyway, the meat tasted of fire and suggested sacrifice. It carried a creaturely flavor; the smell of the stall, of the hide, was still there, and he had to suppress the unwanted feeling of animal intimacy that it gave him. But he ate his steak when it was served and told Gigi how good it was. He knew how much organization it took to get it. Gigi drove herself hard, knocked herself out. A physician cousin would come and put his stethoscope to her, and order her to stay in bed, but she got up to mix a cake for Corde because he had once said he liked her raisin cake, and when she wasn't baking she was otherwise busy. She dragged boxes from the shelves, looking for family records. She answered the telephone on the double. She put a shawl over her back and trotted downstairs to consult with Ioanna, the concierge. Concierges had police connections. You had to keep on the good side of them. If the elevator door had not been completely shut, you might see the top of Gigi's head as she worked her way down step by step. Defensive magic was how Corde described these propitiatory calls Gigi went below to make. The staircase smelled of ancient plaster fallen from the gaps opened by the earthquake, and when you opened the door you were struck by the cold; it was like being thwacked with the flat of a saber.

Fifty years ago Gigi had been sent to study commercial English in London; and she spoke the language well enough, in the hoity-toity way of foreigners when they address Americans in *English* English. "See here, dear Albert, you will find the article you are seeking upon the buffet." But she wasn't being superior, only singing songs from a better time. She wouldn't have dreamed of putting the Dean down. "When this trouble is over," she promised him, "we will have to have a *taita tait.*"

Corde saw how it was. In this oppressive socialist wonderland she had depended on her sister to protect her. Now her sister was dying (although by saying "When this trouble is over" Gigi denied it) and she assumed the senior role. After years as an understudy she was trying to play it. She even took on Valeria's doubts about him. Corde became aware of this when he noticed that Gigi sometimes examined his face silently, dark, warm, brown eyes dilated with female speculation: Could he really, but *really*, be trusted? It was obvious that the question of his stability had been much discussed here. With his record of debauchery (something like Don Giovanni's 1,003 seductions), would he really settle down with their Minna? Corde no longer minded this. It was only fair that Gigi, too, should have a crack at him. American behavior *was* wild by the standards of these old-fashioned Eastern Europeans. Corde might have thrilled her by taking her into his confidence. "I *did* know some wild women, but that's over and done with. I wouldn't worry if I were you."

Tell it to the parole board!

Tanti Gigi in her seventies was still the little sister, and willful, given to fits of goodness, tolerating no resistance to her sacrifices. Corde said to Minna, "Your aunt has all kinds of ideas."

"Yes, I know."

"I find it touching. These sisters."

"In the old days, when she was beautiful, she loved to dress. She was a marvelously fashionable dresser. I remember how people turned to look at her in the street. But then during the forties she began taking in the children of families who died in the war. There were about twenty orphans. My mother helped her. Then her husband died."

The apartment was in Valeria's name. Cousins discussed Gigi's future with Minna. What would she do when she was alone?

Just before Valeria's stroke, Gigi had had her hair done—bobbed, crimped, marcelled at the bottom (Corde didn't have the right word)—and now the whole arrangement was coming apart, standing out stiffly from her slender neck like the dry under-fronds of a palmetto. She fussed over Corde at breakfast especially. "I wish we had a proper toaster, but there is not one. Can this coffee be drunk? It was clever of you to bring a tin of British tea from Chicago. Can we not obtain a foreign newspaper for you at the Intercontinental?" She also said, "What a pity that you cannot see what a beautiful country we have, instead of the dark side, and how frightfully dreary." She must have learned her English from Beatrix Potter's *Tale of Two Bad Mice*. It was pure nanny, in a Balkan version.

Corde said, "At the Intercontinental I saw nothing but *Pravda* and *Tribuna Ludu*. They don't seem to carry the *Her-*

ald Tribune." But he was really in two minds about the news. At home he read too many papers. He was better off without his daily dose of world botheration, sham happenings, without newspaper phrases. Nothing true—really true—could be said in the papers. In the dining room there was a huge shortwave radio which looked as if it could reach Java but gave only jamming squeals. The big TV with its wooden cowl was equally useless. On it you saw nobody but the dictator. He inspected, reviewed, greeted, presided; and there were fanfares, flowers and limousines. People were shown applauding. But if emigration were permitted, the country would be empty in less than a month.

The Dean began to take a special interest in the house plants. It was a good season for cyclamens. The shops were filled with pots of them. He looked up cyclamens in the big Larousse. Observing that Corde went about the apartment watering the plants, Tanti Gigi had her agents bring more flowers. He was glad to have their company. He believed they refreshed his head. The African violets he fussed over at home, those would all be dead by now.

After breakfast he went back to Minna's room, sat at Minna's student table with his coat over his shoulders, tried to write a letter or make a few notes for his new project in collaboration with Beech, read some of the documents Beech had given him; then he discovered that he was in a strange state. Presently he found himself staring at the cyclamens. And often he crept back into bed. The trial of Riggie Hines and Lucas Ebry was now in its second week. His office was supposed to keep him posted. Probably the jurors would be let out to do their Christmas shopping, and nothing would happen until after the holidays. As yet Miss Porson had sent no mail. They'd only been away eight days. So Corde slept a great deal, but not well. The restless ecstasy was what he had.

On some mornings the sun shone—clear winter blue. He looked through the ivy twigs on the porch side of the room. Small frozen berries, dark blue, fell from them. Pigeons descended. They must have been fed by the old ladies. But he was not greatly interested in the birds. It was the cyclamen plants that absorbed him hypnotically—the dark cores of the pink and the more purple circles of the white, the petals turned back, the leaves mottled in many shades of green. They were said by Larousse to belong to the primrose family. They grew from corms. Someone had once suggested to him that these green beings produced their leaves and flowers in a state of sleep, perfection devoid of consciousness, design without nerves. Put a handful of dirt in the pot, and they came up with this beauty. Who had said that, about the sleeping life of plants? Brooding over the cyclamens on the table, he often dozed; he felt too hazy to remember anything. He thought, if you had enough of these plants in a room and watered them with a Nembutal solution, they might cure insomnia, make a dream atmosphere.

His biological clock hadn't caught up. An abnormal sleepiness overtook him in the morning. He didn't fight it. He woke in the chair and found himself leaning back, his arms folded and his face turned upwards like a radar disk. The position made his neck ache. Giving in, he stripped and crawled naked under the covers. As he did this, he sometimes felt how long he had lived and how many, many times the naked creature had crept into its bedding. Minna would say nonsense to this, and that he was, like herself, younger than his years, but the coil in the person, so tight in early life, was certainly much looser. Not so loose as in his mother-in-law—Valeria, in intensive care, was always on his mind—but how could you deny the slippage?

Occasionally Minna woke him from his after-breakfast sleep. She came and asked him urgently (as if he would dream of refusing) to get up and greet special visitors. He heard names like Cousin Cornel, Badia Tich, Dr. Serbanescu, Dr. Voynich, Vlada's brother, relatives and colleagues of her parents. (The word "colleague" had far more weight here than in America. Americans now said "associate," as in "Ali Baba and the Forty Associates.") Most of the callers were elderly ailing people of breeding. They were aware how seedy they were, and seemed to shrug when shaking hands, as if to say, "You see how it is." To Corde they looked as if they were gotten up for a Depression party. They chatted in rusty French, for his sake, sparing him their worse English; and as they talked they tried of course to make out the American husband who sat there, hangloose. He had pulled his clothing on half dazed, and felt insufficiently connected with his collar, socks, shoes, jacket. The Dean had not bought a new suit since getting married, five years ago. He no longer needed to make himself attractive, to divert attention from his thinning hair, long neck, circular face ("something like a sunflower in winter," were his own words). Still not awake, he answered polite inquiries with matching politeness, depending upon the measured bass voice to get him through. At least the Rareshes' only daughter had married an American who spoke some French. French was highly valued here, French was a delicious accomplishment. He explained that he had lived in Paris once, but his conversational powers were limited. He drank a glass of brandy (despite the dishcloth moldiness of the flavor, it had a clean, rousing effect); he ate a slice of Tanti's raisin cake, chased it with a cup of tea. He observed that everybody present was trying to tell him something, to convey by various signs what conditions here were. He gathered, moreover, that the colleagues and cousins were extremely proud of Minna's scientific eminence. He was with them there. It warmed him to think how much there was also on the human side; if it had been appropriate to let himself go, he would have told them how rich she was in human qualities. The visitors would have been glad if the Dean had spoken intelligently about the United States in world politics. After all, he was from the blessed world outside. The West. He was free to speak. For them it was impossible. All conversations with foreigners had to be reported. Few people were bold enough to visit the American library. Those who sat in the reading room were probably secret agents. It was one of the greatest achievements of Communism to seal off so many millions of people. You wouldn't have thought it possible in this day and age that the techniques of censorship should equal the techniques of transmission. Of course, as in France under the Occupation, these captive millions were busy scrounging, keeping themselves alive. In the sadness of the afternoon, the subdued light of the curtailed day, the chill of the room (so disheartening!), the callers would have been grateful to hear something so exotic as an intelligent American; words of true interest, words of comfort, too—this dictatorship could not last forever. But he hadn't the heart to tell them things. Besides, Corde was not altogether with it. Not even the rousing brandy brought him into focus. It was not until Professor Voynich was leaving that mostly silent Corde identified him. Why, this was Vlada's brother. He rose to shake the doctor's hand a second time. "Do you expect Vlada for Christmas?"

"Definitely."

"I'm sorry . . . I'm a little vague today," said Corde. "I think she'll be bringing me news from Chicago."

Professor Voynich was elderly, wasted-looking. His sister was stout, pale, round; very unlike him. But then his sister hadn't been in prison for—for how many years was it? Much of the time the doctor had been in solitary confinement. Voynich said, as Corde was showing him out, "Your wife tells me you haven't seen much of the city. She is unfortunately busy. I should be happy one of these days to show you, before my sister arrives."

"I'd be grateful."

Corde, after he had closed the front door, didn't return to the parlor. He went back to the room and got into the sack again. A temperature of fifty-five degrees was ideal for cyclamens. He took his cue from them and gave up consciousness, he checked out. He was not sorry to feel himself going, surrendering his senses—sound, touch, closing his eyes—something like a swoon, he thought.

But next morning—and it was morning before he knew it—he was lively again. Someone telephoned from the American embassy. One of Corde's friends in Washington must have pulled an important wire. A car would be calling for Mr. Corde at half past ten. Corde shaved carefully, dressed neatly and, went down. Ioanna, the concierge, watching from her *sous-sol* recess, had an event to report to the agents that day—a limousine with the American flag pulling up for Minna's husband.

Corde had sent a note to the cultural attaché. This was Milancey, a smooth-faced man who wore a fur hat; who had a hunched smile; who had seen to their visas when they arrived, had met them at the airport.

Milancey was expert in making the position clear: the U.S. Government had already done its duty by the Cordes and wasn't prepared to put itself out further. The limousine was a surprise, therefore. Milancey would never have sent this Bechstein-style automobile. Maybe the National Science Foundation, maybe a White House adviser familiar with Minna's work, had interceded, and word had come down to Milancey, who had passed it along to the First Secretary or the Minister. Someone at the top had dispatched the Lincoln Continental in which Corde was now riding, warmer than he had been in more than a week, resting his feet on a block of smooth felt that tumbled forward. In spite of these comforts, his eyes were those of a man under extreme pressure. Reaching the blocked, guarded street, the limousine turned into the embassy courtyard. Corde was met by a young woman, who guided him past the Marine sergeant's desk and up the circular marble staircase of the little palace to the Ambassador's office. In the anteroom a secretary rose and opened the door. The Ambassador was standing waiting behind his desk.

"Mr. Corde?"

Corde wondered just why he was being received by this discreet, soft-spoken, almost gentle, mysteriously earnest, handsome black man. Minna's astrophysics was not the explanation, not all of it. The Ambassador said that he had served in the Paris embassy in the mid-fifties, when Corde was writing for the *Herald Tribune*. "I would turn to your pieces first thing." He gestured towards a sofa. It would be an informal conversation. It was possible that there wasn't much official business to do in the holiday gap towards the end of December, but it also occurred to Corde that the Ambassador might have read the articles in *Harper's*. Or perhaps *Time* or *Newsweek* had picked up the story of the Ebry trial from the hometown papers, which were none too friendly. Corde had accused the papers of prejudicing the public against Rufus Ridpath, director of the County Jail, when he was being tried for manhandling prisoners. They did a number on Ridpath. They printed damaging statements by informants who weren't named. Grotesque front-page close-ups made him look like a gorilla. To do this to the only man who had the guts to go into the worst of the tiers and recover control of the jail from the barn bosses and their gangs was an outrage. "Somehow the media are more comfortable with phonies, with unprincipled men," was what Corde wrote. And now, in the Ebry case, the media had a clear shot at him, and they were banging away. A more experienced, craftier man would have anticipated this. But moral excitement (was it because it was so rare?) undermined your practical judgment. Anyway, it was open season on Corde. The papers reported Mason's friendship with Ebry and the charges of the radical students. They hinted that Corde, a racist, was carrying out the racist policies of the college. There was an even more embarrassing complication. Corde's own cousin, Max Detillion, was defending Ebry. Mason had gotten him to take over the case from the lawyer Ebry himself had retained. That was wickedly shrewd of Mason. Oh, how misleading those ingenuous teeth were, and the youth pollen, too, and the long eyelashes! The kid was a devil. Cousin Max, feuding with Corde, called a press conference immediately to announce that he wasn't taking a penny in fees for representing this ghetto dishwasher. Maxie had a passion for publicity, and this time he was good copy. He owed that to his hated cousin, not to his legal talents. The source of Maxie's hatred was love gone sour, family wrangling. He was maddened with imaginary wrongs. Flashy, elderly, corrupt Maxie, with his bold eyes and his illiterate, furiously repetitious eloquence, had a moronic genius for getting attention. He needed the publicity; his practice was declining. The first lawyer was asked to withdraw.

But it was to no purpose that Corde worried himself about Mason and Max and the media in Chicago, for the Ambassador seemed to know nothing about any of it. He had prepared himself for difficulties this polite man had no thought of making. The Ambassador only wanted to talk about Paris in the fifties. "But you don't write for the papers anymore," he said.

"I gave that up. I still publish a piece now and then. There was one recently . . ."

"I must look that up." The Ambassador made a note with a silver ballpoint. "What sort of work have you been doing?"

"Professor of journalism back in my hometown. Even a dean. I'm not a real administrative type. I doubt that I can call myself a real professor, but I was curious to see what it was like."

It was calming to sit with the Ambassador. His office was beautifully furnished. The man was handsome and there was something about him—breeding, delicacy. Also, getting out of

Minna's room was important, a change of scene. Corde had been shut in for too long.

"I suppose you had cultural inclinations you couldn't satisfy by journalism."

"Right you are. It would have to be a very special need to transfer you from Paris to Chicago. I had some reading to do, and wanted to find people to talk to. The right people to talk to—that's the hardest part of all."

"You must be interested in especially difficult things."

"I don't think they're all that difficult or esoteric. I was too busy in Paris. When busyness takes hold of you, then art, philosophy, poetry, those things go out the window. Just before I made the decision to move I was reading Rilke, especially his wartime letters."

"I don't know those."

On the leather sofa with the Ambassador, conversation seemed definitely possible. Mind you, it could never have been easy. When Rilke had complained about his inability to find an adequate attitude to the things and people about him, Corde had thought, Yes, that's very common—that's me, too. Odd that with such a temperament he should have become a newspaperman. A man of words? Yes, but words of the wrong kind. For some years, to cure himself of bad habits, bad usage, he had been mostly silent. And now it seemed he had even forgotten how to open his mouth. Corde's confinement in the silent room where Minna had done her lessons in astrophysics or mathematics, where Valeria kept her relics and wrote her letters, had made him rusty, had shrouded him in mute heart-aching numbness. There was a moment at the beginning of this chat with the Ambassador when he imagined that his face was surfacing, coming up from under like the face that Mason must have seen at the Cape, rising up from the green Atlantic, spectacles lost, back hair floating, big bare brow, French-Irish nose, blind eyes.

It wasn't that subjects were lacking. He was preparing to make an impassioned statement about Valeria. Together with this he wanted to try out on the Ambassador some of his notions about the mood of the West. Oh, he had lots of topics: the crazy state of the U.S., the outlook and psychology of officialdom in the Communist world, the peculiar psychoses of penitentiary societies like this one. The distinguished gentleness of the Ambassador was very encouraging. Corde actually wanted to open up. But he wisely decided to let the Ambassador direct the conversation.

The Ambassador asked for details of Valeria's case, and Corde became more lively as he outlined it. A drink would have helped, but it wasn't a good idea to ask for one. The Ambassador said that he had read his note to Mr. Milancey very carefully. Corde had written slapdash, carelessly, never thinking that the attaché would show it around. Now he tried to remember what he had said.

"There are certain parallels," the Ambassador said. "I have a foreign wife, too. Mine is French. Her mother, an old French lady who lives with us, is very ill."

"I'm sorry to hear it. Yes, I see why you reacted. Can anything be done? We've been here for eight days—I think. I can't even keep track of the dates. My wife has seen her mother twice."

"Only twice . . . ?"

"About twenty minutes each time. For the second visit we didn't have permission from the Colonel—the hospital superintendent."

"How was it arranged, then?"

Corde glanced about. Even here, naming names might be a mistake. The embassy must certainly be bugged. "I don't know how. But my wife was accused of pulling a fast one. That would be completely out of character. She's an unusually . . ."

"She's an astronomer?"

"If we hadn't rushed here, we'd have been at Mount Palomar. The telescope would have been hers part of Christmas week. Now, well, she's never off the phone, trying to find help. You can imagine what a state she's in. She last saw her mother five days ago. She's grieving."

"Of course she is. What's the reason given?"

"Visits are out, no visiting in intensive care," said Corde.

"Yes, you wrote that in your letter. That is unusually rigid. Well, I'm on good terms with the Minister of Health. I'll call him this afternoon, shall I?"

"I assume he runs all the hospitals. He must be the

Colonel's superior. I'd be very grateful. Her mother won't live long. In times like these the whole thing may seem unimportant. I mean," Corde explained himself, "considering what one reads every day—terrorist acts, famine, genocide, events in Latin America, in Cambodia or in Uganda, where a hostage, an old lady at Entebbe who had to be taken to the hospital, was strangled by Amin's people. These brutal, horrible events. In Addis Ababa the regime has been murdering adolescents to crush the opposition, and they leave children's corpses on the parents' doorsteps. That's how things are done now. . . ."

"It's no trifle to Mrs. Corde, nevertheless, that she isn't allowed to see her mother."

"Nor to me. My wife is a simple person. No politics. Her mother wanted her out of it, brought her up that way. No politics, no history. Perhaps too much that way. Back home in Chicago, magazines arrive for her from civil rights organizations, and books by survivors of the camps, refugees. Because she's from Eastern Europe she's on the mailing lists. But she's too busy, so I'm the one that reads all this grim stuff. That's why I have a fairly complete idea of how things are in this part of the world—forced labor, mental hospitals for dissenters, censorship. I've gotten into the habit of reading this mail for her. She asks me to brief her. Anyway, here's the thing in outline: mother-in-law is in the Party hospital, and the superintendent is a colonel in the secret police. Not the type to respond to the humane appeal. I suspect, anyway, that he would like to teach my wife a lesson."

"Because she left the country?"

"That's part of it. Now the lady comes with an American passport and husband, flies in without a visa so that the embassy has to come to the rescue—by the way, she's still a dual citizen—and expects the Colonel to waive the regulations for her. What does she think this is? Besides, her mother was Minister of Health thirty years ago while this man was still very junior, learning his job in prison hospitals. According to the literature I've become addicted to, techniques are different now, according to Amnesty International they inject mind drugs in psychiatric hospitals, and who knows how many people are dying in those places. Electric shocks, sulfadiazine injections. And it was much rawer before, when the Colonel was an apprentice. One of my mother-in-law's colleagues, a Minister of Justice, had his head hacked off in his cell. They decided not to bring him to trial." Corde's excitement was running away with him. He couldn't say why. Well, yes, he could say approximately why. But it was certainly tactless, stupid, to lecture a high-ranking and experienced foreign service officer about atrocities. Tocqueville was dead right when he said that Americans (democrats everywhere) had no aptitude for conversation, they lectured. Bombast, clichés, chewed-up newsprint, naturally made the other party tune out. He had heard what you had heard, read what you had read. The Ambassador was too well bred to cut him off. He listened, he nodded, he waited. And Corde did after all have something to communicate. He tried again. "What I meant earlier when I spoke of trifles is that everybody now follows a scale: A is bad, but B is worse and C worse still. When you reach N, unspeakable evil, A becomes trivial. After thirty years in police work, and having seen whole regiments of corpses, the Colonel must have special views on suffering and death. So what's all the fuss about one old woman? You use the most extreme case to reduce all the rest. It's the same at home. . . . I can imagine what the Colonel would say about the ethical values of the West. So called."

He sensed that he had not altogether turned the Ambassador off by lecturing him. He was getting a polite hearing still. This man, quite black, very slender, had style, class, cultivation. He wore a light gray well-cut suit, and an Hermès necktie (Corde recognized the stirrup motif), and narrow black shoes which could only have come from Italy. Subtly considerate, he listened to Corde's explanations (or bombast), but obviously he didn't care to discuss Western humanism, civilized morality, nihilism East and West. He was a busy official.

"Let's see what the Minister of Health has to say."

"My wife thinks that her mother can't understand why she doesn't come."

"But that's not how you see it—you don't agree?"

"The old woman, with all her experience, must have it figured out."

"Is she fully conscious?"

"She was when we last saw her. They put a ballpoint in her

fingers, and she wrote on a pad that she wanted to be taken home. That is, she wrote the word 'home.' But she can't be unhooked from the machines. The Colonel offered to do that."

"Ah, yes?"

"Yes, he said if she were moved out of intensive care she could be visited every day. But he was only kidding. The respiratory center is gone. She couldn't live ten minutes. This was just his way of sticking it to the daughter. A bonus."

The Ambassador was not altogether comfortable with these details. He was sympathetic, he was exquisitely decorous, but he didn't need to hear it all. But then Corde wasn't transmitting it all. Involuntary memory had passed through his head Goya's painting of Saturn—the naked squatting giant, open-mouthed, devouring. Death swallowing the old woman by the face. Again, the inability to find the adequate attitude. Corde *seemed* sober enough, but his controls were not in dependable working order.

Minna was always asking, "What's Mother thinking? What do you suppose goes through her mind?" And Corde often put it to himself: What would the old woman have felt if she had been able to open her eyes and had seen us standing there in those gowns and surgical masks? He was certain that she had laid her dying plans carefully, but she couldn't arrange Minna's future. There was still the one open question: Could he, Corde, this American, be trusted not to harm, or betray, or even ruin her daughter? The old woman was a very shrewd old woman, but she was a romantic old woman, too. She had loved her husband. When he died, all that was left of him was in their daughter. She sent her daughter directly into cosmic space. Nothing but particle physics, galaxies, equations. Minna had never read the *Communist Manifesto*, had never heard of Stalin's Great Terror. Now then, could Valeria entrust such a daughter to a man like Corde? Suppose Valeria had seen him staring down at her in intensive care, what sort of face did that gauze mask cover—sane, or what? A gentle soul, or a masked killer? Corde was always afraid that that deep old woman knew his worst thoughts, instability, weakness, vices. Oh, Jesus! So must I end up responsible for this life of maternal sacrifice, and the Roman matron purity, and the whole classic achievement!

There's something crazy in this, too. There are people who find you out. And especially old women do. In Pushkin's *Queen of Spades*, maybe it wasn't so much gambler's lust that drove that wild plunger, Hermann; he may have hidden himself in the old woman's room because he needed to face her terrible gaze in a test of his soul. Well, Corde had his disorders, but his reply to Valeria was yes. Yes, she could trust him. He was stable. Yes, he had found his firm point. That was what he would have been ready to tell her. "Don't worry. Don't put me in your agonies. I love your daughter!"

No hint of these reflections (he hoped) was given; nor of what the nearness of death was doing to him, how wide open he was, how near to an emotional eruption.

The Ambassador must have been one of those patrician blacks from Washington or Philadelphia whose ancestors were manumitted slaves before the Civil War. Corde had met some of those before. They had summer homes in Edgartown. This was how, probably mistakenly, he placed him. "I can promise you some news later in the day, Mr. Corde," he said. "And if there's something else the embassy can help with . . ."

"Maybe the information library can let me have the *Tribune* for last week? Last papers I saw were on the plane flying over."

"I think we can find you some of those. There's a journalist in town, by the way, who spoke of you yesterday. Spangler, the columnist."

"What, is Dewey Spangler here?"

"He's on a swing through Eastern Europe. We had him in for a drink and he spoke of you warmly. You're old friends?"

"We were at school together. I haven't seen him in years—ten, maybe."

"May I give him your number?"

"Why, sure."

Spangler never looked him up in Chicago, but there was no need to tell this to the Ambassador. He had already said more than was strictly necessary. Too much comment altogether.

An old-boy reunion here in the Balkans would appeal to Dewey. What—two kids from the sidewalks of Chicago, and one of them now, forty years later, a syndicated big-shot opinion-maker, and meeting in this heavy Communist and Byzantine capital? A great setting! Dewey had in fact become—what?—a public spokesman, a large-scale operator in D.C. For years he had kept his distance from Corde because he didn't like to be remembered as the kinky adolescent who had told preposterous lies, had screaming quarrels with his mother, and wrote violently revolutionary poems.

Corde didn't care greatly for Dewey's column. It was too statesmanlike and doughy. He was trying hard to be a Walter Lippmann. But Lippmann had been the pupil of Santayana and the protégé of potentates at an age when sharp-toothed Dewey in an undershirt was still shrieking and grimacing at his mother.

But we understood each other forty years ago, Corde thought. Of course it was Swinburne, Wilde, Nietzsche, Walt Whitman, in high school. Perfumed herbage, intoxicating lyricism and lamentation, rich music, nihilism and decadence had made them pals. The fat faded pink volume of Oscar Wilde that Corde had found on the lowest shelves, behind Valeria's bed, the pastry-rich hyperboles of sightless souls and red hells, might have been an augury of this reunion. And there was still another connection (he would have thought of it if his wits had been working normally): Max Detillion, his cousin, once had shared their literary interests. He said he did, anyway. A showman even then, Maxie used to recite "The Ballad of Reading Gaol." "For each man kills the thing he loves . . . The poor dead woman whom he loved, and murdered in her bed." Dewey Spangler had made wicked fun of him. "Fat-ass lowbrow . . . gross and dainty . . . Arse Poetica"—these were some of the cracks he used to make. But later Dewey turned tolerant. He said that Maxie had after all shaped up and made something of himself. Dewey respected "achievers," if they didn't achieve too much. Corde's opinion had followed the reverse pattern. He believed that Maxie had lost track of himself altogether. Dewey had had no practical dealings with Max. Max had cost Corde tens of thousands. Even that might have been forgiven if only you had been able to talk openly and reasonably to the man. But the more harm he did you, the more harm he claimed you had done him. He grabbed everything for himself, even the injury. And then you were up against it—no rational judgment, you see, a kind of mystery in itself. Then there were other kinds of craziness, like the one about publicity. Mad for being in the papers, Max hung out with newspapermen, gossiping and buying them drinks. Naturally, he grabbed the Ebry case. It gave him a shot in the arm. And now Maxie, before the jury at Thirteenth and Michigan, swept the courtroom with bold Rooseveltian looks, the statesman-lion, a massive man but falling apart. The cause of the illness was neither virus nor bacteria, but erotic collapse. Maxie was in despair. Perhaps celebrity might be a remedy.

In a way Cousin Albert suffered with Cousin Max. There came to mind (Corde was a terrific reader; he had read far too much) Balzac's sex monsters in *Cousine Bette*, and the pitiable Baron Hulot, a feeble ancient man making passes at the woman who was nursing his dying wife. Corde had his reasons for these thoughts, for if he was going to see Dewey Spangler they would be discussing Cousin Max. Most likely Max had sent Spangler clippings from Chicago, where he was doing so wonderfully. Now they were celebrities, all three.

This was a burden on Corde: sorrow. Cousins, and once playmates, and affectionate, and Max had been a handsome young man, and now . . . some sort of blood trouble, so that Max needed not a literal dialysis but another kind of cleaning up. In his youth Max suffered from frequent nosebleeds; this was why Corde fixed on the corrupted blood.

The Ambassador had mentioned neither *Harper's* nor the Ebry trial, which meant that Spangler hadn't told him what was happening. It figured. Why should Dewey first claim him as an old pal and then louse him up? Corde and Spangler had been rivals thirty years ago. At first he, Corde, had been the more successful of the two. He was still in his early twenties when *The New Yorker* printed his personal account of the Potsdam Conference. The conference had been closed to the press, but Harry Vaughan, who was Truman's aide, had been a friend of Corde's father, and Corde, then a GI, most innocent-looking, with his goggles and cowlick, had wangled his way in. Vaughan was annoyed by the report, or was obliged to say that he was; but for jealous Spangler, who was then stuck in Chicago writing about Planned Parenthood and covering tenement fires for the City News Bureau, Corde's success was a terrible thing. It gave him a gruesome wound. But he was combative, a fierce competitor and an ingenious politician; he made excellent use of his injury and his rage and soon shot ahead. Corde was much less ambitious than Spangler, wrote for a smaller public, seemed sometimes unnecessarily obscure (even, as one of his editors had said, "reclusive"). And when Corde became a professor (no big distinction; by now there were millions of professors), Spangler interpreted it as a victory ("I was too much for him, he's outclassed, no contest, hanging up his gloves") and became more tolerant, more friendly. He sympathized with Corde. Spangler was the worldly one, a shrewder man by far.

To the shrewder man those two articles in *Harper's* must have seemed unaccountable acts of self-destruction. Corde gave up his cover, ran out, swung wild at everyone, made enemies, riled the press most of all—treason to his own trade—virtually asking to be blown away. It was a hell of a strange development. Strangest of all was Corde's regression, for that was how Spangler would describe it. Corde had gone back to an earlier standard, to the days when he and Spangler were reading Shelley and Swinburne together in Lincoln Park. At the age of seventeen they would often quote to each other the line in which Shelley had described George III: "An old mad blind despised and dying king." The wonderful hard music of those words used to stir them. And it was this sort of music that Corde apparently wanted to work into his journalism. If indeed it *was* journalism. If indeed it was Shelley. If it wasn't, instead, Corde as George III himself, old, mad, blind, and sure to be despised in Chicago. Spangler when he had read him would first have been startled, then thrilled by the violence of his self-injury, and finally sorry for the poor guy. It was a wonder the editors of *Harper's* didn't try to restrain him. Here and there he just skirted libel. Crazy with rage, doing himself in.

All these conjectures (Max, Dewey, himself) Corde felt in his silent lips, with the buzzing, tickling sensation one used to get as a kid by playing tunes through cigarette paper on a comb. Wondering: Were these (the personalities, articles, trials, etc.) his own portion of the big-scale insanities of the twentieth century? Did these present thoughts occur because he had been shut up too long in Minna's old room? Or were they the effects of Valeria's dying, or of the death of Rick Lester? Did one turn aside the force of thousands of declines or dooms or deaths and then decide, by some process of selection too remote ever to be known, to fix on certain ones? Yes, and then let those you have chosen paint away in broad visceral strokes until the fiery brushing undermined and overturned your judgment. And at last the superstructure (put together with the protective cunning of the blind) began to totter?

The Ambassador walked out of the office with him to the top of the delicate marble staircase. The embassy must have been a boyar's palace once. The smooth banisters were iridescent and curved again and again like a nautilus shell. The black Ambassador from first to last was very sympathetic: the sympathy may have been no more than highly elaborated propriety, but Corde somehow didn't think so. (No, it wasn't only two, three, five chosen deaths being painted thickly, terribly, convulsively inside him, all over his guts, liver, heart, over all his organs, but a large picture of cities, crowds, peoples, an apocalypse, with images and details supplied by his own disposition, observation, by ideas, dreams, fantasies, his peculiar experience of life.)

"It occurs to me," said Corde to the Ambassador, "since my friend Spangler is here to interview big shots, he may be able to put in a word for my wife."

"It's certainly a possibility. He must have contacts. Yes, I'd ask him if I were you. He's staying at the Intercontinental. I'll see to it that he gets your number. He may be hard to reach."

The Ambassador's secretary had gathered up some recent newspapers for Corde. After the good-bye handshake—what Mencken once had called "the usual hypocrisies"—Corde withdrew into a corner near the desk of the Marine guard and shuffled through the pages. He didn't, to tell the truth, want to find any Chicago items. Some of the papers were held between his knees. No, he didn't look too carefully. But Chicago was nowhere mentioned. He must be nuts ("bubble gum in the brain") to build such extensive and anxious fantasies about the Ebry case. What he did find was one of Dewey Spangler's syndicated columns. He didn't read it, he only glanced through it. To take your oldest friends seriously in their public character was not easy. He generally put it to himself that Dewey had won a brilliant victory over his own handicaps. You had to bear in mind, moreover, that as a kid Dewey had had a mass of handicaps. He had found the most advantageous way of putting them together. You had to hand it to him. He had come a long way, for sure.

Corde walked back from the embassy; he refused the limousine. Minna would have been alarmed, but no one was about to snatch him in the street. You couldn't expect her to be rational now. Earth was strange enough at the best of times. There was nothing too rum to be true. That needed frequent emphasis. Nothing. Under the looping brim of the fedora, as he walked, he arranged the Ambassador's conversation, the promises he had made, in phrases of maximum effectiveness.

He found a group of workmen busy in the lobby of the apartment house, mixing tubs of cement and plaster. It was repair, not restoration. The marble panels that had fallen from the walls during the earthquake had all been stolen, said Gigi. There would be nothing but stucco now. When Corde opened the street door, of wrought iron and glass, Ioanna was on the watch behind the fourfold window of her hutch. Her cheeks were like cold-storage apples, a bandanna was knotted under her chin, she had the shape of a bale. Although she reported on a regular schedule to *securitate*, she seemed nevertheless to consider herself one of the Rareshes, a member of the family. She held on to that. Minna's husband was family, too, of course; but because he and Ioanna had no common language, she reserved a special look of pity for him, as if he were mentally retarded. As he passed her window, he stooped a little, lifting several of his gloved fingers to his hat brim. Idiot is as idiot does. She thought him idiotic? Somebody should.

Tanti Gigi had taken Corde down to Ioanna's quarters on a courtesy call (peculiar forms of protocol, in Eastern Europe), so he knew what was inside. On the walls of the tiny alcove above her head hung official portraits of the dictator and his wife. Nearby was a picture of the beautiful Nadia Comaneci, who didn't need the support of the solid earth and preferred to live in the air, like a Chagall bride. There was also an icon painted on glass with a full flowing brush—red, green and gilt. In this one, Elijah drove into heaven with two horses while saints and angels cried hosannah. By Ioanna's bedside, in the place of honor, was a photograph of Valeria, the Doamna Doctor. Thirty years ago, Ioanna had been the Doamna Doctor's housemaid. She was devoted to Valeria, no doubt about it, but she had to be paid off. Whenever Valeria went abroad, Ioanna's name was high on her shopping list. She was one of those for whom dress materials had to be bought, chocolates, bottles of Arpège, panty hose (the biggest size). All this was depicted as affection. And it *was* affection, who said it wasn't? It was both affection and payola. So there was Ioanna, big on emotion, loyal to the family, fully informed, very potent, dangerous to neglect. The bale figure, the scarlet pippin cheeks, the slow heaving of the big behind, the efficiency of her black-stockinged thick legs, the sincerely pitying face—Corde had taken full note of all of these. The concierge protected, loved and blackmailed the old sisters. How to interpret this? "They that have power to hurt and will do none . . . they are the lords and owners of their faces." No, Shakespeare wasn't thinking of any Ioanna; he had great souls in mind, nobility. But Gigi and Minna and others had assured Corde that the concierge really loved Valeria. He believed them ("I'll buy that"). She was a blackmailer, but she also gave her heart. For there was a love community of women here. The matriarch was Valeria. Ioanna was a member in good standing.

This apartment was the center of an extended feminine hierarchy. There was Tanti Gigi. She had gone to London in the twenties and came back a Mayfair moth in flapper dresses and costume jewelry, covered with eye makeup and speaking Beatrix Potter English. She was Little Sister, at Valeria's right hand. Then there was Minna, in America, but figuring prominently; distance made no difference, even Science didn't; she was a full, willing member and a prominent one. Other members were Viorica, Doina, Cornelia, even Serbian Vlada in Chicago. Vlada in chemistry and Minna in astronomy, both belonged to this emotional union. The ladies consulted Valeria about their husbands, their children, their careers, took her advice in matters of love, education, religion. They made over clothing for one another, raised and lowered hems, repaired zippers, came to sickbeds, waited in queues. There was a small male auxiliary, also. Mihai Petrescu, who had been Valeria's *politruk* in the Ministry, the Party's watchdog, was in it. He seemed, like Ioanna, to work both sides of the street. No outsider could understand these multiple roles and Chinese intricacies. It was beyond Corde, certainly. It was not the American kind of loyalty-duplicity; in America the emotions were different somehow, perhaps thinner. Here you led a crypto-emotional life in the shadow of the Party and the State. You had no personal rights, but on the other hand, the claims of feeling were more fully acknowledged.

He entered the elevator. The thing was made like a china cabinet, and because it knocked when it was in use, you heard a frail wooden echo inside. They had such elevators everywhere in Europe, in buildings of the Haussmann type, had them in Warsaw and in Belgrade, too, these (imitated) vestiges of bourgeois Paris.

He rose to the fifth floor. The talk with the genteel Ambassador, the American papers, the walk home, had stirred him through and through. It seemed to him that he had built up a life of strong mental excitement. Minna, who had been watching at the window, let him in and said, "Why did you walk? They should have sent you home in a car."

"No one thought of it."

"They've done a tracheotomy," said Minna.

"Who has? Oh, I see. I thought they would ask you."

"Dr. Moldovanu said last week that they probably would have to. Well, they did it. It went well, he said. It should help."

"Did he talk to you about a visit? What are the chances?"

"I couldn't discuss that with him on the phone. He recommended it to the Colonel, that I'm sure of. Speaking as her doctor, he said it would help my mother's chances of recovery if she could see me. . . ."

"The Colonel doesn't pay much attention to the doctors. I'd be surprised if Moldovanu mentioned it to him a second time."

"They're all scared. Yes, I think you're right."

Corde and Minna stood talking in the parlor. The peeling, swelling leather armchairs were uninviting. You didn't willingly sit down in them. Big medical volumes from Dr. Cushing's Boston were stacked on the shelves behind the telephone. Corde, too, felt out of date, like the chairs.

"What happened at the embassy? Did you talk to that man Milancey?"

"I was taken to the Ambassador."

"You are kidding! How unusual."

"He'd seen my letter."

"What's he like?"

"Well, he's black. He's handsome. He's a career diplomat. He thought it might help to talk to the Minister of Health. I suppose the M of H runs the hospitals," said Corde. "Well, they've done the tracheotomy. . . ." They've peeled those big tapes from her face, he thought. Those were gone, anyway. To him they were especially oppressive.

"I'll have to ask my contacts about the Minister of Health. And write a note to the Ambassador. Albert, I talked to the lady who has a relationship with Dr. Gherea. I told you, didn't I, that I met her once in Switzerland? She remembered me. In fact, she knew all about my mother. Everybody is talking about it, all over town. I offered to go to Gherea's hospital myself to ask him to examine her. But do you know what the woman said? She said how much Gherea owed both my parents. She was very warm, she talked to me with real feeling. I think she'll arrange it all."

"Let her. She sounds like a good woman."

"Albert, I want to show you a photograph of Gherea. Tanti Gigi found it in a magazine. . . . What do you think?"

The man was stout, hairless. His mouth was set between determined swellings. He was immediately there: that's him.

"I'd say he was a very nice man to have in your corner. I wouldn't be happy to see him on the other fellow's side. There are plenty of pusses like that in Chicago. But if he's so big and important, maybe he can do something about the Colonel."

"Should I talk to him about that?"

"If I were you, I wouldn't go to this particular man with tears in my eyes. Skip the emotions, that's my hunch. If he's like the tough guys he reminds me of . . . It's his trade to scrape tumors out of people's brains."

"So was it my father's."

"From what I hear, your Communist surgeon father got on his knees and prayed before he started cutting. Does this guy look like he sinks to his knees? Didn't you say he socks his anesthetist in the jaw if he crosses him?"

"I'll phone the woman back and ask whether Gherea might try with the Colonel. This is the sixth day I haven't seen my mother."

Without expecting Minna to follow what he was saying (she had too much on her mind; she only wanted to hear the sound of his voice, reassuring if only in the depth of its tones), Corde observed that here was another case of humane cooperation among women in a Communist society. Gigi insisted that Gherea loved his lady friend. Maybe he did. These tough guys always made exceptions. Hitler had had Eva Braun. People in reduced emotional circumstances set their affections on something or other. They were pitted against Eros—against the universe. Total misanthropes, true, absolute ones, were probably as rare as saints. He was trying to divert Minna. She wasn't listening, only staring. Concentration made her face severe. This happened also when she was doing science. With Corde Minna was often cheerful and childlike. When he pleased her, she might jump up and down and clap her hands like a small girl. But when she worked she was a different person entirely. She sat in her corner hours on end with a pad and pencil, writing symbols, her face turned downward, the upper lip lengthened, the chin compressed and dented. She was not an observer; if she had been one she might never have married a man with such a round bare crown and the stare of a Welsh prophet (his own image—it was the eyes he was thinking of). Until now she had had little interest in psychology. Her mother was the psychiatrist; she left all that to her. But now she was forced to study people. He wondered what her powerful intelligence would make of them—of him. He had said often enough that she'd have to come down to earth one day. Not much of a prediction. He was sorry for the satisfaction he had taken in making it. How often people had told *him* that sooner or later he'd have to come down to earth. Well, here she was, anyway, with everybody else, and fighting with childlike passion. "Why do I have to go to Gherea? He should have come to me."

She said this again. "He was a peasant kid with talent. Where would he have been without this family? Even his lady friend says it. My parents took him into the house. He lived right here. My father made him a neurosurgeon. Gherea has never trained anybody. He keeps his monopoly."

"Well, if the clot turns out to be operable, he may move Valeria to his hospital. If he should decide that it was medically necessary, how could the Colonel stop him?"

This was nothing but sophistry, clever comfort, holding the line. Surgery was unthinkable; you couldn't administer an anesthetic if the respiratory center was knocked out. If Gherea was coming to examine Valeria, he had almost certainly discussed the case with Dr. Moldovanu. Hopeless. Anyway, the brain surgeon would have a look at the X-rays, go through all the motions. He'd do that with King Kong delicacy, because his lady wanted the gestures made. It came under the heading of feminine boor-control. But it did Minna good to be angry. Corde himself was angry and trying to increase his anger with people in Chicago who were at this moment trying to do him in—with his cousin Max, for instance. Max was in the courtroom carrying on like John Barrymore in *Counsellor-at-Law*. You could almost see the old movies on which he had formed his character. Corde had studied the geology of his cousin's soul and identified the fossil remains.

Anger was better. In passivity you only deteriorated.

Minna said, "I've been so long in the States that I forgot how things are here. We made such fun of Valeria and her shopping lists, but look how people have to dress. The women are so depressed. They have no food, and there's nothing to wear. One year I washed and ironed the same blouse every night; it was all there was. Now I keep thinking of all the items I could have brought from Chicago. Like the navy dress with the white. I should have left a set of keys with Vlada."

"There was no time for keys. I'll leave my things here, except for this suit to fly back in."

"I'll ask Gigi if Professor Voynich will take your things."

"Better wait till Vlada arrives. She can't bring him to the States, I suppose."

"I'm not sure he wants to go."

"Start a new life? I suppose not. I'd hate it. It's time to stay put, for better or for worse. Voynich said he'd take me for a walk. I'd like to get out, see the city."

"Maybe his French is too rusty, and he feels awkward. He was a social democrat and had a bad time, not much pension. Wait a few days and Vlada will take you. She has to talk to you anyway about the article you're supposed to write with Sam Beech."

"I've by no means decided."

"Why not? Beech is brilliant. You shouldn't refuse. He's a great man."

Minna looked up to great men. She didn't look down on her husband; she didn't quite understand what he was after. But she preferred looking up, definitely. That Corde's articles were approved by an eminent man of science was important to Minna. Now she knew what to think of his critics. The articles themselves hadn't held her interest. Doing her best, she had rattled through the pages while he watched with a certain sympathy—even with envy. Why should slums, guns, drugs, jails, politics, intrigues, disorders matter? Leaving Hell, Dante saw the stars again. Minna saw them all the time. Mason had once said that his new aunt was charming but a little spacy. Uncle Albert was the worldly one, who was supposed to give guidance and support here below. He had come to Europe to interpose himself between Minna and this bughouse country. For clearly the guys in charge were psychopaths. There were no rational grounds for what they did.

But Uncle Albert was not the worldly one, either. Max and Mason were both agreed that he, Corde, wasn't really with it, didn't know the score at all, and that he deserved to be penalized for meddling, for interfering with reality as the great majority of Americans experienced it—to which that majority actually sacrificed itself. As if everybody were saying, "This is life, this is what I give myself to. There is no other deal. No holding back, go with the rest." Then a man like Corde came haunting around. He would never put his chips on the mortal roulette squares, good enough for everybody else. Not on dollars, not on whiskey, not on sexual embraces—but on what? On Swedenborg's angels, maybe? (Swedenborg was Uncle Albert's own addition.) Then Corde remembered how in the office he had wanted to open his heart to Mason, to tell him that under the present manner of interpretation people were shadows to one another, and shadows within shadows, to suggest that these appalling shadows *condemned* our habitual manner of interpretation. Grant this premise and . . . But the kid would never have listened to this. In his opinion (his portion of the prevailing chaos, but let's call it opinion), Uncle Albert was flirting with a delusive philosophy and trying to have an affair with nonexistent virtues. Mason's statement would have been, "Uncle, you're unreal, you're out of it." And Corde, giving in to anger, might have said, "I'm talking straight. Try to listen." But Mason wouldn't—he couldn't. And now he was allied with a longtime ill-wisher. He and Cousin Max would fix Uncle Albert's wagon.

". . . And in my opinion," Minna was saying, "it would be excellent to work with a person like Beech. Excellent."

To bring me within the bounds of higher sanity. Take sanctuary with science.

Like Gigi, Minna was assuming her mother's tone and some of her ways. Well, Valeria's was a role too valuable to lose. It should be filled, no denying that. Minna played it with greater authority than Gigi.

Corde had become attached to Gigi—her distracted, flustered charm, her classic straight nose and full Egyptian eyes. Even the permanent wave, gone wrong at the back. He liked the old girl a lot. As for her, she had noted how he tended the cyclamens. He watered them from beneath, setting the pots in bowls of water. She said to him, "There is not much to offer you. The one thing we can be lavish of is these flowers." He wondered what it might mean about him as a "serious adult" that the flowers should claim so much of his attention.

He mentioned to Minna that Dewey Spangler was in town.

"I've forgotten who he is—remind me."

"You saw him on *Face the Nation*, don't you remember? My buddy from way back. The international celebrity. The Washington columnist."

"He isn't one of the ones I've met."

"No."

"What's he doing here?"

"He's making one of his sweeps of Europe to gather information. I suppose he'll write a series of pieces about the Communist countries."

"Seeing him would make a change for you. You have to sit here day after day."

"I've been thinking—he must have influence in high places."

"Is he so important?"

"In his league, yes. The Ambassador thought so, too. He'll probably have dinner with the dictator. The dictator is another publicity genius, like my cousin Maxie Detillion. Everybody says how progressive and liberal he is."

Minna raised her eyes to the ceiling fixture to warn against listening devices. But Corde had been whispering. She said, "Would your friend put in a word . . . ?"

"Who, Spangler? It can't hurt to ask. . . . Why don't we go to the room and have a drink. It feels like drink time."

"You have a packet of mail from Chicago. It's waiting on the table."

This gave him a start. He had fretted because there was no news from Chicago. Now it was here he wanted no part of it. He decided immediately to put off opening the packet. "From Miss Porson?"

"It looks like it."

"Well, let's have our drink."

He avoided looking too closely at his wife. The tubercular whiteness of her face upset him. Her big shocked eyes were immobile, her lower lip was indrawn, and she was gaunt, stiff. In a single week even her fingers had lost flesh, so that the joints and the nails stood out.

Shortly after they were married, one of Corde's academic friends had congratulated him, saying, "Do you remember that old piece of business from probability theory, that if a million monkeys jumped up and down on the keys of typewriters for a million years one of them would compose *Paradise Lost*? Well, you were like that with the ladies. You jumped up and down and you came up with a masterpiece."

Corde had a mild reflective way of looking at the ground between his feet, his hands gathered behind his back, when people took witty cuts at him. "More like *Paradise Regained*," was his answer. Why was he supposed to have been a wild ladies' man? In others, much greater sexual irregularities weren't even noticed. It was his serious air that made him conspicuous.

He looked moral, gazing Socratically at the ground with large eyes while people teased him about jumping monkeys. Well, he had only himself to blame. If he was going to look so earnest, let him be earnest in earnest. About Minna he *was* earnest.

"Christ! Miss Porson," he said.

"I thought you were waiting for mail."

"I *was* waiting. But facing it is something else."

"You can open it after lunch, if you aren't up to it."

He wasn't up to it at all. He had a stitch, a cramp, thinking about it. But now the telephone began to ring. There was a series of calls. The first was for him. On behalf of Dewey Spangler, the Ambassador's secretary inquired whether Mr. Corde was available to meet him at the Intercontinental. Mr. Spangler would send his car at three o'clock. For Minna's information, Corde repeated, "Mr. Spangler? Drinks at three? Just a moment, please." He covered the mouthpiece, waiting.

"Of course. Of course. Go," said Minna.

"Tell Mr. Spangler that I'll be waiting."

The next call was from Dr. Gherea's obliging lady friend. How decent of her! Her message (there were no short conversations in the Balkans) took twenty minutes to deliver; final arrangements had been made for the consultation. Dr. Moldovanu would phone her about it at ten o'clock tomorrow to report Gherea's opinion.

"That's what we wanted," said Corde, "your old man's protégé."

From the Chicago packet, which he opened with a sigh, he extracted a letter from his sister Elfrida. He galloped through it to see what it was about and then went back and studied it in detail. She was a subtle and tactful woman, good old Elfrida. She might have low tastes in men (that, unfortunately, was common), but she was well-bred. First she wanted to know how Valeria was. She had great respect for Valeria. "That's a superior, dignified woman, not like us mixed hybrid Frenchies from the Midwest." Elfrida, too, had come to England last spring. In London one night, Corde had given all the ladies dinner at the Étoile—sometimes he thought he could live happily ever after on Charlotte Street. Elfrida's letter was particularly circumspect. She was damn careful with him. The word "fond" occurred several times. Why was that necessary? He and his sister loved each other; the "fond" was trivial. Maybe it needed special emphasis because Corde had added lately to her burdens. He was temporarily—humiliatingly—in the Mason category, a troublemaker. So she wanted to assure him that (like Mason!) he had not lost her love. Elfrida had always been gentle with her brother. For his part, Corde had always tried to protect Elfrida, which aggravated Mason's resentment. Elfrida ought not to have had such a turbulent, fanatical son. She ought not to have married such a bully as Zaehner, either. That was her own vulgar streak. But of course Elfrida had no desire for her brother's protection. Nor for his critical analysis, thank you. Naturally, both father and son knew exactly what Corde thought of them. And now by his extreme queerness Mason made an exclusive claim on his mother—but Corde disliked all this psychology. Understanding was at bottom very tiresome.

Elfrida's letter was in part an offering. She wanted to convey affection and kindness to Minna. She did it with a sort of looping, rambling naive charm, not strictly literate, with feminine flourishes. Indirectly she appealed to her brother not to blame her for Mason's behavior, and spoke of "this admittedly difficult stage in Mason's maturing process." He didn't expect a mother to condemn her son. But what did she think existence was, dear girl? How she chose her tones was very odd. In one passage she was soft, in another inappropriately loud. Funny dynamics. She could be hardheaded enough when it was necessary. She was an excellent money manager. One of her paragraphs referred to the difficulties that Paine Webber was having with its computers. She was afraid that they might have lost track of her securities. "I never understood the printouts they sent. How could I? Electronics could make a beggar of me."

Zaehner had left her rich. He had had a big practice, and he used to enjoy quoting a famous Texas lawyer: "I'm just as interested in the poor and oppressed as Clarence Darrow was. If they aren't poor when I meet them, they are when I'm through with 'em."

A few days before the arrival of Gigi's wire, Corde had had a long talk with his sister.

Their meeting came before him now (the sun entered Minna's room, and its walls were relined with warm winter light). Like a colored picture, a carelessly inserted slide, Elfrida's parlor went back and forth, somewhat crooked, and then, right side up and better focused, he saw his sister Elfrida. If Corde's love for Elfrida had an extreme, almost exaggerated character, it was perhaps because she was curiously put together—very slender at the top, with a smooth dark head, and wide in the hips, a narrow profile combined with broad femininity. Her skin was imperfect, pitted on the cheekbones, but it was smooth in the hollows. She had the big mouth of a shouting comedienne and a talent for farcical gestures—she would make exaggerated gestures if she trusted you enough to let herself go. Her breath was acrid with tobacco, perfumed with lipstick; her teeth were irregular and spotty. Her air was that of a woman who had given in to disappointment and ruin. "Oh, to hell with it all!" This was conveyed, however, with a certain cleverness, ruefully amiable and warm. For of course she hadn't withdrawn the feminine claims of a younger woman. "American gals" seldom did. In their fifties they were still "dating." Corde didn't care to be well informed about these dates. She was seeing Stan Sorokin, Judge Sorokin, some years her junior. He courted her, pursued her, although since her husband's death three years ago she seemed to have become swarthier, more lined. But through all the transformations of middle age, the point of her upper lip, that strangely communicative tip, told you (told her brother, at least) what sort of woman she was—patient in disappointment, skeptical, practical, good access to her heart, if you knew where to look. It was all in the rising point of the lip.

Elfrida lived in an expensive hotel apartment near the "Magnificent Mile," just east of Water Tower Place. Corde disliked the commercial and promotional smoothness of the neighborhood, the showiness of the skyscrapers, the Bond Street and Rue de la Paix connections. "The Malignant Mammonism of the Magnificent Mile," he said to his sister. But Elfrida wouldn't acknowledge that it was the restaurants, the name hairdressers, the celebrities in the streets, that attracted her. She needed action, she insisted that she was happiest in a hotel apartment. Their father had been a hotel man. The Cordes had lived for years in a huge old apartment on Sheridan Road, but she preferred to remember the razzle-dazzle hotel life, the banquets, the big kitchens, the jazz bands, the bar gossip, and she told people, with a satisfaction her brother didn't share, "We were a pair of hotel brats." He was more apt to recall the drunks, freaks, noise-makers, check-kiters, the football deadheads, the salesmen and other business dumdums.

She and Zaehner had moved to the suburbs for Mason's sake. "You see how well *that* worked." She said to Corde, "When I'm out of sorts it comforts me that there are people down in the lobby. I don't have to face an empty lawn when my heart is troubled. Thank God I unloaded that big pretentious house."

This was her way of saying that living in Lake Forest had been Zaehner's idea. She seldom spoke frankly to Corde about her husband. The late Zaehner's attitude towards her brother had embarrassed her. She was still decently covering up—foolish wifeliness, Corde thought. There was too much there for tact to cover. Zaehner was tough. His face was charged with male strength in all the forms admired in Chicago. A big fellow, he was forceful, smart, cynical, political, rich, and he had no use for those who weren't. In the city that worked, he was one of those who gave people the works. So he despised his brother-in-law, a man large enough to be forceful, smart enough to be rich, proud enough to be contemptuous. To him Corde was a cop-out, a snob. From his side, Corde was careful to make no trouble for his sister. He let himself be baited, kept to his rule never to tangle with Zaehner. He held aloof, but of course there was tacit comment. The situation was complicated by the fact that in some respects Corde had liked his brother-in-law. He enjoyed his growling wit, his unpressed look, his practical jokes. (Zaehner would send call girls to visit his pals in the hospital, to cock-tease politicians and lawyers just out of the operating room.) Corde told Minna, "Zaehner was a Lyndon Johnson type of bully. When he turned away seven-eighths of his face but was still looking at you—watch out!" Lyndon Johnson was very remote from Minna. She gave Corde a dimpled smile, but he had learned that these smiles (affectionate, intimate, "steal your heart away") didn't signify understanding, only confidence that her husband, if she asked him to explain, could give her his grounds, would show why his remark deserved her smile. He would lay out the whole

American scene, spelling out the similarities he saw between the late Zaehner and the late President: native sons, men of power, devoid of culture, lovers of money, fearlessly insolent. Spelling it all out was a labor. Moreover, none of this meant much to her. Besides, she had no time to listen; she was intensely elsewhere. Nevertheless, she sent him a delightful signal.

So Elfrida had asked him to come, largely because of Mason but also out of sisterly concern, and he was in her apartment, sinking into one of her slipcovered chairs. Her small rooms were over-decorated; she had brought too much stuff with her from the suburbs. On the wall over the sofa were three schlocky watercolors of the Place Vendôme. They belonged in a hospital thrift shop, but they were a Paris gift from Zaehner.

Elfrida wasted no time. Handing Corde a martini and taking her English Ovals, the ashtray and matches into her lap, she began. "Let's see if we can get everything sorted, about you and Mason."

"And Max."

"Yes, Max. He's a nasty bastard. I always warned you about Cousin Detillion. I feel very sorry, Albert, for the heat you're getting."

"Although you'd say I brought it on myself, a good part of it."

"Well, I can't blame Mason on you. Nor Maxie. He always was repulsive. But there were things you could have avoided. You didn't need to publish those articles just before the trial. And then there's the trial itself."

"Well, there was a boy murdered. I didn't have much choice. There's also the young wife."

"But did you have to push so hard?"

"I didn't, not all that hard. The alternative was to accept the death. Just blame the urban situation—hot night, kid pushed out of a window. I could have let it all fade away, and be philosophical about it."

"We don't need to go into that. You had your reasons."

"Of course. You want me to explain why there's a warrant out for Mason's arrest."

"Yes, that's it. Why is there? Did you have anything to do with it?"

"Why would I? To stoke up the publicity fires for Cousin Maxie? I'm getting plenty of heat as it is. You just said it. The facts are in the papers—the real facts, for a change. Grady went before a grand jury and complained that Mason had raised hell with his witnesses. You can't expect a prosecutor to let the kid ruin his case. Hasn't he told you about this himself?"

"Mason?"

"He wouldn't have, naturally. But he threatened those street characters. He said he'd get 'em."

Elfrida said, "It's hard to imagine tough black street people being intimidated by skinny Mason. I can't picture that that Lake Forest schoolboy actually fired a gun at anybody. Do you believe that, Albert?"

"Not necessarily. But I don't necessarily disbelieve it. He's in real earnest about his pal Ebry. By working in the restaurant kitchen, he got to be an honorary black. He cornered those witnesses. . . ."

"They only came out of the woodwork to claim the reward."

Corde said, "One of them had the dead boy's wedding ring. The prostitute asked him to keep it for her. The other fellow put Ebry up that night, and Ebry told him he was in trouble. Mason warned those two. They took fright. . . ."

"Yes," said Elfrida. "That's what I read in the papers. They were shot at, got scared, and hid themselves."

"Without them, Grady had no case. He sent the plainclothesmen into the projects to flush them out, one from Cabrini Green, the other from Robert Taylor Homes. They were taken in custody. . . ."

"Can you see Mason sticking a gun in his pocket and going out at night to shoot anybody?"

"They're capable of making it all up, sure. *If* shots were fired —a doubtful proposition—somebody else might have fired them. There are enough guns around, and plenty of people out to get people. There's an armed population in the city with all kinds of weapons—not just Saturday night specials but machine guns, grenades. I wouldn't be surprised by rockets. Still, Mason did threaten the witnesses, gang style, that does seem to be a fact; and they didn't turn up at the trial, another fact."

Elfrida pulled back strands that had escaped from the tight

black bonds of hair. Her brother almost imagined that the tightness helped her to keep her head in position. With a hint of strain or faintness, Elfrida confessed, "I don't follow. . . . He is a little bastard, isn't he."

"I wouldn't exaggerate," said Corde. "But what's he gone into hiding for? He's not exactly a hunted man. Obstructing justice isn't such a big deal in this case. He must be thrilled to pieces to be a fugitive. It's a terrific luxury for a kid like Mason. You corner two street people. You deliver a death threat. They take you *seriously*—that's a real thrill. It means you're pretty close to being black yourself. You don't have to be ashamed of your white skin."

"Ah, well, I don't have a corner on troubles. You've got your own, Albert."

Wrapped in his coat at Valeria's table, his chair tipped back, Corde reconstructed parts of this conversation. His memory was exceptionally clear. And he could see what a problem he had become to his sister. The last thing she wanted was the sort of "intelligent" discussion he specialized in. There were times when a humoring-the-mad look passed over her face. He knew his sister's mind as he knew her long neck, her characteristic dark female bittersweet fragrance. Mason might be playing a modern version of Tom Sawyer and Nigger Jim. It had an especially nasty twist now. Yes, but what game was Uncle Albert playing?

"You must have discussed this with somebody in the firm. I'd turn it over to Zaehner, Notkin and Delff if I were you."

"Yes, I've talked it over with Moe Delff. He says the indictment won't hold up, the court will dismiss it. But Mason has to surrender first, so I can put up a bond. Moe will go to the police with him. When it comes up for a hearing, Moe thinks the court will give your friend Grady hell for rushing to the grand jury."

"Is this all Delff?" Corde asked.

He was sounding her out about Judge Sorokin. He shouldn't have done this. It was not altogether brotherly amiability. She probably didn't like it. By the lowering of her eyes she confirmed his hunch. Nevertheless he went on. "I assume you've double-checked this with Sorokin."

Sorokin was a minor magistrate, a former precinct captain

who owed his position to the Machine. There were officials in Chicago who didn't much mind being owned. Everybody had to be vetted by the Machine. You didn't get on the ballot unless the Machine put you there. Within the Machine, however, relations were hierarchical and feudal, not necessarily servile. Corde had dealt with this in his articles and Sorokin himself had been one of his informants. Corde liked him, on the whole. Alderman Siblish was said to have Sorokin in his pocket, yes, but the man was cheerful, boyishly good-natured. No really dirty work came his way; he wasn't important enough for that. He had risen from the North Side streets. Wounded at Omaha Beach (Purple Heart), he was far from disabled. For recreation he took Outward Bound survival trips, parachuting from helicopters into the trackless wild. Obviously Elfrida liked Sorokin, but she assumed that her brother, that great reader, journalist, highbrow professor, dean, and intellectual, took a dim view of the Judge, saw him as another Zaehner. Well, she preferred low Chicago male company, people like her own father, a man about town who used to take her to prizefights and nightclubs. Corde's tastes were different altogether. He'd been unwilling to go to the fights with Dad.

"Naturally, I talked it over with Stan Sorokin. Can you blame me? Every morning the papers are at the door. My heart races so, I can't swallow my coffee. It must be even worse for you, reading them."

"They seldom get anything right."

"But how irritating it must be. I'm sure your college isn't happy about it, either."

"So far they've been civilized. *I*'ve been the emotional party. They haven't much use for that. They'd prefer me to be cool. Anyway, they behave like gentlemen. No, they aren't happy—the circus it's turned into, with the Dean's nephew and the Dean's cousin Maxie, the student newspaper, the leftover Lefties of the sixties. Even the Spartacus Youth League from the thirties."

"But Mason, most of all."

Examining his behavior now, Corde thought he had done fairly well on the whole.

"You asked me to stop in on my way home, Elfrida. . . ."

"That's right."

"I didn't invite myself. In fact, I've stayed away deliberately. But I didn't come and complain about Mason. . . ."

"That's true, Albert. . . . I'm sure it is. I believe it. There is an emotional problem. I think Mason has been trying to get at you like this because he wasn't able to reach you otherwise."

So it was to be a session of suburban maternal psychology. He had no use at all for that stuff, but he saw no way to stop it. As he drank his martini, he tuned out, now and again. But if he paid little attention to her words, he listened closely to the sound of her voice, watched her face. She was warm of heart, naturally warm. She spoke of schools and teachers, of psychiatrists, of the loneliness of an only child and the problems of coping with a father like Zaehner, of Mason's lack of success with peer friendships and the effects of marijuana on the brain ("Recent studies show . . ."). Thank heavens Mason didn't have a serious drug problem. Composed, turning the stem of the martini glass, looking into the drink and again at Elfrida's imperfect skin, Corde felt the tidy parlor of the hotel apartment enclosing him—paneled white walls, white silk lampshades, upholstered restfulness, thick carpeting, porcelain cockatoos on the mantel, ornaments of Venetian glass and Meissen, the phony Place Vendôme watercolors, the enormous Hancock Tower with crossed trusses shutting off the westward view—and asked himself where the depth level was. Not in the ladies'-magazine pedagogy or the Lake Forest psychiatry, but in the natural warmth of his sister. In him it was represented if you liked by his feeling for Elfrida—for the length and smoothness of her head, the Vidal Sassoon dye job, the damaged skin, the slender nose with its dark nostrils, the feminized tobacco flavor, her sweet-and-acrid fragrance. All these particulars, the apperceptive mass of a lifetime. Yes, she was heavy in the thighs, big in the hips. There was a perennially strange ultra-familiar contrast between the elongated upper body, the upstream, and the broad estuary of the lower half, the lower flow of womanliness. The depth level he was looking for was in the heat that came from her patchy face, from the art with which she was painted about the eyes, and even from the memories of odors, some of them undoubtedly sexual in origin—from an aching sort of personal history. Perhaps he loved the point of her upper lip most of all. He thought this to be a reading of true feelings and no mere projection. These times we live in give us foolish thoughts to think, dead categories of intellect and words that get us nowhere. It was just these words and categories that made the setting of a real depth level so important. I disagree with my misshapen old sister, we can't talk to each other, yet we have something palpable between us. Mason, somewhere, is aware of this and he doesn't like it. She loves him most, as is quite natural, but that's not enough for him. Maybe he's afraid that I may do him out of his legacy, if she's named me executor. But she's surely too smart to do that. My record with money is bad. I let Detillion swindle me. And I assume the Mason problem comes down to money, somewhere along the line. The form Mason's ambition has taken is downward, for the present. It's as that clever Frenchman said: there's positive transcendence and there's the negative kind. (Corde had stopped thirty years ago trying to discuss theories with Elfrida.) But when Mason's downward ambition stops—and where can it lead?—he'll want his dough. She'll die, he'll get it. He's waiting for that. Elfrida would not be shocked by these parricidal thoughts. Why should she be? If she hadn't read Proust's "Filial Sentiments of a Parricide," she had been married to Mason Zaehner, who had practiced law on La Salle Street for four decades. She had no need of Proust or Freud or Krafft-Ebing or Balzac or Aristophanes. Chicago had it all.

Zaehner the secretive lawyer was big on candor, in a showmanly way. He liked a bold statement over a drink, as when he told Corde that he lived by tipping over garbage cans. "Lived" was his euphemism for the crushing fees he charged. Sometimes he was more Darwinian—the struggle for existence in the Loop jungle. Some jungle! Who were the lions and tigers? It was more like the city dump. Rats were the principal fauna. And it wasn't Zaehner who struggled for existence; he arranged for others to do the struggling. And of course Zaehner sensed how mixed a view his brother-in-law took of him. He couldn't have missed it. You didn't have to be terribly deep for that. Corde had the trick, while keeping his mouth shut, of transmitting opinions. He looked at you with a newspaperman's silent irony. Well, Zaehner was affronted by those opinions. It was people like himself, Zaehner, who lived the life characteristic of the city and of the country, who were realistically connected with its operations, its historical position, its power—the actual American stuff. They were at the center. And who the fuck did this dud dean think *he* was!

Anyway, Zaehner died of heart failure on the expressway while driving back to Lake Forest, and he left a pile of money. And despite her fashionable address among gay bars and executive dining clubs, in these streets of canopies, marquees, doormen, Elfrida was not one of your big spenders. She didn't haunt the boutiques or wear designer dresses. She was increasing Zaehner's dollars, preserving them for Mason!

She was talking money to her brother now, saying that she had been trapped through bad advice with a conservative portfolio. Interest rates had shot up, the bonds declined by thirty percent; the gold hedge hadn't worked, either. About the Paine Webber computers she was rueful, giving him side glances with her slight, smiling dark face as if she were telling him that she had been abused physically, cornered and pinched by gross people. Corde in his polite way, but restive ("Okay, okay, enough!"), said, "SEC is watching this minor Paine Webber mixup, you can be sure. The *Wall Street Journal* said it was trivial." But in matters of money she didn't need his assurances. Sorokin, if she should decide to marry that virile, sleek-headed, nutria-bearded Marlboro Country judge from the North Side, would not come into any of the money. But to do him justice, it didn't appear that he was chasing Elfrida's dollars.

Holding together the ends of his coat collar against the chill in Minna's room and looking out now and then over the bleak Communist capital, or reaching out to the plum brandy, or feeling the soil under the cyclamens (as cyclamens loved low temperatures, they were in heaven here—*he* should be so beautiful at 48 degrees F!), Corde occasionally checked the time on his wrist. Dewey Spangler's car wasn't due yet, and Corde, Elfrida's letter filled with lady phrases before him, continued to reconstruct the last conversation he had had with her. It was important. And somehow he was better able to be objective here; the foreign setting made for more clarity. Or Valeria, dying.

When Elfrida was done with the money—and most of their meetings since she was widowed began like this (the foreground clutter of finance had to be swept away)—Corde claimed the equal time he was entitled to. It was inevitable that they should begin immediately to discuss Maxie Detillion.

Detillion: Why was it that there were people with whom he, Corde, was so tied that his perception of them amounted to a bondage? They were drawn together physically, so tightly that he was virtually absorbed by them. With Elfrida, this absorption was sweet and lucid. But it wasn't always sweet, and liking had nothing to do with it: he didn't *like* his cousin. A kind of hypnotic coalescence was what occurred. Thus he knew the pores of Detillion's face; the close serial waves of his hair descending to a peak felt almost like his own hair—as he remembered it. In action Max's eyes were the eyes of a guru or a star of the German Expressionist movies. When Cousin Max rolled them, Corde took the sensation into his own eyes. Detillion had always had a tang of male acid about him, but now he was beginning to smell like an old man; you got a whiff of unaired clothes closets when he passed by. He had grown side whiskers of macho wool. Rouault would have wanted to paint Maxie—had put other Maxies into his giant studies of corrupt men.

In the courtroom, Maxie and Corde would occasionally look at each other without speaking. Corde's presence may have made things harder for Lydia Lester, whom he had come to protect and support. In fact he saw that his being there aggravated Max's sensationalism, made Max more melodramatic. He sent continual eye messages to the two newspapermen who covered the trial ("Don't miss this, hear?"). He did not give the girl a hard time on the witness stand, because juries sympathized with young women whose husbands had been killed. Knowing this, he intended to be tactful. He did not know that he oppressed her by wooing her. He wasn't at all aware of it—simply didn't know what he was doing. It would never have crossed his mind that she was mourning, sick, shaky, frightened. The message he transmitted was that he was doing his professional best to obtain testimony favorable to his client, but that when this ordeal was over he would show her the other side of his nature, which was tenderly erotic. He sent the same sexual message to all females from a full heart. The innocence of it had in the course of the years become clear to Corde —for it was in a sense innocent—corrupt innocence. Before the jury, Detillion came brandishing papers like Joe McCarthy. He was a brandishing man. What he really flourished was his sex. His once handsome nose was beginning to look damaged, cartilages blasted, and as he aged and grew heavier his cheeks thickened, his color darkened; he looked leaden, he lost height, his pelvis widened, his courtroom pacing was slightly lame. Corde believed he was dying—the old mad blind despised and dying king.

What was it but intimacy to *see* Cousin Maxie Detillion like this? It made no difference that Max cut him, behaving with stupid, cold, waxen hauteur. To see someone like this was to enter into his life. Not necessarily a welcome experience.

Maxie was not a great observer, but it was impossible to remain unaware of so deep a lifetime interest. Detillion had always given this a sexual interpretation. "Albert admired the way I am with women. I was his role model."

Elfrida said, "It looks like you'll have Cousin Max with you at every stage of life."

Corde smiled. "If I die first, don't let him make my funeral arrangements."

"I used to knock myself out trying to understand why you went along with him till he thought he owned you. And when you broke away, he couldn't get it through his head. You betrayed him. *He's* the one with the grievance."

When Grandfather Detillion died, his property down in Joliet had been divided among his three grandchildren. Under the will, Max was executor of the estate. Elfrida had gotten her share of the money—Zaehner saw to that. Zaehner had said to Corde, "What's the matter with you, anyway; can't you see what's happening? The ground floor is rented to McDonald's hamburgers. Have you ever gotten a penny out of it?"

"I got tax write-offs."

"But cash, not one penny, right? He's swindling you. He's milking the property. The phony expenses he puts on the books, I spotted them in the first statement he sent out. When he bought us out he got a two-thirds interest, so he controls it all—what else does he do for you, in the way of business?"

Corde had in fact allowed Cousin Max to make investments for him. Max had obtained from him various powers of attorney, as well as an authorization to trade in securities through the Harris Trust in his name. In his relations with Detillion (and not only Detillion), Corde arranged somehow to persuade himself, however great the quirks of those he trusted, that he wasn't going to be cheated. He had watched Maxie cheating others—shifting and hiding assets, outfoxing creditors, maneuvering to frustrate court orders, claiming preposterous tax deductions. For all his shenanigans he was seldom liquid enough to pay his bills (he lived high), he could never grab as much as he needed. But not from *me*, Corde would tell himself. Max would never cheat me.

"Let me put it on the line to you, brother-in-law. . . ." Zaehner, masterly, prolonged his scowl, silent. Lumps of severity formed at the corners of his mouth. "Unless you hold your cousin's feet to the fire, you'll never see a penny. You must have some idea how much he screwed you out of."

Corde did have an idea, certainly, but he kept it shrouded. It belonged to a group of shrouded objects which he promised himself one day to examine. But on that day a philosophical light would have to shine. Otherwise it wouldn't do to remove the shrouds. He guessed that Max had done him out of something between two and three hundred thousand dollars. This conservative estimate he kept to himself.

"Hold his feet to the fire—how?" Corde said.

"Demand an audit."

"Well, then there'd be an explosion. . . ."

"You wouldn't be *afraid* of that character, would you?"

"I may be, a little. . . ."

"I think I understand. . . . It's not personal fear of your creep cousin, but fear of what will have to come to light about the relationship. Finding out . . . it wouldn't make you happy to look at the picture. Did Max draw your will? Is he going to be in charge when you kick off?"

"Yes, to both questions."

"Tear it up. Make a new will."

"I'd have to find another lawyer."

"A sobering thought, yes? Don't worry, I'll suggest a few safe names. . . . Since you came back to Chicago to be a perfesser, you and your cousin have used each other. He guided you around the Near North and Lincoln Avenue joints, access to the Playboy Mansion, and broads easy to get. Hard to get rid of, but that's a different subject. That's what he did for you. What you did for him was to give him some class. His reputation was really tacky. Not only that he was a rotten lawyer, but his dick was just plain hanging out. Then suddenly he turned into an intellectual. He started dropping intellectual names. People downtown wanted to punch him in the face. But that's no use. You want the bottom line? Detillion is bananas. All you have to do is watch him dancing, there's your proof."

In this Zaehner might have been right. On a dance floor, proud of his technique, Detillion would swing his wide buttocks with crazy grace, mincing out the Caribbean rhythms. In his cha-cha-cha, possessed, he had no eyes for his partner, whom he dominated as a matter of course, like the ringmaster's mare. It was the spectators he danced for. Since Corde was a great reader (who was now convinced that he had read too much, gathered too many associations, idled in too many picture galleries), he frequently saw his performing cousin's massive, ecstatic face in the Rouault version, a sexual oppressor of tragic multitudes of women (possibly also of men). But Detillion's own image when he was in action was of course quite different. He was anything but a screwer of girls. No, he was the agent or personification of Eros, all aflame, all gold, crimson, radiant, experiencing divine tumescence, bringing life. The power to bless womankind was swelling in his pants. Zaehner said his dick was hanging out. His brother-in-law put the matter another way. But he had no intention of discussing Cousin Maxie extensively with Zaehner.

Corde credited Zaehner with high intelligence. He didn't feel superior to him. But Zaehner could not bear hearing Corde's thoughts, and whenever Corde tried to discuss his ideas, he shut him up. "You've lost me, Albert. Can't follow you there. Too mental for me." There was verbal deference, but furious contempt in the modulation of scowl into smile. Yes, this was another interesting relationship, no doubt about it. Another shrouded object in Corde's collection. If Cousin Maxie had affinities with Rouault, Zaehner was associated by Corde with Hermann Göring. This was sobering, severe, unfair—a crushing comparison, and never to be mentioned. Mason senior wore unpressed chalk-striped suits, his pants were low-slung in the seat, he had scuffed shoes. He was your informal Chicagoan. Göring had dressed himself in mountainous medieval velvet robes; he covered his face with pancake makeup; gems were his jelly beans. Still there seemed to be a similarity. Corde, at Valeria's table, tracing the Zaehner-Göring association to its origins, went back as far as a certain Mrs. Wooster, an American society lady in Paris (Rue de Rennes), who had altered her elderly, stern look when Göring's name was mentioned and said, "Why, he was nothing but a teddy bear. I knew him well." Until now inflexible, Mrs. Wooster had smiled with all the sweetness of a stern woman when she relents, and with this smile Göring was reconfirmed in Corde's mind as a great archetype of worldly evil. Zaehner was no great archetype, but to Elfrida, he also had been a teddy bear—anything but a beast of the Chicago jungle dumps.

At all events, Zaehner had kept after Corde and forced him at last, out of "self-respect," to take action against Detillion. It came to that. Detillion was exposed, was unshrouded.

And so Elfrida was saying to her brother in the overheated white rooms of Chicago (rooms which by the completeness of their furnishings, fullness of installation, and convenience, suggested that America had taken care of most outstanding human needs—what more did you want?)—was saying, "I should have told you, Albert, that when you and Cousin Max finally had your big legal hassle, Cousin Max came all the way out to Lake Forest to see me—a special trip. He told me he had to bare his heart to somebody in the family. He said he didn't deserve to be treated like this. He was being pushed too hard. Word was getting out. People were talking around town that he had rooked you, fucked you up with IRS, and he was incompetent. . . ."

"I didn't push him too hard. We settled out of court. What was he trying to get out of you?"

"He wanted me to arrange a conference with Mason, and Mason, as you remember, had just had his first coronary. Max called and left messages, but I wouldn't let Mason call back."

"It would have been worth ten thousand bucks to Max to have Zaehner get him off the hook with me."

"Max said, 'I'll never forgive what Albert did to my image.'"

"His image! And baring his heart! Poor Max. I get sore at

him, but when I look closer or hear what he says, I turn sorry instead."

"You must have been. You let him off easy. What kind of settlement was that?"

"I dropped a lot of dough on him. Let's say I was paying tuition. I had to take a special course."

"Learning what, dear?"

"Things I should have known fifty years ago. A postgraduate seminar in boneheadedness and idiocy."

Corde was trying to get Elfrida to talk with him in *his* way. She was his sister, she ought to be able to do it. She ought to be willing.

"Maybe a quarter of a million wasn't tuition enough."

"I see what you mean. Losing that much dough didn't make me suffer enough. I'm still an idiot, and I haven't got the dough to enroll in another course."

Corde's intent was plain. He was sounding out his sister on the Chicago articles, trying to get her opinion. Did she see those disturbing pieces as his new venture in idiocy? He watched her very closely. When her face darkened, she was flushing. That made her look youthful. Then came tension and reticence and made her look elderly. She was perhaps as sorry for her brother as he was for Cousin Max. She believed he was a very strange man. His hang-ups were not like other people's —identifiable neuroses, alcoholism, bragging. Nothing normal. He had his own most original, incomprehensible way of screwing things up. No, she wasn't going to give an opinion on his articles. So there he had her judgment on them. He couldn't deny that it bothered him, but—he loved his sister just the same. She was actually miffed with him. She had much to say about those Chicago articles but she wouldn't talk. Her black eyes were critical, wistful, canny and angry. She seemed to ask why rock the boat—why push so hard, be so reckless, write so strangely? To Zaehner, Chicago had been the greatest city in the world, no place like it. And Corde's father had agreed with Zaehner, no place like Chicago—big, vital, new, the best! Old Corde, who had cut a figure here as a big hotel man and public personality, would have been bitterly annoyed with a son who knocked Chicago. Of course Elfrida *couldn't* approve.

She turned the discussion again to Cousin Max. "He made

me a long speech, when he came out to see me. He walked up and down with his hands behind his back, spouting about a great evil all around him and drowning his soul, and how you of all people should turn up on the wicked side. All right, Albert—Max mismanaged your money. But you let him do it. And Mason was a devil to go to him with this case—I don't blame you for being sore. But maybe you're being far too sensitive. I doubt that anybody is really paying much attention to Max. They can see what a ham he is. Even if you're down on Chicago, give them *some* credit."

"Did you happen to see him on Channel Two the other night?"

On the tube, unexpectedly, Corde had switched on his cousin. There was Maxie in full color with his cumulus side whiskers and his face blazing with false truthfulness. Corde had been astonished to hear his own name spoken. "Dean Corde, who happens to be my first cousin . . ." Corde had been greatly offended by this. Hearing his name loudly spoken, he was furious. Even now he was angry about it, aware of a large area of atrocious anger very near. He could almost touch it. Detillion made charges of racism, he referred to the college as "a great institution. But its relations with Affirmative Action are troubled." He lied with his eyes and his brows even more than with words. Corde had to admit that he spoke reasonably well, in the unnatural style of the Chicago bar—Corde had commented on this in *Harper's*: "The peculiar, gentlemanly, high-toned illiteracy of lawyers before the Bench . . ."

Corde said, "No, *I* shouldn't be so sensitive about Max. But he comes every day and sprays the girl and the family with untreated sewage. It was me that got her involved, and I feel responsible . . . my family, after all. Even a stronger person couldn't bear this publicity circus, but this isn't a strong young woman. She's inexperienced, she's dazed, and don't forget, the boy's parents are sitting in the courtroom while Max comes on, not with her but with Ebry and other witnesses, about funny sexual practices, and suggesting hadn't the young man gone out that night with a lascivious purpose. Bringing in group sex and hinting at kinkiness with all kinds of esoteric kinks. It's too much."

"Too much for you, I see. You're very emotional about it."

"Well, of course I am, Elfrida. I'm *in* it. Mason knocked on her door last September, to tell her that she'd better not take the stand."

Elfrida said, "Yes, I think I heard that before." As she lowered her eyes, Corde dropped the subject. Elfrida then said, "I can see why she wants those people sent to jail. It's perfectly natural. She must feel she owes it to her husband."

"Grady says it's stupid of Max to push so hard, because if she were to break down in front of the jury it would do his case no good. I almost think Grady is hoping for it. But somehow she's toughing it out. I never thought she could."

"Sorokin's opinion is that Max is making a good defense, purely on the legal side."

Corde said, "Sometimes I think that if Detillion's prayers had been answered and he had become ultra-rich . . ."

"Yes . . . ?"

"Then all this psychopathic suffering of his would have been safely embalmed. He'd be a big giver, a patron of the opera and symphony, he'd be elected to all the boards. Nobody would notice how stupid or how cracked he was. But since he can't even pay his bills, he has to find a way to dress his disaster presentably. But this has to be done in public."

"I get what you're saying," said Elfrida. Her uneasiness was deep. *She* was herself ultra-rich, for one thing. Her moved and distracted brother might at any moment fall into one of his theorizing fits. He saw how it was. He would take off from his elevation, from his butte, in a mad flight of clarity—and heresy. His voice would be equable, deep, harmonious, not a sign of fanaticism, and he would say incomprehensible, ungraspable, glassy, slippery and, finally, terrible, harmful things—things that would have revolted their father and made the late Zaehner look grim. In Elfrida's opinion Albert didn't know what it was to be moderate, he exaggerated everything. But then his love for her also had an exaggerated character. If she was glad to have his love, why did she rule out his "exaggerated" theories? There was a certain amusement in his question. And then—honestly, now!—was it such a distorted theory? He was saying that you became an impregnable monster if you had money, so that if to begin with you felt yourself to be monstrous you could build impregnability by making a fortune. Because then you were a force of nature, although a psychopath. Or if you were without any persona, then you *bought* a persona. And underlying all of this—Corde had had to fly to Communist Europe and sit in his wife's schoolgirl room to understand it—underlying the whole of his recent phase of eccentricity (it wasn't at all eccentric from within) was his continuing dispute with Elfrida's husband, the late Zaehner. *Contra Zaehner* might have been the true title of those articles on Chicago. He hadn't been aware of this at first. The first conception was innocent. Originally period pieces, picturesque, charming, nostalgic, his essays somehow got out of hand. Naturally, he could not expect sympathy from his sister. She couldn't sympathize without disloyalty to Zaehner and to her son. Besides, she disagreed.

"Don't you worry, Elfrida," he had said to her before he left —meaning that he would not molest her, would not try to get her to talk *his* way.

She drew a long, thankful breath, and in her relief she said to him, "I think you ought to know, Albert, that Sorokin thinks you were right about Rufus Ridpath. Ridpath really did do his best at the County Jail. He was the only one who even tried to improve conditions and help the prisoners. And there were people who might have been out to get him. Sorokin agrees that he was basically honest. They not only ganged up to get rid of him but made sure that he had no future in politics around here."

"I don't think Ridpath would ever have run for office, that would be out of character. But did Sorokin tell you this? He was the one who sent me to Ridpath in the first place."

Elfrida made one of her faces. Corde understood exactly what it meant. She said, "You didn't have to go overboard and say that he was such a rare type of black man."

"That wasn't what I wrote. I said he was a rare type in any color. Black or white or ocher or green, there weren't many people in Chicago who bothered their minds with anything like justice. Puzzling, how few. You didn't even realize this until you met a person who did have it on his mind as a primary interest, and then it dawned on you how rare such a primary interest was. . . ."

"The phrase you used was 'a moral life.'"

"That was unfortunate. You've got to be careful about the big word. I realized even then that it would rub everybody the wrong way. This kind of abnormal, professorial Plato-and-Aristotle stuff is the kiss of death. I probably didn't do Ridpath much good, either. Definitely a mistake. . . ."

V

In the adjoining room, Minna was on the telephone. He had heard the ringing and now he became aware (he didn't often tune in) that this was an unusual call. Her voice went up sharply. He listened, and then went around through the corridor to the dining room. The Stambouli-work sofa was near the glass connecting door. He sat bent over, superattentive. The conversation was short. Minna tried to speak but the other party cut her off. Something bad was happening, that was certain. As soon as she rang off, she set out to find Corde. He heard her steps as she moved in the wrong direction, and called out, "Here." She couldn't answer when he asked what it was about, she only stared at him. "That wasn't intensive care?"

Valeria worse? Or dead? No, it hadn't been that sort of news, and it wasn't that sort of shock. Unlike Elfrida, Minna had no repertoire of faces. He had never seen her eyes so black or her skin so lined, so dry and white.

"Well, what was that?" he said.

"Albert, do you know who? It was the Colonel."

"Himself, in person?"

"It was the Colonel. I could murder him."

"What's he done? What did he say?"

"The Ambassador must have gone to work as soon as you left."

"I see. He called the Minister of Health, and the Minister called the Colonel? . . ."

"That's the way it must have been done."

"Well, all right, but what happened? Does the Minister of Health run the hospitals or doesn't he?"

"Not this hospital. The Colonel is in charge. He just told me in no uncertain way. He was terrible to me. Terrible, Albert!"

"I see. It's a power contest—a minister versus the secret police."

"It was no contest. He's the boss."

"That's becoming clear. I'm sorry, Minna. We shouldn't have tried to go over his head if we couldn't go high enough. The usual mistake, doing the thing by halves. Should have realized . . . a secret police colonel doesn't give a damn for a cabinet minister. I think this is why our old friend Petrescu keeps dropping from sight. He gave it a try but he was outranked, and now he stays away. It was the second visit, the one we didn't have permission for, that licked him. I shouldn't have fooled around with the Ambassador. I should have tried to get to the White House on it. A direct call, President to President. It might have been pulled off. Still might. These guys have a favored nation agreement with the U.S., a hell of an important thing to them. They wouldn't have refused."

"He said . . ."

"Yes, what did the Colonel tell you?"

"That I could see my mother one more time. Only once. That was what he said."

"Oh?" said Corde, as if he understood. He didn't understand at all. He had a sharp pang of eyestrain. "Give me that again: he said come and visit her?"

"Once, he said."

"And when?"

"He's going to leave that to me. I couldn't believe it. I tried to talk, but he cut me off. He said, 'Don't you understand Rumanian? I'm allowing you and your husband one visit.'"

Corde by now had taken this in. Come, once, and visit—it was the final visit. He said to Minna, "We started a fight with the Minister, and the Colonel won. I guess he took the dispute upstairs, and upstairs backed him. I should have given this more thought when the Ambassador offered. It was decent of him, but the usual result. You think you're priming the decency pump by pouring decency. It's never real. . . . Did he say, 'You and your husband'?"

"Yes, Albert. What will I tell him? I'm supposed to call back and say when we're coming."

"What about Tanti Gigi?" said Corde. "If this is the one and only visit? . . . No, you can't talk to him about Gigi."

"Albert, answer me: When shall we go? Tomorrow? When?"

"I'd go today—tonight," he said, rising from the settee.

"Are you saying she may die anytime?"

"Tomorrow we may think of more strings to pull. Maybe Gherea can move her. Maybe we can stir up somebody at the White House. We might wire Washington."

"He's waiting for my call."

"Then tell him tonight."

She went back to the telephone.

Corde fetched his coat over his shoulders. These were the shortest days. The afternoon light no sooner came in than it was on its way out. It was cold, too. Brittle scales began to show on the street puddles, a crystalline bitterness setting in. Where the light withdrew, the yellow-brown of the stucco was pocked with mild blue. (They could rub your face into that stucco if they liked.) On the open porches over the way—bottles, wet rags hung out to dry frozen at the points, and vine twigs. The glory of the day carried things easily when the sun shone; but when the sun passed, things seemed abandoned, they became dissociated, and you had to find a way to take them up yourself. Corde followed his wife's voice in the next room. Some languages are spoken, others sung. Even now, fighting the Colonel and the Communist state, she still sounded musical. As he—while pitying his wife; while hating the Colonel; while figuring why the Colonel had made such a decision; and what kind of ploys there had been; or what kind of deal the Colonel had cut with the Minister—still followed thought themes of his own. There was the Colonel in his tall broom-closet office, ruling on this, ruling on that, under a twenty-watt light. And there was personal humanity, a fringe receding before the worldwide process of consolidation. This process might seem too crude to be taken seriously, but don't kid yourself, it was shaping the future. And while this shaping went on, the inmost essence of the human being must be making its own, its necessary, its unique arrangements as it best could.

Now to move to Valeria and the life-support machines. Corde was convinced that the old woman was fully and probably even brilliantly conscious. The life supports were clicking and her mind was (he decided) exquisitely vivid—in a state of hypervividness. She wouldn't die until she had seen her daughter—seen her in a manner of speaking, since she couldn't open her eyes. They made scanning movements under the skin; they might be light-sensitive; they filled out the lids (an involuntary comparison) like ravioli. She was studying her death, that was for sure. Corde thought of her with extraordinary respect. Her personal humanity came from the old sources. Corde had become better informed about these sources in Paris and London. Amid eye pangs that made him pass his fingertips over his forehead from left to right (here in Eastern Europe he felt dehydrated and even conceived of his optic nerves as dry and frayed), he considered those old sources. He remembered that she had taken a serious interest in Structuralism, in Laing's psychiatry. Hell, what did she want to bother for? It must have been alien to her deeper life. In the deeper life she was traditional, even archaic. She had loved her husband, that was why she became a Communist militant: she had loved her husband, loved her daughter, her sister. Then for thirty years she had made up for the Marxism, for the sin of helping to bring in the new regime, by a private system of atonement, setting up her mutual-aid female network. Yet she kept up with sophisticated opinion; the Party had denounced her when she was expelled for "cosmopolitan psychologism," or Freudianism, but that was nothing. She was reading a book on the Hagia Sophia. It was on her desk. Corde was curious about it, but the language was beyond him. This same Valeria, when she visited her husband's grave, and her own burial place, lighted candles in front of the gravestone—there was a big granite stone out there. Gigi said, "When she had to make an important decision, she went to the grave to talk to *him* about it." She brought food for the beggars in the cemetery. It wasn't only the mother-of-pearl inlay that was Stambouli-work. These were the Balkans. Here the deeper life was Byzantine, and even more archaic, never mind the Freud or the Laing—that was for the sophisticated, nervous public. There was no such sophistication here. She stood before the gates of death. And as a physician—but you didn't need to be a physician to know that you were dying. She even suspected perhaps that the authorities might decide to disconnect the life supports when they had had enough of her. Corde definitely thought that the Colonel might have this in mind. He had the authority, definitely. He could say, "Pull 'em," and that would be that. And at this, Corde (himself not so young, not so well) felt a curious affinity for the crystals of brittle ice whose glitter came up to his Balkan window. These badgering perplexities, intricacies of equilibrium, sick hopes, riddling evils, sadistic calculations—you might do worse than to return to that strict zero-blue and simple ice. In all this Corde felt singularly close to the old woman.

Minna when she came back said, "It's settled for tonight."

When Corde began to speak, she reminded him that the place was bugged by pointing to the light fixture.

"Let's walk around the block."

"When is the car coming for you?"

"Not just yet."

There were twenty minutes to spare. Spangler's driver was sure to be punctual. Drivers here, as elsewhere in Eastern Europe, reported to the secret police. For this reason they gave excellent service.

Corde and Minna descended together in the small elevator. He held the heavy wrought-iron-and-glass door for her as she stepped into the street. Towards midafternoon, the December sun was ready to check out. Below the winter beams there were violet shadows; these were collected in the pitted surfaces of the stucco walls, and made Corde think of choppy winter water. A similar color gathered about the pollarded trees. The pigeons afoot on the sidewalk had it, too, with iridescent variations. In midstreet Corde noticed the remains of small rats. They must have run for it during the earthquake, got themselves conked by falling masonry and then rolled flat by trucks and cars. That was how Corde figured them. They were as two-dimensional as weather vanes. Here and there amid the Balkan Haussmann blocks were earthquake ruins or tumuli, and Corde assumed that they must also be graves. The brick heaps exhaled decay. There were unrecoverable bodies underneath. The smell was cold, dank and bad. Coupled rusty-orange tramcars ran with a slither of cables. Pale proletarian passengers looked out. They wore caps, the women kerchiefs. Together with cast-iron sinks and croaking pull-chain toilets, these tramcars belonged to the old days. It was all like looking backwards. You saw the decades in reverse. Even the emotions belonged to an earlier time. The issue of the struggle with the

Colonel was human sentiment—not accepted as an issue under the new order. But the Colonel tacitly admitted it because it gave pain. He knew it *was* an issue. It was Corde's momentary fantasy that these ideas were gathered about his head, as the light gathered, paler, around the pruned trees, each one of which resembled a bouquet.

Minna walked faster than usual. Back home you could do nothing to quicken her pace. She had her own notions of feminine poise, or the appropriate Raresh dignity. But today she moved quickly. She held Corde's arm, and when pedestrians approached, she gave it a tug which meant "shut up." So he was silent, and she looked sternly absentminded. Minna never came to the dinner table, or got into bed at night, or went into the street, without putting on fresh lipstick. But now her lip was drawn thin and the red was hardly visible. She was dry, pale; she looked very sick.

"You understand what the problem is, Albert," she said.

"Gigi."

"Yes, Tanti Gigi, and how we get her in."

"Of course," said Corde. "She has to see her sister. If there are passes for two at the gate, she can take my place."

"No, all three of us have to get in. We must all go. I wish we could turn to Petrescu. He's always been a good friend. You can be sure this is painful for him."

"We'll think about him some other time. He's in another strange branch of experience. We'll go into that later. Right now we have to make a plan."

"The first move is to get cigarettes. We'd better have plenty of them."

"Those I can buy at the Intercontinental valuta shop. King-sized Kents."

"Yes." They were walking through the reduced light and passed a triangular fenced park, palings leaning inward and green benches covered with frost. "There's my old school," she said. "And down that street lived families of boyars." Graceful buildings of the old regime were cut up into flats. In the dark shops where cans of peas and sauerkraut were stacked, you could see no customers. This was a once fashionable neighborhood. No more. The high apparatchiks had their villas elsewhere. "How can we even get to the hospital tonight?"

"You can't phone for a cab?" he said.

"You can phone, but you can't count on anything."

"Gigi says that Ioanna has a nephew who's a driver. You ought to talk to her about him."

"Yes; Traian is his name."

"I think you'd better try this Traian."

"I'll ask Ioanna," said Minna.

"Does he own an automobile?"

"I'll go into it right away."

"You can talk to Ioanna? I mean talk."

"Yes and no. Yes, if you approach it right. She has to be treated like a relation. You don't mention money, but you have to give it to her by and by."

"Hire Traian to drive us. Do you remember the man?"

"Twenty years ago he wasn't a man. He was a fat boy, and he wasn't pleasant."

"Well, you'd better ask whether he can come."

"By seven."

"Once we're in the car—and I'll get a couple of cartons of Kents—you can explain what has to be done. They've got to be on the take here. Can't live on wages."

They turned the corner, and Minna said, "I think your friend's car is coming down the street."

"I should be standing by," said Corde. "I can change the appointment."

"No; you go for the cigarettes, and see your friend. There isn't anything you can do here. I'll go and talk to Ioanna."

She entered the building. Corde, his upper body braced against the cold, waited for the car. Three o'clock, and dusk already, tragic boredom coming with it. The forms of winter trees, the beauty of winter colors, were excepted from this. The trees made their tree gestures, but human beings were faced by the organized prevention of everything that came natural. The smooth limousine stopped and the driver came around and opened the door, let him into the warmth of the back seat. The privileged ride was short. Here was the American embassy again, the street cordoned off, sentries outside. And here was the Intercontinental.

The lobby was luxurious. You could sink deep into those

long sofas—any of them; they were all unoccupied. The atmosphere was that of a mystery novel. From the restaurant came a smell of Turkish coffee. You realized that the Bosporus was just up the line, and that the Orient Express used to steam in here, with Mata Hari in the dining car and Levantine businessmen who were triple agents. In the opulent lobby there were two hard corners of totalitarian organization—a plywood booth where currencies were cashed and a newsstand which sold foreign newspapers. East German magazines hung from a wire by clips, and also *Pravda* and *l'Humanité.*

The valuta shop was on the second floor. Christmas was two days off. A little tree was surrounded by and powdered with cotton batting and mica snow. There were racks of peasant skirts, sheepskins, shelves with table linens and dolls in folk costume, carved wooden flasks, cameras, imported brandy. Among the shoppers were students from Africa. One of them, seeing Corde's passport in his hand, said to him in a crackling British accent, "The clarks here are insolent. They say any damned thing. They think we don't understand their damned language." The black-smocked women were sullen and tired, rushed. Corde thought himself lucky. The girl who sold him the Kents was smiling at him—peculiarly: as if she were about to puff at a dandelion to see what time it was. Nevertheless, it was a sort of smile. She slipped his cigarettes—two cartons of the king-sized—into a Christmas bag with plastic handles.

Was he in a mood for reunion with a high school friend? He felt as though he had been knocked over in the street by a motorcycle, bruised, taped around the chest. What he wanted was to go to the men's room, unbutton his shirt, pull off the adhesive bandages. But there were no bandages. He edged into the crowded restaurant and bar to find Dewey Spangler. Impatient, feeling hampered, feeling bruised, he *seemed* all right, only a little serious (nothing more than a dark mood). He looked about for Spangler. The meeting, the old-pal routine, would have to be brief. If Ioanna's nephew was unavailable, other arrangements would have to be made. Minna and Gigi needed him at home—his supportive presence, his suggestions. And the Kents, too; the Kents most of all, perhaps. The packed bar intensified his caged mood (let me out of here!). Then he saw Spangler, who had risen in his booth and was beckoning with both arms, like an airlines employee signaling a plane to its gate. Spangler's gestures had always been inappropriate, erratic. Unexpectedly, this was endearing. Bossy, fussing little bastard, in spite of his world eminence he was still Screwy Dewey, the starved alley-cat boy intellectual—the same Dewey who had fought a two-hundred-pound Cubs fan in the Wrigley Field bleachers, hitting him with a book of poems. Spangler had been a frightful kid, but Corde had loved him.

"Here, Albert, here," Dewey called.

What was it that made this meeting so rich? Thrilling as hell, wasn't it? Spangler came to Chicago at least ten times a year, a hundred times in the last decade, and he never called Corde. But neither had Corde ever sent him a note to say, "I liked your column of last Wednesday." He liked few or none of the columns. Dewey in the papers never surprised him. Start a Dewey sentence and Corde, with his eyes closed, could finish it for you. The system seldom varied. But in this exotic café, all reservations, judgments, slights and offenses were set aside. Here Spangler could measure the distance he (or both of them) had come. He put an arm about Corde. "Rah, rah, Lakeview!" His figure had expanded and also grown compact. He was fleshy now and dignified by his well-groomed beard. The fat that had gathered in layers under his chin was disciplined, not slovenly, fat. These layers absorbed and even dignified his ducking mannerism, gave it affirmative weight, positive gravity. But he still had that one nervous habit. Although long years of psychoanalysis actually seemed to have helped him. Spangler had been recycled on the couch. He made no secret of it; on the contrary, he frequently mentioned analysis in his column: he liked to reflect on the sense of human worth it gave him, the distinct contribution it had made to his appreciation of the Judeo-Christian value system.

"*Wass willst du haben?*" he said. "You remember that?"

"Yes, indeed. Louie and the Hungry Five, the comic German brass band from Old Heidelberg on Randolph Street, near the Oriental," said Corde.

"Right on."

Come to think of it, what could this meeting give Dewey but the pleasure of nostalgia? He had for many years avoided Corde. Corde embarrassed him: he knew his background, remembered his father and his mother, the Spangler household, its kitchen life, the leonine formation of Mrs. Spangler's face, the flimsy silk bells of her stockings, the thigh portion falling below the gartered knee. They were touching people, especially the father. Old Spangler was bald and ruddy but did not enjoy good health. "In the notions business," he said. But what notions were there late in the Depression? You went down to the wholesale outlets at Twelfth Street and Newberry and took goods "on approval" to peddle door to door—sun visors, for instance, or table runners or combinations or cotton socks. It was the ill-concealed fact that "notions" meant peddling that embarrassed Dewey, and the embarrassment was compounded by grandiose and exuberant fantasies. He used to tell all kinds of stories about his origins. His father had been in a La Salle Street brokerage firm, he sometimes said, and he himself had been educated in a military prep school. But Corde never gave him away. Why should he? He actively sympathized with him. Still he had been distrusted.

"The Heidelberg," said Dewey. "Your formidable memory."

"I'm glad to see you, pal."

Dewey wasted no time. "Albert, we were very close, weren't we, at fifteen and after?" said Dewey. "A consuming association. When you told me—and I told you—damn near everything. And now look at us. Not many peas left in the pod, perhaps, but what of it, since we've made something of ourselves? Consider the origins. . . ." This was a hinted offer of candor.

"I thought of you the other day when I came across a volume of Oscar Wilde in my mother-in-law's flat."

"Mad for Swinburne and Walter Pater. Mad for Wilde. What stuff!

For, lo! with a little rod did I but touch the honey of romance,
And must I lose a soul's inheritance?

Now we can guess what that little rod was. But we didn't guess then, in our innocence."

"No, we loved poetry."

"Odd, in Chicago, where the South Branch of the river, you remember, was Bubble Creek because the blood and tripes and tallow, the stockyards' shit, made it bubble in the summer.

Doctors talk about an alcoholic dying of an *insult* to the brain. Well, that stink could have done it."

"Is it Chicago we're going to talk about?" said Corde.

"It is our native place, as you recently said in print."

The corpulence of his chin and throat, and perhaps also his worldly success, had made the down, down, downward pressure of his chin a movement of unshakable assertion. Like FDR's blinking. FDR's blink on Fox Movietone News meant: "Adversaries, beware." Then Dewey went on (it was predictable): "When you decided to go back, to me that was a sign of lifelong involvement. You were doing so well in Paris." (Was Spangler being patronizing? There was just the hint of a put-down in "doing well." He himself had become such a prodigy and hotshot.) "But when I read the first of your pieces in *Harper's*, I realized that you had scores to settle with the old town."

A waiter brought their drinks. Corde reclined in the booth, but his large hands were thrust deep into his trousers pockets, as far as to the wrists, a sure sign of tension. Dewey would not be taken in by his easy posture, or any of the old disguises. Dewey had the trick of making him an adolescent again. In adolescence Dewey had always had the upper hand. He had been precociously sharp.

Corde rumbled, "Not the old town anymore."

"I suppose it isn't. But you were your old self in your approach. You were eloquent, you were superexpressive. Just the way you used to be—you were metaphorical; you were emotional; you really let yourself go. I recognized lots of the old turns of phrase. Some of them still there."

"They probably are," said Corde.

"Made quite a stir, didn't you?"

Dewey's eyes, pale blue, now set in puffed and wrinkled lids, mocked him. Not unkindly. He was on first-name terms with Kissinger and Helmut Schmidt. Millions read him. In his recent swing through Europe and Asia, he had interviewed Sadat, Margaret Thatcher, Indira Gandhi. No reason to be mean with me, Corde was thinking, in the leisure of this personal, nostalgic hour. Not so long as I admit his superiority. And I do admit it. Why shouldn't I? Corde now decided to make an open concession and to bring this chapter in Spangler's psychic history to a happy close. This syndicated columnist who was a sizable node in the relaying of the tensions that pulsated through the civilized world, made it tremble, saturated it with equivocation, covered its structural outlines with flourishes, filled it with anxieties, happened also to be an old friend. Yes, the same Dewey who at Lakeview had been so self-conscious about the size and shape of his ears that he would give them a nimble tuck under his cap when no one was looking, like an awkward girl; who even tried to fasten them to his head with tape. The Dewey who had tried to grow a mustache to resemble William Powell—William Powell had obsessed him. The pale vinegar worm he had been was now a pundit and an arbiter, his columns anxiously, respectfully read in thirty countries. But it was the original skinny, frantic, striving, screeching Dewey that Corde had liked so much.

"You've been looking at the time, Albert."

"Yes, I'm sorry. I am uptight. There's a lot of trouble here for us."

"So I've been told by the Ambassador. A good fellow, the Ambassador. What's going on?"

"My wife's mother, dying . . ."

"Yes, yes, I remember now what he told me. Your wife can't see her. That's too bad. It must work you up. As your own mother's death did. I can remember that."

"I thought you might," Corde said.

"The Ambassador mentioned that he was calling somebody for you."

"So he did, but the result was negative—double negative."

"Is that so: counterproductive? I wonder if I could put in a word."

"I assume you're meeting the top people here."

"Yes, I am. I am," said Spangler. He drew his chin inward swiftly, two, three, five times against the firm fat of his throat.

"Then you might, if it's convenient. It's very late, though."

"Yes, Albert, I'll try to find an opening. These people have a stake in good relations with Washington. Concerned about their commercial treaties. Besides, they have a liberal image to sustain. Independence from the Soviet bosses, voting against the bloc at the U.N. now and then. All phony, of course."

"They'd like you to report them nicely."

"Correct."

"I've wondered about asking our own President to make a personal call. Combined with Christmas, which is now upon us, it might appeal to his PR people as a pleasant item."

"You serious?" Rotund Spangler passed his hand over his Shavian beard. It made a crisp sound. His hair was tight and vital; Corde envied him that.

"Is that too farfetched?"

"Whom have you got in Washington?"

"There's you for starters, Dewey."

It was much too late for White House intervention. Corde was being wicked, testing old Dewey. How would Dewey react? The reaction was just a little stiff. How could he refuse a humane request by an old friend? You renewed contacts sentimentally and there was an immediate push. You sent your car, made time available, and what did your pal do but ask you for a favor. A favor, what's more, that he'd never be able to reciprocate.

"You *are* troubled about your wife." Then Spangler said, as if abstractly, speculatively, "You must love her."

Corde said, "There's nothing too rum to be true."

"Ho, that's a beauty!" said Spangler. "Is it your own?"

"I heard it years ago on a Channel train from an old English gentleman. He was a lifelong atheist, but maybe God did exist, he said."

"Some Limey told you that? Yes, I think you love the woman. You're just rum enough to do it. You always wanted to love a woman. It's just when the whole world gives up on a thing that it turns you on. That's you." Spangler's pleasure at this meeting began to return. "We can feel out the White House if you like. It's a flaky administration, in case you haven't noticed. The chief executive is what the kids call a nerd. That's a very sanctimonious man. However, we might give it a try. I say might."

"I'd be very grateful."

"No need to be grateful. It gives me a chance to show how influential I've become."

"Still there is a sort of payola or payoff system, isn't there?"

"The quid pro quo? It's not what people usually think. I'd

make it seem an opportunity for the President, not ask him for a favor. But let's not make with the gratitude."

"You don't need anything at all from me."

"I always liked you, Albert. I was a little scarecrow. You were my special friend."

"You had others."

"I was a joke to them. The way I carried on, my fantasies—lies—and so on. You didn't twit me when you caught me in some bullshit."

"It was the poetry and the philosophy," said Corde. "I had to have you. It was the Spinoza and the Walt Whitman. It was the William Blake. Nobody else was interested. Besides, I loved the way you would carry on. You were extravagant. You'd holler and bawl at your poor mother, and call her a whore. . . . It gave me terrific pleasure. I never saw anything like it. You don't mind this reminiscence, do you?"

"Not a whole lot. It's true enough. And it's just you and me in this booth. No use pretending, between us. Anyway, she's been dead so long."

"She'd lose her temper and say, 'You're no kid of mine. You're a criminal's kid. They switched you on me in the hospital.' Lovable moments. I was fascinated. Nobody else like your people around the Lakeview neighborhood. Also, you loved your old man. You'd play checkers. He'd sit in his B.V.D.s, the sweat on his bald head, and study the board through his pop-bottle lenses. And his shaky knuckles with the fur on them. He gave us his streetcar transfers so we could bum around the city. He was a dear, unlucky man. . . . But I have to go, Dewey. I've enjoyed this. Are you taking off soon?"

"Just after Christmas. Don't run. The car will have you there in a few minutes."

"This is a terribly bad time for my wife."

Spangler said sympathetically but knowingly (superknowingly—that had always been a specialty with him): "I can just imagine. For you, too. All kinds of hell in Chicago. I'm damned if I can explain why you wrote those pieces. You might as well have stirred Bubble Creek with a ten-foot pole and forced the whole town to smell it. Then there's the trial you're mixed up in. The young man pushed from the window."

"You've been following that?"

"I always take the Chicago papers. My assistant forwards the clippings. Your fat-ass cousin is going to town on you, too. He's a bad actor."

"I thought you had changed your mind, and he was now okay by you."

"What are you talking about? You were the one who was nice to him in the old days. I didn't want him around. It was you who listened to his bogus poetry."

"Well, we needn't make a contest of it. I did say once that with a slot in his head Max would make a terrific piggy bank."

"Oh! Yes; you did, didn't you. What a gift you always had for those crushing one-liners. At the same time you were in dead earnest much too often. Moralistic. I think it's still there, too. Anyway, your cousin has a super hard-on for you. And what a performance he's giving."

"He gets plenty of help from the media. Ugly. Very hard for the young woman to take."

"What young woman is that? Oh, the girl, the young widow, you mean."

Dewey was not a good drinker. The double Chivas Regal made him talkative. He wanted a good long talk. He said, "What *was* this attack you made on the city!"

"I see no attack. I'm attached to Chicago—I'm speaking quite seriously."

"So am I serious, Albert. Aren't you aware of cutting loose with a lifetime of anger? How strange, for an intelligent man. You should have had some psychoanalysis, Albert. You pooh-poohed me when I recommended it, but you needed it. The Institute is right on Michigan Boulevard and you would have had your choice of the very best. *I* wasn't too good for it. With a little insight, you wouldn't be telling me now that you were *attached*. In *Harper's* you crossed and offended just about everybody. You might have gotten away with it if you had adopted the good old Mencken *Boobus Americanus* approach. Humor would have made a difference. But you lambasted them all. Really—you gave 'em hard cuts, straight across the muzzle. The obscurity of your language may have protected you somewhat—all the theorizing and the poetry. Lots of people must have been mystified and bogged down by it, and just gave up. All the better for you if they didn't read your message clearly. They're all happy, of course, to see you get your lumps. Ill will for ill will. *Harper's* came out of it okay, though. You were good for their circulation, which is pitiful at best. One of their guys in Washington was telling me you were doing yet another provocative piece on a different subject."

"With a man named Beech. But it isn't definite. I haven't decided."

"What's the field, biochemistry?"

"Geochemistry."

"Worse yet. What the hell do you, with your teeth cut on Shakespeare and Nietzsche, know about geochemistry? And you want to put in with the environmentalists? That's an extremely unattractive category of cranks. You're cranky enough already."

"Beech is no crank. There's a powerful scientific mind there."

"The best of them are diapered babies when they go public with a cause. Do you want me to name names? . . . Becoming a professor wasn't the right switch for you, Albert. You've lost some of your realism. You went from active to passive. Now you're tired of the passive and you've gone hyperactive, and gotten distorted and all tied in knots. Wrong for you. So you're a dean, and what next, boy?"

Dutch uncle had always been one of Dewey's favorite roles. And actually Corde didn't much mind; it was the old Dewey scolding away. It was agreeable because it was so characteristic. But Corde didn't have the time for it. He had to go. He downed his drink and collected his things. "Sorry, Dewey."

"Where are you going? I thought we'd have a talk."

"I haven't got the time I expected to have," said Corde. He began to edge out of the horseshoe booth with his sack of Kents. "I've got to go to the hospital with my wife, to see her mother."

"Why, I thought you couldn't."

"They've okayed one visit more."

"One? A last? They think she's dying?"

"They must. She is."

Very thoughtfully, Spangler spread both his hands stiffly on the table. They were braced by his short arms, so that his shoulders were lifted. Grimacing, he said, "Terrible. Terrible on your wife. Very bad. Punitive. Somebody's got it in for those ladies. I can understand why you'd think of taking it to the White House."

"It's too late. It was only a kind of fantasy, anyway. You're locked in, you're tense, and suddenly you remember that you're part of a proud superpower, and you say, 'I don't have to put up with this.' That's baloney, of course. It's from the good old days when an American abroad still got protection from his government. That went out with gunboat diplomacy. There's also the Chicago approach: 'I must know somebody who knows somebody.'"

"Somebody? That's me, for instance. I can still give it a try, if you like. I'm not really effective now. In the Kissinger day it was different. These new guys ain't much, Albert. You might as well talk to Bugs Bunny."

"There's actually nothing that would help now. But it's nice to see you, Dewey. I'll settle for just that. A touch of the old warmth—I'm grateful for it."

"Yes, this must be a hell of a place seen from inside. You're *in* it. I'm just another VIP, passing through. But my impression riding around the city is that it's got to be a miserable damn comfortless life, and scary as well as boring. I wish there were something I *could* do for your missus. It's a shame she's being pushed around. She's a distinguished scientist. These guys have no class. Imagine what it takes to be in power here, the types the Kremlin prefers to appoint. Real dogs. But then" —recollection brightening Spangler's face—"how does it go in *King Lear*? 'A dog's obeyed in office.' Or else what we read in *Zarathustra*: 'Power stands on crooked legs.' Nietzsche must have been thinking of dogs, too. . . . Are there still kids who do that, get together in Lincoln Park and read the way we used to read—wallow in that glorious stuff: the *Zarathustra*, the *Phaedrus*, that *Brigge* book by Rilke?"

Gruff, but looking into Corde's face with a steady smile, Spangler was marveling (teasing) that this juvenilia should still be so influential. Spangler had put it behind him; for some reason Corde had not. If Corde suffered, smarted in this Eastern bloc capital, it was because that glorious stuff made him vulnerable still, because he had failed to put it aside at the proper time. Wasn't that why he became a professor, and why he fulminated in *Harper's*? It wasn't the fault of the masterpieces. It was not knowing when to forget them that was the mistake. A grown man allowing himself to regress? At this moment when the nations, holding off destruction, were convulsed with tensions; when a man needed hardness, patience, maturity, circumspection, craft, real knowledge of diplomacy, economics, science, history? Albert had lost his grip. Of course, it was understandable, regrettable. It was forgivable. All this shone out from Dewey's bearded, understanding, patronizing, forgiving face.

A mysterious metamorphosis had occurred and skinny Dewey had become a bearded dwarf. The tones that came from inside this broad, low figure hadn't changed. He played on the same strings; it was the bowing that was smoother. It was wonderful that the music, coming from the places where the deep tones lived, should still be what it had been forty years ago. He scoffed and he scolded, but now he did it with affection and endearment, soothing poor old nervous Albert. Albert returned his affection. But it was ungrateful in Dewey to depreciate the "glorious stuff." Without the *Zarathustra* and the *Lear*, what would have become of him? Would he ever have risen so high without the cultural capital he had accumulated in Lincoln Park; would he even have gotten out of Chicago? Dewey had never wasted anything in his life; he always got his money's worth. He had made the Shakespeare pay, just as he turned his years of psychoanalysis to use. His bookish adolescence had given him an edge over the guys at the City News Bureau and his competitors in Washington, so that now he could frame his columns in high-grade intellectual plush, passing easily from the President's budget message to John Stuart Mill, transmuting the rattle of the Chicago streetcars into the dark rich tones of political philosophy. Even the idea of filling the shoes of Walter Lippmann (a hell of a nasty ambition to suffer from, Corde thought) went back to the scrolled green benches of Lincoln Park. Corde didn't mean to put Dewey down. But origins were origins. You did the best you could with them. You couldn't turn them in for a better set.

There was something more. What did Dewey have in mind, that he was being so endearing: did he want to resume their vanished connection? Corde, holding his white plastic bag from the valuta shop, saw this possibility descending towards him from a past as remote as a former life on earth. It was, almost, a former life. Were these the boys who had mooched through Lincoln Park with poets and philosophers tucked under their sweaters; who bought caramel corn in the zoo and lounged against the replica of the Viking ship and made themselves at home with Socrates in the *Phaedrus* or with Rilke in Paris? Since then each of them had died at least three or four times. So it *was* a former earth life. Corde's feeling towards his friend was gentle but not particularly sentimental. Did Dewey still long for the old days of poetry and feeling? So did Corde, at times. He reviewed the prospects for a revival of friendship with heartfelt objectivity. There was no question of rejecting Dewey. He'd never do that. But how far he'd admit him depended on his admissibility. They had diverged and diverged and diverged. Each of them had been spoilt, humanly, but in very different ways. Look at Dewey. Dewey grew up among warehouses, garages and taverns on Clark Street, not far from the site of the Valentine's Day massacre, but now he was a great figure in his profession, ten times more important than any U.S. senator you could name. When he discussed plutonium sales to the Third World or Russian natural gas or the diamonds the emperor Bokassa had given to Giscard, he did it with a flavor of art and high thought. He quoted Verlaine or Wittgenstein—in fact he quoted them too much. But those Rilke readings hadn't been wasted: the need for pure being, the fulfillment of the soul in art, *Weltinnenraum*. But then there was the *other* viewpoint, the La Salle Street one that you got from a man like Zaehner—it's a jungle out there. (Correction: a garbage dump!) Now, between these opposites, what ground had Dewey taken? The great public, the consumer of his views, didn't require him to take any ground. He needed only to keep talking. He lived (although Corde doubted that such tension should be called living) in a kind of event-glamour, among the deepest developments of the times, communicating what most concerned serious and responsible opinion. To Corde there was something bogus and grotesque about this. It was only "modern public consciousness." There was no real experience in it, none whatever. The forms that made true experience were corrupted. So Corde asked himself, "What would this wonderful palship of two old boys from Chicago look like if we brought it up to date?" The answer was that it could only look like Dewey's journalism. Dewey in his confident, comforting, but also peremptory way would tell him, "This is what we've got. Lucky us, to have such a bond." Their friendship revived, he would lay it all on you in his newspaper language, and strengthened by those Lincoln Park days, by books and poetry and friendship, by all that Corde had learned meantime, he might become an even more princely "communicator."

And now, with stormier objectivity, himself: How had Albert Corde been spoilt? Well, Albert Corde had illusions comparable to Dewey's, notwithstanding that they were in different fields. Look at him—an earnest, brooding, heart-struck, time-ravaged person (or boob), with his moral desires and taking up the burdens of mankind. He was, more or less in secret, serious about matters he couldn't even begin to discuss with Dewey. There was, for instance, the reunion of spirit and nature (divorced by science). Dewey (Corde happened to have caught this in one of his columns) was rough on writers who talked about "spirit," intellectuals in flight from the material realities of the present age. Corde could name you ten subjects on which they could never agree. And if he himself had been thoroughly clear in his mind, if the subjects had been cleanly thought out and resolved, there would be no difficulty in discussing them. So it was evident that Albert Corde was a spoilt case. Dewey pressed him about his motives for writing those *Harper's* articles. What was the real explanation? Again, the *high* intention—to prevent the American idea from being pounded into dust altogether. And here is our American idea: liberty, equality, justice, democracy, abundance. And here is what things are like today in a city like Chicago. Have a look! How does the public apprehend events? It doesn't apprehend them. It has been deprived of the capacity to experience them. Corde recognized how arrogant he had been. *His* patience was at an end. *He* had had enough. *He* was now opening his mouth to speak. And now, look out!

In the American moral crisis, the first requirement was to experience what was happening and to see what must be seen. The facts were covered from our perception. More than they had been in the past? Yes, because the changes, especially the increase in consciousness—and also in false consciousness—was accompanied by a peculiar kind of confusion. The increase of theories and discourse, itself a cause of new strange forms of blindness, the false representations of "communication," led to horrible distortions of public consciousness. Therefore the first act of morality was to disinter the reality, retrieve reality, dig it out from the trash, represent it anew as art would represent it. So when Dewey talked about the "poetry," pouring scorn on it, he was right insofar as Corde only made "poetic" gestures or passes, but not insofar as Corde was genuinely inspired. Insofar as he was inspired he had genuine political significance.

We were no longer talking about anything. The language of discourse had shut out experience altogether. Corde had accordingly spoken up—or attempted to speak up. I tried to make myself the moralist of seeing. I laid it on them. They mostly hated me for it. My own real consciousness had become intermittent over many years. That's what being spoilt means, in my case; it means fitfulness of vision. Now you have it, now you don't. That leads to exaggeration, also. Anyway, that was what I had in mind. Those Chicago guys may be right to hate me. I may deserve it. But not for this. I was speaking up for the noble ideas of the West in their American form. Which no one was asking me to do, and which I took upon myself without even thinking who the hell was I! A kind of natural effrontery. "This is your city—this is your American democracy. It's also my city. I have a right to picture it as I see it." Or else, "The public doesn't apprehend events which must be apprehended." And I intended to stick it to everybody.

"But you've got to go. Okay," said Dewey. "I'll walk you to the car."

Never again would the gesturing excited adolescent weedy Spangler be seen. There was now a stout dwarfish man awkwardly trying to get out of the booth, pushing on the table with his knuckles. His beard gave him an aspect of decent seniority. But he was half plastered. Corde, waiting for him, was also feeling the drink, for as his friend labored to rise, he looked to him like a kind of human plant—a short, fleshy trunk, and a spherical, overfull, overfructified face, rejoicing in itself.

So go to it. Rejoice. Dewey moved him. Everything seemed to move him now.

"Never mind, pal. I can find my way."

"There's plenty of time. I wish this had been a longer drink. You were putting me on, about the White House, asking me to use my connections, and then it turns out to be too late."

"I guess I shouldn't have. Still, you passed the test."

"No big deal, I suppose. But you are a funny guy. You made a crisis for me with your scoop from Potsdam. I opened *The New Yorker* and was knocked over. My pal Albert, who used to dither about Blake and Yeats, writing a firsthand report about Stalin and Churchill, Truman. Stalin's demonic force. We had the Bomb. Uncle Joe's armies were used up—but he got what he wanted. How come? Anyhow, you hit the ground running. You were made by that piece. Then you turned around and *unmade* yourself. That's mighty peculiar. I can still remember how burned up I was, how I died of envy. It was a class connection that did it for you. You and I may have been intoxicated with the 'monuments of unaging intellect,' but you weren't too intoxicated to use your dad's pull. He had a drag with Harry Vaughan."

"Since, as you say, I unmade myself, you can forget about that now."

"I wanted to have a talk with you, Albert. Can we get together again?"

"*You're* the one with the busy schedule. I'll wait for a call."

"What about Christmas Day?"

"I can't tell you right now."

"Because you don't know when your mother-in-law will die? I see that."

"Most of the time, I'm at your disposal. Free. There's a friend of ours coming over from Chicago—a woman named Vlada. But she'll be here for quite a while. Look, when you talk to your Washington office, ask your staff about the Chicago trial."

Spangler said, "Yes, and I want to discuss that with you, too. It was on my agenda for today."

vi

WHEN Corde returned, Minna said, "Traian will drive us."

"All three?"

"Yes."

They sat down to a dinner of cold leftovers. Little was said at table. For a change, Tanti Gigi was silent. Tonight she was neither the kid sister nor the charming girl who had once lived in London, but a tense old woman, her strained neck with its bobbed hair bent over her plate.

Traian was punctual. He rapped at a pane of the curtained dining room door and asked permission to come in. Obese and Mexican-looking, he had long tufts of hair at the corners of his mouth. He wore his trousers close and tight, especially at the crotch. His many-zippered Hell's Angels leather jacket was reddish, his boots were black and highly polished. He was particularly attentive to Tanti Gigi. Of course, he had known her for most of his life. Probably she had often fed him in the little kitchen, when he was a small boy. They rose from the table and went into the vestibule. Orlon-Dacron fur coats hung there, purplish brown, but even these synthetics were saturated with the fragrance of the ladies, even (so Corde felt) with their personalities. To the right was the primitive kitchen, to the left the old-fashioned water closet. Above were closed cupboards containing boxes of family relics, documents.

Traian handed Gigi into the china-closet elevator, aligned the swinging doors, pressed the button. Squeezed into a corner, Corde lifted up his coat collar, tied the muffler over it tightly, bracing himself for the street. Minna looked sternly absentminded; gracefully dissociated as well. By the small light, her white face was dark under the eyes. The outward curve of her upper lip, the pressure marks of her severe chin, almost made a stranger of her. Corde was carrying the plastic Christmas bag with the Kents in it. Minna got into the front seat of the Dacia while Traian was hooking up the windshield wipers —they would be stolen here if you didn't lock them in the glove compartment. "Albert, give me the cigarettes," she said. When Traian sat behind the wheel, Minna spoke to him, handed him one of the cartons. He opened it and filled the door pocket with Kents. No surprise, no problem; he was on. He drove to the hospital. Gigi, sitting beside Corde in the back seat, seemed incapable of speaking.

Snow might have helped that night, brightened the streets. It had begun to fall earlier but soon petered out. No one went strolling in this blackness. There was only an occasional car. Corde thought he had never seen such street lamps before—something like phosphorescent humus inside the globes.

But at the hospital the porter's lodge was brightly lighted. There were women from the country waiting for passes, peasants in boots and kerchiefs. Then up came Tanti Gigi in the draggled Orlon fur, her bent back and bobbed gray hair, a splash of terror on her face, her wide forehead pure white. She stood staring at the ground. The porter had Minna and Corde on his visitors list and handed them their passes. Traian got him to come outside. The man carried a clipboard; he was booted, a white smock came to his knees, he wore a woolen watch cap. His look was sulky. Primped to say no, thought Corde. Traian took the man by the arm and began to talk to him privately. Next to the porter's lodge there was an outer waiting room, shaped like a trolley car and well lighted. Gigi entered it and sat down.

As they went up the driveway together, Corde said to Minna, "Poor Gigi is scared. Do you think he'll get her in?"

"He seems to know his way around. . . ."

They entered the main building. Just inside the doors was a wide hall, a clerk behind a wicket, another long queue. Then two more spacious dark rooms, and then a door with frosted glass: Intensive Care. Corde recognized the woman who answered their knock; it was Dr. Drur, on duty tonight. Round-faced, speaking softly, she shook Minna's hand with particular warmth. That was significant, the sympathy. Again, Minna and Corde went through the robing routine—sterile gowns, caps, masks, the swelling white overshoes tied with tapes.

"Mammi!" said Minna. Corde followed slowly and stood in the door of the cubicle, but the doctor motioned him to come closer. Valeria's right hand stirred, as much as she could manage. The movement was slight. She knew what was happening, you could see that in the blind face. Also, the monitoring devices speeded up, briefly. Standing by the bed, Corde was much moved, but unsure what to do beyond signifying somehow that he would keep Minna from harm. He bent near and rumbled, "It's Albert, Valeria." She nodded.

Minna drew down the gauze mask to kiss Valeria. Then the quick, plump doctor came up with a pad of paper. She helped Valeria to close her fingers on a ballpoint pen, and the old woman tried to write. No control, thought Corde. Can't manage. She formed a few letters but ended in a big loose spiral that crossed the yellow page. Minna and the doctor tried to make out the word. Corde's guess was that she was asking still to be taken home. But a woman like Valeria would have made alternative preparations—plan A, plan B. Fully aware, and good and ready—that would be characteristic of her. He thought there was no other way to interpret the expression of her face; he derived it even from the posture of her legs and from the old woman's belly, which had risen higher than ever. On both sides of her face, the currents of hair were shining on the bed linen. Consciousness was as clear as it had ever been. No, more acute than ever, for when Minna signaled that he should take her hand (again he noted the blue splayed knuckle, and the blue kink of the vein there), she pressed his fingers promptly. He said, "We came as soon as possible." Then, as if he should not delay the essential message, he said in his deep voice, "I also love you, Valeria."

This had a violent effect. One of her knees came up, her eyes, very full under the skin of the lids, moved back and forth. She made an effort to force them to open. Her face was taken by a spasm. The monitors jumped simultaneously. All the numbers began to tumble and whirl. He might have killed her by saying that. Either because she believed him or because she did not. But she ought to have believed him. So far as he painfully knew, it was the truth. The doctor was startled by the speed of the flashing digits. She motioned to Corde and Minna to step back. No, to go.

They returned to the staff room. He took off his gown. He could hardly bear this. The light was very sharp in this doctors' room.

Minna said, "That was right, what you told her."

Corde was less sure of that.

Then Minna said, "Albert, what kind of state do you think she's in?"

He thought the soul was loosened in Valeria, ready to pull out, and that she could therefore know you for what you were. He answered nothing.

The doctor came in and the women spoke. Minna said, "It's all right on the monitor again." She said she would go out now and fetch her aunt. She was determined to get her in. She said, "Valeria was the big sister; she always took care of her. Tonight I have to do it." Gigi hadn't even asked to be brought. Corde figured that here in the Soviet bloc you learned to refrain from asking. And then, too, Gigi depended on Minna as she had done on Valeria. But it turned out that Minna had promised her aunt—she would have told her with severity: "I'm taking you. You'll see her!"

Minna folded and laid down the sterile gown and the boots —she was even now thorough in her orderliness, absentmindedly ritualistic. She told the doctor that she was going out for a few minutes. She'd be right back. The apprehensive doctor did not question her but shook her head. This was wrong. The rules were being broken. What if the Colonel should burst in?

As Corde helped Minna over the ice of the sloping driveway, the evergreens made a chill sound above them, as if things could simmer also below freezing. Passive, stooped and silent, Gigi sat waiting to see whether Minna would keep her promise. She would. Traian's signal was that the cigarettes had worked, the fix was in. So the two women now went up the slope to the main building, while Corde took Gigi's place beside Traian on the bench. Then the waiting room lights were switched off. The porter, taking no chances, hid them in darkness. As if the Colonel would care much. Now that he had had his way, the matter was closed. The doctors had probably told him that it was all over with Valeria, and the deal with the Minister of Health was, "Let them come."

Meanwhile, Valeria's mind was clear. This was what impressed Corde most deeply. She could still hear and understand everything, and respond. Probably Dr. Drur with the soft face, and the intensive care staff, talked with her, kept her informed. A physician herself (the founder of this hospital),

Valeria had seen plenty of people go. The woman doctor seemed particularly close to her. To have a woman in attendance was a good thing. She had probably said, "Your daughter has permission tonight." Valeria would understand what this signified. There again you saw the extent of the woman connection, its great importance.

Dr. Drur hadn't doped Valeria (professional courtesy) and she was dying in clear consciousness. And Corde contrasted this with the consciousness of that boy Rick Lester, when he realized that he had gone through the window and was falling. The young man had played a kind of game that night, assuming the usual safe conditions, but the conditions were missing—he had a gag in his throat and two or three seconds to recognize that he was finished. He, Corde, had more in common with that boy than with the old woman. She didn't have their sort of mind, the modern consciousness, that equivocal queer condition, working with a net of foolish assumptions, and so much absurd unwanted stuff lying on your heart. He was impressed with Valeria. (Couldn't he attribute it to his equivocal consciousness that he was so much impressed?) She and Dr. Raresh, Marxists, had gone into the streets with roses to greet the Russians, lived to see the prison state, repented. She went back to the old discipline, believed in the good, probably took it all seriously about the pure in heart seeing God, and the other beatitudes. (Nothing too rum?) Her ashes would be placed beside those of her husband.

Though it went against the grain, he suspected that his nephew may have been right, that on the night he was killed Rick Lester had been out for dirty sex, and it was this dirty sex momentum that had carried him through the window. Corde understood this far better than he understood the old woman's beliefs. So what was the pure-in-spirit bit? For an American who had been around, a man in his mid-fifties, this beatitude language was unreal. To use it betrayed him as a man wildly disturbed, a somehow crazy man. It was foreign, bookish—it was Dostoevsky stuff, that the vices of Sodom coexisted with the adoration of the Holy Sophia, cynicism joined with purity in the heart of the paradoxical Russian. He was no Russian but Huguenot and Irish by descent, a Midwesterner flattened out by the prairies, a journalist and a lousy college dean. He suspected that the academic connection had been getting to him. He could feel, with Dr. Faustus, "O would that I had never seen Wittenberg, never read a book"; and it was no wonder that the classroom, the library environment, had driven him finally into the streets of Chicago, or that he had written—well, written that at the Cabrini Green black housing project, some man had butchered a hog in his apartment and had thrown the guts on the staircase, where a woman, slipping on them, had broken her arm, and screamed curses in the ambulance. She was smeared with pig's blood and shriller than the siren. It was illumination from a different side, Chicago light and color, not the Sermon on the Mount.

He was strongly agitated. He thought, Hadn't it been too easy, bribing the porter? Had he let Minna and Gigi walk into a trap, where the Colonel would swoop down on the deathbed and grab them? But what would he want to do that for—why arrest old Gigi? No, Corde saw that he was beginning to think like those women who imagined themselves locked in a mortal struggle with this police colonel, who, right now, must be dining in his luxurious villa, eating delicacies and drinking special vintages. The New Class, or new New Class, lived like Texas millionaires. Corde with his twenty-odd years in Europe understood this. Millions of Americans of his generation had gone out into the world. There were robustious theorists who maintained that this was one of the luckiest developments in history and had done humankind nothing but good. There was a very different point of view. Folks from Trenton, Topeka, Baton Rouge, who lived in Japan, Iran, Morocco, were, as he had read in a magazine, "representatives of the fantasmo imperium of corporate dollars." It was in his dentist's reception room that he had found this piece on American mercenaries and arms salesmen, "high-technology killers operating in Africa and Central America." He had picked up this magazine from the top of the lighted tropical fish tank.

He must ask Dewey Spangler about the "fantasmo imperium." It would amuse him. "Why would corporate dollars be spent on these twerps? Americans living abroad are always supposed to 'represent' something. But there's you, for instance, Albert—what would you be representing?"

That would be a good question. What *did* Corde represent?

Who was this person sharing the bench with Ioanna's nephew Traian? He carried a U.S. passport and money and credit cards. He was dressed in coat, gloves, muffler and an encircling fedora over his radar-dish face, his somewhat swelling eyes and plain mouth. He seemed to be picking up signals from all over the universe, some from unseeable sources. His neck was long; his back, too, seemed to go on longer than was strictly necessary. He was a mid-American of mild appearance. He was aware of that. He called this "the Pullman car gentility" and believed he had inherited it from his Wilson-era grandfather. (Corde didn't admire Woodrow Wilson. Wilson had done great harm.) Anyway, he, Albert, was a Corde. Six generations in Joliet, Illinois, two in Chicago, and he had just told a dying old Macedonian woman in a Communist hospital that he loved her. This was the measure of the oddities life had compiled for him. "I also love you, Valeria." But although she must have been longing to hear this, and although it was true (it was, dammit, one hundred percent true!), she was nevertheless so shocked that the machines began to flash and yammer and the doctor was scared witless. Why had he upset her? He must have reminded her again of her fears, which she would carry into the life to come, or at least up to the gate of death. Perhaps there was no need to take this personally, or to compare himself, as he sometimes did, to a longtime sexual offender still on probation, though the most exacting parole officer would have been satisfied with him. Oh, those sexual offenses! He was by the strictest marital standards decent, mature, intelligent, responsible, an excellent husband. But within the historical currents he could not be viewed from a positive aspect because he was a representative of the rotten West, lacking ballast, the product of an undesirable historical development, a corrupted branch of humanity. One needn't go as far as the extremist Eastern dissidents who called Europe an incorrigible old whore and America her most degenerate descendant, in the stage of general paresis. That was going far. But it was possible to suspect him of being incapable of sustaining a serious relationship, as seriousness was defined by the older, indeed archaic, branch of humanity with its eternal fixtures. Valeria would therefore be thinking that the world Corde came from was the world in which her daughter must live out her life. She must depend now on that world and on this man. So Corde had been moved that in dying she should still be in torment over her daughter, and so Valeria heard his bass voice assuring her, and she was pierced with doubts. This "I also love you," which made her squeeze his hand, might be true, but it might be the truth merely of an agitated moment, no good within an hour. He could see that, yes. It was very painful to him, too.

If we could say what we meant, mean what we said! But we didn't seem to be set up for it. We were set up instead in a habitual state of hypnotic fixity, and this hypnotic fixity was the real fantasmo imperium. Well, never mind the philosophy. But on her deathbed an old woman hears the deep voice of her son-in-law, and it tells her that he loves her. Loves! With what! Nevertheless it *was* true, however queer. There *was* nothing too rum to be true. He depended on that now. Although Valeria—she wasn't going to have time to verify his declaration. She'd have to take his word for it, because for her this world of death was ending. World of death? He surprised himself when he put it that way. More of his poetry, Dewey Spangler would have said, and bared his teeth in a grin—Spangler still had those sharp and healthy teeth. Same dazzling teeth; the ginger marmalade beard was their new setting.

Still Dewey had asked him one really hot question: Why a professor in Chicago? Corde might have answered that the reason was coming, it was on its way. There were hidden and extensive fantasy ambitions and grand designs connected with it. At the moment of decision, it had been convenient that he should have no clear outline. He remembered how surprised his sister had been when he moved back. "Why a college, and why here?" Elfrida inquired.

He couldn't really answer, but he did say, "For me it's more like the front lines. Here is where the action is."

"I wouldn't have left Paris, not with an apartment on Rue Vaneau. Did you sell it for a fortune?"

"No fortune."

"Then getting away from some French broad or other?"

"No, that wasn't it, either, although there are plenty of broads that can inspire leaving—even going into hiding, or taking holy orders."

"Who said, 'When you're tired of Paris you're tired of life'?"

"It was said about London. And the same party said that no man of what he called 'intellectual enjoyment' would immerse himself and his posterity in American barbarism. But that was two hundred years ago."

"That's a real book answer," was Elfrida's comment. "You want to spend the rest of your life reading books in a college? Don't expect me to swallow that. I know you better. You're not a retirement type. You don't look it, but you're a combative type. You just said you were looking for action."

"When I was a kid I had martial instincts."

"You do still. I can't dope you out, Albert. What advantage do you see here?"

"There's the big advantage of backwardness. By the time the latest ideas reach Chicago, they're worn thin and easy to see through. You don't have to bother with them and it saves lots of trouble."

He stopped these thoughts and recollections, for he now caught sight of Minna and Gigi walking carefully, slow, down the slope under the pines. Corde went out to meet them. He asked no questions. No one spoke. It hadn't been a long visit. Maybe the doctor, frightened by Minna's boldness, had asked them to leave. The Colonel hadn't surprised them. No, the Colonel now cared nothing about any of them.

Traian opened the dark green doors of the tub-shaped Dacia. The interior was freezing.

At home, too, it was too cold to get into bed.

"Albert, I can't take my clothes off."

Corde poured from the *pálinca* bottle. "Let's swallow some of this."

They sat in their coats. When Corde removed his hat, he felt the cold on his bald crown. "You didn't stay long. . . ."

"Because of Dr. Drur. I took her completely by surprise with Gigi. I think there were watchers everywhere."

"And what did Gigi say?"

"She didn't say anything, just put her hand on Mother's arm. Lie down with me, Albert."

He pulled the heavy covers from his bed and piled them on hers. Then he turned off the tiny orange-tinted light bulb under the big parchment lampshade. Minna presently fell asleep. Corde, stretched beside her along the edge of the bed, went into a state of blankness for the rest of the night.

vii

In the morning Minna was on the telephone again, trying to reach Dr. Moldovanu, the passionate daughter still fighting for her mother. Corde thought, She can't accept that it's over, the end, she saw Valeria for the last time. But that was a lot to ask. He was being too sensible. It was one of his persistent failings.

And so there he was, as usual. It was morning, and he was sitting in the room. He had swallowed several cups of Gigi's coffee. It was too weak to revive him after his night of blankness. He frowned at the packet of mail from his office. After his catatonic night on the edge of the bed, under the burdensome stiff weight of the Balkan rugs, he was too tired, felt too tender and sore inside, to take on those letters from Chicago. He opened his briefcase instead and looked for the Beech documents. He must get them read before Vlada Voynich arrived. To be idle this morning was a bad idea. If he didn't pull himself together he'd suffer from random thoughts. Those were the worst—they ate you up. Clearing an efficient space on the desk, he set himself to study Beech's scientific papers. He began with Vlada's abstract. Immediately he found his antidote to the distress of random ideas. "Beech picked you, on the basis of those articles in *Harper's*, to be his interpreter," she wrote. "And since I have been part of his team for some years, he requested that I give you a little preliminary guidance. I am glad you had the opportunity to meet him. His reactions to you were very positive." (I liked him, too, thought Corde. Beech was a terrific fellow. Also, to get an eminent man's positive reaction was pleasing.) "The situation is of the most urgent importance," he further read. "Beech wants his case stated not only to the general public but also to the Humanists." This gave Corde pause. Who were these Humanists, and why should Beech imagine that they were a group to whom any case could be stated? And if there was such a group, why should it be inclined to pay attention to Corde? He considered how to discuss this with a geologist like Beech. "You want to understand humanist intellectuals? Think of the Ruling Reptiles of the Mesozoic. . . ." Corde meantime read on. "I think you said that you listened to the tapes he gave you. In those he recorded his personal account of the research that led up to his discoveries and explained what they signified for the future of our species and, consequently, why they presented such an emotional problem for those who drew the inevitable logical conclusions." Yes, Corde had listened to the tapes. In the first minute, Beech said they had been made last summer in a Kansas barn. "Looking through the big open door over the summer wheat fields," the scientist had flatly intoned. "The Great Plains. My native grounds."

Vlada had told Corde in Chicago, "Albert, it was my doing, partly. I brought your articles to Beech's attention because I knew he was looking for somebody who had the necessary skills. Also the brains." Vlada spoke with the fully centered assurance of a stout woman. Her face was wide and pale, the brown Balkan eyes were large—no soft glances, but urgent business, shrewdness. She did not invite you to take part in dream enterprises; she was an extremely shrewd lady. (At moments her eyes did make personal confessions, too, painful ones. But never mind that now.) Beech himself had been more diffident. "After you've listened to these tapes and studied the materials, perhaps you'd consider further discussions leading to eventual collaboration. Naturally, I have a special point of view, as the man who directed the research—in the inside position, right in the middle." Beech's mildness had a special charm for Corde. What a nice man! And when you considered what a terrific charge he carried, the responsibility for such frightening findings (would the earth survive?), how gallant his mildness was. He said to Corde, "You, the author of those special articles, might—you just might—be able to blow the whistle. I want to stop everybody in their tracks and force them to follow. And you can be gripping. As with the blacks you described in public housing and in the jails . . ."

"I didn't please everybody."

"I would assume not. That's exactly it. And when I read

your description of the inner city, I said, 'Here's a man who will want the real explanation of what goes on in those slums.' "

"And the explanation? What is the real explanation?"

"Millions of tons of intractable lead residues poisoning the children of the poor. They're the most exposed. The concentration is measurably heaviest in those old slum neighborhoods, piled up there for decades. It's the growing children who assimilate the lead fastest. The calcium takes it up. And if you watch the behavior of those kids with a clinical eye, you see the classic symptoms of chronic lead insult. I've asked Vlada Voynich to include Needleman's neuropsychiatric findings from the *New England Journal of Medicine* with the other papers. Crime and social disorganization in inner city populations can all be traced to the effects of lead. It comes down to the nerves, to brain damage."

Polite Corde, with silent lips, nodding, doubted this. He wore a look of quiet but high dubiety. Once more, a direct material cause? Everything had a direct material cause? If you gave people employment, money, clothing, shelter, food, protected them from infection and from poison, they wouldn't be criminal, they wouldn't be mad, they wouldn't despair? Sure, the right programs, rightly administered, would fix it. Direct material causes? Of course. Who could deny them? But what was odd was that no other causes were conceived of. "So it's lead, nothing but old lead?" he said.

"I would ask you to study the evidence."

And that was what Corde now began to do, reading through stapled documents, examining graphs.

You couldn't easily hide the sign of the crank from an experienced journalist, and as Spangler had said, these scientists were diapered babies when they went public with a cause. But Beech somehow inspired respect. There was a special seriousness about him. He was even physically, constitutionally serious. His head, for a body of such length, was small, his face devoid of personal vanity. Light hair, grizzled and cropped Marine style, gave him an old-fashioned hayseed look. His cheeks were austerely creased, his glance was dry. Corde had checked on his credentials. He was indeed an eminent man of science. That was unanimous. He had authoritatively dated the age of the earth, had analyzed the rocks brought back from the moon. Corde was beginning to think that with pure scientists, when they turned their eyes from their own disciplines, there were, occasionally, storms of convulsive clear consciousness; they suffered attacks of confusing lucidity.

Therefore Corde had listened closely to the tapes. In his small Chicago study he had switched off the lights, plugged in his headphones.

And here in Bucharest, too, he read with care. Consider: Eastern Europe as a place to read about endangered humanity. Corde was at Valeria's table and sore, rubbed raw within; he could feel the rawness as he bent over Beech's papers. He pressed his hands, for warmth, under his thighs.

What was the message? Three industrial centuries had vastly increased the mining and smelting of lead, and the unavoidable dispersal of lead in air, water, soil, was a danger too little understood. We had been "authoritatively assured" that lead levels were normal and tolerable. Far from it. Official standards are worse than incorrect; they are dangerously false. Investigations are conducted in laboratories themselves heavily contaminated. Only results obtained in ultra-clean sanctuary laboratories are dependable. These are few in number but only their evidence counts, and this evidence tells us that lead levels are about five hundredfold above natural prehistoric levels. The true levels have been established by fossil bone analysis, by the examination of the sediments of fresh and marine waters, of old tree-stem woods, of snow strata in the Antarctic, and of Greenland ice. The "emissions of forest foliage" have also been investigated, together with crustal components of silicate dusts, sea sprays and volcanic sulfurs. This mass of measurements and supporting data ("isotopic compositions") excited Corde, moved him. ("Is there something wrong, that I'm so liable to get agitated?") Radioactivity, of course, and also the depletion of the ozone layer by aerosols he was as familiar with as the next man. But on the midnight tapes recorded in the summer fields of Kansas, Corde had heard also of the chemical saturation of the soil by insecticides and fertilizers. This was why America was the world's greatest food producer. At what a cost! But the lead was far more dangerous than any of these. Beech's voice went on like the plains themselves.

Government agencies assigned the task of measurement and control were incompetent, said Beech. They lacked the necessary instruments and correct procedures. The true magnitude of this deadly poisoning of water, vegetation and air was discovered by the pure sciences of geochronology, cosmology and nuclear geochemistry. A truly accurate method of detecting tiny amounts of lead led to the discovery that the cycle of lead in the earth had been strongly perturbed. The conclusion: Chronic lead insult now affects all mankind. Biological dysfunctions, especially observable in the most advanced populations, must be considered among the causes of wars and revolutions. Mental disturbances resulting from lead poison are reflected in terrorism, barbarism, crime, cultural degradation. Visible everywhere are the irritability, emotional instability, general restlessness, reduced acuity of the reasoning powers, the difficulty of focusing, et cetera, which the practiced clinician can readily identify.

This irritability, this combination of inflammation and deadening—by God, I feel it myself! And I certainly observe it wherever I look! If he had been at home, Corde would have gone to the *Britannica* for more information. Fat medical books jutted from the shelves, within reach, but he was ignorant of Rumanian, weak in German. But for what Beech was getting at he needed no encyclopedia. We couldn't ourselves observe the dulling of consciousness since we were all its victims, and we would be dulled down into the abyss unaware that we were sinking. Tetraethyl fumes alone could do it—engine exhaust—and infants eating flaking lead paint in the slums became criminal morons. Without realizing it, Beech had become a burning moral visionary. He accused the engineers. Applied science, engineering technology, these were the powers of darkness which had poisoned land, air and water, the forests, the animals, the cities, and our own human cells.

Here was an apocalypse—yet another apocalypse to set before the public. It wouldn't be easy. The public was used to doom warnings; seasoned, hell—it was marinated in them. And there are evils, as someone has pointed out, that have the ability to survive identification and go on forever—money, for instance, or war. Those that are most determined to expose them can get no grip upon them. In the current language, that of the mass situation, nothing could be communicated. Nothing was harder to get hold of than the most potent, i.e., the most manifest evils. Here science itself, which was designed for deeper realization, experienced a singular failure. The genius of these evils was their ability to create zones of incomprehension. It was because they were so fully apparent that you couldn't see them. Evidently Beech had begun to feel their power. He couldn't pass through, couldn't get a hearing. He did well to come to Albert Corde, therefore. It was a sound instinct to ask the man who had written those *Harper's* pieces to get him through the blockaded zones. If I were convinced, I could do the job for him. And it wouldn't be by the agitprop, demagogic, haranguing, or the advertising or mystagogic methods; no fantasmo imperium, nothing but unfaltering earnestness, like the Ancient Mariner. You hold 'em with your glittering eye. "The wedding guest he beat his breast, Yet he cannot choose but hear." Beech was not another environmentalist simply. If he had been "one more of those," Corde would never have given him the time of day. What he had learned by listening to his tapes with the closest attention was that the geophysicist had incorporated the planet itself into his deepest feelings, as if it were a being which had given birth to life. Beech was shocked by *Homo sapiens sapiens*, by its ingratitude and impiety. *Homo sapiens sapiens* was incapable of hearing earth's own poetry, or, now, its plea. Man would degrade himself into an inferior hominid. (The biological language was Beech's own.)

Corde felt that they had a lot in common, he and Beech. There was even a physical affinity. Both were plain-looking men from the Midwest, in their late fifties, each with his own stratagem for keeping his noble values out of sight until the moment of disclosure (sometime before the end, and before, one hoped, it was too late). And then to whom did you disclose? Well, you went public, you printed in *Harper's*, or else you chose a spokesman, a Corde, and approached him with a proposition. This process (a scientist's discovery and its sequel) was in itself, taken as an episode in the evolution of the soul, a singularly moving thing. You would never have divined that this dry, long, stooped cactus, this scientific Beech, would at last cough up so large and exquisite a flower. (The earth as a being; earth's own poetry.) So, then, the problem: Deeper realizations were accorded only to the sciences, and there within strict limits. The same methods, the same energies, could not be applied to the deeper questions of existence. It was conceivable, even, that science had drawn all the capacity for deeper realizations out of the rest of mankind and monopolized it. This left everyone else in a condition of great weakness. In this weakness people did poetry, painting, humanism, fiddle-faddle—idiocy.

Terribly moved, restless, clawed within, Corde could not sit still. He heaved himself up from the table (with its history of homework, its treasures of sentiment) and went to look for Minna. He found her with Gigi in the dining room. Of course they were talking about Valeria. He did not interrupt their conversation but stood on the sidelines, in the background. His hands were behind his back and he leaned against the doorframe. Just looking, swell-eyed, through his goggles, and with a silent mouth. Under the thick-legged dining room table the vivid color had gone out of the Balkan carpet, it was sere and wrinkled. The birds in the pattern could scarcely fly. The cyclamens on the sideboard were also worked with faint patterns—the dark leaves had a whitish underpattern, varied with gray, making a smaller heart shape within the heart shape of the leaf. The flowers were white.

"What's up?" said Corde at last. "What's the latest?"

"They can't move her," said Minna. "Dr. Gherea was very sorry."

"Did you talk to the lady friend? Is that who told you?"

"I talked to Dr. Drur."

Gigi looked towards Corde, not directly at him. Her eyes were deep dark brown and fluid. The work of the beauty parlor was undone at the back, where her hair came apart in white straws, like a whisk broom. But her bangs were neatly combed out on her forehead. She had put on a dress today and high heels and lipstick. Maybe she didn't want the news of her sister's death to catch her in the brown dressing gown. This tragic old lady with the tarty, Frenchy name—if grief added weight to the body, it might come out in the curvature of her legs, for today she looked more bandy-legged. Corde also observed—perhaps it was the cut of the dress she wore—how strong her neck was. The neck muscles were heavy.

"Anyhow," said Minna, "surgery is out of the question."

Of course it was. No respiration, no anesthesia.

"Dear Albert! Shall I brew a pot of tea?"

"Thank you, no, Tanti Gigi. I'm doing a bit of paper work. I'll go back."

He was far too restless to sit with the women. He would as soon have had the tea poured over his head.

"There hasn't been any word from your friend Spangler?" said Minna.

"I wouldn't expect much from him."

"*Now* is when I should be with her," said Minna.

There was no answer to make. He muttered only that he would go back to his papers. Again, the room!

There was something in Corde's throat, some East European condensation, and it took East European brandy to clear it. He took two shots from the bottle while he reorganized the desk, putting aside the Beech documents. This mace of lead that was knocking our brains out . . . *Pálinca* left a kind of stale plum aftertaste. He sweetened his mouth with a few brown grapes, the last of them. Waiting for death, you see. There was very little he could do.

And now, at last, he took up the large manila envelope of mail from Chicago. Censorship had obviously unstuck the tapes. He had noticed that yesterday. Disgusted, he lifted the crisscrossed tapes with the point of Valeria's paper knife and shook them off. And Christ! all this stuff, these unwanted clippings and papers; nothing but trouble. Corde's posture was habitually relaxed, and as he went through his mail his body was turned three-fourths aside, askance, in "relaxed" avoidance. He held the sheaf unwillingly, passing paper after paper to the back.

On his own turf, he was at war. He couldn't say why it was necessary to be fighting there. But now, caught up in it, he had to see it through. Hadn't Elfrida told him that he was a combative type?

Miss Porson (or Ms., as she had taken to signing herself) had enclosed an elaborate memorandum, a bulletin from the front. She said she regretted sending him some of these items. He could do without them, where he was. "It must be a bad scene. My heart goes out to Minna." Towards Minna Miss Porson's female generosity and admiration were boundless. "Her wonderful style, the way she walks, her musical speaking voice, her perfect breeding," Miss Porson would say. This Miss Porson of his, Fay Porson, was an old slob (he was at present inclined to call her that) of no little charm. She couldn't have been much younger than Tanti Gigi, but she boasted that she turned on lovers half her age. In her late sixties, she was fleshy, but her bearing was jaunty. Her plump face, heavily made up, was whitish pink, as if washed in calamine lotion, and on some days she painted a raccoon band across her face in blue eye shadow—the mask of a burglar or a Venetian reveler. She kept up her pants with heavy silver-and-turquoise belts. The permanent Miss Porson, the Miss Porson of the deeper strata, turned out to be a bridge-playing Westchester matron. She had come to Chicago with her midlevel executive husband. Here she was widowed and here she preferred to remain. She could swing in Chicago. She was going to "put the sex into sexagenarian," she said. Corde had become fond of her. She was not the supersecretary and faultless organizer she claimed to be; she was overpaid. His dislike of administrative detail had made a hostage of him. Her erotic confidences and boasts set his teeth on edge. But he would not have been able now to replace her.

She wrote that there was only more of the same in the papers. As far as the press was concerned, Mr. Detillion could do no wrong, for the time being, anyway. As her late father would have said, they had Mr. Corde's head "in chancery" and they loved it. ("Chancery," Corde had learned, was a term from the days of John L. Sullivan: You caught your opponent's head under your arm and rubbed it with bare knuckles.) This, she continued, couldn't go on forever; the good guys would have their innings by and by. If the true facts could only be made known—how different it would look! The Dean was still struggling with financial and legal problems created by his cousin. Ms. Porson wished the details could be leaked to reporters. There was, for instance, the IRS matter, originally mishandled by Mr. Detillion when he signed a waiver on the statute of limitations because he was so confident that the government had no case. So now the IRS claim, with interest, was up to $23,000, and although the new lawyer, Mr. Gershenkorn, was doing his best, and would get an extension while the Dean was out of the country, he couldn't promise success. All this information, supplied in pure kindness, stuck in Corde's throat.

For his morale, she enclosed copies of fan letters from his readers. She admitted that some hate mail had also come in. She was saving it for his return. Most of the poison-pen notes were from the suburbs, where the diehard Chicago boosters all lived. Commuters who escaped from race problems and crime were indignant because he had told it as it was. She reported that the Provost had sent a note: The Dean was not to worry about the home front but to take care of Minna in this tragic moment. He expressed himself with great decency and delicacy, said Miss Porson.

There was one message for Minna, from the Mount Palomar Observatory. They would try to rearrange schedules in order to give her some telescope time in January. The rest of Miss Porson's memorandum itemized the notes and letters she was forwarding. He went through the memo again, for it was inconceivable that it should contain no mention of Lydia Lester. He had left Miss Porson in charge of that girl, and most of his last instructions had to do with her protection. He had spent the better part of an hour just before departure spelling it out on the telephone. Fay Porson had *seemed* to see the point. In fact, she had made remarks Corde had had no desire to hear, about the mixture of fatherly solicitude and guilt that motivated him. "Because it was you, Dean, that pushed for the trial? And the girl is so delicate? But she didn't have to go along, did she? In the end she decided that she wanted that pair to pay for what they did to the poor young husband—it was her *own* decision. You take too much on yourself, Dean." Corde had little liking for these psychological insights, but he had let himself in for them. You confided in people, you *had* to. From this came dependency, and then unwanted intimacy, and presently you discovered—horrifying!—that though Porson listened and nodded and looked as clever as Alexander Woollcott (whom she strikingly resembled) and as melting as a mother, that though you moved her to tears, she was an exasperating dumbhead, and lustful old frump. "Not to worry!" was her last word to him, but obviously she hadn't even spoken to Lydia. He made yet another search. No, not a word about the girl. How could a beautiful young woman interest Fay Porson, who had just discovered her own youthfulness. She had her own sexual fat to fry. She wasn't going to give it to the grave. She was like that lascivious old woman in Aristophanes, claiming equal sexual rights with the other "girls," grabbing at all the handsome young men. And those young men wouldn't know what they were getting into until it was time to do the act. . . . But Corde went no further. He relented.

It occurred to him that Lydia Lester might have complained to the Porson about him, said that he had dropped out at the worst moment, abandoned her. Corde had canceled all appointments during the trial. He had never missed a single session at Thirteenth and Michigan, the auxiliary Criminal Courts Building. He had laid on a car to call for Lydia each morning. He wouldn't allow her to take public transportation to that part of the city. Not even a cab was safe. Cabs were filthy and reckless, they stank. Cabbies hustled you, they were known to come on sexually with young women. Corde was taking no chances. Lydia was as delicate as she was tall. Everything possible must be done to protect her from shock. He was on hand well before court convened, sat with her before she was called to the stand, and tried to transmit waves of support while Maxie interrogated her. The Detillion caper had its own special interest. Maxie was taking no fee in this case. True, it was a PR gold mine for him, win or lose. Still, from habit, the legal-fee meter must have been clicking in his head, and he was desperately aware of what it was all costing him, of the drain, the sacrifice, of the outstanding bills he might have paid with a retainer. Yes, thought Corde, and because he conned me down in Joliet and screwed me up in Chicago, he is, by *his* logic, the injured party. That's how it works. You swindle a man and then grab even the sense of injury for yourself. A devouring man devours all there is.

So it was possible that Lydia Lester felt abandoned by the Dean. Maybe she, too, interpreted his solicitude as a proof of guilt. He had dragged her into this. It was the Dean's nephew who molested her and the Dean's cousin who afflicted her; it was the Dean who had published those articles of his at just the wrong moment, and then at the climax the Dean took off. She may well have burst out with this, and the Porson, too tactful to transmit tears and grievances at such a time, wouldn't even mention her name. But he was attributing far too much finesse to the old girl—the usual mistake. She had simply forgotten.

The Cordes had a spare room in Chicago, and Corde had suggested to Minna that Lydia should stay with them. Poor thing, she needed support. Corde had that sort of fervent pity in him. It was more than pity, however; it was also admiration. This girl, who looked as if she would crumble if some cabby propositioned her, if a derelict exhibited himself, who answered Detillion so faintly that he had to say, "Speak up . . . if the Court please, the witness is whispering"—this Lydia was punctual every morning, her blouse freshly ironed, her hair smoothly pinned. Corde said to Minna, "When I first urged her to do this she said absolutely not, she couldn't. Then I wondered whether it would be better not to start only to have her breaking down, but I misjudged her completely. It's like you get to the very limit of your weakness and then you come to a door, and if you have just enough strength to open that door you find all kinds of force inside. The girl found it. If I were still talking to Detillion—and you know how Detillion is with his sex business: if he should ever be elected to office, he wouldn't put his hand on a Bible to take the oath, he'd put it on his cock—if I were talking to that pig, I'd say, 'You're missing the whole point, Cousin.'"

Minna said, "There's one of your troubles. You still want to say things to any lost soul."

"Well, it's only 'just suppose.' I wouldn't think of talking to that meathead. And you're right, you've spotted one of my bad tendencies. I seem to carry this indignation load. But what I wanted to say about Lydia is that it's wonderful when a quality comes out you never would have expected. You look at the girl and she looks pale and ailing. She herself has a faint image—those long defenseless hands, the way she holds them. Lots of nice girls are brought up that way, with too faint an image of themselves. The family tells them they aren't strong. At lunchtime, when the court recesses, she has a small collapse. I drive her over to the Cantonese Chef on Wentworth Street so that she can rest her eyes in a dark booth. She has light-sensitive eye pains, like me. She gets a splitting headache in the courtroom. But after a few spoons of wonton soup she can go back and face Detillion again. Grady prays for her to faint—she *won't faint.*"

But Lydia Lester wasn't invited to sleep in the Cordes' guest room. Minna didn't like having a stranger in the house, opening drawers, reading mail and bank statements. She didn't put it that way. She said, "You mustn't forget, Albert, that we'd have to leave her here alone when we went to Mount Palomar." Corde yielded. He didn't share her sense of privacy, but he didn't argue; he let Minna have her way. He regretted it now. It would have been good for the girl. A protective atmosphere. Maybe another girl of compatible temperament would have been willing to stay with her. They would have looked after the place, watered the plants. (He still thought about his plants.) And if you didn't run the showers the seal dried out in the drains and you had sewer gas coming up. The arrangement would have been compassionate. Practical, too.

In the adjoining room, the women talked—they lived on the telephone. The instrument was warm with continual use. Corde kept his door ajar to hear what was going on. Ignorant of the language, he interpreted Minna's tones. And he was the man of the house. They counted on him. Now and then one of them looked in to tell him the latest; they didn't actually ask him for advice, but he gave them plenty of it, knowing that it would be disregarded for the most part. There was an additional telephone oddity. All calls were monitored. Somewhere in a burrow a man listened in. This agent made no effort to conceal his presence from these unimportant women. You heard him breathing, rattling papers, grumbling. Sometimes he even cut in: "That ain't what you said yesterday." Gigi said, "The man is obstreperous. I believe it possible that he is drinking."

Among the papers from Chicago Corde found a letter from Rufus Ridpath. That pleased him. It was an important gesture, a sign of support. Corde had written passionately about the Ridpath case. No one else had stood up for Ridpath publicly. Of course Ridpath was not rehabilitated, but he had said to Corde,

"At least you put the main facts on record." Mason junior dismissed Ridpath as "*your* kind of black man." There was too much of the freak or crank about Corde (liberal opinion's way of dismissing him). His own way of putting it: "If A. Corde is a man of strength, how come his hands are shaking?" Still the truth about Ridpath (or something like it) was now on record. No, it didn't signify much, unless it signified to make a friend. Corde achieved no practical result. Perhaps it was better for you not to have Corde take up your cause.

One of Corde's respected colleagues at the college, Sam Michaels, had observed, "There's less and less connection between blacks and whites. In the past, in spite of the silent war, there was a connection. Now the blacks don't want it, don't seem to care for white relationships." In Mason you saw an attempted reversal, a connection to be made on black terms. What terms were those? Lucas Ebry's terms? They didn't exist. Unreal! Young Mason's idea of boldness put him in the servile position. Besides, Corde wrote, the effective black "image" had been captured by the black gangs, the Rangers and the El Rukins, and the outlaw chieftains—black princes in their beautiful and elegant furs, boots, foreign cars. They controlled the drug trade. They ruled in the prisons. For young blacks, of all classes, even perhaps for young whites, they provided a powerful model. But Ridpath had nothing to do with images, image-making.

Removed from his post as director of the County Jail, Ridpath may have had to borrow money for his legal defense. He won his case but lost his reputation. People remembered the charges and forgot the acquittal—the usual pattern. Again, Sam Michaels—a supershrewd observer: "They couldn't prove the aggravated battery charge. That might mean that the prosecution was clumsy. Ill-prepared, didn't have the skill to prepare a case. Acquittal doesn't necessarily mean that Ridpath *was* innocent."

But Corde became convinced that powerful persons had been out to get the man. After repeated grand jury investigations—why so many? instigated by whom?—he had been indicted for brutalizing prisoners. Beatings in the cells! The newspapers and networks took out after him as if he had been Chicago's Idi Amin. Having a murdered general's head brought to the banquet table in a silver tureen? Shooting one of your own ministers between the eyes at a state banquet? You would have thought so. But the county couldn't make its charge stick. The defense was able to prove that deals had been arranged with the prosecution witnesses, who were promised shorter sentences. They had nothing to lose. Both were convicted murderers. Corde developed a particular, an intense interest in the Ridpath trial. He had long talks with Wolf Quitman, the defense lawyer. He interviewed people who had had professional dealings with Ridpath. He liked the man. And presently Corde found that he had linked himself with him. One seldom understands quite how such links are formed.

Ridpath wrote: "Hearing from your secretary that you had to leave the country suddenly because of your wife's mother, I thought I would go down to Thirteenth and Michigan and look at what was happening there. When the case broke in the papers, I seemed to remember the defendant. Sure enough, I recognized this man Ebry as soon as I saw him. Over the years he was in and out of County. Petty stuff, same over and over, he had a pattern, mainly street hustling. Not an outstanding sensational personality, in fact kind of a fuzzy outline. The evidence is pretty bad against him and I don't think your cousin will get him off, even acting the way he does in the courtroom. If it hadn't been for you it would have been the usual method of postponement after postponement by the lawyers until the witnesses moved away or died, and three, five, seven years later there would be no case. That's the most common. That's what your nephew hoped for. Where the press is concerned, you caused great resentment by your articles, implying they were lazy and cynical, and now you are their target of opportunity. Quitman and I both tipped you off to the danger when you were doing the research. Now they are in a position to do their number on you. As I look at it, the young man's wife probably couldn't see who pushed him out the window. It could have been either one. The prostitute is a tough gal, really fierce, and has a record of involvement in homicides. The man is low-key, even dull. There is no good way to appraise these people's actions, they all happen in fever-land. . . . I thought my impressions would be useful, knowing how much is riding on the case for you. . . ."

Corde had given a full description of Ridpath in *Harper's.* He was a man of hillocky build, short in the neck, with a powerful intelligent Negro head. His brief arms were widely separated by his cylinder chest; his eyes, also wide-set, measured you with extreme detachment. Under this waiting broad-gauged gaze you were to say why you had asked to see him. He was distrustful at first. Close-shaven, his scalp went into furrows when he raised his brows and began to speak. His ears were small and neat. Although he was completely dressed, coat and tie, nothing seemed in place. After several meetings, Corde concluded that he had no more than two suits, a gray and a brown. He also wore a belted plaid trench coat—if gray on gray could be described as a plaid. The hands, overlapped by shirt cuffs and coat sleeves, were also neat, not big. His arms were, so to speak, crowded apart by the high-breasted width of his body. And his hands were certainly not the hands of a "brutalizer." They couldn't have done much harm to the killers who testified against him—not the hands alone. But of course the indictment was for aggravated battery; bludgeon, blackjack—what weapon he was said to have used Corde couldn't remember.

Ridpath knew what "doing a number" was, because the papers had done a great one on him. Front-page close-ups made him look like Primo Carnera in black, and swelled and distorted his face as if he had acromegaly—they had thrown Ridpath into the distortion furnace.

Corde sometimes said about himself that he was often subject to fits of vividness. In ordinary contact there was a commonsense indifference or inertia in what you saw. But in a vividness fit you had the hillocky man, the obese breast, small hands, short neck, cannonball head—all of it. And then came what Dewey Spangler, tempering sarcasm with sympathy, called "poetry," "impressionism," "exaltation." Corde couldn't say whether this was set off by Ridpath alone or by the Chicago into which his investigation of Ridpath had led him. Whatever the cause, the result was highly nervous, ragged, wild, uncontrolled, turbulent. Corde had tried to clear Ridpath's reputation, but Rldpath's gratitude and loyalty may have been severely tested when he read what Corde had written about black Chicago. The Dean himself may then have seemed to be somewhere in fever-land. And downtown, in higher circles of influence, people may have been saying, "What's with this Professor? What's he talking? His pilot light is gone out."

In this emotional state, "investigative reporting" was utterly out of the question. Wolf Quitman, Ridpath's lawyer, must also have been puzzled by Corde. He couldn't possibly have foreseen—well, who can foresee exaltation? And Quitman wasn't, himself, an exaltation type. He was tough, a very tough man who practiced criminal law. His toughness, however, was not of the repellent downtown Chicago sort. He was a clear-faced, ruddy, muscular, active man. Even his face was muscular. His office was nothing at all like an office, more like a comfortable living room. A woolen shawl, presumably knitted by his wife, was folded on the chintz-and-maple sofa, and there were begonia plants all over the place. The begonias were set on glass shelves across the windows. (Corde was bound to take in the presence of plants.) Evidently Quitman didn't care to see City Hall over the way—a full block of ponderous limestone. Quitman said to Corde, "Professor, do you know what County Jail was like when Ridpath took it over?"

"Some idea."

"It was on the barn boss system. The gang chiefs ran it. Hard for you and me to imagine what went on there. Only by general terms, the catchwords. Damn rough scene. Drugs, rackets, homosexual rape. Plenty of money changing hands. Buy damn near anything you wanted. And people beaten and tortured. Lots of weapons. If you could work loose any piece of metal, you made yourself a knife. If you soaked a rolled newspaper in the toilet and hung it from the window in winter, it froze into a club. You could kill a man with it, and when it thawed where was the evidence? Not exactly the Montessori school. Excuse me if I offend, but professor-criminologists *were* brought in, and they were afraid to go into the tiers and put down the barn bosses, or even look at them. You can't blame them for it, but they sat in the office and wrote reports, or articles for criminology journals, while the suicide figures went up and up, and murders higher and higher. They didn't dare go into the tiers of the jail and they couldn't take charge."

"Ridpath went in?" said Corde.

"Of course. That's just what happened. He's a plain kind of

a man. He goes by duty. The Mayor put him there, so it was his duty to take charge."

"Nobody really expected that?"

"Who could have expected it? He'd probably say he assumed it was the necessary thing to do. No, he wouldn't even say that much. And the barn bosses respected him. He grew up on the streets himself. . . . He's a thoughtful fellow."

Corde said, "Those are his people?"

"It's an attachment he lives for. There are plenty of hustlers around who live off the black crisis. You've met 'em, Professor, we've all met 'em. Now, I've been going almost daily to that jail for years. There's where my clients are, that's a joint I'm totally familiar with. For Ridpath it was a sixteen-hour day, seven days a week, and that's a place that leaves all the rest of them behind."

"So you say he was living in his office?"

"Like a cause, Professor, not like a job. He cut down murders and suicides. I don't think anybody could control the rackets, beatings, stabbings, torture, buggering. He gave it the best try anybody could give. But that didn't impress the political guys much. What do you expect? This is a damn tough city, and damn proud of being tough, and the County is the worst—what you'd expect of Chicago."

"And Ridpath's mission was to clean it up," said Corde.

"Out of the question completely," said Quitman.

"You must have some feeling for that—the savage, subsavage condition. Otherwise you wouldn't be in this kind of practice."

Quitman did not care for this remark. He turned it aside.

"You know what was wrong? The man didn't remember to play ball, and you have to play ball, sir—you have to play it. County jail has a big budget. Suppliers and contractors came to the office (you understand who was sending 'em) and he wouldn't do business. He said, 'If I don't buy your meat boned I can save sixty cents a pound. I'm having it boned right here.' Too many savings. He saved a million dollars out of his budget and refunded it to the county. That money was supposed to be spent. What? Save dough by using the kitchen staff? Fuck the kitchen staff! Rufus got a bad name with the top guys. They thought he might become dangerous politically, too. Why else was he refunding from his budget? That's why they gave him the business."

"Who?"

Plainly, Quitman was startled by the naiveté of this question. He made no answer. Corde later obtained one from a Lakeview alumnus downtown—Silky Limpopo, who had been a star high-jumper ("over the bar like silk") and was now himself a criminal lawyer and a longtime City Hall Watcher. "You asked him who. Quitman wouldn't dream of telling you. Whoever thought Ridpath might be dangerous, that's who. Quitman would be nuts to tell you, and if he told you, you'd be bananas to print it. How do you think those big guys make their moves? They usually do it one on one, over a drink, or while going from the eighth green to the ninth tee. If any money has to change hands, it also is one on one, cash in an envelope which goes into a box at the bank. In Ridpath's case I doubt even if money had to change hands. He was in the way, that was enough. And just in case he did have political ambitions, the best thing was to dump on him. You'd like it very much if Quitman named names and you could take a good hefty cut at them evildoers. I can see that, Professor," said Silky. "You and me, Al, we'd never get anywhere with the politics. That's why I'm only a watcher. The hanky-panky is all going to be secret history, which nobody will ever write, not just because those guys aren't writers, but because they love the secrets. . . . They love 'em! Me, I deal professionally with deviants and sociopaths, like Quitman. *They'll* confide in you, sometimes. But the secrets at the top in politics—never!"

"Oh, I won't be writing any exposé, Silky. No scoops," said Corde.

"What will you be doing?"

"Personalities, scenes, backgrounds, feelings, tones, colors . . . Just between you and me, I wouldn't have been surprised if the strain of sixteen to eighteen hours a day in that place finally got to Ridpath. There must have been plenty of provocation, times when you'd want to lay violent hands on somebody." But Corde discovered that he was only speaking to himself.

Quitman himself would not talk too much. He and Corde had sat silently for a time in the bright office, figuring each other out. The garden of red begonias was now taking the warmth of the sun and the knitted shawl showed its red and iridescent fleece. What did such people make of Corde when he visited them? He was obviously a quiet dean type, no Watergate investigator. During his chat with Quitman, Corde remembered the close-mouthedness of G. O. O'Meara, whom he had interviewed at Meatcutters' Hall just last week. O'Meara, about ninety years old, wouldn't give Corde the time of day. And there had been no talk of the knife or the sledgehammer, the shambles, nor of strikes, nor of scabs, nor of company police. O'Meara was now a public man emeritus. Feeble, not quite with it, he still cut a figure among the big shots of Chicago. Beautifully respectful to the old guy, almost filial, they telephoned him in his meatcutters' palace. He went to board meetings, he attended banquets. There were testimonial plaques and scrolls and inscriptions on silver and bronze all over the place. The O'Meara who received the Dean was proud that he was a poet; full time, now. He presented Corde with a book of his verses—love sonnets to his wife. Yes! How the old boy had preened the last of his feathers. He made Corde listen to a poem he had recited on the Jack Paar show. His breath was perfumed with the penny candy he sucked continually. There were jars of jujubes in front of him. Not one of Corde's questions was answered, and when he got up to leave, the old man said to him, "So you wanted me to talk, but I didn't tell you a thing, did I?" Ancient O'Meara, packed with guile, terribly pleased with himself! Why should an important man in Chicago give information to any punk journalist who came along, calling himself a professor?

"They wouldn't let Ridpath be," said Quitman. "There were five grand jury investigations. One was federal, because he handled government money. There was nothing on him."

"But those people were persistent? . . ."

"His big automobile is about his only valuable asset. Grand juries being so easy to manipulate, it meant he was really clean. Somebody must've been real puzzled."

Corde had had frequent talks with Ridpath. Ridpath at first maintained an attitude of detachment, but presently became warmer. He seemed in the end to make Corde out to be some sort of delicate spirit. He couldn't quite see what he was after, but he said at last, "I might be able to help if I understood what you wanted to do."

"I can send you my notes. They're pretty full. If you have time to read them."

"Oh, plenty of time," said Ridpath.

They had been walking in a cold parking lot to Ridpath's giant automobile. Ridpath put his key, first, not into the door, but into a lock installed in the fender, which turned off the alarm system. The Cordes also had an alarm system. At home their doors and windows were wired.

viii

ABRUPTLY, Bucharest again—Minna burst into the room. All too plainly the news was bad.

"They phoned me from the hospital."

"They, who?"

"The women from intensive care. One of them. What she asked was, did I want them to light a candle."

"I see."

It was the end, then. A matter of hours.

"I told her, Of course! Please."

"Yes. Certainly you did."

"I didn't say anything to Gigi about this. You won't either, will you?"

"No. I'm staying put right here, going nowhere anyway."

Minna wore the maroon or mulberry-colored jersey pants suit. She had lost so much weight that the belt had slipped from the tunic down low on her hips. She gave no sign that she wanted comfort from Corde. She was right to keep her balance in her own way. If he had put an arm about her shoulders it would have been more for his own sake than for hers. Anyway, she went out, again abruptly, as he was preparing to rise, so he sat down again with a sudden sense that the chair cushion under him had been shaped to Valeria's figure. It was the same with the clothes in the armoire; they hung there with the shapes she had given them. If he got into bed for warmth, it would be her bed. All this combined to keep him fixed—stalled. He considered what to do. There seemed nothing to do but what he had been doing. Perhaps more effectively. But what was there to be effective about? He didn't have it in him to conceive how he might do better. He put his fingertips under his glasses and rubbed his eyes. His dependency on these goggles made him recognize how much he was organized for observation and comprehension. The organization, however, was insufficient. The present moment brought this home to him. And just now his thoughts took their shape from Valeria, just as the cushion under him and the clothing in the armoire did. Corde's conjecture was that she was now unconscious. Vital signs must be diminishing, or the women wouldn't have lighted candles. Those must be burning in the outer room, away from the oxygen. Medical technicians offering to light a candle—imagine! And Minna, whose subject was astronomy, so badly wanting it. Please, do!

Despite the great weight of these conjectures, pictures, he leafed again through the papers spread over the desk.

To resume: The notes he had sent to Ridpath had gone into his articles with little revision, in the end. He didn't care to develop them much. They were painful. His motive had been to avoid playing up to readers, making it all too easy for them to say, "You see how bad we've become—all those appalling ghettos."

This was not what the Dean had really felt during the many days he spent in courtrooms and hospitals. Raising the indignation level—*that* easy satisfaction—was not his purpose. No, Dean Albert Corde, exercising his citizen's right to see how justice was administered in his native city—he recorded exotic scenes in the courtrooms at Harrison and Kedzie. However, all the exotics were as native as himself. On his own turf, which was also theirs, he found a wilderness wilder than the Guiana bush. The lawyers had let him sit in the front row with them. These were chicken-feed lawyers waiting for the Bench to assign them to a case. You could pick up a buck here. Some of these were elderly men, down on their luck. The younger ones were built like professional athletes, flashy dressers who went to hair stylists, not to barbers. Beautifully combed, like pretty ladies or dear small boys in Cruikshank's Dickens illustrations, they might have been either thugs or bouncers.

Called up by the court clerk, groups of defendants and

lawyers formed and dissolved all day long from endless dockets—dope pushers, gun toters (everybody had a gun), child molesters, shoplifters, smackheads, purse snatchers, muggers, rapists, arsonists, wife beaters, car thieves, pimps bailing out their whores. People were all dressed up. Their glad rags were seldom clean. Young men wore high-waisted, flaring leatherette coats and high, puffed, long-billed caps; red-and-yellow wooden platform shoes, or Wild Bill Hickok dude boots; or crisscrossed their shins with candy-box ribbons. They wore dashikis, ponchos, cloaks, African amulets, rings and beads—symbolic ornaments symbolizing nothing. There were brash strong women, subtle black small women who had little to say. Their skulls sometimes were terraced, very curious; or else their hair was teased out, dyed, worked into small viper-tangle braids; put up in blue, pink, yellow plastic rollers. For all this gaiety of color, the gloom was very deep. No one seemed able to explain what he had done, who he was. It was all: "You brought us here, you tell us who we are, and what you want with us." Where did this gun come from? It was lying on a shelf. Where? In a burned-out abandoned house where somebody was selling liquor on a plank counter. How did you come to be there? I dunno.

You have before you an offender. This one is white, androgyne in outline, male in dress, open-mouthed, mute, idiotic, frightened, too old to be a boy (the hair is thin). The seat of his pants hangs down, full and dead, and his hands are lame at his sides. The bristles of his dewlaps are shaven in strips. He wears a turtleneck. His lawyer says he has no criminal record, Your Honor, never held a job but keeps house for his father and his brothers, factory workers. It's a motherless household, Your Honor. Regarding the packages of Tums he put in his pockets at the supermarket, he pleads guilty, but it was just one of those once-in-a-lifetime things. The lawyer says, in effect, Look at this poor slob forty-year-old adolescent with these fat tits in a dirty jersey; if you send him to County Jail they'll tear him to bits. They'll beat him, they'll burn him with cigarettes for the fun of it, they'll sodomize him day and night. He'll come out a cripple. Better just give him a scare and send him home. The judge nods, agrees and says, "What if I sentenced you—do you know what they'd do to you in jail?"

The next case is one of the sexual abuse of small children. Pictures are produced of screaming kids whose faces are spattered, covered with gobs of semen. Who would do this? And who had the presence of mind to take such pictures, waiting until the thing had been done? Some undercover-agent photographer?

In his articles, the Dean had had much to say about these "whirling lives." He was sorry now about that. He thought he had interrupted his accounts of County Jail, County Hospital and Robert Taylor Homes far too often with his unwanted and misplaced high-mindedness. On rereading, he himself passed quickly over the generalizing, philosophizing passages. They were irritating. He wouldn't, as a reader, have bothered to figure them out. Straight narrative was a relief and a consolation. "I go with Mr. Ridpath to the Taylor Homes." (Mr. Ridpath, bareheaded, is wearing his gray-within-gray plaid coat. Men who knew him at County Jail wave hello. There are snipers in the upper stories. Also, gangs are operating everywhere.) "He introduces me to Mr. Jones, one of the building engineers in the maintenance department. Vandalism here runs to more than a million dollars a year, one-third of the project's operating budget. 'We had ninety commodes in the warehouse last month, now we are down to two. How do they break the commodes at such a rate? Well, sir, being afraid to go at night to the incinerator drop on each floor, they flush their garbage down the toilet. The large bones stick in the pipes; your plumber tries to snake them out, and there goes your bowl, cracked. Then there're light bulbs. We don't use glass anymore, we use unbreakable plastic. Children hold newspaper torches to them and they melt away. The elevators—those are the biggest headaches of all. They are not built for such hard use or abuse. It's not just that people urinate in them. . . .'" They commit assault, robbery, rape in them. "'We have had young men getting on the top of the elevator cabs, opening the hatch and threatening to pour in gas, to douse people with gasoline and set them afire. Project guards, trapped like this, have had to surrender their guns.'" Mr. Jones, black, a graduate of Tuskegee, is offered the protection of a pseudonym. His large sensitive eyes observe his fingertips on the edge of the desk as he speaks. Then he rearranges his documents. These are facts that should be known, and as Mr. Ridpath vouches for the Dean, Mr. Jones agrees to talk, but he doesn't feel quite safe.

Here in Eastern Europe, the morning's rain had turned to snow. The flakes were large—their shapes made Corde think of contact lenses—but as soon as they touched the pavements it was all over for them.

He turned again to the passages his mother-in-law had evidently read repeatedly. Some of these were items culled from the papers. Nine inmates of County Jail on November 25 sawed their way out of a segregated tier, handcuffed the guards, and then tried to climb down with a ladder of knotted bed sheets. Eight of them had been caught. The ninth, a man named Upshaw, escaped. This Upshaw had been confined to a state mental institution because psychiatrists had found him incompetent to stand trial in the decapitation murders of a man and a woman and the strangling of their young daughter. Escaping from the "mental facility," he had been apprehended and sent to County. Now he was at large. Six of the eight who were caught had been facing murder charges.

You see (Corde saw), you begin to lose contact with human beings and with the world. You experience spiritual loneliness. And of course there are the classics of this condition to study—or rather to mull over: Dostoevsky's apathy-with-intensity, and the rage for goodness so near to vileness and murderousness, and Nietzsche and the Existentialists, and all the rest of that. Then you tire of this preoccupation with the condition of being cut off and it seems better to go out and see at first hand the big manifestations of disorder and take a fresh reading from them. Not quite sufficient to say that at this moment of history the philosophical problems are identical with the political ones. This is true. It's okay. Only it's insufficient. You had better go see in detail exactly what is happening. But there I go again, and never mind that now. He turned the pages of the magazine and found that his mother-in-law had drawn double lines in the margins beside his account of the death of Gene Lewis at Twenty-sixth and California.

Brought from jail to the Criminal Courts Building for sentencing, Lewis was heavily but carelessly guarded by the sheriff's police, so that when his girl friend asked permission to give him a book—to divert him (the legal arguments would be long)—permission was granted, and she handed him a copy of *Ivanhoe*. This had been hollowed out, and there was a gun in it. As Lewis was handcuffed, the book was stuck under his arm. Corde had later been allowed to examine this copy of *Ivanhoe*. It was a boys' edition, with colored, glossy illustrations. The inside had been carved out with razor blades, but smoothly, a work of art, of love. The woman had been described by witnesses as "a high-style Twiggy-type chick with three-inch artificial eyelashes, and orange dust all over her cheeks. She was very slender, about six feet tall, she wore long skinny boots and was gorgeous, out of this world." Why should the armed guards, those Chicago payrollers, bother to open a book—any book? Let the guy have his book. Once seated, Lewis snapped off the rubber bands under the defendant's table. The woman had also put in a key. He unlocked the handcuffs and took out the magnum. He lined up all five beerbellies against the wall and disarmed them. He didn't shoot anyone, but to prove to Judge Makowski that the magnum was not a toy, he fired a single shot into the floor. Then he raced out of the courtroom. He dumped the guards' guns in a trash basket and jumped into an elevator. But the elevator was going up, not down. When he rushed out to change on the next floor, he ran bang into a group of detectives from Area Four. They shot him ten times in the head. Paramedics from the Cermak Hospital came for the corpse with a black plastic bag. The woman was never identified. To look for her was a sheer waste of time.

Students at the college had objected, predictably, to much that Corde had written. He had described broad-daylight rapes and robberies, sexual acts in public places, on the seats of CTA buses, on the floors of public waiting rooms, men on Sheridan Road spraying automobile fenders with their urine. So the students called a meeting to denounce the Dean for writing such things. Miss Porson had gone there, and sat in the hall to take notes. She was pierced with excitement, afraid (she might have been identified as a spy), and she was indignant. But the militant students did not matter much to Corde. He said to Miss Porson, "The usual thing, looking for an issue, trying to catch me out. And I brought it on myself for 'going public.' But by next week I'll be forgotten." Miss Porson was wounded (so deeply wounded, she said) for his sake. They had misunderstood, they didn't know what a good man Mr. Corde was. If you could trust her sympathetic heart, the Dean was an angel. Well, you couldn't trust her sympathetic heart—sorry, but she flattered him with all these flights of generous passion; she flattered herself, too, in her dramatic declarations. The Dean had his vanities. He could count the ways, if you asked. But he was not, if his observations were true, exceptionally vain. Besides, he had a thing about objectivity. Perhaps impartiality was a more accurate term. As age, experience, and wear and tear reduced him physically, they also revealed to him a strong preference for disinterested judgments. It was nothing like nonattachment, not negative objectivity. He was objectivity (no, impartiality) intoxicated. The student militants, a small group now, revolutionary Marxists (like the ones recently murdered in Greensboro by Klan and Nazi riflemen), passed a resolution declaring that the Dean was a racist and that he owed a public apology "to Black, Puerto Rican and Mexican toilers" for making them look "like animals and savages."

Well, you wanted a lead apron and other protective devices when you approached all this dangerous stuff. It gave off deadly radiations and shocks of high voltage. It wasn't as if Corde had been unaware of such dangers, either, as if he had come out of his ivory tower after ten years of seclusion unprepared, innocent, vulnerable, discovering what monstrous destruction the gods had unleashed. It was not like that at all. He had been getting around, reading the papers, keeping up with the criminologists, the economists, the social theorists, the urban analysts, historians, yes, and the philosophers and poets—he was one of our contemporaries, after all, and a wide reader. Wider than most. But he thought he would say something about this Chicago scene drawing on his own experience, making fresh observations, referring to his own feelings, and using his own language. The steps by which he reached this decision were certainly peculiar. When you retraced them, they took you back to sources like Baudelaire and Rilke, even Montesquieu and Vico; also Machiavelli; also Plato. Yes, why not?

He had left the Paris *Herald* in order to give more attention to these great sources. Did he want to write about Chicago? For once, it would be done in style.

Without much success, he had tried to explain this to Minna. She wished him well. Her own interests were mainly astronomical. He was saying to her at breakfast about a year ago that he had been rereading the wartime letters of Rilke. He quoted to her: "Everything visible flung into the boiling abysses to be melted down . . . but hearts—shouldn't they have the power to hang suspended, to preserve themselves in a great cloud?" Minna seemed to be interested in this. But you couldn't be certain that you really had her attention. Still he continued. He said, "Rilke wouldn't discuss the war. He felt betrayed by his friends when they insisted on talking about it. Not just because the present was too brutal and too formless to be talked about, but because you could only talk about it in newspaper expressions. When you did that, he said, you felt disgust and horror at your own mouth. But then there was So-and-so, who said that you departed for the eternal only from Grand Central Station. This was in the day of the trains. What he meant, of course, is that the contemporary is your only point of departure. Hearts, sure, must have the power to hang suspended, but they can't do it indefinitely. Shouldn't . . ." He stopped. The morning must have been ill-chosen. For Minna was astrophysically removed from him. The signs were too plain to miss.

So he tested these truths of his against the blight of Chicago. By no means was it all blight. There was business Chicago sitting in its skyscrapers, monumental banking Chicago, corporate electronic computerized Chicago. There was historical Chicago, about which he wrote many curious things—speaking of the old neighborhoods, their atmosphere, their architecture, the trees, soil, water, the unexpectedly versatile light of the place. He surveyed the views of noteworthy visitors—Oscar Wilde, Rudyard Kipling, the famous Stead, whose book *If Christ Came to Chicago* contained vivid and valuable pages. It wasn't as if Corde had made a beeline for the blight. Nor did he write about it because of the opportunities it offered for romantic despair; nor in a spirit of middle-class elegy or nostalgia. He was even aware that the population moving away from blighted areas had improved its condition in new neighborhoods. But also it was fear that had made it move. Also, it was desolation that was left behind, endless square miles of ruin.

Occasionally he had tried at the breakfast table before they went their separate ways to tell Minna what he was up to. "Rufus Ridpath wants to help out. He thinks it's important. He sends me lists of people to talk to, and places that I should look at."

He should have known from the fixed look of his wife's eyes not to talk to her now. Was he trying to challenge the stars? She was concerned about her husband (he was going into dangerous neighborhoods), but it would have been wiser to postpone this discussion. She took a sharp tone with him. She said, "It's not a good idea to get in so deep with this Ridpath. You may look like two of a kind—out to get the establishment."

"Yes, he took a terrible beating. He's burnt up. He'd like to get back at his enemies. I sympathize with him. His feeling for his people is real. Are they part of American society, or are they going to be eliminated from it? To him this is not a theoretical question. If as many as fifteen million people have already accepted to be stoned out of their minds—and it isn't only the junk use, but the anarchy, which is a sort of narcotic. And it isn't just that he knows this—he *is* it himself, humanly."

"And why is he helping you—because he likes you?"

"Maybe he does. And maybe he has naive respect for academics—thinks they are what they're supposed to be. Morality and justice is their trade. After all, there are libraries filled with marvelous books."

"Are you really talking about him, or about why you should take all this on?"

"Let me see if I can make it clear."

But that was absurd. He couldn't explain himself. It hadn't really been a matter of choice. Something had come over him. He went over the passages marked by Valeria to see whether they formed a pattern. She would have been more interested in his emotions, his character, than in Chicago.

There was, for instance, a long description of County Hospital.

Dr. Fulcher, the hospital's Negro chief, had suggested that Corde might find the kidney dialysis unit interesting. Valeria had heavily underlined his account of it.

The ancient County Hospital, yellow, broad and squat. The surrounding neighborhoods have decayed and fallen down. In the plain of collapse, this mass stands almost alone. Beyond the clearings the giant forms of the business district are gathered close. Between the antennae of the Sears Tower a rotating light blinks out. The weather is gray. The pulsating signal is fluid, evidently made of metals and crystals whose names only engineers might recognize.

I am guided by a Filipino nurse through old tunnels, baked dry by mammoth boilers. The pipes drip rusty water. By the door of the morgue, wheeled stretchers line the walls. The dried blood would be scraped from them if there were staff enough, but there is no money. In these subterranean passages there are alternating zones of heat and chill. Paleotechnic furnaces hugely branching out send warmth up into the ancient wards. The tiny Filipino woman brings me to a room in which reclining chairs are covered with clean sheets. Beside each chair is a complicated device, glass within glass, the inmost compartment filled with blood. We stand and watch the purification process. Hooked into a machine, a large black man in worn work clothes is only semi-conscious. The seaman's watch cap has slipped from his head. His face is hairy, not bearded but unshaven, his big lips cannot close even when he tries to speak. The small woman whispers to me. Kidney patients seldom sleep well, and while their blood is being cleansed they sometimes fall into a stupor. The process takes four hours to complete. Some of the patients, their kidneys destroyed by a variety of diseases, are brought in several times a week. Lives have been extended for as long as ten years.

Kidney patients look puffy. The legs and arms of the veterans are disfigured by surgically produced fistulas. Blood vessels are fused to increase circulation and these conjoined or grafted veins and arteries make great painful lumps which have to be soaked daily. A woman is now brought in who can no longer be treated through the arms or the legs. Her fistula is on the chest. The cabdriver who picks up and returns all these dialysis patients is an enormous black woman in red jersey trousers. Her feet seem quite small. Her shoes have high heels. Her straightened hair hangs to her shoulders. She wears a cabby's cap and a quilted jacket. Solicitous, she supports the sufferer, settles her into her chair. These passenger-patients are her charges, her friends. She wheels forward the television set. The sick woman asks for Channel Two, and sighs and settles back and passes out.

Some of the patients are bald from chemotherapy. One old man has lost his black pigmentation. All that remains of his blackness is an astonishing mole here and there on his naked head, a strange man to see but decent, sensible, and his thoughts in good order. A retired plumber by trade, nonunion, he still takes an occasional job. But then an even older man is brought in who looks altogether senseless. The guide whispers to me: "Dementia—not with it." They seat this old man, and he waits, his jaw undershot, and his head, from which the hair appears to have been scorched, is hanging forward. The technician who takes care of him is a Chinese woman. She works with beautiful skill, washing the lumpy arm with disinfectants, then plugging in the tubes, light and quick, no sign of pain from the old man. But then she blunders. A valve has been left open on the tray, and immediately everything is covered with blood. The suddenness of this silent appearance and the volume of blood with which the tray fills makes my heart go faint. I am almost overcome by a thick and sweet nausea, as if my organs were melting like chocolate in hot weather. But the nurse, working under the blood, plugs the vent, stops the flow, gathers up the soaking napkins, spreads clean ones, wipes the tubes. This act of getting rid of the blood is performed with professional mastery, almost occult. I am astonished by the Chinese woman's lightness and speed. As for the old man, he has noticed nothing. The Filipino nurse says, "You are a little pale. Do you want to go?" As we walk away, she tells me about herself. She is a nun and belongs in a nursing order.

It wasn't just the blood. If it had been ordinary blood. But it was poisoned blood. It is said that these people pin their hopes on kidney transplants. But that will never happen. And these are dead men and women. The metabolic wastes obviously affect their brains. Nevertheless, these nurses and attendants are curiously emotional, extraordinarily tender towards these patients whom their machines keep alive, they manifest a wonderful but also amorphous pity, a powerful but somehow indiscriminate love for these people.

Dr. Fulcher, County's chief, wears a beige silk shirt of Oriental design, open at the throat, anything but negligent in style, and a fawn-colored suit. A big, graceful man, he is bald; the white hairs of his sideburns are wonderfully trimmed. About his neck hangs a pear-shaped pendant of brownish onyx, and his fingers display large, intricate silver rings. He has a great sense of what it means to be at the top. Vividly articulate, he is in command here, he has a presence. Where white men would be diffident, he is exuberant, a regal populist in style. After all, he is at the head of this vast (sinking) institution, and he acts it. He is a great politician, he bears himself like an artist.

No wonder *Harper's* lost millions of dollars, printing this sort of stuff. So Dewey Spangler would have said, much amused. And Corde would have answered—but he didn't answer, after all. The day was almost over, and he thought, I've spent too much time over this stuff. Why don't we go for a walk? There's still an hour of daylight.

He said to Minna, "What about a breath of fresh air?"

But there were cousins expected at four.

Gigi said, "Wouldn't you like a cup of the Twining's tea you brought from Chicago?"

IX

THE thing happened for which, after all, they had come. Well, Corde said to himself, they were here to see Valeria—no? Blunter, to see her off? In spite of the Colonel, the purpose was achieved—no?

The hospital called while they were at breakfast next morning. Old Cousin Dincutza answered the telephone. Corde also came into the small parlor. The old woman stood stooping, holding her lowered head to the phone. She wagged her arm as if to forbid him to come nearer. She made signals with her aged face. Yes, here it was, it had happened. She put down the instrument and said in a low voice, "*Elle est morte. Valeria est morte!*" Then she hurried past him to the room, where he heard her reporting to the women.

When he came in, Minna was looking sternly absentminded. She did not seem to need comfort from her husband. She had made her preparations for this. She said, "You were right, Albert. If we hadn't gone that night I would never have seen her again. Just this morning I talked to Dr. Moldovanu. Mother died a little later, just before nine."

"I see. Well, what is there to do now? I suppose you've thought what to do."

"Yes, of course I have. Tonight is Christmas Eve."

"It is, isn't it. I've lost track."

"We'll try to set the funeral for the day after Christmas. We'll have to make the arrangements immediately. Traian will help. I discussed it with Ioanna last night. Petrescu came to the door just a while ago—before we sat down to breakfast. I talked to him for about five minutes. He already knew she was dead, I think."

"Petrescu?"

"He keeps in touch. He's always been like this. He watches from a distance. He made some suggestions about what to do."

"What needs to be done? Death certificate? Undertaker? I'll make the rounds with you today."

"Petrescu gave me a number where I can reach him during the morning. And there's Dincutza. Being over eighty, she knows a lot about such things. Whatever we have to do, cigarettes will make it easier."

"I must get more Kents."

"That's what I meant. Traian will drive you over to the Intercontinental. But will you see what Gigi's doing?"

Tanti Gigi was in the kitchen with Dincutza. Corde found them sobbing there. Then Gigi told Corde that she wanted to go below to see Ioanna, to tell her that it had happened. The elevator was stuck. On the cold staircase he put a shawl over Gigi's shoulders and helped her down to the concierge's lodge. It didn't make much sense that Gigi should go to Ioanna, whose job it was to tell the police everything. But why should sense be made? In the concierge's cavern, the two women sank to the small bed together, embracing and weeping in the alcove. Valeria's photograph was on the night table, and on the wall were pictures of the dictator and his wife. Corde passed again through the lobby, where workmen with hoes raised a dust, mixing cement for the cracked walls. He climbed back to the apartment. Minna, very thin and stern, staring past everyone, black beneath the eyes, was discussing details of the funeral with Dincutza.

Traian had come upstairs. He sat slumped in a straight-backed chair by the door, buckled up in his fancy multi-zippered leather jacket and being seemly—that is, decently downcast in the house of mourning. He was completely at Minna's disposal. He had plenty of time for her. It was no simple matter to obtain a death certificate. First you had to go to the hospital. You needed releases, authorizations, any number of official papers. "We'll have to drive all over town," said Minna. Corde was grateful to this Traian with the Mexican wisps at the corners of his conspicuous lips. He had taken the whole day off, Minna said. After Christmas he would be available, too.

More cigarettes were bought at the valuta shop. A pack or two of king-sized Kents saved dreary hours of waiting. From the Intercontinental they drove to the hospital, and after that to five or six government buildings—Corde, riding in the front seat of the Dacia, lost count. Traian knew what he was doing. Strange, what an expert he turned out to be. Traian in his leather cap and jacket, and his eyes like the green pulp of Concord grapes, was unbelievably effective. No waiting. He went to the head of the line. He presented himself at the desk boldly, making the essential signals, and putting down the cigarettes. He was a solid young man. His belly gave him more pull with gravitational forces than slighter people had, Corde thought. He took charge of all the papers. Minna paid the fees, signed the papers. She was firm, really very strong. Corde would never have guessed how strong she would turn out to be. She had no practical abilities, she had never needed them. Valeria had done all that. But now Valeria's powers had passad to her (hitherto) absentminded daughter. This is how she'll attend to me, too, Corde thought. It was an entirely commonsensical reflection; it hadn't the slightest emotional weight.

By early afternoon all the necessary documents had been collected. In record time, Corde would have said. Traian drove to the crematorium through a freezing rain. Workers' housing blocks and government buildings were covered with huge pictures of the President. His face, five stories tall, flapped and floated in gusts of rain. This must have been his way of resisting Christmas sentiment. He interposed himself.

Then the crematorium, standing on a hilltop, a huge domed building. Just as you would expect, the grounds were planted with small cypresses. Flanking the doors there were bas-relief figures of Graces in mourning, part Puvis de Chavannes, part socialist realism. Here as elsewhere, Traian seemed to know just what to do. Corde and Minna followed him to the desk (there was no office), where they began to make arrangements with the managing comrade. This man was dressed for the chill of the enormous circular place. He wore sweaters, shawls, an overcoat, an astrakhan hat. The astrakhan was a phony. He was not at all difficult, this official, not gloomy in the least, in fact he was more than normally cheerful, sociable—he was gabby. The paper work was done by his assistant, a young woman in the seventh or eighth month of pregnancy. Pregnancy was said to keep the body warm, the effect of double metabolism, or so Corde had heard. Anyway, she appeared unaffected by the cold—she alone. There was a green Nuremberg stove, but the comrade manager had it all to himself. Another mourner had already come up behind Corde. His coat was buttoned tightly across his belly; he was a stout man, very big, with a red, blustering face, but that was probably an effect of grief aggravated by the terrible cold. His blue bubble eyes were fixed on the tile stove. He reached over Corde's shoulders, trying to warm his distorted large fingers. Meantime the seated comrade manager was receiving slips of paper from his assistant and using two kinds of mucilage to stick them to the documents—documents upon documents—and talking nonstop. He asked whether a priest would perform a service. Priest? Minna turned to Corde. No priest. Valeria was religious but there would be prayers at the cemetery when her ashes were placed in the family headstone. All that had been prepared by Valeria herself. Then did the family want music? There were two choices, the Chopin funeral march or, equally appropriate, Beethoven—the slow movement from the Third Symphony. Four minutes on tape. Minna chose the Beethoven. The astrakhan hat nodded and nodded, writing on diligently, holding the pen in his thumb and two middle fingers, the index pointing forward, riding above the papers. Next, very courteous, anticipating baksheesh from the American husband, he led the way to the center of the hall. This was where services were held. There were two single files of chairs for the principal mourners. Under the center of the dome, in icy gloom, was something that resembled a long metal barrel. It opened longitudinally. This was the bier. When the halves of the barrel closed, the body was mechanically lowered for cremation—same mechanism in double action. In this one spot, heat rose from below. Corde and Minna drew away from it.

There were flowers here, all cyclamens. There wasn't light enough to distinguish their colors. The plants had been placed on the floor. Here they thrived like anything—low temperatures; just what they wanted. Above them, square containers of ashes were stacked like canisters of Twining's tea. Each carried a photograph, and dates of birth and death, and an appropriate legend: "Militant," "Engineer," "Teacher." So many contemporary faces, like pedestrians snapped by a sidewalk photographer. These must have been victims of the earthquake. Witnesses said that tall new buildings had turned to powder as they collapsed. But why were these tea boxes still here? Because there was no consecrated ground prepared for them? Traian explained this to Minna. The regime was short of cemeteries. Graves were at a premium. But why should there be such congestion—wasn't there plenty of land beyond the suburbs? Trembling Dincutza had spoken of this at home. She criticized no one, of course. She only said that Valeria had bought graves in the year of Dr. Raresh's death, when she was still in the government. She had raised the granite monument and built two benches. She owned several other plots as well. One had been promised to Engineer Rioschi, who used to drive her quite often to the cemetery to tend the Doctor's grave. Dincutza stated shrilly (sometimes this kind old woman resembled Picasso's horse in *Guernica*), "*Nous savons combien elle aimait son mari.*" Rioschi, you understand, didn't want to be stacked with these other cans in the crematorium when his time came, so he had been glad to drive Valeria. That had been their deal. He was a single man, you see.

The gray astrakhan now moved more quickly before them. Corde assumed that he was leading them to a chapel of some sort, a place where friends could view the body before the service. But no such thing. He brought them into a curved corridor where there were curtained recesses, tall and dim. Then Corde was astonished to see a pair of shoes sticking through the green-tinted transparent curtains. He was brushed by the soles, by the feet of a corpse. Next were a woman's feet, in high heels. In these cold recesses or cribs, corpses were laid out in their best clothes. Each one lay just visible in a shallow coffin shaped like a small punt and lined with dimity stuff, not much more than cheesecloth or insect netting. One tall corpse with a black Balkan mustache had his homburg set beside his head. He clasped his briefcase to his chest.

Lord, I am ignorant and a stranger to my fellow man. I had thought that I understood things pretty well. Not so.

The comrade manager said that he had wanted to show Minna where Valeria might be brought from the hospital next day. "No, thank you, no," said Minna.

The hour for the service was fixed for ten o'clock on the morning of the twenty-sixth.

The funeral parlor was next. Coordination was the problem —the hearse to be sent to the hospital, the body to be ready for it.

In the dark shop, finished coffins were stacked against the walls. They were only half-coffins, really, lidless. An elderly workman had one on his trestle, tacking in the flimsy two-thread lining. Careful tucks made a simple ruffle along the top. Backed up against the tall tile stove, the place of privilege, an obese old woman in multiple sweaters and a circular fur hat repeated the order hoarsely as she wrote it out. The wisps of her hat matched the hairs of her whiskers. Her lips worked inwards continually. She was not chewing; she had no teeth. She seemed to be tasting her own mouth. She ordered the men about, growling and bullying, but she became happy when Minna paid her off and Traian gave her two packages of American cigarettes. As she shoved the money into the drawer she simultaneously heaved up her clumsy body to reach for the Kents.

Corde said, "Do we go home now?"

"Yes, there's nothing else to do today, except to see if I can place an announcement in the papers. That's the next thing. Then Gigi and I have to choose Valeria's clothes for the funeral. Traian will take them to the hospital."

They steered back through the freezing streets. The only heat he had felt all day came from under the bier. Yesterday he had suggested to Minna that they go out for fresh air. Now he wanted only to get back to his room.

Returning, they found the dining room table surrounded by old cousins. They came with small presents for the mourners. Gigi, wearing a black dress, was unwrapping cakes and bottles at the buffet. The cakes, like the old ladies who had baked them, were dimly spicy. Gigi told Corde, "You had two calls, one from overseas—I think your college in Chicago. They said they would call again." And the other? Dewey Spangler, thought Corde, reporting on his efforts with the White House.

He did not linger among the cousins. He felt used up; the round of offices, the crematorium, the coffin shop, had tired him deeply and the labor of French conversation was too much for him.

The cousins didn't really want to talk to him, anyway; they were only being polite. This was no time to swap French phrases. He went to his refuge, his sanctuary, his cell. He had his private bottle there, and his bed; the flowers also. Towards the flowers he felt slightly negative now, as if they had betrayed him by blooming at the crematorium. An effort of reconciliation might be necessary. The irrationality of this did not disturb him. If this was how he was, this was how he was.

The telephone rang and Minna looked in and said, "For you, my dear."

He picked up the instrument. "Albert? It's Dewey. So far, no luck with those Georgia yokels. I can keep trying. . . ."

"Thanks, Dewey. No point now. . . ."

"Oh? Sorry. When did she pass away?"

"Early this morning. Funeral the day after Christmas."

"You may not want to keep our date," said Dewey. "I'd understand."

"When are you leaving?"

"Evening of the twenty-sixth."

"Why not the same afternoon—after the funeral? I probably won't be needed then. There'll be lots of callers."

"Yes, that makes good sense. Not a bad idea to get away for a while and have a drink. It must all be completely foreign."

"Not completely."

"Not insofar as you liked that old woman."

"I did, yes."

"Foreign—I mean, to be an American in a foreign family. That I call an unusual experience. You didn't tell me that Minna's mother had been a friend of Ana Pauker, and knew Thorez and Tito. I found this out yesterday from an old-timer. He told me about her and that whole Stalinist generation."

"These people were no Stalinists. They were just unpolitical people who got into politics." Corde was beginning to wonder whether Dewey didn't scent a story in Valeria. After all, he owed his syndicate two columns a week.

"How is your wife taking it?" said Dewey.

"At the moment she's busy with arrangements. Doing fine."

"Yes," said Dewey. "It tends to hit one later."

"I've often heard that said."

"Poor girl. Say, before I forget, there's no news out of Chicago about your case. Unless you've heard from other sources."

"It's the holiday lull. Jurors would raise hell if they didn't get their Christmas."

"Well, Albert, I'll check back to see if it's convenient, after the funeral. I'm pretty busy here, but there's always a sort of gap before airport time."

Hanging up, Corde glanced into the dining room but didn't show himself. There were bowls of eggplant salad on the table. Dinner would be late, after the cousins went home. You didn't get much to eat here. Leftovers. But in the West everybody ate altogether too much and sometimes he imagined that overfeeding made people toxic, slowed their thinking. He was trying to account for the recent increase in his own mental acuity. It now seemed to him that he was thinking more clearly here. Evidently fasting and disruption of routine were beneficial. But if his ideas were more clear they were also much more singular. For example: Valeria was certainly dead. She had died, and she was dead, and last arrangements were being made. But he couldn't say that she was dead to him. It wouldn't have been an accurate statement. One might call this a comforting illusion, a common form of weakness, but in fact there was nothing at all comforting about it, he could take no comfort in it. Nor was it anything resembling an illusion. It was more like an internal fact of which he became conscious. He hadn't been looking for it. And he was not prompted to find a "rational" cause for this. Rationality of this sort left him cold. He owed it nothing. It was particularity that interested him. . . .

Again the phone sounded off, and Corde picked it up. He had a hunch that it would be Chicago, and he didn't want Minna to take it. He was right. The Provost was calling. "I wish you a Merry Christmas." He inquired how they were. Ah, bad! Very sorry indeed to hear the news. He asked to have his sincerest condolences conveyed. Corde rumbled, "Thanks. Very thoughtful of you, Alec."

One of the shrewdest operators that ever lived, the Provost was also very strong—the perfect, up-to-date American strongman. You felt his muscle the instant you engaged him. No one was more smooth, more plausible, long-headed, low-keyed than Witt. A man of masterly politeness, ultra-considerate, he had decided (elected in cold blood) to adopt the mild role. That was all right with Corde, by and large. Okay. He was willing to play any man's game and accommodate his needs, if he could, but he was beginning to find the Provost's highly perfected manner hard to take, especially hard since the onset of the troubles.

"I would so like to express my deepest sympathy to Minna. Is she there? I am so sorry to hear about her mother. . . ."

"I'm letting her sleep," said Corde.

"Ah, she must need the rest, poor thing." Minna's high standing, her academic importance, shielded Corde from the Provost. He had never really grasped that, but he understood it fully now.

"I don't suppose there is any way to wire flowers to Eastern Europe," said the Provost.

"There may be; you can find out more easily at your end than I can here."

"Oh, for gosh sakes, I wouldn't dream of troubling you with that, Albert. You must have your hands full."

"Is there anything new on the legal side?"

The Provost said, "You may not have heard that you were subpoenaed by your cousin."

"Is that so?"

"Mr. Detillion wanted to put you on the stand to establish the heavy involvement of the college in this case. I've checked into that with our legal department. . . ."

"With some real lawyers . . ."

"Oh, there's no comparison," said the Provost. "I don't want to downgrade your cousin; you may have residual sentiments about him. But these are *crack* lawyers. Of course, you'd never have to get on the stand. The matter was gone into with the State's Attorney. But the newspapers gave the subpoena some play, which was what your cousin wanted. How come all the French names in your family, Albert?"

"The family explanation is that we were leftovers of the Louisiana Purchase. Napoleon sold us all to Thomas Jefferson so that he could pay for his invasion of Russia. . . . Well, I'm sorry to be a cause of so much trouble to the administration."

"Nonsense, Albert. There's no real trouble, just silliness."

Witt would concede him nothing. The likes of *you* can make us no trouble, was what he was saying. There was nevertheless real bitterness, and Corde could feel it. It came down from the communications satellite perfectly clear, pellucid. Corde was in an odd condition anyway, one that made it possible for him to see the Provost from all sides—the jut of his upper teeth, the gill-like creases under the ears, the continual play of deference and kindliness, command, pressure, threat—back and forth. No, he didn't like Corde. The Dean's appointment had been a mistake, and it was the Provost's job to clear up the mess. Corde was an outsider, he hadn't come up from the academic ranks, hadn't been shaped by the Ph.D. process. It wasn't even clear why he had wanted to become an academic, and even an administrator.

The Provost was still speaking. "Our people have met with Mr. Grady about this crazy subpoena. Since you're out of the country and can't be served, it's all in fun."

"And my nephew?"

"He came in, surrendered, and your sister posted a bond, so the young man is out. The grand jury's indictment probably won't stick, when it's reviewed, because the boy didn't have a preliminary hearing. But all the prosecution wanted was to establish that he had threatened the witnesses, which I'm afraid he really did."

"I doubt that he fired a pistol at them."

"Your guess is better than mine."

"Because I'm his uncle?"

"Oh, no," said Witt, suave again. "We can't be responsible for our relatives; we don't choose them."

"Only I seem to have more bad relatives than the normal person."

"We'll work it out, believe me," said the Provost.

Witt had from the first found it necessary to lead Corde step by step, rehearsing him, instructing him, making certain that he would interpret budgetary, educational, institutional policies appropriately. But (it was Corde himself saying all this for him) there was something unteachable about the Dean, an emotional block, a problem, a *fatum*. One of the permanent human problems, in every age of mankind (Corde saw it now), was the problem of not being a fool. This was truly terrible.

Oh, that oppression, that fool-fear. It pierced your nose, blinded your eyes, split your heart with shame. And to Witt, a man of power, Corde was a fool. To conceal such an opinion was an operational necessity for a Witt. It was the sort of sacrifice (a sacrifice, not to let your opinion dart forth, and scream and mock) you had to make if you were to be a genuine administrator. That sort of thing you had to hold down. But then there was Witt's brutal infrastructure, which could not be covered up. Witt, thought Corde, had a brutal drive to let him know, to transmit by his perfected devices, what a fucking fool he was. The Dean had made Witt very angry. He had bollixed everything up with his muddled high seriousness. It was not so much the Lester case that angered the Provost. The real vexation was that he had published those magazine articles without a clearance from the college. Not to submit them for approval was out of line, unheard of, dangerous to the last degree—wild! Corde had attacked—whom hadn't he attacked: politicians, businessmen, the professions, and he had even loused up the Governor. Maybe suggestions had come to Witt from high places, by discreetest channels, that this was one highly expendable dean. For his part, Corde didn't want to hide behind Minna. But Minna was involved. For Witt there was a delicate tactical problem. But the Provost, Corde believed, took professional satisfaction in his maneuvers, in operations calling for an unusual degree of skill.

He heard the Provost saying, "Lester was one of our graduate students, and we couldn't have backed away from this case, it had to followed up. I authorized the reward, you remember."

Corde did remember that. But he recalled also how plainly the Provost was put off by the Dean's emotionalism, his flushed face, his swollen eyes. "What verdict does the legal department predict?" Corde was asking, really, how the college hoped to come out of the case.

"Not pushing for a death sentence."

"I never had that in mind."

"Yes," said Witt. "You expressed your views in *Harper's* clearly enough. Capital punishment—according to you, nobody's hands are clean enough to throw the switch. What was your expression? Oh, yes, 'the official brutes' . . ."

What Corde had had in mind . . . as if the Provost cared

what position Corde had taken. Witt despised him. Nor, to tell the whole truth, did Corde altogether blame him for it. He was able to admit to himself that he had been out of kilter when he wrote those articles. Dewey Spangler was right, in part. There was a sort of anarchy in the feelings with which those sketches were infused, an uncontrolled flow of "poetry," the truth-passion he had taken into his veins as an adolescent. Those sketches were raw, where was the control of deeper experience? There wasn't any. He had publicly given himself the fool test and he had flunked it. And now came a man like Alec Witt, Witt who represented power, qualified by the higher deviousness, as power usually was. Corde had challenged this "real-world" power without reflective preparation, without taking account of the higher deviousness. He had left himself wide open. And today of all days—Valeria lying in the hospital morgue!—this depressed the Dean fiercely. But oddly enough, when the wave of depression returned from its far low-down horizon it brought back the idea of having another go at the thing. Do it right next time!

But the Provost had not telephoned from the free world in order to discuss capital punishment with a high-principled idiot dean. Both parties now made a pause. Witt was about to disclose the true reason for his call. The deep Atlantic stream brimmed between them. They were—what—seven thousand miles apart? You weren't able to have conversations like this in the old days.

"When do you plan to be back?"

"For the new semester. Minna will have to settle up her mother's affairs—the estate, such as it is. She also needs to get to Mount Palomar; she missed her telescope days."

"You haven't seen Vlada Voynich yet?" said the Provost.

"We've been expecting her. Her brother said she'd be here for Christmas."

"She's been telling what an interest you've developed in Beech's work."

"Purely amateur," said Corde.

"Of course it would be. In the nature of the case. Are you planning, actually, to write about it?"

Corde in his bass voice answered, "That was Beech's idea—*he* proposed it. He sent me the material."

"That's what Vlada told me. You haven't decided yet, though, have you?"

"It hasn't been on my mind much. I've put off thinking about it. I wouldn't want to jump into anything. If there's going to be more controversy . . . I need to be sure I've got a good grasp of the facts."

This should have reassured the Provost somewhat. Instead it made him press a little harder. "These environmental, ecological questions are very complex."

"I wouldn't do it if it were only that. I don't care to get mixed up in environmentalism. But I am interested in Beech himself. The personality of a scientist, his view of the modern world. But I'll have to wait until Minna's able to discuss it. I can't take it up with her now. I'll find out more from Vlada Voynich. She's bringing more material."

"So she told me, and I asked her also to give you copies of letters. . . ."

"What sort of letters?"

"Things that have come in—in connection with those *Harper's* pieces of yours."

"What, complaints to the college, objections?"

"Nothing to disturb you. Lots of curious items. Amazing how worked up people can become and what a variety of responses one can get. You'll find them really thought-provoking. I wouldn't think of upsetting you at a time like this. And you don't need to worry about things here; they're under control. I keep a careful eye on Lydia Lester. She was splendid on the witness stand. But you saw that yourself. So fragile, and turned out to have real guts."

Each of the Provost's final words touched an anxiety in Corde.

"It won't be a happy Christmas for poor Minna. Tell her at least that we think we can get another date for her at Mount Palomar. We'll be looking for you after the first of the year."

Corde explained to Minna under the dim chandelier of the dining room table—the taped black wires hung twisted from the broken plaster. "Alec Witt. Merry Christmas, and condolences. Don't worry about the telescope. And Vlada Voynich is on her way."

Gigi served an early dinner. It was eaten listlessly. For Christmas Eve the table had been laid with linens embroidered in red. Corde went to bed early. The twenty-fourth of December had lasted long enough.

On Christmas morning there were presents beside their coffee cups. The old girls saved gift-wrapping paper and ribbons from year to year. There were treasures of all kinds in the cupboards, boxes of pre-Communist ornaments. Gigi brought to the table the Christmas angels Minna remembered from childhood. They were designed to float slowly on wires radiating from a disk set in motion by the heat of a small candle. The toy would not work. "Valeria always could make it go," Gigi said. She wore deep mourning and her neck was strained as she bent to strike more matches. She had combed out the bobbed hair but at the back it still looked like a hayrick. "It may be the candles," she said. She went through the drawers of the buffet, looking for the right kind. She didn't know where Valeria had put them. Corde tinkered with the wires. Americans were supposed to be mechanically gifted, but he could get nowhere with them. He only bent the toy badly. The four angels hung motionless. That was the end of them. Valeria had taken their secret with her.

"Then open your presents," said Gigi. She had given Minna a peasant blouse. For Corde there was a large gold pocket watch which had belonged to Dr. Raresh. Surprised, he stared at it—graceful numerals, a shapely swell to the tip of the hour hand. To set it you depressed a tiny catch with your thumbnail. Gigi said, "This was the present Valeria decided you should have this year." He slipped it into the pocket of his cardigan and as he bent to sip his coffee he felt the pull of the golden lump near his waist. He reckoned that after London, and especially after the Rowlandson exhibition and dinner at the Étoile, Valeria had accepted him as a full member of the family. When he had tried to take her by the elbow because she was listing, could no longer keep her balance, when she pulled her arm away, it had depressed him (something like the streak of a black grease pencil over his feelings); he felt that she was irritated with him. But that hadn't been what it meant. On the contrary, it was then that his probation had ended.

The morning was sunny. He studied the watch at length in the bedroom. He read Vollard's memoirs and reminiscences of painters—no boards, no back, nothing but a bundle of stitched paper. Minna had no time for him. She and Gigi spent most of the morning deciding how to dress Valeria. Which dress or suit would she have preferred, or shoes, or blouse or ornaments? They decided that she should wear a greeny-blue silk suit Minna had bought in London for her, and a green and black paisley scarf, dark blue shoes. Traian took the clothing to the hospital, together with a photograph to show how Valeria put up her hair.

Gigi, who had been so passive while Valeria was dying, turned assertive and militant, insisting that the government must be "forced" to give her sister a public funeral. She told this to Petrescu when he turned up on Christmas Day. Petrescu surprised Corde by the genuineness of his grief. He carried himself (his swooping belly, his wide undercurves) with soldierly decorum but his eyes were red, tragic pouches under them. He was indulgent with Gigi, he sat sighing and let her talk. She told him (defying the listening devices) that the least the government could do was to acknowledge the fidelity of Dr. Raresh to the Party and the Revolution and the contributions made by this family to surgery, public health, and also astronomy. He answered patiently, his voice rising in spirals until it broke in the higher registers. Minna said to Corde how decent of him it was to come, and how loyal he was to the family. "I think he had no personal secrets from my mother."

Bound to have secrets, in his racket: Corde silently dissented. However, Petrescu's face certainly was ruined. If intensive care doctors could light candles for the dying, secret agents could mourn their adoptive mothers. There was sentiment all over the place. Petrescu had his family side, his soft side. He was delicately, even endearingly attentive to the ladies. He was thoughtful towards Corde, too, and brought him two green bottles of Chenin Blanc, unobtainable except in the commissaries for high-ranking bureaucrats.

Gigi explained to Corde what she was doing. "I am insisting that my sister should not have a commonplace funeral. She ought to be exposed publicly in the great lobby of the Medical School, as her husband was before her. It is only right and proper to give her official recognition."

"Will they give it?"

"We shall insist. I am requesting Mihai Petrescu to approach old members of the Politburo. They remember her. They are aware, as younger ones are not. There was typhus. There was starvation. Valeria asked Truman for supplies. He sent them. The Russians put their own labels on. Requesting drugs and food from America was one of her crimes."

Minna agreed with her aunt, while Corde was thinking that you saw eyes like his wife's in famine photographs. She was starving herself. It would take months to restore her.

"If not the lobby of the Medical School, then the Memorial Hall next door to the crematorium," said Gigi.

Petrescu, downcast, much troubled, nodding, stroked the fuzz of his fedora, stroked the dense hairs growing from his ears. It spite of its wide bottom, his broad body sat uncomfortably. He often pressed his palm over the thin hairs streaking backwards on his skull. His fingers were actually trembling. His pouchy eyes occasionally were lifted to carry silent messages to Corde, to another man. These poor women were *innocent* . . . they didn't *know*, couldn't *understand*. Corde believed that Petrescu had tried to make a stand against the Colonel, had been beaten quickly, clobbered, forced to back off. Now, after Valeria's death, he may have gotten official permission to be helpful to the family. Petrescu's rank in the security forces must have been fairly high. Whatever he had to do in the line of duty (don't ask!) he atoned for in this household by services, by emotional deeds, tender attachments. He was an old-consciousness type in a new-consciousness line of business. Gigi declared, "I assure you, Albert, and I will even swear, that my sister shall have her due. Until now my sister, who was a figure in the history of our country, has been denied notice in the national encyclopedia. But she shall have it. I shall go to the greatest lengths. . . ."

But Minna privately told Corde, "Today I can't even get the newspapers to print a notice of the funeral."

"Why do you suppose . . . ?"

"The obvious reasons. I ran away from them. And my mother was expelled, then refused to rejoin the Party. I think the funeral will be well attended, though. Just word of mouth. The telephone doesn't stop ringing. My mother is a symbol. . . ."

"Of what?"

Minna whispered. "It isn't political, it's just the way life has to be lived, it's just people humanly disaffected." She covered his ear with cupped hands and said, "The government may be afraid of a demonstration at the Medical School."

Corde, who didn't believe this for a moment, nodded. He said, "Sure. I understand. But what would the demonstration be?"

"I told you. It would be sentiment. To approve what Valeria personally stood for. Just on human grounds. . . . Why don't you go and rest for a while, my dear. You're tired. This is hard on you. I can see. Vlada is coming later. She arrived this morning."

A clear Christmas Day. The room was surprisingly warm, the sun heating the windows. It made him feel how badly he needed a breather, "a few minutes of Paris," as he called it—some civilized *calme*, or *luxe*. He picked up the crumbling paperbound Vollard, his *Souvenirs d'un Marchand de Tableaux*, and read a few paragraphs about the testiness of Degas. "You'll see, Vollard, they'll raid the museums for Raphaels and Rembrandts and show them in the barracks and the prisons on the pretext that everybody has a right to beauty!" A crabby old bigot, and he looked so ferociously at a child who annoyed him in a restaurant that he scared the little girl into fits and she vomited on the table. But for this nastiness he gave full compensation in lovely painting and bronze. Whereas a fellow like the Provost . . . But the Provost was no genius-monster, he was only . . . And Corde now tried to protect his sunlit breather, the moment of peace, but he could not beat off Alec Witt and he presently surrendered to Chicago thoughts. The Provost's signal was easy to read: for the sake of the college, he was protecting Beech. Scientists were far too naive to protect themselves, and Corde was especially dangerous because he, too, was in a way an ingenu. Once a man like Witt decided that you were not a man to observe the discreet convention, that you talked out of turn, and that you were a fool, nothing but trouble, you were out. He would do everything possible to stop Corde from writing a piece on Beech—"one of those pieces of his." And you couldn't altogether blame the guy, thought Corde. It's true, I was carried away. Hearts hanging in the dark too long, and going bad, spoiling in suspension, and then having a seizure, an outburst. In most things I don't hold with Dewey, he's too psychoanalytical, but he's clever enough in his own way or he wouldn't have become such an eminence. Give him his due. And he says I was settling scores with Chicago. I must admit that I was retaliating on my brother-in-law, on Max Detillion and on many another.

Tired of false opinions, and of his own distortions most of all, Corde admitted that, yes, he had wanted to give it to them (to a generalized Chicago), to stick it to them. To stick it, and to make it stick so that they couldn't shake it off. Now, a man in a position of real responsibility, a Witt, for instance, he protects his institution from everything immoderate. That's how the silky style is justified. That's his method for dealing with disruption: never lose your cool with the disrupter, gag him with silk, tie him in knots with procedures. Corde would class that as one of the hard, essential jobs of democracy. I gave no sign that I was going to turn disruptive. Dumb thoughtful sweet, was my type, mulling things over. Then I turned out to be one of those excessive, no-inner-gyroscope fellows he can't stand. So he despises me; what of it? I detest him, too. That's neither here nor there.

The publication of his articles had also given Corde a profile of the country, a measure of its political opinions, a sample of its feelings. "I administered my own Rorschach test to the U.S.," Corde said. Before leaving Chicago he had already received a batch of letters forwarded by the editors of *Harper's*. "A flood of mail," one of the assistants wrote. Liberals found him reactionary. Conservatives called him crazy. Professional urbanologists said he was hasty. "Things have always been like this in American cities, ugly and terrifying. Mr. Corde should have prepared himself by reading some history." "The author is a Brahmin. The Brahmins taught us to despise the cities, which accordingly became despicable." "Mr. Corde believes in gemütlichkeit more than in public welfare. And what makes him think that what it takes to save little black kids is to get them to read Shakespeare? Next he will suggest that we teach them Demosthenes and make speeches in Greek. The answer to juvenile crime is not in *King Lear* or *Macbeth*." "The Dean's opinion is that a moral revolution is required. His only heroes are two self-appointed possibly dubious benefactors."

"You should be congratulated for opening up these lower depths of psychology to your readers, giving us an opportunity to look into the abysses of chaotic thinking, of anarchy and psychopathology."

Curious what people will pick on. About *Macbeth* Corde had only noted that in a class of black schoolchildren taught by a teacher "brave enough to ignore instructions from downtown," Shakespeare caused great excitement. The lines "And pity, like a naked newborn babe, Striding the blast" had pierced those pupils. You could see the power of the babe, how restlessness stopped. And Corde had written that perhaps only poetry had the strength "to rival the attractions of narcotics, the magnetism of TV, the excitements of sex, or the ecstasies of destruction."

It was certainly true that Corde had found himself in Chicago looking for examples of "moral initiative," and he had come up with two: Rufus Ridpath at County Jail; and Toby Winthrop, also black, an ex-hit man and heroin addict. He hadn't found his examples in any of the great universities, and there was a large academic population in Chicago. What Alec Witt probably would like to know was why Corde hadn't made his search for moral initiative in his own college. Why, thought Corde, I did look there, up and down, from end to end. Corde was not a subversive, no fifth columnist, nor had he become a professor with the secret motive of writing an exposé. He hadn't been joking when he quoted Milton to his sister Elfrida: "How charming is divine philosophy"—the mosaic motto on the ceiling of the library downtown. And the universities were where philosophy lived, or was supposed to be living. He had never forgotten the long, charmed years in a silent Dartmouth attic, where he had read Plato and Thucydides, Shakespeare. Wasn't it because of this Dartmouth reading that he gave up the *Trib* and came back from Europe? To continue his education, he said, after a twenty-year interruption by "news," by current human business.

It was Ridpath who had sent Corde to Toby Winthrop at Operation Contact. He drove to the South Side on a winter day streaky with snow. You could see the soot mingling with the drizzle. Corde hadn't come to this neighborhood in thirty years. It was then already decaying, now it was fully rotted.

Only a few old brick bungalows remained, and a factory here and there. The expressway had cut across the east-west streets. The one remaining landmark was the abandoned Englewood Station—huge blocks of sandstone set deep, deep in the street, a kind of mortuary isolation, no travelers now, no passenger trains. A dirty snow brocade over the empty lots, and black men keeping warm at oil-drum bonfires. All this—low sky, wind, weed skeletons, ruin—went to Corde's nerves, his "Chicago wiring system," with peculiar effect. He found Operation Contact in a hidden half-block (ideal for muggings) between a warehouse and the expressway. Except on business, to make a sale, who would come to this place? He parked and got out of the car feeling the lack of almost everything you needed, humanly. Christ, the human curve had sunk down to base level, had gone beneath it. If there was another world, this was the time for it to show itself. The visible one didn't bear looking at.

Well, Corde entered the "detoxification center" and climbed the stairs. Two landings, a wired-glass door where you showed your face and were buzzed in. You found yourself in a corridor, and then, unexpectedly, you came into a room furnished with umber and orange sofas. Philodendrons hung in all the corners. Here he met someone who encouraged him, a wiry, whiskery Negro who said, "Go on, man—go, go; you on the right track." The tentative, pale, blundering Dean amused him.

Winthrop's office window was heavily covered in flowered drapes of pink and green. The ex-hit man sat waiting for him. His trunk was enormous, his thighs were huge, his fingers thick. No business suit for him. He was dressed in matching shades of brown—a knitted shirt in beige, a caramel-colored suede jacket, chocolate trousers, tan cowboy boots. He wore a small brown cap with a visor, a boy's cap. His face curved inward like a saddle. He was bearded and, like Dr. Fulcher at County Hospital, he had pendants on his neck and big rings on his hands. He picked up the note Corde had sent him. In the lamplight the folded paper seemed no bigger than a white cabbage moth. "You a friend of Rufus Ridpath, Professor? He asked me to talk to you. Thinks we can do each other some good. Maybe he thinks you might be able to do something for him. Set the record straight."

"What do you think?"

"I think he was the best warden County ever had, and I was a prisoner before and during his time. . . ."

The body of this powerful man was significantly composed in the executive leather chair. If you had met him in the days when he was a paid executioner, if he had been waiting for you on a staircase, in an alley, you would never have escaped him. He would have killed you, easy.

"You can't do much for Ridpath. The guys who did the job on him don't have to worry about you or me, my friend. It's their town. Their names are in the paper every day. No trouble at all to get names. But that's *all* you could get. Rufus doesn't really expect anything from you. He just likes you. Now, what did he tell you about me?"

"He said that you and your friend Smithers founded this center to cure addiction without methadone, as you cured yourself."

This man with the black nostrils, impressively staring under the visor of the childish cap, interrupted him. He said, "You bein' polite. He said I was a hit man, right? I was, too, a hired killer working for very important people in this city. I was tried three times for murder. Those important people got me off. Ask me how, and I identify you as a man who don't know this town."

How many people he had murdered, he didn't care to say. But then he nearly killed himself with an overdose of heroin. Someone should have warned him how strong it was. After he took it he recognized it for what it was. As it began to take effect, he saw that he was dying. This happened in a hotel room near Sixty-third and Stony Island, the end of the el tracks, the tip of rat-shit Woodlawn. "I'm goin' to tell you just a little about this."

A friend came and put him into a tub of cold water, but he saw that Toby was dying and he beat it. "No use hangin' around. But after eighteen hours of death, I came back."

He lifted himself from the tub, and just as he was, in wet clothes, he went down into Sixty-third Street and caught a cab to Billings Hospital, to the detoxification unit. Because of his terrifying looks, the receptionist signaled the police, who grabbed him in the lobby. But they had nothing to hold him on at the station, only vagrancy and loitering. "I bailed myself out. Always a big bankroll in my pocket. I got another cab back to Billings, but this time I stopped in an empty lot and tore the leg off a table. I went in with it under my coat, and I showed it to the receptionist. I said I'd beat her brains out. That's how I got upstairs. They gave me the first methadone shot. I was in a hospital gown, and I went to the toilet and sat on the floor to wait for the reaction. I put my arms around the commode and held tight to it."

"But you didn't go through with the methadone treatment."

"No, sir. I did not. Something happened. When I came in I had the table leg, I was ready to kill. I would have killed the lady if she called the cops again. But in less than an hour I was called to stop a riot. I had to stop a man breaking up the joint. He was a black man, as big as me, and he had delirium tremens. He smashed the chairs in the patients' sitting room. He broke a coffee table, broke windows. The orderlies and nurses were like kindergarteners around him. He was like a buffalo. I had to take a hand, Professor. There was nothing else to do. I separated from the commode and went out and took control. I put my arms around the man. I got him to the floor and lay on the top of him. I don't say he was listening, but he wasn't so wild with me. They gave him a needle and we laid him on a cart and put him in bed."

"That was Smithers?"

"Smithers," said Winthrop. "I wish I could explain what it was all about. I've told this before. It's as if I kept after it till I could find out what happened that moment I took control of him. Maybe it was because I died twenty-four hours before. Maybe because my buddy left me in the bathtub in the hotel—that was all he knew how to do for me. But when they put Smithers in bed, I sat by him and minded him."

"This was when your own treatment stopped."

"I wouldn't leave him. They had to measure his body fluid. I held the man's Johnson for him. You understand what I'm saying? I held his dick for him to pee in the flask. He had a bad ulcer in his leg. I treated that, too. That was his cure, and it was my cure, at the same time. I was his mother, I was his daddy. And we stayed together since."

"And made this center."

"Built it ourselves in this old warehouse—the dormitories, kitchen, shops downstairs to teach trades. We bring in old people from the neighborhood—the old, they're starving on food stamps, scavenging behind the supermarkets. The markets post guards, they say they don't want the old people to poison themselves on spoiled fish. We need those old people here. They teach upholstery, electrical work, cabinetmaking, dressmaking. They teach respect to young hoodlums, too. But it isn't only hoods. We get all kinds here. We take all the kinds—white, black, Indians, whatever color they come in. From the richest suburbs, from Lake Forest . . ."

"You'd call this center a success?"

Winthrop stared at him a moment. Then he said, "No, sir, I don't call it that. They come and go. It takes with some. I could name you a many and a many it never could save."

Until now Winthrop had sat immobile in his chair, but now he turned and, to Corde's great surprise, began to lower himself towards the floor. What was he doing? He was on his knees, his big arm stretched towards the floor, his fingers hooked upward. "You see what we have to do? Those people are down in the cesspool. We reach for them and try to get a hold. Hang on—hang on! They'll drown in the shit if we can't pull 'em out. Some of 'em we'll get out. Some of them will go down. They'll drown and sink in the shit—never make it." With an effort that caused one side of his face to twitch, he labored to his feet and backed himself into the chair again.

"You're telling me that the people who come here . . ."

"I'm telling you, Professor, that the few who find us and many hundred of thousand more who never do and never will—they're marked out to be destroyed. Those are people meant to die, sir. That's what we are looking at."

X

It was at this point, out of earnestness and without seeing how it would be taken by the public, that Corde began to speak in his articles of "superfluous populations," "written off," "doomed peoples." That didn't go down well. You could use terms from sociology or Durkheim or Marx, you could speak of anomie or the lumpenproletariat, the black underclass, of economically redundant peasantries, the Third World, the effects of opium on the Chinese masses in the nineteenth century—as long as it was sufficiently theoretical it went over easily enough. You could discuss welfare politics, medical and social work bureaucracies, without objection. But when Corde began to make statements to the effect that in the wild, monstrous setting of half-demolished cities the choice that was offered was between a slow death and a sudden one, between attrition and quick destruction, he enraged a good many subscribers. Something went wrong. He wrote about whirling souls and became a whirling soul himself, lifted up, caught up, spinning, streaming with passions, compulsive protests, inspirations. He experienced, as he saw when he looked back, a kind of air anarchy. He began to use strange expressions. He wrote, for instance, that Toby Winthrop was a "reconstituted" human being, a "murderer-savior" type; that Winthrop was therefore an advanced modern case. Why? Because the advanced modern consciousness was a reduced consciousness inasmuch as it contained only the minimum of furniture that civilization was able to install (practical judgments, bare outlines of morality, sketches, cartoons instead of human beings); and this consciousness, because its equipment was humanly so meager, so abstract, was basically murderous. It was for this reason that murder was so easy to "understand" (or had he written "extenuate"? Thinness for thinness). He never did get around to explaining how we must reconstitute ourselves. Because of the incompleteness of his argument he confused many readers. Some wrote contemptuously, others were incensed. He hadn't meant to make such a stir. It took him by surprise.

But by far the most controversial part of his article was the interview with Sam Varennes. To this Varennes, the Public Defender in the Spofford Mitchell murder case, Corde had very nearly spoken his full mind. The results, in the lingo people were using nowadays, were "counterproductive."

Corde had gone to see Sam Varennes to discuss the case and to ask permission to interview Mitchell. Varennes was interested in publicity, but in the end he and his defense team decided that any pretrial media coverage would be prejudicial to their client. Corde had, however, reported his conversation with Varennes in full.

The Mitchell case was not exceptional. There were thousands of similar crimes in police files across the country. But there were special circumstances which made it important to Corde.

The victim was a young suburban housewife, the mother of two small children. She had just parked in a lot near the Loop when Mitchell approached and forced her at gunpoint into his own car. The time was about 2 P.M. Spofford Mitchell's Pontiac had been bought from a Clark Street dealer just after his recent release from prison. Corde didn't know how the purchase was financed. (The dealer wouldn't say.) In the front seat, Mitchell forced Mrs. Sathers to remove her slacks, to prevent escape. He drove to a remote alley and assaulted her sexually. Then he locked her into the trunk of his Pontiac. He took her out later in the day and raped her again. By his own testimony, this happened several times. At night he registered in a motel on the far South Side. He managed to get her from the trunk into the room without being seen. Possibly he was seen; it didn't seem to matter to those who saw. In the morning he led her out and locked her in the trunk again. At ten o'clock he was obliged to appear at a court hearing to answer an earlier rape charge. He parked the Pontiac, with Mrs. Sathers still in the trunk, in the official lot adjoining the court building. The rape hearing was inconclusive. When it ended he drove at random about the city. On the West Side that afternoon, passersby heard cries from the trunk of a parked car. No one thought to take down the license number; besides, the car pulled away quickly. Towards daybreak of the second day, for reasons not explained in the record, Spofford Mitchell let Mrs. Sathers go, warning her not to call the police. He watched from his car as she went down the street. This was in a white working-class neighborhood. She rang several doorbells, but no one would let her in. An incomprehensibly frantic woman at five in the morning—people wanted no part of her. They were afraid. As she turned away from the third or fourth closed door, Mitchell pulled up and reclaimed her. He drove to an empty lot, where he shot her in the head. He covered her body with trash.

She was soon discovered. Exceptionally prompt, the police

descended on Mitchell. He was found in the garage behind his father's house, cleaning out the trunk of his Pontiac, hosing out the excrements. He confessed, then retracted, confessed again. He was being held in County jail for trial. These were the facts Corde learned from the papers. He was then preparing his article. What might the real content of these facts be? He made inquiries and was referred to the Public Defender in charge of the case, Mr. Sam Varennes. In *Harper's* he gave an account of his long conversation with Varennes, whom he described as

> . . . a strong bald young man with prominent blond eyebrows and a wide throat, a college athlete in his time. The views we exchanged were enlightened, intelligent, liberal—did us both credit. To be appointed Defender you generally needed some sort of backup or sponsorship, still such appointees are often well-qualified conscientious public servants. Mr. Varennes is a scholarly lawyer, well nigh a Doctor of Jurisprudence. I think he said Stanford.
>
> He asked first what feelings I had about the case. I admitted that I was subject to claustrophobia, and that I believed I might rather be killed than get into the trunk of a car at gunpoint, that sometimes I had fantasies in which I said, "You'll have to shoot me." But if I were pushed in and had the lid slammed on me I would hunt for a tire tool to hit the gunman with at the first opportunity. To lie in a trunk was like live burial. I could never endure it. I then said, "Only think how Mrs. Sathers must have begged the man every time he opened the lid."
>
> He seemed, to my own surprise, slightly surprised by this. "You think she prayed for her life?"
>
> "Begged or prayed—'Let me out!' "
>
> Mr. Varennes did not care for what I was telling him. He had put himself in a posture to make an effective argument for his client (a man, after all, a human being like the rest of us), so he was much disturbed. I think also that I myself—the interviewer—disturbed him. *I* was disturbed. He said, "You suppose? I hadn't thought about that. . . ."
>
> I said, "Oh, but she must have."
>
> "And he was indifferent, are you saying?"
>
> "I wouldn't say indifferent. I'm trying to guess whether he understood her emotions. If you say something in all the earnestness of your heart, and wonder why this doesn't . . . with this earnestness it must—it must get through. If he had understood her pleading he would have been a different kind of murderer."

"The kind who feeds on the victim's pain, like this mass killer Gacy, who specialized in boys? Part of his sexual kick? Subtler and more perverted . . . ?"

"Gacy seems to have tortured and mocked his victims."

"So you don't believe Mitchell was the same?"

"Classification of psychopaths is technically beyond me. My only guess about Mitchell is that he was just bound for death. If you've taken that fast direct track, you may be deaf and blind to something so exotic as the pleading of a woman whom you've locked in your car trunk."

"A more primitive person," said Varennes.

I saw that the Defender was examining me on my social views. Mr. Varennes is a muscular man. Even his throat has muscles, a pillar throat. I think he pumps iron. He said next, "As part of the defense we may argue that Mrs. Sathers accepted the situation."

"Does he say she did?"

"Some of the time she rode in the front seat with him. She was seen by witnesses when he stopped at a bar to buy a bottle of Seven-Up. When he went in to get the drink and left her, she sat and waited. She didn't run away. You might say he had tied her feet."

"I didn't. But it's probable that she was dazed."

"As dazed as all that?"

"Felt she was already destroyed. There must be a sense of complicity in rapes. The sex nerves can stream all by themselves. If people think they're going to be murdered anyway when it's over, they may desperately let go."

"Sexually?"

"Yes. In spite of themselves, spray it all out. They're going to die, you see. Good-bye to life."

"That's quite a theory."

"Maybe. But that's quite a situation," I said. "And with the special confused importance, the peculiar curse of sexuality or carnality we're under—we've placed it right in the center of life and connect it with savagery and criminality—it's not at all a wild conjecture. The truth may even require a wilder interpretation. Our conception of physical life and of pleasure is completely death-saturated. The full physical emphasis is fatal. It cuts us off. The fullest physical joining may always be flavored with death, therefore. This was why I said Spofford Mitchell was on the fast track for death—fast, clutching, dreamlike, orgastic. Grab it, do it, die."

I reminded myself that I was talking with a gymnast. He had backed off his head as if to get a different slant, and took me in again, extremely curious. So I resumed the interviewer's role. "It may be wrong to pry into the last hours of Mrs. Sathers. Well, we were discussing why she didn't make a run for it when he went into the bar. Is it a fact that witnesses saw her waiting alone? . . ."

"I've taken the depositions."

"I'm trying to imagine the despair that kept her from opening the door. And suppose he had chased her down the street; would anybody have helped her?"

"Maybe not, against an armed man. Yes, when you put it that way. I suppose that's what the prosecution would say." His next comment was, "My team and I are on these homicides year in year out. We can't get up the same fervor as an outsider."

I made a particular effort now to recover my interviewer's detachment or professional cool. I am obliged to admit that I never know why I say certain things when I'm agitated. It was nice of him to call it "fervor"; it was far more insidious, a radical disturbance. But he was a nice man. His looks appealed to me. I liked his serious eyes and strong bald head. And this induced me to talk more.

His examination continuing, for he was examining me (as if there were something about me that was not strictly speaking *contemporary*), he tried me on the professional side and invited me to discuss the situation in broader terms—the mood of the country, the inner city, urban decay, political questions. He asked me to describe the pieces I intended to write. Why was I doing them, and what would they be like? I explained that the Cordes had moved up to Chicago from Joliet more than a century ago and that I had been born on the North Side and thought it would be a good idea to describe the city as I had known it, and that my aim was more pictorial than analytical. I had looked up my high school zoology teacher, for instance, whom I had helped with the animals, feeding them and cleaning the cages. Also a self-educated Polish barber who used to lecture boys on Spengler's *Decline of the West* while he cut their hair. I had traced him to Poznan, where he was now living on his Social Security checks from America. I revisited the Larrabee Street YMCA. Also the Loop. The Loop's beaneries, handbooks, dinky dives and movie palaces were wiped out. Gigantic office towers had risen everywhere. Good-bye forever to the jazz musicians, and the boxing buffs who hung around the gymnasiums, to the billiard sharks from Bensinger's on Randolph Street. Then I mentioned a number of contemporary subjects, among them the new housing developments south of the Loop in the disused freight yards; and the mammoth Deep Tunnel engineering project, the Cloaca Maxima one hundred and thirty miles long and three hundred feet beneath the city. Not wishing to ruffle him, I made no reference to my interest in the abuse of "immunities" under federal law by U.S. attorneys (refractory witnesses who rejected the immunity offer were sentenced for contempt of court; judges had the right to send them to jail for a year). It would have done me no good to discuss this with Mr. Varennes. Nor did I mention my interest in the case of Rufus Ridpath, the same people who had dumped Ridpath having perhaps appointed Varennes.

Whether I could be trusted, what my angle was, why I wasn't somehow one hundred percent contemporary in my opinions—these were the Public Defender's questions. I came well accredited—journalist, professor, dean. But in spite of these credentials and the prospect of favorable publicity for his team, I was suspect, he smelled trouble.

He was right, too. A certain instability . . .

Corde laid aside Valeria's copy of *Harper's* and tried again, reframing the interview, as if he intended to write a new version, wider in perspective, closer to the real facts, taking bigger forces into account. The meeting with Varennes was one of those occasions when (if you are like Albert Corde) you are strongly tempted to say what is really on your mind. Very dangerous. In ordinary life you dig far below your real thoughts. But if you come soaring by, why shouldn't the fellow shoot you down? On the other hand, he may be the exceptional case, and perhaps he won't shoot. True, Varennes was running any number of dependability tests. Did I play by Chicago rules or would I cut some exotic caper and embarrass or damage him? For his part, the Provost had decided that I didn't accept the Chicago rules. He had trusted me, and I had brought tons of trouble down on him. But Varennes also buttered me up, you might say. He led me on. He said that on his first undergraduate holiday in Paris he had read my columns in the *Herald Tribune*. He asked whether I was familiar with Solzhenitsyn's Harvard Address. Yes, and here and there I agreed with it. I hedged a little.

Varennes was checking my papers, as it were, to see whether my liberal sympathies were in order. I said that liberalism had never accepted the Leninist premise that this was an age of wars and revolutions. Where the Communists saw class war, civil war, picures of catastrophe, we only saw temporary aberrations. Capitalistic democracies could never be at home with the catastrophe outlook. We are used to peace and plenty, we are for everything nice and against cruelty, wickedness, craftiness, monstrousness. Worshipers of progress, its dependents, we are unwilling to reckon with villainy and misanthropy, we reject the *horrible*—the same as saying we are anti-philosophical. Our outlook requires the assumption that each of us is at heart trustworthy, each of us is naturally decent and wills the good. The English-speaking world is temperamentally like this. You see it in the novels of Dickens, clearly. In his world, there is suffering, there is evil, betrayal, corruption, savagery, sadism, but the ordeals end and decent people arrange a comfortable existence for themselves, make themselves cozy. You may say that was simply Victorianism, but it wasn't—isn't. Modern businessmen and politicians, if they're going to give billions in credit to the other side, don't want to think about an epoch of wars and revolutions. They need to think about contractual stability, and therefore assume the basic seriousness of the authorities in Communist countries—their counterparts, officials, practical people like themselves, but with different titles.

More of this real-sounding discussion, mutually comforting ideas. Those were the stillborn babies of intellect. Dead, really. I realized that long ago. They originate in the brain and die in the brain. Although it's true enough that a simple belief in progress goes with a deformed conception of human nature.

But Varennes got a bang out of this discussion. He didn't want all the time to be thinking about lousy rapes and murders. He knitted his fingers and said he had been reading a new study of the Munich mentality—Chamberlain's inability to dope out Hitler's designs. He asked me, "Where did you get your own catastrophe exposure?"

I said, "In Germany in the forties when I was young. But probably even more by what I read as a young kid in my father's library. He was an artilleryman in the First World War and collected books on the subject. I read a great deal at an impressionable age about trench warfare. In some sectors they paved trenches in winter with frozen bodies to protect the feet of the Tommies. You knew it was spring when the corpses began to cave in under your boots. I didn't stop with Remarque and Barbusse, or Kipling. I went into the memoirs of infantrymen and sappers. I recall an eyewitness account of rats eating their way into corpses, entering at the liver and gnawing their way upwards, getting so fat they had trouble squeezing out again at the mouth. There should be a shorthand for facts of that category. Or maybe there ought to be a supplement to the Book of Common Prayer to cover them. They have rearranged our souls. This *is* Lenin's age of wars and revolutions. The idea has gotten around by now."

The Public Defender said, "Except the Americans? The last of the ideology-negative nations?"

Needing time to think over these propositions, Varennes turned his head to one side, looking out from the big but unopenable window of his air-conditioned office. He was a steady and strong man. He would be steady when he worked out at the gym; also steady and strong while he was cutting his medium-rare New York sirloin at Gene and Georgetti's; presumably he would be strong in the sack, a pillar of muscle on the bosom of some swelling, soft girl. I, instead, was folded skinny into my chair, hands clasped low in my lap (between my cambered thighs—the legs criticized by my nephew), with my swelled eyes, yoked goggles, whitening brow hairs, pale dish face and long, uncomplaisant (only complaisant-looking) mouth. Varennes went on, "Our catastrophe is these inner city slums? Or—tell me if I follow you—the Third World erupting all over?" And as well as I can remember, he went on to say I was suggesting that a man like Mitchell was an unconscious agent of world catastrophe, or an involuntary one. "Do you identify him with terrorists or Third World fanatics? Are you asking whether we—the bourgeois democracies—are capable of coming to grips with the catastrophe mentality?"

The thought I had then I can recall clearly. I said that America no more knew what to do with this black underclass than it knew what to do with its children. It was impossible for it to educate either, or to bind either to life. It was not itself securely attached to life just now. Sensing this, the children attached themselves to the black underclass, achieving a kind of coalescence with the demand-mass. It was not so much the inner city slum that threatened us as the slum of innermost being, of which the inner city was perhaps a material representation. As I spelled this out I felt that I looked ailing and sick. A kind of hot haze came over me. I felt my weakness as I approached the business of the soul—its true business in this age.

Here a dean (or a writer of magazine articles) came to see a public defender to talk about a limited matter and their discussion became unlimited—their business was not being transacted. I was losing Mr. Varennes. Anguish beyond the bounds of human tolerance was not a subject a nice man like Mr. Varennes was ready for on an ordinary day. But I (damn!), starting to collect material for a review of life in my native city, and finding at once wounds, lesions, cancers, destructive fury, death, felt (and how quirkily) called upon for a special exertion —to interpret, to pity, to save! This was stupid. It was insane. But now the process was begun, how was I to stop it? I couldn't stop it.

Varennes seemed to glimpse this and he said, "It's still not clear to me what you have in mind, overall."

I took a different tack for the moment. I said, "You may have seen a long article in the paper recently. Fifty prominent people were interviewed on what Chicago needs to make it more exciting and dynamic."

"I think I saw that."

"Some of these people were lawyers, some were architects, one the owner of a ball club; also, business executives, advertising men, journalists and TV commentators, musicians, artistic directors, publishers, city planners, urbanologists, a famous linebacker, merchandising big shots, et cetera."

"The beautiful people," said Varennes.

"Well, now, some said we needed outdoor cafés like Paris or Venice, and others that we should have developments like Ghirardelli Square in San Francisco or Faneuil Hall in Boston. One wanted a gambling casino atop the Hancock Building; another that the banks of the Chicago River should be handsomely laid out. Or that there should be cultural meeting places; or more offbeat dining places, or discos. A twenty-four-hour deli. A better shake for the handicapped, especially those who use wheelchairs. But no one mentioned the terror. About the terrible wildness and dread in this huge place—nothing. About drugs, about guns. . . ."

"Yes," Varennes said, "but that's hardly a serious matter, the opinions of those people, what the interior decorators are saying, what the feature editors print."

"Quite right, but it made me think it was high time to write a piece, since I grew up here. Several generations of Cordes . . ."

Varennes then said that we had had a very thoughtful exchange, he and I, and that was nice in its way (but what of it? by implication). I had to agree. We sat there explaining evils to each other, to pass them off somehow, redistribute the various monstrous elements, and compose something the well-disposed liberal democratic temperament could live with. Nobody actually said, "An evil has been done." No, it was rather, "An unfortunate crazed man destroyed a woman, true enough, but it would be wrong of us to constitute ourselves judges of this crime since its causes lie in certain human and social failures." A fine, broad-minded conclusion, and does us credit. Although real intelligence is too vigilant to accept this credit and suggests to us all (since it is universal, the common property of all human beings) that this is only a form, and a far from distinguished form, of mutual aid.

Varennes went on, "I don't know what you'd get out of talking with Spofford Mitchell. I'd have to take this up with my team, and I'd have to ask Spofford, too. I have to respect his rights. I guess you would find it interesting to see where he is. The more serious homicide cases are way down below. The officers don't even open their doors at mealtimes down there. They push their trays under the doors. Then the rats come along and lick the icing off the bars."

"Icing?"

Varennes said, "The kitchens bake cake. . . ."

The look we exchanged over the cake was singular. But I broke it off, and backed down. I said, why not—cake and icing, why not? And it was too bad about the extra-security cells. I changed the subject. Of course I didn't want to get in the way, infringe on Mitchell's rights in any way or hamper his defense. He said he aimed to save Spofford Mitchell from the chair. I asked, was this a professional aim or a moral-legal one —was he speaking as a lawyer who didn't like to lose a case or did he have an obligation to save the man's life. He was not glad to hear this question. He was uptight as he said he saw no conflict, and what a bad gang the prosecution was. They kept a tally on their office wall. For a death sentence they chalked up a skull and crossbones.

Then he turned about and took the initiative from me. *He* became the questioner. He said I came down to inspect the Public Defender's office and put him on the defensive as a representative of the educated middle class as if I thought he held a sinecure, and was self-indulgent. At least this mass of trained muscle could speak honestly. The base of his big throat became charged with emotion. He wasn't angry yet, but a certain amount of indignation was developing, and he said that he didn't know yet where *I* stood, or from what point of view I was asking him whether he was being professional or moral.

Well, high feeling was—or might be—a true sign of earnestness. This was better than the first stage of conversation, in which we stated views that might begin to be serious—points for culture and serious concern earned on both sides.

In this phase of the talk I was quite happy, in a whirling disoriented way. I didn't expect him to let me interview Spofford Mitchell (I was a dangerous person), but it was in its way a satisfactory afternoon.

I said, "You're feeling out my racial views. No serious American can allow himself to be suspected of prejudice. This forces us to set aside the immediate data of experience. Because when we think concretely or preverbally, we do see a black skin or a white one, a broad nose or a thin one, just as we see a red apple on a green tree. These are percepts. They should not be under a taboo."

"Well, are they?"

"Yes, we try to stretch the taboo back to cover even these preverbal and concrete observations and simple identifications. Yes, you and I have been playing badminton with this subject for quite a while, with a shuttlecock flying back and forth over the taboo net."

Then he said, "Tell me, Dean, how do you see the two people in this case?"

"I see more than a white mask facing a black one. I see two pictures of the soul and spirit—if you will have it straight. In our flesh and blood existence I think we are pictures of something. So I see a picture, and a picture. Race has no bearing on it. I see Spofford Mitchell and Sally Sathers, two separatenesses, two separate and ignorant intelligences. One is staring at the other with terror, and the man is filled with a staggering passion to *break through*, in the only way he can conceive of breaking through—a sexual crash into release."

"Release! I see. From fever and delirium."

"From all the whirling. The horror is in the literalness—the genital literalness of the delusion. That's what gives the curse its finality. The literalness of bodies and their members—outsides without insides."

Sam Varennes seemed to give this some thought. He must actually have been thinking how to get rid of me. We're usually waiting for somebody to clear out and let us go on with the business of life (to cultivate the little obsessional garden). But my case was more special—I had just exposed myself as a nut, a crank in dean's clothing. That was our conversation seen from his side. Well, you never can tell what conclusions a man may reach when you try especially hard to talk straight to him. Neither party is good at it. No one is used to it. And all individual or true thoughts are essentially queer. But outsides without insides—what did that mean! Metaphysics? Epistemology? What?

We were sitting in his office in the Criminal Courts Building at Twenty-sixth and California. (Here Corde would have added to the printed version in *Harper's* that the sun was shining but even in broad daylight there was a touch of the violet hour. Maybe the architect had put a lavender tint into the glass to cut the glare. Maybe the atmosphere did it, or a metabolic derangement of the senses, a sudden increase of toxicity.) There had been many changes at Twenty-sixth and California since the old Bridewell days. New buildings had risen, a modern wing at County Jail, the achievement of Rufus Ridpath, for which his reward was disgrace, character assassination. Buses rolled up all day long. Prisoners brought from all the lockups in the city were unloaded here. The men hopped out by twos, handcuffed. As they went in pairs down the ramp to be processed in the jail, most were downcast or in a silent rage, but a few were having a hell of a time, reeling with homecoming spirits, yelling to the guards, "Hey, Mack! Look who's back!" They trooped in to be psyched, social-worked, assigned to cells.

Around the courts and prison buildings, viewed from the superb height of Varennes' office, lay huge rectangles, endless regions of the stunned city—many, many square miles of civil Passchendaele or Somme. Only at the center of the city, visible from all points over fields of demolition, the tall glamour of the skyscrapers. Around the towers, where the perpetual beacons mingled their flashes with open day, there was a turbulence of two kinds of light.

Varennes said, "When you talk about whirling you make it sound like the maelstrom—like Edgar Allan Poe."

"You mean apocalyptic. Once you start in with apocalypse you lose your dependable, constructive social frame of reference."

Now, here Corde would have added, in an improved version of his article, that Varennes was healthy, a normal person, with a preference for decent liberal thought. The details of his appointment to the Public Defender's job were normal in Cook County. It was not easy to get in without sponsorship. But he was a symbol, anyway, of the public demand for decency to which even big Clout was obliged to make (limited) concessions. Nevertheless, he was an educated and a decent man—jogged, pumped iron, his hobby was fixing up classic cars. And he was interested in what the Dean had to say. Dean Corde, sitting there, palms upward in his lap, one leg flung over the other. The Dean had an underbrow glance of swerving shrewdness. It seemed to interest Varennes in a theoretical way to hear the Dean talk about turbulence and whirling states, about subhuman incomprehension, about a woman begging for life when the lid of the car trunk was raised. Was his visitor trying to tell him (a middle-class fear) that the county was falling apart or something? Actually the Dean didn't seem to be that sort of Nervous Nellie or commonplace hysteric. Some part of him really was shrewd; at moments he was acute, even hardheaded.

"What would you like?" said Varennes. "Would you give the dead woman's husband a gun and let him take shots at Mitchell through the bars of his cell?"

"Did I suggest anything like that?"

"No, you didn't, Dean. I suppose I'm only fishing."

The Dean said, "Let me make it clear to you what I think. Your defendant belongs to that black underclass everybody is openly talking about, which is economically 'redundant,' to use the term specialists now use, falling farther and farther behind the rest of society, locked into a culture of despair and crime—*I* wouldn't say a culture, that's another specialists' word. There is no culture there, it's only a wilderness, and damn monstrous, too. We are talking about a people consigned to destruction, a doomed people. Compare them to the last phase of the proletariat as pictured by Marx. The proletariat, owning *nothing*, stripped utterly bare, would awaken at last from the nightmare of history. Entirely naked, it would have no illusions because there was nothing to support illusions and it would make a revolution without any scenario. It would need no historical script because of its merciless education in reality, and so forth. Well, here is a case of people denuded. And what's the effect of denudation, atomization? Of course, they aren't proletarians. They're just a lumpen population. We do not know how to approach this population. We haven't even conceived that reaching it may be a problem. So there's nothing but death before it. Maybe we've already made our decision. Those that can be advanced into the middle class, let them be advanced. The rest? Well, we do our best by them. We don't have to do any more. They kill some of us. Mostly they kill themselves. . . ."

Varennes asked, "Is this the conclusion you aim at in your article?"

"Oh, I haven't even begun to reach a conclusion. So far I'm only in the describing stage. What I'm telling you is simply what I see happening. The worst of it I haven't gotten around to at all—the slums we carry around inside us. Every man's *inner* inner city . . . . Some other time we can talk about that."

That was the end of our conversation. The telephone rang. An important call. He excused himself (I was ready to leave) and got rid of me. He promised to discuss the matter with his colleagues. He was a very nice man. Almost talkable-to. Those are the worst. For a while you almost feel you're getting somewhere.

XI

VLADA VOYNICH couldn't make it on Christmas Day. Travel had tired her, she explained to Minna on the telephone, but she would attend the funeral—of course she would be coming—and she'd visit them afterwards at home. Minna was busy with callers. It was Cousin Dincutza who brought this message to Corde. Corde was shut up in the room (by now it was his room). He had a bright winter day to look at. To mingle with visitors and make small talk was definitely beyond him. He didn't even try. Dincutza, replacing Gigi, who was very busy now, had assigned herself to look after him. She brought him a cup of tea occasionally, and she was his informant. He learned from her that Gigi's campaign to bring Valeria to the Medical School had failed—no lying in state. Petrescu had called just now to say that an announcement of the funeral had just appeared in the afternoon paper. It was to be held at the crematorium. No official honors.

In the morning Corde helped his ladies to organize themselves for the funeral. "It'll be cold as hell there," he said to Minna. "Remember what it was like the other day. That dome is a refrigerator." He urged her to wear her own American coat, but she wouldn't, she wrapped herself in her mother's synthetic fur. She had layers of sweaters underneath, so she'd be warm enough, she said. Gigi also wore an imitation fur. To Corde these coats were odd—the lusterless needles mingled brown and purple, they felt soft enough, they had a heavy look but no actual weight; it was up to the wearer to put life into them. Corde's motive, his theme today was to make sure that Minna had everything she might need. She didn't seem to want much. But if he hadn't offered, she would have noticed, abstracted though she was. Thankless work, but necessary.

For the funeral there was funeral weather. No more sun, that was gone, only linty clouds and a low cold horizon. At daybreak there had been frost over the pavements; patches of it remained. It was like the Chicago winter, which shrank your face and tightened your sphincters.

Cousin Dincutza was waiting with Traian beside the small Dacia. In the cold Traian's face was meaty, dense, the color of prosciutto. Under the zippered and belted leather jacket he was built like a small boiler. He wore the legs of his tight blue jeans tucked into his boot tops. At the corners of his mouth, the Mexican wisps, but when you saw him in profile the face turned Byzantine. It was the straight, long nose that did it, the full dark eye. Gigi, too, had this sort of nose, and unlike Traian, she had the classic long Byzantine neck. Age had made it muscular. Because she was so stooped now, the neck detached itself from the collar of the synthetic coat. Beneath her sadly intense brown eyes there were sallow circles. In her own setting Minna, too, looked like a Greek woman. This corner of Europe was after all Macedonian, Roman, Armenian, Turkish —the Eastern empire. If the cold reminded you of Chicago, the faces were from the ancient world. But then in Chicago you had something like a vast international refugee camp, and faces from all over. It was in Chicago after all that he, a Huguenot-Irish-Midwesterner and whatnot else, found the Macedonian-Armenian-Turkish-Slav woman who was exactly what he had been looking for.

Corde was put in the front seat. The three ladies were in the back. Dincutza, the poor relation, sat in a sort of padded Chinese jacket between the two synthetic furs. Traian's first stop was the hospital, where he took a branching driveway to the side of the building. Heavy but quick, a compact man in crunching boots, he slammed the door and walked, efficient, to the service entrance. They watched him go in. Traian, thank God, knew what he was doing. When he returned, he spoke to the bundled passengers through the driver's half-open window. He said Valeria was dressed and ready, and that the hearse was on its way, as arranged. He would stand in the main driveway to wait for it. Then he tipped his cap to Minna—or did he only resettle it on his head?—and handed her a brown envelope containing Valeria's rings, two of them. Corde turned in his seat as Minna shook them from the crumpled paper into her hand. It had been necessary to saw through the gold. They were clotted with blood. Corde drew back a little at the sight of the red drops, but Minna did not appear upset. She said, "This one with the stone was my mother's engagement ring. She never took it off." With her thumbnail she chipped off the dried blood and wiped the rings with a paper tissue. She slipped off her wedding band, put on the sawed rings, and then again the wedding band. Keep them in place.

The undertaker drove up in a panel truck. This was not what Corde had expected—a sort of dry cleaner's van, it would have been in the States. It backed up to the loading platform. The body was put in, and then Traian's little car followed the faded blue van-hearse through the city. In the center of town traffic was already heavy. The three ladies were silent, and Corde, in the fedora, had nothing to say. He looked out, noticing. What a man he was for noticing! Continually attentive to his surroundings. As if he had been sent down to *mind* the outer world, on a mission of observation and notation. The object of which was? To link up? To classify? To penetrate? To follow a sprinting little van-hearse over gloomy boulevards was the immediate assignment.

Around an uphill curve they came up to the mortuary chapel on its hilltop, trickling smoke from the dome into gray air. The panel truck had just parked and Traian pulled up behind it. The attendants were drawing out Valeria's lidless coffin. The technicians had seen to her hair; it was carefully dressed, wouldn't be exposed to the wind for long. Valeria was already being carried up the long flight of stairs in her silk suit, buttoned with silver Macedonian buttons, long in the family. Italian high-heeled shoes. She had been wearing those shoes last spring in London when Corde had noticed that she was stumbling, first in front of the hotel and then at Burlington House. Those were the heels that had gone crooked and tripped her up.

People stood waiting on the broad outer stairs, a beggar's opera crowd of aged friends. Again, the suits and coats, the Sunday-best outfits cut fifty years ago from good prewar material. One old woman was burdened by a real fur coat, so heavy she was hardy strong enough to carry it. She seemed determined to have a close look at Valeria. A ruined old husband supported her as she labored down the stairs to the coffin. They were just in time to see her as she passed. Valeria carried up the stairs by two men looked very much the Roman matron again, Corde thought, not the old woman he had electrified on her deathbed.

Under the center of the dome the crowd was large. The chairs on both sides of the bier were only in the way, no one wanted to use them. They were pushed back. Corde stood between Minna and Gigi; Cousin Dincutza was directly behind him. Friends of the family, coming up, understood only too well that Minna might not be able to recognize them. She had been gone more than twenty years. Some of them could not easily raise their heads for identification, their neck muscles had grown so stiff. Yes, many had the cervical arthrosia. There were splashes of dark pigment on their faces. Old mouths gaped up at you when they spoke. These were "Papa's colleagues," or old Party comrades, busted journalists, onetime boyars, former teachers, distant cousins. They came . . . well, they had their reasons. They were there to signify, to testify. They came also to remind Minna of their existence. "Yes, we're still here, in case you wondered, and we could tell you plenty. And your mother, she got you away, it was one of her great successes. Good for you. And for her. Now it's over for her, and soon for us, too. And this is what turns us out, in this gloom." People had spent extravagantly on flowers. There were only carnations, and those were hard to come by. Dincutza said, "*En hiver on trouve très peu de fleurs. Ils coûtent les yeux de la tête.*" She told Corde how many lei for a single carnation. Several times Valeria's face had to be cleared of flowers. Gigi, from the other side, told him that Petrescu alone was responsible for the wreaths. From official sources. There was a band of color also behind the crowd, on the perimeter. Along the curve of the wall were the square canisters of ashes, and pots of cyclamens with ribbons, lighted candles, burning speckles, fire grains, garnet points in the murk. There were candles, flowers, but it was freezing. Cold consumed Corde under his socks and sweaters. You could feel the fires below. Currents of heat flowed under the floor, but it wasn't the kind of heat you could be warmed by. It came from the openings at the edges of the raised bier, through the metal joints, from under the long bivalve barrel which would close when the coffin sank.

The speeches now began. Corde had lived long enough in Europe to be familiar with Communist oratory, the lame rhythms of questions and answers. "Who was this woman? She was . . . a comrade, a militant . . ." Terrible stuff. Under the dome it sounded exceptionally heavy. He supposed that by now there was no other style of public speaking in any province of the Russian empire, and he blessed his ignorance of the language. The last speech—they were all short—was delivered by Mihai Petrescu, who proved to be by far the most emotional of them all. He could not finish, he broke down. As if to cover him, the slow movement of Beethoven's Third began to vibrate unevenly from loudspeakers. The tapes were frayed, thready, quavering. Minna brushed away the flowers on the step of the bier, knelt by the coffin and kissed Valeria. Next Tanti Gigi bent over her sister's face. The synthetic fur bristled over her back.

Cousin Dincutza just then began whispering to Corde from behind. There was a last formality to attend to. Still one document to be signed. Regulations required that a member of the family go below for final identification of the deceased before cremation.

"By me?"

"Or her sister, or her daughter."

"Not a cousin?"

A cousin was *pas assez proche.* Otherwise, wouldn't she have done it herself? She saw that he was rattled. The thought of going underneath bristled over him. He'd have to go. What alternative was there? The old woman took his arm soothingly, as if to tell him there was nothing to be afraid of. He put his faith in her mottled face, brown buck teeth, sparse hair, goodness of heart. He said okay. This was not the moment to speak to Minna. Quavering, the big Beethoven chords now concluded; the barrel cylinder was closing and simultaneously the coffin began to go down, flowers tumbling after into the gap. The action was quick. The heavy drum grated shut. Valeria had gone below.

Immediately, Minna and Gigi were surrounded by friends. Corde followed Dincutza through the crowd. Traian was waiting at the head of the stairs.

Corde went first, they made way for him. He took air like a diver and trotted down into the increasing heat. It thickened about him. When he reached the bottom he saw Ioanna beside the coffin, which had just arrived. She was kissing Valeria's hand, laying it to her cheek. She wept and spoke brokenly to the dead woman.

"What's she saying?"

"Asking to be forgiven," said Dincutza.

For being a police informer? Just as Petrescu, the only speaker who had choked up, was a member of the security forces? But it wasn't likely that Ioanna would blame herself for having a police connection. If you didn't have one you weren't a concierge, and what was wrong with being a concierge? And if she was going to protect the old sisters it was necessary to be in with the cops. And it wasn't the packets of money, it wasn't the presents from London that she did it for. She would have said, "The Doamna Doctor loved me; I loved her." When Ioanna, crouching by the coffin, liked her eyes to Corde, the blue eyes burnt as if her tears were alcohol. Here was the heat he had felt underfoot in the hall. It was like a stokehold. It went into the tissues, drove all your moisture to the surface. Corde, who had come down shivering, now felt the hot weight of the fedora, his sweatband soaking. He tried by shallow breathing to keep out the corpse smoke, protect his lungs. The heat made you feel all your organs like paper, like the Christmas bell ornaments that used to unfold, all red cells inside and crackling when they were opened. His throat was drying out, and he began to cough. The punt coffin (with flowers) sat on a conveyor belt which moved forward a notch at a time. Weeping, Ioanna followed it. Again a stop. There were other bodies preceding Valeria's. Corde could only think of her as the dead, waiting to be burned. As between frost and flames, weren't flames better?

Traian was convincing the belowstairs official who sat at a high desk that this foreigner was qualified to sign for the family. His credentials had to be examined. He handed over the blue U.S. passport, still looking towards Ioanna. It was right that she should cry over the body, he even owed her something for it. Handed a ballpoint, Corde bent to the register and scrawled his name full across the page. Then he straightened, twitched off his glasses, groped in the inner pocket for the case—for the love of Christ, let's get out of here. There were sweat circles under his arms from the blasting heat. The people here weren't going to open those black steel doors and let them watch a coffin rattling over the rollers, entering, wouldn't show their fires to outsiders.

Dincutza now drew him towards the stairs again and Ioanna helped him as if he were a baby whose incompetence she pitied; but her bulk blocked his way. It was a tight fit in the staircase. Traian spoke sharply to her. On the first landing it was cold again. Corde felt cut in half by the extremes of heat and cold. So, again the freezing dome and the crowd surrounding Minna. Better this cold than that heat. Corde's breast, as narrow as a ladder, was crowded with emotions—fire, death, suffocation, put into an icy hole or, instead, crackling in a furnace. Your last options. They still appeared equally terrible. How to choose between them!

With Dincutza again making a way for him, he was brought back to stand beside Minna.

Ah, the American husband, the Dean. People had been looking for him. They had come to pay their respects, but they were here also to see this couple, the famous astronomer née Raresh and the man she had married. Old guys gave Corde rapid French handshakes, German bows. Gigi's interpretation of the large turnout was that people were telling the regime something. Well, maybe they were, but Corde did not see this as a demonstration. It wasn't because Valeria had fallen from grace, or because she had stood up to the Politburo or the Central Committee, or refused years later to rejoin the Party when they invited her. They came out with a sort of underfed dignity in what was left of their presocialist wardrobe, to affirm that there was a sort of life—and perhaps, as Communists or even Iron Guardists (it was conceivable), they had sinned against it—the old European life which at its most disgraceful was infinitely better than this present one. Most of them were too old to worry about reprisals, and in any case what had they done but dig their Vienna-made suits out of mothballs, put on the balding furs their backs were too weak to support, click heels, murmur French, pay respects to a leading member of their generation, et cetera?

Gigi said to Corde, "While you were away Vlada Voynich passed in the greetings line. But she said she would come later to the house. . . . Many important people are here. I have never seen such an occasion. I did not expect Dr. Gherea. He has had the decency, after all, and there he is in the line. Do you recognize him from the picture?"

Looking for the notorious neurosurgeon, Corde saw instead the heavy figure of his boyhood friend Dewey Spangler, the groomed beard, the full plum flush of his mature face. In moments of excitement he still executed the rapid double nod downward with his chin—charming mannerism, come to think of it. Corde thought, Whattaya know. He took the trouble to come. I didn't realize I meant that much to him. . . . Maybe I don't.

Introduced to Minna, Dewey made an approving grimace to Corde, he gave his okay. Some things hadn't changed—Dewey's expression of face, for instance. The essentials were what they had been, only more condensed. He said, "What about our drink, pal?"

"This afternoon?" said Corde.

"I'll rescue you at two o'clock. It's our last chance."

XII

BY noon, in clear, warmer weather, Corde welcomed the streets after the chill of the domed hall. It took hours to get the ice out of your system. Walking from the apartment with Vlada Voynich, he ventilated his lungs. All that day it felt to him as if he must make an effort to rewarm his blood and clear the smoke from his breathing tubes. He had had just time enough before leaving the house with Vlada to eat a slice of bread and butter and to swallow a large shot of Balkan plum brandy. Powerful stuff, but it went to his extremities rather than his brain; his hands and feet felt tighter, even the surface of his face was tingling as if a helpful pal had given him a few slaps for his own good. He was not entirely himself—the inward fever, ice in the system, he felt disarticulated. But why should he expect to be himself? At the crematorium he had gone through a death rehearsal. You couldn't rehearse death gratis. It had to cost something.

Vlada, glancing at him from the side, evidently saw that he didn't look well and said, "It's all been hard on you, hasn't it?" This was unacceptable, for some reason. He fended off her sympathy.

"You mean the whole December? Oh, I had some time to

myself. I caught up on my sleep. The old apartment is very quiet, except for the telephone. Minna's room was a kind of sanctuary. It's Minna who's having it hard."

"Where shall we go for this talk?"

"If it isn't too cold, and the sun keeps shining, I'd prefer the open air to a café."

"There's a small park just up the street. There used to be."

"It's still there. Minna pointed it out the other day—near her old school."

Vlada was a woman in whom you could have confidence—solid. She was large, her face wide, middle-aged, calm, candid, her complexion very white, the whiteness thick, almost opaque. Because of the length of her smile, her brown eyes, she had something in common with Corde's sister Elfrida. Her hair, like Elfrida's, was unsuitably dyed, far too dark. He would have hesitated to touch it. Dyes and fixative sprays took the life out of hair. But Vlada must have considered this when she made her decision. She was a chemist, after all, she knew what manufacturers put into dyes and sprays.

They settled on a bench in the sun between two pollarded trees—dwarf branches knobbed, knuckled with sealed buds on the bunched twigs, and the trunks wrapped smooth in winter hides. "Ah, how nice." He bent his hat at the back to protect his neck from the chill. A poor park, badly kept; but he was glad to be here with Vlada. He trusted her, he took comfort in her. The large head of hair parted down the middle and coming down in two waves, the wide teeth, the reassuring feminine breath—to him these were elements of stability. She had been married once, many years ago. Her ex-husband had been, by her account, one of the world's permanent and growing population of educated lunatics. Too bad—she would make someone a dependable wife, a good warm embracer, and stable; she would be sympathetic, intelligent, decent. But above all she was stable. Corde often sized up marriageable women in this way, entertained notions about them—maybe illusions was the fitter word. "You haven't got any news for me about the Lucas Ebry trial, have you, Vlada?"

"Only more of the same in the newspapers."

"There ought to be a verdict soon. Did Alec Witt send some messages for me?"

"I brought you an envelope. It's back at the apartment. . . . My brother told me about the Colonel. So now you've had a taste of our country."

"Your country? I thought you were Serbian."

"We are. Voynich is a Serbian name. But my brother married a Rumanian woman. That's how I got here in my twenties."

"What did your brother tell you about the Colonel?"

"Firsthand he doesn't know, but people like this generally are trained in prison administration, sometimes in those so-called psychiatric institutions where they keep dissidents."

"They do everything Russian style. If you're a dissident who can't see the socialist paradise, you must be sick in the head. . . . This Colonel must have lots of clout."

"The decision on a case like this probably was made higher up."

"Because Minna defected? Valeria abhorred that word. The regime did have it in for Valeria. Was it some old class thing?"

"Valeria was not a boyar. The Party is still hard on old boyar families. She was a Communist, all right, but she couldn't get rid of the old distinguished-lady manner. Besides, she was a Dubcek sympathizer. Anyway, she's gone."

"Yes. It puzzled me that they should make so much trouble in a case like this, of no political importance—just a mother and her daughter. Only rubbing it in that nobody has any private rights. Which is not news. But as you say, she's gone. . . . I would have liked to talk to your brother. He said he'd come take me for a walk."

"Oh, he couldn't do that, Albert. He doesn't talk. If you have a conversation with a foreigner, you're supposed to report it to the authorities, and my brother has to be specially careful with the authorities. By the way, if any of Minna's school friends wanted to invite her to their homes they would have to go and get an official clearance from something they call *Protocól.* Without *Protocól* they couldn't give her a cup of tea."

"So your brother couldn't risk it?"

"My brother was in prison for ten years, as a social democrat. Most of the time he was in solitary confinement. But then there was a mission of British Labor Party people coming.

They had met him in the old days. When they were asked whom they would like to see, they named him. So he was taken out of solitary. The cleaned him up, shaved him, gave him a suit of clothes, and he was taken to an apartment. He was supposed to be giving a dinner to the British delegation. It was about six in the evening. The guests were due at seven. At about six-fifteen, they brought in his wife. She had been in prison, too. Ten years. The one didn't know whether the other was still living. She was wearing a nice dress. No time to talk, the cook was an agent, anyway. Any minute, the bell would ring. . . ."

"Ah, what a thing. The visitors never caught on? Like G. B. Shaw in Russia. Like Henry Wallace. The old Potemkin Village trick . . . After which your brother and his wife weren't sent back?"

"They didn't send them back. . . . Last year his wife died." (In the earthquake? I won't ask, Corde decided. I may have passed her canister.) "And my brother lives alone, very quietly. No promenades with foreigners, though. He was sorry. He said you looked *sympa*. I told him he was right. Beech also thinks you're *sympathique*."

"I liked him, too."

"Have you had a chance to read the material I gave you?"

"Oh, I've had nothing but time. I didn't often get out of the house. Minna was afraid of letting me out alone. She thought they might pick me up on some pretext, and that would really complicate things. She may have been exaggerating, but I didn't argue; it was better to stay put. Yes, I read the documents."

"I didn't give you any of the technical material."

"I see that. No point in loading me with chemical data I don't understand."

"How did you feel about it?"

"Let's see—how did I feel? I felt interested. I felt alarmed by the danger. Naturally, I'm a good concerned American. I want bad things to stop, good things to go forward. I want democracy to win, and civilization to survive, but I don't want to become an environmentalist. For me it would be a waste of time, and I haven't the time to waste."

"Beech would never call himself that. He thought you might not quite understand and he asked me to explain more fully. To begin with, he has confidence in you."

"How can he have? We met only twice—or was it three times? That's not enough."

"He's read you."

"It was you that made him."

"Yes, but he thinks you're an artist in your line, not the ordinary kind of journalist."

Corde put down his head to let this pass over. She was trying to calm him with flattery. Were there so many signs of nervousness? Enough, probably. And why shouldn't there be? "Well, if I'm some kind of artist, I must be busy with some kind of art. I wish I knew what it was."

In the wintry sunlight Vlada's face was densely white. She gave him a fully open look. But he didn't have the confidence he had once had in these open looks. It wasn't that he distrusted Vlada, but people were never as sincere as they revved themselves up to be. They couldn't guarantee that their purposes were fixed and constant. Yes, constancy. Love is not love which alters where it alteration finds. What did love have to do with it? She only wanted to show that he could really trust her. And what he thought was, I'm pale, I look unwell, I look rotten, I'm skittish and jumpy—I'm all over the place (quoting Shakespeare out of context). She wants to be nice to me. I had an especially blasting morning. It's still with me. All right, I trust you, Vlada, but you want to get me to take on this job. Probably she's somewhat surprised that I don't jump at the chance. It's an honor. One thing is that her eyes (the chestnut color, this open look) are very handsome. The dark contrast with the white complexion does it. And the eyes are supposed to take me into a proposition I suspect to be dubious. I am willing to yield to the *beaux yeux*, but not necessarily to the proposition. But she's all right, she's a good egg, and I'll hear her out if she'll hear me out. She's devoted to Beech. I envy him that. He's got beautiful support. If he weren't a good guy he wouldn't have won such devotion. No, that might not follow, either.

She said, "I've worked with him for years, and I can recommend him."

"I like the man's looks. He's one of those American hayseed farm types who turn out to be world geniuses. He looks like Ichabod Crane."

Vlada said, "Your looks are misleading, too."

Bass voice, mild manner, plain appearance—yes. He said, "In *Huckleberry Finn* there's a circus clown who falls over his own feet but turns out to be a marvelous equestrian and acrobat. Maybe that's the classic American model—look like a poor stick but turn somersaults on a galloping horse. Well, I won't fence around with you, Vlada, on a day like this."

At this very instant Valeria might be going into the fire, the roaring furnace which took off her hair, the silk scarf, grabbed away the green suit, melted the chased silver buttons, consumed the skin, flashed away the fat, blew up the organs, reached the bones, bore down on the skull—that refining fire, a ball of raging gold, a tiny sun, a star.

He had stopped talking.

"You were saying, a day like this?"

"Yes. I seem to have a headache, something like eyestrain. You wouldn't have a Tylenol in your purse? I can swallow it without water."

"No. Am I giving you a headache by putting pressure on you?"

"The Provost tried to tell me not to mix into this, that it might do Beech harm to associate with me. I shouldn't put Beech in the line of fire; he has troubles enough."

"Yes, the Provost had a chat with Beech."

"And suggested that he might come in for some of the heat I'm getting?"

"Well, are you really so hot as you think? It's just some local unpleasantness. Beech could say his findings affect all Homo sapiens, and the future of the entire species."

"I see that. He talks continually about *Homo sapiens sapiens*, and hominid evolution."

"What impressed him, and it's the word he used, is that you aren't contentious. You didn't look for trouble, but you're capable of fighting. But the antagonism of people in Chicago is insignificant. He has another ball game in mind altogether." (Corde enjoyed hearing slang from these foreign women.) "Besides, Beech and the Provost have never gotten along.

Look, if you go to Washington and testify that the mining and smelting of lead have to stop and that the food and canning industries should be restrained and that the U.S. should lead a world campaign and start immediately to clean up the air and the waters, at a cost of billions . . ."

"It doesn't bring the college much financial support. It gets the FDA into the picture. And Witt would like to keep us apart—a wacko scientist and a cracked dean."

"Why worry about Witt?"

"It isn't worry. The college has been decent to me. Even Witt went out of his way."

"He put up the reward for information in the murder case. So if he feels you'd be bad for Beech you don't want to cross him. But this is merely administration politics. You've got to look beyond that, much further. Beech can't communicate. He says if he were to try to do this himself he'd end up like Bucky Fuller, giving incomprehensible lectures. I say nothing against Fuller—he's wonderful. I only mean there's a special cult public that loves high-minded kook specialists who preach salvation through organic foods . . . how to preserve the shrinking water reserves in a demographic explosion. But try to understand what Beech is up against. He has to start a world discussion at the highest level. You have a gift for getting the attention of a serious public."

"I'm good at sticking it to them, am I? That's probably true, but true because I have my own ends. I couldn't do it for other people. It wouldn't work. No one would pay the slightest attention."

"I see that. I do. But if you understood his ends, they might be yours, too. It wouldn't be a personal matter. It's far from a personal matter with him."

"Yes, he made that clear to me. Liberal humanist culture is weak because it lacks scientific knowledge. He'd communicate some science to me and then we could go forward. Minna also thinks it would *upgrade* me to associate with a man of science. Better than squalid Chicago, as a project."

"I can't really see why you're so skeptical. You're making me argue, fight."

"I don't doubt the nobility of Beech's intentions."

"He's put together a masterpiece of research."

Corde said, "The sun is moving. I'm beginning to feel cold again. Let's walk a little."

"I have enough layers so that I don't feel the frost," said Vlada. "When I'm about to come back to the old country I always begin to eat more. Last year all I could find in the shops here was boxes of salt, jars of garlic pickles, some sauerkraut. Now and then chickens turn up. You stand in line for eggs. Meat is hard to get even on the black market. Fish, never. Other Eastern bloc countries have changed from the original Stalin agricultural plan. This one, never. You can't even buy potatoes. I always fly back slimmer."

They walked in the sun, on the crackling gravel path. "You carry the weight with class," said Corde.

"Among my Serbian family in Chicago, the women say, 'How do you expect to get a husband if you don't reduce?' But I tell them, 'I may not get one even if I stop eating, and then I'm a double loser.'"

"According to your own theory, the more you eat, the more you stupefy yourself with lead."

She laughed and said, "It doesn't build up as fast as that." Corde valued grace in fat women. Vlada walked well, she knew how to place her foot.

"You can't get inured or mithridated?"

She shook her head. That wasn't possible. "Only poisoned. The nervous system is permanently affected. Kids become behavior problems, restless, frantic, and intelligence is permanently impaired."

"Therefore this world—and no matter what we're like, it's a delicious world . . ."

"Yes, is the answer."

"So the bottom line is that we eat and drink lead, we breathe it. It accumulates in the seas, which are getting heavier by the day, and it's absorbed by plants and stockpiled in the calcium of the bones. Brains are being mineralized. The great reptiles with their small brains wore thick armor, but our big brains are being hardened from within?"

He amused Vlada with this survey. More widely smiling, lips large and long, and her white face vividly warm, she said, "I love it when you get going, Albert."

"That's all right," he said. "I'm only thinking aloud. I'm

not talking myself into anything." Then he came near laughing, and when she asked him why, he said, "Well, you see what it's like here. We were at the crematorium just this morning and now we're discussing whether I should join Beech in his campaign to warn mankind against the greatest danger of all. At the moment I feel myself crawling between heaven and earth, and it is a little funny to be offered a big role: the rescuer. Christ, not me! The heart damn near jumped out of my chest when I had to go below to identify Valeria. I was dripping sweat and having fits and convulsions in the guts. And now I'm strolling in this park with you, I'm a gentleman again, taking the grand survey of man's future, the fate of the earth."

"I see that," said Vlada. "It's a bad day to try to get your attention for a project of this kind. Seems unreal and far away in these circumstances."

"No, I admire Beech, and I'd like to go into some of this with him. He probably feels he can't wait, pressed for time. Asked you to sound me out, get me started."

"I never led him to think that because we're friends, and I've been close to Minna since the Harvard days, that I had you in my pocket."

"Of course you didn't. And I'm trying to look as closely as I can at the whole proposition. Sometimes these 'hard' scientists are far out, like a separate species. It makes them especially interesting to me."

"You married one."

"I married one. That's different. That's love. It brings Minna back from outer space. Some I've met never do get back. Some are subject to storms of clear consciousness—my homemade term. Like turbulence, when the pilot asks you to fasten your seat belt. Then there are the ones who have strong musical leanings or are interested in poetry. Now that does appeal to me. And as for those that are far, far out, absorbed in their special complex games—I've often thought it possible that one of them might turn out to be clairvoyant. Just a little. But you have to be careful about this."

"Let me see if I'm following," said Vlada.

"Look at it this way: Lead as a mineral may or may not be the threat that Beech warns us against, but being 'leaden' certainly is a characteristic. Sometimes I say 'earthen'—we often experience this earthenness. Sometimes I say 'sclerotic,' or 'blind,' 'eyes that see not, ears that hear not'—and this leads up to 'the general end of everything' heralded by sclerotic, blind and earthen. 'Lead' is more sinister, maybe because of its color, hue or weight. Lead communicates something special to us about matter, our existence in matter. At Lakeview there was a kid who wrote poems, Joey Hamil, and I remember one of his lines about 'Thy leaden mace flung upon my weathered brow.' He didn't have a weathered brow. He was only sixteen years old."

"So you wonder whether 'lead' is just what Professor Beech has fixed upon but stands for something else that we all sense."

"That's possible, isn't it? The man is in his supersterile lab built for the analysis of moon rocks when it strikes him from both sides that an imbalance in the mineral realm itself threatens mankind, all of life and the world itself. There's poetry in that, isn't there? Man's great technical works, looming over him, have coated him with deadly metal. We can't carry the weight. The blood is sobbing in us. Our brains grow feebler. This disaster also overtook the Roman Empire. It wasn't the barbarians, it wasn't the Christians, it wasn't moral corruption: his theory is that the real cause was the use of lead to prevent the souring of wine. Lead was the true source of the madness of the Caesars. Leaded wine brought the empire to ruin."

"Bones from Roman graves do show extreme concentrations of the metal," said Vlada. "I've examined those in my own lab."

"And that was only Rome. Now it's the whole world. And it isn't the Grand Inquisitor's universal anthill that we have to worry about after all, but something worse, more Titanic—universal stupefaction, a Saturnian, wild, gloomy murderousness, the raging of irritated nerves, and intelligence reduced by metal poison, so that the main ideas of mankind die out, including of course the idea of freedom."

Corde breathed sharply, still ridding himself of (imaginary) smoke inhalation. He drew in the blue icicle-making air of the small park with its fallen fence of iron stakes—collapsed on weeds and bushes.

"I wonder if Beech thinks as romantically as that," said Vlada.

"It's you that work with him—but who knows," said Corde.

"And I'm sure I'm overdrawing it, but if there are mysterious forces around, only exaggeration can help us to see them. We all sense that there are powers that make the world—we see that when we look at it—and other powers that unmake it. And when people shed incomprehensible tears they feel that they're expressing this truth, somehow, one that may be otherwise inexpressible in our present condition. But it's a rare sense, and people aren't used to it, and it can't get them anywhere. Tears may be intellectual, but they can never be political. They save no man from being shot, no child from being thrown alive into the furnace. My late father-in-law would weep when he lost a patient. At the same time he belonged to the Communist underground. The Doctor would weep. I wonder if the Communist ever did. . . ."

"This is an interesting talk," said Vlada. "But I'll have to ask you to set me straight. . . ."

"Why, of course," said Corde. "I'm asking whether certain impulses and feelings which play no part in the scientific work of a man like Professor Beech and lie ignored or undeveloped in his nature may not suddenly have come to life. These resurrections can be gruesome. You can sometimes watch them—clumsy, absurd heart stirrings after decades of atrophy. Sometimes it's the most heartless people who are inspired after forty years of reckoning and calculation and begin to accuse everybody else of being heartless. But as I see Beech, he's innocent of that. The news, let's call it that, reaches him in his lab as he puts the results of his research in order. Like, 'This earth which I've been studying for a lifetime is a being, too. It gave birth to us all, but we are ungrateful, greedy and evil. . . .'"

"And this is news to him—to continue your argument—his feelings are untrained or undeveloped, and he gets carried away. I understand you better now. Even if he cried, which is not his way . . ."

"It wouldn't be a good approach to politics. You can see that I sympathize with him. And how I wish that clear, exquisite brains like his could resolve all our questions. They don't, though. It's endearing, however, that he looks like a hayseed, an Ichabod Crane, but that he's a man of feeling and even a visionary. He wants to protect and to bless. But then he begins to talk—and what neo-Darwinian stuff he expounds: the two-billion-year struggle by organisms in the biosphere. I'd rather eat a pound of dry starch with a demitasse spoon than read this. Truth should have some style."

"That's where you might be of help."

"What—if I tried to speak for him?"

"It would depend upon how it was done."

"It depends upon what he would expect. There would be no difficulty in agreeing that inner city black kids should be saved from poisoning by lead or heroin or synthetic narcotics like the Tees and Blues. The doubtful part of his proposition is that human wickedness is absolutely a public health problem, and nothing but. No tragic density, no thickening of the substance of the soul, only chemistry or physiology. I can't bring myself to go with this medical point of view, whether it applies to murderers or to geniuses. At one end of the scale is Spofford Mitchell. Did he rape and murder a woman because he put flakes of lead paint in his mouth when he was an infant? At the other end, are Beethoven and Nietzsche great because they had syphilis? The twentieth-century Faustus believed this so completely that for the sake of his art he wouldn't have his lesions treated, and the spirochete gave him his awful masterpieces as a reward."

"You'd call that kind of medical interpretation itself 'sclerosis,' or 'lead.'" Vlada followed this.

"Where Beech sees poison lead I see poison thought or poison theory. The view we hold of the material world may put us into a case as heavy as lead, a sarcophagus which nobody will even have the art to paint becomingly. The end of philosophy and of art will do to 'advanced' thought what flakes of lead paint or leaded exhaust fumes do to infants. Which of these do you think will bring us to the end of everything?"

"So that's how you understand this?"

"Real philosophy, not the groveling stuff the universities mainly do. Otherwise: I remember how I used to stare at Mendeleev's chart in the science class. There it all was—Fe, Cu, Na, He. That's what we were made of. I was so impressed! That's what everything was made of. But Pb is licking all the others. Pb is the Stalin of the elements, the boss. . . . Is it true that Beech has measured the age of the planet accurately?"

"Most geophysicists think so."

"I'm full of admiration. That in itself is wonderful—I listened over and over to the tapes he gave me. There are parts I can recall almost verbatim. He never meant to be a crusader. He was only investigating lead levels and this led him into horror chambers. Then he saw vast and terrible things all the way into the depths of hell, and so forth, and the material foundations of life on this earth being destroyed. And if pure scientists had really understood science they would have realized the morality and poetry implicit in its laws. They didn't. So it's all going to run down the drain, like blood in a Hitchcock movie. The Humanists also have flunked the course. They have no strength because they're ignorant of science. They're bound to be weak because they have no conception of what the main effort of the human mind has been for three centuries and what it has found. So Beech is offering me a trade. I must go back to the classroom and learn what it's all about—*really.* When I've understood the beauty and morality contained in the laws of science, I can take part in the decisive struggle—begin to restore the strength of Humanism."

"I see that doesn't sit very well with you."

"I gave up writing for the papers ten years ago because—well, because my modernity was all used up. I became a college professor in order to cure my ignorance. We made a trade. I teach young people to write for the papers and in return I have an opportunity to learn why my modernity was used up. At the college I had time to read scads of books. In Paris I was too busy doing art items and intellectual chitchat. I did have some interesting assignments. For instance, I wrote a few pieces on the poetess Tsvetayeva as she was remembered by the Russian colony in Paris. How her husband, whom she loved deeply, became a member of the GPU and was forced to take part in killings. But there I'm off the subject. I came back to Chicago to continue my education. And then I had to write those articles. There was no way to avoid it. The youngsters would say it was my karma. Well, there's low-down Chicago and there's high-up Chicago. There's Big Bill Thompson, and then there's Aristotle, who has also had a longtime association with the city, which amuses a great many people. Aristotle, believe it or not, became a great influence in certain parts of Chicago. Our great sister institution the University of Chicago revived him. A. N. Whitehead, you know, believed that Chicago had Athenian possibilities. Well, Big Bill, that crook, was a PR pioneer. His slogan was 'Put down your hammer, get a horn—Boost, don't knock!' And then there was Aristotle: A man without a city is either a beast or a god. Well, Chicago was the city. Or was it? *Where* was it, what had become of it? No cities? Then where was civilization? Or was the U.S.A. as a whole now my city? In that case I could move away from this chaos and live with Minna in a quiet place, and we could earn our bread somewhere in the woods, on a computer. The communications revolution could bypass Chicago or Detroit. Cities could be written off—dying generations, the blacks and Puerto Ricans, the aged too poor to move. . . . Let them be ruined, decay, die and eliminate themselves. There are some who seem willing that this should happen. I'm not one of them. Not me."

Corde looked at his watch. It was half past one.

"Yes, you have an appointment at two o'clock," said Vlada. "We'd better start back. I'll try to explain to Beech why you haven't yet made up your mind. But now there's something else. I have another message from Chicago for you; this one is from your sister."

"Oh, you talked with Elfrida. How nice of you, Vlada, to call her."

"She called me. She sent a message. I suppose it's a message."

"What was it that Elfrida wanted you to tell me?"

"She was worried how you would take it, although I said I couldn't see why you would object. . . . She's gotten married."

"What—Elfrida married!" The unexpected news gave Corde a sharp pang. He gave no outward sign of this. He looked away and drew in his lips, thinking, Why should she do *that*! Well, that's Elfrida. He said, "I see. She married Sorokin?"

"Yes, the Judge. Are you surprised?"

He had stopped; his hands were deep in his pockets and his shoulders raised high. He looked sallow.

"You don't like that?"

"She didn't discuss it with me," he said. "But then why should she? She's a mature lady. Am I surprised? Only a little—Sorokin isn't so bad. He's good-natured, virile, he's a lively extrovert. I suppose she did the best she could. What I feel is more like sympathy for her. But among the Chicago types she had to choose from, she might have done worse."

"Isn't she a Chicago type herself?"

"He's a few years younger than Elfrida."

"Yes, she mentioned that."

"Well, there it is. Are they off on their honeymoon? They can't go, I suppose. Not while Mason is still in trouble."

"Mason is very angry with his mother."

"Is he? If he hadn't shaken her up so much she might not have jumped into this. Going it alone was too hard for her. Well, Elfrida . . . she remarried. I dearly love my sister."

"She said that. But she was worried you wouldn't approve."

"Maybe I was standoffish with Sorokin. I doubt that he took much notice. Anyway, I meant no real harm. But why is Mason so miffed? . . . A silly question, come to think of it. Mason came to her one day with a paperback from the drugstore and said she had to read it. It was a how-to book—how the middle-aged woman could manage by herself and be a well-adjusted widow. He put her on notice, she was supposed to keep a holding pattern. He brought her this manual as a Mother's Day present."

"At least she didn't take *that* from him."

"No. I think that clinched it. When I saw her studying this paperback on how to be happy while sad, I was sure she'd marry. And it's foolish to ask why she didn't discuss this match with me. My views are as obvious as Mason's."

"It seemed to me she did the smart thing."

"Well, of course. It was better not to let me put my prejudices on record. Then I'd have to stand by them, she'd feel hurt, et cetera, and she's too intelligent for that."

"So she is—attractive, also," said Vlada. "Well, there's nothing wrong with a husband like the Judge. You said it yourself. I wish I could find one of those. He's good-looking and amusing. He has a plan to ride a raft down a South American river."

"He told me about it. At the time, he planned to do it alone. I can't picture Elfrida rushing through the jungles downstream like the *African Queen*, hanging on to her Samsonite luggage. She's a little old for it. But then there's nobody too old to be young. That's the present outlook. Actually age has been on her mind, naturally it has, but the book Mason ordered her to read—she was supposed to go it alone like a brave modern mother—put her in a furious depression. She saw the handwriting on the nursing home wall."

"Say that she married in self-defense. She's not a young girl like Lydia Lester."

"No, I still think she *might* have talked it over with her only brother. But she and I never could find the common premise. And maybe she thought the Judge would make Mason a good role model—an extrovert who drops from helicopters. Not like an uncle who goes fishing for porgies and falls in the drink. She suspected me of being unsympathetic, of being put off by the boy's resemblance to his father. But I didn't dislike Mason senior. He was the special kind of highly intelligent top-grade barbarian I grew up with—people like my own father and my uncles. People to whom I was affectionately attached. Elfrida's opinion is that young Mason isn't as bad as other sons in her set. He thinks he's one of the black street people, but at least he doesn't burn out his veins with synthetic heroin, the stuff that has to be shot when it's scalding. The addicts become paralyzed. Mason will never really hurt himself. He's not a hijacker, kidnapper, terrorist. He's no Feltrinelli." Here, Corde paused. Then he said, "You can't even talk about your poor sister without getting into broad social questions. That's the worst of it. Now I suppose she'll sell the house on the Cape and invest it in parachutes."

xiii

THE apartment was filled with callers. Some of them came with a second purpose: They wanted to get their children out of the country. You couldn't blame them for that. But how did one find sponsors, and where could you get dollars? You had to have the dollars.

Corde observed some of this. "Your mother was very fond of my daughter. She's an excellent student. She wants to do molecular biology . . ." then pulling a chair closer, urgently whispering, glancing significantly at the Dean. Minna listened in her solemn way. You never knew what she was hearing or whether her large eyes looked at you or through or past you. No, but she saw everything, felt it intensely, took it all to heart. Parents handed her term papers, manuscripts. She accepted them. Nobody was refused. She said she would ask the Dean to read some of them.

Corde said, "Spangler is expecting me."

"Yes, you should go out," she said. "When is the car coming? Yes, it'll be good for you to have a talk with your old pal. But don't stand waiting in the street. Promise you'll stay in the lobby. Please. . . ."

He took the packet from Alec Witt down with him, and had just time enough to see that it was stuffed with letters on his articles, mostly objecting, probably, alumni demanding that he be canned. Corde thought, I could do without crazy mail. Say what you liked about Miss Porson, she might be gross but her feminine instinct was to spare the Dean. You couldn't expect such delicacy from the Provost. But then (self-critical) why look to anyone to spare you? You didn't need to be spared at all, unless you believed that you had a very special and high calling and that right-minded ladies and gentlemen should temper the wind to you (a vocation left you shorn?). Some of the letters were addressed to him personally but Miss Porson had considered it necessary for the administration to see them. She had her own picture of the administration, a vision of the college hierarchy and of who owed what to whom. If you were Dean you reported to the Provost, who reported to the President, who went to the Board. . . .

Cremation or no cremation, a glistening day unfolded—business as usual for the weather. Corde, still bothered by smoke in his lungs, cleared his throat as he hurried into Spangler's limousine. Then the posh Intercontinental café and the big fragrance of the espresso machines. This time Dewey had taken a table by the window, warmed by the sun, an antidote to the horrible gloom of the crematorium. He was suavely solicitous—oh, what a smoothie Dewey had become in the great world! In the indoor sunlight he looked more corpulent —terraces of fat under his shirt, descending over the upswelling belly. He was belted beneath the sunny equator. There was only Corde to remember his skinny adolescence.

"Poor Albert. I'll order you a double Scotch. You were looking green in the mortuary."

"I had to go below and sign papers."

"Odd to see you in a foreign situation, so different from any other setting in the past."

"When you turned up, I had the opposite sensation. Familiarity. Do you remember after my mother's funeral—we were still at Lakeview—you came to the house?"

"No, my memory is dusty on this." (The little bastard. He was lying. But let him.)

"The living room was full of callers. You sat in a corner, behind everyone, and made faces at me."

Spangler was not pleased by this. "I don't remember that."

"Yes," said Corde. "You came to remind me of my duty as a nihilist not to give in to the middle-class hypocrisy of mourning, and the whole bourgeois sham."

"It sounds as though you hadn't forgiven me yet."

"I was angry with you, yes."

"I was an unpleasant kid, I admit. In those days I was the more eccentric one. Seriously, you couldn't hold it against me. This was back in the late thirties."

Skinny, wretched, weak, crowing, angry, Dewey in those days was eager to deal blows left and right. No, of course you couldn't hold it against him. "It's just a recollection—you grimacing and being so kinky when I was grieving so hard, just back from the cemetery. It was one of those winter days of cast-iron gloom, nothing but gray ice."

"It was Chicago winter, all right. But while you're remembering you might also remember that you were going off to Dartmouth that year. My family didn't have the money to send me even to the city college. And your father was sitting there, and he didn't like me."

"I don't think it was dislike. You puzzled my old man. When he found you in a dark corridor of the apartment on all fours, growling and being the wild beast, one of your special behaviors, he was mystified."

"Sure. But your people had money and connections. You got to Potsdam because of your father's pull. You wouldn't have been there if your dad hadn't been a crony of Harry Vaughan, who was one of Truman's guys. Same Harry Vaughan who accepted seven deep-freezers from lobbyists and a medal from Juan Perón."

"Well," said Corde, "all the better that you did it all on your own, without any Vaughans." He knew very well that Dewey had been a talented and tireless career politician. But how Dewey had made it to the top mattered little now. "And you were more eccentric than me."

"*Then* I was," Spangler said. "Okay, it wasn't your fault that your father was a fat cat hotel operator who drove a Packard and belonged to the country club. One thing I remember was that you took me to the family dentist and had him check my teeth and put it on your bill. The dentist was disgusted by all the tartar or plaque in my mouth—I never would brush. In spite of which there wasn't a single cavity. I was very proud."

Yes, a horribly vain and greedy child, Dewey. When he had two bits (on that day Corde was broke) he once ordered a sandwich for himself at the Woolworth counter on Washington Street—roast beef, a scoop of mashed potatoes, peas, a glazed flood of flour gravy or white sauce filling up the plate. Corde watched while Dewey ate it all by himself. He handled the knife and fork with jittering elegance and high breeding—a Chaplin couldn't have duplicated it. His wolfing sharp teeth and famished throat together with the hoity-toity, high-elbowed wielding of the dime store flatware. His ears were tucked under his cap. He offered his pal nothing. It may have been at that time that he shaved back his hairline to increase his resemblance to William Powell. Then the bristles came in, hence the cap. So it was extraordinary how he had civilized himself, somehow. Now he was a substantial public man, what cops in Chicago call "a notable," the companion of statesmen. He had made himself. And now this interesting reflection: Corde, too, had made himself. But then, deliberately, he had *un*made himself. Spangler reckoned that he had done this, that he had stopped writing for the papers, because he conceded Spangler's superiority and withdrew from competition. But this was not how Corde had unmade himself. He had a very different idea about the unmaking. And Spangler despite his theories and for all his world eminence was not entirely sure of himself with his old friend. Sitting with Corde, he felt himself still the squawking green kid, pushing too hard. Big-time deportment had not subdued the struggling punk.

"Yesterday I was received by Mr. and Mrs. President," said Dewey.

"What are they like?"

"He has a fine head of hair, but he looks like a Keystone Kop."

"Was anything said about my mother-in-law?"

"I said I had an old Chicago friend here, the husband of . . . the son-in-law of . . . Say, you are obsessed by those women. You *love* 'em. Mr. President made no comment."

"Still, with so much on your mind . . . Are you writing about the Warsaw Pact? And you remembered to mention it."

"Too late to help," said Spangler. He was modest when thanked, but he'd feel slighted, even outraged, if you failed to acknowledge his influence. Corde therefore acknowledged it. It wasn't flattery; more like charity. From Corde, Spangler needed the right signs. Corde's guess was that he had been a major theme in Spangler's lengthy analysis, the subject of countless groping hours on the couch. Their relationship, accepted at last, must have become an element of Spangler's maturity, his proof, bought with time and suffering effort, that he was indeed mature. In these meetings at the Intercontinental, Spangler was able to test the results of years of psychoanalytic therapy. He was all set now and the cure was firm. Still there was a certain uneasiness between them. Problems, once you conceive of them as problems, never let you alone, thought Corde. All occasions inform against you if you're problem-haunted. He was sorry for Dewey. Dewey still suspects that I know something he doesn't know, have something he just has to have.

His influence acknowledged, Dewey (turnabout) praised Minna. "Just as people said, Albert, your wife is a beauty. I also had a glimpse of the old lady in the coffin. She had quite a face—quite a face!"

Corde refrained from answering. He waited to see what subject Spangler proposed to discuss. Women, love, marriage? No, he'd want to talk about Chicago. Corde himself wanted that.

Dewey said, "That trial will be going to the jury in a few days. Did I hear that your cousin wanted to serve you with a subpoena?"

"That's correct."

"It would have been quite a trick—have a server grab you in the crematorium this morning."

"Maxie still amuses you."

"Not so much in person. I looked him up in Chicago a couple of weeks ago."

"What were you doing there?"

"Seeing my old dad, who's ninety-one years old. Max met me for a drink at the Drake. The cocktail waitress identified him. 'Aren't you the lawyer on that case? I seen you on TV.' Maxie preened. You made him a celebrity. He was just about to ask the girl what she was doing after work. He still has his lascivious hang-up. I remember his idea for sexual comfort stations—like public toilets. Drop four quarters in the slot and enter a private cubicle. If you and your girl friend happen to be walking together and feel hot suddenly, you can get relief at the next corner."

Corde was not to be induced to talk about his cousin's peculiarities. Intermittently he still saw the panel truck hearse, and Ioanna on her knees by the coffin putting Valeria's hand to her cheek; and himself frowning with horror and scrawling his name on the register, freezing, sweating, frantic to escape; and on the stairs the extremes of heat and cold like two faces of an ax, splitting him in halves. He took a large swallow of whiskey. Spangler said, "This erotic stuff doesn't amuse you. . . . You don't believe your cousin can win the case?"

"Anything can happen in a Chicago court."

"You're very hard on the old toddling town. Are things so different elsewhere?"

"I suppose not. Among other discoveries, I found that Chicago wasn't Chicago anymore. Hundreds of thousands of people lived there who had no conception of a place. People *used* to be able to say . . ."

"Ah, yes," said Spangler. "I'm with you there. It's no longer a location, it's only a condition. South Bronx, Cleveland, Detroit, Saint Louis, from Newark to Watts—all the same noplace."

"Why do people decide to live here rather than there?" said Corde.

"Where's their inner reason? you're asking. But that's the modern condition," said Spangler. "That's all old hat. But I have to tell you, Albert. I read those pieces of yours with intense concentration, fascination. They may not have opened my eyes to Chicago, but I learned a lot about you. The old friend revealed. You wrote damn queer things I'm dying to ask you about."

"For example."

"You won't believe it, but I actually made notes. It was on the Concorde and I had a few hours. You said the setting was like the Gobi Desert." Spangler brought out his pocket notebook. "You said that Chicago was part of the habitable globe, of course, the laws of physics apply here as elsewhere, blood circulates in the veins, the same sky is above, but if you grew up in this place there were moments when you felt that it didn't meet nature's full earthly standard. And so on. A curious lack of final coherence, an environment not chosen to suit human needs . . . favorable to manufacture, shipping, construction. Now, I'm not going to argue with you about its charm, but you looked at everything as if the ophthalmologist had put drops in your eyes. I'm frankly surprised that the *Harper's* people let you go on as you did. The language you used from time to time . . ."

"Give me some instances."

"Oh, for example, 'the harsh things of the soul.' How one lives with them. Or, 'Politically is there any salvation for this order?' Many statements of this kind. That's why I said last time how lucky it would be for you if your readers would get impatient and drop the magazine. But for me it's full of curiosities. I have my own favorite passages. One of them is the long paragraph about the tunnel and reservoir project. I wish I had copied it out—a mammoth sewer project costing more than the Alaska pipeline, capacity forty billion gallons, as wide as three locomotives side by side, running for more than a hundred miles deep under the city, maybe weakening the foundations of the skyscrapers. And all those tons of excrement, stunning to the imagination. It won't be the face of Helen that topples those great towers, it'll be you-know-what, and that's the difference between Chicago and Ilium. Now tell me, whom were you writing for? You pushed the poetry too hard."

Corde said, "I don't think I forced poetry on Chicago. Maybe it was Chicago that forced the poetry on me. But then there were also quiet, relaxed passages—descriptions of residential streets. I did quite a lot with domestic architecture."

"Yes, the interiors of the six-flats; that was quite good, quite good. Neighborhood life in the thirties, also. And the lakefront, and the Loop as it was before the war. You had good touches on the parks. I liked the bits about the parks. It's okay to be sentimental. Yes, the good old days when Chicago was a city of immigrants who had found work, food and freedom and a kind of friendly ugliness around them, and they practiced their Old World trades—cabinetmakers, tinsmiths, locksmiths, wurst-stuffers from Cracow, confectioners from Sparta. Those passages had lots of charm." Spangler here was noticeably condescending. He himself faced the big public questions—the Persian Gulf, Russian aims in East Africa, West European neutralism and NATO, the resumption of SALT talks. Such things were truly serious, questions with large, permanent implications. It was after all Dewey the plucked-chicken adolescent, the shrieker, the liar, the problem child, who had attained world distinction. What his blue eyes scanning Corde back and forth were saying was that the old Chicago was far away—Lincoln Park was far away and long ago, the thrills of Shakespeare and Plato, the recitations from "The Garden of Proserpine" and "Lapis Lazuli" and "The Waste Land," the disputes about *The Will to Power*, and what nihilism really meant, all of that, old pal, was boyhood, and one must detach oneself. (Corde hadn't detached himself.) Corde, still filled with feelings about Valeria, Minna, Elfrida (married!), was pleased to be here in the sunshine, however sad. Spangler was pleasant, mostly, garnished with so much beard and his hair in grizzled ginger waves. Why had he ever wanted to look like William Powell?

"One of your better ideas was to hunt up some of the Lakeview classmates. That part was all right. The guy from the central post office, the CPA, the probate court judge—I could take them or leave them. But you got lucky with guys like Billy

Edrix, the Air Force Colonel whose wife tried to murder him. I didn't remember him."

"I happened to. From the track team."

"That was curious," said Spangler. "Even though she was convicted on the evidence of the two hit men she hired. And she tried to poison him, too, and once tried to beat his brains out with the telephone as he slept. With all this proven he still had to go on supporting her by court order and let her occupy the house while the conviction was on appeal. What's *with* the judges?"

"Yes, and all the while Billy was still flying Air Force cargo planes between Germany and O'Hare."

When Corde went out to the far suburbs to talk to him, Billy said he only faintly recalled him. "Track, you say? Hell, I couldn't run across the lawn now."

Billy had built himself a new house, just finished, and they were standing in a raw hole in the ground ("This is gonna be landscaped") drinking beer out of cans. Soldierly Billy wore hunting clothes, well stained. He didn't invite Corde indoors. The jeep was loaded. It was moving day. "Why'd she want to kill you, Billy?"

"You say you want to write about the case. Well, I'll tell you a few facts that weren't in the paper. She first made a deal with one of the neighbors' boys. I finally caught on. I took the boy for a ride in the jeep and said, 'Why are you following me around?' I put a gun to his head and said, 'Tell me why or I'll kill you this minute.' Then he told me. She promised him a thousand bucks to do me in. He told it in court, too." Billy was not deeply angry; he seemed reflective rather. He said, "She even told the Federal Narcotics people I was smuggling opium from Germany and investing the profits in a nightclub, a girlie joint. Every time I landed, they would search my plane. Search? They tore it apart. They must have seen *The French Connection*. Those guys will listen to any crazy broad who wants to put you under. And the court wouldn't let me divorce her even after she was convicted. Not until there was a complete financial fair settlement. Fucking courts are just as crazy as the fucking broads. You want to write about the lawyers and courts, that's what you want to do, Al."

Spangler said, "If she was out to kill him, why did he stay with her?"

"He couldn't bear to leave the children with a murderess, he said."

"Oh, I see, the children. You and I have no kids of our own. You have a nephew, however. Is he an only child?"

"Yes."

"Like myself. But my mother was too poor to spoil me."

"She spoiled you all she could, Dewey."

"You'll never understand about my parents. Your father drove a big Packard. My old man was a straphanger. Your old man didn't want us to be friends, but my mother approved. She hoped your dad would hire me in one of his hotels as a night clerk and then I could save money and go to Wright Junior College. Then you and my mother had trouble. Big trouble, Albert."

So Spangler remembered the trouble and was now capable of speaking about it.

At the age of sixteen the friends had written a book together. "A Death on the El," they had called it. They had finished it during the Christmas holiday and tossed a coin to see which of them would take the manuscript to New York to get it published. Spangler, who had won the toss, tucked the manuscript under his sweater and started immediately for New York. It took him three days, hitchhiking, to get there. Meanwhile Corde, covering for Dewey, had lied to his weeping mother. "I'm sorry, Mrs. Spangler, he didn't say where he was going." Uncle Harold Corde, who was living upstairs at the time, talked with Dewey's mother and took a hand in the matter. Together they forced Corde to go to police headquarters with them. They went there by streetcar. But even the Missing Persons Bureau was unable to break Albert down. He was already receiving letters from Dewey in New York. Dewey wrote, "The reader at Harcourt loves my part of the book, but says that you should go into the hotel business with your dad." Uncle Harold, forcing open the locked drawer of Corde's dresser, called everyone together and read Dewey's letters to the gathered family. Corde's mother was then dying.

Uncle Harold was a Republican politician, whose candidate, Alf Landon, had been defeated by Roosevelt. He was a shouting, bullying old man, not taken seriously by anyone. He called Corde "an aesthetic little sonofabitch" and said he was going to take his books down and burn 'em in the furnace. Corde's mother must have been in considerable pain then, the cancer being far advanced, her face mummified, unrecognizable, and her dark eyes sharp, looking angry. (It was death she was angry with, not her children.) It was impossible to tell what she was thinking when Uncle Harold let Albert have it, but she must have been wounded. Corde remembered how heart-struck he was, and that he had carried his sore injured heart to Lincoln Park. That was always one of the peculiarities of Chicago: Where could you take your most passionate feelings? Carry them into what setting? It was exactly this time of year, Christmas week, getting on for January. The wind came down unchecked from the Arctic—white snow, black chain fences, trees bare, sky blue. Four decades and two continents didn't make much difference, for the present day was much like the other one—freezing blue, the sunlight, and women dying or dead.

Was it possible that Spangler was looking at him with large amusement? Fat face, plump hands, blue eyes, warm lids, brown, swelling and lacy—the sunlight revealed all their intricate puffiness and dark stain. Spangler tucked his laughter under his armpits, where his fingers were inserted, and crossed his smallish feet. Of course (Corde the persistent, almost fixated observer) Spangler now had a drum belly. His sharp teeth were clean, he had accepted the necessity to brush. Psychoanalysis and prestige had sobered him, cleaned him up, he no longer had the screaming-meemies. It was funny how fortunate a man could become, American style. Nietzsche had said that it was better to be a *monstre gai* than an *ennuyeux sentimental*. When Dewey told Miss Starr in the tenth grade that he was an orphan adopted by the cannibals who had eaten his parents and told of his escape on a raft from an African island, he was a *monstre gai*. Now, with Brezhnev and Kissinger and Indira Gandhi, he had still more thrilling real-life adventures. He had every reason to be pleased, therefore. But there was something that he wanted still from Corde. Could it be a heart-to-heart talk? No, not that. Could it be an edifying relationship? Maybe that was closer to the mark.

Spangler said, "You wrote mean things to me about my old lady."

"I felt mean about Uncle Harold."

"That old brute. He gave you a pretty good stab."

"He had your letter to stab me with."

"Yes, that must have been lousy for you, and I suppose your mother did take it hard. But it was just adolescent high jinks. Besides, Albert, that injury only put your back up, just as your Potsdam scoop put up mine. We're a pair of strong-willed and terrifically obstinate guys. For you the enemy was highlighted—Uncle Harold, the vulgar American mind. Wanted to burn your books of philosophy and poetry. It all came out in those *Harper's* sketches of yours. They really are queer work, and completely characteristic of you. I became so absorbed in them on the Concorde that I was in Paris before I knew it. Shortest flight I ever had. There were passages I can't say that I got—too cloudy, and even mystical. But still the old preoccupations. If I were you, I would have steered clear of guys like Vico and Hegel. Hegel saying that the spirit of the time is in us by nature. Where does that get us?"

"It gets us that this world as you experience it is your direct personal fate."

Dewey disliked being mystified. Aggressive and dogged, he made a movement of dismissal. "That doesn't tell me anything."

Corde weighed the matter. Shall I talk? . . . I'll talk. "I meant that we'd better deal with whatever it is that's in us by nature, and I don't see people being willing to do that. What I mainly see is the evasion. But this is a thing that works on the substance of the soul—the spirit of the time, in us by nature, working on every soul. We prefer to have such things served up to us as concepts. We'd rather have them abstract, stillborn, dead. But as long as they don't come to us with some kind of reality, as facts of experience, then all we can have instead of good and evil is . . . well, concepts. Then we'll never learn how the soul is worked on. Then for intellectuals there will be discourse or jargon, while for the public there will be ever more jazzed-up fantasy. In fact, the two are blending now. The big public is picking up the jargon to add to its fantasies. . . ."

"You're going too fast for me," said Spangler. "So you decided to let everybody have it, and force everybody to undergo the facts in some form."

"To recover the world that is buried under the debris of false description or nonexperience."

"It wasn't the material in your pieces that gave me trouble," said Spangler. "Some of that was damned interesting. It was the way you put the facts that was hard to take. Maybe it was your attitude that was intolerable. A modest journalist would have said that he was working up some stuff about Chicago. In the old days he would have said the city was his beat. But you're saying, 'I was assigned to it,' which makes it like a visionary project, or the voice of God saying, 'Write this up, as follows.' Now, believe it or not, you didn't sound much different forty years ago. When I read *Harper's* I was hearing echoes from our youth."

Echoes of youth implied that little or no progress had been made. But Corde was not bothered by this. Spangler, the world-communicator, was a maker of discourse (increasing the debris of false description). Twice weekly, readers all over the U.S. picked up their fresh thick newspapers and turned to Spangler's column to tune up their thinking on world affairs, to correct their pitch. Dewey was quoted often by *Le Monde* and *The Economist*, so why should he be bothered by the opinions of his adolescent sidekick? He had every reason to be confident, relaxing in the plate-glass warmth of the Intercontinental. In the café you saw about you East German trade representatives, members of Chinese missions, costumed, turbaned Nigerian ladies—and as a final bonus two old buddies from Chicago, one of them a figure of international stature. And Corde wondered whether he wasn't being interviewed by Dewey. Interviews were Dewey's great strength. Pressing for true answers, he fixed you with a hard eye, he was in control. "How seriously should I take you?" was his big unspoken question. But this was more than an interview. Spangler was testing whether his old pal was the real thing. Corde had written about Vico and Hegel like a humanist-professor-intellectual. And Spangler, although he had risen so high, gone so far, wanted to rise higher still. Above the Walter Lippmann bracket to which he aspired there was the André Malraux bracket. There you breathed a different air altogether, reviewing with De Gaulle the whole history of mankind, doing Napoleon, Richelieu, Charlemagne, Caesar, touching on the way Christianity and Buddhism, the arts of ancient China, the astronomy of Egypt's priesthood, the Bhagavad Gita. Chicago origin need be no hindrance. A man could pitch himself beyond the Lippmann category, if he hit upon the right combination of forces.

An odd silence came over Spangler. Corde thought, I'm unjust. I'm being too satirical. I'm going to miss something about the man while I gratify my taste for wicked comment.

The impression Spangler now gave Corde was that of a man in a control tower monitoring unusually heavy traffic. He said, "We were boys together, and you may think, Good old Dewey has worked his way to the top and stepped on quite a few fingers and even faces en route; now he wants to enjoy a sentimental hour. And since I was a little creep who turned into a big-time oracle, you may be amused. As much as you can be amused on the day of this funeral, which seems to upset you so much. But what would you say to taking stock, or doing an inventory?" He was agitated, and Corde, too, was anything but calm.

He gave Dewey plenty of time. He himself was under the influence of—well, of Scotch whisky and of strong coffee odors; also of the methyl blue of sharp winter flashing from the beveled corners of the plate glass, the streaming threads of orange, the colors of the spectrum, quivering with heat on the table. Then for some reason, with no feeling of abruptness, he became curiously absorbed in Dewey: blue eyes, puffy lids, tortoise-shell beard, arms crossed over his fat chest, fingers tucked into armpits, his skin scraped and mottled where the beard was trimmed, the warm air of his breathing, his personal odors, a sort of doughnut fragrance, slightly stale—the whole human Spangler was delivered to Corde in the glass-warmed winter light with clairvoyant effect. He saw now that Spangler was downslanted in spirit. The slight wave of his hair, which had always had an upward tendency, apparently had reversed itself. And he used dye, that was perfectly plain. But this was a mere observation and no judgment. *Let* him touch up his hair. Seeing him so actual, vanities were dissipated, you were in no position to judge, and there was no need for judging. Spangler's rays were turned downwards, and his look openly confessed it. He had been a kook, but certainly no coward. Maybe on this death day Corde was receiving secret guidance in seeing life. Perhaps at this very moment the flames were finishing Valeria, and therefore it was especially important to think what a human being really was. What wise contemporaries had to say about this amounted to very little.

"Where would you like to begin?"

"We already have begun," said Spangler, softening his tone. All he wanted, probably, was to feel secure in ordinary human dealings. With an old pal, this should be possible. As a distinguished person, he couldn't afford to take chances, come off looking foolish. "Let's look at the curve of your career, for a minute. You started with a bang, describing Stalin, Churchill, Truman, Attlee. You actually *saw* those guys! But then you settled down on the *Herald Tribune* doing lighter cultural features, very good, no special world perspective. All of a sudden, in your mid-forties, you head back to Chicago and turn into a professor. Well, of course America is where the real action is. This is terrible news to have to tell humankind, but what else is there to say? The action *is* at home! And so you go back." Spangler was earnestly controlling his face and the effort itself had a distorting effect. He was looking almost lewd, but the source of the intensity was mental. "You're back to America, a prof and a dean. Is it a kind of retirement? You're reading books, talking to academics, trying to get the right handle on things, I presume. Then all at once it's: Bam! Here is how things look. Is there any salvation for this order? The harsh things of the soul, what do we do about them in America? You hit Chicago with everything you've got. Mostly, it turns out, you're partial to two black men. One runs a cold-turkey rehabilitation center for heroin addicts and the other is warmly human to derelicts and criminals in County Jail. Everybody else is only trying to contain this doomed population of blacks—the underclass."

"Or to hustle it opportunistically, politically."

"You made that plain enough," said Spangler. "It was when you got apocalyptic about it that you lost me: the dragon coming out of the abyss, the sun turning black like sackcloth, the heavens rolled up like a scroll, Death on his ashen horse. Wow! You sounded like the Reverend Jones of Jonestown. You give yourself the luxury of crying out about doom, and next thing you know you're up to your own neck in squalor. So unless your purpose was to get the discussion into a better key, I can't see what you gained. Actually, I think you were sore as hell with your academic colleagues, because they hadn't found the right key to play all this in. Isn't that what they were supposed to do—and why they got so many privileges?"

Corde lowered his large round head towards the brilliant and twisting prismatic colors of the table, puffing up his hand to stop his unbalanced eyeglasses from dropping, and said, rumbling, "I admit some disappointment there. . . . My late brother-in-law, Zaehner, used to tease me about academic life. He would say a professor with tenure is like a woman on welfare with ten illegitimate kids. They're both set for life, never again have to work." Corde immediately began to regret saying this. It was mischievous. And he had forgotten that they were no longer boys in Lincoln Park. There was a gap in judgment here. They were men now—journalists, at that, quick to see an opening. But Dewey, laughing hard (turned on, ignited), was showing his sharp teeth and putting the heels of his hands to his sides just as he used to do forty years before.

"That's great, Albert, just great. Was Elfrida's husband such a wit? I didn't realize it."

"Her late husband."

"I heard you the first time. He passed away?"

"Three, four years ago. My sister has just remarried."

"Pretty woman, Elfrida. I made a pass at her once. I suppose she told you."

"Yes."

"But you never mentioned it—that's because you were brought up an American gentleman. If I had had that kind of information on you, I would have baited you. You used to say that your people were Pullman car Americans. Not quite accurate. They didn't take an upper berth; they traveled in a drawing room. And wasn't your mother's father governor of the Virgin Islands, or was it the Philippines? You see, you had better breeding than me. So when I propositioned your pretty sister she laughed at me. I *was* a preposterous kid. But I told her preposterous kids were the most uninhibited sex partners. Still, I couldn't get her serious attention. You might not have liked it if she had taken up with me—it would have been quite a test of your breeding to be an uncle to a child of mine. But she snubbed me. Serves her right that her boy is such a twerp and nuisance—what's eating him, anyway?"

Corde lifted his shoulders. "Search me."

"Oh, come on, Albert. . . . It isn't like you not to take a view. Don't deprive an old friend of your interpretation."

"I was saying just a while ago that you couldn't even mention your only sister without broaching all the big social questions."

"Whom did Elfrida marry this time?"

"A judge."

"That'll go down big with her radical son. But since he gives his mother so many legal headaches . . ."

". . . She made an aspirin marriage."

Spangler warmly blinked at him, approving. "Do you say things like that among academic friends? . . . I didn't criticize you for becoming a prof, Albert. I've pushed you about it mainly from curiosity. I myself have thought it would be nice to retire to an academic setting eventually, I never got to go to college. But it shouldn't be too hard, with my record in public life, to become a fellow somewhere."

"You ought to be able to name your own spot, Dewey, like Hubert Humphrey or Dean Rusk."

Spangler received this with a flush of self-congratulation, but he also inclined his head in thanks. Corde thought, I'm not full of rancor and envy, and it pleases him. My mental attitudes, he says, haven't changed in four decades, but then neither have the personal ones, and it may be a pleasant surprise. He may inspire satirical thoughts, but I don't feel like sniping. I have no impulse to pick on him. If he's a fat little obnoxious bastard, which is what I think *he* thinks he is, it doesn't matter, because I evidently love him as I used to do. I can't take it back. I must be immature that way. Affections like this probably seem grotesque to a worldly and psychoanalyzed old party like Dewey.

"I may ask you for advice on universities one of these days, although to judge by your attitudes you may not be the party to turn to."

"When I went off to Dartmouth after my mother died—and

was mourning more than I realized—I had wonderful teachers whom I never forgot, and I read Plato with them, and the poets."

"Yeah, yeah—Chapman's Homer, realms of gold. And that's what you wanted to come back to, more of the same—culture and civilization, the stronghold of humanism. Stupid to expect it. Nevertheless, such a setting would be nice for the declining years, if I have any."

"Why, aren't you well? You look okay."

"I seem more or less normal, I suppose. I guess I can tell you this, although it would hurt me if it got around. But you have too many headaches of your own to start gossiping about me. I went to Chicago to have surgery. Diverticulitis."

"Is that serious? Isn't it what Eisenhower had?"

"It's serious enough for me to be wearing the bag. Do you want to see it?"

"Not particularly."

Dewey showed it to him anyway, impulsively pulling out his shirt. Yes, there was the square plastic envelope. Something dark and warm was inside. Corde's teeth were on edge.

"I'll be back in surgery by and by. They'll try to hook me up again. There's more to see. I have a flap of flesh here."

"I'll take your word for it. What is there to hook up?"

"Two ends of the intestine. The doctors can't promise success."

So this was why Spangler had gone out of his way, had sent his car twice, had made time for Corde in a busy schedule, had come to the crematorium. He's not a man for funerals. He was wrecked, sick, his insides were uncoupled. He stared at Corde. His acquired controls were turned off and the double ducking mannerism returned, as if he could not bring his chin to rest. His expression was angry. But he pushed his shirttail back matter-of-factly.

"They'll sew you together. You'll forget all about it by summer. I'll take you back to Woolworth's lunch counter and buy you a roast-beef-and-white-gravy sandwich."

"Don't talk like a jerk. You're a horse's ass, Albert."

The creature of flesh and blood going through the mill—only one possible outcome. That was Spangler's message. What are you trying to give me! He was flushed, the heat rushing into his blue eyes. His look was fiercely sarcastic. Well, they were on a human footing, at least. Spangler said, "In this condition, what woman will sleep with me?"

"That's a thought. But if it's that important . . ."

"If it's that important, I can get lists of ladies with the same trouble. Or else there are kinky broads enough. Masses of female masochists." He was softening. "Or maybe you think elder-statesmanship has calmed me down and I can't be the horny little bastard I was. You wouldn't be completely wrong. I've had my innings. Well, the bag is depressing, it throws a shadow on my self-image. Otherwise I'm in good health enough. Remember, I never had cavities in my teeth, nor any other complaints until this one, if you don't count complaints of the psyche or character. I can tell how you thought of me, how you *formulated* me, Albert—a near psychopath who was saved by becoming a shaper of public opinion. Sometimes, when driving up to the White House to be recieved by Bugs Bunny himself, I would get weird, deep tingles in the nervous system. I would think of you and some laconic wisecrack you might make in your basso profundo. But with all this your feeling is that I'm not so bad for a comic monster, sort of sweet, in fact. But now, to use a gangland expression, death has me fingered."

Corde said, "That's not such a bad résumé." What he felt was a compression inside, a stirring in certain of his organs; sadness, then faintness, something like "fatedness" and lastly immense pity. This flow of feeling occurred quite slowly. It took its time. It wouldn't do to show the pity. Spangler would be offended, and quite rightly.

"I have to confess to you, there *was* one bit in your articles that agitated me, Albert. It was the patch about your talk with the Public Defender in the case of the rapist who kept the woman in his trunk and killed her. After he killed her he hid the body under trash in a vacant lot. And then you shifted into that Vico of yours. I got sore, I thought what a fucking time to get pedantic! I cursed you for it. But then I saw why you were doing it."

"It was about the human customs that are observed everywhere. And if not, why not. . . ."

"I know what it was about. I don't need your help. Children

born outside the law and abandoned by parents can be eaten by dogs. It must be happening in places like Uganda now. The army of liberators who chased out Idi made plenty of babies. Eaten by dogs. Or brought up without humanity. Nobody teaching the young language, human usages or religion, they will go back to the great ancient forest and be like the wild beasts of Orpheus. None of the great compacts of the human race respected. Bestial venery, feral wanderings, incest, and the dead left unburied. Not that we have any great forests to go back to. There was Jonestown in the Guyana jungle, where they put on public displays of racially mixed cunnilingus as a declaration of equality, and where some cannibalism seems to have occurred, and finally the tub of Kool-Aid poison. But that wasn't the ancient forest, it was the city. . . ."

Corde had pulled his hat and coat towards him.

Spangler said, "We still have so much to talk about."

"You'll be taking off this evening?"

"Back to Paris. Well, this has been an interesting hour. I haven't maintained such a long relationship with anybody else. It would have brought us a lot closer together if you had been an analysand. Believe it or not. But in spite of the barrier, I can't tell you how curious it's been. You were hell-bent from the beginning to unfold your special sense of life. You were blocked. I saw it and I didn't predict much. Then, all of a sudden, it all pours out. There's a passionate but also a cockamamy flowering. You still haven't had a complete deliverance. . . ." Spangler waited for an answer, but Corde was silent, looking over the tops of his glasses into the street, at the first signs of dusk. Spangler said, "I see you've checked out on me. How long do you expect to stay here?"

"I want to leave as soon as we're able. Get my wife out."

"I'll call you from abroad if I see any news. Anything else I can do?"

"Not unless you want to smuggle out a couple of Tanti Gigi's featherbeds, or a few valuable Macedonian heirlooms," Corde said.

XIV

GIGI struggled in the vestibule with a stepladder, much beyond her strength to haul. She wanted the high storage bins opened. Corde took over. You wouldn't have believed how spacious those bins were. They contained boxes and boxes of stuff. "All this was kept for Minna," said Gigi, and she was determined that Minna should have a full inventory, every last doily and cake fork accounted for. Since condolence calls were taken in the dining room, and the parlor was not private enough, the boxes were opened in Minna's room. So out came old letters, diaries, Turkish trays in beaten metal, damask linens, tongs and snuffers, a cut-glass fruit dish, a fifteenth-century treatise in Latin, printed in Germany, a monastic accounts book in Greek sewn with waxed thread which was snarled into lumps, a small Gallé vase, a box of table silver, carved screens, prints and drawings, and also coins and trinkets. No article of real value could leave the country. Everything had to be appraised and taxed. "National treasures" would be confiscated. Now and then Minna came in and looked at these relics, Gigi identifying the photographs. "This is our great-uncle Boulent, who was a trigonometry teacher in Thessalonike." Corde was fascinated by the objects that came out of the boxes. Gigi made Oriental gestures to express their value, circling and stirring with her finger. She wrote on a piece of paper, "I shall show which objects *must* reach Chicago." She then tore up the note and put a match into it in the ashtray. With top-secret significance, she touched the Gallé vase. Next, the cut-glass fruit dish. It was diamond-shaped and narrow and Corde didn't himself much like it, a foolish elaborate object, but that was neither here nor there. She put her finger also on a small Roman landscape in watercolors. "Yes, but how do we pull this off?" said Corde. Gigi tapped him on the breast. She had great confidence in him. Wasn't he a dean? Didn't he contribute to national magazines? The Ambassador sent for him, limousines came to the door.

Corde persuaded Minna to come out into the air for half an hour. Helping her into her fleece-lined brown leather coat, he was aware of her thinness—the *structural* Minna, what you would see on X-ray film, came through. In the sunlight her face was as white as meringue. A small hollow had formed just below her underlip. That was where the grief control seemed concentrated. He couldn't help but think of his own mother, the wasted mummy look of her last days, the big furious stare she would turn on you. He told Minna, "I hope Gigi doesn't get too serious about the relics she's collected."

"My mother hid them away, and I don't want those bastards to take them."

"We may have to pay to get them out."

"The appraisal will be unreal. And with what money?"

"I'll come up with the money. What I really wanted to talk about was going home."

"I can't, right away."

"We'd better, for all kinds of reasons. There isn't much of December left. The new term starts soon. Besides, there's the time at Mount Palomar they're going to reserve for you."

Corde knew what he was doing. Professionally Minna was superconscientious. Nothing was allowed to interfere with duties. Mostly it amused him that this beautiful and elegant woman should behave like a schoolgirl, with satchel and pencil box. When she was getting ready to set out for the day, he sometimes joked with her. "Got your compass and protractor? Your apple for teacher?" Together with her big fragrant purse, a bag of scientific books and papers was slung over her shoulder—ten times more stuff than she needed. But occasionally the gold-star-pupil bit did get him down, and she was cross with him, interpreting his irritation as disrespect for her profession. It had nothing to do with that. She put in a ten-hour day, never missed a visiting lecturer, a departmental seminar. Her tutorials, rehearsed far into the night, must have been like concerts. What he minded was her fanatical absorption. He often had dinner waiting for her, and towards seven o'clock began to listen for the sound of the key in the lock. A lady wrapped up in astronomy going about Chicago after dark? She gave him (it was absurd!) wifely anxieties. But now (manipulative, but it was justifiable) he was using the astronomy to get her back to Chicago.

"Of course we've got to leave," she said. "But I have to

make sure first that Gigi is protected. This isn't even her legal address. The apartment is in Mother's name. Can I let the old girl be put out in the street?"

"It's not a matter of streets. I assumed anyway that we'd bring her to the States."

"I'm glad you assumed it, but that takes time."

"If there's a lease in Valeria's name, you must have inherited it."

"Who knows what kind of law they have here. I need to talk to a lawyer."

"Whatever it may cost—fees, payoffs—that part is easy. Isn't there a lawyer in the family?"

"More than one."

"It's all going to take months. Let somebody dependable take charge right away. We can't—you can't do it."

"In good time," she said. She didn't want him to push, she was resentful.

"As soon as possible. I don't think you should stay. Also I can see that Gigi is winding up to make a big deal out of the glassware, coins, icons, Latin books. . . ."

"It was against the law. Those objects should have been declared. My mother hid them for me."

"Hundreds of thousands of people are hiding glassware, or watches like my Christmas present."

"Maybe, but it's still risky. Mother understood how to do things like this. Gigi will never manage. I'm afraid she'll get into trouble. Besides, Gigi sees herself carrying out Valeria's wishes. She wants me to see everything so she can be in the clear. So there can't be recriminations later. She feels responsible."

"All right. Yes. I can see that. I don't think you care all that much about these items. You don't want the enemy to get them. I assume the officials grab the valuable ones for themselves. As for Gigi's outwitting them, that's just fantasy. And she wants *me* to get the relics out. That's more fantasy."

"Are you sure your journalist friend doesn't travel on a diplomatic passport?"

"We've already gone into that. He couldn't. Newspapermen can't be government agents. Compromising. Terrible idea, especially for a superstar. He might as well be working for the CIA. You can see that."

"He might have good advice, though, if he's as smart as I gather he is."

They walked silent for a while. The street was gray. The piled earthquake rubble smelled moldy, even though refrigerating December checked the decay. Corde found himself looking for the rat silhouettes in the street, flattened like weathercocks by traffic.

He had counted on the good effects of air; his purpose had been to get Minna away from the telephone. A thankless role, the solicitous sensible husband. He was accused of manipulating her. He read this in her brown eyes, plain enough. To invoke the new term and Mount Palomar *was* manipulative, but the aim was to bring her home. His helpfulness rejected, he felt a touch resentful. She was unjust to him. But then, look—"unjust"! Such childish pedantry was a sign that he, too, was dog tired.

She said, "What were you and your friend Spangler talking about yesterday?"

"I think our theme was which of us had done the right thing during the last forty years. Or if either of us had done anything right. We . . ."

But Minna didn't let him continue. She said, "I don't really want to talk about him."

"Let's not, then."

"Albert, I feel absolutely torn to pieces."

"Of course. You are."

"Can you help me to deal with this a little? You're an impartial person, sometimes, and a pretty good psychologist. You won't be judgmental if I tell you. I wake up in the night, and everything good in my life seems to have leaked away. It's not just temporary. I feel as if it can never come back. It's black in the room, and even blacker and worse outside. It goes on and on and on, out there. I'm mourning my mother but I also feel terrible things about her. I'm horribly angry. Can you tell me . . . ?"

What an innocent person! She did stars; human matters were her husband's field. Some division of labor! And swamped with death he was supposed to bail out with a kitchen cup of psychology. His round face crowned with felt hat looked down into her face, which was not only as white as meringue but as finely lined (December daylight was unsparing). What was the case? Her loved and admired mother (how could you not admire an omnipotent Roman matron) had assigned her daughter, for safety, to the physical universe—not exactly the *mysterium tremendum*; that was religion. But science! Science would save her from evil. The old woman protected Minna from the police state. She endured ostracism, she fought the officials, and she finally got her daughter out of the country. But this powerful protection was gone. And now Valeria's disappearance had to be accounted for. Where was the strength on which Minna had always depended? In short, mortal weakness, perplexity, grief—the whole human claim. Minna hadn't made the moves frequently made by scientists to disown this claim: "Don't bother me with this ephemeral stuff—wives, kids, diapers, death." She was too innocent for that. So she turned to her husband for help. She loved him. And as soon as she asked for help the strength drained out of him. But he had only himself to blame for that, because he *had* taken human matters for his province. Neither more nor less. He was justified to Minna the scientist as Albert the human husband. He said, "I may not be able to tell you much."

"But you think about these things all the time. I watch you doing it."

"Then let's see . . . Why do you suppose you feel so angry?"

"On the plane I was frightened that we mightn't get here in time. But the truth is that I didn't actually believe she was going to die."

"I follow that. You thought Valeria had all the strength there was. I mentioned in London that she was falling down."

"I remember. But I couldn't take it in. You'll say this is crazy, but—this is a confession—my mother gave me her word that she'd live to be ninety."

"How could anybody do that?"

"Don't ask me—I'll tell you what happened. The one time my mother came to the U.S., we went to see Pablo Casals at Marlboro, ninety years old, rehearsing an orchestra. We were both terribly impressed, especially Mother. Here was this ancient man, he was shrunk together in a single piece, no waist and no neck. He had to sit down to conduct. He scolded. But how strong he still was in music. If you understand me. Now, there was a girl in the orchestra who played the clarinet, and she was about nineteen. He stopped the music and said to her, 'Can't you get more life into it?' Then Mother and I looked at each other. And when we were leaving the shed—that outdoor hall—she said, 'Why shouldn't I do that, too—live to be his age?' It was put as a joke, but it was serious underneath."

"It would have been better to keep it a joke. But you took it as a promise."

She nodded. "I see I must have."

"So when I warned you that she was slipping, you brushed it off. Your mother kept her word."

He was about to say, "That's like believing in magic," but he refrained. For one thing, everybody followed magical practices of some sort—he could identify a few of his own. And then, too, you didn't reveal to such a woman how cleverly you observed her. She was as intelligent—phenomenally intelligent—as she was childlike. The boundaries between intellect and the rest meandered so intricately that you could never guess when you were about to trespass, when words addressed to the child might be intercepted by a mind more powerful than yours. So the Dean stared at his wife. It was incomprehensible that Valeria should give such a daughter the sort of promise (about death!) you made to a kid, and that the learned daughter should hold her to it. This was Alice in Wonderland: "Drink Me." Mature, highly serious women entering into such an agreement. And it had twelve years more to run. During this time Minna was to get on with her astronomy, equally safe from the decadent West and the decadent East. But Minna now told all, this was a confession. Ah, the poor things, poor ladies! They made him think of one of Rilke's letters: "*Je suis un enfant qui ne voudrait autour que des enfances encore plus adultes.*" The mother, in this case the more adult child, promised not to desert her daughter, and this promise was also to have kept Valeria alive. But the best she could do was to hang in there until Minna arrived from Chicago.

"I wasn't old enough to feel it when my father died. I was sad because everybody else was. But my mother's death is really horrible—being a corpse, and cremated, and tomorrow the cemetery. I can't accept it. And it's even worse to be angry, it's horrible. Not like a grown woman. I feel vicious." White, pinched, Minna was scarcely breathing, and her outraged eyes went back and forth across his face. He put his arm about her waist, but the gesture had to be withdrawn. She didn't want it. She stood too rigid. He then tried to warm his hand in the square pocket of his overcoat.

He said, "I remember being sore, too, feeling abandoned when my own mother died. I was just an adolescent, of course. But . . . I'm not the wise psychologist type. Psychology is out of my line. I even dislike it."

What he was thinking was that Minna's demand was for Valeria. She wanted her mother, and it was impossible to replace Valeria. That was beyond him, beyond any husband. True he had gotten into the habit of attempting whatever Minna needed. He no longer asked whether this suited him, whether he was risking his dignity by pushing a cart in the supermarket, reading recipes, peeling potatoes. Magic practices, yes. But minor ones. But he was no magician; far from it. What he had to offer was active sympathy. Active sympathy should be enough. Why wasn't it! There was a touch of anger in him over this, but the anger was even worse than the inadequacy. He understood, in form, what he should do. The heart of the trouble was in the *form*.

Minna was saying, "All these days we haven't had time to talk. I realize that you're very upset, too, and brooding in the room. I used to think you didn't mind sitting, being by yourself, that you were naturally a quiet person."

"Ready to become a stay-at-home."

"In spite of what people said about you."

"What people said. You listen too much. They said I had raised a lot of hell. Much they know."

"I'm not criticizing, Albert, just reflecting."

Minna marrying Dean Corde: a superclear mind had made a dreamer's match.

She said, "You turned out to be a much more emotional and strange person than I ever expected."

He accepted this, nodding his head. But he wasn't nodding wisely, he was nodding from ignorance. You couldn't fathom Minna's conceptions of strange and normal because she was so astronomical. The hours she spent with you, dear heart, were hours among the galaxies. But she came back from space. There was her mother, and there was her husband to come back for. It was something like Eros and Psyche in reverse. Picturing himself as Psyche, Corde agreed that it was probably better for Eros not to turn on the light. (The Dean was only now discovering how many important things he had neglected to think about.) He was certainly not the man she had supposed she was marrying. Luckily she hadn't made a serious mistake. She had chosen a husband who intended to love her, meant to love her. Yes, she took some pride in having given the marriage due consideration. The truth was that she had done the right thing in spite of it. We knew all kinds of things but not the ones we needed most to know. Modern achievements, the Dean believed, jets, skyscrapers, high technology, were a tremendous drain on intelligence, more particularly on powers of judgment and most of all on private judgment. You could see it in every face, how the depleted wits fought their losing battle with death. Faces told you this. He had learned this from his own face, and he confirmed the discovery by daily observations.

He wasn't merely sorry for his wife, he was horrified. It wasn't only that she was white and drawn but that her features were set in anger, and a kind of accusation. Her mouth was drawn down at one corner and the contraction gave her an expression of face he had learned to dread. He decided, I'd damn well better get her out of here. I never saw anybody go down so fast. This is ruining her.

She thought he was nodding in agreement, and he did agree about being deceptively quiet. He was quiet because he had made so many bad mistakes; he had his work cut out for him, thinking them over. That was the quiet part. He was also misleadingly domestic. She had never noticed how many household duties he took on—the groceries, cooking, vacuuming, washing windows, making beds. He did all this by way of encouraging or conjuring her to change her ways. Let's have a household. Let's not eat frozen TV dinners. But she herself was misleading. It was because people said such things about the wicked Dean that she was attracted to him. She wanted to marry a wickedly experienced but faithful man, a reformed SOB, a chastened chaser, now a gentle husband; and she got what she wanted, all the benefits of his oddity and then some. Earlier women, her unknown rivals, had been defeated. She could believe that she had reformed him. He was even a husband who grieved when she was grieving. He felt like a pity-weirdo. Everything moved him, came back to him amplified, disproportionate, moved him too much, reached him too loudly, was accompanied by overtones of anger. There was some sort of struggle going on. She said she wasn't criticizing, only reflecting, but he couldn't believe that. *You're* supposed to know—*you* tell me. That was how he interpreted the contracted corner of her mouth.

"So you were angry with your mother?" She went back to that.

"It's supposed to be normal, not a sign that there's no love but just the reverse. But I guess the clinicians would say it wasn't the kind of love we'd feel if we were everything we should be. Well, that's standard psychiatry." To himself he added, That's what bothers me about it.

Now what was the position? The position was that Corde had accepted responsibility for keeping his wife posted on sublunary matters. She did boundless space, his beat was terra firma. A crazy assignment, but he enjoyed it most of the time. He liked the fact that she, who had grown up in a Communist country, should have to be told by her American husband who Dzerzhinsky was, a Zinoviev. He had done his homework in Paris while writing on Tsvetayeva. He had done a piece also on Boris Souvarine, so he could describe postrevolutionary Russia. What, never heard of Zinoviev and Kamenev? Nobody had told her about the Moscow trials. "You'll have to fill me in." She wondered whether her father had been aware of Stalin's crimes. She even began to look into Corde's books and to ask, "Who was this Madame Kollontai?" Or, "Tell me about Chicherin." He would say, "Why clutter your mind?" However, it was pleasant at dinner to draw Chicherin for her or to explain what Harry Hopkins had done or describe the members of the brain trust. She was beautifully innocent, a classic case. She also laughed at jokes too old to be told to anybody else. She adored jokes. And when she asked him for the spellings or definitions of words and he gave them in his deep voice without raising his goggled face from the newspaper, she would say, "You're my walking, talking reference book. I don't need to touch a dictionary." But grief, death, these were not your ordinary sublunary subjects. Here he was no authority. Minna was critical, she was angry. What was the point of telling him now that he was not the husband she had thought she was marrying? Was she referring to his Chicago pieces and the fulminations they had touched off? She disliked noise, disorder, notoriety, any publicity. Was this what she referred to? Only a remote possibility, but it all had to be considered, for now that Valeria was dead and she had only him, Corde, to depend upon, total revaluation was inevitable. So, then, who was this man? What have we here? He tried, himself, to see what we had. An elderly person, extensively bald, not well proportioned (Mason was contemptuous of his legs), sexually disreputable; counter, spare and strange maybe, but not in the complimentary sense. And then there was the moral side of things to consider. And the mental, too. Besides, Valeria had had a different sort of husband in mind for her daughter, a younger man, a physicist or chemist, with whom she would have had more in common. Somewhat painful, all this. Although Valeria had changed her opinion; she had come around. And what would a chemist son-in-law have told her on her deathbed—something more scientific, positive, intelligent?

Anyway he was now being reviewed *da capo* by his wife, whom death had put in a rage. He had to submit to it. But since she was going over him so closely, as if seeing him as she had never seen him before, it might be worthwhile to say something useful, or enlightening. What else was there to do in the circumstances? Speak up!

Here goes, however mistaken, was what he said to himself.

She was, in fact, asking him a question just then: "What does that mean, 'If we were everything we should be'?"

"As matters are, people feel free to plug in and plug out," he said. "Whatever it is, or whoever it is, contact can be cut at will. They can pull out the plug when they've had enough of it, or of him, or of her. It's an easy option. It's the most seductive one. You learn to keep your humanity to yourself, the one who appreciates it best."

"I see. . . ."

What was it that she saw? She was far from pleased with what he said.

"Of course you see. It's the position of autonomy and detachment, a kind of sovereignty we're all schooled in. The sovereignty of atoms—that is, of human beings who see themselves as atoms of intelligent separateness. But all that has been said over and over. Like, how schizoid the modern personality is. The atrophy of feelings. The whole bit. There's what's-his-name—Fairbairn. And Jung before him comparing the civilized psyche to a tapeworm. Identical segments, on and on. Crazy and also boring, forever and ever. This goes back to the first axiom of nihilism—the highest values losing their value."

"Why do you think you should tell me this now, Albert?"

"It might be useful to take an overall view. Then you mightn't blame yourself too much for not feeling as you should about Valeria."

"What comfort is it to hear that everybody is some kind of schizophrenic tapeworm? Why bring me out in the cold to tell me this? For my own good, I suppose."

It was no ordinary outburst. She was tigerish, glittering with rage. Her altered face, all bones, turned against him.

"This might not have been the moment," he said.

"I tell you how horrible my mother's death is, and the way you comfort me is to say everything is monstrous. You make me a speech. And it's a speech I've heard more than once."

"It wasn't what you needed. I shouldn't have. The only excuse is that I'm convinced it's central. That's where the real struggle for existence is. But you're right. A lecture . . . it was out of place."

"You lecture me. You lecture. I could make *you* these speeches now. You even put it into your *Harper's* article, about Plato's Cave, and the Antichrist."

He made a gesture of self-defense—it was minimal. He said, "That's not quite it. There's an old book by Stead called *If Christ Came to Chicago*, and what I said was that Chicago looked as if the Antichrist already had descended on it."

"I tell you you lecture about plugs and tapeworms and those sovereign, or whatever it is, human atoms, and how capitalism is the best because it fits this emptiness best, and is politically the safest, for horrible reasons, and so on. I'm tired of hearing it."

"I wasn't aware that you were following so closely. I didn't realize that I said so much about it. I'll stop it."

"I heard you all right, Albert. Against my will. I don't want to hear more of it today."

"Yes, yes, I was wrong."

Her rage now began to fade. The glitter passed off. She said, "It's probably your kind of affection. Besides . . . now you couldn't do much anyway."

"Yes, that was the general idea, but obtuse."

Now she relented altogether. She said, "I understand you're in an emotional state yourself, and you haven't had anybody to talk to except your pal the journalist, and that probably wasn't very satisfactory."

"I suppose we'd better go home. Walking is unpleasant at this time of the evening."

Subdued by his failure with her, he considered how he might do better. It was worse than nothing to be so elementary on such a subject, to misjudge his wife's feelings, to sound like a high-class educated dummy. Academic baby talk. Either you went into it with the full power of your mind or you let it alone.

They had walked as far as the boulevard when they turned back. Lecturing, speechifying, emotional states, she said. Spangler had used different terms—crisis, catastrophe, apocalypse. They concluded, each from his own standpoint, that he was seriously off base, out of line. Naturally, he suspected this himself. He half agreed with Mason senior—almost half. Men like Mason senior went to business. Business was law, engineering, advertising, insurance, banking, merchandising, stockbroking, politicking. Mason senior was proud of his strength in the La Salle Street jungle. Bunk, thought contentious Corde. Those were not animals fighting honorably for survival, they were money maniacs, they were deeply perverted, corrupt. No jungle, more like a garbage dump. Leave Darwin out of this. But—calming himself—these Mason types belonged fully to the life of the country, spoke its language, thought its thoughts, did its work. If he, Corde, was different, the difference wasn't altogether to his credit. So Mason senior believed. Corde's answer was that he made no claim to be different. He was like everybody else, but not as everybody else conceived it. His own sense of the way things were had a strong claim on him, and he thought that if he sacrificed that sense—its truth—he sacrificed himself. Chicago was the material habitat of this sense of his, which was, in turn, the source of his description of Chicago. Did this signify that he did not belong to the life of the country? Not if the spirit of the times was in us by nature. We all belonged. Something very wrong here. He pursued the matter further, probably still feeling the painful reverberations of his obtuseness with his wife. To belong fully to the life of the country gave one strength, but why should these others, in their strength, demand that one's own sense of existence (poetry, if you like) be dismissed with contempt? Because they were, after all, *not* strong? A tempting answer, but perhaps too easy. A critical lady looking at one of Whistler's paintings said, "I don't see things as you do." The artist said, "No, ma'am, but don't you wish you could?" A delicious snub but again too easy. The struggle was not the artist's struggle with the vulgar. That was pure nineteenth century. Things were now far worse than that.

Corde thought that he wasn't advanced enough to be the artist of this singular demanding sense of his. In fact he had always tried to set it aside, but it was *there*, he couldn't get rid of it, and as he grew older it gained strength and he had to give ground. It seemed to have come into the world with him. What, for example, did he know about Dewey Spangler? Well, he knew his eyes, his teeth, his arms, the form of his body, its doughnut odor; the beard was new but that was knowledge at first sight. That vividness of beard, nostrils, breath, tone, was real knowledge. Knowledge? It was even captivity. In the same way he knew his sister Elfrida, the narrow dark head, the estuary hips, the feminized fragrance of tobacco mixed with skin odors. In the case of a Maxie Detillion the vividness was unwanted, repugnant, but nothing could be done, it was there nevertheless, impossible to fend off. With Minna the reality was even more intimate—fingernails, cheeks, breasts, even the imprint of stockings and of shoe straps on the insteps of her dear feet when she was undressing. Himself, too, he knew with a variant of the same oddity—as, for instance, the eyes and other holes and openings of his head, the countersunk entrance of his ears and the avidity expressed by the dilation of his Huguenot-Irish nostrils, the face that started at the base of the hairy throat and rose, open, to the top of his crown. Plus all the curiosities and passions that went with being Albert Corde. This organic, constitutional, sensory oddity, in which Albert Corde's soul had a lifelong freehold, must be grasped as knowledge. He wondered what reality was if it wasn't this, or what you were "losing" by death, if not this. If it was only the literal world that was taken from you the loss was not great. Literal! What you didn't pass through your soul didn't even exist, that was what made the literal literal. Thus he had taken it upon himself to pass Chicago through his own soul. A mass of data, terrible, murderous. It was no easy matter to put such things through. But there was no other way for reality to happen. Reality didn't exist "out there." It began to be real only when the soul found its underlying truth. In generalities there was no coherence—none. The generality-mind, the habit of mind that governed the world, had no force of coherence, it was dissociative. It divided because it was, itself, divided. Hence the schizophrenia, which was moral and aesthetic as well as analytical. Then along came Albert Corde in diffident persistence, but wildly turned on, putting himself on record. "But don't you see . . . !" He couldn't help summarizing to himself what he should have said to Minna.

He would moreover have said (they were now rising in the small china-closet elevator—there was no harm in these unspoken ideas, and when all this was over she might be willing to let her husband tell her his thoughts), he would have told Minna, "I imagine, sometimes, that if a film could be made of one's life, every other frame would be death. It goes so fast we're not aware of it. Destruction and resurrection in alternate beats of being, but speed makes it seem continuous. But you see, kid, with ordinary consciousness you can't even begin to know what's happening."

XV

MINNA couldn't go to the cemetery next morning; she was sick. Nothing by halves, she was violently sick. She could keep nothing on her stomach, not even a cup of tea, and she had woman trouble. Something like a grenade went off within the system. Gigi moved Corde out of the bedroom. She said he would sleep in the "drawing room," where the bulky, peeling leather armchairs were. Well, all right. The old woman took total charge, changing linens, putting soiled things to soak in a tub. Two doctors, a team, came to the house before ten o'clock. They were the ones assigned to the diplomatic corps. "They will charge a lot, but others will not have the drugs," Gigi said. Corde stood by. The physicians were a lady and a gentleman, working together. The lady turned Minna over, the gentleman gave her a shot. You had to admire their professionalism, their dexterity with a needle.

"Can't we put the cemetery off till tomorrow?" Corde asked.

A preposterous question. The announcement was already in the papers.

Vlada Voynich volunteered to sit with Minna. So Corde and Gigi together with one of the feeble old uncles were driven to the cemetery by Traian in the Dacia. Once more slammed within tin doors, and the motor roaring under your feet. It looked like melancholy sunny weather—low winter beams coming through cold haze, the prevailing light russet. As a rule Corde avoided cemeteries and never went near the graves of his parents. He said it was just as easy for your dead to visit you, only by now he would have to hire a hall.

He did not realize that the Dacia had already been to the crematorium and that Traian had picked up the canister of ashes. The Dean failed therefore to understand why Tanti Gigi was doubled up, weeping, in the seat behind him. He reached back to give her comfort. She took his hand and held it. All he could see, half turning, was that Uncle Teo, bolt upright in the corner, preferred to stare at the street with big gray eyes as if to dissociate himself from her keening. Her white head was pushed against the back of the seat. Same old woman who had changed Minna's sheets so efficiently only a while ago, who had shown him cheerful box camera snapshots last night—young Gigi, a high-fashion doll of the twenties in a short dress, leaning against a lion in Trafalgar Square, waving to the folks in Bucharest. Corde didn't learn until Traian had parked the car beside the iron stakes of the cemetery fence that Gigi had been bent double over the tin cylinder of Valeria's ashes. She was pressing it to herself under the coat. But when he helped her to the sidewalk and she came bowed through the door, black shawl slipping from her head, she gave him the long can to hold. He waited until her small feet, the turned heels of scuffed shoes, found the pavement securely; and her strong shoulders found the fit of the coat again—that heavy-looking light coat of synthetic fur (its realism continued to shock him). Her dark purple long bagging mourner's dress overhung her low shoes. Then her cardiac patient's face (her face was full of illness just then) told him that she wanted the cylinder back. And now he identified the object in his hand. The air was cold, but the can was warm. Passing it to her, he heard the sound of larger fragments, bone perhaps, or dental pieces. Perhaps they weren't even Valeria's. Who could tell what the crematorium workers shoveled up.

They went first to the office, where the usual exchange of official forms took place. Fees to be paid, cigarettes to be handed over. Inside the gates, a gang of cemetery beggars waited, more Oriental than European. Then you remembered again that Istanbul was very close, Cairo just over the water. For contrast with the beggars there were the family friends trying to look decorous in their dated Parisian or Viennese suits, shoes, dresses. Standing between beggars and friends was the Greek Orthodox priest. Cousin Dincutza said that he was personally acquainted with Valeria, used to call on her occasionally. The priest was stout, strong; he was sourly masculine, bearded, sallow, sullen; the hem of his rusty cassock was unstitched and coming down. There was a separate committee of sharp, henny ladies. Perhaps it was the black clothing that made them look so very ancient. But if they were old Dincutza types, Corde was for them. Cousin Dincutza was wonderful now. She took total charge of him at the cemetery, protective, advisory. And he greatly needed her advice. This conspicuous foreigner, the man of the family here, was a bit lost. (All the real business, of course, was done by Traian.) And with her jutty teeth, whispering in rudimentary French, Dincutza instructed him continually. As they were setting out from the office she motioned him to go forward and take Gigi's arm.

So they set off in a group. They walked through the cemetery. It was dense with stones and obelisks. The newer monuments were protected from the weather by heavy plastic sheets fastened with belts and ropes, and rattling in the wind. In Chicago, middle-class families covered their furniture with this material; here it was the obelisks and their fresh gilt inscriptions that were protected. No melancholy pleasant winter sunshine now, the weather again turned dark, windy. At the Raresh grave more mourners were waiting.

Considering the season, the color of the grass was surprisingly fresh. Could there be some special source of warmth underneath? There were tapers in large numbers, leaning every which way. Some were sheltered in lanterns but the gusts came down on the rest. The old cousins had seated themselves on benches, and the gypsy beggars crowded up behind—a wild lot, but that was customary, so no special notice was taken of their demented behavior. Dincutza observed (he must have looked rotten, in need of her support) how well Valeria had kept this plot, with *quelle dévotion* flowers were planted. The autumn ones, small asters, had survived the early snow. Now the priest got the service under way. Efficient and gruff, he spoke, sang. Now and then a howl came out. Troubles of his own, obviously. Priests were not pampered in this part of the world. He looked, Corde thought, like a big-bellied tramp in his country boots. In the scuffles of the wind the tapers blew out. Where they fell, there were patches of soot in the grass. Old women rekindled them. Corde shivered because he had respectfully removed his hat while the priest chanted. Dincutza made gestures ordering him to put it on again. Bless the old girl. When the hair was thin you lost heat through the top of the skull. This was elderly knowledge. She had it. She understood.

Now came the traditional cake, white and creamy, huge, swimming loosely and quivering on its platter. The beggars went for it. This was their main course. Dincutza politely offered Corde a taste, but he wanted no part of this death sweet. Anyway, the beggars were helping themselves with their hands. By now the gusts had overcome the last of the tapers, which had tumbled together in the black-spotted grass. It was time to install Valeria's ashes in the waiting socket of the tombstone. This, as you faced the monument, was on the left side. There would be only Valeria and Dr. Raresh here. From all sides a rude rattle of plastics in the wind, the lashed obelisks, those short Cleopatra's needles—there was little open space, the paths were exceedingly narrow.

A cemetery workman pulled out the disk that sealed the socket in the granite and Gigi surrendered Valeria's ashes to him. Corde, on Dincutza's instructions, was holding her up. So Gigi, sobbing, gave up the metal cylinder and the workman tried to push it into the opening.

Regulations must have changed since the stone was raised. The cylinder was too large. Uncle Teo and others moved in to examine the difficulty. There was just a shade of difference in the dimensions and if only a few chips of granite were knocked away from the opening the tube might slide in. On instructions from Uncle Teo and the cousins, the workman applied his chisel, tapped once or twice and then swung his hammer widely—two, three blows. Fragments sprang from the back of the monument, and then the material around the socket crumbled. This was not granite, it was cement. The rounded shoulder of the monument came off, slid down. Gigi did not faint away but she slumped against Corde. He held her up and a space was cleared for her on the bench. Now the lashed sheets of plastic over the surrounding obelisks clattered hard as if to give it away that it was not solid marble they were protecting but a facade. At the core of each obelisk there was cement. Conferring together, Traian and the relatives decided to deposit the cylinder overnight in the ossuary. The socket could be widened, the damage would be repaired by tomorrow.

Then the entire party walked very slowly along the grave-bordered footpath to the principal avenue. Again the line of beggars holding out their hands. The cylinder was left at the low stone building (ossuary? charnel house?), deposited in a box. Then everyone returned to the office by the gate.

The rest of the business was left to solid Traian in his zooty raw tan leather jacket. He went in to arrange for the repairs. The old colleagues and cousins separated quickly, for it now began to rain. Umbrellas were opened.

And suddenly the inner significance of the event (old friends paying last respects, a mourning sister) disappeared. Weather took over, nothing but cloud and rain, gloom over the dark green, old people finding shelter, the priest in his hobo boots striding over gravel, hurrying through the big gates. Corde, feeling empty, guided Gigi to the car. Traian trotted around to open the doors and reattach the windshield wipers. He then turned on the ignition and made a wide U-turn in the vast wet avenue, brown with machine fumes. Corde became aware how much distress had accummulated in him only when the car passed Valeria's mourners, the graveside group, at the tram stop. Dincutza stood among them. Then he said to Tanti Gigi, "Let's back up and take Dincutza home with us. Please tell Traian. . . . We can squeeze her into the back."

"Oh, my dear, what a kind thought, but we have not the space."

"It could be done."

It couldn't. And this was not the time to press Gigi. And by now they were already blocks beyond the tram stop. But it gave him a hard pang. Gigi said, "We are all well accustomed to the trams, Albert. Everybody, but everybody, rides them. And although the steps are too high for elderly passengers, the service, furthermore, is excellent." But Corde was sick at heart, all the same. A grind of two hours, perhaps, on the trolley car. Eighty-year-old Dincutza had looked after him. He went home in style while she waited in the rain. There must in addition be a special kind of fatigue—cemetery fatigue—felt by people who were aware that they would soon be back to stay. He could anticipate that himself.

Miana was asleep when they returned, and Vlada offered him a drink. He took more than one. He filled his glass several times—for the chill, for the cement, for the dark stone, bone, charnel smell, and for Cousin Dincutza. The fermented plum liquor made him smell like a still.

White and full-faced—dark lipstick, dyed hair, wide bosom, bunchy hips—Vlada looked at him with sympathy. "Getting a little thick for you?" she said.

"Getting? It's been all along. How is Minna?"

"Not too well. Before she fell asleep, she wanted to talk about all the things that had to be done yet."

"What is she planning?"

"Not she, so much. Tanti Gigi. Important projects."

If he had encouraged her, Vlada might have made satirical comments about Tanti Gigi. There were hints of that, he saw them, but he kept her honest. She said, "I came to sit in the study when Minna went to sleep, because the telephone had been ringing. I think they gave her Demerol, so she isn't likely to hear it. Poor Minna, she's never had to take this much. . . ."

"Nothing like this, no."

"She forgot what Eastern Europe was like. With her mother's protection, she may never have known it as the rest of us did. As Americans, even if the place is bugged, we can speak freely here. Valeria had plenty of trouble, of course, they almost destroyed her, but she was exceptionally strong and well connected."

"Why shouldn't her mother have protected her?" said Corde.

"Why, of course, it was natural," said Vlada. "And people here all are dying to send their gifted children to the West. A mad desire to get out. What would Minna have amounted to if she had stayed? After it became clear that she wasn't coming back, the Minister of Education called Valeria in. He was a tough old Stalinist. Valeria asked him, 'What were *you* prepared to do for her?' She said, 'My daughter knows how her mother was treated here.' But you've heard this before. Well, here we are, Albert—what?—five thousand, six thousand miles from Chicago? . . . By the way, there was a call for you, earlier, from Paris. A man named Spangler. Is that the columnist? Is he a friend of yours? He said he'd call back within the hour."

"Yes, it is the famous Spangler. Well, well. He must have news for me."

"He didn't tell me anything. I said you'd be back soon from the cemetery."

"There must be a result in the case. He wouldn't call me otherwise. He should have told you something. Just like Spangler. . . ."

"Why don't we chat. It'll help you to bear the suspense,"

said Vlada. "I always hear good things from you when you let yourself go."

"If peculiar."

"All the better when they are. I realize you haven't decided yet about Beech."

"I haven't been able to think about lead. Lead is heavy and I'm feeling light. But I haven't forgotten, it's one of the things I keep at the back of my mind. I still haven't got it clear what Beech expects."

"You think he'll expect total agreement with his views, and that would make you his mouthpiece?"

"He's the scientist. His views would be sound. Mine would only be impressions."

"Why should that enter into it?" said Vlada. "I don't see why there should be a conflict if you limit yourself to reporting."

Corde said, "He takes an apocalyptic view of the poisoning of the earth. If I didn't accept his picture we might not get anywhere. Let's give it a quick inspection: First man conquers nature, and then he learns that conquered nature has lost its purity and he's very upset by this loss. But it's not science that's to blame, it's technocrats and politicians. They've misused science. Yes, I see this is an unfair simplification. I admire the man. But I suspect that if I didn't buy his apocalypse he'd be annoyed, even wounded."

"But your articles had apocalyptic emotions in them," said Vlada. "That's just what got him."

"You can't hitch these two apocalypses together. Doesn't he believe he can straighten me out? Something like, 'I can give the man the real reason for this anarchy he reported. It's lead poisoning, lead insult to the brain.' My friend Spangler was very sharp with me about catastrophes. He told me I went too far, being poetical, mentioning the Antichrist. He's dead against the whole Antichrist business. It's too theological and Moral Majority for his taste. Besides, he's a journalist with a following of millions, masses of people who depend on the press to keep them in balance (what else have they got?). I wouldn't be surprised if he believed that it was up to spokesmen like him—maybe primarily to himself alone—to ensure stability, to put down disorder with his own behind. Fat little Dewey Spangler, as long as he sits tight and bears down with his backside he can suppress evil and save us from anarchy. All he has to do is say all the right things while he prevents the wrong ones from being spoken."

As if to hear better, Vlada moved nearer on the damaged brocade sofa, her cup in her lap. This heavy woman, and pale, eyes large and dark—she was as intelligent as she was stout. Her hair, parted evenly down the center in two symmetrical waves, suggested that the fundamental method of her character was to balance everything out, and that she kept a mysterious, ingenious equilibrium, her fat figure and her balanced thoughts being counterparts. Obviously she wanted to draw him out. She took only tea. The *pálinca* was for him, to drive away the cemetery drizzle and also to make him talk. She said, "You seem to think I have nothing but Beech on my mind. It's not so. I'm interested in what you've seen over here, and what effect it's had on your state."

"I'm in a state?"

"Your state of mind as an American in a place like this."

Yes, Vlada did often ask for his American opinions. She hadn't herself been naturalized for more than five or six years. To her he was an American American. She sometimes led the conversation around to such subjects as Abolition, the Civil War, Mormonism. Not long ago in Chicago, the ladies had had him talking through dinner and until a late hour about buffalo hunters, frontier fighters, Bowie knives, Indian wars. Minna, too, found this wonderfully entertaining, exotic.

"So you want my American standpoint. I wonder if there is such a thing. Maybe I'm not the American you ought to ask."

"Your personal interpretation, then."

He reflected that he had made a speech to Minna in the street yesterday; it hadn't turned out well. That failure (crushing failure of sensitivity) was a stimulant. He wanted to do better, to try again. Vlada was receptive. He was tempted to talk. Her aim was to help him to work off tensions and reduce the anxiety of waiting. He said, "I don't know about interpretations. What about impressions instead, or maybe improvisation. Have you ever read about the Italian *improvvisatori*, mostly from Naples, who used to entertain audiences two hundred years ago? You'd suggest a theme, and they'd give an inspired recitation. Where would you like me to begin? I could start with the little sofa we're sitting on. It's the Orient. But I think you're going to ask about Valeria's death, and what I was thinking when I saw the Colonel."

"What about the Colonel?"

"He was teaching us a lesson. I think a little of it was meant for me."

"What was this lesson?"

"What was the lesson? Well, they set the pain level for you over here. The government has the power to set it. Everybody has to understand this monopoly and be prepared to accept it. At home, in the West, it's different. America is never going to take an open position on the pain level, because it's a pleasure society, a pleasure society which likes to think of itself as a tenderness society. A tender liberal society has to find soft ways to institutionalize harshness and smooth it over compatibly with progress, buoyancy. So that with us when people are merciless, when they kill, we explain that it's because they're disadvantaged, or have lead poisoning, or come from a backward section of the country, or need psychological treatment. Over here the position was scarcely concealed that such and such numbers of people were going to be expended. In Russia, for the building of socialism, that policy was set by Lenin from the first. He would have allowed millions to die in the early famines. More would have died in the early years if the kindly Red Cross and Herbert Hoover hadn't distributed food. Even with us, conservative capitalism has to temper or conceal its position that classic conditions of competition will bring suffering and death—American conservatism has its own difficulties with the pain level. Suppose the public expense of kidney dialysis is ninety thousand dollars a year in a clinic that keeps six or seven dim, unproductive lives going—will we let these old folks watch the television for another year yet?"

"On the other side, it's brutality," said Vlada.

"On the other side, it's the archaic standard, Oriental and despotic, affliction accepted as the ground of existence, its real basis. By that standard we're unformed, we Americans. What do we think the fundamentals are, anyway—the human truth! And this fucking Colonel was running us through the Brief Course, a refresher for Minna and an introduction for me, the represerative of the rival superpower with his unformed character. I've heard Europeans say that the American character doesn't even exist yet. It's still kicking in the womb. The French, the Germans, they know a little more about the archaic pain-level standard. But they live now as we do, comfortably. Only they've had it. They had the trenches in the first war, and the bombing of cities in the second, and the camps. They'd like to retire from history for a while. They're on holiday. They've been on holiday since they cleared away the wreckage in 1945. I don't blame them. I only observed that it prevents rigorous positions from being taken. In that respect they share the American condition. Life is highly enjoyable and there's great reluctance to focus clearly on a pain level. And when a brutal action is necessary—well, think of the scene of our withdrawal from Saigon."

"I thought when you were talking about your friend Spangler that you were going to be a little more amusing."

"When we've worn ourselves out with our soft nihilism, the Russians would like to arrive with their hard nihilism. They feel humanly superior. Even the Russian dissidents, especially the right wing, take the high tone with us. They say, 'We haven't got justice or personal freedom but we do have warmth, humanity, brotherhood, and our afflictions have given us some character. All you can offer us is supermarkets.' Whereas the best defense that liberal democracy can make goes like this: 'True, we're short on charisma and fraternal love, although you have it in debased forms, don't kid yourselves about that. What we do have in the West is a kind of rational citizens' courage which you don't understand in the least. At our best we can be patient, we keep our heads in crisis, we can be decent in a cold steady way. Don't underestimate us.' "

"Do you buy this?"

"No."

"Why don't you?"

"I don't think you can be managerial and noble at the same time. Do you think those Chicago articles are about rational citizens' courage?"

"I somehow expected your inspired recitation would have something to do with Chicago."

Corde said, "You're right. Let me try that now. Here in Bucharest I've been thinking about those articles. Why did I write them? It was late in life for me to act up and sail up the Chicago River to make such a bristling gunboat attack. I even seem to have thought readers would be grateful for this, another sign of immaturity. In middle age I came back to Chicago to make a new start. Ten years later, I may have to do it again. It's like inexhaustible adolescence, a new start every few years. And at the outset I didn't intend to be provoking. I started out in all innocence. I took a light tone. I even thought it might be fun. Like quoting Matthew Arnold about the stockyards in 1884: 'Pigsticking? No, I haven't gone to see the pigsticking.' I wasn't looking for trouble. No sermons to preach about the death of cities or the collapse of civilization. I'm too much of a Chicagoan to feel up to that. Not for me, dear God, to work all this out! I sympathize up to a point with the objections of my friend Spangler. He accused me of abyssifying and catastrophizing. We have a weakness in America for this. Partly it's been first-class show business. We've been brought up for generations on Cecil B. De Mille's 'special effects'—the Sign of the Cross, lions and Christian martyrs, the destruction of Sodom, the last days of Pompeii. This poor make-believe, however, is a dangerous distraction. Because this *is* a time of the breaking of nations. It's all true. Now, Spangler pointed out that you begin with the abyss and end up with Jones of Jonestown, where death was mixed up with 'special effects.' But it doesn't seem to me that *I* was being histrionic. I didn't want to demonstrate or remonstrate or advocate or prophesy. I most certainly did not intend to set myself up as *the* spokesman of the sufferer. But perhaps Spangler's main charge against me was that I was guilty of poetry. And I don't know exactly what to make of that. He himself was keen on poetry in his youth. He's now a spokesman, though, and poets never really were liked in America. Benjamin Franklin said better one good schoolmaster than twenty poets. That's why when we have most need of the imagination we have only 'special effects' and histrionics. But for a fellow like me, the real temptation of abyssifying is to hope that the approach of the 'last days' might be liberating, might compel us to reconsider deeply, earnestly. In these last days we have a right and even a duty to purge our understanding. In the general weakening of authority, the authority of the ruling forms of thought also is reduced, those forms which have done much to bring us into despair and into the abyss. I don't need to mind them anymore. For science there can be no good or evil. But I personally think about virtue, about vice. I feel free to. Released, perhaps, by all the crashing. And in fact everybody has come under the spell of 'last days.' Isn't that what the anarchy of Chicago means? Doesn't it have a philosophical character? Think of a beautiful black chick who spends days with a razor hollowing out a copy of *Ivanhoe* for her desperate lover. Think how symbolic his actions are when he fires a shot into the floor of Judge Makowski's courtroom. He rushes out, they kill him. He dies with histrionic flash. Shot in the head, the head he was probably stoned out of, he leaves us a message. And what's the message? . . . 'You better be more rigorous, man! You better think about the first and last things.' " The telephone was about to ring. It gave its preliminary chirrup.

"Maybe what I've been saying proves that I myself suffer from 'insult.' "

The phone rang and he took the call. "You may have heard already, or am I the first?" said Dewey.

"The first what?"

"Then I am the first. The jury found that man of yours guilty, and he got a sixteen-year sentence. You have a victory."

"How did you hear this?"

"From my office in Washington. Is it exciting? I had my people alerted and they phoned me just a while ago at the Meurice. Do you feel good about it?"

"Sixteen years. I feel worked up."

"Well, it went as you wanted it. I bet your cousin Detillion is disappointed."

"I wonder. Win or lose, it was bound to improve his reputation. Chicago is still more his scene than it is mine. Dewey, listen, I'm grateful to you for taking the trouble, I'm thankful for your call."

"We had a couple of memorable talks," said Spangler. "After forty years, to find out how much you still have in common with a friend is damn important. I hope to stay in touch now."

Corde returned to Vlada, sitting beside her on the orange brocade sofa with the Oriental inlaid back, behind them the drizzling city and in the next room his sick wife, but mercifully, warmly sleeping, her large eyes closed, his pretty lady, lately so ravaged.

"I gather that you are the winner," said Vlada.

"It went as I wanted it. As I suppose I did. . . ."

"That at least is over."

"Going back will be a little simpler now."

"Simpler—you're referring to the college?"

"Partly."

"Was it only the man, or the woman also?"

"She gets a separate bench trial, and with plea bargaining—that's how it was explained to me—she'll get about eight years."

"So . . . there's your justice."

"Nothing comes out neat and even. But those two cost the boy his life. I don't take much stock in the punishment, but the alternative was that they would go scot-free. It's true I used clout and special privileges to nail them. It's true that nobody will change, the jails stink and nothing significant has been added. In jail, out of jail, Lucas Ebry and Riggie Hines are exactly the same. There are millions more where they come from—not attached to life, and nobody can suggest how to attach them. Now listen, Vlada, Minna and I have got to get out of here. If she's going to be really sick."

"Whether it's sickness or mourning . . ."

"In any case, I'll take no chances with Communist hospitals, and I won't wait until she's too sick to travel. Either Zurich or Frankfurt would be a short flight."

"There's your phone again," said Vlada.

It was Miss Porson, speaking from his office. "The man has been sentenced."

"A friend just called from Paris with the news."

"The Provost said I should tell you how well it came out, from his point of view."

"I'm sure he's glad it's over."

"And he sent a message to the poor darling—how is she? The Provost has been in touch with the observatory and she has—you both have—accommodations at Palomar next month, the fifteenth and the sixteenth."

"Now there's a help," said Corde.

"Now then, did Dr. Voynich give you the news about your sister and the Judge?"

"Dr. Voynich is sitting here with me. Of course I've heard about the marriage."

"How nice." Miss Porson had chatted her way to the commanding heights of gossip. "I talked to your sister just now, wondering whether she would have a message for you, and before I could congratulate her she told me that her son had taken off."

"He's gone somewhere?"

"I'm just coming to that. He's been angry. Very angry."

"Over the marriage or the verdict?"

"He's left the country."

"Where did he go—how does she know that?"

"He charged his ticket to her account. He went to her travel agent, and he's now in Mexico, so far as she knows. She didn't discuss it with me, but he's under bond, isn't he?"

"He may have gone to have his sulks in some nice tropical place."

Corde said this not because he believed it but in order to move the conversation to another subject. Mason had little interest in sunny holidays. Already, at the age of twelve, he couldn't have cared less about the porgies and the flounders. Let them stay where they were. Let Uncle Albert, his leg laid open by rows of barnacles, join the fishes in the drink—him with his abstracted look, falling into the sea. Corde was in no mood to chat with Miss Porson and speculate about his unhappy sister on the transatlantic telephone. Miss Porson with her good white hair and her calamine-colored Alexander Woollcott face was warmly sympathetic, but he didn't at all care to bandy civilities with her.

"There's somebody who wants to say hello, Dean. Lydia Lester is standing here."

"Oh! Let me talk to her," said Corde.

Not much was said.

"Well, it's over."

"I'm sorry I had to leave during the trial."

"I understand that. I'm sorry about your wife . . . your mother-in-law."

Slender, nervously pretty, Lydia Lester had long hair to shield her from the world, reticent long hands, pink lips. From the bad side of the tracks unwanted reality had descended on her (how the tracks meandered now!). And which way would she go? Back to maidenliness, he expected. "What are your plans?" he said. She mentioned none. He said he was coming back soon and hoped she would have dinner with them. He did not ask to speak to Miss Porson again, but put the phone down lightly, giving her no time to cut in.

"Do I understand from the conversation that your nephew has taken off?" said Vlada.

"Letting his mother have it because she married without his consent. His new stepfather is political enough to get the case against him dismissed and recover the bond—about five thousand bucks, I think. So Mason has gone to Central America to look over the revolutionary options. Intimidation of witnesses is no big deal, a mere college boy scaring black men who have criminal records. But there is one piece of good news, an open date at the Palomar Observatory."

"Minna won't want to miss that," Vlada said.

"Got any practical advice?"

"Take her away as soon as you can. I have another week here, and I can lend a hand with Gigi. They won't force her out of the apartment; that's not hard to take care of, it's done all the time. And as they'd say in Chicago, the authorities won't make waves. It's nothing to them that you're a dean, but it counts that you're a journalist. Also that you're connected with the Ambassador and with the famous columnist Mr. Spangler. They won't bother your old Tanti Gigi. You be nice to them now and they'll be nice to you, and forget the bygones. Are you so eager to get home, yourself?"

"It's not as if we were going back to order, beauty, calm and peace."

She said, "Still, you'll be glad to see Lake Michigan from your window again, I'm sure of that."

XVI

For some weeks it had been impossible to give the world his full attention—he had been too busy, absorbed, unsteady, unbalanced. But now, thanks be to God, the world began to edge back again, to reveal itself. On the plane when he held his wife's thin hand, she was too ill and bitter to be aware of his touch; she shut him out. But he was minutely aware of things, and the source of this awareness was in his equilibrium, a very extensive kind of composure. Not that this composure didn't have tight areas, crawl spaces, narrow and painful corners where longtime miseries rankled and to which there was no easy access, but this rankling—sometimes an electric prickling in a circle around his heart—couldn't be separated from his sense of improvement, of coming into his own. And in Chicago, when he brought Minna to be examined by Dr. Tyche, he wondered whether the doctor, glancing twice at him—a significant double take—wouldn't order *him* to the hospital, too.

No, it was Minna who was hospitalized at Wesleyan for tests and observation. Careful, judicious old Dr. Tyche said he would not care to offer a diagnosis before the laboratory results were in. A tactful man, he did not intend to discuss Minna's illness with the Dean, but he perfectly understood her state—she was so tormented that it was better to be sick. Let it be a medical problem. On the second day, Tyche was able to tell her that she was anemic, underweight, dehydrated, deficient in potassium. She was helped into a wheelchair by the nurse, X-rays of her chest were taken, she was examined by specialists, given shots. She slept a great deal and her husband, who came twice daily, sometimes studied her—even lying on her side, she appeared purposive, going forward, the black hair spread about her, and in profile her large, female sleeping eye painfully severe under the lid, as if she were getting stern lessons in her sleep. He was driving back and forth along the lakefront afternoon and evening, bringing glycerin and rose water for her hands, nail scissors, plastic tubes of shampoo, scientific papers she wasn't yet able to read. Irritable, she found fault with him, and sometimes he was wounded—that is, the old self would have been wounded.

The habits he had acquired in Eastern Europe were curiously binding, he found. He did not make full use of the double bed but slept on its edge as if he had been laid there like a yardstick. Mornings he sat in his chair just as he had sat in Minna's old-country room. Vlada had been right; he was glad to see the lake from his window and have the freshwater ocean for company. At his back the city, unquiet, the slum and its armies just over the way: blacks, Koreans, East Indians, Chippewas, Thais and hillbillies, squad cars, ambulances, firefighters, thrift shops, drug hustlers, lousy bars, alley filth. In the elevator, Mrs. Morford had told him that she was waiting her turn in the butcher shop when a young man put his hand into her coat pocket. She said, "What are you doing?" and he answered, "What do you *think* I'm doing?" Mr. Vinck, the cop on the fifth floor, was burglarized and his collection of handguns was taken. Teams of thieves ripped off the wheels of cars in the building garage and left them sitting on bricks. The elevators were vandalized, swastikas scratched into the hard metal of the walls and the numbered buttons pried out of the panels. Old people like herself, said Mrs. Morford, her eyes sadly downcast, lived behind locked doors. And, thought Corde (oh, so widely read, what was the good of it), if the good bourgeois of the nineteenth century could loll and dream in his overfurnished Biedermeier coziness, if his drawing room was like a box in the theater of the world, Mrs. Morford on her inflation-shrunk pension, among all the comforts of home, was shut in like a birdie in a cage.

He didn't go to the college; the thought of it repelled him. That would be a bad scene. He wasn't ready for Alec Witt and he didn't notify Miss Porson of his return. He planned to telephone his sister on New Year's Day. To congratulate her wouldn't be too hard, but he preferred to postpone talking to her about Mason. He drove out once to try to find the building where Rick Lester had been killed. He knew the block but not the address. The buildings were all Chicago six-flats in any case, heavy brick, beginning to bow with age, the courtyards miry and gathering litter. It was into one of these courtyards that Lester had fallen. Corde put to himself the question Mason had stuck him with about Lester's death—did it matter so much? Was it King David crying out over Absalom, was it Lear fumbling with Cordelia's button? There was a heavy death traffic which called perhaps for a revision of views. "Can't go through it on the old iambic pentameter," was how Corde formulated it. Must modernize.

But at home he sat usually with his back to the decayed city view. From his corner window he could see the Loop and its famous towers, but he looked directly downward at the working of the water, on bright days a clear green, easing its mass onto the beaches, white. The waters bathing the waters in sun, and every drop having its own corpuscle of light, the light meantime resembling the splash of heavy raindrops on paved surfaces—the whole sky clear, clear but tense. On days of heavy weather you felt the shock of the waves and heard their concussion through the building. Under low clouds you might have been looking at Hudson's Bay and when the floes came close you wouldn't have been surprised to see a polar bear. Only you didn't smell brine, you smelled pungent ozone, the inland-water raw-potato odor. But there was plenty of emptiness, as much as you needed to define yourself against, as American souls seem to do. Cities (this had been impressed on Corde when he pored over Blake—Spangler had not stopped him by kidding him about it)—cities were moods, emotional states, for the most part collective distortions, where human beings thrived and suffered, where they invested their souls in pains and pleasures, taking these pleasures and pains as proofs of reality. Thus "Cain's city built with murder," and other cities built with Mystery, or Pride, all of them emotional conditions and great centers of delusion and bondage, death. It seemed to Corde that he had made an effort to find out what Chicago, U.S.A., was built with. His motive—to follow this through—came out of what was eternal in man. What mood was this city? The experience, puzzle, torment of a lifetime demanded interpretation. At least he was beginning to understand why he had written those articles. Nobody was much affected by them, unless it was himself. So here was the emptiness before him, water; and there was the filling of emptiness behind him, the slums.

Anyway, he slept on the edge of the bed, in a provisional position, feeling something of a stranger in these most familiar surroundings, made his coffee, read the papers, had the waves for company. He did not go in for African violets again; they would only die while he and Minna were at Mount Palomar and visiting colleagues at La Jolla and in the Bay Area. He threw out the dead plants and kept the potting soil in a plastic bag at the bottom of the broom closet, along with shoe polish and floor wax. He went out to the greenhouse on Peterson Road opposite the cemetery and bought a red azalea for Minna's room, a small tree, the finest to be had. This offering, like almost all his offerings, was problematic. In her present condition she was hard to please. Human contact was repugnant to her unless its intent was to heal.

Nevertheless he made the lakefront trip twice daily, and he deliberately confined his conversation with Minna to ordinary subjects. He hadn't washed the car because dust made it less noticeable to car thieves. He had telephoned the laundry. Mail had accumulated in the receiving room, but he hadn't brought it upstairs; he'd wait until the second of January and then have Miss Porson open and sort it. For old times' sake he had stopped at the Lincoln Park Zoo on the way to the hospital, not to look at the animals but to see whether the Viking ship was still there. A team of Norwegians had rowed it across the Atlantic ninety years ago and it had been preserved near the waterfowl pond, where he and Dewey Spangler had had their ignorant arguments about Plato. He was sure that there had been Viking shields hung decoratively along the gunwales. If they had been mere ornaments they had rotted away, but some of the great oars were still there, laid under the ship.

He said, "Will you be starting up your dancing lessons again when we get back from California?"

"You never liked me to go."

"On the contrary, I liked it very much when you came home full of color, lively, pretty. Is there another astronomer in the world who can tap-dance?"

She said, "What about you and your club—have you gone swimming there?"

No, he didn't go to the club. Certain passages in his articles showed why he was wise to absent himself.

In the locker room I tune in on the conversation of a new member (Nick? Jimmy?). Naked, he holds before him a Bacchic belly from which, however, he appears to get no Bacchic pleasure. He is rather gloomy, shortish, curly-haired with large sideburns, hanging red cheeks, springing whiskers. A regretful eye tells you that this vital prosperity is not his fault, is unwanted, does not ensure Nick's happiness. His business? He runs a girlie nightclub in one of the suburbs. Wrapped in a towel, he is one of those useful members who like to give advice. A young executive comes, the black-bearded type with chic eyeglasses, a long slender turtleneck, an attaché case. As he undresses he asks Nick for suggestions. One of the men in his office is being married next week, and the boys want to give him a final stag party. "We're thinking of one of the Rush Street joints." Nick warns him, "You're asking for a rip-off. As soon as a fellow comes in they make him buy a fifty-dollar bottle of stinking champagne. Why don't you fellows rent a good hotel suite. Have dinner served, and if you hire a couple of girls to put on a show, it'll be a nicer evening and much cheaper. You'll get more mileage from the girls on a private arrangement, and it's undignified for professional people to go to Rush Street and be hustled like conventioneers and eat and drink a lot of crap." He warns another member not to patronize the barbershop next door to the club. "They charge you ten bucks for a lousy job—force you to have a shampoo. You just washed your hair in the shower, didn't you? Why should he wash it again and sock you ten bucks, plus a two-dollar tip, and still you'll come out looking like an Eskimo woman chewed on your hairline with her teeth." Nick knows every con there is and he is keen to protect the dignity of the members.

And this one, about another member, a young lawyer, who explained on the telephone why he had to miss an appointment with me at the club.

As he speaks I hear a sort of glad misery or cheerful desperation, his happiness at being where the action is: "I had to go to a closing. My associate prepared the documents while I was out of town, and he screwed up. I had to straighten it out. The first six months the seller was not supposed to get a share of the net from my client, and they dropped this clause from the contract. When I arrived and saw what was going on I said, No way. It wouldn't have been more than fifteen thou, but I wasn't going to let my guy get fucked even that much. The deal was over a restaurant where your average check runs thirty or forty bucks per capita. Not that my client is the type who would keep straight books. But in the meantime, what happens? The cops descend on the restaurant and bust it on account of the liquor license. It's that crazy new captain on Chicago Avenue. He has a special hard-on for the place, because somebody told him it's supposed to be Sinatra's favorite when he's in town, where his whole entourage goes, and that's big business, because when the word is out that you might see Sinatra there's always a crowd of yokels sitting waiting for a glimpse. All that crowd of yokels are on junk and the Chicago Avenue captain has a thing about dopies. He couldn't close the place, the management is entitled to a hearing, but it didn't do business much good when a dozen cops with helmets and riot equipment broke in, like

1968. They did it twice and scared hell out of the diners. There was only me to take care of all this, and it was one of those days. I'm so sorry I stiffed you"—stood you up. All this in a voice that trembles with electrical excitement. The big time. I leave the club and wait at the bank of elevators. The lake wind bellows and rages in the shafts, those long wild gullets. . . .

Corde knew better than to tell Minna why he might be uncomfortable at the club, discreetly avoiding mentioning his articles to her, the troubles he had brought on himself. He saw how it was, undisguised, when she looked at him—the blank of death. Her mother's death had taught her death. Triviality was insupportable to her. Her judgment was rigorous, angry. She wanted no part of his journalism, articles, squalor. Suburban pimps or smart-ass lawyers beneath contempt and the great hordes, even of the doomed, of no concern to her, nor the city of destruction, nor its assaults, arsons, prisons and deaths. And wiping out all fond memories, for the present at least, adopting the universe as a standard.

"I think I should have a talk with Dr. Tyche."

"I wonder if I didn't do the wrong thing by coming back now. I worry about Gigi."

"You were in no condition to help her. Gigi is all right, don't worry about Gigi. And you're better off here, at Wesleyan with Dr. Tyche."

"He's an angelic old man."

"That's exactly what he is. I had him in mind."

"I suppose you were right."

"To insist?"

"To take over when you did."

She had her doubts about Corde's good intentions. About her mother there were no doubts; she came from her womb and they were bound by true bonds. She had no doubts about Dr. Tyche, whose small old face was gentle and healthy. Age and devotion to patients had refined his goodness. But Corde—she loved him but he was suspect. And so he should be. We were a bad lot. For a complex monster like her husband, goodness might be just a mood, and love simply an investment that looked good for the moment. Today you bought Xerox. Next month, if it didn't work out, you sold it. It was an uncomfortable sort of judgment, but Corde was beginning to realize that this was how he wanted to be judged. Minna gave him a true reflection of his entire self. The intention was to recognize yourself for what you (pitiably, preposterously) were. Then whatever good you found, if any, would also be yours. Corde bought that. He wasn't looking for accommodation, comfort.

He had a very short talk with Dr. Tyche in one of the high corners of the hospital—to the south the mighty towers of the city, to the west collapse and devastation.

"What's her condition, really, Doctor?"

"Well, a serious trauma."

"Her mother promised to live a decade yet."

"I see. It's a broken promise, too. Well, the death of a parent does things like that to people."

"Yes, can turn us childish. I've heard, Doc, that in the crucial days of the female cycle a woman can have edema of the brain, and irrational fits? . . ."

The doctor was too canny to answer this, and smiled it away. You didn't give out medical opinions which might later be quoted in disputes. "When you get the curse your brain swells. The doctor told me that!" Tyche would only say, "The iron and potassium levels are very low, and the whole system weakened."

"Will she be able to go to Mount Palomar?"

"She asks me that every day. I don't see why she shouldn't."

Corde drove home, comforted. The weather was bright, keen blue, an afternoon of January thaw. His car had been parked in the sun, so he didn't need to turn the heater on. At home he set a kitchen chair out on the porch. It was mild enough to sit there, on the lee side of the flat. The light was the light of warmer seasons, not of deep winter. It came up from his own harmonies as well as down from above. The lake was steady, nothing but windless water before him. He had to look through the rods of his sixteenth-story porch, an interference of no great importance. Whatever you desired would be measured out through human devices. Did the bars remind you of jail? They also kept you from falling to your death. Besides, he presently felt himself being carried over the water and into the distant colors. Here in the Midwest there sometimes occurred the blues of Italian landscapes and he passed through them, very close to the borders of sense, as if he could do perfectly well without the help of his eyes, seeing what you didn't need human organs to see but experiencing as freedom and also as joy what the mortal person, seated there in his coat and gloves, otherwise recorded as colors, spaces, weights. This was different. It was like being poured out to the horizon, like a great expansion. What if death should be like this, the soul finding an exit. The porch rail was his figure for the hither side. The rest, beyond it, drew you constantly as the completion of your reality.

xvii

THE Cordes, after Minna was discharged from the hospital, attended a party given by Judge Sorokin's brother and his wife. Corde tried to get out of it. He said to Elfrida, through whom the invitation came, "Parties? No. Too tiring." But Elfrida answered, "Don't impose your unsocial habits on her. You're a fusspot, Albert. You want to keep her in a gloomy room and fuss over her. She's naturally a cheerful person and needs to get out. If it were an evening affair it might strain her, but this is only a brunch in lively company." Corde got the message: Elfrida recommended Minna to follow her own example. Grieving daughters like pained mothers should behave with female gallantry. "And I haven't seen Minna at all," said Elfrida. "For that matter, I haven't seen you, Albert, and you're going west soon. Are you on leave, by the way?"

"I'm taking care of Minna. The college thinks I couldn't make better use of my time."

"My brother-in-law and his wife won't bore you, I promise."

"What is he?"

"Ellis Sorokin? Engineering consultants, cybernetics—he runs a big company. His wife is a computer wizard. Or witch. She's a very pretty woman, and fashionable, and a horsewoman. You'd never believe computers were her line."

"Let me talk to Minna about this."

"No brush-off, mind you," said Elfrida.

"I'll get back to you, Elfrida. I can't tell Minna that I've accepted for her, you know that."

"There you're right. She has a mind of her own."

Minna said, "Yes, I'd like to go. I want to see Elfrida. I love her really. And don't you see, Albert, she wants her family to be represented at this party. The new in-laws. And at a time when Mason is being so lousy to her. If we don't attend she'll feel let down." Minna's motives were wholly feminine. But you would be ill-advised to mention your insights to her. Don't be smart. Make no speeches.

"If you think you're up to this," said Corde, deep-voiced.

"If I run out of steam I can leave early."

For the occasion, Minna curled her hair, wore a red knitted suit with a white trim, a mermaid brooch that had been Valeria's, and Valeria's rings, the ones that had been sawed from her fingers—Corde had just brought them back from the jeweler. He himself, never one for soft raiment, looked like a dean on Sunday. He had left his best suit in the old country, together with shirts, sweaters and socks. Minna had rubbed some color into her cheeks. She still looked pinched but her skin was smoother, the hard dints of grief under her lower lip were going. Some would say that this was the will to live, or the natural resilience of the organism. Well, perhaps, but Corde would have said that she had work to do. There was that zone of star formation waiting for her. Minna did not talk much to her husband about stars; he lacked the physics for it. Perhaps she didn't care to discover how ignorant he was of what concerned her most. To try to work the subject up would have been a mistake. He would have pestered her with half-baked, layman's questions, involving her in tedious explanations impossible for him to follow. So he let that alone. But if she would live for the sake of her stars, he didn't ask for more. She, from her side, was clever, too. She let him tell her about Clemenceau or Chicherin or Jefferson or Lenin so that she could exclaim, "Really, I am *so* dumb!" They were even, then, a dumb matching a dumb. Now, that was intelligent, and strategic, and sympathetically graceful. You might love a woman for her tactfulness alone.

At Ellis Sorokin's Lakeshore Drive high-rise apartment building, a Negro took your car in the garage, a Mexican in green uniform was your doorman, and then you rose in a silent elevator to the altitudes of power. When you got out on the fortieth floor you looked as an equal at the Hancock Tower, "Big

John," and at the sugar-cube sparkle of the Standard Oil Building—on all the supershapes of the Loop, in which, perhaps, some sense of common worship was concentrated. The windows of the Sorokin apartment descended nearly to the floor, but though you were so high, you didn't really need to feel that you might fall, and you enjoyed the safe sense of danger.

The Judge's brother resembled him—the same firm, smooth head, tanned creased face and thin mouth and black eyes, a touch of the Indian or the Tartar there. His wife was blond and elegant. Her color was fresh. She had money to spend and—why not?—she spent it, in her innocence, on high fashion. Her elegance was not intimidating, she didn't lay it on you oppressively. Wandering slowly over the ceiling there were green balloons, dozens of them, each one tied with lace ribbon, as expensive as possible. "And what a lot of work," said Corde. The young woman for all her wealth and computer witchery was greatly pleased. "I put in hours and hours blowing them up. But it's a very important occasion, you know."

Corde would have guessed a party for the newlyweds. Not at all; it was the dog's birthday party. Champagne, sturgeon, lobster, Russian eggs for starters, and lunch to follow. The dog was black, huge, gentle—a Great Dane. You were introduced to him in his circular wicker bed, almost a divan, where he lay indolent. Touching, Corde thought as he bent down to stroke the soft animal. The dog sighed under his hand. Wrapped and ribboned birthday presents were stacked beside his bed, and there were congratulatory telegrams.

Elfrida looked somewhat nervous and worn, yes, but also she was deliciously swarthy, discernibly a bride. Her arms, still fine, were heavily braceleted and she carried, as always, the mixed feminine fragrance of perfume and tobacco—almost rank but in the end a good pungency. She embraced Minna, and her brother (no grudges there), and Corde shook the Judge's hand—a rude hand, and all of a piece, as though the fingers were incapable of separate action (outdoor men sometimes have this iron sort of handshake). Congratulations! The bearded Judge was all friendliness. He gave Corde reassuring masculine signals: everything under control, not to worry.

It was a small party. One of the couples owned a Great Dane

from the same litter, so there was a relationship. The husband carried color photos of the dog in his wallet and showed them at the table. These were all church people. The Sorokins, too. Episcopal. Their minister was present. Also a classy old woman, a grande dame, very old (her wrists and ankles appeared lymphatic, and her sleeves were adapted to these swellings at the wrist). Very lively, she was obviously devoted to the worldly minister—*he* knew his way around. The grande dame was a connoisseur of miniature reproductions and knew all the most important collections of Lilliputian rooms. She remembered that the celebrated Mrs. Thorne had commissioned a tiny Jackson Pollock, but it didn't please her and she sent it back. "Imagine what it must be worth now!" Corde could be social enough, when it was necessary. It helped to fondle the Great Dane when the animal came nudging and sighing. What to do with all this animal nature, seemed to be the burden of the dog's groans. He was groomed like a show horse, your stroking told you that—the texture of the short coat, the velvet of the great jowls.

The guests were served chicken Kiev at a glass dining table which was set on a pedestal of contorted wood, something like the trunk of a forest giant flown from the Congo.

Corde had one of the better views: the parks, the winter meadows of drab green cut into geometrical shapes like baize, the big trees like shrubs, the lake too remote to be water, the black-brazen mills at the Indiana end, fizzing out their gray gases.

The birthday tapers when they were lighted reminded Corde of the tapers in the grass before the Raresh grave, and the rings on Minna's fingers made him think of the raspberry grains of blood that had been wiped from them. Then everybody sang "Happy Birthday, Dear Dolphie." Yes, decadence, of course, Corde supposed, though he was almost certainly the only one who supposed it. An all-but-derelict civilization? And the dog, if he represented the Great Beast of the Apocalypse, was also the pal of the Sorokins', on whom the blond wife doted. For her, Corde would have been glad to think, there was no catastrophe and nothing was corrupt, and all living creatures—all!—were equal in her cheerful American heart. She now began to unwrap the great dog's birthday gifts—biscuits, playthings and mock bones, all the carefully packaged products of the billion-dollar pet industry. To oblige his mistress, who stooped with it in her hand, the animal unwillingly licked one of the glazed bones. A high-ranking uncle in the National Guard sent a five-star dog collar, the authentic insignia of a General of the Armies.

And then the balloons, which were of the shade of green poured into the Chicago River on Saint Patrick's Day, were gathered up and set loose from the porches, everybody at play, the clergyman, too, and the aged grande dame, her brittle hair scarfed up in Gucci silk holding these toys by the bands of suggestive lace. On the fortieth floor you were already in the lower stratum of the upper air, out in the naked wind. The balloons, released over the rail, were snatched straight up, out of sight in a vertical updraft, and then they reappeared in flight and you saw them by the dozen spotted over the sky and driven apart, far out over the lake, towards the dark sky-wall where the mills stood. With Sorokin's field glasses you could follow them awhile yet, and then you couldn't see them anymore. The wind had boomed them into Michigan.

Elfrida admitted to Corde, quietly, that Minna wasn't looking well. "You weren't exaggerating. If you're going to California, you should arrange a long weekend in Santa Barbara, rest in one of those good hotels."

Minna was thanking the hostess, in her full, elaborate style —she was strong on etiquette. "We'll be going," said Corde. He kissed his sister with a quick sense of flying through a zone of familiar warmth. She pressed her long cheek to his circular one. "You did right, Elfrida," he said.

"There is the Mason problem, still," said the Judge.

"Where is he now?"

"Down in Nicaragua, the last we heard. He telephoned his mother, but wouldn't say what he was doing or where he was going. He's not ready to forgive her."

"For bringing a white child into the world?" said Corde. "Or however he interprets the primal curse? But I don't think that self-injury is a need of his character."

"That's what his psychiatrist used to say to me," said Elfrida.

"But I wonder," said Corde, "whether he's still in touch with Cousin Maxie."

"Ah, that's just it," said the Judge. "It would give a new publicity boost to old Detillion. But he hasn't put out any statements. And we'll have to wait for the hearing before we can be sure that Mason intended to jump bail."

"Our Uncle Harold was with the Marines who chased out Sandino in the twenties," said Corde.

Elfrida said, "I doubt that Mason was ever told that fact." She now gave the conversation a different turn. "You never said, Albert, that you had met Dewey Spangler overseas."

"No. It never occurred to me to say. How did you hear about it?"

"How did you *not* hear?" said Elfrida. "Haven't you seen the papers?"

"No. We canceled before Christmas and delivery hasn't started again."

"And didn't anybody call you about it? It's unnatural."

"I keep the phones unplugged. I don't want Minna disturbed. She's had enough of telephones."

"I'm astonished. I would have expected somebody, a colleague from the college or a neighbor in the building, to knock at your door."

"Why, what is it in the papers that's so extraordinary?"

"A column by our old friend Dewey, where he lets himself go. How you met behind the iron curtain, the boyhood friendship, Lakeview High, your wife's predicament. I got more information from that little mug than from you."

"I don't know the man myself," said the Judge. "I only hear from Elfrida how he used to be when you were youngsters. I follow his column from time to time, but this article is kind of a departure, unusually personal."

"How personal?" Corde asked Elfrida.

"A certain amount of reminiscence," said Elfrida. "Pretty brief but packed tight, and really pretty curious—full of observations about American society and culture, and Albert Corde of Chicago as a phenomenon. What would you call it—a short study, a personal memoir, and if you ask me, also a love letter. Not in such good taste, either."

Corde's heart sank. He experienced also a kind of vascular

tightening in the legs, like a man who gets to his feet too quickly, momentarily paralyzed.

"We've upset Albert," said Elfrida to her husband. "When the pink turns up on the cheekbones and his lips press together, he's worried or hurt. I didn't find anything so harmful in what Dewey wrote, Albert. Overblown. Pretentious. Here and there he actually slipped into poetry, and I don't think he has a real gift for that kind of thing."

"He said something similar about my articles in *Harper's*," said Corde.

"Oh, what a comparison!" said Elfrida. "But the worst I'd feel in your place is privacy shock. And with Detillion at work we've all been conditioned or immunized to that. Well, Albert, wait at least until you've read him. It isn't so bad. In my opinion, he wanted to join forces with you."

"You've got a copy, haven't you." Corde stated rather than asked this.

"We talked it over before coming," said the Judge, "and decided that on the off chance you had missed it, it was better you should see it, just in case you had to protect yourself."

"But Elfrida was just saying it wasn't so bad."

She was opening her alligator purse. "You certainly could do without this," she said. "Although comparatively it's minor." As she handed him the folded paper she shone her look upon him, but what really—*really!*—her eyes were saying he couldn't have told you.

XVIII

At home, he gave Minna a cup of tea. Then she said she would lie down and read something—what did he recommend? She always consulted him about reading matter. He knew her simple, old-fashioned tastes. Tanti Gigi, from whom she had learned English at the age of ten years, had given her poems to learn by heart: "The Little Black Boy," "The Sick Rose." He said, "I'll give you Blake's Songs. The two contrary states of the human soul. I was reading Blake while you were at Wesleyan."

"And what will you do with the rest of your afternoon?"

"Go over a few items on my desk."

He withdrew to his corner and unfolded Dewey Spangler's double column of print. It was headed "A Tale of Two Cities."

Corde didn't find it poetic. It was written in Spangler's dependable expository prose for the busy reader. It began with a brief nostalgic paragraph: meeting an old friend who had been his rival in Miss Gumbeener's class at Lakeview. In two sentences he did the friendship. Corde described the whole event as an exhibition match—*Monstre Gai* versus *Ennuyeux Sentimental*, five rounds of boxing. The *Ennuyeux* won the first round. Dewey got off to a clumsy start, speaking of "relationships difficult to form with people in public life." He didn't need to mention Kissinger and Nelson Rockefeller, or make them sound like characters out of Plutarch. But he recovered a little towards the end of the paragraph, evoking the friendship of two "inordinately bookish high school kids." He spoke of his gifted pal Albert Corde, "even then a mysterious individual," who later made a considerable reputation in the International *Herald Tribune*, eventually becoming Professor and Dean Corde. The Dean never intended to mystify anybody, but mystify he did, with his mysterious character. One wonders what effect Deep Analysis might have had on such a person, but Albert Corde was inexplicably hostile towards Psychoanalysis. It will portray the man at one stroke to record what he once said about it. "Psychoanalysis pretends to investigate the Unconscious. The Unconscious by definition is what you aren't conscious of. But the Analysts already know what's in it. They should, because they put it all in beforehand. It's like an Easter Egg hunt. You hide the eggs and then you find 'em. That's on the up and up. But Analysis ain't." Dewey went on, "With an attitude like this my old friend therefore remained mysterious.

"As personal idiosyncrasy this warranted no objection, but not long ago Dean Corde went public and wrote two mystifying articles about the City of Chicago, puzzling and disturbing many readers."

Albert Corde, Spangler wrote, had made his debut as a journalist with the only literate firsthand account of the Potsdam Conference. This Dartmouth junior, a GI who had enlisted and served in France and Germany, happened to be in Potsdam and wrote a brilliant piece for *The New Yorker.* He saw Stalin in an armchair as plain as you and me; he saw Churchill's fall from power and watched Harry Truman play poker and drink whiskey. Of course he was only a kid, with no background in history or world politics. Corde was then twenty-two years of age, but his remarkable account of this conference, which had such dark consequences for the world, has been unjustifiably neglected by the anthologist professors and is forgotten. From the first, the Dean's talent was for observation, not for generalization and synthesis (he lacked Spangler's intellectual grand mastery), and he was wise to stay away from international politics.

But just picture it—the two friends from Lakeview High School meeting in a Communist capital during the dismal days of late December. In the hospital, an old woman dying; and in Chicago a jury trial. The Dean had become involved in a disagreeable matter involved the death of a student. There was unpleasant infighting. This was hardly as important as it appeared to a hypersensitive man. "To a friend seasoned in modern politics, covering the world scene in depth for twenty-five years—riot, terrorism, massacre, the strategies of power—Professor Corde's personal distress seemed exaggerated. Temperamentally, he was tender-minded, incapable of grasping the full implications of world transformation, the growth of a new technology for managing human affairs, the new factors, the analytical paradigms which guide the decisions of authority in all postindustrial societies." The Dean was a delicate spirit, a genuinely reflective person. This was why he gave up journalism and took cover in the academy. Coming out again to have a look at the present sociopolitical scene, he went into shock. His particular brand of humanism could not prepare him for what he saw in the streets and skyscrapers. Here was a clear opening (Dewey became very grand in this next passage) for the revival of a humanistic outlook. "Underdefinition of the criteria by which men are defined opened an opportunity to Humanists to introduce their models, as against Economic Man, Psychological Man and other typologies. But the Dean has no bent for such enterprises. He is not a man for models, he is a sensitive and emotional private observer. Trained urbanologists regarded his Chicago articles as excessively emotional."

These "paradigms" and the "underdefinition of the criteria" were Malraux thrusts, Hegelian world history in an updated American form. Who among Spangler's colleagues in Washington or New York could handle such concepts—Reston, Kraft, Alsop in his best days? And what of Walter Lippmann himself?

We were getting into deeper waters now, and Corde's heart took on a monitory heaviness. Warning: Anything can happen here.

The trained urbanologists had found the articles too emotional. "This was predictable in a personality of so rare a type, appalled by the transformation of his native city. For Corde is attached to Chicago by strong feelings and the physical and human destruction he describes in *Harper's* fills him with pain. As a fellow Chicagoan and an old friend I can testify to this. But it should be added that even in his youth Albert Corde, the son of a wealthy and privileged family, did not know the Chicago in which the rest of us were growing up. It takes the most American of all American cities to create this native son who is as unlike his fellow Americans as he can be. When your correspondent and his old friend met for a drink in Bucharest, the Dean repeated the amusing remark an elderly English traveler had once made to him: 'I suppose there's nothing too rum to be true.' I apply this to the Dean himself. He is an American almost too rum to be recognized as such by his fellow citizens. This was why it was hard for them to follow his argument."

As he read this, the Dean discovered that he almost stopped breathing. What a smart little monster Dewey was, and what a keen schemer, and how rivalrous. He disposed of the Dean by describing him as an unwitting alien. How cleverly he got rid of him. Corde had to admit that Dewey had put his finger on an important fact. In touch with the Sadats and the Kissingers, the Brezhnevs and the Nixons, interpreting them to the world, Dewey was a master of the public forms of discourse. If you were going to be a communicator, you had to know the passwords, the code words, you had to signify your acceptance of the prevailing standards. You could say nothing publicly, not if you expected to be taken seriously, without the right clearance. The Dean's problem had been one of language. Nobody will buy what you're selling—not in those words. They don't even know what your product *is.*

"Professor Corde," Dewey went on, "is very hard on journalism, on the mass media. His charge is that they fail to deal with the moral, emotional, imaginative life, in short, the *true* life of human beings, and that their great power prevents people from having access to this true life. What we call 'information' he would characterize as delusion. He does not say this in so many words, but in his recent sketches he tries to outline creatively the right way to apprehend public questions. If he emphasizes strongly the sufferings of urban populations, especially in the ghettos, it is because he thinks that public discussion is threadbare, that this is either the cause or the effect of blindness (or both the cause and effect) and that our cultural poverty has the same root as the frantic and criminal life of our once great cities. He blames the communications industry for this. It breeds hysteria and misunderstanding. He also blames the universities. Academics have made no effort to lead the public. The intellectuals have been incapable of clarifying our principal problems and of depicting democracy to itself in this time of agonized struggle. Reading Dean Corde one is reminded of certain pages of Ortega y Gasset's *The Rebellion of the Masses* (incorrectly translated as *The Revolt*) and also of passages in André Malraux's memorable conversations with General de Gaulle, and of the final work of Malraux's dying days. . . .

"But if the Dean is hard on the media he is even more bitter about the academics. The media are part of corporate America. They are part of the problem, hence their 'impartiality' is meaningless. But the universities are a deep disappointment to him. I gather from his conversation that he thinks academics are not different from other Americans, they are dominated by the same consensus and ruled by public opinion. They were not set apart, with all their privileges, to be like everybody else but to be *different.* If they could not accept difference they could not make the contribution to culture that society needed. The challenge to the Humanists was the challenge to produce new models.

"I am not," Dewey astonishingly wrote, "an admirer of Jean Jacques Rousseau. I would not agree with Immanuel Kant that he was a great man. He did, however, understand that the challenge of modern egalitarian societies would be the creation of high human types, such individuals as would satisfy the human need for stature and love of the beautiful. This would not be elitism in the ordinary acceptance of the term but generosity and love of humankind, the exact opposite of snobbery and false superiority. I assume that this was why my friend Albert Corde gave up a quite successful career in journalism to become a professor. His hopes disappointed, he went out to investigate the surrounding city, and he will forgive me for saying that he went slightly mad. It wasn't only the collapse of urban America that got him but what Julien Benda called the treason of the intellectuals. . . ."

Oh, fuck you, Dewey, and your Julien Benda! Corde, knuckling his eyes, smarting with sweat, read on. There wasn't much left, thank God.

"Dean Corde must have offended his colleagues deeply. They should have been irradiating American society with humanistic culture, and in the Dean's book they are failures and phonies. That's what his articles reveal. I wonder whether my dear old friend realizes this. I am not sure that he has a good idea of what they were up against, the magnitude of the challenge facing them. Who would, who could make high human types of the business community, the engineers, the politicians and the scientists? What system of higher education could conceivably have succeeded? But Dean Corde is unforgiving. Philistinism is his accusation. Philistine by origin, humanistic academics were drawn magnetically back again to the philistine core of American society. What should have been an elite of the intellect became instead an elite of influence and comforts. The cities decayed. The professors couldn't have prevented that, but they could have told us (as the Dean himself somewhat wildly tries to do) what the human meaning of this decay was and what it augured for civilization. Scholars who were supposed to represent the old greatness didn't put up a fight for it. They gave in to the great emptiness. And 'from the emptiness come whirlwinds of insanity,' he writes.

"A little coaching in *realpolitik* would have done the Dean no harm. It was too bad that he was carried away by an earnestness too great for his capacities, because he is a very witty man. In conversation he was charming and amusing about politics and the law in Chicago. When he wasn't sailing in the clouds with Vico and Hegel he was extremely funny. He made some memorable remarks about the varieties of public welfare in the United States. There are high welfare categories as well as low ones. Some professors work hard, said the Dean. Most of them do. But a professor when he gets tenure doesn't *have* to do anything. A tenured professor and a welfare mother with eight kids have much in common. . . ."

The damage that these sentences would do was as clear as the print itself. By a process of instantaneous translation, Corde read them with the eyes of Alec Witt, the Provost. He thought, Dewey has done it to me. Alec Witt has got me now, convicted out of my own mouth. Of course I could try to say that I was only quoting, that this was Mason senior speaking, but Witt isn't going to listen to explanations, nor will he care what actually was said. The trouble is all in the nuances. Oh, the nuances! Dewey and I never did get our nuances together, not in forty years. And the college won't care to hear about the nuances. And here's the progress I've made with the Provost. At first I was suspect, and presently I was distrusted and afterwards disliked. Finally by my own sincere efforts I worked my way down into the lowest category—contempt. And then, "The man is a disaster." And finally, "The sonofabitch is a traitor." Yes, Dewey's done it to me this time. This was the Dewey who never had a college education letting us all have it. And at the same time wanting to draw close. And to take me in his embrace. And hoping to soar far beyond Walter Lippmann. And this is something like the letter he wrote from New York when we were kids, when Uncle Harold, that old goon, jimmied open the drawer and read aloud to the family what Dewey had written, and gave Mother so much pain. That was winter, too, but this is more mean-looking; now the wind is from the north, with rain, and harsh water.

XIX

CORDE did not speak of this to Minna until they had left the Los Angeles airport in the Budget Rent-a-Car. He thought it would be easier to talk in open country. Here at any rate the sun was shining. He had counted on *some* help from the climate. And from astronomy, of course. Whatever, technically, she was thinking was wonderfully good for her. On the plane she had actually chatted with him about the birth of stars from gas clouds, the embryonic form of these suns, their infrared rays and the radio waves they emitted, the past of our own sun, its future. She had mentioned something called FU Orionis. He never bothered her with questions about hydrogen, helium, lithium. He remembered the wise Egyptian who had told Cleopatra, "In Nature's book of infinite secrecy, a little I can read," but she was making such excellent progress that he kept this to himself, although as a rule she liked him to quote her quotes.

When the foothills began he told her what Spangler had written—briefed her quite fully on the consequences. He said, "I didn't want to molest you with all this."

"I see. . . . I wouldn't have been able to do that, keep all that to myself. It was very masculine of you. But stupid! I'm your wife. I'm *supposed* to be told."

"I couldn't predict how you'd take it. Of course, I'm very glad. . . . So then, Dewey really screwed me. It wasn't me that made that crack about professors and welfare mothers . . . Zaehner, poor man."

"Ah, yes, it was Zaehner. But you did quote."

"It was all distorted. Much of the rest I didn't say, either. Although here and there he got me right. But how could he not know what such a column would do to me. Forty years of *almost* communication . . . ."

"And not even forty years is enough? But that's not news to you, either. And why did you talk so openly to him?"

"There's the whole thing—having people to talk to. To be able to say what you mean, mean what you say. Truthfully, it did occur to me at the Intercontinental that Dewey was interviewing me. But I figured it was nothing more than his professional habit."

"If you actually sensed that he was doing an interview, why did you talk?"

"I only said that it had the format of an interview. It didn't cross my mind that I was opening my heart to the press."

"I must read the article. I will, when we get to Palomar. I can understand why you would talk. Talking was about the only desire you had a chance to satisfy, over there."

"Yes, and it was the day of the funeral. Besides, I always did love Dewey. And partly I was affected also by the exotic place, so far from home that somehow it all seemed off the record. I never expected to account to Alec Witt for all that. . . ."

"Alec let you have it."

"Not shouting, of course; that's not his style. His style is to go after you in short rushes. Each one of them is pleasant. But then you begin to see where he's maneuvered you. He hasn't ever been rude to me. He's never been anything except considerate. But there's a grinning glow. And finally at the kill there's a great radiance. He told me I could always say what I liked and say it publicly. Academic freedom protected me. I was, however, involved in a contradiction which, surely, an intelligent man like me couldn't overlook. A tenured professor had no obligations to the institution except minimal adherence to its rules, but the responsibilities of an officer of the administration, once you had accepted them, limited your options. I had made the administration *very* unhappy. While everybody was deeply sympathetic to me, people who had sacrificed for the college, and so on, given their best energies, fought for liberal education as well as for the very survival of the institution, were *deeply* wounded. He beat on my soul, good and hard. He could have been singing *Exsultate, Jubilate* as he kicked hell out of me. His task was to make sure of my resignation without serious offense to you, or blocking any effort I might make to take you away. He executed this like a kind of angel. He bound me while he hit me."

"Then you told him that you would resign as dean?"

"Yes," said Corde. "I told him that. My purpose in going to his office was to tell him. As for you, it was a rule with me not to meddle, I assured him. To find out how you felt he'd have to talk to you."

"That was right," said Minna. "But how disagreeable for you, Albert."

"Not so bad. I'm not much hurt. It's not my game. I wasn't meant to be a dean. I didn't say that to the Provost. I said I was resigning and it wasn't necessary to discuss the motives, but that I did want to say what a valuable institution the college was for the city, along with Northwestern and the University of Chicago, and how important it was for young people learning about painting and poetry, reading history, classics, the sciences, to have libraries and fine instruction. These islands, how badly the country needs them. I almost said, 'If only to counterbalance the S.M. establishments.'"

"What are those?"

"The sadomasochistic shops, where people now go as if to the beauty parlor—with virtually the same carefree attitude."

"You have a really endearing character, but you do somehow work in such strange things," said Minna.

"But I didn't say. I *almost*. I only told him I was grateful to the college. I told him no lies, and I wasn't perverse. Anyway, he wasn't really listening. He accepted my resignation letter and passed to another subject—Beech. Did I intend to write an article about Beech? I said that I guessed I would do more writing."

"Along the lines of *Harper's* pieces?"

"Oh, absolutely. Why not?"

She said, having thought about this for some miles, "It won't be a restful life."

"I won't do articles like the Chicago ones unless I'm stirred in the same peculiar way. That doesn't happen often. I'm quiet enough as a rule. I don't like controversy. I'm good enough at my trade."

"But how are you going to practice it?"

"We'll have to see what happens. Dewey said I had quite a successful career in journalism. I'll take it up again, as quietly as I can."

"Now will you tell me about Beech?"

"I spent a long afternoon with him."

"The best people in Geophysics swear by him."

"I like the man."

"And you've decided to do the article? Wouldn't that be a good way to start over?"

"I arranged to help him with it. Those lead conclusions are his, not mine. *Something* deadly is happening. I'm with him to that extent. So I'll advise him about language only. Then I won't have to agree ignorantly."

She took his hand from the steering wheel, pressed it, kept it in her lap. She said, presently, "We aren't too far from the Indian mission. We can stop there and take a break."

"The trip is tiring you. We didn't make smart arrangements. We should have flown in yesterday and rested overnight in Los Angeles. I can stand that place for about ten hours."

The mission was in a sheltered, warm zone. Corde and Minna looked into the handicrafts shop—beads, turquoise, arrowheads, gloves in the dim showcases, clusters of moccasins gathering dust in the corners. Then they sat in the inner court. "Five minutes in the sun?" said Minna. She followed her schedule. The heavy arches of the cloister formed a small square. In the foreground, flowers; behind the whitewashed arches, darkness, but tranquil darkness.

Corde said, "You know what? It threw Dewey Spangler into a frenzy of happiness to have such crushing wonderful things to say. It put him right on the summits. And best of all, he could blame the mischief on me. He was so delirious that he couldn't think what it might do to his pal. Maybe it was the cuts in his intestines that put him in such a state."

"I wouldn't think any more about him," said Minna.

When they returned to the rental car, Corde reluctant, dragging (but realistically, how long could they stay seated in a mission garden choked with flowers?), Minna said, "Valeria had a high opinion of you, Albert." Her head was down; she clipped the seat belt into place. "She trusted you."

"You think so?"

"What you told her last of all was what she wanted most of all to hear."

No more was said of this. Corde was moved. His wife, unskilled in human dealings, was offering him support from her own main source. What came through Minna's words was that she was alone in the world; and with him; she did have him, with all his troubling oddities; and he had her.

Minna now began to talk about the chances for a clear night. Here on the lower slopes the sun was shining, and that was promising, but conditions changed very rapidly here. When it was cloudy, the dome didn't open. She said that several times.

"I'm sending up prayers for optimum weather," he said. "But I read here and there that the new robots out in space transmit fantastic information, pictures you can't get from the ground."

"That's mostly true. But there's something I need from the two-hundred-inch telescope."

"Even that, I understand, you can see on the TV monitors in the control room."

"Won't do," said Minna. "I have to have the plates."

"You aren't going to sit up there, in the eye of the telescope, or the cage, or whatever it's called? I hope not."

"I've done it a hundred times."

"But this time?"

"I think yes."

"Can't you send up somebody with instructions?"

"No. Last time one of the smart young people made the fine corrections for me, and the results were unusable."

"But you aren't well enough, Minna."

"No? I am, though."

Interference was out of the question. The professional line! How severe she was, drawing it. How he presented himself at the barrier, petitioning. For her own good. It amused them both—each in his own way. "You've lost too much weight," was all that he found to say.

"I'll be wearing the insulated suit. And they keep the cage warmer now than in the old days."

At five thousand feet there was snow on the ground, a thin cover over the huge raw clearing around the dome.

"No clouds at all," said Minna. "We're lucking out. Now, if no fog develops . . ."

To his great relief, she got the weather she wanted, and while she was getting herself ready, talking to colleagues, he explored the enormous dark emptiness of the dome, passing under the gray barrel of the great telescope and hearing the stir of the machines that operated it. He was warmly dressed, he had brought his parka from Chicago. One of the younger assistants in the observatory was assigned to keep him company. "Let's inspect the layout. Have you ever seen it before?"

"Not this particular dome, and never any of them with a guide."

The tall young man, bearded, had the air of a ski instructor, and he talked about right ascension, mirrors, refractions, spectrum analysis. "I can't follow," Corde said at last. They stopped in mid-floor, a vast, unlighted, icy, scientific Cimmerian gloom. The hugeness of the dome referred you—far past mosques or churches, Saint Paul's, Saint Peter's—to the real scale of the night. We built as big as we could build for the purpose of investigating the *real* bigness. The dome's interior was segmented by curved beams. Corde had never been inside an empty space so huge. The floor was endless to cross. Despite his sweaters, coat, double socks, parka, he was cold on the encircling catwalk. They stepped out on the outer gallery—light steel spongework underfoot; you could see through it. The snow extended to the edge of the enormous clearing. He went inside again.

If you came for a look at astral space it was appropiate that you should have a taste of the cold *out there*, its power to cancel everything merely human. That he understood so little of the tall young man's lingo made no difference; he went on talking, but Corde several times refused to go to the rooms below where you could sip coffee, read magazines, practice billiard shots. Minna had said when she was leaving him, "It looks now as if they're sure to open by and by. I'll send for you."

Her messenger found Corde and his guide on the catwalk. Dr. Corde was going to the cage, and would he like to ride up, too? Yes, he did, of course.

He ran down eagerly. The junior colleague who had been guiding him was coming along to help Minna install herself in the eye of the huge instrument. She was wearing the tight-fitting suit. As she went into the open lift, Corde following, he asked again, "You're sure you can take the cold?"

"Don't fuss over me. I'll come down if I can't, my dear."

True, he was foolishly fussing. She had lost her natural insulation. Temporarily emaciated. Permanently excited. She said to the stooping, bearded young man, "My husband has never been up."

"Never?" He pressed the switch and they began to rise.

The lift was attached to one of the structural arches. It didn't go straight up; it followed a curved course. Except in one low corner of the interior, there was no light. And now the vast dome rumbled. Something parted, began to slide above them. Segments of the curved surface opened quickly and let in the sky—first a clear piercing slice. All at once there was only the lift, moving along the arch. The interior was abolished altogether—no interior—nothing but the open, freezing heavens. If this present motion were to go on, you would travel straight out. You would go into the stars. He could make out the edges of the open dome still. And because there was a dome, and the cold was so absolute, he came inevitably back to the crematorium, *that* rounded top and its huge circular floor, the feet of stiffs sticking through the curtains, the blasting heat underneath where they were disposed of, the killing cold when you returned and thought your head was being split by an ax. But that dome never opened. You could pass through only as smoke.

This Mount Palomar coldness was not to be compared to the cold of the death house. Here the living heavens looked as if they would take you in. Another sort of rehearsal, thought Corde. The sky was tense with stars, but not so tense as he was, in his breast. Everything overhead was in equilibrium, kept in place by mutual tensions. What was it that *his* tensions kept in place?

And what he saw with his eyes was not even the real heavens. No, only white marks, bright vibrations, clouds of sky roe, tokens of the real thing, only as much as could be taken in through the distortions of the atmosphere. Through these distortions you saw objects, forms, partial realities. The rest was to be felt. And it wasn't only that you felt, but that you were drawn to feel and to penetrate further, as if you were being informed that what was spread over you had to do with your existence, down to the very blood and the crystal forms inside your bones. Rocks, trees, animals, men and women, these also drew you to penetrate further, under the distortions (comparable to the atmospheric ones, shadows within shadows), to find their real being with your own. This was the sense in which you were drawn.

Once, in the Mediterranean, coming topside from a C-class cabin, the uric smells and the breath of the bilges, every hellish little up-to-date convenience there below to mock your insomnia—then seeing the morning sun on the tilted sea. Free! The grip of every sickness within you disengaged by this pouring out. You couldn't tell which was out of plumb, the ship, or yourself, or the sea aslant—but free! It didn't matter, since you were free! It was like that also when you approached the stars as steadily as this.

The lift stopped and his wife, in the sort of thermal suit she wore, smiled at him. Perhaps his parka amused her. They had reached the top of the telescope. She climbed down into the pit of it, into the cage filled with technical apparatus—gauges, panels glowing, keys to press, wires. The stooped assistant got in with her to help her to hook up. The young man was quick. Agile, he climbed again into the lift. She waved to her husband, cheerful, and closed herself in. She was Corde's representative among those bright things so thick and close.

Corde said, "She'll be all right, I suppose. She's not too long out of the hospital."

The young man pressed the switch for the descent. "Never saw the sky like this, did you?"

"No. I was told how cold it would be. It *is* damn cold."

"Does that really get you, do you really mind it all that much?"

They were traveling slowly in the hooked path of their beam towards the big circle of the floor.

"The cold? Yes. But I almost think I mind coming down more."

CHRONOLOGY

NOTE ON THE TEXTS

NOTES

Chronology

1915 Born Solomon Bellows in Lachine, Quebec, on June 10, fourth child of Abram Bellows and Lescha Gordin, Russian-Jewish immigrants from St. Petersburg. (The family name was changed from "Belo" on arriving in Canada in 1913. Abram Bellows was an importer of dry goods, baker, and junk-dealer. One sister, Zelda, nine years older than Bellow, and two brothers Movscha, seven years older, and Samuel, four years older, were born in Russia.)

1918 Family moves to Saint Dominique Street, in a poor area of Montreal. (Bellow will later write: "The Jewish slums of Montreal during my childhood, just after the First World War, were not too far removed from the ghettos of Poland and Russia. Life in such places was anything but ordinary.") Parents speak Russian and Yiddish; their children speak English and Yiddish at home; French is spoken on the street. Bellow later claims the Armistice parade as one of his earliest memories.

1923 Falls ill with peritonitis and pneumonia, and spends six months in Royal Victoria Hospital, Montreal, where he reads, and is deeply affected by, the New Testament Gospels. Father becomes a bootlegger helping to smuggle liquor into the United States.

1924 Father goes to Chicago to work for cousin's bakery. In July, the rest of family is smuggled across the border to join him. They live on the east side of Humboldt Park. Bellow takes up violin. Attends Lafayette School and Columbus Elementary School. His main source for books is the Budlong branch of Chicago Public Library on North Avenue.

1930 Graduates from Sabin Junior High School. Enters Tuley High School, where he befriends Isaac Rosenfeld, Oscar Tarcov, and Sam Freifeld, all aspiring writers.

1931 Family moves to a more prosperous area of Chicago on the west side of Humboldt Park.

1933 Graduates from Tuley in January. Mother dies of breast cancer in February. Moves out of home in fall, and takes room in a boarding house near the University of Chicago, where he is now enrolled along with his classmate Isaac Rosenfeld.

1934 Father remarries; he is now the successful owner of the Carroll Coal Company.

1935 During the winter the driver of one of the Carroll Company's trucks is killed. Without insurance, father is forced to pay costs, and can no longer afford $100-per-quarter fees of University of Chicago. Bellow is forced to leave university and returns home; in fall transfers to Northwestern University, where he takes dual major in English and anthropology, the latter under Melville J. Herskovits.

1936 First published piece, "Pets of the North Shore," a whimsical sketch about dogs and their owners, appears in *The Daily Northwestern*. Literary editor of university paper rejects one of his short stories. Wins third prize in "Campus in Print" story competition; story appears under a newly adopted name, Saul Bellow: "I wanted to break with everybody, even my own family, so I chose the other name, which was a legitimate name, and belonged to me."

1937 Becomes associate editor of *The Beacon,* a monthly journal, to which he contributes many pieces. Receives B.A. from Northwestern with honors in anthropology and sociology; goes on to graduate fellowship in Department of Sociology and Anthropology at University of Wisconsin, Madison, where Isaac Rosenfeld is a Ph.D. candidate. Works on a thesis on culture of French Canadians, but is soon discouraged ("Every time I worked on my thesis, it turned out to be a story"). Leaves before the end of the year.

1938 Returns to Chicago, where he marries Anita Goshkin. Works in his brother Maurice's coalyard, but is fired for absenteeism. Takes a part-time job in the fall teaching anthropology and English composition at Pestalozzi-Freobel Teachers College on South Michigan Avenue. His assigned reading list (which he will substantially retain through decades of teaching) includes Lawrence, Dostoevsky, Dreiser, and Flaubert. Works on the Federal Writers' Project, part of the New Deal Works Progress

Administration; his job is to compile sketches of contemporary American authors.

1940 Travels to Mexico in summer; reads Lawrence's *Mornings in Mexico* and Stendhal. Arrives in Mexico City on August 21, to find that Trotsky had been assassinated the day before; views body at morgue. Stories rejected by *The Saturday Evening Post* and *The Kenyon Review.*

1941 *Partisan Review* (May–June) publishes short story "Two Morning Monologues." Works on a novel entitled "The Very Dark Trees"; after being rejected by several publishers, it is accepted by William Roth of the Colt Press for $150.

1942 Visits New York, where Isaac Rosenfeld is studying at NYU. Meets Alfred Kazin; spends time with poet Delmore Schwartz. Draft board defers him until end of term at Pestalozzi Teachers College; in June defers him again until mid-July. William Roth, now enlisted, cancels publication of "The Very Dark Trees," sending Bellow consolatory $50. Bellow burns manuscript.

1943 Applies unsuccessfully for a Guggenheim fellowship. During summer, rejected for job at *Time* by Whittaker Chambers, editor of the magazine's books and arts pages. Works as editor on *Encyclopedia Britannica's* "Syntopicon," a two-volume supplement to the "Great Books of the Western World" project. "Notes of a Dangling Man" appears in *Partisan Review* (September–October).

1944 Novel *Dangling Man* published in March by Vanguard Press. Edmund Wilson describes it in *The New Yorker* as "one of the most honest pieces of testimony on the psychology of a whole generation who have grown up during the depression and the war." The book sells a total of 1,506 copies. Son Gregory born in April. Draft board again defers Bellow, who has been diagnosed with inguinal hernia. Studio executive at MGM, seeing author photograph in newspaper, offers to make him a Hollywood star, playing "the guy who loses the girl to the George Raft type or the Errol Flynn type."

1945 Volunteers in April for the Merchant Marine, and is assigned to the Atlantic district headquarters in Sheepshead Bay, Brooklyn. Moves to New York in September. Lives on Pineapple Street, Brooklyn Heights, writing book reviews and reading for publishers; works on novel *The Victim.*

1946 A second Guggenheim application is rejected. In the fall, becomes assistant professor at the University of Minnesota, Minneapolis; meets Robert Penn Warren, who is at work on *All the King's Men.*

1947 Travels to Europe in July, visiting Paris, Madrid, and Granada. Writes "Spanish Letter" for *Partisan Review.* Returns to Minneapolis in September. *The Victim* is published in November by Vanguard Press and sells 2,257 copies.

1948–49 Receives Guggenheim fellowship after third application. With the foundation's $2,500 and a $3,000 advance for his next novel from his new publisher, Viking, travels in the fall to Paris, where he will live for the next two years. Meets Georges Bataille, Maurice Merleau-Ponty, and Albert Camus at the home of his Chicago friend Harold Kaplan. Other Paris friends include Herbert Gold, Mary McCarthy, Lionel Abel, and William Phillips. Works on a third novel, "The Crab and the Butterfly," about two invalids in a Chicago hospital. Abandons novel in progress in October 1949 and begins *The Adventures of Augie March.* (Writes later: "The book just came to me. All I had to do was be there with buckets to catch it.") "From the Life of Augie March" appears in November *Partisan Review.* Visits London in December; meets Cyril Connolly, Henry Green, and Stephen Spender.

1950 In summer, gives lectures at Salzburg Seminar in American Studies. Visits Venice, Florence, and Rome, where he works for six weeks on *Augie March* in the Borghese Gardens. Meets Alberto Moravia and Ignazio Silone. Returns to New York in October; takes a modest apartment in Forest Hills, Queens.

1951 Becomes interested in sexual and emotional therapy of Wilhelm Reich. Begins Reichian therapy with Dr. Chester Raphael; spends hours sitting in "orgone box," supposed to concentrate "orgone energy." Hired as part-time assistant professor at NYU. Applies unsuccessfully for a renewal of Guggenheim fellowship; borrows $500 from Viking. *Commentary* publishes his story "Looking for Mr. Green." Departs for Salzburg Seminar in December, stopping en route in Paris. Reads passages of *Augie March* to his Salzburg students.

1952 Returns to New York in mid-February. Travels west to lecture at universities of Washington and Oregon. Spends time with Theodore Roethke and Dylan Thomas in Seattle. A dramatization of *The Victim* opens off-Broadway in May. Receives a $1,000 grant from the American Academy of Arts and Letters. Spends summer at Yaddo writers' colony in Saratoga Springs, New York. Translates Isaac Bashevis Singer's story "Gimpel the Fool" from the Yiddish (Singer's first appearance in English). In fall, takes creative-writing job at Princeton as Delmore Schwartz's assistant, where he meets John Berryman and wife, Eileen Simpson. Meets Sondra Tschacbasov. Suffers severe case of pneumonia in December. An excerpt from *Augie March* appears in *The New Yorker.*

1953 In September, takes one-year job at Bard College, in Annandale-on-Hudson, New York. At Bard, befriends Keith Botsford and Jack Ludwig. His temporary landlord is Chanler Chapman, later a model for the hero of *Henderson the Rain King. The Adventures of Augie March* is published in September. Gives interview to *New York Times.* In December, receives royalty check for $2,000. Takes temporary apartment on Riverside Drive in New York, where he spends weekends.

1954 Wins National Book Award for *Adventures of Augie March.* Writes "How I Wrote Augie March's Story" in *New York Times* in January: "The book was writing itself very rapidly. I was coming to be strangely independent of place. Chicago itself had grown exotic to me." Separates from Anita Goshkin. Leaves Bard in June; spends summer in Wellfleet, Massachusetts, where friends include Mary McCarthy, Harry Levin, and Alfred Kazin. Applies for another grant from the Guggenheim Foundation. Works on "Memoirs of a Bootlegger's Son," a fictional portrait of Bellows family in Montreal, portions of which will later be incorporated into *Herzog.*

1955 Father dies of an aneurysm in May. The Guggenheim Foundation grants him a second fellowship. In August visits small towns in Illinois for *Holiday* magazine travel piece. Spends next eight months in Reno, Nevada, while waiting for divorce.

1956 Marries Sondra Tschacbasov in Reno in February. Works on novel *Henderson the Rain King*. Visited in April by Arthur Miller and Marilyn Monroe. Finishes novella *Seize the Day*, which appears in the summer issue of *Partisan Review*. In July, childhood friend Isaac Rosenfeld dies of heart attack in Chicago, aged thirty-eight. Buys house in Tivoli, New York, with the help of $8,000 legacy from father. Spends the fall at Yaddo, where he becomes friends with John Cheever. *Seize the Day* is published in November.

1957 Second son, Adam, is born in January. Takes temporary appointment for the spring semester at the University of Minnesota, where he spends time with John Berryman; in Bellow's absence, Ralph Ellison moves into Tivoli house. Meets twenty-three-year-old Philip Roth in Chicago. Spends the fall in Chicago, teaching at Northwestern. In "The University as Villain," published in *The Nation* in November, accuses English departments of being full of "discouraged people who stand dully upon a brilliant plane, in charge of masterpieces but not themselves inspired."

1958 Finishes early draft of *Henderson the Rain King* in March. Dictates the novel's revisions for six weeks to secretary in Tivoli house. In fall, returns to teach at University of Minnesota. Enters therapy with a clinical psychologist.

1959 *Henderson the Rain King* is published in February. Receives $16,000 grant from the Ford Foundation. Returns to Tivoli for summer. Works on play *The Last Analysis*. Separates from Sondra Tschacbasov in November. Stays briefly at Yaddo and then in Herbert Gold's New York apartment before going to Europe for a lecture tour of Poland and Yugoslavia at the invitation of the State Department.

1960 *The Noble Savage*, a journal co-edited by Bellow, Jack Ludwig, and Keith Botsford, appears in February (five numbers will be published); contributors include Harold Rosenberg, Ralph Ellison, and John Berryman. In March, visits Italy, Israel, and England. Returns from Europe and enters therapy with sexologist Dr. Albert Ellis. Spends summer at Tivoli. Divorce becomes final in June. In "The Sealed Treasure," essay published in the July *TLS*, argues against modern Flaubertian aestheticism, and its "disappointment with its human material," in favor of an

American novel that might more optimistically search for the "sealed treasure" of ordinary inner life.

1961 Teaches spring term at the University of Puerto Rico. Marries Susan Glassman in November. Spends fall at the University of Chicago, where he has temporary teaching appointment.

1962 Works steadily on novel *Herzog*. Made honorary Doctor of Letters, Northwestern University. Attends White House dinner for André Malraux in May. An excerpt from *The Last Analysis* appears in the summer issue of *Partisan Review*. Accepts five-year appointment as professor at the Committee on Social Thought of the University of Chicago, and moves into Hyde Park apartment. (Will stay at University of Chicago for thirty years.) John Steinbeck, who has just been awarded the Nobel Prize in Literature, inscribes copy of Nobel lecture to Bellow: "You're next."

1963 Old school friend Oscar Tarcov dies, aged forty-eight. Made honorary Doctor of Letters, Bard College. "Some Notes on Recent American Fiction" is published in *Encounter* in November.

1964 Third son, Daniel, born in March. Spends July and August on Martha's Vineyard, finishing *Herzog* and *The Last Analysis*. *Herzog* is published in September, and reaches top of the best-seller list in October. *The Last Analysis* opens on Broadway the same month; closes within a month. Donates manuscripts of *Augie March* and *Henderson the Rain King* to University of Chicago. Pat Covici, Viking editor and dedicatee of *Herzog*, dies of heart attack in October.

1965 Now increasingly wealthy from *Herzog* sales, gives the Tivoli house to Bard. *Herzog* wins the National Book Award in March. Attends festival of the arts at White House in June, at which he reads from *Herzog*. (Festival is controversial because of Vietnam War, and Edmund Wilson and Robert Lowell return their invitations.) Is interviewed at length for *Paris Review*. Spends summer on Martha's Vineyard.

1966 Receives the Prix International de Litterature (Formentor Prize). Delivers keynote address at PEN Congress in New York in June, declaring: "We have at present a large literary community and something we can call *faute de mieux*, a literary culture, in my opinion a very bad one." *Under the Weather*, a trilogy of one-act plays, opens at the Fortune Theatre in London in the summer; opens in October in New York, where it closes in less than two weeks. Lectures in the fall at the American Embassy in London; travels to Holland and Poland. By the end of the year, marriage has ended. Moves out of Chicago apartment. Begins work on novel *Mr. Sammler's Planet*.

1967 Travels to Israel to cover Six-Day War for *Newsday* in June, writing a series of four articles. Spends summer in rented house in East Hampton, where he sees Saul Steinberg and Harold Rosenberg. Essay "Skepticism and the Depth of Life" published in anthology *The Arts & the Public*.

1968 Is divorced from Susan. Becomes Chevalier des Arts et Lettres in January. B'nai Brith confers Jewish Heritage Award for Excellence in Literature. Gives talk in the spring at San Francisco State College, where he is heckled by novelist Floyd Salas, a faculty member; incorporates detailed description of the incident into his new novel. Spends September at Villa Serbelloni, Rockefeller Foundation villa on Lake Como. A collection of stories, *Mosby's Memoirs*, is published in October. Travels to London in December to see his publisher George Weidenfeld.

1969 Continues to work on *Mr. Sammler's Planet*, describing it as "a dramatic essay of some sort, wrung from me by the crazy Sixties." In March, enters analysis with Heinz Kohut.

1970 *Mr. Sammler's Planet* is published. On his first trip to Africa in February, visits Nairobi and Addis Ababa. In April delivers lecture at Purdue University entitled "Culture Now: Some Animadversions, Some Laughs," in which he attacks 1960s avant-gardism in the arts. Receives honorary degree in May from New York University. Spends June in Israel, attending symposium at Tel Aviv U.S. Cultural Center and a banquet in Jerusalem where Elie Wiesel and Golda Meir speak. Becomes chairman of Committee on Social Thought (will retain position until 1975). In December, *Anon*, a new journal, again co-edited with Keith Botsford, appears for only one issue.

1971 Wins third National Book Award for *Mr. Sammler's Planet*. A revival of *The Last Analysis* opens off-Broadway in June; closes August 1. Travels to London in fall to serve as judge for Booker Prize for Fiction; visits Lisbon, Turin, and Dublin. John Berryman writes to him: "Let's join forces, large and small, as in the winter beginning of 1953 in Princeton, with the Bradstreet blazing and Augie fleecing away. We're promising."

1972 John Berryman commits suicide in January. Visits Japan in April and Europe in August. Delivers lecture "Literature in the Age of Technology" at the Smithsonian in November.

1973 In April, stays for several weeks at Monks House, Rodmell (former home of Virginia and Leonard Woolf), where he works on novel *Humboldt's Gift*. Receives honorary degrees from Harvard and Yale. Begins attending meetings of the Chicago Anthroposophical Society.

1974 Marries Alexandra Ionescu Tulcea, a professor of mathematics at Northwestern, in November.

1975 Attends White House dinner in January for British Prime Minister Harold Wilson. Delivers proofs of *Humboldt's Gift* in June, and travels to London, where he meets Owen Barfield, English scholar of Rudolf Steiner's anthroposophical thought, with whom he will carry on a long correspondence. Spends time at Costa del Sol home of his British publisher Barley Alison. *Humboldt's Gift* is published in August. In October, begins three-month sabbatical in Israel, where, for a projected nonfiction book, he interviews A. B. Yehoshua, Amos Oz, Abba Eban, Jerusalem mayor Teddy Kollek, and Prime Minister Yitzhak Rabin. Louis Simpson attacks *Humboldt's Gift* in *New York Times* in December, claiming that the novel's fictionalized portrait of Delmore Schwartz denigrates American poets.

1976 Visits Stanford, where he renews friendship with John Cheever. Receives Pulitzer Prize in May for *Humboldt's Gift* (prize is mocked in the novel as "the pullet surprise, a dummy newspaper publicity award given by crooks and illiterates—for the birds"). Excerpt from *To Jerusalem and Back* appears in *The New Yorker* in July. First District

Court of Chicago rules that Bellow has misled Susan Glassman about his stated income, and orders him to pay her legal costs of $200,000. *To Jerusalem and Back* is published in October. In the same month Bellow wins the Nobel Prize, following a unanimous decision of the committee. In his Stockholm speech in December, argues against the anti-humanism of the *nouveau roman*, and reasserts his belief that fiction must not "give up the connection of literature with the main human enterprise."

1977 Gives Jefferson Lecture in the Humanities in March. Works on the "Chicago Book," a work of reportage that will later become novel *The Dean's December.* In September, is held in contempt of court by Cook County judge and sentenced to ten days in jail for failing to pay increased alimony to Susan Glassman; sentence is appealed and later voided, and Bellow is never jailed. Spends academic year in Boston, where both he and Alexandra Tulcea teach at Brandeis.

1978 Attends memorial service in July for Harold Rosenberg, along with Dwight Macdonald, Saul Steinberg, and Mary McCarthy. Leaves Viking, his publisher of thirty years, for Harper & Row, with large advance for "nonfiction book about Chicago." Travels to Romania in December, where he attends funeral of his mother-in-law, a former minister of health.

1979 Work in progress shifts from nonfiction "Chicago Book" to *The Dean's December,* which will include Romanian scenes. Rents summer house in West Halifax, Vermont.

1981 Visits London in spring, and in October attends Tuley High School's fiftieth reunion for classes of 1931 and 1932. Continues to work on *The Dean's December*.

1982 Spends spring semester as guest lecturer at the University of Victoria, British Columbia. *The Dean's December* is published in February to mixed reviews. In June, attends John Cheever's funeral; tells mourners, "Our friendship, a sort of hydroponic plant, flourished in the air." In September, visits London and Paris, where he appears on Bernard Pivot's literary television show *Apostrophes.*

1984 At work on short stories; "What Kind of Day Did You Have?" (a fictionalized portrait of Harold Rosenberg) appears in *Vanity Fair* in February. Collection of stories,

Him with His Foot in His Mouth, is published in May. Lachine Public Library in Quebec is renamed after Bellow; he attends building's commemoration on June 10, his birthday, and gives a speech in both French and English: "The human soul has its own way to declare its own freedom and to develop itself in its own way, and it is not true to say: 'Show me where you came from and I'll tell you what you are.'" Visits his birthplace at 130 Eighth Avenue.

1985 Anita Goshkin, first wife, dies in March, followed by his two brothers, Maurice, in May, and Sam, in June. His marriage to Alexandra Tulcea begins to break up. Delivers lecture at the Ethical Culture Society in New York, in which he quips that he meant *Herzog* "as an attack on higher education in America."

1986 Is divorced from Alexandria. In January attends rancorous PEN Congress in New York, where he falls into heated argument with Günter Grass about poverty and the spiritual life in America. Leaves Harper & Row in November for William Morrow.

1987 *The Closing of the American Mind*, by Chicago colleague and friend Allan Bloom, is published in March, with an introduction by Bellow, and becomes a best seller. Has an emotional reunion with Isaac Rosenfeld's son in New York. In April, travels to Israel for a conference on his work at University of Haifa, at which Allan Bloom, Martin Amis, A. B. Yehoshua, and Amos Oz give lectures. Interviewed by *New York Times* about Allan Bloom and controversies over multiculturalism, remarks: "Who is the Tolstoy of the Zulus, the Proust of the Papuans? I'd be glad to read him." Novel *More Die of Heartbreak* appears in June. Spends summer in Vermont.

1989 Returns to Viking with *A Theft*, a novella published in March as a paperback original. In May, sells manuscript of *Mr. Sammler's Planet* to New York Public Library for $66,000. Marries Janis Freedman in August. Takes teaching job at Boston University for fall semester. Has house built near Brattleboro, Vermont, which subsequently becomes summer home. Novella *The Bellarosa Connection* is published in December.

1990 Friends and relatives, including his three sons, Philip Roth, and Saul Steinberg, gather for 75th birthday party in West Dover, Vermont. In October, Mayor Richard M. Daley gives belated birthday party at the Art Institute in Chicago. Receives medal in November from the National Book Foundation for "distinguished contribution to American letters." Allan Bloom falls ill.

1991 *Something to Remember Me By*, a collection of three long stories also including *A Theft* and *The Bellarosa Connection*, is published in fall. Reads title story at Harvard in October to celebrate inauguration of new university president Neil Rudenstine. Travels to Florence in November to give a talk about Mozart at the Teatro Comunale.

1992 Allan Bloom, visited every day by Bellow in his last months, dies in October, probably from complications from HIV; Bellow delivers eulogy at memorial service. Visits Paris, where he sees old Chicago friend H. J. Kaplan.

1993 Becomes University Professor at Boston University in the fall.

1994 Collected essays published as *It All Adds Up*. Ralph Ellison dies. Writes op-ed piece for *New York Times* in March entitled "Papuans and Zulus," an attempt to revise his earlier controversial comments, and praises *Chaka* by Thomas Mofolo, a Zulu novel which he had read as a student, as "a profoundly, unbearably tragic book." Contracts ciguatera poisoning in April from eating contaminated shellfish in St. Martin; suffers heart failure and double pneumonia, and spends three weeks in coma, close to death. Recovers very slowly.

1995 Short story "By the St. Lawrence" appears in *Esquire* (July). At end of year, returns to Chicago, and speaks to a crowd of a thousand in Mandel Hall on "Literature in a Democracy." Begins *News from the Republic of Letters,* a literary journal, with Keith Botsford as co-editor.

1996 In February, ends twenty-five-year relationship with literary agent Harriet Wasserman, and engages Andrew Wylie as his new agent. Susan Glassman dies in December, aged sixty-three.

1997 *The Actual,* a novella, published in April. Attends ceremony in July at National Portrait Gallery, Washington, D.C., for unveiling of portrait. Harriet Wasserman publishes *Handsome Is,* a memoir of her relationship with Bellow.

1999 Works on novel *Ravelstein,* a fictionalized account of his friendship with Allan Bloom. Daughter, Naomi Rose, born in December.

2000 *Ravelstein* is published to warm reviews and controversy stemming from its treatment of Bloom's homosexuality and Bellow's statement in an interview that Bloom's death was AIDS-related (claim is challenged by some, and Bellow revises novel's galleys to omit references to HIV and AIDS in published version).

2001 *Collected Stories* published in March, with a preface by Janis Bellow.

2005 Dies on April 5 at his home in Brookline, Mass., and is buried in Morningside Cemetery, Brattleboro, Vermont.

Note on the Texts

This volume contains Saul Bellow's novels *Mr. Sammler's Planet* (1970), *Humboldt's Gift* (1975), and *The Dean's December* (1982).

The *Atlantic Monthly* published an advanced draft of *Mr. Sammler's Planet* in its entirety in its November and December 1969 issues. After submitting it to the magazine Bellow continued to revise the novel, particularly its ending. It was published in book form early in 1970 by Viking Press in New York and later that year by Weidenfeld and Nicholson in England. (Bellow did not revise the novels in the present volume for their English editions.) This volume prints the text of the 1970 Viking Press edition of *Mr. Sammler's Planet.*

Speaking of *Humboldt's Gift* in an interview with Keith Botsford in November 1975, Bellow remarked that he wrote it in his "usual way": "lots of beginnings, three years on the middle, and then the last third in six weeks flat out." Prepublication excerpts from the novel began appearing when *Playboy* published a selection in January 1974, followed by excerpts in *Esquire* (December 1974) and the *New York Review of Books* (August 7, 1975). *Humboldt's Gift* was published in August 1975 by Viking; the English edition, published by Secker & Warburg, was brought out the same year. The 1975 Viking Press edition of *Humboldt's Gift* contains the text printed here.

In writing *The Dean's December* Bellow drew heavily from a trip to Romania in December 1978–January 1979 to see Florica Bagdazar, the ailing mother of his wife Alexandra Tulcea. Bagdazar died during their visit. The novel also evolved out of his late-1970s "Chicago Book," which was intended to be a book of journalism and commentary about contemporary America. The writing of the novel exhausted him; as he told Philip Roth in a letter dated December 31, 1981, "The Dean took it out of me, I wrote it in a kind of fit and I'm left with a peculiar residue that I don't know how to describe." Bellow having ended his long relationship with Viking in 1978, *The Dean's December* was published by Harper & Row in January 1982; the English edition, brought out by Alison Press/Secker & Warburg, was also published that year. The present volume prints the text of the 1982 Harper & Row edition of *The Dean's December.*

This volume presents the texts of the original printings chosen for inclusion, but it does not attempt to reproduce nontextual features of their typographic design. The texts are presented without change, except for the correction of typographical errors. Spelling, punctuation, and capitalization are not altered, even when inconsistent or irregular. The following is a list of typographical errors corrected, cited by page and line number: 164.3, Jean Jacques; 247.28, Nesbitt,; 263.30, has; 305.9, alone."; 322.18, upen; 340.1, *007*; 348.1, deceased,; 349.37, Rip van Winkle; 354.37, loop; 420.27, miscroscope; 420.30, "This; 420.32, self-sacrifice!"; 435.10, forever—"; 448.34, was get; 458.17, Srole,; 480.21, loom.; 500.9, love the; 506.13, Eriksen; 527.32, school-days; 530.12, *Rip van Winkle*; 530.25, Mrs. van Winkle,; 540.33, laywers; 557.35, this.; 557.40, Chiaramonte; 560.19, Chiaramonte's; 567.31, cirrhus; 583.30, "Liebestod"; 595.25, it affection,; 608.39, men couldn't; 663.4, Toddling; 674.8, all that; 669.10, death."; 684.24, "That's; 776.33, fun; 798.31, unfortunately was; 906.1, Gacey,; 906.4, "Gacey,; 956.35, summer."; 956.36, sandwich.

Notes

In the notes below, the reference numbers denote page and line of this volume (the line count includes headings). No note is made for material included in standard desk-reference books. Biblical quotations are keyed to the King James Version. Quotations from Shakespeare are keyed to *The Riverside Shakespeare*, ed. G. Blakemore Evans (Boston: Houghton Mifflin, 1974). For references to other studies, and further biographical background than is contained in the Chronology, see: Gloria L. Cronin and Blaine H. Hall, *Saul Bellow: An Annotated Bibliography*, 2nd ed. (New York: Garland Publishing, 1987); James Atlas, *Bellow: A Biography* (New York: Random House, 2000).

MR. SAMMLER'S PLANET

5.7–9 Anglophilia . . . Bramble] Spanish critic Salvador de Madariaga y Rojo (1886–1978) lived in England and wrote a generalizing account of English culture in *Englishmen, Frenchmen, Spaniards* (1928); Italian scholar, critic, and translator Mario Praz (1896–1982) taught at the University of Manchester before returning to his native Rome, where he was a professor of English literature and the author of several books on English literary history and culture; French writer André Maurois (1885–1967) made his literary début with the comic novel *The Silences of Colonel Bramble* (1920), a consideration of British manners and characteristics set during World War I.

9.3–4 Vautrin . . . *Trompe-la-mort*] The master-criminal Vautrin, also known as Jacques Collin and Trompe-la Mort ("Cheat Death"), is a recurring character in Honoré de Balzac's Human Comedy novels.

9.19–20 the tale . . . pig] Told in Lamb's "A Dissertation upon Roast Pig," in *Essays of Elia* (1823).

12.8 Hannah Arendt's . . . Evil] From *Eichmann in Jerusalem: A Report on the Banality of Evil* (1963).

18.14 Masada] In 73 C.E., the Roman Tenth Legion occupied the Zealot fortress at Masada, in Judea, after a lengthy siege. According to the account by Jewish Roman historian Josephus Flavius (37 C.E.–c. 100), the defenders of the fortress committed mass suicide rather than submit to the Romans.

20.4–5 *Uccidere? Ammazzare?*] Italian: Kill? Slaughter?

20.23–24 And did . . . upon] From William Blake's preface to *Milton:*

A Poem (1804–10), widely known through the English hymn "Jerusalem" (1916) by Hubert Parry (1848–1918), a musical setting of the poem.

23.9 the open conspiracy] In *The Open Conspiracy: Blue Prints for a World Revolution* (1928), Wells outlined an "Open Conspiracy" led by an intellectual vanguard "against the indignity and absurdity of being endangered, restrained, and impoverished, by a mere uncritical adhesion to traditional governments, traditional ideas of economic life, and traditional forms of behaviour." The movement was to culminate in a single world-state.

23.37 Science . . . race] See Wells, *The World Set Free* (1914): "Science is no longer our servant. We know it for something greater than our little individual selves. It is the awakening mind of the race."

24.28 Baby Jane Holzer] Model and actress (b. 1940), a protégée of artist Andy Warhol.

24.28–29 the Living Theater . . . display] The experimental Living Theatre staged *Paradise Now* in 1968, in which nude actors and audience members performed a "Rite of Universal Intercourse."

24.30 Dionysus '69] *Dionysus in 69*, play loosely based on Euripides' *The Bacchae* that was staged in New York by the Performance Group in 1968–69 and directed by Richard Schechner. Largely improvisatory, it featured nude actors and encouraged audience participation.

25.5–6 Augustine . . . North] See *Confessions*, bk. 10.

25.24 dark satanic mills] From Blake's preface to *Milton: A Poem* (see note 20.23–24).

26.5 Knights Templar] Powerful Christian military order established about 1118, and crushed by the French monarchy in the early fourteenth century.

26.5–7 Lady Stanhopes . . . barbarians] Lady Hester Stanhope (1776–1839), English traveler who journeyed through the Middle East and eventually settled in the village of Joun in present-day Lebanon; Charles Baudelaire (1821–1867), French poet who made a sea voyage to the Indian Ocean as a young man and evoked exotic places in poems such as "Invitation to the Voyage" (1857); Gérard de Nerval, pseudonym of Gérard Labrunie (1808–1855), French Romantic writer whose Middle Eastern travels inspired *Journey to the Orient* (1851); Robert Louis Stevenson (1850–1894), Scottish writer who spent the last four years of his life in Samoa; Paul Gauguin (1848–1903), French artist who emigrated to Polynesia.

27.19–20 *ohne Büstenhalter*] German: braless.

29.7 Max Scheler] German phenomenologist philosopher (1874–1928), author of *On the Eternal in Man* (1960) and *The Nature of Sympathy* (1970).

29.8 Franz Oppenheimer] German political economist and sociologist (1864–1943), author of *The State* (1908).

29.10–11 *Doktor Faustus*] Novel (1947) by Thomas Mann.

29.11 *Les Noyers d'Altenbourg*] *The Walnut Trees of Altenbourg* (1948), novel by André Malraux.

30.18 look like François Premier] French king François I (1494–1547), whose best-known image is a portrait (c. 1535, Louvre) by French painter Jean Clouet (1480–1541).

31.22–23 R. H. Tawney . . . Strachey] Three influential English socialists and writers: economic historian Richard Henry Tawney (1880–1962), Labour Party leader Harold Laski (1893–1950), and Labour MP John Strachey (1901–1963).

31.33 Browning Society] Late-nineteenth-century clubs in Britain and America devoted to the study and discussion of Robert Browning's poetry.

31.38 Mussolini . . . 1936] Fascist Italy invaded Ethiopia in October 1935; the Spanish Civil War began in July 1936 with a military uprising led by General Francisco Franco.

31.38–39 Great Purges in Russia] On Stalin's orders, at least 680,000 people in the Soviet Union were executed and another 635,000 were sentenced to terms in prison or forced labor camps during 1937–38.

31.39–40 Blum, Daladier, the Peoples' Front] The Popular Front, a coalition of Socialists and Radicals (a moderate-left party) that governed with Communist support, held power in France from June 1936 to April 1938. Socialist leader Léon Blum (1872–1950) was the premier of the first (June 1936–June 1937) and third (March–April 1938) Popular Front governments, and served as vice-premier in the second (June 1937–January 1938), which was led by a Radical, Camille Chautemps. The Popular Front was succeeded by a center-right government led by Édouard Daladier (1884–1970), a Radical who served as premier from April 1938 to March 1940. In September 1938 Daladier signed the Munich Pact with Neville Chamberlain, Hitler, and Mussolini.

31.40 Oswald Mosley] A former member of both the Conservative and Labour parties, Mosley (1896–1980) was the founder and leader (1932–40) of the British Union of Fascists.

32.5 mutinous armies . . . Russia] On February 27 (March 12, New Style), 1917, troops in Petrograd (Saint Petersburg) refused to open fire on striking workers. The mutiny of the Petrograd garrison resulted in the abdication of Czar Nicholas II on March 2 (March 15, N.S.) and the end of the Romanov dynasty. Discipline in the Russians armies at the front began to disintegrate following a series of defeats in the early summer of 1917.

32.7 Verdun . . . Tannenberg] Battle sites of World War I.

32.8 fall of Kerensky] Alexander Kerensky (1881–1970) was the minister of justice of the Russian Provisional Government, March–May 1917. He became minister of war in May and premier in July, serving in both positions until the Provisional Government was overthrown by the Bolsheviks on October 25 (November 7, N.S.), 1917.

32.9 Brest-Litovsk] The new Boshevik regime signed the Treaty of Brest-Litovsk with the Central Powers on March 3, 1918. Under its terms, Russia recognized the independence of Finland and the recently proclaimed Ukrainian republic and ceded Russian Poland, Belorussia, and the Baltic states to the control of Germany and Austria-Hungary. The treaty was voided under the terms of the armistice of November 11, 1918, which required Germany to withdraw its troops from all of the territory it had occupied during the war.

32.19–21 Gerald Heard . . . World State] English writers Olaf Stapledon (1886–1950) and Gerald Heard (1889–1971) belonged to a group devoted to Wells's ideas about a utopian world-state (see note 23.9), founded in 1934 as the H. G. Wells Society, renamed the Open Conspiracy, and later Cosmopolis.

40.5–6 A time . . . stones] Cf. Ecclesiastes 3:5.

42.8 Clare Sheridan] English sculptor (1885–1970).

42.31–33 Specialists . . . achieved] From Weber's *The Protestant Ethic and the Spirit of Capitalism* (1920).

43.6–8 *Qu'est-ce que* . . . tragedy] In a letter (1760) to Sophie Volland, French *philosophe* Denis Diderot tells the anecdote of a "cold geometer" who asked, "What does it prove?" after seeing the first scene of the tragedy-ballet *Psyché* (1671) by Molière, Pierre Corneille, and Philippe Quinault.

44.15 *ab initio*] Latin: from the beginning.

45.3–4 *"Et incarnatus est"*] "And was made incarnate" in Latin, the name of an aria in Mozart's Mass in C Minor, K. 427 (1782–83).

45.26–27 *arschenloch*] I.e., German *Arschloch*: asshole.

46.4 fidelity, in his own Cynara-Dowson fashion] See "Non Sum Qualis Eram Bonae Sub Regno Cynarae" (1896) by English poet Ernest Dowson (1867–1900): "Last night, ah, yesternight, betwixt her lips and mine / There fell thy shadow / . . . I have been faithful to thee, Cynara! in my fashion."

47.10 Krafft-Ebing] German psychiatrist (1840–1902), best known for his book *Psychopathia Sexualis* (1886), a study of sexual perversity.

48.9 Freud's Rat Man] The lawyer Ernst Lanzer (1878–1914), whose case was discussed in Freud's "Notes upon a Case of Obsessional Neurosis" (1909).

50.37 Mr. Laird] Melvin Laird (b. 1922), U.S. Secretary of Defense (1969–73).

51.39–52.2 Lingam and Yoni . . . Sanskrit words] For male and female genitals.

54.35 Senator Dirksen] Everett Dirksen (1896–1969), Republican U.S. Senator from Illinois (1951–69), Senate Minority Leader (1959–69).

55.33–35 "Most gladly . . . master."] Quoted in Plato *Republic* 1.329b.

56.18–20 wrinkled faces . . . Hamlet] A compression of Hamlet's exchange with Polonius in *Hamlet*, II.ii.194–204.

60.25 *Ostjude*] German: eastern Jew.

67.7–8 Augustus John] Welsh artist (1878–1961).

68.3 *pruritis ani*] Latin: anal itching.

72.34 *Dans la lune*] French: in the moon.

75.13–16 Jean . . . mathematics] See Rousseau, *Confessions*, bk. 7.

82.24–25 opting out . . . Bull] Mistakenly thought to be ferocious, the hero of Munro Leaf's children's book *The Story of Ferdinand* (1936) and the Disney animated short *Ferdinand the Bull* (1938) prefers smelling flowers to fighting in bullfights.

84.27 poor man's Jean Genet] The early career as petty criminal and prostitute of French novelist, playwright, and activist Jean Genet (1910–1986) was the basis for books such as his autobiographical novels *The Miracle of the Rose* (1946) and *The Thief's Journal* (1949).

84.39 Sorel and Modern Violence] French socialist and political philosopher Georges Sorel (1847–1922), author of *Reflections on Violence* (1908) and *The Illusions of Progress* (1908), advocated the use of violence to achieve political ends.

87.27–29 Carlyle . . . masterpiece] A maid working for John Stuart Mill inadvertently burned the manuscript of the first volume of Thomas Carlyle's *The French Revolution* (1837); T. E. Lawrence lost the manuscript of *Seven Pillars of Wisdom* (1922) at Reading Station, near London.

105.21 *hors d'usage*] French: out of use.

105.26 *sub specie aeternitatis*] Latin: under the aspect of eternity.

105.34 *20,000 Leagues Under the Sea*] Novel (1870) by Jules Verne.

105.36–38 Wells' Time Traveler . . . Eloi maiden] The Time Traveler, protagonist of H. G. Wells's *The Time Machine* (1895), journeys to the year 802,701, and finds a world peopled by the effete, childlike Eloi and the barbaric Morlocks. Soon after his arrival, he befriends an Eloi girl named Weena after saving her from drowning.

107.31 "*Nicht schiessen.*"] German: don't shoot.

110.10 Aqaba crisis] A series of border clashes in the winter and spring of 1967 escalated tensions between Israel and Syria. After receiving false reports from the Soviet Union and the Syrian regime that Israel was preparing to invade Syria, Egyptian president Gamal Abdel Nasser (1918–1970) began reinforcing the Egyptian army in the Sinai Peninsula on May 14 and four days later ordered the expulsion of the United Nations Emergency Force from the Gaza Strip and the Sinai. On May 22 Nasser declared that the Straits of Tiran, the narrow channel connecting the Red Sea with the Gulf of Aqaba and the Israeli port of Eilat, would be closed to Israeli shipping, an act Israel considered cause for war. The Israeli, Egyptian, Syrian, and Jordanian armies mobilized as diplomatic efforts failed to resolve the crisis, and an attempt by the Johnson administration to create a multinational flotilla to challenge the Egyptian blockade failed to receive international or congressional support. Fighting in the Six-Day War began on the morning of June 5, 1967, with a highly successful Israeli surprise attack against Egyptian airfields. The Israel Defense Forces (IDF) reached the Suez canal on June 8 and, in response to Jordanian and Syrian shelling, captured East Jerusalem and the West Bank, June 6–8, and the Golan Heights, June 9–10.

111.20–21 Shukairy's Arabs . . . thousands] In a speech given in East Jerusalem on June 2, 1967, Ahmad al-Shuqayry (1908–1980), first chairman (1964–67) of the Palestine Liberation Organization, warned that Israel and its Jewish inhabitants would be destroyed in the coming war, and that any survivors would be deported.

112.15 Maurasses] French politician and writer Charles Maurras (1868–1952), a leader of the reactionary, anti-Semitic political movement L'Action Française and an editor (1908–44) of its daily newspaper.

116.27–29 priests of Apis . . . bodies] In Memphis in Egypt. See *Histories* 2.37.

121.22 *Le Ventre de Paris*] *The Belly of Paris* (1873), novel by Émile Zola.

121.24–26 *Volupté . . . femme*] French: voluptuousness, breasts, shoulders, hips. On a bed of leaves. The satiny warmth of woman: fragments from Zola's description of La Sarriette, a fruit seller at Les Halles market in *The Belly of Paris.*

126.11–12 *Ô La Reine . . . cascadantes*] Cf. Arthur Rimbaud's poem "Parisian Orgy, or Paris Filling Up Again" (1871): "Avalez, pour la Reine aux fesses cascadantes!" ("Drink up, for the Queen with the cascading buttocks!" in Martin Sorrell's translation.)

140.39 *Timor mortis conturbat me*] Latin: the fear of death troubles me: refrain in "Lament for the Makers" (c. 1508) by the English poet William Dunbar (c. 1465–c. 1530).

140.39–40 *Dies . . . dicturus*] The medieval Latin hymn "Dies Irae"

("Day of Wrath") contains the line "Quid sum miser tunc dicturus" ("What shall I say in my misery?").

141.32 Dr. Piccard's bathysphere] The bathyscaphe, a maneuverable deep-submergence craft designed by Swiss scientist and inventor Auguste Piccard (1884–1962).

147.14–16 Olaf Stapledon . . . years] In Stapledon's *Last and First Men: A Story of the Near and Far Future* (1930), science-fiction novel whose history of humankind extends thousands of years into the future and to other planets, and its sequels *Last Men in London* (1932) and *Starmaker* (1937).

152.4–5, 6–7 "in thy absence . . . moon."] *Antony and Cleopatra*, IV.xv.61–62, 68–69.

152.19 bestrode . . . Colossus] Cf. *Julius Caesar*, I.ii.135–36.

153.2 *kulturnaya*] Russian: cultural.

153.24 *faute de mieux*] French: for lack of anything better.

153.33 *pro bono publico*] Latin: for the public good.

165.3–5 I . . . drab] *Hamlet*, II.ii.585–86.

165.6–7 Words . . . words] *Hamlet*, II.ii.192.

166.36 Rousseau . . . free] See the opening of Rousseau's *The Social Contract* (1762): "Man is born free, and everywhere he is in chains."

167.15–17 *cigale* . . . show] In "La cigale et la fourmi" ("The Grasshopper and the Ant"), French writer Jean de La Fontaine (1621–1695) adapted Aesop's fable about the grasshopper who fiddles and is left starving when winter comes, contrasted with the ant who has stockpiled food during the summer months.

167.31 *gaspillage*] French: waste.

168.32–33 revolutions . . . De Maistre said] See *Considerations on France* (1797) by the conservative French thinker Joseph de Maistre (1754–1821).

169.12–15 The invitation . . . boat] References to Baudelaire's "Invitation to the Voyage" (see note 26.5–7) and Rimbaud's "The Drunken Boat" (1871).

171.3 Oblomov] Title character of novel (1859) by Russian writer Ivan Goncharov (1812–1891).

171.36 sidereal archipelagoes] See Rimbaud, "The Drunken Boat," in Louise Varèse's translation: "I've seen sidereal archipelagoes! Islands / Whose delirious skies open for wanderers: / Is it in such bottomless nights you sleep, exiled, / O countless golden birds, O Force to come?"

172.4 bauernbrot] German: farmers' bread; hearty rye bread.

174.27 *viva voce*] Latin: orally.

175.16 *odi et amo*] Latin: I hate and love: Catullus *Carmina* 85.

177.37–38 *Erst . . . Moral*] "First food, then morality," from act 2 of German playwright Bertolt Brecht's *The Threepenny Opera* (1928).

178.29–30 *Judenältester*] Nazi-appointed Jewish leader, literally "oldest Jew" in German.

179.7 *grand seigneur*] French: great lord.

179.18–19 *Ubu Roi* . . . Pataphysics] *King Ubu* (1896), avant-garde farce by French playwright Alfred Jarry (1873–1907), who outlined the principles of the pseudo-science "pataphysics" in *Exploits and Opinions of Doctor Faustroll, Pataphysician*, written in 1898 and published posthumously.

179.29–35 What . . . dust] Job 7:17–19, 7:16, and 7:21.

181.14 *Dov'è sia* . . . opera?] See Don Alfonso's lines in act 1 of Mozart's opera *Così fan tutte* (1790), with libretto by Lorenzo da Ponte (1749–1838): "E' la fede delle femmine / Come l'araba fenice: / Che vi sia, ciascun lo dice; / Dove sia, nessun lo sa" ("Woman's constancy / Is like the Arabian Phoenix; / Everyone swears it exists, / But no one knows where").

188.32–33 Mass Man . . . arrangements] See *The Revolt of the Masses* (1929), pessimistic cultural analysis by Spanish philosopher and social critic José Ortega y Gasset (1883–1955).

194.9 GORKISKII AUTOZAVOD] Russian: Gorky Motorworks.

214.6–7 But as someone . . . Gadarene swine] In "A Commentary" in *The Criterion* (April 1933), T. S. Eliot wrote that "a Leader may be defined as that one of the Gadarene Swine which runs the fastest." For the biblical story of the herd of Gadarene swine who are driven mad by demons and drown themselves, see Matthew 8:28–34, Mark 5:1–20, and Luke 8:26–39.

218.34 *Kulturny*] Russian: cultured.

228.24 Tallulah's] Actress Tallulah Bankhead (1902–1968).

235.25–26 Tencteri, four hundred and thirty thousand souls] In 55 B.C.E. two tribes, the Usipetes and the Tencteri, crossed the lower Rhine into Gaul. Julius Caesar refused the tribes' request to settle in Gaul and ordered his troops to attack their camp, massacring men, women, and children and driving the survivors back across the Rhine. Led by Cato, a group of Roman senators sharply criticized Caesar for having attacked the tribes while a negotiating truce was in effect. (The number of people killed in this incident is unknown; the figure of 430,000 comes from Caesar's estimate in *Commentaries on the Gallic War* of the population of the tribes as they entered Gaul, and is not reliable.)

237.30–31 *A la lanterne!*] French: to the lamppost! Lynching cry dating back at least as far as the French Revolution.

HUMBOLDT'S GIFT

245.17 Beethoven's *Pastorale*] Symphony No. 6 in F Major, op. 68 (1809), the composer's "Pastoral" symphony.

246.8 Russian ballerina] Lydia Lopokova (1892–1981), married to Keynes from 1925 until his death in 1946.

246.21–22 domes . . . eternity] Cf. Percy Bysshe Shelley, "Adonais" (1821), st. 52: "Life, like a dome of many-colour'd glass, / Stains the white radiance of Eternity, / Until Death tramples it to fragments."

246.22–23 quivering in the intense inane] Cf. Shelley, *Prometheus Unbound* (1820), III.iv.203–4: "The loftiest star of unascended heaven, / Pinnacled deep in the intense inane."

247.27–28 Peaches and Daddy Browning] After a brief marriage, Manhattan teenager "Peaches" Browning, born Frances Belle Heenan (1910–1956), filed for divorce in January 1927 from her fifty-two-year-old husband, real-estate mogul Edward West Browning (1875–1934). The divorce proceedings brought to light his eccentric behavior and were widely publicized.

247.28 Thaw . . . Nesbit] Harry K. Thaw (1880–1947), the wealthy son of a Pittsburgh industrialist, fatally shot architect Stanford White (1853–1906) in the rooftop theater at Madison Square Garden on June 25, 1906. At trial Thaw claimed the shooting was in revenge for White's alleged rape in 1901 of Evelyn Nesbit (1884–1967), the showgirl Thaw had married in 1905. After his first trial ended in a deadlocked jury, Thaw was found not guilty for reasons of insanity in January 1908 and was committed to a mental hospital. He was set free in 1915.

247.33–34 history was a nightmare . . . rest] Cf. James Joyce, *Ulysses* (1922), ch. 2: "History, Stephen [Dedalus] said, is a nightmare from which I am trying to awake."

247.35 Sombart] German sociologist and economist Werner Sombart (1863–1941), author of *Modern Capitalism* (1902) and *Luxury and Capitalism* (1921).

247.36 Rostovtzeff] Russian-born classical scholar and historian Michael Rostovtzeff (1870–1952), author of *Social and Economic History of the Roman Empire* (1926) and the popular two-volume *History of the Ancient World* (1926–27).

248.2 Schliemann] German archaeologist Heinrich Schliemann (1822–1890).

248.12–13 Hack Wilson and Woody English] Hack Wilson (1900–1948) played centerfield for the Chicago Cubs (1926–31); Woody English (1906–1997) played shortstop for the team (1927–36).

248.15–16 John Held, Jr.] American cartoonist (1889–1958) who helped create the image of 1920s Jazz Age youth.

249.2–5 *King Lear* . . . graves] I.ii.107–9 and I.ii.113–14.

250.23–24 great men . . . Tolstoi] See *War and Peace* (1869), bk. 9, sec. 1.

254.2 Potash and Perlmutter] Story collection (1910) and stage comedy (1913) by English Jewish writer Montague Glass (1877–1934) named for Abe Potash and "Mawruss" Perlmutter, fictional Jewish immigrants in the garment business. They were featured in more than a dozen Broadway plays, including *Partners Again* (1922) and *Potash and Perlmutter, Detectives* (1926).

254.7 Genteel Tradition] Phrase coined by Spanish-born American philosopher and critic George Santayana (1863–1952) in his influential critique of American thought, "The Genteel Tradition and American Philosophy" (1911).

254.22–23 Was Santayana . . . barbarous?] Santayana characterized modern poetry, particularly that of Whitman and Browning, as barbarous in his essay "The Poetry of Barbarism" (1900).

255.19–21 Lionel Abel said . . . Russia] See "New York: A Remembrance" (*Dissent*, Summer 1961) by American critic, playwright, and translator Lionel Abel (1910–2001).

255.22 Béla Kun] Hungarian revolutionary and politician (1886–1938), founder (1918) of the Hungarian Communist Party and leader (March–August 1919) of the short-lived Hungarian Soviet Republic. Kun fled to Soviet Russia in 1920 and became a prominent figure in the Comintern. He was arrested in June 1937 during the Great Purge and shot in August 1938.

255.24–26 Zinoviev . . . Moscow trials] Public show trials were held in Moscow in August 1936, January 1937, and March 1938, during which prominent Soviet Communists were falsely accused of conspiring with the exiled Leon Trotsky to overthrow Joseph Stalin and his regime. Among those executed on charges of treason were Grigory Zinoviev (1883–1936), Lev Kamenev (1883–1936), and Nikolai Bukharin (1888–1938). The Smolny Institute in Saint Petersburg served as Bolshevik headquarters during the October Revolution and was later Lenin's residence and headquarters for the Leningrad Communist Party; after Politburo member and Leningrad party chief Sergei Kirov (1886–1934) was assassinated there on December 1, 1934, Stalin falsely accused his political opponents of conspiracy in the murder. In the Shakhty case, fifty-three workers at the Shakhty coal mines in Ukraine were falsely charged with sabotage and treason in 1928; after a show trial, thirty-eight of the defendants were imprisoned and five of the eleven sentenced to death were executed.

255.28–29 how Lenin . . . schwindelt!] German: it makes one dizzy: remark of Lenin to Trotsky during the All-Russian Congress of Soviets on November 8 (October 26, Old Style), 1917, the day after the Bolshevik coup d'état.

256.13–14 finest talkers . . . Gumbein] Art historian, critic, and artist Meyer Schapiro (1904–1996), professor at Columbia University and author of seminal essays on Romanesque and modern art; pragmatist philosopher Sidney Hook (1902–1989), professor at New York University and author of *The Metaphysics of Pragmatism* (1927) and *The Quest of Being* (1961); critic and editor Philip Rahv, born Ivan Greenberg (1908–1973), co-founder of *Partisan Review* in 1934 whose essays are collected in *Image and Idea* (1949), *The Myth and the Powerhouse* (1965), and *Literature and the Sixth Sense* (1969); Huggins, pseudonym for writer, editor, and critic Dwight Macdonald (1906–1982), author of *Against the American Grain* (1962); Gumbein, pseudonym for art critic Harold Rosenberg (1906–1978), best known for coining the term "action painting," author of several monographs on artists and the essay collection *The Tradition of the New* (1959).

256.19 Lenin's dead brother] Vladimir Lenin's older brother Alexander Ulyanov (1866–1887), hanged for his involvement in a plot to assassinate Czar Alexander III.

257.1 Ruggles of Red Gap] Magazine serial (1914) by Harry Leon Wilson (1867–1939), published as a novel (1915) and adapted for stage and screen several times, including the film (1935) starring Charles Laughton (1899–1962) as its eponymous English butler adapting to the boisterous frontier town of Red Gap, Washington.

257.2–3 Mae Murray . . . poorhouse crone] Dancer and actress Mae Murray (1889–1965) appeared in New York's Ziegfeld Follies and enjoyed a successful silent-film career. Shortly before her death she was found living in a Salvation Army shelter in St. Louis.

257.19–20 Morris R. Cohen] Russian-born American philosopher (1880–1947) and an influential professor at City College of New York (1912–38).

260.16 William Blake at Felpham] From 1800 to 1803 Blake lived in the Sussex town of Felpham, near his patron, the English writer William Hayley (1745–1820). He engraved illustrations for Hayley's *Life of Cowper* (1803–4) and wrote *Milton: A Poem* (see note 20.23–24) while there.

260.18–20 basic texts . . . gardening] "Combray," the opening section of *Swann's Way* (1913), first book of Marcel Proust's seven-volume novel *In Search of Lost Time*; Virgil's *Georgics*; English poet Andrew Marvell's poems such as "The Garden" (c. 1650–52) and "Upon Appleton House, to My Lord Fairfax" (c. 1650–52).

261.13 Julien Sorel] Hero of *The Red and the Black* (1830), novel by French writer Stendhal, pen name of Marie-Henri Beyle (1783–1842).

261.13 Balzac's *jeune ambitieux*] The "ambitious youth" of Balzac's Human Comedy novels, such as Eugène de Rastignac, hero of *Le Père Goriot* (1835).

261.14 Marx's portrait of Louis Bonaparte] See the scathing assessment of Louis-Napoléon Bonaparte and his 1851 coup d'état in "The Eighteenth Brumaire of Louis Napoleon" (1852), essay by Karl Marx best known for its observation that history repeats itself "first as tragedy, then as farce."

265.15–16 Tristan . . . *Jaunes*] *The Yellow Loves* (1873), sole collection of poetry by French poet Tristan Corbière (1845–1875).

266.19–20 He then quoted . . . here] *Macbeth*, I.vi.1 and I.vi.5–6.

269.35 Albertine] Protagonist Marcel's lover in Proust's *In Search of Lost Time*, about whom he feels obsessive sexual jealousy even after she is dead.

270.18–20 "There's nothing serious . . . well] *Macbeth*, II.iii.100–101 and III.ii.22–23.

273.14–15 what he allowed . . . Marshall] Senator William Jenner (1908–1985) of Indiana opposed the nomination of George C. Marshall (1880–1959) as secretary of defense in 1950, calling Marshall "a front man for traitors" and a "living lie." In a long diatribe delivered in the Senate on June 14, 1951, Joseph McCarthy (1908–1957) claimed that Marshall's actions formed a "pattern which finds his decisions . . . always and invariably serving the world policy of the Kremlin." Eisenhower made campaign appearances with both senators in 1952 while running for president. A paragraph praising Marshall and criticizing his detractors was deleted from a speech Eisenhower gave at a campaign event held with McCarthy in Wisconsin, an omission made public because the original text had been given to reporters.

273.30 Bronson Cutting] Cutting (1888–1935) was a Republican senator from New Mexico, 1927–28 and 1929–35. In 1934 he won reelection by defeating Democrat Dennis Chavez by 1,261 votes. When Chavez challenged the election in the Senate, Cutting returned to New Mexico to examine contested voting lists. He was killed en route to Washington when his plane crashed in heavy fog at Atlanta, and Chavez was appointed as his successor by the Democratic governor of New Mexico.

273.34–35 J. Edgar Hoover . . . Wheeler] Democratic Senator Burton K. Wheeler (1882–1975), an outspoken critic of corruption in the Department of Justice during the Harding administration, was one of the targets of a harassment campaign by the Bureau of Investigation under the leadership of William J. Burns (1861–1932). Wheeler was placed under surveillance, his office was burglarized, and he was indicted for bribery on trumped-up charges. Burns was dismissed from his position as the bureau's director in 1924 and was succeeded by J. Edgar Hoover (1895–1972), who had served as its assistant director since 1921.

273.37 Dzerzhinsky of the GPU] Feliks Dzerzhinski (1877–1926) led the Cheka, the first Soviet secret police organization, from its founding in 1917 until 1922, and then headed the Cheka's successors, the GPU (1922–23) and the OGPU (1923–26), until his death from a heart attack. Dzerzhinski was praised by Soviet propagandists for his merciless repression of opposition to Soviet rule; under his direction, the Cheka shot at least 140,000 persons and established scores of concentration camps.

273.37–38 Sejanus . . . Empire] The Roman soldier Lucius Aelius Sejanus (20 B.C.E.–31 C.E.) became prefect of the Praetorian Guard in 14 C.E. and made it into a precursor of a modern internal security service. He was eventually executed for plotting against Emperor Tiberius.

274.6 pederasts. . . . Charlus] Baron de Charlus, homosexual character in Proust's *In Search of Lost Time.*

274.8–9 Wheeler-Bennett . . . Hart] English historian John Wheeler-Bennett (1902–1975), author of *The Nemesis of Power* (1953, rev. 1964); Chester Wilmot (1911–1954), Australian journalist and war correspondent, author of *The Struggle for Europe* (1952); Basil Henry Liddell Hart (1895–1970), English soldier, military strategist, journalist, and military historian, author of *The Liddell Hart Memoirs* (1965–66) and *The History of the Second World War* (1970).

274.9–10 Walter Winchell . . . Smith] New York *Daily Mirror* gossip columnist Walter Winchell (1897–1972); New York *Post* show-business columnist Earl Wilson (1907–1987); syndicated columnist Leonard Lyons (1906–1976); New York *Herald Tribune* and *Times* sportswriter Red Smith (1905–1982).

274.19 George Halas] American football coach (1895–1983), a founder of the National Football League and coach (1920–67) and owner of the Chicago Bears franchise.

274.26 Alice] Alice B. Toklas (1877–1967), Gertrude Stein's longtime lover and companion.

274.26 Ferenczi] Sandor Ferenczi (1873–1933), Hungarian psychoanalyst who collaborated with Freud.

279.15–16 Let Rome in Tiber melt] *Antony and Cleopatra*, I.i.33.

284.1–2 *Edel, gebildet, gelassen*] German: refined, educated, composed.

284.6 Big Bill Thompson] Notoriously corrupt Republican politician William Hale Thompson (1869–1944), twice mayor of Chicago (1915–23, 1927–31).

284.21 *nostalgie de la boue*] French: yearning to be back in the mud. From *Le Mariage d'Olympe* (*Olympe's Marriage*, 1855), play by French playwright Émile Augier (1820–1889).

291.33–34 creature with the locks and bolts] In plate 50 of *Los Caprichos* (1799), "The Chinchillas," by Spanish artist Francisco Goya (1746–1828).

292.3–4 stand on your head? . . . William] See *Alice's Adventures in Wonderland* (1865) by Lewis Carroll (1832–1898): "'You are old, Father William,' the young man said, / 'And your hair has become very white; / And yet you incessantly stand on your head— / Do you think, at your age, it is right?'" The poem is a parody of "The Old Man's Comforts and How He Gained Them" (1799) by English poet Robert Southey (1774–1843).

293.11–12 *Radix malorum est cupiditas*] Latin: avarice is the root of all evil. Quoted by the Pardoner in his tale's prologue in Chaucer's *The Canterbury Tales.*

295.24 GPU or the NKVD] NKVD (People's Commissariat of Internal Affairs), Soviet security police organization (1934–43), a successor to the GPU (see note 273.37).

296.15–16 dressed up like Sugar Ray Robinson] Champion American boxer (1921–1989) known for his expensive tailored suits.

302.35 Tönnies] German sociologist Ferdinand Tönnies (1855–1936), author of *Community and Society* (1887).

303.38 Robert Ardrey, the territorial imperative] American novelist and screenwriter Robert Ardrey (1908–1980) published books about anthropology including *African Genesis* (1962) and *The Territorial Imperative: A Personal Inquiry into the Animal Origins of Property and Nations* (1966).

303.39 Konrad Lorenz] Austrian zoologist and animal behaviorist (1903–1989), author of *King Solomon's Ring* (1949) and *On Aggression* (1963).

307.9 Slim Jim and Boob McNutt] Slim Jim, tall character always eluding three hapless policemen in *Slim Jim*, syndicated comic strip (1910–37) illustrated successively by George Frink, Raymond Crawford Ewer, and Stanley Armstrong; Boob McNutt, feckless bumpkin created by Rube Goldberg (1883–1970) in comic strip (1915–34) of the same name.

308.14–15 Music Antiqua . . . Greenberg] New York Pro Musica Antiqua, an early-music ensemble co-founded by conductor Noah Greenberg (1919–1966).

315.12–14 Valéry wrote . . . *même*] "This Apollo ravished me to the heights of my being." From "Introduction to the Method of Leonardo" (1894) by French poet and essayist Paul Valéry (1871–1945). His marginal note means "find before seeking."

317.18 HOY. MUDANZAS. IGLESIA] Spanish: Today. Moving. Church.

318.10 *Un Cœur Simple*] *A Simple Heart* (1877), novella by Gustave Flaubert.

328.25 tear was an intellectual thing] Cf. the final stanza of William Blake, "The Grey Monk" (c. 1805).

322.27–28 too fast . . . Samuel] See 2 Samuel 2:18–23, where the young warrior Asahel, "light of foot as a wild roe," is killed when he persists in pursuing Abner, whose forces had just been defeated in battle.

324.39 all the volumes . . . Zuckerman] *The Mentality of Apes* (1917) by German gestalt psychologist Wolfgang Köhler (1887–1967); *The Great Apes: A Study of Anthropoid Life* (1919) by American psychologist Robert Means Yerkes (1876–1956); *The Social Life of Monkeys and Apes* (1932) by South African–born zoologist Solly Zuckerman (1904–1993).

325.1–2 Marais . . . gorillas] *The Soul of the Ape* (1919, pub. 1969) by South African naturalist and poet Eugene Marais (1871–1936); *The Mountain Gorilla* (1963) and *The Year of the Gorilla* (1964) by American naturalist and field biologist George Schaller (b. 1933).

328.6 the late Colonel McCormick] Robert H. McCormick (1880–1955), publisher of the Chicago *Tribune*.

329.14 1968 riots . . . Hilton] On August 28, 1968, during the Democratic National Convention, police clashed with protestors in front of the Conrad Hilton Hotel on Michigan Avenue across from Grant Park. A government-sponsored independent commission called the response to the protestors a "police riot."

331.8–9 Plato . . . Er] See *Republic* 10.614a–621d. Er was a man killed in battle who revived on his funeral pyre twelve days later to tell of what he saw in the afterlife.

332.27 Bechstein] Prestigious piano manufacturer.

338.17–19 Socrates . . . something about yourself] See *Phaedrus* 230d (trans. Alexander Nehamas and Paul Woodruff): "I am devoted to learning; landscapes and trees have nothing to teach me—only people in the city can do that."

338.32–34 Einstein . . . proved it] English astronomer Arthur Eddington (1882–1944) organized simultaneous expeditions to Sobral, Brazil, and the West African island of Principe to observe a total eclipse of the sun on May 29, 1919. The observations verified that the sun's gravitational attraction would cause starlight to bend, as posited by Einstein's general theory of relativity. The success of the experiment brought widespread acceptance of Einstein's theory and made him a worldwide celebrity.

340.12 Fagin-types . . . addicts] Fagin, a "receiver of stolen goods," is a rapacious criminal in *Oliver Twist* (1838), novel by Charles Dickens (1812–1870).

350.4 Dr. Rudolf Steiner] Austrian philosopher and religious thinker

(1861–1925), founder of the spiritual belief system of Anthroposophy and the Waldorf School education movement.

351.29–30 *Trouve . . .* Picasso.] See note 315.12–14. Spanish artist Pablo Picasso (1881–1973) is attributed to have said, "Je ne cherche pas, je trouve" ("I don't seek, I find").

352.10 *noli me tangerine*] Pun on Latin, *noli me tangere*: don't touch me, Jesus's words to Mary Magdalene when he appears to her after the resurrection (John 20:17).

357.3 Whom . . . chaseneth] Hebrews 12:6.

359.39–40 as General Sarnoff . . . bench] Communications executive David Sarnoff (1891–1971) rose at RCA from commercial manager to president (1930–47) and chairman of the board (1947–70); financier and philanthropist Bernard Baruch (1879–1965) advised several presidents and was often seen discussing affairs of state while sitting on park benches in Washington's Lafayette Square and New York's Central Park.

360.1–3 according to Dr. Johnson . . . curiously] Remark quoted in James Boswell, *Life of Johnson* (1791), entry for July 31, 1763: "A woman's preaching is like a dog's walking on his hind legs. It is not done well; but you are surprised to find it done at all."

360.8 Morris R. Cohen] See note 257.19–20.

363.6 Axel . . . inspiration] *Axel*, Symbolist play (first produced posthumously in 1890) by the French playwright and fiction writer August Villiers de l'Isle-Adam (1838–1889); it was analyzed as representing a type of antisocial, escapist sensibility in Edmund Wilson's *Axel's Castle* (1931).

363.39 Prufrock subtleties] Overly subtle subject of "The Love Song of J. Alfred Prufrock" (1915), poem by T. S. Eliot.

364.33 *The Spoils of Poynton*] Novel (1897) by Henry James.

364.38 Hamilton Wright Mabie] American essayist and editor (1846–1916).

366.35–36 couldn't drink tea . . . Pope] "He hardly drank tea without a stratagem": Samuel Johnson on Alexander Pope in *Lives of the Poets* (1779–81). The phrase is adapted from *Love of Fame* (1728), satire 6, line 90, by English poet Edward Young (1683–1765).

367.10–11 Princeton . . . Panofsky] Influential art historian Erwin Panofsky (1892–1968), author of *Studies in Iconology* (1939) and *Early Netherlandish Painting* (1953), was a professor at Princeton (1935–68).

367.26 Count Mosca] The prime minister of Parma in *The Charterhouse of Parma* (1839), novel by Stendhal.

368.9 the *Kenyon*] *Kenyon Review*, journal based at Kenyon College in Ohio.

372.11–12 *Sailing to Byzantium*] Poem (1928) by William Butler Yeats.

372.27 *heimischer*] Adjectival form of German *heimisch*: homelike, familiar.

379.12 Ickes' *Diaries*] *The Secret Diary of Harold L. Ickes*, 3 vols. (1953). Ickes (1874–1952) was secretary of the interior (1933–46) during the Roosevelt and Truman administrations.

380.24–25 Victor McLaglen . . . of course] When actor and former British Army soldier Victor McLaglen (1886–1959) founded a uniformed riding club, the Light Horse Troop, in California in 1936, he was accused by journalist and historian Carey McWilliams (1905–1980) of having fascist sympathies.

382.34–35 *Ils . . . Me*)] *They Shall Not Have Me (Ils ne m'auront pas): The Capture, Forced Labor, and Escape of a French Prisoner of War* (1943), memoir by French painter Jean Hélion (1904–1987).

383.40 Closerie des Lilas] Café on the Left Bank of Paris frequented by writers such as Ernest Hemingway, F. Scott Fitzgerald, and Samuel Beckett.

384.1 Dr. Moriarty] Professor Moriarty, criminal mastermind created by Arthur Conan Doyle in "The Final Problem" (1894), where Sherlock Holmes refers to him as the "Napoleon of crime."

384.11 Mario Praz he knew] Praz (see note 5.7–9) wrote about the literature of masochism in his most widely read book, *The Romantic Agony* (1930).

384.35 Rudy Vallee . . . Lover"] Hit song from the film *The Vagabond Lover* (1929), sung by Rudy Vallee (1901–1986).

387.29 Hirschfield] American artist and illustrator Al Hirshfeld (1903–2003), whose celebrity caricatures were regularly featured in the *New York Times*, starting in 1928.

392.37–38 Mortimer Snerd] Dummy used by the ventriloquist Edgar Bergen (1903–1978).

395.23–24 He got himself a pistol, like Verlaine] French poet Paul Verlaine (1844–1896) shot poet Arthur Rimbaud, his lover, in the wrist during a drunken quarrel in Brussels in July 1873.

399.2–3 Who says . . . Pardoner?] See note 293.11–12.

400.13–14 Shakespeare . . . trust] *Macbeth*, I.iv.11–14.

400.39–40 genius . . . *Sixpence*] *Moulin Rouge* (1952), film biography of French painter Henri de Toulouse-Lautrec (1864–1901); *The Moon and Sixpence*, film adaptation (1942) of novel (1919) by W. Somerset Maugham

(1874–1965) about a stockbroker who abandons his comfortable life and becomes a painter, ultimately settling in Tahiti.

402.15 what Diotima said . . . love] In Plato's *Symposium.*

402.16 *amor dei intellectualis*] Latin: intellectual love of God.

412.21–22 Fort Dearborn situation] The garrison of Fort Dearborn, located on Lake Michigan at the mouth of the Chicago River, was ambushed by Potawatomi Indians allied with the British during the evacuation of the post on August 15, 1812. More than fifty men, women, and children were killed in the attack.

413.5 Sorel] See note 84.39.

413.18–20 ready to sympathize . . . as Schumpeter says] In *Capitalism, Socialism, and Democracy* (1948), ch. 11, "The Civilization of Capitalism," by Austrian economist Joseph Schumpeter (1883–1950).

415.18–19 Gumbein . . . couch] See Harold Rosenberg, "Couch Liberalism and the Guilty Past" (*Dissent*, Autumn 1955).

414.1 Rameau's nephew] Skeptical, freethinking youth who is the eponymous hero of Diderot's fictional philosophical dialogue, published posthumously in 1805.

414.1 Jean Genet] See note 84.27.

416.18–19 Greek words . . . Tillich the Toiler, expound] German-born theologian Paul Tillich (1886–1965); "Tillich the Toiler" plays on *Tillie the Toiler,* title of a comic strip (1921–67) created by the American cartoonist Russ Westover (1886–1966). Tillie was a flapper who became the stenographer for a wealthy industrialist.

420.9 Sir Patrick Spens] Scottish ballad (c. 1325) about a doomed North Sea crossing from Norway to Scotland in winter.

424.29 Vesco] Financier Robert L. Vesco (1935–2007) fled the United States in 1971 from charges of securities fraud, drug trafficking, and bribery. He had defrauded investors of $200 million and had made illegal contributions to President Richard Nixon's reelection campaign. After spending time in the Bahamas and Costa Rica, he settled in Cuba, where he served a prison term (1996–2005) for a fraud conviction. He is said to have died of lung cancer in Havana.

426.38 Mérite Agricole] French order of merit honoring contributions to agriculture.

427.28–31 old Mr. Karamazov . . . 'The bitch is dead!'] See Fyodor Dostoyevsky, *The Brothers Karamazov* (1879–80), ch. 1. Citrine misremembers Karamazov's words in the street: according to differing accounts given of the scene, he either joyfully commends his wife's soul to heaven, sobs pitifully in grief, or, the narrator suggests, perhaps he does both.

432.2 *affaires de cœur*] French: affairs of the heart.

437.38 *accidia* and *tedium vitae*] Latin: sloth and weariness with life.

438.12 old Binet the psychologist] French psychologist Alfred Binet (1857–1911), who wrote extensively on hysteria.

438.17 *Wille zur Macht*] German: Will to Power, subject and title of book (1888) by German philosopher Friedrich Nietzsche (1844–1900).

438.37 Fronde] Seventeenth-century uprising of landed French aristocrats against the monarchy.

439.5 Manon and Des Grieux] Lovers who are the central characters in *Manon Lescaut* (1731), short novel by the Abbé Prévost (1697–1763), French writer and cleric.

439.27 as Djilas describes them] In *Conversations with Stalin* (1962) by the Yugoslavian revolutionary, politician, and writer Milovan Djilas (1911–1995).

440.1 *Schlag*] German: cream.

442.4–6 Hamlet's kingdom . . . prison] *Hamlet*, II.ii.254–55, II.ii.192, and II.ii.243.

442.14–15 Pascal's advice to stay put] See *Pensées*, 139, by the French philosopher Blaise Pascal (1623–1662): "I have discovered that all human misery comes from one thing alone, being unable to sit quietly in a room."

442.30 Harry Hopkins] American political official and diplomat (1890–1946), administrator of several New Deal agencies, secretary of commerce (1938–40), and a close advisor to President Franklin D. Roosevelt.

443.23–24 Balzac's . . . maid] In his novel *Cousin Bette* (1846).

445.16–17 a follower of Pandour von Trenck] Austrian soldier Baron Franz von der Trenck (1711–1749) commanded an irregular force of mostly Croatian fighters called "pandours," notorious for their marauding and cruelty.

447.33 Clarissa . . . Lovelace] Eponymous heroine of Samuel Richardson's epistolary novel (1748) who is relentlessly pursued and raped by the villainous aristocrat Lovelace.

449.10–11 *Est avis . . . extra*] Latin proverb: a bird in hand is better than four on the loose.

453.10–11 Jacob-Laban . . . Auburn] In Genesis 29:15–30, Jacob agrees to work for Laban for seven years in order to marry Rachel, Laban's youngest daughter. At the end of the seven-year period, Laban tricks Jacob into marrying Leah, his oldest daughter, then allows Jacob to marry Rachel only for a pledge of seven more years of work.

455.10 *fauteuil*] French: armchair.

462.5–8 something Samuel Johnson . . . estimable] Cf. Johnson's remark of June 5, 1781, quoted in Boswell, *Life of Johnson*.

464.16 *dove sia? dove sia? Nessuno sa.*] See note 181.14.

467.36 *res judicata*] Latin: the thing has been adjudicated; an attempted barrier to further legal actions.

469.7 this Maharishi fellow] The Indian guru Maharishi Mahesh Yogi (c. 1911–2008), founder of the Transcendental Meditation movement.

472.4 *ne exeat*] Latin: let him not exit; a legal writ barring a defendant from leaving the jurisdiction of a court.

478.9–10 Cleopatra's words . . . me] *Antony and Cleopatra*, V.ii.282.–83.

481.1 his Dick Whittington's cat] I.e., his fortune, from the English fairy tale "Dick Whittington and His Cat," in which an orphan working as a servant in London is made suddenly wealthy when his cat is sold for a vast sum overseas; he later becomes the city's mayor.

483.18 *bouilli, brulé, farci, fumé*] French: boiled, burned, stuffed, smoked.

489.6 Momigliano] Italian historian and classical scholar Arnaldo Momigliano (1908–1987), author of *The Development of Greek Biography* (1971) and *Alien Wisdom: The Limits of Hellenization* (1976). An Oxford University professor (1951–75), he also taught at the University of Chicago.

489.6–7 Burton of Arabia or T. E. Lawrence] British explorer, diplomat, and scholar Richard Francis Burton (1821–1890) traveled widely throughout Africa and the Middle East and published more than thirty books, including translations of *The Book of the Thousand Nights and a Night* (1885–1888) and *The Kama Sutra* (1883); British military officer T. E. Lawrence (1888–1935), "Lawrence of Arabia," fought with the Arabs during their revolt against the Ottoman Empire, recounted in his autobiography *The Seven Pillars of Wisdom: A Triumph* (1922).

489.7–8 purple genius . . . Venice] Baron Corvo, pseudonym of eccentric English Catholic writer Frederick Rolfe (1860–1913), author of *Hadrian the Seventh* (1904), who spent his last years in dire poverty in Venice.

491.13–15 T.S. Eliot . . . waiting] See *The Waste Land* (1922), pt. 3, lines 215–17.

493.3 the celebrated Dion O'Banion] Irish-born Chicago gangster (1891–1924), one of Al Capone's rivals.

496.20–29 certain words of John Stuart Mill . . . man] See Mill, "On Genius" (1832): "If life were aught but a struggle to overcome difficulties; if the multifarious labours of the *durum genus hominum* were performed for us by supernatural agency, and there were no demand for either wisdom or virtue, but barely for stretching out our hands and enjoying, small would be our enjoyment, for there would be nothing which man could any longer prize in man."

500.5–6 *I am the light of the world*] Jesus's words from John 8:12.

506.12–13 Kinsey or Masters or Erikson] Sex researcher Alfred C. Kinsey (1894–1956), who founded the Institute for Sex Research at the University of Indiana in 1947 and published the first volume of *Sexual Behavior in the Human Male* (popularly known as the Kinsey Report) the following year; sex researcher William H. Masters (1915–2001), who with Virginia E. Johnson (b. 1925) published their findings in the bestselling *Human Sexual Response* (1966); psychoanalyst Erik Erikson (1902–1994), author of *Childhood and Society* (1950).

507.9–10 *American Mercury . . . Occidente*] Influential literary and cultural magazines: *American Mercury* (1923–1981), founded by critics H. L. Mencken (1880–1956) and George Jean Nathan (1882–1958); *The Dial*, founded as a transcendentalist journal (1840–44) and intermittently revived, most notably as a forum for modernist writing in the 1920s; *Revista de Occidente* (*Western Review*, 1923–), Spanish journal founded by philosopher and social critic José Ortega y Gasset.

507.6 a chronicle] *Les nuits de Paris* (*The Nights of Paris*, 1788–94), anecdotal narrative by French novelist Nicolas-Edme Restif de la Bretonne (1734–1806).

511.38 knotted in the Ronald Colman manner] Suave English actor Ronald Colman (1891–1958).

515.14 Murder Incorporated] Gang of hired killers founded by gangsters Louis "Lepke" Buchalter (1897–1944) and Jacob "Gurrah" Shapiro (1899–1947).

520.8 his Peter Wimsey airs] Lord Peter Wimsey, genteel detective featured in several novels and stories by the English mystery writer Dorothy L. Sayers (1893–1957).

520.37 *poubelles*] French: garbage cans.

523.5 *A plus forte raison*] French: all the more reason.

525.27–28 "*Es schwindelt!*" . . . Institute.] See note 255.28–29.

533.22 "*Brutus, thou sleep'st,*" etcetera] *Julius Caesar*, II.i.46–47: "Brutus, thou sleep'st; awake, and see thyself! / Shall Rome, etc. Speak, strike, redress!"

538.39 *tinia crura*] I.e., *tinea cruris*, a fungal infection of the skin of the groin.

542.13–14 'Oh You Beautiful Doll'] Popular ragtime song (1911), words by Seymour Brown, music by Nat Ayer.

545.8 *King Solomon's Mines*] Adventure novel (1885) set in Africa by English novelist H. Rider Haggard (1856–1925).

548.29–33 Gertrude Stein . . . identity] See *The Geographical History of America* (1935): "I am I because my little dog knows me."

548.34–35 as T. S. Eliot said of William Blake] See Eliot's essay on Blake in *The Sacred Wood* (1920).

553.3–4 *I Am Curious Yellow*] *I Am Curious (Yellow)* (1967), Swedish film directed by Vilgot Sjöman (1924–2006), initially banned in the United States because of its sexual content.

555.5–6 Gene Fowler's] American journalist, screenwriter, and biographer (1890–1960).

557.40 Chiaromonte] Italian writer and editor Nicola Chiaromonte (1905–1972), an exile from Mussolini's Italy, author of *The Paradox of History* (1970).

557.40–558.1 Paul Goodman] Social critic, novelist, poet, and prolific writer (1911–1972) whose best-known book is *Growing Up Absurd* (1960).

558.21 Andrei Vishinsky] Soviet government official and diplomat (1883–1954), procurator-general of the Soviet Union and lead prosecutor in the Moscow show trials (see note 255.24–26); later Soviet foreign minister (1949–53).

559.11 Army McCarthy hearings] Televised hearings (April–June 1954) by the U.S. Senate Subcommittee on Investigations addressing Senator Joseph McCarthy's accusations of Communist influence in the U.S. Army.

560.6 Manville . . . broads] Tommy Manville (1894–1967), the heir to an asbestos fortune, was married thirteen times to eleven women.

560.17 Burnham] Writer and editor James Burnham (1905–1987), a Trotskyist who later became a conservative anticommunist; his books include *The Managerial Revolution* (1941), *The Machiavellians* (1943), and *The Struggle for the World* (1947).

560.18 *Encyclopedia of Unified Science*] Series of twenty monographs on science published by the University of Chicago Press from 1937 to 1971. It was the brainchild of its first editor-in-chief, Austrian philosopher of science and political economist Otto Neurath (1882–1945).

560.18–19 Trotsky's Law of Combined Development] Trotsky's view, outlined in *History of the Russian Revolution* (1932), that an underdeveloped country such as Russia could progress rapidly by adopting advanced forms of development while bypassing intermediate stages in the historical process.

561.13–15 old Russian actress . . . Thirties] Russian actress Maria Ouspenskaya (1876–1949) smoked through a long cigarette holder in *The Rains Came* (1939).

561.15 John Held, Jr.] See note 248.15.16.

561.18 René Clair] French director (1898–1981) whose films include the Surrealist short *Entr'acte* (1924), *Le million* (*The Million,* 1931), and *À nous la liberté!* (*Freedom for Us,* 1931).

566.38 "In questa tomba oscura,"] "In This Dark Tomb" (1807), song for bass by Beethoven set to a poem by Giuseppe Carpani (1751–1825).

567.7–8 Tito . . . Galli-Curci] Italian tenor Tito Schipa (1880–1965); Italian baritone Titta Ruffo (1877–1953); American baritone Reinald Werrenrath (1883–1953); Irish tenor John McCormack (1884–1945); Bohemian-born contralto Ernestine Schumann-Heink (1861–1936); Italian coloratura soprano Amelita Galli-Curci (1882–1963).

567.9 Boito] Italian composer Arrigo Boito (1842–1918), best known for his sole opera, *Mefistofele* (1868), and libretti for Verdi's *Otello* (1887) and *Falstaff* (1893).

567.18–19 Paul Ash's sizzling band] Paul Ash & His Merry-Mad Musical Gang, dance band that played in Chicago movie theaters in the 1920s.

576.12–13 words of the crooner . . . still] From "It Had to Be You" (1924), song with words by Gus Kahn, music by Isham Jones.

577.17 Blake . . . Intellect] Cf. Blake's letter to George Cumberland, December 6, 1795: "Enjoyment & not Abstinence is the food of Intellect."

578.11–13 something Keats had said . . . attainable] Cf. Keats's letter to his brother Thomas, July 7, 1818: "How sad it is when a luxurious imagination is obliged in self defence to deaden its delicacy in vulgarity, and riot in thing[s] attainable that it may not have leisure to go mad after thing[s] which are not."

579.30 *donnée*] French: inspiration.

579.32 *Verbum sapientiae*] Latin: word of wisdom.

580.40 idols-of-the-tribe (Francis Bacon)] From aphorism 39 of *Novum Organum* (1620), bk. 1, by Francis Bacon (1561–1626).

581.3 the wicked flee when none pursueth] Proverbs 28:1.

582.31–39 opinion of Blake . . . proportions] From Blake's letter to Rev. John Trusler, August 23, 1799.

585.33–36 Samuel Daniel . . . deed] *Musophilus, or Defence of All Learning* (1602–3), lines 490–91, by English poet Samuel Daniel (c. 1562–1619).

587.1 as Swift says] In "On Poetry: A Rhapsody" (1733), line 42.

595.23–24 *Syndics of Amsterdam*] Painting (1662, Rijksmuseum) by Rembrandt van Rijn (1606–1669).

597.17–18 *avec tout . . . assiette?*] French: with all that's on your plate.

600.27–29 Lydia the Tattooed Lady . . . Lydia'] "Lydia the Tattooed Lady," song with music by Harold Arlen (1905–1986) and words by E. Y. Harburg (1896–1981) in the Marx Brothers' film *At the Circus* (1939), sung by Groucho. The second verse goes: "Lydia, oh, Lydia / That 'encyclopidia' / Oh, Lydia, the queen of tattoo / On her back is the Battle of Waterloo / Beside it the wreck of the Hesperus too / And proudly above waves the red, white, and blue: / You can learn a lot from Lydia."

600.33–34 Sigmund Romberg] Hungarian-born composer (1887–1951) of operettas, film music, and musical theater.

614.25–26 this guy Fromm . . . civilization] In *The Anatomy of Human Destructiveness* (1973) by German psychologist Erich Fromm (1900–1980).

619.4 Herman Kahn] American mathematician and military strategist (1922–1983), founder of the conservative Hudson Institute, author of *On Thermonuclear War* (1962) and *Thinking about the Unthinkable* (1962).

619.11 the Symbionese] The Symbionese Liberation Army, terrorist group best known for their 1974 kidnapping of newspaper heiress Patricia Hearst (b. 1954).

621.1 GAR parade] Grand Army of the Republic.

622.35–36 Ev Dirksen] See note 54.35.

624.7 R. H. Tawney] See note 32.31–23.

624.7–8 Cecil Roth . . . Jewish history] English historian Cecil Roth (1899–1970), prolific author of books on Jewish history; Salo W. Baron (1895–1989), author of eighteen-volume *Social and Religious History of the Jews* (2nd ed., 1952–83).

624.18–19 the Latin word *repax*] Rapacious.

638.33 Goya's *Maja*] Unknown sitter of *La maja desnuda* (*The Nude Maja*, c. 1797–1800, Prado) and *La maja vestida* (*The Clothed Maja*, c. 1805, Prado) by Spanish artist Francisco Goya.

638.34–35 Wallace Stevens' . . . "Pfui!"] In "Anything Is Beautiful If You Say It Is," poem in Stevens's *Parts of a World* (1942).

642.12–13 *Wagon-Lit*] French: sleeping car.

642.36–40 Coleridge . . . deadly sick] Notebook entry, Sept.–Oct. 1796.

646.36–39 tried quoting Shakespeare . . . terrible] Cf. *Julius Caesar*, II.ii.44–48.

647.34–35 I have tremor cordis . . . not joy] *The Winter's Tale*, I.ii.110–11.

651.30 *botónes*] Spanish: bellboy.

655.7–8 Many . . . Misery] Percy Bysshe Shelley, "Lines Written among the Euganean Hills" (1818), lines 1–2.

655.23–25 famous Santayana . . . Genteel America] See note 254.7.

659.35 USIA] United States Information Agency.

660.32–33 *empleadas del hogar*] Spanish: housemaids.

680.14–15 Professor Leakey] English paleoanthropologist and writer Louis Leakey (1903–1972).

684.5 *comedor*] Spanish: dining room.

693.4 *vie quotidienne*] French: everyday life.

693.39 *Time Marches On*] Resounding final line of *The March of Time* (1935–51), series of short films that combined documentary footage with dramatic reenactments of current events.

697.39–40 *Dispute! Bagarre! . . . porte!*] French: Dispute! Fight! Assholes! . . . Outside! Throw them out!

THE DEAN'S DECEMBER

724.35 *doamna*] Romanian: Mrs.

726.6–7 Antonescu] Romanian premier Ion Antonescu (1882–1946), leader of pro-German fascist dictatorship (1940–44).

727.36 *chef de cabinet*] French: principal aide.

728.3 the famous Cushing] American neurosurgeon and writer Harvey Cushing (1869–1939), a pioneer in brain surgery.

728.26–27 Elle . . . moi.] French: she was a mother, a comforter for me.

731.11 Ferenczi] See note 274.26.

731.24 "The Harlot's House,"] Poem (1885) by Oscar Wilde.

735.18 *mysterium tremendum*] Concept of religious awe and mystery defined by German historian of religion Rudolf Otto (1868–1937) in *The Idea of the Holy* (1917).

735.23–25 disabled sheriff . . . rampaging Weathermen] Members of Weatherman (later known as the Weather Underground), a radical splinter faction of the Students for a Democratic Society (SDS), staged a series of violent demonstrations in Chicago, October 8–11, 1969, during which they broke store windows, damaged cars, assaulted bystanders, and fought with police. Richard Elrod (b. 1934), an assistant corporation counsel for the city of Chicago who was accompanying the police, severely damaged his cervical spine on October 11 while attempting to tackle a fleeing Weatherman. Elrod, who eventually regained some use of limbs, served as sheriff of Cook County, 1970–86, and became a judge of the Cook County circuit court in 1988.

740.6 *pálinca*] Plum brandy.

753.18 Brown Decade building] The 1870s was dubbed the "Brown Decade" in architecture because of the dark interiors of the buildings of the period. As with Lewis Mumford's book *The Brown Decade: A Study of the Arts in America, 1865–1895* (1931), the phrase sometimes refers to a wider period.

767.11 Attica riots] A five-day riot by twelve hundred inmates at Attica State Correctional Institution in Attica, New York, ended on September 13, 1971, when the prison was retaken by the state police on the order of Governor Nelson Rockefeller after negotiations with the prisoners broke down. Thirty inmates and nine of their hostages were killed by police bullets during the assault, and another eighty persons wounded.

768.16–17 Potsdam Conference] President Harry S. Truman, Premier Joseph Stalin, and Prime Minister Winston Churchill met in the Berlin suburb of Potsdam on July 17, 1945, to discuss postwar Europe and the war with Japan. The conference lasted until August 2 (Churchill was replaced by Clement Atlee after July 26, following the Labour victory in the British general election).

772.3–4 Don Giovanni's 1,003 seductions] In Mozart's opera *Don Giovanni* (1787), with libretto by Lorenzo da Ponte, Don Giovanni boasts that he seduced 1,003 women in Spain.

772.37–38 Beatrix Potter's *Tale of Two Bad Mice*] Children's book (1904).

772.40 Tribuna Ludu] *Trybuna Ludu* (*People's Tribune*), Polish Communist Party newspaper.

776.29–30 *sous-sol*] French: basement.

781.5 in Uganda . . . Amin's people] Dora Bloch, an elderly British-Israeli citizen, was among the hostages taken in June 1976 when seven members of the Popular Front for the Liberation of Palestine hijacked an Air France flight bound for Tel Aviv and directed it to the airport at Entebbe, Uganda. She was hospitalized after choking on a piece of meat during the standoff. After an Israeli raid rescued the hostages at the airport, Bloch was murdered, reportedly on the orders of Ugandan dictator Idi Amin.

782.7–9 Tocqueville . . . lectured] See *Democracy in America* (1835), trans. Arthur Goldhammer, vol. 1, pt. 2, ch. 6: "Americans do not converse;

they argue. They do not talk; they lecture. They always speak to you as though addressing a meeting."

787.21–22 line in which Shelley had described George III . . . king] Opening line of "Sonnet: England in 1819" (1819).

789.35 Nadia Comaneci] Romanian gymnast Nadia Comăneci (b. 1961), winner of three gold medals and the recipient of a perfect score at the 1976 Montreal Olympics.

790.16–18 They . . . faces] Shakespeare, Sonnet 44, lines 1, 7.

790.40 *politruk*] Russian: police officer.

794.19 *Counsellor-at-Law*] Movie melodrama (1933) about a successful Manhattan attorney threatened with disbarment, directed by William Wyler (1902–1981), with John Barrymore (1882–1942) in the title role.

805.34 Spartacus Youth League] Trotskyist youth organization.

826.33 *Wass willst du haben?*] German: What do you want to have?

827.30–33 Wilde . . . soul's inheritance?] "Helas!" (1881), lines 12–14.

829.11 William Powell] American actor (1892–1894), star of *The Great Ziegfeld* (1936), *My Man Godfrey* (1936), and six movies in the *Thin Man* series (1934–47) playing Dashiell Hammett's detective Nick Charles.

834.28–29 *King Lear* . . . Nietzsche] *King Lear*, IV.vi.158–59; cf. *Thus Spoke Zarathustra*, First Part (1883): "Is it my fault that power likes to walk on crooked legs?"

834.33 *Brigge* book by Rilke] *The Notebooks of Malte Laurids Brigge* (1910).

836.23 diamonds . . . Giscard] French president Valéry Giscard d'Estaing (b. 1926) was embarrassed by revelations that he had accepted gifts of diamonds from the Central African Republic's self-appointed "Emperor," Jean Bédel Bokassa (1921–1996).

836.19 Valentine's Day massacre] Notorious gangland killing (February 14, 1929) by members of Al Capone's gang, who murdered seven men, six of them belonging to George "Bugs" Moran's rival gang, at a garage on North Clark Street.

836.26–27 Rilke readings . . . *Weltinnenraum*] Rilkean concept (literally "world-inner-space") from poem beginning "Nearly all things summon us to feel" (1914).

839.19 'monuments of unaging intellect'] W. B. Yeats, "Sailing to Byzantium" (1928), line 8.

839.21 Harry Vaughan] American army officer (1893–1981), military aide to Truman during his vice-presidential and presidential terms.

845.2–3 could feel . . . . Wittenberg] From Christopher Marlowe, *The Tragical History of Doctor Faustus* (1604), V.ii.20–21.

845.21 New Class] The exploitive class of privileged bureaucrats and Party functionaries in Communist societies, outlined in *The New Class* (1955) by Milovan Djilas (see note 439.27).

848.1–2 Who said . . . London] Samuel Johnson's remark quoted in James Boswell, *Life of Johnson* (1791), entry for July 31, 1763.

848.3–4 that same party said . . . barbarism] Quoted in James Boswell, *Journal of a Tour of the Hebrides* (1785), entry for August 21, 1773.

854.15–17 You hold 'em . . . hear] Cf. Samuel Taylor Coleridge, "The Rime of the Ancient Mariner" (1798), lines 13, 37–38.

857.31 John L. Sullivan] American heavyweight boxer (1858–1918), the last of the bare-knuckles prizefighting champions.

858.38–39 Alexander Woollcott] American critic (1887–1943), member of the Algonquin Round Table of wits.

859.7–9 lascivious old woman . . . "girls,"] In *Ecclesiazusae* (*Assembly-Women*, 390 B.C.E.).

864.24 Primo Carnera] Italian-born American heavyweight boxer and wrestler (1906–1967).

870.38 Cruikshank's] English caricaturist George Cruikshank (1792–1878), best known for his illustrations for Charles Dickens's novels.

874.9 Twiggy] English fashion model born Lesley Hornby (b. 1949), famous for her big eyes and slender figure.

875.17–18 revolutionary Marxists . . . riflemen] Five members of the Communist Workers Party were killed by Ku Klux Klan and neo-Nazi gunmen during an anti-Klan demonstration in Greensboro, N.C., on November 3, 1979.

876.8–11 Everything visible . . . cloud?] From Rilke's letter to Karl and Elisabeth von der Heydt, November 6, 1914.

876.35 the famous Stead] English journalist and editor William Thomas Stead (1849–1912), author of *If Christ Came to Chicago* (1894) and *Satan's Invisible World Displayed; or, Despairing of Democracy: A Study of Greater New York* (1898).

884.16–17 *Nous savons . . . mari*] French: we know how much she loved her husband.

886.31 Ana Pauker] Romanian Communist Party leader (1894–1960), foreign minister (1947–52) removed from office during Stalin's 1952 purge of Jewish officials.

886.32 Thorez] French Communist Party leader Maurice Thorez (1900–1964).

893.39 Vollard's memoirs] *Recollections of a Picture Dealer* (1936), memoirs of French art dealer and publisher Ambroise Vollard (1866–1939).

898.8–9 And pity . . . blast] *Macbeth*, I.vii.21–22.

898.27 "How charming is divine philosophy"] John Milton, *Comus*, line 476.

906.1–2 mass killer Gacy . . . boys] Serial killer John Wayne Gacy (1942–1994), convicted and executed for the murders of thirty-three boys and young men.

907.41 Cloaca Maxima] Name of ancient Roman sewer system.

908.30–31 Solzhenitsyn's Harvard Address] "A World Split Apart," controversial commencement speech delivered by exiled Russian writer Aleksandr Solzhenitsyn (1918–2008) at Harvard on June 8, 1978, in which he criticized the West for materialism, moral decadence, and the loss of civic courage and religious belief.

909.36 Tommies] English soldiers.

909.37–38 Remarque and Barbusse] World War I novels: *All Quiet on the Western Front* (1928) by German novelist Erich Maria Remarque (1898–1970); *Under Fire: The Story of a Squad* (1916) by French novelist and journalist Henri Barbusse (1873–1935).

909.38 Kipling] English poet and novelist Rudyard Kipling (1865–1936), whose son Jack was killed in World War I, wrote several works about the war, including the story "Mary Postgate" (1915) and the poem "Gethsemane" (1918).

920.20–21 *En hiver . . . tête*] French: in winter there are very few flowers. They cost you the eyes in your head.

921.20 *pas assez proche*] French: not close enough.

923.27 Iron Guardist] Romanian fascist movement founded in 1927 and suppressed after a coup attempt in January 1941.

928.33 *beaux yeux*] French: beautiful eyes.

933.29 Grand Inquisitor's universal anthill] See the Grand Inquisitor's speech to Christ in Dostoyevsky, *The Brothers Karamazov* (in Constance Garrett's translation): "All that man seeks on earth . . . [is] someone to bow down to, someone to take over his conscience, and a means for uniting everyone at last into a common, concordant, and incontestable anthill—for the need for universal union is the third and last torment of men."

934.9 Tears may be intellectual] See note 328.5.

936.37 Big Bill Thompson] See note 284.6.

937.3–4 A. N. Whitehead . . . Athenian possibilities] See *Dialogues of Alfred North Whitehead* ed. Lucien Price (1954): "I think the one place where I have been that is most like ancient Athens is the University of Chicago."

937.6–7 Aristotle: A man without a city is either a beast or a god] *Politics* 1253a3–4.

939.25 Feltrinelli] Italian left-wing publisher Giangiacomo Feltrinelli (1926–1972), killed while planting a bomb in an attempted act of sabotage.

946.19 SALT] Strategic Arms Limitation Talks, arms-control negotiations between the United States and the Soviet Union (1969–79) that resulted in the signing of treaties in 1972 and 1979. Following the Soviet invasion of Afghanistan in December 1979, President Jimmy Carter withdrew the unratified SALT II treaty from Senate consideration.

946.26–27 "The Garden of Proserpine"] Poem (1866) by Algernon Charles Swinburne.

946.27 "Lapis Lazuli"] Poem (1938) by W. B. Yeats.

949.30–31 Nietzsche had said . . . *sentimental*] In *The Will to Power*, quoting Voltaire: "It is better to be a gay monster / Than a sentimental bore."

953.40 Reverend Jones of Jonestown] On November 18, 1978, more than nine hundred members of the Peoples Temple, a California cult founded by Jim Jones (1931–1978), were murdered or committed suicide at their settlement, Jonestown, in rural Guyana.

956.4 Chapman's Homer, realms of gold] See John Keats, "On First Looking into Chapman's Homer" (1817), line 1: "Much have I traveled in the realms of Gold."

964.25–26 This was Alice in Wonderland: "Drink me."] Sign on a bottle found by Alice in the first chapter of Lewis Carroll's *Alice's Adventures in Wonderland* (1865).

964.31–33 *Je suis* . . . adultes] French: I am a child who wants only more and more adults around him. From a letter to A. Baumgarten, August 22, 1915.

967.25 Dzerzhinsky . . . Zinoviev] See note 273.37.

967.27 Boris Souvarine] Bolshevik propagandist and Soviet Communist Party leader (1895–1984), expelled for being a follower of Trotsky; author of *Stalin: A Critical Study of Bolshevism* (1939).

967.32 Madame Kollontai] Bolshevik leader and Soviet diplomat Aleksandra Kollontay (1872–1952).

967.33 Chicherin] Bolshevik leader and Soviet diplomat Georgi Chicherin (1872–1936), commissar of foreign affairs (1918–30).

967.35 Harry Hopkins] See note 442.30.

967.35–36 brain trust] Or brains trust, informal circle of advisors to President Franklin D. Roosevelt that included political scientist Raymond Moley (1856–1935), economist Rexford G. Tugwell (1891–1979), and lawyer Adolf A. Berle (1895–1971).

968.24 *da capo*] Italian: from the head, from the beginning.

969.8–10 Fairbairn. And Jung . . . tapeworm] Scottish psychoanalyst Ronald Fairbairn (1889–1964). Jung compared the tapeworm specifically to James Joyce's *Ulysses* in "*Ulysses*: A Monolgue" (1932).

975.24 *quelle dévotion*] French: what devotion.

989.34 King David . . . Absalom] Absalom, son of David, rebelled against his father and was killed in battle when his hair caught in an oak under which he was riding his mule, leaving him suspended in the air. David mourned bitterly (2 Samuel 18:9–33, 19:4).

989.35 Lear . . . button] See *King Lear*, V.iii.310, where Lear says, "Pray you undo this button." It is unclear whether the button is worn by the dead Cordelia or Lear himself.

990.20 "Cain's city built with murder"] William Blake, in the manuscript fragment "Then she bore Pale desire . . ." (before 1777).

1001.33–35 "The Little Black Boy," . . . soul] Poems from Blake, *Songs of Innocence and Experience: Shewing the Two Contrary States of the Human Soul* (1794).

1004.7–8 Reston, Kraft, Alsop] *New York Times* columnist James Reston (1909–1995); syndicated columnists Joseph Kraft (1924–1986) and Joseph Alsop (1910–1989).

1006.17–18 What Julien Benda . . . intellectuals] Title of book (1927) by French philosopher and novelist Julien Benda (1867–1956). (Benda's French title is *La trahison des clercs*; the book's first English translation [1928], by Richard Aldington, is entitled *The Great Betrayal*.)

1008.11 FU Orionis] Class of variable stars that undergo a sudden increase then a gradual diminishment in brightness, named for the star in the Orion constellation that first exhibited this pattern to astronomers in the 1930s.

1008.13–15 wise Egyptian . . . read] *Antony and Cleopatra*, I.ii.11.

1009.32 *Exsultate, Jubilate*] Motet, K. 165 (1773) by Wolfgang Amadeus Mozart.

THE LIBRARY OF AMERICA SERIES

The Library of America fosters appreciation and pride in America's literary heritage by publishing, and keeping permanently in print, authoritative editions of America's best and most significant writing. An independent nonprofit organization, it was founded in 1979 with seed money from the National Endowment for the Humanities and the Ford Foundation.

1. Herman Melville, *Typee, Omoo, Mardi* (1982)
2. Nathaniel Hawthorne, *Tales and Sketches* (1982)
3. Walt Whitman, *Poetry and Prose* (1982)
4. Harriet Beecher Stowe, *Three Novels* (1982)
5. Mark Twain, *Mississippi Writings* (1982)
6. Jack London, *Novels and Stories* (1982)
7. Jack London, *Novels and Social Writings* (1982)
8. William Dean Howells, *Novels 1875–1886* (1982)
9. Herman Melville, *Redburn, White-Jacket, Moby-Dick* (1983)
10. Nathaniel Hawthorne, *Collected Novels* (1983)
11. Francis Parkman, *France and England in North America*, vol. I (1983)
12. Francis Parkman, *France and England in North America*, vol. II (1983)
13. Henry James, *Novels 1871–1880* (1983)
14. Henry Adams, *Novels, Mont Saint Michel, The Education* (1983)
15. Ralph Waldo Emerson, *Essays and Lectures* (1983)
16. Washington Irving, *History, Tales and Sketches* (1983)
17. Thomas Jefferson, *Writings* (1984)
18. Stephen Crane, *Prose and Poetry* (1984)
19. Edgar Allan Poe, *Poetry and Tales* (1984)
20. Edgar Allan Poe, *Essays and Reviews* (1984)
21. Mark Twain, *The Innocents Abroad, Roughing It* (1984)
22. Henry James, *Literary Criticism: Essays, American & English Writers* (1984)
23. Henry James, *Literary Criticism: European Writers & The Prefaces* (1984)
24. Herman Melville, *Pierre, Israel Potter, The Confidence-Man, Tales & Billy Budd* (1985)
25. William Faulkner, *Novels 1930–1935* (1985)
26. James Fenimore Cooper, *The Leatherstocking Tales*, vol. I (1985)
27. James Fenimore Cooper, *The Leatherstocking Tales*, vol. II (1985)
28. Henry David Thoreau, *A Week, Walden, The Maine Woods, Cape Cod* (1985)
29. Henry James, *Novels 1881–1886* (1985)
30. Edith Wharton, *Novels* (1986)
31. Henry Adams, *History of the U.S. during the Administrations of Jefferson* (1986)
32. Henry Adams, *History of the U.S. during the Administrations of Madison* (1986)
33. Frank Norris, *Novels and Essays* (1986)
34. W.E.B. Du Bois, *Writings* (1986)
35. Willa Cather, *Early Novels and Stories* (1987)
36. Theodore Dreiser, *Sister Carrie, Jennie Gerhardt, Twelve Men* (1987)

37A. Benjamin Franklin, *Silence Dogood, The Busy-Body, & Early Writings* (1987)
37B. Benjamin Franklin, *Autobiography, Poor Richard, & Later Writings* (1987)

38. William James, *Writings 1902–1910* (1987)
39. Flannery O'Connor, *Collected Works* (1988)
40. Eugene O'Neill, *Complete Plays 1913–1920* (1988)
41. Eugene O'Neill, *Complete Plays 1920–1931* (1988)
42. Eugene O'Neill, *Complete Plays 1932–1943* (1988)
43. Henry James, *Novels 1886–1890* (1989)
44. William Dean Howells, *Novels 1886–1888* (1989)
45. Abraham Lincoln, *Speeches and Writings 1832–1858* (1989)
46. Abraham Lincoln, *Speeches and Writings 1859–1865* (1989)
47. Edith Wharton, *Novellas and Other Writings* (1990)
48. William Faulkner, *Novels 1936–1940* (1990)
49. Willa Cather, *Later Novels* (1990)

50. Ulysses S. Grant, *Memoirs and Selected Letters* (1990)
51. William Tecumseh Sherman, *Memoirs* (1990)
52. Washington Irving, *Bracebridge Hall, Tales of a Traveller, The Alhambra* (1991)
53. Francis Parkman, *The Oregon Trail, The Conspiracy of Pontiac* (1991)
54. James Fenimore Cooper, *Sea Tales: The Pilot, The Red Rover* (1991)
55. Richard Wright, *Early Works* (1991)
56. Richard Wright, *Later Works* (1991)
57. Willa Cather, *Stories, Poems, and Other Writings* (1992)
58. William James, *Writings 1878–1899* (1992)
59. Sinclair Lewis, *Main Street & Babbitt* (1992)
60. Mark Twain, *Collected Tales, Sketches, Speeches, & Essays 1852–1890* (1992)
61. Mark Twain, *Collected Tales, Sketches, Speeches, & Essays 1891–1910* (1992)
62. *The Debate on the Constitution: Part One* (1993)
63. *The Debate on the Constitution: Part Two* (1993)
64. Henry James, *Collected Travel Writings: Great Britain & America* (1993)
65. Henry James, *Collected Travel Writings: The Continent* (1993)
66. *American Poetry: The Nineteenth Century,* Vol. 1 (1993)
67. *American Poetry: The Nineteenth Century,* Vol. 2 (1993)
68. Frederick Douglass, *Autobiographies* (1994)
69. Sarah Orne Jewett, *Novels and Stories* (1994)
70. Ralph Waldo Emerson, *Collected Poems and Translations* (1994)
71. Mark Twain, *Historical Romances* (1994)
72. John Steinbeck, *Novels and Stories 1932–1937* (1994)
73. William Faulkner, *Novels 1942–1954* (1994)
74. Zora Neale Hurston, *Novels and Stories* (1995)
75. Zora Neale Hurston, *Folklore, Memoirs, and Other Writings* (1995)
76. Thomas Paine, *Collected Writings* (1995)
77. *Reporting World War II: American Journalism 1938–1944* (1995)
78. *Reporting World War II: American Journalism 1944–1946* (1995)
79. Raymond Chandler, *Stories and Early Novels* (1995)
80. Raymond Chandler, *Later Novels and Other Writings* (1995)
81. Robert Frost, *Collected Poems, Prose, & Plays* (1995)
82. Henry James, *Complete Stories 1892–1898* (1996)
83. Henry James, *Complete Stories 1898–1910* (1996)
84. William Bartram, *Travels and Other Writings* (1996)
85. John Dos Passos, *U.S.A.* (1996)
86. John Steinbeck, *The Grapes of Wrath and Other Writings 1936–1941* (1996)
87. Vladimir Nabokov, *Novels and Memoirs 1941–1951* (1996)
88. Vladimir Nabokov, *Novels 1955–1962* (1996)
89. Vladimir Nabokov, *Novels 1969–1974* (1996)
90. James Thurber, *Writings and Drawings* (1996)
91. George Washington, *Writings* (1997)
92. John Muir, *Nature Writings* (1997)
93. Nathanael West, *Novels and Other Writings* (1997)
94. *Crime Novels: American Noir of the 1930s and 40s* (1997)
95. *Crime Novels: American Noir of the 1950s* (1997)
96. Wallace Stevens, *Collected Poetry and Prose* (1997)
97. James Baldwin, *Early Novels and Stories* (1998)
98. James Baldwin, *Collected Essays* (1998)
99. Gertrude Stein, *Writings 1903–1932* (1998)
100. Gertrude Stein, *Writings 1932–1946* (1998)
101. Eudora Welty, *Complete Novels* (1998)
102. Eudora Welty, *Stories, Essays, & Memoir* (1998)
103. Charles Brockden Brown, *Three Gothic Novels* (1998)
104. *Reporting Vietnam: American Journalism 1959–1969* (1998)
105. *Reporting Vietnam: American Journalism 1969–1975* (1998)
106. Henry James, *Complete Stories 1874–1884* (1999)

107. Henry James, *Complete Stories 1884–1891* (1999)
108. *American Sermons: The Pilgrims to Martin Luther King Jr.* (1999)
109. James Madison, *Writings* (1999)
110. Dashiell Hammett, *Complete Novels* (1999)
111. Henry James, *Complete Stories 1864–1874* (1999)
112. William Faulkner, *Novels 1957–1962* (1999)
113. John James Audubon, *Writings & Drawings* (1999)
114. *Slave Narratives* (2000)
115. *American Poetry: The Twentieth Century*, Vol. 1 (2000)
116. *American Poetry: The Twentieth Century*, Vol. 2 (2000)
117. F. Scott Fitzgerald, *Novels and Stories 1920–1922* (2000)
118. Henry Wadsworth Longfellow, *Poems and Other Writings* (2000)
119. Tennessee Williams, *Plays 1937–1955* (2000)
120. Tennessee Williams, *Plays 1957–1980* (2000)
121. Edith Wharton, *Collected Stories 1891–1910* (2001)
122. Edith Wharton, *Collected Stories 1911–1937* (2001)
123. *The American Revolution: Writings from the War of Independence* (2001)
124. Henry David Thoreau, *Collected Essays and Poems* (2001)
125. Dashiell Hammett, *Crime Stories and Other Writings* (2001)
126. Dawn Powell, *Novels 1930–1942* (2001)
127. Dawn Powell, *Novels 1944–1962* (2001)
128. Carson McCullers, *Complete Novels* (2001)
129. Alexander Hamilton, *Writings* (2001)
130. Mark Twain, *The Gilded Age and Later Novels* (2002)
131. Charles W. Chesnutt, *Stories, Novels, and Essays* (2002)
132. John Steinbeck, *Novels 1942–1952* (2002)
133. Sinclair Lewis, *Arrowsmith, Elmer Gantry, Dodsworth* (2002)
134. Paul Bowles, *The Sheltering Sky, Let It Come Down, The Spider's House* (2002)
135. Paul Bowles, *Collected Stories & Later Writings* (2002)
136. Kate Chopin, *Complete Novels & Stories* (2002)
137. *Reporting Civil Rights: American Journalism 1941–1963* (2003)
138. *Reporting Civil Rights: American Journalism 1963–1973* (2003)
139. Henry James, *Novels 1896–1899* (2003)
140. Theodore Dreiser, *An American Tragedy* (2003)
141. Saul Bellow, *Novels 1944–1953* (2003)
142. John Dos Passos, *Novels 1920–1925* (2003)
143. John Dos Passos, *Travel Books and Other Writings* (2003)
144. Ezra Pound, *Poems and Translations* (2003)
145. James Weldon Johnson, *Writings* (2004)
146. Washington Irving, *Three Western Narratives* (2004)
147. Alexis de Tocqueville, *Democracy in America* (2004)
148. James T. Farrell, *Studs Lonigan: A Trilogy* (2004)
149. Isaac Bashevis Singer, *Collected Stories I* (2004)
150. Isaac Bashevis Singer, *Collected Stories II* (2004)
151. Isaac Bashevis Singer, *Collected Stories III* (2004)
152. Kaufman & Co., *Broadway Comedies* (2004)
153. Theodore Roosevelt, *The Rough Riders, An Autobiography* (2004)
154. Theodore Roosevelt, *Letters and Speeches* (2004)
155. H. P. Lovecraft, *Tales* (2005)
156. Louisa May Alcott, *Little Women, Little Men, Jo's Boys* (2005)
157. Philip Roth, *Novels & Stories 1959–1962* (2005)
158. Philip Roth, *Novels 1967–1972* (2005)
159. James Agee, *Let Us Now Praise Famous Men, A Death in the Family* (2005)
160. James Agee, *Film Writing & Selected Journalism* (2005)
161. Richard Henry Dana, Jr., *Two Years Before the Mast & Other Voyages* (2005)
162. Henry James, *Novels 1901–1902* (2006)
163. Arthur Miller, *Collected Plays 1944–1961* (2006)

164. William Faulkner, *Novels 1926–1929* (2006)
165. Philip Roth, *Novels 1973–1977* (2006)
166. *American Speeches: Part One* (2006)
167. *American Speeches: Part Two* (2006)
168. Hart Crane, *Complete Poems & Selected Letters* (2006)
169. Saul Bellow, *Novels 1956–1964* (2007)
170. John Steinbeck, *Travels with Charley and Later Novels* (2007)
171. Capt. John Smith, *Writings with Other Narratives* (2007)
172. Thornton Wilder, *Collected Plays & Writings on Theater* (2007)
173. Philip K. Dick, *Four Novels of the 1960s* (2007)
174. Jack Kerouac, *Road Novels 1957–1960* (2007)
175. Philip Roth, *Zuckerman Bound* (2007)
176. Edmund Wilson, *Literary Essays & Reviews of the 1920s & 30s* (2007)
177. Edmund Wilson, *Literary Essays & Reviews of the 1930s & 40s* (2007)
178. *American Poetry: The 17th & 18th Centuries* (2007)
179. William Maxwell, *Early Novels & Stories* (2008)
180. Elizabeth Bishop, *Poems, Prose, & Letters* (2008)
181. A. J. Liebling, *World War II Writings* (2008)
182s. *American Earth: Environmental Writing Since Thoreau* (2008)
183. Philip K. Dick, *Five Novels of the 1960s & 70s* (2008)
184. William Maxwell, *Later Novels & Stories* (2008)
185. Philip Roth, *Novels & Other Narratives 1986–1991* (2008)
186. Katherine Anne Porter, *Collected Stories & Other Writings* (2008)
187. John Ashbery, *Collected Poems 1956–1987* (2008)
188. John Cheever, *Collected Stories & Other Writings* (2009)
189. John Cheever, *Complete Novels* (2009)
190. Lafcadio Hearn, *American Writings* (2009)
191. A. J. Liebling, *The Sweet Science & Other Writngs* (2009)
192s. *The Lincoln Anthology: Great Writers on His Life and Legacy from 1860 to Now* (2009)
193. Philip K. Dick, *VALIS & Later Novels* (2009)
194. Thornton Wilder, *The Bridge of San Luis Rey and Other Novels 1926–1948* (2009)
195. Raymond Carver, *Collected Stories* (2009)
196. *American Fantastic Tales: Terror and the Uncanny from Poe to the Pulps* (2009)
197. *American Fantastic Tales: Terror and the Uncanny from the 1940s to Now* (2009)
198. John Marshall, *Writings* (2010)
199s. *The Mark Twain Anthology: Great Writers on His Life and Works* (2010)
200. Mark Twain, *A Tramp Abroad, Following the Equator, Other Travels* (2010)
201. Ralph Waldo Emerson, *Selected Journals 1820–1842* (2010)
202. Ralph Waldo Emerson, *Selected Journals 1841–1877* (2010)
203. *The American Stage: Writing on Theater from Washington Irving to Tony Kushner* (2010)
204. Shirley Jackson, *Novels & Stories* (2010)
205. Philip Roth, *Novels 1993–1995* (2010)
206. H. L. Mencken, *Prejudices: First, Second, and Third Series* (2010)
207. H. L. Mencken, *Prejudices: Fourth, Fifth, and Sixth Series* (2010)
208. John Kenneth Galbraith, *The Affluent Society and Other Writings 1952–1967* (2010)
209. Saul Bellow, *Novels 1970–1982* (2010)

To subscribe to the series or to order individual copies,
please visit www.loa.org or call (800) 964.5778.

This book is set in 10 point Linotron Galliard, a face designed for photocomposition by Matthew Carter and based on the sixteenth-century face Granjon. The paper is acid-free lightweight opaque and meets the requirements for permanence of the American National Standards Institute. The binding material is Brillianta, a woven rayon cloth made by Van Heek-Scholco Textielfabrieken, Holland. Composition by Dedicated Business Services. Printing by Malloy Incorporated. Binding by Dekker Bookbinding. Designed by Bruce Campbell.